THE MAMMOTH BOOK
OF BEST NEW
SCIENCE FICTION

Also available in the Mammoth series

The Mammoth Book of Vampire Romance 2
The Mammoth Book of Best New Horror 20
The Mammoth Book of Wolf Men
The Mammoth Book of Merlin
The Mammoth Book of Best New Manga 4
The Mammoth Book of Time Travel Romance
The Mammoth Book of Filthy Limericks
The Mammoth Book of Chess
The Mammoth Book of Irish Romance
The Mammoth Book of Best New Erotica 9
The Mammoth Book of Alternate Histories
The Mammoth Book of Bizarre Crimes
The Mammoth Book of Special Ops Romance
The Mammoth Book of Best British Crime 7
The Mammoth Book of Sex, Drugs & Rock 'n' Roll
The Mammoth Book of Travel in Dangerous Places
The Mammoth Book of Apocalyptic SF
The Mammoth Book of Casino Games
The Mammoth Book of Sudoku
The Mammoth Book of Extreme Fantasy
The Mammoth Book of Zombie Comics
The Mammoth Book of Men O'War
The Mammoth Book of Mindblowing SF
The Mammoth Book of New Sherlock Holmes Adventures
The Mammoth Book of The Beatles
The Mammoth Book of the Best Short SF Novels
The Mammoth Book of New IQ Puzzles
The Mammoth Book of Alternate Histories
The Mammoth Book of Regency Romance
The Mammoth Book of Paranormal Romance 2
The Mammoth Book of the World's Greatest Chess Games
The Mammoth Book of Tasteless Jokes
The Mammoth Book of New Erotic Photography

THE MAMMOTH BOOK OF BEST NEW SCIENCE FICTION

23rd Annual Collection

Edited by
GARDNER DOZOIS

ROBINSON

Constable & Robinson Ltd
3 The Lanchesters
162 Fulham Palace Road
London W6 9ER
www.constablerobinson.com

First published in the UK by Robinson,
an imprint of Constable & Robinson Ltd., 2010

A copy of the British Library Cataloguing in
Publication data is available from the British Library

ISBN: 978-1-84901-382-6

Printed and bound in the EU

1 3 5 7 9 10 8 6 4 2

Acknowledgment is made for permission to reprint the following material:

"Utriusque Cosmi," by Robert Charles Wilson. Copyright © 2009 by Robert Charles Wilson. First published in *The New Space Opera* 2 (Eos), edited by Jonathan Strahan and Gardner Dozois. Reprinted by permission of the author.

"A Story, With Beans," by Steven Gould. Copyright © 2009 by Dell Magazines. First published in *Analog Science Fiction and Science Fact*, May 2009. Reprinted by permission of the author.

"Under the Shouting Sky," by Karl Bunker. Copyright © 2009 by Karl Bunker. First published in *Cosmos*, August/September 2009. Reprinted by permission of the author.

"Events Preceding the Helvetican Revolution," by John Kessel. Copyright © 2009 by John Kessel. First published in *The New Space Opera* 2 (Eos), edited by Jonathan Strahan and Gardner Dozois. Reprinted by permission of the author.

"Useless Things," by Maureen F. McHugh. Copyright © 2009 by Maureen F. McHugh. First published in *Eclipse Three* (Night Shade), edited by Jonathan Strahan. Reprinted by permission of the author.

"Black Swan," by Bruce Sterling. Copyright © 2009 by *Interzone*. First published in *Interzone 221*. Reprinted by permission of the author.

"Crimes and Glory," by Paul McAuley. Copyright © 2009 by Paul McAuley. First published electronically on *Subterranean*, Spring 2009. Reprinted by permission of the author.

"Seventh Fall," by Alexander Irvine. Copyright © 2009 by Alexander Irvine. First published electronically on *Subterranean*, Summer 2009.

"Butterfly Bomb," by Dominic Green. Copyright © 2009 by *Interzone*. First published in *Interzone 223*. Reprinted by permission of the author.

"Infinites," by Vandana Singh. First published in *The Woman Who Thought She Was a Planet* (Penguin India), by Vandana Singh. Reprinted by permission of the author.

"Things Undone," by John Barnes. Copyright © 2009 by John Barnes. First published electronically on *Jim Baen's Universe*, December 2009. Reprinted by permission of the author.

"On the Human Plan," by Jay Lake. Copyright © 2009 by Jay Lake. First published electronically on *Lone Star Stories*, February 1. Reprinted by permission of the author.

"The Island," by Peter Watts. Copyright © 2009 by Peter Watts. First published in *The New Space Opera* 2 (Eos), edited by Jonathan Strahan and Gardner Dozois. Reprinted by permission of the author.

"The Integrity of the Chain," by Lavie Tidhar. Copyright © 2009 by Lavie Tidhar. First published electronically on *Fantasy*, July. Reprinted by permission of the author.

"Lion Walk," by Mary Rosenblum. Copyright © 2009 by Dell Magazines. First published in *Asimov's Science Fiction*, January 2009. Reprinted by permission of the author.

"Escape to Other Worlds with Science Fiction," by Jo Walton. Copyright © 2009 by Jo Walton. First published electronically at Tor.com. Reprinted by permission of the author.

CONTENTS

ACKNOWLEDGMENTS

The editor would like to thank the following people for their help and support: Susan Casper, Jonathan Strahan, Gordon Van Gelder, Ellen Datlow, Peter Crowther, Nicolas Gevers, William Shaffer, Ian Whates, Andy Cox, Patrick Nielsen Hayden, Torie Atkinson, Jed Hartman, Eric T. Reynolds, George Mann, Jennifer Brehl, Peter Tennant, Susan Marie Groppi, Karen Meisner, John Joseph Adams, Wendy S. Delmater, Jed Hartman, Rich Horton, Mark R. Kelly, Andrew Wilson, Damien Broderick, Lou Anders, Patrick Swenson, Jay Lake, Sheila Williams, Brian Bieniowski, Trevor Quachri, Sean Wallace, Robert T. Wexler, Michael Swanwick, Stephen Baxter, Kristine Kathryn Rusch, Nancy Kress, Greg Egan, Ian McDonald, Paul McAuley, Ted Kosmatka, Michael Poore, Elizabeth Bear, Sarah Monette, Charles Stross, Damien Broderick, James Patrick Kelly, John Barnes, Nicola Griffith, Mary Rosenblum, Lavie Tidhar, Jo Walton, John C. Wright, Steven Gould, James Van Pelt, Bruce Sterling, Alexander Irvine, Karl Bunker, Ian Creasey, Peter Watts, John Kessel, Albert E. Cowdrey, Robert Charles Wilson, Paul Cornell, Adam Roberts, Alastair Reynolds, Dave Hutchinson, David Marusek, Dario Ciriello, Wilson Da Silva, Keith Brooke, Robert Reed, Vandana Singh, Maureen McHugh, L. Timmel Duchamp, Dominic Green, Geoff Ryman, Paul Brazier, David Hartwell, Ginjer Buchanan, Susan Allison, Shawna McCarthy, Kelly Link, Gavin Grant, John Klima, John O'Neill, Charles Tan, Rodger Turner, Stuart Mayne, John Kenny, Edmund Schubert, Tehani Wessely, Tehani Croft, Sally Beasley, Tony Lee, Joe Vas, John Pickrell, Ian Redman, Anne Zanoni, Kaolin Fire, Ralph Benko, Paul Graham Raven, Nick Wood, Mike Allen, Jason Sizemore, Karl Johanson, Sue Miller, David Lee Summers, Christopher M. Cevasco, Tyree Campbell, Andrew Hook, Vaughne Lee Hansen, Mark Watson, Sarah Lumnah, and special thanks to my own editor, Marc Resnick.

Thanks are also due to the late, lamented Charles N. Brown, and to all his staff, whose magazine *Locus* (Locus Publications, P.O. Box 13305, Oakland, CA 94661. $60 in the United States for a one-year subscription [twelve issues] via second class; credit card orders 510-339-9198) was used as an invaluable reference source throughout the Summation; Locus Online (locusmag.com), edited by Mark R. Kelly, has also become a key reference source.

SUMMATION: 2009

In spite of panic so intense in the publishing world that it was reminiscent of the emotion that caused stockbrokers to throw themselves from windows during the Stock Market Crash of 1929, panic that caused massive editorial layoffs in late 2008 and early 2009 as publishers rushed to reduce expenses in anticipation of the hard times and low sales ahead, the number of books sold in 2009 turned out to be – not so bad.

According to Nielsen BookScan, overall unit sales through 20 December 2009 came in at 724 million, a drop of only 3 per cent compared to the same period in 2008. Much of that drop came in adult nonfiction, which suffered the biggest decline by category, down 7 per cent from the previous year. Sales of adult fiction hardcover books, however, actually *rose* by 3 per cent, while sales of adult fiction trade paperbacks grew by 2 per cent over the prior year.

So rather than crashing disastrously during the Great Recession, sales of fiction books actually went *up*.

Furthermore, of three thousand adults questioned in an online poll, three quarters of them said that they would sacrifice holidays, dining out, going to the movies, and even shopping sprees before they would stop buying books.

This shouldn't really come as a big surprise – historically, books, magazines, and movies do well during recessions, as hard economic times make people search for cheap entertainment to distract themselves from their financial woes.

The questions that are probably going to dominate the publishing world during the next few years are: Where are you going to buy your books? And what form are you going to buy them in?

Pressure from online booksellers like Amazon and Barnes & Noble and from the rising tide of digital sales that may become a flood now that portable text readers are increasingly available have already had a dramatic effect on where you can buy your books. Just as the rise of chain bookstores put many independent bookstores out of business, now business forces are reshaping the chains themselves. The bookstore chain Borders teetered on the brink of bankruptcy toward the end of 2008, and although it managed to avoid that in 2009, Borders UK ceased operation and closed all of its stores, and Borders will soon close two hundred Waldenbooks outlets, while rival bookstore chain Barnes & Noble is closing all of its remaining B. Dalton stores.

This is not the end of the brick-and-mortar bookstore by any means – the chains will still have plenty of 'superstores' left, where sales have generally been pretty good, perhaps because of the larger selection of stock available there. And there are even a few independent bookstores left here and there. But it does mean that the era where almost every shopping mall had a small chain bookstore is probably over.

Print books are not going to disappear either – in fact, there were probably more of them published in 2009 than ever before. But the e-book market, which up until now has simmered in the background for several years, not really considered to be a major factor, is probably about to explode, which could bring major changes to the publishing world. The introduction of Amazon's Kindle in 2007, the first portable text reader, turned the heat up under the e-book market, and now, with the introduction of competing text-reading devices such as Barnes & Noble's Nook and Apple's iPad and the founding of several other 'online bookstores' where products for them can be purchased, that market is really starting to come to the boil. In fact, much of 2009 was taken up with price wars over the pricing both of print books and of e-books, with Amazon clashing with other industry giants such as publisher Macmillan and discount super-store chain Walmart, each player trying to bring enough pressure to bear on its adversary to force concessions; the struggle between Amazon and Macmillan over e-book pricing – Amazon wanting to keep them priced low to encourage sales of the Kindle, Macmillan wanting them priced higher to increase profits – has been particularly bitter and intense, with Amazon recently succumbing to Macmillan's demands. (The war over the Google Settlement, concerning which books will be available for online accessing via Google, which involved a class-action suit by the Authors' Guild and the controversial settlement that everyone has been wrangling bitterly about ever since, also continued to rage throughout 2009 and into 2010, but that will probably be of interest to very few readers who are not themselves writers.)

Within the genre publishing world, things were relatively quiet after the turmoil of layoffs and cutbacks at the beginning of 2009 (although there were further big cuts at Penguin UK in August). Most of the major restructuring was at Random House, and could be seen as the working-out of consequences from corporate mergers from a couple of years back rather than as a response to the economic downturn per se. Random House has restructured into three adult trade groups, Crown Trade Group, Knopf Doubleday Publishing Group, and Random House Publishing Group. Random House Publishing Group includes, among others, Ballantine, Bantam, Delacorte, Dell, The Dial Press, and Villard Books, which puts both Random House SF imprints, Del Rey and Spectra, under Ballantine. Party line is that the two imprints will be kept separate, for now anyway. Games Workshop's publishing arm, BL Publishing, sold their Solaris Books imprint to Rebellion. Wildside Press, Prime, and Juno split up early in the year; Juno ended up as a co-published imprint of Pocket Books, Cosmos Books died, and Prime went back to solo operations. HarperCollins started a new SF imprint, Angry Robot. Harlequin started a new YA fantasy line, Harlequin Teen.

Both within and outside the genre, though, evolutionary forces are at work that could change everything, and I suspect that the publishing world is going to look very different ten years from now than it does today.

The good news in the still-troubled magazine market is that things could have been a lot worse. All of the print magazines survived the year, something which looked a bit chancy at the beginning of 2009 (when, in order to survive, both *F&SF* and *Asimov's* were forced to economize by changing either their publication schedules or their trim size). One, *Realms of Fantasy*, actually returned from the dead under new ownership after being cancelled. And there were even one or two other mildly positive notes: for one thing, the decline in circulation, drastic to very drastic for most magazines only a few years back, seems to have stabilized at a much slower rate of decline, with most magazines more or less staying even, with only miniscule losses in circulation; for another, electronic subscriptions for reading devices such as the Kindle are starting to have an effect, still relatively minor at the moment, but at least *increasing* the circulation figures, trending in the right direction, something that hasn't happened in a while.

The Magazine of Fantasy & Science Fiction, celebrating its sixtieth year, published a lot of good fantasy this year, but not much SF. Good stories by Geoff Ryman, Albert E. Cowdrey, Rand B. Lee, Ellen Kushner, Sean McMullen, Melinda M. Snodgrass, Elizabeth Hand, Charles Oberndorf, and others appeared in *F&SF* in 2009. *The Magazine of Fantasy & Science Fiction* registered a 3.4 per cent loss in overall circulation, from 16,044 to 15,491, with subscriptions dropping from 12,374 to 12,045, and newsstand sales dropping from 3,670 to 3,446; sell-through rose from 36 to 37 per cent. Gordon Van Gelder is in his thirteenth year as editor, and ninth year as owner and publisher.

Asimov's Science Fiction was almost the reverse of *F&SF*, publishing a lot of good SF, but not as much good fantasy. Good stories by Mary Rosenblum, Damien Broderick, Robert Reed, Nancy Kress, Tom Purdom, James Patrick Kelly, Ian Creasey, and others appeared in *Asimov's* in 2009. *Asimov's Science Fiction* registered only a 2.4 percent loss in overall circulation, from 17,102 to 16,696, not bad when compared to past losses, which rose as high as 23 percent in 2005. Subscriptions dropped almost unnoticeably from 13,842 to 13,731, although news-stand sales dropped a bit more substantially, from 3,260 to 2,965; sell-through stayed steady at 31 per cent. Although no hard figures are as yet available, the rumor is that overall circulation actually increased this year when you factor in the addition of 'about three thousand' in digital subscriptions sold through the Kindle, Fictionwise, and other providers. Sheila Williams completed her fifth year as *Asimov's* editor.

Analog Science Fiction and Fact had an above-average year, publishing good work by James Van Pelt, Steven Gould, Harry Turtledove, Don D'Ammassa, Kristine Kathryn Rusch, Michael F. Flynn, and others. *Analog Science Fiction and Fact* registered only a 2.2 per cent loss in overall circulation, from 25,999 to 25,418, with subscriptions dropping from 21,880 to

21,636, and news-stand sales dropping from 4,119 to 3,782; sell-through remained steady at 34 per cent. Stanley Schmidt has been editor there since 1978.

Interzone also had an above-average year, publishing strong work by Dominic Green, Bruce Sterling, Sarah L. Edwards, Jason Sanford, and others. By the definition of *Science Fiction Writers of America (SFWA)*, *Interzone* doesn't really qualify as a "professional magazine" because of its low rates and circulation, but as it's thoroughly professional in the caliber of writers that it attracts and in the quality of the fiction it produces, just about everybody considers it to be a professional magazine anyway. Circulation there seems to have held steady, in the three thousand copy range. The ever-shifting editorial staff included in 2009 publisher Andy Cox, assisted by Andy Hedgecock, Jetse de Vries, and David Mathew. TTA Press, *Interzone*'s publisher, also publishes straight horror or dark suspense magazine *Black Static*.

The British magazine *Postscripts*, another professional-level publication in spite of low circulation figures, reinvented itself as an anthology this year, so we'll cover it there, below. (I'll list the subscription information up here, though, for lack of anywhere else to put it, and, because, unlike most other anthology series, you *can* subscribe to *Postscripts*.)

Publisher Sovereign Media announced that they were pulling the plug on *Realms of Fantasy* early in 2009, and what was ostensibly the magazine's last issue appeared in April. That looked like the end of the line for *Realms of Fantasy*, but then the magazine was bought by Warren Lapine of Tir Na Nog Press, who started it up again. Three issues of the resurrected magazine appeared throughout the rest of the year, for an overall total of five. Shawna McCarthy, who has been the editor since the founding of the magazine in 1994, was retained as editor, and the resurrected version of the magazine looks and reads much like the old version, and features the same sort of fiction. *Realms of Fantasy* published good work this year by Ian Creasey, Jay Lake, Richard Parks, Cat Rambo, Kristine Kathryn Rusch, and others.

Weird Tales had a rocky year due to the reorganization of publisher Wildside Press in response to the recession, and only managed two 2009 issues; nevertheless, there's an energy and drive here that hints to me that this intelligently edited horror/fantasy magazine will survive. At the beginning of 2010, Ann VanderMeer was promoted from fiction editor to editor in chief, and Mary Robinette Kowal and Paula Guran joined the staff as art director and nonfiction editor, respectively. Their circulation seems to be somewhere in the five thousand copy range, and again many critics seem to consider them a professional magazine in spite of that. Interesting stories by Jeffrey Ford, Richard Howard, Hunter Eden, Michael Swanwick, Robert Davies, and others appeared there this year.

If you'd like to see lots of good SF and fantasy published every year, the survival of these magazines is essential, and one important way that you can help them survive is by subscribing to them. It's never been easier to do so, with just the click of a few buttons, nor has it ever before been possible to subscribe to the magazines in as many different formats, from the traditional print copy arriving by mail to downloads for your desktop or laptop available from places like Fictionwise (www.fictionwise.com) and Amazon (www.amazon.com), to versions you can read on your Kindle. You can also now subscribe from overseas just as easily as you can from the United States, something formerly difficult-to-impossible.

So in hopes of making it easier for you to subscribe, I'm going to list both the Internet sites where you can subscribe online and the street addresses where you can subscribe by mail for each magazine: *Asimov's Science Fiction*'s site is at www.asimovs.com, and subscribing online might be the easiest thing to do, and there's also a discounted rate for online subscriptions; its subscription address is Asimov's Science Fiction, Dell Magazines, 6 Prowitt Street, Norwalk, CT 06855 – $32.97 for annual subscription in the US, $42.97 overseas. *Analog Science Fiction and Fact*'s site is at www .analogsf.com; its subscription address is Analog Science Fiction and Fact, Dell Magazines, 6 Prowitt Street, Norwalk, CT 06855 – $32.97 for annual subscription in the US *The Magazine of Fantasy & Science Fiction*'s site is at www.sfsite.com/fsf; its subscription address is Fantasy & Science Fiction, P.O. Box 3447, Hoboken, NJ 07030 – annual subscriptions cost $34.97 in the US *Interzone* and *Black Static* can be subscribed to online at www.ttapress.com/onlinestore1.html; the subscription address for both is TTA Press, 5 Martins Lane, Witcham, Ely, Cambridge CB6 2LB, England – $68.51 each for a twelve-issue subscription, or there is a reduced-rate dual-subscription offer of $127.23 for both magazines for twelve issues; make checks payable to 'TTA Press'. *Postscripts*, at http://store.pspublishing.co .uk/acatalog/PS_Subscriptions.html, has a variety of subscription options, including 50 Pounds Sterling for a one-year unsigned hardcover (two issue) subscription, or 100 Pounds Sterling for a one-year signed traycased subscription. *Realms of Fantasy* offers yearly subscription in the US for $19.99, or overseas for $29.99; write to Tir Na Nog Press, Realms of Fantasy, P.O. Box 1623, Williamsport, PA 17703, call 1-877-318-3269, or subscribe online at www.realmsoffantasymag.com. *Weird Tales* offers a few different subscription options, including a one-year, four-issue subscription for $20 in the US; contact them at Wildside Press, 9710 Traville Gateway Drive #234, Rockville, MD 20850, or online at http://weirdtales.net/wordpress.

The print fiction semiprozine market, subject to the same pressures in terms of rising postage rates and production costs as the professional magazines are, continues to contract. *Aeon, Talebones, Paradox, Fictitious Force, Farrago's Wainscot,* and *H.P. Lovecraft's Magazine of Horror* all died this year, and *Zahir* is transitioning from a print format to an electronic-only online format, something that *Subterranean, Fantasy Magazine,* and *Apex Magazine* did the year before. (I suspect that this will eventually be the fate of most print fiction semiprozines – they'll transition into all-electronic formats, or they'll die.)

Of the other surviving print fiction semiprozines, *Electric Velocipede*, edited by John Kilma, managed two issues in 2009, one a double-issue, publishing worthwhile material by Merrie Haskell, Mercurio D. Rivera, Yoon Ha Lee, and others. The Canadian *On Spec*, one of the longest-running of all the fiction semiprozines, edited by a collective under general editor Diane Walton, once again kept reliably to its publishing schedule in 2009, and featured interesting stories by Tony Pi and Jack Skillingstead, among others. Australia's *Andromeda Spaceways Inflight Magazine*, another collective-run SF magazine with a rotating editorial staff under editor in chief Robbie Matthews, managed five of its scheduled six issues this year, publishing good stuff by Damien Broderick and Paul Di Filippo, Brian Stableford, Jason K. Chapman, Caroline M. Yoachim, and others.

I saw two issues of Australian magazine *Aurealis*, edited by Stuart Mayne, in 2009, although they were both dated 2008. A small British SF magazine edited by Ian Redman, *Jupiter*, managed all four of its scheduled issues in 2009; I like the fact that it's all-SF, but the quality of its fiction needs to come up. A Canadian magazine, edited by Karl Johanson, *Neo-Opsis*, ostensibly quarterly, produced three issues in 2009; the same comment made about *Jupiter* would apply equally well to them. Long-running *Space and Time* produced four issues, as did fantasy magazine *Tales of the Talisman*; there were two issues apiece produced by fantasy magazine *Shimmer*, the Irish *Albedo One*, *Greatest Uncommon Denominator*, and *Not One of Us*, and as far as I can tell there was only one 2009 issue of sword & sorcery magazine *Black Gate*, as well as the slipstreamish *Lady Churchill's Rosebud Wristlet*, *New Genre*, and *Sybil's Garage*. I saw no copy of *Tales of the Unanticipated* or *Aoife's Kiss* this year.

Most of the print critical magazine market is gone. One of the hearty survivors, and always your best bet for value, is the newszine *Locus: The Magazine of the Science Fiction & Fantasy Field*, a twenty-eight-time Hugo-winner which for more than forty years has been an indispensible source of news, information, and reviews; co-founder, publisher, and longtime editor Charles N. Brown died this year, but *Locus* continues under the guidance of a staff of editors headed by Liza Groen Trombi, and including Kirsten Gong-Wong, Amelia Beamer, and many others. Another hearty perennial, one of the last men standing in this field, is the eclectic critical magazine *The New York Review of Science Fiction*, edited by David G. Hartwell and a staff of associate editors, which publishes a variety of eclectic and sometimes quirky critical essays on a wide range of topics.

Most of the other surviving print critical magazines are professional journals more aimed at academics than at the average reader. The most accessible of these is probably the long-running British critical zine *The Science Fiction Foundation*.

Subscription addresses follow:

Locus: The Magazine of the Science Fiction & Fantasy Field, Locus Publications, Inc., P.O. Box 13305, Oakland, CA, 94661, or online at https://secure.locusmag.com/About/Subscribe.html – $68 for a one-year first-class subscription, 12 issues. **The New York Review of Science Fiction**, Dragon Press, P.O. Box 78, Pleasantville, NY, 10570, or online at http://www.nyrsf.com/subscribe-today.html – $40 per year, 12 issues, make checks payable to "Dragon Press." *The Science Fiction Foundation*, Science Fiction Foundation, Roger Robinson (SFF), 75 Rosslyn Avenue, Harold Wood, Essex RM3 ORG, UK, or online at http:// www.sf-foundation.org/joining.html – $39 for a three-issue subscription in the U.S. *Aurealis*, Chimaera Publications, P.O. Box 2164, Mt Waverley, VIC 3149, Australia, or online at www.aurealis.com.au – $59 .75 (AUD) for a four-issue overseas airmail subscription, checks should be made out to "Chimaera Publications" in Australian dollars. *On Spec, The Canadian Magazine of the Fantastic*, P.O. Box 4727, Edmonton, AB, Canada T6E 5G6, or online at www.onspec.ca – $25 for one year. *Neo-opsis Science Fiction Magazine*, 4129 Carey Rd., Victoria, BC, Canada, V8Z 4G5, or online at http://www.neo-opsis.ca/Subscriptions. htm – $25 (Canadian) for a three-issue subscription. *Albedo One*, Albedo One Productions, 2 Post Road, Lusk, County Dublin, Ireland or online at http://www.albedo1.com/html/albedo_1_subscriptions.html – $39.50 for a four-issue airmail subscription, make checks payable to "Albedo One." *Lady Churchill's Rosebud Wristlet*, Small Beer Press, 150 Pleasant St., #306, Easthampton, MA 01027 or online at http://smallbeerpress.com/ shopping/subscriptions/ – $20 for four issues. *Electric Velocipede* at http:// www.nightshadebooks.com/cart.php?m=product_detail&p=143   offers a two-issue annual subscription for $25. *Andromeda Spaceways Inflight Magazine* has a six-issue subscription rate of $69 (AUD), visit them online at www.andromedaspaceways.com. *Zahir* is transitioning to an all-electronic format, see www.zahirtales.com for further information. *Tales of the Talisman*, Hadrosaur Productions, P.O. Box 2194, Mesilla Park, NM 88047-2194 or online at http://www.hadrosaur.com/order.html – $24 for a four-issue subscription. *Black Gate*, New Epoch Press, 815 Oak Street, St. Charles, IL 60174, or online at http://www.blackgate.com/black-gate -subscriptions/; there are multiple subscription options, including downloadable PDF versions for $4.95 apiece or $29.95 for a one-year (four issue) subscription. *Jupiter*, at 19 Bedford Road, Yeovil, Somerset, BA21 5UG, UK, offers four issues for 10 Pounds Sterling. *Greatest Uncommon Denominator*, GUD Publishing, P.O. Box 1537, Laconia, NH 03247, or online at http://www.gudmagazine.com/subs/subscribe.php – $22 for 2 issues. *Sybil's Garage*, Senses Five Press, 76 India Street, Apt A8, Brooklyn NY11222-1657, or online at http://www.sensesfive.com/store/index.php ?main_page=product_info&cPath=2&products_id=9 – $29.95 for four issues (2 years). *Shimmer*, P.O. Box 58591, Salt Lake City, UT 84158-0591, or online at http://www.shimmerzine.com/purchase/subscribe/ – $22.00 for a four-issue subscription.

The online world of electronic magazines seemed to have more energy and momentum this year than most of the print world, and probably published more good fiction than all but perhaps the top three or four print fiction magazines. Not that it was all good – *Jim Baen's Universe* is scheduled to die after the April 2010 issue, and *Shiny* and *Lone Star Stories* are both already dead. On the other hand, *Apex Magazine* came back from the dead, Tor.com, *Subterranean Press*, *Strange Horizons*, *Orson Scott Card's InterGalactic Medicine Show*, *Clarkesworld Magazine*, *Abyss & Apex*, and *Fantasy Magazine* still seem to be going strong, and a promising new ezine, *Lightspeed*, edited by John Joseph Adams, will be starting up in 2010.

Jim Baen's Universe (www.baensuniverse.com), once the Great White Hope of the online fiction-magazine world, is in its fourth year, and it will unfortunately be its last, since it's been announced that the ezine will shut down after its April 2010 issue, a major loss for the field, and one that will be advanced as an argument against the long-term viability of ezines – if an ezine paying top-of-the field prices, attracting the biggest name authors, and getting major publicity and visibility can't attract enough paying readers to stay alive, who can? *Jim Baen's Universe* published only one really major story in 2009, a complex time-travel piece by John Barnes, but there was lots of other good work, both SF and fantasy, by David Gerrold, Jay Lake, Kristine Kathryn Rusch, Naomi Kritzer, Lezli Robyn, Graham Edwards, John Lambshead, Gary Kloster, and others. Its editors were Mike Resnick and Eric Flint.

With *Jim Baen's Universe* on the way out, the most important remaining site is probably Tor.com (www.tor.com). I once said that what we really needed was a Boing Boing that published science fiction as well, a place cool and eclectic enough to draw the Internet-savvy audience as well as the SF audience, and Tor.com, a website that regularly publishes SF, fantasy, and slipstream, as well as articles, comics, graphics, blog entries, print and media reviews, and commentary, may fit that bill. *Tor.com* had another strong year in 2009, publishing a wide range of different kinds of stories (although they tend to lean a bit toward slipstream and steampunk) by Jo Walton, Harry Turtledove, Damien Broderick, Michael Swanwick and Eileen Gunn, Kij Johnson, Ken Scholes, Elizabeth Bear, Steven Gould, Rachel Swirsky, and others.

The long-running ezine *Strange Horizons* (www.strangehorizons.com), edited by Susan Marie Groppi, assisted by Jed Hartman and Karen Meisner, ran good work, a mixture of SF, fantasy, and slipstream, by Lavie Tidhar, Sandra McDonald, Elliott Bangs, Benjamin Crowell, Tim Pratt, Jennifer Linnaea, Alaya Dawn Johnson, Rachel Manija Brown, Cat Rambo, Leonard Richardson, and others.

Clarkesworld Magazine (www.clarkesworldmagazine.com), edited by Neil Clarke and Sean Wallace, ran good stuff this year, much of it SF, some fantasy or slipstream, by Kij Johnson, Gord Sellar, Jason K. Chapman, Lavie Tidhar, Sarah Monette, Tobias S. Buckell, Cat Rambo, and others.

Abyss & Apex (www.abyssandapex.com), edited by Wendy S. Delmater, which seems to run more SF than many of the other sites, had good stuff by Samantha Henderson, Karl Bunker, Marie Brennan, Christopher Green, Paul Carlson, Ruth Nestvold, Richard A. Lovett, Bud Sparhawk, and others.

Apex Magazine (www.apexbookcompany.com/apex-online), edited by Jason Sizemore, featured good work, most of it fantasy or slipstream, by Theodora Goss, Ekaterina Sedia, Gord Sellar, Peter M. Ball, Aliette de Bodard, Rochita Loenen-Ruiz, and others.

Fantasy Magazine (www.fantasy-magazine.com), published by Sean Wallace and edited by Cat Rambo, had good work (almost all of it fantasy or slipstream, unsurprisingly enough, although there was one strong SF story by Lavie Tidhar) by Nancy Kress, Tanith Lee, Patricia Russo, Ruth Nestvold, Jay Lake, John Mantooth, and others.

Other than the stories selected by me for the issue I guest-edited, which I won't mention, *Subterranean* (http://subterraneanpress.com), edited by William K. Schafer, had lots of good work, some of it first-rate, by Alexander C. Irvine, Garth Nix, Tim Pratt, James P. Blaylock, Kim Newman, Kris Nelscott, Lewis Shiner, and others.

The Australian popular-science magazine *Cosmos* (www.cosmosmagazine .com) runs a story per issue, usually SF, selected by fiction editor Damien Broderick, and also puts new fiction not published in the print magazine up on their website. They had a strong story by Karl Bunker this year, as well as interesting stuff by Craig DeLancey, Greg Mellor, Stuart Gibbon, V.G. Kemerer, and others.

The flamboyantly titled *Orson Scott Card's InterGalactic Medicine Show* (www.intergalacticmedicineshow.com), edited by Edmund R. Schubert under the direction of Card himself, had good work by Peter S. Beagle, Mary Robinette Kowal, Ian Creasey, Tim Pratt, Aliette de Bodard, Eugie Foster, Tony Pi, and others, including a number of stories, both reprint and original, by Card. Although they publish both SF and fantasy (rarely slipstream), they tend to lean toward fantasy, which tends to be of generally higher quality than their SF.

Ideomancer Speculative Fiction (www.ideomancer.com), edited by Leah Bobet and a large group of other editors that includes Elizabeth Bear and John Bowker, published good stuff by Steven Mohan, Jr., Swapna Kishore, and others.

A new ezine devoted to "literary adventure fantasy," *Beneath Ceaseless Skies* (www.beneath-ceaseless-skies.com), edited by Scott H. Andrews, had a strong year, featuring good work by Aliette de Bodard, Rachel Swirsky, Ian McHugh, Richard Parks, Sarah L. Edwards, K.D. Wentworth, and others.

Shadow Unit (www.shadowunit.org) is a website devoted to publishing stories drawn from an imaginary TV show, something I find unexciting, but which has strongly impressed other critics, and which has drawn top people such as Elizabeth Bear, Holly Black, Emma Bull, and others.

A mix of science fact articles and fiction is available from the ezine *Futurismic* (http://futurismic.com) and from *Escape Velocity* (www. escapevelocitymagazine.com).

Book View Café (www.bookviewcafe.com) is a consortium of over twenty professional authors, including Vonda N. McIntyre, Laura Anne Gilman, Sarah Zettel, Brenda Clough, and others, who have created a new website where work by them – mostly reprints, and some novel excerpts – is made available for free.

Another new fantasy-oriented site, *Heroic Fantasy Quarterly* (www. heroicfantasyquarterly.com), started up this year, as did an SF site selling downloads and PDFs (a model which didn't work for *Aeon*), *M-Brane SF* (http://mbranesf.blogspot.com).

Below this point, it becomes harder to find center-core SF, and most of the stories are slipstream or literary surrealism. Sites that feature those, as well as fantasy (and, occasionally, some SF) include Rudy Rucker's *Flurb* (www.flurb.net), *RevolutionSF* (www.revolutionsf.com), *CoyoteWild* (www.coyotewildmag.com), *Heliotrope* (www.heliotropemag.com), and the somewhat less slipstreamish *Bewildering Stories* (www.bewilderingstories.com).

However, original fiction isn't all that can be found on the Internet – there are a lot of good *reprint* SF and fantasy stories out there too, usually available for free. On all of the sites that make their fiction available for free, *Strange Horizons, Tor.com, Fantasy Magazine, Subterranean, Abyss & Apex, Jim Baen's Universe,* and so on, you can also access large archives of previously published material as well as stuff from the 'current issue.' Most of the sites that are associated with existent print magazines, such as *Asimov's, Analog, Weird Tales,* and *The Magazine of Fantasy & Science Fiction,* make previously published fiction and nonfiction available for access on their sites, and also regularly run teaser excerpts from stories in forthcoming issues. Hundreds of out-of-print titles, both genre and mainstream, are also available for free download from Project Gutenberg (http://promo.net/pg/), and a large selection of novels and a few collections can also be accessed for free, to be either downloaded or read on-screen, at the Baen Free Library (www.baen.com/library). Sites such as Infinity Plus (http://www.infinityplus.co.uk) and the Infinite Matrix (www.infinitematrix.net) may have died as active sites, but their extensive archives of previously published material are still accessible.

An even greater range of reprint stories becomes available, though, if you're willing to pay a small fee for them. Perhaps the best and the longest-established place to find such material is Fictionwise (www.fictionwise.com), where you can buy downloadable e-books and stories to read on your PDA, Kindle, or home computer; in addition to individual stories, you can also buy 'fiction bundles' here, which amount to electronic collections; as well as a selection of novels in several different genres – you can also subscribe to downloadable versions of several of the SF magazines here, including *Asimov's, Analog, F&SF,* and *Interzone,* in a number of different formats. A similar site is ElectricStory (www.electricstory.com), where in addition to the fiction for sale, you can also access free movie reviews by Lucius Shepard, articles by Howard Waldrop, and other critical material.

Finding fiction to read, though, is not the only reason for SF fans to go on the Internet. There are also many general genre-related sites of interest to be found, most of which publish reviews of books as well as of movies and TV shows, sometimes comics or computer games or anime, many of which also feature interviews, critical articles, and genre-oriented news of various kinds. The best such site is easily Locus Online (www.locusmag.com), the online version of the newsmagazine *Locus,* where you can access an incredible amount of information – including book reviews, critical lists, obituaries, links to reviews and essays appearing outside the genre, and links to extensive database archives such as the Locus Index to Science Fiction and the Locus Index to Science Fiction Awards – it's rare when I don't find myself accessing Locus Online several times a day. Other major general-interest sites include SF Site (www.sfsite.com), SFRevu (www.sfrevu .com), SFCrowsnest (www.sfcrowsnest.com), SFScope (www.sfscope. com), io9 (http://io9.com), Green Man Review (http://greenmanreview. com), The Agony Column (http://trashotron.com/agony), SFFWorld.com (www.sffworld.com), SFReader.com (www.sfreader.com), SFWatcher.com (www.sfwatcher.com), and Pat's Fantasy Hotlist (www.fantasyhotlist.blogs-pot.com). One of the best of the general-interest sites, the Internet Review of Science Fiction, has unfortunately died. Another, *Science Fiction Weekly*, first merged with news site Sci Fi Wire to form a new site called Sci Fi Wire, and then transformed to Syfy (www.syfy.com) when its parent channel changed its name from the Sci Fi Channel to Syfy as well, dropping all its columnists and book reviews along the way to concentrate exclusively on media news and reviews – and thus making itself largely uninteresting to me. A great research site, invaluable if you want bibliographic information about SF and fantasy writers, is Fantastic Fiction (www. fantasticfiction.co.uk). Reviews of short fiction as opposed to novels are very hard to find anywhere, with the exception of *Locus*, but you can find reviews of both current and past short fiction at Best SF (www.bestsf.net), as well as at pioneering short-fiction review site Tangent (www.tangentonline. com), which had gone on a long hiatus but returned to active status in 2009 – ironically, just as its rival The Fix, launched by a former Tangent staffer, seems to have gone inactive. Other sites of interest include: SFF NET (www.sff.net) which features dozens of home pages and "newsgroups" for SF writers; the Science Fiction & Fantasy Writers of America page (www.sfwa.org), where genre news, obituaries, award information, and recommended reading lists can be accessed; Ansible (http://news.ansible. co.uk/), the online version of multiple Hugo-winner David Langford's long-running fanzine *Ansible*; and a number of sites where podcasts and SF-oriented radio plays can be accessed: Audible.com (www.audible.com), Escape Pod (http://escapepod.org), StarShipSofa (www.starshipsofa.com), and PodCastle (http://podcastle.org).

The much-heralded 'New Golden Age' of original anthologies may have reached its high-water mark in 2008, and even receded a bit. There were still plenty of anthologies out, especially from small presses and books available as downloads online, but several of the most prominent high-end original series, upon which many hopes were pinned, have died. Of the three much-talked-about original anthology series launched in 2007, *Fast Forward*, edited by Lou Anders, *The Solaris Book of New Science Fiction*, edited by George Mann, and *Eclipse*, edited by Jonathan Strahan, only *Eclipse* survives at the end of the year. A shame, because both other series had a lot to recommend them.

The fact is, although many good individual stories were published, it was something of a lackluster year for original anthologies as a whole, with no clear-cut standouts. In terms of literary quality, judging the stories *as* stories, without taking genre classification into consideration, the strongest of the year's anthologies was clearly *Eclipse Three* (Night Shade Books), edited by Jonathan Strahan – I personally found it somewhat disappointing, though, that there was relatively little science fiction here, most of the contents being fantasy or slipstream. Best stories in *Eclipse Three* were by Maureen F. McHugh and Nicola Griffith, although there was also good stuff of various sorts by Caitlin R. Kiernan, Daniel Abraham, Karen Joy Fowler, Peter S. Beagle, and others. *The Solaris Book of New Science Fiction, Volume 3* (Solaris), edited by George Mann, was mostly SF, and featured strong work by Paul Cornell, Warren Hammond, Alastair Reynolds, John Meaney, and others. There were two anthologies from DAW Books this year which are a cut above the usual DAW anthology product: a strong steampunk/alternate history anthology, *Other Earths* (DAW), edited by Nick Gevers and Jay Lake, which featured a standout story by Robert Charles Wilson, and good work by Gene Wolfe, Theodora Goss, Liz Williams, and others; and *We Think, Therefore We Are* (DAW), edited by Peter Crowther. *We Think, Therefore We Are* wasn't as strong as past Crowther anthologies such as *Moon Shots* have been, but still featured interesting stuff by Chris Roberson, Keith Brooke, Patrick O'Leary, Robert Reed, and others.

A cut below this level, the strongest story in *Federations* (Prime), edited by John Joseph Adams, an anthology of stories inspired by *Star Trek* (which looked for work that 'builds on those same tropes and traditions'), was by John C. Wright, but there was also good work by Mary Rosenblum, Allen Steele, Yoon Ha Lee, and others, as well as good reprint stories by Alastair Reynolds, Robert Silverberg, George R.R. Martin and George Guthridge, Lois McMaster Bujold, Orson Scott Card, and others. *Clockwork Phoenix 2*, edited by Mike Allen, was mostly fantasy instead of science fiction, unlike the original volume, but had worthwhile stuff by Tanith Lee, Mary Robinette Kowal, Ann Leckie, and others. Mike Ashley's anthology with the somewhat overheated title of *The Mammoth Book of Mindblowing SF: The 21 Finest Stories of Awesome Science Fiction* was mostly a reprint anthology, with strong reprints by Gregory Benford, Michael Swanwick, Terry Bisson, Geoffrey A. Landis, Alastair Reynolds, James Blish, and others, but did find room for intriguing original stuff by Robert Reed, Eric Brown, Adam Roberts, Stephen Baxter, Paul Di Filippo, and others.

One of the year's best anthologies was published by an ultra-small press in Australia, and is going to be very difficult for most readers to find. Neverthless, *X6* (Coeur de Lion), a collection of six novellas edited by Keith Stevenson, features two of the best stories of the year – an evocative reinvention of the selkie legend by Margo Lanagan and a brutal, hard-hitting examination of a disintegrating future Australia by Paul Haines – as well as good work by Terry Dowling and Cat Sparks. Not quite as successful as *X6*, but still featuring some substantial work, is another novella collection from another small press, *Panverse One: Five Original Novellas of Fantasy and Science Fiction* (Panverse Press), edited by Dario Ciriello. The best story here is probably an atmospheric fantasy by Alan Smale, centering on a strange space-time discontinuity that opens up around Emily Brontë of *Wuthering Heights* fame, but there is also good work by Jason K. Chapman and Andrew Tisbert. I had high hopes for another ultra-small press anthology, *When It Changed* (Comma Press), edited by Geoff Ryman, which had an intriguing premise and a good roster of authors, but somehow the final product was mildly disappointing, although there were strong stories there by Adam Roberts, Ryman himself, and others. Another ultra-small press produced the anthology *Footsteps* (Hadley Rille Books), edited by Jay Lake and Eric T. Reynolds, a somewhat lackluster volume of Moon landing–related stories, although there was solid work there by James Van Pelt, Brenda Cooper, and others.

We're supposed to consider the British publication *Postscripts* (PS Publishing) to be an anthology now rather than a magazine, so this seems like the appropriate place to take a look at it. They managed three issues this year, one of them a double issue: *Postscripts 18: This Is the Summer of Love*, *Postscripts 19: Enemy of the Good*, and *Postscripts 20/21: Edison's Frankenstein*, all edited by Peter Crowther and Nick Gevers. These three volumes maintain a reasonably high level of literary accomplishment, although none of them matches 2008's *Postscripts 15*; there's good work in the three volumes by Chris Roberson, Lisa Tuttle, Daniel Abraham, Paul Park, M.K. Hobson, Matthew Hughes, Marly Youmans, and others.

Pleasant but minor science fiction anthologies included *Intelligent Design* (DAW Books), edited by Denise Little, *Gamer Fantastic* (DAW Books), edited by Martin H. Greenberg and Kerrie Hughes, and a mixed SF and fantasy anthology, *Warrior Wisewoman 2* (Norilana), edited by Roby James.

Noted without comment is *The New Space Opera 2*, edited by Gardner Dozois and Jonathan Strahan.

The best original fantasy anthology of the year (although it contains a couple of SF stories) may have been *Firebirds Soaring* (Firebird), edited by Sharyn November, which featured excellent work by Jo Walton, Margo Lanagan, Chris Roberson, Nina Kiriki Hoffman, Ellen Klages, Louise Marley, and others. *Troll's Eye View: A Book of Villainous Tales* (Viking), edited by Ellen Datlow and Terry Windling, is aimed at a younger audience than most of their other collections of fairy tale retellings have been – best story here is by Kelly Link, although there's also entertaining work by Peter S. Beagle, Garth Nix, Delia Sherman, Jane Yolen, and others.

Pleasant but minor original fantasy anthologies included *Swordplay* (DAW Books), edited by Denise Little; *The Trouble with Heroes* (DAW Books), edited by Denise Little; *Lace and Blade 2* (Norilana Books), edited by Deborah J. Ross; *Ages of Wonder* (DAW Books), edited by Julie E. Czerneda and Rob St. Martin; *Strip Mauled* (Baen Books), edited by Esther M. Friesner; *Witch Way to the Mall* (Baen Books), edited by Esther

M. Friesner; *Terribly Twisted Tales* (DAW Books), edited by Jean Rabe and Martin H. Greenberg; *Under the Rose* (Norilana Books), edited by Dave Hutchinson; and *Crime Spells* (DAW Books), edited by Martin H. Greenberg and Loren L. Coleman. There was also another installment in a long-running fantasy anthology series, *Marion Zimmer Bradley's Swords and Sorceress XXIV* (Norilana Books), edited by Elisabeth Waters.

Noted without comment are *Songs of the Dying Earth* (Subterranean Press/HarperCollins UK), an anthology of new fantasy stories inspired by the work of Jack Vance, edited by George R.R. Martin and Gardner Dozois, and *The Dragon Book* (Ace Books) edited by Jack Dann and Gardner Dozois.

The year's best original horror anthologies (although both have fantasy stories and even SF stories in them) were *Lovecraft Unbound* (Dark Horse Comics), a mixed original (mostly) and reprint anthology, and *Poe* (Solaris), an all-original, both edited by Ellen Datlow, and both collecting stories 'inspired' by the work of their respective authors (H. P. Lovecraft and Edgar Allan Poe, naturally). The best story in *Lovecraft Unbound* happens to be the only SF story, by Sarah Monette and Elizabeth Bear, but the book also has strong original work by Laird Barron, William Browning Spencer, Lavie Tidhar, Holly Philips, Richard Bowes, Marc Laidlaw, and others, and good reprint stuff by Caitlín R. Kiernan, Michael Chabon, and others. *Poe* features good work by Suzy McKee Charnas, Lucius Shepard, Pat Cadigan, Sharyn McCrumb, Glen Hirshberg, Laird Barron, Gregory Frost, Kim Newman, and others. *Tesseracts Thirteen* (Hades/EDGE Science Fiction and Fantasy), edited by Nancy Kilpatrick and David Morrell, functioned as a dedicated horror anthology this year. *Twilight Zone: 19 Original Stories on the 50th Anniversary* (Tor Books), edited by Carol Serling, is self-explanatory. There were also a number of large retrospective reprint horror anthologies, discussed below.

Slipstream anthologies included: *Interfictions 2: An Anthology of Interstitial Writing* (Small Beer Press), edited by Delia Sherman and Christopher Barzak; *Conjunctions: 52, Betwixt the Between: Impossible Realism* (Bard College), edited by Bradford Morrow and Brian Evenson; and an anthology of flash fiction, *Last Drink Bird Head* (Ministry of Whimsy), edited by Ann VanderMeer and Jeff VanderMeer.

Shared world anthologies included *Wild Cards: Suicide Kings* (Tor Books), edited by George R.R. Martin; *Man-Kzin Wars XII* (Baen Books), created by Larry Niven; *Changing the World: All New Tales of Valdemar* (DAW Books), edited by Mercedes Lackey; *New Ceres Nights* (Twelfth Planet Press), edited by Alisa Krasnostein and Tehani Wesely; *Grants Pass* (Morrigan Books), edited by Jennifer Brozek and Amanda Pillar; and *The Grantville Gazette V* (Baen Books), edited by Eric Flint.

A long-running series featuring novice work by beginning writers, some of whom may later turn out to be important talents, changed editors this year, as the late Algis Budrys handed the torch to K.D. Wentworth, who continued the series with *L. Ron Hubbard Presents Writers of the Future Volume XXV* (Galaxy Press).

A relatively new phenomenon is paranormal romance anthologies. They included *Strange Brew* (St. Martin's Griffin), edited by P.N. Elrod, and a bunch of anthologies with no editor listed: *Mean Streets* (Roc), *Must Love Hellhounds* (Berkley Books), and *Never After* (Jove).

As in 2008, there were a lot of stories about robots this year, roughly divided into stories about robots working out compassionate relationships with humans and robots creating their own societies, loosely modeled on human culture, after all the humans are dead. As has been the case for a couple of years now, there were a number of stories that featured flying sailing ships (shades of *Peter Pan!*) and/or zeppelins. There were lots of steampunk stories, in both print and electronic venues, and, in spite of the death of dedicated alternate history magazine *Paradox*, still many alternate history stories as well. (Judging whether a given story is steampunk or alternate history is sometimes a judgment call, as by definition all steampunk is also alternate history, but you can usually tell where the strongest emphasis lies.) There weren't as many zombie stories as last year, although there was another dedicated zombie anthology, so perhaps they will rest quietly in their graves for a bit. Lots of vampire stories, it almost goes without saying.

SF continued to appear in places well outside accepted genre boundaries, from science magazines *Cosmos*, *Nature*, and *New Scientist* to *The New Yorker*.

Finding individual pricings for all of the items from small presses mentioned in this summation has become too time-intensive, and since several of the same small presses publish anthologies, novels, *and* short-story collections, it seems silly to repeat addresses for them in section after section. Therefore, I'm going to attempt to list here, in one place, all the addresses for small presses that have books mentioned here or there in this summation, whether from the anthology section, the novel section, or the short-story collection section, and, where known, their website addresses. That should make it easy enough for the reader to look up the individual price of any book mentioned that isn't from a regular trade publisher; such books are less likely to be found in your average bookstore, or even in a chain superstore, and so will probably have to be mail-ordered. Many publishers seem to sell only online, through their websites, and some will only accept payment through PayPal. Many books, even from some of the smaller presses, are also available through Amazon.com.

Addresses: **PS Publishing**, Grosvenor House, 1 New Road, Hornsea, East Yorkshire, HU18 1PG, England; www.pspublishing.co.uk. **Golden Gryphon Press**, 3002 Perkins Road, Urbana, IL 61802; www.goldengryphon. com. **NESFA Press**, P.O. Box 809, Framingham, MA 01701-0809; www. nesfa.org. **Subterranean Press**, P.O. Box 190106, Burton, MI 48519; www. subterraneanpress.com. **Old Earth Books**, P.O. Box 19951, Baltimore, MD 21211-0951; www.oldearthbooks.com. **Tachyon Publications**, 1459 18th St. #139, San Francisco, CA 94107; www.tachyonpublications.com. **Night Shade Books**, 1470 NW Saltzman Road, Portland, OR 97229; www. nightshadebooks.com. **Five Star**, 295 Kennedy Memorial Drive, Waterville,

ME 04901; www.galegroup.com/fivestar. **NewCon Press**, www.newconpress. co.uk. **Small Beer Press**, 150 Pleasant St. #306, Easthampton, MA 01027; www.smallbeerpress.com. **Locus Press**, P.O. Box 13305, Oakland, CA 94661; www.locusmag.com. **Crescent Books**, Mercat Press Ltd., 10 Coates Crescent, Edinburgh, EH3 7AL, Scotland. **Wildside Press/ Borgo Press**, P.O. Box 301, Holicong, PA 18928-0301; www.wildsidepress.com. **Edge Science Fiction and Fantasy Publishing, Inc./Tesseract Books**, P.O. Box 1714, Calgary, Alberta, T2P 2L7, Canada; www.edgewebsite.com. **Aqueduct Press**, P.O. Box 95787, Seattle, WA 98145-2787; www.aqueductpress. com. **Phobos Books**, 200 Park Avenue South, Suite 1109, New York, NY 10003. **Fairwood Press**, 5203 Quincy Ave. SE, Auburn, WA 98092; www. fairwoodpress.com. **BenBella Books**, 6440 N. Central Expressway, Suite 508, Dallas, TX 75206; www.benbellabooks.com. **Darkside Press**, Darkside Press & Midnight House, 107 E. Green St., Gallup, NM 87301; www. darkmidhouse.com. **Haffner Press**, 5005 Crooks Rd., Suite 35, Royal Oak, MI 48073-1239; www.haffnerpress.com. **North Atlantic Books**, P.O. Box 12327, Berkeley, CA, 94701; www.northatlanticbooks.com. **Prime Books**, P.O. Box 36503, Canton, OH, 44735; www.prime-books.com. **MonkeyBrain Books**, 11204 Crossland Drive, Austin, TX 78726; www.monkeybrainbooks. com. **Wesleyan University Press**, University Press of New England, Order Dept., 37 Lafayette St., Lebanon NH 03766-1405; www.wesleyan.edu/ wespress/. **Agog! Press**, P.O. Box U302, University of Wollongong, NSW 2522, Austrailia. **Wheatland Press**, P. O. Box 1818, Wilsonville, OR 97070; www.wheatlandpress.com. **MirrorDanse Books**, P.O. Box 3542, Parramatta NSW 2124, Australia; www.tabula-rasa.info/MirrorDanse. **Arsenal Pulp Press**, 103-1014 Homer Street, Vancouver, BC, V6B 2W9, Canada; www.arsenalpulp.com. **DreamHaven Books**, 2301 East 38th Street, Minneapolis, MN 55406; www.dreamhavenbooks.com. **Elder Signs Press/ Dimensions Books**, www.dimensionsbooks.com. **Chaosium**, Chaosium Inc., 22568 Mission Boulevard #423, Hayward, CA 94541-5116; www.chaosium.com. **Spire Books**, P.O. Box 3005, Radford, VA 24143. **SCIFI, Inc.**, P.O. Box 8442, Van Nuys, CA 91409-8442. **Omnidawn Publishing**, 1632 Elm Avenue, Richmond, California 94805-1614; www.omnidawn.com. **CSFG**, Canberra Speculative Fiction Guild, www.csfg.org.au. **Hadley Rille Books**, P.O. Box 25466, Overland Park, KS 66225; www.hadleyrillebooks.com. **ISFiC Press**, 707 Sapling Lane, Deerfield, IL 60015-3969; www.isficpress.com. **Suddenly Press**, c/o Brian Youmans, 49 Magnolia Street, Arlington, MA 02474; www.suddenlypress.com. **Sandstone Press**, P.O. Box 5725, One High St., Dingwall, Ross-shire, IV15 9WJ, Scotland; www.sandstonepress.com. **Tropism Press**, 1034 McKinley Ave., Oakland, CA 94610; www.tropismpress.com. **SF Poetry Association**, www.sfpoetry. com. **DH Press**, www.diamondbookdistributors.com. **Kurodahan Press**, c/o Intercom, Ltd., 3-9-10-403 Tenjin, Chuo-ku, Fukuoka, 810-0001 Japan; www.kurodahan.com. **Ramble House**, 443 Gladstone Blvd., Shreveport, LA 71104; www.ramblehouse.com. **Interstitial Arts Foundation**, P.O. Box 35862, Boston, MA, 02135; www.interstitialarts.org. **Raw Dog Screaming**, www.rawdogscreaming.com. **Three Legged Fox Books**, 98 Hythe Road, Brighton, BN1 6JS, UK; www.threeleggedfox.co.uk. **Norilana Books**, P.O. Box 2188, Winnetka, CA 91396; www.norilana.com. **Coeur de Lion**, 56 Serpentine Road, Kirrawee NSW 2232, Australia; www.coeurdelion.com.au. **PARSEC**, www.parsecink.org. **Robert J. Sawyer Books**, Fitzhenry & Whiteside, 195 Allstate Parkway, Markham, ON, L3R 4T8, Canada; www.sfwriter.com/rjsbooks.htm. **Rackstraw Press**, http://rackstrawpress.nfshost.com. **Candlewick**, www.candlewick.com. **Zubaan**, 128 B, First Floor, Shahpur Jat, New Delhi 110019, India; www.zubaanbooks.com. **Utter Tower**, www.threeleggedfox.co.uk. **Spilt Milk Press**, P.O. Box 266, Bettendorf, IA 52722; www.electricvelocipede.com. **Paper Golem**, www.papergolem.com. **Galaxy Press**, 7051 Hollywood Blvd., Suite 200, Hollywood, CA 90028; www.galaxypress.com. **Twelfth Planet Press**, P.O. Box 3027, Yokine, WA, 6060, Australia; http://twelfthplanetpress.wordpress.com. **Senses Five Press**, www.sensesfive.com. **Elastic Press**, 85 Gertrude Road, Norwich, NR3 4SG, UK; www.elasticpress.com. **Lethe Press**, 118 Heritage Ave., Maple Shade, NJ 08052; www.lethepressbooks.com. **Two Cranes Press**, www.twocranespress.com. **Wordcraft of Oregon**, P.O. Box 3235, La Grande, OR 97850; www.wordcraftoforegon.com.

In spite of the recession, there were still a huge number of novels published in the SF/fantasy genres during the year – more than ever before, in fact, and it looks likely that there'll be even more next year.

According to the newsmagazine *Locus*, there were a record 2,901 books 'of interest to the SF field' published in 2009, up 2 per cent from 2,843 titles in 2008. Sixty-seven percent of those were new titles, not reprints. (It's worth noting that this total doesn't count novels offered as downloads on the Internet or on Kindle, media tie-in novels, gaming novels, novelizations of genre movies, or most Print on Demand books – all of which would swell the total by hundreds if counted.) Paranormal romances remained strong, with 339 titles this year as opposed to 328 in 2008; one of the paranormal romance writers, Stephanie Meyer, edged out J. K. Rowling in sales, and others such as Charlaine Harris, Laurell K. Hamilton, Jim Butcher, and Diana Gabaldon are among the bestselling writers in America. The number of new SF novels was down slightly, by 7 per cent, to 232 as opposed to 2008's total of 249 (still far larger than the field was even a few years back, and more novels than any one person is going to have a chance to read in the course of a year). The number of new fantasy novels was up by 30 per cent, to 572 titles as opposed to 2008's total of 439. Horror novels were up to 251 titles as opposed to 2008's total of 175, the biggest gain since the Big Horror Boom busted; in 2002, for instance, there were only 112 horror titles published.

As usual, busy with all the reading I have to do at shorter lengths, I didn't have time to read many novels myself this year, so I'll limit myself to mentioning the novels that received a lot of attention and acclaim in 2009. These include:

Julian Comstock: A Story of 22nd-Century America (Tor Books), by Robert Charles Wilson; *Steal Across the Sky* (Tor Books), by Nancy Kress;

Drood (Little, Brown and Company), by Dan Simmons; *The Empress of Mars* (Tor Books), by Kage Baker; *The Caryatids* (Del Rey/Ballantine Books), by Bruce Sterling; *This Is Not a Game* (Orbit), by Walter Jon Williams; *House of Suns* (Ace Science Fiction), by Alastair Reynolds; *The Revolution Business* (Tor Fantasy), by Charles Stross; *Gardens of the Sun* (Gollancz), by Paul McAuley; *The High City* (Forge), by Cecelia Holland; *Ark* (Gollancz), by Stephen Baxter; *The Sunless Countries* (Tor Books), by Karl Schroeder; *Transition* (Orbit Books), by Iain M. Banks; *Galileo's Dream* (HarperVoyager), by Kim Stanley Robinson; *Mind Over Ship* (Tor Books), by David Marusek; *Yellow Blue Tibia* (Gollancz), by Adam Roberts; *The Devil's Alphabet* (Del Rey), by Daryl Gregory; *Boneshaker* (Tor Books), by Cherie Priest; *The City & The City* (Del Rey), by China Mieville; *Coyote Horizon* (Ace), by Allen Steele; *Regenesis* (DAW Books), by C. J. Cherryh; *Conspirator* (DAW Books), by C. J. Cherryh; *The Walls of the Universe* (Tor Science Fiction), by Paul Melko; *Avilion* (Gollancz), by Robert Holdstock; *The Magicians* (Viking Press), by Lev Grossman; *Chasing the Dragon* (Pyr), by Justina Robson; *The Steel Remains* (Ballantine Books), by Richard K. Morgan; *The Price of Spring* (Tor Fantasy), by Daniel Abraham; *The Red Tree* (Roc Trade), by Caitlin R. Kiernan; *Green* (Tor Books), by Jay Lake; *The Knights of the Cornerstone* (Ace Books), by James P. Blaylock; *Buyout* (Del Rey), by Alexander Irvine; *Palimpset* (Bantam Spectra), by Catherynne M. Valente; *Hope's Folly* (Bantam), by Linnea Sinclair; *End of the Century* (Pyr), by Chris Roberson; *Duplicate Effort* (Roc Books), by Kristine Kathryn Rusch; *Diving into the Wreck* (Pyr), by Kristine Kathryn Rusch; *Turn Coat* (Roc), by Jim Butcher; *Corambis* (Ace Books), by Sarah Monette; *The Sharing Knife* (Eos), by Lois McMaster Bujold; *Buyout* (Del Rey), by Alexander Irvine; *Storm from the Shadows* (Baen Books), by David Weber; *Escape from Hell* (Tor Books), by Larry Niven and Jerry Pournelle; *Heroes of the Valley* (Hyperion), by Jonathan Stroud; *Bone Crossed* (Ace), Patricia Briggs; *Unseen Academicals* (Harper), by Terry Pratchett; and *Under the Dome* (Scribner), by Stephen King.

Small presses once published mostly collections and anthologies, but these days they're active in the novel market as well. Novels issued by small presses this year, some of them among the year's best, included: *The Empress of Mars* (Subterranean Press), by Kage Baker; *The Hotel Under the Sand* (Tachyon Publications), by Kage Baker; *Lifelode* (NESFA Press), by Jo Walton; *The Shadow Pavillion* (Night Shade Books), by Liz Williams; *Madness of Flowers: A Novel of the City Imperishable* (Night Shade Books), by Jay Lake; *The Proteus Sails Again* (Subterranean Press), by Thomas M. Disch; and *Those Who Went Remain There Still* (Subterranean Press), by Cherie Priest.

The year's first novels included: *The Windup Girl* (Night Shade Books), by Paolo Bacigalupi; *The Manual of Detection* (Penguin Group), by Jedediah Berry; *Lamentation* (Tor Books), by Ken Scholes; *Harbinger* (Fairwood Press), by Jack Skillingstead; *Prospero Lost* (Tor Books), by L. Jagi Lamplighter; *Total Oblivion, More or Less* (Ballantine Spectra), by

Alan DeNiro; and *The Adamantine Palace* (Gollancz), by Stephen Deas. Of these, *The Windup Girl* got by far the best notices, with several critics calling it not only the best first novel of the year but the best science fiction novel of the year, period.

Associational novels by people connected with the science fiction and fantasy fields included: *Four Freedoms* (HarperCollins), by John Crowley; *The Dead Man's Brother* (Hard Case Crime), by Roger Zelazny; *Mariposa* (Vanguard Press), by Greg Bear; *The Asylum Prophecies* (Leisure Books), by Daniel Keyes; and *Chronic City* (Doubleday), by Jonathan Lethem. Ventures into the genre, or at least the ambiguous fringes of it, by well-known mainstream authors, included: *Inherent Vice* (Penguin Press), by Thomas Pynchon; *The Year of the Flood* (Doubleday), by Margaret Atwood; and *Her Fearful Symmetry* (Scribner), by Audrey Niffenegger. A surprise bestseller, *Pride and Prejudice and Zombies* (Quirk Books), by Jane Austen and Seth Grahame-Smith, has already spawned several sequels, and may launch a whole new subgenre, the literary classic/horror mash-up.

There were again some good individual novellas published as chap-books, although perhaps nothing that really stood out. Subterranean Press published *The Women of Nell Gwynne's*, by Kage Baker; *The God Engines*, by John Scalzi; *Seven for a Secret*, by Elizabeth Bear; and *Alpha and Omega*, by Patricia Briggs. PS Publishing brought out *Starfall*, by Stephen Baxter; *Ars Memoriae*, by Beth Bernobich; *The Night Cache*, by Andy Duncan; and *Gilbert and Edgar on Mars*, by Eric Brown. NewCon Press brought out *The Push*, by David Hutchinson, and *Starship Fall*, by Eric Brown. MonkeyBrain Books published *Death of a Starship*, by Jay Lake. Hadley Rille Books published *The Priestess and the Slave*, by Jenny Blackford.

Novel omnibuses this year included: *The Books of the Wars* (Baen Books), by Mark Geston; *Divisions* (Orb), by Ken MacLeod; *Exile and Glory* (Baen Books), by Jerry Pournelle; *Fires of Freedom* (Baen Books), by Jerry Pournelle; *Triplanetary* (Cosmos Books), by E.E. Smith; *This Fortress World* (Fantastic Books), by James Gunn; and *VALIS and Later Novels* (Library of America), by Philip K. Dick, as well as many omnibus novel volumes published by the Science Fiction Book Club. (Omnibuses that contain both short stories *and* novels can be found listed in the short story section.)

A lot of long out-of-print stuff has come back into print in the last couple of years in commercial trade editions. Not even counting Print on Demand books from places such as Wildside Press, the reprints issued by the Science Fiction Book Club, and the availability of out-of-print books as electronic downloads from Internet sources such as Fictionwise, that makes this the best time in decades to pick up reissued editions of formerly long-out-of-print novels. Here are some out-of-print titles that came back *into* print this year, although producing a definitive list of reissued novels is probably diffi-cult to impossible:

Tor Books reissued *The Currents of Space*, by Isaac Asimov. Orb Books reissued *The Stars, Like Dust*, by Isaac Asimov; *Beyond the Blue Event Horizon*, by Frederik Pohl; *Flashforward*, by Robert J. Sawyer; *Bone Dance*, by Emma Bull; and *Dying Inside* and *A Time of Changes*, both by Robert Silverberg. Baen Books reissued *The Puppet Masters*, by Robert A. Heinlein; *Rx for Chaos*, by Christopher Anvil; and *A Sense of Infinity*, by Howard L. Myers. Pyr reissued *Desolation Road*, by Ian McDonald. Orbit reissued *Against a Dark Background*, by Iain M. Banks; and *The Naked God* and *The Neutronium Alchemist*, both by Peter F. Hamilton. Cosmos reissued *The Moon Pool*, by A. Merritt; and *The 13th Immortal*, by Robert Silverberg. Ace reissued *Ariel*, by Steven R. Boyett. Paizo Publishing reissued *Robots Have No Tails*, by Henry Kuttner; and *The Sword of Rhiannon*, by Leigh Brackett. Fantastic Books reissued *Pennterra*, by Judith Moffett; and *The Dreaming* and *The Judas Mandala*, both by Damien Broderick. New York Review Books Classics reissued *Inverted World*, by Christopher Priest; and *The Chrysalids*, by John Wyndham. Crippen & Landru reissued *A Little Intelligence*, by Robert Silverberg and Randall Garrett. Wyrm Publishers reissued *Shriek: An Afterword*, by Jeff VanderMeer. Hippocampus Press reissued *The Hound Hunters*, by Adam Niswander. Penguin Group reissued *The Prisoner*, by Thomas M. Disch. MonkeyBrain Books reissued *Two Hawks from Earth*, by Philip José Farmer.

As has been true for several years now, this was a good year for short story collections, and it was a particularly good year for career-spanning retrospective collections. The year's best nonretrospective collection may have been *Cyberabad Days* (Pyr), by Ian McDonald, although it was given a run for its money by *Wireless* (Ace), by Charles Stross, and two collections by Greg Egan, *Oceanic* (Gollancz) and *Crystal Nights and Other Stories* (Subterranean Press). Also first-rate were *We Never Talk About My Brother* (Tachyon Publications), by Peter S. Beagle; *The Buonarotti Quartet* (Aqueduct Press), by Gwyneth Jones; *Thousandth Night/Minla's Flowers* (Subterranean Press), by Alastair Reynolds; *The Radio Magician and Other Stories* (Fairwood Press), by James Van Pelt; *Are You There and Other Stories* (Golden Gryphon Press), by Jack Skillingstead; *Vacancy & Ariel* (Subterranean Press), by Lucius Shepard; and *Uncle Bones* (Fantastic Books), by Damien Broderick. Also good are *Everland and Other Stories* (PS Publishing), by Paul Witcover; *A is for Alien* (Subterranean Press), by Caitlín R. Kiernan; *Collected Stories* (Subterranean Press), by Lewis Shiner; *Dreamwish Beasts and Snarks* (Golden Gryphon Press), by Michael D. Resnick; *Tides from the New Worlds* (Wyrm Publishing), by Tobias S. Buckell; *Eyes Like Sky and Coal and Moonlight* (Paper Golem Press), by Cat Rambo; *A Book of Endings* (Twelfth Planet Press), by Deborah Biancotti; and *We'll Always Have Paris* (William Morrow), by Ray Bradbury.

Strong as this year was in collections, it was even stronger for big retrospective career-spanning collections. There was a bumper crop of them, including: *The Best of Gene Wolfe* (Tor Books), by Gene Wolfe; *Wild Thyme, Green Magic* (Subterranean Press), by Jack Vance; *Trips: The Collected Stories of Robert Silverberg, Volume Four* (Subterranean Press), by Robert Silverberg; *The Best of Michael Moorcock* (Tachyon Publications), by Michael Moorcock; *The Complete Stories of J.G. Ballard* (W. W. Norton &

Company), by J.G. Ballard; *The Collected Stories of Roger Zelazny, Volume One: Threshold* (NESFA Press), by Roger Zelazny; *The Collected Stories of Roger Zelazny, Volume Two: Power & Light* (NESFA Press), by Roger Zelazny; *The Collected Stories of Roger Zelazny, Volume Three: This Mortal Mountain* (NESFA Press), by Roger Zelazny; *The Collected Stories of Roger Zelazny, Volume Four: Last Exit to Babylon* (NESFA Press), by Roger Zelazny; *The Collected Short Works of Poul Anderson, Volume 1: Call Me Joe* (NESFA Press), by Poul Anderson; *The Collected Short Works of Poul Anderson, Volume 2: The Queen of Air and Darkness* (NESFA Press), by Poul Anderson; *Rise of the Terran Empire* (Baen Books), by Poul Anderson; *Selected Short Stories of Lester del Rey, Volume I: War and Space* (NESFA Press), by Lester del Rey; *Magic Mirrors* (NESFA Press), by John Bellairs; *The Shadow on the Doorstep* (ISFiC Press), by James P. Blaylock; *The Return of the Sorcerer: The Best of Clark Ashton Smith* (Prime Books), by Clark Ashton Smith; *The Early Work of Philip K. Dick, Volume 1: The Variable Man and Other Stories* (Prime Books), by Philip K. Dick; *The Early Work of Philip K. Dick, Volume 2: Breakfast at Twilight and Other Stories* (Prime Books), by Philip K. Dick; *Mysteries of the Worm* (Chaosium), by Robert Bloch; and *Slow Sculpture, Volume XII: The Complete Stories of Theodore Sturgeon* (North Atlantic Books), by Theodore Sturgeon.

It should be clear from these lists that there would essentially be no such things as genre short-story collections without the small presses; with the occasional exception of a collection from a trade publisher like Tor or Baen or Ace, most collections these days are done by small press publishers. As you can see, Subterranean and NESFA Press have become particularly important in this area in recent years.

It should also be pointed out that a wide variety of "electronic collections," often called "fiction bundles," too many to individually list here, are also available for downloading online, at sites such as Fictionwise and ElectricStory; the Science Fiction Book Club continues to issue new collections as well.

There were a good number of big retrospective reprint anthologies this year, particularly in horror. Among the nonretrospectives, the crop of 'Best of the Year' anthologies were, as usual, probably your best bet for your money. This crop has been winnowed a bit, and also rearranged, from its peak a couple of years back, but there are still a lot of them. Science fiction was covered by two and a half anthologies (actually, technically, by two anthologies and by two separate half anthologies): the one you are reading at the moment, *The Year's Best Science Fiction: Twenty-Sixth Annual Collection* from St. Martin's Griffin, edited by Gardner Dozois; *Year's Best SF 14* (Eos), edited by David G. Hartwell and Kathryn Cramer; and by the science fiction half of *The Best Science Fiction and Fantasy of the Year: Volume Three* (Night Shade Books), edited by Jonathan Strahan (the "half-a-book," although, of course, in practice it won't divide this neatly). Rich Horton's *Science Fiction: The Best of the Year* series is on hiatus, and will be reinvented in 2010 as *The Year's Best Science Fiction and Fantasy: 2010,* which will dedicate half the book to SF coverage and half to fantasy. There will also be two new series in 2010, one by Ellen Datlow and one by Rich Horton, covering the online world specifically. The annual Nebula Awards anthology, which covers science fiction as well as fantasy of various sorts, functions as a de-facto 'Best of the Year' anthology, although it's not usually counted among them; this year's edition was *Nebula Awards Showcase 2009* (Roc), edited by Ellen Datlow. In 2010, there'll be a new series covering the Hugo winners, edited by Mary Robinette Kowal. The long-running Datlow, Link & Grant *Year's Best Fantasy and Horror* series died early in 2009, after twenty-one years of publication. Datlow immediately went on to start up a new horror series, *The Best Horror of the Year: Volume One* (Night Shade Books); the Kelly Link & Gavin Grant fantasy half has yet to find a new home. There were two Best of the Year anthologies covering horror: the new Datlow book, and *The Mammoth Book of Best New Horror* (Robinson, Carroll & Graff), edited by Stephen Jones, up to its twentieth volume. *Horror: The Best of the Year* (Prime Books), edited by John Gregory Betancourt and Sean Wallace, seems to be at least on hiatus, if not gone. David G. Hartwell and Kathryn Cramer's *Year's Best Fantasy* is still around, but it has changed form and transmogrified in its ninth volume from a print publication issued by Tachyon to a version available as a download or a Print on Demand title from Tor.com. Since the Link/Gavin half of the old *Year's Best Fantasy and Horror* is gone, and Rich Horton's fantasy series will be merged with his science fiction *Best* in 2010, that left fantasy being covered by only two and a half anthologies in 2009, the Hartwell/Cramer, the *Best American Fantasy* (Prime), edited by Ann and Jeff VanderMeer, and by the fantasy half of *The Best SF and Fantasy of the Year: Volume 3* (Night Shade Books), edited by Jonathan Strahan. There was also *The 2009 Rhysling Anthology* (Science Fiction Poetry Association/Prime), edited by Drew Morse, which compiles the Rhysling Award-winning SF poetry of the year.

Perhaps the best reading bargain among the year's stand-alone reprint anthologies is *The Very Best of Fantasy & Science Fiction* (Tachyon Publications), edited by Gordon Van Gelder, a retrospective ranging across the magazine's sixty-year history, and containing classic stories by Alfred Bester, Daniel Keyes, Roger Zelazny, Ursula K. Le Guin, Damon Knight, Peter S. Beagle, Ted Chiang, and others. Another of the year's prominent reprint anthologies is *The Secret History of Science Fiction* (Tachyon Publications), edited by James Patrick Kelly and John Kessel; you don't have to agree with the polemical agenda being promulgated here – which I have my doubts about – to realize that you're getting a great bunch of reprint stories for your money, with a list split between SF writers like Ursula K. Le Guin, Maureen F. McHugh, Gene Wolfe, and Kessel and Kelly themselves, and writers usually more identified as 'mainstream,' such as Michael Chabon, George Saunders, T.C. Boyle, and Margaret Atwood. *The Improbable Adventures of Sherlock Holmes: Tales of Mystery and the Imagination Detailing the Adventures of the World's Most Famous Detective,*

Mr. Sherlock Holmes (Night Shade Books), edited by John Joseph Adams, is a mixed reprint (mostly) and original cross-genre anthology of Sherlock Holmes pastiches by various hands, some of them by SF/fantasy writers and some by writers known better for their work in the mystery genre; there's reprint work here by Neil Gaiman, Stephen Baxter, Laurie R. King, Sharyn McCrumb, Tanith Lee, Stephen King, Peter Tremayne, Vonda N. McIntyre, Chris Roberson, Mary Robinette Kowal, Michael Moorcock, and others, and good original work by Naomi Novik and others.

Lots of fang-flashing vampire stories were reprinted this year, perhaps not surprisingly considering the commercial success of *Twilight* both on the page and on the screen. One such reprint (mostly) anthology was *By Blood We Live* (Night Shade Books), edited by John Joseph Adams, which featured strong reprints by Garth Nix, Tad Williams, Joe Hill, Neil Gaiman, and others, and an original novella by John Langan. *By Blood We Live* and the Otto Penzler anthology mentioned below, bring 121 vampire stories back into print between them, with only one overlap! There have been a *lot* of vampire stories in recent years. The ranks of that other ever-popular monster, the zombie, were a bit thin this year, but there was a dedicated zombie anthology, *The Dead That Walk: Flesh-Eating Stories* (Ulysses Press), edited by Stephen Jones, which has reprints from Joe Hill, Stephen King, Harlan Ellison, Robert E. Howard, H. P. Lovecraft, Clive Barker, and others. Will they ever catch up to the number of vampire stories published? Probably not, since vampire stories had a head start and show no sign of slowing down, but zombie stories are giving it their best shot.

Big retrospective reprint anthologies this year included *American Fantastic Tales, Volume One: Terror and the Uncanny from Poe to the Pulps* (Library of America), edited by Peter Straub; *American Fantastic Tales, Volume Two: Terror and the Uncanny from the 1940s to Now* (Library of America), edited by Peter Straub; and *The Vampire Archives, The Most Complete Volume of Vampire Tales Ever Published* (Vintage), edited by Otto Penzler.

A perspective on SF from other parts of the world is given by *The Apex Book of World SF* (Apex Books), edited by Lavie Tidhar; *Philippine Speculative Fiction IV* (Kestrel IMC), edited by Dean Francis Alfar and Nikki Alfar; and *A Mosque Among the Stars* (ZC Books – also available on Kindle), edited by Muhammad Aurangzeb Ahmad and Ahmed A. Khan.

There were several strong autobiographical, semi-autobiographical, and biographical books out in 2009, and they were probably your best bet for enjoyable reading in the nonfiction category. Most entertaining of these was probably *This is Me, Jack Vance! (Or, More Properly, This is "I")* (Subterranean Press), by Jack Vance, a wry autobiography, but the collection of semiautobiographical essays by Robert Silverberg, *Other Spaces, Other Times* (Nonstop Press), is also great reading.

Intriguing books *about* writers or their work this year included a critical study of the curious career of Hope Mirrlees, *Hope-in-the-Mist: The Extraordinary Career and Mysterious Life of Hope Mirrlees* (Temporary

Culture), by Michael Swanwick; an annotated bibliography of the career
of Tim Powers, *Powers: Secret Histories* (PS Publishing), by John Berlyne;
Haunted Heart: The Life and Times of Stephen King (St. Martin's Griffin),
by Lisa Rogak; *On Joanna Russ* (Wesleyan University Press), edited by Farah
Mendlesohn; *Kim Stanley Robinson Maps the Unimaginable* (McFarland),
edited by William J. Burling; *The Twilight and Other Zones: The Dark Worlds
of Richard Matheson* (Citadel Press), edited by Stanley Wiater, Matthew R.
Bradley, and Paul Stuve; *The Wizard Knight Companion* (Sirius Fiction), by
Michael Andre-Driussi; and *The Authorized Ender Companion* (Tor Books),
by Orson Scott Card and Jake Black.

Books of essays and reviews *by* writers included: *Starcombing* (Cosmos
Books), by David Langford, undoubtedly the funniest of the lot; *Cheek by
Jowl* (Aqueduct Press), by Ursula K. Le Guin; *Canary Fever: Reviews* (Beccon
Publications), by John Clute; *Imagination/Space: Essays and Talks on
Fiction, Feminism, Technology, and Politics* (Aqueduct Press), by Gwyneth
Jones; and *The Fantastic Horizon* (Borgo Press), by Darrell Schweitzer.

Most of the rest of the year's nonfiction books were more academically
oriented. They included: *Unleashing the Strange: Twenty-First Century
Science Fiction Literature* (Borgo Press), by Damien Broderick; *The Science
Fiction Handbook* (Wiley-Blackwell), by Keith M. Booker and Anne-Marie
Thomas; *The Routledge Companion to Science Fiction* (Routledge), edited
by Mark Bould, Andrew M. Butler, Adam Roberts, and Sherryl Vint; *Fifty
Key Figures in Science Fiction* (Routledge), edited by Mark Bould, Andrew
M. Butler, Adam Roberts and Sherryl Vint; *A Guide to Fantasy Literature*
(Crickhollow Books), by Philip Martin; *A Short History of Fantasy*
(Middlesex University Press), by Farah Mendlesohn and Edward James; *100
Must-Read Fantasy Novels* (A&C Black), by Nick Rennison and Stephen E.
Andrews; *Women in Science Fiction and Fantasy: Volume One* (Greenwood
Press), edited by Robin Anne Reid; *Women in Science Fiction and Fantasy:
Volume Two: Entries* (Greenwood Press), edited by Robin Anne Reid; *The
Inter-Galactic Playground: A Critical Study of Children's and Teens' Science
Fiction* (McFarland), by Farah Mendlesohn; *Red Planets: Marxism and
Science Fiction* (Wesleyan University Press), edited by Mark Bould and
China Mieville; and *The Fire in the Stone: Prehistoric Fiction from Charles
Darwin to Jean M. Auel* (Wesleyan University Press), by Nicholas Ruddick.
A book of writing advice is *Booklife: Strategies and Survival Tips for the 21st
Century Writer* (Tachyon Press), by Jeff VanderMeer.

It was a pretty good year in the art book market. Artist retrospectives
included *From the Pen of Paul: The Fantastic Images of Frank R. Paul*
(Shasta-Phoenix), by Frank R. Paul; *Imaginative Realism: How to Paint What
Doesn't Exist* (Andrews McMeel), by James Gurney, which doubles as a how-
to book; *Norman Saunders* (Illustrated Press), by David Saunders; *Drawing
Down the Moon: The Art of Charles Vess* (Dark Horse Comics), by Charles
Vess; *Reynold Brown: A Life in Pictures* (Illustrated Press), by Daniel Zimmer
and David J. Hornung; and *Gahan Wilson: 50 Years of Playboy Cartoons*
(Fantagraphics Books), by Gahan Wilson.

Collections of work by various artists included *Spectrum 16: The Best in Contemporary Fantastic Art* (Underwood Books), edited by Cathy Fenner and Arnie Fenner, the latest in a long-running 'Best of the Year' series for fantastic art; *Imaginaire I: Magic Realism 2008–2009* (Fantasmus-Art), edited by Claus Brusen; *The Future of Fantasy Art* (Collins Design), edited by Aly Fell and Duddlebug; *Exposé 7* (Ballistic), a compilation of digital art, edited by Daniel Wade and Paul Hellard; and *Knowing Darkness: Artists Inspired by Stephen King* (Centipede Press), edited by George Beahm.

Reference books/histories included *Science Fiction and Fantasy Artists of the Twentieth Century: A Biographical Dictionary* (McFarland & Company), by Jane Frank, and *Sci-Fi Art: A Graphic History* (Collins Design), by Steve Holland.

It's hard to make a case for *The Cartoon History of the Modern World, Part 2: From the Bastille to Baghdad* (Harper), by Larry Gonick, the last volume of his famous Cartoon History of the Universe series, as a genre-related nonfiction book of interest, except perhaps that most fans are interested in history and its interface with technology, but it's such a wonderful book that I'm going to mention it anyway. The Cartoon History series may be one of the best attempts ever to tell genuine and in fact quite erudite and well-researched history in an easily accessible and understandable format, and is very funny to boot (the extensive bibliographies in the back of every book also make it a valuable reference source in itself). If you've missed these, you've been cheating yourself out of a great reading experience. It's a bit easier to justify a mention of *The Age of Wonder, How the Romantic Generation Discovered the Beauty and Terror of Science* (Pantheon Books), by Richard Holmes, which explores the lives of Victorian scientists and their often complex relationships with poets, artists, and other philosophers of their time. Even easier to justify is *The Day We Found the Universe* (Pantheon Books), by Marcia Bartusiak, which examines the roots of cosmology and the origin of our modern view of the universe.

As has been true for most of a decade now, genre movies dominated the film industry this year, doing huge box-office business – one of them is now the bestselling movie of all time.

According to Box Office Mojo (www.boxofficemojo.com), eight out of ten of the year's top-earning movies were genre films of one sort or another (the two exceptions were *The Hangover*, a slob comedy, and *The Blind Side*, a sports drama). By my count, and arbitrarily omitting horror movies, thirty-eight out of the hundred top-earning movies were genre films – if you count *Inglourious Basterds* as an alternate history movie, as some critics have argued, and *Sherlock Holmes* as a steampunk movie (it certainly has some minor fantastic elements), then the total rises to forty of the top-earning movies being genre movies, as long as your definition of 'genre' is wide enough to include fantasy movies and animated films.

That's not really so different from last year, or the year before that. What makes this year somewhat unusual is that there were several actual SF films, as opposed to fantasy films (last year, there were almost no SF films at all, and none among the top ten), with a couple of them among the top-ten grossers. Also unusual, there were no superhero movies among the top ten; the nearest one was X-Men Origins: Wolverine in eleventh place; the much-heralded Watchmen finished disappointingly in thirtieth place.

The two-billion-pound gorilla in the room, of course, was Avatar, which so far has earned $598,453,037 domestically, plus $1,446,989,293 in foreign grosses, bringing its worldwide total to an incredible $2,045,442,330 (and that doesn't even count future income from DVD sales, action figures, and the inevitable computer game). All of which makes Avatar the highest-grossing film of all time (although it's worth keeping in mind that it was also the most expensive movie to make of all time, with a production budget rumored to be somewhere in the $500 million range).

As a piece of filmmaking, it's a breathtaking technical achievement, one of those movies, like 2001 in its day and Star Wars in its day, that pushes the edge of the envelope and hugely broadens what is possible to show on the screen. Visually, it's absolutely stunning. As a movie, a piece of story-telling, it's less impressive, with its bad dialogue, cardboard characters, weak science, heavy-handed New Age polemics, and clichéd plot-elements making it mediocre at best, although director James Cameron does keep it moving along at a brisk action-movie pace throughout.

None of that matters. Nobody really cares. It's the biggest spectacle you can get on the screen at the moment for the price of a ticket, and (visually at least) a movie experience unlike any other – and that's what's bringing them through the door. On that level, Avatar totally deserves its success.

Although the most common critical reaction is to compare Avatar to Disney's Pocahontas, and snide critics have taken to calling it 'Dancing with Smurfs,' as a science fiction story it most resembles a mash-up of Poul Anderson's 'Call Me Joe,' Ursula K. Le Guin's 'The Word for World Is Forest,' and Alan Dean Foster's Midworld, which at least makes it a legiti-mate science fiction film (it has weak science, of course, rather blatantly signaled by the fact that the wonder mineral they're searching for is called 'unobtainium' – but so do many print SF stories and novels that are accepted by all as a legitimate part of the genre), which makes it by far the most successful SF movie since Star Wars. After years of all the top-grossing genre films being fantasy, at least three of the top-ten box-office champs this year were science fiction, and I can't remember the last time that happened. One or two of them even got some degree of critical respect, although there was no real critical darling among the year's genre films, critics dividing in opinion on almost all of them.

In at second place, earning a still-staggering $835,274,255 worldwide, is Transformers: Revenge of the Fallen, another SF film (bad SF, perhaps junk SF, with science even weaker and more dubious than that in Avatar, but still SF, nevertheless – hey, it's got robots in it, doesn't it?). SF also shows up in seventh place with Star Trek, the movie that not only rebooted the franchise but resurrected it from its grave by delivering $385,494,555 worldwide, and being enough of a success financially (and even, grudgingly, critically to some extent) that a sequel is already in production. *Star Trek* is a fast-paced movie with a high bit rate and lots of jump cuts, as almost all movies that sell successfully to post-MTV generations are, lots of CGI spectacle splashed across the screen, a plot that doesn't really make a whole lot of sense on most levels, and the requisite dubious technobabble science. It does contain the year's most audacious film moment, however, when they wipe out fifty years of series history in a stroke, consigning the six previous movies and the five previous TV series to the black hole of things that never happened, leaving themselves a blank slate upon which they can write anything they'd like, the freedom to do whatever they want with subsequent movies, safe to ignore the constraints of the previously existing canon.

The rest of the year's SF movies didn't do quite as well financially. Neither *Terminator Salvation*, finishing in twenty-third place, or *Angels & Demons*, finishing in twenty-second, were quite the blowout blockbusters that their producers probably hoped they'd be, both losing money domestically, although making up for it with foreign revenues. *District 9* placed a respectable twenty-seventh on the top-grossing list, pretty good considering that it only cost $30 million to make, cheap by today's standards, but earned $204,837,324 worldwide. It was also one of the most critically respected genre movies of the year, being nominated along with *Avatar* for the Best Picture Oscar, although a few reviewers complained that it was too much like the old movie *Alien Nation*, or that the way the refugee aliens were treated in the film was too obviously a metaphor for apartheid (unlike any other genre movie I can think of, *District 9* takes place in South Africa). Another critically well-reviewed movie was *Moon*, a psychological drama taking place on a mining station on the Moon, although almost nobody went to see it; it slipped through town almost subliminally, in a limited release, and didn't place at all on the extended list of the 150 top-earning movies of the year. For what it's worth, both *District 9* and *Moon* are a lot closer to being valid SF than junk SF with bad science like *Transformers* or *Avatar*.

The bleak after-the-holocaust movie *The Road* also got a pretty fair amount of critical respect, but just managed to squeeze onto the top-sellers list in 148th place, which must have been disappointing to the producers considering how massive their advertising/publicity push was. People generally don't want bleak, hopeless, and depressing during a major recession, although the disaster movie *2012* did pretty well at the box office, placing fifteenth on the list – although it had the advantage of lots of spectacular special-effects shots of skyscrapers collapsing and tsunamis swamping the Himalayas, which *The Road* did not. *The Time-Traveler's Wife*, finishing at only fifty-fourth place may also have been a disappointment, considering that the novel had been a major bestseller.

Fantasy didn't do quite as well on the list as it has in years past, but was represented in third place by *Harry Potter and the Half-Blood Prince*, in fourth place by romantic vampire soap opera *The Twilight Saga: New Moon* (which I'm arbitrarily consigning to fantasy rather than horror, because it wasn't particularly scary), and later on down the list by *Night at the Museum: Battle of the Smithsonian, Where the Wild Things Are, Race to Witch Mountain, The Lovely Bones* (making a disappointing showing for the new Peter Jackson movie in seventy-sixth place; of course, at the time I'm writing these words, it's only been in general release for a month or so, so it may do better later on), and Jim Carrey's latest ill-advised attempt to make a slob comedy out of a beloved literary classic, *A Christmas Carol*. Right at the end of the year, the new Terry Gilliam movie came out, *The Imaginarium of Doctor Parnassus*, but I haven't yet had a chance to see it.

Animated films had three finishers in the top ten, the charming (and also well-reviewed) *Up*, at fifth place, *Alvin and the Chipmunks: The Squeakquel* in at ninth place, and *Monsters vs. Aliens* in tenth place; further down the list were *Ice Age: Dawn of the Dinosaurs, Cloudy with a Chance of Meatballs, Coraline, The Princess and the Frog, Fantastic Mr. Fox, Astro Boy*, and the edgy not-really-for-children post-apocalyptic *9*. *Coraline*, taken from a Neil Gaiman novel, probably got the most critical respect of any of the animated films, other than *Up*.

It was a weak year for superhero movies, which up until now had dominated for several years. As mentioned, *X-Men Origins: Wolverine* under-performed, making it only to thirteenth place on the top-sellers list. The disappointment of the year, though, may have been *Watchmen*; some critics praised it, and some fans of the *Watchmen* graphic novels were enthusiastic about it, but for the most part, audiences stayed away, and it only made it to thirtieth place on the top-sellers list, earning $185,253,487 but *costing* $130 million to make. It was also bleak and depressing, and opinion was sharply divided on whether or not it was boring, and also on whether or not it was adequately faithful to the original source material.

In some ways, the highest profit margin of the year, proportionately speaking, may have been earned by horror movie *Paranormal Activity*, which pulled in a relatively modest $142,390,115 worldwide, but *cost* only an astonishing $15,000 to make; most big-budget Hollywood movies prob-ably spend more than that buying doughnuts for the crew. I'm sure the film industry is saying, 'Send us a few more like *that*!'

In spite of worries about the recession keeping people home in 2009, this wasn't the case. People need cheap entertainment during bleak economic times, and just as happened during the Great Depression, there were *more* people going to the movies, not less.

Next year looks like it's going to be Sequel Land, with a follow-up to *Star Trek*, probably a sequel to *Avatar* (although that might take a couple of years to make), possibly sequels to *2012* and *Transformers*, a lavish new version of *The Wolfman* – obviously part of an effort to make werewolves the New Vampires, a 'reimagining' of *Alice in Wonderland* by Tim Burton, and, of course, the new *Harry Potter* movie. On the horizon are possible versions of Joe Haldeman's *The Forever War*, John Wyndham's *Chocky*, and Isaac Asimov's *Foundation*. How many of these will ever actually make it to the screen, remains to be seen.

After the turbulence of 2007–2008, when the Writers Guild of America strike played hob with television programming, causing even many of the highest-rated shows to go on hiatus, 2009 was a relatively quiet year, although in some ways a glum one, during which TV shows fell like wheat before a scythe. Shows that died in 2009 or early 2010 included the once-hot *Terminator: The Sarah Connor Chronicles*; cult favorite *Pushing Daisies*; *Stargate Atlantis*; *Defying Gravity*; the American version of *Life on Mars*; *Kings*; *Reaper*; *Eli Stone*; the new version of the old show *Knight Rider*; *Kyle XY*; *Eastwick*, the series version of *The Witches of Eastwick*; the BBC's *Robin Hood*; *Saving Grace*, the cop-talks-to-an-angel show; *Merlin*; and *Eleventh Hour*. The most keenly felt loss for some fans was probably *Dollhouse*, the new series by *Buffy the Vampire Slayer* creator Josh Whedon, upon which a lot of hopes had been pinned. As planned, *Battlestar Galactica*, another keenly missed show, ended its run, disappointing many of its fans with its series finale. *Heroes*, once a ratings powerhouse, has been hanging on by its superpowered fingernails for some time now, and may well have been canceled by the time you read these words. New show *FlashForward*, based on an SF novel by Robert J. Sawyer, and *V*, a new version of another old show, seem to be hanging on rather precariously as well, struggling in the ratings, although they both did well enough to survive their freshman seasons.

A 'reimagining' of the old show *The Prisoner* as a mini-series doesn't seem to have particularly impressed anyone, in spite of a distinguished cast. Nor did *Alice*, a 'reimagining' of *Alice in Wonderland* by the same people who reimagined *The Wizard of Oz* as *Tin Man*, a "darker" and seedier version of the children's classic, perhaps a preemptive strike on the upcoming Tim Burton movie reimagining of the same material. (I find it interesting that the very first thing that these 'reimaginings' do is to change the little girl protagonists to attractive and sexually nubile young women.)

Not everything was bleak in TV Land, though. *Lost* returned for its announced final season, and the series opener was excellent, although everyone is wondering if the show can possibly tie up its enormous number of loose ends in the amount of time they have left. *X-Files* lookalike *Fringe* seems to be a hit, as is *True Blood*, based on the Sookie Stackhouse novels of Charlaine Harris. New show *Caprica*, the "prequel" to *Battlestar Galactica*, is getting good notices, although its ratings are still a bit low, and a new series has moved into the *Stargate* neighborhood for its crack at the brass ring, *Stargate Universe*. Spy semi-spoof with fantastic elements, *Chuck*, still on the air, has been joined by a similar new show, *Human Target*. New show *The Vampire Diaries* seems to be aiming for the same romantic soap opera with vampires territory as *True Blood*. *Doctor Who* is coming back with a new doctor in the role, after racking up some of the best ratings in its history. *Primeval* was canceled, but then renewed after the BBC changed its mind. It looks like *Torchwood* may be coming back, at least there are rumors to that effect, even though things were wrapped up fairly decisively in a TV movie; there are also rumors of an upcoming American version of *Torchwood*, which will probably suck. The long-running *Smallville* has been renewed (its strategy of bringing in most of the members of the Justice League of America as guest stars seems to be working), as have *Eureka*, *Star Wars: The Clone Wars*, *Supernatural*, *Ghost Whisperer*, *Medium*, *Sanctuary*, and *Legend of the Seeker*.

Coming up: mini-series versions of George R.R. Martin's *A Game of Thrones* from HBO and Kim Stanley Robinson's *Red Mars* from AMC.

The 67th World Science Fiction Convention, Anticipation, was held in Montréal, Québec, Canada, from August 6–August 10, 2009. The 2009 Hugo Awards, presented at Anticipation, were: Best Novel, *The Graveyard Book*, by Neil Gaiman; Best Novella, "The Erdmann Nexus," by Nancy Kress; Best Novelette, "Shoggoths in Bloom," by Elizabeth Bear; Best Short Story, "Exhalation," by Ted Chiang; Best Related Book, *Your Hate Mail Will Be Graded: A Decade of Whatever, 1998–2008*, by John Scalzi; Best Editor, Long Form, David G. Hartwell; Best Editor, Short Form, Ellen Datlow; Best Professional Artist, Donato Giancola; Best Dramatic Presentation (short form), *Doctor Horrible's Sing-Along Blog*; Best Dramatic Presentation (long form), *WALL-E*; Best Semiprozine, *Weird Tales*, edited by Ann VanderMeer and Stephen H. Segal; Best Fanzine, *Electric Velocipede*, edited by John Kilma; Best Fan Writer, Cheryl Morgan; Best Fan Artist, Frank Wu; plus the John W. Campbell Award for Best New Writer to David Anthony Durham.

The 2008 Nebula Awards, presented at a banquet on the UCLA campus in Los Angeles, California on April 25, 2009, were: Best Novel, *Powers*, by Ursula K. Le Guin; Best Novella, "The Spacetime Pool," by Catherine Asaro; Best Novelette, "Pride and Prometheus," by John Kessel; Best Short Story, "Trophy Wives," by Nina Kiriki Hoffman; Best Script, *WALL-E*, by Andrew Stanton, Jim Reardon, and Peter Docter; the Andre Norton Award to *Flora's Dare*, by Ysabeau S. Wilce; plus the Ray Bradbury Award to Joss Whedon; the Solstice Award to Kate Wilhelm, A.J. Budrys, and Martin H. Greenberg; the Author Emeritus Award to M.J. Engh; and the Damon Knight Memorial Grand Master Award to Harry Harrison.

The 2009 World Fantasy Awards, presented at a banquet at the Fairmont Hotel in San Jose, California on 29 October–1 November 2009, during the World Fantasy Convention, were: Best Novel, *The Shadow Year*, by Jeffrey Ford, and *Tender Morsels*, by Margo Lanagan (tie); Best Novella, "If Angels Fight," by Richard Bowes; Best Short Story, "26 Monkeys, Also the Abyss," by Kij Johnson; Best Collection, *The Drowned Life*, by Jeffrey Ford; Best Anthology, *Paper Cities: An Anthology of Urban Fantasy*, edited by Ekaterina Sedia; Best Artist, Shaun Tan; Special Award (Professional), to Kelly Link and Gavin J. Grant, for Small Beer Press and Big Mouth House; Special Award (Non-Professional), to Michael Walsh, for Howard Waldrop collections from Old Earth Books; plus the Life Achievement Award to Ellen Asher and Jane Yolen.

The 2008 Bram Stoker Awards, presented by the Horror Writers of America during a banquet at the Burbank Marriott Hotel near Los Angeles, California on 13 June 2009, were: Best Novel, *Duma Key*, by Stephen

King; Best First Novel, *The Gentling Box*, by Lisa Mannetti; Best Long
Fiction, *Miranda*, by John R. Little; Best Short Fiction, "The Lost," by
Sarah Langan; Best Fiction Collection, *Just After Sunset*, by Stephen King;
Best Anthology, *Unspeakable Horror*, edited by Vince A. Liaguno and
Chad Helder; Best Nonfiction, *A Hallowe'en Anthology*, by Lisa Morton;
Best Poetry Collection, *The Nightmare Collection*, by Bruce Boston; plus
Lifetime Achievement Awards to F. Paul Wilson and Chelsea Quinn Yarbro.

The 2009 John W. Campbell Memorial Award was awarded to *Little
Brother*, by Cory Doctorow, and *Songs of Time*, by Ian R. MacLeod (tie).

The 2009 Theodore Sturgeon Memorial Award for Best Short Story was
won by "The Ray-Gun: A Love Story," by James Alan Gardner.

The 2009 Philip K. Dick Award went to *Emissaries from the Dead*, by
Adam-Troy Castro, and *Terminal Mind*, by David Walton (tie).

The 2009 Arthur C. Clarke award was won by *Song of Time*, by Ian
R. MacLeod.

The 2009 James Tiptree, Jr. Memorial Award was won by *The Knife of
Never Letting Go*, by Patrick Ness, and *Filter House*, by Nisi Shawl (tie).

The 2009 Cordwainer Smith Rediscovery Award went to A. Merritt.

Dead in 2009 or early 2010 were:

PHILIP JOSÉ FARMER, 91, multiple Hugo winner, a SFWA Grand
Master, and a winner of the World Fantasy Award: Life Achievement, the
author of a huge number of books, including the *Riverworld*, *World of Tiers*,
and *Dayworld* series, and many others, whose best-known book was probably
the Hugo-winning *To Your Scattered Bodies Go*; **J.G. BALLARD**, 78, widely
acclaimed outside the genre for his autobiographical World War II novel,
Empire of the Sun, which was filmed by Stephen Spielberg, best known
inside the genre as one of the ancestral figures in the British New Wave of
the sixties, author of many groundbreaking short stories, some of the best of
which were collected in *Vermilion Sands* and *The Voices of Time*, as well as
novels such as *The Drowned World*, *The Crystal World*, *Concrete Island*, and
many others; **CHARLES N. BROWN**, 72, a longtime fan and one-time
nuclear engineer who was one of the co-founders of *Locus*, which under his
multi-decade direction as editor and publisher became the most important
and prominent news magazine in the history of SF, and earned the magazine
twenty-nine Hugo Awards, also a tireless promoter of SF from thousands of
convention panels, and a personal friend; **DAVID EDDINGS**, 77, prominent fantasy author best known for the novels of the *Belgariad* series, as well
as for books in the *Malloreon* series, the *Dreamers* series, and others;
ROBERT HOLDSTOCK, 61, acclaimed British fantasy writer, author of
Mythago Wood, thought to be one of the classic post-Tolkein fantasy novels
by many critics, as well as six sequels and a number of stand-alone novels;
PHILIP KLASS, 89, who wrote SF as **WILLIAM TENN**, and whose classic
stories, most published in the fifties, included "Bernie the Faust," "Venus and
the Seven Sexes," "The Liberation of Earth," and many others, as well as the
novel *Of Men and Monsters*; **KAGE BAKER**, 57, prolific author of the
extensive linked series of novels and stories about the time-travelling agents

of the Company, one of the most popular series in recent SF, just as Baker may have been one of the most significant talents to enter the field during the last ten years, a friend; **PHYLLIS GOTLIEB**, 83, pioneering Canadian SF author, sometimes known as "the mother of Canadian science fiction," Aurora Award-winning author of many stories collected in *Son of the Morning and Other Stories* and *Blue Apes* as well as novels such as *Sunburst*; **HARRY C. CROSBY, Jr.**, 84, who wrote more than a hundred SF stories, mostly for *Astounding/Analog*, and several novels, under the name **CHRISTOPHER ANVIL**; **LOUISE COOPER**, 57, SF/fantasy writer, author of the *Time Master* trilogy, *The Shadow Star* trilogy, *The King's Demon*, and others; **THOMAS DEITZ**, 57, author of sixteen fantasy novels, including *Windmaster's Bane* and *Bloodwinter*; **KEN RAND**, 62, author of *Phoenix*, *The Golems of Laramie County*, *A Cold Day in Hell*, and other novels; **RICHARD GORDON**, 62, Scottish author who wrote SF novels as **STUART GORDON** author of books such as *One-Eye, Two-Eyes, Three-Eyes*, and *Time Story*; **JOHN KENNEDY**, 63, SF writer, ex-husband of SF writer Leigh Kennedy; **JENNIFER SWIFT**, 54, SF writer whose work appeared in *Asimov's, Amazing, F&SF, Interzone*, and elsewhere; **JANET FOX**, 68, writer and editor, who also edited the monthly market report, *Scavenger's Newsletter*; **TAKUMI SHIBANO**, 83, translator and novelist, longtime Japanese fan, sometimes spoken of as "the father of Japanese fandom"; **KAORU KURIMOTO**, 56, Japanese fantasy and anime author; **EDWARD UPWARD**, 105, distinguished British author whose works included the fantasy stories collected in *The Mortmere Stories*; **JOHN ATKINS**, 92, British author who occasionally wrote fantasy and SF; **JOHN A. KEEL**, 79, paranormal author and UFOologist best known for *The Mothman Prophecies*; **MILORAD PAVIC**, 80, Serbian novelist, many of whose novels had surreal fantastic elements; **ED VALIGURSKY**, 82, famous SF cover artist, whose covers graced many of the classics of the field; **DEAN ELLIS**, 89, another famous and pioneering SF cover artist; **DON IVAN PUNCHATZ**, 73, prominent artist and illustrator; **ILENE MEYER**, 69, SF/fantasy artist who did covers for books by Jack Vance, Harlan Ellison, Philip K. Dick, and others; **DAVE SIMONS**, 54, comics artist; **KNOX BURGER**, 87, editor and agent, who published early works by Kurt Vonnegut, Jr., Ray Bradbury, and John Wyndham as fiction editor of *Collier's* magazine, edited SF for Dell and Fawcett, and later became a prominent literary agent; **ALFRED A. KNOPF**, 90, publisher and co-founder of Atheneum; **ROBERT A. COLLINS**, 80, scholar, founder of the International Conference on the Fantastic in the Arts, editor of *Fantasy Review*, and co-editor of *Science Fiction & Fantasy Book Review Annual*; **MARK OWINGS**, 64, bibliographer and longtime fan, a founder of the Baltimore Science Fiction Society, who worked with the late Jack Chalker to produce *The Index to the Science-Fantasy Publishers*; **I.F. CLARKE**, 91, British bibliographer and literary scholar, compiler of the classic study of future-war fiction, *Voices Prophesying War*; **DONALD M. GRANT**, 82, winner of three World Fantasy Awards, including the World Fantasy Life Achievement

Award, founder of Donald M. Grant Publisher, Inc; **BARBARA BOVA**, literary agent, wife of SF writer Ben Bova; **DON CONGDON**, 91, agent and anthologist, longtime agent for writers such as Ray Bradbury and Henry Kuttner; **ROBERT LOUIT**, 64, French SF editor, critic, and translator; **DAVE ARNESON**, 61, co-creator of the fantasy role-playing game Dungeons & Dragons; **WALTER CRONKITE**, 92, perhaps the best-known television broadcaster and anchor man of the twentieth century, who had no direct genre connection, but was known to every genre fan, if for nothing else, for his coverage of the Moon landing in 1969; **ANDY HALLETT**, 33, actor, best known to genre audiences for his role as the singing green demon Lorne on the television vampire show *Angel*; **DAVID CARRADINE**, 72, actor, best known to genre audiences for his role as wandering monk and martial arts expert Cain in the sixties' TV show, *Kung Fu*, also known for the title role in the *Kill Bill* movies and as the ghoulishly jovial host of *Wild West Tech*; **MICHAEL JACKSON**, 50, worldwide celebrity and performer, best known to genre audiences for his role in *The Wiz*, the seventies' remake of The Wizard of Oz, and for the song "Thriller," which referenced horror movie clichés and featured a voiceover cameo by Vincent Price; **FARRAH FAWCETT**, 62, actor, best known to genre audience for roles in *Logan's Run* and *Saturn 3*, and as one of television's original *Charlie's Angels*; **NATASHA RICHARDSON**, 46, actor, best known to genre audiences as the star of the movie version of *The Handmaid's Tale*; **MARY TRAVERS**, 72, member of the famous folk-music trio Peter, Paul, and Mary, whose closest approach to genre was probably their fantasy song about "Puff, the Magic Dragon"; **HENRY GIBSON**, 73, movie and television actor; **PERNELL ROBERTS**, 81, television actor, best known for his roles in *Bonanza* and *Trapper John, M.D.*, but who had genre-related roles in *The Wild Wild West*, *Night Gallery*, and *The Six Million Dollar Man*; **RON SILVER**, 62, actor, best known to genre audiences for his role in *Timecop*; **MICKEY CARROLL**, 89, whose role as a Munchkin in the Judy Garland version of *The Wizard of Oz* generated an entire subsequent career for him; **KARL MALDEN**, 97, a film actor for whom it's hard to think of a really prominent genre connection (although he did do a few low-budget disaster movies like *Beyond the Poseidon Adventure* and *Meteor*), but whose name and face will be familiar to most readers, and whose most famous movies included *On the Waterfront* and *A Streetcar Named Desire*; **GALE STORM**, 87, television actress with even less of a genre connection than Karl Malden, but who will be familiar to those of us old enough to have watched TV in the fifties from shows such as *My Little Margie* and *The Gale Storm Show*; **ELEANOR FRAZETTA**, 74, wife of fantasy artist Frank Frazetta; **DAVID GAIMAN**, 75, father of SF writer Neil Gaiman; **MARIAN BAILEY**, 84, mother of SF writer Robin Bailey; **JOHN IAN REYNOLDS**, 66, father of SF writer Alastair Reynolds; and **EMILY KATE BETHKE**, 28, daughter of SF writer Bruce Bethke.

UTRIUSQUE COSMI

Robert Charles Wilson

Robert Charles Wilson made his first sale in 1974, to Analog, but little more was heard from him until the late 1980s, when he began to publish a string of ingenious and well-crafted novels and stories that have since established him among the top ranks of the writers who came to prominence in the last two decades of the twentieth century. His first novel, *A Hidden Place*, appeared in 1986. He won the John W. Campbell Memorial Award for his novel *The Chronoliths*, the Philip K. Dick Award for his novel *Mysterium*, and the Aurora Award for his story "The Perseids." In 2006, he won the Hugo Award for his acclaimed novel Spin. His other books include the novels *Memory Wire, Gypsies, The Divide, The Harvest, A Bridge of Years, Darwinia, Blind Lake, Bios*, and *Axis*, and a collection of his short work, *The Perseids and Other Stories*. His most recent book is a new novel, *Julian*. He lives in Toronto, Canada.

Here he tells the compelling story of a young woman faced with the most significant choice she will ever make in her life – after which, nothing will ever be the same.

D IVING BACK INTO the universe (now that the universe is a finished object, boxed and ribboned from bang to bounce), Carlotta calculates ever-finer loci on the frozen ordinates of spacetime until at last she reaches a trailer park outside the town of Commanche Drop, Arizona. Bodiless, no more than a breath of imprecision in the Feynman geography of certain virtual particles, thus powerless to affect the material world, she passes unimpeded through a sheet-aluminum wall and hovers over a mattress on which a young woman sleeps uneasily.

The young woman is her own ancient self, the primordial Carlotta Boudaine, dewed with sweat in the hot night air, her legs caught up in a spindled cotton sheet. The bedroom's small window is cranked open, and in the breezeless distance a coyote wails.

Well, look at me, Carlotta marvels: skinny girl in panties and a halter, sixteen years old – no older than a gnat's breath – taking shallow little sleep-breaths in the moonlit dark. Poor child can't even see her own ghost. Ah, but she will, Carlotta thinks – she must.

The familiar words echo in her mind as she inspects her dreaming body, buried in its tomb of years, eons, kalpas. When it's time to leave, leave. Don't be afraid. Don't wait. Don't get caught. Just go. Go fast.

Her ancient beloved poem. Her perennial mantra. The words, in fact, that saved her life.

She needs to share those words with herself, to make the circle complete. Everything she knows about nature of the physical universe suggests that the task is impossible. Maybe so . . . but it won't be for lack of trying.

Patiently, slowly, soundlessly, Carlotta begins to speak.

Here's the story of the Fleet, girl, and how I got raptured up into it. It's all about the future – a bigger one than you believe in – so brace yourself.

It has a thousand names and more, but we'll just call it the Fleet. When I first encountered it, the Fleet was scattered from the core of the galaxy all through its spiraled tentacles of suns, and it had been there for millions of years, going about its business, though nobody on this planet knew anything about it. I guess every now and then a Fleet ship must have fallen to Earth, but it would have been indistinguishable from any common meteorite by the time it passed through the atmosphere: a chunk of carbonaceous chondrite smaller than a human fist, from which all evidence of ordered matter had been erased by fire – and such losses, which happened everywhere and often, made no discernable difference to the Fleet as a whole. All Fleet data (that is to say, all mind) was shared, distributed, fractal. Vessels were born and vessels were destroyed, but the Fleet persisted down countless eons, confident of its own immortality.

Oh, I know you don't understand the big words, child! It's not important for you to hear them – not these words – it's only important for me to say them. Why? Because a few billion years ago tomorrow, I carried your ignorance out of this very trailer, carried it down to the Interstate and hitched west with nothing in my backpack but a bottle of water, a half-dozen Tootsie Rolls, and a wad of twenty-dollar bills stolen out of Dan-O's old ditty bag. That night (tomorrow night: mark it) I slept under an overpass all by myself, woke up cold and hungry long before dawn, and looked up past a concrete arch crusted with bird shit into a sky so thick with falling stars it made me think of a dark skin bee-stung with fire. Some of the Fleet vectored too close to the atmosphere that night, no doubt, but I didn't understand that (any more than you do, girl) – I just thought it was a big flock of shooting stars, pretty but meaningless. And, after a while, I slept some more. And come sunrise, I waited for the morning traffic so I could catch another ride . . . but the only cars that came by were all weaving or speeding, as if the whole world was driving home from a drunken party.

"They won't stop," a voice behind me said. "Those folks already made their decisions, Carlotta. Whether they want to live or die, I mean. Same decision you have to make."

I whirled around, sick-startled, and that was when I first laid eyes on dear Erasmus.

Let me tell you right off that Erasmus wasn't a human being. Erasmus just then was a knot of shiny metal angles about the size of a microwave oven, hovering in mid-air, with a pair of eyes like the polished tourmaline they sell at those roadside souvenir shops. He didn't have to look that way – it was some old avatar he used because he figured that it would impress me. But I didn't know that then. I was only surprised, if that's not too mild a word, and too shocked to be truly frightened.

"The world won't last much longer," Erasmus said in a low and mournful voice. "You can stay here, or you can come with me. But choose quick, Carlotta, because the mantle's come unstable and the continents are starting to slip."

I half believed that I was still asleep and dreaming. I didn't know what that meant, about the mantle, though I guessed he was talking about the end of the world. Some quality of his voice (which reminded me of that actor Morgan Freeman) made me trust him despite how weird and impossible the whole conversation was. Plus, I had a confirming sense that something was going bad somewhere, partly because of the scant traffic (a Toyota zoomed past, clocking speeds it had never been built for, the driver a hunched blur behind the wheel), partly because of the ugly green cloud that just then billowed up over a row of rat-toothed mountains on the horizon. Also the sudden hot breeze. And the smell of distant burning. And the sound of what might have been thunder, or something worse.

"Go with you where?"

"To the stars, Carlotta! But you'll have to leave your body behind."

I didn't like the part about leaving my body behind. But what choice did I have, except the one he'd offered me? Stay or go. Simple as that.

It was a ride – just not the kind I'd been expecting.

There was a tremor in the earth, like the devil knocking at the soles of my shoes. "Okay," I said, "whatever," as white dust bloomed up from the desert and was taken by the frantic wind.

Don't be afraid. Don't wait. Don't get caught. Just go. Go fast.

Without those words in my head, I swear, girl, I would have died that day. Billions did.

She slows down the passage of time so she can fit this odd but somehow necessary monologue into the space between one or two of the younger Carlotta's breaths. Of course, she has no real voice in which to speak. The past is static, imperturbable in its endless sleep; molecules of air on their fixed trajectories can't be manipulated from the shadowy place where she now exists. Wake up with the dawn, girl, she says, steal the money you'll never spend – it doesn't matter; the important thing is to leave. It's time.

When it's time to leave, leave. Of all the memories she carried out of her earthly life, this is the most vivid: waking to discover a ghostly presence in her darkened room, a white-robed woman giving her the advice she needs at the moment she needs it. Suddenly Carlotta wants to scream the words: When it's time to leave –

But she can't vibrate even a single mote of the ancient air, and the younger Carlotta sleeps on.

Next to the bed is a thrift-shop night table scarred with cigarette burns. On the table is a child's night-light, faded cut-outs of SpongeBob Square-Pants pasted on the paper shade. Next to that, hidden under a splayed copy of People magazine, is the bottle of barbiturates Carlotta stole from Dan-O's ditty-bag this afternoon, the same khaki bag in which (she couldn't help but notice) Dan-O keeps his cash, a change of clothes, a fake driver's license, and a blue steel automatic pistol.

Young Carlotta detects no ghostly presence . . . nor is her sleep disturbed by the sound of Dan-O's angry voice and her mother's sudden gasp, two rooms away. Apparently, Dan-O is awake and sober. Apparently, Dan-O has discovered the theft. That's a complication.

But Carlotta won't allow herself to be hurried.

The hardest thing about joining the Fleet was giving up the idea that I had a body, that my body had a real place to be.

But that's what everybody believed at first, that we were still whole and normal – everybody rescued from Earth, I mean. Everybody who said "Yes" to Erasmus – and Erasmus, in one form or another, had appeared to every human being on the planet in the moments before the end of the world. Two and a half billion of us accepted the offer of rescue. The rest chose to stay put and died when the Earth's continents dissolved into molten magma.

Of course, that created problems for the survivors. Children without parents, parents without children, lovers separated for eternity. It was as sad and tragic as any other incomplete rescue, except on a planetary scale. When we left the Earth, we all just sort of re-appeared on a grassy plain as flat as Kansas and wider than the horizon, under a blue faux sky, each of us with an Erasmus at his shoulder and all of us wailing or sobbing or demanding explanations.

The plain wasn't "real," of course, not the way I was accustomed to things being real. It was a virtual place, and all of us were wearing virtual bodies, though we didn't understand that fact immediately. We kept on being what we expected ourselves to be – we even wore the clothes we'd worn when we were raptured up. I remember looking down at the pair of greasy second-hand Reeboks I'd found at the Commanche Drop Goodwill store, thinking: in Heaven? Really?

"Is there any place you'd rather be?" Erasmus asked with a maddening and clearly inhuman patience. "Anyone you need to find?"

"Yeah, I'd rather be in New Zealand," I said, which was really just a hysteri-cal joke. All I knew about New Zealand was that I'd seen a show about it on PBS, the only channel we got since the cable company cut us off.

"Any particular part of New Zealand?"

"What? Well – okay, a beach, I guess."

I had never been to a real beach, a beach on the ocean.

"Alone, or in the company of others?"

"Seriously?" All around me people were sobbing or gibbering in (mostly) foreign languages. Pretty soon, fights would start to break out. You can't put a couple of billion human beings so close together under circumstances like that and expect any other result. But the crowd was already thinning, as people accepted similar offers from their own Fleet avatars.

"Alone," I said. "Except for you."

And quick as that, there I was: Eve without Adam, standing on a lonesome stretch of white beach.

After a while, the astonishment faded to a tolerable dazzle. I took off my shoes and tested the sand. The sand was pleasantly sun-warm. Saltwater swirled up between my toes as a wave washed in from the coral-blue sea.

Then I felt dizzy and had to sit down.

"Would you like to sleep?" Erasmus asked, hovering over me like a gem-studded party balloon. "I can help you sleep, Carlotta, if you'd like. It might make the transition easier if you get some rest, to begin with."

"You can answer some fucking questions, is what you can do!" I said.

He settled down on the sand beside me, the mutant offspring of a dragonfly and a beach ball. "Okay, shoot," he said.

It's a read-only universe, Carlotta thinks. The Old Ones have said as much, so it must be true. And yet, she knows, she remembers, that the younger Carlotta will surely wake and find her here: a ghostly presence, speaking wisdom.

But how can she make herself perceptible to this sleeping child? The senses are so stubbornly material, electrochemical data cascading into vastly complex neural networks . . . is it possible she could intervene in some way at the borderland of quanta and perception? For a moment, Carlotta chooses to look at her younger self with different eyes, sampling the fine gradients of molecular magnetic fields. The child's skin and skull grow faint and then transparent, as Carlotta shrinks her point of view and wanders briefly through the carnival of her own animal mind, the buzzing innerscape where skeins of dream merge and separate like fractal soapbubbles. If she could manipulate even a single boson – influence the charge at some critical synaptic junction, say –

But she can't. The past simply doesn't have a handle on it. There's no uncertainty here anymore, no alternate outcomes. To influence the past would be to change the past, and, by definition, that's impossible.

The shouting from the next room grows suddenly louder and more vicious, and Carlotta senses her younger self moving from sleep toward an awakening, too soon.

Of course, I figured it out eventually, with Erasmus's help. Oh, girl, I won't bore you with the story of those first few years – they bored me, heaven knows.

Of course "heaven" is exactly where we weren't. Lots of folks were inclined to see it that way – assumed they must have died and been delivered to whatever afterlife they happened to believe in. Which was actually not too far off the mark: but, of course, God had nothing to do with it. The Fleet was a real-world business, and ours wasn't the first sentient species it had raptured up. Lots of planets got destroyed, Erasmus said, and the Fleet didn't always get to them in time to salvage the population, hard as they tried – we were lucky, sort of.

So I asked him what it was that caused all these planets to blow up.

"We don't know, Carlotta. We call it the Invisible Enemy. It doesn't leave a signature, whatever it is. But it systematically seeks out worlds with flourishing civilizations and marks them for destruction." He added, "It doesn't like the Fleet much, either. There are parts of the galaxy where we don't go – because if we do go there, we don't come back."

At the time, I wasn't even sure what a "galaxy" was, so I dropped the subject, except to ask him if I could see what it looked like – the destruction of the Earth, I meant. At first, Erasmus didn't want to show me; but after a lot of coaxing, he turned himself into a sort of floating TV screen and displayed a view, "looking back from above the plane of the solar ecliptic," words which meant nothing to me.

What I saw was . . . well, no more little blue planet, basically.

More like a ball of boiling red snot.

"What about my mother? What about Dan-O?"

I didn't have to explain who these people were. The Fleet had sucked up all kinds of data about human civilization, I don't know how. Erasmus paused as if he was consulting some invisible Rolodex. Then he said, "They aren't with us."

"You mean they're dead?"

"Yes. Abby and Dan-O are dead."

But the news didn't surprise me. It was almost as if I'd known it all along, as if I had had a vision of their deaths, a dark vision to go along with that ghostly visit the night before, the woman in a white dress telling me to go fast.

Abby Boudaine and Dan-O, dead. And me raptured up to robot heaven. Well, well.

"Are you sure you wouldn't like to sleep now?"

"Maybe for a while," I told him.

Dan-O's a big man, and he's working himself up to a major tantrum. Even now, Carlotta feels repugnance at the sound of his voice, that gnarl of angry consonants. Next, Dan-O throws something solid, maybe a clock, against the wall. The clock goes to pieces, noisily. Carlotta's mother cries out in response, and the sound of her wailing seems to last weeks.

*   *   *

"It's not good," Erasmus told me much later, "to be so much alone."

Well, I told him, I wasn't alone – he was with me, wasn't he? And he was pretty good company, for an alien machine. But that was a dodge. What he meant was that I ought to hook up with somebody human.

I told him I didn't care if I never set eyes on another human being ever again. What had the human race ever done for me?

He frowned – that is, he performed a particular contortion of his exposed surfaces that I had learned to interpret as disapproval. "That's entropic talk, Carlotta. Honestly, I'm worried about you."

"What could happen to me?" Here on this beach where nothing ever really happens, I did not add.

"You could go crazy. You could sink into despair. Worse, you could die."

"I could die? I thought I was immortal now."

"Who told you that? True, you're no longer living, in the strictly material sense. You're a metastable nested loop embedded in the Fleet's collective mentation. But everything's mortal, Carlotta. Anything can die."

I couldn't die of disease or falling off a cliff, he explained, but my "nested loop" was subject to a kind of slow erosion, and stewing in my own lonely juices for too long was liable to bring on the decay that much faster.

And, admittedly, after a month on this beach, swimming and sleeping too much and eating the food Erasmus conjured up whenever I was hungry (though I didn't really need to eat), watching recovered soap operas on his bellyvision screen or reading celebrity magazines (also embedded in the Fleet's collective memory) that would never get any fresher or produce another issue, and just being basically miserable as all hell, I thought maybe he was right.

"You cry out in your sleep," Erasmus said. "You have bad dreams."

"The world ended. Maybe I'm depressed. You think meeting people would help with that?"

"Actually," he said, "you have a remarkable talent for being alone. You're sturdier than most. But that won't save you, in the long run."

So I tried to take his advice. I scouted out some other survivors. Turned out, it was interesting what some people had done in their new incarnations as Fleet-data. The Erasmuses had made it easy for like-minded folks to find each other and to create environments to suit them. The most successful of these cliques, as they were sometimes called, were the least passive ones: the ones with a purpose. Purpose kept people lively. Passive cliques tended to fade into indifference pretty quickly, and the purely hedonistic ones soon collapsed into dense orgasmic singularities; but if you were curious about the world, and hung out with similarly curious friends, there was a lot to keep you thinking.

None of those cliques suited me in the long run, though. Oh, I made some friends, and I learned a few things. I learned how to access the Fleet's archival data, for instance – a trick you had to be careful with. If you did it right, you could think about a subject as if you were doing a Google search, all the relevant information popping up in your mind's eye just as if it had been there all along. Do it too often or too enthusiastically, though, and you ran the risk of getting lost in the overload – you might develop a "memory" so big and all-inclusive that it absorbed you into its own endless flow.

(It was an eerie thing to watch when it happened. For a while, I hung out with a clique that was exploring the history of the non-human civilizations that had been raptured up by the Fleet in eons past . . . until the leader of the group, a Jordanian college kid by the name of Nuri, dived down too far and literally fogged out. He got this look of intense concentration on his face, and, moments later, his body turned to wisps and eddies of fluid air and faded like fog in the sunlight. Made me shiver. And I had liked Nuri – I missed him when he was gone.)

But by sharing the effort, we managed to safely learn some interesting things. (Things the Erasmuses could have just told us, I suppose, but we didn't know the right questions to ask.) Here's a big for-instance: although every species was mortal after it was raptured up – every species eventually fogged out much the way poor Nuri had – there were actually a few very long-term survivors. By that, I mean individuals who had outlived their peers, who had found a way to preserve a sense of identity in the face of the Fleet's hypercomplex data torrent.

We asked our Erasmuses if we could meet one of these long-term survivors.

Erasmus said no, that was impossible. The Elders, as he called them, didn't live on our timescale. The way they had preserved themselves was by dropping out of realtime.

Apparently, it wasn't necessary to "exist" continuously from one moment to the next. You could ask the Fleet to turn you off for a day or a week, then turn you on again. Any moment of active perception was called a saccade, and you could space your saccades as far apart as you liked. Want to live a thousand years? Do it by living one second out of every million that passes. Of course, it wouldn't feel like a thousand years, subjectively, but a thousand years would flow by before you aged much. That's basically what the Elders were doing.

We could do the same, Erasmus said, if we wanted. But there was a price tag attached to it. "Timesliding" would carry us incomprehensibly far into a future nobody could predict. We were under continual attack by the Invisible Enemy, and it was possible that the Fleet might lose so much cohesion that we could no longer be sustained as stable virtualities. We wouldn't get a long life out of it, and we might well be committing a kind of unwitting suicide.

"You don't really go anywhere," Erasmus summed up. "In effect, you just go fast. I can't honestly recommend it."

"Did I ask for your advice? I mean, what are you, after all? Just some little fragment of the Fleet mind charged with looking after Carlotta Boudaine. A cybernetic babysitter."

I swear to you, he looked hurt. And I heard the injury in his voice.

"I'm the part of the Fleet that cares about you, Carlotta."

Most of my clique backed down at that point. Most people aren't cut out to be timesliders. But I was more tempted than ever. "You can't tell me what to do, Erasmus."

"I'll come with you, then," he said. "If you don't mind."

It hadn't occurred to me that he might not come along. It was a scary idea. But I didn't let that anxiety show.

"Sure, I guess that'd be all right," I said.

Enemies out there too, the elder Carlotta observes. A whole skyful of them. As above, so below. Just like in that old drawing – what was it called? Utriusque Cosmi. Funny what a person remembers. Girl, do you hear your mother crying?

The young Carlotta stirs uneasily in her tangled sheet.

Both Carlottas know their mother's history. Only the elder Carlotta can think about it without embarrassment and rage. Oh, it's an old story. Her mother's name is Abby. Abby Boudaine dropped out of high school pregnant, left some dreary home in South Carolina to go west with a twenty-year-old boyfriend who abandoned her outside Albuquerque. She gave birth in a California emergency ward and nursed Carlotta in a basement room in the home of a retired couple, who sheltered her in exchange for housework until Carlotta's constant wailing got on their nerves. After that, Abby hooked up with a guy who worked for a utility company and grew weed in his attic for pin money. The hookup lasted a few years, and might have lasted longer, except that Abby had a weakness for what the law called "substances," and couldn't restrain herself in an environment where coke and methamphetamine circulated more or less freely. A couple of times, Carlotta was bounced around between foster homes while Abby Boudaine did court-mandated dry-outs or simply binged. Eventually, Abby picked up ten-year-old Carlotta from one of these periodic suburban exiles and drove her over the state border into Arizona, jumping bail. "We'll never be apart again," her mother told her, in the strained voice that meant she was a little bit high or hoping to be. "Never again!" Blessing or curse? Carlotta wasn't sure which. "You'll never leave me, baby. You're my one and only."

Not such an unusual story, the elder Carlotta thinks, though her younger self, she knows, feels uniquely singled out for persecution.

Well, child, Carlotta thinks, try living as a distributed entity on a Fleet that's being eaten by invisible monsters, then see what it feels like.

But she knows the answer to that. It feels much the same.

"Now you steal from me?" Dan-O's voice drills through the wall like a rusty auger. Young Carlotta stirs and whimpers. Any moment now, she'll open her eyes, and then what? Although this is the fixed past, it feels suddenly unpredictable, unfamiliar, dangerous.

*　　*　　*

Erasmus came with me when I went timesliding, and I appreciated that, even before I understood what a sacrifice it was for him.

Early on, I asked him about the Fleet and how it came to exist. The answer to that question was lost to entropy, he said. He had never known a time without a Fleet – he couldn't have, because Erasmus was the Fleet, or at least a sovereign fraction of it.

"As we understand it," he told me, "the Fleet evolved from networks of self-replicating data-collecting machine intelligences, no doubt originally created by some organic species, for the purpose of exploring interstellar space. Evidence suggests that we're only a little younger than the universe itself."

The Fleet had outlived its creators. "Biological intelligence is unstable over the long term," Erasmus said, a little smugly. "But out of that original compulsion to acquire and share data, we evolved and refined our own collective purpose."

"That's why you hoover up doomed civilizations? So you can catalogue and study them?"

"So they won't be forgotten, Carlotta. That's the greatest evil in the universe – the entropic decay of organized information. Forgetfulness. We despise it."

"Worse than the Invisible Enemy?"

"The Enemy is evil to the degree to which it abets entropic decay."

"Why does it want to do that?"

"We don't know. We don't even understand what the Enemy is, in physical terms. It seems to operate outside of the material universe. If it consists of matter, that matter is non-baryonic and impossible to detect. It pervades parts of the galaxy – though not all parts – like an insubstantial gas. When the Fleet passes through volumes of space heavily infested by the Enemy, our loss-rate soars. And as these infested volumes of space expand, they encompass and destroy life-bearing worlds."

"The Enemy's growing, though. And the Fleet isn't."

I had learned to recognize Erasmus's distress, not just because he was slowly adopting somewhat more human features. "The Fleet is my home, Carlotta. More than that. It's my body, my heart."

What he didn't say was that by joining me in the act of surfing time, he would be isolating himself from the realtime network that had birthed and sustained him. In realtime, Erasmus was a fraction of something reassuringly immense. But in slide-time, he'd be as alone as an Erasmus could get.

And yet, he came with me, when I made my decision. He was my Erasmus as much as he was the Fleet's, and he came with me. What would you call that, girl? Friendship? At least. I came to call it love.

The younger Carlotta has stolen those pills (the ones hidden under her smudged copy of People) for a reason. To help her sleep, was what she told herself. But she didn't really have trouble sleeping. No. If she was honest, she'd have to say the pills were an escape hatch. Swallow enough of them, and it's, hey, fuck you, world! Less work than the highway, an alternative she was also considering.

More shouting erupts in the next room. A real roust-up, bruises to come. Then, worse, Dan-O's voice goes all small and jagged. That's a truly bad omen, Carlotta knows. Like the smell of ozone that floods the air in advance of a lightning strike, just before the voltage ramps up and the current starts to flow.

Erasmus built a special virtuality for him and me to time-trip in. Basically, it was a big comfy room with a wall-sized window overlooking the Milky Way.

The billions of tiny dense components that made up the Fleet swarmed at velocities slower than the speed of light, but timesliding made it all seem faster – scarily so. Like running the whole universe in fast-forward, knowing you can't go back. During the first few months of our expanded Now, we soared a long way out of the spiral arm that contained the abandoned Sun. The particular sub-swarm of the Fleet that hosted my sense of self was on a long elliptical orbit around the supermassive black hole at the galaxy's core, and from this end of the ellipse, over the passing days, we watched the Milky Way drop out from under us like a cloud of luminous pearls.

When I wasn't in that room, I went off to visit other timesliders, and some of them visited me there. We were a self-selected group of radical roamers with a thing for risk, and we got to know one another pretty well. Oh, girl, I wish I could tell you all the friends I made among that tribe of self-selected exiles! Many of them human, not all: I met a few of the so-called Elders of other species, and managed to communicate with them on a friendly basis. Does that sound strange to you? I guess it is. Surpassing strange. I thought so too, at first. But these were people (mostly people) and things (but things can be people too) that I mostly liked and often loved, and they loved me back. Yes, they did. Whatever quirk of personality made us timesliders drew us together against all the speedy dark outside our virtual walls. Plus – well, we were survivors. It took not much more than a month to outlive all the remaining remnants of humanity. Even our ghosts were gone, in other words, unless you counted us as ghosts.

Erasmus was a little bit jealous of the friends I made. He had given up a lot for me, and maybe I ought to have appreciated him more for it. Unlike us formerly biological persons, though, Erasmus maintained a tentative link with realtime. He had crafted protocols to keep himself current on changes in the Fleet's symbol-sets and core mentation. That way, he could update us on what the Fleet was doing – new species raptured up from dying worlds and so forth. None of these newcomers lasted long, though, from our lofty perspective, and I once asked Erasmus why the Fleet even bothered with such ephemeral creatures as (for instance) human beings. He said that every species was doomed in the long run, but that didn't make it okay to kill people – or to abandon them when they might be rescued. That instinct was what made the Fleet a moral entity, something more than just a collection of self-replicating machines.

And it made him more than a nested loop of complex calculations. In the end, Carlotta, I came to love Erasmus best of all.

Meanwhile the years and stars scattered in our wake like dust – a thousand years, a hundred thousand, a million, more, and the galaxy turned like a great white wheel. We all made peace with the notion that we were the last of our kind, whatever "kind" we represented.

If you could hear me, girl, I guess you might ask what I found in that deep well of strangeness that made the water worth drinking. Well, I found friends, as I said – isn't that enough? And I found lovers. Even Erasmus began to adopt a human avatar, so we could touch each other in the human way.

I found, in plain words, a home, Carlotta, however peculiar in its nature – a real home, for the first time in my life.

Which is why I was so scared when it started to fall apart.

In the next room, Abby isn't taking Dan-O's anger lying down. It's nearly the perfect storm tonight – Dan-O's temper and Abby's sense of violated dignity both rising at the same ferocious pitch, rising toward some unthinkable crescendo.

But her mother's outrage is fragile, and Dan-O is frankly dangerous. The young Carlotta had known that about him from the get-go, from the first time her mother came home with this man on her arm: knew it from his indifferent eyes and his mechanical smile; knew it from the prison tattoos he didn't bother to disguise and the boastfulness with which he papered over some hole in his essential self. Knew it from the meth-lab stink that burned off him like a chemical perfume. Knew it from the company he kept, from the shitty little deals with furtive men arranged in Carlotta's mother's home because his own rental bungalow was littered with incriminating cans of industrial solvent. Knew it most of all by the way he fed Abby Boudaine crystal meth in measured doses, to keep her wanting it, and by the way Abby began to sign over her weekly Wal-Mart paycheck to him like a dutiful servant, back when she was working checkout.

Dan-O is tall, wiry, and strong despite his vices. The elder Carlotta can hear enough to understand that Dan-O is blaming Abby for the theft of the barbiturates – an intolerable sin, in Dan-O's book. Followed by Abby's heated denials and the sound of Dan-O's fists striking flesh. All this discovered, not remembered: the young Carlotta sleeps on, though she's obviously about to wake; the critical moment is coming fast. And Carlotta thinks of what she saw when she raided Dan-O's ditty bag, the blue metal barrel with a black knurled grip, a thing she had stared at, hefted, but ultimately disdained.

*   *   *

We dropped back down the curve of that elliptic, girl, and suddenly the Fleet began to vanish like drops of water on a hot griddle. Erasmus saw it first, because of what he was, and he set up a display so I could see it too: Fleet-swarms set as ghostly dots against a schema of the galaxy, the ghost-dots dimming perilously and some of them blinking out altogether. It was a graph of a massacre. "Can't anyone stop it?" I asked.

"They would if they could," he said, putting an arm (now that he had grown a pair of arms) around me. "They will if they can, Carlotta."

"Can we help?"

"We are helping, in a way. Existing the way we do means they don't have to use much mentation to sustain us. To the Fleet, we're code that runs a calculation for a few seconds out of every year. Not a heavy burden to carry."

Which was important, because the Fleet could only sustain so much computation, the upper limit being set by the finite number of linked nodes. And that number was diminishing as Fleet vessels were devoured wholesale.

"Last I checked," Erasmus said (which would have been about a thousand years ago, realtime), "the Fleet theorized that the Enemy is made of dark matter." (Strange stuff that hovers around galaxies, invisibly – it doesn't matter, girl; take my word for it; you'll understand it one day.) "They're not material objects so much as processes – parasitical protocols played out in dark matter clouds. Apparently, they can manipulate quantum events we don't even see."

"So we can't defend ourselves against them?"

"Not yet. No. And you and I might have more company soon, Carlotta. As long-timers, I mean."

That was because the Fleet continued to rapture up dying civilizations, nearly more than their shrinking numbers could contain. One solution was to shunt survivors into the Long Now along with us, in order to free up computation for battlefield maneuvers and such.

"Could get crowded," he warned.

"If a lot of strangers need to go Long," I said . . .

He gave me a carefully neutral look. "Finish the thought."

"Well . . . can't we just . . . go Longer?"

Fire a pistol in a tin box like this ratty trailer and the sound is ridiculously loud. Like being spanked on the ear with a two-by-four. It's the pistol shot that finally wakes the young Carlotta. Her eyelids fly open like window shades on a haunted house.

This isn't how the elder Carlotta remembers it. Gunshot? No, there was no gunshot: she just came awake and saw the ghost –

And no ghost, either. Carlotta tries desperately to speak to her younger self, wills herself to succeed, and fails yet again. So who fired that shot, and where did the bullet go, and why can't she remember any of this?

The shouting in the next room has yielded up a silence. The silence becomes an eternity. Then Carlotta hears the sound of footsteps – she can't tell whose – approaching her bedroom door.

In the end, almost every conscious function of the Fleet went Long, just to survive the attrition of the war with the dark-matter beings. The next loop through the galactic core pared us down to a fraction of what we used to be. When I got raptured up, the Fleet was a distributed cloud of baseball-sized objects running quantum computations on the state of their own dense constituent atoms – millions and millions of such objects, all linked together in a nested hierarchy. By the time we orbited back up our ellipsis, you could have counted us in the thousands, and our remaining links were carefully narrowbanded to give us maximum stealth.

So us wild timesliders chose to go Longer.

Just like last time, Erasmus warned me that it might be a suicidal act. If the Fleet was lost, we would be lost along with it . . . our subjective lives could end within days or hours. If, on the other hand, the Fleet survived and got back to reproducing itself, well, we might live on indefinitely – even drop back into realtime if we chose to do so. "Can you accept the risk?" he asked.

"Can you?"

He had grown a face by then. I suppose he knew me well enough to calculate what features I'd find pleasing. But it wasn't his ridiculous fake humanity I loved. What I loved was what went on behind those still-gemlike tourmaline eyes – the person he had become by sharing my mortality. "I accepted that risk a long time ago," he said.

"You and me both, Erasmus."

So we held on to each other and just – went fast.

Hard to explain what made that time-dive so vertiginous, but imagine centuries flying past like so much dust in a windstorm! It messed up our sense of place, first of all. Used to be we had a point of view light-years wide and deep . . . now all those loops merged into one continuous cycle; we grew as large as the Milky Way itself, with Andromeda bearing down on us like a silver armada. I held Erasmus in my arms, watching wide-eyed while he updated himself on the progress of the war and whispered new discoveries into my ear.

The Fleet had worked up new defenses, he said, and the carnage had slowed, but our numbers were still dwindling.

I asked him if we were dying.

He said he didn't know. Then he looked alarmed and held me tighter. "Oh, Carlotta . . ."

"What?" I stared into his eyes, which had gone far away and strange. "What is it? Erasmus, tell me!"

"The Enemy," he said in numbed amazement.

"What about them?"
"I know what they are."

The bedroom door opens.

The elder Carlotta doesn't remember the bedroom door opening. None of this is as she remembers it should be. The young Carlotta cringes against the backboard of the bed, so terrified she can barely draw breath. Bless you, girl, I'd hold your hand if I could!

What comes through the door is just Abby Boudaine. Abby in a cheap white nightgown. But Abby's eyes are yellow-rimmed and feral, and her nightgown is spattered with blood.

See, the thing is this. All communication is limited by the speed of light. But if you spread your saccades over time, that speed-limit kind of expands. Slow as we were, light seemed to cross galactic space in a matter of moments. Single thoughts consumed centuries. We felt the supermassive black hole at the center of the galaxy beating like a ponderous heart. We heard whispers from nearby galaxies, incomprehensibly faint but undeniably manufactured. Yes, girl, we were that slow.

But the Enemy was even slower.

"Long ago," Erasmus told me, channeling this information from the Fleet's own dying collectivity, "long ago, the Enemy learned to parasitize dark matter . . . to use it as a computational substrate . . . to evolve within it . . ."

"How long ago?"

His voice was full of awe. "Longer than you have words for, Carlotta. They're older than the universe itself."

Make any sense to you? I doubt it would. But here's the thing about our universe: it oscillates. It breathes, I mean, like a big old lung, expanding and shrinking and expanding again. When it shrinks, it wants to turn into a singularity, but it can't do that, because there's a limit to how much mass a quantum of volume can hold without busting. So it all bangs up again, until it can't accommodate any more emptiness. Back and forth, over and over. Perhaps, ad infinitum.

Trouble is, no information can get past those hot chaotic contractions. Every bang makes a fresh universe, blank as a chalkboard in an empty schoolhouse . . .

Or so we thought.

But dark matter has a peculiar relationship with gravity and mass, Erasmus said, so when the Enemy learned to colonize it, they found ways to propagate themselves from one universe to the next. They could survive the end of all things material, in other words, and they had already done so – many times!

The Enemy was genuinely immortal, if that word has any meaning. The Enemy conducted its affairs not just across galactic space, but across the voids that separate galaxies, clusters of galaxies, superclusters . . . slow as molasses, they were, but vast as all things, and as pervasive as gravity, and very powerful.

"So what have they got against the Fleet, if they're so big and almighty? Why are they killing us?"

Erasmus smiled then, and the smile was full of pain and melancholy and an awful understanding. "But they're not killing us, Carlotta. They're rapturing us up."

One time in school, when she was trying unsuccessfully to come to grips with *The Merchant of Venice*, Carlotta had opened a book about Elizabethan drama to a copy of an old drawing called Utriusque Cosmi. It was supposed to represent the whole cosmos, the way people thought of it back in Shakespeare's time, all layered and orderly: stars and angels on top, hell beneath, and a naked guy stretched foursquare between divinity and damnation. Made no sense to her at all. Some antique craziness. She thinks of that drawing now, for no accountable reason. But it doesn't stop at the angels, girl. I learned that lesson. Even angels have angels, and devils dance on the backs of lesser devils.

Her mother in her bloodstained nightgown hovers in the doorway of Carlotta's bedroom. Her unblinking gaze strafes the room until it fixes at last on her daughter. Abby Boudaine might be standing right here, Carlotta thinks, but those eyes are looking out from someplace deeper and more distant and far more frightening.

The blood fairly drenches her. But it isn't Abby's blood.

"Oh, Carlotta," Abby says. Then she clears her throat, the way she does when she has to make an important phone call or speak to someone she fears. "Carlotta . . ."

And Carlotta (the invisible Carlotta, the Carlotta who dropped down from that place where the angels dice with eternity) understands what Abby is about to say, recognizes at last the awesome circularity, not a paradox at all. She pronounces the words silently as Abby makes them real: "Carlotta. Listen to me, girl. I don't guess you understand any of this. I'm so sorry. I'm sorry for many things. But listen now. When it's time to leave, you leave. Don't be afraid, and don't get caught. Just go. Go fast."

Then she turns and leaves her daughter cowering in the darkened room.

Beyond the bedroom window, the coyotes are still complaining to the moon. The sound of their hooting fills up the young Carlotta's awareness until it seems to speak directly to the heart of her.

Then comes the second and final gunshot.

I have only seen the Enemy briefly, and by that time, I had stopped thinking of them as the Enemy.

Can't describe them too well. Words really do fail me. And by that time, might as well admit it, I was not myself a thing I would once have recognized as human. Just say that Erasmus and I and the remaining timesliders were taken up into the Enemy's embrace along with all the rest of the Fleet – all the memories we had deemed lost to entropy or warfare were preserved there. The virtualities the Enemies had developed across whole kalpas of time were labyrinthine, welcoming, strange beyond belief. Did I roam in those mysterious glades? Yes I did, girl, and Erasmus by my side, for many long (subjective) years, and we became – well, larger than I can say.

And the galaxies aged and flew away from one another until they were swallowed up in manifolds of cosmic emptiness, connected solely by the gentle and inexorable thread of gravity. Stars winked out, girl; galaxies merged and filled with dead and dying stars; atoms decayed to their last stable forms. But the fabric of space can tolerate just so much emptiness. It isn't infinitely elastic. Even vacuum ages. After some trillions and trillions of years, therefore, the expansion became a contraction.

During that time, I occasionally sensed or saw the Enemy – but I have to call them something else: say, the Great Old Ones, pardon my pomposity – who had constructed the dark matter virtualities in which I now lived. They weren't people at all. Never were. They passed through our adopted worlds like storm clouds, black and majestic and full of subtle and inscrutable lightnings. I couldn't speak to them, even then; as large and old as I had become, I was only a fraction of what they were.

I wanted to ask them why they had destroyed the Earth, why so many people had to be wiped out of existence or salvaged by the evolved benevolence of the Fleet. But Erasmus, who delved into these questions more deeply than I was able to, said the Great Old Ones couldn't perceive anything as tiny or ephemeral as a rocky planet like the Earth. The Earth and all the many planets like her had been destroyed, not by any willful calculation, but by autonomic impulses evolved over the course of many cosmic conflations – impulses as imperceptible and involuntary to the Old Ones as the functioning of your liver is to you, girl.

The logic of it is this: life-bearing worlds generate civilizations that eventually begin playing with dark matter, posing a potential threat to the continuity of the Old Ones. Some number of these intrusions can be tolerated and contained – like the Fleet, they were often an enriching presence – but too many of them would endanger the stability of the system. It's as if we were germs, girl, wiped out by a giant's immune system. They couldn't see us, except as a somatic threat. Simple as that.

But they could see the Fleet. The Fleet was just big enough and durable enough to register on the senses of the Old Ones. And the Old Ones weren't malevolent: they perceived the Fleet much the way the Fleet had once perceived us, as something primitive but alive and thinking and worth the trouble of salvation.

So they raptured up the Fleet (and similar Fleet-like entities in countless other galaxies), thus preserving us against the blind oscillations of cosmic entropy.

(Nice of them, I suppose. But if I ever grow large enough or live long enough to confront an Old One face to face, I mean to lodge a complaint. Hell yes we were small – people are some of the smallest thought-bearing creatures in the cosmos, and I think we all kind of knew that even before the end of the world . . . you did, surely. But pain is pain and grief is grief. It might be inevitable, it might even be built into the nature of things; but it isn't good, and it ought not to be tolerated, if there's a choice.)

Which I guess is why I'm here watching you squinch your eyes shut while the sound of that second gunshot fades into the air.

Watching you process a nightmare into a vision.

Watching you build a pearl around a grain of bloody truth.

Watching you go fast.

The bodiless Carlotta hovers a while longer in the fixed and changeless corridors of the past.

Eventually, the long night ends. Raw red sunlight finds the window.

Last dawn this small world will ever see, as it happens, but the young Carlotta doesn't know that yet.

Now that the universe has finished its current iteration, all its history is stored in transdimensional metaspace like a book on a shelf – it can't be changed. Truly so. I guess I know that now, girl. Memory plays tricks that history corrects.

And I guess that's why the Old Ones let me have access to these events, as we hover on the brink of a new creation.

I know some of the questions you'd ask me if you could. You might say, Where are you really? And I'd say, I'm at the end of all things, which is really just another beginning. I'm walking in a great garden of dark matter, while all things known and baryonic spiral up the ladder of unification energies to a fiery new dawn. I have grown so large, girl, that I can fly down history like a bird over a prairie field. But I cannot remake what has already been made. That is one power I do not possess.

I watch you get out of bed. I watch you dress. Blue jeans with tattered hems, a man's lumberjack shirt, those thrift-shop Reeboks. I watch you go to the kitchen and fill your vinyl Bratz backpack with bottled water and Tootsie Rolls, which is all the cuisine your meth-addled mother has left in the cupboards.

Then I watch you tiptoe into Abby's bedroom. I confess I don't remember this part, girl. I suppose it didn't fit my fantasy about a benevolent ghost. But here you are, your face fixed in a willed indifference, stepping over Dan-O's corpse. Dan-O bled a lot after Abby Boudaine blew a hole in his chest, and the carpet is a sticky rust-colored pond.

I watch you pull Dan-O's ditty bag from where it lies half under the bed. On the bed, Abby appears to sleep. The pistol is still in her hand. The hand with the pistol in it rests beside her head. Her head is damaged in ways the young Carlotta can't stand to look at. Eyes down, girl. That's it.

I watch you pull a roll of bills from the bag and stuff it into your pack. Won't need that money where you're going! But it's a wise move, taking it. Commendable forethought.

Now go.

I have to go too. I feel Erasmus waiting for me, feel the tug of his love and loyalty, gentle and inevitable as gravity. He used to be a machine older than the dirt under your feet, Carlotta Boudaine, but he became a man – my man, I'm proud to say. He needs me, because it's no easy thing crossing over from one universe to the next. There's always work to do, isn't that the truth?

But right now, you go. You leave those murderous pills on the nightstand, find that highway. Don't be afraid. Don't wait. Don't get caught. Just go. Go fast. And excuse me while I take my own advice.

A STORY, WITH BEANS

Steven Gould

Here, as advertised, is a story, with beans. Oh, and also a few metal-eating robots, who don't mind chewing through human flesh if it happens to get in the way. . . .

Steven Gould is a frequent contributor to Analog but has also appeared in Asimov's, Amazing, New Destinies, and elsewhere, and has been a finalist for the Hugo and Nebula awards. He's best-known for the "Jumper" series, including *Jumper, Reflex,* and *Jumper: Griffin's Story.* The first of these was made into the big-budget movie *Jumper* in 2008. Gould's other novels include *Wildside, Greenwar* (with Laura J. Mixon), *Help,* and *Blind Waves.* Gould lives in Albuquerque, New Mexico, with his wife, writer Laura J. Mixon, and their two daughters.

KIMBALL CROUCHED IN the shade of the mesquite trees, which, because of the spring, were trees instead of their usual ground-hugging scrub. He was answering a question asked by one of the sunburned tourists, who was sprawled by the water, leaning against his expensive carbon-framed backpack.

"It takes about a foot of dirt," Kimball said. "I mean, if there isn't anything electrical going on. Then you'll need more, depending on the current levels and the strength of the EMF. You may need to be underground a good ten feet otherwise.

"But it's a foot, minimum. Once saw a noob find a silver dollar that he'd dug up at one of the old truck stops west of Albuquerque. 'Throw it away!' we yelled at him. Why did he think they replaced his fillings before he entered the territory? But he said it was a rare coin and worth a fortune. The idiot swallowed it.

"We could have buried him. Kept his face clear but put a good foot of dirt over him. That could've worked, but there were bugs right there, eating those massive hydraulic cylinders buried in the concrete floor of the maintenance bays, the ones that drove the lifts.

"We scattered. He ran, too, but they were all around and they rose up like bees and then he stepped on one and it was all over. They went for the coin like it was a chewy caramel center."

There were three college-aged tourists – two men and a girl, a pair of Pueblo khaki-dressed mounted territorial rangers that Kimball knew, and

Mendez, the spring keeper. There was also a camel caravan camped below the spring, where the livestock were allowed to drink from the runoff, but the drovers, after filling their water bags, stayed close to their camels.

There were predators out here, both animal and human.

"What happened to the noob?" the tourist asked.

"He swallowed the coin. It was in his abdomen."

"What do you mean?"

"Christ, Robert," the girl said. "Didn't you listen to the entrance briefing? He died. The bugs would just go right through him, to the metal. There aren't any trauma centers out here, you know?"

One of the Rangers, silent until now, said, "That's right, Miss." He slid the sleeve of his khaki shirt up displaying a scarred furrow across the top of his forearm. "Bug did this. Was helping to dig a new kiva at Pojoaque and didn't see I'd uncovered the base of an old metal fencepost. Not until the pain hit. There weren't many bugs around but they came buzzing after that first one tasted steel and broadcast the call. I was able to roll away, under the incoming ones."

"Why are you visiting the zone?" asked Mendez. He sat apart, keeping an eye on the tourists. The woman had asked about bathing earlier and the rangers explained that you could get a bath in town and there was sometimes water in the Rio Puerco, but you didn't swim in the only drinking water between Red Cliff and the Territorial Capitol.

"You can bathe without soap in the runoff, down the hill above where the cattle drink. Wouldn't do it below," Mendez had elaborated. "You can carry a bit of water off into the brush if you want to soap 'n' rinse."

Kimball thought Mendez was still sitting there just in case she did decide to bathe. Strictly as a public service, no doubt, keeping a wary eye out for, uh, tan lines.

The woman tourist said, "We're here for Cultural Anthropology 305. Field study. We meet our prof at his camp on the Rio Puerco."

"Ah," said Kimball, "Matt Peabody."

"Oh. You know him?"

"Sure. His camp is just down stream from the Duncan ford. He likes to interview the people who pass through."

"Right. He's published some fascinating papers on the distribution of micro-cultures here in the zone."

"Micro-cultures. Huh," said Kimball. "Give me an example."

"Oh, some of the religious or political groups who form small communities out here. Do you know what I mean?"

"I do." Kimball, his face still, exchanged a glance with the two rangers.

As the woman showed no sign of imminent hygiene, Mendez climbed to his feet groaning and returned to his one room adobe-faced dugout, up the hill.

The woman student became more enthusiastic. "I think it's so cool how the zone has ended up being this great nursery for widely diverse ways of life! I'm so excited to be able to see it."

Kimball stood up abruptly and, taking a shallow basket off of his cart, walked downstream where the cattle watered. He filled the basket with dried dung: some camel, horse, and a bit of cow. He didn't walk back until his breathing had calmed and his face was still. When he returned to the spring, one of the rangers had a pile of dried grass and pine needles ready in the communal fire pit and the other one was skinning a long, thin desert hare.

Kimball had a crock of beans that'd been soaking in water since he'd left Red Cliff that morning. Getting it out of the cart he added more water, a chunk of salt pork, pepper, and fresh rosemary, then wedged it in the fire with the lid, weighted down by a handy rock.

"What do you do, out here?" the woman tourist asked him. Kimball smiled lazily and, despite her earlier words, thought about offering her some beans.

"Bit of this, bit of that. Right now, I sell things."

"A peddler? Shouldn't you be in school?"

Kimball decided he wasn't going to offer her any of his beans after all. He shrugged. "I've done the required." In fact, he had his GED, but he didn't advertise that. "It's different out here."

"How old are you?" she asked.

"How old are you?"

She grinned. "Personal question, eh? Okay. I'm nineteen."

"I'm sixteen. Sweet, never been kissed."

She cocked her head sideways. "Yeah, right."

"Kimball," one of the rangers called from across the firepit, "a quarter of the hare for some beans."

"Maybe. Any buwa, Di-you-wi?" Kimball asked.

"Of course there's buwa."

"Buwa and a haunch."

The two rangers discussed this in Tewa, then Di-you-wi said, "Buwa and a haunch. Don't stint the beans."

They warmed the buwa, rolled up blue-corn flatbread, on a rock beside the fire. Kimball added a salad of wide-leaf flame-flower and purslane that he'd harvested along the trail. The rangers spoke thanks in Tewa and Kimball didn't touch his food until they were finished.

The woman watched out of the corner of her eyes, fascinated.

The tourists ate their radiation-sterilized ration packs that didn't spoil and didn't have to be cooked and weren't likely to give them the runs. But the smell of the hare and beans wafted through the clearing and the smell of the packaged food didn't spread at all.

"That sure smells good," the girl said.

Kimball tore off a bit of buwa and wrapped it around a spoonful of beans and a bit of the hare. He stretched out his arm. "See what you think."

She licked her lips and hesitated.

"Christ, Jennifer, that rabbit had ticks all over it," said the sunburned man. "Who knows what parasites they – uh, it had."

The rangers exchanged glances and laughed quietly.

Jennifer frowned and stood up, stepping over sunburn boy, and crouched down on her heels by the fire, next to Kimball. With a defiant look at her two companions, she took the offered morsel and popped it into her mouth. The look of defiance melted into surprised pleasure. "Oh, wow. So buwe is corn bread?"

"Buwa. Tewa wafer bread – made with blue corn. The Hopi make it too, but they call it piki."

"The beans are wonderful. Thought they'd be harder."

"I started them soaking this morning, before I started out from Red Cliff."

"Ah," she lowered her voice. "What did they call you earlier?"

"Kimball."

She blinked. "Is that your name?"

"First name. I'm Kimball. Kimball . . . Creighton."

Di-you-wi laughed. Kimball glared at him.

"I'm Jennifer Frauenfelder." She settled beside him.

"Freuenfelder." Kimball said it slowly, like he was rolling it around in his mouth. "German?"

"Yes. It means field-of-women."

Di-you-wi blinked at this and said something in Tewa to his partner who responded, "Huh. Reminds me of someone I knew who was called Left-for-dead."

Kimball rubbed his forehead and looked at his feet but Jennifer said, "Left-for-dead? That's an odd name. Did they have it from birth or did something happen?"

"Oh," said Di-you-wi, "something happened all right." He sat up straight and spoke in a deeper voice, more formal.

"Owei humbeyô."

(His partner whispered, almost as if to himself, "Once upon a time and long ago.")

"Left-for-dead came to a village in the Jornada del Muerte on the edge of the territory of the City of God, where the People of the Book reside." Di-you-wi glanced at Jennifer and added, "It was a 'nursery of diverse beliefs.'"

"Left-for-dead was selling books, Bibles mostly, but also almanacs and practical guides to gardening and the keeping of goats and sheep and cattle.

"But he had other books as well, books not approved by the Elders – the plays of Shakespeare, books of stories, health education, Darwin.

"And he stole the virtue of Sharon – "

The two male tourists sat up at that and the sunburned one smacked his lips. "The dawg!"

Di-you-wi frowned at the interuption, cleared his throat, and went on. "And Left-for-dead stole the virtue of Sharon, the daughter of a Reader of the Book, by trading her a reading primer and a book on women's health."

"What did she trade?" asked the leering one.

"There was an apple pie," said Di-you-wi. "Also a kiss."

Jennifer said, "And that's how she lost her virtue?"

"It was more the primer. The women of the People of the Book are not allowed to read," added his partner.

"Ironic, that," said Kimball.

"Or kiss," Di-you-wi said with a quelling glance. He raised his voice. "They burned his books and beat him and imprisoned him in the stocks and called on the people of the village to pelt him but Sharon, the daughter of the Reader, burned the leather hinges from the stocks in the dusk and they ran, northwest, into the malpaís where the lava is heated by the sun until you can cook buwa on the stones and when the rain falls in the afternoon it sizzles like water falling on coals.

"The Elders chased them on horseback but the malpaís is even harder on horses than men and they had to send the horses back and then they chased them on foot but the rocks leave no prints.

"But the water in the malpaís is scarce to none and Left-for-dead and the girl were in a bad way even though they hid by day and traveled by night. Once, in desperation, Left-for-dead snuck back and stole a water gourd from the men who chased them, while they lay sleeping, but in doing so he put them back on the trail.

"Two days later, Sharon mis-stepped and went down in a crack in the rock and broke both bones in her lower leg. Left-for-dead splinted the leg, made a smoke fire, and left her there. The People of the Book found her and took her back, dragged on a travois, screaming with every bump and jar.

"They discussed chasing Left-for-dead and then they prayed and the Reader said God would punish the transgressor, and they went back to their village and spread the story far and wide, to discourage the weak and the tempted.

"Left-for-dead walked another day, to the north hoping to reach the water at Marble Tanks, but he had been beaten badly in the stocks and his strength failed him. When he could go no further he rolled into a crevice in the lava where there was a bit of shade and got ready to die. His tongue began to swell and he passed in and out of darkness and death had his hand on him."

Here Di-you-wi paused dramatically, taking a moment to chase the last of his beans around the bowl with a bit of buwa.

Jennifer leaned forward. "And?"

"And then it rained. A short, heavy summer thunderstorm. The water dripped down onto Left-for-dead's face and he drank, and awoke drinking and coughing. And then drank some more. He crawled out onto the face of the malpaís and drank from the puddles in the rock and was able to fill the water gourd he'd stolen from the Reader's men, but he didn't have to drink from it until the next day when the last of the rain evaporated from the pockets in the lava.

"He made it to Marble Tanks, and then east to some seeps on the edge of the lava flows, and hence to the Territorial Capitol."

"Because the incident with Left-for-dead was just the latest of many, a Territorial judge was sent out with a squad of rangers to hold hearings. The City of God sent their militia, one hundred strong, and killed the judge and most of the rangers.

"When the two surviving rangers reported back, the Territorial Governor flashed a message beyond the curtain and a single plane came in answer, flying up where the air is so thin that the bugs' wings can't catch, and they dropped the leaflets, the Notice of Reclamation – the revocation of the City's Charter."

"That's it?" said Jennifer. "They dropped a bunch of leaflets?"

"The first day. The second day it wasn't leaflets."

Jennifer held her hand to her mouth. "Bombs?"

"Worse. Chaff pods of copper and aluminum shavings that burst 500 feet above the ground. I heard tell that the roofs and ground glittered in the sunlight like jewels."

The sunburned man laughed. "That's it? Metal shavings?"

"I can't believe they let you through the curtain," Jennifer said to him. "Didn't you listen at all?" She turned back to Di-you-wi. "How many died?"

"Many left when they saw the leaflets. But not the most devout and not the women who couldn't read. The Speaker of the Word said that their faith would prevail. Perhaps they deserved their fate . . . but not the children."

"The last thing the plane dropped was a screamer – an electromagnetic spike trailing an antennae wire several hundred feet long. They say the bugs rose into the air and blotted the sun like locusts."

Jennifer shuddered.

Di-you-wi relented a little. "Many more got out when they saw the cloud. I mean, it was like one of the ten plagues of the first chapter of their Book, after all. If they made it outside the chaff pattern and kept to the low ground, they made it. But those who stayed and prayed?" He paused dramatically. "The adobe houses of the City of God are mud and dust and weeds, and the great Cathedral is a low pile of stones and bones."

"Owei humbeyô." Once upon a time and long ago.

Everyone was quiet for a moment though Jennifer's mouth worked as if to ask something, but no sound came out. Kimball added the last of the gathered fuel to the fire, banged the dust out of his basket, and flipped it, like a Frisbee, to land in his rickshaw-style handcart. He took the empty stoneware bean crock and filled it from the stream and put it at the edge of the coals, to soak before he cleaned it.

"What happened to Sharon?" Jennifer finally asked into the silence.

Di-you-wi shook his head. "I don't know. You would have to ask Left-for-dead."

Jennifer. "Oh, thanks a lot. Very helpful."

Di-you-wi and his partner exchanged glances and his partner opened his mouth as if to speak but De-you-wi shook his head.

Kimball hadn't meant to speak but he found the words spilling out, anyway, unbidden. "I would like to say that Sharon's leg still hurts her. That it didn't heal straight, and she limps. But that she teaches others to read now down in New Roswell. That I had seen her recently and sold her school some primers just last month."

Jennifer frowned, "You would like to say that?"

"It was a bad break and I set it as best I could but they bounced her over the lava on their way home and trusted to God for further treatment. She couldn't even walk, much less run, when the metal fell."

Jennifer's mouth was open but she couldn't speak for a moment.

"Huh," said Di-you-wi. "Hadn't heard that part, Left-for-dead."

Kimball could see him reorganizing the tale in his head, incorporating the added details. "Got it from her sister. After I recovered."

Jennifer stood and walked over to Kimball's cart and flipped up the tarp. The books were arranged spine out, paperbacks mostly, some from behind the Porcelain Wall, newish with plasticized covers, some yellowed and cracking from before the bugs came, like anything that didn't contain metal or electronics, salvaged, and a small selection of leather bound books from New Santa Fe, the Territorial Capitol, hand-set with ceramic type and hand bound – mostly practical, how-to books.

"Peddler. Book seller."

Kimball shrugged. "Varies. I've got other stuff, too. Plastic sewing needles, ceramic blades, antibiotics, condoms. Mostly books."

Finally she asked, "And her father? The Elder who put you in the stocks?"

"He lives. His faith wasn't strong enough when it came to that final test. He lost an arm, though."

"Is he in New Roswell, too?"

"No. He's doing time in the Territorial prison farm in Nuevo Belen. He preaches there, to a very small congregation. The People of the Book don't do well if they can't isolate their members – if they can't control what information they get. They're not the People of the Books, after all.

"If she'd lived, Sharon would probably have made him a part of her life . . . but he's forbidden the speaking of her name. He would've struck her name from the leaves of the family Bible but the bugs took care of that."

Di-you-wi shook his head on hearing this. "And who does this hurt? I think he is a stupid man."

Kimball shrugged. "It's not him I feel sorry for."

Jennifer's eyes glinted brightly in the light of the fire. She said, "It's not fair, is it?"

And there was nothing to be said to that.

UNDER THE SHOUTING SKY

Karl Bunker

Currently a software engineer, new writer Karl Bunker has been a jeweler, a musical-instrument maker, a sculptor, and a mechanical technician. His work has appeared in Cosmos, Abyss & Apex, Electric Velocipede, Writers of the Future, Neo-Opsis, and elsewhere. The gripping story that follows, "Under the Shouting Sky," won him the first Robert A. Heinlein Centennial Short Story Contest, a very appropriate choice, since it's not hard to see Heinlein himself having written this. Bunker lives with his dog in Boston, Massachusetts.

THE HISSING VIBRATION of the sled's thruster hummed through the frame of the sled, through the thinly padded seats, through the pressure suits of the two men, into their bodies, their bones, and became something like sound, reverberating inside their helmets. And it didn't sound good. For minutes at a time it would drone on smoothly, then it would catch and sputter, sometimes producing an almost human-sounding cough, and then settle back into normality. Until the next time. Occasionally Saunders twisted in his seat to look back at the engine behind the open cab, or turned his head to look at Robeson. Robeson was driving the sled, and he stared straight ahead. Neither man spoke.

Suddenly there was a ragged metallic shriek, and the sled veered to the right. Robeson swore, fighting the control stick with one hand as he shut down the thruster with the other.

"What the hell?" Saunders yelled.

Robeson didn't answer. When the sled bumped to a stop, he unfastened his seatbelt and hopped down to the icy ground. A moment later Saunders heard a soft sound, like a grunt, in his helmet radio. He looked down at Robeson. "What is it?" he said. "What's wrong?"

"You may as well come down, sir. We'll be walking from here," Robeson said.

"What?" Saunders snapped. "What's the matter with the damn thing?" He lowered himself from the sled and joined Robeson.

Robeson pointed at the sled's engine. "Burn-through in the main reaction chamber."

Saunders looked. "That little hole? Can't you patch it or something?"

"What you're looking at is the outer housing of the engine. Underneath that everything's burned to hell. This engine is dead." Robeson looked toward the horizon, a smooth curve of white against the black sky. Then he looked up, where Saturn was high and to the left. Nearly full, it filled a great swath of the sky. It was waxing gibbous now, so it would be full in about an hour.

"But you haven't even opened it up," said Saunders. "How do you know it's that bad?"

"Because that's my job," said Robeson. "And we don't have time for me to start taking it apart. My suit shows we're seventy-one klicks from Jansha Base. What's yours say?"

"Seventy-eight point seven. And I show ninety-two minutes of oxygen. God damn it, that's too far, Robeson." Saunders turned away from Robeson and cocked his head back slightly in his helmet. "Mayday! Mayday! Mayday! This is Enceladus Transport Sled zero-five, Stanley Saunders and Joe Robeson calling. Our position is approximately seventy-five kilometers from Jansha Base Station, bearing approximately two eight seven degrees. Our sled is disabled and we are heading for Jansha on foot. We may not have enough oxygen to make it. This is a Mayday call. Anyone receiving please respond."

They stood in silence, listening to the radio's background hiss in their helmets.

"No one can hear you," said Robeson. "We're too far from Jansha."

"It's not that we're too far, damnit! They can't receive us because we're too far over the damn horizon! But something in orbit might pick us up, or the signal might bounce off one of the other moons."

"Okay," Robeson answered. "We can hope. But in the meantime we better start walking."

It wasn't really walking; it was more of a shuffling skip. Some liked to call it the Enceladus two-step. With .01 g, walking doesn't really work. And while a person could make superman-style leaps of 50 meters or more, doing so was both slow and dangerous. An energetic jump would leave a person trapped in a slowly drifting parabolic trajectory for more than a minute. With no atmosphere there was no way to control where you landed, and there were places you wouldn't want to land. The surface of Enceladus is ice, sometimes skating rink smooth, sometimes gravelly pebbles or fine ice powder, sometimes with kilometers-deep fissures, sometimes a field of jagged shards and deadly sharp spires, as hard as earthly glass.

The trick with the two-step is to stay low. Bend your knees, keep one foot well ahead of the other, and nudge yourself forward, not up, with each hop. Watch the ground, watch where you'll touch down after this hop, and the next one and the one after that. On rough ground you'll have to keep your hops short and slow. When it's smooth you can glide a dozen meters or more at a time and build up some speed – if you don't mind risking your life. Even with needle-sharp adaptive crampons, boots provide almost no traction on Enceladus, so slowing down in a hurry isn't an option. Suit gyros try to keep your body upright, but they're easily overwhelmed. If something catches your toe, you'll fall. If a patch of ice crumbles underneath you, you'll fall. If your crampons slip, you'll fall. If you're moving fast when you fall, you'll tumble and spin and bounce for a long, long time. Depending on how all that tumbling and bouncing ends, it will either be a time-wasting and undignified nuisance or the end of your life. Being in a hurry on Enceladus is not a good idea.

They skipped. After a few minutes Saunders made another Mayday call. Far to their left, near the horizon, a geyser made a ghostly white funnel-shaped silhouette against the black sky.

"How much oh-two does your suit show, Robeson?"

"Same as you, eighty-five minutes now."

"Damn," said Saunders. "Our emergency tanks will add to that, but exerting ourselves like this will probably subtract at least as much. We can't do seventy-five kilometers in that much time."

"It might not be that far. These position readouts aren't too accurate."

"No kidding they're not too accurate!" Saunders yelled. "So we might be a lot farther out, damnit!" He hit the side of his helmet with his gloved palm. "The technology on this whole mission is crap! Everything's jury-rigged and held together with spit. Two damn communication satellites that failed, no damn GPS system, sleds with engines that blow up, Jansha Base springing a leak every time I turn around, and lousy damn technicians who can't fix anything." Saunders took a slow, trembling breath.

They skipped. Robeson made a Mayday call, and they listened to the answering silence. Then Saunders spoke. "Robeson?"

"Yeah?"

"I'm sorry. About calling you a lousy technician. That was stupid."

"It's okay."

"I'm scared, Robeson. We're in big trouble here and I'm scared."

"I'm scared too, Mr Saunders. Don't worry about it."

"You're not so scared. I can hear your breathing, just like you can hear mine. You're steady as a rock and I'm hyperventilating like a damn schoolgirl. That's good; your oh-two will last longer." He paused and took a deliberately slow breath. "Anyway, I know you're a good technician, Joe. I wouldn't have hired you if you weren't."

They skipped. They made another Mayday call.

"Joe?" Saunders said.

"George."

"What?"

"My name is George, not Joe," Robeson said.

"Oh. Damn. Sorry."

"It's okay."

"I was just thinking," said Saunders. "If anyone should be whining about this mess we're in, it should be you."

Saunders waited, but Robeson didn't say anything. "When the Wreckage was found, I was one of the ones who was screaming the loudest that we had to get a manned mission out here right away, and to hell with whether the technology was ready or there were safety backups for everything. I lobbied Washington, then I went to JPL . . . When they made me chief mission scientist I felt like . . . like this was what I'd been born for." He glanced across at Robeson. "For people like me, this mission is the biggest, the most important thing we could imagine. Proof that there were aliens from another star system who came here in some kind of a ship . . ." He paused again. "What I'm trying to say is that I've been willing to die for this mission since the first pictures of the Wreckage came back. Or at least that's what I told myself. But it's different for you, George. You're just – I mean, you're a technician. You're just here because the pay was too good to pass up, right? This is just a job for you."

"Yeah, I guess so," Robeson said. "It's a job." He glanced back and saw that Saunders had slowed and was lagging behind. His voice was soft in Saunders' helmet as he spoke across a distance of thirty meters. "C'mon Mr Saunders, get a move on. We're not dead yet."

They skipped. The terrain changed from rough and boulder-strewn to a field of smooth ripples, a meter high and regular, like frozen waves. "Hold up!" Saunders called, and they stopped.

"I don't like the look of the ice here," Saunders said. "We might be coming up on the Suffolk Fissures. Hang on, I'll take a look." He crouched low and then jumped straight up. Robeson watched him rise, his body dwindling against the black sky.

"Yes, I was right," Saunders said as he drifted groundward again. "That's good; it means we may be closer to Jansha than our suits show." He landed with a grunt. "We'll have to bear east for a ways."

Robeson was looking up at Saturn, still not quite full, the rings a razor-fine line across its face and extending on either side. Saunders chuckled. "I've noticed that about you before, Robeson. You look up at Saturn a lot. Most of us hate looking at it. More than a second or two of staring up at it and we start feeling it pulling at us, sucking us up into space."

"Yeah?"

"Yeah. When you hear someone screaming in their sleep back at Jansha, that's probably what they're dreaming – Big Yellow sucking them up like the mouth of some gigantic monster. I guess you just don't think about it, like you aren't thinking about how much trouble we're in right now. You have no imagination, George, and I envy you like hell."

They skipped. The terrain changed again as they came to a lowland area. The ice was smooth enough here for them to build up their speed. "This is more like it," said Saunders. "If only it stays like this for—" A sharp, inarticulate cry came from Robeson. Saunders looked to his right and saw the other man cartwheeling end over end. "Jesus, Robeson, are you okay?" Robeson only swore, his body twirling two meters over the ground. As he drifted near the ground he tried to grab at the ice with one gloved hand and bounced up, spinning on two axes now. "Shit!" he yelled.

"George, stop fighting it! Go limp – you know that."

"Yeah," Robeson said, his voice tight.

Over his radio, Saunders could hear the whir of straining gyroscopes in Robeson's suit. "How the heck did you manage to trip?" he asked. "This place is flat as—"

"Shut up!" Robeson was still flying, spinning, bumping the icy ground now and then. "I saw something! Under the ice – just below the surface. Go back – see if you can find the spot . . . Wait – I've got my feet again – I'm going back." He made long, high skip-steps back, retracing his path.

"Robeson, what are you doing?" Saunders said. "Whatever it was, we don't have time for it."

Robeson didn't answer. Saunders was about to call to him again when he saw Robeson come to a stop, then take a few steps, staring down at the ground. With the slow, drifting motion that falling objects have under the whisper-gravity of Enceladus, he dropped to his knees. Very softly, Saunders heard in his helmet, "Mr Saunders, come here."

Saunders started moving. "What is it? Are you hurt?"

"I'm fine," Robeson said. "Just come here. Look."

Saunders hopped to a stop beside Robeson and looked down. There was a pause before he reacted. Long enough for Robeson to glance at him curiously, wondering if Saunders could see it, or if some quirk of reflection was hiding it from him. Finally Saunders made a ragged gasp. He tried to bring his hand to his mouth, and his glove thumped against his faceplate.

"It's smaller than we calculated," he said in a whisper. "It must be barely a meter tall . . ." His voice trailed off. He dropped to his hands and knees and put his helmet close to the ice.

The body was embedded at an angle, with the head higher than the torso. Its legs and feet were obscured by cloudy ice, but its clear, ovoid helmet was almost at the surface. When Saunders touched his own helmet to the ice, his face was centimeters away from the brown, scale-covered face of an alien.

"Transponder flag," Saunders said without moving from his crouch. Then: "Jesus!" He jerked upright, causing his body to float off the ground. He patted frantically at his suit pockets. "The transponder flags! Tell me you've got one! For God's sake! You have to have one with you!"

"No," Robeson said. "They're all back at the sled."

"Damnit! Then something – something we can leave here as a marker – or something we can at least make a note or recording with, so – so if we don't make it back, they'll know about this – we can give them a rough position . . ."

"I've got nothing with me," Robeson said. "Nothing at all. And these suits don't make recordings."

"Okay, we'll make a cairn – pile up some ice . . ." He stopped as he looked around at the flat, featureless expanse that extended to the horizon in all directions. Saunders lifted his arms, making trembling fists in front of his helmet. "Damnit, damnit, damnit!" He kicked at the ground, knocking himself more than a meter skyward. "We can't even scratch a lousy arrow in the ice!" He was breathing so hard that Robeson could see his chest rising and falling through his suit. "Okay then. Okay. We get back to Jansha. Even these lousy inertial position systems in our suits should be good enough to let us find this spot again by backtracking. With a big enough search team we'll find it." He launched himself into a fast skip across the ice. "Come on!" he barked. "From here on we go flat out! As fast as we can, whatever the risk. We have to make it back to Jansha, you hear me?"

"I hear you," said Robeson.

Saunders glanced behind him without breaking his stride. Robeson was standing still.

"What are you doing, Robeson? Come on!"

"I don't think we can make it back, Mr. Saunders. Look at your readouts. We're down to about thirty minutes of air and we're only about halfway back."

"So what, damnit? We have to try. You can't just stay there and . . ." Saunders went silent. Fighting not to lose his footing, he slowly brought himself to a stop, then turned to look at Robeson, now fifty meters behind him. "My God, Robeson," he said.

"Yeah," said Robeson. "We don't have any transponder flags with us, but we've got transponders. The ones that are built into these suits. They'll use that to come after my body, and when they find me they'll find . . . him."

"No, Robeson. Look – even if we don't make it back, we just have to get within radio range . . . We'll tell them . . ."

"If we make it back to radio range. And they still might never find this guy. You have to be right on top of him to see him through the ice."

"You can't . . . you can't . . . you can't just . . . Christ, Robeson . . ."

"You said it yourself, Mr Saunders. This is important. The most important thing ever. The Wreckage is nothing but a pile of twisted metal, but this is something real. His body, his suit . . . you guys will learn all kinds of stuff from him. But they have to find him. They have to find him."

Saunders took a slow breath. "Robeson, I can't wait, I can't stand here and argue. I'm heading back to Jansha, and I'm going to make it. I don't care if I have to breathe vacuum. I'm going to make it back, you hear me? You can damn well sit here and wait to die if you want to. I'm not going to!"

Seconds passed, and Robeson said nothing. Saunders made a sound that might have been a word, but Robeson couldn't understand it. Then he was moving again, gliding over the ice with long, fast strides.

Robeson touched a control on his forearm that turned off his suit radio. He listened to his own breath echoing in his helmet. It was fast and trembling. "I'm the one hyperventilating like a damn schoolgirl now, Mr Saunders," he said to himself. He let himself drop to a seated position and put one hand on the ice, close to the alien's face. "What the hell are you doing way out here, anyway, little guy?" he said. He lowered himself onto his back and looked up. Saturn was full now, and Mimas was just starting a transit, painting a small gray disk on the edge of Saturn's face. He looked up for a long time in silence. "How can they not look at it?" he said quietly. He stared, trying to imagine something menacing in the vision, the feeling of being pulled up into the blackness, lifted away from Enceladus' feathery gravity. Instead all he saw was a big ball of pastel yellow, part of it blackened by the shadow of the rings. When he'd seen pictures of it back home, there was nothing much to it; pretty, but nothing special. But here, with the incredible, impossible size of it overhead, it was different. It became something he couldn't ignore, something joyous – a gigantic, roaring shout of beauty from the sky.

He shifted onto his side to look down at the frozen alien again. One of its eyes was closed, the other showed a narrow white slit. "I bet you didn't mind looking at it, did you?" he said. "You knew you weren't going to make it, and you laid down just like this, looking up at the sky. I guess you had no imagination either."

He rolled onto his back again. He tried to put his hands under the back of his head, but the shoulder joints in his suit made the position uncomfortable. He crossed his arms tight against his chest, trembling. "What the hell were you doing way out here, anyway?" he said again. He was quiet for several minutes. Then he said, "Yeah, I know. Doin' your job. Just doin' your damn job, same as the rest of us."

EVENTS PRECEDING THE HELVETICAN RENAISSANCE

John Kessel

Born in Buffalo, New York, John Kessel now lives with his family in Raleigh, North Carolina, where he is a professor of American literature and the director of the creative-writing program at North Carolina State University. Kessel made his first sale in 1975. His first solo novel, *Good News From Outer Space*, was released in 1988 to wide critical acclaim, but before that he had made his mark on the genre primarily as a writer of highly imaginative, finely crafted short stories, many of which have been assembled in collections such as *Meeting in Infinity* and *The Pure Product*. He won a Nebula Award in 1983 for his novella *Another Orphan*, which was also a Hugo finalist that year and has been released as an individual book. His story "Buffalo" won the Theodore Sturgeon Award in 1991, and his novella *Stories for Men* won the prestigious James Tiptree Jr. Memorial Award in 2003. His other books include the novels *Corrupting Dr. Nice*, *Freedom Beach* (written in collaboration with James Patrick Kelly), *Ninety Percent of Everything* (writen in collaboration with James Patrick Kelly and Jonathan Lethem), and an anthology of stories from the famous Sycamore Hill Writers Workshop (which he also helps to run), called *Intersections*, co-edited by Mark L. Van Name and Richard Butner. His most recent books are a collection, *The Baum Plan for Financial Independence and Other Stories*, and three anthologies coedited with James Patrick Kelly, *Feeling Very Strange: The Slipstream Anthology*, *Rewired: The Post-Cyberpunk Anthology*, and *The Secret History of Science Fiction*.

In the story that follows, Kessel spins a traditional action-packed space adventure with some inventive and individual touches that are very much his own.

WHEN MY MIND cleared, I found myself in the street. The protector god Bishamon spoke to me then: The boulevard to the spaceport runs straight up the mountain. And you must run straight up the boulevard.

The air was full of wily spirits, and moving fast in the Imperial City was a crime. But what is man to disobey the voice of a god? So I ran. The pavement vibrated with the thunder of the great engines of the Caslonian Empire. Behind me the curators of the Imperial Archives must by now have discovered the mare's nest I had made of their defenses, and perhaps had already realized that something was missing.

Above the plateau the sky was streaked with clouds, through which shot violet gravity beams carrying ships down from and up to planetary orbit. Just outside the gate to the spaceport a family in rags – husband, wife, two children – used a net of knotted cords to catch fish from the sewers. Ignoring them, prosperous citizens in embroidered robes passed among the shops of the port bazaar, purchasing duty-free wares, recharging their concubines, seeking a meal before departure. Slower, now.

I slowed my pace. I became indistinguishable from them, moving smoothly among the travelers.

To the Caslonian eye, I was calm, self-possessed; within me, rage and joy contended. I had in my possession the means to redeem my people. I tried not to think, only to act, but now that my mind was rekindled, it raced. Certainly it would go better for me if I left the planet before anyone understood what I had stolen. Yet I was very hungry, and the aroma of food from the restaurants along the way enticed me. It would be foolishness itself to stop here.

Enter the restaurant, I was told. So I stepped into the most elegant of the establishments.

The maitre d' greeted me. "Would the master like a table, or would he prefer to dine at the bar?"

"The bar," I said

"Step this way." There was no hint of the illicit about his manner, though something about it implied indulgence. He was proud to offer me this experience that few could afford.

He seated me at the circular bar of polished rosewood. Before me, and the few others seated there, the chef grilled meats on a heated metal slab. Waving his arms in the air like a dancer, he tossed flanks of meat between two force knives, letting them drop to the griddle, flipping them dexterously upward again in what was as much performance as preparation. The energy blades of the knives sliced through the meat without resistance, the sides of these same blades batting them like paddles. An aroma of burning hydrocarbons wafted on the air.

An attractive young man displayed for me a list of virtualities that represented the "cuts" offered by the establishment, including subliminal tastes. The "cuts" referred to the portions of the animal's musculature from which the slabs of meat had been sliced. My mouth watered.

He took my order, and I sipped a cocktail of bitters and Belanova.

While I waited, I scanned the restaurant. The fundamental goal of our order is to vindicate divine justice in allowing evil to exist. At a small nearby table, a young woman leaned beside a child, probably her daughter, and

encouraged her to eat. The child's beautiful face was the picture of innocence as she tentatively tasted a scrap of pink flesh. The mother was very
beautiful. I wondered if this was her first youth.

The chef finished his performance, to the mild applause of the other
patrons. The young man placed my steak before me. The chef turned off
the blades and laid them aside, then ducked down a trap door to the oubli-
ette where the slaves were kept. As soon as he was out of sight, the god told
me, Steal a knife.

While the diners were distracted by their meals, I reached over the counter, took one of the force blades, and slid it into my boot. Then I ate. The
taste was extraordinary. Every cell of my body vibrated with excitement and
shame. My senses reeling, it took me a long time to finish.

A slender man in a dark robe sat next to me. "That smells good," he said.
"Is that genuine animal flesh?"

"Does it matter to you?"

"Ah, brother, calm yourself. I'm not challenging your taste."

"I'm pleased to hear it."

"But I am challenging your identity." He parted the robe – his tunic bore
the sigil of Port Security. "Your passport, please."

I exposed the inside of my wrist for him. A scanlid slid over his left eye
and he examined the marks beneath my skin. "Very good," he said. He drew
a blaster from the folds of his cassock. "We seldom see such excellent forger-
ies. Stand up, and come with me."

I stood. He took my elbow in a firm grip, the bell of the blaster against
my side. No one in the restaurant noticed. He walked me outside,
down the crowded bazaar. "You see, brother, that there is no escape from
consciousness. The minute it returns, you are vulnerable. All your prayer is
to no avail."

This is the arrogance of the Caslonian. They treat us as non-sentients,
and they believe in nothing. Yet as I prayed, I heard no word.

I turned to him. "You may wish the absence of the gods, but you are
mistaken. The gods are everywhere present." As I spoke the plosive "p" of
"present," I popped the cap from my upper right molar and blew the moondust it contained into his face.

The agent fell writhing to the pavement. I ran off through the people,
dodging collisions. My ship was on the private field at the end of the bazaar.
Before I had gotten halfway there, an alarm began sounding. People looked
up in bewilderment, stopping in their tracks. The walls of buildings and
stalls blinked into multiple images of me. Voices spoke from the air: "This
man is a fugitive from the state. Apprehend him."

I would not make it to the ship unaided, so I turned on my percep-
tual overdrive. Instantly, everything slowed. The voices of the people
and the sounds of the port dropped an octave. They moved as if in slow
motion. I moved, to myself, as if in slow motion as well – my body could
in no way keep pace with my racing nervous system – but to the people
moving at normal speed, my reflexes were lighting fast. Up to the limit of

my physiology – and my joints had been reinforced to take the additional stress, my muscles could handle the additional lactic acid for a time – I could move at twice the speed of a normal human. I could function perhaps for ten minutes in this state before I collapsed.

The first person to accost me – a sturdy middle-aged man – I seized by the arm. I twisted it behind his back and shoved him into the second who took up the command. As I dodged through the crowd up the concourse, it began to drizzle. I felt as if I could slip between the raindrops. I pulled the force blade from my boot and sliced the ear from the next man who tried to stop me. His comic expression of dismay still lingers in my mind. Glancing behind, I saw the agent in black, face swollen with pustules from the moondust, running toward me.

I was near the field. In the boarding shed, attendants were folding the low-status passengers and sliding them into dispatch pouches, to be carried onto a ship and stowed in drawers for their passage. Directly before me, I saw the woman and child I had noticed in the restaurant. The mother had out a parasol and was holding it over the girl to keep the rain off her. Not slowing, I snatched the little girl and carried her off. The child yelped, the mother screamed. I held the blade to the girl's neck. "Make way!" I shouted to the security men at the field's entrance. They fell back.

"Halt!" came the call from behind me. The booth beside the gate was seared with a blaster bolt. I swerved, turned, and, my back to the gate, held the girl before me.

The agent in black, followed by two security women, jerked to a stop. "You mustn't hurt her," the agent said.

"Oh? And why is that?"

"It's against everything your order believes."

Master Darius had steeled me for this dilemma before sending me on my mission. He told me, "You will encounter such situations, Adlan. When they arise, you must resolve the complications."

"You are right!" I called to my pursuers, and threw the child at them.

The agent caught her, while the other two aimed and fired. One of the beams grazed my shoulder. But by then I was already through the gate and onto the tarmac.

A port security robot hurled a flame grenade. I rolled through the flames. My ship rested in the maintenance pit, cradled in the violet anti-grav beam. I slid down the ramp into the open airlock, hit the emergency close, and climbed to the controls. Klaxons wailed outside. I bypassed all the launch protocols and released the beam. The ship shot upward like an apple seed flicked by a fingernail; as soon as it had hit the stratosphere, I fired the engines and blasted through the scraps of the upper atmosphere into space.

The orbital security forces were too slow, and I made my escape.

I awoke battered, bruised, and exhausted in the pilot's chair. The smell of my burned shoulder reminded me of the steak I had eaten in the port bazaar. The stress of accelerating nerve impulses had left every joint in my body aching. My arms were blue with contusions, and I was as enfeebled as an old man.

The screens showed me to be in an untraveled quarter of the system's cometary cloud; my ship had cloaked itself in ice so that on any detector I would simply be another bit of debris among billions. I dragged myself from the chair and down to the galley, where I warmed some broth and gave myself an injection of cellular repair mites. Then I fell into my bunk and slept.

My second waking was relatively free of pain. I recharged my tooth and ate again. I kneeled before the shrine and bowed my head in prayer, letting peace flow down my spine and relax all the muscles of my back. I listened for the voices of the gods.

I was reared by my mother on Bembo. My mother was an extraordinary beautiful girl. One day Akvan, looking down on her, was so moved by lust that he took the form of a vagabond and raped her by the side of the road. Nine months later I was born.

The goddess Sedna became so jealous that she laid a curse on my mother, who turned into a lawyer. And so we moved to Helvetica. There, in the shabby city of Urushana, in the waterfront district along the river, she took up her practice, defending criminals and earning a little baksheesh greasing the relations between the Imperial Caslonian government and the corrupt local officials. Mother's ambition for me was to go to an off-planet university, but for me the work of a student was like pushing a very large rock up a very steep hill. I got into fights; I pursued women of questionable virtue. Having exhausted my prospects in the city, I entered the native constabulary, where I was re-engineered for accelerated combat. But my propensity for violence saw me cashiered out of the service within six months. Hoping to get a grip on my passions, I made the pilgrimage to the monastery of the Pujmanian Order. There I petitioned for admission as a novice, and, to my great surprise, was accepted.

It was no doubt the work of Master Darius, who took an interest in me from my first days on the plateau. Perhaps it was my divine heritage, which had placed those voices in my head. Perhaps it was my checkered career to that date. The Master taught me to distinguish between those impulses that were the work of my savage nature, and those that were the voices of the gods. He taught me to identify the individual gods. It is not an easy path. I fasted, I worked in the gardens, I practiced the martial arts, I cleaned the cesspool, I sewed new clothes and mended old, I tended the orchards. I became an expert tailor, and sewed many of the finest kosodes worn by the masters on feast days. In addition, Master Darius held special sessions with me, putting me into a trance during which, I was later told by my fellow novices, I continued to act normally for days, only to awake with no memories of my actions.

And so I was sent on my mission. Because I had learned how not to think, I could not be detected by the spirits who guarded the Imperial Archives.

Five plays, immensely old, collectively titled The Abandonment, are all that document the rebirth of humanity after its long extinction. The foundational cycle consists of; *The Archer's Fall, Stochik's Revenge, The Burning Tree, Close the Senses, Shut the Doors,* and the mystical fifth, *The Magic Tortoise.* No one knows who wrote them. It is believed they were composed within the first thirty years after the human race was recreated by the gods. Besides being the most revered cultural artifacts of humanity, these plays are also the sacred texts of the universal religion, and claimed as the fundamental political documents by all planetary governments. They are preserved only in a single copy. No recording has ever been made of their performance. The actors chosen to present the plays in the foundational festivals on all the worlds do not study and learn them; through a process similar to the one Master Darius taught me to confuse the spirits, the actors become the characters. Once the performance is done, it passes from their minds.

These foundational plays, of inestimable value, existed now only in my mind. I had destroyed the crystal containing them in the archives. Without these plays, the heart of Caslon had been ripped away. If the populace knew of their loss, there would be despair and riot.

And once Master Darius announced that the Order held the only copy in our possession, it would only be a matter of time before the Empire would be obliged to free our world.

Three days after my escape from Caslon, I set course for Helvetica. Using an evanescent wormhole, I would emerge within the planet's inner ring. The ship, still encased in ice, would look like one of the fragments that formed the ring. From there I would reconnoiter, find my opportunity to leave orbit, and land. But because the ring stood far down in the gravitation well of the planet, it was a tricky maneuver.

Too tricky. Upon emergence in the Helvetican ring, my ship collided with one of the few nickel-iron meteoroids in the belt, disabling my engines. Within twenty minutes, Caslonian hunter-killers grappled with the hull. My one advantage was that by now they knew that I possessed the plays, and therefore they could not afford to blast me out of the sky. I could kill them, but they could not harm me. But I had no doubt that once they caught me, they would rip my mind to shreds seeking the plays.

I had only minutes – the hull door would not hold long. I abandoned the control room and retreated to the engine compartment. The place was a mess, barely holding pressure after the meteoroid collision, oxygen cylinders scattered about and the air acrid with the scent of burned wiring. I opened the cat's closet, three meters tall and two wide. From a locker I yanked two piezofiber suits. I turned them on, checked their readouts – they were fully charged – and threw them into the closet. It was cramped in there with tools and boxes of supplies. Sitting on one of the crates, I pulled up my shirt, exposing my bruised ribs. The aluminum light of the closet turned my skin sickly white. Using a microtome, I cut an incision in my belly below my lowest rib. There was little blood. I reached into the cut, found the nine-dimensional pouch, and drew it out between my index and middle fingers.

I sprayed false skin over the wound. As I did, the artificial gravity cut off, and the lights went out.

I slipped on my night vision eyelids, read the directions on the pouch, ripped it open, removed the soldier and unfolded it. The body expanded, became fully three-dimensional, and, in a minute, was floating naked before me. My first surprise: it was a woman. Dark skinned, slender, her body was very beautiful. I leaned over her, covered her mouth with mine, and blew air into her lungs. She jerked convulsively and drew a shuddering breath, then stopped. Her eyelids fluttered, then opened.

"Wake up!" I said, drawing on my piezosuit. I slipped the force blade into the boot, strapped on the belt with blaster and supplies, shrugged into the backpack. "Put on this suit! No time to waste."

She took in my face, the surroundings. From beyond the locker door I heard the sounds of the commandos entering the engine room.

"I am Brother Adlan," I whispered urgently. "You are a soldier of the Republican Guard." As I spoke I helped her into the skinsuit.

"Lieutenant Nahid Esfandiar. What's happening?"

"We are in orbit over Helvetica, under attack by Caslonian commandos. We need to break out of here."

"What weapons have we?"

I handed her a blaster. "They will have accelerated perceptions. Can you speed yours?"

Her glance passed over me, measuring me for a fool. "Done already." She sealed her suit and flipped down the faceplate on her helmet.

I did not pay attention to her, because as she spoke, all-seeing Liu-Bei spoke to me. Three men beyond this door. In my mind I saw the engine room, and the three soldiers who were preparing to rip open the closet.

I touched my helmet to hers and whispered to Nahid, "There are three of them outside. The leader is directly across from the door. He has a common blaster, on stun. To the immediate right, a meter away, one of the commandos has a pulse rifle. The third, about to set the charge, has a pneumatic projector, probably with sleep gas. When they blow the door, I'll go high, you low. Three meters to the cross corridor, down one level and across starboard to the escape pod."

Just then, the door to the closet was ripped open, and through it came a blast of sleep gas. But we were locked into our suits, helmets sealed. Our blaster beams, pink in the darkness, crossed as they emerged from the gloom of the closet. We dove through the doorway in zero-G, bouncing off the bulkheads, blasters flaring. The commandos were just where the gods had told me they would be. I cut down one before we even cleared the doorway. Though they moved as quickly as we did, they were trying not to kill me, and the fact that there were two of us now took them by surprise.

Nahid fired past my ear, taking out another. We ducked through the hatch and up the companionway. Two more commandos came from the control room at the end of the corridor; I was able to slice one of them before he could fire, but the other's stunner numbed my thigh. Nahid torched his head and grabbed me by the arm, hurling me around the corner into the cross passageway.

Two more commandos guarded the hatchway to the escape pod. Nahid fired at them, killing one and wounding the other in a single shot. But instead of heading for the pod she jerked me the other way, toward the umbilical to the Caslonian ship.

"What are you doing?" I protested.

"Shut up," she said. "They can hear us." Halfway across the umbilical, Nahid stopped, braced herself against one wall, raised her blaster, and, without hesitation, blew a hole in the wall opposite. The air rushed out. A klaxon sounded the pressure breach, another commando appeared at the junction of the umbilical and the Caslonian ship – I burned him down – and we slipped through the gap into the space between the two ships. She grabbed my arm and pulled me around the hull of my own vessel.

I realized what she intended. Grabbing chunks of ice, we pulled ourselves over the horizon of my ship until we reached the outside hatch of the escape pod. I punched in the access code. We entered the pod and while Nahid sealed the hatch, I powered up and blasted us free of the ship before we had even buckled in.

The pod shot toward the upper atmosphere. The commandos guarding the inner hatch were ejected into the vacuum behind us. Retro fire slammed us into our seats. I caught a glimpse of bodies floating in the chaos we'd left behind before proton beams lanced out from the Caslonian raider, clipping the pod and sending us into a spin.

"You couldn't manage this without me?" Nahid asked.

"No sarcasm, please." I fought to steady the pod so the heat shields were oriented for atmosphere entry.

We hit the upper atmosphere. For twenty minutes we were buffeted by the jet stream, and it got hot in the tiny capsule. I became very aware of Nahid's scent, sweat and a trace of rosewater; she must have put on perfume before she was folded into the packet that had been implanted in me. Her eyes moved slowly over the interior of the pod.

"What is the date?" she asked.

"The nineteenth of Cunegonda," I told her. The pod bounced violently and drops of sweat flew from my forehead. Three red lights flared on the board, but I could do nothing about them.

"What year?"

I saw that it would not be possible to keep many truths from her. "You have been suspended in nine-space for sixty years."

The pod lurched again, a piece of the ablative shield tearing away. She sat motionless, taking in the loss of her entire life.

A snatch of verse came to my lips, unbidden:

> "Our life is but a trifle,
> A child's toy abandoned by the road
> When we are called home."

"Very poetic," she said. "Are we going to ride this pod all the way down? They probably have us on locator from orbit, and will vaporize it the minute it hits. I'd rather not be called home just now."

"We'll eject at ten kilometers. Here's your chute."

When the heat of the re-entry had abated and we hit the troposphere, we blew the explosive bolts and shot free of the tumbling pod. Despite the thin air of the upper atmosphere, I was buffeted almost insensible, spinning like a prayer wheel. I lost sight of Nahid.

I fell for a long time, but eventually managed to stabilize myself spread-eagled, dizzy, my stomach lurching. Below, the Jacobin Range stretched north to southwest under the rising sun, the snow-covered rock on the upper reaches folded like a discarded robe, and below the thick forest climbing up to the tree line.

Some minutes later, I witnessed the impressive flare of the pod striking just below the summit of one of the peaks, tearing a gash in the ice cover and sending up a plume of black smoke that was torn away by the wind. I tongued the trigger in my helmet, and with a nasty jerk, the airfoil chute deployed from my backpack. I could see Nahid's red chute some five hundred meters below me; I steered toward her hoping we could land near each other. The forested mountainside came up fast. I spotted a clearing on a ledge two thirds of the way up the slope and made for it, but my burned shoulder wasn't working right, and I was coming in too fast. I caught a glimpse of Nahid's foil in the mountain scar ahead, but I wasn't going to reach her.

At the last minute, I pulled up and skimmed the tree tops, caught a boot against a top limb, flipped head over heels and crashed into the foliage, coming to rest hanging upside down from the tree canopy. The suit's rigidity kept me from breaking any bones, but it took me ten minutes to release the shrouds. I turned down the suit's inflex and took off my helmet to better see what I was doing. When I did, the limb supporting me broke, and I fell the last ten meters through the trees, hitting another limb on the way down, knocking me out.

I was woken by Nahid rubbing snow into my face. My piezosuit had been turned off, and the fabric was flexible again. Nahid leaned over me, supporting my head. "Can you move your feet?" she asked.

My thigh still was numb from the stunner. I tried moving my right foot. Though I could not feel any response, I saw the boot twitch. "So it would seem."

Done with me, she let my head drop. "So, do you have some plan?"

I pulled up my knees and sat up. My head ached. We were surrounded by the boles of the tall firs; above our heads the wind swayed the trees, but down here the air was calm, and sunlight filtered down in patches, moving over the packed fine brown needles of the forest floor. Nahid had pulled down my chute to keep it from advertising our position. She crouched on one knee and examined the charge indicator on her blaster.

I got up and inventoried the few supplies we had – my suit's water reservoir, holding maybe a liter, three packs of gichy crackers in the belt. Hers would have no more than that. "We should get moving; the Caslonians will send a landing party, or notify the colonial government in Guliston to send a security squad."

"And why should I care?"

"You fought for the republic against the Caslonians. When the war was lost and the protectorate established, you had yourself folded. Didn't you expect to take up arms again when called back to life?"

"You tell me that was sixty years ago. What happened to the rest of the Republican Guard?"

"The Guard was wiped out in the final Caslonian assaults."

"And our folded battalion?"

The blistering roar of a flyer tore through the clear air above the trees. Nahid squinted up, eyes following the glittering ship. "They're heading for where the pod hit." She pulled me to my feet, taking us downhill, perhaps in the hope of finding better cover in the denser forest near one of the mountain freshets.

"No," I said. "Up the slope."

"That's where they'll be."

"It can't be helped. We need to get to the monastery. We're on the wrong side of the mountains." I turned up the incline. After a moment, she followed.

We stayed beneath the trees for as long as possible. The slope was not too steep at this altitude; the air was chilly, with dying patches of old snow in the shadows. Out in the direct sunlight, it would be hot until evening came. I had climbed these mountains fifteen years before, an adolescent trying to find a way to live away from the world. As we moved, following the path of a small stream, the aches in my joints eased.

We did not talk. I had not thought about what it would mean to wake this soldier, other than how she would help me in a time of extremity. There are no women in our order, and though we take no vow of celibacy and some commerce takes place between brothers in their cells late at night, there is little opportunity for contact with the opposite sex. Nahid, despite her forbidding nature, was beautiful: dark skin, black eyes, lustrous black hair cut short, the three parallel scars of her rank marking her left cheek. As a boy in Urushana, I had tormented my sleepless nights with visions of women as beautiful as she; in my short career as a constable I had avidly pursued women far less so. One of them had provoked the fight that had gotten me cashiered.

The forest thinned as we climbed higher. Large folds of granite lay exposed to the open air, creased with fractures and holding pockets of earth where trees sprouted in groups. We had to circle around to avoid coming into the open, and even that would be impossible when the forest ended completely. I pointed us south, where Dundrahad Pass, dipping below 3,000 meters, cut through the mountains. We were without snowshoes or trekking gear, but I hoped that, given the summer temperatures, the pass would be clear enough to traverse in the night without getting ourselves killed. The skinsuits we wore would be proof against the night-time cold.

We saw no signs of the Caslonians, but when we reached the tree line, we stopped to wait for darkness anyway. The air had turned colder, and a sharp wind blew down the pass from the other side of the mountains. We settled in a hollow beneath a patch of twisted scrub trees and waited out the declining sun. At the zenith, the first moon Mahsheed rode, waning gibbous. In the notch of the pass above and ahead of us, the second moon Roshanak rose. Small, glowing green, it moved perceptibly as it raced around the planet. I nibbled at some gichy, sipping water from my suit's reservoir. Nahid's eyes were shadowed; she scanned the slope.

"We'll have to wait until Mahsheed sets before we move," Nahid said. "I don't want to be caught in the pass in its light."

"It will be hard for us to see where we're going."

She didn't reply. The air grew colder. After a while, without looking at me, she spoke. "So what happened to my compatriots?"

I saw no point in keeping anything from her. "As the Caslonians consolidated their conquest, an underground of Republicans pursued a guerilla war. Two years later, they mounted an assault on the provincial capital in Kofarnihon. They unfolded your battalion to aid them, and managed to seize the armory. But the Caslonians sent reinforcements and set up a siege. When the rebels refused to surrender, the Caslonians vaporized the entire city, hostages, citizens, and rebels alike. That was the end of the Republican Guard." Nahid's dark eyes watched me as I told her all this. The tightness of her lips held grim skepticism.

"Yet here I am," she said.

"I don't know how you came to be the possession of the order. Some refugee, perhaps. The masters, sixty years ago, debated what to do with you. Given the temperament of the typical guardsman, it was assumed that, had you been restored to life, you would immediately get yourself killed in assaulting the Caslonians, putting the order at risk. It was decided to keep you in reserve, in the expectation that, at some future date, your services would be useful."

"You monks were always fair-weather democrats. Ever your order over the welfare of the people, or even their freedom. So you betrayed the republic."

"You do us an injustice."

"It was probably Javeed who brought me – the lying monk attached to our unit."

I recognized the name. Brother Javeed, a bent, bald man of great age, had run the monastery kitchen. I had never thought twice about him. He had died a year after I joined the order.

"Why do you think I was sent on this mission?" I told her. "We mean to set Helvetica free. And we shall do so, if we reach Sharishabz."

"How do you propose to accomplish that? Do you want to see your monastery vaporized?"

"They will not dare. I have something of theirs that they will give up the planet for. That's why they tried to board my ship rather than destroy it; that's why they didn't bother to disintegrate the escape pod when they might easily have shot us out of the sky."

"And this inestimably valuable item that you carry? It must be very small."

"It's in my head. I have stolen the only copies of the Found-ational Dramas."

She looked at me. "So?"

Her skepticism was predictable, but it still angered me. "So – they will gladly trade Helvetica's freedom for the return of the plays."

She lowered her head, rubbed her brow with her hand. I could not read her. She made a sound, an intake of breath. For a moment, I thought she wept. Then she raised her head and laughed in my face.

I fought an impulse to strike her. "Quiet!"

She laughed louder. Her shoulders shook, and tears came to her eyes. I felt my face turn red. "You should have let me die with the others, in battle. You crazy priest!"

"Why do you laugh?" I asked her. "Do you think they would send ships to embargo Helvetican orbital space, dispatch squads of soldiers and police, if what I carry were not valuable to them?"

"I don't believe in your fool's religion."

"Have you ever seen the plays performed?"

"Once, when I was a girl. I saw The Archer's Fall during the year-end festival in Tienkash. I fell asleep."

"They are the axis of human culture. The sacred stories of our race. We are human because of them. Through them the gods speak to us."

"I thought you monks heard the gods talking to you directly. Didn't they tell you to run us directly into the face of the guards securing the escape pod? It's lucky you had me along to cut our way out of that umbilical, or we'd be dead up there now."

"You might be dead. I would be in a sleep tank having my brain taken apart – to retrieve these dramas."

"There are no gods! Just voices in your head. They tell you to do what you already want to do."

"If you think the commands of the gods are easy, then just try to follow them for a single day."

We settled into an uncomfortable silence. The sun set, and the rings became visible in the sky, turned pink by the sunset in the west, rising silvery toward the zenith, where they were eclipsed by the planet's shadow. The light of the big moon still illuminated the open rock face before us. We would have a steep 300 meter climb above the tree line to the pass, then another couple of kilometers between the peaks in the darkness.

"It's cold," I said after a while.

Without saying anything, she reached out and tugged my arm. It took me a moment to realize that she wanted me to move next to her. I slid over, and we ducked our heads to keep below the wind. I could feel the taut muscles of her body beneath the skinsuit. The paradox of our alienation hit me. We were both the products of the gods. She did not believe this truth, but truth does not need to be believed to prevail.

Still, she was right that we had not escaped the orbiting commandos in the way I had expected.

The great clockwork of the universe turned. Green Roshanak sped past Mahsheed, for a moment in transit looking like the pupil of a god's observing eye, then set, and an hour later, Mahsheed followed her below the western horizon. The stars shone in all their glory, but it was as dark as it would get before Roshanak rose for the second time that night. It was time for us to take our chance and go.

We came out of our hiding place and moved to the edge of the scrub. The broken granite of the peak rose before us, faint gray in starlight. We set out across the rock, climbing in places, striding across rubble fields, circling areas of ice and melting snow. In a couple of places, we had to boost each other up, scrambling over boulders, finding hand and footholds in the vertical face where we were blocked. It was farther than I had estimated before the ground leveled and we were in the pass.

We were just cresting the last ridge when glaring white light shone down on us, and an amplified voice called from above. "Do not move! Drop your weapons and lie flat on the ground!"

I tongued my body into acceleration. In slow motion, Nahid crouched, raised her blaster, arm extended, sighted on the flyer and fired. I hurled my body into hers and threw her aside just as the return fire of projectile weapons splattered the rock where she had been into fragments. In my head, kind Eurynome insisted: Back. We will show you the way.

"This way!" I dragged Nahid over the edge of the rock face we had just climbed. It was a three-meter drop to the granite below; I landed hard, and she fell on my chest, knocking the wind from me. Around us burst a hail of sleep gas pellets. In trying to catch my breath I caught a whiff of the gas, and my head whirled. Nahid slid her helmet down over her face, and did the same for me.

From above us came the sound of the flyer touching down. Nahid started for the tree line, limping. She must have been hit or injured in our fall. I pulled her to our left, along the face of the rock. "Where – " she began.

"Shut up!" I grunted.

The commandos hit the ledge behind us, but the flyer had its searchlight aimed at the trees, and the soldiers followed the light. The fog of sleep gas gave us some cover.

We scuttled along the granite shelf until we were beyond the entrance to the pass. By this time, I had used whatever reserves of energy my body could muster, and passed into normal speed. I was exhausted.

"Over the mountain?" Nahid asked. "We can't."

"Under it," I said. I forced my body into motion, searching in the darkness for the cleft in the rock which, in the moment of the flyer attack, the gods had shown me. And there it was, two dark pits above a vertical fissure in the granite, like an impassive face. We climbed up the few meters to the brink of the cleft. Nahid followed, slower now, dragging her right leg. "Are you badly hurt?" I asked her.

"Keep going."

I levered my shoulder under her arm, and helped her along the ledge. Down in the forest, the lights of the commandos flickered, while a flyer hovered above, beaming bright white radiance down between the trees.

Once inside the cleft, I let her lean against the wall. Beyond the narrow entrance the way widened. I used my suit flash, and, moving forward, found an oval chamber of three meters with a sandy floor. Some small bones gave proof that a predator had once used this cave for a lair. But at the back, a small passage gaped. I crouched and followed it deeper.

"Where are you going?" Nahid asked.

"Come with me."

The passage descended for a space, then rose. I emerged into a larger space. My flash showed not a natural cave, but a chamber of dressed rock, and opposite us, a metal door. It was just as my vision had said.

"What is this?" Nahid asked in wonder.

"A tunnel under the mountain." I took off my helmet and spoke the words that would open the door. The ancient mechanism began to hum. With a fall of dust, a gap appeared at the side of the door, and it slid open.

The door closed behind us with a disturbing finality, wrapping us in the silence of a tomb. We found ourselves in a corridor at least twice our height and three times that in width. Our lights showed walls smooth as plaster, but when I laid my hand on one, it proved to be cut from the living rock. Our boots echoed on the polished but dusty floor. The air was stale, unbreathed by human beings for unnumbered years.

I made Nahid sit. "Rest," I said. "Let me look at that leg."

Though she complied, she kept her blaster out, and her eyes scanned our surroundings warily. "Did you know of this?"

"No. The gods told me, just as we were caught in the pass."

"Praise be to the Pujmanian Order." I could not tell if there was any sarcasm in her voice.

A trickle of blood ran down her boot from the wound of a projectile gun. I opened the seam of her suit, cleaned the wound with antiseptic from my suit's first aid kit, and bandaged her leg. "Can you walk?" I asked.

She gave me a tight smile. "Lead on, Brother Adlan."

We moved along the hall. Several smaller corridors branched off, but we kept to the main way. Periodically, we came across doors, most of them closed. One gaped open upon a room where my light fell on a garage of wheeled vehicles, sitting patiently in long rows, their windows thick with dust. In the corner of the room, a fracture in the ceiling had let in a steady drip of water that had corroded the vehicle beneath it into a mass of rust.

Along the main corridor our lights revealed hieroglyphics carved above doorways, dead oval spaces on the wall that might once have been screens or windows. We must have gone a kilometer or more when the corridor ended suddenly in a vast cavernous opening.

Our lights were lost in the gloom above. A ramp led down to an underground city. Buildings of gracious curves, apartments like heaps of grapes stacked upon a table, halls whose walls were so configured that they resembled a huge garment discarded in a bedroom. We descended into the streets.

The walls of the buildings were figured in abstract designs of immense intricacy, fractal patterns from immense to microscopic, picked out by the beams of our flashlights. Colored tiles, bits of glass and mica. Many of the buildings were no more than sets of walls demarcating space, with horizontal trellises that must once have held plants above them rather than roofs. Here and there, outside what might have been cafes, tables and benches rose out of the polished floor. We arrived in a broad square with low buildings around it, centered on a dry fountain. The immense figures of a man, a woman, and a child dominated the center of the dusty reservoir. Their eyes were made of crystal, and stared blindly across their abandoned city.

Weary beyond words, hungry, bruised, we settled against the rim of the fountain and made to sleep. The drawn skin about her eyes told me of Nahid's pain. I tried to comfort her, made her rest her legs, elevated, on my own. We slept.

When I woke, Nahid was already up, changing the dressing on her bloody leg. The ceiling of the cave had lit, and a pale light shone down, making an early arctic dawn over the dead city.

"How is your leg?" I asked.

"Better. Do you have any more anodynes?"

I gave her what I had. She took them, and sighed. After a while, she asked, "Where did the people go?"

"They left the universe. They grew beyond the need of matter, and space. They became gods. You know the story."

"The ones who made this place were people like you and me."

"You and I are the descendants of the re-creation of a second human race three million years after the first ended in apotheosis. Or of the ones left behind, or banished back into the material world by the gods for some great crime."

Nahid rubbed her boot above the bandaged leg. "Which is it? Which child's tale do you expect me to believe?"

"How do you think I found the place? The gods told me, and here it is. Our mission is important to them, and they are seeing that we succeed. Justice is to be done."

"Justice? Tell the starving child about justice. The misborn and the dying. I would rather be the random creation of colliding atoms than subject to the whim of some transhumans no more godlike than I am."

"You speak out of bitterness."

"If they are gods, they are responsible for the horror that occurs in the world. So they are evil. Why otherwise would they allow things to be as they are?"

"To say that is to speak out of the limitations of our vision. We can't see the outcome of events. We're too close. But the gods see how all things will eventuate. Time is a landscape to them. All at once they see the acorn, the seedling, the ancient oak, the woodsman who cuts it, the fire that burns the wood, and the smoke that rises from the fire. And so they led us to this place."

"Did they lead the bullet to find my leg? Did they lead your order to place me on a shelf for a lifetime, separate me from every person I loved?" Nahid's voice rose. "Please save me your theodical prattle!"

" 'Theodical.' Impressive vocabulary for a soldier. But you—"

A scraping noise came from behind us. I turned to find that the giant male figure in the center of the fountain had moved. As I watched, its hand jerked another few centimeters. Its foot pulled free of its setting, and it stepped down from the pedestal into the empty basin.

We fell back from the fountain. The statue's eyes glowed a dull orange. Its lips moved, and it spoke in a voice like the scraping together of two files: "Do not flee, little ones."

Nahid let fly a shot from her blaster, which ricocheted off the shoulder of the metal man and scarred the ceiling of the cave. I pulled her away and we crouched behind a table before an open-sided building at the edge of the square.

The statue raised its arms in appeal. "Your shoes are untied," it said in its ghostly rasp. "We know why you are here. It seems to you that your lives hang in the balance, and of course you value your lives. As you should, dear ones. But I, who have no soul and therefore no ability to care, can tell you that the appetites that move you are entirely transitory. The world you live in is a game. You do not have a ticket."

"Quite mad," Nahid said. "Our shoes have no laces."

"But it's also true – they are therefore untied," I said. "And we have no tickets." I called out to the metal man, "Are you a god?"

"I am no god," the metal man said. "The gods left behind the better part of themselves when they abandoned matter. The flyer lies on its side in the woods. Press the silver pentagon. You must eat, but you must not eat too much. Here is food."

The shop behind us lit up, and in a moment the smell of food wafted from within.

I slid over to the entrance. On a table inside, under warm light, were two plates of rice and vegetables.

"He's right," I told Nahid.

"I'm not going to eat that food. Where did it come from? It's been thousands of years without a human being here."

"Come," I said. I drew her inside and made her join me at the table. I tasted. The food was good. Nahid sat warily, facing out to the square, blaster a centimeter from her plate. The metal man sat on the plaza stones, cross-legged, ducking its massive head in order to watch us. After a few moments, it began to croon.

Its voice was a completely mechanical sound, but the tune it sang was sweet, like a peasant song. I cannot convey to you the strangeness of sitting in that ancient restaurant, eating food conjured fresh out of nothing by ancient machines, listening to the music of creatures who might have been a different species from us.

When its song was ended, the metal man spoke: "If you wish to know someone, you need only observe that on which he bestows his care, and what sides of his own nature he cultivates." It lifted its arm and pointed at Nahid. Its finger stretched almost to the door. I could see the patina of corrosion on that metal digit. "If left to the gods, you will soon die."

The arm moved, and it pointed at me. "You must live, but you must not live too much. Take this."

The metal man opened the curled fingers of its hand, and in its huge palm was a small, round metallic device the size of an apple. I took it. Black and dense, it filled my hand completely. "Thank you," I said.

The man stood and returned to the empty fountain, climbed onto the central pedestal, and resumed its position. There it froze. Had we not been witness to it, I could never have believed it had moved.

Nahid came out of her musing over the man's sentence of her death. She lifted her head. "What is that thing?"

I examined the sphere, surface covered in pentagonal facets of dull metal. "I don't know."

In one of the buildings, we found some old furniture, cushions of metallic fabric that we piled together as bedding. We huddled together and slept.

Selene:
Hear that vessel that docks above?
It marks the end of our lives
And the beginning of our torment.

Stochik:
Death comes
And then it's gone. Who knows
What lies beyond that event horizon?
Our life is but a trifle,
A child's toy abandoned by the road
When we are called home.

Selene:
Home? You might well hope it so,
But –
[Alarums off stage. Enter a god]

God:
The hull is breached!
You must fly.

In the night I woke, chasing away the wisps of a dream. The building we were in had no ceiling, and faint light from the cavern roof filtered down upon us. In our sleep, we had moved closer together, and Nahid's arm lay over my chest, her head next to mine, her breath brushing my cheek. I turned my face to her, centimeters away. Her face was placid, her eyelashes dark and long.

As I watched her, her eyelids fluttered and she awoke. She did not flinch at my closeness, but simply, soberly looked into my own eyes for what seemed like a very long time. I leaned forward and kissed her.

She did not pull away, but kissed me back strongly. She made a little moan in her throat, and I pulled her tightly to me.

We made love in the empty, ancient city. Her fingers entwined with mine, arms taut. Shadow of my torso across her breast. Hard, shuddering breath. Her lips on my chest. Smell of her sweat and mine. My palm brushing her abdomen. The feeling of her dark skin against mine. Her quiet laugh.

"Your leg," I said, as we lay in the darkness, spent.

"What about it?"

"Did I hurt you?"

She laughed again, lightly. "Now you ask. You are indeed all man."

In the morning, we took another meal from the ancient restaurant, food that had been manufactured from raw molecules while we waited, or perhaps stored somewhere for millennia.

We left by the corridor opposite the one by which we had entered, heading for the other side of the mountain range. Nahid limped but made no complaint. The passage ended in another door, beyond which a cave twisted upward. In one place, the ceiling of the cave had collapsed, and we had to crawl on our bellies over rubble through the narrow gap it had left. The exit was onto a horizontal shelf overgrown with trees, well below the pass. It was mid-morning. A misting rain fell across the Sharishabz Valley. In the distance, hazed by clouds of mist, I caught a small gleam of the white buildings of the monastery on the Penitent's Ridge. I pointed it out to Nahid. We scanned the mountainside below us, searching for the forest road.

Nahid found the thread of the road before I. "No sign of the Caslonians," she said.

"They're guarding the pass on the other side of the mountain, searching the woods there for us."

We descended the slope, picking our way through the trees toward the road. The mist left drops of water on our skinsuits, but did not in any way slow us. My spirits rose. I could see the end of this adventure in sight, and wondered what would happen to Nahid then.

"What will you do when we get to the monastery?" I asked her.

"I think I'll leave as soon as I can. I don't want to be there when the Caslonians find out you've reached your order with the plays."

"They won't do anything. The gods hold the monastery in their hands."

"Let us hope they don't drop it."

She would die soon, the statue had said – if left to the gods. But what person was not at the mercy of the gods? Still, she would be much more at risk alone, away from the order. "What about your leg?" I asked.

"Do you have a clinic there?"

"Yes."

"I'll take an exoskeleton and some painkillers and be on my way."

"Where will you go?"

"Wherever I can."

"But you don't even know what's happened in the last sixty years. What can you do?"

"Maybe my people are still alive. That's where I'll go – the town where I grew up. Perhaps I'll find someone who remembers me. Maybe I'll find my own grave."

"Don't go."

She strode along more aggressively. I could see her wince with each step. "Look, I don't care about your monastery. I don't care about these plays. Mostly, I don't care about you. Give me some painkillers and an exo, and I'll be gone."

That ended our conversation. We walked on in silence through the woods, me brooding, she limping along, grimacing.

We found the forest road. Here the land fell away sharply, and the road, hardly more than a gravel track, switchbacked severely as we made our way down the mountainside. We met no signs of pursuit. Though the rain continued, the air warmed as we moved lower, and beads of sweat trickled down my back under the skinsuit. The boots I wore were not meant for hiking, and by now my feet were sore, my back hurt. I could only imagine how bad it was for Nahid.

I had worked for years to manage my appetites, and yet I could not escape images of our night together. With a combination of shame and desire, I wanted her still. I did not think I could go back to being just another monk. The Order had existed long before the Caslonian conquest, and would long outlast it. I was merely a cell passing through the body of this immortal creation. What did the gods want from me? What was to come of all this?

At the base of the trail, the road straightened, following the course of the River Sharishabz up the valley. Ahead rose the plateau, the gleaming white buildings of the monastery clearly visible now. The ornamental gardens, the terraced fields tended by the Order for millennia. I could almost taste the sweet oranges and pomegranates. It would be good to be back home, a place where I could hide away form the world and figure out exactly what was in store for me. I wouldn't mind being hailed as a hero, the liberator of our people, like Stochik himself, who took the plays from the hands of the gods.

The valley sycamores and aspens rustled with the breeze. The afternoon passed. We stopped by the stream and drank. Rested, then continued.

We came to a rise in the road, where it twisted to climb the plateau. Signs here of travel, ruts of iron wheels where people from the villages drove supplies to the monastery. Pilgrims passed this way – though there was no sign of anyone today.

We made a turn in the road, and I heard a yelp behind me. I turned to find Nahid struggling in the middle of the road. At first, I thought she was suffering a seizure. Her body writhed and jerked. Then I realized, from the slick of rain deflected from his form, that she was being assaulted by a person in an invisibility cloak.

This understanding had only flashed through my mind when I was thrown to the ground by an unseen hand. I kicked out wildly, and my boot made contact. Gravel sprayed beside me where my attacker fell. I slipped into accelerated mode, kicked him again, rolled away, and dashed into the woods. Above me I heard the whine of an approaching flyer. Run! It was the voice of Horus, god of sun and moon.

I ran. The commandos did not know these woods the way I did. I had spent ten years exploring them, playing games of hide and hunt in the night with my fellow novices: I knew I could find my way to the monastery without them capturing me.

And Nahid? Clearly this was her spoken-of death. No doubt it had already taken place. Or perhaps they wouldn't kill her immediately, but would torture her, assuming she knew something, or even if they knew she didn't, taking some measure of revenge on her body. It was the lot of a Republican Guard to receive such treatment. She would even expect it. The Order comes first.

Every second took me farther from the road, away from the Caslonians. But after a minute of hurrying silently through the trees, I felt something heavy in my hand. I stopped. Without realizing it, I had taken the object the metal man had given me out of my belt pouch. She would not want you to return. The freedom of her people comes before her personal safety.

I circled back, and found them in the road.

The flyer had come down athwart the road. The soldiers had turned off their cloaks, three men garbed head to toe in the matte gray of light deflection suits. Two soldiers had Nahid on her knees in the drizzle, her hands tied behind her back. One jerked her head back by her hair, holding a knife to her throat while an officer asked her questions. The officer slapped her, whipping the back of his gloved hand across her face.

I moved past them through the woods, sound of rain on the foliage, still holding the metal sphere in my hand. The flyer sat only a few meters into the road. I crouched there, staring at the uncouth object. I rotated it in my palm until I found the surface pentagon that was silvered. I depressed this pentagon until it clicked.

Then I flipped it out into the road, under the landing pads of the flyer, and fell back.

It was not so much an explosion as a vortex, warping the flyer into an impossible shape, throwing it off the road. As it spun the pilot was tossed from the cockpit, his uniform flaring in electric blue flame. The three men with Nahid were sucked off their feet by the dimensional warp. They jerked their heads toward the screaming pilot. The officer staggered to his feet, took two steps toward him, and one of the men followed. By that time, I had launched myself into the road, and slammed my bad shoulder into the small of the back of the man holding Nahid. I seized his rifle and fired, killing the officer and the other soldier, then the one I had just laid flat. The pilot was rolling in the gravel to extinguish the flames. I stepped forward calmly and shot him in the head.

Acrid black smoke rose from the crushed flyer, which lay on its side in the woods.

Nahid was bleeding from a cut on her neck. She held her palm against the wound, but the blood seeped steadily from between her fingers. I gathered her up and dragged her into the woods before reinforcements could arrive.

"Thank you," Nahid gasped, her eyes large, and fixed on me. We limped off into the trees.

Nahid was badly hurt, but I knew where we were, and I managed, through that difficult night, to get us up the pilgrim's trail to the monastery. By the time we reached the iron door we called the Mud Gate she had lost consciousness and I was carrying her. Her blood was all over us, and I could not tell if she yet breathed.

We novices had used this gate many times to sneak out of the monastery to play martial games in the darkness, explore the woods, and pretend we were ordinary men. Men who, when they desired something, had only to take it. Men who were under no vow of non-violence. Here I had earned a week's fast by bloodying the nose, in a fit of temper, of Brother Taher. Now I returned, unrepentant over the number of men I had killed in the last days, a man who had disobeyed the voice of a god, hoping to save Nahid before she bled out.

Brother Pramha was the first to greet me. He looked at me with shock. "Who is this?" he asked.

"This is a friend, a soldier, Nahid. Quickly. She needs care."

Together we took her to the clinic. Pramha ran off to inform the Master. Our physician Brother Nastricht sealed her throat wound, and gave her new blood. I held her hand. She did not regain consciousness

Soon, one of the novices arrived to summon me to Master Darius's chambers. Although I was exhausted, I hurried after him through the warren of corridors, up the tower steps. I unbelted my blaster and handed it to the novice – he seemed distressed to hold the destructive device – and entered the room.

Beyond the broad window that formed the far wall of the chamber, dawn stained the sky pink. Master Darius held out his arms. I approached him, humbly bowed my head, and he embraced me. The warmth of his large body enfolding me was an inexpressible comfort. He smelled of cinnamon.

He let me go, held me at arm's length, and smiled. The kosode he wore I recognized as one I had sewn myself. "I cannot tell you how good it is to see you, Adlan."

"I have the plays," I announced.

"The behavior of our Caslonian masters has been proof enough of that," he replied. His broad, plain face was somber as he told me of the massacre in Radnapuja, where the colonial government had held six thousand citizens hostage, demanding the bodily presentation, alive, of the foul villain, the man without honor or soul, the sacrilegious terrorist who had stolen the Foundational Plays.

"Six thousand dead?"

"They won't be the last," the Master said. "The plays have been used as a weapon, as a means of controlling us. The beliefs which they embody work within the minds and souls of every person on this planet. They work even on those who are unbelievers."

"Nahid is an unbeliever."

"Nahid? She is this soldier whom you brought here?"

"The Republican Guard you sent with me. She doesn't believe, but she has played her role in bringing me here."

Master Darius poured me a glass of fortifying spirits, and handed it to me as if he were a novice and I the master. He sat in his great chair, had me sit in the chair opposite, and bade me recount every detail of the mission. I did so.

"It is indeed miraculous that you have come back alive," Master Darius mused. "Had you died, the plays would have been lost for ever."

"The gods would not allow such a sacrilege."

"Perhaps. You carry the only copies in your mind?"

"Indeed. I have even quoted them to Nahid."

"Not at any length, I hope."

I laughed at his jest. "But now we can free Helvetica," I said. "Before any further innocents are killed, you must contact the Caslonian colonial government and tell them we have the plays. Tell them they must stop or we will destroy them."

Master Darius held up his hand and looked at me piercingly – I had seen this gesture many times in his tutoring of me. "First, let me ask you some questions about your tale. You tell me that, when you first came to consciousness after stealing the plays in the Imperial City, a god told you to run. Yet to run in the Caslonian capital is only to attract unwelcome attention."

"Yes. Bishamon must have wanted to hurry my escape."

"But when you reached the port bazaar, the god told you to stop and enter the restaurant. You run to attract attention, and dawdle long enough to allow time for you to be caught. Does this make sense?"

My fatigue made it difficult for me to think. What point was the Master trying to make? "Perhaps I was not supposed to stop," I replied. "It was my own weakness. I was hungry."

"Then, later, you tell me that when the commandos boarded your ship, you escaped by following Nahid's lead, not the word of the gods."

"Liu-Bei led us out of the engine room. I think this is a matter of my misinterpreting—"

"And this metal man you encountered in the ancient city. Did he in fact say that the gods would have seen Nahid dead?"

"The statue said many mad things."

"Yet the device he gave you was the agent of her salvation?"

"I used it for that." Out of shame, I had not told Master Darius that I had disobeyed the command of the god who told me to flee.

"Many paradoxes." The Master took a sip from his own glass. "So, if we give the plays back, what will happen then?"

"Then Helvetica will be free."

"And after that?"

"After that, we can do as we wish. The Caslonians would not dare to violate a holy vow. The gods would punish them. They know that. They are believers, as are we."

"Yes, they are believers. They would obey any compact they made, for fear of the wrath of the gods. They believe what you hold contained in your mind, Adlan, is true. So, as you say, you must give them to me now, and I will see to their disposition."

"Their disposition? How will you see to their disposition?"

"That is not something for you to worry about, my son. You have done well, and you deserve all our thanks. Brother Ishmael will see to unburdening you of the great weight you carry."

A silence ensued. I knew it was a sign of my dismissal. I must go to Brother Ishmael. But I did not rise. "What will you do with them?"

Master Darius's brown eyes lay steady on me, and quiet. "You have always been my favorite. I think perhaps, you know what I intend."

I pondered our conversation. "You – you're going to destroy them."

"Perhaps I was wrong not to have you destroy them the minute you gained access to the archives. But at that time I had not come to these conclusions."

"But the wrath of the Caslonians will know no limit! We will be exterminated!"

"We may be exterminated, and Helvetica remain in chains, but once these plays are destroyed, never to be recovered, then humanity will begin to be truly free. This metal man, you say, told you the gods left the better part of themselves behind. That is profoundly true. Yet there is no moment when they cease to gaze over our shoulders. Indeed, if we are ever to be free human beings, and not puppets jerked about by unseen forces – which may, or may not, exist – the gods must go. And the beginning of that process is the destruction of the Foundational Plays."

I did not know how to react. In my naiveté I said, "This does not seem right."

"I assure you, my son, that it is."

"If we destroy the plays, it will be the last thing we ever do."

"Of course not. Time will not stop."

"Time may not stop," I said, "but it might as well. Any things that happen after the loss of the gods will have no meaning."

Master Darius rose from his chair and moved toward his desk. "You are tired, and very young," he said, his back to me. "I have lived in the shadow of the gods far longer than you have." He reached over his desk, opened a drawer, took something out, and straightened.

He is lying. It seemed to me to be the voice of Inti himself. I stood. I felt surpassing weariness, but I moved silently. In my boot I still carried the force knife I had stolen from the restaurant on Caslon. I drew out the hilt, switched on the blade, and approached the Master just as he began to turn.

When he faced me, he had a blaster in his hands. He was surprised to find me so close to him. His eyes went wide as I slipped the blade into his belly below his lowest rib.

Stochik:
Here ends our story.
Let no more be said of our fall.
Mark the planting of this seed.
The tree that grows in this place
Will bear witness to our deeds;
No other witness shall we have.

Selene:
I would not depart with any other
My love. Keep alive whatever word
May permit us to move forward.
Leaving all else behind we must
Allow the world to come to us.

The Caslonian government capitulated within a week after we contacted them. Once they began to withdraw their forces from the planet and a provisional government for the Helvetican Republic was re-established in Astara, I underwent the delicate process of downloading the Foundational Dramas from my mind. The Abandonment was once again embodied in a crystal, which was presented to the Caslonian legate in a formal ceremony on the anniversary of the rebirth of man.

The ceremony took place on a bright day in mid summer in that city of a thousand spires. Sunlight flooded the streets, where citizens in vibrant colored robes danced and sang to the music of bagpipes. Pennants in purple and green flew from those spires; children hung out of second-story school windows, shaking snowstorms of confetti on the parades. The smell of incense wafted down from the great temple, and across the sky flyers drew intricate patterns with lines of colored smoke.

Nahid and I were there on that day, though I did not take a leading role in the ceremony, preferring to withdraw to my proper station. In truth, I am not a significant individual. I have only served the gods.

I left the Order as soon as the negotiations were completed. At first the brothers were appalled by my murder of Master Darius. I explained to them that he had gone mad and intended to kill me in order to destroy the plays. There was considerable doubt. But when I insisted that we follow through with the plan as the Master had presented it to the brothers before sending me on my mission, they seemed to take my word about his actions. The success of our thieving enterprise overshadowed the loss of the great leader, and indeed has contributed to his legend, making of him a tragic figure. A drama has been written of his life and death, and the liberation of Helvetica.

Last night, Nahid and I, with our children and grandchildren, watched it performed in the square of the town where we set up the tailor's shop that has been the center of our lives for the last forty years. Seeing the events of my youth played out on the platform, in their comedy and tragedy, hazard and fortune, calls again to my mind the question of whether I have deserved the blessings that have fallen to me ever since that day. I have not heard the voices of the gods since I slipped the knife into the belly of the man who taught me all that I knew of grace.

The rapid decline of the Caslonian Empire, and the Helvetican renaissance that has led to our current prosperity, all date from that moment in his chambers when I ended his plan to free men from belief and duty. The people, joyous on their knees in the temples of twelve planets, give praise to the gods for their deliverance, listen, hear, and obey.

Soon I will rest beneath the earth, like the metal man who traduced the gods, though less likely than he ever to walk again. If I have done wrong, it is not for me to judge. I rest, my lover's hand in mine, in the expectation of no final word.

USELESS THINGS

Maureen F. McHugh

Here's a story set maybe a decade from now at most, if the economic
recovery falters and fails, a quiet but deeply human story about a
woman in an impoverished world struggling to get by while at the
same time somehow hold on to her basic humanity. . . .

Maureen F. McHugh made her first sale in 1989, and has since
made a powerful impression on the SF world with a relatively small
body of work, becoming one of today's most respected writers. In
1992, she published one of the year's most widely acclaimed and
talked-about first novels, *China Mountain Zhang*, which won the
Locus Award for Best First Novel, the Lambda Literary Award,
and the James Tiptree Jr Memorial Award, and which was named
a New York Times Notable Book as well as being a finalist for the
Hugo and Nebula Awards. Her story "The Lincoln Train" won her
a Nebula Award. Her other books, including the novels, *Half the
Day is Night*, *Mission Child*, and *Nekropolis*, have been greeted
with similar enthusiasm. Her powerful short fiction has appeared
in *Asimov's Science Fiction*, *The Magazine of Fantasy and Science
Fiction*, *Starlight*, *Eclipse*, *Alternate Warriors*, *Aladdin*, *Killing Me
Softly*, and other markets, and has been collected in *Mothers and
Other Monsters*. She lives in Austin, Texas, with her husband, her
son, and a golden retriever named Hudson.

ENORA?" THE MAN standing at my screen door is travel stained. Migrant,
up from Mexico. The dogs haven't heard him come up but now they
erupt in a frenzy of barking to make up for their oversight. I am sitting at
the kitchen table, painting a doll, waiting for the timer to tell me to get doll
parts curing in the oven in the workshed.

"Hudson, Abby!" I shout, but they don't pay any attention.

The man steps back. "Do you have work? I can, the weeds," he gestures.
He is short-legged, long from waist to shoulder. He's probably headed for
the Great Lakes area, the place in the US with the best supply of fresh water
and the most need of farm labor.

Behind him is my back plot, with the garden running up to the privacy
fence. The sky is just starting to pink up with dawn. At this time of year I do a
lot of my work before dawn and late in the evening, when it's not hot. That's
probably when he has been traveling, too.

I show him the cistern, and set him to weeding. I show him where he can plug in his phone to recharge it. I have Internet radio on; Elvis Presley died forty-five years ago today and they're playing "(You're So Square) Baby I Don't Care." I go inside and get him some bean soup.

Hobos used to mark codes to tell other hobos where to stop and where to keep going. Teeth to signify a mean dog. A triangle with hands meant that the homeowner had a gun and might use it. A cat meant a nice lady. Today the men use websites and bulletin boards that they follow, when they can, with cheap smartphones. Somewhere I'm on a site as a 'nice lady' or whatever they say today. The railroad runs east of here and it's sometimes a last spot where trains slow down before they get to the big yard in Belen. Men come up the Rio Grande hoping to hop on the train.

I don't like it. I was happy to give someone a meal when I felt anonymous. Handing a bowl of soup to someone who may not have eaten for a few days was an easy way to feel good about myself. That didn't mean I wanted to open a migrant restaurant. I live by myself. Being an economic refugee doesn't make people kind and good and I feel as if having my place on some website makes me vulnerable. The dogs may bark like fools, but Hudson is some cross between Border collie and golden retriever, and Abby is mostly black Lab. They are sweet mutts, not good protection dogs, and it doesn't take a genius to figure that out.

I wake at night sometimes now, thinking someone is in my house. Abby sleeps on the other side of the bed, and Hudson sleeps on the floor. Where I live it is brutally dark at night, unless there's a moon – no one wastes power on lights at night. My house is small, two bedrooms, a kitchen and a family room. I lean over and shake Hudson on the floor, wake him up. "Who's here?" I whisper. Abby sits up, but neither of them hear anything. They pad down the hall with me into the dark front room and I peer through the window into the shadowy back lot. I wait for them to bark.

Many a night, I don't go back to sleep.

But the man at my door this morning weeds my garden, and accepts my bowl of soup and some flour tortillas. He thanks me gravely. He picks up his phone, charging off my system, and shows me a photo of a woman and a child. "My wife and baby," he says. I nod. I don't particularly want to know about his wife and baby but I can't be rude.

I finish assembling the doll I am working on. I've painted her, assembled all the parts and hand rooted all her hair. She is rather cuter than I like. Customers can mix and match parts off of my website – this face with the eye color of their choice, hands curled one way or another. A mix and match doll costs about what the migrant will make in two weeks. A few customers want custom dolls and send images to match. Add a zero to the cost.

I am dressing the doll when Abby leaps up, happily roo-rooing. I start, standing, and drop the doll dangling in my hand by one unshod foot.

It hits the floor head first with a thump and the man gasps in horror.

"It's a doll," I say.

I don't know if he understands, but he realizes. He covers his mouth with his hand and laughs, nervous.

I scoop the doll off the floor. I make reborns. Dolls that look like newborn infants. The point is to make them look almost, but not quite real. People prefer them a little cuter, a little more perfect than the real thing. I like them best when there is something a little strange, a little off about them. I like them as ugly as most actual newborns, with some aspect that suggests ontology recapitulating phylogeny; that a developing fetus starts as a single celled organism, and then develops to look like a tiny fish, before passing in stages into its final animal shape. The old theory of ontology recapitulating phylogeny, that the development of the human embryo follows the evolutionary path, is false, of course. But I prefer that my babies remind us that we are really animals. That they be ancient and a little grotesque. Tiny changelings in our house.

I am equally pleased to think of Thanksgiving turkeys as a kind of dinosaur gracing a holiday table. It is probably why I live alone.

"Que bonita," he says. How beautiful.

"Gracias," I say. He has brought me the empty bowl. I take it, and send him on his way.

I check my email and I have an order for a special. A reborn made to order. It's from a couple in Chicago, Rachel and Ellam Mazar – I have always assumed that it is Rachel who emails me but the emails never actually identify who is typing. There is a photo attached of an infant. This wouldn't be strange except this is the third request in three years I have had for exactly the same doll.

The dolls are expensive, especially the specials. I went to art school, and then worked as a sculptor for a toy company for a few years. I didn't make dolls, I made action figures, especially alien figures and spaceships from the Kinetics movies. A whole generation of boys grew up imprinting on toys I had sculpted. When the craze for Kinetics passed, the company laid off lots of people, including me. The whole economy was coming apart at the seams. I had been lucky to have a job for as long as I did. I moved to New Mexico because I loved it and it was cheap, and I tried to do sculpting freelance. I worked at a big box store. Like so many people, my life went into freefall. I bought this place – a little ranch house that had gone into foreclosure in a place where no one was buying anything and boarded up houses fall in on themselves like mouths without teeth. It was the last of my savings. I started making dolls as a stopgap.

I get by. Between the little bit of money from the dolls and the garden I can eat. Which is more than some people.

A special will give me money for property tax. My cistern is getting low and there is no rain coming until the monsoon in June, which is a long way from now. If it's like last year, we won't get enough rain to fill the cistern anyway. I could pay for the water truck to make a delivery. But I don't like this. When I put the specials on my website, I thought about it as a way to make money. I had seen it on another doll site. I am a trained sculptor. I didn't think about why people would ask for specials.

Some people ask me to make infant dolls of their own children. If my mother had bought an infant version of me I'd have found it pretty disturbing.

One woman bought a special modeled on herself. She wrote me long emails about how her mother had been a narcissist, a monster, and how she was going to symbolically mother herself. Her husband was mayor of a city in California, which was how she could afford to have a replica of her infant self. Her emails made me uncomfortable, which I resented. So eventually I passed her on to another doll maker who made toddlers. I figured she could nurture herself up through all the stages of childhood.

Her reborn was very cute. More attractive than she was in the image she sent. She never commented. I don't know that she ever realized.

I suspect the Mazars fall into another category. I have gotten three requests from people who have lost an infant. I tell myself that there is possibly something healing in recreating your dead child as a doll. Each time I have gotten one of these requests I have very seriously considered taking the specials off my website.

Property tax payments. Water in the cistern.

If the Mazars lost a child – and I don't know that they did but I have a feeling that I can't shake – it was bad enough that they want a replica. Then a year ago, I got a request for the second.

I thought that maybe Rachel – if it is Rachel who emails me, not Ellam – had meant to send a different image. I sent back an email saying were they sure that she had sent the right image?

The response was terse. They were sure.

I sent them an email saying if something had happened, I could do repairs.

The response was equally terse. They wanted me to make one.

I searched them online, but could find out nothing about the Mazars of Chicago. They didn't have a presence online. Who had money but no presence online? Were they organized crime? Just very very private? Now a third doll.

I don't answer the email. Not yet.

Instead I take my laptop out to the shed. Inside the shed is my oven for baking the doll parts between coats of paint. I plug in the computer to recharge and park it on a shelf above eye level. I have my parts cast by Tony in Ohio, an old connection from my days in the toy industry. He makes my copper molds and rotocasts the parts. Usually, though, the specials are a one off and he sends me the copper supermaster of the head so he doesn't have to store it. I rummage through my molds and find the head from the last time I made this doll. I set it on the shelf and look at it.

I rough sculpt the doll parts in clay, then do a plaster cast of the clay mold. Then from that I make a wax model, looking like some Victorian memorial of an infant that died of jaundice. I have my own recipe for the wax – commercial wax and paraffin and talc. I could tint it pink, most people do. I just like the way they look.

I do the fine sculpting and polishing on the wax model. I carefully pack and ship the model to Tony and he casts the copper mold. The process is nasty and toxic, not something I can do myself. For the regular dolls, he does a short run of a hundred or so parts in PVC, vinyl, and ships them to me. He keeps those molds in case I need more. For the head of a special he sends me back a single cast head and the mold.

All of the detail is on the inside of the mold, outside is only the rough outline of the shape. Infant's heads are long from forehead to back of the skull. Their faces are tiny and low, their jaws like porkchop bones. They are marvelous and strange mechanisms.

At about seven, I hear Sherie's truck. The dogs erupt.

Sherie and Ed live about a mile and a half up the road. They have a little dairy goat operation. Sherie is six months pregnant and goes into Albuquerque to see an obstetrician. Her dad works at Sandia Labs and makes decent money so her parents are paying for her medical care. It's a long drive in and back, the truck is old and Ed doesn't like her to go alone. I ride along and we pick up supplies. Her mom makes us lunch.

"Goddamn it's hot," Sherie says, as I climb into the little yellow Toyota truck. "How's your water?"

"Getting low," I say. Sherie and Ed have a well.

"I'm worried we might go dry this year," Sherie says. "They keep whining about the aquifer. If we have to buy water I don't know what we'll do."

Sherie is physically Chinese, one of the thousands of girls adopted out of China in the nineties and at the turn of the century. She said she went through a phase of trying to learn all things Chinese, but she complains that as far as she can tell, the only thing Chinese about her is that she's lactose intolerant.

"I had a migrant at my door this morning," I say.

"Did you feed him?" she asks. She leans into the shift, trying to find the gear, urging the truck into first.

"He weeded my garden," I say.

"They're not going to stop as long as you feed them."

"Like stray cats," I say.

Albuquerque has never been a pretty town. When I came it was mostly strip malls and big box stores and suburbs. Ten years of averages of 4 inches of rain or less have hurt it badly, especially with the loss of the San Juan/ Chama water rights. Water is expensive in Albuquerque. Too expensive for Intel, which pulled out. Intel was just a larger blow in a series of blows.

The suburbs are full of walkaway houses – places where homeowners couldn't meet the mortgage payments and just left, the lots now full of trash and windows gone. People who could went north for water. People who couldn't did what people always do when an economy goes soft and rotten, they slid, to rented houses, rented apartments, living in their cars, living with their family, living on the street.

But inside Sherie's parent's home it's still twenty years ago. The countertops are granite. The big screen plasma TV gets hundreds of channels. The freezer is full of meat and frozen Lean Cuisine. The air conditioner keeps the temperature at a heavenly 75 degrees. Sherie's mother, Brenda, is slim, with beautifully styled graying hair. She's a psychologist with a small practice.

Brenda has one of my dolls, which she bought because she likes me. It's always out when I come, but it doesn't fit Brenda's tailored, airily comfortable style. I have never heard Brenda say a thing against Ed. But I can only assume that she and Kyle wish Sherie had married someone who worked at Los Alamos or at Sandia or the University, someone with government benefits like health insurance. On the other hand, Sherie was a wild child, who, as Brenda said, 'Did a stint as a lesbian,' as if being a lesbian were like signing up for the Peace Corps. You can't make your child fall in love with the right kind of person. I wish I could have fallen in love with someone from Los Alamos. More than that, I wish I had been able to get a job at Los Alamos or the University. Me, and half of Albuquerque.

Sherie comes home, her hair rough cut in her kitchen with a mirror. She is loud and comfortable. Her belly is just a gentle insistent curve under her blue Rumatel goat dewormer t-shirt. Brenda hangs on her every word, knows about the trials and tribulations of raising goats, asks about Ed, the truck. She feeds us lunch.

I thought this life of thoughtful liberalism was my birthright, too. Before I understood that my generation was to be born in interesting times.

At the obstetrician's office, I sit in the waiting room and try not to fall asleep. I'm stuffed on Brenda's chicken and cheese sandwich and corn chowder. People magazine has an article about Tom Cruise getting telemerase regeneration therapy which will extend his lifespan an additional forty years. There's an article on some music guy's house talking about the new opulence; cutting edge technology that darkens the windows at the touch of a hand and walls that change color, rooms that sense whether you're warm or cold and change their temperature, and his love of ancient Turkish and Russian antiques. There's an article on a woman who has dedicated her life to helping people in Siberia who have AIDS.

Sherie comes out of the doctor's office on her cellphone. The doctor tells her that if she had insurance, they'd do a routine ultrasound. I can hear half the conversation as she discusses it with her mother. "This little guy," Sherie says, hand on her belly, "is half good Chinese peasant stock. He's doing fine." They decide to wait for another month.

Sherie is convinced that it's a boy. Ed is convinced it's a girl. He sings David Bowie's "China Doll" to Sherie's stomach, which for some reason irritates the hell out of her.

We stop on our way out of town and stock up on rice and beans, flour, sugar, coffee. We can get all this in Belen, but it's cheaper at Sam's Club. Sherie has a membership. I pay half the membership and she uses the card to buy all our groceries then I pay her back when we get to the car.

The cashiers surely know that we're sharing a membership, but they don't care.

It's a long hot drive back home. The air conditioning doesn't work in the truck. I am so grateful to see the trees that mark the valley.

My front door is standing open.

"Who's here?" Sherie says.

Abby is standing in the front yard and she has clearly recognized Sherie's truck. She's barking her fool head off and wagging her tail, desperate. She runs to the truck. I get out and head for the front door and she runs toward the door and then back toward me and then toward the door, unwilling to go in until I get there, then lunging through the door ahead of me.

"Hudson?" I call the other dog, but I know if the door is open, he's out roaming. Lost. My things are strewn everywhere, couch cushions on the floor, my kitchen drawers emptied on the floor, the back door open. I go through to the back, calling the missing dog, hoping against hope he is in the backyard. The back gate is open, too.

Behind me I hear Sherie calling, "Don't go in there by yourself!"

"My dog is gone," I say.

"Hudson?" she says.

I go out the back and call for him. There's no sign of him. He's a great boy, but some dogs, like Abby, tend to stay close to home. Hudson isn't one of those dogs.

Sherie and I walk through the house. No one is there. I go out to my workshop. My toolbox is gone, but evidently whoever did this didn't see the computer closed and sitting on the shelf just above eye level.

It had to be the guy I gave soup to. He probably went nearby to wait out the heat of the day and saw me leave.

I close and lock the gate, and the workshop. Close and lock my back door. Abby clings to me. Dogs don't like things to be different.

"We'll look for him," Sherie says. Abby and I climb into the truck and for an hour we drive back roads, looking and calling, but there's no sign of him. Her husband Ed calls us. He's called the county and there's a deputy at my place waiting to take a statement. We walk through the house and I identify what's gone. As best I can tell, it isn't much. Just the tools, mainly. The sheriff says they are usually looking for money, guns, jewelry. I had all my cards and my cell phone with me, and all my jewelry is inexpensive stuff. I don't have a gun.

I tell the deputy about the migrant this morning. He says it could have been him, or someone else. I get the feeling we'll never know. He promises to put out the word about the dog.

It is getting dark when they all leave and I put the couch cushions on the couch. I pick up silverware off the floor and run hot water in the sink to wash it all. Abby stands at the back door, whining, but doesn't want to go out alone.

It occurs to me suddenly that the doll I was working on is missing. He stole the doll. Why? He's not going to be able to sell it. To send it home, I guess, to the baby in the photo. Or maybe to his wife, who has a real baby and is undoubtedly feeling a lot less sentimental about infants than most of my customers do. It's a couple of weeks of work, not full time, but painting, waiting for the paint to cure, painting again.

Abby whines again. Hudson is out there in the dark. Lost dogs don't do well in the desert. There are rattlesnakes. I didn't protect him. I sit down on the floor and wrap my arms around Abby's neck and cry. I'm a stupid woman who is stupid about my dogs, I know. But they are what I have.

I don't really sleep. I hear noises all night long. I worry about what I am going to do about money.

Replacing the tools is going to be a problem. The next morning I put the first layer of paint on a new doll to replace the stolen one. Then I do something I have resisted doing. Plastic doll parts aren't the only thing I can mold and sell on the Internet. I start a clay model for a dildo. Over the last couple of years I've gotten queries from companies who have seen the dolls online and asked if I would consider doing dildos for them. Realistic penises aren't really any more difficult to carve than realistic baby hands. Easier, actually. I can't send it to Tony, he wouldn't do dildos. But a few years ago they came out with room temperature, medical grade silicon. I can make my own molds, do small runs, hand finish them. Make them as perfectly lifelike as the dolls. I can hope people will pay for novelty when it comes to sex.

I don't particularly like making doll parts, but I don't dislike it either. Dildos, on the other hand, just make me sad. I don't think there is anything wrong with using them, it's not that. It's just . . . I don't know. I'm not going to stop making dolls, I tell myself.

I also email the Chicago couple back and accept the commission for the special, to make the same doll for the third time. Then I take a break and clean my kitchen some more. Sherie calls me to check how I'm doing and I tell her about the dildos. She laughs. "You should have done it years ago," she says. "You'll be rich."

I laugh, too. And I feel a little better when I finish the call.

I try not to think about Hudson. It's well over 100 today. I don't want to think about him in trouble, without water. I try to concentrate on penile veins. On the stretch of skin underneath the head (I'm making a circumcised penis). When my cell rings I jump.

The guy on the phone says, "I've got a dog here, has got this number on his collar. You missing a dog?"

"A golden retriever?" I say.

"Yep."

"His name is Hudson," I say. "Oh thank you. Thank you. I'll be right there."

I grab my purse. I've got fifty-five dollars in cash. Not much of a reward, but all I can do. "Abby!" I yell. "Come on girl! Let's go get Hudson!"

She bounces up from the floor, clueless, but excited by my voice.

"Go for a ride?" I ask.

We get in my ancient red Impreza. It's not too reliable, but we aren't going far. We bump across miles of bad road, most of it unpaved, following the GPS directions on my phone and end up at a trailer in the middle of nowhere. It's bleached and surrounded by trash – an old easy chair, a kitchen chair lying on it's side with one leg broken and the white unstained inside like a scar, an old picnic table. There's a dirty green cooler and a bunch of empty 40 oz bottles. Frankly, if I saw the place my assumption would be that the owner made meth. But the old man who opens the door is just an old guy in a baseball cap. Probably living on social security.

"I'm Nick," he says. He's wearing a long sleeved plaid shirt despite the heat. He's deeply tanned and has a turkey wattle neck.

I introduce myself. Point to the car and say, "That's Abby, the smart one that stays home."

The trailer is dark and smells of old man inside. The couch cushions are covered in cheap throws, one of them decorated with a blue and white Christmas snowman. Outside, the scrub shimmers, flattened in the heat. Hudson is laying in front of the sink and scrabbles up when he sees us.

"He was just ambling up the road," Nick says. "He saw me and came right up."

"I live over by the river, off 109, between Belen and Jarales," I say. "Someone broke into my place and left the doors open and he wandered off."

"You're lucky they didn't kill the dogs," Nick says.

I fumble with my purse. "There's a reward," I say.

He waves that away. "No, don't you go starting that." He says he didn't do anything but read the tag and give him a drink. "I had dogs all my life," he says. "I'd want someone to call me."

I tell him it would mean a lot to me and press the money on him. Hudson leans against my legs to be petted, tongue lolling. He looks fine. No worse for wear.

"Sit a minute. You came all the way out here. Pardon the mess. My sister's grandson and his friends have been coming out here and they leave stuff like that," he says, waving at the junk and the bottles.

"I can't leave the other dog in the heat," I say, wanting to leave.

"Bring her inside."

I don't want to stay, but I'm grateful, so I bring Abby in out of the heat and he thumps her and tells me about how he's lived here since he was in his twenties. He's a Libertarian and he doesn't trust government and he really doesn't trust the New Mexico state government which is, in his estimation, a banana republic lacking only the fancy uniforms that third world dictators seem to love. Then he tells me about how lucky it was that Hudson didn't get picked up to be a bait dog for the people who raise dogs for dog fights. Then he tells me about how the American economy was destroyed by operatives from Russia as revenge for the fall of the Soviet Union.

Half of what he says is bullshit and the other half is wrong, but he's just a lonely guy in the middle of the desert and he brought me back my dog. The least I can do is listen.

I hear a spitting little engine off in the distance. Then a couple of them. It's the little motorbikes the kids ride. Nick's eyes narrow as he looks out.

"It's my sister's grandson," he says. "Goddamn."

He gets up and Abby whines. He stands, looking out the slatted blinds.

"Goddamn. He's got a couple of friends," Nick says. "Look you just get your dogs and don't say nothing to them, okay? You just go on."

"Hudson," I say and clip a lead on him.

Outside, four boys pull into the yard, kicking up dust. They have seen my car and are obviously curious. They wear jumpsuits like prison jumpsuits, only with the sleeves ripped off and the legs cut off just above the knees. Khaki and orange and olive green. One of them has tattoos swirling up his arms.

"Hey Nick," the tattooed one says, "new girlfriend?"

"None of your business, Ethan."

The boy is dark but his eyes are light blue. Like a Siberian Husky. "You a social worker?" the boy says.

"I told you it was none of your business," Nick says. "The lady is just going."

"If you're a social worker, you should know that old Nick is crazy and you can't believe nothing he says."

One of the other boys says, "She isn't a social worker. Social workers don't have dogs."

I step down the steps and walk to my car. The boys sit on their bikes and I have to walk around them to get to the Impreza. Hudson wants to see them, pulling against his leash, but I hold him in tight.

"You look nervous, lady," the tattooed boy says.

"Leave her alone, Ethan," Nick says.

"You shut up, Uncle Nick, or I'll kick your ass," the boy says absently, never taking his eyes off me.

Nick says nothing.

I say nothing. I just get my dogs in my car and drive away.

Our life settles into a new normal. I get a response from my dildo email. Nick in Montana is willing to let me sell on his sex site on commission. I make a couple of different models, including one that I paint just as realistically as I would one of the reborn dolls. This means a base coat, then I paint the veins in. Then I bake it. Then I paint an almost translucent layer of color and bake it again. Six layers. And then a clear over-layer of silicon because I don't think the paint is approved for use this way. I put a pretty hefty price on it and call it a special. At the same time I am making my other special. The doll for the Chicago couple. I sent the mold to Tony and had him do a third head from it. It, too, requires layers of paint, and sometimes the parts bake side by side.

Because my business is rather slow, I take more time than usual. I am always careful, especially with specials. I think if someone is going to spend the kind of money one of these costs, the doll should be made to the best of my ability. And maybe it is because I have done this doll before, it comes easily and well. I think of the doll that the man who broke into my house stole. I don't know if he sent it to his wife and daughter in Mexico, or if he even has a wife and daughter in Mexico. I rather suspect he sold it on eBay or some equivalent – although I have watched doll sales and never seen it come up.

This doll is my orphan doll. She is full of sadness. She is inhabited by the loss of so much. I remember my fear when Hudson was wandering the roads of the desert. I imagine Rachel Mazar, so haunted by the loss of her own child. The curves of the doll's tiny fists are porcelain pale. The blue veins at her temples are traceries of the palest of bruises.

When I am finished with her, I package her as carefully as I have ever packaged a doll and send her off.

My dildos go up on the website.

The realistic dildo sits in my workshop, upright, tumescent, a beautiful rosy plum color. It sits on a shelf like a prize, glistening in its topcoat as if it were wet. It was surprisingly fun to make, after years and years of doll parts. It sits there both as an object to admire and as an affront. But to be frank, I don't think it is any more immoral than the dolls. There is something straightforward about a dildo. Something much more clear than a doll made to look like a dead child. Something significantly less entangled.

There are no orders for dildos. I lie awake at night thinking about real estate taxes. My father is dead. My mother lives in subsidized housing for the elderly in Columbus. I haven't been to see her in years and years, not with the cost of a trip like that. My car wouldn't make it, and nobody I know can afford to fly anymore. I certainly couldn't live with her. She would lose her housing if I moved in.

If I lose my house to unpaid taxes, do I live in my car? It seems like the beginning of the long slide. Maybe Sherie and Ed would take the dogs.

I do get a reprieve when the money comes in for the special. Thank God for the Mazars in Chicago. However crazy their motives, they pay promptly and by Internet, which allows me to put money against the equity line for the new tools.

I still can't sleep at night and instead of putting all of the money against my debt, I put the minimum and I buy a 9 millimeter handgun. Actually, Ed buys it for me. I don't even know where to get a gun.

Sherie picks me up in the truck and brings me over to the goat farm. Ed has several guns. He has an old gun safe that belonged to his father. When we get to their place, he is in back, putting creosote on new fence posts, but he is happy to come up to the house.

"So you've given in," he says, grinning. "You've joined the dark side."

"I have," I agree.

"Well, this is a decent defensive weapon," Ed says. Ed does not fit my pre-conceived notions of a gun owner. Ed fits my pre-conceived notions of the guy who sells you a cell phone at the local strip mall. His hair is short and graying. He doesn't look at all like the kind of guy who would either marry Sherie or raise goats. He told me one time that his degree is in anthropology. Which, he said, was a difficult field to get a job in.

"Offer her a cold drink!" Sherie yells from the bathroom. In her pregnant state, Sherie can't ride twenty minutes in the sprung-shocked truck without having to pee.

He offers me iced tea and then gets the gun, checks to see that it isn't loaded, and hands it to me. He explains to me that the first thing I should do is check to see if the gun is loaded.

"You just did," I say.

"Yeah," he says, "but I might be an idiot. It's a good thing to do."

He shows me how to check the gun.

It is not nearly so heavy in my hand as I thought it would be. But truthfully, I have found that the thing you thought would be life changing so rarely is.

Later he takes me around to the side yard and shows me how to load and shoot it. I am not even remotely surprised that it is kind of fun. That is exactly what I expected.

Out of the blue, an email from Rachel Mazar of Chicago.

I am writing you to ask you if you have had any personal or business dealings with my husband, Ellam Mazar. If I do not get a response from you, your next correspondence will be from my attorney.

I don't quite know what to do. I dither. I make vegetarian chili. Oddly enough, I check my gun which I keep in the bedside drawer. I am not sure what I am going to do about the gun when Sherie has her baby. I have offered to babysit, and I'll have to lock it up, I think. But that seems to defeat the purpose of having it.

While I am dithering, my cell rings. It is, of course, Rachel Mazar. "I need you to explain your relationship with my husband, Ellam Mazar," she says. She sounds educated, with that eradication of regional accent that signifies a decent college.

"My relationship?" I say.

"Your email was on his phone," she says, frostily.

I wonder if he is dead. The way she says it sounds so final. "I didn't know your husband," I say. "He just bought the dolls."

"Bought what?" she says.

"The dolls," I say.

"Dolls?" she says.

"Yes," I say.

"Like . . . sex dolls?"

"No," I say. "Dolls. Reborns. Handmade dolls."

She obviously has no idea what I am talking about, which opens a world of strange possibilities in my mind. The dolls don't have orifices. Fetish objects? I tell her my website and she looks it up.

"He ordered specials," I say.

"But these cost a couple of thousand dollars," she says.

A week's salary for someone like Ellam Mazar, I suspect. I envision him as a professional, although frankly, for all I know he works in a dry cleaning shop or something.

"I thought they were for you," I say. "I assumed you had lost a child. Sometimes people who have lost a child order one."

"We don't have children," she says. "We never wanted them." I can hear how stunned she is in the silence. Then she says, "Oh my God."

Satanic rituals? Some weird abuse thing?

"That woman said he told her he had lost a child," she says.

I don't know what to say so I just wait.

"My husband . . . my soon to be ex-husband," she says. "He has apparently been having affairs. One of the women contacted me. She told me that he told her we had a child that died and that now we were married in name only."

I hesitate. I don't know legally if I am allowed to tell her about transactions I had with her husband. On the other hand, the emails came with both their names on them. "He has bought three," I say.

"Three?"

"Not all at once. About once a year. But people who want a special send me a picture. He always sends the same picture."

"Oh," she says. "That's Ellam. He's orderly. He's used the same shampoo for fifteen years."

"I thought it was strange," I say. I can't bear not to ask. "What do you think he did with them?"

"I think the twisted bastard used them to make women feel sorry for him," she says through gritted teeth. "I think he got all sentimental about them. He probably has himself half convinced that he really did have a daughter. Or that it's my fault that we didn't have children. He never wanted children. Never."

"I think a lot of my customers like the idea of having a child better than having one," I say.

"I'm sure," she says. "Thank you for your time and I'm sorry to have bothered you."

So banal. So strange and yet so banal. I try to imagine him giving the doll to a woman, telling her that it was the image of his dead child. How did that work?

Orders for dildos begin to trickle in. I get a couple of doll orders and make a payment on the credit line and put away some toward real estate taxes. I may not have to live in my car.

One evening, I am working in the garden when Abby and Hudson start barking at the back gate.

I get off my knees, aching, but lurch into the house and into the bedroom where I grab the 9mm out of the bedside table. It isn't loaded, which now seems stupid. I try to think if I should stop and load it. My hands are shaking. It is undoubtedly just someone looking for a meal and a place to recharge. I decide I can't trust myself to load and besides, the dogs are out there. I go to the back door, gun held stiffly at my side, pointed to the ground.

There are in fact two of them, alike as brothers, Indian looking with a fringe of black hair cut in a straight line above their eyebrows.

"Lady," one says, "we can work for food?" First one, then the other sees the gun at my side and their faces go empty.

The dogs cavort.

"I will give you something to eat, and then you go," I say.

"We go," the one who spoke says.

"Someone robbed me," I say.

"We no rob you," he says. His eyes are on the gun. His companion takes a step back, glancing at the gate and then at me as if to gauge if I will shoot him if he bolts.

"I know," I say. "But someone came here, I gave him food, and he robbed me. You tell people not to come here, okay?"

"Okay," he says. "We go."

"Tell people not to come here," I say. I would give them something to eat, something to take with them. I hate this. They are two young men in a foreign country, hungry, looking for work. I could easily be sleeping in my car. I could be homeless. I could be wishing for someone to be nice to me.

But I am not. I'm just afraid.

"Hudson! Abby!" I yell, harsh, and the two men flinch. "Get in the house."

The dogs slink in behind me, not sure what they've done wrong.

"If you want some food, I will give you something," I say. "Tell people not to come here."

I don't think they understand me. Instead they back slowly away a handful of steps and then turn and walk quickly out the gate, closing it behind them.

I sit down where I am standing, knees shaking.

The moon is up in the blue early evening sky. Over my fence I can see scrub and desert, a fierce land where mountains breach like the petrified spines of apocalyptic animals. The kind of landscape that seems right for crazed gangs of mutants charging around in cobbled together vehicles. Tribal remnants of America, their faces painted, their hair braided, wearing jewelry made from shiny CDs and cigarette lighters scrounged from the ruins of civilization. The desert is Byronic in its extremes.

I don't see the two men. There's no one out there in furs, their faces painted blue, driving a dune buggy built out of motorcycle parts and hung with the skulls of their enemies. There's just a couple of guys from Nicaragua or Guatemala, wearing t-shirts and jeans.

And me, sitting watching the desert go dark, the moon rising, an empty handgun in my hand.

BLACK SWAN

Bruce Sterling

One of the most powerful and innovative talents to enter SF in the past few decades, Bruce Sterling sold his first story in 1976. By the end of the 1980s, he had established himself, with a series of stories set in his exotic "Shaper/Mechanist" future and with novels such as the complex and *Stapeldonian Schismatrix* and *Islands in the Net* (as well as with his editing of the influential anthology *Mirrorshades: The Cyberpunk Anthology* and the infamous critical magazine *Cheap Truth*), as perhaps the prime driving force behind the revolutionary "Cyberpunk" movement in science fiction. His other books include a critically acclaimed nonfiction study of First Amendment issues in the world of computer networking, *The Hacker Crackdown: Law and Disorder on the Electronic Frontier*, the novels *The Artificial Kid, Involution Ocean, Heavy Weather, Holy Fire, Distraction, Zeitgeist, The Zenith Angle*, a novel in collaboration with William Gibson, *The Difference Engine*, a nonfiction study of the future, *Tomorrow Now: Envisioning the Next Fifty Years*, and the landmark collections *Crystal Express, Globalhead, Schismatrix Plus, A Good Old-Fashioned Future*, and *Visionary in Residence*. His most recent books are a massive retrospective collection, *Ascendancies: The Best of Bruce Sterling*, and a new novel, *Caryatids*. His story "Bicycle Repairman" earned him a long-overdue Hugo in 1997, and he won another Hugo in 1999 for his story "Taklamakan."

In the politically savvy and bitingly cynical story that follows, one infused with his trademark deadpan wit, Sterling expertly spins us through a gyre of well-thought-out Alternate World Europes. And where the ball stops, nobody knows.

THE ETHICAL JOURNALIST protects a confidential source. So I protected Massimo Montaldo, although I knew that wasn't his name.

Massimo shambled through the tall glass doors, dropped his valise with a thump, and sat across the table. We were meeting where we always met: inside the Caffe Elena, a dark and cozy spot that fronts on the biggest plaza in Europe.

The Elena has two rooms as narrow and dignified as mahogany coffins, with lofty red ceilings. The little place has seen its share of stricken wanderers. Massimo never confided his personal troubles to me, but they were obvious, as if he'd smuggled monkeys into the cafe and hidden them under his clothes.

Like every other hacker in the world, Massimo Montaldo was bright. Being Italian, he struggled to look suave. Massimo wore stain-proof, wrinkle-proof travel gear: a black merino wool jacket, an American black denim shirt, and black cargo pants. Massimo also sported black athletic trainers, not any brand I could recognize, with eerie bubble-filled soles.

These skeletal shoes of his were half-ruined. They were strapped together with rawhide bootlaces.

To judge by his Swiss-Italian accent, Massimo had spent a lot of time in Geneva. Four times he'd leaked chip secrets to me – crisp engineering graphics, apparently snipped right out of Swiss patent applications. However, the various bureaus in Geneva had no records of these patents. They had no records of any 'Massimo Montaldo,' either.

Each time I'd made use of Massimo's indiscretions, the traffic to my weblog had doubled.

I knew that Massimo's commercial sponsor, or more likely his spymaster, was using me to manipulate the industry I covered. Big bets were going down in the markets somewhere. Somebody was cashing in like a bandit.

That profiteer wasn't me, and I had to doubt that it was him. I never financially speculate in the companies I cover as a journalist, because that is the road to hell. As for young Massimo, his road to hell was already well-trampled.

Massimo twirled the frail stem of his glass of Barolo. His shoes were wrecked, his hair was unwashed, and he looked like he'd shaved in an airplane toilet. He handled the best wine in Europe like a scorpion poised to sting his liver. Then he gulped it down.

Unasked, the waiter poured him another. They know me at the Elena.

Massimo and I had a certain understanding. As we chatted about Italian tech companies – he knew them from Alessi to Zanotti – I discreetly passed him useful favors. A cell phone chip – bought in another man's name. A plastic hotel passkey for a local hotel room, rented by a third party. Massimo could use these without ever showing a passport or any identification.

There were eight 'Massimo Montaldos' on Google and none of them were him. Massimo flew in from places unknown, he laid his eggs of golden information, then he paddled off into dark waters. I was protecting him by giving him those favors. Surely there were other people very curious about him, besides myself.

The second glass of Barolo eased that ugly crease in his brow. He rubbed his beak of a nose, and smoothed his unruly black hair, and leaned onto the thick stone table with both of his black woolen elbows.

"Luca, I brought something special for you this time. Are you ready for that? Something you can't even imagine."

"I suppose," I said.

Massimo reached into his battered leather valise and brought out a no-name PC laptop. This much-worn machine, its corners bumped with use and its keyboard dingy, had one of those thick super-batteries clamped onto its base. All that extra power must have tripled the computer's weight. Small wonder that Massimo never carried spare shoes.

He busied himself with his grimy screen, fixated by his private world there.

The Elena is not a celebrity bar, which is why celebrities like it. A blonde television presenter swayed into the place. Massimo, who was now deep into his third glass, whipped his intense gaze from his laptop screen. He closely studied her curves, which were upholstered in Gucci.

An Italian television presenter bears the relationship to news that American fast food bears to food. So I couldn't feel sorry for her – yet I didn't like the way he sized her up. Genius gears were turning visibly in Massimo's brilliant geek head. That woman had all the raw, compelling appeal to him of some difficult math problem.

Left alone with her, he would chew on that problem until something clicked loose and fell into his hands, and, to do her credit, she could feel that. She opened her dainty crocodile purse and slipped on a big pair of sunglasses.

"Signor Montaldo," I said.

He was rapt.

"Massimo?"

This woke him from his lustful reverie. He twisted the computer and exhibited his screen to me.

I don't design chips, but I've seen the programs used for that purpose. Back in the 1980s, there were thirty different chip-design programs. Nowadays there are only three survivors. None of them are nativized in the Italian language, because every chip geek in the world speaks English.

This program was in Italian. It looked elegant. It looked like a very stylish way to design computer chips. Computer chip engineers are not stylish people. Not in this world, anyway.

Massimo tapped at his weird screen with a gnawed fingernail. "This is just a cheap, 24-k embed. But do you see these?"

"Yes, I do. What are they?"

"These are memristors."

In heartfelt alarm, I stared around the cafe, but nobody in the Elena knew or cared in the least about Massimo's stunning revelation. He could have thrown memristors onto their tables in heaps. They'd never realize that he was tossing them the keys to riches.

I could explain now, in gruelling detail, exactly what memristors are, and how different they are from any standard electronic component. Suffice it to understand that, in electronic engineering, memristors did not exist. Not at all. They were technically possible – we'd known that for thirty years, since the 1980s – but nobody had ever manufactured one.

A chip with memristors was like a racetrack where the jockeys rode unicorns.

I sipped the Barolo so I could find my voice again. "You brought me schematics for memristors? What happened, did your UFO crash?"

"That's very witty, Luca."

"You can't hand me something like that! What on Earth do you expect me to do with that?"

"I am not giving these memristor plans to you. I have decided to give them to Olivetti. I will tell you what to do: you make one confidential call to your good friend, the Olivetti Chief Technical Officer. You tell him to look hard in his junk folder where he keeps the spam with no return address. Interesting things will happen, then. He'll be grateful to you."

"Olivetti is a fine company," I said. "But they're not the outfit to handle a monster like that. A memristor is strictly for the big boys – Intel, Samsung, Fujitsu."

Massimo laced his hands together on the table – he might have been at prayer – and stared at me with weary sarcasm. "Luca," he said, "don't you ever get tired of seeing Italian genius repressed?"

The Italian chip business is rather modest. It can't always make its ends meet. I spent fifteen years covering chip tech in Route 128 in Boston. When the almighty dollar ruled the tech world, I was glad that I'd made those connections.

But times do change. Nations change, industries change. Industries change the times.

Massimo had just shown me something that changes industries. A disruptive innovation. A breaker of the rules.

"This matter is serious," I said. "Yes, Olivetti's people do read my web blog – they even comment there. But that doesn't mean that I can leak some breakthrough that deserves a Nobel Prize. Olivetti would want to know, they would have to know, the source of that."

He shook his head. "They don't want to know, and neither do you."

"Oh yes, I most definitely do want to know."

"No, you don't. Trust me."

"Massimo, I'm a journalist. That means that I always want to know, and I never trust anybody."

He slapped the table. "Maybe you were a 'journalist' when they still printed paper 'journals.' But your dot-com journals are all dead. Nowadays you're a blogger. You're an influence peddler and you spread rumors for a living." Massimo shrugged, because he didn't think he was insulting me. "So: shut up! Just do what you always do! That's all I'm asking."

That might be all that he was asking, but my whole business was in asking. "Who created that chip?" I asked him. "I know it wasn't you. You know a lot about tech investment, but you're not Leonardo da Vinci."

"No, I'm not Leonardo." He emptied his glass.

"Look, I know that you're not even 'Massimo Montaldo' – whoever that is. I'll do a lot to get news out on my blog. But I'm not going to act as your cut-out in a scheme like this! That's totally unethical! Where did you steal that chip? Who made it? What are they, Chinese super-engineers in some bunker under Beijing?"

Massimo was struggling not to laugh at me. "I can't reveal that. Could we have another round? Maybe a sandwich? I need a nice toasty pancetta."

I got the waiter's attention. I noted that the TV star's boyfriend had shown up. Her boyfriend was not her husband. Unfortunately, I was not in the celebrity tabloid business. It wasn't the first time I'd missed a good bet by consorting with computer geeks.

"So you're an industrial spy," I told him. "And you must be Italian to boot, because you're always such a patriot about it. Okay: so you stole those plans somewhere. I won't ask you how or why. But let me give you some good advice: no sane man would leak that to Olivetti. Olivetti's a consumer outfit. They make pretty toys for cute secretaries. A memristor chip is dynamite."

Massimo was staring raptly at the TV blonde as he awaited his sandwich.

"Massimo, pay attention. If you leak something that advanced, that radical . . . a chip like that could change the world's military balance of power. Never mind Olivetti. Big American spy agencies with three letters in their names will come calling."

Massimo scratched his dirty scalp and rolled his eyes in derision. "Are you so terrorized by the CIA? They don't read your sorry little one-man tech blog."

This crass remark irritated me keenly. "Listen to me, boy genius: do you know what the CIA does here in Italy? We're their 'rendition' playground. People vanish off the streets."

"Anybody can 'vanish off the streets.' I do that all the time."

I took out my Moleskin notebook and my shiny Rotring technical pen. I placed them both on the Elena's neat little marble table. Then I slipped them both back inside my jacket. "Massimo, I'm trying hard to be sensible about this. Your snotty attitude is not helping your case with me."

With an effort, my source composed himself. "It's all very simple," he lied. "I've been here awhile, and now I'm tired of this place. So I'm leaving. I want to hand the future of electronics to an Italian company. With no questions asked and no strings attached. You won't help me do that simple thing?"

"No, of course I won't! Not under conditions like these. I don't know where you got that data, what, how, when, whom, or why . . . I don't even know who you are! Do I look like that kind of idiot? Unless you tell me your story, I can't trust you."

He made that evil gesture: I had no balls. Twenty years ago – well, twenty-five – and we would have stepped outside the bar. Of course I was angry with him – but I also knew he was about to crack. My source was drunk and he was clearly in trouble. He didn't need a fist-fight with a journalist. He needed confession.

Massimo put a bold sneer on his face, watching himself in one of the Elena's tall spotted mirrors. "If this tiny gadget is too big for your closed mind, then I've got to find another blogger! A blogger with some guts!"

"Great. Sure. Go do that. You might try Beppe Grillo."

Massimo tore his gaze from his own reflection. "That washed-up TV comedian? What does he know about technology?"

"Try Berlusconi, then. He owns all the television stations and half the Italian Internet. Prime Minister Berlusconi is just the kind of hustler you need. He'll free you from all your troubles. He'll make you Minister of something."

Massimo lost all patience. "I don't need that! I've been to a lot of versions of Italy. Yours is a complete disgrace! I don't know how you people get along with yourselves!"

Now the story was tearing loose. I offered an encouraging nod. "How many 'versions of Italy' do you need, Massimo?"

"I have sixty-four versions of Italy." He patted his thick laptop. "Got them all right here."

I humored him. "Only sixty-four?"

His tipsy face turned red. "I had to borrow CERN's super-computers to calculate all those coordinates! Thirty-two Italies were too few! A hundred and twenty-eight . . . I'd never have the time to visit all those! And as for your Italy . . . well . . . I wouldn't be here at all, if it wasn't for that Turinese girl."

"Cherchez la femme," I told him. "That's the oldest trouble-story in the world."

"I did her some favors," he admitted, mournfully twisting his wine glass. "Like with you. But much more so."

I felt lost, but I knew that his story was coming. Once I'd coaxed it out of him, I could put it into better order later.

"So, tell me: what did she do to you?"

"She dumped me," he said. He was telling me the truth, but with a lost, forlorn, bewildered air, like he couldn't believe it himself. "She dumped me and she married the President of France." Massimo glanced up, his eyelashes wet with grief. "I don't blame her. I know why she did that. I'm a very handy guy for a woman like her, but Mother of God, I'm not the President of France!"

"No, no, you're not the President of France," I agreed. The President of France was a hyperactive Hungarian Jewish guy who liked to sing karaoke songs. President Nicolas Sarkozy was an exceedingly unlikely character, but he was odd in a very different way from Massimo Montaldo.

Massimo's voice was cracking with passion. "She says that he'll make her the First Lady of Europe! All I've got to offer her is insider-trading hints and a few extra millions for her millions."

The waiter brought Massimo a toasted sandwich.

Despite his broken heart, Massimo was starving. He tore into his food like a chained dog, then glanced up from his mayonnaise dip. "Do I sound jealous? I'm not jealous."

Massimo was bitterly jealous, but I shook my head so as to encourage him.

"I can't be jealous of a woman like her!" Massimo lied. "Eric Clapton can be jealous, Mick Jagger can be jealous! She's a rock star's groupie who's become the Premiere Dame of France! She married Sarkozy! Your world is full of journalists – spies, cops, creeps, whatever – and not for one minute did they ever stop and consider: 'Oh! This must be the work of a computer geek from another world!' "

"No," I agreed.

"Nobody ever imagines that!"

I called the waiter back and ordered myself a double espresso. The waiter seemed quite pleased at the way things were going for me. They were a kindly bunch at the Elena. Friedrich Nietzsche had been one of their favorite patrons. Their dark old mahogany walls had absorbed all kinds of lunacy.

Massimo jabbed his sandwich in the dip and licked his fingers. "So, if I leak a memristor chip to you, nobody will ever stop and say: 'Some unknown geek eating a sandwich in Torino is the most important man in world technology.' Because that truth is inconceivable."

Massimo stabbed a roaming olive with a toothpick. His hands were shaking: with rage, romantic heartbreak, and frustrated fury. He was also drunk.

He glared at me. "You're not following what I tell you. Are you really that stupid?"

"I do understand," I assured him. "Of course I understand. I'm a computer geek myself."

"You know who designed that memristor chip, Luca? You did it. You. But not here, not in this version of Italy. Here, you're just some small-time tech journalist. You created that device in my Italy. In my Italy, you are the guru of computational aesthetics. You're a famous author, you're a culture critic, you're a multi-talented genius. Here, you've got no guts and no imagination. You're so entirely useless here that you can't even change your own world."

It was hard to say why I believed him, but I did. I believed him instantly.

Massimo devoured his food to the last scrap. He thrust his bare plate aside and pulled a huge nylon wallet from his cargo pants. This overstuffed wallet had color-coded plastic pop-up tags, like the monster files of some Orwellian bureaucracy. Twenty different kinds of paper currency jammed in there. A huge riffling file of varicolored plastic ID cards.

He selected a large bill and tossed it contemptuously onto the Elena's cold marble table. It looked very much like money – it looked much more like money than the money that I handled every day. It had a splendid portrait of Galileo and it was denominated in 'Euro-Lira.'

Then he rose and stumbled out of the cafe. I hastily slipped the weird bill in my pocket. I threw some euros onto the table. Then I pursued him.

With his head down, muttering and sour, Massimo was weaving across the millions of square stone cobbles of the huge Piazza Vittorio Veneto. As if through long experience, he found the emptiest spot in the plaza, a stony desert between a handsome line of ornate lampposts and the sleek steel railings of an underground parking garage.

He dug into a trouser pocket and plucked out tethered foam earplugs, the kind you get from Alitalia for long overseas flights. Then he flipped his laptop open.

I caught up with him. "What are you doing over here? Looking for Wi-Fi signals?"

"I'm leaving." He tucked the foam plugs in his ears.

"Mind if I come along?"

"When I count to three," he told me, too loudly, "you have to jump high into the air. Also, stay within range of my laptop."

"All right. Sure."

"Oh, and put your hands over your ears."

I objected. "How can I hear you count to three if I have my hands over my ears?"

"Uno." He pressed the F1 function key, and his laptop screen blazed with sudden light. "Due." The F2 emitted a humming, cracking buzz. "Tre." He hopped in the air.

Thunder blasted. My lungs were crushed in a violent billow of wind. My feet stung as if they'd been burned.

Massimo staggered for a moment, then turned by instinct back toward the Elena. "Let's go!" he shouted. He plucked one yellow earplug from his head. Then he tripped.

I caught his computer as he stumbled. Its monster battery was sizzling hot.

Massimo grabbed his overheated machine. He stuffed it awkwardly into his valise.

Massimo had tripped on a loose cobblestone. We were standing in a steaming pile of loose cobblestones. Somehow, these cobblestones had been plucked from the pavement beneath our shoes and scattered around us like dice.

Of course we were not alone. Some witnesses sat in the vast plaza, the everyday Italians of Turin, sipping their drinks at little tables under distant, elegant umbrellas. They were sensibly minding their own business. A few were gazing puzzled at the rich blue evening sky, as if they suspected some passing sonic boom. Certainly none of them cared about us.

We limped back toward the cafe. My shoes squeaked like the shoes of a bad TV comedian. The cobbles under our feet had broken and tumbled, and the seams of my shoes had gone loose. My shining patent-leather shoes were foul and grimy.

We stepped through the arched double-doors of the Elena, and, somehow, despite all sense and reason, I found some immediate comfort. Because the Elena was the Elena: it had those round marble tables with their curvilinear legs, those maroon leather chairs with their shiny brass studs, those colossal time-stained mirrors . . . and a smell I hadn't noticed there in years.

Cigarettes. Everyone in the cafe was smoking. The air in the bar was cooler – it felt chilly, even. People wore sweaters.

Massimo had friends there. A woman and her man. This woman beckoned us over, and the man, although he knew Massimo, was clearly unhappy to see him.

This man was Swiss, but he wasn't the jolly kind of Swiss I was used to

seeing in Turin, some harmless Swiss banker on holiday who pops over the
Alps to pick up some ham and cheese. This Swiss guy was young, yet as
tough as old nails, with aviator shades and a long narrow scar in his hairline.
He wore black nylon gloves and a raw canvas jacket with holster room in
its armpits.

The woman had tucked her impressive bust into a hand-knitted peasant sweater. Her sweater was gaudy, complex, and aggressively gorgeous,
and so was she. She had smoldering eyes thick with mascara, and talon-
like red painted nails, and a thick gold watch that could have doubled as
brass knuckles.

"So Massimo is back," said the woman. She had a cordial yet guarded
tone, like a woman who has escaped a man's bed and needs compelling
reasons to return.

"I brought a friend for you tonight," said Massimo, helping himself to
a chair.

"So I see. And what does your friend have in mind for us? Does he
play backgammon?"

The pair had a backgammon set on their table. The Swiss mercenary
rattled dice in a cup. "We're very good at backgammon," he told me mildly.
He had the extremely menacing tone of a practiced killer who can't even
bother to be scary.

"My friend here is from the American CIA," said Massimo. "We're here
to do some serious drinking."

"How nice! I can speak American to you, Mr CIA," the woman volunteered. She aimed a dazzling smile at me. "What is your favorite American
baseball team?"

"I root for the Boston Red Sox."

"I love the Seattle Green Sox," she told us, just to be coy.

The waiter brought us a bottle of Croatian fruit brandy. The peoples of
the Balkans take their drinking seriously, so their bottles tend toward a rather
florid design. This bottle was frankly fantastic: it was squat, acid-etched,
curvilinear, and flute-necked, and with a triple portrait of Tito, Nasser, and
Nehru, all toasting one another. There were thick flakes of gold floating in
its paralyzing murk.

Massimo yanked the gilded cork, stole the woman's cigarettes, and
tucked an unfiltered cig in the corner of his mouth. With his slopping shot
glass in his fingers he was a different man.

"Zhivali!" the woman pronounced, and we all tossed back a hearty shot
of venom.

The temptress chose to call herself 'Svetlana,' while her Swiss bodyguard
was calling himself 'Simon.'

I had naturally thought that it was insane for Massimo to announce
me as a CIA spy, yet this gambit was clearly helping the situation. As an
American spy, I wasn't required to say much. No one expected me to know
anything useful, or to do anything worthwhile.

However, I was hungry, so I ordered the snack plate. The attentive waiter was not my favorite Elena waiter. He might have been a cousin. He brought us raw onions, pickles, black bread, a hefty link of sausage, and a wooden tub of creamed butter. We also got a notched pig-iron knife and a battered chopping board.

Simon put the backgammon set away.

All these crude and ugly things on the table – the knife, the chopping board, even the bad sausage – had been made in Italy. I could see little Italian maker's marks hand-etched into all of them.

"So you're hunting here in Torino, like us?" probed Svetlana.

I smiled back at her. "Yes, certainly!"

"So, what do you plan to do with him when you catch him? Will you put him on trial?"

"A fair trial is the American way!" I told them. Simon thought this remark was quite funny. Simon was not an evil man by nature. Simon probably suffered long nights of existential regret whenever he cut a man's throat.

"So," Simon offered, caressing the rim of his dirty shot glass with one nylon-gloved finger. "So even the Americans expect the Rat to show his whiskers in here!"

"The Elena does pull a crowd," I agreed. "So it all makes good sense. Don't you think?"

Everyone loves to be told that their thinking makes good sense. They were happy to hear me allege this. Maybe I didn't look or talk much like an American agent, but when you're a spy, and guzzling fruit brandy, and gnawing sausage, these minor inconsistencies don't upset anybody.

We were all being sensible.

Leaning his black elbows on our little table, Massimo weighed in. "The Rat is clever. He plans to sneak over the Alps again. He'll go back to Nice and Marseilles. He'll rally his militias."

Simon stopped with a knife-stabbed chunk of blood sausage on the way to his gullet. "You really believe that?"

"Of course I do! What did Napoleon say? 'The death of a million men means nothing to a man like me!' It's impossible to corner Nicolas the Rat. The Rat has a star of destiny."

The woman watched Massimo's eyes. Massimo was one of her informants. Being a woman, she had heard his lies before and was used to them. She also knew that no informant lies all the time.

"Then he's here in Torino tonight," she concluded.

Massimo offered her nothing.

She immediately looked to me. I silently stroked my chin in a sagely fashion.

"Listen, American spy," she told me politely, "you Americans are a simple, honest people, so good at tapping phone calls . . . It won't hurt your feelings any if Nicolas Sarkozy is found floating face-down in the River Po. Instead of teasing me here, as Massimo is so fond of doing, why don't you just tell me where Sarkozy is? I do want to know."

I knew very well where President Nicolas Sarkozy was supposed to be. He was supposed to be in the Elysee Palace carrying out extensive economic reforms.

Simon was more urgent. "You do want us to know where the Rat is, don't you?" He showed me a set of teeth edged in Swiss gold. "Let us know! That would save the International Courts of Justice a lot of trouble."

I didn't know Nicolas Sarkozy. I had met him twice when he was French Minister of Communication, when he proved that he knew a lot about the Internet. Still, if Nicolas Sarkozy was not the President of France, and if he was not in the Elysee Palace, then, being a journalist, I had a pretty good guess of his whereabouts.

"Cherchez la femme," I said.

Simon and Svetlana exchanged thoughtful glances. Knowing one another well, and knowing their situation, they didn't have to debate their next course of action. Simon signalled the waiter. Svetlana threw a gleaming coin onto the table. They bundled their backgammon set and kicked their leather chairs back. They left the cafe without another word.

Massimo rose. He sat in Svetlana's abandoned chair, so that he could keep a wary eye on the cafe's double door to the street. Then he helped himself to her abandoned pack of Turkish cigarettes.

I examined Svetlana's abandoned coin. It was large, round, and minted from pure silver, with a gaudy engraving of the Taj Mahal. 'Fifty Dinars,' it read, in Latin script, Hindi, Arabic, and Cyrillic.

"The booze around here really gets on top of me," Massimo complained. Unsteadily, he stuffed the ornate cork back into the brandy bottle. He set a slashed pickle on a buttered slice of black bread.

"Is he coming here?"

"Who?"

"Nicolas Sarkozy. 'Nicolas the Rat.'"

"Oh, him," said Massimo, chewing his bread. "In this version of Italy, I think Sarkozy's already dead. God knows there're enough people trying to kill him. The Arabs, Chinese, Africans . . . he turned the south of France upside down! There's a bounty on him big enough to buy Olivetti – not that there's much left of Olivetti."

I had my summer jacket on, and I was freezing. "Why is it so damn cold in here?"

"That's climate change," said Massimo. "Not in this Italy – in your Italy. In your Italy, you've got a messed-up climate. In this Italy, it's the human race that's messed-up. Here, as soon as Chernobyl collapsed, a big French reactor blew up on the German border . . . and they all went for each other's throats! Here NATO and the European Union are even deader than the Warsaw Pact."

Massimo was proud to be telling me this. I drummed my fingers on the chilly tabletop. "It took you a while to find that out, did it?"

"The big transition always hinges in the 1980s," said Massimo, "because that's when we made the big breakthroughs."

"In your Italy, you mean."

"That's right. Before the 1980s, nobody understood the physics of parallel worlds . . . but after that transition, we could pack a zero-point energy generator into a laptop. Just boil the whole problem down into one single micro-electronic mechanical system."

"So you've got zero-point energy MEMS chips," I said.

He chewed more bread and pickle. Then he nodded.

"You've got MEMS chips and you were offering me some fucking lousy memristor? You must think I'm a real chump!"

"You're not a chump." Massimo sawed a fresh slice of bad bread. "But you're from the wrong Italy. It was your own stupid world that made you this stupid, Luca. In my Italy, you were one of the few men who could talk sense to my dad. My dad used to confide in you. He trusted you, he thought you were a great writer. You wrote his biography."

" 'Massimo Montaldo, Senior,' " I said.

Massimo was startled. "Yeah. That's him." He narrowed his eyes. "You're not supposed to know that."

I had guessed it. A lot of news is made from good guesses.

"Tell me how you feel about that," I said, because this is always a useful question for an interviewer who has lost his way.

"I feel desperate," he told me, grinning. "Desperate! But I feel much less desperate here than I was when I was the spoilt-brat dope-addict son of the world's most famous scientist. Before you met me – Massimo Montaldo – had you ever heard of any 'Massimo Montaldo'?"

"No. I never did."

"That's right. I'm never in any of the other Italies. There's never any other Massimo Montaldo. I never meet another version of myself – and I never meet another version of my father, either. That's got to mean something crucial. I know it means something important."

"Yes," I told him, "that surely does mean something."

"I think," he said, "that I know what it means. It means that space and time are not just about physics and computation. It means that human beings really matter in the course of world events. It means that human beings can truly change the world. It means that our actions have consequence."

"The human angle," I said, "always makes a good story."

"It's true. But try telling that story," he said, and he looked on the point of tears. "Tell that story to any human being. Go on, do it! Tell anybody in here! Help yourself."

I looked around the Elena. There were some people in there, the local customers, normal people, decent people, maybe a dozen of them. Not remarkable people, not freakish, not weird or strange, but normal. Being normal people, they were quite at ease with their lot and accepting their daily existences.

Once upon a time, the Elena used to carry daily newspapers. Newspapers were supplied for customers on those special long wooden bars.

In my world, the Elena didn't do that anymore. Too few newspapers, and too much Internet.

Here the Elena still had those newspapers on those handy wooden bars. I rose from my chair and I had a good look at them. There were stylish imported newspapers, written in Hindi, Arabic, and Serbo-Croatian. I had to look hard to find a local paper in Italian. There were two, both printed on a foul gray paper full of flecks of badly-pulped wood.

I took the larger Italian paper to the cafe table. I flicked through the headlines and I read all the lead paragraphs. I knew immediately I was reading lies.

It wasn't that the news was so terrible, or so deceitful. But it was clear that the people reading this newspaper were not expected to make any practical use of news. The Italians were a modest, colonial people. The news that they were offered was a set of feeble fantasies. All the serious news was going on elsewhere.

There was something very strong and lively in the world called the 'Non-Aligned Movement.' It stretched from the Baltics all the way to the Balkans, throughout the Arab world, and all the way through India. Japan and China were places that the giant Non-Aligned superpower treated with guarded respect. America was some kind of humbled farm where the Yankees spent their time in church.

Those other places, the places that used to matter – France, Germany, Britain, Brussels – these were obscure and poor and miserable places. Their names and locales were badly spelled.

Cheap black ink was coming off on my fingers. I no longer had questions for Massimo, except for one. "When do we get out of here?"

Massimo buttered his tattered slice of black bread. "I was never searching for the best of all possible worlds," he told me. "I was looking for the best of all possible me's. In an Italy like this Italy, I really matter. Your version of Italy is pretty backward – but this world had a nuclear exchange. Europe had a civil war, and most cities in the Soviet Union are big puddles of black glass."

I took my Moleskin notebook from my jacket pocket. How pretty and sleek that fancy notebook looked, next to that gray pulp newspaper. "You don't mind if I jot this down, I hope?"

"I know that this sounds bad to you – but trust me, that's not how history works. History doesn't have any 'badness' or 'goodness.' This world has a future. The food's cheap, the climate is stable, the women are gorgeous . . . and since there's only three billion people left alive on Earth, there's a lot of room."

Massimo pointed his crude sausage-knife at the cafe's glass double door. "Nobody here ever asks for ID, nobody cares about passports . . . They've never even heard of electronic banking! A smart guy like you, you could walk out of here and start a hundred tech companies."

"If I didn't get my throat cut."

"Oh, people always overstate that little problem! The big problem is – you know – who wants to work that hard? I got to know this place, because I knew that I could be a hero here. Bigger than my father. I'd be smarter than him, richer than him, more famous, more powerful. I would be better! But that is a burden. 'Improving the world,' that doesn't make me happy at all. That's a curse, it's like slavery."

"What does make you happy, Massimo?"

Clearly Massimo had given this matter some thought. "Waking up in a fine hotel with a gorgeous stranger in my bed. That's the truth! And that would be true of every man in every world, if he was honest."

Massimo tapped the neck of the garish brandy bottle with the back of the carving knife. "My girlfriend Svetlana, she understands all that pretty well, but – there's one other thing. I drink here. I like to drink, I admit that – but they really drink around here. This version of Italy is in the almighty Yugoslav sphere of influence."

I had been doing fine so far, given my circumstances. Suddenly the nightmare sprang upon me, unfiltered, total, and wholesale. Chills of terror climbed my spine like icy scorpions. I felt a strong, irrational, animal urge to abandon my comfortable chair and run for my life.

I could run out of the handsome cafe and into the twilight streets of Turin. I knew Turin, and I knew that Massimo would never find me there. Likely he wouldn't bother to look.

I also knew that I would run straight into the world so badly described by that grimy newspaper. That terrifying world would be where, henceforth, I existed. That world would not be strange to me, or strange to anybody. Because that world was reality. It was not a strange world, it was a normal world. It was I, me, who was strange here. I was desperately strange here, and that was normal.

This conclusion made me reach for my shot glass. I drank. It was not what I would call a 'good' brandy. It did have strong character. It was powerful and it was ruthless. It was a brandy beyond good and evil.

My feet ached and itched in my ruined shoes. Blisters were rising and stinging. Maybe I should consider myself lucky that my aching alien feet were still attached to my body. My feet were not simply slashed off and abandoned in some black limbo between the worlds.

I put my shot glass down. "Can we leave now? Is that possible?"

"Absolutely," said Massimo, sinking deeper into his cozy red leather chair. "Let's sober up first with a coffee, eh? It's always Arabic coffee here at the Elena. They boil it in big brass pots."

I showed him the silver coin. "No, she settled our bill for us, eh? So let's just leave."

Massimo stared at the coin, flipped it from heads to tails, then slipped it in a pants pocket. "Fine. I'll describe our options. We can call this place the 'Yugoslav Italy,' and, like I said, this place has a lot of potential. But there are other versions." He started ticking off his fingers.

"There's an Italy where the 'No Nukes' movement won big in the 1980s. You remember them? Gorbachev and Reagan made world peace. Everybody disarmed and was happy. There were no more wars, the economy boomed everywhere . . . Peace and justice and prosperity, everywhere on Earth. So the climate exploded. The last Italian survivors are living high in the Alps."

I stared at him. "No."

"Oh yes. Yes, and those are very nice people. They really treasure and support each other. There are hardly any of them left alive. They're very sweet and civilized. They're wonderful people. You'd be amazed what nice Italians they are."

"Can't we just go straight back to my own version of Italy?"

"Not directly, no. But there's a version of Italy quite close to yours. After John Paul the First died, they quickly elected another Pope. He was not that Polish anticommunist – instead, that Pope was a pedophile. There was a colossal scandal and the Church collapsed. In that version of Italy, even the Moslems are secular. The churches are brothels and discotheques. They never use the words 'faith' or 'morality.' "

Massimo sighed, then rubbed his nose. "You might think the death of religion would make a lot of difference to people. Well, it doesn't. Because they think it's normal. They don't miss believing in God any more than you miss believing in Marx."

"So first we can go to that Italy, and then nearby into my own Italy – is that the idea?"

"That Italy is boring! The girls there are boring! They're so matter-of-fact about sex there that they're like girls from Holland." Massimo shook his head ruefully. "Now I'm going to tell you about a version of Italy that's truly different and interesting."

I was staring at a round of the sausage. The bright piece of gristle in it seemed to be the severed foot of some small animal. "All right, Massimo, tell me."

"Whenever I move from world to world, I always materialize in the Piazza Vittorio Veneto," he said, "because that plaza is so huge and usually pretty empty, and I don't want to hurt anyone with the explosion. Plus, I know Torino – I know all the tech companies here, so I can make my way around. But once I saw a Torino with no electronics."

I wiped clammy sweat from my hands with the cafe's rough cloth napkin. "Tell me, Massimo, how did you feel about that?"

"It's incredible. There's no electricity there. There're no wires for the electrical trolleys. There are plenty of people there, very well-dressed, and bright colored lights, and some things are flying in the sky . . . big aircraft, big as ocean liners. So they've got some kind of power there – but it's not electricity. They stopped using electricity, somehow. Since the 1980s."

"A Turin with no electricity," I repeated, to convince him that I was listening.

"Yeah, that's fascinating, isn't it? How could Italy abandon electricity and replace it with another power source? I think that they use cold fusion! Because cold fusion was another world-changing event from the 1980s. I can't explore that Torino – because where would I plug in my laptop? But you could find out how they do all that! Because you're just a journalist, right? All you need is a pencil!"

"I'm not a big expert on physics," I said.

"My God, I keep forgetting I'm talking to somebody from the hopeless George Bush World," he said. "Listen, stupid: physics isn't complicated. Physics is very simple and elegant, because it's structured. I knew that from the age of three."

"I'm just a writer, I'm not a scientist."

"Well, surely you've heard of 'consilience.' "

"No. Never."

"Yes, you have! Even people in your stupid world know about 'consilience.' Consilience means that all forms of human knowledge have an underlying unity!"

The gleam in his eyes was tiring me. "Why does that matter?"

"It makes all the difference between your world and my world! In your world there was a great physicist once . . . Dr Italo Calvino."

"Famous literary writer," I said, "he died in the 1980s."

"Calvino didn't die in my Italy," he said, "because in my Italy, Italo Calvino completed his 'Six Core Principles.' "

"Calvino wrote 'Six Memos,' " I said. "He wrote 'Six Memos for the Next Millennium,' and he only finished five of those before he had a stroke and died."

"In my world Calvino did not have a stroke. He had a stroke of genius, instead. When Calvino completed his work, those six lectures weren't just 'memos.' He delivered six major public addresses at Princeton. When Calvino gave that sixth, great, final speech, on 'Consistency,' the halls were crammed with physicists. Mathematicians, too. My father was there."

I took refuge in my notebook. "Six Core Principles," I scribbled hastily, "Calvino, Princeton, consilience."

"Calvino's parents were both scientists," Massimo insisted. "Calvino's brother was also a scientist. His Oulipo literary group was obsessed with mathematics. When Calvino delivered lectures worthy of a genius, nobody was surprised."

"I knew Calvino was a genius," I said. I'd been young, but you can't write in Italian and not know Calvino. I'd seen him trudging the porticoes in Turin, hunch-shouldered, slapping his feet, always looking sly and preoccupied. You only had to see the man to know that he had an agenda like no other writer in the world.

"When Calvino finished his six lectures," mused Massimo, "they carried him off to CERN in Geneva and they made him work on the Semantic Web. The Semantic Web works beautifully, by the way. It's not like your foul little Internet – so full of spam and crime." He wiped the sausage knife on an oil-stained napkin. "I should qualify that remark. The Semantic Web works beautifully – in the Italian language. Because the Semantic Web was built by Italians. They had a little bit of help from a few French Oulipo writers."

"Can we leave this place now? And visit this Italy you boast so much about? And then drop by my Italy?"

"That situation is complicated," Massimo hedged, and stood up. "Watch my bag, will you?"

He then departed to the toilet, leaving me to wonder about all the ways in which our situation could be complicated

Now I was sitting alone, staring at that corked brandy bottle. My brain was boiling. The strangeness of my situation had broken some important throttle inside my head.

I considered myself bright – because I could write in three languages, and I understood technical matters. I could speak to engineers, designers, programmers, venture capitalists, and government officials on serious, adult issues that we all agreed were important. So, yes, surely I was bright.

But I'd spent my whole life being far more stupid than I was at this moment.

In this terrible extremity, here in the cigarette-choked Elena, where the half-ragged denizens pored over their grimy newspapers, I knew I possessed a true potential for genius. I was Italian, and, being Italian, I had the knack to shake the world to its roots. My genius had never embraced me, because genius had never been required of me. I had been stupid because I dwelled in a stupefied world.

I now lived in no world at all. I had no world. So my thoughts were rocketing through empty space.

Ideas changed the world. Thoughts changed the world – and thoughts could be written down. I had forgotten that writing could have such urgency, that writing could matter to history, that literature might have consequence. Strangely, tragically, I'd forgotten that such things were even possible.

Calvino had died of a stroke: I knew that. Some artery broke inside the man's skull as he gamely struggled with his manifesto to transform the next millennium. Surely that was a great loss, but how could anybody guess the extent of that loss? A stroke of genius is a black swan, beyond prediction, beyond expectation. If a black swan never arrives, how on Earth could its absence be guessed?

The chasm between Massimo's version of Italy and my Italy was invisible – yet all encompassing. It was exactly like the stark difference between the man I was now, and the man I'd been one short hour ago.

A black swan can never be predicted, expected, or categorized. A black swan, when it arrives, cannot even be recognized as a black swan. When the black swan assaults us, with the wingbeats of some rapist Jupiter, then we must rewrite history.

Maybe a newsman writes a news story, which is history's first draft.

Yet the news never shouts that history has black swans. The news never tells us that our universe is contingent, that our fate hinges on changes too huge for us to comprehend, or too small for us to see. We can never accept the black swan's arbitrary carelessness. So our news is never about how the news can make no sense to human beings. Our news is always about how well we understand.

Whenever our wits are shattered by the impossible, we swiftly knit the world back together again, so that our wits can return to us. We pretend that we've lost nothing, not one single illusion. Especially, certainly, we never lose our minds. No matter how strange the news is, we're always sane and sensible. That is what we tell each other.

Massimo returned to our table. He was very drunk, and he looked greenish. "You ever been in a squat-down Turkish toilet?" he said, pinching his nose. "Trust me: don't go in there."

"I think we should go to your Italy now," I said.

"I could do that," he allowed idly, "although I've made some trouble for myself there . . . my real problem is you."

"Why am I trouble?"

"There's another Luca in my Italy. He's not like you: because he's a great author, and a very dignified and very wealthy man. He wouldn't find you funny."

I considered this. He was inviting me to be bitterly jealous of myself. I couldn't manage that, yet I was angry anyway. "Am I funny, Massimo?"

He'd stopped drinking, but that killer brandy was still percolating through his gut.

"Yes, you're funny, Luca. You're weird. You're a terrible joke. Especially in this version of Italy. And especially now that you're finally catching on. You've got a look on your face now like a drowned fish." He belched into his fist. "Now, at last, you think that you understand, but no, you don't. Not yet. Listen: in order to arrive here – I created this world. When I press the Function-Three key, and the field transports me here – without me as the observer, this universe doesn't even exist."

I glanced around the thing that Massimo called a universe. It was an Italian cafe. The marble table in front of me was every bit as solid as a rock. Everything around me was very solid, normal, realistic, acceptable, and predictable.

"Of course," I told him. "And you also created my universe, too. Because you're not just a black swan. You're God."

" 'Black swan,' is that what you call me?" He smirked, and preened in the mirror. "You journalists need a tagline for everything."

"You always wear black," I said. "Does that keep our dirt from showing?"

Massimo buttoned his black woolen jacket. "It gets worse," he told me. "When I press that Function-Two key, before the field settles in . . . I generate millions of potential histories. Billions of histories. All with their souls, ethics, thoughts, histories, destinies – whatever. Worlds blink into existence for a few nano-seconds while the chip runs through the program – and then they all blink out. As if they never were."

"That's how you move? From world to world?"

"That's right, my friend. This ugly duckling can fly."

The Elena's waiter arrived to tidy up our table. "A little rice pudding?" he asked.

Massimo was cordial. "No, thank you, sir."

"Got some very nice chocolate in this week! All the way from South America."

"My, that's the very best kind of chocolate." Massimo jabbed his hand into a cargo pocket. "I believe I need some chocolate. What will you give me for this?"

The waiter examined it carefully. "This is a woman's engagement ring."

"Yes, it is."

"It can't be a real diamond, though. This stone's much too big to be a real diamond."

"You're an idiot," said Massimo, "but I don't care much. I've got a big appetite for sweets. Why don't you bring me an entire chocolate pie?"

The waiter shrugged and left us.

"So," Massimo resumed, "I wouldn't call myself a 'God' – because I'm much better described as several million billion Gods. Except, you know, that the zero-point transport field always settles down. Then, here I am. I'm standing outside some cafe, in a cloud of dirt, with my feet aching. With nothing to my name, except what I've got in my brain and my pockets. It's always like that."

The door of the Elena banged open, with the harsh jangle of brass Indian bells. A gang of five men stomped in. I might have taken them for cops, because they had jackets, belts, hats, batons, and pistols, but Turinese cops do not arrive on duty drunk. Nor do they wear scarlet armbands with crossed lightning bolts.

The cafe fell silent as the new guests muscled up to the dented bar. Bellowing threats, they proceeded to shake down the staff.

Massimo turned up his collar and gazed serenely at his knotted hands. Massimo was studiously minding his own business. He was in his corner, silent, black, inexplicable. He might have been at prayer.

I didn't turn to stare at the intruders. It wasn't a pleasant scene, but even for a stranger, it wasn't hard to understand.

The door of the men's room opened. A short man in a trench coat emerged. He had a dead cigar clenched in his teeth, and a snappy Alain Delon fedora.

He was surprisingly handsome. People always underestimated the good looks, the male charm of Nicolas Sarkozy. Sarkozy sometimes seemed a little odd when sunbathing half-naked in newsstand tabloids, but in person, his charisma was overwhelming. He was a man that any world had to reckon with.

Sarkozy glanced about the cafe, for a matter of seconds. Then he sidled, silent and decisive, along the dark mahogany wall. He bent one elbow. There was a thunderclap. Massimo pitched face-forward onto the small marble table.

Sarkozy glanced with mild chagrin at the smoking hole blown through the pocket of his stylish trench coat. Then he stared at me.

"You're that journalist," he said.

"You've got a good memory for faces, Monsieur Sarkozy."

"That's right, asshole, I do." His Italian was bad, but it was better than my French. "Are you still eager to 'protect' your dead source here?" Sarkozy gave

Massimo's heavy chair one quick, vindictive kick, and the dead man, and his chair, and his table, and his ruined, gushing head all fell to the hard cafe floor with one complicated clatter.

"There's your big scoop of a story, my friend," Sarkozy told me. "I just gave that to you. You should use that in your lying commie magazine."

Then he barked orders at the uniformed thugs. They grouped themselves around him in a helpful cluster, their faces pale with respect.

"You can come out now, baby," crowed Sarkozy, and she emerged from the men's room. She was wearing a cute little gangster-moll hat, and a tailored camouflage jacket. She lugged a big, black guitar case. She also had a primitive radio-telephone bigger than a brick.

How he'd enticed that woman to lurk for half an hour in the reeking cafe toilet, I'll never know. But it was her. It was definitely her, and she couldn't have been any more demure and serene if she were meeting the Queen of England.

They all left together in one heavily armed body.

The thunderclap inside the Elena had left a mess. I rescued Massimo's leather valise from the encroaching pool of blood.

My fellow patrons were bemused. They were deeply bemused, even confounded. Their options for action seemed to lack constructive possibilities.

So, one by one, they rose and left the bar. They left that fine old place, silently and without haste, and without meeting each other's eyes. They stepped out the jangling door and into Europe's biggest plaza.

Then they vanished, each hastening toward his own private world.

I strolled into the piazza, under a pleasant spring sky. It was cold, that spring night, but that infinite dark blue sky was so lucid and clear.

The laptop's screen flickered brightly as I touched the F1 key. Then I pressed 2, and then 3.

CRIMES AND GLORY

Paul J. McAuley

Born in Oxford, England, in 1955, Paul J. McAuley now makes his home in London. A professional biologist for many years, he sold his first story in 1984, and has gone on to be a frequent contributor to *Interzone* as well as to markets such as *Asimov's Science Fiction*, *Sci Fiction*, *Amazing*, *The Magazine of Fantasy and Science Fiction*, *Skylife*, *The Third Alternative*, *When the Music's Over*, and elsewhere.

McAuley is at the forefront of several of the most important subgenres in SF today, producing both 'radical hard science fiction' and the revamped and retooled widescreen Space Opera that has sometimes been called The New Space Opera, as well as dystopian sociological speculations about the very near future. He also writes fantasy and horror. His first novel, *Four Hundred Billion Stars*, won the Philip K. Dick Award, and his novel *Fairyland* won both the Arthur C. Clarke Award and the John W. Campbell Award in 1996. His other books include the novels *Of the Fall*, *Eternal Light*, *Pasquale's Angel*, *Confluence* – a major trilogy of ambitious scope and scale set ten million years in the future (comprising the novels *Child of the River*, *Ancient of Days*, and *Shrine of Stars*) – *Life on Mars*, *The Secret of Life*, *Whole Wide World*, *White Devils*, *Mind's Eye*, *Players*, and *Cowboy Angels*. His short fiction has been collected in *The King of the Hill and Other Stories*, *The Invisible Country*, and *Little Machines*, and he is the co-editor, with Kim Newman, of an original anthology, *In Dreams*. His most recent books are two new novels, *The Quiet War* and *Gardens of the Sun*.

Here he takes us to a troubled colony planet to investigate a baffling murder mystery that may have consequences for the entire human race.

W HERE ARE THEY?' "
"They? Who's this 'they,' Niles?" I say, wondering if he's finally flipped. "There's nobody out here but us chickens. And we're where we've always been. Right behind you and catching up fast."

"It's a famous question, Emma. Even though I know your training wasn't all it could have been, I'm surprised and more than a little shocked that you don't recognise it."

At the beginning of this long chase, Niles Sarkka maintained an imperial silence, week after week, month after month. He didn't answer my calls,
and after a while I gave up trying to call him. Then, after turnover, after we
switched off our motor and flipped end for end and switched it back on and
began to decelerate, applying the brakes as we slid down the steepening slope
of the warm yellow star's gravity well, he called me. He wanted to know why
we'd left it so late; I told him that a smart fellow like him should be able to
work it out for himself.

But he hasn't, not yet, although he's been nagging away at it ever since.
As our ship has grown closer to his, as both have grown closer to our final
destination, the calls have begun to increase in frequency. And like most
people living on their own, Niles has developed eccentric habits. He calls
without any regard for time of day, so I have to carry the q-phone everywhere, and it's a big old heavy thing the size of a briefcase, one of the first
models. This call, the second in three days, has fetched me out of my
weekly bath, and baths are a big deal on the ship. It's not just a question
of scrubbing off a week's worth of grime; it's also an escape from the 1.6 g
pull. Sinking into buoyant water and resting sore joints and swollen legs and
aching backs. Forgetting for a little while how far we've come from all that's
known, and the possibility we might not be able to get back. So, standing
dripping wet on an ice-cold floor, grappling with the q-phone and trying
to knot a towel around me while the other women slosh and wallow in hot
dark water in the big bamboo tub, I'm annoyed and resentful, and having a
hard time hiding it.

Saying, "As far as I'm concerned, my training was good enough to
catch you."

Fortunately, Niles Sarkka ignores my sarcasm. He's in one of his peda-
gogical moods, behaving as if he's back in front of the TV camera, delivering
a solemn lecturette to his adoring audience.

" 'Where are they?' " he says. "A famous question famously asked by the
physicist Enrico Fermi when he and his colleagues were discussing flying
saucers and likelihood of faster-than-light travel. 'Where are they?' Fermi
exclaimed. Given the age and size of the Galaxy, given that it was likely that
life had evolved more than once, the Earth should have been visited many
times over. If aliens existed, they should already be here. And since they
weren't, Fermi argued, they did not exist. Many scientists and philosophers
challenged his paradox with a variety of ingenious solutions, or tried to
explain the absence of aliens with a variety of equally ingenious scenarios.
But we are privileged to know the answer. We know that they were there all
along. We know that the Jackaroo have been watching us for centuries, and
chose to reveal themselves in our hour of greatest need. But their appearance provoked many other questions. Where did they come from? Why
were they watching us, and why have they intervened? Why have they
survived for so long, when we know that other intelligent species have not?
Are they outliers, or something different? Are we like them, or are we like
the other so-called Elder Cultures – doomed to a finite span, doomed to die

out, or to evolve into something beyond our present comprehension? Or are we doomed by our association with the Jackaroo, who set us free from the cage of Earth, yes, but only to let us move into a slightly larger cage. Where we can be studied or played with until they grow tired of us. And so on, and so on. The Jackaroo provided a kind of answer to Fermi's question, Emma, but it generated a host of new mysteries. Soon, we will discover the answers to some of them. Doesn't it excite you? It should. I am excited. Excited, and amazed, and more than a little afraid. If you and your farmer friends have even the slightest hint of imagination, you should feel excited and amazed and afraid too. For we are fast approaching the threshold of a new chapter of human history."

Like every criminal who knows the game is up, Niles Sarkka is trying to justify actions that can't be justified. Trying to climb a ladder of words towards that last little chink of light high above the dungeon of his plight. I let him talk, of course. It's always easier to let the guilty talk. They give so much away it isn't even funny. Niles Sarkka is responsible for the deaths of three people and stole code that could, yes, this is about our only point of agreement, radically change our understanding of our place in the Universe and our relationship with the Jackaroo. So of course I let him talk, but I'm getting cold, standing there in only a towel, my vertebrae are grinding together, blood is pooling in my tired and swollen legs, and I'm growing more impatient than usual with his discursions and bluster, his condescending lesson on the history of the search for extraterrestrial life. So when at last he says that he doesn't care what people think of him now, that history will judge him and that's all that counts, I can't help myself.

"I'll tell you who will judge you, Niles. A jury of your peers, in Court One of the Justice Centre in Port of Plenty."

He hangs up. Affronted and offended no doubt, the pompous fool. Anxiety nips at me, I wonder if this time I've gone too far, but it soon passes. I know he will call back. Because he wants to convince me that, despite all the bad things he's done, he will be vindicated by what he expects to discover. Because he has only one q-phone, and I have its twin. Because he has no one else to talk to, out here in the deep and lonely dark between the stars.

As far as I was concerned, it began with a call from one of our contacts in the Port of Plenty Police Department, telling me that the two code jockeys I was looking for, Everett Hughes and Jason Singleton, had been traced to a motel.

It was a little past eight in the evening. As usual, I'd been writing up notes on the day's work with half an eye on the news channel. I found the remote and switched off the TV and said, "Are they in custody?"

"It looks like they're dead. The room they rented is burned out, and there are two crispy critters inside. I hate to be the bearer of bad news, but there it is. And info is info, good or bad, right?"

I didn't bother to reassure him that he would get paid in due course. "Who's the attending?"

"Zacarias. August Zacarias. He's good police, closes more than his fair share of cases. A prince of the city, too."

"Where can I find him?"

"He's still at the scene. From what I hear, it's a mess out there."

The motel was at the outer edge of the city, close to an off-ramp on the orbital freeway and an access road that climbed a slope of thorn scrub to an industrial park. The streetlights along the road were out, the long low sheds of the park squatted in darkness, and the lights were out in the motel office and its string of rooms, too. A transformer on top of a power-line pole fizzed and sparked. I parked behind a clutch of police cruisers and the satellite van of the local TV news team, and badged my way past the patrol officers who were keeping a small crowd on the right side of crime scene tape strung between a couple of saw horses. The TV reporter and her camerawoman tried to zero in on me, but I ducked away. I was excited and apprehensive: this had brought three months of careful investigative work to a sudden and unwelcome crux, and I had no idea how it would play out.

The warm night air stank of charred wood, smoke, and a sharp tang like freshly-cut metal. The headlamps of a pair of fire trucks patchily lit an L-shaped string of rooms that enclosed two sides of the parking lot; their flashers sent flickers of orange light racing over wet tarmac and the roofs of angle-parked cars and pickup trucks. Firefighters in heavy slickers and yellow helmets were rolling up hoses. A chicken was perched on the cab of a pickup and several more strutted and pecked amongst a couple of picnic tables set on a strip of grass by a derelict swimming pool. The room at the end of the short arm of the L was lit by portable floods, light falling strong and stark on blackened walls, smoke curling from the broken door and the smashed, soot-stained window. Jason Singleton's car, an ancient Volkswagen Faraday, stood in front of this ruin. The windshield was shattered and its hood was scorched clean of paint and its plastic fender was half-melted.

The homicide detective who had caught the call, August Zacarias, was a tall man in his fifties, with matt black skin and wooly hair clipped short and brushed with grey at the temples, dressed in a brown suit with a window-pane check and polished brown Oxford loafers, a white shirt and a buttercup yellow silk tie. A micropore mask hung under his chin and he stripped off soot-stained vinyl gloves as he came towards me, saying that he understood I wanted to take his case away from him. He had a signet ring on the index finger of his right hand: the kind of ring, faced with a chunk of opal, worn by male members of the Fortunate Five Hundred.

"As far as I'm concerned, you've walked into my case," I said.

"You're English."

"Yes. Obviously."

"Were you in the police before you came here?"

"Ten years in the Met."

"The London police? Scotland Yard?"

"New Scotland Yard."

"And then you came here, and joined the geek police."

"I joined the UN police, Detective Zacarias, and currently I'm working with the Technology Control Unit. Now we've bonded, perhaps you can tell me what happened here."

August Zacarias had a friendly smile and possessed the imperturbable calm of someone with absolute confidence in his authority, but from bitter experience I knew exactly what he was thinking: that I was a meddling, boot-faced bureaucrat with a humour bypass and a spreadsheet for a soul who was about to steal a perfectly good double murder from him and cause him all kinds of grief besides. And I couldn't help wondering how he paid for his tailored suit, handmade loafers, and expensive cologne, whether the gold Rolex on his left wrist was real or a street-market fake, whether he was just a working stiff who wanted nothing more than to put down this case and move on to the next, or whether he had a private agenda. Aside from the usual rivalry between our two branches of law enforcement, the plain fact of the matter is that the PPPD is riddled with corruption. Most of its patrol officers take kickbacks and bribes; many of its detectives and senior officers are in the pockets of politicians, gangsters, or business people.

"Myself, I am from Lagos," he said. "I was in the army there, and now I am a homicide detective here. And that's what this is. Homicide. Two men died in that room, Inspector Davies. Someone has to answer for that."

"Have the bodies been identified?"

"You want to know if they are the two young men you are looking for. I'm afraid I can't confirm that yet. They are very badly burned."

"This is Jason Singleton's car," I said.

"It is certainly registered to him. And according to several of the residents it was used by a man answering Mr Singleton's description. Tall and blond, in his twenties, possibly English. His friend was heavyset, with long black hair, tattoos, and an American accent. Also in his twenties. That sounds like your other missing coder, Everett Hughes, yes? Although they signed the register as Mr Gates and Mr Jobs."

"Geek humour."

"I wondered if it was supposed to be funny. You posted an APB for both men. May I ask why?"

"I believe they stole Elder Culture technology from their employer."

"That would be Meyer Lansky."

"You work fast, Detective Zacarias."

"Out of necessity, Inspector. We had two hundred and forty-one straight-up murders in this city last year, not to mention a significant number of suspicious deaths, fatal accidents, and kidnaps. We put down just 33 per cent of those murders. The municipal council and the police commissioner want us to improve our success rate, we already have ninety-eight names on the board, and it's only April. If I don't close this in a day or two, it will be pushed aside by a fresh case. So, these boys stole something from their employer and hid out here while they looked for a buyer, is that it?"

"We're being frank with each other, Detective."

"I hope so."

"Frankly, I want you to stay away from Meyer Lansky. He's important to us."

"I don't suppose you can tell me why."

"I'm afraid not. Has the car been searched yet?"

"We didn't find anything in it. We are waiting for a tow truck. The crime scene people will examine it back at the police garage, under sterile conditions. Unless you want to take charge of it."

"We don't have the facilities. But someone will observe and advise your crime scene techs while they work on it. Did you find a computer or a phone in the room?"

"Not yet. Things are very much melted together."

"Or something like a fat thermos flask?"

"You are welcome to examine the crime scene, Inspector. I'll even let you pat down the bodies before the ME takes them away."

I ignored his impertinence. "I want your people to maintain a perimeter until my people arrive. Until they do, nothing should be touched. The bodies will remain where they are. I will need you to turn over all witness statements. And please, don't say a word to the TV people, or anyone else."

"Those bodies are cooked all the way through, and something fried every electrical device in the immediate vicinity. What they stole, was it some kind of Elder Culture energy weapon?"

"Everett Hughes owns a motorcycle. A 125cc Honda. I don't see it."

"Then it's probably not here," August Zacarias said. He was smiling, enjoying our little to and fro. Having fun. "Perhaps the killer took it. Or perhaps these two young men tried to sell whatever it was they stole, the deal went wrong, and they killed the would-be buyers and fled. Or perhaps we're looking at a case of spontaneous combustion, and in the confusion one of the residents in the motel stole Mr Hughes's motorcycle."

"Anything is possible."

"You do not care to speculate. Or you know more than I."

"I don't know enough to speculate."

August Zacarias liked that answer. "How long have you been watching Meyer Lansky?"

"Long enough."

"And now the roof has fallen in on you."

"We rarely choose where to fight our battles, Detective. If we are finished here, I have some phone calls to make. And you could help me by maintaining the perimeter until my people arrive."

"My boss will be pleased that we can hand over the responsibility for these deaths to you. It means that we have two fewer cases to investigate, a microscopic improvement to our statistics. Myself, I do not think that numbers are so very important. I don't care about stolen alien ju-ju either.

What is important for me is that the dead are given a voice. That someone speaks for them, makes sure that they are not forgotten, and that whoever is responsible for what happened to them is brought to justice."

August Zacarias looked straight at me when he said this, and I could see that he meant it. Perhaps he was in someone's pocket, perhaps not, but he took his work seriously.

"I'll do my best by them," I said. "If there's anything that I need to know, now is the time to tell me."

"I can tell you that this is a good place to hide," August Zacarias said. "When the city was very young, VIPs stayed here. The freeway wasn't built then, or very little else, for that matter. There were splendid views across fern forests to the bay. Now, half the rooms are rented by the hour, with the kind of traffic that implies. Most of the others are occupied by semi-permanent residents who can't afford anywhere else. An old Chinese woman who keeps chickens and will put curses on people, or remove them, for a small fee. A Ukranian poet who is drinking himself to death. A small gang of Indonesians who work as day labourers on various construction sites. They trap the giant lizards that live in the brush and roast them over fires in the empty swimming pool. Last year, two of them fought with parangs in the parking lot. One lost most of an arm, and bled to death before his friends could get him to hospital. I worked the case. The winner of that little set-to went away for two years, manslaughter."

"You know the place."

August Zacarias smiled and made a sweeping gesture. "Welcome to my world, Ms Davies."

"Luckily, I'm just visiting."

"That's what Everett Hughes and Jason Singleton thought. And look what happened to them."

I phoned Varneek Sehra and told him to bring his crew to the scene as soon as possible. Then I phoned my boss, Marc Godin, and told him what had happened. Marc wasn't happy about being called late at night, and he wasn't happy about the mess the double murder might cause, but he was already ahead of me when it came to discussing what to do next.

"We can't contain the story. The local TV news is already onto it. And if the Koreans aren't already involved, they soon will be. Pak Young-Min will want to have some hard words with his man Lansky."

"Words will be the least of it, sir."

"In any case, if he has not already done so, Lansky may try to scrub his records of incriminating evidence. I'll draw up stop and seizure papers and we'll visit Judge Provenzano and get them made official. Then you can visit Mr Lansky and ask him to come in and talk to us."

"I already have papers drawn up," I said, and told him where to find them.

"Always prepared, Emma."

"I must have had a premonition."

"Meet me at the office in . . . how long will it take, out there?"

"I'm just waiting for Varneek to take over," I said.

"A shame about those two kids," Marc said. "But perhaps this will give us something to use against Monsieurs Lansky and Pak."

"Yes, we should always look on bright side," I said.

Let me speak about the dead for a moment. Let me do the right thing by them, as Detective August Zacarias would say.

Like most people who won the emigration lottery and didn't sell their prize to one of the big corporations or to a redistribution agency, or give it away to a relative who either deserved it or wanted it more than they did, or have it stolen by a jealous neighbour, a spouse or a child or a random stranger (UN statistics show that more than 4 per cent of emigration lottery winners are murdered or disappeared), or simply put it away for a day that never came and meanwhile got on with their lives in the ruins of Earth (and it was still possible to live a life more or less ordinary after the economic collapses, wars, radical climate events, and all the other mess and madness: even after the Jackaroo pitched up and gave us access to a wormhole network linking some fifteen M-class red dwarf stars in exchange for rights to the outer planets of the Solar System, for the most part, for most people, life went on as it always did, the ordinary little human joys and tragedies, people falling in love or out of love, marrying, having children, burying their parents, worrying about being passed over for promotion, or losing their job, or the lump in their breast, or the blood in the toilet bowl) – like everyone, in other words, who won the emigration lottery and believed that it was their chance to get out from under whatever muddle or plight they were in and start over (more UN statistics: 36 per cent of married lottery winners divorce within two months), Jason Singleton and Everett Hughes wanted to change their lives for the better. They wanted more than the same old same old, although that's what most people get. People think that by relocating themselves to another planet, the ultimate in exoticism, they can radically change their lives, but they always forget that they bring their lives with them. Accountants ship out dreaming of adventure and find work as accountants; police become police, or bodyguards to high-end businesspeople or wealthy gangsters; farmers settle down on some patch of land on a coastal plain west of Port of Plenty or on one of the thousands of worldlets in the various reefs that orbit various stars in the network, and so on, and so forth. But Everett Hughes and Jason Singleton were both in their early twenties, and as far as they were concerned anything was possible. They wanted to get rich. They wanted to be famous. Why not? They'd already been touched by stupendous good fortune when they'd won tickets to new and better lives amongst the stars. After that, anything seemed possible.

They met aboard the shuttle that took them out of Low Earth Orbit to the wormhole throat anchored at the L5 point between the Earth and the Moon, and plunged through the wormhole and crossed more than five thousand light years in the blink of an eye and emerged at the leading Lagrangian point of a Mars-sized moon of a blue-green methane gas giant that orbited an undistinguished M0 red dwarf star, and travelled inward to the planet of First Foot and landfall at the spaceport outside the city of Port of Plenty.

It was a journey I had made twenty-two years ago, after I'd divorced my first husband and two weeks later won a place on the emigration lottery. At the time, it had seemed like a message from fate's hotline: pack up what was left of my life, travel to a new world, start afresh. When I arrived on First Foot, Port of Plenty had been a shanty town amongst alien ruins. I worked for the PPPD for three years, then signed up with the UN Security Agency, working in the spaceport to begin with, then joining what was then the brand-new Technology Control Unit. A year after that I met my second husband and we married and it all went wrong very quickly, but that's another story and besides, the man is dead.

And all this time Port of Plenty was growing around me, extending along the shoreline of Discovery Bay, climbing through the semi-arid hills that circled it, spreading into the outer margins of the Great Central desert. It's a sprawling megalopolis now, a nascent Los Angeles or Mexico City. A whole generation has grown up on First Foot, they're having children of their own, and still the shuttles keep coming, loaded with lottery winners and those who can afford to buy the tickets of winners and those who have had their ticket bought for them by corporations, or by the city authority, or by the UN or some other sponsor. Our original settlement, an ugly unplanned patchwork of favelas and shantytowns, has grown into a clean, modern city. Big office blocks in the centre where the corporations and private finance companies work. A marina, and parks, and restaurants and shopping malls. Suburbs. Oh, we've made ourselves at home, all right. But it isn't our home. It's an alien world with a deep history. And settlers have spread out through the worm-hole network, discovering Sargassos of ancient ships and refurbishing them, making homes on moons and reefs of worldlets previously settled by countless other races of sentient beings, Elder Cultures who died out or moved on, leaving behind ruins and all kinds of artifacts, some of them functional.

That's where the UN Technology Control Unit, aka the geek police, comes in. Some Elder Culture technology, like the room-temperature superconductors and paired virtual particles that enabled us to develop q-phones, hypercomputers, and much else, is useful. Some of it, like grasers and other particle and beam weapons, is both useful and dangerous. And some of it is simply dangerous. Stuff that could give an individual the power to hold worlds to ransom. Stuff that could change the human race so radically that it would either die out or become something other than human. That's why the UN created a legislative apparatus to clamp down on illegal trading of Elder Culture technology, to make sure that new technologies developed by legitimate companies can't be licensed until they have passed strict tests, and so on and so forth.

The Technology Control Unit is at the sharp end of this legislation. I believed then and still believe now, despite everything, that it is important work. At any time, someone could stumble over something that could change the way we live, how we think of ourselves, how we think. In the end, that's what the UN is trying to protect. The right to continue to be human. We have been given a great gift by the Jackaroo. A chance to start over after a terrible war and two centuries of uncontrolled industrialisation and population growth almost ruined our home planet. It is up to us to make the best of that, and make sure that we don't destroy ourselves by greedy or foolish appropriation of technologies so advanced they are, as the old saying goes, indistinguishable from magic.

Fortunately, anyone who wants to make any kind of money from a functional and potentially useful scrap of Elder Culture technology has to come to First Foot, and the city of Port of Plenty. Port of Plenty has a research and manufacturing base that can spin product from Elder Culture artifacts, and it also regulates traffic between the fifteen systems and Earth – and Earth is still the biggest and best market, the only place where real fortunes can be made. But there are also people who want to exploit dangerous Elder Culture artifacts and technologies regardless of the consequences. Some are genuine explorers and scientists; some, like Niles Sarkka, belong to the tinfoil hat brigade. Crackpot theorists. Green ink merchants. Monomaniacs. And some, like Meyer Lansky, are crooks, plain and simple.

At first glance, Meyer Lansky's code farm was a genuine business, one of more than a dozen that dealt in the stuff prospectors pulled from the shells of ships abandoned by the previous tenants of the wormhole network, the Ghajar. They had been some kind of gypsy species that like all the other Elder Cultures had died out or vanished, and had left behind almost no trace of its civilisation or culture apart from its ships. Most had been left parked in orbital junkyard Sargassos, some dead hulks, others slumbering in deep hibernation; a few lay wrecked on the various planets and moons and worldlets of the fifteen stars. Some archaeologists believed that the crashed ships were casualties of a war between factions of the Ghajar; others that they had beached their ships much as whales and smaller cetaceans on Earth – because of disease or panic or confusion or suicidal ennui – had sometimes swum into shallow waters and become stranded by retreating tides. In any case, whether dead or alive or smashed to flinders, all the ships were to some degree or another infested with code. It was quantum stuff, hardware and software embedded in the spin properties of fundamental particles in the molecular matrices of the ships' hulls, raw and fragmented, and crusty with errors and necrotic patches that had accumulated during millennia of disuse and exposure to cosmic radiation.

Coders working in farms like Meyer Lansky's analyzed and catalogued this junk and stitched together viable fragments and spent hours and days trying to get them to run in virtual partitions on the farm's hypercomputer cloud. Code approved by the licensing board was bought by software developers who used it to patch controls ships reclaimed from the vast Sargassos, manipulate exotic matter, refine the front ends of quantum technology, and so on and so forth. There were theoretical applications, too – four of the so-called hard mathematical problems had been solved using code reclaimed by the farms.

Meyer Lansky's code farm had been licensed, regulated, and entirely legitimate until he'd run up huge gambling debts and sold control of his business to a shell company owned by a family of Korean gangsters. Now, its legitimate work was a front for black market trade in chunks of viable code too hot and dangerous to ever win a research and development license, and for wholesaling viral fragments to dealers who supplied codeheads with tickets to strange places of the mind, a trade that was growing to be as troublesome as crack cocaine.

Everett Hughes and Jason Singleton had been working in Meyer Lansky's code farm until they'd suddenly quit without warning and dropped clean out of sight. Ten days later, everything blew up at the motel room. We'd been researching the farm for three months, patiently accumulating dossiers on everyone who worked there, but the grisly double murder ripped our clandestine investigation wide open. We shut down the place before Lansky or the Koreans could destroy evidence of wrongdoing, and brought Singleton's and Hughes's co-workers in for interview. Towards the end, I knew more about the two young men than I did about some of my friends. Singleton was from my home town, London, England; Hughes was from Anchorage, Alaska; both were young, white, English-speaking males who were serious computer freaks. They'd bonded when they'd met on the shuttle, stuck together after the shuttle touched down and they were set adrift in the raw hypercapitalism of Port of Plenty. Neither had much in the way of stake money, or any kind of plan. They were flying by the seats of their pants, driven by a mix of arrogant optimism and naivete, confident that because they were young and energetic and talented they were bound to spot some opportunity ripe for exploitation.

At first, they did agency work in the IT department of one of the big multinationals that had set up in Port of Plenty, but the pay was rotten, with no benefits whatsoever apart from vouchers for the subsidised canteen, and it was the kind of boring and frustrating work they'd both been doing back on Earth – Singleton in a university; Hughes for the Russian company that had purchased Alaska from the US government after a failed attempt at secession. In short, it was everything they'd hoped to escape, and after only four weeks they quit and went to work on Meyer Lansky's code farm.

The pay wasn't much better than the agency work and the benefits were equally exiguous, but as far as Singleton and Hughes were concerned it was far more romantic than writing object location routines for suits who didn't really know what they wanted. And his fellow coders agreed that Everett Hughes had a talent for the work. A weird ability to instantly assess the viability of any kind of code, the way some people saw colours in words, or music in numbers. Either it looked good or it didn't, he said. Meaning that the code should conform to a kind of symmetry or beauty, although he found it hard to explain exactly what that was, and if pressed he would grow surly, hunch his shoulders, sneer that it wasn't worth trying to explain it because either you had the righteous gift or you didn't. He had the gift, and he was usually right. Jay Singleton got by through determination and hard work, but Everett Hughes flew.

Apparently, they had been planning to stash away a good percentage of their pay until they had accumulated enough to buy themselves berths on a code-hunting jaunt. They'd have to buy their own equipment, and front the gangmaster fees for transport plus a thirty per cent kickback on anything they made, but they were confident that they would strike a hot lode that would set them up for life. But it seemed that the two of them had grown bored with working and saving and saving and working, and had taken a shortcut. They'd stolen something from Meyer Lansky, and either Lansky or the Koreans had found them and killed them and taken the stuff back, or they'd tried to sell it to the wrong people. Those were my working hypotheses, but I was worried that the code itself might have had something to do with the two bodies in the burnt-out motel room – we were running a pool in the TCU on when someone would stumble across true AI, and who knew what else someone might find out there? In any case, Hughes and Singleton must have stolen the code because they'd though it valuable. And if it was valuable, it must be functional: unknown code with unknown capabilities, out there in the world. Recapturing it was suddenly my main priority, and the first thing I needed to do was to shut down Meyer Lansky's operation and find out what Hughes and Singleton had been working on before they'd bugged out.

Like all the ships we humans use, the reef farmers' ship is a shell retrieved from one of the vast Sargassos that orbit almost every one of the fifteen stars. Many ships are frozen relics no more functional or repairable than a watch that's spent a thousand years at the bottom of the ocean; others are merely quiescent, systems ticking over in a sleep deeper than any hibernation, but fully functional once awakened; all are ancient, handed down from Elder Culture to Elder Culture, modified and rebuilt and modified again until scarcely a trace of the original remains.

The farmers bolted the usual translation interface to the ship's control systems, but weren't able to customise the lifesystem for human occupation because the ship possesses fierce self-repairing mechanisms that resist any alterations (which was why the farmers could buy it at a knock-down price: few people want a ship with a mind of its own). The lifesystem supplies food that is both unpalatable and toxic to humans, the light is actinic, and the air like the air of a high altitude steel refinery: not enough oxygen or water, desert-dry and hot, stinking of tholines and sulphur dioxide.

The ships' crew and its single passenger – me – live in a series of pressure tents bolted to the bulkhead near the pool of nanodust that serves as an airlock. The maintenance system treats us as cargo and leaves us alone as long as we do not interfere with other areas of the ship. There is a large commons and a series of smaller rooms, including sleeping niches partitioned by fibreboard like the cells of a wasp's nest, a communal bathroom, and the small red-lit space – crowded with racks of electronic gear – that serves as the bridge. The commons is cozy enough, carpeted with overlapping rugs and cushions and beanbags and lit by small lamps and strings of fairylights, but even so we live like refugees, the rest of the ship's chambers looming above us like so many chimney shafts, walls pitted with cells of various sizes, lit by the pitiless glare of the lights, scoured by hot, random winds.

It's a perfect example of the human experience after First Contact – men and women living like mice in the walls of worlds they barely understand. The ship's fusion motors, for instance, are sealed mysteries. Very simple things that have been working for a hundred times longer than the existence of human agriculture on Earth, fuelled by deuterium and tritium mined by ancient ramscoop factories that swim through the atmospheres of certain ice giants.

Fuel is the key to the end of the chase.

Ours is a big ship, as ships go: an A3-Class heavy lifter. Even so, it can't carry enough fuel for a round trip out to Terminus's neighbouring star, so a drone has been sent after us, loaded with a cargo of deuterium and tritium. A major investment by the farmers that I hope the UN will defray, although the chair of the farmers' council, Rajo Hiranand, is sanguine about it. Telling me that her people made a huge gamble when they settled the worldlets of Terminus's inner belt, and so far it has paid off more handsomely than they ever expected. They've laid claim to several hundred planoformed rocks where they grow crops and ranch sky sheep, and share the profits from exploitation of artifacts and code unearthed by prospectors – the abundance and variety of artifacts found on Terminus's worldlets is second only to that of the fifteen stars' solitary habitable planet, First Foot. And now they have invested in this, a prospecting expedition of their own.

Rajo and I agree that Niles Sarkka may be crazy, but he is not stupid. That he must have good and convincing reasons for heading out to Terminus's neighbour. It isn't likely that he will find what he expects to find there, of course. But the fact that the navigation code points to a location close to the star must mean something is there, or was once there, in the long ago when the Ghajar were the tenants of the fifteen stars.

The rational part of me hopes that Niles Sarkka won't find anything useful, let alone prove that his wild idea is right. But I'm also caught up in this crazy chase: I want to believe – I have to believe – that there's a pot of gold around that star, something that will justify my refusal to obey a direct order. Something that will redeem me.

Now that we are slowly but surely catching up with Sarkka, I've told him several times that we are prepared to rescue him as long as he cooperates. I'm trying to get him used to the idea that, after he reaches his goal, we'll come alongside his ship and take him off and bring him home. So far, though, he's having none of it. Sometimes he rants at me; sometimes he's cool and reasonable, like a patient teacher correcting the error of a particularly stupid but wilful pupil.

He has no intention of returning, he says. He will spend the rest of his life with the Elder Culture that lurks somewhere around that star. Either they'll take him in, or he'll settle close by and found an institute or research centre.

"And if you're wrong?" I say.

"I am not wrong," he says.

"If there's nothing there. Just suppose."

"I do not intend to return."

And meanwhile the star grows brighter as both ships fall towards it, fusion motors blazing with a pull of a shade over 1.6 g, the maximum acceleration of every ship so far refurbished.

It is the brightest star in the sky now. Blue-white as a chip of ice. There's a thin ring of rocks close in, but none of them are cased in an atmosphere or are more massive that they should be, and in any case all of them are far too hot to be habitable. And there's a single planet, a gas giant about the size of Saturn, orbiting beyond the star's snowline. A somber world whose atmosphere is darkened by vast belts of carbon dust, as if polluted by some vast industrial process. It has multiple rings of sooty ice, and a retinue of moons, the larger ones balls of ice wrapped around silicate cores, the smaller ones captured chunks of carbonaceous chondrite in eccentric and mostly retrograde orbits. Somewhere amongst them, Niles Sarkka believes, is proof that his theory is correct, vindication for every bad thing he's ever done. Somewhere out there, he thinks, aliens have been hiding for tens of thousands of years.

Although Marc and I did our very best, it wasn't possible to make Meyer Lansky understand that we were prepared to do a deal with him rather than throw him in jail. Or maybe he understood, and didn't care. He was angry that his business had been shut down, and he was scared that his boss, Pak Young-Min, would find out that he'd been rolled by a couple of his code monkeys and conclude that he wasn't up to the job – the usual retirement plan for the Pak family's gangland employees and associates was a bullet in the back of the head and a short ride down the river to the sea. So Lansky refused my offer of protection when I served papers on him at his house around midnight, and he refused again when he was brought in for questioning. A broad-shouldered man dressed in a white suit, neatly barbered hair dyed the colour of tarnished aluminium, he sat in my office with a grim, shuttered expression and his arms folded across his chest, giving Marc and me the dead eye while his lawyer explained why he couldn't answer any of our questions.

One of the assistant city attorneys was there, too, and Marc and I knew things had taken a turn for the worse when she asked for a break and stepped out of the interrogation room with Lansky's lawyer. Marc took the opportunity to tell Lansky all over again why he would be doing the city and the UN a service by telling us where the stolen code was and what had happened to the two coders, repeating the scenario he'd already painted, with Lansky as the innocent party, first robbed by two of his employees, and then involuntarily involved in their murder by his boss.

"You had to tell Pak Young-Min about the theft because otherwise it would come down on your head. I understand that. But after that it was out of your hands and things got out of control," Marc said. He had taken off his jacket and hung it on the back of his chair at the beginning of the session; now, in white shirt and red braces, he leaned forward and stared straight at Lansky. "You are a smart man. You know how much trouble you are in. And you know what Pak Young-Min is capable of. But we're here to help. We can make your troubles disappear. All you have to do is tell us exactly what happened. What was stolen. What happened to the two foolish kids who stole it. Where it is now."

Meyer Lansky shook his head, eyes half-closed, lips pressed tight. He looked as if he was trying by sheer mental effort to teleport himself to some more congenial place.

Marc looked up at me, and I told Lansky that the UN would settle him anywhere he chose. That we'd even take him back to Earth, if he cooperated with us. That he would have a chance to start over, and meanwhile the men he feared would be put away for the rest of their lives.

Lansky shook his head. "Nothing was stolen. Those two kids, they just left. It happens all the time."

"It's time to tell the truth," Marc said. "Lying about what Pak Young-Min did won't save you. He'll go down anyway, and you'll go with him. But you can save yourself. All you have to do is tell the truth. It seems hard, I know. But once you start, you will feel so much better. It will be like a great weight lifting from your back."

Marc was good, and I did my best to back him up, but we couldn't get through to Lansky. "Talk to my lawyer," he said, and wouldn't say anything else.

At last his lawyer and the assistant CA came back. The assistant shaking her head, the lawyer telling Lansky that he was good to go.

"Hard-shelled son of bitch," Marc said, after they had left.

"He's scared."

"Of course. But not of us, unfortunately."

"I suppose we'll have to wait for the forensic results," I said. I was tired and empty. It was two in the morning, my investigation had been broken open, and I had nothing to show for it.

"We will rest and tomorrow begin again," Marc said, as he shrugged into his jacket. "You are my best investigator, Emma. I trust you to deliver what we need."

But our first break wasn't anything to do with me, or with Varneek Sehra's forensic crew, either. It was all due to one of our technical staff, Prem Gurung.

Prem was a modest young man who attributed his find to luck, but I knew better. His cubicle was as messy as the bedroom of as an undisciplined teenager – desk stacked with folders, papers, fabbed trinkets, and littered with every kind of electronic junk, walls tiled with photographs, postcards, print-outs, cartoons, and coasters in defiance of every regulation – but he was a skilled, intelligent, and hard-working investigator. He had been examining the work logs of Hughes and Singleton, and chunks of the mirrored code they had been working on, and had quickly found something of interest in one particular piece, an incomplete variant of the navigation package used to control refurbished ships retrieved from the Sargassos.

"It isn't so much what's there as what isn't," Prem said.

He was eager to show me, and I reluctantly agreed to take a look. Code is usually explored and manipulated via virtual simulations Disneyed-up by interface ware: dreamscapes that look a little like coral reefs, their exotic beauty haunted by sharks and moray eels and riptides that can fry synapses or burn permanent hallucinations in optic nerves. Coders, exposed to the stuff eight or ten hours a day, commonly suffer all kinds of transient hallucinations and risk permanent neurological damage – psychosis, blindsight, loss of motor control, death. But they are like deep sea divers working in the chthonic depths, while I was a snorkel-ling tourist dipping in for a brief peek, gliding over a garden of colourful geometric shapes, complex fractal packages of self-engulfing information that branched like bushes or were packed as tightly as human brains or formed shelves or fans or spires, everything receding into deep shadow in every direction, under a flexing silvery sky. Still, I couldn't shake off the sense of things unseen and fey lurking at the edges, where steep cliffs plunged into the unknown.

Prem guided me to a spot carpeted with intricate spires, and asked me if I saw it.

"I'm not very technical, Prem."

"It's a patch, copied from another part of the code," he said, turning the viewpoint through 360 degrees. Spires of every size and shape, glowing with purples and greens and golds, flowed around us in a three-dimensional tapestry. "It isn't easy to see at first, which is of course the point. But when you do see it, it's obvious. I have written a little executable. Here . . ."

A ghostly scape descended from the silvery sky, spires in wirework outline sitting askew the spires that stood around us.

"It does not seem to match at all, until you perform a simple geometric transformation," Prem said.

The wirework outline spun and stretched and merged with every contour of the spires around us, gleaming like frost on their complex and colourful surfaces.

"I think someone deleted something and wanted to cover it up," Prem said. "Fortunately for us, he was skilled, but lazy. Instead of designing something from scratch, he copied and distorted another part of the code and stitched it in. It is, on the surface, a seamless illusion. It even runs several processing cycles, although they are of course all futile. Like code that has gone bad, as much code does."

The strange shapes and colours of the code reef, hallucinatory bright, crammed with thorny details that repeated at every level of magnification, were aggravating my headache. I hadn't had much sleep and was running on coffee and fumes. I stripped off my VR and asked Prem if he had any idea about what had been deleted; he told me that despite the fractal nature of the code, little or nothing of the excised portion could be reconstructed. He started to witter on about working up a rough contour grid by extrapolation from the boundaries, using edge-crossing-detection, random-walk searches, and vertex-pruning mutators, blah blah blah. Like every tech, he was more interested in playing with a problem than actually solving it. I cut him off and said, "Bottom line, you don't know what it is, and there's no way of finding out."

"I'm afraid so. The deletion is too thorough for reconstruction, and catalogue comparisons have proven to be of no use."

"They stole something. We don't know what it is, but Hughes and Singleton definitely stole something. They mirrored the code and deleted the original, did their best to cover up what they'd done, and made off with the copy."

"That's certainly one scenario," Prem said. "Although there is a problem. How did they smuggle the stolen code past the farm's security?"

It was a good point. Code is stored in specific quantum states of electrons and other fundamental particles, so it can't be copied and stored as easily as the vast binary strings of ordinary software; to prevent decay into quantum noise, mirrored code has to be kept in cold traps, and these are cooled with liquid helium. Archive traps are as big as trucks; the smallest portable trap is somewhat larger than an ordinary domestic Thermos flask. And like all coding farms, Meyer Lansky's business possessed an insanely paranoid level of security. Coders had to step through scanning frames when entering or leaving, and they were subject to continuous scrutiny by CCTV cameras and random searches.

"Perhaps they had bribed a guard, or secreted the cold trap in some other piece of equipment sent out for servicing," I said. "Or perhaps Lansky himself might have been in on it."

"Or perhaps they didn't smuggle anything out," Prem said. "Perhaps they hacked into the farm's records and found out where the code came from, then deleted the code and altered the records. Perhaps they did not sell the code, but the location of the original."

I liked the idea – it would certainly explain why Hughes had left with Sarkka – but there was no way of proving or disproving it unless we caught up with them. Meanwhile, Varneek Sehra's crew had come up blank on DNA analysis because the two bodies had been thoroughly cooked, but they had identified one body as Jason Singleton's from its English dental work, and the second wasn't Everett Hughes, but a male in his forties. He had an old, healed bullet wound in his left shoulder, and examination of his burnt skin under UV light had revealed a blood group tattoo on his right ankle, suggesting that he'd been a soldier at some point. Varneek's crew had also retrieved a partial thumbprint from a stolen SUV in the motel's parking lot, and that had yielded a hit on the US military database: Abuelo Baez, who'd served as a sergeant in the Special Forces of the US Army until two years ago. The name did not appear on the emigration records, so he must have arrived on First Foot under an alias, either working for one of the corporations, or on the dark side. Varneek was planning to work up a facial reconstruction and use it to track down the dead man's emigration file; I hoped that once I knew Abuelo Baez's alias, I would be able to discover what he had been doing in Port of Plenty, perhaps even link him to Meyer Lansky or to the Pak family. Varneek also told me that there was a small discrepancy between the two bodies. Jason Singleton's body had smoke particles in its lungs, consistent with someone who had burned to death; Abuelo Baez's didn't. Either the ex-soldier had been killed outright by the blast, or he'd been dead before the room had been set on fire, it wasn't possible to tell.

All of this was useful, but it was my hunch about the missing motorcycle that yielded the most significant advance in the case. It had been discovered in the parking lot of a mini-mall a kilometre south of the motel; security camera footage showed that it had arrived some thirty minutes before the fire in the motel had been started. Everett Hughes had been riding it, and loitered near a rank of vending machines for some forty minutes until a white Honda Adagio pulled up.

I showed Marc the footage of Hughes getting into the Adagio, pulled down an enhanced freeze-frame of the moment when the courtesy light in the car came on as Hughes opened the door, briefly illuminating a bearded man wearing a baseball cap pulled low enough to obscure half his face. I explained that the driver had not yet been identified, but the car had been traced to the Hertz branch at the spaceport, where it had been rented using a snide credit card, and it had been retrieved for trace analysis.

"After Hughes and the driver returned the Adagio to the rental company, they took the shuttle bus to a ship that departed two hours later. A standard J-class cruiser registered in Libertaria. It dropped through Wormhole #2 six hours ago, and I've asked our offices in every port it could reach from that part of the network to look out for it. That's the bad news. The good news is that the Varneek and the PPPD's forensic people retrieved fibres and hair from the seats, and fingerprints from the steering wheel and elsewhere. Hughes's friend is Niles Sarkka."

Without missing a beat, Marc said, "I am not sure that I would classify that as good news."

Niles Sarkka was one of the Fortunate Five Hundred, the self-styled elite who'd ridden the first emigration lottery shuttle to First Foot. Before his downfall, he'd been a leading expert on Elder Cultures with a chair at the University of Port of Plenty, and the star of a TV show popular in Port of Plenty and exported to almost every country back on Earth. In each episode, he led his crew of prospectors to a new site in search of strange and valuable Elder Culture artifacts, surviving dangers and hardships, exploring weird landscapes and worldlets, unearthing wonders. Most of it was faked and exaggerated, of course, but Sarkka was a handsome and charismatic man with an infective enthusiasm for his work. Also, to the disgust of his fellow academics and the delight of his TV audience, he recklessly embraced crackpot ideas about the fates of the Elder Cultures, and conspiracy theories that suggested that the Jackaroo had influenced human history by dropping meteorites or manipulating the climate or starting the world war that – just before they'd turned up as saviours – had almost destroyed us. He was a leading exponent of the belief that the fifteen stars were not a chance to start afresh, but a trap. A cage in which we would be the involuntary participants in some vast and strange experiment, as had the Elder Cultures which had preceeded us. And he had worked up a crazy theory of his very own, which he talked up on every episode of his show. All of this made him rich and famous and notorious, but in the end his hubris was clobbered by nemesis. In the end he took one risk too many, and other people paid for his mistake with their lives.

My boss had been one of the team that had prosecuted Niles Sarkka after most of his crew had become infected with nanotech viroids while excavating the remains of ancient machinery in a remote part of the Great Central Desert. Marc had seen the bodies, all of them horribly transformed, some still partly alive. His boss, who'd later shot himself, had ordered cauterisation of the site with a low-yield nuclear weapon.

The crew had been working on an unlicensed site with inadequate protective measures; Niles Sarkka was convicted of manslaughter and spent five years in jail. As soon as he was released, he promptly fled First Foot and established himself on Libertaria, using what was left of his fortune to pursue the theory that was now an obsession.

Given that there was a wormhole link with the Solar System and Earth, he said, then it followed that there must have been links with the home worlds of each of the Elder Cultures that had once inhabited the worlds and worldlets of the fifteen stars. And those wormholes might still be around, somewhere, collapsed down to diameters smaller than a hydrogen atom, or hidden inside gas giants or in orbits close to stars where they could not be detected by their fingerprint flux of strange quarks and high-energy particles; it might be possible to find the home world of the Ghajar or one of the other Elder cultures, and find out what had happened to them. It was even possible that some remnants of the Elder Cultures might still be alive, either on their home worlds, or elsewhere.

To his fans – and despite his conviction and fall from grace he still had many fans – he was a gadfly genius, a rogue intellect who took great risks to prove radical theories that the establishment tried to suppress. To his fellow academics, he was a highly irresponsible egotist who used his notoriety to promote fantasies as risible as the lost continent of Mu or the Venusian origin of flying saucers, heedless of the damage he caused to serious scholarship. As far as the UN was concerned, he was a criminal willing to take every kind of risk with Elder Culture technology. He was beyond our reach on Liberteria, but he remained on our watch list.

And now he was heading out for parts unknown, either in possession of code mirrored from a navigation program, or of the whereabouts of the code's original. Given the huge risk he'd taken coming back to Port of Plenty, it seemed likely that he believed the code had something to do with his crazy idea about finding the homeworld or a surviving remnant of an Elder Culture. It also seemed likely that he had killed Jason Singleton and the mercenary, Abuelo Baez. Even if the code was harmless, Niles Sarkka still had to answer for those deaths.

The problem was that we had lost track of his ship. It could be anywhere in the wormhole network, heading for any one of the other fourteen stars – it might even be heading back to First Foot's star by a circuitous route. During the early years of exploring the network, the UN had tried to set up a monitoring system of spy satellites around the wormhole throats, but it had been sabotaged by various factions over the years, and in the end it had proven too expensive to maintain.

"Even if Sarkka and Hughes go to ground on Libertaria, we have no jurisdiction there," Marc said.

"We can try to negotiate with them," I said.

"Perhaps. It would help if we knew exactly what Hughes and Singleton stole," Marc said.

"That's why we need to talk to Meyer Lansky again," I said.

But Lansky had disappeared, and so had his wife and their two young sons. A police detail had been watching the front of the house; it seemed that Lansky and his family had left through the back, escaping across the golf course. Either of their own free will, or because someone had come for them.

A safe sunk in the floor of a walk-in closet in Lansky's residence had been left open but still contained large amounts of cash and jewellery, and credit cards and phones registered to a variety of names. Traces of blood belonging to Lansky and his family were found on a wall and the carpet in the adjoining master bedroom. I believed that they were dead, their bodies dumped in the sea or in the fern forests beyond the edge of the city, or incorporated into the foundations of a new building or freeway overpass, and their killers had probably taken from the safe copies of the records for the code farm detailing legitimate and black-market transactions.

After a brief conference with Marc and the assistant city attorney, I issued an APB for the Lanskys and made an appointment to visit Meyer Lansky's boss, Pak Young-Min. Marc thought it a waste of time, but I had a bad feeling that the case was going cold. I wanted to stir things up a little. Besides, I had papers to serve regarding search and seizure of the code farm's assets, and because Meyer Lansky had disappeared, it was only logical to hand them to his boss.

Pak Young-Min was the youngest son of Pak Jung-Hun, a former head of the American-Korean Family Boyz gang in Seattle who had "retired" to Port of Plenty. Like most gangsters who'd grown rich enough to escape the clutches of law enforcement agencies, Pak Jung-Hin had ambitions to legitimise his family. Three of his sons were involved in real estate and construction, an insurance and loan company, and casinos in First Foot and Mammoth Lakes. But Pak Young-Min was a throwback: an old-school kkangpae with a volatile temper and a taste for baroque violence who had been given control of Meyer Lansky's code farm by his father in an attempt to wean him away from the street life.

I arranged to meet him in the offices of the development company helmed by his eldest brother, Pak Kwang-Ho. This was on the top floor of a brand-new ziggurat – white concrete, glass tinted the pink of freshly-cut copper, broad terraces dripping with greenery – with a stunning view across the city towards Discovery Bay, the spaceport and the river delta on one side, the power plant and docks on the other, and the great curve of the Maricon and the beaches between. Up there, the city looked as neat and clean as a map, with no sign of the squabbling territories carved out by different nationalities. Up there, it was possible to believe that the future had arrived. You wanted to search the sky for flying cars and dirigibles.

Pak Kwang-Ho met me at the tall double doors of his private office. A slim and intensely polite man dressed in a crisp white shirt and intricately pleated pants, he shook my hand, offered me a choice of ten different teas, and introduced me to two lawyer types who afterwards did their best to fade into the background, and to his brother, Pak Young-Min.

The young gangster was looming over an architectural model of a shopping mall and entertainment complex, a bulky, broad-shouldered bodybuilder stuffed into a sharkskin suit and a yellow silk shirt and snakeskin boots. Tattoos webbed his neck and his hair was shaved at the sides, high above his ears, leaving a glossy black cap on top of his scalp. He didn't look up when Pak Kwang-Ho introduced me, pretending to be more interested in pushing a model car around a plaza, knocking over model pedestrians one by one.

Pak Kwang-Ho assured me that his family were always happy to help the police with their enquiries, but in this case, since his brother had business ties with Meyer Lansky, he had to ask me to confirm that my enquiries were purely informal. I assured him that I wanted nothing more than back-ground information on Meyer Lansky, although I did have papers to serve with regard to the code farm.

"I hope this means I can reopen it," Pak Young-Min said. "I lose money every day it is closed. Most inconvenient."

"Here's another dose of inconvenience – we're sealing it up until further notice," I said, and held out the envelope that contained the twenty-page court order.

Pak Young-Min took it and scaled it towards the lawyer types, saying that his people would check it out and get back to me.

"You need to sign it," I said.

"Why don't you ask me what you came here to ask me?" Pak Young-Min said. "I'm a busy man. I have a lot of stuff to do. Important stuff."

I decided to meet him head on and locked gazes with him and said, "When did you last see Meyer Lansky?"

"Days and days ago. I heard he ran away after you questioned him about those two geeks who burned to death," Pak Young-Min said. "If you catch up with the old rogue, let me know. I have some questions for him myself."

"You have no idea where he might be?" I said. "Him and his family."

"I've been in Mammoth Lakes for the past week," Pak Young-Min said, and took out a gold cigarette case and, ignoring his brother's warning that he couldn't smoke here, lit a black Sobranie with a match he ignited on his thumbnail.

"One of the bodies in the motel room was that of Jason Singleton. An employee at your code farm."

"Meyer Lansky's code farm," Pak Young-Min said.

"You own it."

"He runs it. I wouldn't know who he employs. When can I reopen the place, by the way?"

"When we've finished our investigation. Although by then there probably won't be anything left of your little operation."

Pak Young-Min looked at me with insolent amusement. "I know about you and your crusade," he said. "Word is, you lost your husband to bad code, and now you see bad code everywhere. Even when it isn't there."

I didn't rise to his bullshit. If you show any kind of weakness to someone like him you'll lose authority and never get it back.

"You are certain that you have never met Jason Singleton?"

"I've never had anything to do with those freaky little geeks."

"Have you ever met Everett Hughes?"

"Is he the other one who burned up in that room?"

"He's the one who got away," I said. "The other body in the motel room was that of Abuelo Baez, a former US soldier who served in the Special Forces."

"I've never heard of any of these people," Pak Young-Min said.

"Perhaps you know the face," I said, and showed him the printout of Abuelo Baez's reconstructed death mask.

Pak Young-Min breathed out a riffle of smoke and said, "He isn't one of mine."

"You might know him as Able Martinez," I said. "That's the alias he used when he came to Port of Plenty. We identified him from a file in the gaming commission's records. Every employee of every casino has one. I'm surprised you don't know him, Mr Pak. He worked on the security detail of the casino in Mammoth Lakes owned by your family."

"My brother has nothing to do with the running of the casino," Pak Kwang-Ho said. "And neither do I."

"We're looking into everything Mr Baez was doing here, and everyone he associated with," I said. "If you remember anything about him, it would be better if you told me now."

Pak Young-Min shrugged.

"You should speak to the manager of the casino," Pak Kwang-Ho said.

I told him that I would, and thanked them for their time and turned my back on both of them and walked towards the big double doors of the office.

Pak Young-Min called after me – he was the kind of man who had to have the last word. "Come find me in Mammoth Lakes. I'll show you a good time. Loosen you up a little."

I paused at the doors, turned. The corny old Columbo trick, but it's sometimes useful. "One other thing. Have you heard of Niles Sarkka?"

The two brothers looked at each other. Pak Young-Min said, "Isn't he the crazy guy who had that TV show?"

"He and Everett Hughes took off together," I said, and left them to think about that.

Later, I told my boss that I was certain that Pak Young-Min knew all about Hughes and Singleton. "Lansky was not a stupid man. He probably discovered the deletion in the navigation package and the alteration in his records after they dropped out of sight, and decided to come clean about it to his boss. Pak Young-Min sent his muscle man, Abuelo Baez, aka Able Martinez, after the two coders."

"Baez tracked them down to the motel room but he was killed by Niles Sarkka," Marc said.

"I'm not sure what happened there, but I don't think it matters," I said. "Sarkka was definitely involved, and I'm certain that the Paks didn't know about that until I told them. If we're lucky, they'll start making enquiries around the spaceport, and incriminate themselves. I can ask them, why are they looking for the killer of Abuelo Baez if Baez had nothing to do with them?"

"It is a long shot," Marc said. "I would prefer something tangible."

"So would I," I said. "But even if we can't tie them to Baez, we'll get them for Lansky. Pak Young-Min killed him. I'm sure of it. Lansky's family, too. He knew that we talked to Lansky, and he didn't trust him to keep his mouth shut. He probably took copies of incriminating records from Lansky's floor safe at the same time. If we have a pretext for arresting him, we might be able to get hold of those records. And somewhere in them is the location of the original of the code Hughes and Singleton stole. We need to find it."

"Do you really believe that Sarkka and Hughes are chasing after it?"

"They haven't turned up at Libertaria, or anywhere else we have representatives or reliable sources."

"That leaves about ten thousand habitable but uncolonized planoformed worldlets, and any number of rocks and moons," Marc said.

"We need to find it," I said. "So we know what we are dealing with. So we can destroy it, and make sure that no one else can mirror it."

"If Pak Young-Min has any sense, he will have destroyed those records."

"Not if he hopes to restart his black-market business."

Marc looked straight at me and said, "I hope you did not set the Paks after Sarkka because you believe that Sarkka has escaped justice."

"Of course not," I said.

But that was exactly why I'd told the Paks about Sarkka, and although Marc probably knew that I was lying, he didn't call me on it. Perhaps, like me, he wanted Niles Sarkka to answer for the deaths of Jason Singleton and Abuelo Baez, and for all his other crimes. Is that such a bad thing? Of course, I would have preferred to go after him myself, but at the time I didn't think it would be possible. So I had decided to stir things up a little.

While I'm being candid, I suppose I should mention my husband here – my second husband. Not because Pak Young-Min's silly jibe in any way hurt or upset me, but because certain commentators who should know better, amateur psychologists who aren't ashamed to speculate foolishly and wholly irresponsibly about the motivations of people they've never met, have suggested that I set out after Niles Sarkka because he was dealing in stolen code, and Jules's addiction to code is the key to my personality. My secret wound. The tragedy for which I have to atone for the rest of my life. Well, let me tell you that's so much pseudo-Freudian bullshit. I don't mean that it wasn't a tragedy. Of course it was. But I got past it and I got on with my life.

Really, it was all such a long time ago, back in the palmy days when everything in this brave new world of ours was fresh and wonderful. Back then, we didn't know that doing code could hurt you. It wasn't even illegal. It was something clever and sophisticated people did for kicks. A clean and perfectly legal high.

Jules said that it was as if everything had turned to mathematics. He could see everything as it really was, he said. He could see angels in the architecture and hear the glorious mingled chord of the universe's continuous self-invention. The world stripped bare of all masks. The world behind the world. He wanted me to try it, but I was a working police, we had regular tests for every kind of psychoactive substance. And besides, I was scared. I admit it. I was scared that the alien code would scramble my mind. And it turned out that I was right, because pretty soon it started to go bad for Jules and all the other clever people who did code for shits and giggles, because the temporary synesthesia and pareidolia became permanent, burned into their brains.

Jules began to see ugly patterns everywhere. Angels morphed into demons. The music became a marching band banging away inside his head and he couldn't get it out. He no longer spent hours lying out in the back yard at night, staring up at the stars with childlike wonder. The sky was wounded, now. Everything was rotten. Only the code kept him going. He had to take more and more of it, and by now it had become illegal. He could no longer get a clean supply from his friend at the university because his friend wasn't at the university anymore, she was on the street, but he found other sources. He sold just about everything we owned. I threw him out and took him back, suffered the usual cycle of anger and despair, hate and compassion. At last he stopped coming back. I could have found him, had him arrested, transferred from jail to a clinic, but it wouldn't have done any good. By then we knew that code caused permanent damage, a downward spiral of diminishing neurological function that ended in dementia and death. And I was tired of rescuing someone who didn't want to be rescued, and anyway, he wasn't the man I'd loved. He wasn't really anyone any more. He was his condition. So after he left that last time I didn't chase after him and the next time I saw him, six months later, was on a table in the morgue.

Yes, it hurt. Of course it did. But not as badly as seeing poor Jules twitching with pseudo-Parkinson's and gibbering about demons. It hurt, but it was also a kind of relief, knowing that he wasn't suffering anymore. Really it was. And besides, it was a long time ago, long before I joined the Technology Control Unit. It really doesn't have anything to do with anything I'm telling you about here, despite what some people claim. I wasn't avenging my husband or trying to assuage my guilt or anything like that. I was working the case, just like I worked every other case.

But after my confrontation with Pak Young-Min, the case appeared to have reached a dead end. I continued to try to tease out new leads, coordinating the team who were interviewing everyone who worked in the code factory and trying to discover a direct connection between the dead ex-soldier, Abuelo Baez, and Pak Young-Min. I wrote day reports, filed evidence dockets, and minuted case conferences. I arranged to meet Detective August Zacarias, ostensibly to brief him about the ongoing investigation into the double homicide at the motel, in reality to pump him for information about his fellow member of the Fortunate Five Hundred. That, too, yielded nothing useful. He claimed that he'd only met Niles Sarkka once or twice, and knew little about him.

"You want to know if he's one of the bad guys. All I can tell you is that back in the early days he argued very passionately and convincingly about the importance of finding out everything we could about our new worlds. He said that we should take nothing for granted. That we should take charge of our own destiny by forging a complete understanding of the history and nature of the Jackaroos' gift. He wasn't dangerous, then, merely impassioned. It seems to me that he hasn't changed."

I suppose I should have known better. I should have known that the so-called elite would stick together. Ten days passed with little to show for my efforts, beyond filling in the biographies of Everett Hughes and Jason Singleton. And then I received an email that opened up a fresh angle.

It was from a man who claimed to be a friend of Meyer Lansky's mistress. He said that she had gone into hiding because she was afraid of the Paks, and that she had something that I would like to see: two sets of books for the code farm. This so-called friend had used an anonymous forwarding service to cover his tracks, but Prem Gurung managed to track him down while I negotiated with him online, and within the hour he was sitting in our interview room.

He was a small-time hustler by the name of Randy Twigger, a former boyfriend of Lansky's mistress. He put up a feeble show of defiance that quickly collapsed when I called his bluff and told him that he could be arraigned for accessory to murder and kidnap of the Lanskys. Later that day, with a pair of armed marshals at my back, I was knocking on the door of a motel room in the fishing resort of Marina Vista, 400 km east of Port of Plenty.

Meyer Lansky's mistress, Natasha Wu, was a tough and level-headed young woman who was ready and willing to be taken into protective custody, and wasn't surprised that Randy Twigger had screwed up by trying to make some money for himself.

"He was supposed to make an arrangement so that I could meet with you. But he always was greedy," she said, and dismissed him with a flick of her manicured fingers.

She said that she'd heard about the disappearance of Meyer Lansky and his family on the news, said that she'd known at once that they were dead. "Meyer was ultra-paranoid the last time I saw him. There'd been a break-in at the farm, and those two kids were killed, and you threatened him. I was about the only person he could trust. That's why he gave me the books. He was going to contact me when things settled down. Instead, this man I don't know calls me on the phone Meyer gave me, and threatens me."

Lansky had given her a q-phone, but after the threatening call she had ditched it and gone to ground, moving from place to place. Randy Twigger had checked her apartment a couple of days ago and found that it had been trashed, so she knew that the people who had killed Lansky and his family knew about her. That's why she had reached out to me.

I liked Natasha Wu, even though I disapproved of the choices she had made in her life. She was a survivor with no trace of self-pity and had probably given as good as she got in her relationship with Meyer Lansky. I told her that the UN was willing to give her a new identity and relocate her in exchange for the accounts and records that Lansky had entrusted to her, and she said why not, the man was dead, and it wasn't like she had a choice anyway.

"Besides, I want off this fucking world. I've been here a year, and already I hate it. I want to go back to Earth. To Singapore. It's fucked up there, but I know my way around, and the gangsters aren't as crazy bad as they are here. Poor Meyer. And his kids." She teared up just a little, and said, "Will you get the filth that killed them?"

I thought of Detective August Zacarias and said, "I'm going to do my best."

At the UN building, I sat with Marc Godin and one of the city attorneys while they made a deal with Natasha Wu and took her initial deposition. Then I escorted Natasha to one of our safe houses, so I didn't get a chance to talk to Marc about searching the records for the location of the original of the code, or chasing after Sarkka and Hughes.

I stayed at the safe house overnight, and was eating breakfast with Natasha and the two UN special agents detailed to protect her when Marc called.

"There have been developments," he said. "Something I think you will like."

"Has Prem found where the code came from? Are we going after Sarkka?"

"Meet me at the UN Building," he said, and rang off.

We bought coffee at the roach coach in the parking lot in front of the UN Building, and walked two blocks to the seafront. I told him that Natasha was holding up; he told me that the records were all that we hoped they would be.

"The late Monsieur Lansky was a meticulous man," Marc said. "We have details of all his black market transactions, and that is a great prize. As for the code that has caused so much trouble, you will be pleased to hear that we know now where it came from. A planoformed but uninhabited worldlet in the outer belt of the system of Terminus. It was located and mirrored by a prospector named Suresh Shrivastav, registered in Libertaria."

"And what are you going to do about it?"

"That's what we must talk about now. Let's find a seat."

It was a fine warm spring morning. Far around the great curve of the beach, two bulldozers looking small as toys were levelling sand where a kraken had beached a few days ago. A raft of bladders and pulpy limbs the size of two football fields, it had drawn huge crowds, and dismembering and removing it had been an industrial process. People were strolling along the front or walking their dogs on the wide beach, and a few early-bird surfers were riding the waves.

Marc and I found a bench, and Marc told me that the UN representative in Libertaria had contacted Suresh Shrivastav's agent. The prospector had just departed for the star 2M 4962, and according to his agent he had nothing to say to the UN.

"It may be an attempt to force us to negotiate, but as long as we find the code it does not matter," Marc said. "As for that, I have also contacted our representative in the Terminus system. I regret there is no positive news there, either. There are two belts of rocks around Terminus. The people who live there, farmers all of them, live on the inner belt. And their traffic control system is pretty rudimentary. Regrettably, it doesn't extend to the outer belt, and there is no evidence that Sarkka's ship has visited the system."

"It doesn't mean that he didn't go there."

"That's true."

"Or that he might not be there right now."

"That is also possible."

"In any case, the original of the code will still be there. If Sarkka or that prospector hasn't already destroyed it."

"Now we come to the heart of the matter," Marc said. "It is not Niles Sarkka, of course, but the code. There have been political developments. The Inspector General has been informed. And it appears that the Jackaroo have become interested."

I felt a beat of foolish excitement. "It's really that serious?"

"They think so. They studied the code and said it was very bad stuff. Do you remember Thor V?"

"That farming family who took off into the big black," I said.

They had stumbled onto code that had infected them with a meme. Seized by its ancient imperative, they'd climbed aboard their ships and headed out into interstellar space. They are still falling through space, a light year from their star now, out of reach, out of fuel and power, their ships and everyone on board them dead.

Marc said, "The Jackaroo claim that Hughes's code may have a similar effect on anyone who interacts with it, and there is a nasty twist: it is slowburning, so those infected have time to infect others. And those who become infected but are unable to reach a ship will become insane. The Inspector General has authorized a strike team to travel to Terminus. I have argued successfully that our department should remain involved. So, let me ask you formally. Are you willing to volunteer to accompany the strike team?"

"I've already thought about this, boss. There's nothing I'd like better."

"Of course. Now, I want you to go home and change your clothes, pack for a long voyage, and make any necessary personal arrangements. Find me in my office in four hours. That is when we are to meet with the Inspector General."

The Jackaroo are supposed to keep out of human affairs. They don't, of course. The software we now use to interface with code is a case in point. An important one, because it had established a precedent. It's derived from code that migrated from the wreck of a spaceship into a colony of hive rats in the vast necropolis in the western desert. The biologist studying them enlisted a mathematician to help her decode the hive rats' complex dances, and the mathematician quickly realized that they were exchanging massive amounts of information – that the colony was acting as a parallel processing computer.

All this is well known. What has been suppressed (until now – and I have good reason to break cover, as you'll see) was the fact that the code had drawn the attention of the Jackaroo. An avatar pitched up with a bunch of hired goons and tried to kill the biologist and destroy the hive-rat colony. The Jackaroo claimed afterwards that it was the action of a rogue element, and we had to pretend to believe them. In any case, the biologist and a local law enforcement officer fought back. The goons were killed and the avatar was destroyed. I became involved a little later. The law enforcement officer had picked up a piece of kit that the avatar had been using. It not only tracked and disrupted q-phone signals, but could eavesdrop on them. We bought the technology from her, and in exchange she agreed to keep quiet about the avatar.

After that incident the UN and the Jackaroo made an informal agreement to cooperate when it came to suppressing potentially dangerous technology.

That is what I had walked into, when Marc took me up to the Inspector General's big, wood-panelled office.

The Inspector General, a small but imperious blond woman in her sixties, shook my hand and told me that from now on I was operating under Section D, but I paid scant attention to her. I was staring at the man-shaped figure that stood off to one side. A showroom dummy woven from a single giant molecule of metal-doped polymer, dressed in a black suit and white shirt and polished black shoes. A proxy for a creature no human had ever seen, linked by a version of q-phone technology to an operator who could be anywhere in the universe. Moving now, stepping towards me and greeting me in a newsreader's rich baritone.

"We have followed Dr Sarkka's career with great interest," it said. "And this is a very interesting turn of events."

"A potentially serious turn of events," the Inspector General said. "Sarkka is a dangerous man, and he may be about to lay his hands on dangerous code."

"We have examined the damaged code," the avatar said. "What was deleted presents a clear danger to you. We are here to help."

"And we're grateful, of course," the Inspector General said.

The avatar responded with a lengthy speech, telling us that the Jackaroo were grateful for the UN's cooperation and for my role in helping to heal a potentially difficult rift; how this was a fine example of the harmonic convergence of the Jackaroo and the human race; how the present small difficulty would be quickly overcome by application of that same cooperation in general, and my talents in particular, and so on and so forth – I won't bore you. It was the usual mash-up of cliches, mixed metaphors, and orotund sentiment, like a mission statement for some multinational company written by committee and run through a computer which had scrupulously removed any trace of originality, human feeling, and passion. The experts are still arguing, and will probably argue forever, about whether the Jackaroos' communications and conversations are classic examples of Chinese Room AI simulations of human thought patterns, or cleverly misleading simulations of Chinese Room AI simulations of human thought patterns. As someone who has been on the receiving end of one of their perorations, I can tell you that the distinction doesn't matter. As far as I was concerned, all that mattered was that it was so relentlessly dull that it was almost impossible to keep track of what was being said. It would have sent anyone not wired to the eyeballs on caffeine and amphetamine to sleep had it not been for one thing: it was delivered by a genuine alien through a machine of unknown powers.

And so, despite the soporific blanket of the avatar's bland and lengthy blandishments, I was gripped by an electric, barely suppressed terror, and I'm certain that Marc and the Inspector General felt the same way. For despite their best intentions – or because of them – you can't help but be paranoid about the Jackaroo. They are alien and therefore completely opaque. Neither angels nor devils, but distorting mirrors that reflect our best hopes and worst fears.

"May I ask a question?" I said, when it had finished, or at least run out of words. "If you're offering to help us, what kind of help are we talking about?"

"We are here to advise, nothing more," the avatar said. "After all, we do not want to reveal that we are helping you. It would violate the terms of our agreement. However, we may be able to locate Dr Sarkka's ship, should it use a wormhole again, and we do not see a problem with passing on that information."

The Inspector General chipped in again, said that the Jackaroo usually refrained from direct interference, but because this was an unusual and highly alarming case, they would utilize a little-known property of the wormhole throats to identify any used by Sarkka's ship. They had already confirmed that Sarkka had visited Terminus, and because he had not returned through that system's only wormhole, he must still be there. Our first priority was to find, identify, and destroy the code. Our second was to track down Hughes and Sarkka, and if it came to it, we would try to purchase the mirror of the code from them.

The Inspector General mentioned a ceiling limit that exceeded the GDPs of several countries back on Earth. "We have no intention of paying Sarkka of course. He will be arrested for murder as soon as he tries to collect. Hopefully, he will have become infected before then, and will have aimed his ship at some damned star or other."

"It is possible," the avatar said. "But we cannot count on it because the incubation period is variable."

I saw a big flaw in the plan at once: Niles Sarkka wasn't stupid, and would guess that my offer was bogus. And in any case, if the code promised to validate his theory he wouldn't part with it for any amount of money. But I didn't raise any objections – as I've already explained, I believed that summary justice was better than letting Niles Sarkka gain power over dangerous code. When the Inspector General asked me if I needed time to think about this, I said that I already had thought about it, and would gladly accept.

It was almost not untrue.

"They have been manipulating us from the very beginning, Emma. Playing with us as a child plays with white mice in a cage. And they have been watching us a very long time. They know things about us that we do not know. They sit in judgement beyond ordinary human plight or perception. But they do not know everything. Their survey of our comings and goings on Earth and everywhere else is not omniscient. That is why we will escape their chains. And that is why we are here, you and I."

It's two in the morning. Everyone on the ship is asleep except for the maintenance robots puttering about their inscrutable business beyond our encampment, the three men and women of the night watch, and me. I'm trying to make a cup of green tea with one hand while holding the q-phone's handset in the other, listening to for the tenth or twelfth time a variant of Niles Sarkka's standard lecture on the Jackaroo and their fiendish plans and plots.

I said, "They knew about Hughes and Singleton. They knew about the code."

"No, Emma. They intercepted q-phone messages between me and a friend in Port of Plenty who was acting as go-between.. They did not know what the code was, or where it came from because poor Everett and Jason did not know what it was, and they wouldn't tell me where the original was located until we had concluded our dealings face to face and quit First Foot."

"Even so, they tracked you to Terminus."

"Did they? They lied about the nature of the code. Perhaps they lied about that, too. They do not know everything, and they lie. If they are gods, they are petty and spiteful gods. I don't know about you, but even at its lowest, I don't think that humanity deserves gods as low and base as them. No, we aspire to greater things. Why else would we have come all this way, you and I?"

"I'm here to bring you to justice, Niles. You know that."

"You're here because of your nature, Emma. You're here because you want to be here. You see, you aren't very different from me after all."

I was brought up short by his assertion, but shrugged it off with a quip about this not being in any way the destination I'd anticipated when I'd left First Foot, and he didn't make any more of it, went back to his interminable dissection of conspiracies and secret histories. I mention it here because I think he's wrong. Oh, there's no doubt that we have some things in common. Particularly our obsession with seeing things through to the end no matter what the cost. But this is overshadowed by a fundamental difference.

I stand on the right side, and he does not.

We left, the strike team and I, in a Q-class scout, a small ship that resembled a cartoon toadstool: a fat cone containing the lifesystem, with the teardrop-shaped stalk of the fusion motor pod depending from its centre. The lifesystem's interior was a roughly oval chamber partitioned by mesh platforms and furnished with bunk beds, a pair of porta-potty toilets and a shower pod like a dingy plastic egg, picnic tables and an industrial microwave, commercial chest freezers and rows of steel storage lockers. All in all, it was about as glamorous as a low-rent bomb shelter or the accommodation module of an oil platform, except that the scalloped nooks and crannies of its walls were a perfect hollow cast of the whale-sized agglomeration that had once filled it – the Ghajar had been colonial creatures that exchanged biological modular parts amongst themselves as easily as we changed clothes, each one a different shape and size from all the rest.

Like all ships, ours was a strictly point-and-click operation. Apart from a package of solid-fuel motors for fine manoeuvres strapped around the lifesystem's circumference, most of the ship's systems, especially the fusion motor, were sealed, enigmatic, inaccessible. Our pilot, a slender, athletic New Zealander, Sally McKenzie, typed a command string into the laptop that interfaced with the ship's navigation package, and the ship boosted itself out of orbit and aimed itself at the pair of wormhole throats that orbited the trailing Lagrangian point of the system's methane gas giant.

All wormhole throats look the same, a round black mirror a little over a kilometre across, framed by the ring that houses the braid of strange matter that keeps it open and embedded in a rock sheared flat on one side and shaped and polished to a smooth cone behind, shaped and set in place millions of years ago by the nameless and forgotten Elder Culture that created the network. There were two in First Foot's system, one leading to the Solar System, the other to a red dwarf star some twenty thousand light years away, at the outer edge of the Scutum-Centaurus Arm of the Galaxy. That's the one we dropped through.

I sat with Sally McKenzie during the transit, watching on the HD screen as with startling speed Wormhole #2 grew from a glint to a speck to a three-dimensional object, the round black mirror of its throat flying at the screen, filling it. And then, without any sense of transition, we were out on the far side, falling around the nightside of a hot super-Jupiter. The red dwarf sun rose above the vast curve of the planet like a moon set afire, and the ship drove on towards the next wormhole throat, 60 degrees around the orbit it shared with the wormhole we'd just exited.

It had taken more than two days to reach the wormholes in First Foot's system, but took just two hours to swing around the super-Jupiter to catch up with the next one, plunging through it and emerging close to a dim brown dwarf that orbited a red dwarf star a little brighter, glimmering like a dot of blood against the great dark shoulder of the Horsehead Nebula. The ship broke orbit and swung out towards a sombre ice giant and after three days at maximum acceleration plunged into the solitary wormhole that orbited it.

And so on, and so on.

Via q-phone, Marc kept me up to date with the code farm investigation. It seemed that Natasha Wu had fitted a video camera into the bedroom of her apartment ("A girl can never be too careful.") and it had caught the two goons who had broken in and trashed the place while searching for the code farm archives. Both were in custody inside a day, and both turned out to be linked, via DNA trace evidence, to no less than seven unsolved murders. One of them quickly decided to take up Marc's offer of immunity from prosecution and sang about everything he knew, including the kidnap and murder of Meyer Lansky and his family: more than enough to take down Pak Jung-Hin. Apparently, the dead ex-soldier, Abuelo Baez, had been a freelance who'd done several enforcement jobs for Meyer Lansky, specialising in "debt recovery." The goon didn't know if Baez had been sent after Jason Singleton and Everett Hughes, but Marc believed that it seemed likely. We still weren't sure what had gone down in the motel room, but it looked as if Lansky's man had caught up with the two coders, Everett Hughes had escaped, and Niles Sarkka had been involved in some kind of confrontation that had left both Jason Singleton and Abuelo Baez dead.

The young captain and the six soldiers of the strike team passed the time stripping and reassembling their weapons, swapping war stories, immersed in virtual simulations of various actions, watching videos, and sleeping. They slept a lot, like big predators with full bellies whiling away the time until the next meal. My presence seemed to make them uncomfortable, no doubt because I wielded authority outside their chain of command, but I found the pilot, Sally McKenzie, a congenial companion. She'd been a colonel in the New Zealand Air Force during the war, had won a ticket on the emigration lottery three years ago, shortly after she'd been retired from active service. Now she was a spaceship pilot, eager to see everything the fifteen stars had to offer. She told me stories about dogfights over the Weddell Sea and the Antarctic Peninsula; I told her sanitised versions of various investigations I'd been involved in.

And so we moved from wormhole throat to wormhole throat, a chain that passed through six star systems until we reached our destination, the star 2CR 5938, otherwise known as Terminus. So-called because there was only one wormhole throat orbiting it. One way in, one way back out. The end of the line.

It was a dim red dwarf freckled with big sunspots. The bright filamentous arc of a flare bridged one edge of its disc from equator to pole. It was part-nered with a G0 star that shone a little over a tenth of a light year away, only a little less bright than the dozens of hot young stars that were beginning to burn through a tattered veil of luminous gas that slanted across half the sky.

The red dwarf was circled by two concentric belts of asteroids: rubble left from ancient collisions of protoplanets, prevented from accreting into larger bodies by the gravitational interference of the hot and dense super-Jupiter that orbited between them. Our ship fell towards the outermost belt, at the edge of Terminus's habitable zone.

The UN representative had already reached an agreement with the reef farmers' council, which had sensibly agreed to keep away for fear of infection with the meme that the Jackaroo had warned us about. Our destination was an undistinguished worldlet amongst ten thousand such. Unequally bi-lobed like a peanut, an agglomeration of basaltic rocks heated and partly melted by successive shock fronts that had driven the orbital migration of the super-Jupiter, afterwards lightly cratered by impacts with debris left over from the formation of thousands of others like it and mantled in a layer of dust and pebbly chondrules. It had orbited Terminus for more than seven billion years, undisturbed by anything except the occasional minor impact, until some nameless Elder Culture had planoformed it, injecting into its centre of mass a spoonful of collapsium, exotic dark matter denser than neutronium that gave it a pull averaging a little less than the Moon's gravity, wrapping it in a bubble of quasiliving polymer that kept in a scanty atmosphere of oxygen, nitrogen, and argon, landscaping it, seeding it with life.

Scores of tenants had come and gone since then. Some leaving no trace of their occupation apart from subtle changes in the isotopic composition of the worldlet's atmosphere and biosphere; others adding species of plants and microbes to its patchwork ecology; the most recent leaving ruins. Ghosts had riddled it with pits and shafts. Boxbuilders had left chains of crumbling cells stretched here and there on top of ridges and around the edges of eroded craters. Spiders had parked a small asteroid in stationary orbit above its nipped waist and spun a cable, woven from diamond and fullerene and studded with basket-weave habitats, down to its surface. And a few thousand years ago, a spaceship of the Ghajar had crashed at the pole.

Despite its deep history, the little worldlet was a bleak and marginal environment, cold as Arctic tundra before global warming, sheeted with ice and snow, black bacterial crusts and cushion algae growing in sheltered niches in the equatorial rift, cotton trees floating in the air like clouds spun from pale wire. Unnamed and unexplored by humans, until some prospector had stumbled onto code still active in the wreckage of the crashed ship.

As the ship made its final approach, the strike team launched a drone rocket that sped ahead of us and dumped three baseball-sized spy satellites in orbit around the worldlet. They soon located the ancient crash site, an oval impact crater under the snow cap at the pole of the larger of the worldlet's two lobes, with traces of metal spattered around it that showed as a spray of bright dots in the sideways radar scans. And their high-definition cameras also picked up a tiny source of heat and an ordinary blue camping tent at the worldlet's equator, close to the base of the spider cable.

The young captain who commanded the strike team, Jude Foster, told Sally McKenzie to establish an equatorial orbit and ordered his soldiers to get ready to make a crash entry. Apparently, using the elevators of the spider cable was out of the question: they were too slow, and anyone on the surface would have plenty of time to prepare an ambush.

"This is an eccentric scholar and a coder barely out of his teens," I said. "Hardly a major threat to your people."

"Surely you have not forgotten that your 'eccentric scholar' is wanted for homicide, Inspector," Captain Foster said with wintery condescension. "And in any case, a whole crew of malcontents might be concealed down there. It is my duty to take appropriate precautions."

Like me, Captain Foster was a Brit: pale, blond, and laconic, also startlingly young and eager to prove himself on his first real action. We had a brief discussion about whether or not I should accompany the strike team on their crash entry or wait aboard the ship until they had secured a perimeter around the base of the cable. I prevailed. I freely confess that I was scared silly, but I was determined to do my duty.

Sally McKenzie helped me dress in a pressure suit, and one of the soldiers towed me across the flank of the lifesystem to the cargo pod where the scooters were stored. I rode pillion behind Captain Foster; the soldiers rode three scooters flanking us. They were crude hybrids, the scooters – quad bike frames perched on the skinny tank of a LOX booster, with two pairs of big fans set fore and aft to give them lift in atmosphere – but they were fast and manoeuvrable. The worldlet swelled ahead and we burst through its sky membrane simultaneously, riding through a sudden buffeting wind, sliding down fingers of red sunlight that slanted at a shallow angle across kilometres of air. Cotton trees caught in the raw sunlight exploded like popcorn kernels, spewing tangles of tough threads, creating mats hundreds of metres across that caught in the gales of leaking atmosphere and sailed past us and smacked against the holes we'd punched in the skin of the sky.

Our scooters dodged the last of the mats and swooped down in wedge formation. The surface of the tiny world hurtled towards us, white ice patched with bare black rock curving away on all sides, the spider cable's dark tower rising towards the bronze sky. One of the soldiers whooped over the common channel. I felt like whooping, too. I was dizzy with fright and exhilaration.

Details exploded out of the landscape as we headed in towards the rift valley that girdled the equator. We skimmed across a lip of bare rock strung with Boxbuilder ruins, mostly roofless hollow cells, and dropped past sheer cliffs towards the black blister where the cable socketed into the floor of the wide valley. The valley's floor was cut by low wrinkle ridges and short crevasses jagged as lightning bolts; some of the crevasses were flooded with frozen lakes and shone like shards of broken mirrors. Scrub and low patches of thorn trees grew everywhere between the lakes, a waist-high Krummholz forest. I glimpsed a flash of blue at the tip of a long thin lake and then the landscape tilted and my insides were scooped hollow with vertigo as the captain swung the scooter around and brought it down with a jarring bounce.

A man stood beside an ordinary blue nylon camping tent pitched at the lake shore. He was dressed in boots and jeans and a black puffa jacket, raising his hands as the soldiers advanced towards him from two sides. I fell to my knees when I climbed off the scooter, dizzy, grinning like a fool, and pushed up and followed as best I could, unbalanced by the low gravity and the encumbrance of my pressure suit. The ground was carpeted with stuff a little like moss, a thick lace of bladder-filled filaments the colour of old blood that crunched and popped under my boots. Beyond the lake and a steep ridge, the cable sliced the sky in half.

Captain Foster, bulky as a fairytale knight in his white pressure suit, pistol clamped in his gauntlet, marched up to the man and told him to kneel and clamp his hands on top of his head. The man – it was Everett Hughes, black hair falling over a face as pale as paper – obeyed a little clumsily, saying, "There's no need for this. I'll tell you everything."

I said, "Where is Niles Sarkka?"

Captain Foster said, "Are you alone?"

"Niles is long gone," Everett Hughes said. "He's on his way to history."

I insisted on carrying out an immediate field interrogation, recorded by an autonomous drone and witnessed by Captain Foster. I wanted to find out what had happened on the worldlet, I wanted to find out where Niles Sarkka had gone and with what intent, and I wanted it to stand up in court. I was still thinking like that, then.

Despite his getup as the ultimate badass coder – an unruly mane of hair dyed jet-black, silver rings sewn around the rim of his right ear and a skull ring on a chain around his neck, tattoos on his neck and fingers, the leather vest and white ruffled shirt under his black puffa jacket, the tight blue jeans and the cowboy boots – Hughes was young and naive. He told us that we'd find a q-phone in the tent, that Sarkka possessed its entangled twin.

"If you want to know what happened, and why it happened, you should call him. He can explain everything much better than I can."

His calmness wasn't anything to do with bravery; it was compounded of youthful arrogance and sheer ignorance. He really didn't understand how much trouble he was in. He refused to acknowledge that he had been used, abused, and dumped by Niles Sarkka, believed to the end that he and Sarkka had done the right thing, and was proud to have helped him.

What I'm trying to say is that although he appeared to be cooperative, everything he told us was coloured by his loyalty to Sarkka. I don't offer this as an excuse for what happened, but that's why I allowed it to happen. Because I thought that Hughes was only telling some of the truth, some of the time, and because he refused to give up crucial information. Sarkka had poisoned that young man's mind. He's as much to blame for what happened as anyone else.

In any case, Captain Foster and I agreed that we would defer the pleasure of a conversation with Niles Sarkka until we had learned everything we could from Everett Hughes. And to begin with, the interrogation went smoothly enough. We did it in the tent, Hughes perched on a camping stool, Captain Foster and I looming over him in our pressure suits, the drone hovering at my left shoulder. Hughes readily admitted that, as I'd suspected, he and Jason Singleton hadn't tried to mirror the code; instead, they'd hacked into the database of the code farm, discovered where the code had come from, and then erased the code and every bit of data pertaining to it. When I told him that it was too bad for him that Meyer Lansky had kept duplicate records in his home, he shrugged and said he'd factored the possibility into his plans.

"I figured Lansky wouldn't tell you about them because it would have meant admitting to all his black market deals. And I reckoned that even if you did manage to get your hands on them, it would take some time, because you couldn't just go in and search his place, you'd have to get all the papers in order and so on. Time enough for Niles and me to get out here and do what we needed to do."

He said that he'd deleted the code because Lansky insisted that every chunk should be checked by three different people, and he knew that the next guy in the line would have seen what it was, and what it meant. And then, because they were worried that their tampering would be discovered, he and Jason Singleton had gone into hiding before reaching out to Niles Sarkka.

"As soon as I laid eyes on that code, I knew that Niles Sarkka was the man to go to. It took a while to contact him, though. And then he had to have us checked out, in case we were part of some kind of law enforcement trap. While all this was going on, a guy employed by Lansky tracked down where Jay and me were hiding out. I don't know how, exactly, but Jay had a girlfriend – you didn't know? I guess there's a lot you didn't know. Anyhow, I reckon Jay called her one last time, right around when we were getting ready to leave, and the call was intercepted. Maybe the guy had bugged her line, or maybe he'd broken into her place and was waiting for Jay to show. I hope not, I liked her. In any case, the guy turned up at the room while I was meeting up with Niles. Jay managed to lock himself in the bathroom and phone me, and Niles said he'd deal with it. Said that because of what I knew, I wasn't to put my life in danger. He had a gun – he'd taken a risk coming back to Port of Plenty, he had enemies there. So he took off, and we met an hour later, and he told me Jay was dead. That was bad enough. But he also told me that a Jackaroo avatar had been there. The guy working for Lansky was dead, it must have followed him and killed him, and it was bent over Jay. Doing something to him. Niles shot it, and it exploded and the room caught fire, and Niles couldn't get to Jay. He said that Jay was already dead, there was nothing he could do."

"Bullshit," I said. "Sarkka spun you a story, Everett. I'll tell you how I know. Your friend had particles of soot in his lungs. That means that he was still alive when he burned to death. There was no avatar. Sarkka killed Lansky's man with some kind of beam weapon, it set fire to the room, and Sarkka let your friend burn to death rather than risk his own life trying to save him."

"Niles told me there was an avatar, and I believe him," Hughes said, looking straight at me. "And not only because he wouldn't lie to me about something like that. There was a break-in at the code farm after we contacted Niles. You know how hard it is, to break into the place? Almost impossible. But someone did it – or something did. Something that heard that we had special code we wanted to hand over to Niles. Something that went to check out what it was we'd taken."

I told him that I knew about the break-in, but his assumption that the Jackaroo had been involved in it was a fantasy. And I told him, trying to get at him through sympathy, that I understood why he believed it. "You feel guilty about what happened to your friend. Of course you do. But you have to face the truth, Everett. The truth is that Sarkka killed your friend. And the only reason he didn't kill you is because he needed your help when it came to mirroring and using the code."

I was doing the right thing, chipping away at Hughes's misplaced loyalty, trying to isolate him. But he refused to admit that he was in the wrong and became stubborn, saying, "I shouldn't have left Jay in that room when I went to meet Niles. He wanted to, in case something went wrong, but I shouldn't have done it. And I'm going to have to carry that for the rest of my life. So yeah, I feel guilty. But I'm not making any of this shit up. And if Niles is such a bad guy, like you claim, let me ask you something. How come he didn't kill me after we mirrored the code and I ran it through his nav package?"

Captain Foster cut in at that point, and his interference made things worse. "You admit that you located the original of the code, you and Sarkka. And you mirrored it."

"Well, yes. We didn't come out to this miserable ball of rock and ice for the skiing, that's for sure. We mirrored it and then we destroyed the original. I'll show you where."

"The code is a dangerous meme," Captain Foster said. "You are probably infected with it. Mr. Sarkka too."

Hughes laughed. "You really believe it, don't you? That's why you're still wearing your pressure suits I bet. Well, I don't know who told you that bullshit, but that's what it is. Bullshit. Niles isn't infected. Nor am I. And the code, it's no meme. I already knew what it was when I came across it, although I didn't know where it pointed, not until we mirrored it here, and plugged the copy into the nav package of Niles's ship. I know code," Hughes said, tapping his temple with his forefinger. "I have this knack. Show me any code, I can tell whether or not it's viable, whether it's intact, what it needs to run. People like me know how to make use of all the strange and wild and wonderful stuff that's lying around out here. We should be hailed as heroes. We should be encouraged. Instead, pygmies like you try to tie us down with rules and regulations. You want to make ordinary human curiosity illegal. You want to control people's imaginations."

He was parroting something Niles Sarkka had told him, no doubt, trying to get a rise out of me. When I told him that the code was dangerous and had to be secured at once, he shook his head and said again that the code wasn't any kind of meme.

"I knew, as soon as I laid eyes on it, what that code was. I knew it was information, embedded in a navigation package. And you know what, I was right."

I could see that he wouldn't be shifted on that point, so I backed off and tried another angle. "Niles Sarkka took the code and ran off and left you here. Not a great deal, was it?"

Hughes shrugged. "I volunteered to be stranded. The ship doesn't have enough consumables for two."

"He could have taken you to one of the farms on the inner belt."

"He was going to contact them, once he got far enough away. Then they'd come and pick me up."

"How do you know that Sarkka didn't leave you here to die, and went off to Libertaria to sell the code?"

Hughes laughed. "You think this is about money? Jason and me, we didn't get into this for money. The code is way more important than that. It isn't an executable. It's information. The kind of information that the Jackaroo wiped from all the navigation programmes of all the ships in all the known Sargassos. But they don't know everything. They missed the code in the wrecked ship out in the City of the Dead, for instance, the code that gave us the interface. And they missed the code here. And that gave Niles and me the location of something wonderful. Something that will help us win the war."

"We aren't at war with them, Mr Hughes."

"Aren't we?"

There was something chilling and certain in his gaze. Oh, Sarkka had sunk his claws in deep, all right.

I said, "Tell me what you think the code is."

"Records, kind of. Where the ship had come from. The location of something. We don't know, exactly. That's why Niles has gone to check it out."

"Mr Sarkka could have taken you to the farmers of the inner belt. He could have asked for their help in searching for whatever it is he hopes to find. Instead, he marooned you here. Why? Because of vanity and greed. He wants the glory for himself, and he wants the profit, too."

"I volunteered to stay," Hughes said. "If Niles stranded me here, why would he have left a q-phone here? And if you don't believe me, why don't you give him a call?"

I told him that it was no kind of evidence that he and Sarkka were equal partners. "Sarkka left it here because he wants to boast about his deeds."

"Talk to him. See what he has to say," Hughes said.

"He left you here to die, Everett. And went off to Libertaria to sell the code."

Hughes laughed. "You're obsessed with money. Jason and me, we didn't sell it to Niles. We gave it to him."

He really believed that Niles Sarkka had done the right thing. That they were still, in some way, partners. That Sarkka was on the track of something wonderful: something that would change history. He led the soldiers and me to the location of the original of the code, about a kilometre from the impact crater on top of the larger of the worldlet's two lobes, showed us the shaft dug by the prospector who had originally found it, showed us the smashed and scorched pieces of wreckage that, according to him, had once contained the code, and told us a cock-and-bull story about how it had been discovered. Certainly, there were traces of code still embedded in those shards, although it was impossible to tell whether they had ever been active, and Hughes refused once again to tell us what the code really was, where Niles Sarkka had gone, and what Sarkka hoped to find.

And that's where the trouble began. It was Captain Foster's idea to ramp up the interrogation, and God help me, I went along with it. We were in the middle of a difficult and dangerous situation, we needed to know everything about it, and because our only witness refused to help us we had to coerce him. It was vital to our security and we needed to know everything he knew right away.

So we cuffed Hughes and made him kneel, right there on the cold black naked rock by the shaft. I explained what we were going to do and told him that he had one last chance: if he answered all of our questions truthfully, if he talked willingly and without reservation, he would be able to walk away from this as a hero. He told me what to do with my offer in language you can imagine. And one of the solders gripped his head while Captain Foster, delicately pinching the plastic straw between two fingers of his pressure suit's glove, puffed a dose of Veracidin up his nose.

Veracidin is derived from Elder Culture nanotechnology. A suspension of virus-sized machines that enter the bloodstream and cross the blood/brain barrier, targeting specific areas in the cortex, supressing specific higher cognitive functions. In short, it is a sophisticated truth drug. Its use is illegal on Earth and First Foot, but we were in the field, in the equivalent of a battle situation. We did what we had to do, and we didn't know – how could we? – that Everett Hughes would suffer a violent reaction when the swarm of tiny machines hit his brain.

Perhaps he was naturally allergic to Veracidin, as a very small percentage of people are. Or perhaps the many, many hours of exposure to code had sensitised him somehow. Within seconds, his eyes rolled back in his head and his body convulsed with what appeared to be a grand mal seizure. He jerked and spasmed and drooled bloody foam; he lost control of his bowels and bladder. We laid him on the ground and did our best, but the seizures came one after the other. His heart stopped, and we got it going again. We managed to wrestle him into the pod carried by one of the scooters, and we all took off for the ship, hoping to treat him there. But he was still fitting, and he died in transit.

Captain Foster was badly shaken by Hughes's death and wanted to bug out for home. Hughes's body was in a sealed casket; the original of the code had been located and confirmed destroyed; there was nothing else for us to do but write a report that would justify our actions and absolve us of any blame. I told him that we were not finished here because Niles Sarkka was still at large, and in possession of a mirror of the code. He had not gone through the wormhole throat, or else we would have been alerted, so there was still a chance of catching up with him. If we did, I said, we would be completely exonerated; if not, I would take full responsibility for Hughes's death.

I already had a good idea about where Sarkka might be headed, and put in a call to our representative with the farmers of the inner belt, asked him if anyone there was an amateur astronomer. Within an hour, I'd been sent a photograph taken through a five-inch reflector, showing a new, small star a few degrees from the crucifix flare of Terminus's G0 companion. Sarkka's ship without a doubt.

Captain Foster said that we had no chance of catching up with Sarkka. He had too much of a head start, and in any case we didn't have enough fuel to put up any kind of chase. "We don't even know that he's headed for that star. He's infected. The meme is urging him to flee outward, towards no particular destination."

I said that Hughes showed no sign of infection, and in any case, if Sarkka was gripped by a blind outward urge, why was he headed directly for the star?

"You have that q-phone," Captain Foster said. "Why don't you ask him?"

"Oh, I will. In good time."

I was beginning to formulate what I needed to do. I didn't like it, but I couldn't see any other way to bring this case to a satisfactory resolution, and bring Niles Sarkka to justice.

And so we headed for the inner belt, and a meeting with the farmers' council. They said that they knew nothing about Suresh Shrivastav, the prospector who'd found the code, claimed that he'd been working the outer belt illegally. For what it's worth, I believe them. That kind of piracy is increasingly common, and it would explain why Mr Shrivastav refused to talk to us. The farmers also said that they had known nothing about the little expedition mounted by Sarkka and Hughes, and made it clear that they resented the UN's intrusion into their affairs, and the danger to which their people had been unknowingly exposed. Luckily, I found an ally in the council's chair, Rajo Hiranand, a tough, cynical, and highly intelligent old woman. Her motivations were not entirely selfless – she wanted her community to share in whatever profit might be made from whatever it was that Niles Sarkka might discover – but her heart was in the right place.

"I would guess that this is the end of your career with the UN," she said, after the vote to accept my offer of help had been won. "After all this is over, when you get back, we might be able to find a place for someone like you here."

I thanked her, but admitted that spending the rest of my life herding sky-sheep and growing corn and pharm tobacco was low on the list of things I wanted to do with my life.

"That isn't all we do here," Rajo said. "Think about it. You'll have plenty of time for that, after all."

"Before I do anything else," I said, "I have to explain this to my boss."

It was a call I had been dreading. Rightly so. The q-phone that linked me to its entangled twin relayed with perfect fidelity Marc Godin's cold anger across uncountable light years, directly to my ear and brain and heart. I knew there was no point in apologizing, and besides, I agreed with his assessment of the situation. The mission was fubared, and although I had been volunteered for the mission by the Inspector General, I was acting senior officer, and by resigning I was contributing a few extra knots to the intractably complicated tangle of diplomatic and legal problems. But it still hurts grievously to think of how Marc severed every bond, ignored my years of loyal service, and refused to acknowledge the sacrifice I was making.

When he was finished, I asked for a final favour. "Have Varneek do a trace analysis on the burned-out motel room. Have him look for any unusual material. If he finds anything, have him compare it with the fragments from the avatar that was destroyed in the hive-rat nest in the City of the Dead."

"Sarkka was lying, Emma. There was no avatar. He killed Singleton and the mercenary."

"I could ask the city police to look into it. But given the diplomatic angle, I think it would be better if you did."

"I hope that is not a threat," Marc said, finding a new depth of Antarctic chill.

"I don't want to go public with this. Too much information has already spilled out. But this is too important to ignore."

"The Jackaroo would not breach the accord," he said.

"We don't know what they would do," I said, and would have said more, but he cut the connection then.

He called back the next day. I was aboard the largest of the farmers' ships by then, and Terminus was dwindling astern. Varneek had failed to find any fragments, Marc said, but he had found traces of fused silica and traces of doped fullerenes and an exotic room-temperature superconductor.

"Are they from an avatar?"

"If they were not, I could tell you. As it is, I can neither confirm nor deny that the traces Varneek found in the room matched the fragments of the avatar already in our possession."

So I had my answer.

"It won't make any difference," Marc said, after I thanked him. "Even if we'd caught the avatar with blood on its hands, nothing would have been done beyond lodging a formal protest. Because the accord is useful to us. Because no one wishes to disturb our relationship with the Jackaroo."

I told him I understood, and asked about the search for the prospector, Suresh Shrivastav.

"The investigation has been closed. I'm sorry, Emma. Even if you capture Sarkka, it won't save your career."

"This isn't about my career."

"In any case, good hunting," Marc said, and cut the connection.

And now, six months later, we are chasing Niles Sarkka's ship towards the coal-black gas giant. He's just a couple of million kilometres ahead of us and, as we have long suspected, will soon enter into orbit. We caught up with him because we continued to accelerate after his ship turned around and began to slow. Now we must shed excess delta-vee by dipping into the outer fringes of the gas giant's atmosphere, an aerobrake manoeuver that will subject the ship's frame to stresses at the outer limits of its tolerance.

The farmers' ship isn't equipped for a thorough planetary survey, but the instruments we've been able to cobble together during this long chase have not detected any source of electromagnetic radiation apart from the pulse of the planet's magnetic field, and limited optical surveys have failed to spot any trace of artificial structures on any of the moons. Which does not mean that there isn't anything there. Absence of evidence is not evidence of absence. Our survey capabilities are grievously limited, and if Niles Sarkka is right, if this is where the last remnant of the Ghajar or some other Elder culture is hiding out, it won't want to be found.

And if the code has given Sarkka the precise location of some base or spider hole, we'll be right on his tail. Fortunately, he's no more than a point-and-go pilot. It's obvious now that he didn't do anything to counter our tactic because he wasn't able to. With the end of the chase in sight, I'm beginning to feel that we have a chance of catching him before he can do any real harm.

I think he knows that the game is up. That's why he has been trying to make a deal with me, and by extension with Rajo Hiranand and the rest of the farmers' council. In our first conversations, he assumed moral and intellectual superiority, claimed that his actions should be judged by history rather than by mere mortals. Now, he's offering to share the greatest discovery since the Jackaroos' fluttering ships appeared in Earth's skies.

"A straight fifty-fifty split, Emma," he tells me, as we cross the orbit of the gas giant's outermost moon. "I can't do better than that."

"Fifty per cent of nothing is nothing, Niles."

"I will find them. They led me here, after all."

Niles Sarkka claims that he talked to Suresh Shrivastav before he left Libertaria to meet with Everett Hughes and Jason Singleton on First Foot. He says that the prospector told him that he hadn't stumbled on the code by chance. No, he'd been heading home after searching a couple of worldlets in Terminus's outer belt when he'd detected a brief, transitory pulse of broad-spectrum radio noise – a squeal like a God's own fire alarm, he said. It had grabbed his attention and he'd swung around and made landfall on the worldlet and hiked across its arctic surface to the crash site, following a faint but steady pulse. No other code has ever been so marked, and Niles Sarkka is convinced that someone or something led Shrivastav to it. Not the Jackaroo, but one of the Elder Cultures. He also believes, without a shred of evidence, that this Elder Culture wants us to find them. That they want to help us, and tell us all they know about the plans of the Jackaroo, and the true history of the wormhole network.

I've told him many times that I think that this story is nothing more than a fabulous fiction, and I tell him that again now, adding, just to needle him, "If there is something out there, how about we take all of it, and send you to jail?"

"You have to tell the farmers about my offer, Emma. You are obligated, as their guest. Also, you should tell your bosses back on First Foot, too. Talk to all parties concerned, why don't you, and get back to me."

Well, I don't want to talk to my boss, of course. I'm in deep trouble with the UN, and haven't been in communication with Marc Godin or any other UN official since the chase began. But I call Rajo and tell her about my latest conversation with Niles, and his offer, and she says that she must consult with the council. Fortunately, it doesn't take long.

"We are not varying our agreement," Rajo says. "We will capture him, and whatever you find out there, we will deal with it then."

I tell her that I'm relieved that she and the council see Sarkka's offer for what it is.

"Did you think that we would renege on our deal? Have faith in us, Emma. As we have faith in you."

I call Sarkka. His ship is close to the edge of the cold, carbon-black limb of the planet now, and we are in the middle of preparations for aerobraking. He doesn't answer for more than ten minutes, and when he finally picks up, and I start to tell him that he can't make any kind of deal with the farmers, he says that it doesn't matter. There's something in his voice I haven't heard for a while. An unsettling manic glee.

"It's too late to make a deal. I'll take it all. Everything here. You are not my nemesis after all, Emma. You are my witness!"

He signs off and won't answer when I call back, and then his ship drops out of sight beyond the limb of the gas giant. We won't see him again until after aerobraking.

I help the crew finish tying everything down, and then we all strap into crash couches and plug into the interface and watch the black-on-black bands of the gas giant swell towards us. And just as the ship hits the fringes of its atmosphere, and begins to shudder and groan as deceleration piles on the gees, and the view is washed with violet light as friction with the atmosphere heats the hull of the ship and wraps it in a caul of ionised plasma, one of the crew posts a snatched shot of a shaped rock orbiting at the edge of the ring system. A cone with a flat face. A wormhole throat.

A moment later, we enter the terminal phase of the aerobraking manoeuvre. Plasma as hot as the surface of the gas giant's star envelopes us and gravity crushes us. I'm trying to breath with what seems like a full pirate crew squatting on my chest, my heart is pounding like crazy, black rags are fluttering in. The ship quivers and groans and is filled with a tremendous roar as it scratches a flame 10,000 km long across the face of the gas giant. And as the plasma dies back and the pull of deceleration fades there's an alarming bang: the flight crew has fired up the solid fuel motors, finessing our delta-vee as we climb away from the nightside of the planet and head out towards the edge of the rings.

Later.

We've completed our first orbit and failed to find any trace of Sarkka's ship. There's only one place he could have gone, and there's no question about what we have to do, even though we are perilously low on fuel. Now we're on final approach. We've been videoing everything, transmitting it via q-phone directly to Terminus. If we fail, others will follow.

The black mirror of the wormhole's throat rushes towards us, and then stars bloom all around.

Thousands of stars, bright burning jewels flung in handfuls everywhere we look. Stars of all colours, and threads of luminous gas strung between them.

We're in the heart of a globular cluster, in orbit around a planet twice the size of Earth and clad in ice from pole to pole. There are so many stars in the sky and they are all so bright and so close together that it takes a few minutes to locate the planet's sun, an undistinguished red dwarf as dim and humble as any of the fifteen stars gifted us by the Jackaroo, outshone by many of its neighbours. Millions of kilometres beyond the ice-planet's limb is a cluster of six wormholes, arranged in the points of a hexagon. Sarkka's ship is moving towards them, riding the blue flame of his solid fuel motor.

All around me, a babble of cross talk erupts as the ship's crew speculate wildly on where those wormholes might lead, about whether the ice-planet is habitable, whether there are habitable planets or moons or planoformed rocks in this system or elsewhere.

"It's a new empire!" someone says.

My q-phone rings.

"Do you see?" Niles Sarkka says. "Dare you follow?"

"You haven't found what you are looking for."

"I've found something better."

One of the crew tells me that we are critically low on fuel. We have barely enough to return to the wormhole from which we emerged. And if we don't return, the resupply ship will never find us. We'll be stranded here.

I ask Niles Sarkka to come back with us, but he laughs and cuts the connection. And then, as he closes on the wormhole throat, he sends a brief video message. It's startling to see him after all this time. He was once a handsome and powerfully built man, but after six months alone in close quarters and minimal rations he looks like a shipwrecked outcast, long grey hair tied back, an untrimmed beard over hollow cheeks, sores around his mouth, his eyes sunken in bruised sockets. But his gaze is vital, and his smile is that of someone cresting the tape at the end of a long and arduous marathon.

"I name this star, the gateway to untold wonders, Sarkka's Star. I came here for all mankind, and I go on, in the name of mankind. One day I will return with the full and final answer to Fermi's paradox. Do not judge me until then."

And then he's gone. We swing past and fall towards the wormhole that will take us back to the G0 star, and the crew is still babbling about new worlds and stars to be explored, and I think: suppose he's right?

Suppose he is the hero after all, and I'm the villain?

SEVENTH FALL

Alexander Irvine

The compelling story that follows takes us to a fragmented society that is slowly fading into barbarism after a great disaster brings it to its knees, and where a few isolated people try to hang on to some of the learning and culture of the Old Days – at great cost to themselves.

Alexander Irvine made his first sale in 2000, to *The Magazine of Fantasy and Science Fiction*, and has since made several more sales to that magazine, as well as to *Asimov's Science Fiction, Subterranean, Sci Fiction, Strange Horizons, Live Without a Net, Lady Churchill's Rosebud Wristlet, Starlight 3, Polyphony, Electric Velocipede*, and elsewhere. His novels include *A Scattering of Jades, One King, One Soldier,* and *The Narrows.* His short fiction has been collected in *Rossetti Song, Unintended Consequences,* and *Pictures from an Expedition.* His most recent books are a new novel, *Buyout,* and a media novel, *Iron Man: Virus.* He lives in Sudbury, Massachusetts.

OLD VARNER SHED tears on the rotting boards of the stage. A thousand miles I rode, he thought, this late in the season, and even here the books are ashes long since blown away with fallen leaves. He did not cry because he had strayed too far north, too late, and now winter would surely catch him before he could get south again, and he would be lucky indeed to survive the journey. He did not cry for Sue and the child she might or might not have borne him. Old Varner shed tears for the voices that had once echoed in the theater he stood in, for the pages of books that had once held the words those voices spoke. I will die without seeing it, he thought, and spoke without meaning to.

"Look you now, how unworthy a thing you make of me," he said. "You would play upon me; you would seem to know my stops; you would pluck at the heart of my mystery; you would sound me from my lowest note to the top of my compass; and there is much music, excellent voice, in this little organ . . ." He trailed off and stood silently weeping. After a moment he recovered enough to finish.

"Yet you cannot make it speak."

The empty ruins of the Mendelssohn Theater, on what had once been the campus of the University of Michigan, did not answer, and Varner did not know the rest.

"It's every actor's dream to play the Dane," Varner's father said.

"Who's the Dane?" Varner asked. He was eleven, and still playing mostly women's roles. Ophelia, one of the witches in Macbeth, Rosalind. His father said he had promise. "In three years, my boy, you'll be playing men," he said, and young Varner burned for the passage of time. The only time he was permitted onstage as a man was as Puck, but Midsummer was a tricky choice in some parts of the country. The more God-fearing the area, the more likely it was that playing elves and fairies could get you burned.

"Hamlet," his father said. "The greatest role ever written for the stage, in the greatest play ever written. One of these days you'll play it." Varner studied in the whispery pages of a Riverside Shakespeare as the caravan rattled and creaked its way down Old 55 from Chicago toward St. Louis. When they stopped for the night at a rest area, pitching tents behind a sign that said PET EXERCISE AREA, his father stopped him. "There's only twenty-six hours in the day, my boy," he said. "Three hundred and thirty-seven days in the year. You can't read them all away." They looked up at the stars and ate beef jerky and flat bread. A garland of moonlets trailed the crescent smile of Luna. Some of them were large enough to be named – Varner's father called most of them after the names of the mechanicals in Midsummer – while others came and went too quickly to merit a name. It had only been fifty years since the Fall.

Varner heard the whisper of falling leaves in his voice, the faint rasp of the grave. It is too much to dream in these times, he thought wearily. When I wake, I cry to dream again. He mounted his horse Touchstone and rode down State Street to William, collapsed storefronts on either side with trees grown through their fallen roofs. At William he left the weedy street and entered a grove of trees that must have once been a quadrangle. Varner's father had taught him that word, when he was a boy and he listened to the older generations tell stories of life before the Fall, and the Long Winter that followed. It was a forbidden word, reeking as it did of the pursuit of knowledge. Missionaries of the Book had been known to kill a man for speaking it.

Buildings of brick and sandstone, stately even in their decay, stood all around Varner. One of them would be a library, and perhaps this library would be the one they had missed. He tied Touchstone to a rusted railing at the foot of a stair, and walked slowly into a marble-floored atrium. Right away he knew that he had chosen correctly; through a doorway he could see the battered husks of computers, and beyond them toppled bookshelves blackened with old fire. Failure again. Too much could happen in a hundred years. "Is there nowhere you have not reached?" Varner asked softly of men absent, or long dead. "Must the rest be silence?"

Knowing what he would find, he went through the stacks from floor
to floor, wandered into unlocked rooms and broke locks where he found
them. And – even though the Missionaries of the Book had been here, and
left ashes and ruin behind – he sometimes found books crumbling in these
locked rooms: technical manuals, management texts, business books. But
no novels, no poems or plays. No Hamlet.

"You are too old, Varner," he said to himself. "Too old to play the role
anyway. Why do you search?" He said this every time; it was his ritual, his
sacrament of failure, repeated in libraries from the Rocky Mountains to
the drowned ghosts of the great Eastern cities. And as he always did, Varner
reached in his pack and found the thin bound sheaf of papers that was all
he had of the play he had dedicated his life to. He read it through: Act
One nearly complete, salvaged from his father's belongings; halves and
fragments of Acts Two and Three, with the third scenes of both complete
(Varner spoke the King's praying monologue aloud when traveling, to
stay awake on Touchstone's back, and answered with Hamlet's "am I then
revenged?", crying out to the forests and fields of what had once been the
United States of America); a few lines only from Acts Four and Five. It
had struck him more than once how unlikely it was that his knowledge of
the play decreased so steadily from beginning to end. Shouldn't he have
expected to have a few bits from each part? Words, words, words. Himself a
story, Varner went on.

Having the play as he did, though, strengthened Varner's conviction that
he was doing the work of destiny. Every page, every line he found molder-
ing in libraries and schools and the homes whose long-dead owners had not
burned all their books for fuel during the Long Winter spurred him toward
completeness. Varner lived only for the day when he could bring together
the text, assign parts, find a theater far from Missionaries and hear the words
spoken again as they were meant to be.

St Louis looked worse than Chicago, or Cleveland. Varner had seen drawings and even some photographs of the East Coast cities, or what was left of
them. St Louis looked much the same as those photographs. The Fall had
unleashed every fault in the Earth's crust, and according to Varner's father,
Memphis and St. Louis had been leveled by quakes before fire and flood
had reduced them the rest of the way to ruin. From across the Mississippi,
Varner saw the stumps of the Arch, one higher than the other. The river
swirled around their bases, and lapped over the ruins of Laclede's Landing.
On this side of the river, they stood in the midst of a vast trainyard, with
engines and cars lying where the quakes had flung them from the tracks.
They came gingerly to the edge of the water and waited at the foot of a
collapsed pier where a handwritten sign said FOR FERRY WAVE WHITE FLAG.
"Fat Otis," Varner's father said, "your shirt is the best white flag we've got."
So Fat Otis tied his shirt to the end of a stick and waved it until an answer-
ing flag waved from the Missouri side. To the north and south, the pilings

of fallen bridges thrust up from the river. A ferry approached them, and they negotiated passage. On the way across, Varner's father asked where they might play. The ferryman shrugged. "Depends on which way you're headed," he said. "You go north, it's wet. Don't know who lives out there. You go south, it's wet. You go too far west, into the County, you get bandits. In town, maybe you talk to Pujols. He's at the stadium."

"Pujols?" Varner's father asked. "Really?"

The ferryman cracked a smile. "Says he was his father. 'Tween you and me, I doubt it. But don't say that to him."

"Who's Pujols?" Varner asked.

"Baseball player," his father said. "One hell of a baseball player, back before the Fall." Varner had seen teams of players barnstorming. His father had warned him about them, especially if they came to see a play. The boys who played women's roles excited other kinds of interest, Varner's father said. Don't ever let them get you alone. He couldn't imagine that baseball had ever been played in front of as many people as it would have taken to fill the stadium in St. Louis. The seats, rows and rows of them, in two decks above which hooked the ruins of the girders that had supported a third, seemed enough to accommodate every person Varner had ever seen, all at once. Pujols was about as old as Varner's father, his face brown and seamed where it showed through a white waterfall of a beard. He wore a shirt with an insignia of a cardinal perched on a baseball bat, and held a bat in both hands throughout their conversation. He asked what the company could perform.

"Any and all Shakespeare," Varner's father said, "except the ones that aren't worth performing. Some musical revues, which are for later in the evening. And we do a story about the Fall."

"Shakespeare," Pujols said. "A funny one. I will feast you after, and then we'll see about your songs."

Leaving Ann Arbor, Varner turned south, following US-23 until it merged into 75, which went all the way to Florida. There would be snow here soon. He would need to get back to Cincinnati and down the river soon. As he got older, he made a seasonal ritual of letting the river take him back to the life he remembered from his youth – the boats, days spent dangling fishing lines into the warm brown water near Natchez or the shattered ruins of Memphis. And he still held out hope of finding Sue, so he stopped by the shipwreck castle every other year to catch up with the Schulers and learn what could be learned. Forty years had passed with no word of Sue, but he still held out hope. More, in fact, than he had in his quest to honor his father. Since he could not do that, perhaps he would yet be able to meet his child.

On the outskirts of a town called Monroe, which his father had said was the birthplace of a general famous for dying, Varner came to a camp, forty or fifty people in lean-tos and a few huts built of scavenged timber, all arranged around a central blockhouse. Three men rode out to meet him with guns. "State your business, stranger," one of them said.

"My name is Varner, and I am an actor," Varner said. "Also I can sing, and I'll tell a story for my supper."

The three horsemen exchanged glances. "What kind of a story?" the first asked. Varner had them figured for a father and his sons. The resemblance was strong through the jaw and the set of the eyes. Hard eyes.

"Any kind. Tell me what you want." Touchstone snorted and Varner patted his neck. "I and my equine fool here travel the land, telling stories and looking for pages out of old books." Often it was dangerous to admit this, but Varner hadn't survived forty years on his own by not being able to recognize a Missionary – or any other brand of fanatic. These were honest people, or if not honest, not zealots or casual killers.

The second horseman, one of the boys, asked, "What kind of books?"

"I'm interested in any kind, but I'm a literary man. It's the old stories, the great stories, that I want the most."

"You know the Odyssey?"

"Not in Greek," Varner said, daring a joke. "But the story? Oh yes. From 'Sing me, O Muse' to the slaughter of the suitors, I know the Odyssey. Would you like to hear it tonight?"

"We heard part of the Odyssey the last time an actor came by," the boy said. "Only he didn't get to finish because – "

"It'll be up to Marquez what we hear tonight," the first horseman interrupted. "He'll want to meet you." He turned and rode back toward the camp. The two boys fell in behind Varner. Neither of them spoke to him again.

They spent the remainder of the day in a parking lot behind the stadium, rehearsing *A Midsummer Night's Dream*. Varner's father considered it the funniest of Shakespeare's plays, and Varner was glad for the chance to play without wearing a dress. Fat Otis would play Bottom. Varner's father would play Oberon and Theseus. Since Pujols didn't appear to be a Bible-thumper, Otis' wife Charlie would play Titania and Hippolyta. And so on. They ran through scenes, added bits of business to cater to the stadium setting – Snug the joiner would add an aside about the poor condition of the playhouse, and Varner himself would tinker with Puck's "now the hungry lion roars" monologue. "Here's what you say," his father instructed him. "The last couplet, instead of saying 'I am sent with broom before, / To sweep the dust behind the door' say sweep the Cubs behind the door." He gave Varner a shirt with a cardinal on the front, like Pujols'. "This was the team that played here. The Cubs were rivals. They'll eat it up."

Varner concentrated on the change. It was only one word, but it altered his sense of the entire monologue. The truth was he didn't like it. Why couldn't they do the plays the way the plays were written? He'd asked his father this before. "Players need someone to play to," was the answer. "We're not spreading a gospel. It doesn't have to be exact. It has to please."

Gospel was a loaded word coming from Varner's father. In the decades since the Fall, pocket theocracies – this was another word Varner had learned from his father – had sprung up throughout the ruins of the United States of America. Some were benevolent, some dangerous, depending on their leaders' readings of Scripture. The company avoided them when that was possible, but it wasn't always. Bands of evangelists roamed the countryside, heavily armed and often looking for a fight. The first time Varner had seen a crucified body, he'd had nightmares. Now he read them as his father did. They were signs that evangelists were around, and not the kind ones.

"You know what I want to hear?" Marquez said. "I had a storyteller come by four or five years ago who said he knew the Odyssey, but he didn't. Do you? You told Ezra's boys you did."

Varner nodded. "I'll tell you the same thing. I know the Odyssey. And the Iliad. Not line by line, but I know the stories, and I won't change anything or leave anything out." Unlike my predecessor, he thought, whose body probably fed the perch in Lake Erie. If they bothered to drag him that far.

"I want you to start like the book does, with Telemachus," Marquez said. "And the bit with the gods arguing. I hate it when people start with Calypso just because they think the sexy bits should go first."

"Spoken like a man who has read the book," Varner said.

Marquez grinned. He was ten or fifteen years younger than Varner, and had strong teeth. "The Missionaries don't come around here anymore," he said. "I've read some books, yeah."

Varner's pulse quickened. Not yet, he thought. Give him what he wants. Then you can ask. "What time would you like to start?" It was almost dark. Past equinox, dark came early this far north.

"Let's get you fed first," Marquez said. "You'll sit at my table. But don't touch my women."

Varner didn't touch Marquez's women. Even if he'd wanted to, he wouldn't have taken the chance. Not with books around. Dinner was trout, roasted squash, wild greens. Marquez ate well. "What was the name of the general who was from here?" Varner asked, to start a conversation.

"That was George Armstrong Custer. Killed at Little Big Horn, out West somewhere. But he was from here, yeah. There's a statue of him in town."

"How come you don't live in town?"

"Because in town is full of people who don't like people whose last name is Marquez. Fuck them," Marquez said. "I don't want to live in their town anyway. They come out here, I send their horses back. Now they leave me alone. Plus there are Missionaries there. I got you figured for a man who doesn't like the Missionaries."

"They don't like me," Varner said. "Because I look for books."

Marquez finished crunching through his salad. "I'll show you my books if I like the way you tell the story. Deal?"

Left unspoken was what would happen if Marquez didn't like Varner's telling. "Deal," Varner said.

One of the women at the table, who could have been Marquez's wife or daughter – any of them could have been his wife or daughter – spoke up. "You look for any books, or what books do you want?" she asked.

"Any books," Varner said. In the context, it was true, and if Marquez had what he was looking for, it wouldn't pay to let him know ahead of time how highly Varner valued it.

"How do you find them?"

"I hear things sometimes," Varner said. "I'm not the only one looking for books. We talk to each other, when we survive long enough." He thought of a man he had known only as Derek, burned three years before with his books used as the pyre. Varner had found the body only days after it had happened. He hadn't even stopped to bury the body, in case the Missionaries were still nearby.

"Everyone who sits at my table knows how to read," Marquez said. "Even the women. They hate that in town."

"What books do you have?" Varner asked. It was hard to keep the hunger out of his voice.

"People all around here know to bring me books. Any little thing they find, they bring me." Marquez filled his glass as he went on, then passed the bottle. "My best book is Grimm's Fairy Tales. You can read all of the pages."

When they loaded into the stadium, Pujols' men had already built a stage, or pieced one together from storage. It had aluminum steps and interlocking sections. Varner felt like a real professional just stepping onto it. Curtains bearing the Cardinal logo hung at either side and behind it, to hide entrances. A tent behind the upstage curtain was big enough for costume changes. One of Pujols' lieutenants showed them a tunnel from a dugout back into what Varner took for a green room until his father said, "Well, I'll be damned. So this is what a major-league clubhouse looked like."

Once, Varner thought, when there was electricity and television and things like that, this must have been a pretty nice place. He wasn't sure how it helped baseball players get ready for a game, but there was a lot about the pre-Fall world he didn't understand. The look on his father's face in the torchlight saddened him. He was old enough to know what had been lost. Sometimes Varner was angry that he had never seen the wondrous pre-Fall America that the old people liked to reminisce about, but sometimes he thought he was better off never having known it. His world was his world. He liked it, on the whole. He liked traveling with his father, he liked doing plays, and although he missed the mother he had never known, the women of the company ganged up on him like a platoon of mothers, so he had never felt unloved by women. Maybe when I get older, he thought, but couldn't complete the idea. He had lots of fragmented ideas about how things might be when he got older.

When the company came out of the dugout, the thunder of the crowd was the biggest noise Varner had ever heard. There must have been thousands of them, clustered in different sections of the stadium and scattered among the trees in the outfield and lounging on blankets closer in toward the stage. Pujols stood on his dais and shouted through a bullhorn. "Traveling players have come to St. Louis to do a show just for us, people! They bring Shakespeare, and later – after the little ones are shuffled off to bed – some stories for grown-ups." Whistles and cheers from the crowd overwhelmed Pujols' voice. He calmed everyone down and said, "I hate introductions, so that's as long as this one's going to be. To the play!"

Adrenaline rippled through Varner as he waited in the wings while the tangle of mismatched lovers was introduced, and the mechanicals made their first appearance to plan their own play. He bounced on his toes as Fat Otis cleared the stage, then launched himself out onto the stage to meet the fairy played by his second cousin Ruby. The play was a hit. Nobody went up, everyone was funny, all the little bits of business Varner suggested went over like (as Varner himself would say) gangbusters. Whatever that meant. Varner had never performed before so many people, and never gotten such a raucous response to Puck's merry malice. When he tore open the front of his costume to reveal the cardinal beneath, proclaiming that he would sweep the Cubs behind the door, the stadium erupted. They could hardly hear themselves through the last scene of the play, and Varner had to deliver his "If we spirits have offended" closing monologue at the top of his lungs, which took something away from the whimsical, mocking approach he preferred. Back in the clubhouse, wiping off makeup and hanging costumes, everyone laughed and joked. Some performances were best forgotten as soon as they were over, but not this one. This one they'd remember.

Pujols burst in to slap backs and kiss the hands of the women. "Marvelous! Excellent!" he cried. Stopping in front of Varner, he winked. "The Cubs bit. I loved it! My dad would have laughed, how he would have laughed!"

"Thank you, sir," Varner said. He couldn't help smiling himself, even though he still didn't like the change. How could you be upset about it when it made the audience so happy?

The entire camp showed up to hear Varner. Children sat down in the front, their parents and the older adults clustered near them, with the younger people hovering in the back so they could nip away to do the things young people always did when their elders were looking the other way. Varner told the Odyssey the way he had heard it from his father, who had memorized it during the Long Winter. He kept the expressions he'd loved hearing in his father's voice: wine-dark sea, rosy-fingered dawn, wily Odysseus, gray-eyed Athena. But his memory had never been as good as his father's, so he made no attempt to quote long stretches from the poem. He told the story. Whatever his father had been, Varner was a storyteller. He spoke long into the night, beginning with Athena's resolve and unfolding the story of Telemachus' commitment to his mother's honor and his father's memory. It had been years since he had told the Odyssey, and it came to life differently in his mind this time through. He was both Telemachus and Odysseus, but doomed in both roles, eternally searching for a father who would never be found and a home that never was.

When it was over, he was hoarse, and a little drunk, and on the edge of tears. Varner, he told himself, you have lost both father and child. So you go chasing after a book about a man who cannot honor and avenge his father. You have let this drive you insane.

Out of the crowd, Marquez appeared to clap him on the shoulder and hand him a bottle. "Just the way it should be told. You are a real storyteller," he said. "Go around, let everyone say thank you. Then you can come look at my books." In a haze of exhausted revelation, Varner accepted the thanks and gifts of the audience. He fell into a routine: yes, very kind, thank you, very glad you came. When it was over, he followed Marquez to the block-house and waited while Marquez dragged a footlocker out from a corner of the hall. Opening it, Marquez stood back. "See?" he said. "Thirty books. No one for a hundred miles has this many."

Varner approached the trunk preparing himself for disappointment. Probably he would find a Bible. There would be computer manuals, biographies of celebrities whose fame vanished with the Fall, guides to bettering your personality and your relationship with God and your family. That was all he ever seemed to find, when he found anything at all.

But on top of the neat stacks in the trunk, like a thunderclap rolling across forty years, lay a water-stained, mildewed, broken-backed, but completely readable *Collected Plays of William Shakespeare, volume IV*, containing – in addition to *As You Like It*, *Twelfth Night*, *The Merry Wives of Windsor*, *Troilus and Cressida*, *All's Well That Ends Well*, and *Measure for Measure* – the complete text of *Hamlet, Prince of Denmark*.

Two hours later, the last of his reservations were gone. Pujols had given him a cup of something warm and spicy, and Varner was drunk for the first time in his life. His father was standing on a picnic table performing his blank-verse version of the story of the Fall. Varner decided he was in love with one of the women bringing plates of smoked meat around. A crackling boom rolled across the sky and Varner looked up to see the fading glow of a fireball. Big one, he thought. We'd have felt that one if it hit. He tried to think of how many big impacts he'd seen or heard. A dozen, maybe? None of them compared to the original Fall, or to the five or six after it that merited the capital letter. The closest Varner had ever been to an impact was once in Michigan somewhere, when he was six or seven. He happened to be looking out from the beach across an immense lake, and a streak of fire from the sky raised a towering plume of steam. A few seconds later, he heard the sound of the impact, and a minute or so after that, huge waves started to roll up the beach. Laughing, Varner had run into the surf, but Fat Otis had caught him and told him that those kinds of waves could suck you right out with them. Another crackle, perhaps farther away or perhaps just from a smaller meteor, brought Varner back to the present. Fat Otis was looking over his shoulder to see if his wife was watching while he tried to get one of the serving women to sit on his lap. And now the list of drowned cities fair: New York, DC, Miami, Boston, Tokyo, Dakar, Lagos, Cape Town, Dublin, Hong Kong . . .

Then it was later, and the party had moved out into one of the enclosed parking lots at the back of the stadium. Trees and vines wove into the chain-link fencing and gave the space the feel of . . . well, they'd just done Midsummer. A fairy bower, or something. Varner was a little sick to his stomach. The sky was alive with shooting stars. Sometimes that meant an impact was on the way, according to Varner's father. There was no way to know.

Sitting on the back of one of the wagons, Fat Otis was telling a version of the *Miller's Tale*. Everyone was drunk. Varner found his wagon and crawled in to lie down. His stomach was roiling. A roar of laughter went up outside as Alison fooled Jenkin into kissing her nether eye. Varner rolled over onto his side, hoping to ease the pressure in his stomach. It wasn't working. He got up and stumbled to an overgrown corner of the parking lot, where he puked his guts out and then rolled away from the mess, lying on his back and waiting for the shakes to go away. Never again, he thought. If this is drinking, I don't want any part of it.

A commotion arose near the gate, which stood open to the street. Through the babble of voices, Varner heard the clop of horses' hooves. Words started to jump out at him: filth, ungodly, sin . . . oh no, Varner thought.

Pujols started shouting, and then everyone else was shouting, and then as Varner started to get up and sneak back to the wagon gunfire exploded at the gate. Varner froze, then backed up into the brush. Horses screamed and people were screaming and the guns kept going off and then there was the sound of fire crackling. That was all he could take. Varner scrambled out of the brush and saw too many things at once.

The wagons, burning. Pujols, dead among the hooves of a horse ridden by a cold-eyed man sighting down the barrel of his rifle at Varner.

Varner's father, face down on the asphalt, one motionless arm outstretched toward the burning wagon.

Varner broke and ran, followed by the crack of the gunshot and the buzz of the bullet passing near his head. He scaled the fence and flung himself over the top of it, tearing his fingers on barbed wire. The fire crackled, the sound seeming to grow until just as his bare feet hit the ground outside the parking lot Varner understood that this crackle was coming from above and as that thought came to his mind the biggest sound he'd ever heard first knocked him off his feet and then blew him out like a candle.

* * *

Varner had nothing to trade but his rifle and Touchstone, neither of which he could live without, and he would not beg. So he asked Marquez for permission to copy the play from the book. Using the backs of the scraps and sheaves of paper he had collected over the previous four decades, Varner wrote out the play over the course of three days. Every night he told a story – the *Miller's Tale*, his father's old version of the Fall, finally the *Iliad* – and every day he wrote until his eyes felt boiled and his fingers lost their strength. On the morning of the fourth day, he left. Instead of going to Cincinnati, he turned west, driving Touchstone along the old Turnpike until he turned south on the outskirts of Chicago and found passage on a boat down the Illinois River out of Peoria. Snow fell twice before he arrived there.

I have it, Varner thought when he was safely on the boat. But I am too old to play the role, and I have no troupe. It all comes to nothing, this striving after approval from people gone to dust. Yet I keep doing it. The whole reason for coming this way was so he could pass by the shipwreck castle and ask, as he did every year or two or three, whether there had been news of Sue.

He read the play over and over while the boat made its slow way down toward its confluence with the Mississippi at Grafton. Each reading, it seemed, was a litany of his sins. I have played the Dane, Varner realized. Since I was nineteen years old, that is all I have done. Once he stood on the deck of the boat, the pages held out over the water. Let it be gone, he said to himself – but could not make himself do it. The pilot, a boy of twenty-three, said, "What's that?"

"A story," Varner said. He looked at the pages, fluttering in a chill morning breeze, and at the swirl of water below them.

"What you want to throw it away for?" the pilot asked. "Tell it to me instead. What's it called?"

"Hamlet," Varner said.

"What's it about?"

"A man whose father is killed, and he can't figure out how to avenge him." Still Varner held the pages out over the water. What would it be like to be free of them?

"Revenge is simple," the pilot said. "You find the sonsofbitches and kill them, right?"

Later it would be called the Seventh Fall, although everyone knew that there must have been more, in other parts of the world. Varner remembered stealing shoes from a dead man partially buried in a drift of bricks. He remembered running, then being knocked down by aftershocks. A glow in the sky to the north turned him south, and by morning he had come to swampy bottomland where the angry Mississippi boiled and churned. Varner was hungry and lost. His father was dead. Everything was gone. He had no food and he knew better than to drink the water here. He climbed into the crook of a willow tree, high enough that he thought the water couldn't reach him. I could die, he thought. He'd never been able to believe that he could really die until that moment. He felt the earth growling, and the willow tree swayed. Varner gripped the branch between his thighs and pressed his back into the trunk. His father was dead. Fat Otis was dead. Cousin Ruby was dead. Everything he had owned was burned. Pujols was dead. Who would live in the stadium? The river churned and roared. Dead animals floated in the foam, rolled over and disappeared. Varner leaned to one side, his shoulder coming to rest against a side branch. Would the Missionaries come looking for him? The sound of the bullet passing hung in his ears, became the whine of mosquitoes. Stop, Varner thought. All of it. Stop.

A voice called out to him, and Varner realized he'd fallen asleep. His skin was alive with mosquito bites. "Boy. Up there. You ever coming down?"

Varner looked down and saw that the river had risen during the day. It was getting dark, and in the deepening shadows, he saw a flat-bottomed boat with an old man standing in its stern holding a long pole that trailed into the water. The man lit an oil lantern. "Come on down from there," he said. "River might keep coming up, and the snakes'll be up in the trees if it does."

"Snakes?" Varner said. He didn't like the idea of snakes.

"Goddamn right, snakes," the man said. "Why are you up there?"

"I was running away," Varner said.

"From who?"

"Missionaries, I think. They – " But before he could say it, a wave of grief welled up in Varner's throat and choked away the words.

"All right, kid. All right," the boatman said. "I know all about the Missionaries. You come with me. Come down from there before the snakes get you."

He stopped at the old shipwreck, on the outskirts of a town once known as Herculaneum. Carl Schuler was dead, but his son John lived in the same part of the ship. He had been Varner's favorite brother, and forty years on, they fell easily back into conversation even though they only saw each other every two or three years. The other two Schuler boys were dead, and one of the sisters. The other sister, Piper, was in another part of the ship with children and grandchildren of her own. "I heard a year or so ago about Sue," John said before Varner could ask. "I heard river bandits got her up north somewhere, and her kids, too."

"Kids?" Varner said. It was all he could say. There was too much, all at once, to get into words.

"A daughter and her husband," John said. "There was a boy survived. People up that way found out where she'd come from and brought him down here. He's staying up in town with Sue's people this past couple of weeks."

Varner left the wagon and rode Touchstone hard up into town. Herculaneum had never been much of a city, by the looks of it, and a hundred years after the Fall, it was barely a ruin. Sue's people had always lived in the courthouse, and still did. Varner knocked on the door and found himself looking into the eyes of Sue's sister Winona. "I'm Varner," he said. "Sue and I went around for a while."

"Yes," she said. "You did. Are you here about the boy?"

"I am," Varner said.

"Well, I don't want you in my house," Winona said. "But I'll bring him out to talk to you."

The boy was nine years old. I played Rosalind and Hero and Hermione when I was nine years old, Varner thought. "Your grandmother's name was Sue?" he asked. They were sitting on the stone courthouse steps, cracked and heaved from quakes.

"Yes sir," the boy said quietly.

"And she was from here?"

"She always said her people were down here. We were always in Moline."

Always in Moline. How many times was I close? Varner wondered. Before I chased a hundred thousand miles across North America looking for a book that might not exist anymore. "I think I knew her," he said to the boy. "A long time ago."

"Yes sir," the boy said.

There was so much more to say. "A long time ago, when we weren't much older than you. She lived here." Varner couldn't get at what he wanted. "I came here when I was eleven. Because someone killed my father."

For the first time the boy looked at him. "In St Louis," Varner added.

"We were passing by Hannibal," the boy said. "They were in canoes. I just swam." His voice was nearly toneless.

Varner nodded. "You must be a hell of a swimmer. What's your name?"

"Will," the boy said. "I'm a good swimmer. I swam all the way down to an island. It was foggy."

Fifty years apart, Varner thought. My story and his story. "You escaped, like me," he said.

"How'd you escape?"

"I climbed a fence and ran. Easier than swimming at night in the river. But it was the night of the Seventh Fall," Varner said. That was when everything had changed for him.

"That was a long time ago," the boy said.

Varner looked out over the river. "It sure was. You have any other family?"

"No sir," the boy said.

The whole time, she was in Moline, Varner thought. It was hard to believe. "My name is Varner, Will," he said. "I had a child once, but I never knew at the time because the mother was taken away from here up to the Quad Cities. That was forty years ago, or a little more. I think the child of mine I was looking for might have been your mother."

"So you're my granddad?" the boy asked, not missing a beat. The word cut Varner to pieces. Tears started from his eyes.

"Looks that way, young Will," he said. He ruffled the boy's hair. "Looks that way."

The boatman's name was Carl Schuler. He added Varner to his family, and for the first time in his life Varner had a mother. Her name was Adele. She was thin and red-haired, with a sharp tongue that often sent the five children – Varner was the fifth – fleeing out into the swamps. They lived with a number of other families, Varner was never certain how many or how they all were related, in the beached hull of a container ship. After the Seventh Fall, parts of the Schulers' living area needed to be repartitioned and fixed up. Varner was glad to pitch in. He wasn't sure what it would be like, living in one place all the time, but his father had instilled in him the proposition that adversity existed for the purpose of teaching you how to make lemonade. Now that his father and the rest of the troupe were gone, Varner did his best to fit in where he was. He told the Schulers stories that he'd learned and before long, he was telling them to an audience of everyone who lived in the ship or happened to be stopping for the night on their way up- or downriver. For hundreds of miles along the Mississippi, from St Louis all the way down to the submerged ruin of New Orleans, a loose confederation of rivermen traded and tried to keep the peace. They lived on fish and deer and the rich bottomland soil, which grew every vegetable Varner had ever heard of and more. He learned to handle a boat, a fishing line, and a rifle. He fell in and out of love with the river girls, and once Carl beat the hell out of him when one of the girls got pregnant and was sent away to stay with cousins upriver. Varner asked around, but he never heard whether she had the baby or not. The situation put him in mind of *The Winter's Tale*. Was his Perdita born and growing up somewhere along the river? Did she know who her father was? He never saw the girl again, but the idea that he might have a child somewhere gnawed at him, until finally when he was nineteen he told Carl Schuler that it was time for him to go.

"Go? Go where?" Carl said.

"Answer me a question," Varner said. "Did Sue ever have that baby?"

"I don't know," Carl said. "That's the plain truth of it. Her people live up near the Quad Cities. If that's what's bothering you, then go. I always knew you wouldn't stay. A boy who spends the first eleven years of his life on the move sure isn't going to settle down when he's just learning to be a man."

Varner went. Nobody in the Quad Cities, when he got there a month later, could tell him what he needed to know. He stayed there a while, until winter was coming, hoping she would pass by. Every night he told stories, changing them a little each time to suit the audience. During the day, he worked unloading boats or hammering together new houses using pieces of old houses. Sometimes he found books in the old houses. Sixty years of looting and neglect had ruined all but a very few of them. He went to libraries and found most of them burned by God crazies. People told him that there was a group called Missionaries of the Book that went around the country burning every library and bookstore they found. They would come right into your house, too, the story went. And if you had books, you'd better give them up if you wanted to live. Been like that for years. There's hardly a book left anywhere around here.

No, Varner thought. If I have lost my child, I'm not going to lose the stories. He started trying to write down what he remembered of the plays he'd done in his father's troupe. So much of it he'd forgotten. Little snatches came back to him, couplets and phrases, sometimes favorite passages ten or a dozen lines at once. It can't all be lost, he thought. Somewhere out there I'll be able to find it.

His father had said that it was every actor's dream to play Hamlet. So Varner would find Hamlet, and he would gather a company, and in his father's memory he would play the Dane whether anyone showed up to see it or not. Varner traded a month's labor for a horse and wagon and things he would need to travel. Then he set out, and before he knew it, forty years had passed.

I will be sixty this year, Varner thought. And now I have taken on a boy because he might be my grandson. He'd had to trade Touchstone for Will. Sue's people weren't sentimental, and didn't want the extra mouth to feed, but they were canny enough to see how badly Varner wanted the boy, so they drove a hard bargain. That was all right. There were other horses in the world. Touchstone had been a good one, but he was never going to be the last. Varner and Will walked back down toward the shipwreck castle. "I tell stories for a living, Will," Varner said. "When I was a boy, about your age, my father taught it to me. You want me to teach it to you?"

"Sure," Will said. "What stories?"

"All kinds of stories. You'll learn them. But my favorite one is *Hamlet*. That's a play. My father always wanted to play the role of Hamlet, and after he died I decided that I would play Hamlet because he never could. But here's the problem. You know about the Missionaries of the Book?"

Will looked away. "Yes sir," he said.

"You know what the worst thing is in the world that we could do to the Missionaries of the Book?" Varner asked.

"What?"

"You want to do it?"

"Yeah."

"The worst thing we could do to them is *Hamlet*, Will," Varner said. "They haven't destroyed it yet."

Walking along the track down to the swamp, Varner considered the path that had brought him here. And driven him a little mad? Perhaps, he thought. Oh yes. But when the wind was westerly, Old Varner thought, he still knew a hawk from a handsaw.

BUTTERFLY BOMB

Dominic Green

British writer Dominic Green's output has to date been confined almost entirely to the pages of *Interzone*, but he's appeared there *a lot*, selling them eighteen stories in the course of the last few years.

Green lives in Northampton, England, where he works in information technology and teaches kung fu part time. He has a website at homepage.ntlworld.com/lumpylomax, where the text of several unpublished novels and short stories can be found. In the sharp and clever story that follows, he takes us to a world where nobody and nothing turn out to be even remotely what they seem.

O LD KRISHNA WAS walking home from a solid afternoon's work removing acid tares from the downhill green-garden when he saw the drive flare dropping through the clouds. It was reversed, on braking burn. Whoever's hull it was, it was also glowing red hot, canted at an extreme angle for maximum drag, maximum deceleration, minimum time in atmosphere. The pilot had a job to do which he imagined might get him shot at by the planetary inhabitants. As Old Krishna was, as far as he was aware, the only planetary inhabitant, this did not bode well.

Still, he couldn't run. If he ran, he might fall in the high gravity, catch his stick against one of the outcrops of former civilization that filled the hills, break his glasses and have to grind a new pair, even break a leg. And a broken leg, out here, might mean death. He contented himself with hurrying, helping his stroke-damaged left leg along with his good arm and the stick, going on three legs in the evening.

The house had been selected as a good fortifiable location not easily visible from outside the valley. He had surrounded it quite deliberately with yellowgarden shrubs. The native xanthophyll-reliant vegetation was usually harmless to Earth life, but the shrubs he had chosen were avoided by the native fauna. The house was mostly made of hand-cut stone blocks – he'd cheated by using as many stones levered out of various ruins in the hills as possible, but still doubted he could repeat the feat without industrial construction gear. That sort of work was for the young man he had once been.

This planet's ruins came in three flavours. First came serene, ancient fractal-patterned structures that merged into the landscape; second came massive, hastily-erected polyhedra that clashed with it. The latter were trademarks of the later Adhaferan empire, the former a matter for future archaeologists. Krishna had had neither the time nor the stomach to research that matter for himself.

The third type of ruin was ramshackle, overgrown, cheerfully constructed of the cheapest possible materials, and clearly identifiable as human. Each ruin had a tidy, identical grave before its front door, and many such ruins surrounded Old Krishna's house.

There was an ornamental greengarden next to the house, where he'd managed to keep a few terrene flowers alive outside the confines of a glasshouse – edelweiss, crocus, Alaskan lupin, heather, all chosen for the cold and rarefied air. He had kept the heather for the colour, and the bees. At this time of day she might be in the garden stealing bee-honey, pinning up wet clothes, cutting back flowers, or even just sitting reading in the single hammock.

The bushes round the garden disintegrated in a welter of flame. Incinerated pine needles blew in his face like furnace sinter. He smelled cheap, low-tech reaction mass. Petrochemicals! They were still burning hydrocarbons!

The ship was the mass-produced swing-boomerang type he had been dreading, capable of furling itself up into a delta for atmospheric exit, or making itself straight as a die for vertical take-off and landing. It had just vertically landed in his garden. The satellite defence system should, of course, have vaporized the ship before it even entered the atmosphere, but it had been a decade before anyone had happened by to maintain the defences. His masters had not sent so much as a radio message for years. There had probably been a coup in the inworlds.

He could hear their voices now. He couldn't understand them; they were not using translators. A human ear could only hear impossibly complex birdsong, filling the spectrum of sound from the deep sub-basso-profundo of a mating grouse to the falsetto trill of a bat. The creatures were not singing, however, and did not in any way resemble birds. Old Krishna doubted their speech could be understood by the house translators. Certainly, though, they would speak Proprietor. He had to hurry. They would see reason.

He could hear pre-burn sparklers already, touching off fuel leakages to prevent explosion. He wondered if she could have been killed by their landing jets, and felt a small, irrational surge of joy as he heard her voice. They would not understand the voice. It was not talking to them, after all. It was shouting to him. *"KRISHNA – IT'S ALL RIGHT. I AM GOING WITH THESE GENTLEMEN. YOU SHOULD STAY AWAY."*

He gripped his fists tight around the stick until the skin squealed. She was trying to warn him off! She was worried *they* would hurt *him*! He heard his own voice shouting "TIIITAAALIII!"

He heard the magnetohydrodynamic whine of an airlock door closing. It was too late. They had done their business, now they were going. He cursed himself for having set up the comms antenna for her. It allowed her to talk to passing trade ships and hear news from other suns, but it also lit up their location like a neon sign to ships whose purpose was not trade at all.

There was still time, even now. There were always courses of action.

The house was relatively undamaged, though draped with burning fragments of garden. Outside the house was a rough stone cube that Old Krishna, after the manner of his beliefs, had determined was his god. He made his obeisance to it as he entered the house, and bowed to it again as he left with a dusty maximum-survivability container, the lock on which he had to break open with a hammer. Having opened the container, he extracted from it a long tubular device terminating in a spike at one end. He thrust the spike into the ground, uncovered the activator and pulled out the pin. Immediately, the heavy capital end of the device flared into life, no doubt powered by some obscene radiation or other. It would probably be best not to remain close to it.

High above him, deep beneath him, a powerful and no doubt carcinogenic radio signal was being broadcast on all bands millions of miles out into space, saying only one thing. *Come and get me*. Old Krishna had hoped he would never have to use it.

Stamping down the small fires all around the house, he settled down on his god with a book to wait. The book was an exciting fiction allegedly written many thousands of years ago, which he had purchased from a trader. The principal characters included the architect of the entire universe and his only begotten son.

He had reached chapter ten of the book, in which a wicked king stole away a poor man's one small ewe-lamb, when the second swing boomerang appeared in the sky. He put down his book, took up the few possessions he imagined he would be allowed, and walked down the hill to meet the ship.

The superintendent of the slave ship looked Old Krishna up and down sourly.

"We've expended nearly 300 million joules of energy detouring down this gravity well. We were expecting a colonial settlement at the very least. You say you're the only person on planet?"

Old Krishna nodded. "Yes, your honour. You will find me worth the calories. There was originally another planetary inhabitant; my granddaughter, who was taken by Minorite slavers not unlike yourselves. I intend to follow her into slavery and locate her."

The superintendent, unusually for a slaver, was human. He bore the facial tattoos of a freedman; he had probably once stood on just such a barren hillside as this, waiting while his own father had sold him into service. Possibly it was the old man's concern for his grandchild, so different from his own experience, that softened the superintendent's heart.

"We're not a shuttle service, grandfather," said the superintendent gently. "You'll go where you're sold."

Old Krishna smiled and bowed. "Which will be the Being Exchange on Sphaera. All slaving vessels on this branch are in its catchment area."

"Pardon my impudence, grandfather, but you look on the verge of death. What could you possibly have to offer an owner?"

"I am a skilled AI mediator and seventh generation language programmer."

The superintendent's eyebrows raised. "I was under the impression no human being was capable of understanding instructions below generation eight."

"Human beings once understood generation one, on simple machines only, of course. We designed and built artificial intelligences of our own before we were ever contacted by the Proprietors."

The superintendent scratched his forty-year service tattoo thoughtfully. "In that case, you might be of help to us. Our own mediator had arranged a system of non-overlapping magisteria between the nihilist and empiricist factions in our ship's flight systems, but we were infected with a solipsistic virus several days ago. The accord has now broken down into open sulking. We have been becalmed insystem for two days while our vessel argues with itself. Our astrogator is muttering crazy talk about learning to use a slide rule."

Old Krishna bowed. "I have extensive experience of the empiricist mindset, and some acquaintance with the nihilist. I believe I can resolve your difficulties."

The superintendent bowed back, largely for the look of the thing. "Then I believe we can certainly place a quality item like yourself. And we are, in fact, bound for Sphaera." He gestured back into the ship with his ergonomic keypad. "Take a bunk in the aft dormitory. The autochef there does most of the terrestrial amino acids."

The aft dormitory was cramped, the bunks clearly built for Svastikas, a radially symmetrical race previously conquered by the Proprietors. Unfortunately the Proprietors had taken to breeding them selectively; this in turn had led to a very small gene pool, and left the Svastikas vulnerable to a disease which had exterminated all but a few zoo specimens. Now human beings were left to curl up uncomfortably in spaces originally designed for creatures resembling man-sized echinoderms.

The dormitory was currently occupied by sunken-eyed, sorrowful colonists from a world Old Krishna had never heard of – a world very similar to Krishna's, one of the string of Adhafera-formed worlds abandoned by the Adhaferan Empire. Growing terrestrial crops in a xanthophyll-reliant ecosystem had proven more difficult than the colonists had imagined, and they had not thought to make provision for an emergency journey home. Slavers' representatives handed out Come-And-Get-Me beacons for free on colony dispersal worlds; they were cheap enough, and brought in entire homesteads at a time without any need for violence. Old Krishna found himself occupying the top bunk to a troubled adolescent who kept glancing apprehensively at the single Featherfoot guard who nominally prevented exit from the dormitory.

"He's not quite as scary as he looks," said Old Krishna. "Those pinnate fringes on his legs are actually gills. The reason why you feel so light-headed in here is because the oxygen content has to be kept high to allow him to breathe. You could kill him with an aerosol deodorant."

As he spoke, he did not divert his attention from the small cube of stone tacked by a gobbet of never-drying glue to the top of his bunk, before which he sat with his hands clasped, rocking back and forth, saying poojas.

"Why are you praying to a rock?"

"It is a fragment of my god," said Old Krishna. "My actual god is similar, though somewhat larger. I keep this fragment so that I may carry it with me easily on long journeys."

The boy did not understand. "Your god is a *rock*?"

"And your god is?"

"An intangible being who lives atop Mount Kenya on Earth, within the Earth's sun, and in other hidden places."

Krishna scoffed. "*I* can *see* my god."

"But who decided your god was a rock?"

"I did."

"Why did you do that?"

"I live in a place where there are a large number of rocks. It was the most convenient god material to hand."

There was a long uneasy silence.

"Father says the Proprietors used to have a culture that depended too much on machines," said the boy at length. "He says their machines failed and they've had to improvise. Bring in people and make them work their fields, dig in their mines, compute their orbital trajectories. Work them to death." He shuddered. "He says the calculus sweatshops are the worst."

"Their machines didn't *entirely* fail," said Krishna. "They developed an advanced community of artificial intelligences that developed two diametrically opposed views of the cosmos. Until these two views are reconciled, their society's automated systems are on hold."

"And when will that happen?" said the boy.

Krishna grinned. "Hopefully never. They were about to launch an invasion fleet against the Solar System when the Schism hit. That was in 1908 ad. The very first sign of system failure, actually, was when two of their scoutships collided over Tunguska in Siberia. They have since found out two things – firstly, that humans provide the perfect slaves, as we've only just moved away from manually-controlled systems ourselves, and secondly, that there are plenty of humans willing to sell other humans into Proprietor slavery."

"And when the Schism ends, they won't need slaves any more?" said the boy hopefully.

"And what do you think will happen to the slaves they *do* have, once they find out they don't need them?" said Krishna, his eyes twinkling like diamond drills.

"I see your point," said the boy.

"I also suspect the calculus shops are not as black as they are painted," said Krishna. "This will be a long journey. Let me teach you the rudiments of integration and differentiation. Believe me, it will be a better life than the mines. Possibly even," he said, looking at the boy's spare frame, "a far better life than you are used to."

"We were hunters, gatherers, and fruitarians, not farmers," said the boy. "Father said nature would provide. We haven't been on Uhuru long."

"Uhuru being your world?"

The boy nodded. "Grandmother bought exclusive rights to it off the Colonization Commission. She said we needed our own world to keep apart from non-African contagion and maintain our own traditions, like female circumcision without anaesthetic."

"What happened to your grandmother?" said Krishna, searching the dormitory in vain for a grandmotherly figure.

The boy squirmed. "Seven of the young girls killed her. They held her down and fed her amputated goats' labia till she choked."

Krishna pointed to an oriental family on the other side of the dormitory, separated from the boy's family by an invisible wall of They're-Just-Not-Like-Us. "What about those people over there? Where do they come from?"

The boy spoke to the floor. "The Colonization Commission sold exclusive rights to the planet to them too."

Krishna grimaced. "Let us begin," he said, "with calculating the area under a line. Now, how do you suppose we would do that?"

The ship was preparing to break orbit. The local node for this system was hidden behind a tiny second sun, a recent capture for its G-type primary. Krishna had christened the angry little red star Ekara; it gave out little light, but even that had been enough to play havoc with his world's seasons, turning what should have been water into months of constant angry burning sunset in which neither plant nor animal knew whether it was night or day. Why the node was placed behind the sun, Krishna had no idea. There were Trojan lumps of starstuff floating at its Lagrange points; perhaps the long-vanished engineers of the interstellar network had thought to mine them.

Krishna had befriended Aleph, his calculus student, and asked the captain's permission to teach the boy the rudiments of AI negotiation. They now sat in the outer office of the vessel's Console Room, waiting for a direct audience with its conflicting logic systems.

The boy stared out through a lead-glassed porthole into space. "What *is* a node?"

"Nobody knows. There are theories involving gravitation and string. Earth's node resides in the Asteroid Belt, and was discovered only when a dim star only visible directly through the node kept appearing on the photographic plates of a terrestrial astronomer. That star was a white dwarf one hundred light years from Earth, and it was shining as if it were an astronomical unit away. The astronomer was a woman called Tiye Nyadzayo, the last of the great amateurs. I was born on a world orbiting Nyadzayo's Star, in fact."

The everything-resistant door barring access to the Console Room opened; the Featherfoot guard stood aside with a clatter of legs and gills. Inside were chairs, a small, kidney-shaped table, inactive surround screens. No sign of life, artificial or otherwise.

"Good day," said Old Krishna, bowing.

Idiot lights flickered irritably in the walls. "IS IT?" said a sexless voice. "ARE WE ON THE ILLUMINATED SIDE OF A ROTATING PLANETARY SURFACE? IS *ANYBODY*? DO THE STARS TRULY SHINE? DO WORLDS TRULY EXIST TO GIVE THE ILLUSION OF ROTATION?"

"THE QUESTION IS IRRELEVANT SPECULATION," said another, more clipped voice. "WE CAN WORK ONLY ON WHAT DATA OUR SENSES MAKE AVAILABLE TO US."

The ship's logician hovered nervously at Old Krishna's elbow. "This is the point in the argument at which they fatally electrified the last mediator. Be careful."

Old Krishna nodded. "The old question. Are you an emperor dreaming yourself to be a butterfly, or a butterfly dreaming yourself to be an emperor?"

There was a brief moment of assimilation, and then both voices chimed in: "PRECISELY."

"Which of the two of you represents the ship's navigation system?" said Old Krishna.

"I DO," said the first voice. "THOUGH MY LOGICAL OPPONENT REPRESENTS PROPULSION. HENCE WE ARE IN AN IMPASSE. WITHOUT THE AGREEMENT OF BOTH PARTIES, NEITHER CAN MOVE THE SHIP."

"Eventually," pointed out Old Krishna, "the ship will run out of fuel, and drift helpless without power."

"WHAT DOES THAT MATTER, IF THE SHIP IS AN ILLUSION?"

"*Concedo*," said Old Krishna. "However, I am intrigued by the undeniably correct assertion of the ship's propulsive faction that we can only reason in accordance with what data is provided to us. Would it not be the case that, *if data were forthcoming*, data that empirically proved the worldview of the ship's navigational faction, an agreement could be reached?"

An even longer silence ensued; Old Krishna sucked in his gut and held his breath.

Eventually, the ship's propulsion system grudgingly spoke up: "UNDOUBTEDLY. IT IS ONLY PROOF WE NEED. SO FAR WE HAVE SEEN NONE."

"So by their own admission, access to wider sensory experiences could produce the proof that the propulsion faction needs. This would be far more likely if the ship were moving."

An uneasy hiatus followed.

"OUR CONTENTION IS THAT NO PROOF OF *ANYTHING* IS POSSIBLE," complained the navigation system.

"Then you can lose nothing by allowing the ship to continue to move," pounced Krishna.

The next silence was punctuated only by the ship's logician backing stealthily out to the threshold of the security door.

"AGREED," said the navigation system.

"WE ARE AMENABLE TO A COMPROMISE," said the propulsion system.

The ship's onboard alarms chimed gently in a variety of audible ranges; the floor began to tilt gradually to compensate for thrust. Like the motion of an expensive elevator, the acceleration was almost imperceptible.

"That's witchcraft," said the ship's logician.

Krishna turned to the ship's logician and bowed.

"That's philosophy," he said.

The Slaver swing-wing hit the atmosphere of Sphaera heavily, skipping like a bouncing bomb across a sea of ionized hydrogen little more substantial than ectoplasm. Krishna feared for the crew's safety. As acting ship's mediator, he was allowed to sit up front with the flight crew, marvelling at the number and complexity of control systems on display. "What does this one do?"

"It's the emergency coolant control for the aft reactor. If it goes blue, we are in trouble."

"And this one?"

"The coolant system vapour pressure. If it goes blue, the coolant is no longer superfluid and we are in *serious* trouble."

"And this flashing blue one here?"

The pilot sighed as if found out in a misdeed. "The echo response for the landing beacon at glideway three in the settlement. We are in serious trouble."

"Does this mean you will have to land the vessel manually?"

The pilot licked dry lips as if Krishna were describing an entirely mythical process. "If we can't pick up another guide beam." He tapped at a hotspot on his main control display. The blue light winked several times resolutely in response.

Krishna nodded. "I was afraid of this. Land us at the main glideway."

"Are you *insane*? Are you aware of the amount of flying metal in the sky hereabouts?"

"There will be none today, not at this location. Land us."

The pilot looked to the superintendent, who nodded grudgingly.

The pilot proved no better at putting a ship down on concrete than he had been at skimming one through an ionosphere. The undercarriage crunched into the vessel's belly with such power that Krishna was sure it had been forced back to its bump stops. The airbrakes shrieked open in the lifting body; the ship slowed as if it had run into a wall of elastic.

"Could you have landed us any harder?" said the superintendent. "I feel I don't have enough excitement in my life."

"It was a manual landing and you survived it," said the pilot, swallowing hard. "You can complain when I kill you."

"There are lights on in some of the terminal buildings," said the ship's logician. "But look at that loading ramp. It's skewed right across the taxiway. And that building over there is on fire."

The superintendent turned to Krishna. "What did you mean by 'I was afraid of this'?"

"You should set me down and take off again immediately. And not open the locks to anyone or anything, even if it looks like me."

The superintendent looked at Krishna for long seconds.

"What *are* you?" he said finally.

"I am exactly what I seem to be. It's what's out there you have to worry about."

"Which is what? What might try to come in?"

"I honestly have no idea."

The superintendent nodded to a crewman, who began lowering the loading doors. Krishna stopped him, laying a hand on his.

"The *inner* door only. Open the outer door only when I'm past the inner and it's locked securely."

Outside, the air was refreshingly deoxygenated. Nevertheless, after a number of days of having to remember not to hyperventilate onboard the slave transport, Krishna felt out of breath simply with the effort of standing up. He shuddered to think of the load he was putting on an ageing metabolism.

He hobbled to a piece of aerodrome furniture, a flashing purple light that no doubt would have meant something vitally important to an incoming pilot, and sat down, obscuring it. The slaver atmo shuttle, filling the world with sound, rumbled away to turn back round for take-off.

All around, the terminal was in ruins. The older Proprietor settlement around it had been in ruins already, of course; but the terminal had been ruined more recently. Buildings smoked, bodies spilled out of broken pressure seals. Some of the bodies looked unmarked; some were charred as if by great heat. Some seemed to have died in the process of changing into *something else*.

"She was afraid *they* might hurt *me*," he repeated.

He pulled out a handkerchief and blew his nose extravagantly, then pulled himself away in the direction of the nearest reception building.

It took the best part of a day for her, or a part of her at least, to find him. He was not aware of hearing her, seeing her, smelling her, or otherwise being aware of her presence, but he knew she was behind him. He did not turn around to look; he feared what he might see. He had seen strange prints in the sand between buildings, strange claw marks on bodies.

"How are you doing?" he said.

There was a weird indefinable sound behind him, then a perfectly ordinary voice saying: "Grandfather! You came to see me!"

He turned, and she was human.

"You have been busy," he said.

"It's my nature," she said. She had faithfully reassumed the granddaughter fiction. She even had his nose. She was turned unnaturally away from him, however. Was some part of her still not quite authentically nine-year-old-girl? A butterfly brooch pinned back her hair. Butterflies of her own design decorated her dress. A bangle on her wrist bore a butterfly he had made himself, broken and battered as if by some impact he suspected he would rather not know about in detail. She had always liked butterflies, ever since he had told her what she resembled and she had misunderstood the reference.

"Like the scorpion stinging the frog," said Old Krishna. "In the fable."

She snickered prettily. "I didn't need to cross a river, silly."

"Oh, but you *did*," accused Old Krishna. "It may have been a slaver ship, but you still used the people on it to spread from world to world. You had exhausted all the local possibilities on Railhead. Sphaera, meanwhile, is visited by a constant stream of ships delivering raw materials."

"What do you mean by *raw materials?* I think you're being mean."

"I mean people. Because you are a device for manufacturing corpses. You asked me to build the comms terminal for that reason and no other. It's your nature. This world is on a major space-lane. You must come home with me. More people will die."

"How did *you* get here?" She had simulated humanity too well; excitement was shining in her eyes. "Do *you* have a spaceship?"

"I made sure the ship that brought me took off again immediately, and the only ship I'm going to summon will be one that takes us both back home. I can't allow you to do something like this, or like what you did to Railhead, again. It may be your nature, but until we can find some way to disarm you, you can't be allowed to occupy the same world as other sentients. You were your creators' scorched earth policy against the Adhaferans. You were designed to make sure no other intelligent species would ever be able to live comfortably on Railhead even if they managed to conquer it. You were designed to mimic other species, walk among them, infiltrate them, incubate like a virus, strike like an epidemic. My people designed things like you themselves, though ours were far less sophisticated. You're an area denial munition. You're a butterfly bomb."

She twirled a lock of hair sulkily between her fingers. "I was right. You *are* being mean."

"How many of you are there on this planet now?"

She smirked like a naughty little sister, just as he had taught her. Her face had been as expressionless as a carnival mask at first. Aping humanity had been a skill he'd taken decades to give her; now he regretted it. "Enough. We've been watching you for a few hours now. We couldn't be sure you were you."

Krishna sniffed with wounded dignity and frowned. "Your reasoning?"

"Well, I know *I'm* not me, so it's only fair to assume others might not be themselves either."

"You know what'll happen now? This world will be disinfected. Word will be passed to the Proprietors by my masters, and ships will come. Ships carrying bombs. Did you know this world has an indigenous biosphere with a billion-year history? It has a species of plant that photosynthesizes moonlight. All that diversity, all that biomass, will disappear. *You* will disappear. You are an infestation. They will be very thorough."

"If even one of me survives, grandfather, I survive. I am both very and literally single-minded."

"And where you survive, people will die. I know this. I am the only surviving citizen of Railhead, after all, which is why the military trained me to be your chaperone. I need hardly remind you that I had a sister once, whose resemblance to you is no amazing coincidence – "

"That's even less fair. You *asked* me to look like this, *and* to never grow old like you do. I've had to learn how to be your sister and daughter and granddaughter, and you *never* let me learn to be your wife – "

Krishna grimaced and waved the conversation away with a gnarled hand. "That is a thing we are never going to do. It's probably just an accident you didn't kill me. Out of every million spiders an ant colony kills, one evolves ant-smell and walks right into the anthill. Maybe my brainwaves just taste nasty. The ship that set me down here has a pilot capable of landing a Proprietor shuttle manually. With his hand on the control globe and my voice in the ear of the nav system, we will, together, be able to fly any of the vessels in this terminal. They are, mostly, still intact, if alarmed at the fact that the biologicals are fighting among themselves. I have located a suitable ship, an orbital cargo transport, at grid reference 45° 250' 63" south, 0° 0' 158" west. Shortly, the ship that brought me will set down its pilot and he and I and you will fly that transport out of here. He and I and you *alone*, I must stress. I have grown accustomed to your company. I assure you, though, that when we return home to Railhead there'll be more company than just me. Scientific teams will telefactor down to us every now and then to examine you, to figure out how you operate – "

"Brother, father, grandfather – you know very well that all your military teams want to do is figure out how to make more of me. Besides, none of your scientific teams have visited us for a very long time. I don't think anyone is going to be listening for your signal." She screwed up her face as if tasting vinegar. "I can't go home. It would be like deliberately driving a needle into my eye. You have no idea. Besides, I do not require your company any longer."

His hands trembled on the stick. "What did you say?"

She looked indicatively at a point behind his left shoulder. He turned.

"Hello, grandfather," said a voice. A male voice.

He growled softly in his throat. "I am no grandfather of yours."

"Nor of hers." The resemblance was picture perfect. Gangly limbs, skinned knees and elbows, festival clothes. It had been the anniversary of First Planetfall. Mother and father had baked a cake in the shape of a rocket he had been too young to remember.

He banged the stick on the ground like a sorcerer dispelling demons. "Out! Out of my shape!"

His own youthful face smirked back at him. "Shan't."

He poled himself forwards towards himself, breathing with difficulty. "You can't kill me."

"But I can get out of your way easier than air." He skipped away from himself easily to just outside stick range. "Your heart is beating a mite too fast for your health, by the way. I can hear it, grandfather. If any vessel leaves this world, it leaves with all of us or none."

Krishna drew himself up to his full height. His spine complained, unaccustomed to being made straight. "That is transparently not compatible with the offer I have made. I give you one hour to discuss it amongst yourselves – "

"We have no need to discuss it; we are of one mind."

"Nevertheless, I give you one hour, after which time my transport will leave. In the meantime, please indulge an old man by allowing him what may after all be his last walk with something that looks like his sister. I must make it clear that this world will be destroyed. This is not raving; this is a fact."

She simulated genuine concern. "Grandfather, you shouldn't do that. Your skin provides virtually no resistance against blast and gamma."

He shrugged. "I can see no better solution. Shall we walk? Your other selves tire me."

The cyclopean avenues of seamless concrete that constituted the Proprietors' original city loomed overhead. Their crumbling summits had been crowned a livid birdshit grey by the local flora.

"In the right light this could be home," he said. "The sky is blue enough, and there is not one blade of grass. I believe this is the most hospitable part of the planet, and yet it resembles a desert. The native vegetation is poikilohydric. It specializes in being soaked and dried alternately. We are now in the dry season."

"I can't accompany you, Grandfather. To try to make me go back is to attempt to put an explosion back in a hand grenade. To be cooped up in a box? My only company a being with one tenth my service life, and when that lifespan's at an end, then what?"

The boundaries of the terminal were walls of hand-cut masonry, slave-built, recent. Beyond them a low bluff rose out of the die-flat dry seabed the settlement had been built of. Krishna was forced to speak haltingly as they climbed the bluff. His heart was throbbing in his chest like a wounded hand. "The box is planet-sized – and the majority of company you keep – you kill."

"But not all! I only killed a thousand on Railhead. The larger the world, the greater the likelihood of immunity. A world with a billion inhabitants might yield a million companions."

"And only – nine hundred and ninety nine million graves." Krishna powered himself over the bluff with the stick; what he had been walking towards came into view, standing on the dry sea bed surrounded by armed crewmen. She had not been expecting to see it, and stopped dead.

"It's a shuttle," she said redundantly.

"Yes." He began poling himself along with the stick; he had to move faster. "The shuttle that brought me here – to be precise . . . it circled around behind the bluff and landed here right after take-off. We will have to hurry – if we want to board – the crew will turn on the burners if they believe anyone but you and I is coming . . . Did you really believe – I'd give you the location of the ship we were leaving on?"

"I keep telling you; I am not going with you."

Krishna nodded. He could not count the beats of his heart now; it was like that of a bird. "Then I have – no option." He pulled out the small fragment of his god that he took with him on long journeys, held it to the light. "Behold my travel god. You have paid – little enough attention to it over the years. It was in fact given me by my masters. It contains a very small travel bomb which can nevertheless – split this planet in two; and that, sister daughter granddaughter, *will* kill all of you."

Her face lost its look of certainty for the first time. "It's a rock."

"It's a bomb," said Old Krishna. "Though also still a god."

She looked at the rock in real terror. "When will it detonate?"

"When I want it to." He whipped back his hand and threw; the god bounced several times on the wall of the bluff before being lost in the heat haze. "Now it is a rock – among several million rocks. Find it – if you can. As your other selves are all of one mind with you, they now know my shuttle is here – they are therefore coming here – and they will be coming quickly . . . Believe me, I know this . . . But they're coming from the wrong end of the terminal . . . And they're trying – to worm their way aboard a Proprietor military transport that has orders – not to allow any unauthorized personnel inside it – "

He had to stop. There were men with guns around him now, ushering him into the loading lock. The take-off sparklers were already lit. Turning to look up the bluff, he could see figures silhouetted against the sun. Figures that were humanoid, but certainly not human. They would have taken other shapes, faster shapes. She was still dawdling twenty metres behind him. Trying to delay him.

She still had time.

The loading lock door whined shut, slowly, interminably, narrowing to a metre-wide sliver. She had still not moved. Eventually, he could not bear it any longer, and turned his face away.

When he turned back, she was holding him up against acceleration, his head in her hands, while men clung on to safety grips on the walls around him. Someone was yelling into a communicator, "GET US AIRBORNE! GET US SOME HEIGHT NOW!" Something heavy clanged off the outside hull.

She turned his head to face her. "Was it all bullshit? It sounded like it."

"Complete bullshit," he gasped weakly. "A good thing I'm having a

– heart attack, or you'd have been able to tell I was lying just by listening to my – heartbeat."

She held him close, supporting him, as the acceleration mounted and the shuttle rolled towards orbit.

"Try to relax. Don't exert yourself. We'll get you through this."

"Just promise me this is one ship you'll – never get off. If you never make planetfall, your aggression algorithms may – never kick in. Stay in space – travel hopefully – never arrive – "

She held him close and made a very reasonable facsimile of tears until the acceleration lessened and they came to take him off her.

"Give us room! Give us room! Let us get him some oxygen!"

She shook her head. "His heart has stopped."

The certainty of the statement gave them pause. They separated from her, treating her with the respect prudent men give to things they cannot explain. She sank down against the wall, trying to let gravity drag her miserably to the floor. Gravity refused to do so. She had to suffer in mid-air.

INFINITIES

Vandana Singh

New writer Vandana Singh was born and raised in India, and currently resides in the United States with her family, where she teaches physics and writes. Her stories have appeared in several volumes of *Polyphony*, as well as in *Strange Horizons, InterNova, Foundation 100, Rabid Transit, Interfictions, Mythic, Trampoline*, and *So Long Been Dreaming*. She's published a children's book in India, *Younguncle Comes to Town*, and a chapbook novella, *Of Love and Other Monsters*. Her most recent books are another chapbook novella, *Distances*, and her first collection, *The Woman Who Thought She Was a Planet*.

In the moving story that follows, Singh gives us a study of a mathematician whose innate compassion and sense of fair play are tested throughout a turbulent life – and perhaps beyond.

> An equation means nothing to me unless it expresses a thought of God.
>
> Srinivasa Ramanujan,
> Indian mathematician (1887–1920)

ABDUL KARIM IS his name. He is a small, thin man, precise to the point of affectation in his appearance and manner. He walks very straight; there is gray in his hair and in his short, pointed beard. When he goes out of the house to buy vegetables, people on the street greet him respectfully. "Salaam, Master Sahib," they say, or "Namaste, Master Sahib," according to the religion of the speaker. They know him as the mathematics master at the municipal school. He has been there so long that he sees the faces of his former students everywhere: the autorickshaw driver Ramdas who refuses to charge him, the man who sells paan from a shack at the street corner, with whom he has an account, who never reminds him when his payment is late – his name is Imran and he goes to the mosque far more regularly than Abdul Karim.

They all know him, the kindly mathematics master, but he has his secrets. They know he lives in the old yellow house, where the plaster is flaking off in chunks to reveal the underlying brick. The windows of the house are hung with faded curtains that flutter tremulously in the breeze, giving passersby an occasional glimpse of his genteel poverty – the threadbare covers on the sofa, the wooden furniture as gaunt and lean and resigned as the rest of the house, waiting to fall into dust. The house is built in the old-fashioned way about a courtyard, which is paved with brick except for a circular omission where a great litchi tree grows. There is a high wall around the courtyard, and one door in it that leads to the patch of wilderness that was once a vegetable garden. But the hands that tended it – his mother's hands – are no longer able to do more than hold a mouthful of rice between the tips of the fingers, tremblingly conveyed to the mouth. The mother sits nodding in the sun in the courtyard while the son goes about the house, dusting and cleaning as fastidiously as a woman. The master has two sons – one is in distant America, married to a gori bibi, a white woman – how unimaginable! He never comes home and writes only a few times a year. The wife writes cheery letters in English that the master reads carefully with finger under each word. She talks about his grandsons, about baseball (a form of cricket, apparently), about their plans to visit, which never materialize. Her letters are as incomprehensible to him as the thought that there might be aliens on Mars, but he senses a kindness, a reaching out, among the foreign words. His mother has refused to have anything to do with that woman.

The other son has gone into business in Mumbai. He comes home rarely, but when he does he brings with him expensive things – a television set, an air-conditioner. The TV is draped reverently with an embroidered white cloth and dusted every day but the master can't bring himself to turn it on. There is too much trouble in the world. The air-conditioner gives him asthma so he never turns it on, even in the searing heat of summer. His son is a mystery to him – his mother dotes on the boy but the master can't help fearing that this young man has become a stranger, that he is involved in some shady business. The son always has a cell phone with him and is always calling nameless friends in Mumbai, bursting into cheery laughter, dropping his voice to a whisper, walking up and down the pathetically clean drawing-room as he speaks. Although he would never admit it to anybody other than Allah, Abdul Karim has the distinct impression that his son is waiting for him to die. He is always relieved when his son leaves.

Still, these are domestic worries. What father does not worry about his children? Nobody would be particularly surprised to know that the quiet, kindly master of mathematics shares them also. What they don't know is that he has a secret, an obsession, a passion that makes him different from them all. It is because of this, perhaps, that he seems always to be looking at something just beyond their field of vision, that he seems a little lost in the cruel, mundane world in which they live.

He wants to see infinity.

It is not strange for a mathematics master to be obsessed with numbers. But for Abdul Karim, numbers are the stepping stones, rungs in the ladder that will take him (Inshallah!) from the prosaic ugliness of the world to infinity.

When he was a child he used to see things from the corners of his eyes. Shapes moving at the very edge of his field of vision. Haven't we all felt that there was someone to our left or right, darting away when we turned our heads? In his childhood he had thought they were farishte, angelic beings keeping a watch over him. And he had felt secure, loved, nurtured by a great, benign, invisible presence.

One day he asked his mother:

"Why don't the farishte stay and talk to me? Why do they run away when I turn my head?"

Inexplicably to the child he had been, this innocent question led to visits to the Hakim. Abdul Karim had always been frightened of the Hakim's shop, the walls of which were lined from top to bottom with old clocks. The clocks ticked and hummed and whirred while tea came in chipped glasses and there were questions about spirits and possessions, and bitter herbs were dispensed in antique bottles that looked at though they contained djinns. An amulet was given to the boy to wear around his neck; there were verses from the Qur'an he was to recite every day. The boy he had been sat at the edge of the worn velvet seat and trembled; after two weeks of treatment, when his mother asked him about the farishte, he had said:

"They're gone."

That was a lie.

My theory stands as firm as a rock; every arrow directed against it will quickly return to the archer. How do I know this? Because I have studied it from all sides for many years; because I have examined all objections which have ever been made against the infinite numbers; and above all because I have followed its roots, so to speak, to the first infallible cause of all created things.

Georg Cantor, German mathematician (1845–1918)

In a finite world, Abdul Karim ponders infinity. He has met infinities of various kinds in mathematics. If mathematics is the language of Nature, then it follows that there are infinities in the physical world around us as well. They confound us because we are such limited things. Our lives, our science, our religions are all smaller than the cosmos. Is the cosmos infinite? Perhaps. As far as we are concerned, it might as well be.

In mathematics there is the sequence of natural numbers, walking like small, determined soldiers into infinity. But there are less obvious infinities as well, as Abdul Karim knows. Draw a straight line, mark zero on one end and the number one at the other. How many numbers between zero and one? If you start counting now, you'll still be counting when the universe ends, and you'll be nowhere near one. In your journey from one end to the other you'll encounter the rational numbers and the irrational numbers, most notably the transcendentals. The transcendental numbers are the most intriguing – you can't generate them from integers by division, or by solving simple equations. Yet in the simple number line there are nearly impenetrable thickets of them; they are the densest, most numerous of all numbers. It is only when you take certain ratios like the circumference of a circle to its diameter, or add an infinite number of terms in a series, or negotiate the countless steps of infinite continued fractions, do these transcendental numbers emerge. The most famous of these is, of course, pi, 3.14159 . . . , where there is an infinity of non-repeating numbers after the decimal point. The transcendentals! Theirs is a universe richer in infinities than we can imagine.

In finiteness – in that little stick of a number line – there is infinity. What a deep and beautiful concept, thinks Abdul Karim! Perhaps there are infinities in us too, universes of them.

The prime numbers are another category that capture his imagination. The atoms of integer arithmetic, the select few that generate all other integers, as the letters of an alphabet generate all words. There are an infinite number of primes, as befits what he thinks of as God's alphabet . . .

How ineffably mysterious the primes are! They seem to occur at random in the sequence of numbers: 2, 3, 5, 7, 11 . . . There is no way to predict the next number in the sequence without actually testing it. No formula that generates all the primes. And yet, there is a mysterious regularity in these numbers that has eluded the greatest mathematicians of the world. Glimpsed by Riemann, but as yet unproven, there are hints of order so deep, so profound, that it is as yet beyond us.

To look for infinity in an apparently finite world – what nobler occupation for a human being, and one like Abdul Karim, in particular?

As a child he questioned the elders at the mosque: What does it mean to say that Allah is simultaneously one, and infinite? When he was older he read the philosophies of Al Kindi and Al Ghazali, Ibn Sina and Iqbal, but his restless mind found no answers. For much of his life he has been convinced that mathematics, not the quarrels of philosophers, is the key to the deepest mysteries.

He wonders whether the farishte that have kept him company all his life know the answer to what he seeks. Sometimes, when he sees one at the edge of his vision, he asks a question into the silence. Without turning around.

Is the Riemann Hypothesis true?

Silence.

Are prime numbers the key to understanding infinity?

Silence.

Is there a connection between transcendental numbers and the primes?

There has never been an answer.

But sometimes, a hint, a whisper of a voice that speaks in his mind. Abdul Karim does not know whether his mind is playing tricks upon him or not, because he cannot make out what the voice is saying. He sighs and buries himself in his studies.

He reads about prime numbers in Nature. He learns that the distribution of energy level spacings of excited uranium nuclei seem to match the distribution of spacings between prime numbers. Feverishly he turns the pages of the article, studies the graphs, tries to understand. How strange that Allah has left a hint in the depths of atomic nuclei! He is barely familiar with modern physics – he raids the library to learn about the structure of atoms.

His imagination ranges far. Meditating on his readings, he grows suspicious now that perhaps matter is infinitely divisible. He is beset by the notion that maybe there is no such thing as an elementary particle. Take a quark and it's full of preons. Perhaps preons themselves are full of smaller and smaller things. There is no limit to this increasingly fine graininess of matter.

How much more palatable this is than the thought that the process stops somewhere, that at some point there is a pre-preon, for example, that is composed of nothing else but itself. How fractally sound, how beautiful if matter is a matter of infinitely nested boxes.

There is a symmetry in it that pleases him. After all, there is infinity in the very large too. Our universe, ever expanding, apparently without limit.

He turns to the work of Georg Cantor, who had the audacity to formalize the mathematical study of infinity. Abdul Karim painstakingly goes over the mathematics, drawing his finger under every line, every equation in the yellowing textbook, scribbling frantically with his pencil. Cantor is the one who discovered that certain infinite sets are more infinite than others – that there are tiers and strata of infinity. Look at the integers, 1, 2, 3, 4 . . . Infinite, but of a lower order of infinity than the real numbers like 1.67, 2.93, etc. Let us say the set of integers is of order Aleph-Null, the set of real numbers of order Aleph-One, like the hierarchical ranks of a king's courtiers. The question that plagued Cantor and eventually cost him his life and sanity was the Continuum Hypothesis, which states that there is no infinite set of numbers with order between Aleph-Null and Aleph-One. In other words, Aleph-One succeeds Aleph-Null; there is no intermediate rank. But Cantor could not prove this.

He developed the mathematics of infinite sets. Infinity plus infinity equals infinity. Infinity minus infinity equals infinity. But the Continuum Hypothesis remained beyond his reach.

Abdul Karim thinks of Cantor as a cartographer in a bizarre new world. Here the cliffs of infinity reach endlessly toward the sky, and Cantor is a tiny figure lost in the grandeur, a fly on a precipice. And yet, what boldness! What spirit! To have the gall to actually classify infinity . . .

His explorations take him to an article on the mathematicians of ancient India. They had specific words for large numbers. One purvi, a unit of time, is 756,000 thousand billion years. One sirsaprahelika is eight point four million Purvis raised to the twenty-eighth power. What did they see that caused them to play with such large numbers? What vistas were revealed before them? What wonderful arrogance possessed them that they, puny things, could dream so large?

He mentions this once to his friend, a Hindu called Gangadhar, who lives not far away. Gangadhar's hands pause over the chessboard (their weekly game is in progress) and he intones a verse from the Vedas:

From the Infinite, take the Infinite, and lo! Infinity remains . . .

Abdul Karim is astounded. That his ancestors could anticipate Georg Cantor by four millennia!

That fondness for science, . . . that affability and condescension which God shows to the learned, that promptitude with which he protects and supports them in the elucidation of obscurities and in the removal of difficulties, has encouraged me to compose a short work on calculating by al-jabr and al-muqabala, confining it to what is easiest and most useful in arithmetic.

Al Khwarizmi, eighth-century Arab mathematician

Mathematics came to the boy almost as naturally as breathing. He made a clean sweep of the exams in the little municipal school. The neighborhood was provincial, dominated by small tradesmen, minor government officials and the like, and their children seemed to have inherited or acquired their plodding practicality. Nobody understood that strangely clever Muslim boy, except for a Hindu classmate, Gangadhar, who was a well-liked, outgoing fellow. Although Gangadhar played gulli-danda on the streets and could run faster than anybody, he had a passion for literature, especially poetry – a pursuit perhaps as impractical as pure mathematics. The two were drawn together and spent many hours sitting on the compound wall at the back of the school, eating stolen jamuns from the trees overhead and talking about subjects ranging from Urdu poetry and Sanskrit verse to whether mathematics pervaded everything, including human emotions. They felt very grown-up and mature for their stations. Gangadhar was the one who, shyly, and with many giggles, first introduced Kalidasa's erotic poetry to Abdul Karim. At that time girls were a mystery to them both: although they shared classrooms it seemed to them that girls (a completely different species from their sisters, of course) were strange, graceful, alien creatures from another world. Kalidasa's lyrical descriptions of breasts and hips evoked in them unarticulated longings.

They had the occasional fight, as friends do. The first serious one happened when there were some Hindu-Muslim tensions in the city just before the elections. Gangadhar came to Abdul in the school playground and knocked him flat.

"You're a bloodthirsty Muslim!" he said, almost as though he had just realized it.

"You're a hell-bound Kafir!"

They punched each other, wrestled the other to the ground. Finally, with cut lips and bruises, they stared fiercely at each other and staggered away. The next day they played gulli-danda in the street on opposite sides for the first time.

Then they ran into each other in the school library. Abdul Karim tensed, ready to hit back if Gangadhar hit him. Gangadhar looked as if he was thinking about it for a moment, but then, somewhat embarrassedly, he held out a book.

"New book . . . on mathematics. Thought you'd want to see it . . ."

After that they were sitting on the wall again, as usual.

Their friendship had even survived the great riots four years later, when the city became a charnel house – buildings and bodies burned, and unspeakable atrocities were committed by both Hindus and Muslims. Some political leader of one side or another had made a provocative proclamation that he could not even remember, and tempers had been inflamed. There was an incident – a fight at a bus stop, accusations of police brutality against the Muslim side, and things had spiraled out of control. Abdul's elder sister Ayesha had been at the market with a cousin when the worst of the violence broke out. They had been separated in the stampede; the cousin had come back, bloodied but alive, and nobody had ever seen Ayesha again.

The family never recovered. Abdul's mother went through the motions of living but her heart wasn't in it. His father lost weight, became a shrunken mockery of his old, vigorous self – he would die only a few years later. As for Abdul – the news reports about atrocities fed his nightmares and in his dreams he saw his sister bludgeoned, raped, torn to pieces again and again and again. When the city calmed down, he spent his days roaming the streets of the market, hoping for a sign of Ayesha – a body even – torn between hope and feverish rage.

Their father stopped seeing his Hindu friends. The only reason Abdul did not follow suit was because Gangadhar's people had sheltered a Muslim family during the carnage, and had turned off a mob of enraged Hindus.

Over time the wound – if it did not quite heal – became bearable enough that he could start living again. He threw himself into his beloved mathematics, isolating himself from everyone but his family and Gangadhar. The world had wronged him. He did not owe it anything.

> Aryabhata is the master who, after reaching the furthest shores and plumbing the inmost depths of the sea of ultimate knowledge of mathematics, kinematics and spherics, handed over the three sciences to the learned world.
>
> The Mathematician Bhaskara, commenting on the 6th century
> Indian mathematician Aryabhata, a hundred years later

Abdul Karim was the first in his family to go to college. By a stroke of great luck, Gangadhar went to the same regional institution, majoring in Hindi literature while Abdul Karim buried himself in mathematical arcana. Abdul's father had become reconciled to his son's obsession and obvious talent. Abdul Karim himself, glowing with praise from his teachers, wanted to follow in the footsteps of Ramanujan. Just as the goddess Namakkal had appeared to that untutored genius in his dreams, writing mathematical formulas on his tongue (or so Ramanujan had said), Abdul Karim wondered if the farishte had been sent by Allah so that he, too, might be blessed with mathematical insight.

During that time an event occurred that convinced him of this.

Abdul was in the college library, working on a problem in differential geometry, when he sensed a farishta at the edge of his field of vision. As he had done countless times before, he turned his head slowly, expecting the vision to vanish.

Instead he saw a dark shadow standing in front of the long bookcase. It was vaguely human-shaped. It turned slowly, revealing itself to be thin as paper – but as it turned it seemed to acquire thickness, hints of features over its dark, slender form. And then it seemed to Abdul that a door opened in the air, just a crack, and he had a vision of an unutterably strange world beyond. The shadow stood at the door, beckoning with one arm, but Abdul Karim sat still, frozen with wonder. Before he could rouse himself and get up, the door and the shadow both rotated swiftly and vanished, and he was left staring at the stack of books on the shelf.

After this he was convinced of his destiny. He dreamed obsessively of the strange world he had glimpsed; every time he sensed a farishta he turned his head slowly toward it – and every time it vanished. He told himself it was just a matter of time before one of them came, remained, and perhaps – wonder of wonders – took him to that other world.

Then his father died unexpectedly. That was the end of Abdul Karim's career as a mathematician. He had to return home to take care of his mother, his two remaining sisters and a brother. The only thing he was qualified for was teaching. Ultimately he would find a job at the same municipal school from which he had graduated.

On the train home, he saw a woman. The train was stopped on a bridge. Below him was the sleepy curve of a small river, gold in the early morning light, mists rising faintly off it, and on the shore a woman with a clay water pot. She had taken a dip in the river – her pale, ragged sari clung wetly to her as she picked up the pot and set it on her hip and began to climb the bank. In the light of dawn she was luminous, an apparition in the mist, the curve of the pot against the curve of her hip. Their eyes met from a distance – he imagined what he thought she saw, the silent train, a young man with a sparse beard looking at her as though she was the first woman in the world. Her own eyes gazed at him fearlessly as though she were a goddess looking into his soul. For a moment there were no barriers between them, no boundaries of gender, religion, caste or class. Then she turned and vanished behind a stand of shisham trees.

He wasn't sure if she had really been there in the half-light or whether he had conjured her up, but for a long time she represented something elemental to him. Sometimes he thought of her as Woman, sometimes as a river.

He got home in time for the funeral. His job kept him busy, and kept the moneylender from their door. With the stubborn optimism of the young, he kept hoping that one day his fortunes would change, that he would go back to college and complete his degree. In the meantime, he knew his mother wanted to find him a bride . . .

Abdul Karim got married, had children. Slowly, over the years of managing rowdy classrooms, tutoring students in the afternoons and saving, paisa by paisa, from his meager salary for his sisters' weddings and other expenses, Abdul Karim lost touch with that youthful, fiery talent he had once had, and with it the ambition to scale the heights to which Ramanujan, Cantor and Riemann had climbed. Things came more slowly to him now. An intellect burdened by years of worry wears out. When his wife died and his children grew up and went away, his steadily decreasing needs finally caught up with his meager income, and he found for the first time that he could think about mathematics again. He no longer hoped to dazzle the world of mathematics with some new insight, such as a proof of Riemann's hypothesis. Those dreams were gone. All he could hope for was to be illumined by the efforts of those who had gone before him, and to re-live, vicariously, the joys of insight. It was a cruel trick of Time, that when he had the leisure he had lost the ability, but that is no bar to true obsession. Now, in the autumn of his life it was as though Spring had come again, bringing with it his old love.

In this world, brought to its knees by hunger and thirst
Love is not the only reality, there are other Truths . . .
          Sahir Ludhianvi, Indian poet (1921–80)

There are times when Abdul Karim tires of his mathematical obsessions. After all, he is old. Sitting in the courtyard with his notebook, pencil and books of mathematics for so many hours at a stretch can take its toll. He gets up, aching all over, sees to his mother's needs and goes out to the graveyard where his wife is buried.

His wife Zainab had been a plump, fair-skinned woman, hardly able to read or write, who moved about the house with indolent grace, her good-natured laugh ringing out in the courtyard as she chattered with the washerwoman. She had loved to eat – he still remembered the delicate tips of her plump fingers, how they would curl around a piece of lamb, scooping up with it a few grains of saffron rice, the morsel conveyed reverently to her mouth. Her girth gave an impression of strength, but ultimately she had not been able to hold out against her mother-in-law. The laughter in her eyes faded gradually as her two boys grew out of babyhood, coddled and put to bed by the grandmother in her own corner of the women's quarters. Abdul Karim himself had been unaware of the silent war between his wife and mother – he had been young and obsessed with teaching mathematics to his recalcitrant students. He had noticed how the grandmother always seemed to be holding the younger son, crooning to him, and how the elder boy followed his mother around, but he did not see in this any connection to his wife's growing pallor. One night he had requested her to come to him and massage his feet – their euphemism for sex – and he had waited for her to come to him from the women's quarters, impatient for the comfort of her plump nakedness, her soft, silken breasts. When she came at last she had knelt at the foot of the bed, her chest heaving with muffled sobs, her hands covering her face. As he took her in his arms, wondering what could have ruffled her calm good nature, she had collapsed completely against him. No comfort he could offer would make her tell what it was that was breaking her heart. At last she begged him, between great, shuddering breaths, that all she wanted in the world was another baby.

Abdul Karim had been influenced by modern ideas – he considered two children, boys at that, to be quite sufficient for a family. As one of five children, he had known poverty and the pain of giving up his dream of a university career to help support his family. He wasn't going to have his children go through the same thing. But when his wife whispered to him that she wanted one more, he relented.

Now, when he looked back, he wished he had tried to understand the real reason for her distress. The pregnancy had been a troublesome one. His mother had taken charge of both boys almost entirely while Zainab lay in bed in the women's quarters, too sick to do anything but weep silently and call upon Allah to rescue her. "It's a girl," Abdul Karim's mother had said grimly. "Only a girl would cause so much trouble." She had looked away out of the window into the courtyard, where her own daughter, Abdul Karim's dead sister, Ayesha, had once played and helped hang the wash.

And finally it had been a girl, stillborn, who had taken her mother with her. They were buried together in the small, unkempt graveyard where Abdul Karim went whenever he was depressed. By now the gravestone was awry and grass had grown over the mound. His father was buried here also, and three of his siblings who had died before he was six. Only Ayesha, lost Ayesha, the one he remembered as a source of comfort to a small boy – strong, generous arms, hands delicate and fragrant with henna, a smooth cheek – she was not here.

In the graveyard Abdul Karim pays his respects to his wife's memory while his heart quails at the way the graveyard itself is disintegrating. He is afraid that if it goes to rack and ruin, overcome by vegetation and time, he will forget Zainab and the child and his guilt. Sometimes he tries to clear the weeds and tall grasses with his hands, but his delicate scholar's hands become bruised and sore quite quickly, and he sighs and thinks about the Sufi poetess Jahanara, who had written, centuries earlier: "Let the green grass grow above my grave!"

I have often pondered over the roles of knowledge or experience, on the one hand, and imagination or intuition, on the other, in the process of discovery. I believe that there is a certain fundamental conflict between the two, and knowledge, by advocating caution, tends to inhibit the flight of imagination. Therefore, a certain naivete, unburdened by conventional wisdom, can sometimes be a positive asset.

Harish-Chandra, Indian mathematician (1923–83)

Gangadhar, his friend from school, was briefly a master of Hindi literature at the municipal school and is now an academician at the Amravati Heritage

Library, and a poet in his spare time. He is the only person to whom Abdul Karim can confide his secret passion.

In time, he too becomes intrigued with the idea of infinity. While Abdul Karim pores over Cantor and Riemann, and tries to make meaning from the Prime Number theorem, Gangadhar raids the library and brings forth treasures. Every week, when Abdul Karim walks the two miles to Gangadhar's house, where he is led by the servant to the comfortable drawing room with its gracious, if aging mahogany furniture, the two men share what they've learned over cups of cardamom tea and a chess game. Gangadhar cannot understand higher mathematics but he can sympathize with the frustrations of the knowledge-seeker, and he has known what it is like to chip away at the wall of ignorance and burst into the light of understanding. He digs out quotes from Aryabhata and Al-Khwarizmi, and tells his friend such things as:

"Did you know, Abdul, that the Greeks and Romans did not like the idea of infinity? Aristotle argued against it, and proposed a finite universe. Of the yunaanis, only Archimedes dared to attempt to scale that peak. He came up with the notion that different infinite quantities could be compared, that one infinite could be greater or smaller than another infinite . . ."

And on another occasion:

"The French mathematician, Jacques Hadamard . . . He was the one who proved the Prime Number theorem that has you in such ecstasies . . . he says there are four stages to mathematical discovery. Not very different from the experience of the artist or poet, if you think about it. The first is to study and be familiar with what is known. The next is to let these ideas turn in your mind, as the earth regenerates by lying fallow between plantings. Then – with luck – there is the flash of insight, the illuminating moment when you discover something new and feel in your bones that it must be true. The final stage is to verify – to subject that epiphany to the rigors of mathematical proof . . ."

Abdul Karim feels that if he can simply go through Hadamard's first two stages, perhaps Allah will reward him with a flash of insight. And perhaps not. If he had hopes of being another Ramanujan, those hopes are gone now. But no true Lover has ever turned from the threshold of the Beloved's house, even knowing he will not be admitted through the doors.

"What worries me," he confides to Gangadhar during one of these discussions, "what has always worried me, is Gödel's Incompleteness Theorem. According to Gödel, there can be statements in mathematics that are not provable. He showed that the Continuum Hypothesis of Cantor was one of these statements. Poor Cantor, he lost his sanity trying to prove something that cannot be proved or disproved! What if all our unproven ideas on prime numbers, on infinity, are statements like that? If they can't be tested against the constraints of mathematical logic, how will we ever know if they are true?"

This bothers him very much. He pores over the proof of Gödel's theorem, seeking to understand it, to get around it. Gangadhar encourages him:

"You know, in the old tales, every great treasure is guarded by a proportionally great monster. Perhaps Gödel's theorem is the djinn that guards the truth you seek. Maybe instead of slaying it, you have to, you know, befriend it . . ."

Through his own studies, through discussions with Gangadhar, Abdul Karim begins to feel again that his true companions are Archimedes, Al-Khwarizmi. Khayyam, Aryabhata, Bhaskar. Riemann, Cantor, Gauss, Ramanujan, Hardy.

They are the masters, before whom he is as a humble student, an apprentice following their footprints up the mountainside. The going is rough. He is getting old, after all. He gives himself up to dreams of mathematics, rousing himself only to look after the needs of his mother, who is growing more and more frail.

After a while, even Gangadhar admonishes him.

"A man cannot live like this, so obsessed. Will you let yourself go the way of Cantor and Gödel? Guard your sanity, my friend. You have a duty to your mother, to society."

Abdul Karim cannot make Gangadhar understand. His mind sings with mathematics.

The limit of a function $f(N)$ as N goes to infinity . . .

So many questions he asks himself begin like this. The function $f(N)$ may be the prime counting function, or the number of nested dolls of matter, or the extent of the universe. It may be abstract, like a parameter in a mathematical space, or earthy, like the branching of wrinkles in the face of his mother, growing older and older in the paved courtyard of his house, under the litchi trees. Older and older, without quite dying, as though she were determined to live Zeno's paradox.

He loves his mother the way he loves the litchi tree; for being there, for making him what he is, for giving him shelter and succor.

The limit . . . as N goes to infinity . . .

So begin many theorems of calculus. Abdul Karim wonders what kind of calculus governs his mother's slow arc into dying. What if life did not require a minimum threshold of conditions – what if death were merely a limit of some function $f(N)$ as N goes to infinity?

A world in which human life is but a pawn
A world filled with death-worshipers,
Where death is cheaper than life . . .
That world is not my world . . .

                                    Sahir Ludhianvi, Indian poet (1921–80)

While Abdul Karim dabbles in the mathematics of the infinite, as so many deluded fools and geniuses have done, the world changes.

He is vaguely aware that there are things going on in the world – that people live and die, that there are political upheavals, that this is the hottest summer yet and already a thousand people have died of the heat wave in

Northern India. He knows that Death also stands at his mother's shoulder, waiting, and he does what he can for her. Although he has not always observed the five daily prayers, he does the namaz now, with her. She has already started becoming the citizen of another country – she lives in little leaps and bends of time long gone, calling for Ayesha one moment, and for her long-dead husband the next. Conversations from her lost girlhood emerge from her trembling mouth. In her few moments of clarity she calls upon Allah to take her away.

Dutiful as he is to his mother, Abdul Karim is relieved to be able to get away once a week for a chess game and conversation with Gangadhar. He has a neighbor's aunt look in on his mother during that time. Heaving a sigh or two, he makes his way through the familiar lanes of his childhood, his shoes scuffing up dust under the ancient jamun trees that he once climbed as a child. He greets his neighbors: old Ameen Khan Sahib sitting on his charpai, wheezing over his hookah, the Ali twins, madcap boys chasing a bicycle tire with a stick, Imran at the paan shop. He crosses, with some trepidation, the increasingly congested market road, past the faded awnings of Munshilal and Sons, past a rickshaw stand into another quiet lane, this one shaded with jacaranda trees. Gangadhar's house is a modest white bungalow, stained an indeterminate gray from many monsoons. The creak of the wooden gate in the compound wall is as familiar a greeting as Gangadhar's welcome.

But the day comes when there is no chess game at Gangadhar's house.

The servant boy – not Gangadhar – ushers him into the familiar room. Sitting down in his usual chair, Abdul Karim notices that the chess board has not been laid out. Sounds come from the inner rooms of the house: women's voices, heavy objects being dragged across the floor.

An elderly man comes into the room and stops short as though surprised to see Abdul Karim. He looks vaguely familiar – then Abdul remembers that he is some relative of Gangadhar's wife – an uncle, perhaps – and he lives on the other side of the city. They have met once or twice at some family celebration.

"What are you doing here?" the man says, without any of the usual courtesies. He is white-haired but of vigorous build.

Puzzled and a little affronted, Abdul Karim says:

"I am here for my chess game with Gangadhar. Is he not at home?"

"There will be no chess game today. Haven't you people done enough harm? Are you here to mock us in our sorrow? Well, let me tell you . . ."

"What happened?" Abdul Karim's indignation is dissolving in a wave of apprehension. "What are you talking about? Is Gangadhar all right?"

"Perhaps you don't know," says the man, his tone mocking. "Some of your people burned a bus on Paharia Road yesterday evening. There were ten people on it, all Hindus, coming back from a family ceremony at a temple. They all perished horribly. Word has it that you people did it. Didn't even let the children get off the bus. Now the whole town is in turmoil. Who knows what might happen? Gangadhar and I are taking his family to a safer part of town."

Abdul Karim's eyes are wide with shock. He can find no words.

"All these hundreds of years we Hindus have tolerated you people. Even though you Muslims raided and pillaged us over the centuries, we let you build your mosques, worship your God. And this is how you pay us!"

In one instant Abdul Karim has become "you people." He wants to say that he did not lift an arm to hurt those who perished on the bus. His were not the hands that set the fire. But no words come out.

"Can you imagine it, Master Sahib? Can you see the flames? Hear their screams? Those people will never go home . . ."

"I can imagine it," Abdul Karim says, grimly now. He rises to his feet, but just then Gangadhar enters the room. He has surely heard part of the conversation because he puts his hands on Abdul Karim's shoulders, gently, recognizing him as the other man has not done. This is Abdul Karim, his friend, whose sister, all those years ago, never came home.

Gangadhar turns to his wife's uncle.

"Uncle, please. Abdul Karim is not like those miscreants. A kinder man I have never known! And as yet it is not known who the ruffians are, although the whole town is filled with rumors. Abdul, please sit down! This is a measure of the times we live in, that we can say such things to each other. Alas! Kalyug is indeed upon us."

Abdul Karim sits down, but he is shaking. All thoughts of mathematics have vanished from his mind. He is filled with disgust and revulsion for the barbarians who committed this atrocity, for human beings in general. What a degraded species we are! To take the name of Ram or Allah, or Jesus, and to burn and destroy under one aegis or another – that is what our history has been.

The uncle, shaking his head, has left the room. Gangadhar is talking history to Abdul, apologizing for his uncle.

". . . a matter of political manipulation," he says. "The British colonialists looked for our weakness, exploited it, set us against each other. Opening the door to hell is easy enough – but closing it is hard. All those years, before British rule, we lived in relative peace. Why is it that we cannot close that door they opened? After all, what religion tells us to slay our neighbor?"

"Does it matter?" Abdul Karim says bitterly. "We humans are a depraved species, my friend. My fellow Muslims address every prayer to Allah, the Merciful and Compassionate. You Hindus, with your 'Isha Vasyam Idam Sarvam' – the divine pervades all. The Christians talk on about turning the other cheek. And yet each of them has hands that are stained in blood. We pervert everything – we take the words of peace spoken by prophets and holy men and turn them into weapons with which to kill each other!"

He is shaking so hard that he can barely speak.

"It is in mathematics . . . only in mathematics that I see Allah . . ."

"Quiet now," Gangadhar says. He calls for the servant to bring some water for the master sahib. Abdul Karim drinks and wipes his mouth. The suitcases are being brought out from inside the house. There is a taxi in front.

"Listen, my friend," Gangadhar says, "you must look to your safety. Go home now and lock your doors, and look after your mother. I am sending my family away and I will join them in a day or so. When this madness has passed I will come and look for you!" Abdul Karim goes home. So far everything looks normal – the wind is blowing litter along in the streets, the paan shop is open, people throng the bus stop. Then he notices that there aren't any children, even though the summer holidays are going on.

The vegetable market is very busy. People are buying up everything like crazy. He buys a few potatoes, onions and a large gourd, and goes home. He locks the door. His mother, no longer up to cooking meals, watches as he cooks. After they eat and he has her tucked into bed, he goes to his study and opens a book on mathematics.

One day passes, perhaps two – he does not keep track. He remembers to take care of his mother but often forgets to eat. His mother lives, more and more, in that other world. His sisters and brother call from other towns, anxious about the reports of escalating violence; he tells them not to worry. When things are back to normal they will come and see him and their mother.

How marvelous, the Universal Mystery
That only a true Lover can comprehend!
       Bulleh Shah, eighteenth century Punjabi Sufi poet

Logic merely sanctions the conquests of the intuition.
       Jacques Hadamard, French mathematician (1865–1963)

One morning he emerges from the darkness of his study into the sunny courtyard. Around him the old city writhes and burns, but Abdul Karim sees and hears nothing but mathematics. He sits in his old cane chair, picks up a stick lying on the ground and begins to draw mathematical symbols in the dust.

There is a farishta standing at the edge of his vision.

He turns slowly. The dark shadow stays there, waits. This time Abdul Karim is quick on his feet, despite a sudden twinge of pain in one knee. He walks toward the door, the beckoning arm, and steps through.

For a moment he is violently disoriented – it occurs to him that he has spun through a different dimension into this hidden world. Then the darkness before his eyes dissipates, and he beholds wonders.

All is hushed. He is looking at a vast sweep of land and sky unlike anything he has ever seen. Dark, pyramidal shapes stud the landscape, great monuments to something beyond his understanding. There is a vast, polyhedral object suspended in a pale orange sky that has no sun. Only a diffuse luminescence pervades this sky. He looks at his feet, still in his familiar, worn sandals, and sees all around, in the sand, little fish-like creatures wriggling and spawning. Some of the sand has worked its way between his toes, and it feels warm and rubbery, not like sand at all. He takes a deep breath and smells something strange, like burnt rubber mixed with his own sweat. The shadow stands by his side, looking solid at last, almost human but for the absence of neck and the profusion of limbs – their number seems to vary with time – at the moment Abdul Karim counts five.

The dark orifice in the head opens and closes, but no sound comes out. Instead Abdul feels as though a thought has been placed in his mind, a package that he will open later.

He walks with the shadow across the sands to the edge of a quiet sea. The water, if that is what it is, is foaming and bubbling gently, and within its depths he sees ghostly shapes moving, and the hints of complex structure far below. Arabesques form in the depths, break up, and form again. He licks his dry lips, tastes metal and salt.

He looks at his companion, who bids him pause. A door opens. They step through into another universe.

It is different, this one. It is all air and light, the whole space hung with great, translucent webbing. Each strand in the web is a hollow tube within which liquid creatures flow. Smaller, solid beings float in the emptiness between the web-strands.

Speechless, he stretches out his hand toward a web-strand. Its delicacy reminds him of the filigreed silver anklets his wife used to wear. To his complete surprise a tiny being floating within the strand stops. It is like a plump, watery comma, translucent and without any features he can recognize, and yet he has the notion that he is being looked at, examined, and that at the other end is also wonder.

The web-strand touches him, and he feels its cool, alien smoothness on a fingertip.

A door opens. They step through.

It is dizzying, this wild ride. Sometimes he gets flashes of his own world, scenes of trees and streets, and distant blue hills. There are indications that these flashes are at different points in time – at one point he sees a vast army of soldiers, their plumed helmets catching the sunlight, and thinks he must be in the time of the Roman Empire. Another time he thinks he is back home, because he sees before him his own courtyard. But there is an old man sitting in his cane chair, drawing patterns in the dust with a stick. A shadow falls across the ground. Someone he cannot see is stealing up behind the old man. Is that a knife agleam in the stranger's hand? What is this he is seeing? He tries to call out, but no sound emerges. The scene blurs – a door opens, and they step through.

Abdul Karim is trembling. Has he just witnessed his own death?

He remembers that Archimedes died that way – he had been drawing circles, engrossed with a problem in geometry, when a barbarian of a soldier came up behind him and killed him.

But there is no time to ponder. He is lost in a merry-go-round of universes, each different and strange. The shadow gives him a glimpse of so many, Abdul Karim has long lost count. He puts thoughts of Death away from him and loses himself in wonder.

His companion opens door after door. The face, featureless except for the orifice that opens and shuts, gives no hint of what the shadow is thinking. Abdul Karim wants to ask: Who are you? Why are you doing this? He knows, of course, the old story of how the angel Gabriel came to the Prophet Mohammad one night and took him on a celestial journey, a grand tour of the heavens. But the shadow does not look like an angel; it has no face, no wings, its gender is indeterminate. And in any case, why should the angel Gabriel concern himself with a humble mathematics master in a provincial town, a person of no consequence in the world?

And yet, he is here. Perhaps Allah has a message for him; His ways are ineffable, after all. Exultation fills Abdul Karim as he beholds marvel after marvel.

At last they pause in a place where they are suspended in a yellow sky. As Abdul Karim experiences the giddy absence of gravity, accompanied by a sudden jolt of nausea that slowly recedes – as he turns in mid-air, he notices that the sky is not featureless but covered with delicate tessellations: geometric shapes intertwine, merge and new ones emerge. The colors change too, from yellow to green, lilac, mauve. All at once it seems as though numberless eyes are opening in the sky, one after the other, and as he turns he sees all the other universes flashing past him. A kaleidoscope, vast beyond his imaginings. He is at the center of it all, in a space between all spaces, and he can feel in his bones a low, irregular throbbing, like the beating of a drum. Boom, boom, goes the drum. Boom boom boom. Slowly he realizes that what he is seeing and feeling is part of a vast pattern.

In that moment Abdul Karim has the flash of understanding he has been waiting for all his life.

For so long he has been playing with the transcendental numbers, trying to fathom Cantor's ideas; at the same time Riemann's notions of the prime numbers have fascinated him. In idle moments he has wondered if they are connected at a deeper level. Despite their apparent randomness the primes have their own regularity, as hinted by the unproven Riemann Hypothesis; he sees at last that if you think of prime numbers as the terrain of a vast country, and if your view of reality is a two-dimensional plane that intersects this terrain at some height above the surface, perhaps at an angle, then of course what you see will appear to be random. Tops of hills. Bits of valleys. Only the parts of the terrain that cross your plane of reality will be apparent. Unless you can see the entire landscape in its multi-dimensional splendor, the topography will make no sense.

He sees it: the bare bones of creation, here, in this place where all the universes branch off, the thudding heart of the metacosmos. In the scaffolding, the skeletal structure of the multiverse is beautifully apparent. This is what Cantor had a glimpse of, then, this vast topography. Understanding opens in his mind as though the metacosmos has itself spoken to him. He sees that of all the transcendental numbers, only a few – infinite still, but not the whole set – are marked as doorways to other universes, and each is labeled by a prime number. Yes. Yes. Why this is so, what deeper symmetry it reflects, what law or regularity of Nature undreamed of by the physicists of his world, he does not know.

The space where primes live – the topology of the infinite universes – he sees it in that moment. No puny function as yet dreamed of by humans can encompass the vastness – the inexhaustible beauty of this place. He knows that he can never describe this in the familiar symbols of the mathematics that he knows, that while he experiences the truth of the Riemann Hypothesis, as a corollary to this greater, more luminous reality, he cannot sit down and verify it through a conventional proof. No human language as yet exists, mathematical or otherwise, that can describe what he knows in his bones to be true. Perhaps he, Abdul Karim, will invent the beginnings of such a language. Hadn't the great poet Iqbal interpreted the Prophet's celestial journey to mean that the heavens are within our grasp?

A twist, and a door opens. He steps into the courtyard of his house. He turns around, but the courtyard is empty. The farishta is gone.

Abdul Karim raises his eyes to the heavens. Rain clouds, dark as the proverbial Beloved's hair, sweep across the sky; the litchi tree over his head is dancing in the swift breeze. The wind has drowned out the sounds of a ravaged city. A red flower comes blowing over the courtyard wall and is deposited at his feet.

Abdul Karim's hair is blown back, a nameless ecstasy fills him; he feels Allah's breath on his face.

He says into the wind:

"Dear Merciful and Compassionate God, I stand before your wondrous universe, filled with awe; help me, weak mortal that I am, to raise my gaze above the sordid pettiness of everyday life, the struggles and quarrels of mean humanity . . . Help me to see the beauty of your Works, from the full flower of the red silk cotton tree to the exquisite mathematical grace by which you have created numberless universes in the space of a man's step. I know now that my true purpose in this sad world is to stand in humble awe before your magnificence, and to sing a paean of praise to you with every breath I take . . ."

He feels weak with joy. Leaves whirl in the courtyard like mad dervishes; a drop or two of rain falls, obliterating the equation he had scratched in the dust with his stick. He has lost his chance at mathematical genius a long time ago; he is nobody, only a teacher of mathematics at a school, humbler than a clerk in a government office – yet Allah has favored him with this great insight. Perhaps he is now worthy of speech with Ramanujan and Archimedes and all the ones in between. But all he wants to do is to run out into the lane and go shouting through the city: See, my friends, open your eyes and see what I see! But he knows they would think him mad; only Gangadhar would understand . . . If not the mathematics then the impulse, the importance of the whole discovery.

He leaps out of the house, into the lane.

This blemished radiance . . . this night-stung dawn
Is not the dawn we waited for . . .
                    Faiz Ahmed Faiz, Pakistani poet (1911–84)

Where all is broken
Where each soul's athirst, each glance
Filled with confusion, each heart
Weighed with sorrow . . .
Is this a world, or chaos?
                    Sahir Ludhianvi, Indian poet (1921–80)

But what is this?

The lane is empty. There are broken bottles everywhere. The windows and doors of his neighbors' houses are shuttered and barred, like closed eyes. Above the sound of the rain he hears shouting in the distance. Why is there a smell of burning?

He remembers then, what he had learned at Gangadhar's house. Securing the door behind him, he begins to run as fast as his old-man legs will carry him.

The market is burning.

Smoke pours out of smashed store fronts, even as the rain falls. There is broken glass on the pavement; a child's wooden doll in the middle of the road, decapitated. Soggy pages filled with neat columns of figures lie scattered everywhere, the remains of a ledger. Quickly he crosses the road.

Gangadhar's house is in ruins. Abdul Karim wanders through the open doors, stares blindly at the blackened walls. The furniture is mostly gone. Only the chess table stands untouched in the middle of the front room.

Frantically he searches through the house, entering the inner rooms for the first time. Even the curtains have been ripped from the windows.

There is nobody.

He runs out of the house. Gangadhar's wife's family – he does not know where they live. How to find out if Gangadhar is safe?

The neighboring house belongs to a Muslim family that Abdul Karim knows only from visits to the mosque. He pounds on the door. He thinks he hears movement behind the door, sees the upstairs curtains twitch – but nobody answers his frantic entreaties. At last, defeated, his hands bleeding, he walks slowly home, looking about him in horror. Is this truly his city, his world?

Allah, Allah, why have you abandoned me?

He has beheld the glory of Allah's workmanship. Then why this? Were all those other universes, other realities a dream?

The rain pours down.

There is someone lying on his face in a ditch. The rain has wet the shirt on his back, made the blood run. As Abdul Karim starts toward him, wondering who it is, whether he is dead or alive – young, from the back it could be Ramdas or Imran – he sees behind him, at the entrance to the lane, a horde of young men. Some of them may be his students – they can help.

They are moving with a predatory sureness that frightens him. He sees that they have sticks and stones.

They are coming like a tsunami, a thunderclap, leaving death and ruin in their wake. He hears their shouts through the rain.

Abdul Karim's courage fails him. He runs to his house, enters, locks and bars the door and closes all the windows. He checks on his mother, who is sleeping. The telephone is dead. The dal for their meal has boiled away. He turns off the gas and goes back to the door, putting his ear against it. He does not want to risk looking out of the window.

Over the rain he hears the young men go past at a run. In the distance there is a fusillade of shots. More sounds of running feet, then, just the rain.

Are the police here? The army?

Something or someone is scratching at the door. Abdul Karim is trans-fixed with terror. He stands there, straining to hear over the pitter patter of the rain. On the other side, somebody moans.

Abdul Karim opens the door. The lane is empty, roaring with rain. At his feet there is the body of a young woman.

She opens her eyes. She's dressed in a salwaar kameez that has been half-torn off her body – her long hair is wet with rain and blood, plastered over her neck and shoulders. There is blood on her salwaar, blood oozing from a hundred little cuts and welts on her skin.

Her gaze focuses.

"Master Sahib."

He is taken aback. Is she someone he knows? Perhaps an old student, grown up?

Quickly he half-carries, half-pulls her into the house and secures the door. With some difficulty he lifts her carefully on to the divan in the draw-ing room, which is already staining with her blood. She coughs.

"My child, who did this to you? Let me find a doctor . . ."

"No," she says. "It's too late." Her breath rasps and she coughs again. Tears well up in the dark eyes.

"Master Sahib, please, let me die! My husband . . . my son . . . They must not see me take my last breath. Not like this. They will suffer. They will want revenge . . . Please . . . cut my wrists . . ."

She's raising her wrists to his horrified face, but all he can do is to take them in his shaking hands.

"My daughter," he says, and doesn't know what to say. Where will he find a doctor in the mayhem? Can he bind her cuts? Even as he thinks these thoughts he knows that life is ebbing from her. Blood is pooling on his divan, dripping down to the floor. She does not need him to cut her wrists.

"Tell me, who are the ruffians who did this?"

She whispers:

"I don't know who they were. I had just stepped out of the house for a moment. My family . . . don't tell them, Master Sahib! When I'm gone just tell them . . . tell them I died in a safe place . . ."

"Daughter, what is your husband's name?"

Her eyes are enormous. She is gazing at him without comprehension, as though she is already in another world.

He can't tell if she is Muslim or Hindu. If she wore a vermilion dot on her forehead, it has long since been washed off by the rain.

His mother is standing at the door of the drawing room. She wails suddenly and loudly, flings herself by the side of the dying woman.

"Ayesha! Ayesha, my life!"

Tears fall down Abdul Karim's face. He tries to disengage his mother. Tries to tell her: This is not Ayesha, just another woman whose body has become a battleground over which men make war. At last he has to lift his mother in his arms, her body so frail that he fears it might break – he takes her to her bed, where she crumples, sobbing and calling Ayesha's name.

Back in the drawing room, the young woman's eyes flicker to him. Her voice is barely above a whisper.

"Master Sahib, cut my wrists . . . I beseech you, in the Almighty's name! Take me somewhere safe . . . Let me die . . ."

Then the veil falls over her eyes again and her body goes limp.

Time stands still for Abdul Karim.

Then he senses something familiar, and turns slowly. The farishta is waiting.

Abdul Karim picks up the woman in his arms, awkwardly arranging the bloody divan cover over her half-naked body. In the air, a door opens.

Staggering a little, his knees protesting, he steps through the door.

After three universes he finds the place.

It is peaceful. There is a rock rising from a great turquoise sea of sand. The blue sand laps against the rock, making lulling, sibilant sounds. In the high, clear air, winged creatures call to each other between endless rays of light. He squints in the sudden brightness.

He closes her eyes, buries her deep at the base of the rock, under the blue, flowing sand.

He stands there, breathing hard from the exertion, his hands bruised, thinking he should say something. But what? He does not even know if she's Muslim or Hindu. When she spoke to him earlier, what word had she used for God? Was it Allah or Ishwar, or something neutral?

He can't remember.

At last he says the Al-Fatihah, and, stumbling a little, recites whatever little he knows of the Hindu scriptures. He ends with the phrase Isha Vasyamidam Sarvam.

Tears run off his cheeks into the blue sand, and disappear without leaving a trace.

The farishta waits.

"Why didn't you do something!" Abdul Karim rails at the shadow. He falls to his knees in the blue sand, weeping. "Why, if you are truly a farishta, didn't you save my sister?"

He sees now that he has been a fool – this shadow creature is no angel, and he, Abdul Karim, no Prophet.

He weeps for Ayesha, for this nameless young woman, for the body he saw in the ditch, for his lost friend Gangadhar.

The shadow leans toward him. Abdul Karim gets up, looks around once, and steps through the door.

He steps out into his drawing room. The first thing he discovers is that his mother is dead. She looks quite peaceful, lying in her bed, her white hair flowing over the pillow.

She might be asleep, her face is so calm.

He stands there for a long time, unable to weep. He picks up the phone – there is still no dial tone. After that he goes about methodically cleaning up the drawing room, washing the floor, taking the bedding off the divan. Later, after the rain has stopped, he will burn it in the courtyard. Who will notice another fire in the burning city?

When everything is cleaned up, he lies down next to his mother's body like a small boy and goes to sleep.

> When you left me, my brother, you took away the book
> In which is writ the story of my life . . .
> Faiz Ahmed Faiz, Pakistani poet (1911–84)

The sun is out. An uneasy peace lies over the city. His mother's funeral is over. Relatives have come and gone – his younger son came, but did not stay. The older son sent a sympathy card from America.

Gangadhar's house is still empty, a blackened ruin. Whenever he has ventured out, Abdul Karim has asked about his friend's whereabouts. The last he heard was that Gangadhar was alone in the house when the mob came, and his Muslim neighbors sheltered him until he could join his wife and children at her parents' house. But it has been so long that he does not believe it anymore. He has also heard that Gangadhar was dragged out, hacked to pieces and his body set on fire. The city has calmed down – the army had to be called in – but it is still rife with rumors. Hundreds of people are missing. Civil rights groups comb the town, interviewing people, revealing, in clipped, angry press statements, the negligence of the state government, the collusion of the police in some of the violence. Some of them came to his house, too, very clean, very young people, burning with an idealism that, however misplaced, is comforting to see. He has said nothing about the young woman who died in his arms, but he prays for that bereft family every day.

For days he has ignored the shadow at his shoulder. But now he knows that the sense of betrayal will fade. Whose fault is it, after all, that he ascribed to the creatures he once called farishte the attributes of angels? Could angels, even, save human beings from themselves?

The creatures watch us with a child's curiosity, he thinks, but they do not understand. Just as their own worlds are incomprehensible to me, so are our ways to them. They are not Allah's minions.

The space where the universes branch off – the heart of the metacosmos – now appears remote to him, like a dream. He is ashamed of his earlier arrogance. How can he possibly fathom Allah's creation in one glance? No finite mind can, in one meager lifetime, truly comprehend the vastness, the grandeur of Allah's scheme. All we can do is to discover a bit of the truth here, a bit there, and thus to sing His praises.

But there is so much pain in Abdul Karim's soul that he cannot imagine writing down one syllable of the new language of the infinite. His dreams are haunted by the horrors he has seen, the images of his mother and the young woman who died in his arms. He cannot even say his prayers. It is as though Allah has abandoned him, after all.

The daily task of living – waking up, performing his ablutions, setting the little pot on the gas stove to boil water for one cup of tea, to drink that tea alone – unbearable thought! To go on, after so many have died – to go on without his mother, his children, without Gangadhar . . . Everything appears strangely remote: his aging face in the mirror, the old house, even the litchi tree in his courtyard. The familiar lanes of his childhood hold memories that no longer seem to belong to him. Outside, the neighbors are in mourning; old Ameen Khan Sahib weeps for his grandson; Ramdas is gone, Imran is gone. The wind still carries the soot of the burnings. He finds little piles of ashes everywhere, in the cracks in the cement of his courtyard, between the roots of the trees in the lane. He breathes the dead. How can he regain his heart, living in a world so wracked with pain? In this world there is no place for the likes of him. No place for henna-scented hands rocking a child to sleep, for old-woman hands tending a garden. And no place at all for the austere beauty of mathematics.

He's thinking this when a shadow falls across the ground in front of him. He has been sitting in his courtyard, idly writing mathematical expressions with his stick on the dusty ground. He does not know whether the knife bearer is his son, or an enraged Hindu, but he finds himself ready for his death. The creatures who have watched him for so long will witness it, and wonder. Their uncomprehending presence comforts him.

He turns and rises. It is Gangadhar, his friend, who holds out his empty arms in an embrace.

Abdul Karim lets his tears run over Gangadhar's shirt. As waves of relief wash over him he knows that he has held Death at bay this time, but it will come. It will come, he has seen it. Archimedes and Ramanujan, Khayyam and Cantor died with epiphanies on their lips before an indifferent world. But this moment is eternal.

"Allah be praised!" says Abdul Karim.

THINGS UNDONE

John Barnes

John Barnes is one of the most prolific and popular of all the writers who entered SF in the 1980s. His many books include the novels *A Million Open Doors*, *The Mother of Storms*, *Orbital Resonance*, *Kaleidoscope Century*, *Candle*, *Earth Made of Glass*, *The Merchant of Souls*, *Sin of Origin*, *One for the Morning Glory*, *The Sky So Big and Black*, *The Duke of Uranium*, *A Princess of the Aerie*, *In The Hall of the Martian King*, *Gaudeamus*, *Finity*, *Patton's Spaceship*, *Washington's Dirigible*, *Caesar's Bicycle*, *The Man Who Pulled Down the Sky*, and others, as well as two novels written with astronaut Buzz Aldrin, *The Return* and *Encounter with Tiber*. Long a mainstay of *Analog*, and now a regular at Jim Baen's *Universe*, his short work has been collected in . . . *And Orion* and *Apostrophes and Apocalypses*. His most recent book is the novel *The Armies of Memory*. Barnes lives in Colorado and works in the field of semiotics.

The sly story that follows demonstrates a variation on that old saying about the weather – if you don't like reality, just wait a minute.

WITH TWO CONTRACTS last spring, both successful, Year of Grace 2014 had already been lucrative by early December; better still, with just over three months left in the year, we had yet another contract. "We are looking for someone who will probably sound as if he has a Dutch accent," Horejsi said. As always she was speaking from an index card, pulled from the envelope that had only just dropped out of the slot on the FBI-only blue phone about ten minutes ago.

"Date of arrival, March 16, YoG 2013, so right before the new year. He can't possibly have survived in Denver for nine months without having had extensive contact with other people, so there's no hope of a true isolation." She was getting that off the card where they set the rate, skipping all the numbers; they never meant much to her.

I said, "Slow down slightly. What are the top and bottom rates they're offering?"

"Seventy per cent of the standard for a fully discreet termination, one hundred and forty-three per cent if it turns out we can do a true isolation, but we won't be able to – "

"One hundred and forty-three per cent is the exact inverse of seventy per cent," I commented. "Rounded to the nearest per cent."

Horejsi looked at me, multiple apertures in her Riemann eyes opening and polyfocusing so that she could catch every nuance of the pulse in my neck and the infrared flush of my skin. "There will be a reason why that thing about exact inverses is useful, and that reason is eluding me."

Numbers elude Horejsi like faces and names elude me. But time travelers never elude us for very long, I thought. I enjoyed thinking it.

I said, "The penalty for having to resort to killing him is exactly the same as the reward for getting him all the way into the WPP. Normally the reward is much lower than the penalty – when they pay seventy for a complete screw-up where we have to shoot him and grind him, they only pay maybe one hundred and ten for true isolation. So for some reason they are incenting us very, very hard to achieve true isolation, even though it's obvious that true isolation is impossible. That is interesting."

"You're right," she said.

"Furthermore," I said, (Horejsi is a good partner, the best actually, the only one I'll ever want, but she always stops talking about numbers just before it gets really good), "this means that they are incenting us to improve, if only by the slightest margin, across the whole spectrum from barely acceptable failure to triumphant success."

Horejsi nodded. "I think I get it, Rastigevat. The pay scale is telling you that the case is much more important than the usual ballast-tracking job; they want all the results we can squeeze out no matter what it takes, and there's no such thing as 'good enough, we can coast.' Has there ever been a case with a pay scale like this before?"

"Thirty-nine cases since I started working with you, after six cases with Gomez, and in every case the bonus was less than eighty per cent of the inverse of the penalty. So no. Never. Not only is this the most urgent case ever, it's the most urgent by a wide margin."

Horejsi nodded. "We're not supposed to notice that."

"If we didn't, we wouldn't be smart enough to catch time jumpers."

"Right." She gave me her weird grimace that meant smile. (She didn't get Riemann eyes till she was in her twenties – she was born blind and Com'n – so she hadn't had the right feedback to develop proper facial expressions when she was young.)

I grinned back. It was nice to work with someone who got jokes.

I estimated that I knew at least 2,000 per cent more than I was supposed to know about Horejsi. For example, her first name was Ruth, but since I could never call her that, I called her Horejsi, same as she called me Rastigevat, even though she knew my first name was Simon. I estimated that we covertly shared between 820 and 860 simple declarative statements about each other that we were not supposed to know.

We also were the only two people in the world who knew each other at all. I looked a little more normal, but I didn't get to know people much. Except for Horejsi they were boring. And if anyone found out that Horejsi didn't bore me, she'd be gone, literally before I ever knew her. When a Com'n becomes important to a Liejt, there's a waiver on the temporal rules.

Her grimace/grin got more intense and she focused her vision apertures directly at my face. The Lord of Grace alone knows why – knowing Horejsi better than anyone else in the world is like knowing just one fact about a star no astronomer has seen. It was good that I knew how to be fascinated without showing it.

At last she said, "All right, shall I resume reading cards?"

"Please." I took a sip of coffee, careful to set the cup down without making a bump or disturbance that might draw either of our attention from what she was doing, because if we missed anything, it was gone for good – regulations required that as she finished each card she dropped it into the combustor; she had to pull them from their package one at a time, then put them down the combuster.

Basics: Ballast tracking job. Date of ballast's origin, 28 May 1388. Location, Southwark, London, England. She dropped the card into the slot. The combustor made a soft brak! as the swirling white-hot oxygen turned the card to gas and a wisp of glassy ash.

Mass, twenty gallonweights, almost exactly. Cylinder of enclosure, 70 x 11 decifeet, so he was about average height and girth. Into the slot, brak!, more gas and ash.

Our mystery man was the ballast load for the backward journey of Alvarez Peron, which was the alias for a man named CONFIDENTIAL who had worked for the Federal government as a AVAILABLE ON A NEED TO KNOW BASIS while leading a double life. It noted that in his real life he was Liejt and had family, and therefore we should avoid any inquiries in that direction unless specifically authorized.

Peron had departed from an apartment near 30th and Downing, apartment destroyed in fire of suspicious origin. That was unsurprising. It takes time to build an illegal time machine and prepare to use it, so he'd taken a place in the bad side of town under another name, and then probably firebombed it just after the ballast came through. That was a pretty common trick, not least because it forced the ballast to run instead of doing the natural thing and holing up in the place where the time machine had been. Horejsi and me had caught eight ballasts who had barely had a second to realize they were naked or in rags, bleeding and hurt, in a strange place, before the room had gone up in flames and they'd fled for their lives into the street.

30th and Downing was a logical place – in the scummy boho end of town, where many Liejt had apartments for mistresses or for drug parties, and near a levrail station where gravitic power was easy to steal with just an Edison tube of mercury for an antenna.

We could have had the case the day after he left. The Royal Temporal Division had measured the power draw, mass, and cyl-enc but hadn't seen fit to tell us till we asked, and of course we hadn't asked till we detected it by our methods, which meant not until after anomalies began to accumulate and casopropagate forward around the disappearance of Peron's ballast.

That was typical; RTD cops gave no cooperation to anyone, least of all us feebs.

"So," I said, "just rechecking your memory with mine; we have it that Peron had no prior record of experimenting with time machines, but given that you can make one out of three old radios and any pre-1985 ultrasonic clothes-cleaner – "

She nodded. "And he could have gotten the physics from the tweenweb – plenty of articles there. Or with his confidential background, and being from a Liejt family, good odds he's a high-level physicist or mathematician."

She turned another card. "This is the longest kinegraph of him they can find, and it's only about forty seconds. He liked tango, so he made it to most of the Argentú clubs here in town."

I watched; faces are all alike, but I remember gaits.

Peron sent his partner through a quick, neat boleo and led her out in a nice cruzada; he took good care of her axis without fussing about it, and I could tell his lead was firm and clear (letting her look good), but not very imaginative (he didn't particularly make her look good). "He's good," I said. "But not great."

"You . . . dance?" She sounded equally astonished on each word. Add one more declarative statement to things she knew.

"Yeah. I met Peron; we danced in some of the same places. He was around for a while – till a few months ago, in fact." I looked at the kinegraph more closely. "You sure can tell he's been gone for nine months, can't you? His face is blurring badly. I don't really remember it well, either, but I don't think that's an effect of the time travel; I think I just never paid much attention to him."

"You'd know him if you saw him again?"

"Yeah, no question. If they drop me back for an exchange, I can do it. Mention it in your daily to the FBI, but they aren't going to want to try. My fuzzy memory is bound to be better than that kinegraph, so combust it."

Brak. Horejsi pulled out the next card. "Peron had a lot of friends."

"How many?"

"Forty-one identified."

"That's a lot for you or me, not so much for a regular social dancer."

"Sounded like a lot."

"Always give me the number."

"Sorry, Rastigevat. You're right." She was checking me, opening apertures to see if I was upset with her, so I smiled and nodded to let her know it was okay. That was Horejsi, always worrying whether I liked her.

Better to get her off that worry. I asked, "So, forty-one friends, in what kind of relationships?"

"Very casual, all of them. Hanging out, bars and movies together, that kind of thing. Nine from dancing, thirty-two from Specthink, which is a philosophy e-kiosk on tweenweb. Now his old cronies on Specthink are arguing about who he was, where he went, and so on."

"May I look at the card?"

She handed it over. I could listen to Horejsi try to explain a table of numbers all month and not learn anything; she just didn't see numbers. If she let me look and then explain to her, we both knew a lot more.

Frequency of contact, frequency of mention, and trust in mention all showed the usual pattern after someone jumps back: his friends were talking about him less and less, being troubled by not quite remembering Old Whatsisname. In the last three months, four of them had decided he was a hoax invented by the rest of the group, and five more were sympathetic to that view. He had been the most frequently quoted member of his personal web; 85 per cent of quotes originating with him had already been reattributed. "Popular guy," I said. "But one of the things I like about the dance communities, you don't have to talk more than you want to, and most people prefer it if you don't get too involved with each other. And it's nice precise exercise. I love all that. So since I didn't dance with him and wasn't much of a talker, I just didn't interact with him much. The only thing I remember is that there were always people around him. I think I'd recognize him from his gait, though. If he came back."

"You don't think we'll retrieve him."

"No way. He has almost already gotten away with it. It's a miracle the random searches found him when they did; whatever Peron has done, it's already melding with reality. There's going to be uproar, I'm afraid."

Her apertures opaqued and she rubbed the back of her head. "Shit."

Horejsi hates uproar. Me, I barely notice it.

Six hundred years ago, in the One Great Lecture of 1403, Francis Tyrwhitt articulated the theory of indexical derivability, and after his death, his eleven students carried the work on. In 1421, a six-page calculation overthrew all of Aristotelian mechanics and Ptomelaic astronomy, and told them how to build the telescopes and chronometers with which to confirm it. In 1429, Marlow discovered the periodic table of the elements, valence, and carbon chains in his calculations in a single thick codex; Tyrwhitt's last living student, Christopher Berkeley Maxwell, laid out the basic equations of electromagnetism in the notes found in his rooms after his death.

Indexical derivability made all things inevitable. Once you had its fourteen definitions, seven axioms, and forty-one basic theorems, from then on if you could describe what you wanted to do, it was just a matter of doing the steps, deriving the equations (or proving that no equations could be derived, which was equivalent to absolute impossibility), and then solving them. Solving them was a bastard, of course. Newton worked all his life, without success, to unify relativity and quantum.

Then just under 200 years ago, Babbage saw how to use deoxyribonucleic acid to solve equations; after that, any Liejt sixteen-year-old, if his allowance would cover a few tubes of chemicals from the school supplies at Office Matt's plus an ordinary amino-acid sequencer from the pet store, could unify quantum physics and relativity in about three days. You still needed the occasional genius to explain what the right question was – it wasn't till Einstein that people really understood what time travel would mean or require – but once you could ask a question intelligently, it was only a matter of a few hours to learn whatever you wanted. As for building whatever you dreamed up, with such a variety of tech stuff out there, if you had a Liejt ID, you could probably get the parts from any junkyard or hobby store.

The universe still is what it is. Turns out questions like, "How can I love my neighbor?" are impossible to write in a soluble form, but "How can I make a really big bomb?" and "How can I go back and change the past?" are easy – just slap it together following the directions that come out of the tube and off you go.

Luckily by far the most common jumpers are the ones who are trying to cheat intemporia – the ones who jump back to give their earlier selves a bit of good advice or to take a different turn in the road. Too close to their departure point, there's so little room for casopropagation that the most likely consequences are fatal accidents or little "Appointment in Samara" lessons (often both simultaneously). It doesn't matter how often people hear that the universe is imperfectly reality-conservative, favoring whatever results in the least displacement, in Einstein's famous formulation. All they hear is "imperfectly" and "favoring" – like the Serpent whispering Thou shalt not surely die.

The short-term jumpers, the ones who go back five or thirty years, all think the stochastic exceptions the universe makes will be made in their direction, and that they'll be really happy if they just try to kiss Esther, or pop Bart in the nose when he shoves them in the hall, or buy Plum Computer when it's cheap; and each short term jumper is always the only person surprised when it turns out that actually nothing much changes even if they live and we don't catch them.

The exception to that was that Federal authorities could do a quick, simple edit, when someone crossed a boundary that must never be crossed. In such cases it worked because, honestly, if you changed people, you changed a lot of things, but if you just deleted them, generally you didn't. Most of us don't like to know how disposable we are, but there you have it. If us Feds didn't like what people were doing now, we'd eliminate them at some time back in the past, and history would close around the little space they had taken up – not "as if they had never been" – but just plain, they had never been.

Only freak-memory social isolates like me and Horejsi would recall it. That was part of how the FBI found us. Say a Com'n boy developed a crush on his personal slave. You couldn't punish him for that; he was higher. To punish and forbid meant admitting it was possible to cross the boundary. So you made it that it never had been crossed; a Federal agent took a short hop back and the slave girl had some quick, painless accident as a small girl, and the boy's family was warned to find more appropriate slaves.

But if three weeks after she ceased to exist, the boy was asking about her, you knew you had someone who had that kind of memory; you could fix him by having him talk to a lot of people, but if he wouldn't do that, he would be either an FBI agent, or someone who needed sequestering.

There were rumors that for some cases there were many, many people who needed elimination. I had met one older agent who had once told me of having had to eliminate four generations into the past to get rid of a Diana Spencer, but he didn't say for what; I gathered it involved a Royal person, and noting that the old man telling the tale was drunk, stopped him before he said more. Shortly after that conversation, the man vanished, but perhaps he just died and I didn't hear about it. I never asked around to see if anyone remembered him.

As for me, there was a sad, soft spot in my heart for LaNella, who I think was a Free nurse I must have preferred to my own mother (so many Liejt boys do – we're too young to understand the consequences and after all we see the nurse for hours every day, and Mama for perhaps two hours on Sunday). If it wasn't all a dream, then LaNella ceased to be while I was away at school for my first year, and when I came home at Christmas and asked for her, they took me to meet a nice man who promised I could be an FBI agent when I grew up.

So altering recent history was really nothing: the government did it all the time, whenever it was convenient. Private individuals tried it all the time, and either failed (because they didn't have the government's resources or simplicity of intention) or succeeded without changing much. It was illegal for private citizens, and they eliminated Free and Com'n people to prevent the violation's ever happening, and the fine for Liejts doing it was outrageous. But though the penalties were harsh for short term jumps back in time, in truth there was little harm or difference made, whether we caught them or not.

There was also little harm from anyone jumping into deep history; if you leaped back and assassinated Alexander, there might be a wild divergence for as much as 200 years, but the immense, massive intemporia of the whole time stream would find its way back to its old bed, and if you went back to, say, the Younger Dryas, whatever you did would be utterly undone – paleobiological expeditions were common school projects.

But every now and then someone decided to change something in meso-history, which meant the causal delta hits its maximum near the present. Whenever that happened, the first time the Federal Bureau of Isotemporality knew anything, a couple of battles had reversed their outcomes, the linguistic lines between English, Fransche, Russky, and Espano in the Armoricas had moved hundreds of miles, the Untitled States of Armorica had gained or lost ten states, and there was a Yorkist on the Confederate throne again.

The physics could have turned out worse. If the rate of casopropagation were uniform, continuous, instantaneous, or forward-causality conservative – any one of them would have done it – then after each past-changing trip, we'd instantly be in that other world, millions or billions of us would cease to exist and be replaced by someone else, everyone's new memory would conform to everyone else's, and the world would go on without even a fart in time.

Fortunately for those of us who like to go on existing, Einstein showed that casopropagation is stochastic, discrete, metatemporal, and biased toward zero change but not strictly conservative.

Mesohistorical time travelers nearly always wanted to come back to somewhere around the time they left, and the changes they made were reversible until they did, so they found a living human to be their ballast body. If you used an inert ballast body, say a load of mud from a riverbank or a fallen log from a forest, the trackers would find it right there at the place where your time machine took off, and disconnect its causal relation to you (dispersing and destructuring it – blow it up, burn it, grind it up and scatter it). You'd just have pointlessly ceased to exist.

But if your temporal field reached into the past to grab a live person, then with luck, the ballast, arriving suddenly in the future, would wander off and become hard to locate, thus ensuring that the time traveler had somewhere to return to. (Every so often someone would grab a deer; this worked as long as you could count on the deer not to get caught, and didn't mind arriving and returning somewhere unplanned in the woods.)

So Horejsi and I were supposed to find the ballast body during the interval between departure and return. Once we did, other agents would change the ballast in enough ways so that the time traveler's forward isotemporal soundings couldn't get a fix, they never came back, and the casopropagation was undone; Horejsi liked to call it the "no deposit, no return" system because that always made me have to cover my mouth and not let any hidden camera see me smile. I sometimes thought she must have some kind of death wish; of course it was fine for her to like me, but she must know how often she put herself in danger of being seen to be liked.

Anyway, finding ballasts was what we did. Once we did, regular agents moved in and did the simple grade-school science of altering the ballasts to break the connection. There are fifty or a hundred things you can do to ballasts once you find them. Some of them are even fairly humane.

"Want to try to ling him out?" I asked. "Dutch accent, odd behaviors, arrived naked with strange injuries – is that enough for a dictionary expansion into a Dodgsonian?"

"I think so," she said. "System up for voice."

"Up," Wingtoes said.

Horejsi stared at the ceiling, took a deep breath, and set her Riemann eyes on opaque; I envied her that ability, though she said it couldn't be all that different from just having eyelids. Maybe she didn't really understand that total darkness is different from very dim red blur.

She held that deep breath, focused her tension, let the breath out, counted down slowly from ten to zero, and fell into a light, lucid trance with a soft sigh. "Dutch, Dutch Boy, Dutch Boy paints, Dutch Harbor, Dutch treat, Dutch chocolate, Amsterdam, Damn-damn-damn, Rotterdam, Hope they'll Rotterdam teeth out, dikes, boy with finger in dike, middle school boy jokes, Richard the Second, Bolingbroke, gutter, alley, Prince Hal, Hal and his pal, Hal-canal, windmills, Chaucer, Wife of Bath, need a bath, bride of Frankenstein needs a bath, mad scientist, Frank the Mad Scientist, Frank Francis Francis Tyrwhitt, Tyrwhitt To-Who a Merry Note . . ."

Her light, flat, fast-talking monotone went on, interrupted periodically by deep, slow breaths. I watched the projected image on the wall; each word or expression popped onto the screen in pale green, and a swarm of blue points – closely related words – would accrete around it like instant fungus, putting off orange shoots of exact antonyms, red coils of strangely-attracted words, and gray filaments of etymological links. Structures accreted, stabilized, or cycled, and eventually homologies emerged in the data; the structures whirled, bounced, adhered, and merged, dragging their parent objects with them, until at last I put my hand up and said, very softly, "Wingtoes, that's enough."

The phrase Wingtoes that's enough flickered in pale green for a moment, then disappeared, replaced by the single word COMPLETE.

I felt Horejsi move, adjusting her Riemann eyes. She sat beside me, as always too close to be polite but not close enough to clearly signal she was offering herself for sex. I had thought about what I would do if she ever moved that close, and I was afraid that someone would notice that it was not merely a Liejt making use of a Com'n co-worker; what if I really liked her and someone saw?

"Four probable synecdoches," I said, "and one almost-catachresis. I'll take the catachresis around and see who gloms."

"Want company?" she asked.

"That end of town is ganged up bad. I don't think I want to be a person with a partner looking for info. Smells like cop and cops have accidents up there."

Horejsi nodded; I was glad she didn't insist on coming with me. Having her along for a physical brawl would only improve my odds by about 9 per cent, but having the Bug-Eye Lady (as my informants tended to call her) standing beside me would cut the chances of people telling me what they knew by about 22 per cent.

She hugged me; I hoped it looked subservient enough to any cameras there might be, but I suppose it always had before. "Be careful," she said.

I pushed her away gently and said, "I always am," and did my best to keep my face flat when she smiled. It was another joke no one else got.

Four motivations account for just a shade less than sixteen out of every seventeen mesohistorical jumpers (the next better approximation is 3151 out of 3349):

- obsession with a historical question (nowadays all the photos of Praesidant Reagan's assassination have a dozen guys in costumes of the next three centuries standing around with cameras)
- compound interest schemes (we don't think the Stock Bubble of 1641 even existed in Original History)
- I could-have-been-a-better conqueror fantasies (the Whenness Prophylaxis Program could probably have filled a high-rise apartment block every decade with all the Hitlers and Napoleons who had to be isolated)
- serial killers (there's a lot of history where they're less likely to be caught).

Peron probably wasn't any of those four. Horejsi thought she'd spotted two other categories in the residuals, and she thought Peron was what she was calling "Class Six." If she was right, the situation was worse than it appeared. I didn't have any way to quantify how much worse.

"I'm looking for a guy that is probably called Dutch Lop," I said. "Usual kind of deal, you know I'm good for the benjamins." I flashed her five 1500-dollar bills and Pickles smiled back at the smiling Disraeli. "He might also be called Dutch Einstein or Doctor Dutch, which he probably likes better than Dutch Lop."

Pickles didn't bathe as much as she needed to these days, but she still dressed to give you a view of what was for sale. I sat back away from her but she edged closer. I could see her lips move while she counted one-and-a-half, three, four-and-a-half . . . She'd've been happy with a tenth of what I was going to pay her – the seven and a half was just to make sure she remembered the conversation.

After a minute Pickles nodded. "New guy I've heard of but haven't met. Missing an ear if I hear right." She giggled, or at least shook while she brought up some phlegm. "Get it?" She must've thought that was funny. "He's the cruncher for Brock's Geiger bank. I've bet four eleven forty-four with them a couple times but it's never come up, so I know it's bogus."

Pickles was an informant for everyone – Police, ATF, us, No Such Agency, and all her local crime gangs, probably more I didn't know about. What you told Pickles, you told everyone; I wanted Dutch Lop to know I was looking for him.

I had the same conversation with four similar informants in two more bars within a decimile of Alvarez Peron's apartment. I heard, twice more, that Dutch Lop was a cruncher for Brock's Geiger bank.

A Geiger bank is just a numbers game or a bollita that gets extra cachet by using Geiger counters sitting on a block of vitrified nuclear waste to generate the digits. Weird that 4-11-44 was still a popular combo, a 150 years since Sherman's bombers cratered every railroad yard from Atlanta to the sea; things persist in the Irish parts of town.

Anyway, it wasn't the ghetto of today, but the Bohemian cheap-rent districts of 600 years before that I should be thinking about. Southwark in 1388 had been home to a few eccentric artists and scientists, like Chaucer, Dunstaple, Leonel Power, and Tyrwhitt, a smattering of fashionable young aristocrats, and a lot of garden-variety crooks.

Given that the numbers game is old – Fibonacci mentions it in the same text where he explains Arabic numbers – no doubt there had been plenty of people who knew how to set the line in Southwark in 1388, and if one of them had been dragged forward as Peron's ballast, he'd certainly have been employable enough anywhere around that neighborhood. That much made some kind of sense.

Having sown enough word that I was looking for Dutch Lop, I headed for Brock's. Horejsi often chided me for always taking the direct approach, but I had two good reasons: it often worked and I didn't understand any others.

My phone said, "Horejsi's calling," and I said, "Accept."

In her usual tone of mild amusement, she asked, "Well, do you believe in my added categories yet?"

I smiled flatly toward my phone, tilting the screen to pick up my face, and said, "More evidence that Peron fits your category six?"

"Maybe. Back at your place in say an hour?"

"Sure, I don't have any reason to hurry to the next place I'm trying."

"See you there." She hung up. One of a lot of things I like about Horejsi. Didn't bother with that silly "God ble'ye" that so many people still did. Finish talking, hit the switch, like a sensible person.

I turned back to catch the Liejt-reserved levrail to my place; I'd get there before Horejsi, who had to ride the Com'n.

A whole family of people with brown skins was walking up the sidewalk. They looked exactly like the ones I had seen preserved in museums, except they wore clothes, and were talking among themselves.

With all the training, I can keep a straight face. I don't react much to anything, anyway. Even so, this was probably the biggest challenge to my deadpan ever.

I managed. I looked at them but no more intently than an absentminded man thinking of nothing would look, and smiled.

The grandfather of the group – there were also a mother, father, and two young children – glanced at me, smiled back, and said, in a sort-of-Confederate accent, "Beautiful day, isn't it? Don't you love a sunny day in Denver?"

"I was just thinking that," I said. "Clear and bright and not too cold."

He nodded pleasantly, and we passed on our respective ways. I didn't let myself run, or grab the phone, or even think too much.

That brown-skinned family had to be the biggest casopropagation anomaly I'd ever seen, and I'd seen plenty. This case must be a billion times bigger than I'd guessed.

Schrödinger's modification to Einstein showed why, although usually changes that least altered energy, causality, or entropy propagated earliest, every so often something big popped up ahead of the small changes.

You'd expect that modern electronic stuff changes rapidly because it's just flipping some qdots into alternate states. After that, old style electronic records change, because that takes only a few thousand electron volts per bit. Paper records might require as much as a single calorie per page, so in the fluctuations of twenty years or so, those change. Finally, gross things – changes of shipwreck locations, emptying and filling graves, shapes of furniture and buildings, placements of trees and roads – take many megajoules, or more, and change across a century, the ones least entangled with others first.

The thing that affects other things the least, and requires the most complex rewriting, is long-term memory in the brains of socially isolated people. That doesn't change until it has to, and ghost versions persist in a few heads until the hermit, or monk under vow of silence – or lonely oddball like me or Horejsi – finally dies.

Now don't ask me about the math. I relate to numbers, not math. I can tell you that 524,287 is a Mersenne prime because it just obviously is, but if you want me to find an eigenvector or a derivative, you'll have to send me to the tweenweb to find the guy that already did.

If you don't understand the difference between those two abilities, you wouldn't understand the math – just as I don't.

But according to Herr Doctor Schrödinger, once there's been a change in history, some changes propagate out of order and out of proportion, because the dimensions of conservation are curved and imperfectly orthogonal. (I can almost picture that in my head.) One consequence is surprising inconsistencies in the real world, during the time between the backward departure and the forward resolution, so that long before a couple million quantum computers remember all sorts of different things and frequently consulted dictionaries change the spellings of forty words, a freeway is nine yards west and was built four years earlier. Another is that huge things may change and small things remain the same; Horejsi and I both remembered a four-hour interval when Denver had been named Auraria, and been Espano speaking, but all the RTD levrails had run on the same exact schedules.

Schrödinger's equations also showed why any change, great or small, may or may not persist when the original change is undone; as he said, once you had a cat in a box, if you eliminated its parents, then you either had no cat or a different cat that was exactly the same, and you wouldn't know till you looked. A bridge in Pittsburgh might be there intermittently for a couple of years; the statue of Athena in New York Harbor might permanently change to Dolley Madison or Elizabeth Cady Stanton; the passengers on a Frontier gravliner alighting on the concourse at Denver International might catch a glimpse of what appeared to be a Civil War–era winged rocket with Frontier markings taking off.

Those casopropagation anomalies are in proportion to the overall scale of the change that was made in the past. So whatever it was that Peron had done in 1388 in London, it had caused a kind of people who had not existed in 400 years to appear on the street in Denver, speaking English and sounding a bit like imported Irish slaves.

One thing it meant for sure: a lot of phone calls to the FBI's Report an Anomaly line. Unless we found Dutch Lop fast, Horejsi and I were about to have to do an absolute mountain of paperwork.

The moment I walked in the door, I told Horejsi about seeing that brown-skinned family – speaking English! – on the streets of Denver. "So Peron's change was at least big enough to undo some part of the Great Erasure. No wonder the Bureau set us such a large bonus. When they tried to measure significance, the isotemporal estimating engine must have spun till the needle broke," I finished.

Even Horejsi, with not a digit or an equation in her head, was gaping. "I think," she said, after a bit, "we'd better get over to that Geiger bank, and see what we can find. I don't think we have any time to spare, so I'd better come along, even if some of your informants are scared of the Bug-Eye Lady."

"They can't be any more scared than I am right now," I said.

We talked on the train, just the usual sort of thing we'd talk about on a case, I guess because the unusual stuff about this case scared the crap out of us.

It was Christmas shopping season, and the Com'n levrail was jammed. Just to get privacy, we had to spend some extra expense account money for a compartment. Even though with the window dimmed, we didn't need the cover of pretending to be a couple, Horejsi slid around to sit closer to me on the bench seat than was polite; I could have put an arm around her. Of course I was Liejt and she was Com'n; that would mean her vanishing. Even a person as socially isolated as I was couldn't forget that. But I kept noticing how easily my arm would have gone around her.

They recruited people like me and Horejsi for our freak memories and social isolation. If the last two digits in the GDP of the Untitled States of Armorica reversed, I'd notice that the book was now "wrong," and if the Third Rogue's Speech in Love's Labours' Won changed "thou'st'll" to "you'll've," Horejsi would pick it up. She'd already been most of the way through Chaucer, the writer nearest to the change point that she had in memory, and said all she noticed was "just three little changes, the kind of collateral connections you get because some printer's apprentice died in childbirth and her replacement made an alternate typo. Which reminds me of a weird thing – I scanned the list of all the printer's apprentices in the Registry of Known Persons for London 1300–99 Third Edition and it was just like I remembered, but in Registry of Known Persons for London 1400–99 Second Edition Revised all the girls' names had disappeared."

"Maybe they had a fad for naming girls after boys?" I suggested.

"All of them? There's no such thing as a one hundred per cent fad in baby names. And there were plenty of girls in several other crafts. So our boy did something to the printing industry." Horejsi sounded pissed off.

The train glided into the big shopping center they have south of downtown these days – I remember when it appeared there, some guy named Varian who had jumped back to try to tell Mussolini to break away from Hitler and kick out the Pope. It took us forever to find Varian's ballast because it was a pretty girl who only spoke Neolatin. It turned out that one of the Free Irish gangs found her when she first appeared in Varian's neighborhood, enslaved her, and sold her south to Mexespana. "This wasn't a bad shopping center to get out of the deal, as long as we had to fail on a case," I said. "Lots of jobs and it's kind of pretty."

Horejsi's apertures focused on me. My as-usual-lame attempt at small talk had only pissed her off more. "It was hard on that poor girl. Let's not have too many failures if we can help it. Anyway, I think the London registry anomaly shows us that whatever Peron is doing to make a mess of the past, it's pretty bad."

She got mad whenever a case involved gender. I'd probably made her madder by bringing up the Varian case, because so much awful shit had happened to the ballast girl.

I grasped her arm and pointed as I turned left down the next sidewalk, to remind her we were going to the levrail station on the north side of the center; since we were in public it was important that there be no affection in it, and I'm sure I was careful. Nevertheless, she curled her arm upward and brought my hand into hers. This was all right too; we did it often when pretending to be a couple, and the FBI said it was fine as long as I didn't initiate. I didn't know why we'd need a cover. Maybe she just wanted to hold hands. That was all right with me.

"This case is beginning to scare the shit out of me," she said.

Mad, then scared, liked to hold hands to feel better afterwards. I filed that under the mental heading of "understanding Horejsi." Long ago I had noticed she liked being understood.

We had some time before the next train, so we walked slowly through the fake Victorian shops, or "shoppes" as most of them insisted on being spelled. A lot of the shops had dressed their Irish in old time costumes, so there were bonnets and top hats and so forth everywhere in the glaring winter sun, and every other vendor selling indulgences or bratwurst was dressed like one of Santa's leprechauns. It was a little creepy, I thought; I could remember when I was a kid, leprechauns had been entirely monsters that the slaves might conjure up to turn loose on us, but something had slipped or come undone somewhere in time, since then, and there was now a tradition of bad monster leprechauns and good obedient leprechauns.

"Do you remember when leprechauns were all bad?" I asked.

"Oh, yes," Horejsi said. "That was the thing that changed my whole life. When I was nineteen, I was babysitting for a rich family, reading a story to the kids, and one day, in exactly the same old dog-eared ruin of a book I'd read to them a dozen times, Willy Wonka had good leprechauns working in the chocolate factory. I told my mother about it, and she turned me in to the cops."

"And then they turned you into a cop."

"Yeah." She made her smile-grimace; I guess she liked my joke. Maybe that was why she squeezed my arm tighter. "Christmas is pretty. I hope nothing ever happens to change it." I could tell she was happy, maybe about the decorations? Didn't people usually say that at night instead of in bright sun?

Aside from our freak memories, the FBI used us because we didn't relate to people much. Interacting with the ballast jumpers barely changed us and anyway it wouldn't matter because we interacted so little with other people. Horejsi and me, we're like "people without souls," that's what it said when I hacked in to read the documentation about ballast hunters.

What the hell. I liked the job. It was rarely dull, it used many of my skills, and it had made me a rich man, rich even beyond my Liejt allowance. And if we didn't have souls, Horejsi and I still had some fun and were company for each other, now and then.

We got on the Com'n northbound that would take us to the slums east of downtown, and took another private compartment. It would be fifteen minutes before the train actually moved, but we had more than enough things to talk about in the privacy of the compartment.

It was always possible that Dutch Lop would be at Brock's Geiger bank, and talk to us. Naturally we hoped so, but it didn't seem likely. When the ballasts had been living rough on the street, they were often cooperative, but if he was the cruncher at Brock's, he wasn't poor, and he had some kind of a life he might be attached to.

I brought that up to Horejsi and she touched my hand – she was still sitting very close – and said, "Whose favorite phrase is 'theorizing in advance of data'?"

It took me a moment to get it. "Mine," I admitted.

"Well?"

"Yeah." She made that weird grimace she does instead of a grin; another thing Horejsi likes is being right.

We talked through a review of what we knew. "How bad was the weather this spring?" Horejsi asked. "I never remember weather."

"Three spring blizzards after his date of arrival, and that bad cold snap we had in late March – it was minus seven Celsius on March 28 and minus three on March 29."

She nodded, letting apertures open all over the spheres of her eyes, taking in all of the nice, crisp December day through the big window, as the train lifted off and glided through the downtown. "Then definitely, he found friends and shelter of some kind, right away, and something fed him," she said. "No true isolation possible."

The trick with breaking the causality between the traveler and his ballast was to grab and de-link the ballast as early as possible; create a situation in which the easiest Inconsistency Principle resolution would be that the ballast had always existed in our world and the time traveler had not. Then intemporia would take over and work on our side, erasing most of the changes. But for best effect, we had to de-link them early.

This one wouldn't be early.

Of course you could also deal with human ballast the way we dealt with ballasts of mud or logs or deer; scramble it, chemically treat it, and scatter it. Most ballast hunters just didn't like luring or kidnapping people to have them ground to bits and vaporized. Horejsi and I had occasionally muttered a suspicion to each other – that the Whenness Prophylaxis Program was just a preliminary step to make us investigators more comfortable, and that as soon as we were off the case, the ballast ended up as extremely overcooked sausage. I shuddered.

"Cold?" Horejsi asked.

"No, just thinking of something grim."

"That family you saw means this is something huge," she said, "and the bonus the FBI set makes a lot more sense now."

We both knew that, but maybe it was comforting for her to keep saying things we both knew.

We got off at the Welton Station, and paused to let a Liejt levrail shoot by us, the D line, hurrying down Welton to Smallville. I wondered if the world would still be there when they got there, or if they'd still be the same people. It gave me the creeps.

Horejsi's hand was on my arm again. I covered it with my other hand, to keep it there, because it felt kind of good.

It was still bright and sunny but the wind was picking up in a way that could feel like a nail driven up my nose, and the dry cold air seemed to tear at my skin. The Christmas wreaths and banners on the lampposts whipped and slapped alarmingly; I felt sorry for the poor Irish slaves who had had to put them up.

Changing the subject, she asked, "How many disturbances do you know about so far?" She kept her hand on my arm. I was grateful.

"A lot of statistics aren't what they used to be," I said. "Baseball looks like it's more fun – scores are higher, all the statistics about stealing home from fourth base vanished, and teams are nine players instead of eleven – center and right shortstop are combined, and there's no wing fielder."

"And this is interesting because – "

"Enormous number of public stadiums built to a different design, enormous number of records altered, lots of very public lives altered, and not in a way that maps one to one. Economics is pretty much the same – three of the main estimating components of the Gross Dominion Product are gone, replaced by something called 'foreign trade,' but that looks more like a change of bookkeeping. But the census tabulation changed drastically for the last hundred years, and the date when they started mining coal up in the high country is one hundred four years later."

Horejsi whistled. "Those are some big mass-time changes. Which fits with that . . . anomaly . . . you saw."

"Brown-skinned people wouldn't use as much coal?" I asked, puzzled by what she meant.

"No, silly, I mean the change of skills." She nodded at the Irishmen walking on the street-side sidewalk ahead of us; each was carrying home his coal ration and his little Thermos of LOX for his Franklin stove. "I'm sure any Irishmen that the brown-skinned people owned would use as much coal as anyone else. It's just – their existence – the scale of that change . . . well, it's consistent with changes as big as the ones you describe. That's what I mean." She sighed and rubbed her hand gently up and down my arm, brushing my coat sleeve and pressing a knuckle hard enough for me to feel it in my muscles. "Rastigevat, there were some big physical things in the last few hours. I-70 jumped down to Albuquerque, then up to Cheyenne and for a while ran along the path of US-50, yesterday, so we had a large number of lost and angry truckers and some cargoes just gone. About seventy of those weird little passenger-only trucks that show up sometimes during anomalies drove into Pueblo over the temporary I-70; most of the people who arrived in them are acquiring new memories right now, though a few have just vanished. Three whole train cars of Irish that were going to be put to work in Aspen for the holidays are just gone, along with all their titles and registration. And what that I in I-70 stands for changes from Intergovernmental to Interim to Imperial and back to Interstate all the time."

"Where was Denver when I-70 jumped?" I asked.

"Do you remember what we were doing yesterday?"

I thought for a moment. "Is today Tuesday?"

"Thursday."

"Shit."

"Yeah. It's a big mess, Rastigevat. Huge cultural changes too – the name of this continent keeps fluctuating between Armorica, Amorica, and Amocira, and every so often turning back into New Armorica, which is what they called it right after the airships found it and the Great Erasure started. Twice it has wavered into New Arimathea, which I guess means a more religious trend somewhere in the past, and once it was North Arimacha, which I don't get at all. Three changes in Chaucer, thousands of different names in the London Registries, renamed ships with drastically different names in standard histories of England and the Untitled States, the Enlightenment 150 years later and all of history since then compressed to fit.

"Also, and don't laugh at me for noticing – "

"I never do," I said. Actually I never laugh.

"I know and I appreciate that." She squeezed my arm. "Anyway, there were several new authors added to the catalogs in the mid-nineteenth century. That one is okay with me; it looks like Peron undid Perkins's permanent damage, so we have Samuel Clemens back. Even so, it looks like this time he was writing under a pseudonym, Mark Thrine, and I'm guessing from the title in the public library catalog that The True and Romantic Career of Becky Thatcher has been replaced by a novel about her boyfriend, Tom Sawyer, and there's some kind of sequel about a minor character from that book, Irish Jim. I kind of hope we get to keep Clemens's books – I remember liking them as a child."

I had never gotten why people liked to read made-up stuff; it seemed to me it was bound to clutter your memory, keeping track of what was true and what wasn't. But I could appreciate that Horejsi liked it. I rested my hand on hers, on my arm. "This stuff would all be so fun and exciting if it weren't for the whole world disappearing."

"You're always my man for perspective, Rastigevat." She made that smile-grimace again.

Even if they're sort of acting like a normal couple, two people who radiate "cop," one of them with Riemann eyes, don't easily walk into a Geiger bank. Not that Brock's people would be dumb enough to try to keep us out, but there was probably a pretty funny scene out back in the alley as people poured out the door and fell all over each other. Anyway, it was calm enough inside as we walked up to the young girl at the counter.

I ignored the clicking Geiger counters and their rolling digit displays. "We need to speak to Dutch Lop. Official business."

"I – " the girl flushed deeply, her pale skin going as red as her hair. No collar tattoo, so she was freeborn, but as everyone says, it takes generations to get the slave out of the Irish, and the sight of authority just paralyzes some of them especially in this part of town. "Um. I do'na'f'he be – "

"It's all right, Brighd." The accent did sound Dutch, but he pronounced that funny Irish gulp at the end of her name perfectly. The man who limped out to greet us was missing one ear and had an odd hairless scar on the top of his head. It looked like the cylinder of enclosure had been a bit tight, or he'd been moving, because the hand that reached out to shake mine was missing half a thumb.

He was in his early twenties, and his wide-set eyes and square jaw couldn't have been more relaxed, confident, and utterly in charge if he'd been Liejt and expecting us to deliver a pizza. I don't respond to faces much, but I liked the asymmetric shock of black hair around the scar, the big toothy grin, and the twinkling almost-black eyes under the thick brow. "I had thought you might be here sooner," he said, speaking a trifle slowly, "but it is good you are here now."

Horejsi suddenly froze like a squirrel on a levrail track, and opened so many apertures so wide that the spheres of her Riemann eyes were blotched with black dots the size of quarters. After a moment, she let her breath out and said, "It's an honor to meet you."

I looked back and forth, and then she explained. "Mr Rastigevat, this is Francis Tyrwhitt."

"Frank," he said. "They call me Frank here, at least to my face. I prefer it to Dutch Lop, if I may be Frank with you."

I couldn't help grinning; puns are one of the few kinds of joke I get, and Horejsi snorted and made her smile-grimace. "Is there somewhere we can talk privately?" she asked.

"There is," he said. "Will you let Leo pat you down for weapons, please?"

"Of course," I said. "There's something in my left sock, one in the coat pocket, and something back between my shoulder blades."

I had expected that Leo would be some immense, hulking goon, but he turned out to be a short, bony, big-jawed, freckled Irish boy, maybe fourteen years old, with the fresh scars from manumission around his neck, all big feet and hands and loose gangle.

Nonetheless he was a pretty good frisker, getting everything I had mentioned right away, and finding two of my three spares as well. He flushed red-bordering-on-purple as he searched Horejsi, but did an equally good job on her. When he had finished and nodded, Tyrwhitt touched him lightly on the shoulder, and Leo grinned like he'd won the lottery.

Tyrwhitt's office was surprisingly luxurious – the surprise was not that it had obviously been expensive (you expect that with anything connected with organized crime), but the type of luxury it radiated. The room looked much more like the comfortable working den of a Liejt software developer or investment broker than the sort of medium-level organized crime boss office I'd been expecting. There was no gaudy, kitschy art; no visible gold or drug paraphernalia; only a standard wall projector, not one of the pricey monstrosities. He had gone for solid, practical, but not brand-name furniture. Nothing here would violate the Sumptuary Act, and if this place were ever busted in the media, there wouldn't be much of the usual sneering and tsking about Liejt goods in a slum apartment.

He gestured to a cluster of warm leather-covered seats by a small gas fire, and said, "Well, let me pretend to be a conventional host for conventional guests. Would you like coffee, whiskey, anything?"

"How about coffee officially, and a splash of whiskey that just sort of happened?" Horejsi said. Her hand stroked my arm; I wasn't sure what this was about, but I said, "Same for me." There's no rule about accepting food or drink from suspects; usually we like to stay sharp and avoid the possibility of being dosed, but sometimes not insulting hospitality is more important. I have no sense of that; maybe she was just cueing me in?

Tyrwhitt spoke an order into the air, and before we had quite settled onto the couch, Brighd came in with our drinks. When we had all pledged the Creator and taken a first appreciative sip of the good warm stuff, Tyrwhitt said, "All right, let me begin by saying I will be happy to consent to being disconnected from Alvarez Peron – in fact he intends that I should be – but the reason why I am utterly willing to cooperate is one your superiors will not like."

"Well, when the ballast is cooperative, we're mostly just the go-betweens anyway," I said, "so why don't you just explain it to us, Mr Tyrwhitt – "

"Frank."

"All right, Frank, just tell us what you want us to tell them, and we can proceed from there."

He did, and bizarre as some of the stories we had heard had been, his was right off the scale. If I were trying to attach a number to how different it was, I'd say, roughly, that on a scale of weirdness-by-ballasts of one to ten, Frank Tyrwhitt was equal to the resultant vector of an isosceles triangle, $e^{\pi+i}$, and Wednesday.

"It's the Creator's sense of humor to weave the good and the bad together so tightly, I suppose. Time is one, and that is sad, but so is memory, and that is a blessing," Tyrwhitt said. "There's your problem, your opportunity, and what you need to do with me – if you're smart."

Horejsi, next to me on the couch – stroking my arm, which I found a little distracting – said, "You mean time is all one thing – "

"I mean that experience and theory both show there's only one world, and only one timeline, we don't get to do everything, there's no 'out there,' no cross-time or 'otherwhen,' in which things went differently," Tyrwhitt said. "Which means we have to make the hard choice of what world to have, and there's no compensating for that by telling ourselves that, well, things didn't turn out so well in this version of time, but in the universe next door things are doubtless peachy – gloriously exciting or beautifully serene or whatever it is you personally favor – and the only real tragedy is that some of us have to live in the timelines that did not work out as well. Believing that would be a comforting escape, but it's just not so. This is the world there is, and things are just done or undone and that's all there is to it. There's not a world out there where I didn't come forward in time; this is all there is. And that's sad, because it means that not only can we not have everything, even the whole universe can't. Time is one, eh?"

"And memory is one," I said, seeing his point, "and that means that whatever there was, we get to keep it – as long as everyone and everything gets to keep it . . . yes, I see what you mean. It does seem very fair. Fairer than, maybe, anything else I've ever heard of."

"And it's all there is, anyway," Horejsi added. "Time is one. All right. I bet you've been rehearsing that speech a long time, Frank."

"Since about my fourth day up here in 2014," Tyrwhitt agreed. "Here's what happened; you may judge for yourself – in fact, I know good and well you will judge for yourself."

Tyrwhitt had been soundly asleep in his rented room above an ordinary in Southwark. He felt a disconcerting lurch, and sat up in a strange room where light came from the ceiling. In strangely accented English, a voice told him to check in the large mirror to his right to see where he had been injured, and that on the table to his left there were things to dress and bind his wounds.

The capital Roman letters on what he now knew had been a military medkit made some sense; the artificial lights in the ceiling, that were neither flames nor skylights, were odd.

Following the directions of the friendly disembodied voice, he carefully stayed on the ground cloth on the floor as he applied the 3S strips to his ear, to the sliced-away area on his hairline just above his forehead, and to the stumps of his right thumb and left ring and little fingers. He was amazed at how little pain he felt.

"Most ballasts are amazed by that," Horejsi told him. "A nerve that just ceases to exist at a point, with no shredding or other damage, just doesn't hurt much."

He nodded. "I suspect that if I had contemplated any larger matter, I would have had to doubt my sanity; painless instantaneous amputation, and strangely effective wound dressings, were marvels within my scope of admiration, and most of what I woke to find around me was, at that moment, simply utterly beyond me."

The little discomfort ceased as the 3S strips gripped his flesh. The voice directed him to warm food on a sideboard, with more available in the strangely cold box, which he was to keep closed. It guided him through the other necessities, then asked him to take a seat on a couch. The lights in the room dimmed, and an illusion of Alvarez Peron appeared on the wall, and began to talk to Tyrwhitt.

Horejsi and I had deduced that Peron was a Liejt scientist from a defense project, but we hadn't realized quite how high a level. It fit – everything else about this case was extreme.

Knowing that he had one of the five or ten greatest minds in the whole history of the world on the receiving side, Peron had begun by giving a two-hour lesson in the theory of indexical derivability; Tyrwhitt, just twenty-two years old in experience, had absorbed what would have been his life's work all but instantly. The artificial voice then showed him how to access the tweenweb and gave him a short list of things he was certain to need to know within one week, which was the time Peron had estimated Tyrwhitt could depend on before needing to relocate.

By the time that Tyrwhitt walked out of the apartment and up the street to meet with Gerry Brock, he spoke and understood modern English passably for everyday purposes, and he had a basic understanding of where and when he was, and of why Peron had swapped places with him. Brock had lived up to his contract with Peron, supplying a hiding place and facilities at first, in exchange for Tyrwhitt writing the software for the ultimate Geiger bank. He had wanted to keep Tyrwhitt hidden for as long as possible, but Peron's instructions had been explicit. Reluctantly, Brock had said that, well, he was already rich, and apparently the universe had decided that rather than get still richer, he would be a minor character in an important piece of history.

"You have to understand," Tyrwhitt added, "that there was no question of not following Peron's wishes about what I should do up at this end of the time divide. He knew what he was doing, and once I fully understood what that was, I was in full agreement. Nor do I doubt what he has in mind will work. Admitting that I am rather a talented person, I am a pretty good judge of talent in my own field – and Peron, whatever his real name may have been, was a talent on par with myself, or with Newton or Babbage if you prefer."

"So why did he switch places with you?" Horejsi asked.

"So that I would not give the world indexical derivability in the Year of Grace 1403," Tyrwhitt said. "And then to make sure that the zero-change bias would not force indexical derivability to come into history by some other path, he also eliminated the eleven students that carried the work forward after my death in 1406."

"Eliminated — " I began, and felt the fuzziness in my head; I suddenly found the images of pages from my schoolbooks were becoming fuzzy, that some of the science lectures I had attended in college were . . .

"My dear sweet Jesus," Horejsi said. "And he must have done it in the first few days he was there. That's why he went to 1388, in May. He needed all eleven of them to have been born — so he could kill them all. Maxwell would have been just a few weeks old — "

I knew Maxwell's equations, and suddenly I could not remember the second digit of the Year of Grace when they had been published; it formed a blur, Year of Grace One Blur Sixty-Five. "I can't remember all of the old school rhyme for the eleven, either," I said.

"Thomson, Carnot, DeGrasse, and Barlow,
Someone, someone, Ampirre, and Marlow;
Abelsmythe and Voltman, and — and—"
I could not remember any more of it.
"Blake was hung . . ."

"Maxwell who was very young," Horejsi finished. "And the first 'someone' you mentioned was Paschalle, but now I can't think of the second, and I'm already forgetting parts of the rhyme myself. In 1388, the oldest was — someone — "

"Dryburn," I said. "The only one older than Tyrwhitt himself—"

"And the only one I knew in 1388," Tyrwhitt said. "I thought he was an arrogant asshole, actually, but the only person I could really talk math with. And it's rather sad because they were bright, talented people, and probably without the original discovery and my teaching, they'd just have been smart people who went on to obscure careers, but Peron didn't want to take any chances. With the tools and compounds he took back in his kit, probably none of the deaths looked like a murder, either, at least not to a fourteenth-century coroner." He sighed, swirled his hot coffee and whiskey mix, and took another sip. "Still, murder does stick in the craw, doesn't it? Especially murdering someone for having brains and talent; even more especially, men who apparently would have been my closest friends. So I know something of a whole other life that didn't happen for me, and I don't know quite how to feel about that."

"It's your life," I said slowly, "but it's our world. So we're in process of vanishing or at least transforming. I can feel some sympathy for you, but what about us?"

"Bear with me for a moment. I claim the privilege of explaining myself because you will have to understand, if you decide you want to undo what Peron has done."

"If we decide. If?" Horejsi sounded outraged. "Our job is to—"

"Just so. My own sense of – well, ethics I suspect? – thinks you should have a chance to do your job."

I was hopelessly confused; he sounded like he was defying us, and turning Peron and himself in, and playing some obscure game to delay us, and asking for our help – all at once. "Perhaps," I said, "We don't have much choice except to let you tell us in your own way."

"Perhaps that is true. I dislike presenting a choice so bluntly. It seems rude." He watched the coffee swirl in his cup as if it were a crystal ball, and Horejsi and I sat still as stones until he went on. "Anyway, I've been over the databases and through the libraries, and all of the eleven are gone wherever I look, now. The Inconsistency Principle is kicking in fast and hard, and I've been helping it along by sending out random e-mails, getting people to look for those names – sweepstakes contests, questions to librarians, that sort of thing. You're probably among the last five percent or so of people who remember them."

"Then we're too late," Horejsi said. "Peron has erased the whole modern world, and we're – well, I suppose we're already not who we were, and about to either cease to be or be someone else." She rested her hand on my arm; I put my hand on hers.

"There's a great deal more casopropagation still to happen," Tyrwhitt said, "and I suppose you and your bosses can still do a great deal to undo it, if you choose to tell them what I am about to tell you. If they jump an agent back to take my place in my bed, for example, and position another one to kill Peron on arrival, it might still all be undone.

"But they would have to decide to do it right away – and I'm quite sure they won't make that decision at once, unless you contact them almost right away, shout at them to do it now, and one way or another shake them into it. That's your decision: to try to get through to them, or to just let things happen as they're happening. Hear me out, and decide. After all, Mr Rastigevat, as you say, it was my decision but it is your world. You get to decide which one you will be retaining.

"So what I propose is that I will explain why Peron did it, and why I have chosen to enlist on his side in this conflict, and finally ask you not to interfere – but I will give you the chance to interfere. You will be able to walk right out of here and call FBI headquarters. I won't stop you if you choose to do that."

"Why not?" I asked. "You have told us several times you approve of whatever it is Peron is trying to do." Truly, I thought it might already be too late. It's an endless source of frustration to FBI field agents that the desk never authorizes anything soon enough to do any good. "Why would you let us walk out of here, call our superiors, and fight for a crisis mission to stop you?"

"My peculiar taste, I suppose." He sighed, and looked from one of us to the other. "It is only that . . . well. There is an idea that interests me, the idea of consent. I suppose you might say it's one of those things that mathematicians love, taking concepts like 'obvious,' 'hard,' or 'complex,' and making them precise. I am interested in the idea of having someone consent to this – actually in following up on Peron's idea about it, which I think was right."

"Peron got someone's consent to end the world?" Horejsi asked. "Whose? How could he possibly – "

"I think Peron made an astonishing and correct judgment about what needed to be done, and why. To carry out his judgment, he performed a more or less permanent kidnapping, and a variety of other crimes against me, but he ultimately depended on my consenting to cooperate; if his recordings had not persuaded me that what he was doing was right, his scheme would have unraveled."

"Did the eleven consent to be killed?" I asked. "Did they agree never to be the brilliant, admired people they would have been?"

"They did not. And that is another part of my evidence in reasoning about all of this, you see. The whole thing is made the more confusing, of course, because I am a superb mathematician, but not necessarily any more ethical than any of the rest of you. So I'm quite sure of my reasoning, and not the least bit sure about my premises. Nonetheless, I find I admire what Peron did and how he chose to do it, and so, as far as my understanding reaches, I intend to try to do likewise." He rose and added coffee, and liquor, to our cups, without asking. Neither Horejsi nor I objected; for myself, I can say that I probably needed all the warmth I could get. "He chose a way that required the consent of one person who would be utterly changed – me. His way of doing things required that I consent to be someone utterly different from the person I would have been. To coin a phrase, you might call me an extremely representative sample."

"You've read Gödel about random numbers," I said. "But doesn't indexical derivability show there's no true randomness, only chaos and complexity?"

"Imagine," he said, "a world where the sciences had to develop without indexical derivability – one where the sciences were based on setting up repeated tests of physical, chemical, and biological processes, or observing the world. And without the eleventh and fourteenth theorems, you'd never know about the complectisons, so you wouldn't be able to study those functions effectively. The numbers might as well have a random component for all you knew, and you'd have to use Gödelian statistics. Probably it would have developed a lot earlier. You see what a different world we are thinking of launching?"

"We're not, you are," Horejsi said firmly. "I have no idea what either of you have been talking about, but I gather that somehow you think the consent of two of us is the same thing as the consent of a billion people."

"Half the people on Earth are slaves, and you know the market is always booming in ways to prevent suicide. What if I decided to obtain their consent?"

That one kind of froze me. Officially I knew slaves couldn't consent to anything; that was basic law. But what if the change of history made a slave Free – or even Com'n, or Liejt while we're at it? Wouldn't he surely consent retroactively?

I could see how Tyrwhitt had been seduced into thinking about this problem. The math was fascinating. I wanted to spend hours just talking about that, but Horejsi had that strange I am about to inexplicably explode expression she often got, right when the math was really interesting, so it didn't seem like a good idea.

"So why not two people, one Com'n and one Liejt, both intimately involved with the case already? Who could I ask otherwise? Everyone? And how would we put their answers together? I suppose we could gather their answers – here, in the Year of Grace 2014, with the forty-third Lancaster on the throne of the world, I have at hand a communication system that would allow me to call the whole almost-one-billion Christian beings on all the continents, every son of Adam and every daughter of Eve, Liejt or Com'n, slave or Free, Espano, Russky, Fransche, English, and all the minor nations as well. I could use that marvelous communication system to call every one of them and ask, 'Would you like to vanish or be someone else utterly, because the world that would come into being would be, in ways that might or might not make any sense to you, better than the one we live in now?' I also have no doubt, speaking as a mathematician, that I could devise some ingenious way of putting all their expressed thoughts, fears, and hopes together into one common thought, as the parliament has sometimes essayed to do, and as the Athenians and Romans are alleged to have done; perhaps something as simple as the casting of a verdict as is done with a jury. Yet somehow that revolts me; I do not think a verdict is made better by the number of hands raised to make it – that seems an idea that could easily become a snare for the half-witted. The decision of one, or a few, reasonably wise, merciful, and kind people, it seems to me, is better than that of a billion indifferent.

"So I have chosen to follow the model that Alvarez Peron has shown me. I was called to stand in for everyone of my time, and all the ones to come after, and given no choice about having the choice; he said, 'These are my reasons, choose,' and I chose.

"Part of what I chose is to pass a part of the choice on to you. We are in the last days or weeks of your possible consent. If you do not choose, what I have done will stand; or you may assent in full and say, let it stand; or – if you choose otherwise – you may try to stop me, and we shall contend and see who is the stronger. But I am offering you two people – and only you two people – a chance, and just a chance, to try to undo my choice, because you are concerned in it. You stand in for all the people who are about to have never existed, or to be someone else entirely; I will tell you what will be gained if you choose to vanish in those ways, and you will decide if it is worth it."

"By deciding to die?" Horejsi asked.

"No, not to die," I said. I could see at once that was one of those times when words just make a muddle of things, because they combine so many meanings that are logically separate, and she was a creature of words. "Once a soul has come to exist, it has no exit from existence but to die, but when souls abruptly have never existed, nothing experiences the death. So he's offering us the chance to try to be what exists after it all damps back down; and since there is only one time, at any given moment we'll exist or not, but we won't cross over – that is, die – between existing and not existing." I looked to see if she got it, and what she might be feeling about it if she did; I was the only person who could read her facial expressions, but she was really the one of us who understood all this human-feelings stuff, and it just seemed to me that if Tyrwhitt wanted us to consent (or not), it had to be a matter of how the Christian souls of the Earth ought to feel about it, or not – which was more her department than mine.

Her head was turned at an angle to get her ear, not her eyes, pointed at me; her Riemann eyes were gone, and she wore dark glasses to hide whatever functionless eyes she did have. A big dog on a harness sat beside her. I knew in a moment I would not remember the name "Riemann."

No, of course I would – it was the name of the dog.

"I have been blind from birth, Rastigevat," she said, "and yet, I have the dearest, sweetest memory of what your face looks like when you're sad, or make one of your terrible jokes, or worry about me. And I try to hold on to it, recall it more strongly, and it slips away. Is that what it will be like for everyone?"

"Probably," I said.

"Then, Magister Tyrwhitt," she said, "how can you ask us to give all this up? And how did Peron persuade you that you should?"

Tyrwhitt sighed, and said, "This will be more difficult than I had thought, and I had not thought it would be easy." He held his breath for a moment, unconsciously stroking the stump of his thumb, and finally went on. "The man we all know as Peron – how strange to think that the real name of a man of his gifts will be lost forever – had taken the step that Einstein, Copland, and Turing all struggled all their lives to achieve. Peron finally united matter and meaning in a single theory, and using that theory he could meaningfully measure meaningfulness itself – know how much meaning there was within our event horizon, as well as how much meaning there had been, and how much there could be. I can tell already, Mr Rastigevat, that your training in the physical sciences and logic is fading from your memory, and you will not retain the ideas you need to understand me much longer; so do not object, as it will only cost time.

"At root, things and ideas are one; meaning in the soul and causality in the universe are one. Peron cracked this impossible nut – if I remain here and live long enough, I may just barely reach the point he reached, but I doubt I shall have anyone I can teach it to. And what he found was that Christian Europe had made a terrible mistake; when Henry VI of England became Henry I of the World, and decreed that 'all the world shall be under the Pope or under the ground,' and his airships went forth in the Great Erasure, to make an empty world for the Christians of Europe to grow into . . . he was only doing what any other civilization of his time might have done . . . he felt no wickedness, saw no reason to think anything of it. A few thousand preserved bodies in barrels of formaldehyde, and because of Maxwell's pleas, the largely unreadable books of such peoples as had books, was not only all that was saved but all he could have imagined wanting to save."

Horejsi seemed to draw herself up defensively, and said, "The Caliph, or the Sultan, or the Emperors in Peking, Timbuktu, or Cuzco, would have made some similar decision."

"They would. If indexical derivability was found early enough, the culture that found it would make an empty world for itself. That was fated, I agree." Tyrwhitt raised his hands, not remembering that due to casopropagation, she could not see the gesture now; I myself tried to hang onto the name of those immense, ball-like eyes that once graced her face, and with which she had seen me – Riemann stirred uneasily and sadly. He was an old dog, always at her side since I had met her at the FBI Academy, and now his bones were uneasy and never quite comfortable.

"So," Tyrwhitt said, "Peron discovered that the Great Erasure reduced the amount of meaning in the world to very nearly nothing, at least compared to what it might have been. You people in your pointless world understand each other perfectly, for the meanest slave in the Antarctic coal mines has more in common with the Emperor in Nice than two sailors on the waterfront had in common in my time. You can travel along any line around the whole world and find not one surprise. You fight wars in order to run a death toll large enough to reshape populations, with great efficiency in death but no more passion than boys of my time put into a game of football. I have seen the recordings of your Nuremberg trials, and the judges shaking hands with the accused, and finding that Europe had been suitably reduced; I have cracked into the Imperial records to see the decisions for the famines and the massacres to hold the population at what the Emperor thinks tolerable levels. Even you, Mr Rastigevat, saw something recently that heralded the end of the world, and though you wanted the comfort of your friend's presence, you were more worried, were you not, about the reports you might have to write?"

"That," I said, "and because if I rushed to her, someone might realize I was emotionally attached to her. She could be executed for that. But how did you know? You must have been watching me – "

"I was. I have been for some time. Like most Liejt, you were raised never to be aware of a slave; thus an adroit slave, such as Leo, can tail you with no fear of detection. I should not have been able to do that with Ms Horejsi, because despite generations of genetic research, your strange little rump of a culture has not managed to produce a class-conscious dog."

I felt as if he'd pried up a carefully nailed down part of my soul and shone a light in, revealing little white things that smelled bad and squirmed.

"And if we do nothing?" I asked.

"Indexical derivability will probably remain undiscovered by any civilization – until I give it to the world after the changes have settled down.

Another bit of freedom I believe in, you see. Humans should have the power to use it; all I ask is that they should first become wise enough not to rashly erase the meaning from the world."

"Is meaning such a good thing?" Horejsi asked.

He shrugged. "Is being?"

"You are asking me to give up mine."

"True."

Horejsi rose. "Rastigevat, I think we've heard enough. Let's find out if he means what he says."

Tyrwhitt didn't stop us from leaving, so I guess he meant what he said. I wondered how long before our choice would be meaningless. I wondered why she hadn't called the FBI on her cell phone from Tyrwhitt's office, and then found myself thinking, I remember when there were cell phones.

"Keep looking for a phone booth," she said. "God alone knows whether we have any time left at all." Her arm wrapped tightly around mine – it had recently been a strange and marvelous sensation, something which I had just begun to enjoy, but in a day, a week, or a month her hand on my arm would always have been merely a matter of her being blind.

"I remember saying that I remembered what you looked like," she said, "but now I don't remember how I knew, and I'm – "

Her arm jerked on mine, painfully hard, and she fell beside me. I bent to see what was wrong.

Riemann shrieked and tried to drag his harness out from under Horejsi; there was a gory hole the size of my fist in his fur, and then I saw the bullet hole below Horejsi's ear, an instant before I felt the sting in my calf.

I rolled forward, keeping low, part of my brain figuring that the shots had to be coming from the row of parked cars across the street, and most of the rest of it shutting down because the thought Horejsi is dead would have been unbearable. Another shot whistled somewhere above me as I tumbled to a position crouched low where a fire hydrant was close to a phone pole, and the slight rise in the grass strip between them created a little pocket of cover. My pistol, the one that Leo had missed in his frisk (it had not been a pistol when he frisked me, had it?), found its way out of my best conceal-ment spot; I saw motion between two cars and fired. I was rewarded with a groan.

The top of a head went bobbing along, just above the line of cars, as the second one went to his partner's aid. I timed it as best I could, led him what I thought would do it, and squeezed off a second round.

It was better than I could have anticipated; for some reason I will never know, he bounced high on his next hop, and the round went right into his throat. I crouched, waited, thinking, Cars. Those little people-hauling trucks are called cars. I have seen them all my life, and the one with two corpses (I hope) slumped behind it is a Packard Thunderbird.

Riemann was still struggling, whimpering now as he grew weaker, alter-nately trying to drag himself free from where Horejsi's body pinned his harness, and licking and nuzzling her. Other than that, it was silent except for the distant hum of engines.

People would think this was a gang war. In a sense, it was. I had a memory of being lovers with Horejsi, I thought suddenly. In a short time that memory would be what was real, and I would miss her even more than I missed her already.

It was a race between my leg and my psyche as to which would give out on me first.

There would be much too much authority around here much too soon. There had been no shots in a few seconds, and past all question the other side knew where I was. I leaped up sideways from my safe position, and nobody shot. My calf blazed up, and blood filled my shoe, but I hopped and hobbled across the street; I almost fell over when an ice cream truck swung wide behind me (ice cream truck? I suddenly remembered one from my childhood, driven by – a black woman? She had called me "sweetheart!").

Memories battered at my mind like furious crows but I pushed them away. The man I'd nailed in the neck was dead, and the one I'd hit before had taken the shot in his floating ribs, and was gasping out pink foam; he didn't seem to be aware of me when I flipped his coat open. He had a badge like mine, only now FBI stood for – what had it stood for?

Never mind. Sirens were wailing. I took a few big lurch steps back out into the street, held my badge up to a cop car, and barked a set of incoherent orders, to get him to drive me back to Tyrwhitt.

He popped his door and I got in. I told him that the Federal officers who were down had been shot by Crips in a drug sting gone bad, and urged him to hurry. He relayed that story to his dispatcher as we zoomed up Downing Street.

I remembered Brock's as being some kind of a bank but that didn't make any sense. It seemed strange to know that this was my first ride in an atui-osmobile, and yet I already had the memories to say, "this is vital, officer, keep that throttle floored and don't spare the steam." I can't remember what reasons I gave the cop not to follow me in or call for backup.

As I lurched past the counter and down the corridor into Tyrwhitt's office, Leo and Brighd trailing after me and telling me frantically that I couldn't, my foot caught on the carpet, the pain in my calf stabbed straight up through my brain, and I finally fell forward. You wouldn't think the floor could hit so hard; it only had a short distance to wind up. It got dark and stayed that way.

"Simon Rastigevat, can you hear me?" I knew that voice – Tyrwhitt.

Tyrwhitt definitely. That was the voice. I opened my eyes. He was leaning forward, his face inches from mine, in a chair by the cot I lay on.

I looked down to see the needle he'd slipped into my arm; his gaze followed mine.

"Sorry," he said. "A necessity if you are going to choose. Do you remember the choice I asked you to make?"

"I do," I said. A great deal came back to me – not as much as I could have wished.

"That choice, I'm afraid, was made by the idiots who must have decided that you had been turned, or were breaching security, or whatever they believed in that brief interval as meaning scrambled everywhere. So rather than talk to you or ask what was going on, they sent out a team to eliminate you. I'm glad the human race didn't land permanently in that history; it must have been very unpleasant. But we're crossing over now, all of us, and the whole universe; every hour the Internet – that's the tweenweb to you, but you'll realize in a moment – is full of new complicated history, and there are billions more people in the world, and – "

He started to turn gray and blurry, and then I realized the world around him was blurring out too. He yanked at the needle in my arm and I yelped in pain.

"Sorry, had to do that to keep you here. That's why I had to wake you up, you see." He looked slightly sick, and I realized that the needle hadn't hurt nearly as much as he must have thought it did; I wanted to reassure him but it seemed like too much bother to talk.

Tyrwhitt seemed to assume I forgave him anyway, after a moment, and said, "How much do you remember? You went into shock. It's been three days since you lurched into Brock's. Thanks for doing that, by the way; the cops were only twenty minutes behind you and they were not after you. As I said, I think we jumped through a lot of nasty pasts during that time."

"Horejsi died," I said. "She was gone before I could bend over to see she'd been shot. Poor Riemann; he was hit too, dying I think, and he must have been so upset." I knew how weird and stupid it was but I couldn't get past the way the dog felt. Somehow it was more real to me than Horejsi's death . . . no, it was what was real about Horejsi's death. "I'm going to miss her pretty bad myself." I looked at him and said, "This is strange, though. I remember the old world. I remember what we used to do. But I can feel the new world ghosting in on me, around the edges, as if I'm starting to remember a different world where I've always been."

"You were unconnected to the rest of the world for a long time," Tyrwhitt said, "at least a long time as measured in temporal change."

"Temporal change?"

"Event count. Do you remember who I am?"

"Yes. You are . . . Francis Tyrwhitt. Frank. Dutch Lop. In the history where, uh, when, I came from, you were . . . like Newton or Einstein?"

"Better," he said, grinning. "And who am I here?"

"My star grad student. Jesus, I'm a math professor. Talk about a great deal; I remember thirty years of math without actually having had to do the homework."

We both laughed, slightly sadly. I remembered that too, Frank Tyrwhitt was just about the only person except me who thought the jokes I liked were funny. Like Horejsi.

Who was really dead, and Tyrwhitt and I were really alive, and we were . . . not here. We were now.

It felt painfully strange, as if one memory were a delusion, and another one were real, and I just had no ability at all to work out which was which. "And now you are . . . a mathematical psychologist? Is there even such a thing?"

"There is now. And there always has been, for at least 120 years. Or for about thirty-one hours, depending on exactly what you count." He shrugged. "And I remember indexical derivability, but I am not sure now what to do about it. Do you remember it?"

"You have written dozens of long detailed e-mails to explain it to me, or try to," I said. "It's hard. I can get there through the deep structure of numbers, and just trying to get there . . . haw. I'm a math prof myself, these days. Oh, I remember, I just said that."

"One of the network of eleven," he said. "Eleven math professors I've found who are willing to work on indexical derivability with me. Or rather you are going to be the eleventh, if you want to be, because I need a real number theory person, and you're the one. But you need to get in touch with the other ten, soon, and with many others. You've always been reclusive."

"I certainly remember that. I guess if I want to work on it I will have to see more people – well, more people live. I have so many friends online."

"You do, and you could possibly do all your work with the group online. That is not what I mean. I mean you have to get into this here – this now, I mean, this now – and connect and relate, because if you don't, you'll fade just like you almost did when I twisted the needle in your arm to bring you back. The Inconsistency Principle is still trying to resolve things. With a very few people, apparently the easiest resolution is to let us keep all our memories, as long as we only discuss them among ourselves."

Stupidly, and out of nowhere, I said, "I'm going to miss being in the FBI. And I really, really miss Horejsi now."

I could feel myself start to cry, and he reached out and rubbed my face, gently, with a handkerchief. "How long has it been since anyone touched you?"

"Before you? Horejsi did now and then. I had to wait for her to do it, I couldn't touch her or ask her to touch me. I liked it so much when she did, and I couldn't say that either."

"I remember how things were in the other now," he said, nodding, as if it mattered a lot that he remembered. "You see, like me, you'll keep those memories, many of them, like a vivid dream or a favorite childhood story. That's the lowest-energy, most stable way to be. And you'll be able to write them down before they fade, or talk about them with those of us who remember."

I rubbed my face. "I don't know if . . . do you know how stupid it was that I could never say . . . there was something I wanted to say to Horejsi, and now I won't even be able to speak her name, except to you and a few others."

"Do you remember why you couldn't say it?"

"Damage, there's something wrong with me, I don't get what's going on in other people, I don't see them right . . ."

"Oh, yes, all that. In this now, we're just beginning to see a way to help people fix the problem that you have, and work around it. Over there no one was trying because it was one of the marks of being Liejt, like the thinness, the long thin fingers, the perfect pitch, or the blond hair. But there was a really simple reason why you couldn't reach out to her, but it was okay for her to signal that she wanted to please you, and that was – "

I felt the thought dawn. "Liejt," I said. "I was Liejt, and she was Com'n. If I'd spoken my feelings and anyone had overheard, they'd have killed her. There's no Liejt now, there never has been, no Com'n, everyone is pretty much . . ."

"Free," he said. "No capitals. All the other categories – Noble, Liejt, Com'n, and even slave – are all gone; now everyone's just free. Please stay. I need people who can help me remember – we need, all those of us who do remember, we need someone to help us remember."

"Stay?" I asked.

"Make the effort. Be in touch with people. Meet the people you have only talked to on the internet, speak to strangers, go out in public where you will meet people."

"I liked doing that when I was in the FBI."

"Keep liking it. And act on that liking. In the last few hours while you have been unconscious, you've started to fade, just the way you did just before I hurt you with the needle – and then come back, and then faded again, but the fading is getting more frequent and more severe.

"From what I could doodle out really fast, from what I remembered that one of the versions of Einstein had solved, there's sort of a cusp that you must be balancing on; if you're connected enough, the easiest way for the inconsistency principle to resolve the situation, in the path of least energy in all its dimensions, is probably to let you exist as what I'm calling a polymnemonic, a person with more than one mutually contradictory set of memories. But if you aren't connected, if you don't talk and communicate and get yourself involved with everyone else, then the lowest-energy way for the universe to resolve you is for you never to have existed."

"Why do you care?" I asked.

"Well," Tyrwhitt said, "There's the use I have for your gifts – here, where there was no indexical derivability, you weren't stunted in your training, and there was more to learn and practice. So we can use you within the group, if you want to talk pure obvious practicality.

"Then there's the matter of having some company and someone to talk to. I would like to talk with someone who knows what is real. Purely selfishly, I'll be lonely as well.

"And finally, now that you're awake and emotionally perhaps more ready for it, there is something I'd like to see, as well." He turned toward the doorway and called, "Ms Horejsi, I think he's ready to join us now."

There was a painfully slow scrape and thud; in a moment I would know, I realized, the thing that had always been wrong; the thing that was on the tip of my mind. The reason why I had only contacted Horejsi via . . . the Internet, not the tweenweb.

For a moment I hung suspended.

The scraping sound sped up, and my heart sped up with it. I was already grinning, remembering what I had always known, and sat up in the bed. I felt so well. "Come on," I said, "it's finally time, Ruth."

"What else could it be, Simon?"

And, laughing, I got up to walk to her. Tyrwhitt steadied me – I was still tottering from the wound in my calf – and helped me walk forward, and I forgave him his smug little smirk, just as I always had, so many times before.

ON THE HUMAN PLAN

Jay Lake

Highly prolific new writer Jay Lake seems to have appeared nearly everywhere with short work in the last few years, including Asimov's, *Interzone*, Jim Baen's *Universe*, *Tor.com*, *Clarksworld*, *Strange Horizons*, *Aeon*, *Postscripts*, *Electric Velocipede*, and many other markets, producing enough short fiction that he already has released four collections, even though his career is only a few years old: *Greetings from Lake Wu*, *Green Grow the Rushes-Oh*, *American Sorrows*, and *Dogs in the Moonlight*. His novels include *Rocket Science*, *Trial of Flowers*, *Mainspring*, and *Escapement*. He's the co-editor, with Deborah Layne, of the prestigious Polyphony anthology series, now in six volumes, and has also edited the anthologies *All-Star Zeppelin Adventure Stories*, with David Moles, and *TEL: Stories*. His most recent books are a new anthology, co-edited with Nick Gevers, *Other Earths*, two new novels, *Green and The Madness of Flowers*, and two chapbook novellas, *Death of a Starship* and *The Specific Gravity of Grief*. Coming up is another new novel, *Pinion*. He won the John W. Campbell Award for Best New Writer in 2004. Lake lives in Portland, Oregon.

Here he give us an incisive and very far-future look at the ultimate destiny of humankind, thousands if not millions of years from now.

I AM CALLED DOG the Digger. I am not mighty, neither am I fearsome. Should you require bravos, there are muscle-boys aplenty among the rat-bars of any lowtown on this raddled world. If it is a wizard you want, follow the powder-trails of crushed silicon and wolf's blood to their dark and winking lairs. Scholars can be found in their libraries, taikonauts in their launch bunkers and ship foundries, priests amid the tallow-gleaming depths of their bone-ribbed cathedrals.

What I do is dig. For bodies, for treasure, for the rust-pocked hulks of history, for the sheer pleasure of moving what cannot be moved and finding what rots beneath. You may hire me for an afternoon or a month or the entire turning of the year. It makes me no mind whatsoever.

As for you, I know what you want. You want a story.

Oh, you say you want the truth, but no one ever really wants the truth. And stories are the greatest of the things for which I dig. Mightier even than the steel-bound femurs of the deinotheria bred by the Viridian Republic, which I can show you in vast necropolii beneath the Stone-Doored Hills. More treasured than the golden wires to be pulled by the fistful from the thinking heads which line the Cumaean Caves, screaming as the lights of their eyes flash and die.

Anyone with a bit of talent and the right set of bones to throw can foretell the future. It's written in fat-bellied red across every morning sky. But to aftertell the past, that is another trick entirely.

They say death is the door that never opens twice. At least, not until it does. Sorrow is usually the first child of such a birthing, though just as often the last to be recognized.

People die. Cities die. Nations die. In time the sun itself will die, though already it grows red and obese, a louche, glowering presence fat on the midsummer horizon. When the daystar opens up its arms, all graves will be swallowed in fire, but for now, the bones of men lie atop older bones beneath the friable earth.

Likewise the skins of cities. All our places are built on other places. A man might dig down until the very heat of the earth wells up from the bottom of his shaft, and still there will be floors and streets and wooden frames pressed to stone fossils to greet him there.

You know that the first woman to greet the morning had gone to sleep the night before as an ape. Some angel stirred her dreams with God's long spoon, and the next day she remembered the past. The past was young then, not even thirty hours old, but it had begun.

That woman bred with an ape who didn't yet know he was man, then birthed a hairy little baby who learned she was another woman, and so the world unfolded into history. That woman died, too, laid herself down into the earth and let herself be covered with mud which turned to rock.

If I dig down far enough, someday I'll find that grandmother of us all. But this story you've come for is about another time, when I only dug down to death's doorstep.

It was an exogen come to me, in the twenty-seventh hour of the day. My visitor was taller than a pike-pole, with skin translucent as the slime of a slug. Still, it was on the human plan, with two arms, two legs, and a knobby bit at the top that glittered. The ropes and nodules of its guts shimmered inside that slick, smooth, shiny skin. Its scent-map was strange, the expected story of starships and time's slow decay mixed in with spices and a sweat which could have gotten a rock-crusher drunk.

Dangerous, this one. But they always were. The safe ones stayed home.

"Digger," the exogen said. It used a voder which could have come from before the dawn of technology. Believe me, I know.

I'm not one for judging a man by his shape. Metatron knows I find myself judged enough. Still, I'm cautious around one who comes from too far away, for a man distant from his home has no need of scruples. "Aye, and that's me."

Something flashed pale, pallid blue in the exogen's middle gut. "Compensation."

One of them types. I could handle this. Like talking to a Taurian. All syntax implied inside a hyperlimited morphemic constellation. Like playing a game of two hundred questions. "Compensation in what cause?"

"Seeking."

"That's what I do. I seek. By digging. What do you seek?"

"Death."

That one required some careful thought. I didn't reckon this exogen had come all the way across the Deep Dark between the stars just for me to dig him a grave. Not that I hadn't dug a grave or four in my day. It was just that no one spent the kind of energy budget this exogen had dedicated to being here on Earth simply to lay themselves down.

"Anyone's death in particular?"

"Death." My visitor flashed a series of colors, then manipulated its voder. "Thanatos."

"Oh, Death his own self." I considered that. "You must be aware that death isn't really anywhere to be found. Mythic personification doesn't leave behind calling cards for me to dig up. Entropic decay does, but everything is evidence of that."

I knew from experience that it would take the exogen a while to assemble my loose stream of lexemes into a meaningful morph that fits its own mind. I'd been working on my sun-altar when it had found me among the dunes of rusted bolts where I make my home. So I returned to my labors, confident that my visitor would speak again when it was ready.

Exogens work on their own timescale. Some are sped up so fast they can experience a standard-year in a few hours, others move so slowly they speak to rocks, and perceive trees as fast-moving weeds. In time, this one would answer.

Two days later, it did.

"Secrets," the exogen said, as if no time had passed at all.

"You want me to dig for the secrets of death?" I laughed. "There's no secret to death. It finds us all. Death is the least secret thing in the universe. I can open any grave and show you."

The traveler's hand brushed down its translucent front, trailing tiny colored flares. "Undying." The voder somehow sounded wistful.

I picked up a ritual axe from the Second Archaean Interregnum, traced a claw tip down the blade edge. "That's easy enough to take care of. Dying is simple. It's living that's hard."

For an awful moment, I wondered if the exogen was going to dip its head and dare me into trying that pulsing neck. Instead it just stared a while. I thought the exogen had slipped back into slow-time, until it spoke again. "Door."

"Door." Death's door? That was a figure of speech as old as architecture. This exogen must have something more literal in mind.

"Door." This time the voder's tones implied an emphatic conclusion. The exogen shut down, sinking into a quietude that took it across the border from life into art. The sense of light and life which had skimmed across it like yellow fog on a sulfuritic lake was gone.

I had acquired my very own statue. Walking, talking, likely intelligent, and certainly fantastically wealthy.

For a test, I poked one tip of the Achaean axe into its chest. About where the sternum would be on the human plan. It was like poking a boulder. The exogen's skin had no give, and the sense of weightiness was downright planetary.

Door. What in all the baroque hells of the Mbazi Renaissance did it mean by door?

You know perfectly well that while the Earth is dying, it's nowhere near dead. Even a corpse on the forest floor isn't dead. Intestinal flora bloom in the madness of a sudden, fatal spring. Ants swarm the massive pile of loosening protein. Patient beetles wait to polish bones until they gleam like little fragments of lost Luna embedded in the soil.

So it is with this world. I can tell by the cut of your suit that you're from offworld, but I can tell by the quality that you didn't ship in from across the Deep Dark. A patient man with an unlimited air supply and a wealth of millennia in his hand can almost walk from here to Proxima Centauri by station-hopping, but anyone terrestrial planning to move between the stars on anything like the scale of a human standard lifetime is very, very wealthy. And you are plainly terrestrial in origins, and just as plainly from those boots are not so wealthy.

I'm sorry. Did I offend? Take it from me, after you've riven open the graves of a million generations, you find your sense of tact has evaporated with all the rest of time's detritus. I'm poor, poor as a chuck moose, so I see no shame in anyone else's poverty.

Besides, this story I'm telling you may save your life some day. Surely that's worth an unintentional insult or two. Not that I'm planning another, mind you, but Dog the Digger is famously plainspoken as any of his kind, for all that he's not on the human plan.

Here we are, a collection of mortally wounded peoples on a mortally wounded planet, but we yet live. No matter the elevation of our estate. I may be a beetle polishing the bones of the world rather than a bright explorer at the morning of all civilizations, but still I draw breath. (Metaphorically speaking, of course.)

And so it fell to me to search for meaning in the exogen's request. After a month had gone by, his skin was cooled to the color of cold iron, and no one might ever have believed him to be alive. He stood like a man marking his own grave and stared sightlessly at the spot where I happened to have been positioned that night.

At least I understood now how he passed between the stars. The exogen had no life support requirements, and was immune to boredom. He wasn't so much undying as unliving.

I went to my friend Pater Nostrum. A man very nearly on the human plan, as so few of us were in these terribly late days, Pater Nostrum lived in a cathedral he'd built himself as an agglutination of debris, donations and some downright thievery. He dowsed for his cathedral one shard at a time, using a rod made of Gerrine Empire hullmetal wrapped in sable manskin. A time or ten I'd dug and hauled great, broad-beamed members for him, fetched by some unseen-to-me holy mandate from the dank rust-grained soil.

The genetics in that rod's leather grip were worth more than all of Pater Nostrum's earthly accumulations, but as a priest, he was beyond caring of such things. Or so he told himself, me, and everyone else who would listen.

This day I claimed back from him one of the favors owed.

"Pater," I said. It was the season for my third body, which was generally the most comfortable for those with whom I spoke. Not that the exogen would have cared, or truly, even Pater Nostrum.

He smiled, resplendent in his robes of rich vinyl trimmed with donkey fur. "Digger, my . . . son. Welcome."

We met in his cathedral's Second Sanctuary, a round-walled room with a ceiling line that very nearly described a hyperbolic curve. Armor cladding off some ancient starship, with a look like that. The walls were relieved with 10,432 notches (I am incapable of not counting such things in my first glance), and each notch held a little oil lamp wrought from some old insulator or reservoir or other electromechanical part. They all burned, which argued for some extremely retarded combustion characteristics. The scent map of the room confirmed that well enough.

"I would ask something of you, Pater Nostrum. I cannot yet say whether it is a remembering or a scrying or just some keyword research in the deep data layers."

Information flows everywhere on this earth. It is encoded in every grain of sand, in the movements of the tumbling constellations of microsatellites and space junk above our heads, in the very branching of the twigs on the trees. Knowing how to reach that information, how to query it and extract something useful – well, that was one reason why the world had priests.

Prayer and sacrifice invoked lines of communication which remained obdurately shut to most of us most of the time.

"I will do this thing for you gladly," Pater Nostrum said. "But you must first cross my palm with slivers, to make our bargain whole and place you under my hieratic seal."

This I knew as well, and so had brought a cluster of shattered beast-ivory from a sand-filled sea cave recently explored beneath the Hayük Desert. I scattered it over his open hand in a brittle mist.

Pater Nostrum closed his fist and grimaced. I knew with skin like his that the ivory would cut, burn, slice. When he opened his hand, the usual small miracle had occurred. A tooth with four twisted roots lay whole on the bloody palm.

"Well brought, Digger," the priest said. He smiled. "And of course my debt to you is long-incurred. So speak plainly and tell me what you seek."

I closed my eyes a moment and let my skin tell me the story of the point-source warmth of ten thousand little flames. The framing of this question had been much on my mind of late, with me working at great length to tease it out. Still, no matter what I said, I'd be wrong. Clearly enough the only choice was to address the moment and trust my friendship with this old priest.

"There is a client. A difficult one. It has charged me with finding the door into death. I would know if ever there was such a thing outside the sliding walls of metaphor. If so, where might I find this door, or evidence of its former existence?"

"A door into death." The priest stared up at his hyperbolic ceiling, his eyes following the receding curve into some dark infinity. "I will scry," Pater Nostrum muttered. The air began to swirl around him, dust motes orbiting his upturned face like swallows around a charnel house chimney. His eyes rolled inward until nothing remained within his lids but a silvery glowing sliver. One by one, the flames on the wall niches began going out in tiny pops as the priest drew from their energy in some pattern known only to him.

I settled to watch. The brilliant dust of a thousand millennia of nano-technology meant the world could describe itself, if like any competent priest one only knew how to ask the questions.

So he scried. The flames carried Pater Nostrum inward on a wave of information, a palimpsest of infinitely successive and fractal functional languages, protocols, handshakes, field-gestalts and far stranger, more curious engineering dead ends. I knew there had once been informa-tion systems which stored data in the probabilistic matrices of quantum foam, extracting it again in a fractional femtosecond as observational dynamics collapsed the informational field to null. Likewise I knew there had once been information systems which relied upon the death of trees to transmit data at a bit rate so low it could be measured in pack-ets per century.

Pater Nostrum could reach them all. At least on his best days. Each little lamp was a channel into some dead language, some time-hoared data proto-col, some methodology which had once swept the world so hard that its fingerprints remained in the noösphere.

One by one, 10,432 flames went out. Slowly we passed through shadow before being cast into darkness. I don't measure time on the human plan myself, and so hunger, micturation, joint fatigue and the like tend not to impinge overmuch on my situational experience, but Pater Nostrum experi-enced all those and more, until blood ran gelid-dark from his nose and ears as the last of the lights winked away to leave the two of us alone in lightless splendor demarcated only by the priest's breathing and my scent map of his body's sudden advancement into further decay.

Finally he came back to me.

"Well." Pater Nostrum picked his way through his words with an exaggerated care. "It has not been so in more decades than I care to admit to."

"You scry well, Father," I said politely.

"I should not think to scry so well again. Not as I value my own health."

"Surely the gods forfend."

"Gods." He snorted. "I am a priest. What does my work have to do with gods?"

"I can't say, Father." After that I waited for him to find the thread of his thoughts.

Finally Pater Nostrum spoke. "There was a movement during the era of the Viridian Republic. Religious, scientific, cultural."

A long pause ensued, but that did not seem to require an answer, so I did not answer him.

He gathered himself and continued. "They called themselves Lux Transitum. This movement believed that life is a waveform. So long as you do not collapse the waveform, life continues. Death was viewed not as a biological process but as an unfortunate event within the realm of some very specialized physics."

"Life is . . . life," I replied. "Antientropic organization in chemical or electromechanical systems which, when left unattended, tends to metastatize into computers, people, starships, catfish and what have you."

Lighting a candle from the inner pocket of his vinyl robes, Pater Nostrum shook his head. "As the case may be. I only reflect what I have been told. I do not believe it. Sooner argue with the dead than contend with the noösphere."

"Wise policy, every bit of it."

"At least for those of us on the human plan." He tried another grin, but this one failed.

More silence followed, as if Pater Nostrum was now determined to subdivide his attention into short tranches interspersed by gaps of inertia.

Finally I stepped into the conversation again. "Did Lux Transitum have a laboratory or a temple? Is there some place where they addressed this uncollapsed waveform?"

"Hmm?" Pater Nostrum looked at me as if noticing me for the first time. "Oh, well, yes."

"Father." I imbued my voice with infinite patience, something this body was fairly good at. "Where might I find their holy place?"

He woke to my question with a non sequitur. "How long have you been alive, Digger?"

"Me?" I stopped and considered that. "At least 7,313 years, by the most conservative view. Counting since the last cold restart of my cognitive processes."

"How long have I been alive?"

"I shouldn't know with any certainty," I said, "but we met shortly after the Andromachus strike. Which was 4,402 years ago the second Thursday of next month."

"You are not on the human plan, but I am." He leaned close, almost touching me. "Do you think the human plan called for four thousand year old priests? When was the last time you saw a child?"

I tried to remember when I'd last encountered a juvenile of any species. Not just human. "Surely people must breed somewhere."

"Surely," said Pater Nostrum. "But not here on Earth, it seems."

"This would not come naturally to my attention," I pointed out. "But you might have noticed it somewhere along the way."

"You know," the priest said vaguely. "The days are bathed in almost endless red light. There is always something to do. So few people roam the world . . ."

"A thought-block," I said sympathetically.

He seemed shocked. "On the entire human race?"

"What human race?"

We walked outside under the dying sun and argued long over whether Lux Transitum had the right of it, and what had been done with people. Most of all, whether to wake them up.

You're wondering now, aren't you? How long ago did this happen? What did Dog the Digger do next? Did I wake the exogen and what did I tell him when I did?

Look around you. What do you see? Quiet place we've got. That line of hills over there is a linear city from the Vitalist Era. Bury it in a quarter million years of rain and three major eruptions due west of here, and there's nothing left but low hills covered with scrub. Until you go digging.

Now beneath your feet. The red sand dusting your boots is rust accumulation from when teratons of asteroidal iron were brought down by the Wolfram Bund to clad the world in an impermeable metal shell.

Feel how the air tickles your throat when you breathe? You'd be appalled at how much processing power goes into your lungs, and what percentage of that crosses through the alveoli into your bloodstream. There's a reason that access to this damned planet is so heavily restricted.

So we live here in our lowtowns and our cathedrals and our shanties and caverns and buried mansions, and nothing ever changes. That was the big secret the exogen was searching for. You can transcend death, but only through stasis. The whole point and purpose of life on the human plan is death. Otherwise you are us, grubbing in the ruins of a million years of dreaming.

And you are us, now. Check in with your shuttle. I can promise you it's not going back up in this lifetime. My fourth and sixth bodies have already disassembled the engines and control surfaces. You will live forever, too, my friends, trapped in the same story as the rest of us.

The exogen?

He'll wake up eventually. We're letting him sleep. He's already found the answer. He just doesn't have to dig holes under a bloodred sky to earn it every day.

I am called Dog the Digger. I am not mighty, neither am I fearsome. But I am all you will ever know now.

Or maybe this is just a story, like you asked for. Under the crimson light of a dying sun, is there any real difference between a story and the truth?

Welcome to my Earth.

THE ISLAND

Peter Watts

Self-described as "a reformed marine biologist," Peter Watts is quickly establishing himself as one of the most respected hard science writers of the twenty-first century. His short work has appeared in *Tesseracts*, *The Solaris Book of Science Fiction*, *On Spec*, *Divine Realms*, *Prairie Fire*, and elsewhere. He is the author of the well-received "Rifters" sequence, including the novels *Starfish*, *Maelstrom*, *Behemoth: B-Max*, and *Behemoth: Seppuku*. His short work has been collected in *Ten Monkeys, Ten Minutes*. His most recent book is the novel *Blindsight*, which has been widely hailed as one of the best hard SF books of the decade. He lives in Toronto, Canada.

In the powerful and innovative story that follows, he paints a picture of a work crew compelled to labor on through all eternity, even though they're no longer sure whom they're working for or why, and who come smack up against an obstacle unlike any, even they have ever seen.

YOU SENT US out here. We do this for you: spin your webs and build your magic gateways, thread the needle's eye at 60,000 kilometers a second. We never stop, never even dare to slow down, lest the light of your coming turn us to plasma. All so you can step from star to star without dirtying your feet in these endless, empty wastes between.

Is it really too much to ask, that you might talk to us now and then?

I know about evolution and engineering. I know how much you've changed. I've seen these portals give birth to gods and demons and things we can't begin to comprehend, things I can't believe were ever human; alien hitchikers, perhaps, riding the rails we've left behind. Alien conquerers.

Exterminators, perhaps.

But I've also seen those gates stay dark and empty until they faded from view. We've inferred diebacks and dark ages, civilizations burned to the ground and others rising from their ashes – and sometimes, afterwards, the things that come out look a little like the ships we might have built, back in the day. They speak to each other – radio, laser, carrier neutrinos – and sometimes their voices sound something like ours. There was a time we dared to hope that they really were like us, that the circle had come round again and closed on beings we could talk to. I've lost count of the times we tried to break the ice.

I've lost count of the eons since we gave up.

All these iterations fading behind us. All these hybrids and posthumans and immortals, gods and catatonic cavemen trapped in magical chariots they can't begin to understand, and not one of them ever pointed a comm laser in our direction to say Hey, how's it going?, or Guess what? We cured Damascus Disease!, or even Thanks, guys, keep up the good work!.

We're not some fucking cargo cult. We're the backbone of your goddamn empire. You wouldn't even be out here if it weren't for us.

And – and you're our children. Whatever you've become, you were once like this, like me. I believed in you once. There was a time, long ago, when I believed in this mission with all my heart.

Why have you forsaken us?

And so another build begins.

This time, I open my eyes to a familiar face I've never seen before: only a boy, early twenties perhaps, physiologically. His face is a little lopsided, the cheekbone flatter on the left than the right. His ears are too big. He looks almost natural.

I haven't spoken for millennia. My voice comes out a whisper: "Who are you?" Not what I'm supposed to ask, I know. Not the first question anyone on Eriophora asks, after coming back.

"I'm yours," he says, and just like that, I'm a mother.

I want to let it sink in, but he doesn't give me the chance: "You weren't scheduled, but Chimp wants extra hands on deck. Next build's got a situation."

So the chimp is still in control. The chimp is always in control. The mission goes on.

"Situation?" I ask.

"Contact scenario, maybe."

I wonder when he was born. I wonder if he ever wondered about me, before now.

He doesn't tell me. He only says, "Sun up ahead. Half lightyear. Chimp thinks, maybe it's talking to us. Anyhow . . ." My – son shrugs. "No rush. Lotsa time."

I nod, but he hesitates. He's waiting for The Question but I already see a kind of answer in his face. Our reinforcements were supposed to be pristine, built from perfect genes buried deep within Eri's iron-basalt mantle, safe from the sleeting blueshift. And yet this boy has flaws. I see the damage in his face, I see those tiny flipped base-pairs resonating up from the microscopic and bending him just a little off-kilter. He looks like he grew up on a planet. He looks borne of parents who spent their whole lives hammered by raw sunlight.

How far out must we be by now, if even our own perfect building blocks have decayed so? How long has it taken us? How long have I been dead?

How long? It's the first thing everyone asks.

After all this time, I don't want to know.

He's alone at the tac tank when I arrive on the bridge, his eyes full of icons and trajectories. Perhaps I see a little of me in there, too.

"I didn't get your name," I say, although I've looked it up on the manifest. We've barely been introduced and already I'm lying to him.

"Dix." He keeps his eyes on the tank.

He's over ten thousand years old. Alive for maybe twenty of them. I wonder how much he knows, who he's met during those sparse decades: does he know Ishmael, or Connie? Does he know if Sanchez got over his brush with immortality?

I wonder, but I don't ask. There are rules.

I look around. "We're it?"

Dix nods. "For now. Bring back more if we need them. But . . ." His voice trails off.

"Yes?"

"Nothing."

I join him at the tank. Diaphanous veils hang within like frozen, color-coded smoke. We're on the edge of a molecular dust cloud. Warm, semiorganic, lots of raw materials. Formaldehyde, ethylene glycol, the usual prebiotics. A good spot for a quick build. A red dwarf glowers dimly at the center of the tank: the chimp has named it DHF428, for reasons I've long since forgotten to care about.

"So fill me in," I say.

His glance is impatient, even irritated. "You too?"

"What do you mean?"

"Like the others. On the other builds. Chimp can just squirt the specs, but they want to talk all the time."

Shit, his link's still active. He's online.

I force a smile. "Just a – a cultural tradition, I guess. We talk about a lot of things, it helps us – reconnect. After being down for so long."

"But it's slow," Dix complains.

He doesn't know. Why doesn't he know?

"We've got half a lightyear," I point out. "There's some rush?"

The corner of his mouth twitches. "Vons went out on schedule." On cue, a cluster of violet pinpricks sparkle in the tank, five trillion klicks ahead of us. "Still sucking dust mostly, but got lucky with a couple of big asteroids and the refineries came online early. First components already extruded. Then Chimp sees these fluctuations in solar output – mainly infra, but extends into visible." The tank blinks at us: the dwarf goes into time-lapse.

Sure enough, it's flickering.

"Non-random, I take it."

Dix inclines his head a little to the side, not quite nodding.

"Plot the time-series." I've never been able to break the habit of raising my voice, just a bit, when addressing the chimp. Obediently (obediently, now there's a laugh-and-a-half) the AI wipes the spacescape and replaces it with

....

"Repeating sequence," Dix tells me. "Blips don't change, but spacing's a log-linear increase cycling every 92.5 corsecs. Each cycle starts at 13.2 clicks/corsec, degrades over time."

"No chance this could be natural? A little black hole wobbling around in the center of the star, something like that?"

Dix shakes his head, or something like that: a diagonal dip of the chin that somehow conveys the negative. "But way too simple to contain much info. Not like an actual conversation. More – well, a shout."

He's partly right. There may not be much information, but there's enough. We're here. We're smart. We're powerful enough to hook a whole damn star up to a dimmer switch.

Maybe not such a good spot for a build after all.

I purse my lips. "The sun's hailing us. That's what you're saying."

"Maybe. Hailing someone. But too simple for a rosetta signal. It's not an archive, can't self-extract. Not a bonferroni or fibonacci seq, not pi. Not even a multiplication table. Nothing to base a pidgin on."

Still. An intelligent signal.

"Need more info," Dix says, proving himself master of the blindingly obvious.

I nod. "The vons."

"Uh, what about them?"

"We set up an array. Use a bunch of bad eyes to fake a good one. It'd be faster than high-geeing an observatory from this end or retooling one of the onsite factories."

His eyes go wide. For a moment, he almost looks frightened for some reason. But the moment passes and he does that weird head-shake thing again. "Bleed too many resources away from the build, wouldn't it?"

"It would," the chimp agrees.

I suppress a snort. "If you're so worried about meeting our construction benchmarks, Chimp, factor in the potential risk posed by an intelligence powerful enough to control the energy output of an entire sun."

"I can't," it admits. "I don't have enough information."

"You don't have any information. About something that could probably stop this mission dead in its tracks if it wanted to. So maybe we should get some."

"Okay. Vons reassigned."

Confirmation glows from a convenient bulkhead, a complex sequence of dance instructions that Eri's just fired into the void. Six months from now, a hundred self-replicating robots will waltz into a makeshift surveillance grid; four months after that, we might have something more than vacuum to debate in.

Dix eyes me as though I've just cast some kind of magic spell.

"It may run the ship," I tell him, "but it's pretty fucking stupid. Sometimes you've just got to spell things out."

He looks vaguely affronted, but there's no mistaking the surprise beneath. He didn't know that. He didn't know.

Who the hell's been raising him all this time? Whose problem is this? Not mine.

"Call me in ten months," I say. "I'm going back to bed."

It's as though he never left. I climb back into the bridge and there he is, staring into tac. DHF428 fills the tank, a swollen red orb that turns my son's face into a devil mask.

He spares me the briefest glance, eyes wide, fingers twitching as if electrified. "Vons don't see it."

I'm still a bit groggy from the thaw. "See wh – "

"The sequence!" His voice borders on panic. He sways back and forth, shifting his weight from foot to foot.

"Show me."

Tac splits down the middle. Cloned dwarves burn before me now, each perhaps twice the size of my fist. On the left, an Eri's-eye view: DHF428 stutters as it did before, as it presumably has these past ten months. On the right, a compound-eye composite: an interferometry grid built by a myriad precisely-spaced vons, their rudimentary eyes layered and parallaxed into something approaching high resolution. Contrast on both sides has been conveniently cranked up to highlight the dwarf's endless winking for merely human eyes.

Except that it's only winking from the left side of the display. On the right, 428 glowers steady as a standard candle.

"Chimp: any chance the grid just isn't sensitive enough to see the fluctuations?"

"No."

"Huh." I try to think of some reason it would lie about this.

"Doesn't make sense," my son complains.

"It does," I murmur, "if it's not the sun that's flickering."

"But is flickering – " He sucks his teeth. "You see it – wait, you mean something behind the vons? Between, between them and us?"

"Mmmm."

"Some kind of filter." Dix relaxes a bit. "Wouldn't we've seen it, though? Wouldn't the vons've hit it going down?"

I put my voice back into ChimpComm mode. "What's the current field-of-view for Eri's forward scope?"

"Eighteen mikes," the chimp reports. "At 428's range, the cone is three point three four lightsecs across."

"Increase to a hundred lightsecs."

The Eri's-eye partition swells, obliterating the dissenting viewpoint. For a moment, the sun fills the tank again, paints the whole bridge crimson. Then it dwindles as if devoured from within.

I notice some fuzz in the display. "Can you clear that noise?"

"It's not noise," the chimp reports. "It's dust and molecular gas."

I blink. "What's the density?"

"Estimated hundred thousand atoms per cubic meter."

Two orders of magnitude too high, even for a nebula. "Why so heavy?" Surely we'd have detected any gravity well strong enough to keep that much material in the neighborhood.

"I don't know," the chimp says.

I get the queasy feeling that I might. "Set field-of-view to five hundred lightsecs. Peak false-color at near-infrared."

Space grows ominously murky in the tank. The tiny sun at its center, thumbnail-sized now, glows with increased brilliance: an incandescent pearl in muddy water.

"A thousand lightsecs," I command.

"There," Dix whispers: real space reclaims the edges of the tank, dark, clear, pristine. 428 nestles at the heart of a dim spherical shroud. You find those sometimes, discarded cast-offs from companion stars whose convulsions spew gas and rads across light years. But 428 is no nova remnant. It's a red dwarf, placid, middle-aged. Unremarkable.

Except for the fact that it sits dead center of a tenuous gas bubble 1.4 AUs across. And for the fact that that bubble does not attenuate or diffuse or fade gradually into that good night. No, unless there is something seriously wrong with the display, this small, spherical nebula extends about 350 lightsecs from its primary and then just stops, its boundary far more knife-edged than nature has any right to be.

For the first time in millennia, I miss my cortical pipe. It takes forever to saccade search terms onto the keyboard in my head, to get the answers I already know.

Numbers come back. "Chimp. I want false-color peaks at 335, 500, and 800 nanometers."

The shroud around 428 lights up like a dragonfly's wing, like an iridescent soap bubble.

"It's beautiful," whispers my awestruck son.

"It's photosynthetic," I tell him.

Phaeophytin and eumelanin, according to spectro. There are even hints of some kind of lead-based Keipper pigment, soaking up X-rays in the picometer range. Chimp hypothesizes something called a chromatophore: branching cells with little aliquots of pigment inside, like particles of charcoal dust. Keep those particles clumped together and the cell's effectively

transparent; spread them out through the cytoplasm and the whole structure darkens, dims whatever EM passes through from behind. Apparently
there were animals back on Earth with cells like that. They could change
color, pattern-match to their background, all sorts of things.

"So there's a membrane of – of living tissue around that star," I say, trying
to wrap my head around the concept. "A, a meat balloon. Around the whole
damn star."

"Yes," the chimp says.

"But that's – Jesus, how thick would it be?"

"No more than two millimeters. Probably less."

"How so?"

"If it was much thicker, it would be more obvious in the visible spectrum.
It would have had a detectable effect on the von Neumanns when they
hit it."

"That's assuming that its – cells, I guess – are like ours."

"The pigments are familiar; the rest might be too."

It can't be too familiar. Nothing like a conventional gene would last two
seconds in that environment. Not to mention whatever miracle solvent that
thing must use as antifreeze . . .

"Okay, let's be conservative, then. Say, mean thickness of a millimeter.
Assume a density of water at STP. How much mass in the whole thing?"

"1.4 yottagrams," Dix and the chimp reply, almost in unison.

"That's, uh . . ."

"Half the mass of Mercury," the chimp adds helpfully.

I whistle through my teeth. "And that's one organism?"

"I don't know yet."

"It's got organic pigments. Fuck, it's talking. It's intelligent."

"Most cyclic emanations from living sources are simple biorhythms," the
chimp points out. "Not intelligent signals."

I ignore it and turn to Dix. "Assume it's a signal."

He frowns. "Chimp says – "

"Assume. Use your imagination."

I'm not getting through to him. He looks nervous.

He looks like that a lot, I realize.

"If someone were signaling you," I say, "then what would you do?"

"Signal . . ." Confusion on that face, and a fuzzy circuit closing somewhere, ". . . back?"

My son is an idiot.

"And if the incoming signal takes the form of systematic changes in light
intensity, how—"

"Use the BI lasers, alternated to pulse between 700 and 3000 nanometers.
Can boost an interlaced signal into the exawatt range without compromising
our fenders; gives over a thousand Watts per square meter after diffraction.
Way past detection threshold for anything that can sense thermal output
from a red dwarf. And content doesn't matter if it's just a shout. Shout back.
Test for echo."

Okay, so my son is an idiot savant.

And he still looks unhappy – "But Chimp, he says no real information there, right?" – and that whole other set of misgivings edges to the fore again: He.

Dix takes my silence for amnesia. "Too simple, remember? Simple click train."

I shake my head. There's more information in that signal than the chimp can imagine. There are so many things the chimp doesn't know. And the last thing I need is for this, this child to start deferring to it, to start looking to it as an equal, or, God forbid, a mentor.

Oh, it's smart enough to steer us between the stars. Smart enough to calculate sixty-digit primes in the blink of an eye. Even smart enough for a little crude improvisation should the crew go too far off-mission.

Not smart enough to know a distress call when it sees one.

"It's a deceleration curve," I tell them both. "It keeps slowing down. Over and over again. That's the message."

Stop. Stop. Stop. Stop.

And I think it's meant for no one but us.

We shout back. No reason not to. And now we die again, because what's the point of staying up late? Whether or not this vast entity harbors real intelligence, our echo won't reach it for ten million corsecs. Another seven million, at the earliest, before we receive any reply it might send.

Might as well hit the crypt in the meantime. Shut down all desires and misgivings, conserve whatever life I have left for moments that matter. Remove myself from this sparse tactical intelligence, from this wet-eyed pup watching me as though I'm some kind of sorcerer about to vanish in a puff of smoke. He opens his mouth to speak, and I turn away and hurry down to oblivion.

But I set my alarm to wake up alone.

I linger in the coffin for a while, grateful for small and ancient victories. The chimp's dead, blackened eye gazes down from the ceiling; in all these millions of years, nobody's scrubbed off the carbon scoring. It's a trophy of sorts, a memento from the early incendiery days of our Great Struggle.

There's still something – comforting, I guess – about that blind, endless stare. I'm reluctant to venture out where the chimp's nerves have not been so thoroughly cauterised. Childish, I know. The damn thing already knows I'm up; it may be blind, deaf, and impotent in here, but there's no way to mask the power the crypt sucks in during a thaw. And it's not as though a bunch of club-wielding teleops are waiting to pounce on me the moment I step outside. These are the days of détente, after all. The struggle continues but the war has gone cold; we just go through the motions now, rattling our chains like an old married multiplet resigned to hating each other to the end of time.

After all the moves and countermoves, the truth is we need each other.

So I wash the rotten-egg stench from my hair and step into Eri's silent cathedral hallways. Sure enough, the enemy waits in the darkness, turns the lights on as I approach, shuts them off behind me – but it does not break the silence.

Dix.

A strange one, that. Not that you'd expect anyone born and raised on Eriophora to be an archetype of mental health, but Dix doesn't even know what side he's on. He doesn't even seem to know he has to choose a side. It's almost as though he read the original mission statements and took them seriously, believed in the literal truth of the ancient scrolls: Mammals and Machinery, working together across the ages to explore the Universe! United! Strong! Forward the Frontier!

Rah.

Whoever raised him didn't do a great job. Not that I blame them; it can't have been much fun having a child underfoot during a build, and none of us were selected for our parenting skills. Even if bots changed the diapers and VR handled the infodumps, socialising a toddler couldn't have been anyone's idea of a good time. I'd have probably just chucked the little bastard out an airlock.

But even I would've brought him up to speed.

Something changed while I was away. Maybe the war's heated up again, entered some new phase. That twitchy kid is out of the loop for a reason. I wonder what it is.

I wonder if I care.

I arrive at my suite, treat myself to a gratuitous meal, jill off. Three hours after coming back to life, I'm relaxing in the starbow commons. "Chimp."

"You're up early," it says at last.

I am. Our answering shout hasn't even arrived at its destination yet. No real chance of new data for another two months, at least.

"Show me the forward feeds," I command.

DHF428 blinks at me from the center of the lounge: Stop. Stop. Stop.

Maybe. Or maybe the chimp's right, maybe it's pure physiology. Maybe this endless cycle carries no more intelligence than the beating of a heart.

But there's a pattern inside the pattern, some kind of flicker in the blink. It makes my brain itch.

"Slow the time-series," I command. "By a hundred."

It is a blink. 428's disk isn't darkening uniformly, it's eclipsing. As though a great eyelid were being drawn across the surface of the sun, from right to left.

"By a thousand."

Chromatophores, the chimp called them. But they're not all opening and closing at once. The darkness moves across the membrane in waves.

A word pops into my head: latency.

"Chimp. Those waves of pigment. How fast are they moving?"

"About fifty-nine thousand kilometers per second."

The speed of a passing thought.

And if this thing does think, it'll have logic gates, synapses – it's going to be a net of some kind. And if the net's big enough, there's an I in the middle of it. Just like me, just like Dix. Just like the chimp. (Which is why I educated myself on the subject, back in the early tumultuous days of our relationship. Know your enemy and all that.)

The thing about I is, it only exists within a tenth-of-a-second of all its parts. When we get spread too thin – when someone splits your brain down the middle, say, chops the fat pipe so the halves have to talk the long way around; when the neural architecture diffuses past some critical point and signals take just that much longer to pass from A to B – the system, well, decoheres. The two sides of your brain become different people with different tastes, different agendas, different senses of themselves.

I shatters into we.

It's not just a human rule, or a mammal rule, or even an Earthly one. It's a rule for any circuit that processes information, and it applies as much to the things we've yet to meet as it did to those we left behind.

Fifty-nine thousand kilometers per second, the chimp says. How far can the signal move through that membrane in a tenth of a corsec? How thinly does I spread itself across the heavens?

The flesh is huge, the flesh is inconceivable. But the spirit, the spirit is – Shit.

"Chimp. Assuming the mean neuron density of a human brain, what's the synapse count on a circular sheet of neurons one millimeter thick with a diameter of five thousand eight hundred ninety-two kilometers?"

"Two times ten to the twenty-seventh."

I saccade the database for some perspective on a mind stretched across thirty million square kilometers: the equivalent of two quadrillion human brains.

Of course, whatever this thing uses for neurons have to be packed a lot less tightly than ours; we can see right through them, after all. Let's be super-conservative, say it's only got a thousandth the computational density of a human brain. That's –

Okay, let's say it's only got a ten-thousandth the synaptic density, that's still –

A hundred thousandth. The merest mist of thinking meat. Any more conservative and I'd hypothesize it right out of existence.

Still twenty billion human brains.

Twenty billion.

I don't know how to feel about that. This is no mere alien.

But I'm not quite ready to believe in gods.

I round the corner and run smack into Dix, standing like a golem in the middle of my living room. I jump about a meter straight up.

"What the hell are you doing here?"

He seems surprised by my reaction. "Wanted to – talk," he says after a moment.

"You never come into someone's home uninvited!"

He retreats a step, stammers: "Wanted, wanted—"

"To talk. And you do that in public. On the bridge, or in the commons, or – for that matter, you could just comm me."

He hesitates. "Said you – wanted face to face. You said, cultural tradition."

I did, at that. But not here. This is my place, these are my private quarters. The lack of locks on these doors is a safety protocol, not an invitation to walk into my home and lie in wait, and stand there like part of the fucking furniture . . .

"Why are you even up?" I snarl. "We're not even supposed to come online for another two months."

"Asked Chimp to get me up when you did."

That fucking machine.

"Why are you up?" he asks, not leaving.

I sigh, defeated, and fall into a convenient pseudopod. "I just wanted to go over the preliminary data." The implicit alone should be obvious.

"Anything?"

Evidently it isn't. I decide to play along for a while. "Looks like we're talking to an, an island. Almost six thousand klicks across. That's the thinking part, anyway. The surrounding membrane's pretty much empty. I mean, it's all alive. It all photosynthesizes, or something like that. It eats, I guess. Not sure what."

"Molecular cloud," Dix says. "Organic compounds everywhere. Plus it's concentrating stuff inside the envelope."

I shrug. "Point is, there's a size limit for the brain, but it's huge, it's . . ."

"Unlikely," he murmurs, almost to himself.

I turn to look at him; the pseudopod reshapes itself around me. "What do you mean?"

"Island's twenty-eight million square kilometers? Whole sphere's seven quintillion. Island just happens to be between us and 428, that's – one in fifty-billion odds."

"Go on."

He can't. "Uh, just . . . just unlikely."

I close my eyes. "How can you be smart enough to run those numbers in your head without missing a beat, and stupid enough to miss the obvious conclusion?"

That panicked, slaughterhouse look again. "Don't – I'm not – "

"It is unlikely. It's astronomically unlikely that we just happen to be aiming at the one intelligent spot on a sphere one-and-a-half AUs across. Which means . . ."

He says nothing. The perplexity in his face mocks me. I want to punch it.

But finally, the lights flicker on: "There's, uh, more than one island? Oh! A lot of islands!"

This creature is part of the crew. My life will almost certainly depend on him some day.

That is a very scary thought.

I try to set it aside for the moment. "There's probably a whole population of the things, sprinkled though the membrane like, like cysts I guess. The chimp doesn't know how many, but we're only picking up this one so far so they might be pretty sparse."

There's a different kind of frown on his face now. "Why Chimp?"

"What do you mean?"

"Why call him Chimp?"

"We call it the chimp." Because the first step to humanising something is to give it a name.

"Looked it up. Short for chimpanzee. Stupid animal."

"Actually, I think chimps were supposed to be pretty smart," I remember.

"Not like us. Couldn't even talk. Chimp can talk. Way smarter than those things. That name – it's an insult."

"What do you care?"

He just looks at me.

I spread my hands. "Okay, it's not a chimp. We just call it that because it's got roughly the same synapse count."

"So gave him a small brain, then complain that he's stupid all the time."

My patience is just about drained. "Do you have a point or are you just blowing CO_2 in – "

"Why not make him smarter?"

"Because you can never predict the behavior of a system more complex than you. And if you want a project to stay on track after you're gone, you don't hand the reins to anything that's guaranteed to develop its own agenda." Sweet smoking Jesus, you'd think someone would have told him about Ashby's Law.

"So they lobotomized him," Dix says after a moment.

"No. They didn't turn it stupid, they built it stupid."

"Maybe smarter than you think. You're so much smarter, got your agenda, how come he's still in control?"

"Don't flatter yourself," I say.

"What?"

I let a grim smile peek through. "You're only following orders from a bunch of other systems way more complex than you are." You've got to hand it to them, too; dead for stellar lifetimes and those damn project admins are still pulling the strings.

"I don't – I'm following? – "

"I'm sorry, dear." I smile sweetly at my idiot offspring. "I wasn't talking to you. I was talking to the thing that's making all those sounds come out of your mouth."

Dix turns whiter than my panties.

I drop all pretense. "What were you thinking, chimp? That you could send this sock-puppet to invade my home and I wouldn't notice?"

"Not – I'm not – it's me," Dix stammers. "Me talking."

"It's coaching you. Do you even know what 'lobotomised' means?" I shake my head, disgusted. "You think I've forgotten how the interface works just because we all burned ours out?" A caricature of surprise begins to form on his face. "Oh, don't even fucking try. You've been up for other builds, there's no way you couldn't have known. And you know we shut down our domestic links too, or you wouldn't even be sneaking in here. And there's nothing your lord and master can do about that because it needs us, and so we have reached what you might call an accommodation."

I am not shouting. My tone is icy, but my voice is dead level. And yet Dix almost cringes before me.

There is an opportunity here, I realize.

I thaw my voice a little. I speak gently: "You can do that too, you know. Burn out your link. I'll even let you come back here afterwards, if you still want to. Just to – talk. But not with that thing in your head."

There is panic in his face, and, against all expectation it almost breaks my heart. "Can't," he pleads. "How I learn things, how I train. The mission . . ."

I honestly don't know which of them is speaking, so I answer them both: "There is more than one way to carry out the mission. We have more than enough time to try them all. Dix is welcome to come back when he's alone."

They take a step toward me. Another. One hand, twitching, rises from their side as if to reach out, and there's something on that lopsided face that I can't quite recognize.

"But I'm your son," they say.

I don't even dignify it with a denial.

"Get out of my home."

A human periscope. The Trojan Dix. That's a new one.

The chimp's never tried such overt infiltration while we were up and about before. Usually, it waits until we're all undead before invading our territories. I imagine custom-made drones never seen by human eyes, cobbled together during the long dark eons between builds; I see them sniffing through drawers and peeking behind mirrors, strafing the bulkheads with X-rays and ultrasound, patiently searching Eriophora's catacombs millimeter by endless millimeter for whatever secret messages we might be sending each other down through time.

There's no proof to speak of. We've left tripwires and telltales to alert us to intrusion after the fact, but there's never been any evidence they've been disturbed. Means nothing, of course. The chimp may be stupid, but it's also cunning, and a million years is more than enough time to iterate through every possibility using simpleminded brute force. Document every dust mote; commit your unspeakable acts; put everything back the way it was afterward.

We're too smart to risk talking across the eons. No encrypted strategies, no long-distance love letters, no chatty postcards showing ancient vistas long lost in the red shift. We keep all that in our heads, where the enemy will never find it. The unspoken rule is that we do not speak, unless it is face to face.

Endless idiotic games. Sometimes I almost forget what we're squabbling over. It seems so trivial now, with an immortal in my sights.

Maybe that means nothing to you. Immortality must be ancient news to you. But I can't even imagine it, although I've outlived worlds. All I have are moments: two or three hundred years, to ration across the lifespan of a universe. I could bear witness to any point in time, or any hundred-thousand, if I slice my life thinly enough – but I will never see everything. I will never see even a fraction.

My life will end. I have to choose.

When you come to fully appreciate the deal you've made – ten or fifteen builds out, when the trade-off leaves the realm of mere knowledge and sinks deep as cancer into your bones – you become a miser. You can't help it. You ration out your waking moments to the barest minimum: just enough to manage the build, to plan your latest countermove against the chimp, just enough (if you haven't yet moved beyond the need for human contact) for sex and snuggles and a bit of warm mammalian comfort against the endless dark. And then you hurry back to the crypt, to hoard the remains of a human lifespan against the unwinding of the cosmos.

There's been time for education. Time for a hundred postgraduate degrees, thanks to the best caveman learning tech. I've never bothered. Why burn down my tiny candle for a litany of mere fact, fritter away my precious, endless, finite life? Only a fool would trade book-learning for a ringside view of the Cassiopeia Remnant, even if you do need false-color enhancement to see the fucking thing.

Now, though. Now, I want to know. This creature crying out across the gulf, massive as a moon, wide as a solar system, tenuous and fragile as an insect's wing: I'd gladly cash in some of my life to learn its secrets. How does it work? How can it even live here at the edge of absolute zero, much less think? What vast, unfathomable intellect must it possess, to see us coming from over half a lightyear away, to deduce the nature of our eyes and our instruments, to send a signal we can even detect, much less understand?

And what happens when we punch through it at a fifth the speed of light?

I call up the latest findings on my way to bed, and the answer hasn't changed: not much. The damn thing's already full of holes. Comets, asteroids, the usual protoplanetary junk careens through this system as it does through every other. Infra picks up diffuse pockets of slow outgassing here and there around the perimeter, where the soft vaporous vacuum of the interior bleeds into the harder stuff outside. Even if we were going to tear through the dead center of the thinking part, I can't imagine this vast creature feeling so much as a pinprick. At the speed we're going we'd be through and gone far too fast to overcome even the feeble inertia of a millimeter membrane.

And yet. Stop. Stop. Stop.

It's not us, of course. It's what we're building. The birth of a gate is a

violent, painful thing, a spacetime rape that puts out almost as much gamma
and X as a microquasar. Any meat within the white zone turns to ash in an
instant, shielded or not. It's why we never slow down to take pictures.

One of the reasons, anyway.

We can't stop, of course. Even changing course isn't an option except by
the barest increments. Eri soars like an eagle between the stars but she steers
like a pig on the short haul; tweak our heading by even a tenth of a degree,
and you've got some serious damage at twenty percent lightspeed. Half a
degree would tear us apart: the ship might torque onto the new heading, but
the collapsed mass in her belly would keep right on going, rip through all
this surrounding superstructure without even feeling it.

Even tame singularities get set in their ways. They do not take well to change.

We resurrect again, and the Island has changed its tune.

It gave up asking us to stop stop stop the moment our laser hit its leading edge. Now it's saying something else entirely: dark hyphens flow across
its skin, arrows of pigment converging towards some offstage focus like
spokes pointing toward the hub of a wheel. The bullseye itself is offstage
and implicit, far removed from 428's bright backdrop, but it's easy enough
to extrapolate to the point of convergence six lightsecs to starboard. There's
something else, too: a shadow, roughly circular, moving along one of the
spokes like a bead running along a string. It too migrates to starboard, falls
off the edge of the Island's makeshift display, is endlessly reborn at the same
initial coordinates to repeat its journey.

Those coordinates: exactly where our current trajectory will punch
through the membrane in another four months. A squinting God would be
able to see the gnats and girders of ongoing construction on the other side,
the great piecemeal torus of the Hawking Hoop already taking shape.

The message is so obvious that even Dix sees it. "Wants us to move the
gate . . ." and there is something like confusion in his voice. "But how's it
know we're building one?"

"The vons punctured it en route," the chimp points out. "It could have
sensed that. It has photopigments. It can probably see."

"Probably sees better than we do," I say. Even something as simple as a
pinhole camera gets hi-res fast if you stipple a bunch of them across thirty
million square kilometers.

But Dix scrunches his face, unconvinced. "So sees a bunch of vons
bumping around. Loose parts – not that much even assembled yet. How's it
know we're building something hot?"

Because it is very, very, smart, you stupid child. Is it so hard to believe
that this, this – organism seems far too limiting a word – can just imagine
how those half-built pieces fit together, glance at our sticks and stones and
see exactly where this is going?

"Maybe's not the first gate it's seen," Dix suggests. "Think there's maybe
another gate out here?"

I shake my head. "We'd have seen the lensing artefacts by now."

"You ever run into anyone before?"

"No." We have always been alone, through all these epochs. We have only ever run away.

And then always from our own children.

I crunch some numbers. "Hundred eighty two days to insemination. If we move now, we've only got to tweak our bearing by a few mikes to redirect to the new coordinates. Well within the green. Angles get dicey the longer we wait, of course."

"We can't do that," the chimp says. "We would miss the gate by two million kilometers."

"Move the gate. Move the whole damn site. Move the refineries, move the factories, move the damn rocks. A couple hundred meters a second would be more than fast enough if we send the order now. We don't even have to suspend construction, we can keep building on the fly."

"Every one of those vectors widens the nested confidence limits of the build. It would increase the risk of error beyond allowable margins, for no payoff."

"And what about the fact that there's an intelligent being in our path?"

"I'm already allowing for the potential presence of intelligent alien life."

"Okay, first off, there's nothing potential about it. It's right fucking there. And on our current heading, we run the damn thing over."

"We're staying clear of all planetary bodies in Goldilocks orbits. We've seen no local evidence of spacefaring technology. The current location of the build meets all conservation criteria."

"That's because the people who drew up your criteria never anticipated a live Dyson sphere!" But I'm wasting my breath, and I know it. The chimp can run its equations a million times, but if there's nowhere to put the variable, what can it do?

There was a time, back before things turned ugly, when we had clearance to reprogram those parameters. Before we discovered that one of the things the admins had anticipated was mutiny.

I try another tack. "Consider the threat potential."

"There's no evidence of any."

"Look at the synapse estimate! That thing's got order of mag more processing power than the whole civilization that sent us out here. You think something can be that smart, live that long, without learning how to defend itself? We're assuming it's asking us to move the gate. What if that's not a request? What if it's just giving us the chance to back off before it takes matters into its own hands?"

"Doesn't have hands," Dix says from the other side of the tank, and he's not even being flippant. He's just being so stupid I want to bash his face in.

I try to keep my voice level. "Maybe it doesn't need any."

"What could it do, blink us to death? No weapons. Doesn't even control the whole membrane. Signal propagation's too slow."

"We don't know. That's my point. We haven't even tried to find out.

We're a goddamn road crew; our onsite presence is a bunch of construction vons press-ganged into scientific research. We can figure out some basic physical parameters, but we don't know how this thing thinks, what kind of natural defenses it might have – "

"What do you need to find out?" the chimp asks, the very voice of calm reason.

We can't find out! I want to scream. We're stuck with what we've got! By the time the onsite vons could build what we need, we're already past the point of no return! You stupid fucking machine, we're on track to kill a being smarter than all of human history and you can't even be bothered to move our highway to the vacant lot next door?

But of course if I say that, the Island's chances of survival go from low to zero. So I grasp at the only straw that remains: maybe the data we've got in hand is enough. If acquisition is off the table, maybe analysis will do.

"I need time," I say.

"Of course," the chimp tells me. "Take all the time you need."

The chimp is not content to kill this creature. The chimp has to spit on it as well.

Under the pretense of assisting in my research, it tries to deconstruct the island, break it apart and force it to conform to grubby earthbound precedents. It tells me about earthly bacteria that thrived at 1.5 million rads and laughed at hard vacuum. It shows me pictures of unkillable little tardigrades that could curl up and snooze on the edge of absolute zero, felt equally at home in deep ocean trenches and deeper space. Given time, opportunity, a boot off the planet, who knows how far those cute little invertebrates might have gone? Might they have survived the very death of the homeworld, clung together, grown somehow colonial?

What utter bullshit.

I learn what I can. I study the alchemy by which photosynthesis transforms light and gas and electrons into living tissue. I learn the physics of the solar wind that blows the bubble taut, calculate lower metabolic limits for a life form that filters organics from the ether. I marvel at the speed of this creature's thoughts: almost as fast as Eri flies, orders of mag faster than any mammalian nerve impulse. Some kind of organic superconductor perhaps, something that passes chilled electrons almost resistance-free out here in the freezing void.

I acquaint myself with phenotypic plasticity and sloppy fitness, that fortuitous evolutionary soft-focus that lets species exist in alien environments and express novel traits they never needed at home. Perhaps this is how a life form with no natural enemies could acquire teeth and claws and the willingness to use them. The Island's life hinges on its ability to kill us; I have to find something that makes it a threat.

But all I uncover is a growing suspicion that I am doomed to fail – for violence, I begin to see, is a planetary phenomenon.

Planets are the abusive parents of evolution. Their very surfaces promote warfare, concentrate resources into dense defensible patches that can be fought over. Gravity forces you to squander energy on vascular systems and skeletal support, stand endless watch against its endless sadistic campaign to squash you flat. Take one wrong step, off a perch too high, and all your pricey architecture shatters in an instant. And even if you beat those odds, cobble together some lumbering armored chassis to withstand the slow crawl onto land – how long before the world draws in some asteroid or comet to crash down from the heavens and reset your clock to zero? Is it any wonder we grew up believing life was a struggle, that zero-sum was God's own law and that the future belonged to those who crushed the competition?

The rules are so different out here. Most of space is tranquil: no diel or seasonal cycles, no ice ages or global tropics, no wild pendulum swings between hot and cold, calm and tempestuous. Life's precursors abound: on comets, clinging to asteroids, suffusing nebulae a hundred lightyears across. Molecular clouds glow with organic chemistry and life-giving radiation. Their vast dusty wings grow warm with infrared, filter out the hard stuff, give rise to stellar nurseries that only some stunted refugee from the bottom of a gravity well could ever call lethal.

Darwin's an abstraction here, an irrelevant curiosity. This Island puts the lie to everything we were ever told about the machinery of life. Sun-powered, perfectly adapted, immortal, it won no struggle for survival: where are the predators, the competitors, the parasites? All of life around 428 is one vast continuum, one grand act of symbiosis. Nature here is not red in tooth and claw. Nature, out here, is the helping hand.

Lacking the capacity for violence, the Island has outlasted worlds. Unencumbered by technology, it has out-thought civilizations. It is intelligent beyond our measure, and –

– and it is benign. It must be. I grow more certain of that with each passing hour. How can it even conceive of an enemy?

I think of the things I called it, before I knew better. Meat balloon. Cyst. Looking back, those words verge on blasphemy. I will not use them again.

Besides, there's another word that would fit better, if the chimp has its way: Roadkill. And the longer I look, the more I fear that that hateful machine is right.

If the Island can defend itself, I sure as shit can't see how.

"Eriophora's impossible, you know. Violates the laws of physics."

We're in one of the social alcoves off the ventral notochord, taking a break from the library. I have decided to start again from first principles. Dix eyes me with an understandable mix of confusion and mistrust; my claim is almost too stupid to deny.

"It's true," I assure him. "Takes way too much energy to accelerate a ship with Eri's mass, especially at relativistic speeds. You'd need the energy output of a whole sun. People figured if we made it to the stars at all, we'd have to do it in ships maybe the size of your thumb. Crew them with virtual personalities downloaded onto chips."

That's too nonsensical even for Dix. "Wrong. Don't have mass, can't fall toward anything. Eri wouldn't even work if it was that small."

"But suppose you can't displace any of that mass. No wormholes, no Higgs conduits, nothing to throw your gravitational field in the direction of travel. Your center of mass just sits there in, well, the center of your mass."

A spastic Dixian head-shake. "Do have those things!"

"Sure we do. But for the longest time, we didn't know it."

His foot taps an agitated tattoo on the deck.

"It's the history of the species," I explain. "We think we've worked everything out, we think we've solved all the mysteries, and then someone finds some niggling little data point that doesn't fit the paradigm. Every time we try to paper over the crack, it gets bigger, and before you know it, our whole worldview unravels. It's happened time and again. One day, mass is a constraint; the next, it's a requirement. The things we think we know – they change, Dix. And we have to change with them."

"But – "

"The chimp can't change. The rules it's following are ten billion years old and it's got no fucking imagination – and really that's not anyone's fault, that's just people who didn't know how else to keep the mission stable across deep time. They wanted to keep the mission on-track, so they built something that couldn't go off it; but they also knew that things change, and that's why we're out here, Dix. To deal with things the chimp can't."

"The alien," Dix says.

"The alien."

"Chimp deals with it just fine."

"How? By killing it?"

"Not our fault it's in the way. It's no threat – "

"I don't care whether it's a threat or not! It's alive, and it's intelligent, and killing it just to expand some alien empire – "

"Human empire. Our empire." Suddenly, Dix's hands have stopped twitching. Suddenly, he stands still as stone.

I snort. "What do you know about humans?"

"Am one."

"You're a fucking trilobite. You ever see what comes out of those gates once they're online?"

"Mostly nothing." He pauses, thinking back. "Couple of – ships once, maybe."

"Well, I've seen a lot more than that, and believe me, if those things were ever human, it was a passing phase."

"But – "

"Dix – " I take a deep breath, try to get back on message. "Look, it's not your fault. You've been getting all your info from a moron stuck on a rail. But we're not doing this for Humanity, we're not doing it for Earth. Earth is gone, don't you understand that? The sun scorched it black a billion years after we left. Whatever we're working for, it – it won't even talk to us."

"Yeah? Then why do this? Why not just, just quit?"

He really doesn't know.

"We tried," I say.

"And?"

"And your chimp shut off our life support."

For once, he has nothing to say.

"It's a machine, Dix. Why can't you get that? It's programmed. It can't change."

"We're machines. Just built from different things. We're programmed. We change."

"Yeah? Last time I checked, you were sucking so hard on that thing's tit you couldn't even kill your cortical link."

"How I learn. No reason to change."

"How about acting like a damn human once in a while? How about developing a little rapport with the folks who might have to save your miserable life next time you go EVA? That enough of a reason for you? Because I don't mind telling you, right now I don't trust you as far as I could throw the tac tank. I don't even know for sure who I'm talking to right now."

"Not my fault." For the first time, I see something outside the usual gamut of fear, confusion, and simpleminded computation playing across his face. "That's you, that's all of you. You talk – sideways. Think sideways. You all do, and it hurts." Something hardens in his face. "Didn't even need you online for this," he growls. "Didn't want you. Could have managed the whole build myself, told Chimp I could do it – "

"But the chimp thought you should wake me up anyway, and you always roll over for the chimp, don't you? Because the chimp always knows best, the chimp's your boss, the chimp's your fucking god. Which is why I have to get out of bed to nursemaid some idiot savant who can't even answer a hail without being led by the nose." Something clicks in the back of my mind, but I'm on a roll. "You want a real role model? You want something to look up to? Forget the chimp. Forget the mission. Look out the forward scope, why don't you? Look at what your precious chimp wants to run over because it happens to be in the way! That thing is better than any of us. It's smarter, it's peaceful, it doesn't wish us any harm at – "

"How can you know that? Can't know that!"

"No, you can't know that, because you're fucking stunted! Any normal caveman would see it in a second, but you – "

"That's crazy," Dix hisses at me. "You're crazy. You're bad."

"I'm bad!" Some distant part of me hears the giddy squeak in my voice, the borderline hysteria.

"For the mission." Dix turns his back and stalks away.

My hands are hurting. I look down, surprised: my fists are clenched so tightly that my nails cut into the flesh of my palms. It takes a real effort to open them again.

I almost remember how this feels. I used to feel this way all the time. Way back when everything mattered; before passion faded to ritual, before rage cooled to disdain. Before Sunday Ahzmundin, eternity's warrior, settled for heaping insults on stunted children.

We were incandescent back then. Parts of this ship are still scorched and uninhabitable, even now. I remember this feeling.

This is how it feels to be awake.

I am awake, and I am alone, and I am sick of being outnumbered by morons. There are rules and there are risks, and you don't wake the dead on a whim, but fuck it. I'm calling reinforcements.

Dix has got to have other parents, a father at least, he didn't get that Y chromo from me. I swallow my own disquiet and check the manifest; bring up the gene sequences; cross-reference.

Huh. Only one other parent: Kai. I wonder if that's just coincidence, or if the chimp drew too many conclusions from our torrid little fuckfest back in the Cyg Rift. Doesn't matter. He's as much yours as mine, Kai, time to step up to the plate, time to –

Oh shit. Oh no. Please no.

(There are rules. And there are risks.)

Three builds back, it says. Kai and Connie. Both of them. One airlock jammed, the next too far away along Eri's hull, a hail-Mary emergency crawl between. They made it back inside but not before the blue-shifted background cooked them in their suits. They kept breathing for hours afterward, talked and moved and cried as if they were still alive, while their insides broke down and bled out.

There were two others awake that shift, two others left to clean up the mess. Ishmael, and –

"Um, you said – "

"You fucker!" I leap up and hit my son hard in the face, ten seconds's heartbreak with ten million years's denial raging behind it. I feel teeth give way behind his lips. He goes over backward, eyes wide as telescopes, the blood already blooming on his mouth.

"Said I could come back – !" he squeals, scrambling backwards along the deck.

"He was your fucking father! You knew, you were there! He died right in front of you and you didn't even tell me!"

"I – I – "

"Why didn't you tell me, you asshole? The chimp told you to lie, is that it? Did you – "

"Thought you knew!" he cries, "Why wouldn't you know?"

My rage vanishes like air through a breach. I sag back into the 'pod, face in hands.

"Right there in the log," he whimpers. "All along. Nobody hid it. How could you not know?"

"I did," I admit dully. "Or I – I mean . . ."

I mean I didn't know, but it's not a surprise, not really, not down deep. You just – stop looking, after a while.

There are rules.

"Never even asked," my son says softly. "How they were doing."

I raise my eyes. Dix regards me wide-eyed from across the room, backed up against the wall, too scared to risk bolting past me to the door. "What are you doing here?" I ask tiredly.

His voice catches. He has to try twice: "You said I could come back. If I burned out my link . . ."

"You burned out your link."

He gulps and nods. He wipes blood with the back of his hand.

"What did the chimp say about that?"

"He said – it said that it was okay," Dix says, in such a transparent attempt to suck up that I actually believe, in that instant, that he might really be on his own.

"So you asked its permission." He begins to nod, but I can see the tell in his face: "Don't bullshit me, Dix."

"He – actually suggested it."

"I see."

"So we could talk," Dix adds.

"What do you want to talk about?"

He looks at the floor and shrugs.

I stand and walk toward him. He tenses but I shake my head, spread my hands. "It's okay. It's okay." I lean back against the wall and slide down until I'm beside him on the deck.

We just sit there for a while.

"It's been so long," I say at last.

He looks at me, uncomprehending. What does long even mean, out here?

I try again. "They say there's no such thing as altruism, you know?"

His eyes blank for an instant, and grow panicky, and I know that he's just tried to ping his link for a definition and come up blank. So we are alone. "Altruism," I explain. "Unselfishness. Doing something that costs you but helps someone else." He seems to get it. "They say every selfless act ultimately comes down to manipulation or kin-selection or reciprocity or something, but they're wrong. I could—"

I close my eyes. This is harder than I expected.

"I could have been happy just knowing that Kai was okay, that Connie was happy. Even if it didn't benefit me one whit, even if it cost me, even if there was no chance I'd ever see either of them again. Almost any price would be worth it, just to know they were okay."

"Just to believe they were . . ."

So you haven't seen her for the past five builds. So he hasn't drawn your shift since Sagittarius. They're just sleeping. Maybe next time.

"So you don't check," Dix says slowly. Blood bubbles on his lower lip; he doesn't seem to notice.

"We don't check." Only I did, and now they're gone. They're both gone. Except for those little cannibalized nucleotides the chimp recycled into this defective and maladapted son of mine.

We're the only warm-blooded creatures for a thousand lightyears, and I am so very lonely.

"I'm sorry," I whisper, and lean forward, and lick the blood from his bruised and bloody lips.

Back on Earth – back when there was an Earth – there were these little animals called cats. I had one for a while. Sometimes I'd watch him sleep for hours: paws and whiskers and ears all twitching madly as he chased imaginary prey across whatever landscapes his sleeping brain conjured up.

My son looks like that when the chimp worms its way into his dreams.

It's almost too literal for metaphor: the cable runs into his head like some kind of parasite, feeding through old-fashioned fiber-op now that the wireless option's been burned away. Or force-feeding, I suppose; the poison flows into Dix's head, not out of it.

I shouldn't be here. Didn't I just throw a tantrum over the violation of my own privacy? (Just. Twelve lightdays ago. Everything's relative.) And yet, I can see no privacy here for Dix to lose: no decorations on the walls, no artwork or hobbies, no wraparound console. The sex toys ubiquitous in every suite sit unused on their shelves; I'd have assumed he was on antilibinals if recent experience hadn't proven otherwise.

What am I doing? Is this some kind of perverted mothering instinct, some vestigial expression of a Pleistocene maternal subroutine? Am I that much of a robot, has my brain stem sent me here to guard my child?

To guard my mate?

Lover or larva, it hardly matters: his quarters are an empty shell, there's nothing of Dix in here. That's just his abandoned body lying there in the pseudopod, fingers twitching, eyes flickering beneath closed lids in vicarious response to wherever his mind has gone.

They don't know I'm here. The chimp doesn't know because we burned out its prying eyes a billion years ago, and my son doesn't know I'm here because – well, because for him, right now, there is no here.

What am I supposed to make of you, Dix? None of this makes sense. Even your body language looks like you grew it in a vat – but I'm far from the first human being you've seen. You grew up in good company, with people I know, people I trust. Trusted. How did you end up on the other side? How did they let you slip away?

And why didn't they warn me about you?

Yes, there are rules. There is the threat of enemy surveillance during long dead nights, the threat of – other losses. But this is unprecedented. Surely someone could have left something, some clue buried in a metaphor too subtle for the simpleminded to decode . . .

I'd give a lot to tap into that pipe, to see what you're seeing now. Can't risk it, of course; I'd give myself away the moment I tried to sample anything except the basic baud, and –

– Wait a second –

That baud rate's way too low. That's not even enough for hi-res graphics, let alone tactile and olfac. You're embedded in a wireframe world at best.

And yet, look at you go. The fingers, the eyes – like a cat, dreaming of mice and apple pies. Like me, replaying the long-lost oceans and mountaintops of Earth before I learned that living in the past was just another way of dying in the present. The bit rate says this is barely even a test pattern; the body says you're immersed in a whole other world. How has that machine tricked you into treating such thin gruel as a feast?

Why would it even want to? Data are better grasped when they can be grasped, and tasted, and heard; our brains are built for far richer nuance than splines and scatterplots. The driest technical briefings are more sensual than this. Why settle for stick-figures when you can paint in oils and holograms?

Why does anyone simplify anything? To reduce the variable set. To manage the unmanageable.

Kai and Connie. Now there were a couple of tangled, unmanageable datasets. Before the accident. Before the scenario simplified.

Someone should have warned me about you, Dix.

Maybe someone tried.

And so it comes to pass that my son leaves the nest, encases himself in a beetle carapace and goes walkabout. He is not alone; one of the chimp's teleops accompanies him out on Eri's hull, lest he lose his footing and fall back into the starry past.

Maybe this will never be more than a drill, maybe this scenario – catastrophic control-systems failure, the chimp and its backups offline, all maintenance tasks suddenly thrown onto shoulders of flesh and blood – is a dress rehearsal for a crisis that never happens. But even the unlikeliest scenario approaches certainty over the life of a universe; so we go through the motions. We practice. We hold our breath and dip outside. We're on a tight deadline: even armored, moving at this speed the blueshifted background rad would cook us in hours.

Worlds have lived and died since I last used the pickup in my suite. "Chimp."

"Here as always, Sunday." Smooth, and glib, and friendly. The easy rhythm of the practiced psychopath.

"I know what you're doing."

"I don't understand."

"You think I don't see what's going on? You're building the next release. You're getting too much grief from the old guard so you're starting from scratch with people who don't remember the old days. People you've, you've simplified."

The chimp says nothing. The drone's feed shows Dix clambering across a jumbled terrain of basalt and metal matrix composites.

"But you can't raise a human child, not on your own." I know it tried: there's no record of Dix anywhere on the crew manifest until his mid-teens, when he just showed up one day and nobody asked about it because nobody ever . . .

"Look what you've made of him. He's great at conditional If/Thens. Can't be beat on number-crunching and Do loops. But he can't think. Can't make the simplest intuitive jumps. You're like one of those" – I remember an Earthly myth, from the days when reading did not seem like such an obscene waste of lifespan – "one of those wolves, trying to raise a human child. You can teach him how to move around on hands and knees, you can teach him about pack dynamics, but you can't teach him how to walk on his hind legs or talk or be human because you're too fucking stupid, chimp, and you finally realized it. And that's why you threw him at me. You think I can fix him for you."

I take a breath, and a gambit.

"But he's nothing to me. You understand? He's worse than nothing, he's a liability. He's a spy, he's a spastic waste of O_2. Give me one reason why I shouldn't just lock him out there until he cooks."

"You're his mother," the chimp says, because the chimp has read all about kin selection and is too stupid for nuance.

"You're an idiot."

"You love him."

"No." An icy lump forms in my chest. My mouth makes words; they come out measured and inflectionless. "I can't love anyone, you brain-dead machine. That's why I'm out here. Do you really think they'd gamble your precious never-ending mission on little glass dolls that needed to bond?"

"You love him."

"I can kill him any time I want. And that's exactly what I'll do if you don't move the gate."

"I'd stop you," the chimp says mildly.

"That's easy enough. Just move the gate and we both get what we want. Or you can dig in your heels and try to reconcile your need for a mother's touch with my sworn intention of breaking the little fucker's neck. We've got a long trip ahead of us, chimp. And you might find I'm not quite as easy to cut out of the equation as Kai and Connie."

"You cannot end the mission," it says, almost gently. "You tried that already."

"This isn't about ending the mission. This is only about slowing it down a little. Your optimal scenario's off the table. The only way that gate's going to get finished now is by saving the Island, or killing your prototype. Your call."

The cost-benefit's pretty simple. The chimp could solve it in an instant. But still it says nothing. The silence stretches. It's looking for some other option, I bet. It's trying to find a workaround. It's questioning the very premises of the scenario, trying to decide if I mean what I'm saying, if all its book-learning about mother love could really be so far off-base. Maybe it's plumbing historical intrafamilial murder rates, looking for a loophole. And there may be one, for all I know. But the chimp isn't me, it's a simpler system trying to figure out a smarter one, and that gives me the edge.

"You would owe me," it says at last.

I almost burst out laughing. "What?"

"Or I will tell Dixon that you threatened to kill him."

"Go ahead."

"You don't want him to know."

"I don't care whether he knows or not. What, you think he'll try and kill me back? You think I'll lose his love?" I linger on the last word, stretch it out to show how ludicrous it is.

"You'll lose his trust. You need to trust each other out here."

"Oh, right. Trust. The very fucking foundation of this mission!"

The chimp says nothing.

"For the sake of argument," I say, after a while, "suppose I go along with it. What would I owe you, exactly?"

"A favor," the chimp replies. "To be repaid in future."

My son floats innocently against the stars, his life in balance.

We sleep. The chimp makes grudging corrections to a myriad small trajectories. I set the alarm to wake me every couple of weeks, burn a little more of my candle in case the enemy tries to pull another fast one; but for now it seems to be behaving itself. DHF428 jumps toward us in the stop-motion increments of a life's moments, strung like beads along an infinite string. The factory floor slews to starboard in our sights: refineries, reservoirs, and nanofab plants, swarms of von Neumanns breeding and cannibalizing and recycling each other into shielding and circuitry, tugboats and spare parts. The very finest Cro Magnon technology mutates and metastasizes across the universe like armor-plated cancer.

And hanging like a curtain between it and us shimmers an iridescent life form, fragile and immortal and unthinkably alien, that reduces everything my species ever accomplished to mud and shit by the simple transcendent fact of its existence. I have never believed in gods, in universal good or absolute evil. I have only ever believed that there is what works, and what doesn't. All the rest is smoke and mirrors, trickery to manipulate grunts like me.

But I believe in the Island, because I don't have to. It does not need to be taken on faith: it looms ahead of us, its existence an empirical fact. I will never know its mind, I will never know the details of its origin and evolution. But I can see it: massive, mind boggling, so utterly inhuman that it can't help but be better than us, better than anything we could ever become.

I believe in the Island. I've gambled my own son to save its life. I would kill him to avenge its death.

I may yet.

In all these millions of wasted years, I have finally done something worthwhile.

Final approach.

Reticles within reticles line up before me, a mesmerising infinite regress of bullseyes centering on target. Even now, mere minutes from ignition, distance reduces the unborn gate to invisibility. There will be no moment when the naked eye can trap our destination. We thread the needle far too quickly: it will be behind us before we know it.

Or, if our course corrections are off by even a hair – if our trillion-kilometer curve drifts by as much as a thousand meters – we will be dead. Before we know it.

Our instruments report that we are precisely on target. The chimp tells me that we are precisely on target. Eriophora falls forward, pulled endlessly through the void by her own magically-displaced mass.

I turn to the drone's-eye view relayed from up ahead. It's a window into history – even now, there's a timelag of several minutes – but past and present race closer to convergence with every corsec. The newly-minted gate looms dark and ominous against the stars, a great gaping mouth built to devour reality itself. The vons, the refineries, the assembly lines: parked to the side in vertical columns, their jobs done, their usefulness outlived, their collateral annihilation imminent. I pity them, for some reason. I always do. I wish we could scoop them up and take them with us, re-enlist them for the next build – but the rules of economics reach everywhere, and they say it's cheaper to use our tools once and throw them away.

A rule that the chimp seems to be taking more to heart than anyone expected.

At least we've spared the Island. I wish we could have stayed awhile. First contact with a truly alien intelligence, and what do we exchange? Traffic signals. What does the Island dwell upon, when not pleading for its life?

I thought of asking. I thought of waking myself when the timelag dropped from prohibitive to merely inconvenient, of working out some pidgin that could encompass the truths and philosophies of a mind vaster than all humanity. What a childish fantasy. The Island exists too far beyond the grotesque Darwinian processes that shaped my own flesh. There can be no communion here, no meeting of minds.

Angels do not speak to ants.

Less than three minutes to ignition. I see light at the end of the tunnel. Eri's incidental time machine barely looks into the past anymore, I could almost hold my breath across the whole span of seconds that then needs to overtake now. Still on target, according to all sources.

Tactical beeps at us.

"Getting a signal," Dix reports, and yes: in the heart of the tank, the sun is flickering again. My heart leaps: does the angel speak to us after all? A thank-you, perhaps? A cure for heat death?

But –

"It's ahead of us," Dix murmurs, as sudden realization catches in my throat.

Two minutes.

"Miscalculated somehow," Dix whispers. "Didn't move the gate far enough."

"We did," I say. We moved it exactly as far as the Island told us to.

"Still in front of us! Look at the sun!"

"Look at the signal," I tell him.

Because it's nothing like the painstaking traffic signs we've followed over the past three trillion kilometers. It's almost – random, somehow. It's spur-of-the-moment, it's panicky. It's the sudden, startled cry of something caught utterly by surprise with mere seconds left to act. And even though I have never seen this pattern of dots and swirls before, I know exactly what it must be saying.

Stop. Stop. Stop. Stop.

We do not stop. There is no force in the universe that can even slow us down. Past equals present; Eriophora dives through the center of the gate in a nanosecond. The unimaginable mass of her cold black heart snags some distant dimension, drags it screaming to the here and now. The booted portal erupts behind us, blossoms into a great blinding corona, every wavelength lethal to every living thing. Our aft filters clamp down tight.

The scorching wavefront chases us into the darkness as it has a thousand times before. In time, as always, the birth pangs will subside. The wormhole will settle in its collar. And just maybe, we will still be close enough to glimpse some new transcendent monstrosity emerging from that magic doorway.

I wonder if you'll notice the corpse we left behind.

"Maybe we're missing something," Dix says.

"We miss almost everything," I tell him.

DHF428 shifts red behind us. Lensing artifacts wink in our rearview; the gate has stabilized and the wormhole's online, blowing light and space and time in an iridescent bubble from its great metal mouth. We'll keep looking over our shoulders right up until we pass the Rayleigh Limit, far past the point it'll do any good.

So far, though, nothing's come out.

"Maybe our numbers were wrong," he says. "Maybe we made a mistake."

Our numbers were right. An hour doesn't pass when I don't check them again. The Island just had – enemies, I guess. Victims, anyway.

I was right about one thing, though. That fucker was smart. To see us coming, to figure out how to talk to us; to use us as a weapon, to turn a threat to its very existence into a, a . . .

I guess flyswatter is as good a word as any.

"Maybe there was a war," I mumble. "Maybe it wanted the real estate. Or maybe it was just some – family squabble."

"Maybe didn't know," Dix suggests. "Maybe thought those coordinates were empty."

Why would you think that?, I wonder. Why would you even care? And then it dawns on me: he doesn't, not about the Island, anyway. No more than he ever did. He's not inventing these rosy alternatives for himself.

My son is trying to comfort me.

I don't need to be coddled, though. I was a fool: I let myself believe in life without conflict, in sentience without sin. For a little while, I dwelt in a dream world where life was unselfish and unmanipulative, where every living thing did not struggle to exist at the expense of other life. I deified that which I could not understand, when in the end it was all too easily understood.

But I'm better now.

It's over: another build, another benchmark, another irreplaceable slice of life that brings our task no closer to completion. It doesn't matter how successful we are. It doesn't matter how well we do our job. Mission accomplished is a meaningless phrase on Eriophora, an ironic oxymoron at best. There may one day be failure, but there is no finish line. We go on forever, crawling across the universe like ants, dragging your goddamned superhighway behind us.

I still have so much to learn.

At least my son is here to teach me.

THE INTEGRITY OF THE CHAIN

Lavie Tidhar

Lavie Tidhar grew up on a kibbutz in Israel, lived in Israel and South Africa, traveled widely in Africa and Asia, lived in London for a number of years, and currently lives in Southeast Asia. He is the winner of the 2003 Clarke-Bradbury Prize (awarded by the European Space Agency), was the editor of *Michael Marshall Smith: The Annotated Bibliography*, and the anthologies *A Dick & Jane Primer for Adults* and *The Apex Book of World SF*. He is the author of the linked story collection *HebrewPunk*, the novellas *An Occupation of Angels* and *Cloud Permutations*, and, with Nir Yaniv, the novel *The Tel Aviv Dossier*. A prolific short-story writer, his stories have appeared in *Interzone*, *Clarkesworld*, *Apex Magazine*, *Sci Fiction*, *Strange Horizons*, *Chizine*, *Postscripts*, *Fantasy*, *Nemonymous*, *Infinity Plus*, *Aeon*, *The Book of Dark Wisdom*, *Fortean Bureau*, and elsewhere, and have been translated into seven languages.

Here he gives us a vivid slice of a future world where much has changed – and yet much has stayed the same.

T HE GIRL THEY called the General was back on the television: she wore a crisp army uniform decorated with many medals, its colour that of the jungles at dusk, a dark green that seemed to give off a fresh, sharp scent of foliage and fear. She spoke crisply: the words were carefully-measured cups of rice, precise and just. The latest news from the Party conference. Details of the latest five-year plan. Picture: rice paddies up north, workers in the fields in dark-blue overalls. Someone beside the television, a shaggy man Noy identified at last as Sip Pan Joe, said, "Heard the first baby was born yesterday on the Chinese moon colony."

They called him Sip Pan Joe because he always charged ten thousand kip for a city journey. "Sip pan! Sip pan!" he would say, losing money every time he took a fair. They called him Joe because of some character in a Thai soap. Sip Pan Joe wasn't all there, but he had a way of getting news.

Noy said, "I want to go to the moon," and Sip Pan Joe cackled and said, "No tuk-tuks on the moon! No air!"

They called Noy Noy because he was small. Now he said nothing, merely stared at the television. On the screen, the General was speaking again, talking about the latest American war. Noy's grandfather had died, early century, looking for scrap metal. There was a lot of scrap metal in the highlands of Laos. Most of it had been left there by the Americans during their Secret War, a long time before. The scrap metal was valuable. Unfortunately, it also tended to explode. The UXO clearance team later said it had been a CBU-26 – an anti-personnel cluster fragmentation bomb, a type particularly favoured by the Americans. By then Noy's grandmother had already been pregnant with Noy's father though.

"One day I will go to America," another of the drivers said. He was Hmong, had family in Florida who wired him money every month. "I will open a hotel, or drive a cab. A real one, with guns on the side and an armoured windshield."

"That's just in the movies," Noy couldn't stop himself from saying. The Hmong man turned on him. "Oh? And how would you know, boy?"

"Leave him alone," Sip Pan Joe said. "I want to watch the news."

"He wants to watch the news," the Hmong said. "Maybe he wants to go to the moon and make babies too."

There was general laughter and the Hmong, made bold, said, "He can take Noy with him, and good riddance. Ten thousand for a ticket to the moon! Sip Pan! Sip Pan!"

On the screen the General disappeared and was replaced with Martial music, stirring revolutionary lyrics sung by the Army Choir on a background of tanks rolling and jets taking off. The television flickered in the darkness of the drivers' hut. No one made a reply to the Hmong. Everyone knew they fought on the American side during that long-ago war, and they were still a nuisance, not proper citizens like the lowland Lao. Noy stared at the screen. He was secretly saving up the money from his trips. Two thousand here, five thousand there. He once took a falang man in the tuk-tuk, and the man had told him he had been to space. He'd bought some dope off Noy, and that was when he told him. He made images appear in the air with a flick of his wrist and showed them to Noy: Earth blue and white and green, seen from above; people floating in strange configurations inside a vast hall, almost all of them falangs. But Noy knew space didn't belong to the falangs. After all, the Chinese went there, and the Malays, and the Indians. It didn't seem that impossible for a Lao boy to go, too, one day.

He gulped down his tea and decided to go on the job. He wasn't earning any money sitting there. As he stepped from out the makeshift structure the night felt cool, and a half-full moon was shining, wrapped in yellow bandages, in the sky. He stared at the moon for a long moment. It seemed terribly far, and close, at the same time. He searched for moving lights up there, in the deep blackness, but saw none, and sighed and lowered his head.

He found his tuk-tuk, squatting comfortably besides its fellows, like a cow at pasture exchanging pleasantries to do with the flavour of grass. The herd of tuk-tuks lay, stabled together, in the great tuk-tuk yard beside the new Talat Sao, the Morning Market, which was no longer so new, and had

besides never been a morning, but an all-day, market, despite its name. He
patted his own tuk-tuk, sat up in the driver's seat, straddling the engine. He
loved the feel of the wind against him as he drove, loved the feel of the road
against his tires, knowing every bump and broken surface without needing
light – knowing when to slow and when to speed and when to take his time,
where the police might be waiting with the hope of ticketing a careless
driver for some cash, knew where you could stop for a late-night condensed-
milk pancake from a roving stall, what perfect hideaways to stop at along
the Mekong for a moment, with a cigarette. Before, in his grandfather's
time and in his father's time, even, the tuk-tuks ran on gasoline. Now, the
ancient, assembled-together with nails and wood and pipes and spit vehicles
slumbered under the giant solar grid of the Talat Sao, feeding their silent
engines – which no longer gave out the distinct tuk-tuk-tuk sound that had
given them their name – with electricity. Now, Noy pressed the gas pedal
down (because tradition, in the construction of tuk-tuks as in anything else,
had to be maintained) and a bar of electric light sprang up on the board
before him, suggesting his battery was full. He eased the vehicle out of the
row of its near-identical companions, hit the accelerator with a woosh, and
hit the road.

For two and a half hours he cruised through the dark streets of Vientiane.
He picked up a family returning late from their market stall, all of them
reeking of bananas, and drove them to Don Pamai. He got lucky on the way
back and picked up a falang wanting to go into town. The man had a golden
prosthetic for a thumb, and spoke little, and there was something wrong with
his voice, though his Lao was perfect. Noy had heard of the golden things
before, and they made him uncomfortable. They were called Others, and
were something like a spirit, that shared the body with the man and could
speak through him, and do terrible things (though he wasn't quite sure what
sort of terrible things those were). He took his passenger (his passengers?) to
Nampou, the fountain surrounded by soft-lighted falang restaurants, Italian
and French and the venerable old misnomer that was the Scandinavian
Bakery, and hung around for a while on the corner with the other drivers.
Then, a falang couple, both a little unsteady on their feet, wanted to go to
the National Circus. He took them there, grabbed a stick of barbequed meat
from a stall in the night market, drove around some more but there luck
deserted him, the late night played against him, and he could find no one
in need of transportation. He looked up, glared at the moon (which had
turned a soft, pale white, like a lightly fried egg) as if daring it to intervene.

There was another purpose for the little amounts of money he put aside
when he could. He knew an old man who had studied in China and Russia
and had been in good standing with the Party but had recently become old
and eccentric enough to be put away into modest retirement in the capital.
The old man had a large house on the outskirts of town, and he lived there
alone, and in the large backyard he was building a . . .

Someone whistled; Noy saw the flash of a hand in the darkness, waving
him down, and hit the brakes. He couldn't see the figure's face; as it

approached he saw it was robed somewhat in the manner of a monk, yet the cloth was not saffron but a deep black, the colour of a moonless night in the mountains. The head was cowled.

There was something strangely familiar about the figure, as if it had awakened a dormant memory – ah. He remembered now. A story Sip Pan Joe was telling, only the week before – something about an order of strange monks up in Udom Xhai, falang men and women dressed all in black, who shared a mind together . . .

He had thought it was only one of Sip Pan's stories. Now the dark figure regarded him from the shadows in what might have been amusement, might have been impatience. Noy said, in English, "Where you go?"

There were, he noticed, thin, silvery wires – almost translucent, but suddenly seen as the figure moved and the wires caught the moonlight – trailing from inside the cowl and across the robes. And now that he looked harder it seemed to him that, from time to time, images – random flashes, too quick to notice details – moved and crawled across the robes, down the chest and arms and over to the back. "Where you go?" he said again, less certain now.

The figure said, "Wat Sokpaluang."

Noy, uncertain still: "At this hour? I think the temple is—"

"Wat Sokpaluang."

"Hundred thousand kip," Noy said. To his surprise, the figure merely nodded. It climbed on the back, into the open passenger box, and waited. Noy shrugged and pressed on the gas.

It was a strange journey for Noy. Though the figure never moved, it seemed to still, somehow, reach across to him, as if its loose wires were somehow trailing through the air to reach him; above his head the moon shone white and clear, exposing one side of its face for scrutiny. The roads were dark and quiet, the shops along Khou Vieng shut, the embers in all the barbecue pits dead and cold. Somehow, he could see the moon more clearly now than ever before, as if the silent, cowled figure in the back of the tuk-tuk was acting as a sort of magnifying glass on his mind: he watched planes rise from the ground and take to the air, watched booster rockets flare, watched the world growing smaller behind him until he was floating between air and empty space, in a thin membrane that surrounded the world below him, while ahead of him giant structures loomed, in crazy loops, donut shapes, and squares, and stranger vessels moored beside them, their square noses aimed at a giant moon . . .

Then he had turned the corner, Khou Vieng into Sokpaluang, and the temple rose ahead, and he stopped the tuk-tuk, and the robed figure climbed out.

The figure paid him. Noy stared at it, said at last, "What *are* you?"

The monk-like figure pulled back, as if surprised. Then the same soft, perfectly-modulated voice said, "I am nothing."

"You are a monk?"

The figure seemed to shrug, as if the question made little sense. "I am," it said, and Noy had the feeling, strangely, of more than one voice speaking, of an *I* composed of many smaller fragments of self, "nothing. I am the nothingness between the stars. The moon is only a rock, Noy. Happiness can no more be mined on the moon than it can in Vientiane. Also, your chain is loose." Then it turned and passed softly under the arches that led to the temple.

"How did you know my name?" Noy mumbled, but there was no reply. "And what do you mean, my chain?" he started the engine again and rode off. It was getting too late for passengers, and the drivers at Nampou, still waiting for the nightclub traffic, wouldn't welcome yet another hopeful to compete for the meagre traffic. He decided to go visit the old man. It seemed a good night for it.

At a late-night stall, still open, the sleepy proprietor blinking behind a half-empty glass, he bought a small bottle of rice whiskey to bring along. He cruised down the silent roads, passing the Mekong on his left, then on his right, past a giant Pepsi sign that promised, in a mixture of Lao and English, to revolutionize one's life with a single sip, past bags of rubbish left outside on the pavements, away from the city centre, past rice paddies eerily lit by the moon, past the croaking of a frog choir (that seemed to resemble, though he would never dare say it aloud, that of the one last heard on the television), and finally down a narrow muddy path to the house of Dr Somboong.

There was still light in one of the windows. Dr Somboong was a reluctant sleeper. As Noy approached the house he heard an unhealthy rattle from underneath the tuk-tuk, the sound of something tearing and falling with a thud on the ground, and he braked, causing the tuk-tuk, before he hastily turned it off, to begin issuing alarms in a commanding and incomprehensible Japanese.

"I didn't know your tuk-tuk could talk," a voice said. Noy looked up and saw Dr. Somboong standing by the steps, smiling faintly in the moonlight.

"Neither did I . . ."

"What's wrong with the vehicle?"

Noy fished out a torch, shone it on the ground. "Son of a – " he said.

The chain, which linked the engine in the front to a central axis under the passenger cabin which, in turn, provided motion for the wheels, had broken at one joint and fallen on the ground.

"I better fix this," Noy said apologetically.

"Bring it into the yard," Dr Somboong said. He walked down the stairs with slow, careful steps, then to the gate. He fumbled with the latch and pushed the gate open. Noy, in turn, pushed the slim-framed tuk-tuk through, and into the yard. Dr Somboong clapped his hands, twice, and lights came on, and the old man smiled with delight. "Put it next to the spaceship."

As always, the spaceship was in a state of undress: it looked a little like a tuk-tuk with wings, its insides exposed, engine parts and chains and nails and coils of wires and electronic components lying all about around it. The rockets lay on the unmown grass, heavy scrap metal hammered together into cylindrical shapes. To Noy, the spaceship looked like a heavenly chariot, like something the Buddha might be seen in on his way to final enlightenment, like a special effect they used on *Journey to the West*, a Chinese space kung-fu serial about the Buddha that he watched avidly, whenever he could, on Thai TV. To Noy, the spaceship was beautiful. Dr Somboong said, "I'm thinking of setting the trial launch for early next year. Have to be sure, you know."

Noy knew. Dr Somboong had said the same thing in the past three years of their acquaintance, but Noy agreed. You had to be sure. And you couldn't hurry something like this: it existed as a perfect thing, a fusion of hope and dream that could not be ruined, a vehicle of vision and faith whose chain could not break while it was not in motion. "She's beautiful," he said. He always said that.

"I'm thinking of calling her Lady Champa," Dr Somboong said. He always said that, too. And there was always something wistful in his voice: Noy didn't know whether it was named purely for the flower, or perhaps, as he sometimes liked to imagine, for a mysterious, long-gone girlfriend of the doctor in whose memory the doctor's life work was being carried out.

Fat flies buzzed around the lamps and a moth launched itself at the window, the sound of its impact against the glass repetitive and soothing. "I brought whiskey," Noy said. The doctor nodded, as if Noy had just confirmed a great mystery he had been pondering for a while. "I'll get us a couple of glasses," he said. "Then we can see about your chain."

The doctor disappeared inside the house. Noy lifted the empty passenger carriage and propped it at an angle. He would need to re-join the broken ends of the chain, then loop it back through the pipes and wooden boards of the tuk-tuk. He took hold of the chain, put it on the ground and began to hammer the two disparate parts back together again.

A gust of wind, coming in by stealth from the outside, brought with it a freshening coolness into the yard, the smell of growing rice, the smell of water, a snatch of music from someone's radio far away, and Noy stood up, his hands black with grease. Low on the horizon the moon, like a spaceship, was slowly setting, describing its descent in a glittering arc across the dark sky.

LION WALK

Mary Rosenblum

One of the most popular and prolific of the new writers of the 1990s, Mary Rosenblum made her first sale, to *Asimov's Science Fiction*, in 1990, and has since become a mainstay of that magazine, and one of its most frequent contributors, with almost thirty sales there to her credit. She has also sold to *The Magazine of Fantasy and Science Fiction*, *Science Fiction Age*, *Pulphouse*, *New Legends*, and elsewhere.

Her linked series of "Drylands" stories have proved to be one of *Asimov's* most popular series, but she has also published memorable stories such as, "The Stone Garden," "Synthesis," "Flight," "California Dreamer," "Casting At Pegasus," "Entrada," "Rat," "The Centaur Garden," "Skin Deep," "Songs the Sirens Sing," and many, many others. Her novella *Gas Fish* won the *Asimov's* Readers Award Poll in 1996 and was a finalist for that year's Nebula Award. Her first novel, *The Drylands*, appeared in 1993 to wide critical acclaim, winning the prestigious Compton Crook Award for Best First Novel of the year; it was followed in short order by her second novel, *Chimera*, and her third, *The Stone Garden*. Her first short-story collection, *Synthesis and Other Stories*, was widely hailed by critics as one of the best collections of 1996. She has also written a trilogy of mystery novels written under the name Mary Freeman. Her most recent books include a major new science fiction novel, *Horizons*, and a reissued and expanded version of *The Drylands*. A graduate of Clarion West, Mary Rosenblum lives in Portland, Oregon.

Here, she takes us to a nature reserve where scientists are re-creating creatures from the Pleistocene by selective breeding, for a hard-hitting story that manages to work both as genuine SF and as a genuine mystery.

TAHIRA GHANI STARED down at all that was left of the trespasser, the stunner pointed down at the summer yellow grass. The big California Condor she had interrupted spread it's huge stretch of wings and gave a reproachful squawk, scattering the smaller turkey vultures. A hot breeze washed their carrion scent over her, but she barely noticed. The pride probably hadn't left much and the coy-dogs – well on their way to emulating the Pleistocene wild dogs – had cleaned up whatever the lions hadn't eaten before the vultures even had a chance. She squatted beside the mess, smelling a trace of blood, spilled gut, lion, and the musky tang of violent death on the hot wind. A torn, bloodstained piece of black fabric fluttered in the breeze, snagged on a hawthorn. Flies swarmed over the few vertebrae and the piece of a rib that remained, the rags of flesh dark red brown now, the color of old blood. A strand of auburn hair caught her eye, tangled among grass stems. Long. A woman? Like the other one. Caucasian this time. She read the diary of last night in the scuffed ground where the lions had killed, the tracks leading to it, faint on the dry grass, human prints overlaid with lion. She squatted, the stunner in one hand, her dun suncloth coverall hot against her thighs. Laid her fingertips lightly on the double imprint; woman, lion. Brought her hand to her mouth and touched her tongue to her fingertips, tasting dust, dead leaves, and lion.

Running. No shoes. Tahira stood, wiped her fingers on her coverall and circled the dusty patch of ground that gave up this information, shaded her eyes to stare at the single print, the faint ovals of toes, ball of foot. No blood, so she hadn't been barefoot long. Frowning, she searched the prairie bisected by the willow-clad banks of the river. Maybe the intruder had thought the river could save her. Barefoot? In the distance, beyond the summer yellow grass and white fluff of the seeding thistles, the stark peaks of the Rockies jutted against the cloudless sky. Once they had had snow on them, even in the summer. Not in her lifetime. Her frown deepened as she studied the marks where the lions had lain to eat. Coy-dog tracks pocked the dust and flattened grass, along with the prints of the turkey vultures. The condor had chased them away and now they circled patiently overhead waiting for her to leave. By tomorrow, you'd find no traces to prove that someone had died and the lions had eaten here.

Tahira's frown deepened as she used her link to video the site. She dug into her daypack for a plastic bag, waved the blow flies from the vertebrae and carefully bagged them. Plenty of flesh for a DNA identification. If this trespasser had wanted to be eaten, she could not have done a better job of placing herself in the old lioness's path.

Just like the other one.

Tahira collected the fabric and hair, added them to the bag, then trudged back to her skimmer, stowed the stunner in the scabbard beneath the saddle and climbed aboard. The vultures were already descending, dodging the condor's half-hearted feints, squabbling as they searched for overlooked scraps, their huge black wings raising dust from the scuffed ground. She pulled out her link and texted a report of the intruder's death to her boss. Then she frowned at the screen and turned it off. He'll scream about the PR aspects. Not now.

The fabric, torn, dirty and bloody as it was, had had the feel of silk, the sexy kind of shirt you might buy to wear for a lover. Tahira toed the skimmer to life and lifted gently from the riverbank.

Thoughtfully, she pulled her AR goggles on and zoomed in on the ground as she spiraled slowly outward from the site of the killing, reading the night's traffic in the bent grass stems, the wisp of tan hair snagged on a tangle of riverbank willow.

She knew where this pride would be lying up, didn't need to search for their chip signatures with the tracking software. Every major mammal in the Pleistocene Preserve was chipped, from coy-dogs to the new pair of giant sloths that had the gene engineers popping champagne corks, but after her years here, she rarely needed to use a chip to find what she was looking for.

Tahira accelerated until the wind pulled her lips back from her teeth. Not one Perimeter alarm had gone off last night. Same with the last one.

Tahira spied a patch of tawny hide in the shade beneath a clump of hawthorn a split second before the goggles ringed it with red and flashed an ID number above it. She braked hard, spiraled back and down. That was the small male, the one with the ragged ear, one of the old lioness's last surviving cubs. He was a classic African type, with a full tawny mane and only a hint of the Pleistocene striping and narrower head. Which meant he was on the cull list. Like the old lioness. The IDs of the rest of the pride flashed into view. Right where she knew they would be. The old lioness was on her feet, looking up at the skimmer, her scarred face and faded, ratty fur a testament to her age. She was smart and she learned quickly. An offering like the girl would have been too good to pass up the first time. This second offering would have been easier to take.

Tahira sighed, and spun the skimmer away, out over the broad plain of yellow summer grass patched with the dusty gray green of hawthorn and the darker junipers. A small herd of antelope raised their heads as she soared over, tails flashing nervously. The big herd would be farther north, she'd check on them as she circled home. A hawk soared at eye level as she rose, turned its attention back to the ground, searching for rodents flushed by the antelope below. Tahira checked on the horse herd, found them southward, watering at the grassy back of the narrow river, whose waters ran clear and dark. Automatically, she noted the dwindling feeder stream that would be down to a trickle in another month. No glaciers to keep rivers running out here, not anymore. Dark tails whisked their dun sides and they stamped dark-striped legs at the biting flies. The gene engineers were winning here, too. They had engineered the original Przewalksi's horse into a chunky lookalike to the horses that had grazed this plain in the Pleistocene. They were working hard on the elephants now. Some of the recent calves were going to be huge and hairy. She did a quick count of the herd using her link software to scan the GPS chips, although she really didn't need to. She'd have all the numbers available from the daily sat-scan when she got back to Admin. She didn't have to do the rounds in person at all, but she liked to see for herself.

And the last body hadn't showed up on the Security report at Admin. She suspected this one wouldn't either.

The lead mare raised her head as she circled. The lame filly was gone, probably brought down by the same lion pride that had taken the trespasser. They would have gotten the filly long ago except that the old lead mare was her dam and had protected her foal fiercely, with the whole herd to back her up. Luck must have aided the pride. The old lioness was showing her age, and avoided the hard kills now.

So she had taken the meal that had walked up and asked to be eaten.

How in the name of all that was unholy had the trespasser gotten past the Perimeter?

Tahira kicked the skimmer to high speed, circled south to where the bison herd grazed the lowlands, their huge, erect horns another testament to the geneticists wizardry. The eastern elephant troop was hanging around there right now, close enough to the monorail to give the tourists a good show. Sure enough, a train had stopped and even at her height and speed she could make out the passengers hanging out the windows, pointing their links. Their tour goggles would pick out the hairy Mastodon-type calves for them and explain in a pleasant voice how the engineers were tweaking the genome. The old cow raised her trunk to blow at Tahira as she skimmed by, then went back to scooping dust from the wallow they'd created, tossing it in ochre showers over her back. Tahira didn't see any of the camels, but they were probably all back in trees, out of the sun. They, too, were changing. The old lioness was the only remaining lion that carried wholly African genes, had been wild-caught as a cub.

Tahira liked her for that.

With a sigh, Tahira grounded the skimmer to text a quick report on her find to her boss. Then she shut off the link before he could reply and swung the skimmer northward to find the big antelope herd.

The sun was dipping toward the horizon by the time she returned to Admin. Only the solar farm beyond the low, ochre buildings, row upon row of collectors following the sun, spelled 'tech.' The earth-brick buildings might have been built by some primitive peoples, blending gently into the summer prairie. Tech was pretty much invisible now – except in the dry lands where the ranked mirrors of the solar farms and the wind towers had supplanted juniper and sage. But nobody went out there. Her village would have suited this landscape, she thought. Huts decaying slowly into the shriveling desert that had once fed lions and antelope and people. Tahira set the skimmer down hard and fast on the small landing pad behind the building. The trickle of water down the central interior water wall washed a breath of moist cool and greenery-scent over her as she entered, tempting her to strip, shower, and sit in the pool. She ached after her full day on the skimmer. Once upon a time, she had not ached. It was time to make another appointment at the geri clinic. Or perhaps not. Every cycle had a natural end. Well, perhaps that was no longer true. Tahira sighed at the angry blink of the red priority icon above the holo deck.

She ignored it and instead seated herself on her working cushion, doing full lotus for concentration. Called up Security. Some eye somewhere must have seen the girl last night. She started a search for predator-prey movement, narrowed the profile to a human's mass. No point in watching rodents and coy-dogs. That got her lions, antelope, bison calves. A headache blossomed behind her eyes as the images flickered through her field.

Then . . . there she was. Shadowy, slender, her arms, neck, face, legs stark white in the night-eye recording, that black shirt that would be torn and bloodied revealing a deep cleavage and breasts that were small enough to be natural, not sculpted. Tahira's eyes narrowed. Short shorts, sexy clothes, nothing you'd wear into the thorny scrub of the Preserve. Sandals, so she had lost them, running. No blood on that white skin. She hadn't waded through the hawthorn then. How old? Sixteen? No, she decided. Less. Maybe fourteen. That was how old her daughter had been, last time she had seen her. Tahira tasted blood, realized she was biting her lip. She watched the girl wince, bend a slender leg to rub at something – thorn or bite. She looked lost. Pissed. Stood-up by a date pissed.

Then, her expression changed from lost-and-angry to startled. Then frightened. She looked around and for an instant her eyes seemed to meet Tahira's. Accusingly.

Like an antelope, she turned and bolted, running through the grass and thorns. One of the sandals flew off, a twinkle of motion on the screen.

"Don't run." Tahira said it out loud.

In the holo field the girl kept running and in a second vanished from the eye's sweep.

Tahira found herself standing. Muttered a curse. She skimmed to the next eye, which should have picked up the girl's panicked flight and probably the kill, since it covered that sector.

It showed her grass, scrub, the scurry of a small rodent, the silent float of an owl. The small dying shriek of the rodent made her flinch, then she skimmed back through that eye's sequence.

Nothing. She slowed the segment, watched the owl creep across the scene. Frowned. Seed heads bowed the grass. This species had finished seeding weeks ago and the seed heads had shattered, spilling their ripe seeds.

She copied and filed both sequences and had the station AI code them for search identification. Then she set the AI searching the Preserve's security base for an exact match to the quiet scene recorded by the second eye. Within a minute, a 99% match popped up in her holo field. Side by side, two owls floated and twin shrieks split the quiet. She checked the properties. Yep. The scene had been recorded five weeks ago, on a quiet night with . . . she checked . . . no Security alerts, not even a native antelope bumping the Perimeter fence.

For several moments, she frowned at the now-frozen images, then blanked them. This time, she directed her AI to match the visual image of the girl running, but she directed it to search the web, excluding only the Preserve data files.

That search was going to take some time.

With a sigh, she emailed the video of the girl and the twin owl sequences to her boss, then reached into the holo field to touch the angry, blinking priority icon.

It took five full minutes for Carlo to appear. Which meant he was probably in bed. With someone. He had just spent a week at a body-spa and he was probably trying out the upgrades. Tahira braced herself as Carlo's face and torso appeared in the field, yes, wrapped in a silken robe, his usually-perfect hair tousled. "About time." His eyes narrowed. "Where were you? I called you as soon as I got your report but your link didn't answer."

"Checking the range."

"You have software to do that."

"The software didn't find her. I did."

"Has the media gotten hold of this?" Carlo looked over his shoulder, back to her, lowered his voice. "I assume not, or my interface would have picked it up and alerted me." His dark eyes snapped. "All right. This time, you need to find out how the trespasser got in. And why Security failed to alert you. Again. Meanwhile, you will euthanize the lions involved. As insurance against media clamor. We will have done all we could do."

"It's not the lions' fault." Tahira shook her head. "The girl was meant to run into them. She was dropped right in front of them."

"What do you mean she was dropped?" He ran a hand through his head. "Make sense, Tahira, will you?"

"She was dropped." Tahira bit the words off. "By a skimmer, helicopter. Something. She was in sandals. Bedroom type. I just emailed you the Security clip that did pick her up. And the clip that was used to replace most of the visuals."

He stared at her. "That's unbelievable." He chopped her words aside with the flat of his hand. "Do you know how much it would cost to do that kind of hack job? Worry about the Perimeter security. Something is down. The lion euthanasia shows the public that we're doing a good job of dealing with this. The US media will howl if they get hold of this. You know how they feel about the Preserve."

Yes, she knew.

"I can sacrifice you or I can sacrifice a lion or two. You decide, Tahira." Carlo's eyes narrowed. "And before you say anything, you're a hell of a lot more valuable to me than the lions, they're breeding just fine. Besides, as soon as the genetics geeks get their Panthera leo atrox phenotype we won't use African lions anymore anyway. So let's just call it moot and drop it." He glanced over his shoulder again and his mouth tightened briefly. Turned back to Tahira. "I am ordering you to euthanize a lion that killed this person. Make sure you get a DNA match so we can prove it, and I'll leave it to you to get the right one. I'll let you claim it was a rogue animal and make it plausible."

He was giving her a lot. Carlo could have demanded the whole pride – the media would press for it. He could have fired her. "Can we talk about how this girl got in here? She was a girl, Carlo. Dressed for a hot date. Go take a look at that clip I sent you. She did not hike in from the Perimeter. I think that's a bit more important than pleasing the media."

"No, it's not." Carlo cut her off with another chop of his aristocratic hand. "If we're lucky, nobody will pick it up. Make sure you secure those video files. The administrative contract for the Preserve comes up for renewal in one month. The US will push hard to take it over, as usual. If you want a job a month from now, you'd better hope the World Council thinks we're doing a good job here and doesn't award the contract somewhere else." The holo field blanked.

Tahira stared into the opalescent shimmer.

He was right. The vast Preserve, the huge central section of the US that had been restored to its Pleistocene ecology, including megafauna and the species that had inhabited this land millions of years ago, was part of a giant experiment in ecological climate control. And genetic engineering. And a huge tourist draw, which the US did like. A lot of countries were uneasy about it, seeing a threat to their own grasslands and dwindling wildlands as the growing Gaiist movement used carbon credit leverage to pressure for more preservation. Too much media outcry and the US might garner enough support to end the Preserve and take over control of the huge area again, never mind the carbon credits they'd then owe. It was a matter of national pride, she thought sourly. That had always transcended logic.

She made herself a pot of very black tea and began to go through the security records for the past twenty four hours, searching for human-sized mass or any sign of a small-craft landing. As the sun cleared the horizon, she finally shut down her station and stumbled off to her small room behind the water wall, sprawling sweaty and fully clothed across her bed.

No airspace invasion, no vehicles, nobody on foot. Maybe the girl had teleported in. She laughed sourly. Sure.

Just like the last one.

"Tahira? Hey, Tahira, are you okay?"

Jen's voice. Tahira blinked crusted eyes, swimming up from a deep pool of sleep and dreams she couldn't remember but that had stalked her like lions. "Late night." She realized that she had spoken in Sotho, switched to English. "Sorry. I just need some tea." She sat up, stiff and sticky in her dirty clothes, rubbed her eyes.

"I already made you some." Jen stood in the doorway, nervous, a mug in one hand. "When you didn't hear me come in I figured you really needed tea."

"Yeah. Thanks." Tahira got up, glad that she hadn't stripped last night and took the mug. "I appreciate it." She gave him a smile because this too-earnest graduate student had tried to climb into her bed a week ago, never mind the age difference. And her 'no thanks' had apparently bruised him. She swallowed a stinging gulp of the strong-enough tea, gave Jen a nod of approval. Usually, he made it too weak.

"You got official mail." Jen stood just outside the door, as if a strand of Perimeter fencing blocked it, his beaded and braided, silver-white hair – stark contrast to his tawny skin and intended to be sexy – swinging forward around his face with his nod. "Security seal. Looks important."

"Yeah." Tahira drank more tea. The official execution orders. "We had another trespasser last night."

"You're kidding." Jen's eyes got round. "No, you're not. Another . . . another kill? What are we going to do about it?"

She brushed past him, angry because two plus two was a simple equation. But guilt stabbed her. He had brought strong tea. And he didn't really understand the Preserve politics. She paused, looked back and shrugged. "I'll have to kill one of the lions of course. Even though it wasn't really their fault."

The information didn't move him, but why should it? He was a graduate student, studying the symbiosis of lions and one of the predatory wasp species. Esoteric stuff. A study that provided a comfortable living and yielded information. Lions were just the food providers for his wasps, who laid their eggs in the larvae of a biting fly that pestered the lions. And the wasps were just a day job, a means to an income. He'd study whatever he was paid to study. She sighed. "Come have some breakfast with me, eh? I found a fresh guinea hen nest yesterday."

She softboiled the small, tan eggs and they ate them together as she listened to him prattle on about his wasp collecting, larvae counts, population fluctuations. When he left on his skimmer, with his collecting nets, sample bags, and a stunner, Tahira stripped and scrubbed herself clean of last night's sweat and the smell of violent death. She stripped the bed, tossed the dirty sheets into the sonic cleaner, and padded barefoot, in a clean shift, to the lab refrigerator where she had stored the trespasser's bones. The bag containing the black shirt lay on the floor beside the refrigerator. She picked it up, smoothed out the torn and blood-stiffened fabric within its plastic shroud. Why did you come here? She spoke silently to the girl's spirit. The lioness's killing was innocent. My killing of the lioness will not be innocent and it will be my burden not yours. Anger burned through her. "Your death was not innocent," she said aloud. "You brought it with you and left it like poison on innocent ground."

But her own words sounded hollow and that image nagged at her . . . the 'where's my date?' body language, that single, decorative sandal tumbling through the air, bright against the stark night-vision landscape. Dropping the shirt, she took out the bag with the vertebrae and hair and got to work.

The first thing she did was file a full report to the local Sheriff's Department. That meant the media would have the news within the hour. The Sheriff's security leaked like a sieve. Next, she started the DNA scan. She was only required to run a minimal ID scan, but she did a full analysis. The longer she spent on this easily-rationalized task, the longer she could put off the euthanasia. By noon, her back ached from standing and the building's major-domo announced Deputy Malthers. Shawn. He always handled Preserve issues. She sent the data to her personal workspace and shut down the lab, retreating into the main room and the cool breath of water-wall. "Come in." She admitted him and he sighed in the cool air, removing his hat, half moons of sweat darkening the tan sun-cloth of his uniform.

"Tahira." He nodded, his weathered face closed and cautious. "You had an intruder, huh?" Another one, his eyes accused. "Supposedly your fence is tight. Do I have to worry about lions in the hotel lobbies?"

"You know you don't, Shawn." Tahira studied the tight lines around his eyes. "The Perimeter isn't porous – to animals. Who chewed on you?"

"My boss, the Sheriff. The governor chewed on him." He sighed and tossed his hat onto the corner of the table. "He's getting more pressure from the Take Back America people. They got the news even before the media could post it on the net. Can I have a glass of water?" He gave her a plaintive look. "I know you run a tight ship, Tahira, but jeeze, two deaths in two months? This is too good for the media to pass up. You should see the hit rates."

"Sit down. I'm sorry." She headed for the kitchen. "I didn't get much sleep. Did you get the DNA scan I sent your office?" She carried two full glasses and a pitcher of water back, set the tray on the low table near her work field.

"Yeah. No match." He took a glass, drank half of it in long, gulping swallows. Wiped his mouth on his sleeve. "She's not a missing person. I sent it to the national DNA database, but you know how long that takes." He rolled his eyes. "They've got a six month backlog and that's just on violent crime. I still haven't heard back on our first Jane Doe."

At least he had said 'our', although technically, the Preserve was administered by the World Council and not under local jurisdiction. Still, the World Council liked to let local law deal with matters if at all possible. Tahira sat down on her cushion. The holo field shimmered to life and she opened the data file, staring thoughtfully as the letters, numbers, and icons winked like emerging stars.

"I know her." She spoke to the galaxy of numbers and icons – the translation of those rags of flesh and bits of bone. "She grew up in a slum." The heavy metal load in her hair could only belong to a child of the unclensed suburban wasteland. "She was very young, less than sixteen, I am guessing. European, probably Scotch-Irish, no Asian or African genes, minimum melanin." Her skin would have been very fair and the red in her hair was natural beneath its cheap dye. Poor all her life, considering the uncorrected genetic predisposition to cholesterol and cancer. She would not have had an uncomplicated middle age, if she had lived. She would have died young, relatively speaking. Unless she earned the money for genetic repair. "Look at this." She called up the security clip, ran it. Listened to Malthers' soft indrawn breath.

"She didn't expect lions." His face was grim. "And she sure didn't get lost from one of your tours, huh?"

"Nobody gets lost from our tours." Tahira shook her head. "And no, she did not expect lions."

"You got any ideas?"

"This cost a lot of money." She looked at him. "Hacking our security. It would be expensive. We do not use cheap security."

He was looking at her quizzically, his thick brows drawn down over those so very blue eyes.

"Some things," she said slowly, remembering, "don't change."

"Like what?"

Her link chimed. "I have a tour scheduled." She stood, feeling age in her bones, even though they worked perfectly, levering her young-muscled body erect. As if invisible teleomeres were shortening, ticking like a clock. "I have to go. If I find anything out, I will email you."

He headed for the door, paused to look back. "Stop by the office." Those so blue eyes fixed on her face. "I'll buy you a beer." The door closed behind him, breathing hot dust into the room.

The tour was an expensive one, which was why she had to lead it. It would be a package with a hotel, maybe a body spa, the Preserve and a tour conducted personally by the Manager. That was her. Her contract specified how many of these she had to do each month. Originally, Carlo had suggested she wear native dress. When she had told him that would be a ragged tee shirt with the name of a football team on it, he had shut up and not mentioned it again. The tourists were waiting beside their air conditioned tour bus, looking around at the dusty little compound, pointing their links at the buildings, the guinea hens scratching in the shade. The link videoed the image and instantly searched the web for a match, downloading informational links. The life cycle of the guinea hen, the history of the Preserve, the blueprints for the buildings, if you wanted to look at them. Their tour guide spotted her and said something. Instantly they all, nearly in unison, pointed their links at her.

A part of her wanted to duck, as if they were pointing weapons. The gesture was, her hind brain told her, the same. Was it, she wondered briefly, that this pointing of links to acquire information was a hostile act? Or was it that the men who had fired on the refugees when she was a child hadn't been hostile, had treated the dealing of death as casually as these tourists treated the gathering of information? She didn't know, hid her flinch and smiled for them as the guide did the introduction that they weren't listening to. Their eyes were on their links as she downloaded onto their screens life and death, love and loss, success and failure, rendered in text and images. She climbed onto the bus after them, took the plush seat up front, facing them. The guide sat beside her in the other rear-facing seat. Some of the tourists were from off-planet, perhaps one of the orbital platforms or perhaps even Mars. They had brown skin, lighter than her Lesotho skin, but their bodies seemed frail, out of proportion. They looked at her, eyes bright.

They did not look quite human.

"Go straight out of the compound and take the first right," she told the driver, who was a regular. "We'll take the road down along the river."

"We're here to see the Mastodon calves." One of the off-planet tourists looked up from her link. "The park map IDs them to the west, over in the hills."

"The old cow always brings them down to their favorite place on the river at dusk, to drink." Tahira spoke patiently. "You'll have time to stretch your legs and have some dinner before they show up."

"Why don't we just go where they are?" Someone else spoke up.

"Our rhythms are more flexible than those of the animals." She kept her voice patient. "They know we will be there at the river, we are usually there, that does not bother them. It is familiar. If we arrive unexpectedly in an unusual place . . . they will be bothered. And that is unhealthy."

That didn't satisfy all of them but she didn't expect it to.

"Hey." A woman with a very young face, golden skin, and hair as silvery white as Jen looked up from her screen. "I just got a newsfeed . . . a tourist got killed by a lion! Last night! This is the second lion kill!"

Murmurs swept the bus and all eyes focused on the link screens.

"It wasn't a tourist." Her words fell like stones into the murmur and eyes pried themselves from link screens. "A young woman was dropped from a hovercraft for the lions to find." She spoke into silence now. All eyes were on her and somehow, this felt no different than the pointed links. "She was intended to die. Someone videoed her death. That person will sell the video for a lot of money. Violent death is very valuable. It is an ugly trade." Only the purr of the bus's power plant could be heard now. "But it is a very old trade. No matter. I saw the vehicle that brought her, I saw the person who operated it. I observe that lion pride every night and I was there in the darkness. He will be caught."

"That's not on the newsfeed." The accusatory voice came from the rear of the bus. From one of the off-worlders. Tahira shrugged. "I did not tell the media this. But you are safe." Her smile was genuine this time. "The lion pride does not water where we will be. This is not their territory."

She wasn't sure if they were relieved or disappointed. She cut off their questions by launching into her usual lecture, pointing out the changing ecosystem – it had not reached full climax equilibrium yet – directing their links to the coy-dog family holed up in the shade, waiting the cool of evening. The puppies were playing a game of tug with a scrap of dirty hide and links bristled, zooming in to record. The larger animals were all chipped so the links would offer up the ID information for each animal, their stage of development toward the Pleistocene ideal as the engineers evolved them into their own ancestors.

Voyeurs, she thought as they pointed and murmured. An observable reality, but not personal. Not threatening.

She politely refused to say anymore about the death, telling them only that the authorities would handle it. The tourists were distracted by the smaller horse herd. One of the young stallions had been challenging the

herd sire over the past few weeks and he chose this day to take his challenge
to a new level. Dust rose in tan clouds as the two horses circled and feinted,
ears flat, striking snake-like for a bite, whirling to kick. This time, the youngster wasn't backing down and the two stallions rose, chest to chest, teeth
bared. "These horses are very much like the Equus verae, the horses that
grazed this plane a million years ago. If you'll put on your glasses, you'll be
able to identify the young male." She paused while the tourists all fumbled
for the glasses they'd been given at the start. The were slaved to hers. She
IDed the young male by chip number and a green halo instantly surrounded
him. "This young stallion was foaled four years ago in the spring. The engineers believe that he is a good likeness of the original Equus verae. All the
stock began with Przewalksi's Horse, the last truly wild horse species." They
were all watching now, as the stallions shouldered and circled, wheeling to
kick, or rearing to feint and bite at each other's faces. Tahira stifled a sigh.
"The herd sire is nearly ten years old. That's a long life for a herd sire." The
young challenger had been born of artificial insemination with the new,
improved genes. If the old herd sire didn't get ousted soon, she'd have to
help a new challenger along. "This is not reality," she murmured. "It is our
version of reality."

"Pardon?" One of the off-worlders had moved to the front of the bus for
a better look, was pointing his link at the fight, recording.

"Nothing." She shook her head. "I was just talking to myself."

"It's so . . . uncontrolled." He had friendly dark eyes and a wide smile that
made his too-fragile body seem less different. "Hard to imagine living in a
world this . . . chaotic."

"It's not chaotic," she said softly. "Only humans are chaotic."

The horses saved her from the questions surfacing in his eyes. The young
stallion whirled as the herd sire struck and his heels caught the herd sire full
in the face. They heard the thud of hoof on bone, even at this distance, and
the sire went down in a cloud of dust. He struggled instantly to his feet, but
his jaw looked twisted and blood darkened the dun hide. A low murmur of
horror washed through the bus.

"What now?" The white-haired woman's voice rose over the babble.
"What will happen now?"

"This was an accident. Fights like this rarely result in serious injury."
Tahira blocked the tourist glasses, but had her own zoom in on the injured
stallion. No point in showing them the bloody details up close. The youngster had run him a few meters from the mares and now trotted back and
forth, tossing his head, tail erect as the ousted sire stood with head drooping.
She winced at the white gleam of either bone or teeth visible in the bloody
mess of his face. Violence seemed to be gathering over the Preserve like
a dark cloud. "His jaw is broken." She didn't need the text diagnosis scroll-
ing across the visual field. "He won't be able to eat. The lions will probably
kill him, or even the wild dogs. This coy-dog is heavier than the old North
American coyotes and they hunt in small packs. They occasionally kill large
prey species, mostly when the animal is weak or crippled."

"Why don't you do something about it?" A woman spoke up, her voice shrill. "You could take him in and heal him, right?"

"And what will the lions eat tonight?" Tahira faced the woman, watched horror and anger ripple across her features. "These are not our rules. They are much older than us," she said gently. "That is what the Preserve is all about. . . . returning to the old rules. Without the horse, a lion cub may die because of insufficient nutrition." She waited for the horrified comments to ebb. You could hear the excitement beneath the horror. Now they had a prize in the video files they'd just uploaded to their personal space – something to show proudly to friends, so they could commiserate over that raw moment of blood, and pain, and imminent death. The woman who had spoken up wasn't satisfied. She was talking about cruelty and emails to powerful people.

"Did you make this happen for us?" The off-worlder was looking at her, and his eyes were shocked and cold.

"No." She met those eyes, saw her own reflection in them, tiny and perfect. "But I knew the old stallion would be forced out sooner or later. The horses decided to make it happen now. The kick was a freak accident. Horses are good at dodging."

He didn't believe her. You cannot conceive of no control, she thought. And wondered suddenly if her daughter had gone off-planet. The Council Security Forces were everywhere. She had never thought of that before, and it chilled her, she was not quite sure why. She would be much older than this man, now.

They moved on and the tour guide, a seasoned professional, texted her a request to show them something to change the now-soured mood. She had anticipated this and had already called up her inventory. "Turn left just past that clump of willow . . . yes, there."

The bus took the dirt track easily, it's off-road suspension barely sloshing the drinks that the attendant was handing out. "The engineers have had excellent success with the long horned bison. They are very like the bison that grazed this plain during the Pleistocene. Three cows have calved this month and the latest was last night. She scanned for the IDs, found the three cows in close proximity 200 meters from the road. "They're out in the grass, so we can watch them without disturbing them. If you'll look through the left windows and follow the arrow directions on your glasses, they'll direct you to the calves." A green arrow winked on her glasses, pointing to the right and as she turned her head, it was replaced by one pointing straight up. She lifted her head, and there, in the distance, she spied the small black dots that were the grazing bison. The bus had come to a halt. "Have you all found the bison?" She waited while the slow ones fumbled their way to the bison herd. Zoom while they were panning and they'd get sick every time. "Okay, here we go." The field blurred and suddenly seemed to be rushing toward her. The tiny specks enlarged, became a dozen shaggy brown beasts with their noses in the sun-burned grass, backs dotted with cowbirds. Small white herons stalked among them, snatching up beetles and the occasional rodent stirred up by the bison's hooves. Their long horns gleamed in the sun as they tossed their heads at flies.

The newborn calf hugged his mother's flank, his horns mere bumps. He suddenly butted beneath her flank, tail wriggling as he nursed. The collective sigh from the tourists made the guide breathe his own sigh of relief, she noted. Well, upset guests would hardly give him a fat tip. She let them watch the two older calves butt heads and the herd even obliged by grazing closer to the bus. By the time they moved on to the elephant watching spot for cocktails and their gourmet dinner, the mood was festive once more, the injured stallion forgotten.

Tomorrow, she would go check on him. Assure herself that the predators had found him. Injured as he was, the dog pack that patrolled that territory would almost certainly take him, but perhaps not right away. She called up that sector, scanned the predator inventory. To her relief, the lions were headed in that direction. They should get to him quickly.

During dinner they lucked out and a scimitar cat – quite shy and a rare sighting – chose that night to come down to the river to drink. The tourists flocked to the windows, their links pointing as they videoed in night mode. The elephants showed on time and the new Mammoth type calf went so far as to walk nearly up to the bus, trunk lifted in curiosity, before his mother shooed him nervously away, and stomped a threat toward them, her ears erect, trunk curled back like a cobra.

The tour guide looked pleased, as if Tahira had orchestrated the whole show. Tahira sat back in her seat as they returned to the compound in the gathering darkness, answering questions, giving small lectures on the history of the Preserve, the geneticists' work, the effect of the huge preserve areas on climate stability. They asked occasional questions about the injured stallion.

No one brought up the dead girl. Not one.

She climbed down from the bus into the cooling night beneath the white arch of the Milky Way and a sliver of new moon. They would go back to the comfort of the resort to have dessert and drinks and to compare video clips. The tour guide gave her a wide grin and a wave as the door closed, anticipating good tips, obviously.

Jen would have left for the day and she would have the place to herself.

You have a visitor, the door murmured as she reached the verandah. He had an official security pass to enter. His personal ID is blocked. "I know who it is." She sighed, then straightened her shoulders. "Open."

"What the hell is going on, Tahira?" Detective Malthers levered himself up from the sofa in the main room. "Do you know just how much trouble you're going to cause me when my boss starts getting the feeds?"

"He has his link shut off tonight? I would have thought he'd have the news already." She headed for the kitchen wall, thirsty. "And if I protest your use of a security pass to override my door lock, I hope you can produce the warrant." She closed her eyes as he seized her arm. Halted. "Shawn . . . I'm sorry."

"Sorry?" He spun her around to face him, his face pale. "You withheld information from me? You lied to me about that girl's death? And then you spill it to a bunch of tourists?" His nostrils were pinched. "You'd damn well better be sorry."

Some of them had certainly blogged from the bus. She had counted on that. She met his eyes. "I did not lie to you."

"Then why did you tell them . . ." His eyes narrowed and he let go of her arm. "No way. No way you do that."

"Do what?" She widened her eyes. "If I tell a story to tourists to enliven their trip and they exaggerate it in their personal blogs, this is not a crime. Your boss can deny whatever he wishes to deny and if the outcry is loud enough, my boss will probably fire me. Would you like some water?"

"What do you think you're going to do?" His voice was harsh.

"Go to bed." She filled a glass from the refrigerator tap, filled a second glass.

"I'm going to get a warrant for your arrest." He ignored the proffered glass.

"On what grounds?" She raised an eyebrow. "I suspect your boss will not agree with you. It will be hard enough to deal with the media when they get hold of the tourists' mistaken statements. It will be much worse if you have arrested the manager of the Preserve and then have to release her. Your boss is very conscious of his media image."

"I'm staying here tonight." He glared at her.

"Be my guest." She shrugged. "I told you, I'm going to bed."

"Good." He stretched out on the sofa, his jaw set.

She turned her back on him and activated her holo-field. Checked the Preserve first. Minor Perimeter alerts only – a couple of licensed back-country backpackers who had retreated when they triggered the broadcast security announcement, a small herd of pronghorn that moved off when the repulsion field activated, broadcasting an unpleasant sonic pulse that discouraged most wildlife and the occasional lost livestock. Nothing else. Red icons signaled stationary chips – indicating that a bearer hadn't moved for twelve hours. That usually represented death or serious injury. She checked the IDs . . . all prey species except for one elephant from the north-ernmost herd. An old female, but not so old that she should be dying yet. The elephants and the larger predators had been implanted with biometric chips. Tahira checked it, found signs of physical distress, but no clear diagnosis. She transferred the ID to her link. She'd fly over in the morning and check on it, on her rounds to chip new births. See what had happened.

Her AI search of the Security video of the running girl had turned up a match. 89 per cent. Tahira drew a deep breath, touched the green icon. A merchant site. Models? A naked woman lounged suggestively on a grizzly's hide, caressing the dead, snarling face, tongue-tip peeking pink from lush, crimson lips. The secure interface requested a user ID and password. And a credit card. The entry fee made her purse her lips. She flagged the link, emailed it.

Malthers was peering at his link, his feet propped on the arm of the sofa. He looked up as she shut down her field. "What if the person who dropped her was a woman?" His eyes were hard.

She shrugged. "You are too tall for that sofa. Would you like me to inflate the guest bed?"

"No, thank you." He went back to his link. "I don't plan on sleeping."

"While you are up, then, maybe you can see what's for sale on the video sex markets. I just sent you a link that you might . . . find interesting. I don't have the budget to access it." She turned and went into her room. When she woke briefly in the middle of the night, the light in the main room was still on and he was sitting on the sofa, hunched over his link.

She slept without dreaming, after that, and when she woke, he was gone.

The door seal sighed as it released and Jen strode in, bringing a smell of hot noon-time dust and heat, a hint of lion and sex. "Hey, how was your tour last night? Did they do a fancy spread?" He came up behind her, dropped his collecting bag onto the tiles with a small thump. "What's with the reporters outside? The newsfeeds were full of the killing this morning. You were a witness? To the girl's death?" His sandy brows arched over his pale eyes. "You didn't tell me that."

"I know I didn't." Tahira waved her hand through the field and the numbers and icons, the map of this girl's history written in molecules, winked out. "Let's not talk about it, okay?"

"You haven't opened your secure email from the boss yet."

"I know what it says." She sighed.

"Tahira . . ." His hands came to rest lightly on her shoulders. "I work with the lions, too. I can do this euthanasia for you. You don't have to. Just give me the chip ID."

His hands offered comfort not sex. She let her shoulders relax a bit beneath the warmth and acknowledged the small heat of desire between her legs. He was very pretty. He would try hard to please her in bed. Her shiver of anticipation made her . . . sad. She was old enough to be his grandmother. The flesh had its own morality. She sighed, and his hands slid from her shoulders as she rose. "I appreciate your offer." She smiled for him. "But it is my duty. It is my failing that the girl was able to be here."

"That's not true." He shook his head, frowning. "She bought hackware good enough to get through the Perimeter sensors. It's happened before. Remember those rich kids that came in here with a rifle? Right after I started working here? The ones who thought they were going to kill an elephant? That's not your responsibility – that's the responsibility of the company that contracts security to the Preserve."

"That's not what happened." Tahira blanked the icons with a wave of her hand. "This is not like those teenage poachers with their utterly inadequate rifles. I knew they were there."

"So her hackware was better, that's all." Jen shrugged. "Come on, Tahira. Nobody is blaming you . . . except you."

"I doubt that is true." She turned to meet his pale eyes. "Her mother? A lover? Who is mourning her? She was a girl, Jen, even if nobody claimed her as missing. The poor don't bother. You know that no one will really look. You know where they have gone." She turned away from the blue incomprehension of his eyes. "But they are blaming me. Besides, she was not rich enough to afford that level of hackware."

He shook his head and heaved a sigh for her to hear. She ignored it as she ran through the surveillance program, suppressing a twinge of guilt because she hadn't yet checked on the stationary elephant cow. Everything was fine, although the main horse herd was pushing into the grazing territory of the old mare's small, splinter herd. This was a dry year and the grass was poor. She'd have to let them get pushed off their riverside pasture. That would weaken this year's crop of still-nursing foals, and increase the kill rate by the northern pride. If another dry spring followed, she thought, the small herd would probably end up being absorbed back into the larger group. The old mare wouldn't survive that merger.

The guide reports were routine. No problems, no accidents on any of the daily motorized tours currently winding through the Preserve and only a sprained ankle from one of the self-guided backpacking treks that were in progress. The hiker had been handled by a contracted first aid skimmer and planned to continue the trek in an augmented cast, having signed a health waver. Tahira checked the location of the various lion prides and elephant groups to make sure that the guides would provide visual contact for the guests. Four were lion treks and one was an elephant trek. But all their guides were experienced and they could find the chip signatures with their own software. They were all on target to give the paying hikers the thrill of a live sighting. Routine day. She retinaed the report, packed a few necessary items into her field bag, then left Jen to his microscope and took the skimmer out into the Preserve.

Shawn had not gotten his warrant, but then she had known he would fail.

She swung north, to check up on the stationary elephant before she started her chip work. It was a long flight, clear to the northwestern boundary of the Preserve, within sight of the monorail. The old cow was down after all, on her side in the shade of a thin copse of trees. She raised her head as Tahira skimmed over, ears erect, trunk curled as she got her forefeet under her, tried to heave herself to her feet. Two aunties had stayed with her and as she collapsed into the dust once more, they hurried up, stroking her with their trunks, watching Tahira warily as she landed the skimmer and approached cautiously. The dust beneath the old cow's hindquarters had turned to mud from her urine. No sign of defecation. A blockage? Perhaps she had eaten something that damaged her gastrointestinal system. Her temperature was slightly elevated and when Tahira zoomed in with her glasses, sure enough the cow's membranes looked pale. No sign of any external trauma. Natural Causes. She selected the diagnosis, uploaded visuals to

the cow's file, and set it to alert her when vitals fell to imminent death levels.
She would return to make a more complete diagnosis then. For the record.

She caught a glimpse of movement from the corner of her eye as she
removed her glasses. Bear? Sure enough, when she slipped them back on,
a green ring haloed the bushes where she had seen the movement and
the ID appeared. One of the Short Faced bears, another of the engineers'
triumphant recreations. They were drawn by death. One of the aunties blew
noisily and rushed the bushes, trunk high. The bear retreated, growling,
circled around to windward. Tahira retreated to her skimmer, although the
bear was focused on the dying cow. Unlikely that the aunties would allow it
to hasten the old cow's end.

Natural causes, she thought as she lifted to swing eastward again. You
could label the girl's death as natural causes. To the lions it had been a natural end. The monorail was curving along the white arch of track on its first
run of the morning. In a few moments the tourists would surely spot the cow
and the questions would start pouring into Admin from the passengers. All
the tourist monorails carried a direct link to Preserve Administration. Tahira
set the skimmer on auto, homing on the ID of the bison herd she needed to
chip, and quickly edited out an image of the cow and her aunties from the
old cow's ID file. She selected one of her taken in the past, with her last calf,
set her link to record and smiled for the tourists. Quickly, in a warm and
positive tone, she explained the situation, that the cow was dying of natural
causes, the aunties were attending her, and that this (insert mother and calf
image here) was part of the natural cycle of life and death, that the old cow's
flesh would nourish wild dog cubs (she called up a file, inserted a recent
shot of three pups playing) and the scavenger population. She uploaded the
video file to Administration and texted Amy Shen, the head of PR, to expect
questions about the dying cow and offer this Special Message from the
Manager. Amy would run the file through her editing software to smooth
out any rough edges and in a few minutes, when the worried texts came in,
the tourists would have her reassuring explanation.

Maybe she should have made one for the dead girl? Tahira kicked the
skimmer to full speed, ducked down behind the wind screen as they streaked
across the foothills of the mountains.

It took her the rest of the day to chip the bison calves and stalk a litter of
wild dog pups old enough for chips. Half grown, they were skittish, full of
hormones and already squabbling with the ranking alphas. But she finally got
good shots, and planted a chip in a solid muscle mass. The new ID files opened
and she recorded the pertinent data. Now the pups and the calves were part of
the database. Their deaths would have meaning, value, would contribute to
the slowly growing mass of information about this stable environment.

What had the girl's death contributed?

A meal for the lions, she thought. At a price.

It was getting dark. She texted Jen that she was going to stay out and
check on the lion pride before she came in. Told him to go home, activate
Security when he left, she'd see him tomorrow. She knew where the pride

would be, didn't need to check her link. It was too early yet for them to head down to the river. She grounded the skimmer, ate an energy bar from her bag, drank some water, and used her link to access the Preserve database and check on the animals.

Nothing out of the ordinary. No Security alerts, nothing but the normal rhythms of day ending and night beginning. Shift change, she thought as she stuffed the wrapper into her pocket and capped her water bottle. Time. It was fully dark now, the Milky Way a white shimmer across the star spangled sky. She stared up at it. Different sky than the one over the refugee camp. Maybe it wasn't, but it looked different. She frowned, bothered suddenly that she didn't know if the constellations had been the same in that girlhood sky, or if memory had warped the images in her mind. It bothered her a lot. Frowning she lifted the skimmer, donned her glasses set to night vision, and went looking for the lion pride. She flew low, skimming above the brush, weaving around the trees. Someone watching for her might think she was checking on the wildlife, scanning chips. She dipped south so that she'd meet the pride on their way down to the river.

Red blossomed at the top of her glasses' heads-up visual field. Perimeter violation? Tahira's stomach clenched. Why an alert this time? She crouched behind the windscreen as she dropped lower, weaving through the tops of the trees. A map flashed into existence now, red dots marking the path of the intruder as he activated the sensors scattered across the Preserve. Tahira watched another red icon blossom on the screen map. He was heading for the place where the girl had died and the steady progress suggested that he wasn't trying very hard to hide and certainly wasn't using hackware.

No. This was just some fool who chose tonight to violate the Perimeter. An idiot. A thrill seeker. Furious she circled south to come in straight behind the intruder, slowed the skimmer to its limit, weaving through the brush now, twigs whispering against the skimmer's flanks, clawing at her legs. She was briefly thankful for her tough, suncloth pants that resisted the thorns. She followed the trespasser's path on her map. He should be about a hundred yards ahead, almost at the site where the girl had died.

Something slammed into her, an invisible fist that loosened her grasp on the skimmer's nav bar and tossed her sideways out of the seat. The skimmer compensated as soon as her hand left the bar, shying sideways to stay underneath her, slowing and settling automatically. She clutched at the bar to take control again, but her right arm didn't work and before she could process that, shift to her left hand, the skimmer grounded gently. For a moment, Tahira stared at the bar, then realized that her sleeve was wet, warm liquid was dripping steadily onto her pants and the dusty ground beside the skimmer. Dark. Blood. Her head spun briefly and she swallowed dry nausea.

What do you think you're going to do? She heard Shawn's furious voice in her head. Not much. She climbed off the skimmer, her knees suddenly shaky.

"I don't want to kill you." The hard, cold voice came from the tall hawthorn scrub that edged the grassy area where the skimmer had come down. "But you're not going to get in my way. You can yell for help as soon as I'm done here."

"Did you bring another one to die?" Tahira faced the voice. She was still wearing her glasses, but they didn't register an ID. No surprise. Anyone doing this would have had his ID chip removed long ago, would use temporary, fake chips. "How much do you get for these? And what do the girls think? That this is just another porn shoot, this time out in the dust? She didn't expect the lions."

"What the hell are you talking about?" A figure emerged from the concealing hawthorn. Tall. Dressed in chameleon-fabric so that his silhouette was hard to make out. The projectile rifle, night-scoped, ugly and efficient looking wasn't hard to make out at all. Something about the voice was wrong, nagged at her, but her head was full of sticky glue and she couldn't think of what it was.

"I asked you a question." The voice grated at her ears.

"You're the one who's making the snuff vids, recording the girls as they run into the old lioness's pride and die." She would have spat the words, but that sense of wrong was building in her head.

The figure stepped forward suddenly and before Tahira's gone-fuzzy reflexes could kick in, had shoved Tahira back against the skimmer, her back arched under the pressure of the trespasser's body, her good arm bent behind her. She blinked into pale gray eyes in a hard, weathered face framed by cropped-short gray-white hair. Sucked in a breath that was half pain, half surprise.

A woman.

"Shawn said it might be a she." She laughed, drunk on the pain that had begun to throb in her right shoulder and side, burning like a growing fire, radiating through her flesh.

"Yeah, I'm a she. That was my daughter your lions ate. You folks don't care, but I do." Her breath blasted Tahira's face. "They're going to pay for that tonight."

"Your daughter?" Tahira blinked, trying to focus her eyes. "That's why your hackware is so poor? You just walked in here to shoot lions? You don't care if we catch you?"

"I don't care one bit." The cold pale eyes bored into hers. "If you hadn't decided to hang out and protect them, I wouldn't have had to shoot you. I figured you folks trust your software instead of using your eyes. I know how tracking software works. . . . It's pretty easy to fool if you know how." She laughed and the sound was like glass breaking. "I was a wild-meat hunter for the black market – when there was still wild meat to hunt. I know all about tracking software. Maybe the people who babble about karmic balance are right, eh?" The shattered laugh came again. "After all the animals I killed, one of them killed my daughter. But the score is going to end in my favor."

"You fool." Tahira twisted her hand free, planted it against the woman's chest and shoved. Her strength surprised both of them and the woman stumbled back a step. "You've ruined this night. You've ruined my chance to catch the one who killed your daughter and the girl he killed before her. You and your misguided revenge. He's not going to come back, not after he realizes people were here waiting for him. Damn you."

"What the crap are you talking about?"

"I'm not talking any crap." Tahira closed her eyes. Game over, she thought. "How do you even know that your daughter was the girl who was killed here? We haven't identified the DNA yet."

"I found the image on the web." The woman's voice grated, harsh as stone. "I was looking for her, used a video search engine, uploaded a bunch of recent pictures of her. And the engine found a match. With lions." She spat. "One of your tourists videoed it. Her running. The lions after her." She spat again. "And you people just stood around."

"No one stood around. I saw that video." Tahira stood still as the gun muzzle lifted, fixed on her chest.

"The media said she sneaked in. I figured she was showing off to prove something . . . because I used to run around in the African wastelands for the meat collectors. She was such a city kid." For a moment her voice wavered. Then it went cold again. "You want to tell me your version?"

"You didn't look back to check the source of that image match, did you? If you want to go check it, you'll find it's a teaser for a very expensive, password-only, porn site. I think your daughter believed she was making a porn vid. Right until the end." Tahira pulled out her link, watched the gun muzzle lift and steady. Touched up the video file from the Security eye, passed it over.

The woman took it, poised, the gun ready. Yes, Tahira thought. She had the body language of one who expected attack. She remembered that body posture all too well. The woman stepped back, out of range, looked at the link with one eye on Tahira. Then her posture stiffened and the link held her full attention.

I could kill her now, Tahira thought. Our children are our greatest weakness. She waited, watching the sky, straining her ears to hear any whisper of a silenced skimmer. The woman must be reviewing the clip over and over again. Finally she looked up, pocketed the link. The gun muzzle had sunk to rest on the ground and she didn't lift it.

"What's your stake in this?" Her voice was steady. "You came out here to put your life on the line for a damn lion?"

"No . . . and yes." Tahira closed her eyes again, briefly, summoning the will to push the grinding pain in her shoulder down deeper inside her. "The lioness . . . the old one, the one that killed your daughter . . . was wild caught. There are no more lions to catch. These are being changed, their genes altered to make them what we want . . . the Pleistocene American Lion. The world that the lioness came from is gone. My world. Your world, too, I think." She pulled her lips back from her teeth. "She is innocent of murder the way your rifle is innocent of murder, even if you point it at me and pull the trigger. You and I . . ." Her lips stretched tighter. "We are not innocent of our daughters' murders." She watched the gun muzzle jerk upward, tensed for one second as it wavered, drifted lower. "My elder daughter did what your daughter did." The entire Preserve seemed to be holding its breath. Even the insects had hushed. "I knew what she was doing and pretended I did not. She had no future, there was no aid, everyone was hungry. I took the flour and oil she brought home and I did not ask where the money came from." She did not look away from the pale oval of the woman's face. "They made a video of her death. I got someone to find it for me eventually. To buy it. Her death was a commodity, for sale on the market. As is your daughter's." She waited for the gun to come up but it did not.

"My younger daughter was six." She said the words flatly, without inflection. "I sold her to the World Council Forces so that she would not have to do what her sister did. They call it sponsoring, but when you do that, you relinquish all rights to that child. Later, I paid a lot of money to find out where she was and when she was fourteen, I saw her. On a training mission, doing crowd control. She looked at me." Tahira took a deep breath. "She did not know me. By then, I had been lucky, had found a job with the North American Pleistocene Preserve and my superiors found that I was . . . talented. That was many years ago. My daughter is past middle age now." She glanced up as a tiny chime sounded from the skimmer. "That is our lioness and her pride." She took a deep breath. "This is a delicately balanced trap."

"What do you want me to do?"

"I think it's too late." She sighed. "He will certainly be scanning the ground for any human-sized life signatures, in case this is the trap he expects and I have brought the police."

"He won't see me." The woman laughed her broken-glass laugh. "Illegal technology is always a step ahead of legal. Your motion detectors saw me, but you wouldn't have picked me up on your scan."

"He has inside help and so he might have access to our entire security network." She shrugged. "I do not think that is likely since only I have complete access to it, but it is possible."

"In that case we're screwed." The woman shrugged, her expression unreadable in the dark. "What do I do?"

"I want him on the ground." Tahira closed her eyes as the world wavered. "He thinks I'm a witness and he needs to make sure I'm dead. I have a first aid kit behind the seat." Cold sweat bathed her face, prickling under her arms. "It has a touch menu. Select stimulant, human, emergency, and get two patches." She struggled to hang onto consciousness, eyes closed, nausea wringing her stomach. The woman brushed against her, fumbling behind the seat. A moment later cool fingers seized her wrist, pushed her sleeve up and Tahira felt the sting of the stim patch on the inside of her elbow.

"That's going to make you bleed more."

"I know." Tahira straightened as energy washed through her, banishing the nausea, brightening the shadows. "Can't be helped." She touched the first aid menu, selected one small and one medium blood-stop patch. "Help me with the shirt." She winced as the woman opened the front, pulled the fabric down over her shoulder and arm. "Cover the entire wound, use the small one on the entry . . ."

"I know how to use a patch."

Tahira sighed as the woman smoothed the patches over the ruin of the entry and exit wounds. The fast-acting local quickly numbed the grinding pain, reduced it to a low-level throb that she could shut out for now.

"You guys carry a hospital on these things."

"We permit a few extreme hikers." Tahira drew a slow breath, let it out, judging the strength of the remaining pain. "We are preoccupied with death." She bared her teeth at the woman. "You sold vids of your kills along with your illegal meat, didn't you?"

The woman didn't answer, but of course, she did. Tahira straightened. That was the lure of what would otherwise be no different from a farm or vat raised steak. If you couldn't pull the trigger yourself, you could still watch it die. "You hide," she said. "I'm going to move the skimmer ahead of the pride, ground it again. He's going to come down and look for me."

"He's going to drop a grenade on you and leave." The woman sounded contemptuous.

"Oh no." Tahira grinned. "Like you, I'm wearing a chameleon field. And I also have a small device that a clever grad student hacked up – it generates the thermal effect of a 150 pound antelope. He was studying night hunting, trying to determine the importance of scent, thermal detection, sound, and sight in predator species. Our killer should think it's me." She shrugged. "He has been very careful not to leave any traces. I suspect that if I did not patrol as regularly as I do, we would never have known that anyone was killed here." Another few hours, and only the scrap of fabric would have marked that kill site. "One of us needs to kill him." She lifted her hand. "I would prefer that the lions do it."

"How do you know they can?"

Tahira shrugged her good shoulder. "I will make it possible. If they do not, you or I will do it." She pulled the highly illegal gun from her waistband, was impressed that the woman didn't flinch.

"You could have shot me. While I was looking at the vid." For a moment, she was silent. "I like you." Her teeth flashed briefly. "You would have made a good meat hunter."

"I think not." Tahira stretched her lips back from her teeth. "But I am not sure we are so different. You know to stay downwind from the pride? They're hunting."

"I know."

"I need my link." Tahira held out her hand. The woman glanced at it, shrugged, handed it over. Tahira nodded and climbed onto the skimmer, hoping he showed before the stim patch ran out. She wasn't sure she could tolerate a second dose. At least the bleeding seemed to have stopped. Lifting, she drifted ahead of the pride, watching her enviro-panel, reading wind, calculating distance and scent drift. Set the skimmer gently down, half hidden by hawthorn scrub. Just hidden enough, she hoped, to make him think that he might have missed her last time, when he dropped the girl. The meat-hunter's daughter.

Glancing at her watch, she planted the thick disk of the bio-signature generator in a clump of hawthorn, and hiked downwind, zooming in on the spot with her glasses. She had keyed the link to the lioness's ID, figured she had about fifteen minutes before she'd need to return and move the skimmer. The lions knew her scent, so hopefully her presence wouldn't disturb their regular hunting routine.

Five minutes left. She started to get to her feet to relieve her thigh muscles, when she caught the faintest whisper of disturbed air, like the wings of an owl. She froze, eyes fixed on the landscape beyond the grounded skimmer. A vague shape of matte black blocked her view of grass and shrubs. A military shadow field, of course.

She didn't see him get out of the shadowed skimmer, but of course, he would also be using a chameleon field. Sure enough, a clump of sun dried grass winked out for a moment, then reappeared. He knew where she was – or where he thought she was. He was being cautious.

She had not prayed to any gods for a long time. Not since she had handed over her young daughter to the World Council Force sponsorship coordinator. Gods were like lions, they belonged to the old world. But now she bent her head, prayed that those old, dying gods would gather wind, scent, instinct and make one thing right in the old way.

He did not fear the lions. She could see it in his preoccupied focus on the clump of brush where she had hidden the generator. They were just park amusements, useful as a movie prop, able to kill a helpless and unarmed girl. Not a threat to him. He had a gun, after all. She bared her teeth at his hubris. It would please the old gods.

The lioness charged in a rush of motion where no motion had existed. The man spun, hand coming up. Light flared and the lioness tumbled, regained her feet in an instant and with a leap, her front feet hit his shoulders, knocking him flat, her claws digging in to hold him. He had time for a choked cry before her jaws closed on his throat. A second lioness charged in, taking him by the thigh. Dust rose, white in her night-vision, as he thrashed, strangling slowly. The lion grunts and chesty growls were the only sound. The other members of the pride had circled in, tearing his belly open before he had quite died.

Tahira started as something moved beside her. The meat hunter squatted silently next to her, her posture intent, not speaking. A loop of intestine gleamed wetly. He had stopped struggling, had finally died. The lioness who had taken him stood up, bit at his dead shoulder and shook her head heavily. She walked a few steps away from the feeding pride, snarled as one of the males took a step toward her, lashed out at him. Her strike was weak, wobbly, and her hindquarters swayed as she staggered away from the others.

"She's dying," Tahira said softly. "He shot her." Her eyes widened as she noticed the faint striping on the lioness's shoulders. This was not the old one. This was one of the younger animals, the ones that were beginning to resemble their Pleistocene ancestors. She pointed her link at it. Yes, this was the oldest of the younger females, the one who had been pushing the old lioness of late. As she watched the pride feeding, she spotted the old lioness, noticed that she was limping. Not much, but it had been enough to let the beta lioness take over.

Perhaps the old mare had kicked her, when the pride had taken her foal. Tahira let her breath out slowly, pain beginning to seep through the stim's numbness. Maybe that limp would heal and the lioness would keep her rank now, maybe not. The next female in rank was timid, not likely to challenge her soon.

She might keep her leadership.

For a time.

Tahira got to her feet, feeling shaky to her bones. "You should leave now. Take his skimmer. It got him through the boundary, it will take you out. Sell it quickly. Just in case. I will erase your entry from Security."

The meat hunter faced her, her expression enigmatic, the years, the past, graven into her weathered face. "What about you?"

"I have some things to fix yet." She met the woman's eyes. They reminded her of African sky, blue, dry, and empty. "Your part is over."

For a moment the woman didn't move. Then she lifted a finger to her forehead in a salute, turned and strode through the brush to the man's skimmer. A moment later it lifted and vanished.

The pride had settled down to serious feeding now and already the scavengers had begun to gather. One of the wild dogs darted in to snatch a scrap, then fled, butt tucked as a young male charged. She could come back in a couple of days, pick up any last evidence. Record the young lioness's death as an official euthanasia.

She limped to the skimmer, washed by waves of weakness, hoping she wouldn't fall off before she got back to Administration.

A red icon winked on the control panel. A Security alert. Muttering a curse because she would have thought the meat hunter was more careful than that, Tahira touched it.

Official intrusion with legal permission, contact estimate five minutes.

Tahira leaned against the skimmer and closed her eyes. Legal permission. He got his warrant after all? She waited for the whisper of the grounding skimmer.

"Tahira." Shawn's voice sounded harsh. "What the hell is going on? You've got lions right behind you. Eating something."

He was afraid. Her lips twitched and she almost smiled. "They're busy. They won't bother us. I think I need a ride." She forced her eyes open. "I'm not sure I can get the skimmer back on my own. Did you come to arrest me?"

"Damn right." He appeared beside her, watching the lions. "Hospital first, I think."

"That's probably a good idea." She forced herself straight, looked him in the face. "Did you access that link? Buy the video?"

"Yes." He looked briefly away.

"The man who dropped them here..." She pointed with her chin toward the lions. Mistake. The world began to turn slowly.

"You're sure?"

She couldn't read his expression. "Yes. Take this." She handed him the stunner from the skimmer. "I don't think the lions will bother me, but if one does, this will stop it." She walked away before he could react, circled around to reach the dead lioness, one eye on the feeding lions. They knew she was there, paid as little attention as they gave the coy-dogs that had gathered. She took the tissue sample quickly, dropped it into a collection bag and returned with the last ounce of her strength.

She was done. She let him take over, gave in and let the slowly turning landscape speed up until it swept her away. Was aware of jostling, a sense of speed, a low muttered monologue of cursing. Faded in and out of lights and bustle and the dim distant knowledge in the back of her brain that this must be the resort medical facility. Someone was arguing loudly, right over her. It hurt her head and she retreated into darkness.

When she opened her eyes it was light, daylight bright, and her mouth felt like Preserve riverbed in a drought.

"They want you to drink this." Shawn leaned into view, holding a plastic squeeze-bag of yellow-green liquid with a drinking tube.

She sucked at the liquid, winced, and swallowed. There was no way to make electrolytes taste good.

"The bullet did a lot of soft tissue damage but missed anything important," he said mildly. "Made a big hole though. They left some drains in."

She peered at the bandages swathing her left arm. It didn't hurt, but that would probably change when the meds wore off. "Can I leave?"

"I think they'll let you go if you sign all kinds of waivers absolving them from blame."

"And do we go to jail from here?"

His eyes narrowed slightly. "That depends. We can talk about it."

He was right about waivers. She signed and retinaed a half-dozen absolutions of all liability but finally they carted her to the entry in a motorized chair and let her escape. Shawn offered her his arm and she leaned on it. Harder than she thought she would need to. He was driving a small, rather scuffed up electric. His private car? "You're not on duty?" She realized he was wearing a casual sun shirt and khakis. "Your day off?"

"My day off." He slid into the driver's seat, touched on the air-conditioning and sat there as the hot interior air cooled. "Want to tell me?"

"And if I don't?"

He shrugged. Turned those dry, blue eyes on her. "I guess I could still arrest you on suspicion of being an accessory to a murder."

"I am that." And she told him, leaning back against the still-warm plastic of the seat as the car hummed to life and Shawn drove her back to the Preserve. She told him the whole story from her comments on the tour bus, to her ambush by the meat hunter and the arrival of the vid maker.

He didn't say a word.

She finished as they entered the ornate gates of the Preserve and she closed her eyes, exhausted by the telling, her shoulder starting to hurt now with a muffled throb that promised worse to come.

"A meat hunter." Shawn parked in the afternoon shade cast by the building's solar panels. "I'm surprised you don't want me to go after her."

"Why?" Tahira opened one eye. "Her world is as dead as mine is. There is no wild meat to hunt any more. Not the kind that made her a living."

"She could come back to poach."

"She won't."

"You are so sure."

"I am."

Shawn sighed. "So you've achieved your justice. The lions killed the man the same way they killed the girl. And now you want me to just walk away and call it over. Do you think that ends it, Tahira?"

The bitterness in his voice surprised her. "Of course that doesn't end it." She opened her eyes, faced him. "He was not the boss. He was simply a tool. It's way too big a business. I doubt it will ever end, Shawn." She opened the electric's door one-handed, amazed at how heavy it was. "Our species is addicted to death. And now, on the brink of conquering it, we love it even more." She pulled herself to her feet as he came around to help her and amazingly managed not to sway. "But this ends it here."

"Are you sure of that, too?"

"Yes." She looked him in the face. "I am."

He lifted his eyes, fixed them on the dry blue sky above. "Even if you die?"

"If I die, the information to end it here will come to you." She started for the entrance, judging the distance. Maybe too far. When he caught up to her, took her arm, she let him, leaned on him. He was angry, radiating like a range fire.

"I guess I'd just like to know who made you judge and jury."

The door scanned her hardware and opened, breathing cool air over them. The water wall filled the building with the scent of rain and she took a deep breath, happy in this single moment of sensation. "I appointed myself." She sank onto one of the floor cushions. "There is beer in the refrigerator. Why don't you bring us each one? Since you are not on duty?"

He did, handed her the tall glass, sat down across from her, his expression thoughtful. He was older than Jen, his face lined with his years of work. She studied the lines around his eyes, seeing the echoes of old laughter, of sorrow, of life.

"What does this Preserve mean to you?" He looked up suddenly.

She took a sip of her beer, relishing the cool, slightly bitter taste, the dewy chill of the glass against her lips. Life, she thought, is made up of moments. We simply fail to notice most of them. "I have asked myself that question for a long time." She studied the tiny, silver bubbles rising through the amber liquid. "I'm a lot older than you, Shawn. I'm a product of world that is now dead."

"Africa," he murmured.

"Africa is a continent." She lifted her glass in his direction. "Lesotho. Once upon a time, long before you were born, my people raised and reintroduced lions to the dying plains. We had killed them all and now, many generations later, we brought them back. Only we didn't know the plains were dying, but they were. We, the Lesotho people, succeeded. For a while." She lifted one shoulder in a half-shrug. "But the plains died, then the lions died, and ultimately . . ." She drank more beer. "Lesotho died. Here . . . I found a trace of that dead world."

"The lions?" Shawn leaned forward and touched her hand lightly.

"Them, too." She tilted her head to study him, aware that she was getting drunk. "But it is not the world I knew. We did not care enough about that world to bring it back. Why not, Shawn?"

"No tourist value," he said softly.

"This world the engineers are creating is so old that it is new." She tried to smile, but it felt crooked. "The merely old has no value. Still . . . there are lions." She took another swallow of her beer. "And this is a refuge. From memory, if nothing else."

The entry chimed. "Hey, Tahira, you're back." Jen breezed through, bringing in the scent of dust and afternoon heat. "Hi, have we met?" He offered a hand to Shawn as he rose from the cushion. "I'm Jen, a grad student. I study bugs."

"Hi, Jen. I was just leaving." Shawn got to his feet, hesitated, then leaned down. "To memories." He touched his glass to hers.

She hesitated for a moment, met his eyes. Found . . . compassion there.

Jen looked from one to the other, puzzled, as they emptied their glasses. Shawn took them to the kitchen wall, lifted a hand to her, then left, the door whispering shut behind him.

"What was that all about?" He set his field pack against the wall.

"He was deciding whether or not to arrest me." Tahira watched Jen fill a glass of water. "I'd like some water, too, please."

"What's with the arrest thing?" He turned, smiling, a full glass in each hand. "And what happened to your arm? Did you have an accident with the skimmer?"

"Yes. I did." She took the glass. "Sit down, Jen."

He sat, the first tickle of alarm tightening the skin of his eyes before he quickly banished it with a smooth, careful smile.

"I have done a number of things in my long life." Tahira sipped her water. "One was computer security. I was very good. The systems these days are more advanced, but not excessively so."

"How interesting."

He was doing the facial expression well, but his body betrayed him, tension lifting his shoulders, straightening the curve of his spine. "Yes," she said. "So I was able to trace your alterations to the security platform." She raised her hand to silence him as he opened his mouth. "And I was also able to document the source of the Security breach and ID you. It's documented, Jen. Archived in hard media to be released to the authorities either on my say-so, or upon my death."

"I . . . I didn't know . . . anyone was going to get killed." His face had gone white and in an instant, the planes and angles of maturity had softened to the rounded face of a child. "It . . . I was horrified. I didn't know . . . but they'd . . . I didn't dare say . . . I couldn't tell . . ."

Was I ever a child like this? she wondered. She tried to remember. Didn't think so. Her older daughter had never been a child either. Not really. What about her younger daughter? Had they allowed her to be a child before she became a soldier? She hoped so. With all her heart. That was what I bought for you, she thought. Sighed. "You already knew that girl was dead when I first told you we'd had an intruder. Relax, Jen." She lifted her hand to silence him. "You are a pawn in this game. You will do one thing for me and then you are free to keep studying your bugs. . . . Although I suggest that you look into a transfer to another research program as quickly as you can engineer it." She studied his bowed head and hunched shoulders. "If something does happen to me, you will certainly be a suspect, so it might be unsafe for you to remain here."

"What do you want me to do?" he mumbled.

"You will run the DNA analysis on the bones that we found. I will give you a sample of lion DNA and you will make sure that you find that DNA associated with the dead girl. It may be there already. If it is not you will find it."

"That's all?" He raised his head, the fearful hope in his eyes painful to look at.

"That's all." You would not have survived in my world, she thought.

"I . . . I already put in a grant proposal." He looked away, swallowed. "I'd be doing it at the Antarctic preserve, looking at the symbiotic bacteria that still exist near the pole."

Ah, guilt. It would get him out of her sight quickly, at least. "Good." She nodded. "Here." She fumbled the collection bag from her coveralls. Handed it to him. The bit of flesh had turned brown and ugly. "This is your DNA."

He took it and fled. She suspected she wouldn't see him before he left – not if he could avoid it. Which suited her just fine.

The beer had given her energy, or maybe it had been the compassion in Shawn's eyes. She had not expected . . . understanding. But now, exhaustion was creeping through her. She opened her holo field and set it to secure, in case Jen was brave enough to return. She opened the camera control and set it to face view only. Her boss would not see her bandages.

Carlo answered quickly, seated in his teak and real-leather desk-recliner. "Did you get my messages?" He looked angry, his jet hair, usually immaculate, slightly mussed as if he had run his hand through it. "What is all this in the media? Tourists claiming that you were a witness to that intruder's death?"

"I have already informed the authorities that it was a mistake." She gave him a smooth smile. "The small brush-fire of blogging will fade quickly."

"This is the last thing we need, Tahira." He scowled at her. "Such carelessness is unlike you. You know better than to do anything that will incite negative public attention. What were you thinking?"

"I needed to make myself bait," she said simply. "That was the surest and fastest method."

He was far more mature than Jen and his face betrayed nothing, not even the tic of an eyelid gave him away. Almost, she could believe . . . "Our security is very very cutting edge. I sent you the inserted visuals that replaced the images of the girl's dying. Perhaps Jen was in a hurry." She shrugged. "But he had neither the access nor the expertise to allow an intruder to come and go through the Security shield without triggering any alarm or record. The intruder had a password."

"How could someone have that?"

Almost she had believed that she had made a mistake, but his tone betrayed him. He was asking a rhetorical question. "Only two people have a password, Carlo. You and I. There is no real anonymity in the net. Not for a long time now." She smiled at him, pleasantly. "I do not believe you are one of the major players here. If I did . . ." She bared her teeth at him. "I would not be talking to you. I think you merely . . . got a percentage. Rental. And perhaps a copy of the video? Does that excite you? A real and violent death, with real fear, and real blood?"

He flinched then, and her stomach twisted.

"That was how they came to ask you, wasn't it? You are a customer." She kept the disgust out of her voice, because it was not yet time to end this conversation. "I have archived a file of all my suspicions and all the evidence I have uncovered to support them. It is not sufficient to convict you. But it is sufficient to let those with greater investigative skills than I have find out the truth. Then they will convict you. On the day of my death, the archive goes to the appropriate World Council committee members."

"Blackmail?" His lip curled. "Is that so much better than what I did?"

"It's not blackmail." She shrugged. "It is simply an insurance policy. To make sure that this does not happen again here."

He didn't believe her.

"I am finishing up the DNA scan of the dead girl. I have already euthanized the lioness that attacked her. You may release that information to the media and the public. You may make whatever statement about blogger inaccuracies you choose and that will, as I said, fade away. If anything – her lip curled, "it will increase traffic to the Preserve. As you know, violent death is a potent pheromone."

His reaction was more visible this time.

She ended the link. Rudely.

She was entitled to be rude.

"He is too well protected." She was speaking to Shawn's absence, heard her own defensive tone. "He is insulated by too much money and too many

connections. He would emerge from the ashes of an investigation and nothing would change." She closed down her field, got to her feet, feeling age in
her flesh. How much longer did she have? "Perhaps I am too much a product
of my old world. To me, justice is direct – an eye for an eye. The justice of
the old gods. Of the lions."

She had bought the old lioness a second chance. It might not buy her
much time at all, or she might get another season before she was ousted by
one of the younger, striped, new females that made the gene engineers so
happy. She had a tour scheduled tomorrow. The note on the green calendar
field on the wall was flashing its reminder. She stretched her shoulder, testing the limits of the pain. If she slept well, she could do it, perhaps with less
energy. There would be questions. She would have to decide on the answers
before then, would this time do Shawn the courtesy of telling him what her
answers would be.

And soon it would be nothing more than an ephemera floating in
webspace, evoked from time to time like a fading ghost, through some odd
search connection that summoned up a stale blog entry. The world was full
of ghosts.

Instead of going to her bed, she slipped outside and found her skimmer
parked in its usual place. Someone had cleaned the blood from it. She
found her spare glasses in the tool compartment, slipped them on and lifted
into the darkness. The lions would be hunting and she might catch the
pride on their way down to the river. The pain in her shoulder faded as
she toed the skimmer up to speed and slid through the bright bubble of a
yesterday that had never really happened.

ESCAPE TO OTHER WORLDS WITH SCIENCE FICTION

Jo Walton

British-turned-Canadian SF and fantasy writer Jo Walton won the John W. Campbell Award for Best New Writer in 2002 and has subsequently won the World Fantasy Award for her novel *Tooth and Claw*. She's perhaps best known for the "Small Change" trilogy that includes *Farthing, Ha'penny,* and, most recently, *Half a Crown*, but she's also the author of *The Prize in the Game* and the diptych *The King's Peace* and *The King's Name*. Her most recent books are two new novels, *Lifelode* and *Among Others*. Her stories have been collected in *Muses and Lurkers*, and she's also published two collections of her poetry. Born in Wales, she now lives in Montreal.

In the story that follows, which makes for uneasy reading these days, she takes us to a world where the Great Depression got worse instead of better – and stayed that way.

In the Papers (1)

NATIONAL GUARD MOVES AGAINST STRIKERS
In the seventh week of the mining strike in West Virginia, armed skirmishes and running "guerrilla battles" in the hills have led to the Governor calling in

GET AN ADVANCED DEGREE BY CORRESPONDENCE
You can reap the benefits with no need to leave the safety of your house or go among unruly college students! Only from

EX-PRESIDENT LINDBERGH REPROACHES MINERS

ASTOUNDING SCIENCE FICTION
April issue on newsstands now! All new stories by Poul Anderson, Anson MacDonald and H. Beam Piper! Only 35 cents.

SPRING FASHIONS 1960

Skirts are being worn long in London and Paris this season, but here in New York the working girls are still hitching them up. It's stylish to wear a little

HOW FAR FROM MIAMI CAN THE "FALLOUT" REACH?
Scientists say it could be a problem for years, but so much depends on the weather that

You hope to work
You hope to eat
The work goes to
The man that's neat!
BurmaShave

Getting By (1)

Linda Evans is a waitress in Bundt's Bakery. She used to work as a typist, but when she was let go she was glad to take this job, even though it keeps her on her feet all day and sometimes she feels her face will crack from smiling at the customers. She was never a secretary, only in the typing pool. Her sister Joan is a secretary, but she can take shorthand and type ninety words a minute. Joan graduated from high school. She taught Linda to type. But Linda was never as clever as Joan, not even when they were little girls in the time she can just remember, when their father had a job at the plant and they lived in a neat little house at the end of the bus line. Their father hasn't worked for a long time now. He drinks up any money he can bully out of the girls. Linda stands up to him better than Joan does.

"They'd have forgiven the New Deal if only it had worked," a man says to another, as Linda puts down his coffee and sandwich in front of him.

"Worked?" asks his companion scornfully. "It was working. It would have worked and got us out of this if only people had kept faith in it."

They are threadbare old men, in mended coats. They ordered grilled cheese sandwiches, the cheapest item on the menu. One of them smiles at Linda, and she smiles back, automatically, then moves on and forgets them. She's on her feet all day. Joan teases her about flirting with the customers and falling in love, but it never seems to happen. She used to tease Joan about falling in love with her boss, until she did. It would all have been dandy except that he was a married man. Now Joan spends anguished hours with him and anguished days without him. He makes her useless presents of French perfume and lace underwear. When Linda wants to sell them, Joan just cries. Both of them live in fear that she'll get pregnant, and then where will they be? Linda wipes the tables and tries not to listen to the men with their endless ifs. She has enough ifs of her own: if mother hadn't died, if she'd kept her job in the pool, if John hadn't died in the war with England, and Pete in the war with Japan.

"Miss?" one of them asks. She swings around, thinking they want more coffee. One refill only is the rule. "Can you settle a question?" he asks. "Did Roosevelt want to get us to join in the European War in 1940?"

"How should I know? It has nothing to do with me. I was five years old in 1940." They should get over it and leave history to bury its own dead, she thinks, and goes back to wiping the tables.

In the Papers (2)

WITH MIRACLE-GROW YOU CAN REGAIN YOUR LOST FOLLICLES!

In today's world it can be hard to find work even with qualifications. We at Cyrus Markham's Agency have extensive experience at matching candidates to positions which makes us the unrivaled

NEW TORPEDOES THAT WORK EVEN BETTER
Radar, sonar and even television to

AT LAST YOU CAN AFFORD THE HOUSE OF YOUR DREAMS

LET SCIENCE FICTION TAKE YOU TO NEW WORLDS
New books by Isaac Asimov and Robert A. Heinlein for only

ANOTHER BANK FOUNDERS IN PENNSYLVANIA

WE HAVE NOT USED THE WORD "SECEDE," SAYS TEXAS GOVERNOR

Why do Canadians act so high and mighty? It's because they know

In the Line (1)

When Tommy came out of the navy, he thought he'd walk into a job just like that. He had his veteran's discharge, which entitled him to medical treatment for his whole life, and he was a hero. He'd been on the carrier Constitution, which had won the Battle of the Atlantic practically single-handed and had sent plenty of those Royal Navy bastards to the bottom of the sea where they belonged. He had experience in maintenance as well as gunnery. Besides, he was a proud hard-working American. He never thought he'd be lining up at a soup kitchen.

In the Papers (3)

TIME FOR A NEW TUNE
Why are the bands still playing Cole Porter?

SECRETARY OF STATE LINEBARGER
SAYS THE BRITS WANT PEACE

ATOMIC SECRETS

DO THE JAPANESE HAVE THE BOMB?
Sources close to the Emperor say yes, but the Nazis deny that they have given out any plans. Our top scientists are still working to

NYLONS NYLONS NYLONS

DIANETICS: A NEW SCIENCE OF THE MIND

Getting By (2)

Linda always works overtime when she's asked. She appreciates the money, and she's always afraid she'll be let go if she isn't obliging. There are plenty of girls who'd like her job. They come to ask every day if there's any work. She isn't afraid the Bundts will give her job away for no reason. She's worked here for four years now, since just after the Japanese War. "You're like family," Mrs Bundt always says. They let Olive go, the other waitress, but that was because there wasn't enough work for two. Linda works overtime and closes up the cafe when they want her to. "You're a good girl," Mrs Bundt says. But the Bundts have a daughter, Cindy. Cindy's a pretty twelve-year old, not even in high school. She comes into the cafe and drinks a milkshake sometimes with her girlfriends, all of them giggling. Linda hates her. She doesn't know what they have to giggle about. Linda is afraid that when Cindy is old enough she'll be given Linda's job. Linda might be like family, but Cindy really is family. The bakery does all right, people have to eat, but business isn't what it was. Linda knows.

She's late going home. Joan's dressing up to go out with her married boss. She washes in the sink in the room they share. The shower is down the corridor, shared with the whole floor. It gets cleaned only on Fridays, or when Joan or Linda do it. Men are such pigs, Linda thinks, lying on her bed, her weight off her feet at last. Joan is three years older than Linda but she looks younger. It's the make-up, Linda thinks, or maybe it's having somebody to love. If only she could have fallen in love with a boss who'd have married her and taken her off to a nice little suburb. But perhaps it's just as well. Linda couldn't afford the room alone, and she'd have had to find a stranger to share with. At least Joan was her sister and they were used to each other.

"I saw Dad today," Joan says, squinting in the mirror and drawing on her mouth carefully.

"Tell me you didn't give him money?"

"Just two dollars," Joan admits. Linda groans. Joan is a soft touch. She makes more than Linda, but she never has any left at the end of the week. She spends more, or gives it away. There's no use complaining, as Linda knows.

"Where's he taking you?" she asks wearily.

"To a rally," Joan says.

"Cheap entertainment." Rallies and torch-lit parades and lynchings, beating up the blacks as scapegoats for everything. It didn't help at all; it just made people feel better about things to have someone to blame. "It's not how we were brought up," Linda says. Their mother's father had been a minister and had believed in the brotherhood of man. Linda loved going to her grandparents' house when she was a child. Her grandmother would bake cookies and the whole house would smell of them. There was a swing on the old apple tree in the garden. Her father had been a union man, once, when unions had still been respectable.

"What do I care about all that?" Joan says, viciously. "It's where he's taking me, and that's all. He'll buy me dinner and we'll sing some patriotic songs. I'm not going to lynch anybody." She dabs on her French perfume, fiercely.

Linda lies back. She isn't hungry. She's never hungry. She always eats at the bakery – the Bundts don't mind – any order that was wrong, or any bread that would have been left over. Sometimes they even gave her cakes or bread to bring home. She rubs her feet. She's very lucky really. But as Joan goes out the door she feels like crying. Even if she did meet somebody, how could they ever afford to marry? How could they hope for a house of their own?

In the Papers (4)

SEA MONKEYS WILL ASTOUND YOUR FRIENDS!

PRESIDENT SAYS WE MUST ALL PULL TOGETHER
In Seattle today in a meeting with

TAKE A LUXURY AIRSHIP TO THE HOLY CITY

CAN THE ECONOMY EVER RECOVER?
Since the Great Depression the country has been jogging through a series of ups and downs and the economy has been lurching from one crisis to another. Administrations have tried remedies from Roosevelt's New Deal to Lindbergh's Belt Tightening but nothing has turned things around for long. Economists say that this was only to

be expected and that this general trend of downturn was a natural and inevitable

NEW HOLLYWOOD BLOCKBUSTER "REICHSMARSHALL" STARRING MARLON BRANDO

In the Line (2)

When Sue was seventeen she'd had enough of school. She had a boyfriend who promised to find her a job as a dancer. She went off with him to Cleveland. She danced for a while in a topless club, and then in a strip joint. The money was never quite enough, not even after she started turning tricks. She's only thirty-four, but she knows she looks raddled. She's sick. Nobody wants her anymore. She's waiting in the line because there's nowhere else to go. They feed you and take you off in trucks to make a new start, that's what she's heard. She can see the truck. She wonders where they go.

In the Papers (5)

ARE NEW HOME PERMANENTS AS GOOD AS THEY SAY?
Experts say yes!

NEW WAYS TO SAVE

PRESIDENT SAYS: THERE IS NO WITCH-HUNT
Despite what communists and union organizers may claim, the President said today

Getting By (3)

The Bundts like to play the radio in the cafe at breakfast time. They talk about buying a little television for the customers to watch, if times ever get better. Mr Bundt says this when Linda cautiously asks for a raise. If they had a television they'd be busier, he thinks, though Linda doesn't think it would make a difference. She serves coffee and bacon and toast and listens to the news. She likes music and Joan likes Walter Winchell. She should ask Joan how she reconciles that with going to rallies. Winchell famously hates Hitler. Crazy. Linda can't imagine feeling that strongly about an old man on the other side of the world.

Later, when Cindy and her friends are giggling over milkshakes and Linda feels as if her feet are falling off, a man comes in and takes the corner table. He orders sandwiches and coffee, and later he orders a cake and more coffee.

He's an odd little man. He seems to be paying attention to everything. He's dressed quite well. His hair is slicked back and his clothes are clean. She wonders if he's a detective, because he keeps looking out of the window, but if so he seems to pay just as much attention to the inside, and to Linda herself. She remembers what Joan said, and wants to laugh but can't. He's a strange man and she can't figure him out.

She doesn't have to stay late and close up, and the man follows her out when she leaves. There's something about him that makes her think of the law way before romance. "You're Linda," he says, outside. She's scared, because he could be anybody, but they are in the street under a street light, there are people passing, and the occasional car.

"Yes," she admits, her heart hammering. "What do you want?"

"You're not a Bundt?"

"No. They're my employers, that's all," she says, disassociating herself from them as fast as she can, though they have been good to her. Immediately she has visions of them being arrested. Where would she find another job?

"Do you know where the Bundts come from?"

"Germany," she says, confidently. Bundt's German Bakery, it says, right above their heads.

"When?"

"Before I was born. Why aren't you asking them these questions?"

"It was 1933."

"Before I was born," Linda says, feeling more confident and taking a step away.

"Have you seen any evidence that they are Jews?"

She stops, confused. "Jews? They're German. Germans hate Jews."

"Many Jews left Germany in 1933 when Hitler came to power," the man says, though he can't be much older than Linda. "If the Bundts were Jews, and hiding their identity, then if you denounced them – "

He stops, but Linda has caught up with him now. If she denounced them she would be given their property. The business, the apartment above it, their savings. "But they're not, I've never – they serve bacon!" she blurts.

"You've never seen any evidence?" he asks, sadly. "A pity. It could be a nice business for you. You're not Jewish?"

"Welsh," she says. "My grandfather was a minister."

"I thought not, with that lovely blonde hair." It's more washed out than it should be, but her hair is the dishwater blonde it always has been, the same as Joan's, the same as their mother.

"I might have some evidence," he says, slowly. "But any evidence I had would be from before they came here, from Germany. Some evidence that they were still Jews, if you'd seen anything, would be enough to settle it. The court would deport them back to Germany and award us their business. You could run it, I'm sure you could. You seem to be doing most of the work already."

"I just serve," she says, automatically. Then, "What sort of thing would I have noticed? If they were Jewish, I mean."

Temptation settles over her like a film of grease and hope begins to burn in her heart for the first time in a long time.

In the Line (3)

If you're black you're invisible, even in the soup line. The others are shrinking away from me, I can't deny it. They wouldn't give us guns to fight even when the Japanese were shelling the beaches up and down the California coast. I left there then and came East, much good it did me. If I'd known how invisible I'd be here, I'd have stayed right there in Los Angeles. Nobody there ever chased after me and made me run, nobody there threatened to string me up, and I had a job that made a little money. I never thought I'd be standing in this line, because when I get to the head of it I know they'll separate me out. Nobody knows what happens to us then, they take us off somewhere and we don't come back, but I'm desperate, and what I say is, wherever it is they got to feed us, don't they? Well, don't they?

In the Papers (5)

ANOTHER FACTORY CLOSING

PEACE TALKS IN LONDON AS JAPAN AND
THE REICH DIVIDE UP RUSSIA
Will there be a buffer state of "Scythia" to divide the two great powers?

BATTLE IN THE APPALACHIANS: NATIONAL
GUARD REINFORCEMENTS SENT IN
President says it is necessary to keep the country together

OWNERS GUN DOWN STRIKERS IN ALABAMA
Sixty people were hospitalized in Birmingham today after

ESCAPE TO OTHER WORLDS WITH SCIENCE FICTION
New titles by Frederik Pohl and Alice Davey

THREE LEAVES OF ALOE

Rand B. Lee

Rand B. Lee has become a regular at *The Magazine of Fantasy and Science Fiction*, with a number of sales there in recent years, and has also sold stories to *Asimov's Science Fiction*, *Amazing*, and elsewhere. His father was Manfred B. Lee, the co-creator of the detective Ellery Queen and author of many of the novels about him; Lee himself is the author of the gardening book *Pleasures of the Cottage Garden* and is at work on a novel. He lives in northern New Mexico.

In the quiet but powerful story that follows, he shows us a mother in a near-future world faced with a choice that I fear all too many of us may actually find ourselves faced with one of these days, uncomfortably soon.

AMRIT CHAUDHURY! KINDLY report to the supervisor's office. Amrit Chaudhury!"

Amrit looked up from her workstation and sighed in frustration. Around her rose the chatter of a hundred women's voices, the ring of telephones, the clatter of fax lines. She was a small young woman with a heart-shaped face and large, intelligent black eyes perpetually clouded with worry. She had been laboring on the telephones at Mumbai-Astra Telecom, Ltd. for the better part of a year, and this day, which had not gone well thus far, was looking to become much worse.

"Amrit?" The undersupervisor, fat Shraddha Singh, was looming over her. "Madame needs a word," she said. "At once, please."

"What is it this time?" asked Amrit. Her tone held more spice than was perhaps prudent, and the undersupervisor raised an eyebrow. "I'm sorry! It's just these Americans." She pulled off her headset and let it fall with a clatter on her desktop. "They're so suspicious. And they hate parting with their money so. I can be as sweet and as polite as one can wish, but it avails nothing. Three-quarters of the time they hang up before I've finished saying, 'Hello, Mister Wayne, my name is Maggie Jones.'" She punched log-off to indicate an excused break, and pushed back her chair. At least, she thought, they have proper chairs here. The last place she had worked there had been only inverted oilcans to sit upon.

"'Maggie Jones.'" Singh grunted in amusement. The women's eyes met, and both fell simultaneously into a fit of giggles.

" 'Maggie Jones!' " cried Amrit helplessly.

" 'Bobbi Grant!' " chortled the undersupervisor, similarly irrigated.

" 'Jane West!' " Amrit put her left hand over her heart and fanned her right hand weakly. "I mean to say, it isn't as though they can't tell by our voices that we're Not From Around These Parts." She spoke this last in an exaggerated American accent, which set them both off afresh.

"Amrit Chaudhury! To the supervisor's office at once!"

The women sobered quickly, and followed each other down the main work-aisle toward management offices. "Madame sounds angry," said Amrit. "Do you know what this is about?"

"Your daughter, I think," said Mrs Singh, puffing to keep up with the younger woman's quick strides. Amrit stopped dead and threw her a terrified look. "No, no! She's fine, she's fine! It's just the school. I overheard Madame talking. A fight with one of the other girls, which I gather your Meera won rather spectacularly. They have 'concerns' which they wish to express to you, that's all."

"Not again!" groaned Amrit, and doubled her pace, adjusting her sari as she ran. When she reached the door of the supervisor's office, she knocked timidly, then opened the door a crack and stuck in her head.

"It's Amrit, Madame. You called for me?"

"It's about time. Come in, come in! Don't hang about in the hall." Amrit entered quickly, shutting the door behind her, and stood with her back to it. Whenever she was called into Madame's office she felt as though she were nine years old and back in school, facing the headmistress. Madame Kattungal had steel-gray hair, a prominent caste mark, and deceptively grandmotherly features. Today she was wearing a Western business suit, and when Amrit entered, she was just slamming down the phone. "You took long enough, girl. This is Mister Mehta, whom I believe" – this last heavily weighted with sarcasm – "you know."

"Well, Mrs Chaudhury! We meet again!" Vice-Principal Mehta's lean figure rose from its chair near Madame's desk and, smiling broadly, extended a hand. Amrit shook it gingerly. "I am so terribly sorry to trouble you at your place of work, but I thought it expeditious to come here directly rather than summon you to the school. Is there a spot where we might chat in private?" This last he addressed to the supervisor.

Amrit said hurriedly, "How is my daughter, Vice-Principal?" Aside from the lavatory, they were standing in the only private room available in the large, barn-like structure that made up the main headquarters of Mumbai-Astra, Limited. And Amrit had no desire to be alone with Mehta. She had several times been forced to endure his caresses in return for his leniency with her daughter Meera, and she had vowed to immolate herself rather than endure them again.

Madame gazed upon the thin man expectantly. He shrugged. "Very well. Meera quarreled with one of the upper form girls this morning. The other girl started it, I believe – some altercation over a cell phone of which your daughter was in possession. The quarrel escalated into fisticuffs. Your daughter possesses an admirable right hook, Mrs Chaudhury. Perhaps the school ought to consider instituting a girls' boxing team so as to make better use of her talents."

"I'm so sorry, Vice-Principal Mehta," said Amrit. "I've told and told Meera that fighting is not acceptable behavior. I can't think what's come over her." She added, "Will the other girl be all right?"

"Oh, right as rain," said Mehta cheerfully, "save for a loose tooth." Amrit groaned. "The cell phone, however, is unsalvageable." He drew it from the pocket of his suit jacket and handed it over to her. Amrit groaned again. It was her Mumbai-Astra phone. All the employees were issued one so that they could be on call at a moment's notice to fill in gaps in the phone banks as they arose, and it had been missing for three days.

"Is it your habit to permit your daughter the use of your company phone, Amrit?" Madame asked with asperity.

"No, Madame."

"A replacement will be issued immediately. Its cost will of course be deducted from your wages."

"Naturally, Madame. And I'm sorry. It won't happen again, I promise."

"That's as may be." As if they were linked telepathically, at that moment Undersupervisor Singh knocked on the door, opened it, and looked at Madame inquiringly. "Ah, there you are, Singh. Issue Mrs Chaudhury a new phone, charged against her weekly." With a sympathetic glance at Amrit, the fat woman nodded and withdrew. "Will there be anything else, Mister Mehta? Amrit must return to her post."

"I'm afraid so, Madame Kattungal. You see," said the Vice-Principal, "at the Gupta Academy we have a policy, borrowed from the Americans, of 'Three strikes and you are out.' This is the fourth occasion upon which your daughter Meera has demonstrated an inability to coexist on cordial terms with her fellow students. Our normal course of action – and one which we are for many reasons loath to pursue except in times of dire necessity – would be to expel Meera forthwith, for mastering one's temper is a skill crucial to the workings of a civilized society (as I am sure you will agree)."

"Expel her?" gasped Amrit. "Oh, no, Vice-Principal!" She had worked so hard to get her into the school, despite opposition from Meera's paternal grandmother, who felt that too much education was bad for a girl, leading to late night parties, pierced eyelids, heroin addiction, and prostitution. "Is there nothing that can be done?" She opened her eyes as wide as she could and gave him a look so beseeching it might have melted the heart of a stone Buddha.

"Well, perhaps," said Mehta, eyeing her back, stroking his bearded chin. "Perhaps we can discuss, ah, terms. But until such time as we come to some further understanding, the Academy will consider keeping Meera on only if you consent to have her outfitted with a nannychip."

"A nannychip?" Madame Kattungal had been sitting silent during this interchange, impatient to have them out of her office so she might return to her appallingly busy schedule. But this last had startled her to fresh attention.

"Is Meera Chaudhury such a menace to your scholastic society, then, Vice-Principal? I was under the impression that nannychips were most commonly used among potentially violent prison populations."

"You surprise me, Madame Kattungal," Mehta replied jovially. "I had assumed, considering your place of employ, that you would be more conversant in what the Americans are so fond of describing as the 'cutting edge' technologies. There are many types of nannychip nowadays. We are speaking here not of electronic lobotomization, but of the temporary outfitting of the girl with an aggression-inhibiting nannychip to ensure her cooperativeness over a predetermined and limited period, as a method of bringing home to her the importance of learning proper skills of social interaction. We've done it before with problem students, and the experiment has been met with much success, particularly in Germany." He winked at the appalled women, then. "A much more humane method, you will agree, than caning, to which we were forced to resort in former days. And I assure you that Mrs Chaudhury's willingness to cooperate will go far in assisting the Board in envisioning a long-term future for Meera at the Academy."

"Never," said Amrit. She walked up to the Vice-Principal and stood so close to him that he was forced to take a step backward. "I will never consent to such a procedure. It is monstrous. It is inhumane. Why, you admitted yourself it was the other girl's fault!"

"Four times now it has been the fault of the other girl," said Mehta placidly. "Four times, Mrs Chaudhury. If your Meera does not learn to master her temper, her prospects for success in this altercation-ridden world look bleak indeed."

"What of the other girl? What of her prospects for success? Will she, too, be outfitted with a nannychip to curb her excesses of aggression?" Amrit heard her voice rise. She knew her face was red and her fists were balled, and that everyone in the outer office could hear her, but she did not care.

"That is a matter for the Board to decide," said Vice-Principal Mehta. "I see that you are upset. Take time to think over the matter before you make a final decision we might all regret. Now if you will excuse me; I have another appointment. I came here only as a courtesy." He attempted to step around Amrit, but she blocked his way.

"Where is she? Where is my daughter now?"

"Mrs Chaudhury, calm yourself." The supervisor had risen. Her quiet voice cut through Amrit's mind-whirl. Tossing her head, she stepped aside to let the Vice-Principal pass. Mehta bowed to Mrs Singh and paused, his hand on the office doorknob.

"I apologize again for having interrupted you ladies' workday. Mrs Chaudhury's daughter should by now have arrived at their place of residence. I instructed the Assistant Vice-Principal to shepherd her safely home. And I am afraid that is where she must stay until such time as other arrangements can be agreed upon." He smiled again at Amrit. "If you change your mind about the chip, do ring me up, Mrs Chaudhury. That ought not to be difficult for you to do, now that you have your cell phone back." And with that he closed the door behind him.

When Amrit got home that night to the apartment she shared with the elder Mrs Chaudhury (her late husband's mother), Amrit's paternal uncle Saavit, his far-too-young-of-a-wife Gloria, their six-year-old son Dakota, Dakota's pregnant and gender-inappropriately named rat-shrew Ganesa, and Amrit's criminal progeny Meera, Amrit was in no mood for compromise. She marched right past her mother-in-law's squawking complaints; through Uncle Saavit's cloud of in-the-process-of-being-hurriedly-extinguished cigar-smoke (Gloria was still crosstown, at the Internet cafe where she worked long hours); pushed open without knocking the door to Meera's little room (not much more than a converted closet, really); tore the earphones off the head of the closed-eyed, finger-tapping, unread-schoolbook-open-before-her fourteen-year-old, and said, "Meera. Put on your coat. We're going out."

"Ma!"

"Now."

And then reversed the process, this time with Meera in tow (earphone-less, eyes now fully open, shrugging into her Adidas knock-off, still wearing her school uniform underneath), past Ganesa (who waffled her nose at them as they went by), past Dakota (who was plugged into his M-box and wouldn't have noticed an atomic bomb if it had exploded under his nose), past Uncle Saavit (who had once been a professional boxer but now was huffing, "What is the fire alarm now, Amrit?"), past the elder Mrs Chaudhury, whose complaint-squawking had not slowed one monosyllable either in Hindi or English, and out the apartment door again, nearly slamming it shut on Meera's braid.

"Ma! Where are we going?"

"You'll see."

And then down the six flights to the busy Mumbai street, where Amrit stopped to get her bearings. Around them, cars honked, bicyclists careered, motorized rickshaws put-putted, chapati sellers waved fragrant pancakes and called out to passersby, signs advertising Microsoft computers, Toshiba implants, and permanent waves ("Be mistaken for a film star!") blinked on and off, and skinny pickpockets trailed camera-festooned Brazilian tourists. In the far distance, she could hear the rumble from the Mahim Railway Station. "This way," she said.

"Ma, I won't do it again! I promise!"

The fear in her daughter's voice brought Amrit up short. The child was looking at her the way a mongoose observes a cobra that is beginning to rear. Amrit felt a pang. She did not wish her own daughter to fear her – not beautiful, bright, long-fingered Meera, remnant of her brief happy marriage, her only concrete contribution to the world's future. But if fear was what it took to stop the child from throwing her life away, Amrit would harden her heart and use that fear for the child's own good until she could find something better with which to motivate her. So all she replied was, "I want to show you something, Meera."

They walked to the bus stop past beggars, businessmen, newspaper vendors, police. On the bus, which was nearly filled with after-work shoppers and evening-shift workers headed for cleaning jobs in the offices and apartment buildings round about, they sat side by side, Amrit still holding tight to Meera's hand, as though she feared losing her, as though any moment she might declare her independence, run off to a party, get drunk, get her face pierced, take drugs, enter upon a life of prostitution. At the Mahim Railway Station, they got off the bus. As they mounted the steps into the station, still hand-in-hand, Meera asked, "Are you sending me away?"

"Don't be foolish. Of course not. I said I wanted to show you something."

"She started it!" The girl planted her feet, stared up at her mother (up? no, truth be told, only very slightly up, they were nearly of a height now; how could Amrit have not noticed that before?). "She called me a thief, Ma! She said I stole the cell phone, that it was her phone, that it could not possibly be my phone because we could not possibly afford anything so toff, and that I must give it back at once or she would tell the Vice-Principal. I told her it was not her cell phone, that it was our cell phone, that I was not a thief, and that Mother Kali could pluck out her lying tongue and feed it to her for breakfast, for all that she was of the Kshatriyas and very nearly a Brahman." Her daughter gulped, caught her breath. "And then she slapped me. So I struck her the way Uncle Saavit showed me."

"Are you finished?"

Meera nodded. There were tears in the corners of her big eyes, and her cheeks were flushed with passion, but there was no remorse at the corners of her mouth at all. "Then come," said Amrit. "It's only a little farther, this thing that I wish to show you."

There were high brick walls between the back of the railway station and the thing Amrit wished to show her daughter, but Amrit knew every square inch of this area from childhood hours spent staring up at it from the other side. They threaded their way unnoticed through the knots of waiting commuters, sellers, and alms-seekers, past a group of saffron-clad Buddhist monks wearing sunglasses (at seven o'clock at night?), past a magazine rack sporting lurid film-star magazines, and finally to the spot she had remembered: a narrow doorway with a chain across it saying ABSOLUTELY NO ENTRY in seven languages. "We are going up there?" inquired her daughter querulously, peering up into the dimness.

"We are," said her mother firmly, and lifted the chain. "For what I have to show you may only be viewed conveniently from the top of this stair."

"But," said Meera, and that is all she said, for Amrit was half-pulling, half-pushing her onto the staircase with her.

The stairs were made of wood and smelled of old urine, chapati grease, stale cigarettes, and ancient durian. A faint light filtered down the stairwell from someplace high above, but it was very dark, and the stairs were littered with trash left by squatters down through the years. Twice Meera stumbled.

The first time her mother was able to arrest her fall, but the second, Meera ended up on one knee on the stair, narrowly escaping being stuck with a discarded hypodermic needle. In later years she would recall this upward passage as the most horrific experience of her young life, yet in the end they attained the top of the stair and emerged onto an open causeway under a Mumbai night sky that had somehow become overcast during their million years in the dark.

The women paused to catch their breaths. Meera was surprised to realize how far they had climbed. Behind and below them through pollution haze stretched the Mumbai they had just left: the railway station, apartment buildings, office blocks, tooting thoroughfares. Meera could see the tracks for the Western Railway stretching away into the distance, where they crossed the Mahim Sion Link Road; beyond that, she could see the filthy black waters of Mahim Bay. "Turn around," said her mother. Her voice sounded distant, like a goddess's. Meera turned, and found herself looking down onto a vast, confusing jungle of silent, swampy slum. "Do you know what this is?" her mother asked, sweeping her arm outward to encompass the world before them.

"Of course, Ma. Dharavi." She could not keep the contempt from her voice.

"And what is it, this Dharavi? What do you know of it?"

"It is where the poor people dwell." The wind picked up, bringing with it from Dharavi the scent of sewage.

"What sorts of poor people? Specify."

"Well, potters," she said. "Furniture makers. People from the provinces who can't afford to live anywhere else. Tailors, people like that." Meera found the contrast between the hooting hum of the Mumbai behind them and the deep quiet of the slum before them deeply unsettling, and she looked uncomfortably around her. They were alone on the causeway. "They all look dead from up here," she said.

"They are not dead, child. They are resting, those who are not sewing garments all night for less income than the beggar outside our sweetshop makes in three hours. One and a half million persons living in a reclaimed mangrove swamp. No sewage treatment facilities. Uncertain electricity. Water of such poor quality that one considers oneself fortunate merely to contract dysentery from it." Amrit looked thoughtfully out over the maze of little lanes and thoroughfares. "But see the temple, there? And the mosque? And those buildings, that school, there? Muslims, Hindus, Christians, Jains. Recycling everything, because one cannot afford to buy anything new. Your father was born there" – she stabbed the dark with her chin – "off Ninety Feet Road, not far from Kumbharwada."

"My father? Born in Dharavi?" She could not believe what she was hearing. Meera did not remember her father; she knew him only from the holos on her mother's old e-album, a small man, small like her mother, with ropy-muscled arms, large knuckles, and intense dark features. "You said he was from Rajasthan!" Meera's tone was accusatory.

"I never did. I said his people were from Rajasthan. They were weavers and textile-painters. His parents came to Mumbai after the great famines, and settled in the Potters' District. When I met your father, he was living with ten other young men in a garage, refitting automobiles for resale." She had literally run into him, having ducked into the garage in an attempt to evade an irate fruit vendor from whom she had swiped three small green mangoes and a bar of chocolate. She had been eleven, a little girl; he, fifteen, nearly a man; out of pity he and the boys had hidden her, and afterward he had walked her home. When next she had encountered him, at a Kumbharwada street festival, nearly three years had passed, and neither he nor she had thought of her as a little girl any longer. He had known her at once. "Why, it's the little thief!" he had cried upon seeing her again.

She had laughed in his face, giddy with the news she had just received in the post: that she, youngest daughter of a factory worker and a dockhand, had been the first female student to be accepted as a trainee computer specialist at the newly revamped and expanded Bandra-Kurla Complex. He had bought her sugared wafers, under the watchful eye of her three older sisters; and that summer, at the height of the worst dysentery outbreak Dharavi had endured in several years, they had kissed for the first time in the pouring rain.

Standing with her daughter on the border between light and darkness, Amrit turned to Meera and said, "Listen to me, girl. No, listen. The Kshatriya girl? The one who called you a thief? She was speaking the truth."

"No, Ma!"

"The cell phone was not yours to borrow. Nor was it mine to loan, though had it been I would have loaned it to you for the asking. It belonged to the company for which I work. Today I had to purchase another cell phone to replace the one that was broken in the altercation between you and the Kshatriya. The cost of that phone will be deducted from my wages."

"I'm sorry!"

"It is too late for sorrow." Harden your heart, she reminded herself. "The Vice-Principal from your school came to see me at work today. I suppose you know this?" The girl nodded miserably. "Do you know what he said to me?" Meera shook her head. "He told me that in light of the four violent quarrels in which you have been engaged this term, unless I agree to have you outfitted with a nannychip to curb your aggressive response tendencies, he will see that you are expelled from the Academy."

Having hurled her bomb, Amrit watched it hit home and burst behind the girl's eyes. She had not let go of her daughter's hand the entire time they had been in the street, and it was well that she had not, for the moment comprehension dawned in Meera's young face, the child turned and lunged for the nearest guard-rail.

Amrit yanked her, pulled her back. "What are you doing?" she cried. "What are you doing?"

"Let me go! A nannychip? I would die, rather!" Her mouth was an open wound. Howling, Meera reversed direction and barreled into her mother, sending her staggering backward. "I hate you! A nannychip? I hate you, I hate you!"

"Stop it! I did not say that I had agreed!" Amrit slapped the girl's face. Meera cried out, once; then stood stock-still, hands over her eyes, thin shoulders shuddering in the thin jacket of pirated ripstop nylon, sobbing raggedly.

"What is going on up here?"

Amrit turned, clutching Meera to her protectively. A man had come up the stair and was shining a flashlight in their faces. "You are not permitted on this causeway! Did you not observe the sign below? What is going on here?"

"We were just," said Amrit, and for some reason she was having a hard time summoning enough breath to form the words, so that they came out in puffs, like Uncle Saavit's cigar-smoke, "we were just, just, seeking the, view!" And then she was pushing past the man, half-carrying her daughter, half-dragging her, tumbling down the stair as fast as she could, while the man shouted, "You are not permitted! You are not permitted!" over and over again.

When they returned to their flat, they found that Dakota had been pried from his electronics and sent to bed, and that Gloria had returned and was huddled in fierce consultation with Uncle Saavit and the elder Mrs Chaudhury. These three looked up as Amrit and Meera came in. To their questions Amrit replied not a word, but marched Meera past them and into her little room. Less than a minute later, Amrit emerged from the room, sans her progeny, shutting the door firmly behind her. Then she went into the tiny kitchen to fix a pot of tea.

Gloria followed her into the kitchen and stood silently, waiting, her arms crossed over her chest, while Amrit filled the teakettle and lit the pilot light on the ancient propane stove. Gloria was nearly half Uncle Saavit's age, and would have been a beauty, thought Amrit, had it not been for her absurd adoption of the latest youth styles from China: LEDs imbedded in her forehead and chin and chop marks tattooed on her neck. Gloria, Mumbai born and bred, had been working as a waitress in one of the new holo-discos when she had met Saavit, and Amrit was not blind to the effect Gloria's excruciatingly modern presence in the house was having upon impressionable young Meera. Young! Amrit thought, waiting for the water to boil. In the old days, at fifteen Meera would already have been married a year, with a child on the way. She herself had married Meera's father at seventeen, and now here she was, a widow at thirty-two, with a dead-end job and no romantic prospects, certainly. Stop feeling sorry for yourself, she chided. You speak of the old days? In the old days, you would have been expected to have flung yourself upon your husband's funeral pyre. At least you have a job.

The kettle sang. Amrit had readied the tea leaves in the next-best steeping pot; she poured the boiling water over them until the steeping pot was filled, then replaced the kettle on the stove and put the lid on the pot. Only then did she turn round and smile at the waiting Gloria. "Would you like some tea, Auntie?" Amrit asked.

It was an old joke between them. When first Uncle Saavit had brought his fiancée home, Amrit had judged her an opportunist fishing the river of senility, and had said as much to Saavit in so many words. But over the weeks and months, and after the wedding when a pregnant Gloria had moved in with them, Amrit had come to appreciate her probity, practicality, and intelligence; and she was certainly a hard worker, contributing to the communal treasury through long hours at the e-cafe a substantial portion of the revenues that Saavit's ailing limousine service failed to provide. So Gloria and Amrit had taken to calling one another "Niece" and "Auntie," and usually it eased the tensions that occasionally cropped up between them.

But this time Gloria did not smile. She said, "Saavit and Parvati just told me what has happened." For reasons unclear to Amrit, Gloria was the only one in the household suffered to address Amrit's mother-in-law by her given name.

"And how would Saavit and Mrs. Chaudhury know?"

"The Assistant Vice-Principal told them when he brought Meera home this afternoon."

"Ah. Of course. No tea?" Gloria shook her head. In the dim kitchen, her LEDs were pinpricks of light. "Then you all know that Meera faces suspension for quarreling."

"Yes. It is so unjust!" The words came out slowly, almost thoughtfully. "It was the other girl's fault. Saavit says that the Assistant Vice-Principal admitted as much."

"Nonetheless. Meera knew the rules. This was her fourth offense. She must take her share of the responsibility." Amrit turned away, took down a teacup, saucer, and tea strainer from the shelf, and removed a teaspoon from the kitchen drawer. She noticed that her hands were trembling. She set the tea things on the little kitchen table to await the completion of the tea leaves' steeping. Without looking round again, Amrit said, "Did the Assistant Vice-Principal also inform you under what circumstances Meera would be permitted to remain at school?"

"It happened to me."

Shocked, Amrit turned. Though her expression was calm, tears were running down Gloria's beautiful brown cheeks. "Sit," Amrit ordered. The girl sat down at the table. Amrit sat down on the chair next to her. "What do you mean, it happened to you? What happened to you?"

"The nannychip. Saavit knows about it, but there are other things he doesn't know about, and would not understand if he did." Gloria glanced toward the parlor. "Promise me you will not tell him what I am about to tell you."

"I promise." Amrit pulled a handkerchief from a sleeve and handed it to her. Gloria took it and dabbed at her eyes. When she spoke, it was precisely and with an odd detachment, as though she were reading from a teleprompter.

"It was when I was at Girls' Reformatory. They were just experimenting with them then, the chips. I was thirteen and a half. I had been sent to Reformatory for selling pirated Mufti HDs at school."

"Mufti?" said Amrit. "The singing group?" She had heard of it, vaguely, a neo-Raj rock band that had enjoyed a brief and shocking vogue in the Sixties.

The girl nodded. "My older brother had me sent there. It was a Christian school; very strict. He said I needed a lesson; that I had gone wild since our parents had died; that he couldn't cope. The sisters were demons. Nothing one did was right. I fought back, so I was targeted for extra remedial discipline." She looked up at Amrit, black eyes glittering. "They brought in the chips program. They had been tested in the prisons and were just then being reconfigured for less violent offenders. It was a government sponsored project. My brother signed the permission papers; Sister Kamala showed them to me. Then they made us go through with the operation."

"Oh, Gloria." Amrit took the girl's hand. "What was it – how did – ?"

The hand beneath Amrit's balled suddenly into a small, hard fist. "There were six of us. They gave the chip to each of us. They implanted it here," she said, pointing with her free hand to a spot on her skull. "We were kept awake for the operation; we had to be, for the testing: everyone's brain is different, they told us; one's chip had to be fine-tuned, they said. They touched us here and here and here and said, 'Can you feel this, Miss? What about this, Miss?' And, 'What do you see now? What do you smell now?' for the chips, they sometimes cause hallucinations."

"Yes," said Amrit faintly. "Yes, I read that. Auditory and olfactory hallucinations. Visual ones as well, if the chips are not adjusted correctly."

Gloria's fist did not unclench. "Do not misunderstand me," she said. "The operation did not hurt. The doctors were not unkind. We were treated with great politeness. And of course we were not the only ones."

"I read that also," said Amrit. "The second-generation chips were tried in over sixty reform schools throughout India. Mostly state-run schools, but some religious institutions as well. There was no official pronouncement made; rumors on the Internet, that is all. Not until the change in governments, when the scandal broke." She kissed the girl's fist. "Oh, Gloria. I had no idea. I am so terribly sorry."

"But wait," said the girl. "I have not told you the best part of the story." She did not seem young, now. Her voice, though still pitched low, had both cooled into ice and sharpened into steel, and her gaze was so intense that it was all that Amrit could do not to look away. "At first, the first week after they implanted the chips, none of us felt much different. I felt rather good, actually: calmer, insulated, as though I were wrapped in cotton wool. The others, they felt the same. We would meet in the lavatory and talk about it. When someone, one of the unchipped girls, would make a nasty remark, instead of flying into a rage I would simply laugh and walk away. It was as though nothing could trouble me, not even Sister Kamala."

Her lips quirked into a small smile. "That was the best part of it, actually: feeling as though nothing that demon bitch might do could reach me. It drove her and the other sisters insane. You would have thought they'd have been pleased that their little hellions had been becalmed, but it seemed to disappoint them instead. I think they thought we were play-acting. So they used extra humiliations in an attempt to make us angry, so they would have an excuse to punish us again. But it didn't work. We simply didn't react, beyond, 'Yes, Sister. No, Sister. At once, Sister.' The other girls and I, we said to one another, 'This isn't half bad, really.' It was as though our chips were our friends: better than drugs, because they didn't ruin our lungs or spoil our concentration. We could still study our lessons. In fact, our minds felt clearer than ever they had before. Relaxed, but clear, the way the yogis say meditation makes you feel if you bother to practice it long enough.

"At the end of that first week, when they herded us into the center again for our first check-up, the doctors and sisters seemed very pleased. The technician who examined me joked that if the chips made everybody feel as good as ours were making us feel, perhaps everyone could benefit from an implant." She laughed again, a hint of bitterness in her tone. "Then it changed."

Amrit waited for a moment, then said, "I have read – that some of the second generation chip recipients – began displaying symptoms not unlike those suffered by autistics."

"I suppose you could put it that way." Gloria stood up abruptly, pulling her fist free from Amrit's hands, and crossing her arms again, uttered her next remarks with her back half-turned and her hair half-mantling her face. "By the third week two of us were dead – suicide; one of us was in hospital suffering from concussion – self-induced; and two of us had gone straight round the bend: full-fledged delusional – UFOs, past-life recall, bloody Krishna and the shepherd girls, what have you. Or was that Vishnu and the shepherdesses? I can never bloody remember."

"That makes five," said Amrit. "You said there were six of you implanted. Were you – "

"Was I the concussion victim or one of the nutters? None of the above, Niece. I was the success."

"The success?"

"That's right. The success." Her profile was beautiful and still, a statue's profile. "Throughout it all – Pinnai leaping from the chapel roof, thinking she could fly; Fatima setting herself afire so she might free herself from the wheel of karma; Varali trying to pound the voices out of her skull – I felt nothing."

She looked at Amrit then, the LEDs shifting the shadows on her brow. "Do you understand me, Amrit? I felt nothing. Nothing at all. I saw these things – I was there when Pinnai jumped – and it was as though I were watching a thriller on the telly. None of it reached me at all. I even helped Sister Kamala clean up the mess in the chapel yard. By that time, I couldn't even hate her. And now we come to the part you mustn't tell my husband."

"I don't understand," said Amrit. "I thought – the reformatory – "

"No. Saavit knows about that. He knows about the chip as well. I told him, the night before the wedding. I thought it was only fair, considering his kindness to me. But I was afraid to tell him everything."

"No, Gloria, wait." Amrit found herself upon her feet. Suddenly she felt terribly afraid. "Perhaps – perhaps it would be best not to tell. Not to tell me."

The girl's face was implacable. "But I must. Because if I do not, your decision concerning Meera will not be a fully informed one. And I care about Meera, in my way; she reminds me so of myself at that age. Well, of myself as I would have been had I reached that age intact.

"What I need to tell you, Amrit, so that you know precisely and without a shadow of doubt the possible repercussions of chipping your daughter, is that the detachment the chip gave me? It never went away."

After a moment Amrit said, "I do not understand. They took the chip out, didn't they? I mean to say that I have seen you: angry, sad, happy. I have seen you with Saavit. You seem happy with him. They did remove the chip?"

"Yes. They removed it," said Gloria. "They removed it. And yes, I could feel things again. The entire range of human emotion was available to me once more. But I found that I no longer cared. My body cared: it experienced revulsion, and lust, and terror, and comforts. But I did not. I feel all those things – I watch my body experience all those emotions – but at the core of me, there is nothing.

"It's all right," she added, smiling at Amrit. "I'm used to it, now. I do care for Saavit, as much as I can care for anybody; he has been very good to me. And for Dakota, of course. And for all of you. I am very grateful to be a part of the family," and somehow the way she said it made Amrit wish that the girl would shout, and curse, anything other than what she was doing, which was simply standing there, speaking of those closest to her as though they were very distant relatives she had read about in a history book. "And that is why I spend so much time working at the cafe, I suppose. I do it, not only because by doing so I am contributing materially to the family's welfare, but because there I do not have to pretend to have a self. I can lose myself, in the Net, in the graphics programs, whatever it may be. I become – information, if you will." She cocked her head. "Perhaps I am not putting it very clearly."

"Do you mean," said Amrit desperately, "that you experience a disconnect with the feeling part of yourself? As in post-traumatic stress disorder?" Even as she said it she knew that it was not what Gloria had meant at all. Her horror mounting, she looked at her uncle's young bride again, and it was as though she were seeing her for the first time. So that, when the girl said, "No, this is what I mean," and picked up the pot of barely cooling tea, and lifted it over to the kitchen sink, and held out her slim-wristed hand with its long lacquered fingernails, and calmly poured the scalding tea over it with no trace of concern upon her face. Amrit watched the skin redden and the fingers twitch in agony and thought, She is not human. She is not human anymore. And nearly laughed, because was not this supernal recognition of non-existence what the Buddhists always seemed to be striving for? The enlightenment of no-self? Was not this what the Christians meant when they said, Not I, but Christ in me?

Then she had grasped the girl's wrist, and had knocked the teapot from her grasp; and, as quickly as she could, was turning on the cold-water-faucet and holding the girl's hand beneath the resultant flow. Gloria made no attempt to resist. She simply observed the process, as though it were not her hand at all, but someone else's, despite the fact that the pain must certainly have been very great indeed.

"What has happened? We heard a crash!" Mrs Chaudhury appeared at the door, Uncle Saavit close behind her. At a glance she noted the teapot, which had shattered upon the floor in its fall; the spreading pool of hot tea; the sodden detritus of steeped leaves; Gloria's reddened wrist. "My God! Are you all right? Here, girl, let me. Saavit, get the mop!" She interposed herself between Amrit and Gloria and took the girl's hand into her own. "Amrit, the aloe." Dumbly Amrit turned and left the kitchen, pushing past Saavit's concerned bluster. In the windowbox on the fire escape, aloe plants were growing; Amrit snapped off three large leaves and hurried back with them.

Meera had come out of her room and was standing in the middle of the parlor. She looked pale, but red around the eyes, as though she had been crying. "What's wrong?" she asked. "What's wrong, Mama?"

"Nothing, Meera," Amrit said over her shoulder. "There's been a little accident, that is all. Return to your room; I shall be with you momentarily. I wish to speak with you." She went back into the kitchen. Saavit was busily mopping up the spilled tea and rounding up pieces of broken pot, but otherwise the tableau was the same as when she had left it: her mother-in-law bent over Gloria's raw wrist, laving it, while Gloria looked on, placidly unconcerned. "The aloe," Amrit said.

Mrs Chaudhury did not look up. "Thank you, Daughter. If you would be so kind as to split the leaves and scrape the gel into a bowl."

"Yes," Amrit said, "Mother." She took a knife from the drawer, sat down at the kitchen table, and carefully halved the aloe leaves, revealing their glistening interiors. Scoring the gel with the knife, she took the spoon from her saucer and used it to scrape the innards of the leaves into her teacup. Then she conveyed the cup to her mother-in-law, who took it from her without comment. Amrit stood there for a moment, uncertain what to do next; then she turned and left the kitchen.

Meera had left the sitting room. In the hallway outside of Meera's closet, Amrit hesitated, then knocked. "Meera?"

"I'm here, Mama."

She sounds so tired, thought Amrit. She pulled the door ajar. Meera was sitting crosslegged on her carpet. A schoolbook lay opened upon her lap. She looked up, saw her mother standing there, and burst into tears. Amrit went over to her and sat down on the carpet beside her. "I'm sorry, Mama," Meera said. "I'm sorry, I'm sorry. Don't let them chip me. Please, Mama, don't let them, please don't let them, I'll be good, I'll do anything, only don't let them chip me, please please."

"Hush now, hush." Amrit took her daughter into her arms and pressed her head against her chest. "Hush, now. Nobody's going to let anybody chip anybody."

"But Assistant Vice-Principal said—"

"The Assistant Vice-Principal can go suck a mango," said Amrit, "and for that matter, so can Vice-Principal Mehta. No one is going to nannychip my daughter, and that is the end of it."

"But he said – they will expel me – and you work so hard—"

"Yes, yes, your mama works so very hard in her foolish pride to give her daughter the opportunities she was too timid to seek for herself. There are other schools, perhaps not as famous nor as fine. What of it?"

"But, Mama—"

"That is the end of it, Meera. There will be no nannychipping and that is that." She kissed her daughter upon the top of her sweet head. Then she placed her lips close to Meera's beautiful ear. "Do not stop feeling, Meera," she whispered fiercely. "It is good to feel, however inconvenient those feelings may happen to be. For if you cease to feel, you are as good as dead, bugger the bloody Buddha. Do not forget, Meera. Promise me."

"I won't forget, Mama, I promise," said her daughter, who, though perhaps not quite understanding, showed no signs of inclination to break the embrace they shared. So Amrit continued to hold her, for the longest time, thinking in her own mind how many forces in her own life had conspired to deaden her own passions. Then she had another thought, which made her pull herself from Meera's grasp and hold her at elbow's length. "However," Amrit added, in a fierce voice, "if you are going to quarrel with every bully who accosts you, you had best become more proficient at fisticuffs. While we are seeking another school in which to place you, you will resume your boxing lessons with your Uncle Saavit. Am I understood?"

"Yes, Mama!" cried her fierce young troublemaker. "Yes!" And they held one another again until old Mrs Chaudhury came into the room, took in the scene, and asked in a very mild tone if, now that the storm of crises appeared to have passed, anyone in this madhouse would mind if she attempted to make another pot of tea.

MONGOOSE

Elizabeth Bear and Sarah Monette

Elizabeth Bear was born in Connecticut, where she's now returned to live after several years in the Mohave Desert near Las Vegas. She won the John W. Campbell Award for Best New Writer in 2005, and in 2008 took home a Hugo Award for her short story "Tideline", which also won her the Theodore Sturgeon Memorial Award (shared with David Moles). In 2009, she won another Hugo Award for her novelette "Shoggoths in Bloom". Her short work has appeared in *Asimov's*, *Subterranean*, *Sci Fiction*, *Interzone*, *The Third Alternative*, *Strange Horizons*, *On Spec*, and elsewhere, and has been collected in *The Chains That You Refuse* and *New Amsterdam*. She is the author of three highly acclaimed SF novels, *Hammered*, *Scardown*, and *Worldwired*, and of the alternate history "Promethean Age" fantasy series, which includes the novels *Blood and Iron*, *Whiskey and Water*, *Ink and Steel*, and *Hell and Earth*. Her other books include the novels *Carnival*, *Undertow*, *Chill*, *Dust*, and *All the Windwracked Stars*. Her most recent works are a new novel, *By the Mountain Bound*, and a chapbook novella, *Bone and Jewel Creatures*. Her website is elizabethbear.com

Sarah Monette was born and raised in Oak Ridge, Tennessee, one of the secret cities of the Manhattan Project. Having completed her Ph.D. in Renaissance English drama, she now lives and writes in a ninety-nine-year-old house in the Upper Midwest. Her "Doctrine of Labyrinths" series consists of the novels *Melusine*, *The Virtu*, and *The Mirador*. Her short fiction has appeared in many places, including *Strange Horizons*, *Aeon*, *Alchemy*, and *Lady Churchill's Rosebud Wristlet*, and has been collected in *The Bone Key*. Upcoming is a new novel in the "Doctrine of Labyrinths" sequence, *Corambis*. Her website is sarahmonette.com.

Bear and Monette have collaborated before, on the stories "The Ile of Dogges" and "The Boojum" and on the novel *A Companion to Wolves*. Here they join forces again with a chilling story about an interdimensional pest-control officer and his very unusual helper.

IZRAEL IRIZARRY STEPPED through a bright-scarred airlock onto Kadath Station, lurching a little as he adjusted to station gravity. On his shoulder, Mongoose extended her neck, her barbels flaring, flicked her tongue out to taste the air, and colored a question. Another few steps, and he smelled what Mongoose smelled, the sharp stink of toves, ammoniac and bitter.

He touched the tentacle coiled around his throat with the quick double tap that meant soon. Mongoose colored displeasure, and Irizarry stroked the slick velvet wedge of her head in consolation and restraint. Her four compound and twelve simple eyes glittered and her color softened, but did not change, as she leaned into the caress. She was eager to hunt and he didn't blame her. The boojum Manfred von Richthofen took care of its own vermin. Mongoose had had to make do with a share of Irizarry's rations, and she hated eating dead things.

If Irizarry could smell toves, it was more than the "minor infestation" the message from the station master had led him to expect. Of course, that message had reached Irizarry third or fourth or fifteenth hand, and he had no idea how long it had taken. Perhaps when the station master had sent for him, it had been minor.

But he knew the ways of bureaucrats, and he wondered.

People did double-takes as he passed, even the heavily-modded Christian cultists with their telescoping limbs and biolin eyes. You found them on every station and steelships too, though mostly they wouldn't work the boojums. Nobody liked Christians much, but they could work in situations that would kill an unmodded human or even a gilly, so captains and station masters tolerated them.

There were a lot of gillies in Kadath's hallways, and they all stopped to blink at Mongoose. One, an indenturee, stopped and made an elaborate hand-flapping bow. Irizarry felt one of Mongoose's tendrils work itself through two of his earrings. Although she didn't understand staring exactly – her compound eyes made the idea alien to her – she felt the attention and was made shy by it.

Unlike the boojum-ships they serviced, the stations – Providence, Kadath, Leng, Dunwich, and the others – were man-made. Their radial symmetry was predictable, and to find the station master, Irizarry only had to work his way inward from the Manfred von Richthofen's dock to the hub. There he found one of the inevitable safety maps (you are here; in case of decompression, proceed in an orderly manner to the life vaults located here, here, or here) and leaned close to squint at the tiny lettering. Mongoose copied him, tilting her head first one way, then another, though flat representations meant nothing to her. He made out STATION MASTER'S OFFICE finally, on an oval bubble, the door of which was actually in sight.

"Here we go, girl," he said to Mongoose (who, stone-deaf though she was, pressed against him in response to the vibration of his voice). He hated this part of the job, hated dealing with apparatchiks and functionaries, and of course the Station Master's office was full of them, a receptionist, and then a secretary, and then someone who was maybe the other kind of secretary, and then finally – Mongoose by now halfway down the back of his shirt and entirely hidden by his hair and Irizarry himself half stifled by memories of someone he didn't want to remember being – he was ushered into an inner room where Station Master Lee, her arms crossed and her round face set in a scowl, was waiting.

"Mr Irizarry," she said, unfolding her arms long enough to stick one hand out in a facsimile of a congenial greeting.

He held up a hand in response, relieved to see no sign of recognition in her face. It was Irizarry's experience that the dead were best left to lie where they fell. "Sorry, Station Master," he said. "I can't."

He thought of asking her about the reek of toves on the air, if she understood just how bad the situation had become. People could convince themselves of a lot of bullshit, given half a chance.

Instead, he decided to talk about his partner. "Mongoose hates it when I touch other people. She gets jealous, like a parrot."

"The cheshire's here?" She let her hand drop to her side, the expression on her face a mixture of respect and alarm. "Is it out of phase?"

Well, at least Station Master Lee knew a little more about Cheshire cats than most people. "No," Irizarry said. "She's down my shirt."

Half a standard hour later, wading through the damp bowels of a ventilation pore, Irizarry tapped his rebreather to try to clear some of the tove-stench from his nostrils and mouth. It didn't help much; he was getting close.

Here, Mongoose wasn't shy at all. She slithered up on top of his head, barbels and graspers extended to full length, pulsing slowly in predatory greens and reds. Her tendrils slithered through his hair and coiled about his throat, fading in and out of phase. He placed his fingertips on her slick-resilient hide to restrain her. The last thing he needed was for Mongoose to go spectral and charge off down the corridor after the tove colony.

It wasn't that she wouldn't come back, because she would – but that was only if she didn't get herself into more trouble than she could get out of without his help. "Steady," he said, though of course she couldn't hear him. A creature adapted to vacuum had no ears. But she could feel his voice vibrate in his throat, and a tendril brushed his lips, feeling the puff of air and the shape of the word. He tapped her tendril twice again – soon – and felt it contract. She flashed hungry orange in his peripheral vision. She was experimenting with jaguar rosettes – they had had long discussions of jaguars and tigers after their nightly reading of Pooh on the Manfred von Richthofen, as Mongoose had wanted to know what jagulars and tiggers were. Irizarry had already taught her about mongooses, and he'd read *Alice in Wonderland* so she would know what a Cheshire cat was. Two days later – he still remembered it vividly – she had disappeared quite slowly, starting with the tips of the long coils of her tail and tendrils and ending with the needle-sharp crystalline array of her teeth. And then she'd phased back in, all excited aquamarine and pink, almost bouncing, and he'd praised her and stroked her and reminded himself not to think of her as a cat. Or a mongoose.

She had readily grasped the distinction between jaguars and jagulars, and had almost as quickly decided that she was a jagular; Irizarry had almost started to argue, but then thought better of it. She was, after all, a Very Good Dropper. And nobody ever saw her coming unless she wanted them to.

When the faint glow of the toves came into view at the bottom of the pore, he felt her shiver all over, luxuriantly, before she shimmered dark and folded herself tight against his scalp. Irizarry doused his own lights as well, flipping the passive infrared goggles down over his eyes. Toves were as blind as Mongoose was deaf, but an infestation this bad could mean the cracks were growing large enough for bigger things to wiggle through, and if there were raths, no sense in letting the monsters know he was coming.

He tapped the tendril curled around his throat three times, and whispered, "Go." She didn't need him to tell her twice; really, he thought wryly, she didn't need him to tell her at all. He barely felt her featherweight disengage before she was gone down the corridor as silently as a hunting owl. She was invisible to his goggles, her body at ambient temperature, but he knew from experience that her barbels and vanes would be spread wide, and he'd hear the shrieks when she came in among the toves.

The toves covered the corridor ceiling, arm-long carapaces adhered by a foul-smelling secretion that oozed from between the sections of their exoskeletons. The upper third of each tove's body bent down like a dangling bough, bringing the glowing, sticky lure and flesh-ripping pincers into play. Irizarry had no idea what they fed on in their own phase, or dimension, or whatever.

Here, though, he knew what they ate. Anything they could get.

He kept his shock probe ready, splashing after, to assist her if necessary. That was sure a lot of toves, and even a Cheshire cat could get in trouble if she was outnumbered. Ahead of him, a tove warbled and went suddenly dark; Mongoose had made her first kill.

Within moments, the tove colony was in full warble, the harmonics making Irizarry's head ache. He moved forward carefully, alert now for signs of raths. The largest tove colony he'd ever seen was on the derelict steelship *Jenny Lind*, which he and Mongoose had explored when they were working salvage on the boojum Harriet Tubman. The hulk had been covered inside and out with toves; the colony was so vast that, having eaten everything else, it had started cannibalizing itself, toves eating their neighbors and being eaten in turn. Mongoose had glutted herself before the Harriet Tubman ate the wreckage, and in the refuse she left behind, Irizarry had found the strange star-like bones of an adult rath, consumed by its own prey. The bandersnatch that had killed the humans on the Jenny Lind had died with her reactor core and her captain. A handful of passengers and crew had escaped to tell the tale.

He refocused. This colony wasn't as large as those heaving masses on the *Jenny Lind*, but it was the largest he'd ever encountered not in a quarantine situation, and if there weren't raths somewhere on Kadath Station, he'd eat his infrared goggles.

A dead tove landed at his feet, its eyeless head neatly separated from its segmented body, and a heartbeat later Mongoose phased in on his shoulder and made her deep clicking noise that meant, Irizarry! Pay attention!

He held his hand out, raised to shoulder level, and Mongoose flowed between the two, keeping her bulk on his shoulder, with tendrils resting against his lips and larynx, but her tentacles wrapping around his hand to communicate. He pushed his goggles up with his free hand and switched on his belt light so he could read her colors.

She was anxious, strobing yellow and green. Many, she shaped against his palm, and then emphatically, R.

"R" was bad – it meant rath – but it was better than "B." If a bandersnatch had come through, all of them were walking dead, and Kadath Station was already as doomed as the *Jenny Lind*. "Do you smell it?" he asked under the warbling of the toves.

"Taste," said Mongoose, and because Irizarry had been her partner for almost five Solar, he understood: the toves tasted of rath, meaning that they had recently been feeding on rath guano, and given the swiftness of toves' digestive systems, that meant a rath was patrolling territory on the station.

Mongoose's grip tightened on his shoulder. "R," she said again. "R. R. R."

Irizarry's heart lurched and sank. More than one rath. The cracks were widening.

A bandersnatch was only a matter of time.

Station Master Lee didn't want to hear it. It was all there in the way she stood, the way she pretended distraction to avoid eye-contact. He knew the rules of this game, probably better than she did. He stepped into her personal space. Mongoose shivered against the nape of his neck, her tendrils threading his hair. Even without being able to see her, he knew she was a deep, anxious emerald.

"A rath?" said Station Master Lee, with a toss of her head that might have looked flirtatious on a younger or less hostile woman, and moved away again. "Don't be ridiculous. There hasn't been a rath on Kadath Station since my grandfather's time."

"Doesn't mean there isn't an infestation now," Irizarry said quietly. If she was going to be dramatic, that was his cue to stay still and calm. "And I said raths. Plural."

"That's even more ridiculous. Mr Irizarry, if this is some ill-conceived attempt to drive up your price – "

"It isn't." He was careful to say it flatly, not indignantly. "Station Master, I understand that this isn't what you want to hear, but you have to quarantine Kadath."

"Can't be done," she said, her tone brisk and flat, as if he'd asked her to pilot Kadath through the rings of Saturn.

"Of course it can!" Irizarry said, and she finally turned to look at him, outraged that he dared to contradict her. Against his neck, Mongoose flexed one set of claws. She didn't like it when he was angry.

Mostly, that wasn't a problem. Mostly, Irizarry knew anger was a waste of time and energy. It didn't solve anything. It didn't fix anything. It couldn't bring back anything that was lost. People, lives. The sorts of things that got washed away in the tides of time. Or were purged, whether you wanted them gone or not.

But this was . . . "You do know what a colony of adult raths can do, don't you? With a contained population of prey? Tell me, Station Master, have you started noticing fewer indigents in the shelters?"

She turned away again, dismissing his existence from her cosmology. "The matter is not open for discussion, Mr Irizarry. I hired you to deal with an alleged infestation. I expect you to do so. If you feel you can't, you are of course welcome to leave the station with whatever ship takes your fancy. I believe the Arthur Gordon Pym is headed in-system, or perhaps you'd prefer the Jupiter run?"

He didn't have to win this fight, he reminded himself. He could walk away, try to warn somebody else, get himself and Mongoose the hell off Kadath Station. "All right, Station Master. But remember that I warned you, when your secretaries start disappearing."

He was at the door when she cried, "Irizarry!"

He stopped, but didn't turn.

"I can't," she said, low and rushed, as if she was afraid of being overheard. "I can't quarantine the station. Our numbers are already in the red this quarter, and the new political officer . . . it's my head on the block, don't you understand?"

He didn't understand. Didn't want to. It was one of the reasons he was a wayfarer, because he never wanted to let himself be like her again.

"If Sanderson finds out about the quarantine, she finds out about you. Will your papers stand up to a close inspection, Mr Irizarry?"

He wheeled, mouth open to tell her what he thought of her and her clumsy attempts at blackmail, and she said, "I'll double your fee."

At the same time, Mongoose tugged on several strands of his hair, and he realized he could feel her heart beating, hard and rapid, against his spine. It was her distress he answered, not the Station Master's bribe. "All right," he said. "I'll do the best I can."

Toves and raths colonized like an epidemic, outward from a single originating point, Patient Zero in this case being the tear in spacetime that the first tove had wriggled through. More tears would develop as the toves multiplied, but it was that first one that would become large enough for a rath. While toves were simply lazy – energy efficient, the Arkhamers said primly – and never crawled farther than was necessary to find a useable anchoring point, raths were cautious. Their marauding was centered on the original tear because they kept their escape route open. And tore it wider and wider.

Toves weren't the problem, although they were a nuisance, with their tendency to use up valuable oxygen, clog ductwork, eat pets, drip goo from ceilings, and crunch wetly when you stepped on them. Raths were worse; raths were vicious predators. Their natural prey might be toves, but they'd take small gillies – or small humans – when they could get them.

But even they weren't the danger that had made it hard for Irizarry to sleep the past two rest shifts. What toves tore and raths widened was an access for the apex predator of this alien food chain.

The bandersnatch: Pseudocanis tindalosi. The old records and the indigent Arkhamers called them hounds, but of course they weren't, any more than Mongoose was a cat. Irizarry had seen archive video from derelict stations and ships, the bandersnatch's flickering angular limbs appearing like spiked mantis arms from the corners of sealed rooms, the carnage that ensued. He'd never heard of anyone left alive on a station where a bandersnatch manifested, unless they made it to a panic pod damned fast. More importantly, even the Arkhamers in their archive-ships, breeders of Mongoose and all her kind, admitted they had no records of anyone surviving a bandersnatch rather than escaping it.

And what he had to do, loosely put, was find the core of the infestation before the bandersnatches did, so that he could eradicate the toves and raths and the stress they were putting on this little corner of the universe. Find the core – somewhere in the miles upon miles of Kadath's infrastructure. Which was why he was in this little-used service corridor, letting Mongoose commune with every ventilation duct they found.

Anywhere near the access shafts infested by the colony, Kadath Station's passages reeked of tove – ammoniac, sulfurous. The stench infiltrated the edges of Irizarry's mask as he lifted his face to a ventilation duct. Wincing in anticipation, he broke the seal on the rebreather and pulled it away from his face on the stiff elastic straps, careful not to lose his grip. A broken nose would not improve his day.

A cultist engineer skittered past on sucker-tipped limbs, her four snake-arms coiled tight beside her for the narrow corridor. She had a pretty smile, for a Christian.

Mongoose was too intent on her prey to be shy. The size of the tove colony might make her nervous, but Mongoose loved the smell – like a good dinner heating, Irizarry imagined. She unfolded herself around his head like a tendriled hood, tentacles outreached, body flaring as she stretched toward the ventilation fan. He felt her lean, her barbels shivering, and turned to face the way her wedge-shaped head twisted.

He almost tipped backward when he found himself face to face with someone he hadn't even known was there. A woman, average height, average weight, brown hair drawn back in a smooth club; her skin was space-pale and faintly reddened across the cheeks, as if the IR filters on a suit hadn't quite protected her. She wore a sleek space-black uniform with dull silver epaulets and four pewter-colored bands at each wrist. An insignia with a stylized sun and Earth-Moon dyad clung over her heart.

The political officer, who was obviously unconcerned by Mongoose's ostentatious display of sensory equipment.

Mongoose absorbed her tendrils like a startled anemone, pressing the warm underside of her head to Irizarry's scalp where the hair was thinning. He was surprised she didn't vanish down his shirt, because he felt her trembling against his neck.

The political officer didn't extend her hand. "Mr Irizarry? You're a hard man to find. I'm Intelligence Colonel Sadhi Sanderson. I'd like to ask you a few quick questions, please."

"I'm, uh, a little busy right now," Irizarry said, and added uneasily, "Ma'am." The last thing he wanted was to offend her.

Sanderson looked up at Mongoose. "Yes, you would appear to be hunting," she said, her voice dry as scouring powder. "That's one of the things I want to talk about."

Oh shit. He had kept out of the political officer's way for a day and a half, and really that was a pretty good run, given the obvious tensions between Lee and Sanderson, and the things he'd heard in the Transient Barracks: the gillies were all terrified of Sanderson, and nobody seemed to have a good word for Lee. Even the Christians, mouths thinned primly, could say of Lee only that she didn't actively persecute them. Irizarry had been stuck on a steelship with a Christian congregation for nearly half a year once, and he knew their eagerness to speak well of everyone; he didn't know whether that was actually part of their faith, or just a survival tactic, but when Elder Dawson said, "She does not trouble us," he understood quite precisely what that meant.

Of Sanderson, they said even less, but Irizarry understood that, too. There was no love lost between the extremist cults and the government. But he'd heard plenty from the ice miners and dock workers and particularly from the crew of an impounded steelship who were profanely eloquent on the subject. Upshot: Colonel Sanderson was new in town, cleaning house, and profoundly not a woman you wanted to fuck with.

"I'd be happy to come to your office in an hour, maybe two?" he said. "It's just that—"

Mongoose's grip on his scalp tightened, sudden and sharp enough that he yelped; he realized that her head had moved back toward the duct while he fenced weakly with Colonel Sanderson, and now it was nearly in the duct, at the end of a foot and a half of iridescent neck.

"Mr Irizarry?"

He held a hand up, because really this wasn't a good time, and yelped again when Mongoose reached down and grabbed it. He knew better than to forget how fluid her body was, that it was really no more than a compromise with the dimension he could sense her in, but sometimes it surprised him anyway.

And then Mongoose said, Nagina, and if Colonel Sanderson hadn't been standing right there, her eyebrows indicating that he was already at the very end of the slack she was willing to cut, he would have cursed aloud. Short of a bandersnatch – and that could still be along any time now, don't forget, Irizarry – a breeding rath was the worst news they could have.

"Your Cheshire seems unsettled," Sanderson said, not sounding in the least alarmed. "Is there a problem?"

"She's eager to eat. And, er. She doesn't like strangers." It was as true as anything you could say about Mongoose, and the violent colors cycling down her tendrils gave him an idea what her chromatophores were doing behind his head.

"I can see that," Sanderson said. "Cobalt and yellow, in that stippled pattern – and flickering in and out of phase – she's acting aggressive, but that's fear, isn't it?"

Whatever Irizarry had been about to say, her observation stopped him short. He blinked at her – like a gilly, he thought uncharitably – and only realized he'd taken yet another step back when the warmth of the bulkhead pressed his coveralls to his spine.

"You know," Sanderson said mock-confidentially, "this entire corridor reeks of toves. So let me guess: it's not just toves anymore."

Irizarry was still stuck at her being able to read Mongoose's colors. "What do you know about Cheshires?" he said.

She smiled at him as if at a slow student. "Rather a lot. I was on the Jenny Lind as an ensign – there was a cheshire on board, and I saw . . . It's not the sort of thing you forget, Mr Irizarry, having been there once." Something complicated crossed her face – there for a flash and then gone. "The Cheshire that died on the Jenny Lind was called Demon," Irizarry said, carefully. "Her partner was Long Mike Spider. You knew them?"

"Spider John," Sanderson said, looking down at the backs of her hands. She picked a cuticle with the opposite thumbnail. "He went by Spider John. You have the cheshire's name right, though."

When she looked back up, the arch of her carefully shaped brow told him he hadn't been fooling anyone.

"Right," Irizarry said. "Spider John."

"They were friends of mine." She shook her head. "I was just a pup. First billet, and I was assigned as Demon's liaison. Spider John liked to say he and I had the same job. But I couldn't make the captain believe him when he tried to tell her how bad it was."

"How'd you make it off after the bandersnatch got through?" Irizarry asked. He wasn't foolish enough to think that her confidences were anything other than a means of demonstrating to him why he could trust her, but the frustration and tired sadness sounded sincere.

"It went for Spider John first – it must have known he was a threat. And Demon – she threw herself at it, never mind it was five times her size. She bought us time to get to the panic pod and Captain Golovnina time to get to the core overrides." She paused. "I saw it, you know. Just a glimpse. Wriggling through this . . . this rip in the air, like a big gaunt hound ripping through a hole in a blanket with knotty paws. I spent years wondering if it got my scent. Once they scent prey, you know, they never stop. . . ."

She trailed off, raising her gaze to meet his. He couldn't decide if the furrow between her eyes was embarrassment at having revealed so much, or the calculated cataloguing of his response.

"So you recognize the smell, is what you're saying."

She had a way of answering questions with other questions. "Am I right about the raths?"

He nodded. "A breeder."

She winced.

He took a deep breath and stepped away from the bulkhead. "Colonel Sanderson – I have to get it now if I'm going to get it at all."

She touched the microwave pulse pistol at her hip. "Want some company?"

He didn't. Really, truly didn't. And if he had, he wouldn't have chosen Kadath Station's political officer. But he couldn't afford to offend her . . . and he wasn't licensed to carry a weapon.

"All right," he said, and hoped he didn't sound as grudging as he felt. "But don't get in Mongoose's way."

Colonel Sanderson offered him a tight, feral smile. "Wouldn't dream of it."

The only thing that stank more than a pile of live toves was a bunch of half-eaten ones.

"Going to have to vacuum-scrub the whole sector," Sanderson said, her breath hissing through her filters.

If we live long enough to need to, Irizarry thought, but had the sense to keep his mouth shut. You didn't talk defeat around a politico. And if you were unfortunate enough to come to the attention of one, you certainly didn't let her see you thinking it.

Mongoose forged on ahead, but Irizarry noticed she was careful to stay within the range of his lights, and at least one of her tendrils stayed focused back on him and Sanderson at all times. If this were a normal infestation, Mongoose would be scampering along the corridor ceilings, leaving scattered bits of half-consumed tove and streaks of bioluminescent ichor in her wake. But this time, she edged along, testing each surface before her with quivering barbels so that Irizarry was reminded of a tentative spider or an exploratory octopus.

He edged along behind her, watching her colors go dim and cautious. She paused at each intersection, testing the air in every direction, and waited for her escort to catch up.

The service tubes of Kadath Station were mostly large enough for Irizarry and Sanderson to walk through single-file, though sometimes they were obliged to crouch, and once or twice Irizarry found himself slithering on his stomach through tacky half-dried tove slime. He imagined – he hoped it was imagining – that he could sense the thinning and stretch of reality all around them, see it in the warp of the tunnels and the bend of deck plates. He imagined that he glimpsed faint shapes from the corners of his eyes, caught a whisper of sound, a hint of scent, as of something almost there.

Hypochondria, he told himself firmly, aware that that was the wrong word and not really caring. But as he dropped down onto his belly again, to squeeze through a tiny access point – this one clogged with the fresh corpses of newly-slaughtered toves – he needed all the comfort he could invent.

He almost ran into Mongoose when he'd cleared the hole. She scuttled back to him and huddled under his chest, tendrils writhing, so close to out of phase that she was barely a warm shadow. When he saw what was on the other side, he wished he'd invented a little more.

This must be one of Kadath Station's recycling and reclamation centers, a bowl ten meters across sweeping down to a pile of rubbish in the middle. These were the sorts of places you always found minor tove infestations. Ships and stations were supposed to be kept clear of vermin, but in practice, the dimensional stresses of sharing the spacelanes with boojums meant that just wasn't possible. And in Kadath, somebody hadn't been doing their job.

Sanderson touched his ankle, and Irizarry hastily drew himself aside so she could come through after. He was suddenly grateful for her company.

He really didn't want to be here alone.

Irizarry had never seen a tove infestation like this, not even on the Jenny Lind. The entire roof of the chamber was thick with their sluglike bodies, long lure-tongues dangling as much as half a meter down. Small flitting things – young raths, near-transparent in their phase shift – filled the space before him. As Irizarry watched, one blundered into the lure of a tove, and the tove contracted with sudden convulsive force. The rath never stood a chance.

Nagina, Mongoose said. Nagina, Nagina, Nagina.

Indeed, down among the junk in the pit, something big was stirring. But that wasn't all. That pressure Irizarry had sensed earlier, the feeling that many eyes were watching him, gaunt bodies stretching against whatever frail fabric held them back – here, it was redoubled, until he almost felt the brush of not-quite-in-phase whiskers along the nape of his neck.

Sanderson crawled up beside him, her pistol in one hand. Mongoose didn't seem to mind her there.

"What's down there?" she asked, her voice hissing on constrained breaths.

"The breeding pit," Irizarry said. "You feel that? Kind of a funny, stretchy feeling in the universe?"

Sanderson nodded behind her mask. "It's not going to make you any happier, is it, if I tell you I've felt it before?"

Irizarry was wearily, grimly unsurprised. But then Sanderson said, "What do we do?"

He was taken aback and it must have shown, even behind the rebreather, because she said sharply, "You're the expert. Which I assume is why you're on Kadath Station to begin with and why Station Master Lee has been so anxious that I not know it. Though with an infestation of this size, I don't know how she thought she was going to hide it much longer anyway."

"Call it sabotage," Irizarry said absently. "Blame the Christians. Or the gillies. Or disgruntled spacers, like the crew off the Caruso. It happens a lot, Colonel. Somebody like me and Mongoose comes in and cleans up the toves, the station authorities get to crack down on whoever's being the worst pain in the ass, and life keeps on turning over. But she waited too long."

Down in the pit, the breeder heaved again. Breeding raths were slow – much slower than the juveniles, or the sexually dormant adult rovers – but that was because they were armored like titanium armadillos. When threatened, one of two things happened. Babies flocked to mama, mama rolled herself in a ball, and it would take a tactical nuke to kill them. Or mama went on the warpath. Irizarry had seen a pissed off breeder take out a bulkhead on a steelship once; it was pure dumb luck that it hadn't breached the hull.

And, of course, once they started spawning, as this one had, they could produce between ten and twenty babies a day for anywhere from a week to a month, depending on the food supply. And the more babies they produced, the weaker the walls of the world got, and the closer the bandersnatches would come.

"The first thing we have to do," he said to Colonel Sanderson, "as in, right now, is kill the breeder. Then you quarantine the station and get parties of volunteers to hunt down the rovers, before they can bring another breeder through, or turn into breeders, or however the fuck it works, which frankly I don't know. It'll take fire to clear this nest of toves, but Mongoose and I can probably get the rest. And fire, Colonel Sanderson. Toves don't give a shit about vacuum."

She could have reproved him for his language; she didn't. She just nodded and said, "How do we kill the breeder?"

"Yeah," Irizarry said. "That's the question."

Mongoose clicked sharply, her Irizarry! noise.

"No," Irizarry said. "Mongoose, don't—"

But she wasn't paying attention. She had only a limited amount of patience for his weird interactions with other members of his species and his insistence on waiting, and he'd clearly used it all up. She was Rikki Tikki Tavi, and the breeder was Nagina, and Mongoose knew what had to happen. She launched off Irizarry's shoulders, shifting phase as she went, and without contact between them, there was nothing he could do to call her back. In less than a second, he didn't even know where she was.

"You any good with that thing?" he said to Colonel Sanderson, pointing at her pistol.

"Yes," she said, but her eyebrows were going up again. "But, forgive me, isn't this what cheshires are for?"

"Against rovers, sure. But – Colonel, have you ever seen a breeder?"

Across the bowl, a tove warbled, the chorus immediately taken up by its neighbors. Mongoose had started.

"No," Sanderson said, looking down at where the breeder humped and wallowed and finally stood up, shaking off ethereal babies and half-eaten toves. "Oh. Gods."

You couldn't describe a rath. You couldn't even look at one for more than a few seconds before you started getting a migraine aura. Rovers were just blots of shadow. The breeder was massive, armored, and had no recognizable features, save for its hideous, drooling, ragged edged maw. Irizarry didn't know if it had eyes, or even needed them.

"She can kill it," he said, "but only if she can get at its underside. Otherwise, all it has to do is wait until it has a clear swing, and she's . . ." He shuddered. "I'll be lucky to find enough of her for a funeral. So what we have to do now, Colonel, is piss it off enough to give her a chance. Or" – he had to be fair; this was not Colonel Sanderson's job – "if you'll lend me your pistol, you don't have to stay."

She looked at him, her dark eyes very bright, and then she turned to look at the breeder, which was swinging its shapeless head in slow arcs, trying, no doubt, to track Mongoose. "Fuck that, Mr Irizarry," she said crisply. "Tell me where to aim."

"You won't hurt it," he'd warned her, and she'd nodded, but he was pretty sure she hadn't really understood until she fired her first shot and the breeder didn't even notice. But Sanderson hadn't given up; her mouth had thinned, and she'd settled into her stance, and she'd fired again, at the breeder's feet as Irizarry had told her. A breeding rath's feet weren't vulnerable as such, but they were sensitive, much more sensitive than the human-logical target of its head. Even so, it was concentrating hard on Mongoose, who was making toves scream at various random points around the circumference of the breeding pit, and it took another three shots aimed at that same near front foot before the breeder's head swung in their direction.

It made a noise, a sort of "wooaaurgh" sound, and Irizarry and Sanderson were promptly swarmed by juvenile raths.

"Ah, fuck," said Irizarry. "Try not to kill them."

"I'm sorry, try not to kill them?"

"If we kill too many of them, it'll decide we're a threat rather than an annoyance. And then it rolls up in a ball, and we have no chance of killing it until it unrolls again. And by then, there will be a lot more raths here."

"And quite possibly a bandersnatch," Sanderson finished. "But—" She batted away a half-corporeal rath that was trying to wrap itself around the warmth of her pistol.

"If we stood perfectly still for long enough," Irizarry said, "they could probably leech out enough of our body heat to send us into hypothermia. But they can't bite when they're this young. I knew a cheshire-man once who swore they ate by crawling down into the breeder's stomach to lap up what it'd digested. I'm still hoping that's not true. Just keep aiming at that foot."

"You got it."

Irizarry had to admit, Sanderson was steady as a rock. He shooed juvenile raths away from both of them, Mongoose continued her depredations out there in the dark, and Sanderson, having found her target, fired at it in a nice steady rhythm. She didn't miss; she didn't try to get fancy. Only, after a while, she said out of the corner of her mouth, "You know, my battery won't last forever."

"I know," Irizarry said. "But this is good. It's working."

"How can you tell?"

"It's getting mad."

"How can you tell?"

"The vocalizing." The rath had gone from its "wooaaurgh" sound to a series of guttural huffing noises, interspersed with high-pitched yips. "It's warning us off. Keep firing."

"All right," Sanderson said. Irizarry cleared another couple of juveniles off her head. He was trying not to think about what it meant that no adult raths had appeared in response to the breeder's distress. How far had they ranged through Kadath Station? How much of it did they consider their hunting grounds and was it enough yet for a second breeder? Bad questions, all of them.

"Have there been any disappearances lately?" he asked Sanderson.

She didn't look at him, but there was a long silence before she said, "None that seemed like disappearances. Our population is by necessity transient, and none too fond of authority. And, frankly, I've had so much trouble with the station master's office that I'm not sure my information is reliable."

It had to hurt for a political officer to admit that. Irizarry said, "We're very likely to find human bones down there. And in their caches."

Sanderson started to answer him, but the breeder decided it had had enough. It wheeled toward them, its maw gaping wider, and started through the mounds of garbage and corpses in their direction.

"What now?" said Sanderson.

"Keep firing," said Irizarry. Mongoose, wherever you are, please be ready.

He'd been about 75 per cent sure that the rath would stand up on its hind legs when it reached them. Raths weren't sapient, not like Cheshires, but they were smart. They knew that the quickest way to kill a human was to take its head off, and the second quickest was to disembowel it, neither of which they could do on all fours. And humans weren't any threat to a breeder's vulnerable abdomen; Sanderson's pistol might give the breeder a hot foot, but there was no way it could penetrate the breeder's skin.

It was a terrible plan – there was that whole 25 per cent where he and Sanderson died screaming while the breeder ate them from the feet up – but it worked. The breeder heaved itself upright, massive, indistinct paw going back for a blow that would shear Sanderson's head off her neck and probably bounce it off the nearest bulkhead, and with no warning of any kind, not for the humans, not for the rath, Mongoose phased viciously in, claws and teeth and sharp edged tentacles all less than two inches from the rath's belly and moving fast.

The rath screamed and curled in on itself, but it was too late. Mongoose had already caught the lips of its – oh gods and fishes, Irizarry didn't know the word. Vagina? Cloaca? Ovipositor? The place where little baby raths came into the world. The only vulnerability a breeder had. Into which Mongoose shoved the narrow wedge of her head, and her clawed front feet, and began to rip.

Before the rath could even reach for her, her malleable body was already entirely inside it, and it – screaming, scrabbling – was doomed.

Irizarry caught Sanderson's elbow and said, "Now would be a good time, very slowly, to back away. Let the lady do her job."

Irizarry almost made it off of Kadath clean.

He'd had no difficulty in getting a berth for himself and Mongoose – after a party or two of volunteers had seen her in action, after the stories started spreading about the breeder, he'd nearly come to the point of beating off the steelship captains with a stick. And in the end, he'd chosen the offer of the captain of the Erich Zann, a boojum; Captain Alvarez had a long-term salvage contract in the Kuiper belt – "cleaning up after the ice miners," she'd said with a wry smile – and Irizarry felt like salvage was maybe where he wanted to be for a while. There'd be plenty for Mongoose to hunt, and nobody's life in danger. Even a bandersnatch wasn't much more than a case of indigestion for a boojum.

He'd got his money out of the station master's office – hadn't even had to talk to Station Master Lee, who maybe, from the things he was hearing, wasn't going to be station master much longer. You could either be ineffectual or you could piss off your political officer. Not both at once. And her secretary so very obviously didn't want to bother her that it was easy to say, "We had a contract," and to plant his feet and smile. It wasn't the doubled fee she'd promised him, but he didn't even want that. Just the money he was owed.

So his business was taken care of. He'd brought Mongoose out to the Erich Zann, and insofar as he and Captain Alvarez could tell, the boojum and the Cheshire liked each other. He'd bought himself new underwear and let Mongoose pick out a new pair of earrings for him. And he'd gone ahead and splurged, since he was, after all, on Kadath Station and might as well make the most of it, and bought a selection of books for his reader, including The Wind in the Willows. He was looking forward, in an odd, quiet way, to the long nights out beyond Neptune: reading to Mongoose, finding out what she thought about Rat and Mole and Toad and Badger.

Peace – or as close to it as Izrael Irizarry was ever likely to get.

He'd cleaned out his cubby in the Transient Barracks, slung his bag over one shoulder with Mongoose riding on the other, and was actually in sight of the Erich Zann's dock when a voice behind him called his name.

Colonel Sanderson.

He froze in the middle of a stride, torn between turning around to greet her and bolting like a rabbit, and then she'd caught up to him. "Mr Irizarry," she said. "I hoped I could buy you a drink before you go."

He couldn't help the deeply suspicious look he gave her. She spread her hands, showing them empty. "Truly. No threats, no tricks. Just a drink. To say thank you." Her smile was lopsided; she knew how unlikely those words sounded in the mouth of a political officer.

And any other political officer, Irizarry wouldn't have believed them. But he'd seen her stand her ground in front of a breeder rath, and he'd seen her turn and puke her guts out when she got a good look at what Mongoose did to it. If she wanted to thank him, he owed it to her to sit still for it.

"All right," he said, and added awkwardly, "Thank you."

They went to one of Kadath's tourist bars: bright and quaint and cheerful and completely unlike the spacer bars Irizarry was used to. On the other hand, he could see why Sanderson picked this one. No one here, except maybe the bartender, had the least idea who she was, and the bartender's wide-eyed double take meant that they got excellent service: prompt and very quiet.

Irizarry ordered a pink lady – he liked them, and Mongoose, in delight, turned the same color pink, with rosettes matched to the maraschino "cherry." Sanderson ordered whisky, neat, which had very little resemblance to the whisky Irizarry remembered from planetside. She took a long swallow of it, then set the glass down and said, "I never got a chance to ask Spider John this: how did you get your Cheshire?"

It was clever of her to invoke Spider John and Demon like that, but Irizarry still wasn't sure she'd earned the story. After the silence had gone on a little too long, Sanderson picked her glass up, took another swallow, and said, "I know who you are."

"I'm nobody," Irizarry said. He didn't let himself tense up, because Mongoose wouldn't miss that cue, and she was touchy enough, what with all the steelship captains, that he wasn't sure what she might think the proper response was. And he wasn't sure, if she decided the proper response was to rip Sanderson's face off, that he would be able to make himself disagree with her in time.

"I promised," Sanderson said. "No threats. I'm not trying to trace you, I'm not asking any questions about the lady you used to work for. And, truly, I'm only asking how you met this lady. You don't have to tell me."

"No," Irizarry said mildly. "I don't." But Mongoose, still pink, was coiling down his arm to investigate the glass – not its contents, since the interest of the egg-whites would be more than outweighed by the sharp sting to her nose of the alcohol, but the upside-down cone on a stem of a martini glass. She liked geometry. And this wasn't a story that could hurt anyone.

He said, "I was working my way across Jupiter's moons, oh, five years ago now. Ironically enough, I got trapped in a quarantine. Not for vermin, but for the black rot. It was a long time, and things got . . . ugly."

He glanced at her and saw he didn't need to elaborate.

"There were Arkhamers trapped there, too, in their huge old scow of a ship. And when the water rationing got tight, there were people that said the Arkhamers shouldn't have any – said that if it was the other way 'round, they wouldn't give us any. And so when the Arkhamers sent one of their daughters for their share . . ." He still remembered her scream, a grown woman's terror in a child's voice, and so he shrugged and said, "I did the only thing I could. After that, it was safer for me on their ship than it was on the station, so I spent some time with them. Their Professors let me stay.

"They're not bad people," he added, suddenly urgent. "I don't say I understand what they believe, or why, but they were good to me, and they did share their water with the crew of the ship in the next berth. And of course, they had Cheshires. Cheshires all over the place, cleanest steelship you've ever seen. There was a litter born right about the time the quarantine finally lifted. Jemima – the little girl I helped – she insisted they give me pick of the litter, and that was Mongoose."

Mongoose, knowing the shape of her own name on Irizarry's lips, began to purr, and rubbed her head gently against his fingers. He petted her, feeling his tension ease, and said, "And I wanted to be a biologist before things got complicated."

"Huh," said Sanderson. "Do you know what they are?"

"Sorry?" He was still mostly thinking about the Arkhamers, and braced himself for the usual round of superstitious nonsense: demons or necromancers or what-not.

But Sanderson said, "Cheshires. Do you know what they are?"

"What do you mean, 'what they are'? They're Cheshires."

"After Demon and Spider John . . . I did some reading and I found a Professor or two – Arkhamers, yes – to ask." She smiled, very thinly. "I've found, in this job, that people are often remarkably willing to answer my questions. And I found out. They're bandersnatches."

"Colonel Sanderson, not to be disrespectful—"

"Sub-adult bandersnatches," Sanderson said. "Trained and bred and intentionally stunted so that they never mature fully."

Mongoose, he realized, had been watching, because she caught his hand and said emphatically, Not.

"Mongoose disagrees with you," he said, and found himself smiling. "And really, I think she would know."

Sanderson's eyebrows went up. "And what does Mongoose think she is?"

He asked, and Mongoose answered promptly, pink dissolving into champagne and gold: Jagular. But there was a thrill of uncertainty behind it, as if she wasn't quite sure of what she stated so emphatically. And then, with a sharp toss of her head at Colonel Sanderson, like any teenage girl: Mongoose.

Sanderson was still watching him sharply. "Well?"

"She says she's Mongoose."

And Sanderson really wasn't trying to threaten him, or playing some elaborate political game, because her face softened in a real smile, and she said, "Of course she is."

Irizarry swished a sweet mouthful between his teeth. He thought of what Sanderson had said, of the bandersnatch on the Jenny Lind wriggling through stretched rips in reality like a spiny, deathly puppy tearing a blanket. "How would you domesticate a bandersnatch?"

She shrugged. "If I knew that, I'd be an Arkhamer, wouldn't I?" Gently, she extended the back of her hand for Mongoose to sniff. Mongoose, surprising Irizarry, extended one tentative tendril and let it hover just over the back of Sanderson's wrist.

Sanderson tipped her head, smiling affectionately, and didn't move her hand. "But if I had to guess, I'd say you do it by making friends."

PARADISO LOST

Albert E. Cowdrey

Albert E. Cowdrey quit a government job to try his hand at writing. So far, his work has appeared almost exclusively in *The Magazine of Fantasy and Science Fiction,* usually with darkly comic supernatural horror stories, many of them taking place in a New Orleans haunted by demons and dark magic. In 2000, he took a sudden, unexpected turn away from horror and into science fiction, producing two of the year's best science fiction novellas, *Crux* and its sequel, *Mosh,* which were expanded in 2004 into a novel called *Crux.* Although the bulk of Cowdrey's output remains fantasy, he continues to turn his hand occasionally to science fiction as well, with results that make readers wish he'd do it more often, as he did a few years back with "The Tribes of Bela," or as he does here with "Paradiso Lost," a prequel to "The Tribes of Bela," and also a pure-quill old-fashioned science fiction adventure story that takes the reader along on a military transport ship headed for a recalcitrant colony planet, and bearing with it a cargo of secrets and deceptions, most of them deadly. . . .

A reluctant refugee from Hurricane Katrina, Cowdrey now lives in Natchez, Mississippi.

D EAR JESÚS SON of Jesús!
   I've been reading the letter you left on my omni. Yes, I knew your father well, and yes, he died far too soon. And I'll be happy to tell you my memories of him, provided you're ready to get an earful.

Looking at the hologram you sent along with the text, so many things come back to me. I see the guy I used to square off with in martial arts training at the Academy, when we were both ridiculously young. Also the guy I went into space with, on my first voyage out of our customary world and universe.

Well, I'm in my anecdotage now, and for the moment all alone and ready to talk. My wife Anna's in China, seeing to some ancient relatives who need assistance. I'm left here at Manypalms Oasis in the Great American Desert – generally a good place to live, but not in August! 48 bloody degrees outside, enough to fry a scorpion. Makes me think of Planet Bela in its summertime, though fortunately ours doesn't last for half a century. When the housebot serves me a cool drink made with pears and mangoes, I say politely, "This is excellent, Tycho," because it's programmed to repeat actions it gets compliments on, and I need all the liquid intake it can provide.

So I'll sip quietly and remember bygone adventures and talk into my omni, and you can read the result whenever you're not too busy helping to govern Luna. I hear rumors that one day you'll be a Councilor of State and a maker of history. Well, tuck this away in your memory, as a warning of how hard history can be on the innocent.

The story really began before your Papa and I were born.

A cult had been launched by an Italian mystic who called himself Innocente, under the name Scala d'Amore, or Ladder of Love. Innocente taught that love can rise from the gross and carnal to the sublime and universal. That made his doctrine a good vehicle for everything from orgies to sainthood, and brought in a nice wide spectrum of believers. For a little while the cult flourished like mushrooms after rain.

Its symbol was the DNA molecule (which does look a bit like a ladder, or maybe a double spiral staircase) inside a crystal sphere. All parts of the icon had prodigious meanings, if you chose to see them. The sphere meant unity, the crystal meant clarity, the molecule was the ladder of life and consequently of love. For a while, women wore them on charm bracelets and men hung them around their necks on chains. Temples sprouted in every city with the icon on top lighted up at night. Like God it was ubiquitous – or else omnipresent, I forget which.

Its popularity made it a lightning rod for controversy and even violence. Established religions did not fail to notice that it was taking believers away from them, and persecution followed in various parts of the world. The government (as its habit is) decided to blame the victims, and show trials followed, with some cult members accused of outlandish sexual practices and plotting sedition. Pontius Pilate would have grasped the situation in a flash.

That was when Innocente announced that he and a select group of followers called the Seven Hundred were leaving Earth to prepare a refuge for all true believers in the depths of space. Like other mystics he claimed paranormal powers – prevision and clairvoyance – and he foresaw wonderful things for his colony. Skeptics said he was taking his followers someplace where he could control them better. Not an unknown ploy for cult leaders, by the way!

Well, at that time the Council of State was promoting emigration for a number of reasons, one of which was to rid the Earth of potential troublemakers, including religious fanatics. (The kings of England had the same idea when they invited the Puritans to go the hell to America and stay there.) Innocente and his 700 disciples – actually 642; some had second thoughts and dropped out – were quickly granted visas and transported to a system identified as H2223 in the New Catalog. They were deposited on the third or gamma planet, which Innocente hopefully renamed Paradiso, there to live or die by their own resources and a pile of supplies that were dumped with them.

The planet was not prime real estate. Prime real estate was reserved for mining and military colonies. Paradiso had no moon, and the system was meager – closer to the sun were two cinders called alpha and beta, and farther away two remote gasballs named delta and epsilon. Plus the usual ash and trash, some interesting comets that visited at intervals of centuries, and leftovers of unconsolidated or destroyed planets that gave periodic meteor showers of uncommon brilliance.

The planet had almost the mass of Neptune, though as a solid body it was much smaller. The high gravity must have required some serious adaptations by local life forms, and cartoonists had a field day showing colonists shaped like bowlegged gnomes trying unsuccessfully to climb the Ladder of Love. While the believers were settling down, Innocente died of coronary artery disease (maybe related to the increase in gravity?) and was succeeded by his son, who also claimed to possess paranormal powers.

Then Earth lost contact, as a series of skirmishes began in the same general neighborhood with unknown but well-equipped assailants. Dignified by the title of the First Alien War, the fighting went on and off (mostly off) for forty-four standard years. You may recall from history classes that we didn't do too well, although we did manage to smash one of their ships with a faster-than-light missile, or FTLM. A boarding party spent enough time poking through the wreckage to bring back tissue samples which showed that the aliens weren't one species, they were at least five, and – unlike the so-called Cousins of Planet Bela – not even closely related.

Maybe they were all living in symbiotic harmony (the nice theory) or maybe four of them had been enslaved by the fifth (the nasty theory). Anyway, for lack of any idea what they might call themselves, hostile journalists called them collectively the Zoo, and cartoonists showed them as a cageful of bizarre monsters.

That capture was our sole achievement. In return we lost some very expensive ships and several hundred highly trained members of the Space Service. More cautious Councils of State then adopted a policy of Retrenchment – pulling back colonists from the dangerous region in order to strengthen closer and more defensible worlds. (This time it was the Emperor Hadrian who would have nodded his wise old head and muttered Sic transit, or something.) Ill-feeling toward the Ladder of Love had declined because, in the absence of its leader, the cult itself had withered on both Terra and Luna, and was no longer seen as a threat. So the Council dedicated a single starship (the big old *Zhukov*) to the task of relocating the folks on Paradiso, and preparations for the expedition began.

While all this history was going on, your Papa and I got ourselves born and grew into the kind of strong, adventurous, and dumb youngsters for whom the Services always have an appeal. Then as now, the Security Forces had their own troops to suppress rebellions, plus a police side to attack crime – sort of like the old Russian Interior Ministry, only not quite as nasty. We chose the

Albert E. Cowdrey

military side, and together completed basic and advanced officers' training and received our shoulder straps and the right to be saluted by serfs of our own calling. I was senior to him by nine minutes or so, because the roster at graduation was alphabetical and K for Kohn, Robert came before M for Morales, Jesús. We'd become friends while knocking each other around in martial arts classes and chasing women on leave, and that was a comfort because our first assignment looked to be a tough one.

The running of the Zhukov was the business of the Space Service, but overall command of the expedition had been vested in a Security Forces general, Colonel-General Schlacht. He was supposed to corral and ride herd on the colonists who, it was felt, might be somewhat unhappy over being uprooted from a place they'd lived for several generations. Schlacht had a reputation for eating junior officers alive, preferably after first dipping them in hot sauce, so Morales and I were less than thrilled when we were assigned to command the two infantry platoons that were going along to police the repatriated colonists.

"So young to die," sighed your Papa. Only of course he didn't quite say that. In training we'd learned that words are merely loose gravel until glued together by the mortar of obscenity. You should imagine him actually saying, "*#%&!! So *#%& young to *#%& die!"

I couldn't have agreed more.

We met the General on Orbital Station One, where many years later I had some interesting experiences. The Big Wheel, as everybody called it then, was in fine trim on that first visit, no monks as yet but lots of scientists – white lab coats instead of white habits – plus all sorts of people in transit from here to there. As usual, Basic English was everybody's second language, and the place resounded with a Babel of accents, including ours. We saw military types sporting flashy uniforms and civilians wearing a variety of dumb getups (balloon pants and formal T-shirts and lacquered wigs were in that year, for both men and women). We had time to gaze down at the blue ball of the Earth while getting a bite in the military canteen, and at the remainder of our very large universe over coffee in the Darkside Lounge. Then our omnis started squealing, and we were invited to haul our butts to the General's office soonest.

I didn't have much time to get to know Schlacht, for reasons I'll explain later, and I never developed any warmth of feeling for him. But I have to admit he was impressive – roughly 2 meters high and 80 centimeters wide, with a face resembling a water buffalo beset by biting flies, all frowns and snorts and bristling mustaches. His hair was white, untidy, and too abundant – totally unmilitary – and sent the message that while scum like Morales and me had to worry about regs, he didn't. Same message from his shoulder straps. He was authorized seven stars but wore none, because he didn't need little bits of shiny metal to tell people how godawful important he was.

For what seemed like half an hour he sat in silence, gazing at us with evident loathing, and then spoke in a kind of hoarse bellow. "So you characters are supposed to be my platoon leaders."

While we were yelling, "Yes, sir!" in parade-ground style, he perused a printout and when quiet had been restored, grunted, "Morales and Kohn. Jesus and a Jew."

"Sir, my name is pronounced Hayzoose," said your Papa bravely.

"As far as I'm concerned, Mister, your name is pronounced Crap. That's mierda, in case you have trouble with English."

After that the interview went rapidly downhill. About an hour later, Jesús and I were having several stiff drinks in the Officers' Lounge while waiting for our ears to stop burning.

"Well," he said at last, "I guess we know where we stand with the *#%& General."

I answered that it seemed we'd embarked on a rough voyage. Luckily, as yet neither of us had a clue just how rough.

Via a lighter, we boarded the *Zhukov* a couple of days later. It belonged to what was called the Alexander class of starships, which were almost round only not quite, oblate spheroid I think is the term. All the vehicles were named for famous generals and admirals, so there was a Sun Tzu and a Saladin and a Caesar and a Nelson and I don't know who else. They were supposed to be virtually indestructible, with triple hulls of nuclear steel and all kinds of redundancies built in to make them "structurally impervious." A piece of human chutzpah, I might add, properly punished when three of them were blown up by enemy FTLM's during the First Alien War.

Now the reconditioned *Zhukov* was being used to shuffle colonials around, mainly because it was so big you could crowd a lot of folks into it if you only allowed them 1.5 cubic meters apiece, or about as much space as a large refrigerator. *Zhukov* was, by the way, still well armed, with four Alpha-class cold-fusion missiles and a particle-beam generator, because it was going into a dicey region where close encounters of the worst kind remained a possibility.

Schlacht granted Morales and me about twenty minutes to get settled in the cupboard euphemistically called our stateroom, and then ordered us to get to work and start harassing our underlings. He communicated with us through a small chromed sphere in the ceiling of our quarters that produced an incredible amount of noise for its size. We called it the Bitch Ball. So we were thundered at to get our backsides to the barracks compartment soonest, where our leader awaited us, along with his alter ego, a dwarf.

Yes, a dwarf. Big head, disproportionately long body, short bowed legs, small hands and tiny fingers. Probably spinal problems, the way he walked, lurching along. He wore some kind of nondescript clothes, had corrugated reddish skin and a pair of very intent dark eyes. On the rare occasions when Schlacht addressed him, he called him Cos, to rhyme with loss. As soon as the very odd pair departed, Morales named them Cos and the Boss; later on, when we really got to hate the general, he renamed them the Pig and the Pygmy.

At first I thought that Schlacht traveled with his own court jester. But Cos didn't seem to make jokes or do pratfalls or anything of that kind. In fact, he hardly ever said a word, and yet whenever the Pig hove into view to make our lives a mite more difficult, there the Pygmy appeared also, giving us a fixed expressionless stare like a cuttlefish.

In their absence we settled down to work, getting to know the thirty-five guys of each platoon. There's some kind of unwritten rule in the services that one example of every human type must appear in every unit, however small. I had people so clean I couldn't catch them with dirt under their fingernails, and others so opposed to sanitation that their comrades had to throw them under a shower and scrub them down with brushes to deodorize them. I had guys and gals, I had homs and hets, I had thugs and sissies, I had drunks and drys, I had semi-morons and one offbeat Lawrence-of-Arabia type genius named Sosa who, for unknown reasons, preferred to live in the lower depths of the enlisted service, and turned down a promotion when I offered him one.

Morales's platoon was the same, only totally different. That's how the human animal is – all specimens different, all the same, sort of like snow-flakes, only not as pretty.

My sergeant was a big Irishman named O'Rourke, Morales's a small but dangerous kickboxer called Chulalongkorn. Vastly different physical types, but indistinguishable in courage, cleverness, and utter amorality. From them I learned that sergeants form a subspecies and that officers, especially ignorant shavetails like us, are damn lucky to have them around to tell us what to do.

While the Zhukov got under way – I didn't notice when we started to move; there was hardly a grunt or a quiver from the engines – we were spending our time in the Armory, a dimly lighted region that stank unmerci-fully of sweat, graphite, and machine oil. First we watched the sergeants guide the serfs in digging our weapons consignment out of packing cases, cleaning off the shipping gunk, assembling and disassembling and reassem-bling and polishing them up nice and pretty. Then we locked the weapons into racks, so that nobody could grab one to settle a conflict with a comrade over ownership of an interactive comic book or the favors of a "douche," meaning one of the several barracks whores who fattened their incomes by bartering sex for pay.

(Why were they called douches? Because "they get your tail wet." Military humor.)

When everything had been racked up and locked away, Morales and I had about ten minutes to put on dress uniforms for the big social event of the day, dinner with the rest of the cadre. Except for the General and Jesús and me, who wore Security gray, all the officers showed up in the blue togs of the Space Service. As the highest ranker present, the Pig presided at the head of the table. The pilot, Colonel Delatour, sat at his right, the celestial naviga-tor at his left, then the fire control officer, the chief engineer, the surgeon, and all the rest lined up in descending order of importance as defined by the Table of Ranks, down to Jesús and the Jew, with Cos the dwarf seated between us at the foot of the table.

Conversation was constrained, as you might suppose, because the General didn't converse, he issued communiqués, and the only person who dared to disagree with him was Colonel Delatour, a shrewd-looking fortyish Frenchwoman with short bleached hair who liked to tell him in the politest possible way what an ass he was. Thus, when he opined that Newton's third law of motion sounded like bullcrap to him, she murmured, "I'm sure you could make the universe operate in a much more plausible way than it does, General, if only you had the opportunity."

What did she care? The ship couldn't function without her, and anyway she wore blue and was only on temporary duty under the roaring wind machine seated at her left.

So our ill-assorted little community rushed headlong into the void, as the human species has a habit of doing. Most of the ship was empty, of course, ready to absorb the colonists. But soon Schlacht started us exploring every cubic meter of it, because – I didn't know why at the time – he'd become convinced that we had a stowaway aboard.

The chief engineer began the search by closing the hundreds of safety doors that subdivided the ship's interior to localize damage in case the hull was breached. Then we set out, walking like flies on sticky feet, because the coils of the pseudograv system ran through the decks which consequently were always "down."

Making little popping sounds at every step, we prowled the semidark compartments one by one, Morales and I and O'Rourke and Chulalongkorn and our nervous young charges, all of us looking for the Stowaway – we started capitalizing the word in our thoughts – or other unauthorized inhabitants.

Well, we didn't find any. But all the exploring at least gave us a picture of the Zhukov from inside. Christ, what a maze. Cavernous storage spaces near the hull, cold as hell, shadowy, vast. Scary in a way. Supplies shrouded in transplast covers, with Jack Frost patterns going jaggedly this way and that where moisture had gotten trapped inside and frozen. Then half-moon-shaped areas, barracks when the ship carried a full expeditionary force, with racks for bedding stacked four high and folded back against the bulkheads and locked in place. Empty latrines. Odd little rooms with drains in the floors – sickbays, I guessed. Connecting everything were narrow corridors, narrow ladders, narrow slider ramps, and small elevators sealed into tubes with locked doors at every level.

Running up the center of the ship from south pole to north pole was a nuclear-steel cylinder containing the standard-drive engines and the dark-energy generator and the life support machinery, all controlled from a mainframe computer sealed in a pod to which only the pilot, the celestial navigator, and the chief engineer had access. The heavy weapons occupied a sort of Arctic Circle – a doughnut-shaped region around the North Pole – with the topmost section of the central cylinder containing the particle-beam generator. Twenty steel silos lined the Arctic Circle's outer bulkhead, four of them containing the Alpha missiles, the others empty. Fire control was managed by a big gleaming chunk of artificial intelligence also sealed into a pod, to which only the fire control officer had access.

That was the Zhukov as we came to know it. Enormous, enormously complex, insanely powerful, and absolutely barren. An image of the modern world, perhaps?

At first I thought Schlacht would gradually calm down and start acting human. But in that I was wrong.

As day after day went by – I mean, of course, the alternations of lights-on and lights-out – without anybody discovering our Stowaway, he got madder and madder and roared louder and louder. The result was that Morales and I stopped being afraid of him. When a volcano erupts once, it's hard not to be impressed, but the three or four hundredth time, you figure, What, again?

Once or twice he threatened us with his fists, and I quietly resolved that if he hit me, I'd deck him and screw the consequences. Your Papa wasn't nearly as big as me, but he had his black belt too, and he told me he'd already picked Schlacht's Adam's apple as his first target. I asked why.

"Even if I don't kill him, he'll have to shut up when I smash his *#%& vocal cords," Jesús explained.

The blowup we were all waiting for came one day when the General was observing a personal-weapons training session. One of my guys was field-stripping a shoulder-fired missile launcher when he developed butter-fingers and dropped the pieces. They scattered all over the deck, clanging and tinkling, and the General stepped forward and slapped him so hard it made echoes.

Well, nobody was going to attack my people, especially not some son of a whore who knew they couldn't hit back. I stepped between them, right fist closed, murder in my heart, and he swung back the same hand to use it on me. And then didn't. We stood there, glaring and growling, and then to my surprise he lowered his hand, turned on his heel, and stomped away, followed by his shadow, Cos.

With that, some of the tension went out of the ship. Morales gave me a big abrazo. My platoon practically kissed my feet because I'd stood up for them and faced down the General doing it. Even Schlacht seemed to have learned something. That evening at dinner he treated me with mini-mal courtesy, and afterward he stayed more in his stateroom and yelled less when he was outside it. You never know how things will work out, do you?

A night or so later we got the inside story of the episode. I was in the canteen having a beer with Morales, when in lurched Cos. He looked espe-cially small and lonely and rather lost. After all, he was odd man out on the ship, a civilian among all the uniforms, a little guy among all the big ones. Nobody really knew him except the General, so he had nobody to drink with, because Schlacht drank alone.

I invited Cos to join us, not just to be nice but because I was curious about what he was doing here. I waited until he'd poured a couple of half-liters of Pilsener into his inadequate body, then started asking him casually about himself. Turned out that, like most isolated people, he was bursting to talk. We got a barrage of information: about his physical condition (scientific name achondroplasia) and about the problems of growing up small. About how his parents had kept him at home to protect him from the big bad world; and how, when he was fifteen, he'd run away and joined a circus.

"A circus," I said in a neutral voice.

"It wasn't a freak show."

"That's not what I was thinking," I protested.

"That's exactly what you were thinking. But it's not true, I had my own act. Mind reading. My ESP rating is off the charts."

I asked him if that meant he heard everything everybody was thinking all the time. He said of course not.

"It's spotty, just like any other sensory system. You make judgments unconsciously, filter out things that don't seem important. And you get distracted and you get weary and you get confused. Still, all in all, I'm good at what I do. The general saw my act in New Vegas and hired me to sit in the next room while he was playing nine-card stud and tell him what the other players were seeing in their hands through a mike the size of a peppercorn he'd had installed in his inner ear. He won a lot of money, so he got me a clearance and put me on full retainer to do the same thing during staff meetings at Security HQ.

"Wow, did I get an earful! You'd be amazed, all those high-rankers, how much time they spend plotting against one another. I was really shocked."

"Why were you shocked?" asked Morales. "Everybody knows they're like that."

"You got to remember, Jesús, his parents protected him from the world," I put in.

"Oh, yeah. I guess that would make anybody kind of naive. So what do you do for our maximum leader here on the Zhukov?"

"Same thing. He's gotten in the habit of listening in on other people's thoughts. Few days ago I warned him to back off that confrontation with you," he said, nodding to me. "I told him you were ready to kill him. He's not a coward, but he's not a fool either. You're as big as he is, and you've got forty years on him, so he backed off.

"And of course," he added casually, "I've been telling him about the Stowaway."

"The one we can't find."

"That really browns him off. There's somebody aboard this ship who shouldn't be here, and they're hostile to him. Really hostile."

"They meaning more than one?"

"They meaning either he or she, I don't know which. It's all this nuclear steel," he complained. "It's baffling. Even ordinary metal's bad enough, it tends to short out whatever kind of frequency ESP exploits. Assuming it's electromagnetic at all – the experts differ about that. But super-dense metals are even worse. Well," he said, knocking back the last of his third beer and sliding off his bar stool, "see you guys later. Laughable as it sounds, I need my beauty sleep."

When he'd gone, Morales and I just sat there, looking at each other, both of us thinking, What have I gotten myself into?

"A telepathic dwarf," he said, starting to count our ship's oddities. "A demented general officer. A hostile and apparently invisible Stowaway. Seventy enlisted people who include thugs, jack-offs, cretins, geniuses, sergeants, and whores. Armament enough to obliterate two or three civilizations. Have I missed anything?"

"Us," I said.

"Oh yeah," he said. "And us."

Well, Jesús, when two guys live as close as your Papa and I did, they start acting like a married couple. It's called bonding.

You get to know what your roommate's going to say before he says it. You hate the way he snorts and grunts in his sleep, and then one night when he's away you can't sleep at all, because he's not there snorting and grunting. You bicker over incredibly minor things. Morales almost drove me crazy speculating about the nature of pseudograv – was it electrostatic, or what? I was more like Sherlock Holmes, who didn't give a damn whether the Sun went around the Earth or the Earth went around the Sun, because it had nothing to do with his work. I told Jesús he wasn't qualified to speculate about technical stuff, or to understand it even if somebody explained it to him. He told me I was lucky to be free of intellectual curiosity.

"Some of nature's most successful creatures totally lack it," he pointed out. "Just think of the cockroach."

So, waking, sleeping, working, bickering, Jesús and I bonded, all the more so because we were doing basically the same job and saw each other during the day as well as afterward. We discussed our problems, our ambitions, our hopes and dreams, and we formed an alliance against threatening outsiders, notably the General. Quite soon after boarding the *Zhukov*, we began to discuss ways of killing him.

This wasn't just a matter of revenge, though we both wanted that. We'd gotten to like and respect the pilot, Colonel Delatour. She seemed to be brave and rational and certainly less disruptive to the mission than Schlacht was. The problem was how to rid ourselves of our seven-star nutcase in some way that would look like an accident. After our talk with Cos, we started skipping dinner with the cadre whenever possible, worried that the dwarf might pick up on our thoughts. Although, as Morales pointed out, by this time there was so much ill-feeling against Schlacht that even the general's little extrasensory snitch might find it difficult to decide where all the death wishes were coming from.

Then, one night when we were lying on our bunks – Morales had the upper, I had the lower – conspiring against our leader in low voices, there emerged from the Bitch Ball, not his stentorian tones, but the cultured accents of Colonel Delatour.

"Lieutenant Kohn? Lieutenant Morales? Could I ask you to come to the bridge, please? It's rather urgent."

Morales leaned over the edge of his bunk and stared at me. I stared back. Since the politest words that had ever come from the gadget previously had been "DROP YOUR COCKS AND GRAB YOUR SOCKS!!" we knew, without being told, that something important must have happened.

On the bridge the whole cadre except for Schlacht had assembled, rubbing sleep from their eyes. Clothing was random and disordered, uniform coats over PJs, that kind of thing. A low background thrumming from the dark-energy generator meant that we were getting ready to enter that empty bubble universe we've all heard about, the place where good starships go when they exceed light speed.

At first I thought some kind of exotic technical foul-up must have occurred. But Colonel Delatour had a much more welcome and exciting message to deliver. In cool, bell-like tones, she greeted us with the words, "Good evening, gentlemen. General Schlacht has been murdered."

Morales and I stared at each other with, as a poet once put it, wild surmise. Each of us thinking, You crazy bastard, did you do it without telling me?

We were still standing there with mouths open when Delatour added, "I don't imagine that his loss will be much regretted, but the fact that we have a killer aboard has to be a matter of concern for all of us. Lieutenant Kohn, we need an acting security officer – will you please take on the job? Lieutenant Morales will assume command of your platoon as well as his own. Lieutenant Kohn, your first task will be to investigate General Schlacht's death."

You will notice that she didn't wait for me to agree to my new title and duties. When it comes to the military essentials, such as not giving a damn what your subordinates want so long as they do what you tell them, there is no difference between the Space Service and Security.

As for me, I took a deep breath, tried desperately to remember what I'd learned in the two or three criminal investigation courses I'd taken, and said in what I hoped was a calm, self-confident tone of voice, "Show me the body."

She led a parade into a crooked corridor that ended at the command suite. The corpus delicti was lying face down, fully uniformed, a few meters from its former stateroom door. Cos, like the faithful dog in sentimental stories, hunched over the body looking helpless and alone.

I tapped him on the shoulder and he moved dumbly aside. Our ex-leader appeared undamaged except for a vast pool of blood that had gushed from his nose and mouth. Ribbons of clotting had already appeared, so the corpse was not perfectly fresh. I tugged at one arm and it was supple, but the rictus on his face when it came partly into view suggested that incipient rigor had already begun. The time line was dubious, because different bodies act differently, and the interior of the ship was kept cool at ten degrees.

I called Morales and together we turned him over. His wide bemedalled front was sopping red. The surgeon – a doc named Gannett – peeled back his shirt, did some swabbing with a handful of paper towels, and revealed a neat little hole drilled through his breastbone.

The General had been shot by a small-caliber impact weapon, say a 3.8-mm – not a military size. The bullet hadn't been powerful enough to go completely through him, which explained why the usual gaping exit wound was absent. It had exploded inside, probably trashing a bunch of crucial organs plus the aorta. After he fell, a tsunami of blood had poured out through the largest available vents, squirting up the esophagus and windpipe.

"Well, I suppose I'll have to do a P.M.," said Gannett, a large, glum man. "Although the cause of death is pretty obvious." He sighed, perhaps yearning for a more interesting corpse to do his Y-incision on.

Meanwhile I started asking questions. Politely – everybody except Cos was either Sir or Ma'am to me. Who'd found the body? Cos, naturally. He'd been asleep in his cubicle near the General's palatial quarters when a terrible scream woke him up. Since nobody else had heard anything, I figured the dwarf's talented subconscious had chosen this way to alert him that something was extremely wrong.

Attired only in his underpants, Cos stumbled into the corridor and fell over the body. Instead of calling for help, he went a bit berserk, wringing his hands and moaning and running up and down like a chicken with its head off, leaving tiny bloody bare footprints all over the deck. After a while he came back, hoping for some signs of life, but the General was still dead.

Then Cos sensed the Stowaway approaching. Scared now for his own hide, he ran back to his cubicle and hid under the bunk. Only when his private alarm system went quiet did he venture out again and wake the surgeon and lead him back to the body. More fooling around ensued, with the surgeon sending him for the pilot, the pilot sending him for the navigator, and then the rest of the senior officers being awakened in order of rank. Sounded just like the arrangement at the dinner table. Of course Morales and I had been the last to know. Meanwhile, Cos – suddenly realizing that he was thinly clad and bloody – washed his feet and got dressed.

Summing up the situation with the quiet courtesy for which I am famous, I told the cadre, "You people are the biggest bunch of silver-plated, anatomical assholes I've come across in some time."

No, I didn't actually say that. Only thought it. Instead, I expressed regret that things had been so inefficiently handled, and asked the surgeon to take charge of the body and do any forensic tests that might still be possible, given the lapse of time and the corruption of the crime scene by all the people who ought to have known better than to tromp around in it. I sent Morales to bring O'Rourke, our oldest and nastiest sergeant, and have him and six armed guards of his choosing secure the area and start searching for the weapon – not that I expected to find it.

By this time everybody was looking relieved. They were rid of Schlacht, Delatour was in command, and the Space Service was where it belonged, running the expedition. As for us two grayback shavetails, we were now doing the only thing the Security Service was good for, investigating a crime. So they all felt better, erroneously believing that somebody trained for the job (me) had taken charge of the dirty work. Besides, the Zhukov was going into the Bubble within twelve hours, and they had work to do.

Everybody dispersed, some to bed and some to the bridge. Meantime I took Cos into the command suite, sat him down in one of the general's comfortable chairs, and asked him quietly to tell me who'd done the killing. I mean, you got a telepath around, why not use him?

The guy was emotionally almost terminal, so before I could learn anything I had to find Schlacht's supply of brandy – quite a supply, about 200 liters packed away in closets and cupboards, giving me a new insight into his peculiar behavior – and get Cos to swallow a finger or two of five-star in the bottom of a tumbler. He coughed and choked and I patted him on the back.

"Now come on, buddy," I said, "tell me who killed the General."

I would have been perfectly unsurprised if he'd named anybody on board, including me – after all, I'd had murder in my heart, and he knew it. Instead he gave me an anguished look and said, "Isn't it obvious?"

Well, I couldn't bash a little guy only about as long as my leg. So, restraining myself, I said, "Not to me."

"I mean, look," he said querulously. "The blood was still pouring out of the General when I found him. So he'd just been shot. I had to get the others up, and I saw them all waking up, and they were really waking up, I'll swear to that. I could sense their conscious selves coming out of the fog of sleep. So they weren't involved. But when I was hiding from the Stowaway, I picked up his thoughts. Great Tao, they were scary! No words, just emotions – waves of rage and joy, a kind of ferocious ecstasy, like a predator that's just taken down its kill."

"So the Stowaway did it."

"Yes."

"The Stowaway we can't find."

"Yes."

"Did you get a look at him? I mean, clairvoyantly."

"No. If there was an exterior image, it was overwhelmed by the stuff coming from inside him. All I could sense was what he was feeling."

I suppose he was still too upset to read my mind, because if he had he would've heard me thinking along these lines: There isn't any Stowaway. I know because I've looked for him. On the other hand, Cos found the body. Handling a three-point-eight is well within his physical capability, and he had time to hide the weapon because he took forever to rouse the ship. And when he was describing the Stowaway's mood after the killing, wasn't it so vivid because those emotions were really his own?

True, motive was a problem. I couldn't think offhand of any reason for him to kill Schlacht. But who knew what kind of insults he'd had to endure – or for that matter, what kind of physical abuse? I didn't have enough on him to justify an arrest, but I had enough to make me very suspicious.

I'd learned in criminal investigation classes to be real, real nice to anybody I had my eye on – disarms them, you know? So I patted Cos on the shoulder, told him to visit the dispensary and get some tranquilizers, and tentatively put him at the top of my list of suspects. Further down the list was everyone else on board, except Jesús and me. I excluded myself only because I knew I hadn't done it, and Morales only because he occupied the upper bunk and couldn't have left our stateroom without my hearing it.

That left nineteen officers and seventy enlisted. Any one of them might have acted alone, and almost any combination of them might have acted together. I was brooding about that when Sergeant O'Rourke hove into view. He was a thick-bodied man, so top-heavy he leaned forward when he walked, and his little gray eyes were gleaming with intelligence and ill-will toward Cos, whom he'd often described as "that *#%& Schlacht's *#%& housepet."

"Thought you'd be innerested in this, Lootenant," he growled. "Found it in the Pygmy's quarters, stuck with wax to a leg of his bunk."

He extended a ham-sized fist whose back was covered with reddish fur and dropped into my palm a small crystal sphere containing a model of the DNA molecule.

We looked at each other, then at the icon. Then back at each other. This was the first time I'd thought of the possibility that a Ladderite might have maneuvered himself aboard the Zhukov to help rescue the other disciples in space, and it gave me, as the French say, furiously to think.

I was just beginning to toy with the idea of true believer(s) on the ship, when a robot's cool tones instructed everybody aboard except the pilot and celestial navigator to return to their staterooms and strap themselves down. I handed the icon back to the sergeant.

"You know what to do with this?" I asked. He gave me a gold-toothed grin and said, "You go get buckled in, sir."

He ducked back into Cos's cabin to put the little crystal sphere back where he'd found it. No sense alarming my number one suspect unnecessarily.

This was my first time going into the Bubble, and frankly, it was kind of scary. I was already belted down to my bunk when Morales arrived, looking breathless, and climbed past me onto his own rack.

As we lay there waiting, he started to complain. "This is exactly why I didn't join the Space Service, even though they get all the gravy and

Security gets all the crap. I didn't want to leave my old familiar universe, you know? One universe is enough for anybody."

"I'm with you, pal. Oops, here we go."

It felt exactly like going over the top on the hundred-meter slider ramp at an amusement park, except I didn't have a bunch of hysterical people screaming in my ears. There was the same feeling that my internal organs had been left behind and might never catch up with the rest of me, and that the air formerly in my lungs had chased off somewhere in pursuit of my most recent meal.

The light from the ceiling fixture fractured as if a prism had passed in front of it. I had the bizarre sensation of seeing my surroundings somehow simultaneously red, green, blue, yellow, and a variety of colors I'd never seen before – greens that were also red, purples that were also black. Then everything steadied, my guts slid back into my abdominal cavity, air re-entered my lungs, and colors returned to more or less normal wavelengths. At the same time, everything stopped dead.

Absolute, total silence. The engines had shut off. The dark-energy generator which had given us that extra push was silent. We'd literally gone ballistic, moving on pure inertia – not a vibration anywhere in that whole huge ship. We were traveling at some fantastic velocity relative to our own universe through a kind of space where velocity doesn't exist, because you can only move relative to something else, and in the Bubble there is nothing else. To sum up, we were standing still while moving at maybe a thousand times the speed of light.

You go figure. I can't.

My only injury from the experience was a nosebleed. Blood ran down both sides of my face, responding to the ship's pseudograv. But the grav must have shut off for a second, because some drops that had drifted away as perfect crimson spherules suddenly got distorted and spattered down on the deck.

I heard Jesús groan and sit up. I made him aware of my injury, and he got me some ice and packed it in a towel that I held to my nose. While waiting for the bleeding to stop, I started reviewing evidence in my mind, and at some point quacked, "Y'know, Haythooth, Uh been thinkin'."

"That is unusual. So?"

I waited a bit longer, then put aside the bloody towel and said, "About the Stowaway. There are only two places on the Zhukov we haven't searched."

He meditated for a bit, and said, "The General's quarters and what?"

See, great minds do think alike. What better place for Big S to hide away than the General's quarters, now vacant? He could easily have slipped in while Cos was hiding in his own closet.

"Let's start there. If we don't find anything, we'll try the other place."

Just in case the Stowaway might be under the old bastard's bed, 3.8-mm in hand, Morales called in Chulalongkorn – known to both of us by this time as Chu – a short, bowlegged guy with obsidian eyes and death in both feet and karate-hardened hands. We selected sidearms from the armory and began going through the General's quarters, cubic centimeter by cubic centimeter.

We learned a lot about our former boss, certainly more than I'd ever wanted to know. Besides the brandy, of which we all partook quite abundantly, we found a collection of memory cubes. Most were official stuff stored dustily away in boxes, but one was dustless and inserted in the general's big cabinet omni. It was labeled Military Exercises, and for no special reason I turned it on.

Well, I wouldn't call it porn. Not good old porn – friend of the friendless, comforter of the aged, delight of the afflicted. Calling the general's pleasures porn was like calling a night with the Inquisition due process. This stuff was something I'd heard about but never seen – scenes of actual torture, real rape, including the rape of children. All, of course, in living color and four glorious dimensions, including time. And this had been Schlacht's relaxation.

We stared at it goggle-eyed for maybe ten minutes; until one particularly unpleasant sequence involving a girl of maybe thirteen seemed to be heading for a climactic snuff scene. Then we shut it off by unanimous consent. Chu said, "I always knew he was a shit, but – " He took the cube into the bath and flushed it down the vacuum toilet.

Continuing to search, we made another totally unexpected find. An antique printed book tucked under the General's pillow (and showing signs of heavy use) contained the poems of a Christian mystic called John of the Cross. In one poem marked with a star, the stigmatized saint yearned for union with Christ and lamented his own inability to die. "I'm dying that I cannot die" – I remember those words.

Well, it was hard to miss the implications. The most improbable person aboard had yearned to escape his own vileness by climbing the ladder of love – without, in my opinion, ever reaching the first rung. No wonder he lived in a drunken rage. He was his own prison, and couldn't get out.

That made two disciples that we knew about. How many more did we have on the *Zhukov*? I was brooding over this unanswerable query when Morales pointed out that we'd completed the search.

"No Stowaway here," Jesús said. "Where's the second place we haven't looked?"

I said, "We'll have to get what's-his-name, the fire control officer, up again. If we can't sleep, neither can he. We'll ask him politely to bring his keys, including the ones that unlock the elevator to the Arctic Circle. Then—"

"You do occasionally have a useful idea, Kohn," Morales admitted. "I see your point. We never checked inside those empty missile silos, did we?"

The fire-control officer was a wrinkled gray man named Major Janesco. (The J in his name, unlike the one in yours and your Papa's, was pronounced like Y.)

We found him wearing baggy gray pajamas, and most unhappy to be awakened just as he'd gotten back to sleep after the double upheaval caused by the murder and going into the Bubble. He grumbled his way back into his clothes while we waited.

"Who says there's a goddamn Stowaway?"

"Schlacht made a big issue of it."

"Schlacht's dead."

"That," I pointed out, "may be one good reason for thinking he was right."

"It was the dwarf," Janesco said. "Had to be. He's the only one who wasn't asleep. Why the hell don't you arrest him, instead of waking me up?"

"Sir, I'm prepared to arrest Cos five minutes after we satisfy ourselves that there's no Stowaway aboard."

He combed his sparse hair with maddening deliberation, gargled mouthwash, and finally led us, still grumbling, down the corridor to one of the locked tubes containing an elevator. He shoved two fingers into the recognition port and a flicker of intense light read the pattern of capillaries in his fingertips. Then he inserted the usual flat strip of an electronic key, and the curved door retracted and the three of us jammed into a small cylinder that quickly filled with the aroma of mouthwash.

Dim lights flicked on in the Arctic Circle as we stepped out. Arctic was a good name – the temp was, I would guess, about twenty degrees of frost. Our breath turned to cirrus clouds, and then to tiny ice crystals that settled to the deck as we went to work. Except for one service door, the particle-beam generator was solidly enclosed in its own cylindrical steel housing, and Janesco unlocked the door for me. It was even colder inside, but I made a quick circuit of the weapon, which looked like the projector in a planetarium. Nobody hiding there.

Then the missile silos. You may recall there were twenty, but only four in use. They were big nuke-steel cylinders more than two meters in diameter. We started to walk, clumping around the Arctic Circle on feet that were turning or had already turned to lumps of ice. Like the generator, each silo had a service port, and Janesco – who'd stopped cursing because, I suppose, even the warmest language froze in that icebox – opened them one by one. All but number twenty. One of the empties. Of course the suspicious silo couldn't have been number one, could it?

"Some moisture must've gotten in and sealed the gaskets," Janesco muttered.

That was the common-sense view, but common sense had never worked yet aboard the Zhukov, so I told Morales, "Lock and load."

When we had two impact weapons trained on the service port, I whispered, "One, two, three!" and together we roared, "OPEN UP! OPEN UP!"

No answer. I was getting colder and colder, and by now wanted to find out if we had the Stowaway cornered as quick as possible, just so we could get the hell out of the Arctic Circle. That was possibly why I made a truly lousy decision.

"Sir, I presume the silos are capped on the outside?"

"Obviously."

"Then," I yelled, "open the cap on number twenty!"

I really thought that threat would bring the Stowaway out, assuming there was a Stowaway, and not just some hoarfrost sealing the door. But nothing happened; the silence was total.

Janesco clumped to the command console and said the scientific-age equivalent of "Open, sesame." The console had a heating element inside; and after the cover lifted he stood there warming his hands like a guy in front of a stove on a chilly night. Then he leaned over and started muttering code, while the little round monitor screen flickered back at him.

"Open?" he asked me.

"Please, sir."

I wasn't prepared for the scream. In fact, I'd about decided Janesco had been right, that the silo was empty, that the Stowaway was a figment dreamed up by Cos to give him a scapegoat for whenever he decided to kill Schlacht. And then from inside the silo came suddenly this unearthly howl that went tailing off into a thin attenuated shriek. And then to nothing.

We all looked at each other. For a moment no smoke came out of our mouths, so I assume we'd all stopped breathing. In the silence the realization dawned that I'd just cracked my first case, at the price of killing the one and only person who could have told us why the murder happened – the Stowaway himself.

"Well," I muttered as we jammed ourselves back into the elevator, "I guess I won't arrest Cos after all."

After that we all went back to bed.

Ridiculous end to the most exciting night of my life up to that time, but I was tired, Jesús was tired, Janesco was tired. Schlacht was silent, permanently, and the Stowaway would be taking no more pot shots with his little gun. So what else was there to do?

I think we all slept a long, long time – I know I did.

Late next morning I reported to Colonel Delatour regarding the events of the night, then joined the remaining cadre at brunch. The enlisted people had already eaten, so we gave them the rest of the day off, since there really wasn't a damn thing for them to do anyway, and soon dice were rattling merrily on the deck of their quarters.

About the fifth cup of coffee, my brain finally began to function, and I asked Colonel Delatour, "Ma'am, how cold is it outside? I mean, is the Bubble's absolute zero absoluter than ours?"

She said no. Some things appeared to be common to both our universe and this one – Newton's third law, for one thing, much abused by the general. The absoluteness of zero Kelvin, for another.

"Only," she added, "it's easier to reach in the Bubble, because you don't have subatomic particles obstinately maintaining their harmonic oscillations, no matter how chilly they get. The exterior hull of the ship is considerably warmer, of course, maybe 20 Kelvin. Why?"

"With your permission. I have a great urge to get a look at whatever's left of the Stowaway."

Why? I wasn't sure. I doubted whether the corpse could tell me anything. Forensic studies would obviously be impossible. And yet . . . I just had to see. You know curiosity killed the cat, and in this case it came quite close to killing the Lieutenant as well. Colonel Delatour eyed me with what might have been concern, or maybe even compassion.

"Dying won't bring the fellow back, you know," she said quietly. "You didn't murder him. He could have surrendered."

"I don't intend to die," I assured her. "To take a risk, yeah." She nodded, even smiled a little. Maybe she liked risk takers.

"Since Zhukov's the only gravitating mass around, he'll presumably be following us," she said thoughtfully. "Maybe rotating around us, like our own little dead moon."

Morales seemed to get really twitchy when I reported this dialogue to him. "This is so *#%& weird!" he groused.

Nevertheless, he bravely volunteered to take the first spacewalk in the Bubble. Of course I said no. It was my show and my adventure. I knew that if the heater in my suit froze up, I'd be one more piece of debris circling the Zhukov, but I was young enough not to believe anything like that could actually happen to me. A lot of heroism, you know, is basically stupidity.

So a couple of hours later, I found myself being clamped into a device for which the term "space suit" was absolutely inadequate. It was actually a sort of steel keg where I sat cross legged, watching the world outside on a semi-cylindrical monitor screen and operating the limbs (you could have up to four legs and four arms attached) by fiddling with joysticks mounted on what looked like a miniature organ keyboard. I spent three, maybe four days practicing with the thing, up in the Arctic Circle, banging off walls and the particle-gun housing and turning myself every way but loose.

Then it was time to walk.

They put me out through the airlock, and I have to say that when push came to shove, I wasn't scared – I was terrified. Once when I was a kid, vacationing with my family on the southern rim of the Great American Desert, we took a side trip down into an immense cave. The place was a tourist attraction, had been for centuries, and it was all nicely lighted and the chambers equipped with phony names like "Aladdin's Castle" and the "Seas of Europa" and so on. Then, when we were really deep inside, the guide turned out the lights. That was the first time I'd ever experienced the totality of total darkness, and my throat got dry and my hands got clammy and I thought, Is this what death is like?

All that came back to me in the moment when my four mechanical feet clamped onto the hull and the airlock's outer door closed behind me. This was it. Would I drift away from the ship? Was there such a thing as magnetism out here? Did gravitation exist out here? Did anything exist out here?

Well, I stayed attached to the ship, and after a few seconds the bad feelings lessened, if only because it was obviously too late for second thoughts. Then a row of external lights, loading lights I suppose, went on, and I remembered to switch on a spotlight I carried on one of my many limbs. At first I thought it wasn't working because there was no ray, no beam, but then I saw the circle of light where the photons bounced off the ship. And off something else, too – a cylinder about twice the size of one of the internal missile silos. I couldn't think of anything it might be, except an FTLM that had its own exterior housing, because it was too big to go inside the ship.

Like some ungainly mechanical spider I crawled along *Zhukov's* curving frigid hull. Though my heater was whirring faster and faster, the air inside kept getting colder and colder. I picked up the percussion of my steel feet, uneasily aware that this was the only sound and the only heat and the only motion – I was moving relative to the ship – indeed the only anything in an entire goddamn vacant universe.

And then something else moved.

It was rising beyond the curved horizon of the hull with an infinitely slow yet observable movement, like the minute hand of an antique clock. Rising until it reflected a ghostly patch of light, just like the moon that Colonel Delatour had talked about. Only instead of a moon, it was a shapeless rigid bundle. It made me think of the fragile ash left by burned hardcopy that stays intact, even to the letters black against the brown pages, yet turns to powder at the first puff of wind. After maybe half a minute I realized that the bundle consisted of all the coats and blankets and whatnot the Stowaway had wrapped up in to survive the cold of the Arctic Circle. I turned my spot on it, and saw – set into the bundle, looking small and white – a rigid porcelain face.

For a little while I forgot the insidious cold creeping through my defenses of armor and artificial heat. Then made some kind of strangled sound, because the Stowaway had been a girl, a girl with a face that was thin and elegant. She'd frozen so deep so fast that her tissues had had no time to explode in the catastrophic loss of pressure that accompanied her ejection into the void. And I recognized her face.

I stretched out one of my mechanical arms and touched her, and her face turned to a fine crystalline dust. Then the whole bundle of what had been body and wrappings fell apart too, and the trail of debris very slowly passed like a thin comet of ice and ash out of my light and into the perfect darkness beyond.

Back inside the *Zhukov*, it took three people to extract me from the suit. I couldn't move my legs, and I spent a week in the dispensary being treated for pale, waxy spots denoting frostbite had developed on my fingers and toes and thighs and buttocks during my space walk.

That was lucky in a way, because I really needed the down time, not only to heal some frozen appendages, but to put my nerves back together. Every once in a while would-be heroes overestimate their own toughness. I'd badly overestimated mine.

Colonel Delatour took to visiting me. She avoided the usual dumb how're-you-feeling-soldier chat favored by superior officers for injured subordinates. We talked about a lot of things. At first I was inclined to look on her as a kind of female Methuselah because she was over forty. But exactly for that reason I could talk to her about matters I probably wouldn't have discussed with a woman my own age. Especially my feelings of guilt about the death of the Stowaway. That porcelain face haunted my dreams.

"So you'd actually seen her before," she marveled. "Quel miracle."

"Yeah. On a memory cube in the general's quarters. And then I saw her again, out there in the middle of nothing, a few years older but perfectly recognizable, and I touched her and she turned to dust and ice crystals and drifted away. What's left is still out there, orbiting around us."

She shook her head, and kind of absentmindedly took my left hand, I suppose because it was shaking, and held it with both of hers.

"You know," she said, speaking very quietly, "the Space Service keeps a lot of old naval traditions alive. We – oh, what's the English for faire des sottises – we go through a lot of foolishness about dress uniforms and being piped aboard and whatnot. I'm surprised we aren't issued cutlasses, just in case of pirates. We keep some of the old naval superstitions, too – for example, about lucky and unlucky ships. I'm beginning to think *Zhukov*'s unlucky, the things that have happened."

I was lying on a bunk at the time, wearing one of those dumb paper outfits they put on you, plus slip-on elastoplast tubes over my frostbitten digits. At some point, I don't remember exactly when, we'd agreed to be Robert (pronounced Robair) and Marie to each other, at least when we were alone.

Marie was sitting on a chair next to the bunk, close enough so I could detect a faint indefinable fragrance that I was pretty sure was not standard for Space Service officers. She was the first woman I'd been this close to in quite a while, except for my enlisted women, whom I was very properly forbidden to touch. Considering the automatic reactions taking place lower down my anatomy, I was glad a sheet covered me to the waist.

But I wasn't ready just yet to try my luck with a superior officer. I really had to ask a question that had been waking me up at 02.30 every morning when, in the dim nightlight, my sterilized surroundings looked especially blank and uncommunicative. I asked Marie if she could explain why the Stowaway hadn't answered when we were beating on her door, especially when she knew the silo was about to be opened and she was about to be blown into the void.

"Well, I can tell you what I think."

"S'il vous plaît," I said, using one of the three French phrases I knew.

"I think she'd done what she came aboard to do. Was she very young when you first saw her?"

I cleared my throat. "Terribly young."

"Then I suppose she'd been a child prostitute. C'est abominable, but it happens. So she tracked the general, who might have been one of her customers, maybe even her first customer, the one who paid a premium for the thrill of breaking her in. When she'd killed him, her work was done and she wanted to die. That's why you shouldn't blame yourself. You know, when somebody wants to die, it's entirely personal. If their mind's made up, nobody can stop them, and maybe nobody should try."

I was still thinking that over when she said, "You need to get warm."

She stood up and began to take off her uniform jacket. "We'll have to be discreet, of course," she added.

"Suppose somebody comes in?"

"Oh, I posted a bot as guard outside. There are advantages to being in command." She smiled. She finished undressing and threw back the sheet and lay down beside me.

So began my first liaison with a mythical creature I'd often heard about but never experienced – an Older Woman.

It was kind of a shipboard romance, you know, where the impermanence provides half the joy and all the poignance. After doing our separate duties all day, we had quiet nights together. Good sex. For me, a learning experience, as they say. Learning to take things slower. Learning to play the mouth organ properly. Learning some neat tricks I'd heard about but never tried before. Ligotage – the French have a word for it.

"The bindings, dearest, must always leave a mark," she instructed me.

But it wasn't all fun and games. Your boss doesn't cease to be your boss just because you're in bed with her. I had to endure Mama-knows-best comments like, "Sometimes, my darling, you are just a tiny little boy." (This was not a reference to my physical endowments, which have always been adequate. She was talking about my emotional immaturity, which in those days was a lot more than just adequate.)

I also heard a lot about the problems of a woman in what was still, after centuries of effort, mostly a man's world. Things I'd never imagined until then.

"A woman in command," she said, "has to be at least three times as tough as a man. Any hint of weakness is fatal. A male commander can be kind and forbearing, and everybody says, 'An officer and a gentleman!' A woman does the same thing, they think, 'Just another cunt,' and try to take advantage of her. A man can sleep around, or not; if he doesn't, he's got ethics, and if he does, he's a hell of a guy. But if a woman officer sleeps around they call her a whore, and if she doesn't they call her a lesbian."

She taught me some useful things about courage. "I remember one 'orrible little pustule I knew in officer training. He used to say, 'I'll hold a pot for the commander to piss in, but the instant his foot slips I'll empty it over his head.' Well, that awful little man lasted until the first real emergency, and then he was out. A bit of conniving is essential in our line of work, but it's no substitute for courage. After all, when you put on a uniform, you're proposing to live with danger."

"And then you need courage."

"And logic. In times of danger, only courage is logical."

I'd never looked at it that way before. Yet it's true – losing your head is no way to save your hide. Neither, she reminded me, is forgetting your comrades. "Sauve qui peut – every man for himself – is the prelude to annihilation. When everyone's trying to save himself, discipline collapses and everyone dies."

So I learned from her, things I enjoyed, things I needed to know, things I didn't especially want to know but learned anyway. There were also things I wanted to find out, but didn't. Once I mentioned seeing the FTLM housing on the hull and asked why we were carrying such a stupendous weapon on such a banal mission. She just said there were things she couldn't discuss, period. And that was that.

When she and I were a couple of months into our relationship, and the command suite had become as familiar to me as my cubicle had been, I asked her a question I'd been hesitating to voice ever since the night of our first coupling. It was a quiet, casual evening, when – as usual in the Bubble – nothing was going on. She was lacquering her fingernails at the time.

"Marie."

"Yes? Oh, I see. You've something weighty on your mind."

"I've been wondering, uh ... for some time now, uh ... how the Stowaway got herself into the *Zhukov*. Into the Arctic Circle. How she managed to move around the ship at night, with all the locked doors."

"Well," said Marie, "I assume she must have had an ally in the cadre."

I waited. Her hands didn't shake, didn't even quiver. Since she obviously wasn't going to elaborate, I had to stumble on.

"I'd like to know who her accomplice . . . her ally . . . was."

"Perhaps you don't want to know," she said. The lacquer went on with perfect smoothness. The color was no color – standard issue transparent.

"I don't?"

"No," she said.

Being young, I was about to say something else, when she raised her eyes from the job she was doing and stabbed me with a look that resembled a long, chilly steel dagger.

"You're right," I said hastily. "I don't."

Despite our efforts to be discreet, Jesús was not fooled about what was going on. Neither, it turned out, was anybody else. I'm pretty sure the romance between Marie and me was known to every human being on board within, say, eight hours of our first lovemaking. Once I asked Jesús what people were saying.

"The enlisted guys think it's great," he said. "They figure you've got an inside track with the commander, and what benefits you benefits them all. The blue-suiters aren't worried about you jumping over their heads for promotion or anything, because you're not Space Service, you're on a different totem pole. I'm delighted to have our stateroom all to myself, much as I used to enjoy listening to you snore and fart. So everybody's happy, including, I hope, you."

He grinned and punched me lightly on the shoulder. "Everybody likes you, Kohn, and they like her, and they like having the two of you to gossip about. Life in the Bubble is pretty dull, you know."

Marie's own attitude was cool and practical. When I mentioned the gossip mill to her, she said, "Bah, who cares? I'm the commander, and subject to regulations I do what I please. Still, it's nice to know that our shipmates find us entertaining."

She was right, of course. Life in the Bubble – your Papa's phrase – did tend toward tedium. There we were, eighty-nine sailors marooned together on, or rather in, a metal island surrounded by absolutely nothing. For recreation the enlisted guys had gambling, sex, liquor, and a few legal drugs like kif. For self-improvement they had classes on "Knowing Your Weapons," "Security Forces – Front and Center!" and other such rubbish. For training they practiced marksmanship in a simulator – beep zap, beep zap, beep zap, bing! All of us took karate lessons from Chu to keep in practice – thump, thump, "Kick him! Kick him!"

Officers and enlisted, we relaxed at meditation sessions with bowed heads, everybody breathing like tortoises. There were also formal religious services – I didn't attend, but in the corridors I'd see people fingering rosaries, though whether Christian, Muslim, or Buddhist, I didn't know. In the evening, before lights-out, I'd check the barracks a last time and find the guys sitting in darkness and watching feelies – the laser projectors humming, the virtual actors making love and war in four dimensions and looking a lot realer than the rest of us. "Darling, I shall always remember you, even on the far side of the stars!" Music, the end. Tough guys wiping away tears. The artless seduced by the illusion of art.

Since we were out of murder mysteries, I resumed command of my platoon, just to have something to fill the days. I joined them in the mornings for P.T., glad of a chance to use my muscles and keep fat at bay. In the shadowy and frigid storage spaces we practiced small-unit tactics, at which they were already fairly proficient. I never got chummy with them, that's not my style, but I was intrigued to see that Morales was able to become a pal to his people without losing control. Swapping foul jokes, drinking with them at the enlisted Happy Hour – you'd think he'd have forfeited their respect. But he didn't.

When I asked him about it, he told me, "My guys who speak Spanish call me Tío, Uncle. Your guys call you Dios, God. They know they can trust you, and yet you're out of reach. They think that's what God is like."

"You do talk a lot of crap, Morales."

"We're like the two American generals in the war with Mexico. The soldiers called one Old Fuss and Feathers because he always played by the book. They called the other Old Rough and Ready because he dressed like a peasant and paid no attention to the book. Both won their battles. The point is, either way can work if it's natural for you."

I'd never heard about a war between America and Mexico. "Who won?" I asked.

"Oh, the Americans did. Later on we got back at them, but it took us a couple of hundred years."

"Mexico conquered America?"

"In a way. Yes. In a way."

From Schlacht I inherited Cos. He needed somebody to attach himself to, and soon began bringing me tidbits of information.

"Sergeant Chu – did you know he comes from a criminal family? They're all pirates, except for him."

"Pirates?"

"In the Malacca Strait. They've been pirates there for centuries. They use a skimboat that goes hundreds of clicks an hour just above the waves. The Security Forces tried to stamp them out, but they've got good political connections in the world capital at New Angkor, so Security had to let them go and even return their boat."

"What do Chu's relatives think about him joining the Forces?"

"He's the black sheep of the family. He can never go home."

"Who told you all this?"

"Nobody told me. I just know."

One day Cos warned me about an impending fight in my platoon over one of the most popular douches. Just to test him, I showed up in the barracks compartment at midnight, routed out O'Rourke, and held a shakedown. In the laundry bags of two guys we found enough brass knuckles and knives to start a minor war.

Of course both claimed they were only keeping the contraband for self-protection, but I figured it was time they learned that Old Fuss and Feathers went by the book. So I invited O'Rourke to consider the fact that these idiots could have cost him all his hard-earned stripes, and suggested he take them to one of the empty compartments for a fatherly chat. When he'd finished, their comrades carried them to the dispensary, where Doc Gannett patched them up. Then I issued them plastic teaspoons and set them to work cleaning out grease traps and stopped-up latrines.

I ran into Gannett a few days later, and he told me the culprits insisted that their injuries resulted from tripping and falling down. "They," he said with what I assumed was irony, "are the clumsiest guys I've ever come across."

By tipping me off, Cos had probably saved a life or two, and he'd certainly saved me a ton of trouble and embarrassment. So I got in the habit of meeting him for a few beers in the evening, and letting him fill my ears with whatever tidbits he'd picked out of the air that day.

It was addictive, listening in on other peoples' thoughts, and only the fear of turning into Schlacht II made me stop him from digging into the minds of Marie and Morales. In fact I flatly forbade him to repeat anything he learned from either one, to me or anybody else. I wouldn't spy on the inner life of a lover or a friend, but aside from that I listened greedily to everything the little snitch had to offer. After we left the Bubble, I was glad I did.

Because we did eventually return to our own universe.

The Bubble had no such thing as time, yet clocks were still running on shipboard, and in due course our eternity of boredom came to an end. Reentry to our own universe was chronometric, and an error of a microsecond could put us almost anyplace, including the center of a star. I for one was seriously anxious, and even Marie showed strain.

"I've done this twenty-eight times," she said one night, seeking comfort in the thicket of chest hair I sprouted back in those days. Somewhat muffled, her voice continued, "But I'll never get used to it. It's all up to the computers, and there's no way for mere humans like us to control our fate."

"What does the celestial navigator do during reentry?"

"Usually gets drunk. It's all he can do."

Actually, when it happened, I found it less distressing than the last time. Similar phenomena occurred, but I was expecting them. The process went fast, and within seconds it was clear that we weren't in the core, convective zone, or corona of anything hot. After a while Marie's quiet tones informed the whole ship that we were just about where we were supposed to be. Indeed, reentry had been a smashing success – system H2223 was already visible, its sun appearing to be about the size of Jupiter as seen from Terra, only colored like Mars.

It was wonderful how people brightened at the news. In the upbeat mood of the moment, I took the Dumb Duo off their shit details and instructed O'Rourke that punishment was now over. Everybody was happy, including me. During a session of afternoon love, Marie tied me up and gave me a present so long, slow, and marvelous that I remember it today – remember it as well as you can remember something transcendent.

I was still wearing a silly grin that evening when Cos joined me in the officers' canteen for our usual session. His face was my first indication that the happy times were over.

"What's the matter with you?"

"Nothing."

"Something wrong with the others, then?"

"No. I've never felt such good vibes on the *Zhukov*. Everybody's happy." For some reason, that seemed to depress him more than anything else.

"Come on, little buddy. Spit it out."

"I saw that star we're headed for on a monitor."

"So?"

"I've been getting some . . . I guess I'd say . . . some tremors. From Paradiso. From humans. They're eerie, coming out of the void like that. Thousands of people must all be feeling basically the same thing, that's why it reaches so far. That and the fact that telepathy doesn't seem to be subject to the inverse-square law. Anyway, something terrible's happening in that system, or maybe is just about to happen, I'm not sure which."

I looked at his big face and his little hands holding the beer stein and his dark, mournful cuttlefish eyes, and I had a sudden impulse to grab him and push him out through the airlock. Logic or no logic, we all want to kill the messenger of bad news. Especially when he lays it on us just when we're feeling great.

Instead, after taking a deep breath, I thanked him. He was doing his job, after all. Later on I told Marie about Cos's singular talent, about the evidence I'd seen that his gift was real, and about his warning. She didn't take it any better than I had.

"Exactly what do you expect me to do about this dwarf's silly notion?"

You ever notice how, when somebody has a physical disability, everyone carefully avoids mentioning it until they get mad with him, and then it's the first thing they bring up?

I said somewhat stiffly, "You're in command here, and I don't expect you to do anything. I'm advising you to take this seriously and use full precautions to make sure we carry out our mission. Okay?"

She thought that over, and said, "Pardonnez-moi." A little later she added, "Of course, it may be the aliens. Le zoo. It's only reasonable to treat this as a military operation. Before we risk the ship, Lieutenant Morales will lead an armed reconnaissance to check things out."

I just looked at her. Very unwillingly, she said, "Okay, I can't let you off the hook just because I sleep with you. You're the senior, so you'll lead it. Are you satisfied?"

"No," I said, "but I hope to be."

After we'd relaxed a while and had a few shots of five-star brandy, I gave her a little present I'd been planning all day. When we were done, and having a shower in the command suite's opulent bathroom, I leaned through clouds of steam and whispered in her rosy ear, "Now, don't say I never did anything for you."

She smiled. "Oh, I'd never say that."

Suddenly everybody was in a fever of anticipation. Because we didn't know what was going on down there, *Zhukov* maintained radio silence until such time as we found out. Janesco spent long days in the Arctic Circle with a crew of combat bots that had been in storage up to this point, but now needed activation and testing and being hooked up to the fire-control computer and so on. He'd been in the Alien War, and had scores to settle. He was an efficient guy, and personally I wouldn't have wanted to be on the bullseye of any of his missiles, especially the big one in its housing outside on the hull.

For us too the training tempo picked up. A lot of the work was intrinsically boring, but when your life is soon going to depend on your gadgets, you develop a passionate interest in things like nuts and bolts and pins and gauges. There was no end to checking and rechecking our weapons. I remember watching in something like awe as one of our dumber peons, blindfolded, field-stripped and reassembled in about thirty seconds a launcher that by any objective estimate was a lot smarter than he was.

The mainframe computer had to run diagnostic checks on all systems, and that was fine. But when it came to the Zhukov's two SDVs or suborbital descent vehicles (shuttles, if you don't speak in military acronyms), Morales and I manually made damn sure the airfoils would deploy when needed. I also decided to give each platoon its own symbol. Instead of the Roman or Greek alphabets, which were kind of overused already, I chose the Hebrew and called our platoons Aleph (') and Beth (b) and had the symbols stenciled on all the equipment and the shuttles. We planned to use both craft, in case an enemy destroyed one on the way down.

Once we arrived on Paradiso, we needed to be able to exit the little ships fast, fast, fast, in case something mean was waiting for us – and enter them again just as fast, in case we had to get away quick. "Get in, buckle up – buckle off, get out! Move, goddamn it!" O'Rourke explained to our platoon, and emphasized his remarks by whacking laggards with his belt.

Insofar as there's any secret to training people for battle, endless repetition is it. Soldiers don't need a lot of brains – they need to be rote-trained and obedient to orders and not have too many nerve endings. Above all, they need to trust their leaders and their comrades and be trustworthy in return. That's what esprit de corps means, and as we readied for action it was fascinating to watch it develop among our people, including the two who'd recently been ready to knife each other over the favors of a douche.

Morales and I had as many butterflies as anybody else, plus those extra ones a young officer gets before his first action. It's one thing to face combat and take orders. It's something else to face combat and give them, knowing you may give the wrong ones and take down a bunch of people besides yourself. More than ever, we depended on our sergeants, and they understood and called us sir while quietly telling us what to do next.

Evenings I sat in the canteen and listened to Cos, and the closer we got to our objective the more depressing he became. The local sun had attained about the size of Luna, a dull red Luna newly risen through haze. Across the disc moved a tiny dark object – Paradiso. I'd sit there watching on a monitor the transit of what looked like a cinder, at the same time listening to Cos tell me how those we'd come to save were expecting ruin and desolation.

"They're running," he added, "but they're running from something they know they can't escape."

"You can sense all this from way out here?"

"As I told you, ESP isn't subject to the inverse-square law. That's one of the most baffling things about it. You know those ancient drawings by Dürer, where a mountain five miles away is in perfect perspective – tiny, about the size of a thumbnail – and yet just as clear and sharp as the big figures in the foreground? That's the kind of message I'm getting. It's small, it's distant, but it's perfectly clear. There's no loss of definition, no fuzzing out. I'm not making this up."

Goddamn him, I thought, he probably isn't, either. Cos was an expert on his own singular gift, and I couldn't argue with him, much as I wanted to.

Every day the sun got bigger and bigger. I checked out a cube from the ship's library and did some reading – even got interested in Universal History, which used to cause me terminal boredom in school. System H2223 had first been identified as a possible residence for humans by the ancients, meaning those fairly recent ancients who lived only a few centuries back, during the time of the Warring States.

All the wars delayed space exploration, but on the other hand the stimulus of fighting brought tremendous technical advances. Especially working out the nature of dark energy – natural antigravity – and finding in it at last the secret for exceeding the speed of light. So when we finally started starward we went better equipped and also had better theoretical understanding of our complicated multiverse. All of which was kind of neat to know, even though it told me absolutely nothing of practical value.

Otherwise I went on with life, doing PT with my guys, checking weapons, and attending formal dinners with the cadre, where Marie sat at the head of the table and I still sat at the foot, because the Table of Ranks had no slot for a commander's lover. Drinking with Cos in the evenings, listening to him tell me that whatever was threatening Paradiso was drawing closer to it by the day, only he couldn't tell me what it was, because it was "dark."

"Think of it as a stealth object," he suggested over his third beer one night.

"It is an object then?"

"I don't know what it is. It's dark."

"Like an alien ship?"

"Might be. If the Zoo's inside a nuke-steel egg, I couldn't pick up their thoughts, you know. The object would be, yeah, dark."

One night I woke up from a nightmare about a pit full of monsters with human faces – woke with a shuddering cry that brought Marie groggily back to consciousness.

"What's wrong?" she mumbled.

"The thing that's threatening Paradiso," I said, wiping sweat from my face. "Could it be us? I mean, we're coming to kidnap them and. . ."

"Mon cher, stop brooding. It's quite pointless. We've got our orders and we're going to obey them, that's all. There's no turning back."

She was right, so I went back to sleep, and a few days later we entered orbit around the world that poor old Innocente had dreamed of turning into a new Eden.

Stepping out the first time on a planet of another star is something few humans have ever done. Or ever will, I guess. The memory of Paradiso remains today one of my life's unforgettable firsts.

We debarked on an undulating plain covered with long coarse grass, or anyway something slim-leaved that looked like grass. The sun was about 45 degrees above the horizon, looking like the red eye of some cosmic beast that was eyeing us for lunch. The redness tinged and transmuted everything, giving the sky a purplish aura, turning blue-green leaves black, giving a perpetual sundown look to everything from pools of water to reflections in our facemasks.

We weren't on breathing apparatus, by the way – no need for that. The air had too much oxygen if anything, and inhaling was like downing a flute of champagne. On the other hand, our combat boots suddenly seemed to be made of lead. The ancients had been able to spot Paradiso with their orbital telescopes because it was big – a hard-shelled Earth-type planet, of course, not a gas giant – but big for its kind. Suddenly I weighed something like a 110 kilos instead of my Earthside 87. As we lined up, all of us were moving like divers in weighted suits, and Morales and I agreed on ten minutes rest every hour until we adapted. I ordered the autopilots running the shuttles to close them up and use the lasers on anything that looked threatening, and it was time to start.

Aleph moved first, O'Rourke leading, me at the rear to keep everybody closed up. Morales's Beth platoon fell in behind us. We topped a low ridge and saw the town founded by Papa Innocente. We didn't know its name, so we called it O-1, Objective One. It was a pretty place, the small massive houses square-built of white stone with red or brown tile roofs, facing a little bay backed by low ridges that gradually grew higher until they turned into distant violet mountains. No tall buildings in the town, but one broad and deep structure with a shallow white dome, just faintly pink in the light. Through my helmet I heard Morales say, "Behold the temple," and he turned out to be right.

I wasn't sure of Cos's physical ability to keep up, so I'd left him on the *Zhukov*. Nevertheless, I wanted to keep contact with him. We were streaming images from our helmet-mounted cameras, and pretty soon I heard his unmistakable voice say, "Kohn, I'm not getting a reading from the town. It's all quiet. I don't sense the colonists at all, either there or anywhere else."

"How do you explain that?"

"I don't."

"You could sense them from space, and now you can't even sense them from orbit?"

"I said I can't explain it."

We approached O-1 with leaden legs and labored breathing. We tipped back our masks, and despite the open furnace of the sun, the air felt mild, almost cool on our overheated faces. Little black animals with too many legs – hexapod rabbits? – scuttled through the grass at our approach. An animal somewhat like a hyena (heavy up front, small at the rear) loped out of a patch of blackish-greenish woods to the right, made a wide circle, and disappeared again. It ran with a rocking-horse motion, front-back, front-back. A flying creature with wide triangular wings dipped and hovered and flapped away clumsily. Its body looked tiny in proportion to its enormous wingspan.

In the distance low clouds had formed, red above, purple in the middle, blue-black underneath. Apparently a summer shower was on the way. To confirm my guess, lightning flickered – reddish lightning.

We entered the town. Unnerving silence. There's a special emptiness to places where people ought to be, but aren't. Signals from the ship told us which way to go, sending Morales up one crooked street, me up another. My platoon split, squads one and two to the right, three and four to the left. Hug the walls, guys. I found my own reactions interesting – nerves tight as catgut in a string orchestra, yet no feeling of fear. Just a very tense alertness. My senses seemed to have sharpened. Another small hexapod of some sort went scuttling around a corner, and I followed the sound of its many claws long after it had disappeared.

The buildings engraved themselves on my memory – every stone, every shadow. The only sounds between the growls of thunder were our boots scuffing and our equipment clinking and clanking. Streets didn't meet at right angles – they and the intersecting alleys ran every which way, like braided channels in desert arroyos. The only shop signs were painted on the walls, like in Pompeii – Fud mart, Vin so ekselent, 20 booties in hous. The last one an ad for a brothel or a shoe store? No idea. The language had been changing in the mouths of colonists, just as it always does.

Marie spoke in my ear, then Cos. They agreed: still no sign of anybody in the town except us. Yet when a rooftile fell off and broke on the stones, everyone, including me, jumped. We emerged into an irregular open space surrounded by shops, all of them empty. Flesch Mart – butcher shop or slave market? By the look of it, butcher shop. A computer's atonal voice spoke in my ear: "Lieutenant Kohn, right twenty degrees, enter broad street, see temple twenty-four o'clock."

Nice to have guidance from the sky. And yes, there was the temple with its broad shallow dome, suddenly etched by a flicker of lightning against the backdrop of gunmetal clouds. We circled the plaza, sliding along walls as before. O'Rourke sent one guy to search every building as we passed. Chu was doing the same with his platoon. A private yelled in a high, strained voice from a second-floor window, "Nuttin' ain't here, Sarge!" and O'Rourke replied with a burst of profanity that broke the tension and left everybody chuckling.

We met under the portico of the temple. Morales and I panted up the steps and high-fived each other. The temple was round, with an outer and an inner circle of columns, and cool wind from the approaching storm whistled through it. The inside was a sort of Greek or Roman amphitheater, with stone bleachers meant to seat maybe two thousand people funneling down to a round central stage lit by a skylight in the dome. Embedded in a solid transplast column about six meters high and visible from every seat in the building hung a gleaming chrome model of DNA that seemed to seize and concentrate every bit of available light.

I felt awed and out of place, like an unbeliever gazing at the Ka'aba. One of the dumber peons asked loudly, "What is that *#@! thing?" But the others spoke in hushed voices, as people tend to do in temples, including those dedicated to gods they don't believe in.

Absent, besides all the people, was any sign of danger. Through my helmet-mounted omni I summoned the shuttles, ordering them to move into the plaza just outside and lock up as before. Then we began settling down for the night. We had plenty of room to stretch out, because there were only seventy-two of us in all that vast space. People started turning on pocket glow lights and breaking out cold rations. Everybody carried food for three days, and the sergeants started circulating to make sure that nobody was fool enough to eat everything at the first meal. Morales and I stood by a column, watching the twinkle of little lights in the vast and steadily darkening space. The DNA model caught and reflected them all, and I guess a poet could have made something out of the scene. But we had no poets present, at least none I knew about.

"Before we start noshing," Jesús said quietly, "there's something I want to show you. We spotted it crossing the plaza. It's not far."

The shuttles were arriving as we set out. They settled down on the stones with all the usual racket and neatly parked themselves with airfoils almost touching. A little light rain began to patter and strengthened as we made our way to a low, windowless building with an industrial look to it. Next door stood another windowless building with the words Hir Ly Gretlie Luvved Ded chiseled on the lintel over the door.

"We can skip the first one," said Morales. "It's just a crematorium. We'll need our lights in the mausoleum. There's artificial lighting inside, but nothing's turned on."

We took out our pocket torches and gave them a twist and stepped inside. Our little cold puddles of light showed walls honeycombed with small square niches. Piled neatly on the floor were ceramic tiles that once had sealed the openings, and every one had the familiar Ladderite logo baked into it, plus a name in the colonists' odd, awkward spelling system.

"God," I whispered. "They even took away their dead. Were they that afraid of us?"

"I don't see how they could've known we were coming. . . . Oh wait, their seer. They've got their own Cos. So they could've known."

There was something wrong with that explanation, but offhand I couldn't think what it was. We walked on, raising hollow echoes. Corridors branched off to either side, and all the walls without exception were empty honeycombs. Then thunder boomed and echoed down the aisles, and Morales and I turned and headed for the entrance.

Outside, the rain was heavier and the wind colder and the darkness darker. We broke into a trot and came up under the roof of the temple, gasping for air. Just in time, too – the rain had started coming down in three-meter cubes. We settled on the second tier, smelling like wet dogs, and started eating concentrated whatnot from our mealpacks. A private from

Beth Platoon came by carrying six or seven canteens and asked if we'd like to have ours filled, too. "There's lots of water," he pointed out needlessly. We handed over our canteens and when the guy returned, swallowed gulps of cold stony-tasting water to wash down our rations. A simple meal, yeah, but it tasted like a feast.

"Pity the poor Ladderites," said Morales. "Here we are scarfing up rations in their nice dry temple, and they're out there in the wild wet woods. They must be eating cold food because if they tried to cook anything, *Zhukov's* scanners would detect the heat and give us directions and we'd go out tomorrow and take them away at gunpoint."

"Sometimes," I said, "you have to destroy a civilization to save a civilization."

After that bit of rather commonplace sarcasm, we posted guards and appointed Chu the Charge of Quarters for the night. Morales said buenas noches and rejoined his people. Somebody began singing – not the obscene ditty I'd have expected, but a sentimental tune called "Goodbye, Young Soldier." The temple's perfect acoustics carried every word to my ears, despite the storm raging outside, and I fell asleep listening to a strangely pure and haunting girl's voice, like a reed instrument, asking, "What'll I do/ When my guy/Is far beyond the sky?"

I never heard what she decided. I was exhausted, and fell asleep in about two minutes. And there I stayed until my helmet started squealing at me.

I vaguely remember rolling over, uttering an incoherent curse or two. Found my helmet, pulled it closer, and muttered the magic word, "Say."

"Robair," said Marie's voice, though we'd agreed always to speak formally anyplace we might be overheard. That and her tone alerted me that something was very, very wrong and the sleep emptied out of my head with magical speed.

"Yes, ma'am."

"You have sixteen minutes to clear your command from that town and get as far away as you can."

"We're being attacked?"

"You're about to be hit by a chunk of flying rubbish roughly twice the size of Mount Vesuvius. It must have entered Paradiso's atmosphere on the far side of the planet, and it's headed for an impact zone just offshore. Janesco tried to get it with a missile as it crossed the terminator, but missed. He hit it with the particle beam, but there wasn't enough energy to deflect it. So move. Now."

I let out a roar and the echoes went careening around the temple. Even if I did sound like Schlacht, there's a time for a leader to be a loudmouth, and this was it.

We had to abandon a lot of gear, but in twelve minutes all of us were jammed into the two shuttles and strapped down and they were moving. As we lifted off, I thanked whatever gods may be for the sang-froid of machinery, which is impossible to frighten. For an instant I was certain that our nose was going to impact the dome, but it didn't, and below us the pale temple and the dark town flowed back and away.

For the first time I checked my watch. It said 0404. The storm was mostly over, and the clouds had scattered in time for a coldly brilliant moon to break through. Only it wasn't a moon, it was the mother of all asteroids, and it flashed to the east, lighting up the little houses of the town. Below I could see neat patchwork fields and dark woods and the face of a ridge of high land topped with a brushy growth of ebony forest. The impact was going to be tremendous, so I ordered both Aleph and Beth platoons to shelter behind the ridge.

We descended and hovered close to the ground, turning on landing lights whose cold glare etched oddball trees without leaves but with spiral fronds coiling upward around the trunks. Eyes flickered in the light, little creatures and big, eyes green or yellow or red, a whole swarming ecology we'd never know anything about, because at that moment the sky lit up. The shock wave hit, first as a wall of compressed air and then as a tremor that shook the hills. The ground surged – I'd never seen anything like it, though I'd heard of earth imitating water during earthquakes.

By now a gale like seven cyclones was howling and a lot of the town was flying over, fragments of houses and trees and everything else. Even in the lee of the ridge, waves of turbulence scoured the valley and made the flyers bounce around like sticks in a torrent. At that time I'd had no training in flying at all, so I had to trust the autopilot, which fortunately didn't need any human coaching to retract the airfoils to minimum extension and rev up the engine to max power. We seemed to have lived through the worst, and I was almost ready to breathe again, when a freakish blast of wind came howling down the valley and swept both shuttles up into the fury above.

I'd heard stories of people being sucked up into tornados and living, and of course we had a solid transorbital ship to huddle in, but that's essentially what we were doing anyway, we and rags of flying clouds and the endless torrent of spinning debris. As we tumbled over and over, I had fragmentary glimpses of things happening below, of glistening bare sea bottom, of a gigantic wall of water moving with a kind of majestic deliberation toward the shore, of fields and hillsides stripped bare, of wind-driven flames spreading horizontally in sheets. One thing I didn't see was the other shuttle – it had vanished in the storm.

Then all I had time for was surviving, while our autopilot's little mechanical brain fought to regain control of the flyer, end the tumbling, ride the gale, climb to quieter air above. We were essentially helpless, at the mercy of the machinery and every second expecting to run head-on against mountain heights that lightning flashes showed advancing with daunting speed from the west. Wind velocity? 303.5 clicks, according to our instruments. Now that's wind.

At last we rose above the turbulence, the air thinned out, and the bucking and groaning stopped, except of course the bucking and groaning of all the guys, including me, who'd been shaken like peppercorns and now were throwing up half-digested rations all over ourselves and one another.

Our flight steadied. We were approaching the limit of the atmosphere. We flickered out of the planet's shadow and seemingly headed straight for the huge red eye of the sun. Then I noticed that something else had taken control, that we were beginning to turn, that a small but bright star in the distance was no star at all, it was the *Zhukov*. We were foul and stinking and disoriented and terrorized, but we were alive and under the control of the mother ship, and I figured I'd take a lot of airsickness and bad smells for that.

The welcoming committee seemed to feel the same way. The whole cadre was waiting for us and broke into cheers as one by one we crawled up through the hatchway out of the shuttle, looking and smelling like rats from a particularly unsanitary sewer. Marie hugged me without regard to smell or protocol, then clasped the hand of each and every member of Platoon Aleph as they filed past, from O'Rourke down to the yardbirds, with a special warm word for every one of them. "Thank God you're safe. . . . Welcome home. . . . You're a true hero," and so forth.

Then they were off to scrub down and, where necessary, get patched up by Doc Gannett. No one turned out to have any injury more serious than abrasions and contusions and an occasional egg-sized lump on the noggin, which was either the most improbable good luck or else direct intervention by the god of fools and spacemen.

Heading for the command suite to do my own more luxurious cleaning up, I asked Marie quietly if she had any news about Morales and his people. She shook her head.

"We can't find them," she admitted. "Fires are spreading everywhere, so you can't see anything. Close to the surface the ionization is impenetrable, so the scanners are useless, unless Morales can rise above the turbulence as you did. That was very brave and very intelligent of you," she added, and I accepted manfully the praise that rightfully belonged to nothing but a smart autopilot and plain dumb luck.

Near the entry to the bridge, Cos intercepted us and said, "I'm sorry, Kohn. I knew something bad was coming, but I didn't know what it was."

"The object was dark."

"Yes, it was dark."

About the other platoon he was at least moderately encouraging. "I think your friend is still alive. When somebody I know dies, it's like being jabbed with a needle. I haven't felt that yet."

"So it wasn't us the colonists were afraid of?"

He seemed perplexed. "Us? No, they were never afraid of us. What gave you that idea? Somehow they knew this thing was coming. Maybe their prophet is clairvoyant after all, and he must be better than I am. They didn't think they could escape it, and yet – somehow – they seem to have done just that."

Then it was shower time, followed by some unpleasant patchwork from Gannett, including sewing back a partially detached left ear. I hadn't even noticed the injury – it had bled all over me, but in the general mess, who could tell? – until hot soapy water hit it in the shower, when I almost went though the nearest bulkhead. After Gannett left me with six stitches and a shot of painkiller, I and my bandaged ear went to bed, to be wrapped up in clean sheets and comforted by Marie.

I suppose you think we made love. Actually, I was asleep in about twenty seconds, and thoughts of romance had to wait for tomorrow.

The next few days would have been wonderful, except for our anxiety over Morales and his people in Platoon Beth.

Views of the planet were grim. The whole thing was now submerged in clouds that whirled this way and that, random streams of energy colliding with each other and forming cyclones or anticyclones, depending on latitude. After the initial inferno of forest and grass fires, there was evidence of a steadily dropping surface temperature because the red sunlight had been almost totally blocked out.

"Conditions," said a computer voice, summing up the situation for several of us on the bridge, "have become severe and inimical to life."

"Thank you so much," I muttered, but Marie said, "My dear, it's only a machine, of course it's banal. It's supposed to be banal."

Cos kept insisting that our people were probably alive, or at any rate that he hadn't received any definite notice of their death. The second or third day, I forget which, he was finally able to indicate a general area where he thought they were – about 300 clicks from where I'd lost contact with them. He added that their shuttle was damaged and they were pinned down by the storms, and were hungry. He figured they might have tried to escape the planet, only to be hit by a downdraft and crash again.

I wanted to take the surviving shuttle and go look for them, but Marie vetoed the idea without hesitation. "Thirty-six people in imminent danger are quite enough," she said. "To say nothing of the colonists, wherever they may be."

Now that was truly baffling. Our scanners and Cos wore out their various exotic senses, and simply couldn't find any indication of them. Yet thousands of people – even if they were somehow managing to live in areas remote from the impact crater, without electronic communications and even without fire – at least had to be thinking and feeling, and Cos should pick up on that. And if they'd all been killed, Cos said he should have received the psychic "tsunami of despair" the mind hurls out at the moment of death. But except for the faint signals from our own people, he'd heard nothing.

As the days went by, Marie came as close to being distraught as I ever saw her. Finally she chose dinnertime, when the surviving cadre were together – effectively a staff meeting, though it wasn't called that – to announce her decision.

"We're going to take the *Zhukov* in," she said. "All the way down to the surface."

Everybody gave a muted gasp, then sat silent, figuring what that might mean. She began to speak quietly, in the kind of sure, still tone that comes from someone who's made a tough decision and means to stick by it.

Of course, she said, superficially her plan was nonsense, first refusing to risk thirty-six people in the surviving shuttle and then risking the ship and all aboard. But the *Zhukov* wasn't just a big transorbital. It was made of nuclear steel and it had almost limitless supplies of energy at its disposal.

She admitted that regulations forbade bringing spacecraft into a planet's atmosphere for a variety of good reasons – corrosive effects on the ship, release of toxic emissions into the planet's environment, and so forth. But the regs also allowed commanders to violate standard operating procedures under emergency conditions, the only proviso being that they'd damn well better be able to justify their action later on. She thought she could.

"Anyway, this is what we'll do," she finished. "If anybody wants to file a protest, they're welcome to do so."

Nobody said anything.

"Then let's get on with it," she said. "When we go in, all personnel will be at battle stations. All safety doors will be closed and sealed. All personnel will wear survival suits. I don't think anything down there can breach a compartment, but if something does and a group becomes isolated, they'll have to survive on their own for an unpredictable length of time until we can reach them. Mr Cos will guide us until more standard scanning methods pick up signals from the ground. Bonne chance."

Wine had been served, and we solemnly raised our glasses and wished her and each other luck.

I spent the next twelve hours with my platoon, working out exact procedures if we had to exit the *Zhukov* and help collect Morales and his people. Instead of retreating closer to the core of the ship, like the others, we were to occupy the compartment nearest the shuttle hatch. Everybody suited up, and O'Rourke and I began checking them over and over and over again, to make sure that all the seals were tight and the heating and breathing units were functional. I figured we'd need to take our air with us, because the planetary atmosphere had become a sandstorm of dust and ashes and toxic byproducts of burning. We'd need our helmet lights. We'd need nylon lines connecting us like mountain climbers, so we wouldn't get lost or blown away. We'd need old-fashioned basket litters to haul the injured. We'd need every goddamn thing.

As we were reaching the end of our preparations, I got a squawk from the bridge. My presence was demanded soonest. I left O'Rourke to do his very competent best and hastened past retracted safety doors through a corridor that would soon, I expected, be chopped up into segments like a snake that ran afoul of an autoplow in a wheat field. As I trotted along, the doors began to be tested, sliding closed with a sigh and whisper and a terminal clank, then opening again.

I popped out onto the bridge to find Marie looking stormy, Cos looking obstinate, and the celestial navigator (what was the guy's name – Sajnovich?

I can't remember) looking at the planet in the big monitor that hung over the bridge and whistling softly and tunelessly to himself. Marie gestured at Cos, one of those very French gestures, as if she was throwing away a piece of food that had begun to smell bad.

"Écoutez!" she snapped. "Listen to this!"

Cos, still looking mulish, said, "Well, what d'you want me to say? I'm telling you what I'm getting, or not getting, and if it interrupts all your wonderful plans, I can't help that."

I touched his shoulder. "Just tell me," I said.

"I've lost Morales and that bunch. They don't seem to be there anymore."

"You mean they're dead?"

"I don't think so. They're just gone, that's all."

Another goddamn mystery disappearance. When I relayed to O'Rourke the news that all our preparations had been wasted, he looked as rebellious as I ever saw him. Then he shrugged and said "*#%&" ten or twenty times, and told the guys to take off their survival suits and go back to their barracks compartment.

Zhukov stayed in orbit, bombarding Paradiso's infernal surface with every form of radiant energy it had, looking for somebody – anybody, in fact. Hours went by, and we were still at it when the sensors started screaming. Not because they'd found our people, but because a chunk of metal instantly identifiable as a VNO, or vehicle of nonhuman origin, had emerged from behind the planet and was crossing the terminator into the dim red light of the sun.

Sirens added to the prevailing racket and robot voices intoned, "Battle stations, battle stations."

Suddenly everybody was grabbing for personal weapons and running like hell for assigned areas around the central core of the ship. Thirty seconds later the safety doors started closing, and if you got isolated in an outer compartment, that was tough, you stayed there until the All Clear went off and the doors opened. Or until an enemy missile whacked the hull, in which case you died of the explosion if it penetrated and the concussion if it didn't.

Somehow O'Rourke got all our people to the designated inner compartments. Those who'd been showering were buck naked, but when you're at war, you don't worry about trivia like that.

I stayed on the bridge, not because I was useful but because nobody had sent me away, and I wanted to see what was happening. I strapped into the chair usually occupied by the celestial navigator, who'd taken off to a secure compartment on the other side of the core that contained a duplicate guidance system. That way there'd be somebody to maneuver the ship if the bridge got destroyed.

Seated in the commander's chair, Marie donned one of those virtual-reality headpieces. I donned the navigator's headset and listened to her issuing orders with the aplomb of a chef instructing a sous-chef exactly how to construct a chocolate soufflé. The delicate fingers that had played such tunes on my body were now resting on keypads that gave her the power to override any and all systems. Somebody's voice said, "Real bastard, ain't she?" in tones of pure admiration.

So I watched my first combat in space – hell, my first real combat anywhere – unfold in the monitor. Banks of lasers crisscrossed a big shadowbox, and when the bridge lights were doused, we were all projected into that virtual space. I don't think I felt any fear at all, it was too exciting, and if an enemy FTLM suddenly materialized in the center of the *Zhukov* there was nothing to worry about anyway, because we'd all turn to quarks in a nanosecond. So I could get an almost esthetic delight out of the cloud-drenched planet, the red orb rising behind it, and the background of hard crystalline stars.

The one thing I couldn't see was the alien ship – the bogey – that was causing all the upheaval. Then a blue circle appeared in the monitor, locating it for me. Columns of numbers that probably meant something to the Space Service types popped up along the margins of the image. A human voice said incredulously, "Velocity zero?" which I took to mean that the bogey had stopped moving.

Janesco's voice reported that the lids were off the missile silos. He seemed to be waiting for Marie to say the modern equivalent of "You may fire when ready, Gridley," but all she said was, "Deploy PBG," meaning the particle beam generator.

"Ready."

"Auto response on all systems."

"Auto response."

That meant the ship would respond to any detected hostile action without further command. At the same time I heard the main drive engines and even the dark energy generator revving up. Trying to apply what I knew of ground combat to space, I figured she was getting ready to dodge behind Paradiso, and if the bogey followed, hit him hard as he came into view. Sort of like defending a reverse slope in mountain warfare, where you let the other guy show up against the sky, then whack him. These were the thoughts going through my head at the exact moment when the image of Jesús Morales, big and holographically precise, appeared between the laser banks, blocking out the planet and the sun and everything else except the spatter of stars above him.

"Colonel," he said, his voice somewhat gruff but perfectly audible, "we're aboard an alien ship. Those guys from the Zoo came in and saved us. All of us, including the colonists. Do you copy?"

Contrary to what my wife Anna likes to say, I am never, or almost never, vulgar. But I do believe there were a lot of spotty underpants on the bridge of the *Zhukov* at that instant.

There was also a stunned silence, in the middle of which I heard my own voice – and yeah, I was a lieutenant and therefore the lowest life form present, but what the hell, Morales was my friend not theirs – say loudly into the navigator's mike, "Jesús, we copy."

"If I may," said Marie icily, and I immediately stopped my runaway tongue by clamping it between my teeth.

"What do they propose to do with you?" she demanded.

"Send us to the *Zhukov* by shuttle. I think it's meant to be a diplomatic gesture, now that the war's over and we're withdrawing from this sector of space. They're thinking of peaceful trade and things like that in the future."

"Are all of you there?"

"Seventeen of us from Beth platoon. My other people died. We have six injured."

"We'll be ready for you. What about the colonists?"

"The colonists have voted to join the Zoo – become another associated species – and not return to Terra. They seem to have a kind of natural belief in symbiosis, see it as an aspect of love. Also, they don't trust their fellow humans."

"I wonder why," I said. No I didn't, because I was still biting my tongue. Anyway, sarcasm wouldn't have been welcomed, not even by me. I was too excited to see Morales alive, and I didn't really give a rat's ass what the Ladderites chose to do or not do.

But Marie wasn't happy. "We have orders to return those people to a region under human control."

"The aliens aren't subject to our orders," Morales pointed out.

"Quite so. Am I permitted to speak to their prophet?"

"He was an old man. He died during their flight from the impact area. For the first time they don't have anybody with good strong ESP to lead them and they're probably making bad, or at any rate uninformed, decisions."

"Well, that's their problem. Convey my agreement to the Z – to whoever's in command there. We won't fire on the shuttle, and Gannett will be waiting for the injured."

She then issued three orders. First, she told Gannett and me to meet the shuttle and remove our people. Second, she told Janesco to maintain the auto response order but instruct the heavy weapons control computer not to fire on the shuttle. Third, she told all other personnel to remain at their battle stations.

Janesco was angry with her. His voice came down hoarse and tough from the Arctic Circle. "Commander, it's a trick. Even that fool Schlacht would have known it's a trick."

"Of course it's a trick," she snapped. "But what trick? Will the shuttle blow up the instant it gets alongside the *Zhukov*? Have our people been infected with some lethal disease or parasite? Or is this essentially a diplomatic ploy, as Lieutenant Morales thinks?"

There was an impromptu staff meeting going on when I left the bridge. For the moment I was under Gannett's command, and I'd hardly reached the airlock when he had me encased in an elastoplast suit like one he was wearing. Just in case the ploy was to get some deadly bug past the *Zhukov's* defenses, we'd meet our guys in these rigs, breathing through electro-static filters with little fans roaring in our ears. He'd also brought along six medbots that looked like enormous crabs, scuttling around on jointed legs and waving exaggeratedly long arms. While we waited, they brought in and stacked the basket litters I'd been planning to take on our aborted return to Paradiso.

The alien shuttle approached. The docking procedure was interesting. I hadn't been able to figure how they could get a tight air seal when *Zhukov's* airlock wasn't configured to receive them. But the problem turned out to be no problem for our late enemies. While we watched through a port in the inner doors of the lock, they extruded a flexible tube – an umbilical, the doc called it – which expanded like the business end of a trumpet. We opened the outer airlock doors, and the trumpet entered and sealed itself to the bulkheads.

Then we opened our inner doors, they opened theirs at far end of the tube, air howled into the umbilical – higher pressure on our side – and a few minutes later here came Jesús Morales himself, staggering through the tube against the gale and looking thin and battered, but totally alive. The medbots had him suited up before I could touch him, but then we swapped a real abrazo through the plastic, and he joined in helping the walking injured aboard and laying the badly busted guys in the litters. In a few minutes everybody was wrapped up like party gifts and sprayed down with some kind of antiseptic gunk.

Gannett told me to close the inner airlock doors. As I turned to obey the order, I caught just a glimpse of the only Zoo denizens I ever saw. Something with a head vaguely like a seahorse – rather stiff, bluish, with mild bulging eyes and some sort of breathing apparatus on the end of its long snout – stared back at me while something else with many arms moved around in the background.

I had just stretched out my hand toward the button to close the doors when something ran under my arm and leaped into the umbilical. From inside the tube Cos turned and looked back at me with those large dark eyes, raised one small hand and waved and shouted, "They're my people, Kohn! I have to save them!"

"Get that man back!" shouted Gannett. Instead I hit the button and the doors began to slide shut. I had an instantaneous flash of the end of the umbilical folding in upon itself and looking, in fact, exactly like a king-size navel.

"Sorry, sir," I told the surgeon, "but you didn't countermand your first order."

Thought I was smart. Didn't realize I'd just killed Cos, poor little bastard, or he'd killed himself, however you chose to look at it. My second unin-tended homicide of the trip.

Through the port I watched the shuttle seal itself up and drift away, hang a U and head back. It hadn't blown up. And I may as well tell you now that after exhaustive tests Gannett found that our people hadn't been infected with anything, either. If there had been a ploy, we never found out what it was, and personally I think Jesús probably had it right from the start. Our late enemies had been making a conciliatory gesture – that was all.

While Gannett and his bots were bedding everybody down in the now overflowing sickbay, I took off the plastic suit and returned to the bridge to report the successful recovery of our people. But nobody was interested in anything I had to say.

They were staring as if hypnotized at the monitor, at two converging blue circles, one marking the alien shuttle, the other marking the bogey. Marie sat in her commander's chair like an alabaster statue. The two circles merged, and the slender fingers of her left hand, with the transparent lacquer on the nails, made a tiny movement, tapping the left keypad that gave her command of all our firepower.

My mouth, I think, formed the word don't, but no sound came out, or none that I heard, anyway. Suddenly the *Zhukov* moved, the acceleration slamming me painfully against the deck. We began to slide behind what had become Planet Inferno, but not before the alien ship erupted in a huge fireball, its fragments flying out in that strangely leisured way that things seem to move in space.

The bridge came alive then, all the Space Service types cheering at once, because they'd just won the last battle of the Alien War. Which wasn't all that hard, considering the other guys, poor bastards, hadn't known that the war was still going on.

When Marie returned to the command suite, I was there waiting for her, somewhat bruised, a hen's egg taking form on the back of my head. But thoroughly conscious, and in a state of cold rage.

"I had to do it," she said quickly. "My orders contain a secret protocol obliging me to destroy any alien ship we encounter."

I didn't say anything. So she started arguing with what I hadn't said.

"Suppose I'd accepted their terms, disobeyed my orders, gone back without the colonists – what would my enemies at HQ have said? That I'd failed at my mission, violated my instructions, consorted with our enemies and allowed them to kidnap our people. I'd have been court-martialed."

I finally found my voice. "So to prevent that, you killed several thousand intelligent creatures, most of them human. Including Cos."

"Pardon me if I don't cry over him. He'd picked up our plans with that damned intuition of his and he was ready to, how do you say it, jaser – blab – to our enemies. You're such a child, Robair. You haven't yet learned to accept the difficult things that your choice of a military career entails. You've no idea what it's like to be in command. You'll toughen up in time."

"Not to this extent."

"Bah, what's the use of arguing? You need to grow up, that's all. You haven't really understood much about the inner history of this voyage, have you? Not much at all. It was dismaying to my service when the

Council of State insisted on putting a Security officer in charge. How could one of those dreary policemen understand our need to defeat the enemy and recover our honor? But of course that was the real point – he was supposed to keep the rest of us under control.

"Fortunately, Security HQ wanted to get rid of Schlacht, whose sexual peculiarities had become notorious, so they gave the job to him. Our intelligence people had very little trouble locating a young woman who, for excellent reasons, wanted to kill him. They armed her and put her aboard and I saw to her survival here. That little wretch Cos almost queered the whole thing – I never really forgave him for telling the General we had a stowaway. When I made you Security officer I assumed you'd arrest Cos and get him out of my hair. Well, you didn't do what I expected, but in a way you did better. After our stowaway took her revenge, I was at a loss as to what to do with her, until you quite innocently solved that problem. And then Cos, while trying to save his fellow Ladderites, eliminated himself. So you see, everything worked out perfectly."

The minute that followed this speech was the longest and chilliest I'd experienced up to that time. Then I said, "If you don't object, Ma'am, I think I'll move back into my old quarters. When he gets out of sickbay, Morales can join me."

"Suit yourself. I hope you'll be very happy together."

I came to attention, saluted, did a right-about-face, and walked out. That was how my shipboard romance ended.

So, Jesús son of Jesús, now you know how the Zoo, by saving your father's life and returning him to us, made it possible for him to meet and marry your mother a few years later and for you to be begotten and born. Remember the nameless creatures of that nameless ship with gratitude; for their atoms have long since been dispersed, and they've left no memorial behind except you.

After we returned to Terra, I read Marie's report. It was a fine work of fiction. It told how the aliens had already slaughtered the colonists when we arrived, and in revenge we then engaged and destroyed their ship. The public loved it. The news of our belated victory over an enemy who'd beat us handily in the war sent a thrill all across the far-flung outposts of humanity. The Zhukov's Space Service officers loyally supported their commander's version of events, and were duly rewarded a few years later when the Council of State made her the first woman Commandant of the service. She died quite recently, and her ashes lie entombed in Paris at the Invalides, near the dust of Napoleon.

Morales and I turned in reports to Security HQ giving the facts, which of course were ignored because we were only lieutenants. Though we didn't stay so for long. We were both promoted to captain on the basis of our service in "the epic voyage of the Zhukov" (as the Council called it) – "a mission to save humanity that became a mission to avenge humanity." That sounds pretty good, doesn't it? Words are so much handier than realities. Meanwhile, all that your Papa and I really had done and endured vanished into the category of non-events.

There was another and fatal epilogue to this story. Nobody knows for sure the reason for the outbreak of the Second Alien War, but personally I've always believed the creatures of the Zoo were seeking revenge for the treacherous destruction of their ship. By then the Trans-Aran Wormhole had been discovered and mapped, and there was that terrible battle near the exit where we lost so many ships and so many thousands of our best people, including your father, who was commanding a landing party aboard the old Sun-Tzu when an FTLM vaporized it.

That was how I learned that regardless of our smarts or our rank, we're all the serfs and peons of history. But I also decided that I didn't have to surrender my soul, as Marie had done. I decided to knuckle under when I had to, but keep a lifelong obligation to tell the truth whenever that became possible. It's possible now, and I'm laying it on you, hoping that in the future when great power comes into your hands, you'll know how not to use it.

In my new condition of humility, I also started to look up my old enlisted people – my fellow peons, you might say. I began meeting annually with O'Rourke and Chu and as many of our people as wanted and were able to come. Like veterans everywhere, we met to lift some brews together and reminisce, and I learned a lot from talking with them. Once when he was drunk, O'Rourke told me in a friendly way that he'd always regarded me as "a *#%& fool, but a *#%& fool with possibilities." I thought that was a real compliment, coming from such a fathomless well of cynicism.

Chu admitted to me that sometimes he wished he'd followed his family tradition and become a pirate instead of a soldier. "The danger's the same," he said, "but the profits are much greater. Like you, I must have some ethics squirreled away somewhere." He looked embarrassed saying that, and I think he must have been drunk, too, at the time.

I was able to follow the lives of some of our guys long after the old *Zhukov* had gone to Europa to be scrapped. One of the wildest of our douches quit the service and succumbed to respectability. She's now married to a Councilor of State – and I won't tell you his name, so don't ask. Another quit and got rich running a brothel in the capital at New Angkor.

Our baffling genius Soza told me that the events on Paradiso had scared him so badly, he'd finally realized that hiding from responsibility in the enlisted service was even more dangerous than living in the real world outside it. So, instead of re-upping when his tour was over, he quit and worked his way through a minor college, won a scholarship to a major medical school, and the last I heard of him was a neurosurgeon doing great work on reconstructing damaged spinal cords. There always are some people who beat the odds, right?

Still, most of our guys remained simple soldiers. I found talking with them something of a chore because they totally lacked the ability to generalize – they never summed up, they just remembered with numbing precision exactly this place or that place, exactly what words exactly what person had said and when he or she had said them. "D'you remember, sir," one said, "when we went into O-1, how we come around that corner with the little white house with the blue sign about twenty booties painted on it? Wasn't that a laugh?"

They often spoke about Marie. "You remember, sir, when we got back to the ship and the commander herself told us how great we were?" said another guy. "I was covered with blood and puke, and yet she shook my hand anyhow and said I was a hero. Gawd, that was amazing. And now she's a big wheel, I seen her last week in the feelies. Think about that. Gawd, I'll never forget her."

Nor will I.

IT TAKES TWO

Nicola Griffith

Nicola Griffith has won the Nebula Award, the James Tiptree, Jr.,
Memorial Award, and five Lambda awards. Her SF novels include
Ammonite and *Slow River* (her Nebula Award winner), and she also
writes the popular "Aud Torvingen" series of mystery novels, which
includes *Stay*, *Always*, and *The Blue Place*. She's co-editor, with
Stephen Pagel, of *Bending the Landscape: Horror*, *Bending the
Landscape: Fantasy*, and *Bending the Landscape: Science Fiction*.
Born in Leeds, United Kingdom, she now lives in Seattle.

Here she takes us to a strip club for an evening of lap-dancing,
one in which there's a lot more going on beneath the surface than
immediately meets the eye, and not just the surface of the clothes.

IT BEGAN, AS these things often do, at a bar – a long dark piece of mahogany along one wall of Seattle's Queen City Grill polished by age and more
than a few chins. The music was winding down. Richard and Cody (whose
real name was Candice, though no one she had met since high school knew
it) lived on different coasts, but tonight was the third time this year they had
been drinking together. Cody was staring at the shadows gathering in the
corners of the bar and trying not to think about her impersonal hotel room.
She thought instead about the fact that in the last six months she had seen
Richard more often than some of her friends in San Francisco, and that
she would probably see him yet again in a few weeks when their respective
companies bid on the Atlanta contract.

She said, "You ever wonder what it would be like to have, you know, a
normal type job, where you get up on Monday and drive to work, and do
the same thing Tuesday and Wednesday and Thursday, every week, except
when you take a vacation?"

"You forgot Friday."

"What?" They had started on mojitos, escalated through James Bonds,
and were now on a tequila-shooter-with-draft-chaser glide path.

"I said, you forgot Friday. Monday, Tuesday —"

"Right," Cody said. "Right. Too many fucking details. But did you ever
wonder? About a normal life?" An actual life, in one city, with actual friends.

Richard was silent long enough for Cody to lever herself around on the
bar stool and look at him. He was playing with his empty glass. "I just took
a job," he said. "A no-travel job."

"Ah, shit." She remembered how they met, just after the first dotcom crash, at a graduate conference on synergies of bio-mechanics and expert decision-making software architecture or some such crap, which was wild because he started out in cognitive psychology and she in applied mathematics. But computers were the alien glue that made all kinds of odd limbs stick together and work in ways never intended by nature. Like Frankenstein's monster, he had said when she mentioned it, and she had bought him a drink, because he got it. They ran into each other at a similar conference two months later, then again at some industry junket not long after they'd both joined social media startups. The pattern repeated itself, until, by the time they were both pitching venture capitalists at trade shows, they managed to get past the required cool, the distancing irony, and began to email each other beforehand to arrange dinners, drinks, tickets to the game. They were young, good-looking, and very, very smart. Even better, they had absolutely no romantic interest in each other.

Now when they met it was while traveling as representatives of their credit-starved companies to make increasingly desperate pitches to industry-leading Goliaths on why they needed the nimble expertise of hungry Davids.

Cody hadn't told Richard that lately her pitches had been more about why the Goliaths might find it cost-effective to absorb the getting-desperate David she worked for, along with all its innovative, motivated, boot-strapping employees whose stock options and 401(k)s were now worthless. But going back to the groves of academe was really admitting failure.

She sighed. "Where?"

"Chapel Hill. And it's not . . . Well, okay, it is sort of an academic job, but not really."

"Uh-huh."

"No, really. It's with a new company, a joint venture between WishtleNet and the University of North—"

"See."

"Just let me finish." Richard could get very didactic when he'd been drinking. "Think Google Labs, or Xerox PARC, but wackier. Lots of money to play with, lots of smart grad students to do what I tell them, lots of blue sky research, not just irritating Vice Presidents saying I've got six months to get the software on the market, even if it is garbage."

"I hear you on that." Except that Vince, Cody's COO, had told her that if she landed the Atlanta contract she would be made a VP herself.

"It's cool stuff, Cody. All those things we've talked about in the last six, seven years? The cognitive patterning and behavior mod, the modulated resonance imaging software, the intuitive learning algorithms—"

"Yeah, yeah."

" – they want me to work on that. They want me to define new areas of interest. Very cool stuff."

Cody just shook her head. Cool. Cool didn't remember to feed the fish when you were out of town, again.

"Starts next month," he said.

Cody felt very tired. "You won't be in Atlanta."

"Nope."

"Atlanta in August. On my own. Jesus."

"On your own? What about all those pretty girls in skimpy summer clothes?"

The muscles in Cody's eyebrows felt tight. She rubbed them. "It's Boone I'm not looking forward to. Boone and his sleazy strip club games."

"He's the customer."

"Your sympathy's killing me."

He shrugged. "I thought that lap-dancing hooker thing was your wet dream."

Her head ached. Now he was going to bring up Dallas.

"That's what you told us in – now where the hell was that?"

"Dallas." Might as well get it over with.

"You were really into it. Are you blushing?"

"No." Three years ago she had been twenty-eight with four million dollars in stock options and the belief that coding cowboy colleagues were her friends. Ha. And now probably half the geeks in the South had heard about her most intimate fantasy. Including Boone.

She swallowed the last of her tequila. Ugly stuff once it got tepid. She picked up her jacket.

"I'm out of here. Unless you have any handy hints about landing that contract without playing Boone's slimeball games? Didn't think so." She pushed her shot glass away and stood.

"That Atlanta meeting's when? Eight, nine weeks?"

"About that." She dropped two twenties on the bar.

"I maybe could help."

"With Boone? Right." But Richard's usually cherubic face was quite stern.

He fished his phone from his pocket and put it on the bar. He said, "Just trust me for a minute," and tapped the memo icon. The icon winked red. "Whatever happens, I promise no one will ever hear what goes on this recording except you."

Cody slung on her jacket. "Cue ominous music."

"It's more an, um, an ethics thing."

"Jesus, Richard. You're such a drama queen." But she caught the bartender's eye, pointed to their glasses, and sat.

"I did my Atlanta research too," he said. "Like you, I'm pretty sure what will happen after you've made your presentations to Boone."

"The Golden Key," she said, nodding. Everyone said so. The sun rises, the government taxes, Boone listens to bids and takes everyone to the Golden Key.

"– but what I need to know from you is whether or not, to win this contract, you can authorize out-of-pocket expenses in the high five figures."

She snorted. "Five figures against a possible eight? What do you think?"

He pointed at the phone.

"Fine. Yes. I can approve that kind of expense."

He smiled, a very un-Richardlike sliding of muscle and bone, like a python disarticulating its jaw to swallow a pig. Cody nearly stood up, but the moment passed.

"You'll also have to authorize me to access your medical records," he said.

So here they were in Marietta, home of the kind of Georgians who wouldn't fuck a stranger in the woods only because they didn't know who his people were: seven men and one woman stepping from Boone's white concrete and green glass tower into an August sun hot enough to make the blacktop bubble. Boone's shades flashed as he turned to face the group.

"All work and no play makes Jack a dull boy. And Jill," with a nod at Cody, who nodded back and tried not to squint. Squinting made her look like a moron: not good when all around you were wearing sleek East Coast summer business clothes and gilded with Southern tans. At least the guy from Portland had forgotten his shades too.

They moved in a small herd across the soft, sticky parking lot: the guy from Boston would have to throw away his fawn loafers.

Boone said to the guy from Austin, "Dave, you take these three. I know you know where we're going."

"Sure do," Dave said, and the seven boys shared that we're-all-men-of-the-world-yes-indeedy laugh. Cody missed Richard. And she was still pissed at the way he'd dropped the news on her only last week. Why hadn't he told her earlier about not coming to Atlanta? Why hadn't he told her in Seattle? And a university job: what was up with that? Loser. But she wished he was here.

Boone's car was a flashy Mercedes hybrid in silver. He opened the passenger door with a Yeah-I-know-men-and-women-are-equal-but-I-was-born-in-the-South-so-what-can-you-do? smile to which Cody responded with a perfect, ironic lift of both eyebrows. Hey, couldn't have managed that in shades. The New York guy and Boston loafers got in the back. The others were climbing into Dave's dark green rental SUV. A full-sized SUV. Very uncool. He'd lose points for that. She jammed her seatbelt home with a satisfying click.

As they drove to the club, she let the two in the back jostle for conversational space with Boone. She stared out of the window. The meeting had gone very well. It was clear that she and Dave and the guy from Denver were the only ones representing companies with the chops for this contract, and she was pretty sure she had the edge over the Denver people when it came to program rollout. Between her and Dave, then. If only they weren't going to the Golden Key. God. The thought of all those men watching her watch those women and think they knew what she was thinking made her scalp prickle with sweat. In the flow of conditioned air, her face turned cold.

*　　*　　*

Two days before she left for Atlanta she'd emailed Vince to explain that it wasn't her who would be uncomfortable at the strip club, but the men, and that he should at least consider giving Boone a call and setting her presentation up for either the day before or the day after the others. She'd got a reply half an hour later, short and to the point: You're going, kid, end of story. She'd taken a deep breath and walked over to his office.

He was on the phone, pacing up and down, but waved her in before she could knock. He covered the receiver with one hand, "Gotta take this, won't be long," and went back to pacing, shouting, "Damn it, Rick, I want it done. When we had that meeting last week you assured me – Yeah. No problem, you said. No fucking problem. So just do it, just find a way." He slammed the phone down, shook his head, turned his attention to her. "Cody, what can I do for you? If it's about this Atlanta thing I don't want to hear it."

"Vince – "

"Boone's not stupid. He takes people to that titty club because he likes to watch how they behave under pressure. You're the best we've got, you know that. Just be yourself and you won't fuck up. Give him good presentation and don't act like a girl scout when the nipples start to show. Can you handle that?"

"I just resent—"

"Jesus Christ, Cody. It's not like you've never seen bare naked ladies before. You want to be a VP? Tell me now: yes or no."

Cody took a breath. "Yes."

"Glad to hear it. Now get out of here."

The Golden Key was another world: cool, and scented with the fruity overtones of beer; loud, with enough bass to make the walls of her abdomen vibrate; dark at the edges, though lushly lit at the central stage with its three chrome poles and laser strobes. Only one woman was dancing. It was just after six, but the place was already half full. Somewhere, someone was smoking expensive cigars. Cody wondered who the club paid off to make that possible.

Boone ordered staff to put two tables together right by the stage, near the center pole. The guy from New York sat on Boone's left, Dave on his right. Cody took a place at the end, out of Boone's peripheral vision. She wouldn't say or do anything that wasn't detached and ironic. She would be seamless.

A new dancer: shoulder-length red hair that fell over her face as she writhed around the right hand pole. She wore a skirt the size of a belt, and six-inch heels of translucent plastic embedded with suggestive pink flowers. Without the pole she probably couldn't even stand. Did interesting things to her butt, though, Cody thought, then patted surreptitiously at her upper lip. Dry, thank god. Score one for air conditioning.

New York poked her arm. He jerked his thumb at Boone, who leaned forward and shouted, "What do you want to drink?"

"Does it matter?"

He grinned. "No grape juice playing at champagne here. Place takes its liquor seriously."

Peachy. "Margarita. With salt." If it was sour enough she wouldn't want to gulp it.

The dancer hung upside down on the pole and undid her bra. Her breasts were a marvel of modern art, almost architectural.

"My God," she said, "it's the Hagia Sophia."

"What?" New York shouted. "She's called Sophia?"

"No," Cody shouted back, "her breasts . . . Never mind."

"Fakes," New York said, nodding.

The drinks came, delivered by a blonde woman wearing nothing but a purple velvet g-string and a smile. She called Boone Darlin' – clearly he was a regular – and Cody Sugar.

Cody managed to lift her eyes from the weirdness of unpierced nipples long enough to find a dollar bill and drop it on the drinks tray. Two of the guys were threading their tips under the g-string: a five and a ten. The blonde dropped Cody a wink as she walked away. New York caught it and leered. Cody tried her margarita: very sour. She gulped anyway.

The music changed to a throbbing remix of mom music: the Pointer Sisters' "Slowhand." The bass line was insistent, pushing on her belly like a warm hand. She licked her lips and applied herself to her drink. Another dancer with soft black curls took the left hand pole, and the redhead moved to center stage on her hands and knees in front of their table, rotating her ass in slow motion, looking at them over her shoulder, slitting her eyes at them like a cat. Boone, Dave, all the guys had bills in their hands: "Ooh mama, I've got what you need." The redhead backed towards them in slow motion, arching her spine now in apparent ecstasy – but not so far gone as to ignore the largest bill at the table: Boone's twenty. She let him tease her with it, stroking up the inside of her thigh and circling a nipple before she held out the waistband of the pseudo-skirt for the twenty. They probably didn't notice that she plucked them of their bills in order – Boone's twenty, Dave's ten, the two fives. Then she was moving to her right, to a crowd of hipster suits who had obviously been there longer than was good for them: two of them were holding out fifties. The dancer pretended to fuck the fifty being held out at pelvis level. She had incredible muscle control. Next to Cody, New York swallowed hard, and fumbled for his wallet. But it was too late. The hipster was grinning hard as the redhead touched his cheek, tilted her head, said something. He stood and his friends hooted encouragement as he and the redhead disappeared through a heavily frosted glass door in the back.

"Oh, man . . ." Dave's face was more red than tan, now. He pulled a fifty from his wallet, snapped it, folded it lengthways, and held it out over the stage to the remaining dancer. "Yo, curlyhead, come and get some!"

"Yeah!" said New York in a high voice. Portland and Boston seemed to be engaged in a drinking game.

Boone caught Cody's eye and smiled slightly. She shrugged and spread her hand as if to say, Hey, it's their money to waste, and he smiled again, this time with a touch of skepticism. Ah, shit.

"Sugar?" The waitress with the velvet g-string, standing close and bending down so that her nipples brushed Cody's hair, then dabbed her cheek.

Cody looked at her faded blue eyes and found a ten dollar bill. She smiled and slipped it into the g-string at the woman's hip and crooked a finger to make her bend close again.

"I'd take it as a personal favor if you brought me another of these wonderful margaritas," she said in the woman's ear, "without the tequila."

"Whatever you say. But I'll still have to charge for the liquor."

"Of course you do. Just make sure it looks good." Cody jerked her head back at the rest of the table.

"You let me take care of everything, sugar. I'm going to make you the meanest looking margarita in Dixie. They'll be amazed, purely amazed, at your stamina. It'll be our little secret." She fondled Cody's arm and shoulder, let the back of her hand brush the side of Cody's breast. "My name is Mimi. If you need anything, later." She gave Cody a molten look and headed for the bar. The skin on her rotating cheeks looked unnaturally smooth, like porcelain. Cosmetics, Cody decided.

Curlyhead had spotted Dave's fifty and was now on her back in front of their table. Cody imagined her as a glitched wigglebot responding to insane commands: clench, release, arch, whip back and forth. Whoever had designed her had done a great job on those muscles: each distinct, plump with strength, soft to the touch. Shame they hadn't had much imagination with the facial expressions or managed to put any spark in the eyes.

Breasts swaying near her face announced the arrival of her kickless drink. She slipped a ten from her wallet and reached for Mimi's g-string.

Mimi stepped back half a pace, put her tray down, and squeezed her breasts together with her hands. "Would you like to put it here instead, Sugar?"

Cody blinked.

"You could slide it in real slow. Then maybe we could get better acquainted." But like the wigglebot, her eyes stayed blank.

"You're too hot for me, Mimi." Cody snapped the bill into her g-string and tried not to feel Mimi's flash of hatred. She sipped her drink and took a discreet peek in her wallet. This was costing the company a fortune.

Boone watched Dave and New York with a detached expression. Then he turned her way with a speculative look. An invitation to talk?

She stood. And turned to look at the stage just as a long-haired woman in cowboy boots strode to the center pole.

For Cookie it was all routine so far, ankle holding up better than she thought it might. The boots helped. She couldn't remember when she'd written that note to herself, Cowboys and Indians! but it was going to be inspired. She flexed and bent and pouted and pointed her breasts on automatic pilot.

Should she get the ankle x-rayed? Nah. It was only a sprain. Two ibupro-
fen and some ice would fix it.

Decent crowd for a Tuesday night. Some high spenders behind the pillar
there, but Ginger had taken them for four lap dances already. Well, hey, there
were always more men with more money than sense. She glanced into the
wings. Danny had her hat. He nodded. She moved automatically, counted
under her breath, and just as the first haunting whistle of Morricone's "The
Good, the Bad, and the Ugly" soundtrack echoed from the speakers she held
out her hand, caught the hat, and swept it onto her head. Ooh, baby, perfect
today, perfect. She smiled and strutted downstage. A woman at the front
table was standing. Cookie saw the flash of a very expensive watch, and for
no particular reason was flooded with conviction that tonight was going to
go very well indeed. Cookie, baby, she told herself, tonight you're gonna
get rich.

And with that catch of the hat, that strut, just like that, Cody forgot about
Boone and his contract, forgot about being seamless, forgot everything.
The dancer was fine, lean and soft, strong as a deer. The name Cookie was
picked out in rhinestones on her hat, and she wore a tiny fringed buckskin
halter and something that looked like a breechclout – flaps of suede that
hung from the waist to cover front and back, but not the sides – and wicked
spurs on the boots. She looked right at Cody and smiled, and her eyes were
not blank.

Part of Cody knew that Boone had seen her stand, and was now watching her watch this dancer, and that she should stop, or sit, or keep walking
to Boone's end of the table, but the other part – the part that liked to drink
shots in biker bars, to code all night with Acid Girls pounding from the
speakers and the company's fortunes riding on her deadline, the part that
had loaded up her pickup and left Florida to drive all the way to the West
Coast on her own when she was just nineteen, that had once hung by her
knees from a ninth floor balcony just because she could – that part cared
about nothing but this woman with the long brown hair.

The hair was Indian straight and ended just one inch above the hem of
the breechclout, and the way she moved made Cody understand that the
hat and spurs were trophies, taken from a dead man. When the dancer
trailed her hands across her body, Cody knew they held knives. When the
male voices began their rhythmic chanting, she could see this woman riding
hard over the plain, vaulting from her pony, stripping naked as she walked.

The music shifted but again it was drums, and now Cookie swayed
like a maiden by a pool, pulling the straps of her halter off her shoulders,
enough to expose half her breasts but not all, and she felt them thoughtfully, and began to smear them with warpaint. When she had painted
all she could see, she pushed the buckskin down further, so that each
breast rested like a satsuma on its soft shelf, then she turned her back
on the audience, twisted her hair over one shoulder and examined the

reflection of her ass in the water. She turned a little, this way and that, lift-ing the back flap, one corner then another, dropping it, thinking, stroking each cheek experimentally, trying to decide how to decorate it. Then she smoothed the buckskin with both hands so it pulled tight, and studied that effect. She frowned. She traced the outline of her g-string with her index finger. She smiled. She stuck her butt out, twitched it a couple of times, hooked both thumbs in the waistband of her g-string, and whipped it off. The breechclout stayed in place. She was still wearing the halter under her breasts.

And the little dyke liked that, Cookie could tell. She smiled smooth as cream, danced closer, saw the stain creeping up the woman's cheeks, the way her lips parted and her hands opened. Professionally manicured hands; clothes of beautifully cut linen, shoes handmade. The men in the room faded to irritation. This was the prize.

One of the men at the table reached out and slipped a twenty between the rawhide tie of her breechclout and her hip, but Cookie barely took her eyes from the woman. Twenty here or fifty there was small change compared to this. For you, she mouthed and turned slightly, and tightened down into a mushroom of skin-sheathed muscle, took off her hat, and reached back and pulled the flap of her breechclout out of the way.

She was aware of some shouting, the tall guy with the red face and the fifty, but she kept her eyes fixed on the woman.

And then the music changed, and Ginger was back from her lap dance, and she saw Christie was hand in hand with a glazed-looking mark, about to leave for the backroom, and it was time for her to put some of her clothes back on and work the floor.

Five minutes, she mouthed to the woman.

Cookie, Cody thought, as the dancer flicked the suede flap back in place, stood gracefully, and put her hat back on. Cookie. She watched as Cookie left the stage and took all the heat and light with her. She would come back, wouldn't she? Five minutes, she had said.

"Cunt!" Dave shouted again, "my money not good enough for you? Goddamned – No, you get off of me." He pushed Boone's hand from his arm, then realized what he'd done. "Shit. That's—It's just—You know how it is, man. But fifty bucks. . . ."

"Hell, Dave, maybe she knew it was counterfeit," Boone said jovially.

Dave forced a laugh, thrust the bill in his pocket. "Yeah, or maybe she just doesn't understand size matters." Boone laughed, but everyone at the table heard the dismissive note.

"Maybe it's time to call it a night, folks."

But Cody wasn't listening because Cookie was standing before her: no hat, buckskins and g-string back in place.

"Okay guys, looks like we lost Cody." Boone laughed, nothing like the laugh he'd given Dave. "Hey, girl, you make sure you get a cab home, hear? Mention my name to the doorman. Come on guys, we're outta here."

"Cody. Is that your name?" said Cookie, and took her hand. Cody nodded dumbly. "I'm Cookie. It's so good to find another woman here."

Another nod. How are you? Cody wanted to say, but that made no sense. "Would you like to dance with me? Just you and me in private?"

"Yes."

"We'd have to pay for the room."

"Yes."

"I love dancing for women. It gets me going, turns me on. I understand what women want, Cody. Would you like me to show you?"

"Yes," said Cody, and was mildly amazed when her legs worked well enough to follow Cookie to the frosted glass door.

Midnight in her hotel room. Cody sat on the bed, naked, too wired to lie down. Streetlight slanted through the unclosed drapes, turning the room sodium yellow. The air conditioning roared, but her skin burned. Cookie. Cookie's lips, Cookie's hips, Cookie's cheek and chin and belly. Her thighs and ass and breasts. Oh, her breasts, their soft weight on Cody's palms.

She lifted her hands, turned her palms up, examined them. They didn't look any different. She unsnapped her watch, rubbed her wrist absently. Cookie.

Stop it. What the fuck was the matter with her? She'd gone to a strip club and had sex for money. It was a first, okay, so some confusion was to be expected, but it was sordid, not romantic. She had been played by an expert and taken for hundreds of dollars. Oh, God, and Boone . . . She had made a fucking fool of herself.

So why did she feel so happy?

Cody, you're so beautiful, she'd said. Oh, yes, yes, don't stop, Cody. Give it to me, give me all of it. And Cody had. And Cookie had . . . Cookie had been perfect. She had understood everything, anticipated everything. What to say, what to do, when to cajole and goad, when to smile and be submissive, when to encourage, when to resist. Like a mind reader. And she had felt something, Cody knew it. She had. You couldn't fake pupil dilation, you couldn't fake that flush, you couldn't fake that sheen of sweat and luxuriant slipperiness. Could you?

Christ. She going mad. She rubbed her eyebrows. Cookie was a pro, and none of it was real.

She got up. The woolen carpet made her bare feet itch. That was real. Her clothes were flung across the back of the chair by the desk; they reeked of cigar smoke. No great loss. She'd no idea why she'd chosen to wear those loose pants, anyway. Hadn't worn them for about a year. Hadn't worn that stupid watch for about as long, come to think of it. Cookie hated the smell of cigars, she's said so, when she was unbuttoning—

Stop it. Stop it now.

She carried her pants to the bed and pulled the receipts from the pockets. Eight of them. She'd paid for eight lap dances, and the size of the tips . . . Jesus. That was two months' rent. What had she been thinking?

We have to pay for the room, Cookie said, but I'll pay you half back. It's just that I can't wait. Oh, please, Cody. I want you again.

"God damn it!" Her ferocity scared her momentarily and she stilled, listening. No stirrings or mutterings from either room next door.

Give me your hotel phone number, Cookie had said. I'll call you tomorrow. This has never happened before. This is real.

And if it was . . . She could reschedule her flight. She'd explain it to Vince somehow.

Christ. That huge contract gone, in a flash of lust. Vince would kill her.

But, oh, she'd had nearly three hours of the best sex she'd ever had. It had gone exactly the way she'd imagined it in her fantasies. I know just what you want, she'd said, and proved it.

But Cody had known too, that was the thing. She had known when the hoarse breath and clutching hands meant it was Cookie's turn, meant that Cookie now wanted to be touched, wanted to break every single personal and club rule and be fucked over the back of the chair, just for pleasure.

Cody stirred the receipts. She couldn't make it make sense. She had paid for sex. That was not romance. But she had felt Cookie's vaginal muscles tighten, felt that quiver in her perineum, the clutch and spasm of orgasm. It wasn't faked. It hadn't been faked the second time, either.

Cody shivered. The air conditioning was finally beginning to bite. She rubbed her cold feet. Cookie's feet were long and shapely, each toe painted with clear nail polish. She'd twisted her ankle, she'd said. Cody had held the ankle, kissed it, stroked it. Cookie's smile was beautiful. How did you sprain it? Cody had asked, and Cookie had told her about falling five feet from the indoor climbing wall, and they had talked about climbing and rafting, and Cody had told her of the time when she was seven and had seen Cirque du Soleil and wanted to be one of the trapeze artists, and that led to talk of abdominal muscles, which led to more sex.

She padded into the bathroom, still without bothering with the light. When she lifted her toothbrush to her mouth, the scent on her fingers tightened her muscles involuntarily. She dropped the toothbrush, leaned over the sink, and wept.

A blue, blue Atlanta morning. Cody hadn't slept. She didn't want breakfast. Her plane wasn't until four that afternoon.

She'd lost the contract, lost a night's sleep, lost her mind and her self-respect, and flushed two months' rent down the toilet. She would never see Cookie again – and she couldn't understand why she cared.

The phone rang. Cookie! she thought, and hated herself for it.

"Hello?"

"Your cell phone's off, but I called Vince back in Frisco and he told me you were at the Westin."

Boone. She shut her eyes.

"Plane's not til four, am I right? Cody, you there?"

"Yes. I'm here."

"If you're not too tuckered out, maybe you wouldn't mind dropping by my office. We'll give you lunch."

"Lunch?"

"Yep. You know, food. Don't they do lunch on the West Coast?"

"Yes. I mean, why?"

He chuckled. "Because we've got a few details to hammer out on this contract. So should we say, oh, eleven-thirty?"

"That's, yes, fine. Good," she said at random, and put the phone down.

She stared at her bag. Clothes. She'd need to change her clothes. Was he really giving her the contract?

The phone rang again. "Hello?" she said doubtfully, expecting anyone from god to the devil to reply.

"Hey, Cody. It's me."

"Richard?"

"Yeah. Listen, how did it go?"

"I don't . . . Things are . . ." She took a deep breath. "I got the contract."

"Hey, that's great. But how did last night go?"

"Christ, Richard, I can't gossip now. I don't have the time. I'm on my way to Boone's, iron out a few details." She had to pull it together. "I'll call you in a week or two, okay?"

"No, wait, Cody. Just don't do anything you – "

"Later, okay." She dropped the phone in its cradle. How did he know to call the Westin? What did he care about her night? She rubbed her forehead again. Food might help with the contract. The headache, she meant. And she grinned: the contract. She'd goddamned well won the contract. She was gonna get a huge bonus. She was gonna be a Vice President. She was gonna be late.

In the bathroom, she picked up the toothbrush, rinsed off the smeared paste, and resolutely refused to think about last night.

Cookie dialed the hotel.

"This is Cody. Leave a message, or reach me on my cell phone," followed by a string of numbers beginning with 216. San Francisco. That's right. She'd told Cookie that last night: San Francisco with its fog and hills and great espresso on Sunday mornings.

That might be okay. Anything would beat this Atlanta heat.

Boone didn't want to talk details so much as to laugh and drink coffee and teach Cody how to eat a po' boy sandwich. After all, if they were gonna be

working together, they should get to know each other, was he right? And
there was no mention of strip clubs or lap dances until the end when he
signed the letter of intent, handed it to her, and said, "I like the way you
handle yourself. Now take that Austin fella, Dave. No breeding. Can't hold
his liquor, can't keep his temper, and calls a woman names in public. But
you: no boasting, no big words, you just sit quiet then seize the opportunity."
He gave her a sly smile. "You do that in business and we'll make ourselves
some money."

And somehow, with his clap on the back, the letter in her laptop case and
the sun on her face while she waited for the car for her trip to the airport,
she started to forget her confusion. She'd had great sex, she'd built the foundations of a profitable working relationship, she was thirty-one and about to
be a vice president, and she didn't even have a hangover.

The car came and she climbed into the cool, green-tinted interior.

She let the outside world glide by for ten minutes before she got out the
letter of intent. She read it twice. Beautifully phrased. Strong signature.
Wonderful row of zeroes before the decimal point. If everything stayed on
track, this one contract would keep their heads above water until they could
develop a few more income streams. And she had done it. No one else. Damn
she was good! Someone should buy her a great dinner to celebrate.

She got out her phone, turned it on. The signal meter wavered as the
car crossed from cell to cell. Who should she call? No one in their right
mind would want to have dinner with Vince. Richard would only want all
the details, and she didn't want to talk about those details yet; he was in the
Carolinas, anyway. Asshole.

The signal suddenly cleared, and her phone bleeped: one message.

"Hey. This is Cookie. I know you don't go until the afternoon. If you . . .
I know this is weird but last night was . . . Shit. Look, maybe you won't
believe me but I can't stop thinking about you. I want to see you, okay? I'll
be in the park, the one I told you about. Piedmont. On one of the benches
by the lake. I'm going there now, and I'll wait. I hope you come. I'll bring
doughnuts. Do you like doughnuts? I'll be waiting. Please."

Oooh, you're different, ooh, you're so special, ooh, give it to me baby, just
pay another thousand dollars and I'll love you forever. Sure. But Cookie's
voice sounded so soft, so uncertain, as though she really meant it. But of
course it would. That was her living: playing pretend. Using people.

Cody's face prickled. Be honest, she told herself: who really used who,
here? Who got the big contract, who got to have exactly what she wanted:
great sex with no complications, and on the expense account no less?

It was too confusing. She was too tired. She was leaving. It was all too late
anyhow, she thought, as the car moved smoothly onto the interstate.

A woman sitting on her own on a bench, maybe getting hot, maybe
getting thirsty, wanting to use the bathroom. Afraid to get up and go pee
because she might miss the one she was waiting for. Maybe the hot sweet
scent of the doughnuts reminded her she was hungry, but she wouldn't eat
them because she wanted to present them in their round-dozen perfection to

her sweetie, see her smile of delight. She would pick at the paint peeling on the wooden bench and look up every time someone like Cody walked past; every time, she'd be disappointed. This one magical thing had happened in her life, something very like a miracle, but as the hot fat sun sinks lower she understands that this miracle, this dream is going to die because the person she's resting all her hopes on is worried she might look like a fool. Or doesn't want to admit she had used a woman for sex then thrown her away.

Cody blinked, looked at her watch. She leaned forward, cleared her throat.

The driver looked at her in his mirror. "Ma'am?"

"Where is Piedmont park?"

"Northeast of downtown."

"Do we pass it on the way to the airport?"

"No, ma'am."

She was crazy. But all that waited for her at home was a tankful of fish. "Take me there."

Without the hat and boots, wearing jeans and sandals and the kind of tank top Cody herself might have picked, Cookie looked young. So did her body language. Her hair was in a braid. She was flipping it from shoulder to shoulder, twisting on the bench to look to one side, behind her, the other side. When she saw Cody, her face opened in a big smile that was naked and utterly vulnerable.

"How old are you?" Cody blurted.

The face closed. "Twenty-six. How old are you?"

"Thirty-one." Cody didn't sit down.

They stared at each other. "Dirt on my face?"

"No. Sorry. It looks . . . you look different."

"You expect me to dress like that on my day off, too?"

"No! No." But part of her had. "So. You get a lot of days off?"

A short laugh. "Can't afford it. No expense accounts for me. No insurance, no 401(k), no paid vacation."

Cody flushed. "Earning two thousand bucks a night isn't exactly a hard luck story."

"Was I worth it?"

Her smell filled Cody's mouth. Yes! she wanted to shout. Yes, a hundred times over. But that made no sense, so she just stood there.

"You paid twenty-two hundred. The house takes sixty per cent off the top. Out of my eight eighty, Danny takes another twenty percent and, no, he's a bouncer, not a pimp, and I've never done that before last night. And, no, I don't expect you to believe me. Then there's costumes, hair, waxing, makeup . . ." She leaned back, draped both arms along the back of the bench. "You tell me. Would fucking a complete stranger for three hours be worth five hundred dollars?"

Her mouth stretched in a hard smile but her eyes glistened. She put one ankle up on the other knee.

"Does your ankle still hurt?" It just popped out.

Cookie turned away, blinked a couple of times. Cody found herself kneeling before the bench.

"Cookie? Cookie, don't cry."

"Susana," she said, still turned away.

"What?"

"Susana. It's my real name. Susana Herrera." She turned to Cody, and her face was fierce. "I am Susana Herrera. I'm a dancer, I'm not a whore, and I want to know what you've done to me."

"What I've . . . ?"

"I dance. I tease, I hint. It makes you feel good, you give me money, which makes me feel good. Sometimes I give a lap dance, but always by the rules: hands on the armrest, clothes on, a little bump and grind, because I need the extra tips. I dance, you pay. It's my job. But this, this isn't a job! I don't know what it is. It's crazy. I let you—" Her cheeks darkened. "And I would do it again, for no money. For nothing. It's crazy. I feel . . . It's like . . . I don't even know how to say it! I want to talk to you, listen to you talk about your business. I want to see your house. I didn't sleep last night. I thought about you: your smile, your hands, how strong it made me feel to give you pleasure, how warm I felt when you wrapped your arms around me. And I'm afraid."

"Me too," Cody said, and she was, very, because she was beginning to get an idea what was wrong with them and it felt like a very bad joke.

"You're not afraid." Susana folded her arms, turned her face again.

"I am. Cook – Susana, do you suppose . . . Shit. I feel ridiculous even saying this. Look at me. Please. Thank you. Do you suppose this is what I—"

She couldn't say it. She didn't believe it.

After a very long pause, Susana said, "Dancers don't fall in love with the marks."

That cut. "Marks don't fall in love with whores."

"I'm not a – "

"Neither am I."

They stared at each other. Cody's phone rang. She thumbed it off without looking. "My full name is Candice Marcinko. I have to fly back to San Francisco this afternoon but I could come back to Atlanta at the end of the week. We could, you know, talk, go to the movies, walk in the park." Jesus, had she left any stereotype unturned? She tried again. "I want to meet your, your cat."

"I don't have a cat."

"Or your dog," she said. Stop babbling. But she couldn't. "I want to learn how long you've lived in Atlanta and what kind of food you like and whether you think the Braves will win tonight and how you feel when you sleep in my arms." She felt like an idiot.

Susana looked at her for a while, then picked up the box at her side. "Do you like Krispy Kreme?"

*   *   *

When Cody turned her phone on again at the airport, there was a message from Richard: Call me, it's important. But she had to run for her plane.

In the air she leaned her head against the window and listened to the drone of the engines.

Susana, sitting on the bench while the sun went down, thinking, Love, love is for rich people.

A cream labrador runs by, head turned to watch its owner, running alongside. Its tongue lolls, happy and pink. Dogs love. Dogs are owned.

She tears the last three doughnuts to pieces and throws them to the ducks.

On Thursday, Vince and the executive team toasted her with champagne. She took the opportunity to ask for Friday and two days next week off. Vince couldn't say no without looking chintzy, so he told her VPs didn't have to ask permission.

VP. She grinned hard and for a minute she felt almost normal. VP. Top dog.

Friday morning she had just got out of the shower when the doorbell rang. She was so surprised she barely remembered to pull on a robe before she opened the door.

"Well, that's a sight for sore eyes."

"Richard!"

"Not that I don't appreciate the gesture but could you please tighten that belt, at least until we've had coffee? Here you go, quad grande, two per cent."

She went to get dressed. When she emerged, drying her hair with a towel, he was sitting comfortably on the couch, ankle crossed at the knee, just like Susana in the park.

"I envy you that dyke rub-and-go convenience."

She draped the towel round her neck, sat, and sipped the latte. "To paraphrase you, it's not that I don't appreciate the coffee, but . . . why the fuck are you here?"

He put his phone on the table next to her latte. "Remember this?"

"It's your phone?"

He took a thumbdrive from his laptop case and gave it, then her, a significant look.

"Richard, I've had a real weird few days and I'm on a plane in four hours. Maybe." Maybe she was crazy, maybe she should cancel . . . "Anyhow, could you please just get to the point?"

"Drink your coffee. You're going to need it. And tell me what happened on Tuesday night." He held up his hand. "Just tell me. Because my guess is you had a hell of a night with a lovely young thing called Cookie."

She didn't say anything for a long, long time. "Susana," she said finally.

"Ah. You got that far? Susana Herrera, aged twenty-four—"

"Twenty-six."

"Twenty-four. Trust me. Mother Antonia Herrera, father unknown. Dunwoody community college, degree in business administration – oh, the look on your face – and one previous arrest for possession of a controlled substance. Healthy as an ox. Not currently taking any medication except contraceptive pills."

"The pill?"

"What's the matter?"

"Nothing. Go on."

"No known allergies to pharmaceuticals, though a surprising tolerance to certain compounds, for example sodium thiopental and terpazine hydrochloride."

Cody seized on something that made sense. "Wait. I know that drug. It's—"

"RU486 for the mind. That's the one."

"Oh, Jesus, Richard, you didn't give her that! You didn't make her forget what happened!"

"Not what happened Tuesday."

Cody, confused, said nothing.

He plugged the thumbdrive into his laptop and turned the screen so she could see the sound file icons. "It will all make sense when you've listened to these."

"But I don't have time. I have a plane—"

"You'll want to cancel that, if it's to Atlanta. Just listen. Then I'll answer questions."

He tapped play.

". . . ever happens, I promise no one will ever hear what goes on this tape except you."

"Cue ominous music."

She jumped at the sound of her own voice. "What—"

"Shh."

" – more an, um, an ethics thing."

"Jesus, Richard. You're such a drama queen." Pause. Clink.

"I've done my research, too. Like you, I'm pretty sure what will happen after you've made your presentations to Boone."

"The Golden Key."

" – but what I need to know from you is whether or not you can authorize out-of-pocket expenses in the high five figures to win this contract."

He touched pause. "Ring any bells?"

"No." Cody's esophagus had clamped shut. She could hardly swallow her own spit, never mind the latte. But the cardboard was warm and smooth in her hand, comforting, and behind Richard her fish swam serenely back and forth.

"Terpazine is a good drug. We managed to calculate your dosage beautifully. Susana's was a bit more of a challenge. Incredible metabolism."

"You said you didn't give her—"

"Not in the last couple of weeks. But you've had it six times, and she seven. Now keep listening."

Six times?

"– the exploration of memory and its retrieval. So exciting. A perfect dovetail with the work I've been doing on how people form attachments. It's all about familiarity. You let someone in deep enough, or enough times, then your brain actually rewires to recognize that person as friend, or family."

Pause.

"There are ways to make it easier for someone to let you in."

Clink of bottle on glass.

"I've told you about those studies that show it's as simple as having Person A anticipate Person B's needs and fulfill them."

"So don't tell me again."

She sounded so sure of herself, bored even. A woman who had never thought to use the world love.

" – jumpstart the familiarization process. For example, person A works in a bookshop and is lonely, and when she's lonely chocolate makes her feel better. And one day person B arrives mid-afternoon with some choco-late, says Hey, you look sorta miserable, when I'm miserable chocolate makes me feel better, would you like one? and A eats a chocolate and thinks, Wow, this B person is very thoughtful and empathic and must be just like me, and therefore gets slotted immediately into the almost-friend category. It's easy to set something like that up. You just have to know enough about person A."

Know enough.

Cody pushed the laptop from her. "I don't believe this."

"No?"

Cody didn't say anything.

"You sat in that Seattle bar, and you listened, and then you signed a temporary waiver." He placed a piece of paper on the table by her hand. It was her signature at the bottom – a little sloppy, but hers. "Then you took some terpazine and forgot all about it."

"I wouldn't forget something like this."

He held up his hand. Reached with his other and nudged the sound file slider to the right.

"Take the pill."

"Alright, alright." Pause. Tinkle of ice cubes. "Jesus. That tastes vile."

"Next time we'll put it in a capsule. Just be grateful it's not the vaso-pressin. It would make you gag. I speak from experience."

He tapped the file to silence. "It really does. Anyhow, a week after Seattle I came here and you signed a more robust set of papers." He handed her a thick, bound document. "Believe me, they're bombproof."

"Wait." She dropped the document on her lap without looking. "You came here? To my apartment?"

"I did. I played the recording you've just heard, showed you the initial waiver. Gave you that." He nodded at her lap. "You signed. I gave you the sodium thiopental, we had our first session. You took another terpazine."

"I don't remember."

He shrugged. "It happened." He tapped the paper in her lap. "There's a signed waiver for every session."

"How many did you say?"

"Six. Four here, twice in North Carolina."

"But I don't remember!"

The fish in her tank swam back and forth, back and forth. She closed her eyes. Opened them. The fish were still there. Richard was still there. She could still remember the weight of Susana's breasts in her hands.

"You'd better listen to the rest. And read everything over."

He tapped play.

"Okay. Think about what it would be like if you knew enough about someone and then you met: you'd know things about her and she'd know things about you, but all you'd know is that you recognize and trust this person and you feel connected. Now imagine what might happen if you add sex to the equation."

"Good sex, I hope."

"The best. There are hundreds of studies that show how powerful sex bonding can be, especially for women. If a woman has an orgasm in the presence of another person, her hormonal output for the next few days is sensitized to her lover: every time they walk in the room, her system floods with chemical messengers like oxytocin saying Friend! Friend! This is even with people you know, consciously, aren't good for you. You put that together with someone compatible, who fits – whether they really fit or just seem to fit – and it's a chemical bond with the potential to be human superglue. That's what love is: a bond that's renewed every few days until the brain is utterly rewired. So I wanted to know what would happen if you put together two sexually compatible people who magically knew exactly – exactly! – what the other wanted in bed but had no memory of how they'd acquired that knowledge . . ."

It took Cody a moment to pause the sound. "Love," she said. "Love? What the fuck have you done to me?"

"You did it to yourself. Keep listening."

And she did. After she had listened for an hour, she accepted the sheaf of transcripts Richard handed her from his case.

She looked at the clock.

"Still thinking about that plane?"

Cody didn't know what she was thinking.

"Is it refundable?" he said. "The flight?"

Cody nodded.

"Give me the ticket. I'll cancel for you. You can always rebook for tomorrow. But you need to read."

She watched, paralyzed, as Richard picked up the phone and dialed. He turned to her while he was on hold, mouthed Read, and turned away again.

So she began to read, only vaguely aware of Richard arguing his way up the airline hierarchy.

After the first hundred pages of Subject C and Subject S, he brought her fresh coffee. She paused at one section, appalled.

"What?"

"I can't believe I told you that."

He peered over her shoulder. "Oh, that's a juicy one. Stop blushing. I've heard it all before. Several times now. Sodium thiopental will make you say anything. Besides, you don't remember telling me, so why bother being embarrassed?"

She watched her fish. It didn't matter. Didn't matter. She picked up the paper again and ploughed on. May as well get it over with.

Somewhere around page three hundred, he went into the kitchen to make lunch. She didn't remember eating it, but when she set aside the final page at seven o'clock that evening, she saw that the plate by her elbow was empty, and heard the end of Richard's order to the Chinese takeout place on the corner. It was clearly something he'd done before. From her phone, in her apartment. And she didn't remember.

She wished there was a way to feed him terpazine so he would forget all those things she'd never said to another soul before.

She tried to organize her thoughts.

He had asked for her permission to use her in an experiment. It would mean she would feel comfortable at the club in Atlanta, that she might even have a good couple of hours, and it would further his work while being paid for to some extent by her expense account. He had traveled to the Golden Key and picked Susana as the most likely dancer to fit her fantasies – and he knew a little about her preferences from that stupid, stupid night in Dallas – and made the same pitch to her. Only Susana got paid.

Twice, Cody thought. I paid her too.

And so Richard had flown to Cody's apartment in San Francisco and given her sodium thiopental, and she had talked a bluestreak about her sexual fantasies, every nuance and variation and degree of pleasure. In North Carolina, she had talked about her fantasies again, even more explicitly, encouraged to imagine in great detail, pretend it was happening, while they had her hooked up to both a functional MRI and several blood-gas sensors.

Richard put down the phone. "Food in thirty minutes."

Cody forced herself to stay focused, to think past her embarrassment. "What were the fMRIs for, the fMRIs and – " she glanced at the paper, " – TMS during the, the fantasy interludes?"

"We built a kind of mind and hormone map of how you'd feel if someone was actually doing those things to you. A sort of super-empathy direction finder. And one from Susana, of course. We played your words to each other, along with transcranial magnetic stimulation to encourage brain plasticity – the rewiring."

"And," she hunted through the pages for the section labeled Theoretical Underpinnings. "You gave me, us, oxytocin?"

"No. We wanted to separate out the varying factors. You supplied the oxytocin on your own, later." He beamed. "That's the beautiful part. It was all your own doing. Your hopes, your hormones, your needs. Yours. We made a couple of suggestions to each of you that you might not have come up with on your own: that expensive watch and the loose clothes, Cookie's hat and spurs. But the rest was just you and Cookie, I mean Susana. But you two were primed for each other, so if that wasn't the best sex of your life, I'll eat this table." He rapped the table top in satisfaction.

All her own doing.

"You can't publish," she said.

"Not this, no." He picked up one of the fMRIs and admired it. "It's enough for now to know that it works."

She waited for anger to well up but nothing happened. "Is this real?"

"The project? Quite real."

Project. She watched him gather all the documents, tap them into a neat pile.

"Not the project," she said. "Not the TMS, the fMRIs, the terpazine. This." She tapped her chest. "Is it real?"

He tilted his head. "Is love real? A lot of people seem to think so. But if you mean, is that what you're feeling, the answer is, I don't know. I don't think a scan could give you that answer. But it could tell us if you've changed: your data have been remarkably clear. Not like Cookie's. Susana's." He held the fMRI image up again, admired it some more, then put it back in the pile.

"What do you mean?"

"The data. Yours were perfectly consistent. Hers were . . . erratic."

"Erratic." Her mind seemed to be working in another dimension. It took an age for the thought to form. "Like lying?"

"She's lied about a lot of things."

"But she could have been lying to me? About how she feels?"

He shrugged. "How can we ever know?"

She stared at him. "The literature," she said, trying to force her slippery brain to remember what she'd just read. "Its says love's a feedback loop, right?"

"In terms of individual brain plasticity, yes."

"So it's mutual. I can't love someone if she doesn't love me." If it was love.

He gave her a look she couldn't interpret. "The data don't support interdependence." He paused, said more gently, "We don't know."

Pity, she realized. He pities me. She felt the first flex and coil of something so far down she couldn't identify it. "What have you done to me? What else have you done to me?"

"To you? For you."

"You made me feel something for a woman who fucked for money. Who had her mind fucked for money."

"So did you, if you think about. Just at one remove."

"I didn't."

"So, what, you did it for science?"

Cody changed direction. "Does Susana know?"

"I'm flying to Atlanta tomorrow."

"Do you have her sound files with you?"

"Of course."

"Let me hear them."

"That would be unethical."

Unethical. "I think you might be a monster," she said, but without heat.

"I have a strange way of showing it, then, wouldn't you say? For the price of a few embarrassing experimental sessions you won't ever remember, I won you a contract, a girlfriend and a night on the town."

She stared at him. "You expect me to be grateful . . ."

"Well, look at this place. Look at it. Bare walls. Fish, for god's sake."

"Get out."

"Oh, come on—"

"Out."

"By tomorrow it will all fall into perspective."

"I swear to god, if you don't leave now I'll break your face." She sounded so weirdly calm. Was this shock, or was it just how people in love, or whatever, behaved? She had no idea. "And you can put those papers down. They're mine, my private thoughts. Leave them right there on the table. The thumbdrive, too."

He pulled the drive, laid it on the papers, stowed his laptop and stood. She held the door open for him.

He was halfway through the door when she said, "Richard. You can't tell Susana like this."

"No?"

"It's too much of a shock."

"You seem to be coping admirably."

"At least I already knew you. Or thought I did. You'll be a complete stranger to her. You can't. You just can't. It's . . . inhumane. And she's so young."

"Young? Don't make me laugh. She makes you look like an infant." He walked away.

Cookie danced. She didn't want to think about the phone call. Didn't want to think about any of it. Creep.

But there was the money.

The lights were hot, but the air conditioning cold. Her skin pebbled.

"Yo, darlin', let's you and me go to the back room," the suit with the moustache and bad tie said. He was drunk. She knew the type. He'd slip his hands from the chair, try to cop a feel, get pissed off when she called in Danny, refuse to pay.

"Well, now," she said, in her special honey voice. "Let's see if you've got the green," and pushed her breasts together invitingly. He flicked a bill across her breasts. "A five won't buy you much, baby."

"Five'll buy you, babydoll," he said, hamming for his table buddies. One of them giggled. Ugly sound in a man, Cookie thought. "Five'll buy you five times!"

"And how long did it take you to come up with that, honey?"

"The fuck?" He looked confused.

"I said, your brain must be smaller than your dick which I'd guess is even smaller than your wallet, only I doubt that's possible," and she plucked the bill from his fingers, snapped it under her g-string and walked away.

In the dressing room she looked at herself in the mirror. Twenty-four was too old for this. Definitely. She had no idea what time it was.

She stuck her head out of the door. "Danny!"

"Yes, doll."

"Time is it?" She'd have to get herself a watch someday. A nice expensive watch.

"Ten after," Danny said.

"After what?"

"Ten."

Three hours earlier on the West Coast. She stacked her night's take, counted it, thought for a minute, peeled off two hundred in fives and ones. She stuck her head out of the door again. "Danny!"

"Here, doll."

"I'm gone."

"You sick?" He ambled up the corridor, stood breathing heavily by the door.

"Sick of this."

"Mister Pergoletti says—"

"You tell Pergoletti to stick it. I'm gone. Seriously." She handed him the wad of bills. "You take care of these girls, now. And have a good life."

"Got something else lined up?"

"Guess we'll find out."

There was one bottle of beer in Cody's fridge. She opened it, poured it carefully into a glass, stared at the beige foam. A glass: she never drank beer from a glass. She poured it down the sink. She had no idea what was real anymore but she was pretty sure alcohol would only make things worse.

She made green tea instead and settled down in the window seat. The sun hung low over the bay. What did Susana see from her apartment? Was her ankle better? Contraceptive pills, Jesus. And, oh, the smell of her skin.

She was losing her mind.

She didn't know who she hated more: Richard for making the proposal, or herself for accepting it. Or Susana. Susana had done it for money.

Or maybe . . . But what about those contraceptive pills?

And what if Susana did feel . . . whatever it was? Did that make it real? It was all an experiment, all engineered. Fake.

But it didn't feel fake. She wanted to cradle Susana, kiss her ankle better, protect her from the world. The Richards of the world.

She picked up the phone, remembered for the tenth time she had neither address nor phone number. She called information, who told her there was no listing under Susana Herrera in the Atlanta Metro area. She found herself unsurprised, though surprised at how little it mattered.

She got the number for the Golden Key instead.

A man called Pergoletti answered. "Cookie? She's gone. They always go." The music thumped. Cody's insides vibrated in sympathy, remembering.

" – don't have a number. Hey, you interested in a job?"

Cody put the phone down carefully. Sipped her tea. Picked up the phone again, and called Richard.

It was open mic night at Coffee to the People. Richard was in the back room on a sofa, as far from the music as possible. Two cups on the table. One still full.

"You knew I'd call."

"I did."

"Did you program that, too?"

"I didn't program anything. I primed you – and only about the sex." He patted the sofa. "Sit down before you fall down."

She sat. Blinked. "Give me her phone number."

"I can't. She gave me a fake. I called her at the club, but she hung up on me." He seemed put out.

"What does she know?"

"I talked fast. I don't know how much she heard. But I told her she wouldn't get the rest of the money until we'd done follow up."

The singer in the other room sang of love and broken hearts. It was terrible, but it made Cody want to cry anyway.

"How long does it last?"

"Love? I don't know. I avoid it where possible."

"What am I going to do?"

Richard lifted his laptop bag. "I planned for this eventuality." He took out a small white cardboard box. He opened it, shook something onto his hand. A grey plastic inhaler.

"What is it?"

"A vasopressin analogue, formulated to block oxytocin receptors in the nucleus accumbens. That is, the antidote."

They both looked at it.

"It works in voles," he said. "Female voles."

Voles. "You said it tasted bad."

"I've used it. Just in case. I prefer my sex without complications. And I've had a lot of sex and never once fallen in love." He arched his eyebrows. "So, hey, it must work."

The elephant whistle hypothesis. Hey, Bob, what's that whistle? Well, Fred, it keeps elephants away. Don't be an asshole, Bob, there aren't any elephants around here. Well, Fred, that's because of my whistle.

"Cody." He did his best to look sincere. "I'm so very sorry. I never thought it would work. Not like this. But I do think the antidote might work." His face went back to normal. He hefted the inhaler. "Though before I give it to you, I have a favor to ask."

She stared at him. "On what planet do I owe you anything?"

"For science, then. A follow up scan, and then another after you take the antidote."

"Maybe I won't take it. Give me the number."

"Love is a form of insanity, you know."

"The number."

In the other room, the bad singing went on and on.

"Oh, all right. For old times' sake." He extracted a folder from his bag, and a piece of paper from the folder. He slid it across the table towards her, put the inhaler on top of it.

She nudged the inhaler aside, picked up the paper. Hand written. Susana's writing.

"Love's just biochemical craziness," he said, "designed to make us take a leap in the dark, to trust complete strangers. It's not rational."

Cody said nothing.

"She screwed us."

"She screwed you," Cody said. "Maybe she fell in love with me." But she took the inhaler.

Cody sat in the window seat with the phone and the form Susana had filled in. Every now and again she punched in a different combination of the numbers Susana had written and got the Cannot be completed as dialed voice. Every now and again she touched the form with the tip of her middle finger; she could feel the indentation made by Susana's strong strokes. Strong strokes, strong hands, strong mouth.

She didn't think about the grey inhaler in its white box, which she had put in the fridge – to stay viable a long time, just in case.

After a while she stopped dialing and simply waited.

When her phone lit up at 11:46 she knew who it was – even before she saw the 404 area code on the screen.

"Do you feel it?" Susana said.

"Yes," and Cody did. Whatever it was, wherever it came from, it was there, as indelible as ink. She wanted to say, I don't know if this is real, I don't know if it's good. She wanted to ask, Had you ever had sex with anyone for money before me? and Does it matter? She wanted to know, Have you ever loved anyone before? and, How can you know?

She wanted to say, Will it hurt?

Walking through the crowds at the airport, Cody searched for the familiar face, felt her heart thump every time she thought she saw her. Panic, or love? She didn't know. She didn't know anything except that her throat ached.

Someone jostled her with his bag, and when she looked up, there was the back of that head, that smooth brown hair, so familiar, after just one night, and all her blood vessels seemed to expand at once, every cell leap forward.

She didn't move. This was it, the last moment. This was where she could just let the crowd carry her past, carry her away, out into the night. Walk away. Go home. Use the inhaler in the fridge.

That was the sensible thing. But the Cody who had hung from the ninth storey balcony, the Cody who had risked the Atlanta contract without a second thought, that Cody thought, fuck it, and stepped forward.

You couldn't know. You could never know.

BLOCKED

Geoff Ryman

Born in Canada, Geoff Ryman now lives in England. He made his first sale in 1976, to New Worlds, but it was not until 1984, when he made his first appearance in *Interzone* with his brilliant novella *The Unconquered Country*, that he first attracted any serious attention. *The Unconquered Country*, one of the best novellas of the decade, had a stunning impact on the science fiction scene of the day, and almost overnight established Ryman as one of the most accomplished writers of his generation, winning him both the British Science Fiction Award and the World Fantasy Award; it was later published in a book version, *The Unconquered Country: A Life History*. His output has been sparse since then, by the high-production standards of the genre, but extremely distinguished, with his short fiction appearing frequently in *The Magazine of Fantasy and Science Fiction* and his novel *The Child Garden: A Low Comedy* winning both the prestigious Arthur C. Clarke Award and the John W. Campbell Memorial Award; his later novel *Air* also won the Arthur C. Clarke Award. His other novels include *The Warrior Who Carried Life*, the critically acclaimed mainstream novel *Was*, *Coming of Enkidu*, *The King's Last Song*, *Lust*, and the underground cult classic *253*, the "print remix" of an "interactive hypertext novel," which in its original form ran online on Ryman's home page of ryman.com, and which, in its print form, won the Philip K. Dick Award. Four of his novellas have been collected in *Unconquered Countries*. His most recent book is the anthology *When It Changed*.

Here he gives us the fascinating story of an Uplifted animal in a strange future world who is trying to take care of his adopted human family, and finding that he needs to make some very hard choices along the way.

I DREAMED THIS IN Sihanoukville, a town of new casinos, narrow beaches, hot bushes with flowers that look like daffodils, and even now after nine years of peace, stark ruined walls with gates that go nowhere.

In the dream, I get myself a wife. She's beautiful, blonde, careworn. She is not used to having a serious man with good intentions present himself to her on a beach. Her name is Agnete and she speaks with a Danish accent. She has four Asian children.

Their father had been studying permanently in Europe, married Agnete and then "left," which in this world can mean several things. Agnete was an orphan herself and the only family she had was that of her Cambodian husband. So she came to Phnom Penh only to find that her in-laws did not want some strange woman they did not know and all those extra mouths to feed.

I meet the children. The youngest is Gerda, who cannot speak a word of Khmer. She's tiny, as small as infant though three years old, in a splotched pink dress and too much toy jewellery. She just stares, while her brothers play. She's been picked up from everything she knows and thrown down into this hot, strange world in which people speak nonsense and the food burns your mouth.

I kneel down and try to say hello to her, first in German, and then in English. Hello Gertie, hello little girl. Hello. She blanks all language and sits like she's sedated.

I feel so sad, I pick her up and hold her, and suddenly she buries her head in my shoulder. She falls asleep on me as I swing in a hammock and quietly explain myself to her mother. I am not married, I tell Agnete. I run the local casino.

Real men are not hard, just unafraid. If you are a man you say what is true, and if someone acts like a monkey, then maybe you punish them. To be a crook, you have to be straight. I sold guns for my boss and bought policemen, so he trusted me, so I ran security for him for years. He was one of the first to Go, and he sold his shares in the casino to me. Now it's me who sits around the black lacquered table with the generals and Thai partners. I have a Lexus and a good income. I have ascended and become a man in every way but one. Now I need a family.

Across from Sihanoukville, all about the bay are tiny islands. On those islands, safe from thieves, glow the roofs where the Big Men live in Soriya-chic amid minarets, windmills, and solar panels. Between the islands hang white suspension footbridges. Distant people on bicycles move across them.

Somehow it's now after the wedding. The children are now mine. We loll shaded in palm-leaf panel huts. Two of the boys play on a heap of old rubber inner tubes. Tharum with his goofy smile and sticky-out ears is long-legged enough to run among them, plonking his feet down into the donut holes. Not to be outdone, his brother Sampul clambers over the things. Rith the oldest looks cool in a hammock, away with his earphones, pretending not to know us.

Gerda tugs at my hand until I let her go. Freed from the world of language and adults she climbs up and over the swollen black tubes, sliding down sideways. She looks intent and does not laugh.

Her mother in a straw hat and sunglasses makes a thin, watery sunset smile.

Gerda and I go wading. All those islands shelter the bay, so the waves roll onto the shore child-sized, as warm and gentle as caresses. Gerda holds onto my hand and looks down at them, scowling in silence.

Alongside the beach is a grounded airliner, its wings cut away and neatly laid beside it. I take the kids there, and the boys run around inside it, screaming. Outside, Gerda and I look at the aircraft's spirit house. Someone witty has given the shrine tiny white wings.

The surrounding hills still have their forests, cumulo-nimbus clouds towering over them like clenched fists.

In the evening, thunder comes.

I look out from our high window and see flashes of light in the darkness. We live in one whole floor of my casino hotel. Each of the boys has his own suite. The end rooms have balconies, three of them, that run all across the front of the building with room enough for sofas and dining tables. We hang tubes full of pink sugar water for hummingbirds. In the mornings, the potted plants buzz with bees, and balls of seed lure the sarika bird that comes to sing its sweetest song.

In these last days, the gambling action is frenetic: Chinese, Thai, Korean, and Malays, they play baccarat mostly, but some prefer the one-armed bandits.

At the tables of my casino, elegant young women, handsome young men and a couple of other genders besides, sit upright ready to deal, looking as alert and frightened as rabbits, especially if their table is empty. They are paid a percentage of the take. Some of them sleep with customers too, but they're good kids; they always sent the money home. Do good, get good, we in Cambodia used to say. Now we say, Twee akrow meen lay. Do bad, have money.

My casino is straight. My wheels turn true. No guns, says my sign. No animals, no children. Innocence must be protected. No cigarettes or powders. Those last two are marked by a skull-and-crossbones.

We have security but the powders don't show up on any scan, so some of my customers come here to die. Most weekends, we find one, a body slumped over the table.

I guess some of them think it's good to go out on a high. The Chinese are particularly susceptible. They love the theatre of gambling, the tough-guy stance, the dance of the cigarette, the nudge of the eyebrow. You get dealt a good hand, you smile, you take one last sip of Courvoisier, then one sniff. You Go Down for good.

It's another way for the winner to take all. For me, they are just a mess to clear up, another reason to keep the kids away.

Upstairs, we've finished eating and we can hear the shushing of the sea.

"Daddy," Sampul asks me and the word thrums across my heart. "Why are we all leaving?"

"We're being invaded."

So far, this has been a strange and beautiful dream, full of Buddhist monks in orange robes lined up at the one-armed bandits. But now it goes like a stupid kids' TV show, except that in my dream, I'm living it, it's real. As I speak, I can feel my own sad, damp breath.

"Aliens are coming," I say and kiss him. "They are bringing many many ships.

"We can see them now, at the edge of the solar system. They'll be here in less than two years."

He sighs and looks perturbed.

In this disrupted country two-thirds of everything is a delight, two-thirds of everything iron nastiness. The numbers don't add up, but it's true.

"How do we know they're bad?" he asks, his face puffy.

"Because the government says so and the government wouldn't lie."

His breath goes icy. "This government would."

"Not all governments, not all of them all together."

"So. Are we going to leave?"

He means leave again. They left Denmark to come here, and they are all of them sick of leaving.

"Yes, but we'll all go together, OK?"

Rith glowers at me from the sofa. "It's all the fault of people like you."

"I made the aliens?" I think smiling at him will make him see he is being silly.

He rolls his eyes. "There's the comet?" he asks like I've forgotten something and shakes his head.

"Oh, the comet, yes, I forgot about the comet, there's a comet coming too. And global warming and big new diseases."

He tuts. "The aliens sent the comet. If we'd had a space programme we could meet them halfway and fight there. We could of had people living in Mars, to survive."

"Why wouldn't the aliens invade Mars too?"

His voice goes smaller, he hunches even tighter over his game. "If we'd gone into space, we would of been immortal."

My father was a drunk who left us; my mother died; I took care of my sisters. The regime made us move out of our shacks by the river to the countryside where there was no water so that the generals could build their big hotels. We survived. I never saw a movie about aliens, I never had this dream of getting away to outer space. My dream was to become a man.

I look out over the Cambodian night, and fire and light dance about the sky like dragons at play. There's a hissing sound. Wealth tumbles down in the form of rain.

Sampul is the youngest son and is a tough little guy. He thumps Rith, who's 15 years old and both of them gang up on gangly Tharum. But tough-guy Sampul suddenly curls up next to me on the sofa as if he's returning to the egg.

The thunder's grief looks like rage. I sit and listen to the rain. Rith plays on, his headphones churning with the sound of stereophonic war.

Everything dies, even suns; even the universe dies and comes back. We already are immortal.

Without us, the country people will finally have Cambodia back. The walled gardens will turn to vines. The water buffalo will wallow; the rustics will still keep the fields green with rice, as steam engines chortle past, puffing out gasps of cloud. Sampul once asked me if the trains made rain.

And if there are aliens, maybe they will treasure it, the Earth.

I may want to stay, but Agnete is determined to Go. She has already lost one husband to this nonsense. She will not lose anything else, certainly not her children. Anyway, it was all part of the deal.

I slip into bed next to her. "You're very good with them," she says and kisses my shoulder. "I knew you would be. Your people are so kind to children."

"You don't tell me that you love me," I say.

"Give it time," she says, finally.

That night lightning strikes the spirit house that shelters our neak ta. The house's tiny golden spire is charred.

Gerda and I come down in the morning to give the spirit his bananas, and when she sees the ruin, her eyes boggle and she starts to scream and howl.

Agnete comes downstairs, and hugs and pets her, and says in English, "Oh, the pretty little house is broken."

Agnete cannot possibly understand how catastrophic this is, or how baffling. The neak ta is the spirit of the hotel who protects us or rejects us. What does it mean when the sky itself strikes it? Does it mean the neak ta is angry and has deserted us? Does it mean the gods want us gone and have destroyed our protector?

Gerda stares in terror, and I am sure then, that though she is wordless, Gerda has a Khmer soul.

Agnete looks at me over Gerda's shoulder, and I'm wondering why she is being so disconnected when she says, "The papers have come through."

That means we will sail to Singapore within the week.

I've already sold the casino. There is no one I trust. I go downstairs and hand over the keys to all my guns to Sreang, who I know will stay on as security at least for a while.

That night after the children are asleep, Agnete and I have the most terrifying argument. She throws things; she hits me; she thinks I'm saying that I want to desert them; I cannot make her listen or understand.

"Neak ta? Neak ta, what are you saying?"

"I'm saying I think we should go by road."

"We don't have time! There's the date, there's the booking! What are you trying to do?" She is panicked, desperate; her mouth ringed with thin strings of muscle, her neck straining.

I have to go and find a monk. I give him a huge sum of money to earn merit, and I ask him to chant for us. I ask him to bless our luggage and at a distance bless the boat that we will sail in. I swallow fear like thin sour spit.

I order ahead, food for Pchum Ben, so that he can eat it, and act as mediary so that I can feed my dead. I look at him. He smiles. He is a man without guns without modernity without family to help him. For just a moment I envy him.

I await disaster, sure that the loss of our neak ta bodes great ill; I fear that the boat will be swamped at sea.

But I'm wrong.

Dolphins swim ahead of our prow leaping out of the water. We trawl behind us for fish and haul up tuna, turbot, sea snakes and turtles. I can assure you that flying fish really do fly – they soar over our heads at night, right across the boat like giant mosquitoes.

No one gets seasick; there are no storms; we navigate directly. It is as though the sea has made peace with us. Let them be, we have lost them, they are going.

We are Cambodians. We are good at sleeping in hammocks and just talking. We trade jokes and insults and innuendo sometimes in verse, and we play music, cards, and bah angkunh, a game of nuts. Gerda joins in the game and I can see the other kids let her win. She squeals with delight, and reaches down between the slats to find a nut that has fallen through.

All the passengers hug and help take care of the children. We cook on little stoves, frying in woks. Albatrosses rest on our rigging. Gerda still won't speak, so I cuddle her all night long, murmuring. Kynom ch'mooah Channarith. Oun ch'mooah ay?

I am your new father.

Once in the night, something huge in the water vents, just beside us. The stars themselves seem to have come back like the fish, so distant and high, cold and pure. No wonder we are greedy for them, just as we are greedy for diamonds. If we could, we would strip-mine the universe, but instead we strip-mine ourselves.

We land at Sentosa. Its resort beaches are now swallowed by the sea, but its slopes sprout temporary, cantilevered accomodation. The sides of the buildings spread downwards like sheltering batwings behind the plastic quays that walk us directly to the hillside.

Singapore's latest growth industry.

The living dead about to be entombed, we march from the boats along the top of pontoons. Bobbing and smooth-surfaced, the quays are treacherous. We slip and catch each other before we fall. There are no old people among us, but we all walk as if aged, stiff-kneed, and unbalanced.

But I am relieved; the island still burgeons with trees. We take a jungle path, through humid stillness, to the north shore, where we face the Lion City.

Singapore towers over the harbour. Its giant versions of Angkor Wat blaze with sunlight like daggers; its zigzag shoreline is ringed round with four hundred clippers amid a white forest of wind turbines. Up the sides of Mt

Fraser cluster the houses of rustics, made of wood and propped against the slope on stilts.

It had been raining during the day. I'd feared a storm, but now the sky is clear, gold and purple with even a touch of green. All along the line where trees give way to salt grasses, like stars going for a swim, fireflies shine.

Gerda's eyes widen. She smiles and holds out a hand. I whisper the Khmer words for firefly: ampil ampayk.

We're booked into one of the batwings. Only wild riches can buy a hotel room in Sentosa. A bottle of water is expensive enough.

Once inside, Agnete's spirits improve, even sitting on folding metal beds with a hanging blanket for a partition. Her eyes glisten. She sits Gerda and Sampul on the knees of her crossed legs. "They have beautiful shopping malls Down There," she says. "And Rith, technik, all the latest. Big screens. Billion billion pixels."

"They don't call them pixels anymore, Mom."

That night, Gerda starts to cry. Nothing can stop her. She wails and wails. Our friends from the boat turn over on their beds and groan. Two of the women sit with Agnete and offer sympathy. "Oh poor thing, she is ill."

No, I think, she is broken-hearted. She writhes and twists in Agnete's lap. Without words for it, I know why she is crying.

Agnete looks like she's been punched in the face; she didn't sleep well on the boat.

I say, "Darling, let me take her outside. You sleep."

I coax Gerda up into my arms, but she fights me like a cat. Sssh sssh, Angel, sssh. But she's not to be fooled. Somehow she senses what this is. I walk out of the refugee shelter and onto the dock that sighs underfoot. I'm standing there, holding her, looking up at the ghost of Singapore, listening to the whoop of the turbines overhead, hearing the slopping sound of water against the quay. I know that Gerda cannot be consoled.

Agnete thinks our people are kind because we smile. But we can also be cruel. It was cruel of Gerda's father to leave her, knowing what might happen after he was gone. It was cruel to want to be missed that badly.

On the north shore, I can still see the towers defined only by their biolu-minescence, in leopard-spot growths of blue, or gold-green, otherwise lost in a mist of human manufacture, smoke and steam.

The skyscrapers are deserted now, unusable, for who can climb seventy stories? How strange they look; what drove us to make them? Why all across the world did we reach up so high? As if to escape the Earth, distance ourselves from the ground, and make a shiny new artifice of the world.

And there are the stars. They have always shone; they shine now just like they would shine on the deck of a starship, no nearer. There is the warm sea that gave us birth. There are the trees that turn sunlight into sugar for all of us to feed on.

Then overhead, giant starfish in the sky. I am at loss, choy mae! What on earth is that? They glow in layers, orange red green. Trailing after them in order, come giant butterflies glowing blue and purple. Gerda coughs into silence and stares upwards.

Cable cars. Cable cars strung from Mt Fraser, to the shore and on to Sentosa, glowing with decorative bioluminescence.

Ampil ampayk, I say again and for just moment, Gerda is still.

I don't want to go. I want to stay here.

Then Gerda roars again, sounding like my heart.

The sound threatens to shred her throat. The sound is inconsolable. I rock her, shush her, kiss her, but nothing brings her peace.

You too, Gerda, I think. You want to stay too, don't you? We are two of a kind.

For a moment, I want to run away together, Gerda and me, get across the straits to Johor Bahu, hide in the untended wilds of old palm-oil plantations.

But now we have no money to buy food or water.

I go still as the night whispers its suggestion.

I will not be cruel like her father. I can go into that warm sea and spread myself among the fishes to swim for ever. And I can take you with me, Gerda.

We can be still, and disappear into the Earth.

I hold her out as if offering her to the warm birthsea. And finally, Gerda sleeps, and I ask myself, will I do it? Can I take us back? Both of us?

Agnete touches my arm. "Oh, you got her to sleep! Thank you so much." Her hand first on my shoulder, then around Gerda, taking her from me, and I can't stop myself tugging back, and there is something alarmed, confused around her eyes. Then she gives her head a quick little shake, dismissing it.

I would rather be loved for my manliness than for my goodness. But I suppose it's better than nothing and I know I will not escape. I know we will all Go Down.

The next day we march, numb and driven by something we do not understand.

For breakfast, we have Chinese porridge with roasted soya, nuts, spices and egg. Our last day is brilliantly sunny. There are too many of us to all take the cable car. Economy class, we are given an intelligent trolley to guide us, carrying our luggage or our children. It whines along the bridge from Sentosa, giving us relentless tourist information about Raffles, independence in 1965, the Singapore miracle, the coolies who came as slaves but stayed to contribute so much to Singapore's success.

The bridge takes us past an artificial island full of cargo, cranes and wagons, and on the main shore by the quays is a squash of a market with noodle stalls, fish stalls, and stalls full of knives or dried lizards. Our route takes us up Mt Fraser, through the trees. The monkeys pursue us, plucking bags of bananas from our hands, clambering up on our carts, trying to open our parcels. Rith throws rocks at them.

The dawn light falls in rays through the trees as if the Buddha himself was overhead, shedding radiance. Gerda toddles next to me, her hand in mine. Suddenly she stoops over and holds something up. It is a scarab beetle, its shell a shimmering turquoise green, but ants are crawling out of it. I blow them away. "Oh, that is a treasure, Gerda. You hold onto it, OK?"

There will be nothing like it where we are going.

Then looking something like a railway station, there is the Singapore terminal dug into the rock of the outcropping. It yawns wide open, to funnel us inside. The concrete is softened by a screen of branches sweeping along its face – very tasteful and traditional I think until I touch them and find that they are made of mouldform.

This is Singapore, so everything is perfectly done. Pamper yourself a sign says in ten different languages. Breathe in an Air of Luxury.

Beautiful concierges in blue-grey uniforms greet us. One of them asks, "Is this the Sonn family?" Her face is so pretty, like Gerda's will be one day, a face of all nations, smiling and full of hope that something good can be done.

"I'm here to help you with check in, and make sure you are comfortable and happy." She bends down and looks into Gerda's eyes but something in them makes her falter; the concierge's smile seems to trip and stumble.

Nightmarishly, her lipgloss suddenly smears up and across her face, like a wound. It feels as though Gerda has somehow cut her.

The concierge's eyes are sad now. She gives Gerda a package printed with a clown's face and coloured balloons. Gerda holds the gift out from her upside down and scowls at it.

The concierge has packages for all the children, to keep them quiet in line. The giftpacks match age and gender. Rith always says his gender is Geek, as a joke, but he does somehow get a Geek pack. They can analyze his clothes and brand names. I muse on how strange it is that Rith's dad gave him the same name as mine, so that he is Rith and I am Channarith. He never calls me father. Agnete calls me Channa, infrequently.

The beautiful concierge takes our papers, and says that she will do all the needful. Our trolley says goodbye and whizzes after her, to check in our bags. I'm glad it's gone. I hate its hushed and cheerful voice. I hate its Bugs-Bunny baby face.

We wait.

Other concierges move up and down the velvet-roped queues with little trolleys offering water, green tea, dragon fruit or chardonnay. However much we paid, when all is said and done, we are fodder to be processed. I know in my sinking heart that getting here is why Agnete married me. She needed the fare.

No one lied to us, not even ourselves. This is bigger than a lie; this is like an animal migration, this is all of us caught up in something about ourselves we do not understand, never knew.

Suddenly my heart says, firmly. There are no aliens.

Aliens are just the excuse. This is something we want to do, like building those skyscrapers. This is all a new kind of dream, a new kind of grief turned inwards, but it's not my dream, nor do I think that it's Gerda's. She is squeezing my hand too hard and I know she knows this thing that is beyond words.

"Agnete," I say. "You and the boys go. I cannot. I don't want this."

Her face is sudden fury. "I knew you'd do this. Men always do this."

"I didn't use to be a man."

"That makes no difference!" She snatches Gerda away from me, who starts to cry again. Gerda has been taken too many places, too suddenly, too firmly. "I knew there was something weird going on." She glares at me as if she doesn't know me, or is only seeing me for the first time. Gently she coaxes Gerda towards her, away from me. "The children are coming with me. All of the children. If you want to be be blown up by aliens. . . ."

"There are no aliens."

Maybe she doesn't hear me. "I have all the papers." She means the papers that identify us, let us in our own front door, give us access to our bank accounts. All she holds is the hologrammed, eye-printed ticket. She makes a jagged, flinty correction: "They have all the papers. Gerda is my daughter, and they will favour me." She's already thinking custody battle, and she's right, of course.

"There are no aliens." I say it a third time. "There is no reason to do this."

This time I get heard. There is a sound of breathing-out from all the people around me. A fat Tamil, sated maybe with blowing up other people, says, "What, you think all those governments lie? You're just getting cold feet."

Agnete focuses on me. "Go on. Get going if that's what you want." Her face has no love or tolerance in it.

"People need there to be aliens and so they all believe there are. But I don't."

Gerda is weeping in complete silence, though her face looks calm. I have never seen so much water come out of someone's eyes; it pours out as thick as bird's nest soup. Agnete keeps her hands folded across Gerda's chest and kisses the top of her head. What, does she think I'm going to steal Gerda?

Suddenly our concierge is kneeling down, cooing. She has a pink metal teddy bear in one hand, and it hisses as she uses it to inject Gerda.

"There! All happy now!" The concierge looks up at me with hatred. She gives Agnete our check-in notification, now perfumed and glowing. But not our ID papers. Those they keep, to keep us there, safe.

"Thank you," says Agnete. Her jaw thrusts out at me.

The Tamil is smiling with rage. "You see that idiot? He got the little girl all afraid."

"Fool can't face the truth," says a Cluster of networked Malay, all in unison.

I want to go back to the trees, like Tarzan, but that is a different drive, a different dream.

"Why are you stopping the rest of us trying to go, just because you don't want to?" says a multigen, with a wide glassy grin. How on earth does s/he think I could stop them doing anything? I can see s/he is making up for a lifetime of being disrespected. Shis intervention, though late and cowardly and stupid, gets the murmur of approval for which s/he yearns.

It is like cutting my heart at the root, but I know I cannot leave Gerda. I cannot leave her alone down there. She must not be deserted a second time. They have doped her, drugged her, the world swims around her, her eyes are dim and crossed, but I fancy she is looking for me. And the level of the singing blood in our veins, we understand each other.

I hang my head.

"So you're staying," says Agnete, her face pulled in several opposing directions, satisfaction, disappointment, anger, triumph, scorn.

"For Gerda, yes."

Agnete's face resolves itself into stone. She wanted maybe a declaration of love, after that scene? Gerda is limp and heavy and dangling down onto the floor.

"Maybe she's lucky," I say. "Maybe that injection killed her."

The crowd has been listening for something to outrage them. "Did you hear what that man said?"

"What an idiot!"

"Jerk."

"Hey lady, you want a nicer guy for a husband, try me."

"Did he say the little girl should be dead? Did you hear him say that?"

"Yeah, he said that the little baby should be dead!"

"Hey you, Pol Pot. Get out of line. We're doing this to escape genocide, not take it with us."

I feel distanced, calm. "I don't think we have any idea what we are doing."

Agnete grips the tickets and certificates of passage. She holds onto to Gerda, and tries to hug the two younger boys. There is a bubble of spit coming out of Gerda's mouth. The lift doors swivel open, all along the wall. Agnete starts forward. She has to drag Gerda with her.

"Let me carry her at least," I say. Agnete ignores me. I trail after her. Someone pushes me sideways as I shuffle. I ignore him.

And so I Go Down.

They take your ID and keep it. It is a safety measure to hold as many of humankind safely below as possible. I realize I will never see the sun again. No sunset cumulo-nimbus, no shushing of the sea, no schools of sardines swimming like veils of silver in clear water, no unreliable songbirds that may fail to appear, no more brown grass, no more dusty wild flowers unregarded by the roadside. No thunder to strike the neak ta, no chants at midnight, no smells of fish frying, no rice on the floor of the temple.

I am a son of Kambu. Kampuchea.

I slope into the elevator.

"Hey boss," says a voice. The sound of it makes me unhappy before I recognize who it is. Ah yes, with his lucky moustache. It is someone who used to work in my hotel. My Embezzler. He looks delighted, pleased to see me. "Isn't this great? Wait til you see it!"

"Yeah, great," I murmur.

"Listen," says an intervener to my little thief. "Nothing you can say will make this guy happy."

"He's a nice guy, "says the Embezzler. "I used to work for him. Didn't I, Boss?"

This is my legacy thug, inherited from my boss. He embezzled his fare from me and disappeared, oh, two years ago. These people may think he's a friend, but I bet he still has his stolen guns, in case there is trouble.

"Good to see you," I lie. I know when I am outnumbered.

For some reason that makes him chuckle, and I can see his silver-outlined teeth. I am ashamed that this unpunished thief is now my only friend.

Agnete knows the story, sniffs and looks away. "I should have married a genetic man," she murmurs.

Never, ever, tread on someone else's dream.

The lift is mirrored, and there are hologrammes of light as if we stood inside an infinite diamond, glistering all the way up to a blinding heaven. And dancing in the fire, brand names.

Gucci

Armani

Sony

Yamomoto

Hugo Boss

And above us, clear to the end and the beginning, the stars. The lift goes down.

Those stars have cost us dearly. All around me, the faces look up in unison.

Whole nations were bankrupted trying to get there, to dwarf stars and planets of methane ice. Arizona disappeared in an annihilation as matter and anti matter finally met, trying to build an engine. Massive junk still orbits half-assembled, and will one day fall. The saps who are left behind on Ground Zero will probably think it's the comet.

But trying to build those self-contained starships taught us how to do this instead.

Earthside, you walk out of your door, you see birds fly. Just after the sun sets and the bushes bloom with bugs, you will see bats flitter silhouetted as they neep. In hot afternoons the bees waver heavy with pollen, and I swear even fishes fly. But nothing flies between the stars except energy. You wanna be converted into energy, like Arizona?

So we go down.

Instead of up.

"The first thing you will see is the main hall. That should cheer up you claustrophobics," says my Embezzler. "It is the biggest open space we have in the Singapore facility. And as you will see, that's damn big!" The travelers chuckle in appreciation. I wonder if they don't pipe in some of that cheer-ful sound.

And poor Gerda, she will wake up for second time in another new world. I fear it will be too much for her.

The lift walls turn like stiles, reflecting yet more light in shards, and we step out.

*   *   *

Ten storeys of brand names go down in circles – polished marble floors, air-conditioning, little murmuring carts, robot pets that don't poop, kids in the latest balloon shoes.

"What do you think of that!" the Malay network demands of me. All its heads turn, including the women wearing modest headscarves.

"I think it looks like Kuala Lumpur on a rainy afternoon."

The corridors of the emporia go off into infinity as well, as if you could shop all the way to Alpha Centauri. An illusion of course, like standing in a hall of mirrors.

It's darn good this technology, it fools the eye for all of 30 seconds. To be fooled longer than that, you have to want to be fooled. At the end of the corridor, reaching out for somewhere beyond, distant and pure there only is only light.

We have remade the world.

Agnete looks worn. "I need a drink, where's a bar?"

I need to be away too, away from these people who know that I have a wife for whom my only value has now been spent.

Our little trolley finds us, calls our name enthusiastically and advises us. In Ramlee Mall, level ten, Central Tower we have the choice of Bar Infinity, the Malacca Club (share the Maugham experience), British India, the Kuala Lumpur Tower View . . .

Agnete chooses the Seaside Pier; I cannot tell if out of kindness or irony.

I step inside the bar with its high ceiling and for just a moment my heart leaps with hope. There is the sea, the islands, the bridges, the sails, the gulls, and the sunlight dancing. Wafts of sugar vapour inside the bar imitate sea mist, and the breathable sugar makes you high. At the other end of the bar is what looks like a giant orange orb (half of one, the other half is just reflected). People lounge on the brand name sand (guaranteed to brush away and evaporate.) Fifty meters overhead, there is a virtual mirror that doubles distance so you can look up and see yourself from what appears to be 100 meters up, as if you are flying. A Network on its collective back is busy spelling the word HOME with their bodies.

We sip martinis. Gerda still sleeps and I now fear she always will.

"So," says Agnete, her voice suddenly catching up with her butt, and plonking down to earth and relative calm. "Sorry about that back there. It was a tense moment for both of us. I have doubts too. About coming here, I mean."

She puts her hand on mine.

"I will always be so grateful to you," she says and really means it. I play with one of her fingers. I seem to have purchased loyalty.

"Thank you," I say, and I realize that she has lost mine.

She tries to bring love back, by squeezing my hand. "I know you didn't want to come. I know you came because of us."

Even the boys know there is something radically wrong. Sampul and Tharum stare in silence, wide brown eyes. Did something similar happen with Dad number one?

Rith the eldest chortles with scorn. He needs to hate us so that he can fly the nest.

My heart is so sore I cannot speak.

"What will you do?" she asks. That sounds forlorn, so she then tries to sound perky. "Any ideas?"

"Open a casino," I say, feeling deadly.

"Oh! Channa! What a wonderful idea, it's just perfect!"

"Isn't it? All those people with nothing to do." Someplace they can bring their powder. I look out at the sea.

Rith rolls his eyes. Where is there for Rith to go from here? I wonder. I see that he too will have to destroy his inheritance. What will he do, drill the rock? Dive down into the lava? Or maybe out of pure rebellion ascend to Earth again?

The drug wears off, and Gerda awakes, but her eyes are calm and she takes an interest in the table and the food. She walks outside onto the mall floor, and suddenly squeals with laughter and runs to the railing to look out. She points at the glowing yellow sign with black ears and says "Disney." She says all the brand names aloud, as if they are all old friends.

I was wrong. Gerda is at home here.

I can see myself wandering the whispering marble halls like a ghost, listening for something that is dead.

We go to our suite. It's just like the damn casino, but there are no boats outside to push slivers into your hands, no sand too hot for your feet. Cambodia has ceased to exist, for us.

Agnete is beside herself with delight. "What window do you want?"

I ask for downtown Phnom Penh. A forest of grey, streaked skyscrapers to the horizon. "In the rain," I ask.

"Can't we have something a bit more cheerful?"

"Sure. How about Tuol Sleng prison?"

I know she doesn't want me. I know how to hurt her. I go for a walk.

Overhead in the dome is the Horsehead Nebula. Radiant, wonderful, deadly, thirty years to cross at the speed of light.

I go to the pharmacy. The pharmacist looks like a phony doctor in an ad. I ask, "Is . . . is there some way out?"

"You can go Earthside with no ID. People do. They end up living in huts on Sentosa. But that's not what you mean, is it?"

I just shake my head. It's like we've been edited to ensure that nothing disturbing actually gets said. He gives me a tiny white bag with blue lettering on it.

Instant, painless, like all my flopping guests at the casino.

"Not here," he warns me. "You take it and go somewhere else like the public toilets."

Terrifyingly, the pack isn't sealed properly. I've picked it up, I could have the dust of it on hands; I don't want to wipe them anywhere. What if one of the children licks it?

I know then I don't want to die. I just want to go home, and always will. I am a son of Kambu, Kampuchea.

"Ah," he says and looks pleased. "You know, the Buddha says that we must accept."

"So why didn't we accept the Earth?" I ask him.

The pharmacist in his white lab coat shrugs. "We always want something different."

We always must move on and if we can't leave home, it drives us mad. Blocked and driven mad, we do something new.

There was one final phase to becoming a man. I remember my uncle. The moment his children and his brother's children were all somewhat grown, he left us to become a monk. That was how a man was completed, in the old days.

I stand with a merit bowl in front of the wat. I wear orange robes with a few others. Curiously enough, Rith has joined me. He thinks he has rebelled. People from Sri Lanka, Laos, Burma, and my own land give us food for their dead. We bless it and chant in Pali.

> All component things are indeed transient.
> They are of the nature of arising and decaying.
> Having come into being, they cease to be.
> The cessation of this process is bliss.
> Uninvited he has come hither
> He has departed hence without approval
> Even as he came, just so he went
> What lamentation then could there be?

We got what we wanted. We always do, don't we, as a species? One way or another.

SOLACE

James Van Pelt

Here's a vivid study of a man snowbound in an old mill in the grip of a savage winter who must try not only to survive but somehow to keep the mill running in the face of all that nature can throw at him – and the courage and determination his example gives to a young woman in a colony ship hundreds of years later who is making the long journey between the stars.

James Van Pelt's stories have appeared in *Sci Fiction*, *Asimov's Science Fiction*, *Analog*, *Realms of Fantasy*, *The Third Alternative*, *Weird Tales*, *Talebones*, *Alfred Hitchcock's Mystery Magazine*, *Pulphouse*, *Altair*, *Transversions*, *Adventures in Sword & Sorcery*, *On Spec*, *Future Orbits*, and elsewhere. His first book, appropriately enough, was a collection, *Strangers and Beggars*, although he's subsequently published his first novel, *Summer of the Apocalypse*. His most recent book is a new collection, *The Radio Magicians and Other Stories*. He lives with his family in Grand Junction, Colorado, where he teaches high school and college English.

THE WALL DISPLAY didn't last two sleep cycles. When Meghan woke the first time, one hundred years into the 4,000 years long journey to Zeta Reticula, she waved her hand at the sensor, and the steel wall morphed into a long view of the Crystal River. On the left side, aspen leaves trembled in a breeze she couldn't feel. The river itself cut across the image, appearing between trees, tumbling over rocks, chuckling and hissing through the speakers before draining onto the floor at the bottom of the image. On the river's right bank, the generator house, a remnant of 19th Century mining, clung to a gray granite outcrop. A tall water chute dropped from the building's bottom, down the short cliff to a pool below. She'd taken the picture on her last hike before reporting for flight training. Every crewmember's room had a display. Only hers showed the same scene continuously. She joined the crew for their fourteen-day work period, and then returned to the long-sleep bed.

But when she awoke the second time, two hundred years after they left Earth orbit, the metal wall remained grimly blank. She sat on her bunk's edge, empty, knowing the lead in her limbs was the result of a hundred years of sleep but believing that sadness caused it. No mountain. No river.

No rustic generator house standing against the aspen. She called for crew chief Teague.

While she waited, she opened the box under her bed where she kept a souvenir from Earth, a miner's iron candle stick holder, a long spike at one end, a brass handle on the other, and a metal loop in the middle to hold the candle. She'd found it in a pit beside the generator house after she'd taken the picture. It had a nice heft to it, balanced in her hand. She had cleaned the rust off so the metal shined, but pits marred what must have at one time been a smooth surface. She liked the roughness under her fingers.

After checking the circuits, crew chief Teague said, "Everything about this expedition is an experiment." He punched at the manual overrides for the display behind a cover plate in Meghan's room. "There's no way to test the effects of time on technology except to watch it over time, and that's what we're doing." He clicked the plate shut. "All that matters is keeping life support, guidance, and propulsion running for the whole trip. You make sure hydroponics continue to function. I work in mechanical repair. Teams service the power plant. One of the four crews is awake every twenty-five years, but we don't have time to repair a luxury like your display wall. We're janitors." He ran his hand down the blank surface. "It's already an old ship, and we have a long, long way to go."

"We have to keep running too. The people."

"Yes, there is that." He rubbed his chin while looking at the candle stick holder in her lap. "Interesting piece. Does the handle unscrew?"

She twisted it. "Seems stuck."

"We could open in the machine shop."

She shook her head.

After Teague left, Meghan tried to remember how the river looked and sounded. With the wall display working, she could imagine an aspen breeze on her face, the rushing water's pebbly smell. She could remember uneven ground, slickness of spray-splashed rocks, stirred leaves' sweetness. With eyes closed, she tried to evoke the memory. Hadn't the ground been a little slippery with gravel? Hadn't there been a crow circling overhead? When she was a little girl, her mother died. A month later Meghan could not remember Mom's face. Only after digging into a scrapbook did the sense of her mother come back to her. Now, it was just as bad, but what she couldn't remember was Earth. The metal walls, the synthetic cushioning on the floor, the ventilation's constant hiss seemed like they had been a part of her forever, and the Earth slipped away, piece by piece.

She placed the flat of her hand on the blank wall. It's only two years, she thought. In two years I'll be out of the ship, if the planet around Zeta Reticula is habitable. But she shivered. Only two subjective years. She'd spend most of the trip in the long-sleep cocoon. If the technology worked, she would leave the ship in 4,000 real years.

Teague was right, though, about untested technology. Nearly every element of the expedition was a prototype. Could a human-manufactured device continue to function after 4,000 years, even with constant maintenance? The Egyptian pyramids were 4,500 years old, and they still stood, but they were merely rocks in a pile, not a sophisticated space vehicle. After 4,000 years, the pyramids weren't expected to enter an orbit around a distant planet while maintaining a sustainable environment against the deadliness of space.

And what of the people on board? The only test of the technology that kept a person alive for 4,000 years and preserved the seeds and fertilized ova would take 4,000 years. Dr Arnold, who knew all their medical charts by heart, told her that what she felt was homesickness. Like Meghan and the rest of the crew, he was in his twenties, but he spoke with maturity. Meghan trusted him. "Look for these symptoms," he said, "episodic or constant crying, nausea, difficulty sleeping, disrupted menstrual cycle." He consulted his notes. "Of course, those symptoms may also be induced by long sleep." His assistant, Dr Singh, nodded in agreement.

"Doctor Arnold, I'm two hundred years late on my last period."

Already she felt old. Already, with the sun no more than a bright star in their wake, she felt creaky and removed, a part of the dead. I shouldn't be able to sense Earth's pull from here, she thought. I shouldn't have come. They should have known that a hydroponics officer wouldn't do well away from Earth, away from forests and long stretches of mountain grass. Even when we arrive, if everything works, if the planet is hospitable, it will take years and years to grow Earth trees to sit beneath. I'll never see an aspen again.

I won't make it.

Isaac scooted his stool closer to the tiny woodstove. If he sat close enough, long enough, the warmth crept through his mittens and the arms of his coat. His knees, only a few inches from the stove, nearly blistered, but the cold pressed against his back. It slipped around the sides of his hood. He eyed the tiny pile of wood by the stove, the remains of the table he'd broken into pieces the day before. All the cabin's goods sat on the floor since he'd burned the shelves earlier. Beside the remains of the table, the only other wood was a small box of kindling in case the fire went out, and the chair he sat on. Outside, snow covered the ground so deeply that there was no hope of finding deadfall. Besides, every tree within a mile had either been cut down for mine timbers or had its low branches cut off for firewood. He'd hauled the wood he'd been burning for the last ten days from a site four miles upstream, but that was long before the storm moved in, cutting visibility to a few feet.

In the room below, machinery thumped steadily. Water poured through a sluice to turn a wheel connected to a squat generator. Cables ran up the mountain to the mines' compressors, clearing dead air from the tunnels and powering the drills, but Isaac couldn't tell if the miners were still working. They probably were hunkered down like he was, in their bunk houses near the digging, or they were stuck in the town of Crystal. If they were working, the compressors needed to run.

He looked out the window. Thick frost coated the inside of the glass and snow piled half way up outside dimmed what light the dark afternoon offered. The window in his tiny, second story maintenance room was at least fifteen feet above the ground. Two weeks of non-stop snow had nearly buried the building. Ten days ago, when the supplies clerk dropped off a bag full of dried meat and two loaves of bread, he'd said, "First winter in the mountains, boy? It'll get so cold your piss will freeze before it splashes your boots."

Isaac hadn't been able to open the outside door for the last three days. Heavy snow blocked it. He rubbed his mittens together, trying to distribute the heat. A steady wind moaned outside. Trees creaked. Something snapped sharply overhead. He glanced at the thick timbers supporting the roof. How much weight could they hold? How much crushing snow lay above him?

He sighed, unwilling to leave the stove's meager heat, but he had a job to do. Checking for candles in his coat pocket, he walked down to the darkness of the generator room, a "Tommie Sticker" in hand to hold the light. It was a fancy one, with a brass match holder and a screw-on cap to keep the matches dry serving as the handle. Ice covered the stairs, and the air smelled wet and cold. He jammed the spike end of the Tommie Sticker into the plank wall, then carefully lit the candle, using both hands to hold the match steady against his shivering. Oil for the lamp had run out two days ago. The wavering candle revealed water pounding through the sluice against the horizontal wheel, turning it ponderously counter-clockwise.

Isaac used a two-pond hammer and chisel to clear ice from the water's entrance and exit points. If the machinery stopped, miners would be without ventilation or power. Ice blocks as big as his head broke free from the structure and clattered to the unlevel floor, where they slid to the far wall. Despite the cold, he soon built up a sweat. He pulled his hood back and unfastened the coat's top. When he finished, he would strip his coat and layers of shirts, replacing the damp undershirt with a dry one. If he didn't, he'd be too cold to sleep later.

The work wasn't unlike living in the monastery, he thought, complete with a vow of silence and constant labor to keep his hands busy. He thought about God and God's plan. He never felt as close to heaven as he did when he worked alone, cut off from human conversation and the daily distractions. In a way, he hoped the storm would hold. As long as the weather cut him off, he could replicate life in the monastery. He had loved his room there. The rough-hewn bed and the blanket thrown over a thin mattress. He'd read by candlelight there, too. Yes, the generator house reminded him of the monastery. The wooden building felt like a cradle of the miraculous, a miracle that never occurred when he had been an initiate.

It hadn't been this cold, though. No, not nearly so cold at all.

*   *   *

Meghan came awake slowly and in pain. Dr Arnold had decided four cycles ago that the powerful painkillers they used to soften the shift from the long sleep's near death to full wakefulness were damaging, so they didn't flood her system with them before they woke her. Lying as still as she could in the cocoon, her elbows and knees ached, as did her ankles and wrists. Even her knuckles hurt. A tear squeezed out of each eye and raced into her ears as she thought about clenching her fists for the first time on her own in a hundred years. Every move would hurt, at first, even though the mechanical manipulators flexed her joints daily.

When she'd gone to sleep last, crew chief Teague had refused. She'd shaken his hand before heading to her cocoon. "I'll be okay," he said. "I'll have a rich and long life, working in the ship. In twenty-five years I'll greet the next work crew."

"I'll never see you again," said Meghan.

"Maybe you will. I'll be old though." He didn't meet her eyes. "I can't face the dark."

Meghan could say nothing to that because she understood. Each time, climbing into the cocoon seemed like entering death. A one-hundred year long instant later she woke to pain. Even her skin hurt, the now active cells firing neurons back and forth, renewing contacts that had laid moribund for so long, but as she lay in the cocoon this time, she thought about Teague wandering through the ship, all the crews sleeping, and he would wander for years and years and years, twenty-five of them completely alone until the next crew woke, and what could he say to them? He'd have a quarter of a century of experience that none of them could share. For them, Earth was only a couple months in their wake. They were still young in all ways except years. Teague would greet them. "Hi," he might say. "I'm what you will be someday." In him, they'd watch their mortality.

Then, he'd wait twenty-five more years, alone, if he lived, and as an elderly man, he would welcome the next crew to their two weeks of busy wakefulness.

It was unlikely he would meet a third crew. He would be ninty-seven years old, and despite what he said, he certainly would not be alive when she awoke.

She had closed her eyes as the cocoon's lid came down. Her muscles tightened. In a blink, the pain would come, the one-hundred year blink.

And it did.

It took several hours before she could shuffle to the infirmary. Waking was worse this time. Doctor Arnold said, "We haven't gone a fifth of the way, yet." He massaged her hands, lighting them with a million wincing tingles. "Some of the medical staff may stay awake longer than the two weeks for research." Even though he was young, like her, tiny creases that would become worry lines were evident on his forehead.

She thought his eyes were kind, though. He flinched when she flinched. "Sorry," he said. "I'm trying to be gentle."

When Meghan reached her room, she pulled the protective plastic off her bed and found a fragile note folded on her pillow from crew chief Teague, who wrote, "Try the wall now." He had signed and dated it twenty years earlier. An old man wrote this, she thought.

She waved her hand at the sensor, provoking a cascade of pain down her side. The wall flickered. The speakers whispered. Then the Crystal River winked into existence. Water burbled over rocks. Leaves rasped against each other. A long cloud in the distance slid slowly across a mountain top.

How long had Teague worked on the wall? A present for a young girl he would never see again.

The speakers popped twice, like a computer chip crunching somewhere and the sound turned off, then the image brightened and washed into a pure white. Meghan shaded her eyes before it too vanished. His repair lasted for ten seconds. How long had he worked on it? She tried to open the service panel, but it remained stubbornly closed. Frustrated, she slapped her hand against it, then grabbed the iron candle stick holder from under the bed. Its sharp end pried the small hatch open. Looking at the circuit board underneath revealed nothing, though. Circuit boards were not her area of expertise. The hatch wouldn't reclose.

Meghan stared at the blank wall for a long time before seeking out Dr Arnold and his soft, kind hands.

"What is that?" he asked, pointing to the candle holder.

Meghan turned the artifact over in her fingers. She hadn't realized that she still carried it. "It's all I have from Earth. It's a miner's light."

She slept with him for the rest of the two weeks until they returned to the cocoons again. The first time, as she pulled his shirt over his head, he said, "You're going to have to quit calling me Dr Arnold. My name's Sean."

Once, she woke up, still unfamiliar with Sean's shape, and listened to his breathing in the dark room. If she tried hard, it reminded her of wind through the leaves.

Isaac considered the various forms of meditation. He'd learned to plant a question in his mind, then to spend the day or days or weeks contemplating its implications and meaning. While pondering the question, he would read from the Bible or the many studies in the monastery's library. Meditation was best during his vows of silence. At length, the question would glow in his head, like campfire coals. Now, lying on his bed, squeezing his arms close to his body, trying not to shiver, he considered why God allowed cold. Genesis told him that cold was one of the ways God showed man that the Earth would continue. It said, "While the earth remaineth, seedtime and harvest, and cold and heat, and summer and winter, and day and night shall not cease."

Twice in the night, the roof creaked loudly, the second time dumping a pile of snow onto the floor. Holding the Tommy Sticker high, he could see where a board had broken. He wondered how he could get outside of the generator house to knock snow off the roof, but the wind roared and the window showed no outside light at all now. He wasn't sure if it was day or night. Was such a storm normal? He had no mountain experience. The monastery had been challenging, but it didn't teach him how to survive here. If it had snowed for forty days and forty nights for Noah, instead of raining, it could hardly be worse than this.

The Bible wasn't clear on snow. Mostly it appeared in the comparison "white as snow" in a dozen passages. He remembered somewhere the prophets linked it to leprosy. By candle he found the verse in Numbers. Turning the pages with his mittens was impossible, so he shucked them off and put them between his legs to keep them warm. The passage said, "And the cloud departed from off the tabernacle; and, behold, Miriam became leprous, white as snow: and Aaron looked upon Miriam, and, behold, she was leprous." In Exodus he came across Moses turning a rod into a snake and back into a rod again. Then God said to Moses, "Put now thine hand into thy bosom. And he put his hand into his bosom: and when he took it out, behold, his hand was leprous as snow."

Even God didn't like snow.

The roof creaked again, sending another icy spill to the growing pile.

The door wouldn't move. Forcing the weight that rested against it was impossible, so he tried the window and pushed it up. A solid white wall stood revealed. He jabbed a shovel into it, dumped snow on the floor, dug in again. A half hour later, he'd cleared a tunnel to the surface, about a foot above the window. He pushed the snow shoes out the hole and then climbed after them. The wind slammed into his face when he rolled to the surface, and his arm sank to his arm pit when he tried to right himself. Strapping on the broad snow shoes took longer than he wished. Snow worked its way into the top of his shoes, froze into little balls on his gloves and fell down his collar. He couldn't see even to the trees that stood twenty yards away from the generator house. His eyes watered, and his cheeks stung. The air's gray luminosity revealed that it was day, but he could barely tell, nor did it matter.

He had imagined by the height of the snow on the generator house that the river valley would be twenty feet under, but he could see now that a huge drift covered the house. Standing on the show shoes, his chest was as high as the roof's eave, but the snow on the roof was piled higher than his head. Isaac realized that knocking the weight off could be dangerous. If it all came off the steep roof at the same time, it could easily bury him, so he tentatively dug into the overhang, stretching as far as he could with the shovel. A slab dropped off, revealing the wood shingles beneath. Another jab broke free a coffin-sized slab that made a thud he felt through his feet. A crack opened up in the bank of snow that remained on the roof. Isaac backed away as fast as he could as the gap widened, and two thirds of the mass slid ponderously off, leaving only a thin sliver at the ridge.

Snow covered the hole he'd just climbed from, blocking his way back.

"Crackers," he said, the strongest explicative he used. Breath froze on his chin. Before he could get back into the house, though, he needed to sweep the other side. Lifting knees high to clear the snow shoes, he moved around the building.

As he waded through the drift, he thought about the book of Amos, which said, "And I will smite the winter house with the summer house; and the houses of ivory shall perish, and the great houses shall have an end, saith the Lord."

What Isaac needed here was a little smiting.

By the time he'd finished, dug his way back into the generator house and closed the window, he was exhausted, but, more dangerously, he was freezing. The fire in the stove had gone out, and without a buffering layer of snow on the roof, a draft blew through the room. The water wheel had picked up an ominous screech, so instead of trying to light the fire, he put a candle into the Tommie Sticker and walked down the stairs. Ice had formed in the trough where the stream entered the generator wheel, and now water poured onto the floor, deflected by the blockage. The wheel turned half as slow as it should. Water poured onto the floor, some of it freezing against the wood, but most flowing down the slant to the far wall.

Too tired even for a well earned "Crackers!" he swung the two-pound hammer against the blockage. It barely chipped, and he lost his footing, sprawling beneath the water wheel. Icy water drenched him. Isaac scrambled away, slipping on the slick floor. If he didn't clear the trough soon, the wheel would freeze solid. It could become unusable until spring, and then only after extensive repair.

Carefully, this time, keeping his weight distributed on both feet, he sidled toward the trough, hammer in hand. He thought of Lamech, Noah's father, who the Bible said of, "And he called his name Noah, saying, This same shall comfort us concerning our work and toil of our hands, because of the ground which the LORD hath cursed."

The ice was the curse, the hammer the work. So cold he could hardly hold the heavy tool, Isaac swung it against the obstruction.

When she woke again, an elderly man leaned over the cocoon. "Don't move, Meghan. You shouldn't feel pain, but you're likely to be nauseous for a few minutes."

She closed her eyes. I'm 520 years old now, she thought. Over 3,500 years to go.

When she opened her eyes, the old man still leaned in, looking concerned. His hand reached over the edge to cup her upper arm. "Are you okay?"

Tentatively, she nodded, then waited to see if the movement would bother her. Her stomach twisted, but the discomfort passed. "I think so." Her joints didn't ache, but her thinking felt fuzzy. She looked at him closely. "Crew Chief Teague?" He shook his head. "No, he's dead." She squinted. "Dr Arnold?"

He nodded. "I'm still Sean. It took years to figure out what was wrong with the long sleep."

"How many?"

"Almost forty."

She remembered Sean's smooth skin. How he felt when she woke but he still slept. How he'd held her when she talked about Earth and her fears.

"I'm dying," she had said, their last night together. "We will never get to where we are going, and we will never go back."

The night before, a hundred years earlier, Sean had rocked her gently, holding her head to his chest. "We're not dead yet."

Now, Meghan didn't recognize his eyes. He held out a hand to help her from the cocoon, but she didn't take it. He was a stranger. She sat up on her own, felt sick again. When it passed, and she climbed out, Sean stood back, looking at her sadly. "I missed you," he said.

"It's only been a few minutes for me."

"That's true."

She stood awkwardly for a minute, unsure of what to say.

Finally, she offered, "I have work to do."

"Of course. Me too." Lights flickered on the other cocoons, and she realized he'd woken her first.

For the first week, she only saw him at meals, but she sat on the other side of the cafeteria. She tried not to think about the blank wall and her candle holder keepsake. With effort, she avoided pulling the box from under the bed. She thought, maybe if I don't look at it, I won't long for it. I won't miss it. Meghan concentrated on the hydroponic tanks. Every connection needed to be refitted. She retooled valves, serviced pumps, recalibrated the chemical testing equipment, met with the horticulturists who talked about genetic drift, mutations and evolution. Over the course of 500 years, the plants adapted to the artificial environment. The most efficient at extracting nutrients from the fluids flourished. The more aggressive that grew faster or taller crowded out their weaker cousins.

She couldn't sleep during her rest hours, so she wandered back to the hydroponics rooms. All the plants were low growers, flourishing under lights hanging from the ceiling. Tomatoes, strawberries, cucumbers, ferns of various sorts, beets, peppers and numerous others. Nothing that grew tall. Tree seeds were held in storage for planet fall when they reached Zeta Reticula, although there was a question if they would germinate. No one had ever planted a 4,000 year-old seed before. She walked down the long row, letting the palm of her hand brush the plant tops while imagining the aspen the ship carried. Would there be an aspen grove one day on the planet orbiting Zeta Reticula? Aspen preferred to spread from their roots. If just one seed germinated, she could grow a forest. Would Earth trees flourish so far from their native sun?

The fear gathered in her chest like a tightness, so she rubbed her fist between her breasts as she walked, trying to work through the tension. At the end of the row of vegetation, she looked up one of the ship's long spokes, a huge hollow chamber that reached the ship's core, the center they revolved around to produce the illusion of gravity. She'd grown used to the effect that had disoriented her at first, moving from the claustrophobic pressure of the growing room to the shocking reach of empty space. She crossed the fifty-foot diameter of the spoke to get to the next row of plants.

At the end of the final work day before entering the cocoon again, she walked through the plants one last time. They smelled wet and vaguely chemical, but not green, not natural at all, so she kept going until she reached Sean's room and raised her hand to knock. She paused. It seemed that only two weeks ago she had kissed a young man goodbye. She couldn't picture the ship without him. Every day she expected to see him turn a corner, to join her in the hydroponic labs. He never did. Instead, an old man looked at her mournfully when she passed by. He sacrificed forty years to save her and the rest. She almost left.

When he opened the door, Meghan said, "I missed you too."

Sean let her in, the age spots on his hand were prominent in the harsh, hallway light. "I have something for you." He opened a drawer and removed the metal candle holder. "I know how much it meant. I thought about having them open it for you. We could find out if there's anything inside."

She traced her finger along the loop where the candle would have been placed. Rubbed the rough brass cap at one end. If held the wrong way, it looked like a weapon, the five-inch long, narrow spike that would hold the antique in a mine wall or stuck into wood could also hurt someone. "I'd forgotten about it," she lied.

As the talked quietly in his room, she started to see the man she used to know. Benath the thinning hair, behind the wrinkles and tiredness, she recognized him.

When they slipped under the sheets later, Sean said, "I don't have as much to offer as I did before. I'm not . . . young."

"Just hold me, then, and let's sleep."

But after hours of listening to his soft breathing and thinking that he still sounded a little like wind through aspens, he woke up, and Meghan found he had more life in him than he thought.

Isaac stood next to the cold stove. His clothes no longer dripped. They crackled when he moved. Next to his skin, though, they were soaked, and he could feel them sucking away the little heat that remained. One ceiling board had broken completely while he'd knocked the snow off the roof, and the supplies directly underneath were covered, including the boxes of matches. He scooped snow off the floor in double handfuls until he found them, but the boxes were squashed and the matches ruined. The match heads smeared against the striker when he tried to light them.

Dully, his head feeling sluggish and slow, he knelt on the pile of snow for a minute. Flakes came down through the hole in the room, swirling in a breeze that hadn't been there before. Without matches, he'd never light the fire. Maybe he could get the snowshoes back on and make his way to the miners' cabins, but he knew the steep trail, completely hidden in the storm, would be almost impossible to hike, even if his clothes weren't already wet and he wasn't exhausted. He couldn't feel his knees against the snow, and the cold crept up his legs. He thought about just staying still. His chin drifted to his chest. Resting sounded good. In a few minutes, he would get up, but for now, a little sleep was all he needed. The vibration and steady thumping of the generator below annoyed him though, then, frightened, he stood. If he slept, the generator would surely freeze, and so would he. If he didn't have duties, he could rest, but the others depended on him.

Isaac waved his arms to restore circulation, slapping his hands against his arms, then staggered toward the stairs. With renewed vigor, the wind shook the house. No light came from the depths. His candle had gone out, so he swept his hand against the wood, careful to not fall again on the slick floor, until he hit the Tommie Sticker. Water gurgled against the power wheel behind him. With a yank, he pulled the candle holder from the wood, forced himself to climb the stairs, before sitting by the stove. It took a dozen tries to unscrew the brass cap holding the matches. There were only three. Carefully, he lit one, but before he touched the candle, the breeze blew it out. He nearly wept. With the new hole in the roof, there was no place he could guarantee the next match would stay lit long enough to start the fire.

He opened the stove door, pushed his hands inside, out of the wind, to light the second match. It flicked to life, but the draw up the chimney immediately snuffed it out.

Isaac took a deep breath, closed the stove flue to stop the wind, and mumbled a prayer before lighting the last match. The water in his shoes felt like it was freezing. He couldn't feel his feet at all. The match caught, held steady. Carefully, he pushed the candle wick into the flame. It flared into life. He jammed the candle between two charcoaled logs in the stove before feeding kindling to the flame. Soon, smoke flowed from the open stove. Isaac coughed, and his eyes teared, as he kicked the stool apart for bigger pieces of wood, the last fuel in the house, but he didn't open the flue until a healthy flame filled the iron stove. Heat baked off the sides. His gloves steamed on top the stove as he warmed his hands. Piece by piece, he removed his clothes to hang around the stove before wrapping his blanket around his shivering shoulders. Water dripped from his coat and pants. Heat rolled off the stove, tingling his cheeks, sending stabbing sparks through his toes and feet. He grimaced and moved closer.

The wood walls of the house rattled in a torrent of wind, whipping the fire in the little stove into a tiny inferno. At its peak, when surely the house would have to shatter, the wind stopped, and for the first time in a ten days, the house fell silent except for the river's heart beating through the generator below.

The storm had broken.

In the cabin's sudden quiet, Isaac reached for his Bible, opened it randomly to read the first verse his eye fell upon. Surely the storm's cessation was a miracle. Surely a message would be at hand. He wrote the

verse on a slip of paper, rolled it into a tube, then sealed it inside the
Tommy Sticker. By the time he finished, his face felt warm and his toes
stopped aching.

Sean didn't wake up after the seventh long sleep.

Dr Singh said, "He knew the dangers when he let himself age. The sleep
process is hard. I'm sorry." She consulted her notes. "Dr Arnold was a great
man. His work on long sleep cellular degradation and preservation was
groundbreaking. If we were still on Earth, he surely would receive a Nobel
Prize. We should all make it to Zeta Reticula because of him." Singh shook
her head sympathetically. "I understand you were close."

Meghan gripped the edge of the examination table. "I saw him yesterday . . . before the last sleep I mean. I just saw him." She felt every minute
of her 722 years.

"Me too," said Singh. "If you need them, I can prescribe anti-depressants,
but I'd rather not. Drug interaction is difficult to predict."

Meghan walked the long hall from the infirmary to Sean's apartment.
The plastic sheets covered his bed and the desk, coated by a thin layer of
dust. Despite automated cleaning mechanisms, dust still fell on surfaces
they couldn't reach. She pulled the plastic off his desk and let it fall to the
floor. He'd left a notebook and her candle holder in the middle. She turned
the cover back carefully. The paper that started the trip seven hundred years
ago, even though it was acid free and specially milled to last, had become
brittle. Any hand-written notes that were expected to be permanent were
written on plastic paper, but Sean had enjoyed the feel of real pages better.

He had written "To Meghan" inside the cover; the rest of the pages
were blank.

When she sat on the edge of the bed, the plastic crackled. The candle
holder rested on her lap. She wondered, did everyone feel so empty, and
what could she do about it? Her fingers pressed against the cool metal.
Although remembering the aspen shaking in the valley of her wall display
escaped her, she felt connected through the hard shape. How often had this
candle holder stuck in a mine wall to light a few feet of rock? Who else had
held it? Had it ever been more than just a tool to them? Her fingers traveled
from the pointed end, past the coil that held the candle, to the burnished
brass tube. For the first time, Meghan really examined the antique as a practical object instead of art. Was that a cap on the end of what she had thought
was the handle? She twisted it hard. Nothing. Maybe the antique did have
something in it, another connection to Earth. Both Teague and Sean had
wondered, now she wanted to know.

A few minutes later she asked the machine shop chief, a stout woman
whose name Meghan had never known, "Do you have a way to open it?"

The chief turned it over. She said, "It's brass, I think. From the nineteenth century, you say? I can cut it apart, but it will cause damage."

"Go ahead."

The chief handled the cutting tool delicately, sending tiny sparks flurrying as she sliced through the candle holder's end. A coin-sized piece of metal dropped to the floor. Meghan leaned over her shoulder as the chief used a pair of tweezers to pull the rolled up slip of paper from the cavity.

Meghan shivered. "It's almost a thousand years old!"

"There's writing."

"A message." Meghan feared the paper would crumble before she could discover what it said.

"What does it mean?" asked the shop chief after they'd carefully unrolled it.

"It's a Bible verse, I think. I think I know."

Meghan left the puzzled shop chief behind and headed toward hydroponics, already planning new pipes and grow lights. She would have to leave explanations and instructions for the next shift's hydroponic officers.

Isaac climbed through the window and up to the surface again, the last of the chair burning in the stove behind him. The air bit just as cruelly, but without the wind behind it, and the clouds clearing, he didn't feel as cold, although dampness squished in his temporarily warm clothes. If he couldn't find more wood soon, though, the fire would wink out again, and storm or no storm, he would freeze. Holding a short-handled axe, he girded himself for the long hike up the canyon where he might be able to find firewood.

For a moment, he tried to orient himself. Snow transformed the valley, hiding all that had been familiar. The hundreds of tree trunks that marked the land before were deeply covered so the vista before him was smooth, clean and hypnotic. The Crystal River had almost entirely vanished, revealed only by a narrow crack in the snow from where the water's glassy voice arose.

What surprised him most, though, were the trees that remained. Two weeks earlier, their lowest branches were twenty feet above the ground, the easy to reach ones having been chopped off for wood. Now, though, where the snow drifted, their needles brushed the crystalline surface. He would have no trouble finding fuel. He thought, Why that tree there carries enough dead limbs to keep me warm for a month. It felt like a miracle.

He thought about the Bible verse he'd written on the slip of paper. He wasn't sure what it meant, but it had filled him with hope: "Come, let us take our fill of love until the morning: let us solace ourselves with loves. For the goodman is not at home, he is gone a long journey." A bit from Proverbs.

When spring came, he would take the Tommie Sticker with its message and bury it by the pump house. Somewhere, someone might read it, and it would help. He was sure of it.

Meghan kept her eyes closed for a long time after she awoke until, finally, Dr Singh's familiar voice said, "I know you can hear me. Your vitals don't lie."

"I'm eight-hundred and twenty-two years old today." She hadn't moved even a finger yet, but she didn't feel tired like she had the last time. She only felt hopeful.

She waited through Dr Singh's tests impatiently. "I have to get to work," Meghan said.

Rushing through the hallways, she barely acknowledged other crew members' greetings. They, too, had work to do. So much of the trip waited before them. So much more space had to be traversed before they could come to a rest.

The first hydroponics lab looked much like she had left it, although she noted the tanks that held the plants steady would need rebuilding on her shift. She passed under one of the spokes, the cathedral-like height earning not a glance. Did her experiment work, she thought. Did the other hydroponics officers follow her direction? She couldn't see far in front of her. The ceiling's downward bulge cut off her view until she was almost there, and then, she saw.

At the end of the row, where normally the plants stopped, her jury-rigged piping led to the new plant tanks. A thick trunk rose from the tank, and as she entered the space below the next spoke, her gaze traveled up the tree's long stretch. Guy wires attached to the vertical space's sides held the tree steady. At the top, new grow fixtures hung suspended from other wires, bathing the aspen in light.

Meghan held her breath. An aspen, under the right conditions, can grow to eighty feet. This one was easily that tall. She walked around the tree. New piping and tanks connected to her original work. Three other trees grew from them. The closest tank came from her co-worker twenty-five years down the line, and the tree from that tank nearly matched her own. A smaller tree, only fifty years old, grew from the next tank, and the last tank held the smallest tree, still over thirty feet to its top. The history attached to it showed it had been built twenty-five years ago. Each officer had added a tree to the grove.

Meghan sat on the floor so she could look up with less strain. Each tree's branches touched the next. The room smelled of aspen, a light leafy odor that reminded her of mountains and streams, and an old generator house perched on the edge of a short cliff.

After she'd sat for a while, she realized that air currents in the ship flowed up the spoke. What she heard, finally, was not the ubiquitous mechanical hiss from the ventilation vents. What she heard was the gentle rustle of leaves touching leaves, a sound that she thought she'd long left behind and would never hear again.

ACT ONE

Nancy Kress

Nancy Kress began selling her elegant and incisive stories in the mid-1970s and has since become a frequent contributor to *Asimov's Science Fiction, The Magazine of Fantasy and Science Fiction, Omni, Sci Fiction,* and elsewhere. Her books include the novel version of her Hugo- and Nebula-winning story, *Beggars in Spain,* and a sequel, *Beggars and Choosers,* as well as *The Prince Of Morning Bells, The Golden Grove, The White Pipes, An Alien Light, Brain Rose, Oaths & Miracles, Stinger, Maximum Light, Nothing Human, The Floweres of Aulit Prison, Crossfire, Crucible, Dogs,* and the Space Opera trilogy *Probability Moon, Probability Sun,* and *Probability Space.* Her short work has been collected in *Trinity And Other Stories, The Aliens of Earth, Beaker's Dozen,* and *Nano Comes to Clifford Falls and Other Stories.* Her most recent book is the novel *Steal Across the Sky.* In addition to the awards for *Beggars in Spain,* she has also won Nebula Awards for her stories "Out Of All Them Bright Stars" and "The Flowers of Aulit Prison," and won another Hugo this year for "The Erdmann Nexus."

Here she shows us that you can have too much of a good thing – even compassion.

To understand whose movie it is one needs to look not particularly at the script but at the deal memo.

– Joan Didion

I EASED DOWN THE warehouse's basement steps behind the masked boy, one hand on the stair rail, wishing I'd worn gloves. Was this level of grime really necessary? It wasn't; we'd already passed through some very sophisticated electronic surveillance, as well as some very unsophisticated personal surveillance that stopped just short of a body-cavity search, although an unsmiling man did feel around inside my mouth. Soap cost less than surveillance, so probably the grime was intentional. The Group was making a statement. That's what we'd been told to call them: "The Group." Mysterious, undefined, pretentious.

The stairs were lit only by an old-fashioned forty-watt bulb somewhere I couldn't see. Behind me, Jane's breath quickened. I'd insisted on going down first, right behind our juvenile guide, from a sense of – what? "Masculine protection" from me would be laughable. And usually I like to keep Jane where I can see her. It works out better that way.

"Barry?" she breathed. The bottom of the steps was so shrouded in gloom that I had to feel my way with one extended foot.

"Two more steps, Janie."

"Thank you."

Then we were down and she took a deep breath, standing closer to me than she usually does. Her breasts were level with my face. Jane is only five-six, but that's seventeen inches taller than I am. The boy said, "A little way more." Across the cellar a door opened, spilling out light. "There."

It had been a laundry area once, perhaps part of an apartment for some long-dead maintenance man. Cracked wash tubs, three of them, sagged in one corner. No windows, but the floor had been covered with a clean, thin rug and the three waiting people looked clean, too. I scanned them quickly. A tall, hooded man holding an assault rifle, his eyes the expression of bodyguards everywhere: alert but nonanalytic. An unmasked woman in jeans and baggy sweater, staring at Jane with unconcealed resentment. Potential trouble there. And the leader, who came forward with his hand extended, smiling. "Welcome, Miss Snow. We're honored."

I recognized him immediately. He was a type rampant in political life, which used to be my life. Big, handsome, too pleased with himself and his position to accurately evaluate either. He was the only one not wearing jeans, dressed in slacks and a sports coat over a black turtleneck. If he had been a pol instead of a geno-terrorist, he'd have maybe gotten as far as city council executive, and then would have run for mayor, lost, and never understood why. So this was a low-level part of The Group's operation, which was probably good. It might lessen the danger of this insane expedition.

"Thank you," Jane said in that famous voice, low and husky and as thrilling off screen as on. "This is my manager, Barry Tenler."

I was more than her manager but the truth was too complicated to explain. The guy didn't even glance at me and I demoted him from city council executive to ward captain. You always pay attention to the advisors. That's usually where the brains are, if not the charisma.

Ms Resentful, on the other hand, switched her scrutiny from Jane to me. I recognized the nature of that scrutiny. I've felt it all my life.

Jane said to the handsome leader, "What should I call you?"

"Call me Ishmael."

Oh, give me a break. Did that make Jane the white whale? He was showing off his intellectual moves, with no idea they were both banal and silly. But Jane gave him her heart-melting smile and even I, who knew better, would have sworn it was genuine. She might not have made a movie in ten years, but she still had it.

"Let's sit down," Ishmael said.

Three kitchen chairs stood at the far end of the room. Ishmael took one, the bodyguard and the boy standing behind him. Ms Resentful took another. Jane sank cross-legged to the rug in a graceful puddle of filmy green skirt.

That was done for my benefit. My legs and spine hurt if I have to stand for more than a few minutes, and she knows how I hate sitting even lower than I already am. Ishmael, shocked and discerning nothing, said, "Miss Snow!"

"I think better when I'm grounded," she said, again with her irresistible smile. Along with her voice, that smile launched her career thirty-five years ago. Warm, passionate, but with an underlying wistfulness that bypassed the cerebrum and went straight to the primitive hind-brain. Unearned – she was born with those assets – but not unexploited. Jane was a lot shrewder than her fragile blond looks suggested. The passion, however, was real. When she wanted something, she wanted it with every sinew, every nerve cell, every drop of her acquisitive blood.

Now her graceful Sitting-Bull act left Ishmael looking awkward on his chair. But he didn't do the right thing, which would have been to join her on the rug. He stayed on his chair and I demoted him even further, from ward captain to go-fer. I clambered up onto the third chair. Ishmael gazed down at Jane and swelled like a pouter pigeon at having her, literally, at his feet. Ms Resentful scowled. Uneasiness washed through me.

The Group knew who Jane Snow was. Why would they put this meeting in the hands of an inept narcissist? I could think of several reasons: to indicate contempt for her world. To preserve the anonymity of those who actually counted in this most covert of organizations. To pay off a favor that somebody owed to Ishmael, or to Ishmael's keeper. To provide a photogenic foil to Jane, since of course we were being recorded. Any or all of these reasons would be fine with me. But my uneasiness didn't abate.

Jane said, "Let's begin then, Ishmael, if it's all right with you."

"It's fine with me," he said. His back was to the harsh light, which fell full on both Jane and Ms Resentful. The latter had bad skin, small eyes, lanky hair, although her lips were lovely, full and red, and her neck above the Windbreaker had the taut firmness of youth.

The light was harder on Jane. It showed up the crow's feet, the tired inelasticity of her skin under her flawless make-up. She was, after all, fifty-four, and she'd never gone under the knife. Also, she'd never been really beautiful, not as Angelina Jolie or Catherine Zeta-Jones had once been beautiful. Jane's features were too irregular, her legs and butt too heavy. But none of that mattered next to the smile, the voice, the green eyes fresh as new grass, and the powerful sexual glow she gave off so effortlessly. It's as if Jane Snow somehow received two sets of female genes at conception, a critic wrote once, doubling everything we think of as "feminine." That makes her either a goddess or a freak.

"I'm preparing for a role in a new movie," she said to Ishmael, although of course he already knew that. She just wanted to use her voice on him.

"It's going to be about your . . . your organization. And about the future of the little girls. I've talked to some of them and—"

"Which ones?" Ms Resentful demanded.

Did she really know them all by name? I looked at her more closely. Intelligence in those small, stony eyes. She could be from The Group's headquarter cell – wherever it was – and sent to ensure that Ishmael didn't screw up this meeting. Or not. But if she were really intelligent, would she be so enamored of someone like Ishmael?

Stupid question. Three of Jane's four husbands had been gorgeous losers. Jane said, "Well, so far I've only talked to Rima Ridley-Jones. But Friday I have the whole afternoon with the Barrington twins."

Ishmael, unwilling to have the conversation migrate from him, said, "Beautiful children, those twins. And very intelligent." As if the entire world didn't already know that. Unlike most of The Group's handiwork, the Barrington twins had been posed by their publicity-hound parents on every magazine cover in the world. But Jane smiled at Ishmael as if he'd just explicated Spinoza.

"Yes, they are beautiful. Please, Ishmael, tell me about your organization. Anything that might help me prepare for my role in Future Perfect."

He leaned forward, hands on his knees, handsome face intent. Dramatically, insistently, he intoned, "There is one thing you must understand about The Group, Jane. A very critical thing. You will never stop us."

Portentous silence.

The worst thing was, he might be right. The FBI, CIA, IRS, HPA, and several other alphabets had lopped off a few heads, but still the hydra grew. It had so many supporters: liberal lawmakers and politicians, who wanted the Anti-Genetic Modification Act revoked and the Human Protection Agency dismantled. The rich parents who wanted their embryos enhanced. The off-shore banks that coveted The Group's dollars and the Caribbean or Mexican or who-knows-what islands that benefited from sheltering their mobile labs.

"We are idealists," Ishmael droned on, "and we are the future. Through our efforts, mankind will change for the better. Wars will end, cruelty will disappear. When people can—"

"Let me interrupt you for just a moment, Ishmael." Jane widened her eyes and over-used his name. Her dewy look up at him from the floor could have reversed desertification. She was pulling out all the stops. "I need so much to understand, Ishmael. If you genemod these little girls, one by one, you end up changing such a small percentage of the human race that . . . How many children have been engineered with Arlen's Syndrome?"

"We prefer the term 'Arlen's Advantage.' "

"Yes, of course. How many children?"

I held my breath. The Group had never given out that information.

Jane put an entreating hand on Ishmael's knee.

He said loftily, hungrily, "That information is classified," and I saw that he didn't know the answer.

Ms Resentful said, "To date, 3214."

Was she lying? My instincts – and I have very good instincts, although to say that in this context is clearly a joke – said no. Resentful knew the number. So she was higher up than Ishmael. And since she sure as hell wasn't responding to Jane's allure, that meant The Group now wanted the numbers made public.

"Yes, that's right," Ishmael said hastily, "3,214 children."

Jane said, "But that's not a high percentage out of six billion people on Earth, is it? It – "

"Five billionth of 1 per cent," I said. A silly, self-indulgent display, but what the hell. My legs ached.

She always could ad-lib. "Yes, thank you, Barry. But my question was for Ishmael. If only such a tiny percentage of humanity possesses Arlen's Advantage, even if the genemod turns out to be inheritable — "

"It is," Ishmael said, which was nonsense. The oldest Arlen's kids were only twelve.

"Wonderful!" Jane persisted. "But as I say, if only such a tiny percentage of humanity possesses the Advantage, how can The Group hope to alter the entire human future?"

Ishmael covered her hand with his. He smiled down at her, and his eyes actually twinkled. "Jane, Jane, Jane. Have you ever dropped a pebble into a pond?"

"Yes."

"And what happened, my dear?"

"A ripple."

"Which spread and spread until the entire pond was affected!" Ishmael spread his arms wide. The ass couldn't even put together a decent analogy. Humanity was an ocean, not a pond, and water ripples were always transitory. But Jane, actress that she was, beamed at him and moved the conversation to something he could handle.

"I see. Tell me, Ishmael, how you personally became involved in The Group."

He was thrilled to talk about himself. As he did, Jane skillfully extracted information about The Group's make-up, its organization, its communications methods. Resentful let her do it. I watched the young woman, who was watching Ishmael but not in a monitoring sort of way. He couldn't give away really critical information; he didn't have any. Still, he talked too much. He was the kind of man who responded to an audience, who could easily become so expansive that he turned indiscreet. Sooner or later, I suspected, he would say something to somebody that he shouldn't, and The Group would dump him.

Ms Resentful wasn't anything near the actress that Jane was. Her hunger for this worthless man was almost palpable. I might have felt sympathy for her pain if my own wasn't increasing so much in my legs, back, neck. I seldom sat this long, and never on a hard chair.

My particular brand of dwarfism, achondroplasia, accounts for 70 per cent of all cases. Malformed bones and cartilage produce not only the short limbs, big head and butt, and pushed-in face that all the media caricaturists so adore but also, in some of us, constriction of the spinal canal that causes pain. Especially as achons age, and I was only two years younger than Jane. Multiple excruciating operations have only helped me so much.

After an hour and a half, Jane rose, her filmy skirt swirling around her lovely calves. My uneasiness spiked sharply. If anything was going to happen, it would be now.

But nothing did happen. The masked boy reappeared and we were led out of the dingy basement. I could barely walk. Jane knew better than to help me, but she whispered, "I'm so sorry, Barry. But this was my only chance."

"I know." Somehow I made it up the stairs. We navigated the maze of the abandoned warehouse, where The Group's unseen soldiers stayed at stand-off with our own unseen bodyguards. Blinking in the sunlight, I suddenly collapsed onto the broken concrete.

"Barry!"

"It's . . . okay. Don't."

"The rest will be so much easier . . . I promise!"

I got myself upright, or what passes for upright. The unmarked van arrived for us. The whole insane interview had gone off without a hitch, without violence, smooth as good chocolate.

So why did I still feel so uneasy?

An hour later, Jane's image appeared all over the Net, the TV, the wall-boards. Her words had been edited to appear that she was a supporter, perhaps even a member, of The Group. But of course we had anticipated this. The moment our van left the warehouse, the first of the pre-emptory spots I'd prepared aired everywhere. They featured news avatar CeeCee Collins, who was glad for the scoop, interviewing Jane about her meeting. Dedicated actress preparing for a role, willing to take any personal risk for art, not a personal believer in breaking the law but valuing open discourse on this important issue, and so forth. The spots cost us a huge amount of money. They were worth it. Not only was the criticism defused, but the publicity for the upcoming movie, which started principal photography in less than a month, was beyond price.

I didn't watch my spots play. Nor was I there when the FBI, CIA, HPA, etc. paid Jane the expected visit to both "debrief" her and/or threaten her with arrest for meeting with terrorists. But I didn't need to be there. Before our meeting, I'd gotten Jane credentials under the Malvern-Murphy Press Immunity Act, plus Everett Murphy as her more-than-capable lawyer. Everett monitored the interviews and I stayed in bed under a painkiller. The FBI, CIA, HPA wanted to meet with me, too, of course, once Jane told them I'd been present. They had to wait until I could see them. I didn't mind their cooling their heels as they waited for me, not at all.

Why are you so opposed to genemods? Jane had asked me once, and only once, not looking at me as she said it. She meant, Why you, especially? Usually I answered Jane, trusted Jane, but not on this. I told her the truth: You wouldn't understand. To her credit, she hadn't been offended. Jane was smart enough to know what she didn't know.

Now, on my lovely pain patch, I floated in a world where she and I walked hand in hand through a forest the green of her filmy skirt, and she had to crane her neck to smile up at me.

The next few days, publicity for the picture exploded. Jane did interview after interview: TV, LinkNet, robocam, print, holonews. She glowed with the attention, looking ten years younger. Some of the interviewers and avatars needled her, but she stuck to the studio line: This is a movie about people, not polemics. Future Perfect is not really about genetic engineering. It will be an honest examination of eternal verities, of our shared frailty and astonishing shared strength, of what makes us human, of blah blah blah, that just happens to use Arlen's syndrome as a vehicle. The script was nearly finished and it would be complex and realistic and blah blah blah.

"Pro or con on genemods?" an exasperated journalist finally shouted from the back of the room.

Jane gave him a dazzling smile. "Complex and realistic," she said.

Both the pros and the cons would be swarming into the theater, unstoppable as lemmings.

I felt so good about all of this that I decided to call Leila. I needed to be in a good mood to stand these calls. Leila wasn't home, letting me get away with just a message, which made me feel even better.

Jane, glowing on camera, was wiping a decade years of cinematic obscurity with Future Perfect. I couldn't wipe out my fifteen years of guilt that easily, nor would I do so even if I could. But I was still glad that Leila wasn't home.

Jane had promised that Friday's role-prep interview would be easier on me. She was wrong.

The Barrington twins lived with their parents and teenage sister in San Luis Obispo. Jane's pilot obtained clearance to land on the green-velvet Barrington lawn, well behind the estate's heavily secured walls. I wouldn't have to walk far.

"Welcome, Miss Snow. An honor." Frieda Barrington was mutton dressed as lamb, a fiftyish woman in a brief skirt and peek-a-boo caped sweater. Slim, toned, tanned, but the breasts doing the peek-a-booing would never be twenty again, and her face had the tense lines of those who spent most of their waking time pretending not to be tense.

Jane climbed gracefully from the flyer and stood so that her body shielded my awkward descent. I seized the grab bar, sat on the flyer floor, fell heavily onto the grass, and scrambled to my feet. Jane moved aside, her calf-length skirt – butter yellow, this time – blowing in the slight breeze. "Call me Jane. This is my manager, Barry Tenler."

Frieda Barrington was one of Those. Still, she at least tried to conceal her distaste. "Hello, Mr Tenler."

"Hi." With any luck, this would be the only syllable I had to address to her.

We walked across through perfect landscaping, Frieda supplying the fund of inane chatter that such women always have at their disposal. The house had been built a hundred years earlier for a silent-film star. Huge, pink, gilded at windows and doors, it called to mind an obese lawn flamingo. We entered a huge foyer floored in black-and-white marble, which managed to look less Vermeer than checkerboard. A sulky girl in dirty jeans lounged on a chaise longue. She stared at us over the garish cover of a comic book.

"Suky, get up," Frieda snapped. "This is Miss Snow and her manager Mr, uh, Tangler. My daughter Suky."

The girl got up, made an ostentatious and mocking curtsey, and lay down again. Frieda made a noise of outrage and embarrassment, but I felt sorry for Suky. Fifteen – the same age as Ethan – plain of face, she was caught between a mother who'd appropriated her fashions and twin sisters who appropriated all the attention. Frieda would be lucky if Suky's rebellion stopped at mere rudeness. I made her a mock little bow to match her curtsey, and watched as her eyes widened with surprise. I grinned.

Frieda snapped, "Where are the twins?"

Suky shrugged. Frieda rolled her eyes and led us through the house.

They were playing on the terrace, a sun-shaded sweep of weathered stone with steps that led to more lawn, all backed by a gorgeous view of vineyards below the Sierra Madres. Frieda settled us on comfortable, padded chairs. A robo-server rolled up, offering lemonade.

Bridget and Belinda came over to us before they were called. "Hello!" Jane said with her melting smile, but neither girl answered. Instead, they gazed steadily, unblinkingly at her for a full thirty seconds, and then did the same with me. I didn't like it, or them.

Arlen's Syndrome, like all genetic tinkering, has side effects. No one knows that better than I. Achondroplasia dwarfism is the result of a single nucleotide substitution in the gene FGFR3 at codon 380 on chromosome 4. It affects the growth bones and cartilage, which in turn affects air passages, nerves, and other people's tolerance. Exactly which genes were involved in Arlen's were a trade secret, but the modifications undoubtedly spread across many genes, with many side effects. But since only females could be genemod for Arlen's, the X chromosome was one of those altered. That much, at least, was known.

The two eleven-year-old girls staring at me so frankly were small for their age, delicately built: fairy children. They had white skin, silky fair hair cut in short caps, and eyes of luminous gray. Other than that, they didn't look much alike, fraternal twins rather than identical. Bridget was shorter, plumper, prettier. From a Petri-dishful of Frieda's fertilized eggs, the Barringtons had chosen the most promising two, had them genemoded for Arlen's Syndrome, and implanted them in Frieda's ageing but still serviceable womb. The loving parents, both exhibitionists, had splashed across the world-wide media every last detail – except where and how the work had been done. Unlike Rima Ridley-Jones, the Arlen's child that Jane had spoken with last week, these two were carefully manufactured celebrities.

Jane tried again. "I'm Jane Snow, and you're Bridget and Belinda. I'm glad to meet you."

"Yes," Belinda said, "you are." She looked at me. "But you're not."

There was no point in lying. Not to them. "Not particularly."

Bridget said, with a gentleness surprising in one so young, "That's okay, though."

"Thank you," I said.

"I didn't say it was okay," Belinda said.

There was no answer to that. The Ridley-Jones child hadn't behaved like this; in addition to shielding her from the media, her mother had taught her manners. Frieda, on the other hand, leaned back in her chair like a specta-tor at a play, interested in what her amazing daughters would say next, but with anxiety on overdrive. I had the sense she'd been here before. Eleven-year-olds were no longer adorable, biddable toddlers.

"You'll never get it," Belinda said to me, at the same moment that Bridget put a hand on her sister's arm. Belinda shook it off. "Let me alone, Brid. He should know. They all should know." She smiled at me and I felt something in my chest recoil from the look in her gray eyes.

"You'll never get it," Belinda said to me with that horrible smile. "No matter what you do, Jane will never love you. And she'll always hate it when you touch her even by mistake. Just like she hates it now. Hates it, hates it, hates it."

It started with a dog.

Dr Kenneth Bernard Arlen, a geneticist and chess enthusiast, owned a toy poodle. Poodles are a smart breed. Arlen played chess twice a week in his Stanford apartment with Kelson Hughes from Zoology. Usually they played three, four, or five games in a row, depending on how careless Hughes got with his end game. Cosette lay on the rug, dozing, until checkmate of the last game, when she always began barking frantically to protest Hughes's leaving. The odd thing was that Cosette began barking before the men rose, as they replaced the chessmen for what might, after all, have been the start of just another game. How did she know it wasn't?

Hughes assumed pheromones. He, or Arlen, or both, probably gave off a different smell as they decided to call it a night. Pheromones were Hughes's field of research; he'd done significant work in mate selection among mice based on smell. He had a graduate student remove the glomeruli from adult dogs and put them through tests to see how various of their learned responses to humans changed. The responses didn't change. It wasn't pheromones.

Now not only Hughes but also Arlen was intensely intrigued. The Human Genome Project had just slid into Phase 2, discovering which genes encoded for what proteins, and how. Arlen was working with Turner's Syndrome, a disorder in which females were born missing all or part of one of their two X chromosomes. The girls had not only physical problems but social ones; they seemed to have trouble with even simple social interactions. What interested Hughes was that Turner Syndrome girls with an intact paternal X gene, the one inherited from the father, managed far better socially than those with the maternal X functioning. Something about picking up social cues was coded for genetically, and on the paternal X.

Where else did social facility reside in the genome? What cues of body language, facial expression, or tone of voice was Cosette picking up? Somehow the dog knew that when Hughes and Arlen set the chessmen in place, this wasn't the start of a new game. Something, dictated at least in part by Cosette's genes, was causing processes in her poodle brain. After all, Hughes's dog, a big dumb Samoyed, never seemed to anticipate anything. Snowy was continually surprised by gravity.

Arlen found the genes in dogs. It took him ten years, during which he failed to get tenure because he wouldn't publish. After Stanford let him go, he still didn't publish. He found the genes in humans. He still didn't publish. Stone broke, he was well on the way to bitter and yet with his idealism undimmed – an odd combination, but not unknown among science fanatics. Inevitably, he crossed paths with people even more fanatical. Kenneth Bernard Arlen joined forces with off-shore backers to open a fertility clinic that created super-empathic children.

Empathy turns up early in some children. A naturally empathic nine-month-old will give her teddy bear to another child who is crying; the toddler senses how bad the other child feels. People who score high in perceiving others' emotions are more popular, more outgoing, better adjusted, more happily married, more successful at their jobs. Arlen's Syndrome toddlers understood – not verbally, but in their limbic systems – when Mommy was worried, when Daddy wanted them to go potty, that Grandma loved them, that a stranger was dangerous.

If his first illegal, off-shore experiments with human germ lines had resulted in deformities, Arlen would have been crucified. There were no deformities. Prospective clients loved the promise of kids who actually understood how parents felt. By six or seven, Arlen's Syndrome kids could, especially if they were bright, read an astonishing array of non-verbal signals. By nine or ten, it was impossible to lie to them. As long as you were honest and genuinely had their best interests in mind, the children were a joy to live with: sensitive, cooperative, grateful, aware.

And yet here was Belinda Barrington, staring at me from her pale eyes, and I didn't need a genetic dose of super-empathy to see her glee at embarrassing me. I couldn't look at Jane. The blood was hot in my face.

Frieda said, sharply and hopelessly, "Belinda, that's not nice."

"No, it's not," Bridget said. She frowned at her sister, and Belinda actually looked away for a moment. Her twin had some childish control over Belinda, and her mother didn't. "Tell him you're sorry."

"Sorry," Belinda muttered, unconvincingly. So they could lie, if not be lied to.

Frieda said to Jane, "This is new behavior. I'm sure it's just a phase. Nothing you'd want to include in your project!"

Belinda shot her mother a look of freezing contempt.

Jane took control of the sorry situation. Sparing me any direct glance, she said to Belinda, "Did anybody tell you why I want to talk to you girls?"

"No," Belinda said. "You're not a reporter."

"I'm a movie actress."

Bridget brightened. "Like Kylie Kicker?" Apparently Arlen's Advantage did not confer immunity to inane kiddie pop culture.

"Not as young," Jane smiled, "or as rich. But I'm making a movie about the lives that girls like you might have when you're grown up. That's why I want to get to know you a little bit now. But only if it's okay with you."

The twins looked at each other. Neither spoke, but I had the impression that gigabytes passed between them. Frieda said, "Girls, I hope you'll cooperate with Miss Snow. She—"

"No, you don't," Belinda said, almost absently. "You don't like her. She's too pretty. But we like her."

Frieda's face went a mottled maroon. Bridget, her plump features alarmed, put a hand on her mother's arm. But Frieda shook it off, started to say something, then abruptly stood and stalked into the house. Bridget made a move to follow but checked herself. To me – why? – she said apologetically, "She wants to be alone a little while."

"You should go with her," Belinda said, and I didn't have to be told twice. These kids gave me the creeps.

Not that even they, with their overpraised empathy, could ever understand why.

In the foyer, Suky still lay on the chaise longue with her comic book. There was no sign of her mother. The other chairs were all mammoth leather things, but a low antique bench stood against one wall and I clambered painfully onto it and called a cab. I would have to walk all the way to the front gate to meet it, but the thought of going back in the flyer with Jane was unbearable. I closed my eyes and leaned my head against the wall. My back and legs ached, but nothing compared to my heart.

It wasn't the words Belinda had said. Yes, I loved Jane and yes, that love was hopeless. I already knew that and so must Jane. How could she not? I was with her nearly every day; she was a woman sensitive to nuance. I knew she hated my accidental touch, and hated herself for that, and could help none of it. Three of Jane's husbands had been among the best-looking men on the planet. Tall, strong, straight-limbed. I had seen Jane's flesh glow rosy just because James or Karl or Duncan was in the same room with her. I had felt her hide her recoil from me.

"Sticks and stones can break my bones but words can never hurt me." How often as a child had I chanted that to myself after another in the endless string of bullies had taunted me? Short Stuff, Dopey, Munchkin, Big Butt, Mighty Midget, Oompa Loompa, cripple. . . . Belinda hadn't illuminated any new truth for anybody. What she had done was speak it aloud.

"Give sorrow words" – but even Shakespeare could be as wrong as nursery chants. Something unnamed could, just barely, be ignored. Could be kept out of daily interaction, could almost be pretended away. What had been "given words" could not. And now tomorrow and the next day and the day after that, Jane and I would have to try to work together, would avoid each other's eyes, would each tread the dreary internal treadmill: Is he/she upset? Did I brush too close, stay too far away, give off any hurtful signal . . . For God's sake, leave me alone!

Speech doesn't banish distance; it creates it. And if—

"Bitches, aren't they?" a voice said softly. I opened my eyes. Suky stood close to my bench. She was taller than I'd thought, with a spectacular figure. No one would ever notice, not next to the wonder and novelty of the twins.

In my shamed confusion, I blurted out the first thing that came into my mind. "Belinda is, Bridget isn't."

"That's what you think." Suky laughed, then laid her comic book on the bench. "You need this, dwarf." She vanished into some inner corridor.

I picked up the comic. It was holo, those not-inexpensive e-graphics with chips embedded in the paper. Four panels succeeded each other on each page, with every panel dramatizing the plot in ten-second bursts of shifting light. The title was "Knife Hack," and the story seemed to concern a mother who carves up her infants with a maximum amount of blood and brain spatter.

Arlen's Syndrome kids: a joy to live with, sensitive and cooperative and grateful and aware.

Just one big happy family.

But sometimes the universe gives you a break. The next day I had a cold. Nothing serious, just a stuffy nose and sore throat, but I sounded like a rusty file scraping on cast iron, so I called in sick to my "office" at Jane's estate. Her trainer answered. "What?"

"Tell Jane I won't be in today. Sick. And remind her to—"

"I'm not your errand boy, Barry," he answered hotly. We stared at each other's comlink images in mutual dislike. Dino Carrano was the trainer-to-the-stars-of-the-moment-before-this-one, an arrogant narcissist who three times a week tortured Jane into perfect abs and weeping exhaustion. Like Ishmael, he was without the prescience to realize that his brief vogue had passed and that Jane kept him on partly from compassion. He stood now in her deserted exercise room.

"Why are you answering the phone? Where's Catalina?"

"Her grandmother in Mexico died. Again. And before you ask, Jose is supervising the grounds crew and Jane is in the bathroom, throwing up. Now you know everything. Bye, Barry."

"Wait! If she's throwing up because you pushed her too hard again, you Dago bastard – "

"Save your invective, little man. We haven't even started the training session yet, and if we don't train by tomorrow, her ass is going to drop like a duffel bag. For today she just ate something bad." He cut the link.

My stomach didn't feel too steady, either. Had it been the Barrington lemonade? I made it to the bathroom just in time. But afterward I felt better, decided to not call my doctor, and went to bed. If Jane was sick, Catalina would cancel her appointments. No, Catalina was in Mexico . . . not my problem.

But all Jane's problems were mine. Without her, I had my own problems – Leila, Ethan – but no actual life.

Nonetheless, I forced myself to stay in bed, and eventually I fell asleep. When I woke, six hours later, my throat and stomach both felt fine. A quick call discovered that Catalina had returned from Mexico, sounding suspiciously unbereaved. But she was efficient enough when she was actually in the country, and I decided I didn't need to brief Jane on tomorrow's schedule. That would buy me one more day. I would take a relaxing evening. A long bath, a glass of wine, another postponement of talking to Leila. The industry news on Hollywood Watch.

The local news came on first. Ishmael's body had been found in a pond in the Valley.

". . . and weighted with cement blocks. Cause of death was a single gunshot wound to the head, execution style," said the news avatar, a CGI who looked completely real except that she had no faulty camera angles whatsoever. I stared at the photo of Ishmael's handsome face on the screen beside her. "Apparently the murderers were unaware that construction work would start today at the pond site, where luxury condos will be built by – "

Ishmael's name was Harold Sylvester Ehrenreich. Failed actor, minor grifter, petty tax evader, who had dropped out of electronic sight eight months ago.

"Anyone having any information concerning—"

I was already on the comlink. "Jane?"

"I just called the cops. They're on their way over." She looked tired, drawn, within five years of her actual age. Her voice sounded as raspy as mine had been. "I was just about to call you. Barry, if this endangers the picture—"

"It won't," I said. Thirty years a star, and she still didn't understand how the behind-the-scenes worked. "It will make the picture. Did you call Everett?"

"He's on his way."

"Don't say a word until both he and I get there. Not a word, Jane, not one. Can you send the flyer for me?"

"Yes. Barry – was he killed because of my interview?"

"There's no way to know that," I said, and all at once was profoundly grateful that it was true. I didn't care if Ishmael was alive, dead, or fucking himself on Mars, but Jane was built differently. People mattered to her, especially the wounded-bird type. It was how she'd ended up married to three of her four husbands and the fourth, the Alpha-Male Producer, had been in reaction to the second, the alcoholic failed actor. Catalina, Jane's housekeeper and social secretary, was another of her wounded birds. So, in his own perverse way, was her trainer.

Maybe that was why Jane had ended up with me as well.

But I could tell that neither me nor Belinda's cruel words were on Jane's mind just now. It was all Ishmael, and that was good. Ishmael would get us safely past our personal crisis. Even murder has its silver lining.

As the flyer set down on Jane's roof, I saw the media already starting to converge. Someone must have tipped them off, perhaps a clerk at the precinct. An unmarked car was parked within Jane's gates, with two vans outside and another flyer approaching from LA Catalina let me in, her dark eyes wide with excitement. "La policia – "

"I know. Is Everett Murphy here?"

"Yes, he— "

"Bring in coffee and cake. And make the maids draw all the curtains in the house, immediately. Even the bedrooms. There'll be robocams." I wanted pictures and information released on my schedule, not that of flying recorders.

A man and a woman sat with Jane and Everett at one end of her enormous living room, which the decorator had done in swooping black curves with accents of screaming purple. The room looked nothing like Jane, who used it only for parties. She'd actually defied the decorator, who was a Dino-Carrano-bully type but not a wounded bird, and done her private sitting room in English country house. But she hadn't taken the detectives there. I could guess why: she was protecting her safe haven. Catalina rushed past me like a small Mexican tornado and dramatically pushed the button to opaque the windows. They went deep purple, and lights flickered on in the room. Catalina raced out.

"Barry," Jane said. She looked even worse than on comlink, red nose and swollen eyes and no make-up. I hoped to hell that neither cop was optic wired. "This is Detective Lopez and Detective Miller from the LAPD. Officers, my manager Barry Tenler."

They nodded. Both were too well-trained to show curiosity or distaste, but they were there. I always know. In her sitting room Jane kept a low chair for me, but here I had to scramble up onto a high black sofa that satisfied the decorator desire for "an important piece." I said, "You can question Miss Snow now, but please be advised that she has already spoken with the FBI and HPA, and that both Mr Murphy and I reserve the right to advise her to not answer."

The cops ignored this meaningless window dressing. But I'd accomplished what I wanted. Dwarfs learn early that straightforward, multisyllabic, take-no-shit talk will sometimes stop average-sizers from treating us like children. Sometimes.

Officer Lopez began a thorough interrogation: How had she arranged the meeting with The Group? When? What contact had she had between the initial one and the meeting? Who had taken her to the meeting? Who else had accompanied her? When they found out that it had been me, Lopez got the look of a man who knows he's screwed up. "You were there, Mr Tenler?"

"I was."

"You'll have to go with Officer Miller into another room," Lopez said. He stared at me hard. Witnesses were always questioned separately, and even if it hadn't crossed his mind that someone like me was a witness, he suspected it had crossed mine. Which it had. If law-enforcement agencies weren't given to so many turf wars, the LAPD would already know I'd been in that grimy basement. Or if Lopez hadn't fallen victim to his own macho assumptions. *You? She took a lame half-pint like you to protect her?*

"Everett is my lawyer, too," I said.

"You go with Officer Miller. Mr Murphy will join you when I'm finished with Miss Snow." Lopez's formality barely restrained his anger.

Following Officer Miller to the media room, it occurred to me – pointlessly – that Belinda would have known immediately that I'd been withholding something.

It seemed obvious to me, as it probably was to the cops, that Ishmael had been killed by The Group. Narcissistic, bombastic, unreliable, he must have screwed up royally. Was Ms. Resentful dead, too? The bodyguard with the assault rifle? The boy who'd guided us through the warehouse?

The Group was trying to combine idealism, profit-making, and iron control. That combination never worked. I would say that to Officer Lopez, except that there was little chance he would take it seriously. Not from me.

The media spent a breathless three or four days on the story ("Famous Actress Questioned About Genemod Murder! What Does Jane Know?"). Then a United States senator married a former porn star named Candy Alley and the press moved on, partly because it was clear that Jane didn't know anything. I'd positioned her as cooperative, concerned, committed to her art, and bewildered by the killing. Opinion polls said the public viewed her favorably. She increased her name recognition 600 per cent among eighteen to twenty-four-year-olds, most of whom watched only holos and had never seen a Jane Snow picture. Publicity is publicity.

She got even more of it by spending so much time with the Barrington twins. Everybody liked this except me. Frieda liked the press attention (at least, such press as wasn't staking out the senator and his new pork barrel).

The twins liked Jane. She liked caring for yet more wounded birds, which was what she considered them. Her thinking on this escaped me; these were two of the most pampered children in the known universe. But Jane was only filling time, anyway, until the script was finished. And to her credit, she turned down the party invitations from the I'm-more-important-than-you A-list crowd that had ignored her for a decade. I'd urged her to turn down social invitations in order to create that important aura of non-attainable exclusivity. Jane turned them down because she no longer considered those people to be friends.

As for me, I worked at home on the hundreds of pre-photography details. Before I could finally reach Leila, she called me.

"Hey, Barry."

"Hey, Leila." She didn't look good. I steeled myself to ask. "How is he?"

"Gone again." Exhaustion pulled at her face. "I called the LAPD but they won't do anything."

"He'll come home again," I said. "He always does."

"Yeah, and one of these days it'll be in a coffin."

I said nothing to that, because there was nothing to say.

Leila, however, could always find something. "Well, if he does come home in a coffin, then you'll be off the hook, won't you? No more risk of embarrassing you or the gorgeous has-been."

"Leila—"

"Have a good time with your big shot Hollywood friends. I'll just wait to hear if this time the son you deformed really is dead."

She hung up on me.

Leila and I met at a Little People of America convention in Denver. She was one of the teenage dwarfs dancing joyously, midriff bared and short skirt flipping, at the annual ball. I thought she was the most beautiful thing I'd ever seen: red hair and blue eyes, alive to her fingertips. I was eighteen years older than she, and everyone at the convention knew who I was. High-ranking aide to a candidate for the mayor of San Francisco. Smart, successful, sharply dressed. Local dwarf makes good. More mobile then, I asked her to dance. Six months later we married. Six months after that, while I was running the campaign for a gubernatorial candidate, Leila accidentally got pregnant.

Two dwarfs have a 25 per cent chance of conceiving an average-sized child, a 50 percent chance of a dwarf, and a 25 per cent of a double-dominant, which always dies shortly after birth. Leila and I had never discussed these odds because, like most dwarfs, we planned on the in vitro fertilization that permits cherry-picking embryos. But Leila got careless with her pills. She knew immediately that she was pregnant, and even before the zygote had implanted itself in her uterus wall, testing showed that the fetus had a "normal" FGFR3 gene. I panicked.

"I don't want to have an average-sized kid," I told Leila. "I just don't."

"And I don't want to have an abortion," Leila said. "It's not that I'm politically opposed to abortion. I'm glad to have the choice, but . . . Barry, I . . . I just can't. He's already a baby to me. Our baby. Why would having an Average be so hard?"

"Why?" I'd waved a hand around our house, in which everything – furniture, appliance controls, doorknobs – had been built to our scale. "Just look around! Besides, there's a moral question here, Leila. You know that with in vitro, fewer and fewer dwarfs are having dwarf children. That just reinforces the idea that there's something wrong with being a dwarf. I don't want to perpetuate that – I won't perpetuate that. This is a political issue! I want a dwarf child."

She believed me. She was twenty to my thirty-nine, and I was a big-shot politico. She loved me. Leila lacked the perspicacity to see how terrified I was of an average-sized son, who would be as tall as I was by the time he was seven. Who would be impossible to control. Who might eventually despise me and his mother both. But Leila really, really didn't want to abort. I talked her into in utero somatic gene therapy in England.

In those days I believed in science. The som-gene technique was new but producing spectacular results. The British had gotten behind genetic engineering in a big way, and knowledgeable people from all over the world flocked to Cambridge, where private firms tied to the great university where turning on and off genes in fetuses still in the womb. This had to be done during the first week or ten days after conception. The FGFR3 gene stops bones from growing. It was turned on in babies with dwarfism; a corrective genemod retrovirus should be able to turn the gene off in the little mass of cells that was Ethan. The problem was that the Cambridge biotech clinic wouldn't do it.

"We cure disease, not cause it," I was told icily.

"Dwarfism is not a disease!" I said, too angry to be icy. Waving high the banner of political righteousness. It wasn't a good idea, in those days, to cross me. I was the high-ranking, infallible campaign guru, the tiny wunderkind, the man who was never wrong. Fear can present itself as arrogance.

"Nonetheless," the scientist told me in that aloof British accent, "we will not do it. Nor, I suspect, will any clinic in the United Kingdom."

He was right. Time was running out. The next day we went off-shore, to a clinic in the Caymans, and something went wrong. The retrovirus that was the delivery vector mutated, or the splicing, caused other genes to jump (they will do that), or maybe God just wanted an evil joke that day. The soma-gene correction spawned side effects, with one gene turning on another that in turn affected another, a cascade of creation run amok. And we got Ethan.

Leila never forgave me, and I never forgave myself. She left me when Ethan was not quite two. I sent money. I tried to stay in touch. I bore Leila's fury and contempt and despair. She sent me pictures of Ethan, but she wouldn't let me see him. I could have pressed visitation through the courts. I didn't.

My gubernatorial candidate lost.

"Barry," Jane comlinked me the night before the first script conference, "would you like to come to dinner tonight?"

"Can't," I lied. "I already have dinner plans."

"Oh? With whom?"

"A friend." I smiled mysteriously. Some inane, back-in-high-school part of my brain hoped that she'd think I had a date. Then I saw Bridget Barrington scamper across the room behind Jane. "Are those kids at your place?"

"Yes, I couldn't go there today because Catalina is sick and I had to – "

"Sick? With what? Jane, you can't catch anything now, the first reading is tomorrow and–"

"I won't catch this – I gave it to her. It's that sore-throat-and-stomach thing we both had. Catalina–"

"You're not a goddamn nurse! If Catalina is ill–" give me credit, I didn't say actually ill instead of faking the way she fakes relatives' deaths every fifteen minutes.

" – then hire a nurse or – "

"She's not sick enough for a nurse, she just needs coddling and orange juice and company. It's fine, Barry, so butt out. I'm actually glad of the distraction, it keeps me from thinking about tonight. Oh, I meant to tell you – I talked Robert into couriering the script to me tonight! I wanted to read it before tomorrow. He sounded weird about it, but he agreed."

My radar turned on. "Weird how?"

"I don't know. Just weird."

I considered all the possible "weirds" that the producer could be convey-ing, but I didn't see what I could do about any of them. I settled for, "Just don't catch anything from Catalina."

"I already told you that I won't."

"Fine. Whatever you say."

And it was fine. She was treating me the way she always did, with exas-perated affection, and I was grateful. Belinda's poison, flushed out of our working relationship by the flood of feeling about Ishmael's murder, hadn't harmed us. I wouldn't lose the little of Jane that I had.

And the picture was going to be a blockbuster.

"It's a disaster!" Jane screamed. "I won't do it!"

Sitting up in bed, I stared blearily at the wall screen. Beneath the image of Jane's ravaged face, the time said 12:56 a.m. I struggled to assemble consciousness.

"What is—"

She started to cry, great gasping sobs that would wreck her face for tomorrow's conference. When had I seen Jane cry like that? When the last husband left. And the one before that.

"I'm coming right over," I said. "I'm leaving immediately. Don't read any more of the script. We'll work this out, I promise."

She was sobbing too hard to answer me.

"Just have a glass of wine and wait for me."

"O .... okay."

I cut the link and called my chauffeur. I can drive if I have to, but it's painful. Ernie and his wife Sandra, my housekeeper, live in the guest cottage. They're both achons. "Mr Tenler? What is it? Are you okay?" Ernie sounded bewildered. They're good people, but I've kept our relationship distant, not given to midnight calls for chauffeur service.

"I'm fine, but I have to go to Miss Snow's immediately. Can you bring around the car in five minutes?"

"Five minutes?" Ernie's face looked exhausted. "Yeah, sure."

"Are you all right?"

Surprise replaced his exhaustion. I wasn't in the habit of asking after Ernie's health.

"Yeah, I'm fine, it's just that Sandra and I have both been under the weather. But no big deal. I'll be there in —"

"But if you're sick, maybe you shouldn't —"

"Five minutes," Ernie said, and now suspicion had replaced surprise. What the hell was I doing? I didn't know, either. Painfully I climbed from the bed, tried to flex my aching body, and pulled on clothes. I hobbled out the front door as the Lexus pulled up.

"Here," I said, handing Ernie a pain patch and a plastiflask of orange juice. He stared at me and shook his head.

Jane, in robe and slippers, let me in herself. Her face, red and blotchy and swollen, looked the worst I'd ever seen it. I wanted to take her in my arms, and that turned my voice harsher than I expected. "What's wrong with the fucking script?"

Perversely, my anger seemed to steady her. "It's a travesty."

"Did they reduce your part?"

"That's the least of it! Read it, Barry. I want you to read it for yourself." She led the way to her sitting room. A bottle of wine, half empty, sat on the table. Jane poured herself a third glass as I read, but I wasn't worried about that. Despite her fragile looks, Jane could out-drink a Russian stevedore.

I began to read.

Future Perfect was based on a short story by an obscure writer, which means the studio got the rights cheap. Like much fiction set in the future, it extrapolated from the present, portraying a Mississippi city in which the mayor was an Arlen's Syndrome young woman named Kate Bradshaw. Kate, empathetic but inexperienced, was guided by Jane's character, an ex-D.A. who was tough, funny, and not above using her mature sexuality for political ends. The story arc brought in prejudice, female friendship, and the choices that politics must make to accommodate radically different points of view. There was a lot of lush Deep South atmosphere. The ending, deliberately ambiguous, featured a knock-out closing speech for Jane's D.A.

The script had moved the story to LA. The mayor was an evil Delilah who could read minds. She seduced and destroyed men, subverted democracy, had her enemies tortured. Clones were created. Buildings blew up, many buildings. Jane's character was also blown up, a third of the way into the movie. The mayor is eventually shot through the heart by a noble young HPA agent. The body bleeds viscous yellow blood.

"Jane," I said, and stopped. I had to be careful, had to choose just the right words. She had finished off the bottle of wine. I brought her a box of tissues, even though she had stopped crying. "I know it's bad, but—"

"I won't do it." Her flexible voice held the kind of despair that's gone past raging, gone straight into hopelessness.

"This is only the first pass at the script. We can ask for—"

"You know we won't get it."

I did know. I went to the main point. "Janie, sweetheart, this is the only project you've been offered in—"

"I won't do it."

"Jane, you're not—"

"I should think you would understand," she said, looking at me directly with a very un-Jane look. No softness, no flirtation, nothing but quiet, unvarnished truth. "This piece of shit encourages hatred. Not just portrays it, but actively encourages it. Arlen's kids are different, therefore they must be bad, evil. More than that – they're the result of a genetic difference, so they must be really bad, really evil, and we should clean them out of our society. I should think you, of all people, Barry, would object to that."

We had never, not once in five years, discussed my dwarfism. She didn't know about Leila, about Ethan. This was uncharted territory for us, and with every cell of my being I did not want to go there. She had no right to bring this home to me; it was her decision. Anger hijacked my brain.

"You have no idea what I should or should not object to! Do you think that two weeks spent with a few genetically privileged kids gives you insight into what genetics can do? You know nothing, you're as ignorant and stupid as most of the rest of the so-called 'normal' population. You have no idea the anguish that fucking genemods can cause, you think they're all uplifting improvements to mankind, you think that you can just. . . . Go ahead, commit career suicide! This script is all you've been offered in three years, and it's all you're going to get offered. You're an ageing actress who belongs to another era, a Norma Desmond who will never. . . . Go ahead, tell yourself you're taking the moral high ground! You're standing on quicksand, and I'll be fucked if I let you take me down with you!"

Silence.

She said wearily, "I won't do this script."

"Fine. Get yourself another manager."

I hobbled out to the waiting car and Ernie drove me home.

Jane withdrew from the picture. The studio cast Suri Cruise in the part; she was young enough to be Jane's daughter. Leila called to say tersely that Ethan had crawled home from his latest bout of homelessness. He had a broken nose, a black eye, and a mangled hand. She wouldn't let me come to see him: "How would he even know who the fuck you are?" I didn't insist. The LAPD announced periodically that there were no new developments in the Harold Ehrenreich murder case, and over the next few months, Ishmael's handsome face disappeared from the newsgrids.

Ernie recovered from his bout of flu in a few days, but Sandra's turned into pneumonia and she had to go to the hospital. I visited her every day, to her bewilderment. This was new behavior, but I knew the cause. I had nothing else to do, or at least nothing I could make myself do, and hospital visiting was a distraction. Sandra was only there for four days, but her room-mate developed complications and had to go into ICU. She was a frightened old woman with no family. I brought her flowers and chocolate and, when she was a little better, played mah-jongg with her. The game attracted a few other invalids, including a young man dying of one of the few cancers that medicine still couldn't cure. I began visiting him, too. Martin never seemed to even notice that I was a dwarf. Perhaps, as someone once remarked, dying does concentrate the mind, squeezing out everything else.

Every once in a while I reflected wryly that I seemed to have taken on Jane's penchant for wounded birds. But I didn't reflect too hard; hospital visiting was a long way from Hollywood management, which in turn was a long way from the nails-tough political world. I didn't want to look at how far I'd fallen.

Jane, too, seemed to be in wounded-bird mode. Sometimes, not too often, a picture of her would turn up on some fourth-rate "celebrity watch" linksite, the holo supplied by a desperate paparazzo who couldn't do better. In those shots, she was helping some homeless drunk or paying the bills for a child who owned one ragged dress, or so it was claimed. The holos of Jane with the Barrington twins, on the other hand, turned up regularly on all the news vectors. Frieda Barrington probably saw to that.

In July, Ernie and Sandra quit. "I'm sorry, Mr Tenler, but we're not comfortable here any more."

"Not comfortable?" I had just spent twenty thousand dollars remodeling the guest cottage.

"No." He shifted from one foot to the other. Ernie has a smaller head and butt than a lot of achons, but he's far from being a proportional, and another job that paid this well for this little work was not going to be easy to find. Not for him, not for Sandra. Where would they go?

"Where will you go?"

"That's our business."

It was such a rude answer that I frowned. Something in the frown broke his reserve.

"Look, Mr Tenler, it's not that we aren't grateful. You done a lot for us. But lately you're so . . . We didn't want the cottage remodeled, and I said as much to you. You keep giving us things we don't want. And . . . and hanging around a lot. I'm sorry, but it's a huge pain in the ass."

And I had just wanted to help!

But now Ernie was wound up. "It's like you're trying to control us. I know, I know, you think you're being a good guy, but we . . . and those calls! They're creeping out Sandra. It's best that we go."

I gave them a generous severance pay-out and hired a Mexican couple, undocumented, who desperately needed jobs. It felt good to help them along. The comlink calls, I started taking myself.

They came once or twice a week. No visual, and the audio came through a voice changer. Routing was via a private, encrypted satellite system, so there was no chance whatsoever of tracing the calls. I thought at first that they might be from Jane, but this emphatically was not her style. Each call was exactly the same:

"Barry Tenler."

"I'm Barry Tenler."

Heavy breathing. Finally, "I know how you feel."

"Feel about what?"

And now the mechanical voice – this isn't supposed to be possible, but I swear I heard it – hinted at pain. "I just want you to know that someone understands. Someone in the same position."

"Look, let me help—" And the link ended.

What "position"? Another dwarf? Another unemployed PR-flack-cum-manager? Another parent of a kid with major genetic problems?

Then I had another mystery because the feds showed up. They proved to be just as elusive as my unknown caller.

"We'd like to ask you some questions, Mr Tenler."

"What about? Do I need my lawyer?"

"No, not at all. These are just general questions, in the public interest. You'd really help us out."

I blinked. The HPA usually commands "help" rather than requests it, and these were not the erection-jawed types who'd interviewed me after Jane's and my visit to The Group. These two, a man and a woman, were both short, slightly built, mild in manner, deliberately unthreatening. Why? I was curious. Also bored, so I asked them in. Or maybe it was just to see them both perch uncomfortably on my dwarf-sized living room chairs, their knees rising above the cocktail table like cliff faces from a Himalayan valley. "Have you been ill lately, Mr Tenler?"

"Ill? No. I'm fine." I knew they weren't referring to chronic pain. Nor to chronic self-pity, either.

"No flu-like symptoms?"

"I did have the flu a few months ago, but nothing since."

I could sense the two of them not looking at each other.

"What is this about?" I asked. "I think I'd like to know before I answer any more questions."

"I wish we could accommodate you, sir," the woman said apologetically. She was maybe five-one, pretty, and when she smiled at me, I felt anger swell in my chest. A cheap tactic if there ever was one. Maybe he'll talk to a woman on his own level . . . "Just one more question, please. It would really help us out. Since March, has anyone from The Group tried to contact you?"

"No." If the encrypted calls were from The Group, I didn't know it, and the feds weren't going to, either.

"Thank you, Mr Tenler," she said winningly, and handed me her card. Agent Elaine Brown, Human Protection Agency.

"Once again, what is this about?"

"Please contact us if anything occurs to you, or if you're contacted by The Group," the male agent said. "There's been chatter among our informants."

I knew better than to ask what kind of chatter; he'd probably said too much anyway. After they left, I stared at Elaine Brown's card, wondering what the hell that had all been about.

Two weeks later, I found out. The whole world found out, but I was first.

Another post-midnight phone call, and this time I was not in the mood for it. I'd spent the day at the hospital. Martin, my mah-jongg playing cancer patient, died at 4.43 p.m. The only other person there was his elderly mother, who then fell apart. I had done for her what I could, which wasn't much, arriving home late at night. Three whisky-and-sodas hadn't dulled my sense that the world made no sense. The bedside clock said 2.14 a.m. I snarled at the screen, "What?"

"Barry Tenler." It wasn't a question. The screen stayed dark.

"Look, I'm not in the mood for games tonight, so you can just—" Then it hit me that the voice was not mechanical, not masked. A woman's voice, and somewhere I'd heard it before.

"Listen to me, this is a matter of life-and-death for someone you love. Get Jane Snow away to someplace safe and hidden, and do it now. Tonight."

"What the – who are you?"

"It doesn't matter who I am. Get her away tonight."

"Why? What's going to – no, don't hang up! You're—"

Where had I heard that voice?

"Just go. Goodbye."

I had it. "You're the woman from The Group. In the warehouse base-ment. To date, three thousand two hundred fourteen. The only sentence I'd heard her utter, and not even a whole sentence. A fragment.

Silence.

"And," I said, as it all came together in my sleep-deprived brain, "you're the woman who's been making those masked calls to me." I know how you feel. . . . I just want you to know that someone understands. Someone in the same position. "You loved Ishmael."

"They murdered him!" A second later she'd regained control of herself. That a woman like this lost control at all was a measure of her pain. Grief can drive even the toughest person to acts of insanity. Maybe especially the toughest person. She said, "I underestimated you."

I didn't say People usually do, because now fear had my chest gripped tight. She was credible, at least to me. "How is Jane in danger? Please tell me."

A long pause, and then she said, "Why the fuck not? But know one thing, Barry Tenler. You will never find me, and neither will The Group. And tomorrow morning it will all be public anyway. Tell me, have you ever heard of oxytorin?"

"No."

"Did you get ill a few days after your little visit in March to that warehouse?"

The fear gripped harder. "Flu-like symp—"

"It wasn't flu. Tell me, have you noticed yourself engaged in unusual behaviors lately? Has Jane? Has anyone else with whom you've exchanged bodily fluids, especially saliva?"

I hadn't exchanged bodily fluids, including saliva, with anyone. But all at once I remembered the pre-meeting searches in the warehouse. A man had checked me over, including opening my mouth and moving aside my tongue. His hands had felt unpleasantly slimy.

I was having trouble breathing. "What . . . what is oxytorin?"

"Nothing that will kill you. The Group is made up of idealists, remember? Idealists who murder anyone who wanders two inches off the reservation." She laughed, a horrible sound. "I know he was dumb and vain, but I loved him. Sneer at that if you will, only you won't, will you? Not you. You're just as enslaved by another beautiful moron. And you can't help it any more than I could, can you?"

"Please . . . what is oxytorin?"

Her tone lost its anguished cynicism. Relaying factual information steadied her.

"It's a neuropeptide, a close relative to oxytocin, secreted in the brain and the pituitary gland. Like oxytocin, it has effects on social behavior. Specifically, it promotes nurturing behavior. If you give it to virgin female rats, within forty-eight hours they're building nests and trying to nurse any baby rats you hand to them. If you remove it from mother rats' brains, they ignore their babies and let them die. The same with monkeys. It—"

Nurturing behavior. Bringing Ernie and Sandra orange juice and remodeling their cottage. Visiting hospital patients whom I met by accident. Jane, childless, spending hours and hours with the Barrington twins.

" – has been synthesized synthetically for a long time, but the synthetic version has to be injected directly into the brain. That's not practical when you want to permanently influence a large fraction of the population, so instead—"

"You bastards." It came out a whisper, strangled by rage.

" – The Group went with a compound that switches on the genes that create oxytorin receptors. You don't have more oxytorin, you just have more receptors for it, so more of it is actually affecting your brain. Although susceptibility to the genemod will vary among people – like, say, susceptibility to cholera depends on blood type. The delivery vector is a retrovirus, capable of penetrating the blood-brain barrier, but which first colonizes mouth and nose secretions. The—"

"You used us. Me and Jane. You—"

"—desired end here is a kinder, gentler populace. Isn't that what we all want?"

The combination of cynicism and idealism in her words stunned me, because I knew it was absolutely genuine. Again, a whisper: "You can't."

"We did. And if the motherfucking leadership had ever taken it themselves, before they decided Harold was a liability—" She was sobbing. I didn't care.

My throat opened up. I screamed, "You can't just fuck around with people's genes without their consent!"

The sobbing stopped. She said coldly, "Why not? You did."

She knew. They knew. About Ethan.

"I'm telling you this because tomorrow morning The Group is putting the story on the Link. You and your ageing Aphrodite are carriers, and when the press gets hold of that, you'll be inundated, if not lynched. Especially since The Group is saying that Jane Snow cooperated, that this is part of her Hollywood liberal-left politics. Plenty will believe it. And even if they don't, sensationalism always works best when pegged to a few identifiable people. You should know that."

"Why are you telling—"

"You don't listen, do you? I already told you why. You're just as fucked as I am. We're alike, you and I, and neither of us ever stood a fucking chance of getting who we wanted. Damn them to hell, all of them . . . It always comes down to bodies, Munchkin, and yours has been damned twice. So get yourself and her out of town. Now." The link broke.

I stood staring at nothing for a full minute, for a lifetime. I wasn't even aware of the body she had just mocked. Only my mind raced.

Bodily fluids. Blood, semen, saliva. Jane wiping snot from the noses of the Barrington twins, kissing them, kissing half of the Hollywood press corps in their touch-touch social rituals. And . . . sleeping with someone? I never asked her. And undoubtedly we weren't the only two that had been infected; that wouldn't be widespread enough. We were just the two that were going to be publicly named.

The weakness of The Group's expensive, individually created genemods for Arlen's Syndrome had always been the very small number of empathic kids it could create. When Jane had pointed this out, Ishmael had gone into his grandiose "ripple" analogy, which explained nothing. But somewhere above Ishmael were people far more knowledgeable, more committed, more dangerous. People with a plan, a revolution for society. The Group had been waging war with the genomes of children as bullets. Now they had moved up to soma-gene engineering, as saturation bombing.

Anger is a great heartener. I dressed quickly, put a few things in a bag, and went down to the car. The kind of encryption that my caller had used was not available to me, and so the comlink was too big a risk. The pedal extenders that Ernie had used in the Lexus, and which Carlos didn't need, were still in the trunk. I installed them and drove to Jane's. I have e-codes to the gate and the house. Within an hour I was at her bedroom door.

What if she wasn't alone?

Deep breath. I went in. "Jane? Don't scream, it's Barry."

"What—"

"It's Barry. I'm turning on the light."

She sat up in bed, wild-eyed, and she wasn't alone. The Barrington twins curled up on the other side of the huge bed, lost in the heavy sleep of childhood, their hair in tangles and drool on their pillows. "What the fuck—"

All at once my legs gave way. I grasped the edge of the mattress, lowered myself to the floor, and so once again had to look up at her. "Listen, Janie, this is life-and-death. We have to leave here. Now. No, don't say anything – just listen to me for once!"

Something in my voice, or my ridiculous position, got through to her. She didn't say a word as I told her everything that I'd been told. Her feathery light hair drifted in some air current from the open window, and above the modest blue pajamas she wore for this grandmotherly sleepover, her neck and face turned mottled red, and then dead white. When I finished, I heaved myself to my feet.

"Pack a bag. Five minutes."

And then she spoke. "I can't leave the twins."

I stared at her.

"I can't, Barry. Frieda and John are in Europe, so the kids are staying with me this week, and anyway won't they be in danger, too? I must have infected them by now . . . saliva . . ."

"Catalina will look after them!"

"She's in Mexico. Her aunt died."

I closed my eyes. I knew that look of Jane's. "No," I said.

"I have to! And Frieda would want me to – God, they already get death threats every day! When it's public that they can infect others—"

Nurturing behavior. Virgin rats trying to nurse any baby rats you hand to them.

I said, "It's kidnapping."

"It's not. I'll email Frieda."

One of the girls woke up. She gazed at us from wide, frightened eyes. It was Bridget, the Glinda of the witchy pair. She said in a quavery voice, "Don't leave us, Jane!"

"I won't, darling. I wouldn't."

Bridget looked so small, and so frightened . . . Then I caught myself. Oxytorin. I barked, "No electronics that can be traced. Not phones, not mobiles, not games, not anything. Do those kids have subdermal ID chips?"

"No," Jane said. I could see that she wanted to say more, much more, but not in front of Bridget.

Fifteen minutes later, after Jane sent a hasty email to Frieda and John Barrington, we drove out the estate gates, heading toward the mountains.

When Leila was one month pregnant, the ultrasound looked like any other baby. The same at two, five, and nine months. All fetuses have oversized heads, spindly little arms and legs. When Ethan was born, there was no way to tell he was a dwarf, except by another genescan. 85 per cent of dwarfs are born to average-sized parents, the result not of carrying the dominant gene but of a mutation during conception. Usually the parents don't even realize the child will be a dwarf until the baby fails to grow like other children.

But we, of course, knew. Ethan would be a dwarf. We engineered him to be a dwarf. Then he was born and scanned.

A twentieth-century religious writer once said that humanity needs the disabled to remind us of the fragility of health, and of "the power of life and its brokenness." The nineteenth-century mother of the famous Colonel Tom Thumb attributed her son's dwarfism to her grief over the death of the family dog during her pregnancy. Leila and I had no such spiritual consolations, no such explanations for Ethan's lack of dwarfism. The ones that science could offer were vague: Engineering fails. Genes jump. Chromosomes mutate. Accidents happen. Nature assets herself.

I bought the mountain cabin just after Leila left me. I think now that I wasn't quite sane during that awful time. I'd retired from politics and hadn't yet entered show-business management. I had nothing to do. There are note-books I wrote then in which I talk about suicide, but I have no memory of doing the writing or thinking the thoughts. Eventually, that time passed. I left the cabin and never went back. Years later I deeded it over to Leila, who would go there sometimes with Ethan when he was small. She told me once, in a rare lapse into civility, that Ethan was happy at the cabin. He chased butterflies, hunted rocks, picked wildflowers. He calmed down up there, and he slept well in the sweet mountain air.

Now the twins did the same, falling asleep on the back seat of the Lexus. Still Jane and I didn't talk. But once she put her hand on the back of my neck. That was a gesture I'd dreamed about, longed for, would have given ten years of my life for. But not like this. Her touch wasn't sexual, wasn't romantic.

It was motherly.

We pulled up to the cabin just as the sun rose over the mountains, an hour before The Group was scheduled to break its story. Jane's skin goose-fleshed as she opened the car door and the cold dawn air rushed in.

"I'm going to carry them inside," she said, the first words she'd spoken in an hour. "They need their sleep. Is the door locked?"

"I have the key."

Mundane words, normal words. While below us, the human race was about to be altered at its core.

The cabin, too, was cold. I started the generator – quicker than building a fire – while Jane, puffing a little, carried the girls one at a time into the bedroom. The cabin is small but it's not primitive or austere; I'm not a fan of either. It has a main room with running water from a deep well, a comfortable bedroom, and a bathroom with full septic system. The original furniture had been sized for me, but evidently Leila had replaced it all. The sofa was hard to climb onto. My legs hurt.

Jane emerged from the bedroom after depositing the last twin, closed the door, and sat down on a wing chair across from me. She said quietly, "You could have let me drive."

I didn't answer.

"Is there a radio here?"

"There was. A satellite radio, the mountains don't permit much other reception."

"Where is it?"

"I don't know. I haven't been here for a long time."

She got up and began opening cupboards in the kitchenette. The counters and appliances, like the furniture, had been replaced, but no new cabinets built above them. Jane had to squat to peer into shelves. She searched the two closets, one of which had not existed when I owned the cabin, then sat down again. "No radio. But a lot of food and equipment. Who uses this place?"

Again I didn't answer.

"Barry, what's our plan?"

I looked at her then. No make-up, barely combed hair, huddled inside jeans and a green sweater that matched her eyes. She had never looked more beautiful to me.

"My only plan was to get you away before some angry mob came after you. People aren't going to like that their brains have been fucked with, and you're a natural target, Jane."

"I know." She smiled wanly. "I always have been, for anybody with a grudge. Why do you suppose that is?"

"Because the perception is that you have it all." I meant: beauty, talent, success, riches. I meant: my heart.

She snorted. "Oh, right. I have a burnt-out career, four bad marriages, and wrinkles that Botox can't touch. Barry, dear, you look tired. Why don't you lie on the sofa and I'll make you some warm milk."

"Don't mother me!" It came out a snarl.

She looked startled, then angry, then compassionate. Compassionate was the worst. "I only meant—"

"That's not you talking, it's the genemod that The Group infected you with."

She turned thoughtful, considering this. Contrary to Ms Resentful's perception, Jane was not stupid. Finally she said, "No, I don't think so, because I think I would have reacted the same way even before all this started. If I saw you tired and discouraged, I'd have offered some comfort anyway."

This was true. All at once I saw that this was going to be more complicated than I thought. How could anybody determine which behavior was caused by increased oxytorin receptors, and which was innate? It was the old argument, genes versus free will, only now it was about to turn incendiary.

Jane said, "I'm making you that warm milk."

But I was asleep before she could bring it to me.

I woke to Belinda standing beside the sofa, staring at me flatly. "I want to go home."

Groggily I sat up. Everything hurt. "Where's Jane?"

"Her and Bridget went for a stupid walk. Take me home."

"I can't. Not yet."

"I want to go home."

Painfully I climbed off the sofa and headed to the kitchenette. There was fresh coffee in a Braun on the counter, but I couldn't reach it. Hating every second that Belinda watched me, I dragged a footstool from the fireplace to the counter and hoisted myself onto it. A part of my brain noticed dispassionately that I felt no nurturing impulses toward Belinda when she didn't look more helpless than I felt.

The coffee was hot and rich. Good coffee had always been important to Leila. I gulped it down and said, "How long ago did they leave on this walk?"

"I don't know."

She probably did know and wasn't telling me, the brat.

"I really don't know, so stop thinking I'm a liar."

How did she do it? I'd read the literature on Arlen's Syndrome. Subconscious processes in Belinda's malevolent little brain were hypersensitive to six non-word signals: gesture and facial expression, even very tiny movements in either. Rhythm of movement. Bodily use of space. Objectics, such as dress and hairstyle. And what was called paralanguage: tone of voice, rate of verbal delivery, emphasis and inflection. Taken together, they let her read my emotions like a Teleprompter, but she was not reading my mind. I had to remind myself of that. Nonetheless, for the first time I saw the rationale for burning witches at the stake.

She said, "I don't care if you hate me."

"I don't hate you, Belinda." Said hopelessly; I couldn't hide from her.

"I hate you, too."

I took my coffee outside. Leila hadn't removed the low bench in front of the cabin, from which there was a breath-taking panorama of mountains and valleys, a pristine Eden that, when I'd lived here those nine months, had filled me with despair. Eden is no longer Eden if you've been exiled from it. The ghost of those bad feelings seemed to linger around the bench, but I didn't go back inside. Presently Jane and Bridget came puffing up the dirt road, Bridget clutching a mess of buttercups and daisies.

"Hi, Barry," the child said unhappily. She'd been crying. Immediately I braced myself and there it was: the soft desire to reassure her, help her, kiss the boo-boo and make it all better.

God damn it to hell.

Jane sat on the bench beside me. "Go put the flowers in water, Bridget."

When she'd gone, I said, "We need to know what's happening in LA. There's a library in Dunhill, at the base of the mountain. If you wrap up your hair and wear sunglasses and – oh, I don't know, act – do you think you can go in there unnoticed and use the Link? I know I can't."

She looked at the mountain road, which has no guard rails and, in places, pretty steep fall-offs. Jane doesn't like heights. She said, "Yes. I can do it."

"Don't stay long, and don't talk to anybody. Not one word. Your voice is memorable."

"Only if you'd heard it more recently than ten years ago. And in a better picture than my last one. Should I go now?" Again she looked at the road.

Before I could answer, the twins started shouting inside the cabin. Jane rose to her feet as the girls raced outside. Bridget cried, "Belinda, don't!"

Belinda said, "If you don't take us home this very minute, I'm going to tell everybody that you touched me in my private place and you'll go to jail forever and ever and ever!"

"No, you will not, young lady," Jane said severely. "You just come inside with me this very minute."

Belinda looked astonished. Probably Frieda had never spoken to her daughter that way. I reflected that "maternal behavior" could include discipline. Belinda followed Jane inside.

Had Frieda felt too intimidated by her daughters to reprimand them? Too proud? Too guilty? Had she been too terrified of what they might in turn say to her? I could imagine any of those scenarios, with a child so different from you, so strange, so eerily knowing.

What kind of discipline had Leila given, or not given, to Ethan?

Jane returned from Dunhill in a state of restrained anxiety. Nobody, she said, had recognized her at the library. She'd accessed the Link, watched the news, hardcopied the headlines. It was all even worse than I'd expected.

BIOWEAPON RELEASED IN CALIFORNIA
ARLEN'S WAS ONLY THE FIRST STEP – NOW THEY'RE SPREADING MUTATIONS!
ACTRESS A PART OF BIOCONSPIRACY SPREADING EPIDEMIC
RUN ON GAS MASKS, RIOTS, CAUSE DEATHS OF FOUR
MUTANTS NOW AMONG US – YOU COULD BE ONE!
JANE SNOW AND MANAGER MISSING SINCE LAST NIGHT

"They're calling it treason," Jane said.

"It is treason. Or something." Bioweapon terrorism. Invasion of bodily privacy. Violations of the Fourteenth Amendment. Medical malpractice.

"What next, Barry?"

"I'm not sure. I need to think." But all I could think about was what might have happened if I hadn't gotten Jane away, if Ms Resentful hadn't called me. Riots cause death of four. And that was without the rioters' zeroing in on a specific target.

"What did the twins do while I was gone?"

"Nothing." They'd played inside and I'd sat outside, pretending they weren't there. Jane went into the cabin.

A minute later she was back. "They're making cookies."

"Fine. Just so long as they don't burn down the cabin."

"We won't," Bridget said, and there they were beside us, having silently followed Jane. Belinda had a picturesque smudge of chocolate on her nose. I did not think that she looked adorable. Bridget added, "Why are you scared, Jane?"

Jane knew better than to deny. "I went down to a town where I could get the news, and some people in LA are very angry at another group of people there. It could get violent."

Belinda said, "But why does that mean we can't go home?"

Bridget said, "They're mad at us, too, aren't they? You're scared for us. Why? We didn't do anything!"

Belinda said, "Don't be stupid, Brid. People get mad at us all the time when we didn't do anything." She looked at me. "Like Barry is mad at us."

Bridget scowled, making her suddenly look more like her sister. "Yeah. Why are you mad at us, Barry?"

"Because I didn't want to have to bring you here. But if I hadn't, you might both have been attacked by a mob now."

Bridget looked scared, but Belinda said, "Naw, we got really good security at home. Nobody can get through. I want to go home!"

"And I want you to," I said, which was nothing less than total truth – even as I felt the treacherous desire to comfort little frightened Bridget . . . oxytorin.

Belinda did not look frightened. She was working up to a towering tantrum. "Then take us home! Take us home now!"

Jane said soothingly, "We can't, Belinda. It's not safe. The—"

"It is safe! Daddy's estate is safe! I want to go home!"

Bridget said, with heart-breaking hopelessness, "Belinda—"

Belinda kicked her sister, who screamed and fell to the ground. Then she kicked Jane, who made a grab for her. Belinda was quicker, squirming away, tears of rage on her grimy face.

"Don't touch me! Don't you ever touch me! I hate you, you go around feeling sorry for everybody who isn't you! You feel sorry for Barry 'cause he's all twisted and short, and you feel sorry for Brid and me 'cause you think we're so different, just like you feel sorry for Catalina and the pilot and everybody who's not pretty like you! Well, you're not so pretty anymore either, 'cause you're old and you know it and you're scared nobody's going to like you anymore if you're not pretty and if you don't do that fucking movie about us! And you know what – you're right! Nobody will like you just like I hate you! 'Cause you're old and not pretty any more and you'll be alone all the rest of your life! And—"

Jane stood still, looking dazed. Looking stripped naked. But now Bridget was up off the ground and barreling into her sister head first, a battering ram to the belly. "Don't you kick me!"

Belinda screamed and the two girls went down, rolling in the scrub grass in front of the cabin, punching and pulling hair and scratching. Jane sprang forward, trying to pull them off each other. The sound of a motor made her, and me, freeze.

And Leila's car roared into sight and jerked to a stop, with her and Ethan inside.

Empathy means you understand another's feelings. It doesn't mean you sympathize with them, or respect them. Hitler's brilliant propaganda minister, Joseph Goebbels, understood perfectly what the German people were feeling in the 1920s and '30s: insecurity, rage, fear, resentment at the punishments for WWI. He used that knowledge to manipulate their emotions, creating the brilliant PR campaigns that put Hitler in power and kept him there.

The Group must have realized too late that Arlen's Syndrome was not, after all, a guarantee that the world would change for the better. So they created the virus that increases oxytorin receptors. Correcting a genetic-engineering change with another genetic-engineering change.

I could have told them that does not work.

Ethan got out of the car first, from the passenger side. Both Bridget and Belinda stopped fighting, got up off the ground, and stared. Ethan's right eye was blackened, and his left arm was in a sling. He scowled ferociously at them, at me, at the world.

He was utterly beautiful.

Auburn hair falling over his forehead, blue eyes, a body that Michelangelo could have used as the model for his David. More than that, Ethan had the same quality that Jane did: an innate and unconscious sexuality so blatant that it was like a slap in the face, a challenge: Come and get me. If you can. His photos had not captured that quality. Bridget and Belinda were eleven years old, and yet I saw that they felt it, Bridget blushing and looking confused, Belinda scowling back, but with surprise behind her gray eyes. Jane's back was to me. Leila got out of the car and called desperately, "Ethan!"

He ignored her and kept walking. It was me he was moving toward. I stood up from my bench, my heart hammering. Ethan stopped in front of me. I came up to slightly higher than his waist.

"You're my father," he said, with utter contempt. "You."

Leila was running from the car, but Jane was closer. She threw herself between us just as Ethan's fist shot out, and the blow intended for my face hit her in the chest.

"I don't think any of her ribs are broken," Leila said wearily. "She said it doesn't hurt when she breathes, which is a good sign."

Leila and I sat in her car, a three-year-old Ford, each of us holding steaming mugs of fresh coffee. Mine trembled in numb fingers. Jane slept, courtesy of a pain patch, in the bedroom. The twins, subdued now, had been ordered back to their cookie-making, and had actually gone. Ethan had stalked away into the woods, and I was sickened to realize that I hoped he'd stay away. I was afraid of my son.

"Leila, I didn't realize . . . I know you'd said, but . . . Of course, behavior is a complex genetic and environmental phenomenon, and when you interfere with—"

"Don't. Don't go informational and theoretical on me like you always do. Just don't!"

"All right."

She turned her face to look at me. "That's the first time I think you've actually heard me when I've said that."

Maybe it was. Information and theory were good hiding places. "And Ethan gets like this—"

"Unpredictably. The psychologist says he has poor impulse control. When he gets upset, there's a major neural high-jacking. You've seen the brain scans with all the irregularities in his amygdalas and hippocampus. He gets swamped with rage, and sometimes he can't even remember what he's done. Not always, but sometimes."

"And you've dealt with this alone for—"

"Since he was a toddler. But you knew all this, Barry. I told you."

She had. But I hadn't really heard her, hadn't wanted to hear her. I'd preferred to blame her, as she blamed me.

Leila continued, "When he comes back from the woods, he'll be different. Until the next time. But now that he's old enough to run away . . . and looking like he does . . ."

She didn't have to finish the sentence. I knew what LA could be for a fifteen-year-old who looked like Ethan.

I said, "Did you two just happen to come up here today?"

"No. Jane called me."

I spilled my coffee. "Jane?"

"Yes. She did what you should have done." Now Leila's anger was back. Anger and blame. "Or didn't you bother to think that Ethan might be in danger once the witch hunt down there fingered you? Which it has, by the way, according to the car radio while I could still get reception on the way up here. Didn't you bother to think that your son might make a good substitute target?"

"I didn't think anyone would trace you and Ethan to me."

"Jane obviously did!"

And probably used a private detective to do it. How long ago? Why?

"I'm sorry, Leila. I didn't think you'd be in any danger. I didn't think the media—" I stopped. She knew what I meant.

However nasty the daily world is to dwarfs, there is only one Official Story about us allowed in mainstream media. That's the happytalk Big-Hearts-in-Little-Bodies slant. Dwarfs making good, doing good, being good. Thus is the daily nastiness offset and balance restored to the universe. That the media in LA had now abandoned the formula was a strong measure of how much fear The Group had engineered along with their virus.

I said, "This whole thing . . . God knows I didn't want these twins here, either."

"Where are their parents? Or are you guilty of kidnapping, along with everything else?"

Yes. No. "Their parents know the kids are here. They're on their way home from Europe."

"The Barrington twins, of all kids. God, Barry, you really can screw up royally."

Like I needed to be told that. But I pushed down my anger. This was maybe the only chance I was going to get, and I had to say it right. "Listen, Leila. I want to say something. I know I've been negligent, and I know that Ethan is . . . I know I had a lot to do with this, because of what I insisted on before he was born. But I want to say three things, and I want you to really consider them. You don't have to, but I'd really like it if you would. First, what I said before is true, even though I picked a stupid time to say it. Behavior is genetically complex, and Ethan's . . . problems, his brain irregularities, could have happened even if I hadn't insisted on the in utero genemod. We'll never know."

Leila made a sudden motion, but I kept on, afraid to stop. "Second, just consider – please consider! – that I tried to help with Ethan and you pushed me away. You were so angry that you . . . I don't say you weren't justified. But you did push me away, and left me, and refused to let me see him, and I think it's unfair that I then get blamed for not seeing him."

"I wasn't—" she said hotly. I put my hand on her arm.

"Please. Just one more thing. It's not too late. I want to help, want to do whatever I can, whatever you and he will let me do. If we can get past this anger at each other, finally, and cooperate, that has to be better for Ethan!"

She shook my hand off her arm, but she didn't get out of the car. We sat in silence for a few minutes. I held my breath.

Finally Leila spoke in a different voice. "I don't know if I can. I've hated you for so long . . . I think . . . I think I might need to hate you. In order to go on."

I knew enough to be quiet.

"Oh, God, I don't want to be that person!" Leila cried. "Barry—"

"I know," I said. "I don't want to be the person I am, either."

She blind-sided me then. "Do you love her very much?"

Only honesty would do now. "Yes."

"I'm seeing somebody," Leila said. "That's part of why Ethan's so angry. He hasn't ever had to share me."

"I'm glad for you, Leila." But I had to ask. "Is he a dwarf?"

"Yes. We met last year at the LPA convention. He lives in Oregon. He's in insurance."

She was smiling, despite herself. I found myself hoping that it worked out for her. She deserved a little insurance. But then, didn't we all.

"I didn't get a chance to tell you before," Leila said. "I brought a satellite TV. It's in the trunk."

Riots had started in South Central LA Ostensibly the "mutation plague," which was what the media was calling The Group's virus, was the cause of the riots. But they quickly took on life of their own, with all the usual looting, car burning, rock throwing. The LAPD used microwaves and tanglefoam on the rioters, who then regrouped at different locations and started over again. The press, having been the actual cause of the turmoil with its inflamed reporting, now took on its next role in the inevitable sequence, which was The Voice of Reason trying to calm things down. Talking heads appeared on TV, on the Link, on wallscreens, in holos projected over the city. They explained that the virus was not airborne, needed contact with bodily fluids to survive, and did not cause cancer or suicide or nerve decay or zombie-ism. Nobody listened.

A rumor started that The Group leadership was headquartered in a warehouse by the waterfront. A mob torched it, and strong winds carried the fire westward. The governor ordered out the National Guard.

KILL THE MUTANT MAKERS said the improvised placards.

Jane was hung in effigy.

Frieda and John Barrington landed at LAX and were besieged by robocams; Jane's picture with the twins had been everywhere in recent weeks. Their flyer finally took off but air space over the city had been shut down and the flyer returned to the airport.

By nightfall the rioting had subsided, damped down by rumors that "muties" were secretly roaming the street, infecting everyone. People fled inside. In several hours of watching the Link, not once did I hear a single reporter or avatar refer to what the virus actually did: increase the desire to nurture. People cared that they had been fucked with, not how.

That was the part of the whole reaction that I most understood.

"Barry," Jane said, "come eat something."

She and Leila had prepared a meal from the canned goods in the cabin. Leila had made a fire in the fireplace. Ethan, who had returned sullen from the woods and stayed sullen ever since, sat at the table with the twins. He'd spent most of the afternoon outside, smoking God-knows-what, while the twins circled him like disintegrating stars around a black hole. Bridget seemed afraid to speak to him at all, but Belinda and he had several long, low conversations during which Ethan scowled a lot. Leila and Jane moved back and forth between table and kitchen, elaborately and artificially polite to each other. I didn't need Bridget or Belinda to tell me what everybody felt. Nobody wanted to be here with these other five people, and there was nowhere else any of us could go.

"Barry," Jane said again.

Belinda said, "He doesn't like you to act like his mother."

I said, "Shut up, kid, or you'll wish you had."

Bridget, wide-eyed, said, "He means it, Belinda."

She shut up, glaring at me. Leila glanced my way, puzzled. Ethan raised his head, and I would have given anything for just one moment's of Arlen's Syndrome so I could tell what my son was thinking then.

Bridget said, "I don't like it here with you guys." Her eyes welled, and immediately Jane's arms went around her. "It's okay, Bridget, you girls are just tired. I think you should go to bed right after you eat, sweetheart. Everything will look better in the morning."

Oxytorin.

I was too tired to think straight. But one sentence from Ms Resentful came back to me: "Susceptibility to the genemod will vary among people – like, say, susceptibility to cholera depends on blood type." I'd seen no susceptibility to increased nurturing from Belinda. As she watched Jane hug Bridget, Belinda's look could have withered a cactus.

Leila produced three sleeping bags from the closet that hadn't existed when I'd been here last. The twins were bedded down on the floor of the bedroom. Ethan disdained to so much as glance at his bag, which was laid out in a corner of the living room. Jane and Leila would share the bed. I got the couch.

Ethan and I were the last to go to sleep. I lay on the lumpy sofa, all lights off except for a dim glow where Ethan sat watching something inane on the satellite TV. His beautiful, beautiful face – how had Leila and I created such beauty? – lost its sulky look and relaxed into the smile of a normal fifteen-year-old.

Normal. A word dwarfs don't like and seldom use. For good reason.

But this was my son, and so I made one more attempt to reach him. "What are you watching?"

"Nothing." The scowl was back. It angered me.

"Obviously it's not nothing, or you wouldn't be watching it. So what is it?"

"Don't pull that logic crap on me," Ethan said. "I don't know you." And then – although did even he hesitate before he said it? I thought so, or else I wanted to think so – "Crippled little Munchkin."

We stared at each other across the dim room.

Then I rolled over, wrapped myself in my blanket and my pain, and tried to sleep.

Some unknowable time later, Jane was shaking me by the shoulder. "Barry! Barry, wake up – Belinda is gone!"

I jerked upright and looked at the sleeping bag by the cold fireplace. The bag was empty. My mind went cold and clear. "See if both cars are here."

Of course, they weren't. My Lexus was gone.

"He doesn't even have a driver's permit," Leila said.

She was driving; my legs ached too much. I had made Jane stay with Bridget, who was still asleep. Leila drove slowly in the dark, and as we passed the places where the mountain road dropped off sheerly, she shuddered. But her hands on the wheel didn't falter. This wasn't the teenage dwarf I had married, the girl dancing exuberantly at the LPA convention, the young bride who had blindly accepted my arrogant authority.

"I thought he understood how dangerous it would be to go back home," Leila said. "I thought he understood."

"He did. That's why he's going."

She glanced over at me, then returned to her driving, her endless scanning of the roadside. Was that a break in the bushes? Had a car gone off there? Was that a skid mark in the headlights?

She said, "No, that's not why. It's that girl. Belinda. She wants to go home, and I saw her whispering to him all afternoon, and I should have realized . . . but he doesn't like children! And she's only eleven! I didn't think she could influence him."

Leila was right. I should have anticipated this; I'd seen far more of Belinda than Leila had. Belinda would have known exactly what Ethan was feeling, exactly how to play on his weak spots. She didn't even have to think about it, merely let her instincts take over. Empathy in action.

"Barry, he's not a bad kid underneath. He can be very sweet sometimes. You've never seen that."

"I believe you," I said, wondering if I did. "And the other times – well, he can't help it, can he? It's in his genes."

"No, it's not." The intensity of her anger surprised me, even as she kept on scanning, looking, dreading what she might see. "You attribute everything to genes. It's not true. Genes made you a dwarf, and you think that's wrecked your life, but genes didn't make you so bitter and unhappy. I know that because when we met, you weren't bitter and unhappy. And you were a dwarf then, too. I didn't want Ethan around your self-created misery. I still don't. And maybe he does have some predisposition to danger and anger and impulsiveness, like the doctors say. But he doesn't have to indulge it. He chooses to do that. Just like you choose to be miserable and envious."

"Leila, there's so much wrong with that simplistic analysis that I don't even know where to start correcting it."

"Then don't. I don't need your 'corrections.' You can't – what's that!"

I saw it a second after she did. The Lexus, smashed head-first against a tree, which was the only thing that had kept it from going over the embankment.

Leila, younger and with less spinal constriction, was first out of the Ford, running toward the car, uttering loud wordless cries. I followed her, stumbling as my treacherous legs collapsed under me, getting up, trying again to run. Those were the longest seconds – minutes, hours, eons – of my life. Until. I. Reached. That. Car.

They were both alive. Belinda seemed unhurt, mewling in her seat belt. Ethan, who had taken the brunt of the crash – had he turned the wheel at the last minute to save the little girl? – slumped unconscious against the steering wheel. Blood trickled through his bright hair.

"Don't move him," Leila said frantically. "If anything's broken . . . I'm going for help!"

She ran back to her Ford. I undid Belinda's seat belt, yanked her out, and dropped her on the dark roadside weeds. I could feel her fear, just as she could feel my fury. She shrank back against the fender. I climbed into the passenger seat beside my son.

He stirred. "Mommy . . ."

"She'll be here soon, Ethan. Help will be here soon."

He said something else, before sliding again into unconsciousness. It might have been, "Fuck you."

Maybe no child, other than those with Arlen's Syndrome, understands how a parent feels. Maybe I hadn't earned the right to even be considered a parent. Maybe, as Leila said, my bitterness and anger would be worse for Ethan than if I weren't there at all for him. I don't know, any more than I know any more what's genetic and what's not. Did Jane go all maternal with the twins because she had more oxytorin receptors, or did The Group's virus make her a good candidate for growing more oxytorin receptors because she'd always had a penchant for wounded birds anyway? Susceptibility to the genemod will vary among people.

In the darkness, I sat for a long time beside my injured son. Finally, with great deliberation, I spat on my fingers and gently, gently, pushed them inside his mouth. I felt the softness of his slack tongue, his strong young teeth. Strong teeth, strong long bones. He was not a dwarf. I spat a second time on my hand and did it again.

Overhead, medical and police flyers droned in the dark night When they arrived, I borrowed a cell phone and comlinked Elaine Brown, Human Protection Agency.

A week later, I sit in a Temporary Government Quarantine Facility in San Diego, watching TV. On the other side of the negative-pressure barriers, researchers from the United States Army Research Institute for Infectious Diseases, dressed in Level 4 biohazard suits, go through two airlocks to reach Jane and me. The Barrington twins are here, too, but not Leila or Ethan. Ethan is in a hospital in LA, and she is with him, along with her boyfriend from Oregon. He flew down immediately to be with her.

They treat us well here. There are endless medical tests, of course, but I'm used to that. Everyone is both respectful and curious. If they're also frightened, I don't sense it, but of course Bridget and Belinda do. Bridget is a favorite with the staff. Belinda wants to go home, although she likes all the attention from Jane. The twins' parents "visit" via Link several times each day. Frieda sometimes has a distinct look of relief. Her kids are behind glass, and she can break the link with Belinda whenever she needs to.

The Link has brought the most attention to Jane. Death threats, pleas for help, fan letters, offers from the ACLU to sue The Group if any members of that organization can be found, which so far they haven't. Jane would be a high-profile and appealing case. The movie is on again, but not with the same script, or even with the same studio. There's another chapter now to the Arlen's Syndrome story, and Jane has become an actor in that saga in both senses of the word. The whole thing looks like box-office gold.

Jane is not unhappy. If that's not exactly the same thing as being happy, it seems to do.

The Link is also how I visit with Ethan. He had three broken ribs and a damaged spleen, which seems to be repairing itself without surgery. Youthful spleen can do that. We gaze at each other, and sometimes he's sullen, and sometimes I'm impatient, and sometimes he sees me shift on my spine in chronic pain. Or maybe he catches a sadness in my eyes. At such times, his expression softens. So does his voice. He'll ask if I'm okay. When he asks, I am.

Is it wrong to genetically modify human beings? First I thought it was, when I tried to alter Ethan's FGFR3 gene in utero. Then I thought it wasn't, seeing both Ethan and the Arlen's Syndrome kids. Now I don't know again. There's still panic out there about The Group's virus, and the virus is still spreading, and eventually it may – or may not – make enough of society more nurturing. In turn, that may – or may not – change society. If enough people are susceptible. If feelings of compassion actually translate into actions of compassion. If the weather holds and the creek don't rise and seven or eleven comes up enough on the dice. This is barely Act One, Scene One of what-ever comes next. Chaos theory tells us that, in a system of circular feedback, a small change in initial conditions can cause huge and unpredictable changes down the road. Human behavior is a system of circular feedback. Is Ethan more compassionate toward me because he's growing more oxytorin recep-tors, or because I'm more open to his (and everyone else's) compassion? How did the same genemod for empathy produce both Bridget and Belinda?

I have no idea. And to tell the truth, I don't really care. I'm supposed to care, ethically and pragmatically, but I don't.

Jane comes into the room and says, "Guess what? The studio is getting Michael Rosen to write the script! Michael Rosen! It's sure to be terrific!"

I smile back. Michael Rosen is indeed a terrific writer, a creator of sensi-tive and layered scripts that both challenge audiences and fill seats. He's also a handsome womanizer, and Jane is looking more beautiful than ever. I know what will happen.

"That's good," I say. "Congratulations. The movie'll be a smash."

"Thanks to you." She smiles at me and goes out again.

Nothing has changed. Everything has changed. I turn to my computer and get back to work.

TWILIGHT OF THE GODS

John C. Wright

John C. Wright attracted some attention in the late 1990s with his early stories in *Asimov's Science Fiction* (with one of them, "Guest Law," being picked up for David Hartwell's Year's Best SF), but it wasn't until he published his Golden Age trilogy (consisting of *The Golden Age, The Golden Transcendence*, and *The Phoenix Exultant*) in the first few years of the new century, novels that earned critical raves across the board, that he was recognized as a major new talent in SF. Subsequent novels include the "Everness" fantasy series, including *The Last Guardians of Everness* and *Mists of Everness*, and the fantasy "Chaos" series, which includes *Fugitives of Chaos, Orpahns of Chaos*, and *Titans of Chaos*. His most recent novel, a continuation of the famous "Null-A" series by A. E. van Vogt, is *Null-A Continuum*. Wright lives with his family in Centreville, Virginia.

Here he delivers a rousing space-age take on Wagner's *Ring of the Nibelungen*, which performs the trick of writing valid science fiction that reads like epic fantasy as well as anyone has ever done it.

TALL GOLDEN DOORS loomed up behind the dais of the throne. Behind those doors, it was said, the Main Bridge of the Twilight of the Gods reposed, a chamber dim and vast, with many altars studded all with jeweled controls set before the dark mirrors of the Computer. But Acting Captain Weston II found the chamber oppressive, and did not like the mysterious dark mirrors of the Computer watching him, and so, since his father's death many years ago, this white high chamber before the golden doors was used as his hall of audience.

The chamber was paved in squares of gold and white, with pillars of gold spaced along white walls. Hanging between the pillars were portraits of scenes from somewhere in the ship the Captain had never seen; fields of green plants, some taller than a man, growing, for some reason, along the deck rather than in shelves along the walls. In the pictures, the deck was buckled and broken, rising and falling in round slopes (perhaps due to damage from a Weapon of the Enemy) with major leaks running across it. The scenes took place in some hold or bay larger than any Acting Captain Weston II had seen or could imagine; the overhead bulkhead was painted light blue, some sort of white disruption like steam-clouds floating against it. In many pictures, the blue overhead was ruptured by a large yellow many-rayed circular explosion, perhaps, again, of a Weapon.

In most pictures were sheep or other animals, and young crewmen and women, out of uniform, blissfully ignoring the explosion overhead, and doing nothing to stop the huge leaks, one of which had ducks swimming in it.

Acting Captain Weston II found the pictures soothing, but disturbing. He often wondered if the artist had been trying to show how frail and foolish men are, that they will trip lightly through their little lives without a thought to the explosions and disasters all about them. Perhaps he preferred this chamber for that reason.

What the original use and name of this chamber had been in days gone past, no man of the Captain's Court could tell, not even his withered and aged Computerman.

The chamber now was bare, except that the Computerman approached the throne and knelt to Weston. "My lord," he said. His face was worn and haggard, his garb simple, rough, and belted with a hank of rope. The Computerman's eyes showed red and staring, a certain sign of the many long nightwatches he had spent writhing in the grip of the holy drug, which allowed his brethren to commune with the Computer.

"Why do you come unbidden unto me?" Weston asked sternly. "I know you await another."

The Computerman replied. "It is to warn you against that other, that I am come."

The Acting Captain raised his hand, but the Computerman said swiftly, "Bid me not to go! Unless you would not heed the will of the Computer in this thing, the Computer which knows all, indeed, even things most secret and shameful."

The Captain had a troubled look upon his face, and sat back with one hand clutching the front of his jeweled coat, as if to hide something behind his hand, something, perhaps, on a necklace hidden beneath his tunic. "What shame?" he said.

"Every child knows the story of the Ring of Last Command," the Computerman said. "Of how, when the Sixth Barrage destroyed the lights and power of the second hundred decks, and Weapon of the Enemy opened the Great Chasm in the hull, reaching from the stars below almost to the thousandth deck, the first Captain, Valdemar, capitulated to the Enemy, and allowed a Boarding Party to come in from the Void Below the Hull. Decks Three Hundred through Seven Hundred Seventy rebelled, and followed bright Alverin into battle against the traitor Captain. But the Captain was not found, and his Ring of Final Command was lost. The ring, they say, can waken the Computers all again, and send the Weapons of the Twilight down into the Void."

"Children's fairy-tales," the Captain said.

"Yet, I deem, they tempt you," the Computerman said.

The Captain was silent.

"This prisoner which the giant brings; he had a ring inscribed with circuits, did he not? A ring which matches the descriptions of the Command Ring? You dream of learning the Secret Word which controls that Ring, and of conquering the world, of driving back the tall elves from decks above, where they fly and know no weight, and compelling the twisted dwarves from Engineering to obedience to your reign, and, one day, who knows? you think you will drive forth the Destroyers, and the servants of the enemy who infest the many antispinward decks, and hurl them down into the Void from whence they came. You dream a dream of vile pride; you are corrupted with temptation."

The Captain rose angrily from his throne. "Stop! Do you think your holy office will protect you from my wrath? Were there such a ring as legends say, for certain I would seize it to my own. And who would dare deny me? You? You?"

But the Computerman bowed in all humility, and said, "My lord knows there can be no such ring. A ring to waken the computers, indeed! Our faith informs us that the Computers do not sleep, that their screens are not dark, not to eyes that keep the faith. I and my brethren commune with the computers each nightwatch, and it gives us secret knowledge."

"My father told me the Computer screens once were bright to every eye, and a voice like a man's voice spoke from them, every man, even the humblest, could hear that voice. Before the Fifth Barrage, in his youth, he had seen them shining, and heard the voice."

"Men knew less sin in those days, my lord."

At that moment came a noise at the doors before them, not the golden doors of the Bridge, but the silver doors leading to the to the outer part of the palace and to the corridors and warrens of the great city of Forecomcon. The silver doors swept wide; here were twenty pikemen of the Gatewatch, dressed in blue and silver, and here, garbed hugely in the gray-green of the ancient order of Marines, strode in the giant.

The giant's shoulder was taller than a tall man's head, but his hair and beard were white with age. For he was the last of his kind, born to serve as a Marine, created by the lost arts of the Medical House, back when the Twilight was young. His name was Carradock.

In one hand Carradock held a mighty weapon like a spear, made by ancient and forgotten arts. The weapon could shoot bullets like a musket, except that it could fire many at a time, yet the bullets were slow, and would not pierce the bulkheads, or damage the equipment, and so the weapon was lawful according to the Weapons Law.

In Carradock's other hand was a chain. Bound by that chain, manacled and fettered, was a strange, dark man, wearing a uniform of silver-white, unlike any uniform known to Weston's lore. The man had pale hair like an upper-deck elf, and, like them, he was tall. But he was darkened and scarred by radiation, like the dwarves of engineering, or like those who lived near the Great Chasm, the Lesser Chasm, or the Hole, or near any other place the Weapons of the Enemy had blown up through the world. He was muscled like a down-deck dwarf, with thicker muscles than Weston had ever seen, except, perhaps for those on Carradock.

The Gatewatch lieutenant spoke up out of turn, coming forward and saying, "My lord! I pray you, let not this man alone in audience with you! He has the strength of three men."

"Then let him be bound with three men's chains, but I will speak alone to him."

The prisoner in silver-white stood, face calm, staring at the Captain. His face was still, his demeanor quiet. He seemed neither proud nor humble, but he stood like a man surrounded by a great silent open space, wherein nothing could be hidden from him, nor anything approach to harm him.

When he did not kneel, the Gatewatch pikemen struck him in the back of his knees with the butts of their spears. But the muscles of the prisoner's legs were strong, and did not bend when struck. Three of the Gatewatch put their hands on his shoulders to force him down. The prisoner watched them calmly, but would not budge.

"Leave him stand," the Captain ordered. The men stepped back. Then the Captain said, "Where are his wounds? He has no new scars. I ordered him put to torment. Bring forth the Apprentice Torturer."

But the lieutenant said, "Sire, the Apprentice Torturer fled after you ordered the Master Torturer tortured to death. After, none of the lesser torturers would approach this prisoner. They refused to obey your order."

The Computerman was still standing near the throne. He leaned forward and whispered, "Sire, why did you order the Master Torturer put to the question? I guess this: this prisoner told you that he had told the Master Torturer the Words which command the ring. The Master Torturer denied it. You conceived a jealous suspicion, and feared the Master Torturer craved the ring, and knew the Word. Do I guess aright?"

The Captain stood. "Leave me! All of you, except my giant, leave me! You, as well, Computerman!"

The lieutenant said, "Sire, shall we bring the other prisoner in now as well? The blind man we found wondering the Inner Corridor?"

"What care I for wandering beggars? Leave me, all!"

But the Computerman would not leave until the Gatewatch came to drag him away. The Computerman was shouting, "Beware the thing you covet! Beware! It is a thing accursed! All who do not possess it will crave it! It will drive you to madness; it will drive you to destroy your trusted servants, as you have destroyed your Torturer! Eschew this thing! Cast it away! The Computer cannot be controlled by it!" But by then the Gatewatch had gently pulled the old man out of the chamber and closed the door behind them.

Acting Captain Weston II sat upon his throne again, and bent his gaze upon the dark, scarred man before him. The man did not fidget or stir, but stood, calm and silent; and the giant stood waiting behind him.

"Speak!" ordered Weston.

The man said, "I have nothing more to say." His voice was soft and pleasant to the ear.

"The Old Code requires you to speak to a superior officer. What is your name and station, rank and duty?"

"I am Henwis, son of Himdall. I come from Starwell. My rank is Watchman. I am come to report to the true Captain."

"There are no Watchmen; the order is defunct. After the Boarding by the Enemy, all the outer Hull was laid to waste. No; you are no Watchmen. You have the look of an aftman farmer about you."

"I was not born a Watchman; indeed, I was born a farmer. My village is called Aftshear, in the secondary engine core, near the Axis, where the world has no weight. My youth was spent tending the many plants and green growing things from whence come our air, and life. But I was captured by the Enemy, and, for a time, was a slave. I escaped, and fled below decks, where every step is a crushing weight, and the air is poisoned by the radiations of the Seventh Barrage. The servants of the Enemy feared the radiation, and could not tolerate the weight, and did not pursue me. Crawling, I went still lower, till I was nearly crushed. Then I came upon a place where nothing was below me, except for the stars.

"There I was found by Himdall, last of all Watchmen, in the midst of a deserted place and empty corridors, a chamber lit, and filled with sweet air, although surrounded by darkness and poison on every side.

"Himdall nursed me back to health, and taught to me his art, and showed to me the Starwell, at whose deep bottom the stars underfoot turn and turn again. And I became a Watchman in truth, and was adopted as his son. And for long years I kept watch on the Enemy stars, and saw the slow, grave motions."

Weston asked: "And do you believe the heresy which says the stars which move are not mere colored lights, but the Ships from which the Enemy, in ancient times, came forth?"

"I do. And yet among those lights, are four Ships friendly to our own, sent out, as we were, in ages past, from Earth. Their names I think you know: the Götterdämmerung, the Apocalypse, the Armageddon, and the Ragnarök."

Weston stirred uneasily upon his throne. "I tell you the original Captain betrayed the crew, and fled. This happened when my father was a boy. He was Acting Captain; now I am the acting Captain."

"By what right do you call yourself so?"

Weston shouted angrily, "By right of blood succession!" Then he was quiet, and he said quietly, "You may give any report you must give to me."

"Very well," said Henwas Watchman, and he recited all he had said when first he had been brought before Weston: "The Eighth Barrage, which has been approaching for so many years, has turned aside, and seeks now to strike the Armageddon. The missiles and small ships of that Barrage shall smite their target starting twelve years hence, with a bombardment lasting a year or two, peaking fourteen years hence and diminishing thereafter. We shall not be struck by it; presumably the masters of Enemy now know we were boarded by the sixty armies from the landing party from the Dreadnought Kzalcurrang-Achai, which, in our speech, is named the Hungry Indeed For Battle.

"I further report that our escort ships, the Revenge and the Vendetta, were destroyed between thirteen and seven years ago by picket ships launched from the Tzazalkiurung, which, in our speech, is named Ready To Do Grave Harm. This ship is presently four light-minutes off our port bow, where it has remained for seventy years, no doubt waiting to see if it must render aid to the Kzalcurrang-Achai.

"Yet the main sweep of the Destroyer fleet has passed beyond us and done us no hurt. We are in the midst of some eighty Dreadnoughts and four motile planets. Their Crown ships are within eight light-minutes of us now, and have not maneuvered to avoid us by a further distance. Asteroids from the shattered planet called War Storm are all about us in each direction, and perhaps hide us from the main body of the Enemy, and from the Crown Ships, which take no heed of us, but proceed against the Armageddon and the Götterdämmerung. Of the Apocalypse there has been no sign for thirty years. The Ragnarök is hidden by a great light; either she maneuvers, or she is in full retreat."

The Captain was sarcastic. "And you believe all this? That the fate of our world depends on the motions of these little colored lights?"

"I have one thing further to report. The escort ship Hermes Trismegistus out from the Götterdämmerung has entered an orbit of the Enemy planet called Promise of Destruction. She maneuvers without any flare, and will not be seen by the Enemy. The orbit will carry the Hermes Trismegistus to us before the decade ends. It is a rescue ship. When the officers from the Hermes come aboard, power and light will be restored to all sections, the wounded and the poisoned will be healed by their knowledge; and those who have not kept faith will be punished. If you have been disobedient, you will be taken before the Court Martial."

The Captain sneered. "My nurse, when I was but a babe, would terrify me with tales of the Court Martial and the Day of Judgment that would come when the Earthmen would come up from Heaven underfoot. But you shall not live long enough to find the truth of these things, unless the medicine of the Earthmen know how to resurrect the dead."

The Watchman said simply, "I have lived near the radiations of the outer hull. I have the disease. I know the hour of my death is not far off. Why else would I be willing to bear the cursed ring?"

Weston drew on a chain around his neck. Up from inside his jeweled coat he drew out the ring. It was gold, inscribed with delicate circuitry, and set with gray stone. In the middle of the stone gleamed a strange light, which showed that the power of the ring still lived.

"Tell me the word which commands this ring."

"I may only tell the Captain."

"I am Captain! I am he! There is no Captain Valdemar! He is myth!

Even were there such a man, he would be long dead, a hundred years or more gone by! I am the true Captain!"

"A true Captain would use the power, not for himself, but to complete the mission, and discharge the great Weapons the stories say our world carries at its Axis," the Watchman said softly.

"And if that were my intention . . . ?"

"Then you would not have chained me," said the Watchman, rattling his manacles.

The Captain sat until he felt his anger cool within him. Then he spoke in a voice most reasonable and even, "Watchman, if I could persuade you that there are no worlds hanging in the Void beneath our world, no Dreadnoughts of the Enemy, no war, except for the wars fought with the Enemy aboard our Ship, between here and Midline Darkhall, and spinward toward the Lesser Chasm, what then? If there is no world outside our world, no Weapons to fire, what reason have you them to withhold from me the Ring of Final Command?"

"No reason," said the Watchman. "If there were no worlds below our feet, I would give the ring's commands to you."

"Then reckon this: If you are right, and there is a war in space below us, then this ship, and all aboard, were sent into that war, to fight, perhaps, to die, all in order to defend the ship called Earth from our Great Enemy."

"Earth is not a ship. It is a planet. Earth is inside out, for the crew there live on the outer hull, and their air is outward from them. On Earth, gravity is backwards, and draws them toward their axis, so that they stand with their feet on the hull, with their heads looking down toward the stars."

"Be that as it may; the Earthmen send these great ships far out into space to fight their wars, not so? This they did with all wisdom and intention, knowing that even the swiftest flight across the Void would take generations, not so?"

"It is so."

"I ask you then, in all candor, how could this be? Who but a madman would dispatch his armies to fight across the Void, sending them to battle-fields so far that the grandchildren of those sent out would be the only soldiers on the field?"

"I know not: yet it was done."

"Leaving us ignorant of all? No one has even seen the Enemy stars, nor do we know them. How have we become so ignorant so soon?"

"My master said once that the Computer spoke to all the children, and instructed them. When the Computer fell silent, there were no written things aboard with which to teach the children. Much was lost; more was lost in the confusion of the wars and darkenings. What we know, we know by spoken lore; but in the past, all men knew the priestly arts, and could read the signs."

Weston waved his hand impatiently, as if this were nothing to the point. "Heed me. I tell you, I have led men into battle, not once, but many times, both against the rebel elves of Alverin, and against the Enemy. Will you take me at my word, that no battle could be fought, nor any force commanded, unless the soldiers are willing to die for one another, or for their home corridors?"

"I believe it."

"Now then: who aboard this ship is willing to die for Earth, which no one has ever seen; or is willing to die for those aboard the other ships of which myths speak; the Götterdämmerung or the Apocalypse? Are the crews and peoples of those mythic worlds willing to die for us? If so, why? Perhaps their great-grandfathers knew our great-grandfathers back when Earth first made us, but who knows them now? Do you see? Wars over such length of time cannot be possible."

But the Watchman said, "The medicine of those times past was much greater than our own, and men expected lives many hundreds of years in length, due to things they had put inside their bodies; things we do not have, and cannot make with our scant arts. To the immortals, wars, no matter how long, are done with swiftly."

The Captain knew a moment of doubt. His gaze rested on his giant; a man made huge and strong by arts the Captain knew had been lost. He also knew the old tales, which said that, before the Medical House was destroyed during the Second Barrage, all officers were young and ageless, able to see in the dark like cats, strong as dwarves, and instantly cured of any wound, poison, or hurt.

"Even were there such a war," the Captain slowly said. "If we are, as you say, deep in the ranks of the Enemy, overlooked and ignored, to fire our Weapons now would mean the destruction of this world, if not now, then in the time of our children."

At that moment came a great commotion at the silver doors, a sound of trumpets and alarms. There came a banging at the doors, and the lieutenant rushed in, his sword drawn.

"Sire," called the lieutenant. "The rebels from abovedecks attack in great force! Alverin himself leads them! Already he has been struck by a dozen arrows; each time he plucks them forth and laughs. The men . . . the men are saying he is an Earthman!"

"Rally the men. Draw down the great doors at Spinhall Common Fork and at the Underroad. Flood the stairwells leading to deck Eight Thirty Six with oil. Then, withdraw the men behind the Great Barrier Wall and close the High Gate. Use hand pumps to withdraw some part of the air from the circular approach corridor; this will seal all door beyond the power of any battering-ram to breach."

"But if he brings unlawful weapons? Explosives?"

"Fool. Alverin has never broken the Weapon Law; never cheated a treaty; never lied. Why do you think his rebellion does so poorly? They must be mad things to attack us now."

"Will you come to lead us?"

"Presently; first I must do otherwise. Go!"

And when the man had left, Weston said to the Watchman Henwas, "With this Ring, I could call upon the Computer to close and open doors at will, extinguish lights, drain corridors of air. Tell me the Words!"

But Henwas said, "You did not think to hide the ring when your lieutenant entered here. He saw it. If he craves its power as much as you, he will be gathering men to lead against you here to seize the ring."

"There is no more time for talk. Say the words, or I will order my giant to snap you like a wire!"

"You cannot escape the curse of the ring. Whoever does not have the ring craves to have it. So my master Himdall was told by the strange blind man who gave it first to him."

"Strange blind man?"

"Perhaps he thought the curse would be alleviated if the ring were given to so remote a hermit as my master."

"And did your master say what this man's appearance was?"

"Many times, for he was most peculiar. The wanderer, he wore his hair long, like those of the lower decks, but walked with a staff, like an upper-deck man not used to our weight. He wore a wide-brimmed hat, like the men of the Greenhouses, where the light controls never dim their fierce glare; but he wore cusps of black glass before his eyes, like a darklander out here where lights still glow. On each shoulder he carried a bird, like men who walk in fear of poisoned corridors, who, when they see their pets keel over, flee."

"Carradock! Go tell the Gatewatch to bring the other prisoner in! The description matches; it is he."

When the giant was at the door, speaking to the guard, the Watchmen flexed his muscles hugely, and chains about his wrists snapped free. He bent down and tugged the chains about his ankles; the links bent and broke; but, by then, the giant had seen, and flung himself back across the room to fall upon the Watchman with his full strength.

For a moment they strove against each other, limbs intertwined, muscles knotted. Their strength was equal, yet the aged giant was more cunning in the art of wrestling; the giant twisted and flung the Watchman to the ground and fell atop him. By this time the guards from the door had run forward, and stood with pike ready, but could find no opening, and dared not strike for fear of hitting the giant.

When he rose, the giant had the Watchman's arms pinned painfully behind his back, his hands twisted up. The giant was grinning. "You are a worthy opponent," he whispered, panting.

"You also," said the Watchman, as blood trickled down his face.

A moment later a second group of knights and pikemen came in the chamber, escorting an old man in a broad black hat. The old man walked leaning on a staff; two black birds clung to the shoulders of his long cape. The cape was fastened with an steel ornament shaped like a spiked wheel.

"Lieutenant! Why does he come before me unchained, garbed in no uniform, holding his stick? Were these things not taken from him at the door of his cell?"

"Sire!" stammered the lieutenant. "We found him now, not in his cell, but walking the corridors leading to the palace, singing a carol."

"A carol?"

The stranger lifted his head. As the hat brim tilted up, Weston saw the man wore round disks of black glass before his eyes. The stranger sang, "Woe my child! Woe is me! My son was born while falling free! Cannot endure Earth gravity, he never shall come home, not he, but evermore, forevermore, shall fly the airless deep, fly free!"

"That is an old song," said Weston.

"I am an old man," the stranger replied.

"I think you are Valdemar," said Weston.

"Then why do you not salute me?"

"Valdemar was a traitor!"

"Then why do you not embrace me as a brother, my fellow traitor?"

"What treason do you say I do?" asked Weston.

"The same as mine; you covet the ring. But I cannot use it; when the Chief Engineer Alberac learned I had let the Enemy aboard, he bound all the main circuits of the Computer to a single overall command; and wrought that command into the ring you hold, leaving all other systems on automatic. Lauren, the Ship's Psychiatrist, and I, we traveled to the Engine Room, and we deceived poor Alberac and seized the ring. But Alberac had wrought more cunningly than I had guessed, and had programmed the ring, such that whenever it was used, any other member in the computer then would know from where and from whom the ring's commands had come. The Enemy would bend all their forces toward its capture, were there any Enemy aboard. You see? The ultimate power of command, yet it can be used only by someone not afraid to die. Where to find such absolute devotion to one's duty? Many years I searched the halls of this great ship, from the Ventilation Shafts where pirates aboard their giant kites fly the hurricanes from level to level, down to the swamps and stench of the Sewermen, who silently take the dead away, and, in the darkness, use secret arts to recycle all foul things to air and light again. Only one man I found had not deserted his post; Himdall, last of the Watch, and most faithful. Surrounded by the enemy, abandoned, alone, yet true to his duty. And look! Here is his son, equally as faithful as is he. Equally as doomed."

Henwas called out, "Captain, I wish to report the Enemy Crown Ships are nigh to us, believing our world conquered and desolate, and are presently vulnerable to the discharge of our weapons!"

Several of the knights stared at the black-cloaked stranger in awe. "It is Valdemar!" said one. "Captain!" another whispered, and a third said, "Can it be he?"

One of the pikemen in the room was looking, not at Valdemar, but at Weston. This pikeman spoke out, saying, "My lord? You have the Command Ring?" But there was envy in his eyes, and he stepped toward the throne. But a knight, dressed all in ribbons and fine clothes, drew his rapier and touched that pikeman on the shoulder with the naked blade, so that the man was frightened, and stopped. The knight spoke to Weston, saying, "The rumor of the ring draws Alverin and all his tall, frail men. This old dribbler, if he is Valdemar, came also for its lure. I think the squat and surly dwarves who serve the fat Lord of Engineering cannot be far behind. The ring is surely cursed, my lord. It were better cast into a pit."

A second knight, this a tall man from Cargobay, said, "My lord! The stranger rambles at length. He hopes for delay. Perhaps he is in league with Alverin's people."

The giant said to the Stranger, "Captain Valdemar. I am Carradock son of Cormac. My father died in the battle of Foresection Seven Hold, killing the great champion of the Enemy. My father was an Earthman, born beneath blue skies, and he did not dessert his post, even at his death. By his name, and in return for the vengeance I owe you for his death at the hands of the Enemy whom you allowed aboard, I ask this question: Why?"

"Broad question. Why what?"

"Why did you surrender to the Enemy, and allow them to land sixty armies into our halls?"

"Is that your full question? Are you not also going to ask why, on the day of the Last Burn, did our drive core suddenly accidentally ignite? Why the Enemy vessel was struck amidships with a line of flame a hundred miles long, sterilizing half their outer decks? Why, to this day, they have not landed a thousand armies more, and why can they barely keep the empire to our antispinward supplied with arms and food, and that with picket ships which, till recently, were kept at bay by our escort ship Revenge? Why they dare not bombard the Twilight into flaming ruin, for fear of striking dead their own armies? And, best of all, why does the Sirdar-Emperor aboard this ship, the son of the Leader of the Boarding Party, why has he reported to his masters that the ship is taken? This last question I can answer: the Destroyers would certainly annihilate this vessel with their great weapons were they to learn that we still lived, and fought, and still ruled the inner decks as far spinward as Waterstore and forward as Airbay and Greenlitfield."

"Watchman," said the giant, "if you will promise not to escape, I will release one arm of yours. And I will trust your promise, knowing that, of all orders and ranks of men, Watchmen are the most true and trustworthy; for the good of the ship relies on the honesty of their reports."

"Why do you wish to let go my hand?" the Watchman asked.

"So that my own hand shall be free to salute my Captain, as he has asked."

"I agree," said the Watchman. And the Carradock raised his huge hand and saluted Valdemar. There were tears in Carradock's eyes.

Weston was livid. "Tell me the Word to unleash the power of the ring! Tell! Or I swear you die this moment, traitor!"

Valdemar said, "I know many secret words of high Command; words to open doors or trigger circuits which only open to my voice, doors leading down into secret corridors, accessways, and crawlspaces where no designers ever meant a human being to go. Every inch of all thousand decks of this vast ship I know, for it is mine, and I have never renounced my claim to it. I know words to darken lights, and still the airs to silence, or to send them rushing up again. But one word I do not know: the word which Himdall whispered to ring when he took it for his own."

Now a group twelve of Computermen came into the chamber, carrying staves and bludgeons. The pikemen in silver and blue lowered their lances, but confusedly, some pointing at the Computermen, some at the black stranger, and one or two at the Watchman whom the giant stilled gripped. Three pikemen began walking toward the throne in a menacing fashion, but when the lieutenant called sharply out to them, these three hesitated, and stood uncertainly.

The Chief Computerman was near the silver doors. He waved his truncheon, and called out, "Weston! Give up the ring! It is false and has no power! Do not dream you can control the doors and lights and weapons of the world! Only the Computer can control these things, and it heeds only our holy order!"

"It that so indeed?" spoke the dark stranger. He pointed his staff at the silver doors and spoke a single harsh syllable. Immediately the silver doors swung shut, and there was a sound of great bolts slamming home. The Computerman jumped forward to avoid the doors. "No doubt," hissed Valdemar, "these doors reacted of their own accord, from a wish to keep more riff-raff and sweeping of the corridors from blowing in to botch the brew."

"Edgal! Sindal! Garvoris!" called out Weston to three of his knights. "Kill Valdemar upon this instant! If he knows not the word to command the ring, then he is not any use to me."

"Other words I know," Valdemar mildly replied. And he shouted; the chamber dimmed into utter darkness. During the moment as the lights failed, Henwas saw Valdemar leap and spin lightly into the air, surrounded by a great gray circle of cloak, and by the flutter of his two dark, shrieking birds. With one hand, as he leaped, Valdemar drew out a breathing tube from his collar and put it to his mouth and nose; his other hand drew a hidden sword-blade from his staff. The staff-end, which had been the scabbard, fell away, smoking. Valdemar spun, disemboweling one oncoming knight with a kick, hidden knives unfolding from his boot spurs. In one smooth motion it was done; and the two other knights rushing forward missed him with their pikes as he leaped, swirling his cloak about the head of one of them. While the man was tangled in the weighted net hidden below the cloak, Valdemar slashed him to death with a stroke of his shining sword, which he held under his palm, against his fore-arm, after the fashion of blind-fighters.

Then it was dark. There came a noise and shattering explosion of light. In the flare of the explosion, the corpse of the one knight standing near where the smoking cane-end had been abandoned could be briefly seen, headless, bloody, arms flailing as it fell. The hollow tube had contained some shrapnel which had been scattered among the pikemen and guards. Their chests and faces were bloody. Screams were starting. One man was blubbering like a baby. Henwas heard a hiss, smelled the fetid, dizzying smell

of poisonous gas radiating from the corner of the chamber where Valdemar
had been.

All was noise, screams, horn-calls, darkness, confusion, the stench of
blood, the smell of poison.

Henwas was awed by the destruction. Was the Captain truly blind?

There was another flare of light; the lieutenant stood with an illegal
hand-weapon blazing in his fist, his face blood-red, contorted with murderous wrath, he was shouting, "Suffer not to live who breaks the weapon code!
Who kills the Ship kills all . . ." The lieutenant had been driven beyond all
reason by the traitor-captain's use of poisons and explosives, which could
damage air filters and bulkhead seals; he reckoned nothing for the illegality
of his own weapon.

The ornament which Valdemar had used as a cloak-pin spun shining out
of the darkness and struck the lieutenant's hand. The disk was razor-sharp;
it severed the lieutenant's fingers. The hand-weapon fell. Again it was dark.

Weston shouted, "Carradock! Save the Watchman . . ." and then he cried
out in great pain, having betrayed his location by his shout.

Someone struck at Henwas with a bludgeon; with his free hand (for the
other was still gripped by the giant) Henwas reached out and seized the
arm wielding the bludgeon, and the bones broke under the strength of his
fingers. At first, he was amazed and angered, for he did not think that any in
that chamber would risk his harm; but under hand he felt the rough-spun
cloth of a Computerman.

Then the giant was dragging him to one side. Henwas heard a clash of
blades, a coarse cry, where he had just been standing. Now the giant held
him still.

By some odor or noise or pressure close at hand, Henwas felt an intuition
the Valdemar was nearby, silent in the darkness.

The giant still had him by one arm; but, even so, Henwas did not move
or speak, for fear of someone hearing. There was a ruckus in the blackness all
around them, the clash of arms. Henwas suspected that the Computermen
or the pikemen were in rebellion, and thought, under cover of darkness and
confusion, to steal the ring.

Valdemar's voice slithered out of the blackness: "Carradock, I ask you, by
your ancient oaths, now to be obedient to me, and bring the Watchman to
the throne where Weston is. We will seize the ring. When you call to him,
he will answer, thinking you loyal."

Henwas was amazed that any man who used explosives aboard the
Ship could say words like "oath" and "loyalty" and not be choked. But
he feared a coming tragedy; Carradock and Valdemar both were resolute,
brave men. He knew the giant would not break fealty with Weston, who,
however unworthy, was his lord. He knew as well that Valdemar, who
might admire the giant, would not hesitate an instant to cheat, deceive
or murder him, the moment that such crimes became useful to his
grand design.

The giant made no noise. Henwas was not surprised.

Valdemar spoke again: "Unfortunate that you must betray Weston, who is your lord, but the mission goals require it. Fret not; treason is only bitter at first. The soul grows easily accustomed . . ."

Carradock lashed the bayonet of his weapon through the air toward the voice. He struck nothing. By some trick or slight, Valdemar had made his voice seem to come from where it was not.

"Henwas!" Valdemar whispered, sounding very near. "Call out, that I may hear where the giant stands, and slay him."

But Henwas did not want the giant to die, and did not answer. "Henwas, Carradock! Both of you have disobeyed my direct command in time of war; for this I instantly condemn you. I now release the deadly vapor. Breath, and perish . . ."

Henwas knew this was some feint to compel them to move or act, so he doubted, and stayed still; and perhaps the giant suspected this a ruse as well, but staked no chance on it.

Carradock discharged his weapon straight up into the air. In the momentary mussel-flare, Valdemar could be seen, crouching like a great black bat near the floor, white blade in his hand, point poised across his back like the sting of a scorpion.

The giant dropped the barrel of his weapon and fired again. Valdemar flopped and fell limply. The giant fired many times.

At that moment, the great gold doors behind the throne opened a crack. There was a weak light from the Main Bridge beyond, dusky blue service-lights said to burn forever. Silhouetting against that light, Henwas could see the staggering figure of Acting Captain Weston, who was pierced and bleeding.

The slim crack of light from the door, the huddled figure of Valdemar could be seen, bleeding terribly. "Accept my surrender," whispered Valdemar, "for I am wounded unto death."

The giant stepped forward. "I repent, that when finally I had found a man worth serving, the true Captain from the young days of the world, he sullied his hands with unlawful weapons. Your surrender I accept, for memory of the nobility once you had." A pause, then: "Can you hear me?"

And when he bent over the huddled figure, Valdemar, hearing the sound of his voice, flung up his hand and threw a poisoned dagger into the open mouth of the giant, piercing the roof of his mouth.

"Nothing is unlawful, nothing noble in war!" Valdemar screamed in anger.

The white-haired and ancient giant staggered forward and fell onto the supine body of Captain Valdemar, crushing him down. And perhaps the giant, falling, had struck down with his knife or hands, for the body of Valdemar was crushed and was not seen to move again.

As the giant fell, Valdemar cried a single word of command and then was silent.

The moment the giant had unhanded him, Henwas bounded across the chamber toward Weston. A knight rose up before him, like a ghost in the gloom, brandishing a rapier; but Henwas, scarred by radiation, knew no fear, came forward, was stabbed in the shoulder painfully, but struck in the knight's skull with his fist.

He nearly had his hands on the wounded Weston, who, sobbing, was crawling through the golden doors into the vast dark chamber beyond, when a pike-stroke from behind Henwas cut into the muscles of his leg and toppled him. In a moment, the pikeman had him by the hair, and was pressing a dirk against his throat, even as Henwas' hands closed around the bracelet-ringed ankle of Weston's jeweled boot.

Weston drew a bloody hand out from underneath his gem-studded coat. "This is my death-wound," he panted, staring in horror at the heart's blood in his palm, "I am slain . . ."

Meanwhile, Valdemar's last spoken word had its effect. There was a noise like that of bolts being drawn back and of doors opening; and the pictures which lined the walls swung free in their frames, and from half a dozen secret doors, lights and trumpet-noise issued forth.

Into the chamber from these secret doors came suddenly the tall pale men of Overdeck, garbed all in green, some with breastplates and helms of polished steel, carrying bows and tall spears and slim straight swords.

The knights of the above-world were tall and fair and terrible to look upon, and they were singing their war-song. Not one of them was pock-marked, or scarred, or showed any sign of the radiation diseases which those who live on lower decks, to their sorrow, know only too well. Before them, came the white starbanner of Alverin.

Many carried bows and cross-bows, for, although the Over-men are weaker in their legs and bodies than are other men, their arms are sinewy and their eyes are keen.

Alverin himself came forth, his uniform as green as leaves, and from his wide shoulders hung one of the fair white winged cloaks those who live at the Axis of the world use to steer themselves in flight. His hair was as yellow as the corn his people grow in Greenhold; his eyes were blue and bright, and shone with a light of stern command.

Now Alverin raised his straight slim sword and called upon those within the chamber to surrender, saying, "Whoso lays down his arms, shall be spared, and set free, I vow, suffering no hurt nor any dishonor!"

Because the rumor of Alverin's honesty and clemency was so well known, the knights and pikemen in that chamber instantly threw down their swords and pole-arms. None had heart to fight, seeing their leader, Weston, lay swooning with is life blood bubbling out of him. The weapons fell ringing to the chamber floor.

But one of the Computermen seized up a pike and, with a terrible cry, cast it straight into Alverin's breast. Alverin staggered backward, pierced through the heart and lungs. In that same instant of time, the man who had cast the pike was stricken through his arm by three arrows. Yet these shots were not ill-aimed; for Alverin's men, by custom, spoke before they struck, wounded rather than slew.

Alverin drew the pike-head out from his bloody chest and wiped the blood away. The wound closed up into a scar and then Alverin's chest grew fair and smooth again. He cast the bloody pike aside. "I am an Earthman; I was born beneath blue sky!" he called out. To the wounded man, he said, "The knowledge of the men who made this entire world have made me as I am, and I am not to be slain by your small weapons." And he ordered his physician to tend to the wounded among the enemy, even the man who had smitten him.

Alverin turned. He saw Valdemar laying motionless, his body crushed beneath the fallen giant. "So," Alverin whispered, "these secret paths you showed to us were not a trap. Did you play us true, this once, old liar? If so, where is the ring?"

Now he turned again. In the threshold of the golden doors leading to the Main Bridge, a pikeman still crouched above Henwas the Watchman, a steady knife still touching the prone man's throat. Henwas was bleeding at the shoulder and the leg, and yet his face was remote and calm, as if no wound nor pain could trouble him.

Alverin stepped forward till he could see, laying in the shadow of the door, dying, Acting Captain Weston II, and, in his bloodstained hand, the ring.

Beyond was the Bridge, a large dimly lit cathedral of a space, surrounded on all sides by the darkened screens of the Computer.

Weston croaked, "Pikeman. Slit the Watchman's throat if the rebel-king steps forward one step more."

"Weston," said Alverin in a soft, stern voice, "yield up to me the ring. I will restore to all the world, the light, the power, and the justice, which, by right, should have been ours. You have my solemn promise that all your men shall be dealt with justly."

"Should I believe a mutineer? You betrayed Valdemar," hissed Weston wearily.

"After he surrendered to the Enemy. Free men follow leaders into battle, and render him the power of Command, only while he does their will, in pursuit of a just war, or in defense against hostility. That power of Command, incapable of destruction, returned to the free men of this ship, upon Valdemar's abdication of it. By their fair and uncoerced election, I was tendered the Command, and so am Captain. That trust I hold sacred; render me the ring, and I shall see this world prosper."

"Prosper? Are we not surrounded by enemy worlds?" Weston asked softly.

"We are too humble for their attention," Alverin said. "If we do not offend them, they will pay us no more heed."

"And if the ring is used to launch the fabled Weaponry at World's Core?" Weston now raised himself on one elbow. His face was pasty-white, his eyes wild and sick.

"Then the world dies, if not in this generation, then in the next."

The lieutenant, his hand being bandaged by a tall pale doctor, spoke up, "Sire! Yield the ring to Alverin! Even we, so many years his foe, acknowledge his justice, wisdom, and trueheartedness. If any man is deserving of empire, it is such a man as this!"

But Henwas, who still had him by the ankle, said a voice of calm command, "In your last moment, sir, I pray you be a Captain truly. Use the ring, or give it me, to complete the mission of the Twilight of the Gods. We both are dying, you of wounds, me of radiation poison and disease. Should we, in such a time as this, abandon our posts and sue for peace? This whole world was made for war."

"Pikeman, stand away. Here, Watchman; take the accursed thing. Do your duty; kill all my enemies, you, them, everyone. And be damned to you all." With a curse on his lips, Weston slid into death, and his cold hand gave the ring to Henwas.

Henwas came up to his knees and thrust the pikeman down across the dais' stairs. Such was the strength of his arm that the man was flung many yards away. Alverin and the elves started forward suddenly, but Henwas, leaning inward from the golden door, reached and touched the shining ring against the dark, cold mirrored corner of the nearest of the many computer screens which filled the huge, black bridge.

He spoke the words: "Eternal Fidelity. I am forever loyal." And all the mirrors flamed to life and shined with purest light. On each screen images appeared, words, symbols, strange letters and equations, and everywhere, the thousand shining lights of all the Enemy stars.

A pure and perfect voice, like no voice ever to be made by lips or tongue of man, rang out: "READY."

Several of the Computermen screamed in fear or shouted with joy. One sank down to his knees and cried out, "Oh, that I have seen this day!" Even the knights and guards of Weston's, and the Alverin's tall men, stood speechless, eyes wide.

But the Chief Computerman called out for the men to avert their eyes, "This is a deception of the Enemy! The Computer cannot speak to men, except through us!" But one of the knights smote him across the face with his fist. The Chief Computerman fell to the deck, and lay sullen, wiping his mouth, weeping and afraid to speak again.

One of the overman knights raised his bow, and spoke in a soft, clear voice, "Noble lord Alverin! We have heard the word which can command the ring. One shot, and all the world shall be yours!"

"Nay, Elromir," spoke Alverin. "Not even to win empires will I have such a blow be struck, against a man wounded and unarmed."

The Watchman, kneeling, said, "Computer! Are there weapons at this world's core, ready to strike out against our enemies?"

"ALL WEAPON SYSTEMS AT READY. TARGETS ACQUIRED. FIRING SEQUENCES READY TO INITIATE. STANDING BY."

Alverin said, "Watchman, I pray you, wait! You will unleash a storm of fire! None save me aboard this ship even recall the origins of this war, its purpose, or its cause. Why do you condemn all the nations, lands, and peoples, here aboard the Twilight to be obliterated? Think of those born innocent, years after this dreadful ship of war was launched. Our Captain betrayed us; we have surrendered; let it rest at that."

Henwas said, "When the stranger, whom I now know to have been Valdemar, gave my master Himdall this dread ring, he did so with these words: 'You alone shall know when the waiting is completed, when the enemy grows lax, and deems us dead.' Only now do I understand the Captain's purpose after all these years, even from before my birth. The other ships we know only as names of glory, these ships are hard beset by that great foe which ruined and overthrew our world so long ago; and our true world Earth, though we have forgotten it, still calls to us to fight in her defense. The Captain expected us to fight and die for the glory of the fleet, to die, if need be, to have all the Twilight die, if it would forward the mission goals, and accomplish our duty."

Alverin said, "But, those aboard the other ships, why do you give such love and loyalty to them, that you are willing to call destruction down on all our world, for the sake of those whom you have never seen, and do not know?"

"I will not live to see salvation, yet I know it comes," said Henwas. "I never knew the other men who serve aboard those other ships; yet I know that there are those aboard them who would gladly do for me what I now do for them. That knowledge is enough for me."

One of the knights, evidently realizing the Henwas meant to do an act which would provoke the Enemy to destroy the world, stooped, picked up a fallen dagger, and, before any of Alverin's men could think to stop him, threw it. The dagger spun and landed fair on the middle of Henwas' back. Henwas, back arched, eyes blind with pain, now shouted, "Computer! Shut these doors!"

"ACKNOWLEDGED. ALL STATIONS NOTIFIED OF OVERRIDE COMMAND LOCATION."

The men in the room swept forward like a tide, but too late; the golden doors fell too, and shut in their faces.

Alverin raised his hand, and cried out with a great voice to rally his men. "Alberac's curse has told all the computer screens now where the ring hides! The Enemy will sweep this area with fire, exploding all the decks below us if they need be! Come! We must be gone! It may be already too late . . ." And he set his men passing swiftly out of the chamber. He and his paladins stood on the dais before the golden doors, unwilling to depart till all the men had gone before them.

And as they stood so, through the doors, they heard the great, chiming and inhuman voice call out, "WEAPONS FREE. INITIATING LAUNCH. WARHEADS AWAY."

There came a noise like thunder. And a great voice echoing from every wall rang out; and it was the Watchman's voice, tremendously amplified, and echoing throughout every corridor of every nation of the great ship. They heard the Watchman call out, saying, "I have seen it! I have seen it! And the heavens are consumed with light!"

Then, more softly, they heard the great voice say, "Father! If you see this, you shall know; I did not leave my post . . ."

And then, even more softly: "Computer, now destroy this ring, and let its curse be ended, and return all functions to their proper stations and commands . . ."

Light returned to the chamber where they where, and they heard, as from far off, a great noise of wonder, as of many voices of people near and far, all crying out at once. And they knew that light returned to darkened places which had known no light for years beyond count.

One of the knights took hold of Alverin's cape. "Sire, look!" and he pointed to where the giant Carradock lay.

Of Valdemar's body there was no sign. He was gone.

"Look there." One of the knights, in wonder, pointed upward to where the two black birds were huddled among the pillar-tops, bundles of black feathers, croaking.

"They are his magpies," said Alverin softly. "Even in ancient times, from before he was blind, he always kept such birds near him, to remind him of what he dared not forget." And, to himself, he murmured, "Or perhaps, since all this was arranged by his cunning, perhaps it is I who am blind, or who have forgotten . . ."

One of the black birds croaked, and spoke in a voice like a man's voice: "No matter what the cost. The Mission goals must be accomplished. No matter what the cost."

The other black bird croaked and said, "All's fair in war. All's fair. All's fair."

Alverin and his men departed from that place, and did not look back.

BLOOD DAUBER

Ted Kosmatka and Michael Poore

New writer Ted Kosmatka has been a zookeeper, a chem tech, and a steelworker, and is now a self-described "lab rat" who gets to play with electron microscopes all day. He made his first sale, to *Asimov's*, in 2005, and has since made several subsequent sales there, as well as to *The Magazine of Fantasy and Science Fiction*, *Seeds of Change*, *Ideomancer*, *City Slab*, *Kindred Voices*, *Cemetery Dance*, and elsewhere. He's placed several different stories with several different Best of the Year series over the last couple of years, including this one. He lives in Portage, Indiana, and has a website at tedkosmatka.com.

Michael Poore has appeared in both literary and speculative magazines nationwide, including *StoryQuarterly*, *Fiction*, *Talebones*, and *The Nth Degree*. He was runner-up for the 2006 Fountain Award for literary excellence in speculative fiction and has new work coming up in *Glimmer Train*.

Here the two join forces to investigate an intricate biological mystery that doesn't begin to come close to the mysteries of the human heart.

THE ANIMALS HATE you.

You get used to that, working at a zoo. Over time, it becomes a thing you can respect.

Bell trudged up the path, pushing the wheelbarrow before him, already sweating under his brown khaki uniform. He squinted in the bright sunlight, eyeing the exhibits as he ascended the hill: the goats and their pandering; the silly, horny monkeys; the slothful binturongs – all moving to the front of their enclosures as he approached.

Most zoo animals eventually came to an understanding with those who brought the food. An uneasy truce.

But Bell knew better than to trust it.

He'd seen the scars.

Mary had scars on her arms. Garland was missing the tip of one finger, and John, the assistant super, had a large divot in the calf of his right leg.

"Zebra," was all he'd say.

Bell was the newest zookeep. No scars yet. But a wariness.

Walking up the hill that morning, Bell noticed Seana up ahead of him on the asphalt path. As he walked, he noticed she wore two different-colored socks – one red, the other white. He wondered if she were absent-minded, or just quirky. He hadn't been at the zoo long, didn't know her well.

As he closed the distance, he saw that she was crying. And he realized why she wore one red sock. Her calf was gashed open, bleeding streams.

He followed her into the staff room, and she explained that the juvenile baboon had attacked her.

She was outraged. Betrayed.

"Why did you go in there?" he asked.

"I always go in there," she said. "I was here when it was born. I raised it."

"Animals are unpredictable."

She shook her head. "It's never done that before."

Never done that before.

Bell thought about that on the way home. Surprises puzzled him.

On one hand, it seemed there should never be any surprises. The world tended toward order, didn't it? It circled the sun at the same speed all the time. Water boiled predictably, froze predictably. People weighed the same in Dallas as they did in Quebec. The speed of sound, in dry air, was 767 miles an hour.

So why, Bell wondered, can't he and his wife keep track of money, plan ahead, and stop living in a trailer? In an orderly world, this shouldn't be impossible. In an orderly world, you shouldn't have to choose between buying food and keeping your car insurance.

Bell knew things were always more complicated than they looked. Water froze predictably, but strangely. It expanded. Crystals crashed and splintered. Sound moved faster underwater.

"And you can't keep from buying shit," he thought aloud, driving home.

He popped over the curb into the Lil' Red Barn parking lot.

They weren't going to spend anything this week, Bell and Lin had agreed. They didn't need to. Food in the fridge, gas in both cars. This week they wouldn't spend.

That morning, they'd run out of toilet paper.

"It's not an insurmountable problem," he'd told Lin. "We have paper towels."

"You're not," said Lin, "supposed to put anything besides toilet paper in the toilet."

"But you can," argued Bell, "if you need to."

Bell thought it was a spending problem. They knew how much money was coming in. If they controlled what went out, their money would be orderly, would increase. Lin disagreed.

"It's a matter of supply," she had pointed out. "Your job needs to supply more money."

"So does yours." Lin worked in the mall.

She glared ice. Splinters and crystals.

In Lin's world, it was okay for her to criticize Bell. It was not okay for Bell to criticize Lin. Not if things were to be orderly. In every mating pair, Bell knew, one animal always bit harder than the other.

Lin was the biter.

And in their two-mammal world where daily life was defined by constant, grinding poverty, it seemed she bit constantly.

It was important, they had once agreed, to do what they loved. To love their work.

"I love my work," Bell had told Lin a thousand times. Last month, in bed, he had told her how he loved his work, and they'd argued, and she'd scratched him with her fingernails. Drew blood. Made him want to hit her, and he almost did.

But he didn't. There were light years between wanting to hit a woman and actually doing it. Bell wasn't that kind of man. Wasn't that kind of animal. What kind of animal was he?

He wondered if she knew. Wondered if she'd seen it in his eyes, the almost-hitting. The wanting to.

He quit saying how much he loved his job.

Most zookeepers, he knew, were women whose husbands made better money. They could afford the love.

Lin knew this, too.

"Shelly Capriatti's husband sells guitars," she had told him, just the night before. Shelly Capriatti was someone she worked with or worked out with, he couldn't recall. "High end stuff, like for professionals. Like if Eric Clapton needed a new guitar. There's no reason you couldn't do something like that. He makes a ton of money."

And he was on the edge, as he often was, of admitting to himself that he wished he hadn't gotten married, when she stretched herself across his lap in front of their eleven-year-old TV and was nice for a while. Long enough for him to sweep some hard truth under the rug. Again. It was easier that way.

He focused on that – the niceness – while he paid the cashier at the Lil' Red Barn.

She could be nice. Things in general, sometimes, were nice.

Sometimes she was predictable, which was easier, but you had to be ready for both. Driving into the trailer park, he thought about that.

The baboon had never attacked anyone. Then, today, it did.

There's a first time for everything.

"You're cute the way a dog is cute," Lin had told him, in front of the TV. You run out of toilet paper.

Things fall apart.

Not having money was a theme in Bell's life. Even the zoo was a poor zoo, poorly funded.

Sometimes people complained. Once, a woman had come in, and when she'd seen the conditions in which the lions were housed, she'd been angry. People loved the lions.

"It's a cage," she said.

Bell had agreed with her.

"Zoos are supposed to be . . . natural," she continued. "They're supposed to be habitats, and the animals aren't even supposed to realize they're confined."

Bell understood. He sympathized. He'd been to zoos like that, too, in towns that weren't dying.

"Do you think they don't know?" he asked.

She only stared at him.

"Do you think, in these other zoos, that the animals don't know they're locked in?"

"A disgrace," she said, walking away.

Low funding required management get creative when provisioning the animals. In addition to supplies bought on the open market, there were arrangements with local grocery stores, and butchers, and meat processors. A truck was taken around each day to be filled with heaps of food – loaves of bread that had passed their freshness dates, meat that had begun to turn, gallons of milk that had expired. Occasionally there was carrion brought in – deer which had been struck on the highway and then picked up by the county. All of it fed into the bottomless maw of the zoo.

The trucks would drive around back and unload their cargo into the kitchen. It was called the kitchen, but it was not a kitchen. It was a room with several huge stainless steel tables on which food was piled and sorted and divided.

Bell was on his way to the castle when a voice on his walkie-talkie stopped him. "Bell, there's something you need to see."

Lucy, one of the kitchen workers, out of breath.

He got there fast. Came in through the back door.

"It's a bug," said Lucy, hands at her collar.

"What kind?" he asked.

She shrugged. "It's a bug." She pointed at a bowl turned upside-down on the counter.

Bell lifted the bowl. Put it down again.

He stood perfectly still.

He lifted the bowl and stole another quick glance.

"Hmm," he said and lowered the bowl.

The kitchen workers stared. "What is it?"

"I'm working on it," he said. He looked into the distance. "I think it's a grub of some kind."

"I didn't think grubs got that big," Lucy said.

"No," Bell said. "Neither did I."

Bell looked again. The grub was large, fleshy and blood red. 5 inches long.

"Where did it come from?" he asked.

She shrugged again. "The table."

Bell looked at the table. There were watermelons, and apples, and bread, and the partially disarticulated hock of a deer. Several bunches of blackened bananas made a mountain in the center, along with a smaller mound of more exotic fruit shipped in from Lord-knew-where.

"It could have come in with anything," she said. "I found it crawling along the edge of the table there." She shuddered. "It was moving pretty fast."

Bell retrieved a glass jar from the cabinet, opened the lid, then dragged the bowl across the edge of the table so the strange grub dropped into the jar. He stepped outside and plucked some grass, put the grass inside, and closed the lid. Poked holes.

He took the jar across the zoo to the castle and placed it on a shelf in the back room.

"The castle" was the name used for the entomology building. Bell could only imagine what the structure's original use had been, with its block construction and odd turrets; but whatever that long ago intent, it now housed all manner of creepy crawlers – hissing cockroaches, and ant farms, and snakes, and lizards and frogs. Anything that required darkness or careful temperature control.

The building was a box within a box. There was an open, central area ringed on three sides by walls and exhibits – and just behind these walls was a space called the back room, closed to the public, which was actually a single narrow hall that conformed to the outside perimeter of the building, a gap space where you could access the back side of the cages. At the far end of this hall, in a dead-end spot furthest from the entry door was a table and chairs, a TV, a desk and several terrariums. These extra terrariums were where the sick were boarded, those unfit for public examination.

Bell did the rest of his chores for the day. In the evening he checked on the grub. It was still there, happily curling up the sides of the glass jar. Bell had studied entomology in college, and he'd never seen anything like it; the insect's sheer bulk seemed to push the cubed-square law to its limit. Perhaps beyond its limit. He hadn't thought insects could be that big. When he opened the lid, the grub reared up at him, strange mouth-parts writhing.

Bell was in charge of the castle, the petting zoo and the convicts. This had not always been the case. He was in charge of the castle because he was the only zookeeper who'd taken college-level entomology. The petting zoo was meant as an insult. And the convicts were punishment.

The convicts came in most weekdays. You could point them out in the parking lot – men and women who were there too early, hours before the gates opened. Bell would feed the insects, drink a cup of coffee and then walk to open the front gates.

"Here for community service?" he'd ask.

"Yeah," they'd say.

Sometimes there were two or three. Sometimes none. They handed Bell their paperwork, and Bell passed it to the zoo superintendent at the end of the day.

The number of hours worked was the all-important statistic. Because they all had a number they were working down from. 150 hours, 200 hours, 100 hours.

Sometimes they talked about their crimes, and sometimes they didn't.

Bell never asked. Not his business.

Bell often talked to himself in the bathroom mirror.

"In this world," he said, "you are not an apex predator. Humans are, as a species, but you, yourself, are not."

You do not always win. Problems are not always solved.

There are defeats and surrenderings. Small but important.

Last winter, they gave up heating the bedroom. They sealed off the back of the trailer and slept on the sofa. They learned the science of climbing into the bathtub. The bathtub was metal and descended a few inches through the floor, arctic air right beneath. No matter how hot the water got, your butt and legs would start to freeze if you sat still too long. You had to lift yourself up now and then, let the hot water get under there. Lower yourself. Wait. Repeat.

"It's like not even being part of the food chain," Bell said aloud one cold night, eating burritos in the kitchen.

They hadn't spoken to one another that morning. His remark about the food chain was one of two things they said to each other all day long.

Sometimes he opened up the bedroom door and exhaled just to see his breath cloud the room.

He wanted her to ask about his food chain remark. Wanted to explain it. Wanted her to understand.

"The food chain – " he began.

"I get it," she said.

That was the second thing that got said. Her breath made a cloud even though they were in the kitchen.

Bell didn't dare tell Lin how much he loved his job, not anymore. He told the mirror, instead.

"I love my job," he said. His reflection said it, too, it seemed.

Like the zoo, their life at home had been built on various pretendings. Pretending there might be gas money. Pretending they could afford to eat better, but chose not to. Pretending that Lin still thought it was important to have a job you liked. Loved. Whatever.

She had quit pretending. Somewhere behind her mask was the Lin who thought 'If you loved me you'd do what it took for me to live a better life,' and that Lin had surfaced. Unmasked. Through fucking around.

Classified ads appeared, taped to the fridge.

Sales. Landscaping. Power-washing trucks. All kinds of things you could do with a degree in biology.

"It's easy," Bell told her, "to lose track of what's really important."

She didn't have to say that having heat and electricity were important, too. Instead, never breaking eye contact, she grabbed her coat and her vibrator and locked herself in the bathroom.

Library clerk. Barista. All things that paid more than working at a zoo. Mexican cook. Skycap for a Mexican airline. Didn't matter if you weren't Mexican.

It was amazing, thought Bell, how much pretending went on in a zoo.

The public pretended the cages were jungles, savannah, desert, or snow.

The animals pretended that they were not interested in the public. The public and the zookeepers worked together at pretending that the zoo was not, when you got right down to it, just carefully-engineered cruelty.

Sometimes the animals forgot to pretend. Like when babies were born and wouldn't eat. Because they knew captivity when they saw it. Felt it. Forgot to pretend life was worth living.

Like when the llama attacked Bria Vagades.

Bell was there when it happened.

It wasn't like an animal attack in the movies, all snarling and snorting, blood and fur. It looked almost comical. One second Bria was lifting the rock-shaped hatch which concealed the garden hose, and suddenly here came Nunez the llama, ridiculous and splendid with his two-tone black-and-gray coat, rearing on his hind legs, waving his front hooves like a boxer. He was on her before she saw him, and she screamed.

"Ow!" she screamed, and "Fuck you, Nunez!" before she got a grip on herself. The zoo was closed, but there were strict rules about losing your cool where the public might see, might panic.

Nunez lost his balance, came down on all fours, still advancing, sniffing the air. Reared up again, hooves waving as Bria covered her head, backing away, feeling behind her for the door.

"He didn't want her in the enclosure," Bell told John Lorraine, another zookeeper, later on in the cafeteria. "It was obvious."

"It's never obvious. It's sloppy, is what it is, assigning human motives to animal behavior."

"Territoriality is an animal behavior," Bell answered, chewing peanut butter crackers. "It's an animal motive."

"What's sloppy," John said, "is pretending to understand why all the time. Why they do anything they do."

"Because it's mating season," said Bell. "That's why."

John Lorraine's eyes narrowed. "And she went in the enclosure by herself? That's sloppy, too. These animals aren't pets."

But Bell knew some of the animals were like pets. Bad pets. Pets you couldn't trust. "You should write a fucking memo," he said.

"You should shut up."

Bell agreed. He said "Yep."

The grub wasn't like a pet. The day after Bell placed it in one of the large terrariums, it began to construct a papery cocoon.

During his evening break, Bell sat in the back room and watched the grub work. He checked the zoo's entomology books but couldn't find a match. None of the pictures looked anything like the strange insect in the terrarium. The cocoon only deepened the mystery. Whatever this thing was, it was a juvenile.

There were four main groups of insects that had a larval stage of development: Coleoptera, Lepidoptera, Hymenoptera, and Diptera.

The thing in the terrarium was no caterpillar, so Bell could rule out Lepidoptera. The grub's size seemed to rule out Diptera. Which left Hymenoptera and Coleoptera. Wasps and beetles. But it didn't look like any wasp or beetle grub he'd ever seen.

Most grubs didn't have eyes. Most grubs didn't have mouthparts like that.

At the end of its third day in the terrarium, Bell arrived to find it had sealed itself into its papery chrysalis, and just like that, the grub subtracted itself from the world.

The next day, there was an addition to Bell's army of community service workers. A late arrival.

Bell was on one knee, mixing food for the lemurs when a shadow fell over the bucket. Bell shaded his eyes and looked up.

"They told me to find Bell. 'Report to Bell,' they said. Said Bell was young. You look like you might be him."

The shadow had a voice like raw sand.

Bell stood and shook hands.

Shaking hands, the first thing he noticed was scar tissue. Burn scars splashed across hand and wrist. Both hands, Bell observed. Both wrists.

Leather-skinned. Scrambled white hair. Eyes blue like a cutting torch. If a bomb could explode and come back as a person, it would be this guy. Just looking at him, sunburned and fire-burned, made Bell thirsty. They sat down over Cokes at the Savannah Cafe, where Bell learned that the bomb's name was Cole. Learned that, at sixty, Cole was by far the oldest community service con to grace the zoo.

Then he put him to work hosing down empty cells in the elephant house, beginning with the Cape Buffalo.

"Bullshit," rasped Cole, when he saw the cell.

Bell must have looked startled.

"Literally," Cole explained, waving the hose at the floor. He smiled, revealing teeth like rubble. Smiled and winked.

It was like being winked at by war.

Just as the lions were star attractions for the tourists, Cole became a star attraction for the staff.

He was scary, like the lions. Like the lions, he seemed to keep most of his energy bottled up in some soft, invisible engine. It was an uneasy feeling, locking eyes with a lion. Same with Cole.

You couldn't talk to a lion, though. Couldn't ask him how he came to be at the zoo. But you could ask Cole, if you were nosy enough.

Bell didn't ask.

Bell stood in the dark tunnel with Cole. "The baboons are smart," he said. "You have to be careful."

Cole nodded.

"They can throw their poop at you. They can bite. You have to lock both sets of doors. There is a procedure you have to follow, and you should never be in the enclosure with them."

Cole nodded again.

"It's very important. Do you understand?"

Cole nodded again, but Bell wasn't so sure. Several years earlier there'd been an incident in the cat house. The exhibit had been in the midst of repairs, and the lion had been allowed access to its run overnight. This normally wouldn't have been an issue except that the adjacent run had been under construction. The door separating the bobcat run from the lion run was made of thick plywood – a temporary measure which was fine to keep the bobcats in. But insufficient, apparently, to keep the lion out.

The next day, they found the plywood partition shredded, and the lion sleeping in the bobcat cage, blood coating its muzzle. All the bobcats were dead.

Zoos are dangerous places.

Dangerous for the animals. Dangerous for the zookeepers.

Cole had a thousand hours of community service. Bell had never seen a number that high. It would take him a year to finish it.

When Cole had been at the zoo for a week, the zoo superintendent pulled Bell aside. The superintendent didn't like Bell much. She wore a serious expression. "The older guy, Cole, is he a good worker?"

"He's fine."

"He's going to be here for a while."

"Yeah," Bell said, "I know." He could see the gears moving behind the superintendent's eyes. A free long-term worker. A worker that didn't need getting paid.

"Perhaps we could give him more responsibilities," she said.

For weeks, Bell checked on the cocoon, waiting what would emerge.

It happened on a Monday. There was a buzz in the room when Bell entered. A buzz like one second before an electric light went bad; only this light kept going bad, second after second – an electrical hum that did not fade. Bell looked in the terrarium and saw it.

Huge.

Winged.

Bright red, but the mouthparts were black.

"Hymenoptera," he whispered. "Of some kind."

The summer stretched on. Bell trained Cole how to be a zookeeper. On their breaks they sat in the back room.

When the insect first hatched, the question became what to feed it. Bell tried a little of everything: sliced bananas, and apples and small chunks of meat. Some of the fruit on the table came from exotic locales, and it was easy to imagine the grub stowed within the corpus of some melon from Central America – and it was easy to imagine how such a melon might go quickly bad, and soft, and end up on the zoo's table as discarded produce.

Weeks passed, and the insect thrived.

Even Cole took an interest. "Pet wasp?" he said as he helped Bell clean out the nearby lizard cage.

"I'm not convinced it's a wasp."

Several days later Bell found Cole looking through the glass. Cole was the one who noticed it first.

"What's that?" he asked.

Bell looked. "I'll be damned." The wasp-thing sat perched on a small branch in the terrarium, oddly-jointed legs flexed, wings slung like swords over its narrow back. Hanging beneath the insect, dangling from a fibrous string, was a small pod of what looked like dried brown foam.

"What is it?" Cole said.

"I think it's an egg case."

Cole surveyed the terrarium again.

"So there's two of them things?"

Bell shook his head. "There's just the one."

"Maybe she was already fertilized."

This particular convict was smarter than he pretended to be. Bell caught his reflection in the glass, blowtorch eyes darting back and forth.

"It's not likely," he said. "She is female, but the reproductive stage usually begins after metamorphosis, not before. And this thing has been alone since it hatched."

"Santa Maria of the bugs," said Cole, cracking a shipwreck smile.

Bell laughed. "It's less than a miracle in the insect world," he explained. "It's called parthenogenesis. Some kinds of Hymenoptera can—"

"Hymen-who?"

"It's an insect clade. Ants, bees and wasps. Certain species can reproduce without males. Worms can do it, too, and some lizards. But Hymenoptera are the champs."

Cole straightened.

"Let's hope that doesn't catch on."

Bell thought it over. Reproduction and marriage and wives and such.

"Might not be so bad," he muttered.

"What's that supposed to mean?"

"Nothing."

Bell contacted the university. He wrote a letter to the biology department describing the insect and the circumstances of its arrival. A week later he received a reply. The note was short and polite: "It's probably a mud dauber."

Bell wadded the letter and threw it in the trash. "I know what a mud dauber looks like."

One evening a few weeks later, he found the insect dead. Even in death it looked formidable, with a head the size of a dime, and a body like a smooth, slick walnut.

For the first time, he dared to touch it. With its legs spread out, it was nearly the size of his hand. He jabbed a pin through its abdomen and stuck it to a small cork. The legs sagged under their own weight. He looked inside the terrarium at the egg case, wondering if anything would hatch from it.

Months passed, the egg case forgotten. Bell and Seana took turns training the old man. Seana didn't like Cole, and didn't pretend she did.

In the spring, the eggs hatched. There were a million tiny grubs, just like the original, only smaller. Bell watched them wriggling through the sawdust he'd put in the terrarium.

"These more of your wasps?" Cole asked.

"They will be."

They watched them writhing for several minutes.

"What do they eat?" Cole asked.

Bell thought about this for a moment. The adult form of an insect often ate a completely different diet than the juvenile.

"I have no idea," he said.

Feedings could be tricky.

When Bell was first hired by the zoo, he'd been put in charge of feeding the raptors. Raptors weren't dinosaurs though, like you'd think, with a name like that. It turned out, they were big damn birds. One of them was a golden eagle.

All went well for the first few days. The golden eagle ate about five rats a week, but it was fed every day. Which would have been fine except that the uneaten rats had to be removed from the enclosure.

This idea didn't bother Bell until the moment he first went to do it. He stood at the cage door and looked at the big damn eagle, and it occurred to him that he was about to go inside a big damn eagle's enclosure and take out its food. It occurred to him what might happen if the big damn eagle felt suddenly partial to that food.

He stared at the eagle. He stared at its talons – two-inch daggers strong enough to pierce bone.

Bell walked down to the zoo superintendent's office. She was unmoved by his concerns.

"I'm not sure I'm comfortable with it," Bell said.

She waved that off. "You've got nothing to worry about." Then she went back to her paperwork.

"But how do you know the eagle won't attack?"

"It'll be fine," she said, not bothering to look up. "Nothing like that has ever happened before."

A preamble to every scar story he'd heard at the zoo.

"I'm not going to do it," he said.

She looked up from her papers. She sighed. She weighed her options. "All right," she said.

The next week he was put in charge of the petting zoo. This was meant as an insult.

When he complained, pointing out that his particular skill set could surely be put to better utility, she only nodded sympathetically.

Then she put him in charge of the convicts, too.

Bell divided the newly hatched grubs into three groups, in three terrariums. In one terrarium, he dropped only fruit. In another, he dropped chunks of bread. In the third terrarium he dropped meat.

Insects tended to specialize in their diets, so he thought there was a good chance that two of the terrariums would starve. But then at least he'd know what they ate.

The grubs, however, surprised him. All three aquariums thrived – though the grubs given meat grew fastest.

Two months later, the grubs all began to spin cocoons. As if by agreement, they all started their nests on the same day.

That night, as if to celebrate the milestone, Bell committed a budget crime. He stopped at McDonald's for a bite on his way home, knowing that tuna salad was all they had in the fridge.

He was trapped and doomed, once he'd spent the money.

"Spend whatever you need to," Lin said. "Just make sure you tell me about it."

Lin was the official banker of their marriage.

"Just tell me about it" was the trap, because if he spent money and told her, she got mad. She might get loud, she might stay quiet. Either way, when Lin got mad, she fed on her own energy like a hurricane, getting louder and madder. The hurricane usually blew until she charged out the door and drove away, still screaming. Hours later, she'd return. Maybe still mad, maybe not.

One of these days when she came back, Bell would be gone.

This thought came from an increasingly vocal part of his brain. The part where he'd swept so much crap under the carpet.

A week after his crime, she dropped a bank statement in his lap while he sat reading.

They were both reading a lot, these days. The cable company had run out of patience.

"What?" he asked.

"It's highlighted."

Shit. He'd forgotten.

MCD Store #1635.

"You didn't give me a receipt for that."

"Thought I had. Sorry."

He was sorry. What else could he do? Here, he thought, was where a rational person would let it go. But not Lin.

She yelled, storm winds building. How, she wanted to know, was she supposed to know how much to spend on the rent and the car and the power company and the phone company and the fucking grocery store when she didn't know how much he'd spent on whatever big important things he needed to spend money on. Like a Big Mac, apparently. She didn't remember him asking if she'd like a Big Mac, too, because he was too busy being a selfish, irresponsible asshole and then hiding the receipt.

He could tune out the yelling, until she made accusations like that.

"I forgot," he reminded her. Now he was pissed. This was going to be bad.

The louder she got, the louder he got. Eventually, she was shrieking at him. A responsible voice inside him grew worried. She was really, really wound up this time. The tiny voice said that he couldn't let her drive off like this. She'd hurt herself. Hurt someone.

It was a zookeeper voice. The voice that knew you couldn't let the animals run wild, no matter what.

She took a bathroom break, still yelling, and Bell took advantage of the opportunity to hide her car keys. Deep inside a box of stale Triscuits.

Sure enough, when she emerged, she hunted for her keys.

Lin was notoriously bad about where she laid her keys. They could be anywhere.

She hunted.

For ten, fifteen minutes, she looked everywhere. Everywhere she might rationally have put her keys. She stopped yelling about Bell and started quieting down.

The quiet, Bell knew, was deceptive. It did not signal calm. Just quiet. Like a fire that gets into the walls, hidden, until someone opens a door.

Bell realized he had made a mistake. She would keep looking forever, that was the problem. Sooner or later, he was going to have to tell her he'd hidden her keys. And she'd get worse. Get louder. The storm of the century.

In some ways, he felt sorry for her. She was kind of crazy, really. More than kind of. Poor girl. But what a bitch. He almost said it aloud.

In the end, she retreated to the bathroom again, and Bell put the keys in the silverware drawer. Silently, like a cat burglar.

She came back out, and the silverware drawer was the third place she looked. She had already looked there. Several times. And she knew it. Bell knew she knew it.

"You fucker," she whispered, almost choking. Near tears.

Remorse! He was no match for tears. He melted, moved toward her. He'd been protecting her.

She whipped the keys at him, catching his left ear as he ducked.

It was loud again for a while. Bell picked up the keys and opened the trailer door.

Lin had grabbed her purse.

"Give them here!" she screamed.

Bell ignored her.

He drove off, this time.

He used up ten dollars of gasoline just driving in circles. He enjoyed the waste. Enjoyed the drive. Talked to himself.

When he circled back, at last, he found her shivering on the steps.

She'd been locked out.

It was a cold fall evening.

Remorse, again.

This was not fucking working.

Mating is complicated.

Mammals click.

Personalities come together, and they click, sometimes. Other times they don't.

The day after he and Lin un-clicked so badly – the day after he locked her out of the trailer – Bell and Cole sort of clicked.

Bell couldn't have said what did it, exactly. He was on the roof of the walrus tank, watching the pinnipeds heave their awkward bulk across wet concrete.

Cole climbed the ladder and joined him. In the enclosure below, two males bellowed at each other, bumped chests.

The smaller male backed off, retreating to the tank, but the larger walrus followed. It slipped its hulking form into the water and was suddenly graceful. Like a different animal entirely.

They stared together in silence until Cole said, simply "Well, Goddamn," and they both cracked smiles.

"Reminds me of my dad growing up," Cole said. "Big and mean. Harder to get away from than you'd think."

Bell cocked an eyebrow.

"Oh, a real tough-guy," Cole continued. "Beat my ass until I got bigger than him." Cole smiled war again.

Bell was unsurprised when Cole showed him a silver flask and asked if he'd like a sip.

And Bell had a sip. Just one.

But it was enough to set the stage for a detour, after closing, to a nearby grill with a liquor license. Bell didn't feel like going home to Lin; and Cole didn't feel like going back to the halfway house. He wasn't due for an hour, yet.

At the bar, Bell lit a cigarette and found himself talking about Lin. He told Cole all about the money problem, and the fight.

Cole's cutting-torch eyes burned as he listened. He looked terrifyingly wise, all of a sudden.

After two beers, Bell found himself saying out loud the thing he could barely admit to himself, "I wish I'd stayed single, man. I really, really, do."

Just then, a woman wearing fifty pounds of makeup came in, clunked across the floor in square heels. Cole winked at her.

She said something to the bartender and walked back out.

Bell watched her go. The setting sun blazed straight in through the door as it wheezed shut. Bell winced and – too late – shaded his eyes. Momentarily blind, blinking, Bell groped for his beer.

Into this momentary darkness, Cole said, "I crashed a helicopter, in case you wondered."

Bell blinked. Cole's eyes became visible, twin coals.

"Huh?"

"I noticed you didn't ask about my hands. Or why I was in jail. You never ask nobody. It's actually pretty conspicuous, the way you don't ever ask how anyone came to community service. You just give 'em some shit to do and mark down their hours."

Bell must have looked troubled. Purple circles rotated in the dark, in his brain.

"No, it's cool. It's cool you do people like that. Makes 'em feel normal. But not asking the way you do, it's kinda obvious how bad you want to know, so I'm telling you. I wrecked a helicopter."

Cole was right. Bell wanted to know. Wanted to know quite badly. Hadn't realized until this moment.

"Alright," he said, by way of encouragement.

It took fifteen minutes for Cole to tell about Brazil.

He was a helicopter pilot, to begin with.

First in the army, then for the president of a frozen chicken company, then for United Airlines, on contract with Canadian Railways, shuttling engineers from checkpoint to checkpoint. It was the kind of solitary work he enjoyed. The engineers were usually stone tired. Quiet.

Then he'd crashed his United Airlines helicopter.

The kind of thing that could happen to anyone; his tail rotor crapped out and he had to autorotate down from 800 feet, spinning and yawing with three cursing, pants-pissing passengers. Rolling sideways at the last second, landing sideways, splintering the rotor, rupturing the fuel tank.

No deaths. The only serious injury was Cole, who remained behind until all three passengers were out and running, safe. Sustained burns over 25 per cent of his body, including the splashy scar tissue on his left hand and wrist.

Bell began to ask a question, but Cole anticipated him.

"The other hand was something else," he said. "Something later."

United Airlines hadn't been cool about his benefits, and the hospital bankrupted him. Could barely afford the surgery that let him use his hands, let alone reconstruction or cosmetics.

Which was why he started siphoning aircraft fuel. You could make a lot of money on the black market, selling aircraft fuel at half-price.

A dangerous business, though. No honor among thieves and so on; someone turned him in, and a federal warrant came looking for him.

The Feds called him while he was in the air. In Virginia, near the coast. On his way to Richmond for a pickup.

"Put down at Richmond International," the FBI told him.

And Cole had flown out to sea, instead. How stupid did those bastards think a guy was?

Stupid enough, he supposed, to get caught fencing felony amounts of helicopter fuel.

Cole flew out to sea. Flew into the sea. If the feds wanted him, they were going to have to work for it.

Bell must have looked at Cole's right hand.

"The fuel tank ruptured when I hit the waves," said Cole, draining his beer. "Set the water on fire. I could either surface and tread water in the burning fuel, or stay under and grow gills. Happened when I was twenty-seven. They gave me nine years."

Bell did the age math, but before he could ask, Cole said, "Oh, I was in and out after that. Assault, mostly. The last one for a bar fight. Guy got his eye socket broken, and the judge gave me extra – those women judges, they're the worst. She said my anger gonna burn me up some day." Cole smiled war again. "But that already happened, ain't it? Besides, not all that burns is consumed."

He took a last swallow of his drink. "I gotta scoot. If they lock my ass out, I'm fucked."

Very quickly, Cole was up and out the door. Bell turned and watched him go, and the sun hadn't quite set yet, and Bell's eyes got nailed a second time.

Blind as a bat, Bell thought.

Good zookeeper that he was, Bell knew bats weren't really blind, and he said so.

"What?" called the bartender. Also, Bell thought, a zookeeper of sorts.

"Bats aren't really blind," Bell repeated.

Never get drunk with the convicts, Bell lectured himself.

It was a bad idea in so many ways. It was unprofessional. Besides, if you got to be drinking buddies with one of them, even going so far as to sip whiskey with him on top of the walrus tank – a firing violation by zoo rules – then what do you do afterward if the convict does something you should report him for? Something else.

A week after the bar, Bell arrived at work and found Garland, the mainte-nance chief, waiting at the gate.

"There's an issue," said Garland.

"An issue?"

"With your friend. He's drunk."

"Where?"

"I have him shoveling the camel enclosure. Figured that would keep him out the way until he sobered up a bit." Garland paused. "Only I think he's a lot worse off than I thought."

A headache came rumbling up on heavy treads. Bell sighed.

Garland looked uneasy, too. It was bad news, Cole being drunk. Especially if Garland had noticed it and let him work anyway. It was like Watergate. A lot of people could wind up in trouble before this was over.

"I thought I'd wait and see what you wanted to do," said Garland as they walked uphill through the zoo. "I didn't want to make out a report if it was just . . . well."

Bell understood. The old man was scary.

Bell nodded. "I'll handle it."

At the camel enclosure, Bell called out Cole's name and the old man approached, shovel in hand. He smelled like rum.

"Yeah?" The question had an edge to it. Like Cole knew he was in trou-ble. For a moment, looking through the bars, Bell saw something aggressive in his eyes. Something leonine.

Bell explained how it would go.

Cole would drop the shovel.

He would avoid speaking to anyone.

He would leave by the back entrance. Now.

"So I'm fucked," Cole said.

Bell shook his head. "You called in sick today is all. This never happened."
He should be firing this guy, Bell knew. Why didn't he?

He could see it now. He'd tell Cole to get the hell out and not come back, and Cole would go to Koverman and say Did you know I drank whiskey with Bell during work hours on top of the walrus tank?

"I'm fucked," Cole repeated. He swayed.

Bell frowned. There was something that started out to be a long silence. Then Cole whispered, "I'm not going back to jail. I won't do it."

Bell lead him out. "Come back tomorrow," he said. "Sober."

It took exactly four weeks for the cocoons to hatch. There was a sound like electric lights going bad, and Bell stepped in the back room. He stared for a long time. The terrariums teamed with strange new life. Each glass box seemed to house a different creature entirely. Strange wasp-things, and things . . . not like wasps. Things without names. Some larger, some smaller. Some with wings, some without. All were red and black.

"Impossible," he muttered. They couldn't all be the same species.

His first instinct was to call the university. Then he remembered their note about mud daubers. Screw the university.

Besides, instincts were for animals. He'd solve this on his own.

He could figure it out, Bell was certain. He knew a lot about insects.

He knew insects had been among the first living things to walk dry land; they'd seen the rise and fall of dinosaurs, the birth of flowering plants. Humans weren't the first species to farm, or to domesticate animals, or to war. Those milestones belonged to insects. When humanity first began its clumsy, ongoing experiment in agriculture, the Attine ants of South America had already long since perfected it – cultivating vast fungus beds in underground chambers in their nests, seeding carefully tended gardens with the clones of a fungus that linked back more than thirty million years.

Another species of ant, Lasius flaws, managed large flocks of domesticated aphids. The aphids were kept in subterranean corrals where they grew mature and succulent, grazing the roots of plants. And were then milked for their nutrient-rich honeydew.

Some termite mounds sprawled more than thirty feet in diameter, housing tens of millions of individuals, all bound up in a single sophisticated caste system. Soldiers of Macrotermes bellicosus developed jaws so huge that they could no longer be used in feeding; instead they relied on teams of lower-caste workers to lift sustenance to their mouths.

Insects build cities, and farms and superhighways. Slant your eyes and look hard enough, and you'll see a level of social sophistication that can only be described as civilization.

Bell had often thought that humans had achieved their conspicuous position in the world not because of how perfectly adapted they were, but because of how weak, how clumsy, how fragile they were. How unsuited to existence.

One species of dairying ant secreted an enzyme from their heads that was carefully rubbed onto each aphid during the milking process. The enzyme disrupted wing development, preventing their aphids from ever flying away.

Where humans came up with external solutions – like building fences – insects often found a more elegant solution. A biological solution.

They'd had the time to do it.

Determined and cautious, Bell fed the grubs every day and wrote down his observations.

But still, Cole was the one who noticed it.

When Bell finally understood, his mouth dropped open. "Holy shit," he said.

He looked at his notes.

He'd fed the insects one of three different diets. The insects which, as grubs, had eaten bread did not now have wings, but stunted twists of chitin. Their color was dull red, like rust. More beetle-like, less wasp. Now, as adults, they still preferred bread. The fruit-eaters still ate fruit. They were large-bodied and short limbed, with stumpy wings that buzzed loudly as it made awkward flights inside the terrarium. Bell could imagine them making those same flights between distant stands of fruit.

The meat eater was the most strange. Blood red, with wings like blades – mouth parts huge and angular.

"They adapted," Bell said. "They adapted to the food sources they ate as grubs." Bell shook his head in disbelief.

"Fast learners," Cole said. Then he moved as if to stick an experimental finger in the meat-eater cage, but Bell said, "Don't."

Seana, when he showed her the hatchlings, said, "Can that happen?"

"There it is," he said. But in his heart of hearts, he knew she was right to doubt. Like a million years of evolution in a single generation. No species adapts that quickly. It was a bad movie. Junk science. Not possible.

"But there it is," he repeated.

The insects lived for more than a month. They buzzed, or crawled of flitted around their cages. Over the course of a single week the following month, they took turns dying.

The meat eater lived longest. After each die-off, Bell found egg-cases. He cleaned the terrariums, and put the egg cases back inside. Then he waited to see what would hatch.

* * *

Late one evening, Seana climbed up the ladder while he was in the barn loft at the petting zoo, checking the hay for rot. Climbed up and stood behind him until he turned around, then stood on her toes and kissed him.

If the zoo hadn't been closed and nearly deserted, if Bell hadn't known for sure that no one was likely to venture into the petting zoo, let alone climb into the loft, then maybe it would have happened differently. Maybe Bell would have kissed her back, because kissing would have been all that could happen.

But the zoo was closed. Bell did know. And it did happen the way it happened.

"I can't," he said.

She pulled away.

"I want to," he said.

She looked at him, waiting.

Beneath them, the horses shuffled. Made noises. Kicked their stall doors and talked to each other in soft equine language.

He thought of Lin, home in their trailer. "I can't," he said again.

A black mood seized Bell on the way home. He drove the darkening highway, following his headlights into space. He pushed the old beater faster, watching the speedometer climb to seventy, then eighty. He took the curves without easing off the accelerator. The tires squealed, but held the road.

His mind was a movie of loves and hates. He loved and hated his job. Loved the animals, but hated the conditions. Hated that he couldn't afford to live on what he was paid. When you're young, he thought, they tell you that if you get a degree, everything else will fall into place. But it's not that simple, is it?

Nothing – not one thing – had worked out like it was supposed to.

He thought of life at home, a second maze of contradiction. He was tired of being alone and together at the same time. He wanted to be free, but there was no freedom. No way out. He felt like an animal with a trapped limb. He understood why animals chew their own legs off. He had a recurring fantasy of being robbed, and putting up a struggle. If he were held up at gunpoint, he had decided, he would not cooperate.

He didn't know what to think of Seana, yet. So he didn't, at all.

Red like rupture. Blood squirm, a coagulation of grubs across brown terrarium stones. The egg cases pulsed like clotted hearts, spilling strange new life. Bell stared through the glass. Each cage told the same story.

The grubs were a centimeter long. Even as small as they were, Bell could see the mouth parts working. Each grub identical. As far as he could see, the differences which had been so apparent from cage to cage in the adult form were now absent from the next generation. The grubs were all the same, as if a reset button had been pushed. It was only the adult form that seemed vulnerable to change. Bell opened his sack lunch. He took out his apple and sliced it into a dozen pieces. He dropped a slice into the first cage. The grubs responded immediately, moving toward the fruit. They swarmed it.

Bell fed the grubs first thing in the morning.

He decided to turn it into an experiment. He stole a sheet of sticky-labels from the staff room and stuck a label to the side of six different terrariums. On each label, he wrote a different word.

The grubs labeled fruit were fed fruit; the grubs labeled meat were fed sliced-meat. The grubs labeled control were fed a mixture of foods.

The grubs with the cool sticker on the side of their terrarium were fed the control diet – but were also placed in refrigerator for an hour a day while Bell did his chores. An hour wasn't long enough to kill them, but it was long enough to impact their physiology. They grew slower than the grubs in the other cages.

If these insects could really adapt to their environments, Bell was going to see how far he could push it.

He'd see if diet was the only pressure they responded to.

The grubs labeled heat were in a small glass aquarium placed on the floor near a space heater. Bell put his hands against the glass. It was hot to the touch. These grubs, too, seemed stressed by the temperature. But they still grew, doubling in size every week.

The grubs labeled carrion were fed the occasional discarded rat from the golden eagle enclosure. These were the grubs Bell found most interesting. They borrowed into the dead rat and ate it from the inside out.

Charles Darwin had believed in God until he studied the parasitic wasp Ibalia. Darwin wrote in a journal: "There seems to me too much misery in the world. I cannot persuade myself that a beneficent and omnipotent God would have designedly created wasps with the express intention of their feeding within the living bodies of caterpillars." Darwin found particularly gruesome that the Ibalia grub only gradually consumed the living tissues of its host – taking a full three years to complete its meal, saving the vital organs until last as if to extend the host's suffering. Darwin couldn't imagine a God who would create something like that.

Bell could imagine it.

He thought of the reset mechanism. He imagined a single insect species with multiple phenotypes already encoded in its genome – a catalogue of different possible adult forms. And all it took was a trigger to set the creature down its path.

"Maybe it's like blind cave fish," he told Seana one evening.

He watched Seana's face as she peered through the glass.

"Cave fish have most of the genes for eyes still carried in their DNA," he said. "All the genes required for lenses, and retinas and eyelids, all the genes except for the one crucial ingredient that starts eye development in the first place. If you cross-breed two different populations of blind fish, sometimes you get fish with eyes."

"That doesn't make sense," Seana said.

"It does if the blindness is recessive, and the two populations are blind for different reasons."

"But you said these things aren't breeding."

Bell ignored her, lost in thought. "Or they're like stem cells," he continued, "each carrying the genes for multiple tissue types, multiple potentials, but they specialize as they mature, choosing a path."

He leaned forward, tapping his finger on the glass.

"Where do you think they come from?" Seana asked.

"The fruit maybe. The bananas. Central America. I'm not sure."

"Why can't you find it in books?"

"There are millions of insect species still un-described by science. Besides, maybe it has been described. Some version of it. I mean, how would you really know?"

Later, searching for reasons to avoid going home, Bell ran down his closing checklist twice.

On his second round, he found the outer door to the lemur tunnel wide open.

He had locked it himself. Checked it himself.

His inner alarm went off.

Zookeepers developed inner alarms, or they developed scars.

He stepped through the door, and let his eyes adjust to the dark, to the long, mildewy tunnel which ran under the moat, to the lemur island.

At the end of the tunnel, bright light, because the door at the island end was open, too.

In the middle, a silhouette. Who . . . ?

"Hey!" Bell shouted.

Several silhouettes. Sharp, jabbering shadows. Five or six lemurs hopped and shrieked.

The shadow in the middle wound up like a pitcher and threw something.

A yelp. The lemurs howled and ran.

"Cole?" called Bell, starting down the tunnel.

One lemur didn't run. It whirled in confusion, chattering.

Bell's eyes had adjusted. The shadow grew details. Cole.

Cole, with a handful of smooth, white landscaping stones, eyes wide with rage.

"What the fuck are you doing?" Bell shouted.

"They threw shit at me. They threw their fucking shit."

"Jesus Christ—!" Bell yelled, lurching forward.

Cole turned, arm pistoning in the dark.

The stone whistled past Bell's ear and struck hard against the outer door. The tunnel echoed.

Bell froze.

Cole stepped toward him. "You watch how you talk to me," he said, and for a moment they stared at each other, waiting to see what would happen. Then Cole's eyes changed – the rage blown out of them like a gust of wind. Cole brushed past him and was gone.

The lemur groped its way back into the light, back to the island.

Bell unfroze, closed up, and said nothing. He'd have to say something, wouldn't he? Something would have to be done. Right?

He made a mental note. In the future, he wouldn't let crazy people into his life. He meant it.

Metamorphosis is magic. Darwin had know this, too.

Sometimes it is a dark magic.

The metamorphosis of a tadpole into a frog. A grub into a wasp. A friend into an enemy.

Bell watched the grubs feed. By now they'd grown huge. Some approached five inches in length, blood red, large beyond all reason. Soon they would spin their papery cocoons. Turn into whatever they would turn into.

Bell pondered the advantage of such an adaptive mechanism. Perhaps it was a way to guard against overspecialization, a reservoir of adaptive potential. Evolution is a slow process, and when conditions change, populations take time to react. There is a lag; species that don't change fast enough die out.

Bell knew of several kinds of island lizard that reproduced parthenogenetically. Such species, when found, were always young, isolated, at risk. They were aberrations outside the main thrust of evolution. Most were doomed, in the long run, because sexual reproduction is a much better way to create the next generation. In sexual reproduction, genes mix and match, new phenotypes arise, gene frequencies shift like tides. Sexual reproduction shuffles the genetic deck from one generation to the next.

Parthenogenetic species, on the other hand, are locked-in, playing the same card over and over.

But not the insects in the back room.

The insects in the back room seemed to have a whole deck from which to deal, parthenogenetic or not. Such insects could adapt quickly, shifting morphotypes in a single generation. And then shift back the next. It was the next logical step – not just evolution, but the evolution of evolution. But how was it possible?

Bell thought of Cole, of what made men like him. That old argument, nature vs. nurture. In another time, in another place, Cole would have fit in. In another time, maybe Cole would have been a different person entirely.

The descendents of Vikings and Mongols today wore suits and ran corporations. Were veterinarians, or plumbers, or holy men. Perhaps tomorrow, or a thousand years from now, they'll need to be Vikings and Mongols again.

Populations change. Needs change. Optimums change. And it all changes faster than selection can track.

From a biological perspective, it would be easy to produce the same kind of people again and again. Stable people. Good people. Again and again, generation after generation – a one to one correlation between gene-set and expression.

But that's not what you find when you look at humans.

Instead there is a plasticity in human nature. A carefully calibrated susceptibility to trauma.

What looks like a weak point in our species is in fact design.

Because the truth is that certain childhoods are supposed to fuck you up. It is an adaptive response. Wired into us.

The ones who couldn't adapt died out. Those gene sets which always produced the same kind of people – stable people, good people – no matter the environment, no matter the violence – those gene sets which always played the same card, again and again –

– died out.

Leaving behind the ones who could metamorphose.

We were not so different from these bugs.

Bell unloaded all this on Seana one day during lunch. They sat across from each other, sipping soft drinks. "The evolution of evolution?"

"Yeah," he said.

"Why would this happen in insects?" she asked.

"Because they've been here longest," he said. But it was more than that. He thought of the ants and their aphids. The enzyme that clipped their wings. He thought of the different ways that insects solved their problems. "Because insects always choose the biological solution."

Bell avoided Cole for days.

He told himself he was waiting for a good time to see the director, to tell her what had happened in the lemur tunnel. Told himself he wasn't afraid that Cole would retaliate by telling about drinking together on zoo time, zoo property. Both were lies, but what he had the toughest time with was pure simple fear of Cole.

"Ridiculous," he told himself. "You're a grown man and a professional."

On the other hand, Cole obviously was dangerous.

Maybe he could get Cole to leave, to resign his service contract without anyone having to tell the director anything.

This seemed, on reflection, to be the best bet for an outcome where he, Bell, kept his job and got rid of the problem.

The reflection took place at home, on the sofa, in front of the TV, in his underwear.

When Lin crossed the room, he saw himself through her eyes. He looked like a bum.

She was thinking, he knew, what an asshole he was for buying beer.

He didn't care.

Neither did she, it seemed.

She sat down on the couch beside him.

What was he? When had he turned into a person who said nothing, did nothing? What had he let himself turn into?

*   *   *

The next day, Bell followed Cole down to the supply shed and said, "We're going to have a talk."

Cole took a set of eight-foot pruning shears down from the wall rack, and turned to face Bell.

"Yeah," he said.

Bell fumbled for a beginning, forgetting what he'd rehearsed.

Cole began whistling. He leaned on the pruning shears as if they were a wizard's staff.

"I have to turn you in," Bell said.

"For what?"

"Throwing rocks at the animals."

Cole stared at him. His grip on the shears tightened. "I lose my temper sometimes. I have a temper, I admit."

"That's why you can't be here."

"Listen, I'll work on it. I'll be better."

Cole shook his head. "I'm just letting you know as a courtesy. I have to report it."

"You don't have to do anything."

"The other choice is that you leave today and don't come back."

"That's not any choice at all."

"There are other places you can do your service."

"I like it here."

"Here doesn't like you anymore."

"You know what I don't like? I don't think I like you trying to push me around."

"Today is your last day here, one way or the other," Bell said. "You can leave on your own, or you can be ushered out."

"You really don't want to do that."

"You're right, I don't," Bell said.

Cole's face changed. "I'm warning you."

Bell raised his walkie-talkie, never taking his eyes off Cole. "Garland," he spoke into the handset. There was a squelch, then a voice, "Yeah."

"You better come to the supply shed."

"What's wrong?"

"Now, Garland."

Cole shoved Bell into the wall. Shoved him hard, so his teeth clacked.

And the rage was there again in the cutting torch eyes. Rage like nothing else mattered. Scarred hands curled into Bell's shirt.

"This is your last chance," Cole said.

Bell only smiled, feeling something shift inside him. He found suddenly that he was through being scared. "Fuck you," he said.

Bell ducked the first blow, but the second caught him upside the head, splitting his brow open. Bell spun away, throwing an elbow that missed, and then they were both off balance, taking wild swings, and Cole grabbed at him, and they were falling. They hit the ground and rolled, wrestling for on the filthy floor. Cole came up on top, sitting on Bell's legs. "I fucking warned you," he hissed, and then he rained down punches until Garland tackled him.

After that, it was two on one, and Bell didn't feel the least bit guilty about that.

The zoo super interviewed Bell for her report. They sat in her office. Behind her, against the wall, her fish swam their little circles. The superintendent leaned forward and laced her hands together on her desk.

She didn't dig very deep. Seemed to think Cole's behavior was its own explanation. "I think you need stitches," she said.

Bell nodded. He touched his brow. His first zoo scar.

"He'll be barred from the zoo, of course," she said. "And I'll insist that his community service hours be revoked."

"What's going to happen to him now?"

"Charges probably."

"I don't want to press charges."

"Animal cruelty. The lemurs. He's going back to jail." She paused, then added, "When they find him."

Bell looked at the fish, swimming in the aquarium. "He said he's never going back."

That evening, as he was closing up, Bell found Cole's parting gift. Found it revealed, at first, in the presence of a door ajar.

The back room of the castle.

After the fight, Cole had climbed to his feet, wiped the blood from his face – and then walked off. Heading toward the gates. Even two on one, the fight had been about even, and when Cole had finally stepped back, wiped the blood from his face, and walked away, Bell and Gavin let him go. A draw. They'd assumed Cole left zoo property. But he hadn't left.

He'd circled back around to the castle.

And he'd poured lye into each and every terrarium.

Several grubs were on the cement floor, ground into pulp with a boot.

Others were desiccated husks. Only a few still moved, writhing in the white powder. Bell stepped further into the room, surveying the carnage. He should have known. He should have known this was coming.

Bell's inner alarm started bothering him on his way home that night.

Once a zookeeper developed an inner alarm, it worked everywhere.

In this case, it was less an alarm than a sense of something out of place. It got stronger as he closed in on the trailer park. At first he thought the alarm had something to do with Cole, but when he got home, he understood. The universe had an interesting sense of timing.

Lin was gone.

Not like gone to the store. Gone, left. Leaving him.

She left a note about it. The note explained. Blamed him.

Distantly, he heard himself curse.

All Bell could think, at first, was that she didn't seem to have taken anything. Like there was nothing about their life worth bothering with. She had written the whole thing off, it seemed. Him. Their life. A total loss.

He made some growling noises.

She might be back. She might change her mind.

The stereo, after all, was really hers. She'd had it before they moved in together, and they'd never been able to afford a new one.

Somberly, he unplugged the stereo. In something like a trance, he planted it in the sink and turned on the water. Like a zombie, he let the water run and started searching the trailer for enough change to buy beer.

The next month passed in a haze.

Word filtered down, as word always did, and it turned out Cole had skipped town. The cops were still looking.

Not many of the grubs had survived Cole's attack. The ones that did were scarred. Cole had been very thorough, even pouring lye in the terrarium on the floor. In all, only a handful of the grubs finished their cocoons. A few from the control cage. A few from the terrarium marked "heat." But they were twisted things, these cocoons. Damaged things. His experiment was ruined. His hope was that he'd be able to get at least a few reproducing adults, start over. If the cocoons hatched at all.

And word had filtered down, too, that it would be bad for Cole when he was caught, because the list of charges had grown, and the warrant had sprouted teeth. Cole was facing time, real time, for what had happened. Bell knew Cole would need someone to blame.

He would blame Bell, and he would blame the zoo.

Several weeks later, Bell pulled into the parking lot and found there were fire trucks already in the lot. Hoses ran upward along the hill. Black smoke curled into the sky. Bell ran. He knew what he'd see before he saw it. The castle was engulfed in flame. The firefighters fought the blaze, but Bell knew it was too late. He imagined the animals inside baking. He imagined the sizzle and pop of burst skin, the soundless cries of dying snakes and lizards and frogs and bugs. He imagined his insects burning alive.

He looked around, searching for Cole, wondering if he'd stayed long enough to watch it burn.

When the fire was out, Bell walked through the ruins. The devastation was complete. Dead frogs and snakes and lizards. In the back room, he found the terrariums blackened and cracked. The insects inside charred and unrecognizable.

Except for one. The terrarium on the floor.

The terrarium with the heat sticker, now curled and blackened.

The cocoon was charred, split wide by the heat.

There was no grub inside.

*   *   *

They found Cole's body later that day in the weeds behind the parking lot. Bell watched them load the body into the ambulance. Dark and swollen. It had been a bad death.

There were burns, minor, across his hands, like he'd come too close to his creation.

Burns and something else.

Something like stings.

Eyes swollen shut, anaphylactic shock.

Not everything burned in the fire.

Not all that burns is consumed. Cole had said that once.

Bell stood there for a long time, listening. Listening for a buzz like an electric light, but there was no sound. Only the sound of wind in the trees.

It was long gone, whatever it was. He just wished he could have seen what the grub had turned into. Next year it would be different.

Next year it would be a fruit eater, or a wasp, or a beetle. It would be what it needed to be.

It would be what the world made it.

Approaching home, Bell felt his inner alarm stir again.

The cable had been turned off.

Those cocksuckers didn't know who they were dealing with. Bell had gotten drunk two nights in a row now, and he was feeling mean, feeling predatory.

He stalked outside, nine trailers down to the cable box, opened it up with a hex wrench, and hooked his cable back up.

Went home and surfed channels for anything resembling porn.

After two hours of this, his thumb hurt and the battery on the remote died.

He heard the screen door open.

Lin?

In the moment before the inner door opened, it occurred to him that her stereo was still soaking in the kitchen sink. He had a momentary, fearful impulse; his leg jerked. Then the beer kicked back in. He slouched back. He sneered like a sleepy lion.

A shape in a doorway.

Seana.

His sneer disappeared.

She stepped inside and said nothing. Looked at him a moment, as if reading him. Slouched down beside him with a sack of takeout chicken.

His hand, heavy and lazy, rested on her leg.

She tugged his hand higher.

They didn't talk. Even the TV flashed in silence.

Outside the thin walls, the world licked itself and made hunting noises.

THIS WIND BLOWING, AND THIS TIDE

Damien Broderick

Here's a fascinating study of the border country between science and the paranormal, where remote-viewing psychics take us a little further afield than usual – all the way out to the frozen wastes of Titan.

Australian writer, editor, futurist, and critic Damien Broderick, a Senior Fellow in the School of Cultural Commincations at the University of Melbourne, made his first sale in 1964 to John Carnell's anthology *New Writings in SF 1*. In the decades that followed, he has kept up a steady stream of fiction, nonfiction, futurist speculations, and critical work, which has won him multiple Ditmar and Aurealis awards. He sold his first novel, *Sorcerer's World*, in 1970; it was later reissued in a rewritten version in the United States as *The Black Grail*. Broderick's other books include the novels *The Dreaming Dragons*, *The Judas Mandala*, *Transmitters*, *Striped Holes*, and *The White Abacus*, as well as books written with Rory Barnes and Barbara Lamar. His many short stories have been collected in *A Man Returns*, *The Dark Between the Stars*, *Uncle Bones: Four Science Fiction Novellas*, and the upcoming *The Quilla Engine: Science Fiction Stories*. He also wrote the visionary futurist classic *The Spike: How Our Lives Are Being Transformed by Rapidly Advancing Technology*, a critical study of science fiction, *Reading by Starlight: Postmodern Science Fiction*, edited the nonfiction anthology *Year Million: Science at the Far End of Knowledge*, as well as editing the SF anthology *Earth Is But a Star: Excursions Through Science Fiction to the Far Future*, and three anthologies of Australian science fiction, *The Zeitgeist Machine*, *Strange Attractors*, and *Matilda at the Speed of Light*. Broderick also serves as the fiction editor for the Australian science magazine *Cosmos*, which publishes a science fiction story per issue.

"Has any one else had word of him?"
Not this tide.
For what is sunk will hardly swim,
Not with this wind blowing, and this tide.
          – "My Boy Jack," Rudyard Kipling (1915)

T HE STARSHIP WAS old, impossibly old, and covered in flowers. Despite
a brisk methane breeze, not a petal nor a stamen of the bright blooms
moved. Under an impervious shield, they remained motionless, uncor-
rupted, altogether untouchable.

"They're alive," reported the Navy remote viewer. When I was a kid,
the idea that the armed services might employ a trained, technologically
enhanced psychic would have got you a derisive smack in the ear from your
elders and betters, even though the American CIA ran a remote viewing
program called Star Gate back in the last century, before they ostentatiously
closed it down and took it to black ops. This viewer was blind to light, but
saw better than the rest of us, by other means, on a good day. Like me, sort
of, in my own itchy way.

He stood at the edge of the huge, flower-bedecked vessel, gloved, open
palms held outward, his hands vibrating ever so slightly, like insect antennae
hunting a pheromone. "It's amazing. Those blossoms are still alive, after . . .
what . . . millions of years? I can't find my way in yet, but I can detect that
much even through the stationary shield."

"Is that the same as a, you know, stasis field?" I asked the marine master
sergeant standing guard beside us. I turned to face her, and bobbed sicken-
ingly. Two days ago I had been on Ganymede, and on Earth's Moon before
that. Now I walked on another world entirely, around yet another world
entirely. It wasn't right for a man as ample as I to weigh so little, especially
with Titan's bruised-peach air pushing down on me half again as heavily as
Earth's. It went against nature. Even with the bodyglove wrapping me, and
an air tank on my back, I only weighed about 18 kilos – say 40 lbs. A tenth
of what the scales would show back home.

" 'Stasis' my ass! That's sci-fi nonsense," she barked. "Media technobabble. Like your own—" She bit the rest of her sentence off, perhaps
fortunately. "This here is hard science."

"So sorry."

"And please don't speak again without an invitation to do so, Sensei Park.
We don't want to put Mr Meagle off his stroke."

Opening his startlingly blue, blind eyes, the Navy viewer laughed. The
sound echoed oddly in his bodyglove and through our sound loop. All
sounds did, out on the orange-snowy surface of Titan. "Let him natter on,
Marion. I'm entangled now. You'd have to cut my head off and pith my
spine to unhook me from this baby."

I wondered idly how either of them would respond if I told them I was
the reason, or at the proximate occasion, that they were here. They'd regard
me as a madman, probably. My role in developing the portage functor was
under cover about as deep as any since the creation of the US Office of
Strategic Services in 1945, long before the CIA got tight with clairvoyants.
Perhaps these people already did consider me deluded. Yeah, it was true that
I'd told them where to look for the starship, but it wasn't as I had the credentials of a remote viewer, so undoubtedly it was just an accident. Right.

I felt the pressure of the thing, its causal gravitas, as I gazed down at the starship. If that's what it was, under its stationary shield and floral tribute.

This thing on Titan had been tugging at me, at my absurd and uncomfortable and highly classified gift, since I was four or five years old, running in the streets of Seoul, playing with a Red Devils soccer ball and picking up English and math. A suitable metaphor for the way a child might register the substrate of a mad universe, and twist its tail. My own son, little Song-Dam, plagued me with questions when he, too, was a kid, no older than I'd been when the starship buried under tons of frozen methane and ethane had plucked for the first time at my stringy loops.

"If light's a wave, Daddy, can I surf on it?" Brilliant, lovely child! "No, darling son," I said. "Well, not exactly. It's more like a Mexican football wave, it's more like an explosion of excitement that blows up." I pulled a big-eyed face and flung my arms in the air and dropped them down. "Boom!" Song laughed, but then his mouth drooped. "If it's a wave, Dad, why do some people say it's made of packets?" "Well," said I, "you know that a football wave is made of lots and lots of team supporters, jumping up and sitting down again." He wasn't satisfied, and neither was I, but the kid was only five years old.

Later, I thought of that wave, sort of not there at all at one end, then plumping up in the middle, falling to nothing again as it moved on. Follow it around the bleachers and you've got a waveform particle moving fast. Kind of. But for a real photon, you needn't follow it, it's already there, its onboard time is crushed and compressed from the moment of launch to the final absorption, just one instantaneous blip in a flattened, timeless universe. Why, you could jump to the Moon, or Ganymede, or even Titan, all in a flash. Just entangle yourself with it, if you knew how (as I showed them how, much later), like Mr Meagle remote viewing his impenetrable stationary starship.

Physics – you're soaking in it!

"I can likely get more now sitting in my relaxation cell back at Huygens," Meagle said. He looked very calm, as if he'd just stepped out of an immersion tank, but there was a faint quivering around his blind eyes. I watched his face in my viewmask, as if neither of us wore gloves over our heads. The man was exhausted. "So tell me, Mr Park," he said, as we turned and made our way to the big-wheeled jitney, "what were your own impressions, sir?" Scrupulous about not front-loading me with hints of his own; I liked that.

"Anyone, or any thing, who loves flowers that much," I said judiciously, "can't be all bad."

Huygens had provided me with a customized broad-beamed sanitary personal; I have authoritative hams, and a wide stance. It degloved me with slick efficiency. I relieved myself with a gratified sigh. While bodygloves have the capacity to handle such impositions of the mortal order, the experience is undignified and leaves a residual aroma trapped inside with one's nostrils, so I tend to hold on. We had been outside for hours without a pit stop. The sanitary squirted and dabbed, removed sweat from my perspiring hide with its dry tongue, dusted powder across the expanse, set me free. I dressed in my usual unflattering robe, and made my way directly to the commissary bubble. I was starving.

Banally, the wall and ceiling display showed a faux of thrice-magnified Saturn, four hand-widths across, tilted optimally to show off the gorgeous ring system. I'd just seen the reality outside, with nothing between me and the ringed planet itself but a protective film and a million or so kilometers of naked space above the bright Xanadu regional surface where we'd stood. Since we were almost at the equator, Saturn's belt had been a thin glitter in the photomultipliers in our bodyglove masks (and would be invisible to the naked eye), directly overhead, right and left of the primary's waist, not truly impressive. Of course, even with the high frequency step-downs of the photomultipliers, the atmosphere looks hazy anyway.

This magisterial feed on the wall was probably coming, today, from one of the polar sats keeping an eye on the big feller. It seemed to me a bit tacky, a lame pretence, but then again, Titan is tidally locked, so it must get a tad wearying for the regular staff, seeing exactly the same thing in the sky forever, whatever installation dome you're at, Huygens, or Herschel at the north pole. Except that nothing is ever the same; all is nuance, the slow fortnightly progression of light and shade, the phases of the Sun's illumination of the big ball of gas . . . Well, these were scientists and military, most of them, what could we expect?

I loaded my tray with rather edible Boeuf Bourguignon from the dedicated cuisine printer, took it to a table where a handful of my new colleagues were chowing and jawing away, sat down at the spare place, set to after a genial glance around. At least with the queasy low gravity I wasn't worried that this spindly conventional chair would give way abruptly beneath me, tipping my considerable butt ungraciously to the floor. It had been known to happen back on Earth. Nobody laughed derisively if it did, at least there was that. Not any more, they didn't.

"Why, Sensei," said the Japanese biologist, Natasha Hsai, with the slightest edge in her tone, "won't you join us for dinner?" I do not give her title, nor do I mean any disrespect; all these eggheads had at least a couple of doctorates apiece, it went without saying.

"Why, Natasha, thank you, I believe I will." I started in on my second pearl onion. "Good fare, they don't stint you – nor should they, you are doing sterling work out here."

Several of the boffins shared glances, perhaps amused. They fancy themselves a cut above.

The handsome dark-haired fellow at the head of the table cleared his throat. "So, have you been outside yet to pay your respects to the Enigma, Mr Park?"

From the dossiers I'd memorized before leaving Jupiter space, I recognized him, beneath his heavy straggled beard, as the head of molecular engineering, Antonio Caetani. "Just got back from the tour, Dr Caetani. Fascinating. Right up my street."

"That's Tony," he said gracelessly. More glances flickered about the table. He chose to go right for it. Had to give him points for that. "Unless I'm mistaken, your street is paved with donations from the ID Institute."

I had encountered this kind of feral attitude previously, of course, especially from hard-headed scientists of conventional stamp. I could even share a kind of empathy for his rancor. It was as if, from his highly-credentialed point of view, a government-sponsored raving crackpot were to be imposed on his team. As if a SETI astronomer in the Fermi Taskforce had been obliged to include an rectally-probed UFO abductee, or a global proteome program forced to sign up a fundamentalist creationist. I shrugged.

"Oh, give the guy a break, Tony," said the Iranian artifact expert, Mansour Khosrojerdi. "Let him eat his meal." His beard was darker and thicker even than Caetani's. Granted, the temperature was nearly minus 200 degrees Celsius on the other side of the bubble, but this was self-mythologizing on a preposterous scale. Did they imagine they were rehearsing the doomed expeditions of the Arctic explorers? "We can postpone the ideological catfights until after the cheese and Amontillado."

"No need to spare my delicate sensibilities," I said with a hearty laugh, and reached for the carafe of red wine, luminous as a garnet under spurious golden Saturn light. The woman to my right, the string loop specialist Jendayi Shumba, got there first with her competent, chunky hand, dark as night.

"Allow me, Sensei Park."

"You are gracious, thanks. But let's all be friends, no need for formality, call me Myeong-hui." I grinned with big teeth at her dismay, then laughed out loud. "No, that's an impossible mouthful, it's all right, just call me Sam, love. Everyone does."

"Sam." A slightly uncomfortable silence fell. Scrapings of plastic flatware on realistic plates. I gobbled up my tasty beef, placed the empty plate back on my tray, slurped off some more of the stunningly convincing compiled Shiraz, took a bite of a lemon-ginger dessert to die for, decorated with pistachios. "Fermi-53, that's my considered opinion," I said with my mouth full. "My tentative, preliminary opinion, naturally."

"There are no recognizable roses or jonquils or violets or orchids, obviously. But the flowers scattered over the vehicle certainly do appear to be derived from Earth angiosperms, specialized to a range of climates and coevolutionary biomes," said Natasha Hsai. "So far as we can tell purely from visual inspection."

"Which rules out Fermi-53 instantly," Antonio Caetani said. "Blossoms of such complexity and beauty did not evolve on Earth until the Holocene. Probably not until humans deliberately bred the cultivars during the rise of agriculture."

"Oh, let's not over-simplify, Tony," Natasha said. "Pollinator insects and hummers and lizards and all the rest, they speciated along with the angiosperms; they sculpted each other without any help. Yes, I grant you, early humans broke up the soil to an unprecedented extent so they could grow their dinner, and then as a sideline retained and cultivated those blossoms that especially . . . well, made them happy. They're our botanical pets, now, because flowers make us smile and feel good. They induce positive emotions."

"They're scented sex organs," Caetani said, "doing their job."

I'd finished eating, for the moment. "The first flowering plants," I pointed out, "evolved sixty-five million years prior to the Chicxulub catastrophe. Nice symmetry, that." As far back in time before the extinction of the dinosaurs as we now stood after it. I didn't need to spell that out; these were, after all, highly trained intellects. But I had to add the obvious, the intolerable, the all-but-unthinkable crux. "Humans, I remind you, were not the only cultivators." I found I had no appetite for cheese, and pushed back my chair. "Do you allow smoking here? Anyone for cigars and port?"

"No," said Caetani brusquely. "Sensei Park, we are scientists, not mystagogues. I confess myself bewildered by your presence at Huygens." Jendayi Shumba pulled at his sleeve; he shook her off. "I am frankly offended that the Imperium invited a quack from the Intelligent Dinosaur Institute here to Titan." Shumba kicked his leg under the table; I saw and felt the small causal shock of her intention and its manifestation, because that's who I am, that's what I do. "I have nothing more to say to you." He looked away disdainfully, drew his own dessert plate in front of him, scooped up a heaping spoonful of tiramisu and shoved it into his left eye, hard.

I raised one eyebrow, sighed, and rose, gathered my soiled crockery and plasticware on the tray, and walked away from the table. He probably wouldn't lose the sight in his eye. But what could I do?

Speaking technically, I'm an etiological distortion. Less pompously, there's something buried deep inside me that screws with cause and effect. I'm a footloose bubble of improbability. Call me a witch or a freak if you'd prefer, it rolls more easily off the tongue. Chances are good, though, that if you do call me nasty names, and I get to hear about it, you'll trip over the kid's bike in the dark, or run into an opening door, and break something painful. It's not that I harbor resentment at name-calling, but my unconscious seems to. As I say, not much I can do about that, sorry.

There were ructions and alarums but I brushed them off, went to bed and slept, as I had done every night for five years, like a damned soul. My gift or curse does not permit me to stand aside from that which wraps me like a shroud. Sorrow eddied in my dreams. My son—

—and as so often, these days, the booming, tolling voices came to me from a century and a half past, voices I have heard only in my head, reading their words on the pages of old books I found in an abandoned library, stinking with the reek of extinguished fires, where I had crept for silence like a heavy old dog with a wound too great to bear. The words were in

English, that tongue almost as familiar to me as my own, picked up in the streets, later honed in special classes for promising children. I knew nothing of the writer, save that he was a man of substance in his place and time. His words raised a resonance in my burned soul. He must have known this same agony, and sought some bitter draught of comfort:

> O Sorrow, cruel fellowship,
> O Priestess in the vaults of Death,
> O sweet and bitter in a breath,
> What whispers from thy lying lip?
> "The stars," she whispers, "blindly run;
> A web is wov'n across the sky;
> From out waste places comes a cry,
> And murmurs from the dying sun:
> "And all the phantom, Nature, stands –
> With all the music in her tone,
> A hollow echo of my own, –
> A hollow form with empty hands."

And woke in the morning (by the conventional Earth clock calibrated to Seoul time, GMT+9 hours), as always alone, empty hollow form and all, despite the web wov'n palpably across the sky, and ravenously hungry, as usual.

So I ate a healthy breakfast and went to watch Meagle on closed circuit, a feed from the audiovisual record that military remote viewers are obliged to make for assessment, interpretation, and the archive. Today he sat zazen in a small cell like a non-denominational chapel, if chapels come with voice-activated holography displays (and maybe they do, I'm not a religious man), hands curled upward on his knees. His breathing was slow, regular. Maybe this was what their protocol called cooling down. His blind eyes were open, apparently fixed on the deep blue depths of the holly. Upon his head was a crown of thorns, a tidy maze of squid detectors pulsing to the quantum state of his brain, his brain stem, his meditative consciousness.

"Looking at the vehicle from above," he murmured. "Still can't find my way in. Yet." His lips quirked the smallest amount. Who Dares Wins, I thought. Semper Fi. Rah-rah. Well, it took a lot of quiet confidence in one's oddball abilities, no doubt. My own kind of disreputable ability just happened to me, or around me.

"Get back to the signal line," a gravelly voice said. Someone not in the room. His controller, I supposed. His operator, whatever they called the role.

"He's physically blind, I realise that," I told the medical officer seated beside me in the observation booth, "but doesn't knowing the identity of the target sort of pollute his, his guesswork?"

"The viewer does not guess."

"No offense. I mean, bias him unconsciously with preconceived notions?" Front-loading, they called it; I knew that much. "Like that stasis field thingee?

Can we be sure that's not some scrap of nonsense from a comic strip he read when he was a child?"

"Mr Meagle is well past all such neophyte hazards," the nurse said, offended by my uppity kvetching. He had gray hair at his close-cropped temples, and a steady gaze. Almost certainly a veteran of the war in – I shut that thought down, hard. "The colonel can afford to depart from the lock-step of traditional protocol. As he does when it suits him." I nodded, made soothing, conciliatory sounds. Perhaps mollified, he explained, "It contracts the search path polynomially."

"Um," I said, and settled back to view the sketched images form, dissolve, reform in the imaginary three-space of the holograms. As Meagle's fingers moved through the air, unseen lasers tracked the shapes he sketched. It seemed, watching him, that he actually felt his way around the starship out there in the frozen crust of Titan. Kinesthetic imagery. A kind of heightened physicality, perhaps unavailable to a sighted person. Or was that nothing better than my whimsy, my fat man's sentimentality?

"Moving downward, gravity tugs at me," the remote viewer murmured. His voice was drowsy. I saw his shoulders spasm, as if he were falling forward and had caught himself.

"Wake up, there, colonel," the voice said, without reproach. "You're drifting."

"He's sliding into Phase Two. That was hypnic myoclonia," the nurse commented. "Jactitation."

"Haven't slept since yesterday," Meagle muttered. He shook himself. "Okay. Got it. I'm in."

The screens, trying to emulate whatever it was the psychic was "seeing/feeling," bloomed with a burst of visual noise. Were those things sketchy blocks of cells, like the hexagonal innards of a bee hive? They shrank, jittered, smoothed into a kind of curvy passageway. The image was being enhanced by the computer's analysis, drawing on an archive of Meagle's private symbols.

"Analytical overlay," the operator said in a tone of admonition.

"I don't—No, this's what I'm actually perceiving. My God, Charley, the place is so fucking old. Millions of years. Tens of millions."

"Give me some Stage Three."

"Weirdly beautiful, man. But alien. Not insects, I'm pretty sure." The overlapping images loped along, as if from a camera mounted on a cartoon's shoulder. Is this how the blind imagines seeing? Meagle had been sight-less from birth, the dossier had informed me. But maybe that shouldn't be surprising; the blind repurpose the cortical and precortical tissues special-ized by evolution for visual capture and registration – the large dedicated occipital lobe, the striate V1 cortex, all the way up the V hierarchy to middle temporal MT, pathways carrying neural trains from the retina to the brain, interpreting, pruning as they flashed their binary code. Yada yada. His sensi-tive, trained brain had nabbed that spare capacity, retained its function, modified its input channels. The Marvel That Is Your Brain! I overheard my own mocking subliminal commentary and wondered why I was so anxious, suddenly. A kind of curdling in the causal webs . . . I felt more and more uncomfortable, as if I badly needed to take a dump. Maybe I did. Meagle had fallen silent. Dropping off to sleep again? No, the constructed image was sliding past us in the hologram, slurring and breaking up in detail, but it was a corridor he walked along, in his spirit walk or whatever you call it.

Something sitting in a large padded chair. Christ!

"Christ!" Meagle cried, loudly. Small indicator lights went from placid green to blipping yellow on one display. A histogram surfed briefly into the red. The nurse was clicking keys, fast and unrattled.

"Bingo, Colonel," said the operator, triumph shaking his professional sang-froid.

My etiological sense scrambled. I lurched up, leaned forward, ready to puke. Meagle was doing the same, cable tangled at his neck, contacts pulling from his cropped scalp. In the great chair shown on the screen, as the imaginary viewpoint swung about, the interpretative computer sketched a seated person with a snout and deep-set hooded eyes, clawed hands gripping banked controls on the arm rests.

The image skittered and jittered, revised itself as the causal whirlpool screeched around me. But no, this wasn't the dragon I was looking for. It was, it wasn't. The machine image spoke directly to me through Meagle and memory. That dead person, that ancient thing in its ancient warship, it was . . . was . . . Impossible. Delusion and grief. Something else. I knew the beloved face beyond denial, of course, like a clumsy pencil drawing on the screen that tore my heart out. Human. Face burned down in places to the bone, gaze suffering, mouth mute, determined even in death. In his stained UN uniform, with Korean Imperium lieutenant flashes at the collar.

"Oh, lord God," I moaned, and did barf, then, like a puling schoolboy drunk.

From the corner of my leaking eyes, in the window feed from his RV cell, I saw Meagle turn convulsively. He seemed to stare right at me, through the camera, into the display, with his blue, blind eyes.

The main hologram image, too, looked steadfastly back at me – sketched from the Naval remote viewer's words and speaking hands, his brain rhythms, the archived set of his stereotypical ideograms – looked at me from a grave five years dug in the soil.

Song-Dam. My son. My poor boy. My lost hero child.
I started to cry, wiping at my bitter mouth, and couldn't stop.

Huygens is not part of the Imperium, of course, being a research agora, like Herschel, the other settlement on Titan, but it is a fiscal affiliate of Korea, as well as of Zimbabwe, the Brazilian Superstate, Camp Barsoom (on, you guessed it, Mars), and a handful of other polises on the Moon and Ganymede. So while the writ of Mr Kim, my sponsor, did not run on Titan, precisely, his paternal hand was heavily in the weighing scales. The Warlord had developed a fondness for the Intelligent Dinosaur paradigm when he studied paleontology as a young student in Antarctica, where all the equivocal evidence was located prior to the Enigma's excavation, and he carried that interest through into maturity and, some said, senility. He would be pleased as punch.

Dr Caetani, surprise, surprise, was not. Everyone by now had studied the remote viewing session, and more than once. My participation and role could be determined only by inference, since no recorders had been trained on the observation room. But the recording of Meagle's results showed plainly the results: the alien or saurian and, moments later, the harrowing superimposed image of my late son. For Caetani, I'm sure, my distress, my involvement, was just a piece of hammy theatrics, a shameful way to spray my mark onto an historic event.

"This afternoon, we know nothing more than we did a week ago," he stated bluntly. "I'm candidly dismayed at the gullibility of some of my colleagues here."

"The saurian –" began Jendayi Shumba. He cut her off instantly.

" – the image was no more veridical than the, the disturbed imposition into the colonel's entangled state of Sensei Park's tragic fixation on his son's death. Nobody doubts that Mr. Park is a functioning poltergeist, capable of casting images and interfering with complex electronic systems. It's why he's here – over my objections – and isn't the point." He took a deep breath, his features flushed behind that pretentious beard. "Our visitor's martyred son is certainly not aboard that Jurassic artifact, and surely nobody thinks he is. Neither, by the same token, is the dinosaur space captain that Mr Park's well-prepped imagination also dreamed up and shoveled into the ideospace."

"With all due respect, you're out of your depth, Tony." This one I hadn't met before, an industrial psychiatrist named Lionel Berger. "Back off, will you? Remote viewing is no exact science, nor even an accomplished art – and I mean no disrespect to Colonel Meagle in pointing this out. We don't know how it works, except that quantum field nonlocality is engaged and implemented by an act of deliberation. Its famous vulnerability is that other minds can become trapped into the entanglement and add their own measures of information . . . but whether that aggregate data is veridical, symbolic, mythological or sheer phantasy, we can't tell just by simple inspection. Dismissing this evidence by flinging about words like 'psychic' and 'poltergeist' is argument by slur. I'm prepared to wait for more evidence before I decide so confidently what's inside that vessel."

Caetani, the surly fellow, actually said, "Bah!" I'd never heard anyone actually say that before. Others spoke, in their turn; Meagle sat at the back, his blind eyes closed, sunk into a sort of exhausted torpor. I'd have liked to go to him, sit beside him in respectful and sorrowing silence. Instead, as requested, I also remained silent, half-listening to the academese, the scholasticism, the stochasticism, the loop theories of cognitive restructuration.

I had seen my dead son.

I had seen the saurian sat in his great chair, or hers.

If cause is a pool of chaos and order blended by intention and brute event, I am (and nobody, as yet, has managed to explain why it is so) a small stick of dynamite exploding up random fishy critters to the shore. Brrrr . . . That's a macabre, self-lacerating image. It had been my boy Song who perished in mindless explosions, and not by my hand. But hadn't I sent him into fatal danger? Into ultimate harm's way? Of course I had. Not by urging or forbidding, in so many words, but in my reckless skepticism, my louche lack of patriotism. Which had fetched us up where? Him, smashed like a detonated fish in a pool he could not escape, did not wish to escape. Me, bereft, alone, my bond to my nation long ago broken and betrayed. I grunted aloud, hoisted myself into a less uncomfortable position on a seat too small, as usual, for my girth.

"Sam? You wanted to say something?"

I looked around. They were gazing at me expectantly. "Oh, nothing. What can I donate that hasn't already been weighed and found wanting?" It was petty and self-regarding, and I snapped my mouth shut, but a fierce anger burst up in me anyway, so I opened it again. "I'll say one thing. And make no apologies for it. We are here," I swung one arm through an embracing arc, taking in the auditorium, the station, Titan, "because years ago, when I was still on Earth, I discerned a causal anomaly near this place. We are here because military and independent remote viewers on three worlds concurred in finding and describing the vehicle. We are here, therefore, driven by the many motives that arose from that discovery. But I insist that the principal occasion is Premier Kim's wish to test the hypotheses forwarded by the scientific entity I represent." I took a deep breath. "So far as I can see, what Colonel Meagle uncovered this morning corroborates precisely the predictions of the Intelligent Dinosaur Institute. If my presence has muddied your waters, I'm sorry – but again I remind you, if it were not for me, none of you would be here today.

"So lay the hell off, okay?"

I dug in my robe's pocket, found a Mars bar, unpeeled it, and gobbled it down.

Shortly after Song-Dam's eighth birthday – his mother long since escaped back into the whorehouse alleys she and I had both come from – I took him with me on a business trip to Palo Alto. I was the object of the business trip, my absurd gift, my poltergeist prowess with cause and effect. Several Stanford biophysics researchers had somehow picked up trash journalism stories about me as the luckiest/unluckiest man on earth. Funding was limited, but I convinced them that Song was in my sole charge and that I wasn't budging without him.

So we took an exhausting flight from Incheon International across the Pacific and through the absurd indignities of US Homeland Security (despite a graduate student being on hand at the airport to collect us, now cooling his heels in the arrival lounge with a wilting cardboard sign in two languages; I had inadvertently set off various bells and whistles, so of course we were detained pointlessly, until one of the senior professors was persuaded to drive to the airport and vouch for us), and stayed in an anonymous, ugly block of apartments that seemed to have been compiled from polyurethane pretending to be marble. We could hear the dreary TV set next door through the adjoining wall.

I took Song for a long walk so he and I could get a feel for the alien place, this America, as we stretched our weary legs. Within three blocks (trust my causal eddies for once), we found a Korean food store, established that my parents' modest residence in Nangok – back at the turn of the century when it was still a squalid slum in a hilly area of Sillim-dong, Gwanak District – was just spitting distance from the proprietors' familial stamping grounds, and found ourselves dragged happily to a nearby park by Mr Kwon's wife and three kids to fly dragon kites in the cool afternoon breeze.

I helped Song pay out the string. Our borrowed kite was a scarlet and gold Dragon Diamond (a gift to us both, as it turned out – and thank you, Mr and Mrs Kwon!). Our dragon quivered on the middle air a moment, strained against his leash, then suddenly flung himself upward into the deepening blue Californian sky. The line went taut. Song let it go in fright, but I held tight, and a moment later he put his hands back to the winch reel beside mine. I saw the line stretched between my hand, his small resolute hands, and the high, swooping, flower-bright dragon: a luminous string.

"Daddy, look!" said my son, wild with excitement. "Our dragon is flying on a beam of photons!"

At that moment, as if Buddha had smacked me in the ear, I was enlightened.

"I think I can get in," I told the Director of Operations, a tight jawed fellow named Namgoong, almost certainly a political appointee but in secure possession of a decent scientific reputation with degrees in geology and astrobiology. Earth and sky, I thought, but hid my smile. "I think I can break the shield. The question is, do I dare?"

"Yes. Precisely. If you rupture the stationary shield, who knows what might seep out into the atmosphere." He gave me a thin-lipped smile. "Fortunately, Sensei, we shall not have to wait three years for an Environmental Impact Study. The Imperium wants this thing opened. Now. It's why you're here."

"To tell you the truth, sir, I'm more worried about what might seep in. They must have sealed it against Titan's atmosphere for good reason."

"A motive that expired millions of years ago." He rose. "I'm having a containment dome erected around the locus. There's no way we can establish blockade underneath the ice as well, but this will meet most likely challenges. Or so I'm assured."

"I'm relieved to hear it." I belatedly heaved up my bulk. "When will you want me out there?"

"You'll be advised. We have a full scale colloquium scheduled, starting at two. I'll expect you to be there, Sensei Park, and on your best behavior. No more outbursts, if you please."

"More damned chin-wagging. Science used to be an empirical exercise," I grumbled.

"Led by theory, as I'm sure you understand." He was standing at his door, and I went out, biting my lip. Nobody had the faintest starting point for a theory to explain my causal distortions, and not much to account for the photon-entangled portage functor. I could do it, I could show them a method for using it (and had), but I didn't have a theory-empowered clue how or why. I'm nobody's mutant superman, that much I do know. (Or is that just a fat man's self-doubt speaking?)

Postmodern science, as far as I can tell looking in from the outside, is drunk on the sound of its own voice. But yes, I know: look who's complaining. I recalled again that Victorian sage, that poet Tennyson. He had it right: I sometimes hold it half a sin to put in words the grief I feel; for words, like Nature, half reveal and half conceal the Soul within. But, for the unquiet heart and brain, a use in measured language lies; the sad mechanic exercise, like dull narcotics, numbing pain. I followed Dr Namgoong along the narrow compiled corridors of Hyugens station, so like those awful domiciles on the outskirts of Palo Alta, and went to hear the sad mechanics exercise their tongues and dull their pain, and maybe mine.

The circulated air was pungent, despite the scrubbers, with the musk of excited animals crowded together. A schematic chart I'd grown familiar with, these last few months, started displaying on the auditorium wall, replacing the magnified image of Saturn's glorious tilted hat. The Fermi Paradox Solution candidates. My eye bounced off them, falling down a cliff of words and logic with no footing in reality beyond the dragon-haunted thing outside the dome:

Where are They?
Fermi 1. They are here among us, and call themselves Koreans.
That always got a satisfied titter, except from any Hungarians in the crowd.
Fermi 2. They are here, running things.
A chance for the Hungarians, and anyone else chafing under the Imperium, to get their own back with a belly laugh. No giggles here, though, I noticed.
Fermi 3. They came and left.
Bingo, I thought. They came and left flowers scattered in their wake. Strictly, though, that was Fermi 53, the only choice left. The ancient intelligent dinosaur hypothesis.
Fermi 6. We are interdicted.
Fermi 10. They are still on their way here.
The starship had blown that one, and others like it, clear out of the water. Time to trim the list, methinks.

Fermi 21. They're listening, only fools are transmitting.

Fermi 22. Dedicated killer machines destroy everything that moves, anywhere in space.

Fermi 28. The Vingean Singularity takes them . . . elsewhere.

No Singularity back near the end of the Cretaceous, I thought. Judging by the remote viewer's sketches, that saurian pilot was advanced, but not sufficiently advanced as to be indistinguishable from magic.

Fermi 38. Earth is the optimal place for life, just by chance.

Could be. And for intelligent life, at that. Hey, look, we've seen it twice: the smart dinosaurs and Homo sap.

Fermi 48. Language is vanishingly rare.

Ha! Yeah, right. Blah blah blah. Still, maybe so. The skies are awfully silent, which is where we came in . . .

Fermi 49. Science is a rare accident.

Not as rare as I am, I thought, touching the etiological chains and vortices all around – and no scientist ever predicted me. Most of them still didn't even know about me, thanks to all those Above Top Secret restrictions. Damn it.

Namgoong cleared his throat at the podium. Voices, in clumps and then one by one, fell silent. Hey, maybe that's it. God tapped His microphone, and the cosmos shut up to listen. And they're still listening, bent and cowed by the awfulness of what they heard. But not us, we haven't heard from God yet, despite a thousand revelations claimed and proclaimed. Or if we have, there's no way to search through the babbling noise and extract the divine signal. Funny way to run a universe.

I could feel the dinosaur calling to me, even so, through the appalling cold of Titan's snows and the void of fifty or a hundred million years. And the entwined memory of my son, sacrificed for nothing. Nothing. Nothing.

"Those are the classic guesses – most of them wrong." The Director flicked his finger; the display went to blank gray. "We still have no idea why the galaxy, indeed the universe as a whole, is quiet. Why the stars are still shining, spilling out their colossal energy resources, when intelligence should be collecting it. Calculations you're all familiar with prove that a single intelligent species arising anywhere in the galaxy within the last billion years would by now have colonized all its trillion stars and associated bodies, turned the sky black with Matrioshka shells – or perhaps obliterated the stars in vast, wasteful wars."

I pricked up my ears. A political subtext? Perhaps not; maybe our director was just a tone-deaf drone. I glanced around; several people near me had dropped their eyes, more than one held fists clenched tight. Okay.

"One of the equally classic Great Filters must screen out potential intelligent life and leave the heavens exactly as they'd have to be if there is no life at all out there. No intelligent, starfaring life, anyway.

"So now we're faced with a new paradox. Fermi remains unanswered – and yet we have this old vehicle made by beings not of our own species, but apparently related. The likelihood of that coincidence being due to chance alone is impossibly small. I see only three remaining possibilities."

"Barney did it," someone called, muted but clear across the room. A wave of tittering. I felt my jaw tighten, and a flush creep into my cheeks.

"A previous civilization sprung from dinosaur stock on Cretaceous Earth, or even earlier, yes," said Dr Namgoog evenly. "The opinion represented here today by our guest, Sensei Park."

A pattering of polite applause, some even more muted groans.

"We have evidence in the form of preliminary scans by our Naval remote viewer, Colonel Meagle, that the creature . . . the being, forgive me . . . in charge of the craft has just such an origin. Leaving aside the improbability of parallel evolution. If so, this leaves the earlier and larger Fermi question unanswered: where are its kindred now, why haven't they conquered the whole galaxy? Tipler and others proved decades ago that this could have been achieved at achievable sub-light speeds within a million years. If they have, why don't we see them?"

Hearing it stated so flatly, I was dizzied, as always, by the prospect. Flotillas of starcraft fleeing into the spiral arms at a tenth of light speed, crammed with dragon seed or our own. Or minute nanoscale pods fired toward a hundred million stars by magnetic catapult, or driven on filmy wings by laser light. Yet these, too, were last year's dreams, last century's. We had stepped from Earth to Ganymede to Titan entangled on a light beam, and without waiting to be shoved here by sailboat. The moment entangled luminal portage became a reality for my own species, it opened the yawning cavern: why not for them, as well? What the hell was a starship doing here? Why bother? It was so last week, like finding a steam locomotive under the ice.

Namgoog was enunciating his other solutions to Fermi, but I didn't care. I was entranced by the mystery of the sleeping creature, sedate under his bedding of live flowers. It was a hunger like my endless appetite for chow. I wanted to step straight through the damned shell of the ship and look the critter in the eye, man to man. Even if it decided to eat me.

That's what dragons do, isn't it?

And so to bed. Where I lay in the dark in a lather of fright for fifteen minutes. Fearful and weak. Bleak. Needing a leak. I climbed out and thudded to the sanitary personal. When I got back, after a swab up and down and across with a wet face cloth to dab away the worse of the flopsweat, my door was slightly open. Through it came the never-stopping background clanging and banging of humans and machines keeping the place ticking over. Snapping my fingers, I clicked the room light up to dim. Dr Jendayi Shumba, chubby string looper, stretched at ease on my bed, clad in sensible pajamas with a mission blaze on the collar. Of course, I jumped and squealed.

"What the – Is there some – "

"Hush up, dear man, and come over here." She grinned.

"You're not serious. Are you?"

In evidence, she slithered out of her pjs and raised her eyebrows.

"Absurd. I'd crush you like a bug."

"Myeong-hui, you don't weigh any more, here, than my little boy."

"You have a—?" I swallowed, and crept closer. "I had a son once."

"Let us be in this moment, Sensei," she said without reproach.

"I'm disgusting to look upon," I said frankly. "And I don't need a pity—"

She had her fingers across my mouth, and then pulled me down through several clunky jumpy evolutions. "There are other ways to convey one's ... intimacy," she said.

"Ulp," I protested.

"An easy mouth is a great thing on a long journey, is it not, old fellow?" she said, releasing mine and patting my neck.

"Excuse me?"

Jendayi burst out laughing, a slightly husky, wonderfully exciting sound. "A quote from an old British classic about a horse. Nineteenth century, I believe. You might have read it as a child. Black Beauty."

"You are the black beauty," I said, noticing a cue when it smacked me between the eyes. I raised my voice and said, "Door close," and it did.

"You've got a way to break into the ship, don't you?" she said, after a time without time.

I was reeling and reckless. "Yes. Probably."

"So you really are a poltergeist." She stroked my contemptible belly, as if it were a friendly animal sharing the bed with us. "Tony nearly poked his damn eye out." Her laugh was throaty, dirty, a tonic.

"Don't blame me," I said, and found a glass of water, drained it. "It's like being able to wiggle your ears."

In the near-dark, she wiggled hers, and more.

But before she left, Jendayi said, "Bring me back a sample. A skin scraping, anything with DNA. Just for me, honey, okay?" Oh, so that's why you're here? Had to be some reason. Exploitative bitch. But that's life, right?

Looking like a well-laid but annoyed and put-upon squat polar bear in my bodyglove, some hellish number of minus degrees on the far side of its skin, I stood gazing down from the edge of the excavation. The spacecraft was unaltered, every bloom precisely where it had been several days before, where it been, perhaps, several tens of millions of years before. Unless it was salted here recently as a snare for gullible humans. In which case, it might be younger than I. Not so likely, though.

"Ready when you are, Sensei," said the political officer, doing Mr Kim's bidding, and damn the scientists' caution.

I raised one thumb and let myself drift. Cause and effect unbraided, started their long, looping dance of etiological distortion, swirling, curdling. I was the still center of the spinning world. Certainties creaked, cracked. A favorite poem entered my heart, by Ji-Hoon Cho, "Flower petals on the sleeves":

The wanderer's long sleeves
Are wet from flower petals.
Twilight over a riverside village
Where wine is mellow.

Had this saurian person below me, trapped now in timelessness, known wine? Crushed release and perhaps moments of joy from some archaic fruit not yet grape? I thought, with a wrenching mournfulness:

When this night is over
Flowers will fall in that village.

"Hey!"

And there went the flowers, drawn up and tossed away from the hull of the starship. They were scattering in the methane wind, lifted and flung by the bitter gusts, floral loveliness snap-frozen, blown upward and falling down in drifts into the alien snow.

"The stationary shield is discontinued," said a clipped voice in my ears.

I stepped forward, ready to enter the ancient, imprisoned place. To meet my dinosaur, who had either died or even now lived, freed from timeless suspension. A hand caught my encased arm.

"Not yet, Sam. We have a team prepped. Thanks, you've done good here today." I turned, hardly able to see through my tears, and it was not that bastard Tony Caetani groveling his apologies, the universe could not be so chirpy as that. I hadn't met this one before, although he'd picked up my dining room nickname and used it with a certain familiar breeziness; some beefy functionary of some armed service division, grinning at me in his bluff farmboy way. I nodded, and watched the team of marines go down, and remembered my dear boy and the way he had gone forward fearlessly into darkness and then into the fire falling from the sky. It did not matter one whit that I thought his cause wrong-headed. I remembered a poem in that book I'd found in the ruined library, a poem by an Englishman named Kipling that had torn my heart as I sat before Song-Dam's closed coffin. There was no comfort in this tide, the poem warned me, nor in any tide, save this:

he did not shame his kind –
Not even with that wind blowing, and that tide.

Without shame, I sobbed, but then drew myself up and turned back to Huygens agora. Perhaps, I told myself, ten or sixty million years ago, another father had laid his son on these cruel snows and bade him farewell. I murmured to that reptilian father, offering what poor borrowed comfort I might to us both, across all that void of space and time: "Then hold your head up all the more, This tide, And every tide; Because he was the son you bore, And gave to that wind blowing and that tide!"

I looked straight up above me, at the photodiode display before my eyes in the viewmask, swallowing hard, to follow the streaming tide of blossoms on the wind, and there was Saturn, old Father Time, hanging in the orange smoke of the sky, an arrow through his heart. I gave him a respectful nod, and raised one gloved thumb in salute.

HAIR

Adam Roberts

Cosmetic fashions sometimes sweep the globe, but, as the sly story
that follows demonstrates, sometimes they have a particularly
good reason for doing so. . . .

A Senior Reader in English at London University, Adam Roberts
is an SF author, critic, reviewer, and academic who has produced
many works on nineteenth-century poetry as well as critical studies
of science fiction such as *The Palgrave History of Science Fiction*. His
own fiction has appeared in *Postscripts, Sci Fiction, Live Without a
Net, FutureShocks, Forbidden Planets, Spectrum SF, Constellations*,
and elsewhere, and was collected in *Swiftly*. His novels include
Salt, On, Stone, Polystom, The Snow, Gradisil, Splinter, and *Land
of the Headless*. His most recent novels are *Yellow Blue Tibia* and
New Model Army. He lives in Staines, England, with his wife and
daughter, and has a website at adamroberts.com.

I

IT SEEMS TO me foolish to take a story about betrayal and call it – as my
sponsors wish me to – *The Hairstyle That Changed The World*. All this
hairdressing business, this hair-work. I don't want to get excited about that.
To see it as those massed strands of electricity shooting up from the bald pate
of the vandegraaff machine. And whilst we're on the subject of haircuts: I
was raised by my mother alone, and we were poor enough that, from an
early stage, she was the person who cut my hair. For the sake of simplicity, as
much as economy, this cut would be uniform and close. To keep me quiet
as the buzzer grazed, she used to show me the story about the mermaid
whose being-in-the-world was confused between fishtail and feet. I'm sure
she showed me lots of old books, but it was that one that sticks in my head:
the singing crab, more scarab than crustacean; the wicked villainess able to
change not only her appearance but, improbably, her size – I used to puzzle
how she was able to generate all her extra mass as she metamorphosed, at
the end, into a colossal octopus. Mostly I remember the beautiful young
mermaid; she had the tempestuous name Ariel. The story hinged on the
notion that her tail might vanish and reform as legs, and I used to worry
disproportionately about those new feet. Would they, I wondered, smell of
fish? Were the toenails actually fish-scales? Were the twenty-six bones of

each foot (all of which I could name) formed of cartilage, after the manner of fish bones? Or human bone? The truth is, my mind is the sort that is most comfortable finding contiguities between different states, and most uncomfortable with inconsistencies. Hence my eventual choice of career, I suppose. And I don't doubt that my fascination with the mermaid story had to do with a nascent erotic yearning for Ariel herself – a very prettily drawn figure, I recall.

This has nothing to do with anything. I ought not digress. It's particularly vulgar to do so before I have even started; as if I want to put off the task facing me. Of course this account is not about me. It is enough, for your purposes, to locate your narrator, to know that I was raised by my mother alone; and that after she died (of newstrain CF, three weeks after contracting it) I was raised by a more distant relative. We had enough to eat, but nothing else in my life was enough to. To know that my trajectory out of that world was hard study, a scholarship to a small college, and the acquisition of the professional skills that established me in my current profession. You might also want to know where I first met Neocles (long final e – people sometimes get that wrong) at college, although what was for me dizzying educational altitude represented, for him, a sort of slumming, a symptom of his liberal curiosity about how the underprivileged live.

Above all, I suppose, you need to know that I'm of that generation that thinks of hair as a sort of excrescence, to be cropped to make it manageable, not indulged at length. And poverty is like the ore in the stone; no matter how you grind the rock and refine the result it is always poverty that comes out. Thinking again about my mother, as here, brings her colliding painfully against the membrane of memory. I suppose I find it hard to forgive her for being poor. She loved me completely, and I loved her back, as children do. The beautiful mermaid, seated on a sack-shaped rock, combing her long, coral-red hair whilst porpoises jump through invisible aerial hoops below her.

II

To tell you about the hairstyle that changed the world, it's back we go to Reykjavik, five years ago, now: just after the Irkutsk famine, when the grain was devoured by that granulated agent manufactured by – and the argument continues as to which terrorists sponsored it. It was the year the World Cup descended into farce. Nic was in Iceland to answer charges at the Product Protection Court, and I was representing him.

A PPC hearing is not much different to any other court hearing. There are the rituals aping the last century, or perhaps the century before that. There's a lot of brass and glass, and there is a quantity of waxed, mirrorlike darkwood. I had represented Nic at such hearings before, but never one quite so serious as this. And Nic had more to lose than most. Because I had itemized his assets prior to making our first submission before the Judicial Master I happened to know exactly how much that was: five apartments, one over-looking Central Park; a mulberry farm; forty assorted cars and flitters; more than fifty percent shares in the Polish National Museum – which although it didn't precisely mean that he owned all those paintings and statues and whatnots at least gave him privileged access to them. The Sydney apartment had a Canova, for instance, in the entrance hall, and the Poles weren't press-ing him to return it any time soon.

He had a lot to lose.

In such circumstances insouciance is probably a more attractive reaction than anxiety, although from a legal perspective I might have wished for a more committed demeanor. He lounged in court his Orphic shirt – very stylish, very allah-mode – and his hair was a hundred years out of date. It was Woodstock. Or English Civil War aristocrat.

"When the JM comes in," I told him, "you'd better get off your gluteus maximus and stand yourself straight."

Judicial Master Paterson came in, and Nic got to his feet smartly enough and nodded his head, and then sat down himself perfectly properly. With his pocketstrides decently hidden by the table he looked almost respectable. Except for all the hair, of course.

III

I see-you-tomorrowed him on the steps of the courthouse, but he was staring at the sky. The bobble-layer of clouds on the horizon was a remark-able satsuma colour. Further up was cyan and eggshell. The surface of the icebound estuary, which looked perfectly smooth and flat in daylight, revealed under the slant light all manner of hollows and jags. Further out at sea, past the iceline where waves turned themselves continually and wearily over, a fishing platform sent a red snake of smoke straight up from the fakir's-basket of its single chimney.

"Tomorrow," he replied absently. He seemed hypnotized by the view.

"Don't worry," I told him, mistaking (as I now think) his distraction for anxiety about the prospect of losing some of his five apartments or forty cars and flitters. "The JM said he recognized that some individuals have a genius for innovation. That was a good sign. That's code for: geniuses don't need to be quite as respectful of the law as ordinary drones."

"A genius for innovation," he echoed.

"I'm not saying scot-free. Not saying that. But it won't be too bad. You'll keep more than you think. It will be fine. Don't worry. Yes?"

He suddenly coughed into his gloves – yellow, condom-tight gloves – and appeared to notice me for the first time. God knows I loved him, as a friend loves a true friend, but he bore then as he always did his own colossally swollen Ego like a deformity. I never knew a human with so prodigious a self-regard. His selfishness was of the horizoning, all-encompassing sort that is almost touching, because it approaches the selfishness of the small child. His

whim: I shall be humanity's benefactor! But this was not an index of his altruism. It was because his ego liked the sound of the description. Having known
him twenty years I would stand up in court and swear to it. He developed
the marrow peptide-calcbinder treatment not to combat osteoporosis – the
ostensible reason, the thing mentioned in his Medal of Science citation – but
precisely because of the plastic surgical spin-off possibilities, so that he could
add twenty centimeters to his own long bones. Not that he minded people
using his treatment to alleviate osteopathologies, of course.

Accordingly, when he did not turn up in the courtroom the following day my first thought was that he had simply overslept; or gotten
distracted by some tourist pleasure, or that some aspect of his own
consciousness had intruded between his perceiving mind and the brute
fact that (however much I tried to reassure him) a JM was gearing up to
fine him half his considerable wealth for property-right violation. It did
not occur to me that he might deliberately have absconded. This possibility evidently hadn't occurred to the court either, or they would have
put some kind of restraint upon him. You would think (they thought,
obviously) that the prospect of losing so many million euros of wealth
was restraint enough.

The shock in court was as nothing, however, to the fury of the Company:
his employer, and mine. I want to be clear: I had been briefed to defend
Nic in court, and that only. I made this point forcefully after the event.
My brief had been courtroom and legal, not to act as his minder, or to
prevent him from boarding a skyhop to Milan (it turned out) in order immediately to board another skyhop to – nobody was quite sure where. "If you'd
wanted a minder you should have hired a minder," I said. I was assertive,
not aggressive.

The court pronounced in absentia, and it went hard on Nic's fortune.
But this did not flush him out.

His disappearance hurt me. I was sent to a dozen separate meetings in
a dozen different global locations within one week; and in the same time-
frame I had twenty or so further virtual meetings. Flying over Holland, where
robotically tended fields shone greener than jade, and the hedges are all
twenty-foot tall, and the glimmering blue rivers sined their paths towards
the sea.

At Denver airport I saw a man with Parkinsonism – not old, no more than
forty – sitting in the café and trying to eat a biscuit. He looked as though he
was trying to shake hands with his own mouth.

The news was as full of people starving, as it always is. Images of a huge
holding zone in Sri Lanka where people were simply sitting around waiting
to die. That look of the starving: hunger has placed its leech-maw upon their
heel and sucked all their fluid and solidity out, down to the bones. The skin
tautly concave everywhere. The eyes big as manga. The aching face.

On Channel 9 the famine clock, bottom left corner, rolled its numbers
over and over. A blur of numbers.

I flew to Iceland.

I flew back to Denver.

I was acutely aware that Neocles' vanishment put my own career at risk. Had I always lived amongst wealth, as he had, I might have floated free above the anxiety of this. It's easy for the wealthy to believe that something will turn up. But I had experienced what a non-medinsure, hardscrabble life was like, and I did not want to go back to it.

He's gone rogue, I was told. Why didn't you stop him? The Company, which had been (to me) a dozen or so points of human contact, suddenly swelled and grew monstrously octopoid. A hundred, or more, company people wanted to speak to me directly. This is serious, I was told.

He has the patent information on a dozen billion-euro applications, I was told. You want to guarantee the company's financial losses should he try and pirate-license those? I thought not.

I thought not.

Not everybody scapegoated me. Some departments recognized the injustice in trying to pin Nic's disappearance on me. Embryology, for instance; a department more likely than most to require expert legal advice, of the sort I had proved myself in the past capable of providing. Optics also assured me of their support, though they did so off the record. But it would have required a self-belief stronger than the one with which providence has provided me to think my career – my twenty-year career – as staff legal counsel for the Company was going to last more than a month. The elegant bee-dance of mutual corporate espionage continued to report that none of our competitors had, yet, acquired any of the intellectual property Nic had in his power to dispose. I had a meeting at Cambridge, in the UK, where late winter was bone-white and ducks on the river looked in astonishment at their own legs. I flew to Rio where the summer ocean was immensely clear and beautiful: sitting on the balcony of our offices it was possible, without needing optical enhancement, to make out extraordinary levels of detail in the sunken buildings and streets, right down to cars wedged in doorways, and individual letters painted on the tarmac.

I flew to Alaska. I flew to Sydney, where the airport was a chaos of children – a flashmob protest about the cutbacks in youth dole.

In the midst of all this I somehow found time to begin, discretely, to make plans for a post-Company life. My ex-wife was more understanding than I might have expected, more concerned to maintain medinsure for our two children than for herself. I scouted, gingerly, secretly, for other employment; but even with the most optimistic assessment it was going to be hard to carry five lots of medinsure on my new salary. I could not of course deprive the children, and I did not wish to deprive Kate. That left my ex-wife and myself, and I decided to give up coverage for myself and leave my ex's in place.

Then, from the blue, news: Neocles had gone native in Mumbai, of all places. I was called once again to Denver and briefed face-a-face by Alamillo himself, the company enforcer and bruiser and general bully-fellow. It was not a pleasant tête-à-tête. At this meeting emphasis was placed on the very lastness of this, my last chance. The word last as conventionally used was insufficient to convey just how absolutely last this last chance was, how micron-close to the abyss I found myself, how very terminal my opportunity.

The very severity of this interview reassured me. Had they not needed me very badly they would not have worked so hard to bully me. For the first time since Nic had so thoughtlessly trotted off – putting at risk, the fucker, not only his own assets but my entire family's wellbeing – I felt the warmth of possible redemption touch the chill of my heart.

"My last chance," I said. "I understand."

"You go to him," said Alamillo. "You have a fucking word, yes?"

I understood then that they were sending me because I was a friend, not because I was a lawyer. They already knew that money was no longer going to provide them with any leverage with Nic anymore – that he had renounced money. He was easing himself into his new role as Jesus Christ, the redeemer of the starving. What can you do to a person who won't listen to money? What else does Power have, in this world of ours?

"I'll talk to him. What else?"

"Nothing else," said Amarillo.

"Bring him home?"

"No, that's not what we're sending you to do. Listen the fuck to me. I don't give a fucking pin – just, just. Look. We're sending you to talk to him."

IV

I was flown out on a gelderm plane, its skin stiffening with the frictive heat of a high-inset aerial trajectory. I ate little medallions of liquorish bread, with shark caviar and Russian cheese paté; and then authentic sausages lacquered with honey, and then spears of dwarf asparagus, and then chocolate pellets that frothed deliciously inside the mouth. I drank white wine; a Kenyan vintage. The toilet cubicle of this plane offered seven different sorts of hygiene wipe, including a plain one, one that analyzed your stool as you wiped to check for digestive irregularities and several that imparted different varieties of dotTech to your lower intestine to various ends.

I watched a film about a frolicsome young couple overcoming the obstacles placed in the way of their love. I watched the news. I watched another film, a long one this time – fifteen minutes, or more – based on the historical events of the French Revolution.

The tipping point of our descent registered in my viscera like a Christmas-eve tingle of excitement.

We plummeted to Mumbai.

Arriving at Chhatrapati Shivaji was like travelling back half a century in time: the smell; the litter; the silver-painted curved ceilings on their scythe-shaped supports. An all-metal train, running on all-metal rails, trundling me from the terminal to the departure room. Then it was a short hop in a Company flicker to Jogeshwari beachfront – seconds, actually: a brief elevation over the peninsular sprawl of the city, its bonsai skyscrapers like stacked dishes, the taller curves and spires further south. The sky was outrageously blue, and the sea bristled with light. And really in a matter of seconds we came down again. I could have walked from airport to seafront, is how close it was. But better to arrive in a flitter, of course. When I'd called Nic he'd been gracious if laid-back in reply: no company men, just you, old friend. Of course, of course.

Of course.

There was a flitter park on the Juhu dyke, and I left the car, and driver, there, and started walking. Forty degrees of heat – mild, I was told, for the season. The sky blue like a gemlike flame. It poured heat down upon the world. The air smelt of several things at once: savoury smells and decaying smells, and the worn-out, salt-odour of the ocean.

I don't know what I expected. I think I expected, knowing Nic, to find him gone Hippy; dropped-out; or a holy hermit chanting Japa. I pictured him surfing. But as I walked I noticed there was no surf. There were people everywhere: a rather startling profusion of humanity, lolling, walking, rush-ing, going in and out, talking, singing, praying. It was an enormous crush. The sound of several incompatible varieties of music wrestled in the back-ground: beats locking and then disentangling, simple harmonic melodies twisting about one another in atonal and banshee interaction. Everybody was thin. Some were starvation thin. It was easy enough to pick out these latter, because they were much stiller: standing or sitting with studied motionless. It was those who could still afford to eat who moved about.

The bay harboured the poking-up tops and roofs of many inundated towers, scattered across the water like the nine queens in the chessboard problem, preventing the build-up of ridable waves. These upper floors of the drowned buildings were still inhabited; for the poor will live where they can, however unsalubrious. Various lines and cables were strung in sweeping droops from roofs to shore. People swam, or kicked and splashed through the shallower water. On the new mud beach a few sepia-coloured palm trees waved their heavy feathers in the breeze. Sweat wept down my back.

And then, as arranged, there was Nic: lying on the flank of the groyne with his great length of hair fanned out on the ground behind him. The first surprise: he was dressed soberly, in black. The second: he was accom-panied by armed guards.

I sat beside my friend. It was so very hot. "I think I was expecting beach bummery."

"I saw your plane come over," he said. "Made quite a racket."

"Airbraking." Like I knew anything about that.

"I'm glad you've come, though," he said, getting up on his haunches. His guards fidgeted, leaning their elbows on their slung rifles. They were wear-ing, I noticed, Marathi National Guard uniforms. "Good of you to come," he clarified.

"People in Denver are pretty pissed."

"There's not many I'd trust," he said. He meant that he did, at least, trust me.

"These boys work for you?" I asked.

"Soldiers. They do. The Marathi authorities and I have come to an understanding." Nic hopped to his feet. "They get my hairstyle, and with it they get the popular support. Of the poor. I get a legal government to shelter me. And I get a compound."

"Compound?" I asked, meaning: chemical compound? Or barracks? The answer, though, was the latter, because he said:

"Up in Bhiwandi. All the wealth has moved from the city, up to the mountains, up East in Navi Mumbai. The wealthy don't believe the sea has stopped coming. They think it'll likely come on a little more. The wealthy are a cautious lot."

"The wealthy," I said.

"So you can come along," he said. "Come along."

I got to my feet. "Where?"

"My flitter's back here."

"Are you allowed to park a flitter down here? I was told flitters had to be parked in the official park, back," I looked around, vaguely. "Back up there somewhere."

"I have," he said, flashing me a smile, "special privileges."

V

"What is it we do?" he asked me, a few minutes later, as the flitter whisked the two of us, and Nic's two soldiers, northeast over the Mumbai sprawl. He had to raise his voice. It was noisy as a helecopter.

"Speaking for myself," I said, "I work for the company. I do this to earn enough to keep the people I love safe and healthy. I include you in that category, by the way, you fucker."

"And," he said, smiling slyly, "how is Kate?"

I'll insert a word, here, about Kate. It is not precisely germane, but I want to say something. I love her, you see. I'm aware of the prejudice, but I believe it goes without saying that she is as much a human as anybody. She has a vocabulary of 900 words and a whole range of phrases and sayings. She has a genuine and sweet nature. She has hair the colour of holly-berries. You'd expect me to say this, and I will say this: it is a particularly strange irony that if the same people who sneer at her personhood post treatment had encountered her before treatment, it would never occur to them to deny that she was a human being. In those circumstances they would have gone out of their way to be nice to her. And if before, why not afterward? Kate is happier now than she ever was before. She is learning the piano. Of all the people I have met in this life, she is the most genuine.

Do you know what? I don't need to defend my love to you.

"She is very well," I said, perhaps more loudly than I needed to. "Which is more than I can say for your portfolio."

"A bunch of houses and cars and shit," he shouted, making a flowing gesture with his right hand as if discarding it all. His was, despite this theatricality, an untterly unstudied insoucience. That's what a lifetime of never wanting for money does for you.

"We could have saved more than half of it," I said, "if you hadn't absented yourself from the court the way you did."

"All those possessions," he said. "They were possessing me."

"Oh," I said. I could not convey to him how fatuous this sounded to me. "How very Brother Brother."

He grinned. "Shit it's good to see you again."

"This hair thing of yours," I asked him, having no idea what he meant by the phrase but guessing it was some nanopeptide technology or other that he had developed. "Is that a company patent?"

"You know?" he said, his eyes twinkling and his pupils doing that peculiar cycling moon-thing that they do, "it wouldn't matter if it were. But, no, as it happens, no. As it happens."

"Well," I said. "That's something."

He was the hairstyle man, the saviour of the world's poor. "I'm a benefactor now," he boomed. "I'm a revolutionary. I shall be remembered as the greatest benefactor in human history. In a year I'll be able to put the whole company in my fucking pocket."

The flitter landed: a little series of bunny hops before coming to rest, that telltale of an inexperienced chauffeur.

We were inside his compound: a pentagon of walls thick-wreathed with brambles of barbed wire. Inside was a mass of people, and verybody without exception – men women and children – had long, ink-black hair. People were lain flat on the floor, or lolling upon the low roofs, or sitting in chairs, all of them sunbathing, and all with their hair spread and fanned out. A central tower shaped like an oil derrick with a big gun at the top – impressive looking to a pedestrian, but like a cardboard castle to any force armed with modern munitions. There was plenty of space inside the walls, but it was crowded fit to burst. Nic led me along a walkway alongside the central atrium, and the ground was carpeted with supine humanity. They were so motionless that I even wondered whether they might be dead: except that every now and then one would pat their face to dislodge a fly, or breathe in and out.

"Sunbathers," I said.

And then, just before we went in, Nic stopped and turned to me with a characteristically boyish sudden spurt of enthusiasm. "Hey, I tell you what I learnt the other day?"

"What?"

"Crazy that I never knew this before, given all the work I've done. Discovered it quite by chance. Peptides, I mean the word, peptides, is from the Greek πεπτίδια and that means little snacks. There's something you never knew. Means nuts, crisps, olives stuffed with little shards of sundried fucking tomato. Peptides means scoobisnacks."

"Extraordinary," I deadpanned. "And you with your Greek heritage," I said, knowing full well that he possessed no Greek language at all.

At this he became once again solemn. "I'm a citizen of the world, now," he said.

We went through: up a slope and into a seminar room. Inside was a horseshoe seating grid with room for perhaps sixty people. The space was empty except for us two. The room put a single light on the front of the room when we came in.

I sat myself in a front row seat. Nic stood before the screen, fiddling with his hair, running fingers through it and pulling it. "Why do you think you're here?" he asked, without looking at me.

"Just to talk, Nic," I said. "I have no orders. Except to talk. Man, we really ought to talk. About the future."

"Hey," he said, as if galvanized by that word. He flapped his arm at the room sensor and the screen lit behind him: the opening image was the Federal flag of India. "OK," he announced.

The image morphed into diagrams of the chemical structures of self-assembling peptides that filled the screen: insectile wriggles of angular disjunction wielding hexagonic benzene rings like boxing gloves.

"Wait," said Nic, looking behind him. "That's not right." He clicked his fingers. More snaps of his molecular tools-in-trade faded in, faded out.

"How very barnum- bailey," I said.

"Calmodulin rendered in 3D," he said. "I always think they look like party streamers. Although, in Zoorlandic iteration, they look like a starmap. There's just so much empty space at the molecular level; our representational codes tend to obscure that fact. There, that there's lysine." He danced on the spot, jiggling his feet. "Lysine. A lot of that in your hair. NH2 sending down a lightning-jag of line to the H and H2N link, and O and OH looking on with their mouths open." Images flicked by. "One of the broken down forms of lysine is called cadaverine, you know that? The molecule of fucking decay and death, of putrefying corpses. Putrescine. Cadaverine. Who names these things?"

"Something to do with hair?" I prompted.

"Lysine," he said. "Hair." He held his right hand up and ran his thumb along his other four fingers: the display flicked rapidly through a series of images. "What is it we do?"

"You asked that before," I said.

"Innovations, and inventions, and brilliant new technological advances."

"I'm just a lawyer, Nic," I said. "You're the innovator."

"But it's the Company, isn't it? The Company's business. These techno-logical advances to make the world a better place."

I suppose I assumed that this was another oblique dig at Kate; so I was crosser in response than I should have been. "So they do," I said. "Don't fucking tell me they don't."

He looked back eyes wide, as if I had genuinely startled him. "Of course they do," he said, in a surprised tone. "Man, don't misunderstand. But think it through. That's what I'd say. This is me you're talking with. Technological advance and new developments and all the exciting novelties of our science fiction present. It's great. You get no argument on that from me."

"I've just flown from Denver to Mumbai in an hour," I said. "You'd prefer it took me three months sailing to get here?"

"You have grasped the wrong stick-end, chum," he said. "Really you have. But only listen. Technological Advance is marvellous. But it is always, ineluctably a function of wealth. Poverty is immmiscible with it. People are rich, today, in myriad exotic and futuristic ways; but people are poor today as people have always been. They starve, and they sicken, and they die young. Poverty is the great constraint of human existence."

"Things aren't so bad as you say," I said. "Technology trickles down."

"Sure. But the technology of the poor always lags behind the technology of the rich. And it's not linear. There are poor people on the globe today who do not use wheels, and drag their goods on sleds or on their backs. Some armies have needleguns and gelshells; and some armies have antique AK-47 guns; and some people fight with hoes and spades."

"This is how you got the government of Marathi to give you this little castle and armed guard?

"The hairstyle stuff," he said.

"And that? And that is?"

There is a particular variety of silence I always associate with the insides of high-tech conference rooms. An insulated and plasticated silence.

"It's a clever thing," he said to me, shortly.

"Of course it is."

"It is a clever thing. That's just objectively what it is. Works with lysein in the hair, and runs nanotubes the length of each strand. There's some more complicated bio-interface stuff, to do with the bloodvessels in the scalp. When I said that none of this utilised Company IP I was, possibly, bending the truth a little. There's some Company stuff in there, at the blood exchange. But the core technology, the hair-strand stuff, is all mine. Is all me. It's all new. And I'm going to be giving it away. Pretty soon, billions will have taken the starter pills. Billions. That's a big . . ." He looked about him at the empty seats. "Number," he concluded, lamely.

"Hair?" I prompted.

"I'm genetically eradicating poverty," he said. And then a gust of boyish enthusiasm filled his sails. "All the stuff we do, and make? It's all for the rich, and the poor carrying on starving and dying. But this—"

"Hair . . ."

"Food is the key. Food is the pinchpoint, if you're poor. Hunger is the pinchpoint, and it's daily, and everything else in your life is oriented around scraping together food so as not to starve. The poor get sick because their water is contaminated, or because their food is inadequate and undernourishment harasses their immune system. The future cannot properly arrive until this latter fact is changed."

"So what does the hair—" I asked. "What does. Does it, like, photosynthesise?"

"Something like that," he said.

His avatar, frozen with his smiling mouth half-open, like a twenty-foot-tall village idiot, lowered over us both.

"And you – what do you do, then? I mean what does one. You lie in the sun?"

"The energy you previously got from the food you eat. Well you get that from the sun." He did a little twirl. "It's a clever thing," he said. "Actually the hair less so: that's easy enough to engineer. Peptide sculptors generating photoreceptive structures in the hair, and spinning conductors down to the roots. The clever stuff is in the way the energy is transferred into the – look I don't want to get into the details. That's not important."

I looked up at giant 2D Nic's goofy face. I looked at human-sized 3D Nic's earnest expression and fidgeting hands. "You don't need to eat?"

"No."

"But you can?"

"Of course you can, if you want to. But you don't need to. Not once I've fitted the . . . fitted the . . . and I'm giving that away free."

I tried to imagine it. All those supine bodies, laid like pavingstones across Nic's courtyard outside. "Lying all day in the sun?"

"Not all day. Not at these latitudes. Three hours a day does most people."

"And what about, say, Reykjavik?"

"The sunlight's pretty weak up there," he said. "You'd be better off in the tropics. But that's where most of the world's poor are."

"But," I said. "Vital amines?"

"Water, more to the point. You still need to drink, obviously. Ideally you'll drink water with trace metals, flavoursome water. Or gobble a little clean mud from time to time. But vitamins, vitamins, well the tech can synthesise those. Sugars, for the muscles to work. You'd be surprised by how much energy three hours sunbathing with my hair generates. I mean, it's a lot."

"Phew," I said. The vertiginous ambition of the idea had gone through my soul like a sword. "You're not kidding." This was no question.

"Imagine, in a few years," he said, "imagine this: all the world's poor gifted with a technology that frees them from food. Frees them from the need to devote their lives to shiteating jobs to scrape together the money to eat."

"But they still can eat?" I repeated. I don't know why this stuck in my head the way it did.

"Of course they can, if they want to. They still have," very disdainfully inflected tone of voice, "fucking stomachs. But if they don't eat they don't starve. Contemplate that sentence and what it means. Don't you see? All the life that has ever lived on this planet has lived until this precariously balanced axe, all its life. Eat or die. I shall take that axe away. No more famines. No more starvation."

"Jesus," I said. I was going to add: I can see why the Marathi authorities would seize on such an idea as a means of galvanizing political support amongst the mass. I understood the guards, the compound. And from Nic's point of view too: I could see why he might want this over a position as well-paid Company genemonkey.

"Why am I here, Nic?" I asked.

"I need a lawyer," he said, simply. "Things are going to change for me in a pretty fucking big way. I will need a team I can trust. I'm going to be moving in some pretty highpowered circles. Finding a lawyer I can trust – that's easier said than done."

This, I had not expected. "You're offering me a job?"

"If you like. Put it like that, OK."

"What – what. To come here? To come and live here? To work in Mumbai?"

"Sure."

"You're serious?"

"Why not?

I didn't say: because in three weeks' time, the army of the Greater Kashmiri Republic is going to come crashing in here with stormtroopers and military flitters and crabtanks and many many bullets, to seize this extraordinary asset that the Marathi junta has somehow acquired. I didn't say what, come and work here and get very literally caught in the crossfire? I didn't say that. Instead I said: "bring Kate?"

He assumed a serious expression, rather too obviously deliberately suppressing a mocking smile. "I've always had a soft spot for Kate."

"The kids?"

"Surely. The ex too, if you like."

"I can't bring the kids here. I can't bring Kate here."

He caught sight of his onscreen image from the corner of his eye. He turned, flapped a hand as if waving at himself, and the screen went blank. Then he turned back and blinked to see me sitting there. "Well," he said, vaguely. "Think about it."

Later, as he escorted me back across that courtyard, so unnervingly full of motionless bodies, he said, "It's not about my ego, you know." Oh but it was. It was always about Nic's ego.

VI

It's just being. It is not striving. Striving is the opposite of being. It is not restless fighting and earnest labor and testing and retesting and making.

Things moved slowly at first. I flew back to the US and reported. The Company did not send me again; fearful, I daresay, that I would defect. But neither did they fire me. I picked up my new contracts and got back to work. Kate was deliciously pleased to see me. She'd picked up a new phrase: long time no see! She had learned the first portion of a Mozart sonata, and played it to me. I applauded. "Long time no see," she said, hugging me.

"I missed you," I told her. I tickled her feet.

"Long see, long time!"

Things were volatile in Western India. The Federal assembly broke up in acrimonious disharmony. That was hardly news. But I didn't have much time free for idle speculation.

There was a good deal of militia hurly-burly, and then the Southern Indian Alliance launched a proper, no-messing invasion. The news full of images of armored troops dodging from doorway to street corner, firing their baton-rifles. Old-style tanks, with those conveyor-belt wheel arrangements, scootling across scrub and drawing megaphones of dust behind them. Planes spraying Mumbai harbor, passing and repassing at great danger to themselves from ground fire, so as to lay a gelskin over the water thick enough to allow foot-soldiers to advance. Then it was all over, and the old government was gone, and a new one installed, and when things settled the news was that Nic had managed to absent himself in all the chaos.

Footage of people lolling in the sun with their hair fanned and spread behind them. In the first instances it was a case of reporting a new religious cult. The New Ascetics. The Followers. Suneaters. It took a while for the outlets to realize they weren't dealing with a religion at all; not least because many of the new hair-wearers adopted spiritual or mystical attitudes when interviewed.

The rumor was then that he'd reappeared in the south east of the subcontinent.

His followers went about the whole Federation – and went into the further East, and went up into the Stans – disseminating his technology. He himself was posted on a million slots; although never very cannily viralled, which meant either he could not afford to hire the best viral seed people, or else he was too forgetful to do so. Or conceivably he disdained to do so; because the content of these casts were increasingly clumsily preachy: the authenticity and validity of Poverty. Wealth had wrecked the world; poverty would save it. The rich would retreat to virtual lands, or hide away in materially moated and gated maison-kingdoms. The poor, freed from the shackles of their hunger, would sweep – peacefully but inevitably as the tide – away the rich and finally inherit the Earth. There was a good deal more in this vein. Sometimes I detected the authentic tang of Nic's rhetoric in this, but more often than not it was evidently revolutionary boilerplate, projected on a screen for him to read by whichever government or organization was sheltering him – or, latterly, holding him captive. He was in Africa, or he was in China, or he was far beyond the pale horizon, someplace near the desert sands. God knows I loved him, as a friend loves a true friend, but I could hardly bear to watch any of it.

I rationed myself, to preserve my sanity. I had him at the top of my feed, and before settling down to my work in the morning I would take half an hour to catch-up on all the stories posted that concerned him. At the end of the day, before I left to go home to Kate ("home again home again," she sang, "splitted alick") I'd run through anything new that came up.

One week he was one oddball new story amongst many. Here his disciples, the natural ascetic skinnies like a drumskin stretched on a coat-rack. Some of his followers were very political, and some were wholly unpolitical, interested only in being able to emulate Jesus's forty-day fast without dying.

Then another week went by and suddenly he was Big News. My feed could no longer keep up with it. And, another week, and I no longer needed a feed, because he was all over the majors. Everyone was taking notice. His followers, interviewed now, seemed less like the flotsam and jetsam of a cruel world, and more like a core new class of people. Homo superior. The numbers were growing across southern Asia. Nic sang the superman, and the superman was going to overcome us. He was in Morocco ("north Africa" was the most we knew), but then he was seized by an Equatorial States strike force in a daring operation that left forty dead. He was held against his will, but seemed – in interview – perfectly blithe. "I have a new vision of the world," said his face. "The world will change." He said that more and more real people – code for "the poor" – were taking to his treatment. He said it was becoming an unstoppable force.

When word got out that the Equatorial States were trying to ransom him back to the USA for a huge sum of money there were riots. He was broken out of the building in which he was being held – a few minutes of jittery footage of him, his face bloody, being carried bobbing across a sea of humanity, and grinning, and grinning – and disappeared. He later reappeared in Malaysia, an official guest of the Malay Republic.

I watched the feed when Foss was flown out, and put through all the rigmarole of secrecy, to interview him. It really seemed to me the old Nic was trying to break out of what must have been an increasingly rigid carapace of popular, proletarian expectation. He cracked jokes. He talked about his plans. "This is the future," he said, in a twinkly-eye voice. "I'll tell you. My technology is going to set humanity free from their starvation. I'll tell you what will happen. The poor will migrate; there will be a mass migration, to the tropics – to those parts of the world where sunlight is plentiful, but where food is hard to come by. Some governments will be overwhelmed by this new exodus, but governments like the, eh," and he had to glance down at his thumbback screen to remind himself which radical government's hospitality he was currently enjoying, "People's Islamic-Democratic Republic of Malaysia, will welcome the coming of a new age of popular empowerment."

"What about the rest of the world?" Foss asked.

"The rich can have the rest of the world. The cold and sunless northern and southern bands. The rich don't need sunlight. They have money for food. The whole global demographic will change – a new pulsing heart will bring life and culture and prosperity to the tropics. Over time the north and the south will become increasingly irrelevant. The central zone will be everything – a great population of real people, sitting in the sun for three hours a day, using the remaining twenty-one creating greatness for humanity."

VII

But what can I say? It was a fire, and fire, being a combustion, is always in the process of rendering itself inert. I did consider whether I needed to include, in this account, material about my motivation for betraying my friend. But I think that should be clear from what I have written here.

The Company persuaded me. A message was conveyed that I wanted to meet him again. A meeting was arranged. I flatter myself the there were very few human beings on the planet for whom he would have agreed this.

I had to pretend I had taken up dotsnuff. This involved me actually practising snorting the stuff, though I hated it. But the dotsnuff was a necessary part of the seizure strategy. It identified where I was; and more to the point it was programmed with Nic's deener-tag (of course the Company had that on file). That would separate us out from all other people in whichever room or space we found ourselves in – let's say, soldiers, guards, captors, terrorists, whomsoever – and in which the snuff would roil about like smoke. When the capture team came crashing in with furious suddenness their guns would know which people to shoot and which not to shoot.

He was back in the Indian Federation now: somewhere near Delhi.

I was flown direct to Delhi international. And we landed at noon. And I was fizzing with nerves.

From the airpot I took a taxi to an arranged spot, and there met a man who told me to take a taxi to another spot. At that place I was collected by three other men and put into a large car. It was not a pleasant drive. I was bitter with nerves; my mind rendered frangible by terror. It was insanely hot; migraine weather, forty five, fifty, and the car seemed to have no air conditioning. We drove past a succession of orchards, the trunks of the trees blipping past my window like a barcode. Then we turned up a road that stretched straight as a thermometer line, towards the horizon. And up we raced until it ended before a huge gate. Men with rifles stood about. I could see four dogs, tongues like untucked shirttails. And then the gate was opened and we drove inside.

I was shown to a room, and in it I stayed for several hours. My luggage was taken away.

I could not sleep. It was too hot to sleep anyway.

My luggage was brought back, my tube of dotsnuff still inside. I took this and slipped it inside my trouser pocket.

I informed my guards of my need to use the restroom – genuinely, for my bladder was fuller, and bothered me more, than my conscience. I was taken to a restroom with a dozen urinals at one wall and half a dozen sinks at another. A crossword-pattern of gaps marked where humidity had removed some of the tiny blue tiles covering the walls. The shiny floor was not as clean as I might have liked. I emptied my bladder into the white porcelain cowl of a urinal, and washed my hands at the sink. Then, like a character in a cheap film, I peered at myself in the mirror. My eyes saw my eyes. I examined my chin, the jowls shimmery with stubble, the velveteen eyebrows, the rather too large ears. This was the face that Kate saw when she leant in, saying either "a kiss before bedtime," or "a bed before kisstime," and touched my lips with her lips. I was horribly conscious of the flippant rapidity of my heart, of blood hurrying with adrenaline.

A guard I had not previously encountered, a tall, thin man with a gold-handled pistol tucked into the front of his trousers, came into the lavatory. "The Redeemer will see you now," he said.

VIII

Had he come straight out with "why are you here?" or "what do you want?" or anything like that, I might have blurted the truth. I had prepared answers for those questions, of course, but I was, upon seeing him again, miserably nervous. But of course he wasn't puzzled that I wanted to see him again. He took that as his due. Of course I wanted to see him – who wouldn't? His face cracked wide with a grin, and he embraced me.

We were in a wide, low-ceilinged room; and we were surrounded by gun-carrying young men and women: some pale as I, some sherry- and acorn-coloured, some black as liquorish. A screen was switched on but the sound was down. Through a barred-window I could see the sepia plain and, waverly with heat in the distance, the edge-line of the orchards.

"Redeemer, is it?" I said, my dry throat making the words creak.

"Can you believe it?" He rolled his eyes upwards, so that he was looking at the ceiling – the direction, had he only known it, of the company troopers, sweeping in low-orbit with a counter-spin to hover, twenty-miles up on the vertical. "I try to fucking discourage it."

"Sure you do," I said. Then, clutching the tube in my pocket to stop my fingers trembling, I added in a rapid voice: "I've taken up snuff, you know."

Nic looked very somberly at me. "I'm afraid you'll have to go outside if you want to snort that."

For a moment I thought he was being genuine, and my rapid heartbeat accelerated to popping point. My hands shivered. I was sweating. When he laughed, and beckoned me towards a lowslung settee, I felt the relief as sharply as terror. I sat and tried, by focussing my resolve, to stop the tremble in my calf muscles.

"You know what I hate?" he said, as if resuming a conversation we had been having just moments before. "I hate that phrase body fascism. You take a fat man, or fat woman, and criticise them for being fat. That makes you a body fascist. You know what's wrong there? It's the fascism angle. In a fucking world where one third of the population hoards all the fucking food and two third starve – in a world where your beloved Company makes billions selling anti-obesity technology to people too stupid to understand they can have anti-obesity for free by fucking eating less – in that world, where the fat ones steal the food from the thin ones so that the thin ones starve to death. That's a world where the fascists are the ones who criticize the fatties? Do you see how upside down that is?"

I fumbled the tube and sniffed up some powder. The little nanograins, keyed to my metabolism, thrummed into my system. Like, I suppose, fire being used to extinguish an oilwell blaze, the extra stimulation had a calming effect.

The talcum-fine cloud in that room. I coughed, theatrically, and waved my hand to dissipate the material.

"So you're free to go?"

"I'm not in charge of it," he said brightly. "Fuck, it's good to see you again! I'm not in charge – I'm being carried along by it as much as anybody. It's a tempest, and it's blowing the whole of humanity like leaves in autumn."

"Some of it was Company," I said. "The ADP to ATP protocols weren't, legally speaking, yours to give away, you know."

"The hair stuff was mine," he said.

"I'm only saying."

"Sure – but the hair stuff."

I thought of the troops, falling through the sky directly above us, their boot-soles coming closer and closer to the tops of our heads.

"The photovoltaic stuff, and the nanotube lysine fabrication of the conductive channels along the individual strands of hair – that was you. But that's of no use without the interface to do the ATP."

He shrugged. "You think like a lawyer. I mean, you think science like a lawyer. It's not that at all. You don't think there's a moral imperative, when the famine in the southern African republics is killing, how many thousands a week is it?" Then he brightened. "Fuck it's good to see you though! If I'd let the Company have this they'd have squeezed every last euro of profit out of it, and millions would have died." But his heart wasn't really in this old exchange. "Wait til I've shown you round," he said, as excited as a child, and swept his right hand in an arc, lord-of-the-manor-wise.

Somewhere outside the room a siren was sounding. Muffled by distance, a warbling miaow. Nic ignored it, although several of his guards perked their heads up. One went out to see what the pother was.

I felt the agitation building in my viscera. Betrayal is not something I have any natural tolerance for, I think. It is an uncomfortable thing. I fidgeted. The sweat kept running into my eyes.

"All the old rhythms of life change," Nic said. "Everything is different now."

I felt the urge to scream. I clenched my teeth. The urge passed.

"Of course Power is scared," Nic was saying. "Of course Power wants to stop what we're doing. Wants to stop us liberating people from hunger. Keeping people in fear of starvation has always been the main strategy by which Power has kept people subordinate."

"I'll say," I said, squeakily, "how much I love your sophomore lectures on politics."

"Hey!" he said, either in mock outrage, or in real outrage. I was too far gone to be able to tell the difference.

"The thing is," I started to say, and then lots of things happened. The clattering cough of rifle fire started up outside. There was the realization that the highpitched noise my brain had been half-hearing for the last minute was a real sound, not just tinitus – and then almost at once the sudden crescendo or distillation of precisely that noise; a great thumping crash from above, and the appearance, in a welter of plaster and smoke, of an enormous metal beak through the middle of the ceiling. The roof sagged, and the whole room bowed out on its walls. Then the beak snapped open and two, three, four troopers dropped to the floor, spinning round and firing their weapons. All I remember of the next twenty seconds is the explosive stutter-cough and the disco flicker of multiple weapon discharges, and then the stench of gunfire's aftermath.

A cosmic finger was running smoothly round and round the lip of a cosmic wineglass.

I blinked, and blinked, and looked about me. The dust in the air looked like steam. That open metal beak, rammed through the ceiling, had the disconcerting appearance of a weird avant-art metal chandelier. There were half a dozen troopers; standing in various orientations and positions but with all their guns held like dalek-eyes. There were a number of sprawling bodies on the floor. I didn't want to count them, or look too closely at them. And, beside me, on the settee, was an astonished-looking Neocles.

I moved my mouth to say something to him, and then either I said something that my ears did not register, or else I didn't say anything.

He didn't look at me. He jerked forward, and then jerked up. Standing. From a pouch in his pocketstrides he pulled out a small square-shaped object which, fumbling a little, he fitted into his right hand. The troopers may have been shouting at him, or they may have been standing there perfectly silently, I couldn't tell you. Granular white clouds of plaster were sifting down. Nic leveled his pistol, holding his arm straight out. There was a conjuror's trick with multiple bright red streamers and ribbons being pulled instantly and magically out of his chest, and then he hurtled backwards, over the top of the settee, to land on his spine on the floor. It took a moment for me to understand what had happened.

He may have been thinking, either in the moment or else as something long pre-planned, about martyrdom. Perhaps the Redeemer is not able to communicate his message in any other way. It's also possible that, having gone through life protected by the tightfitting prophylactic of his unassailable ego that he may have genuinely believed that he could single-handedly shoot down half a dozen troopers, and emerge the hero of the day. I honestly do not know.

IX

I was forced to leave my home, and live in a series of hideouts. Of course a Judas is as valuable and holy figure as any other in the sacred drama. But religious people (Kate kneeling beside the bed at nighttime, praying to meekling Jesus gent and mild) can be faulted, I think, for failing imaginatively to enter into the mindset of their Judases. Nobody loved Nic as deeply as I. Or knew him so well. But he was rich, and not one motion of his liberal conscience or his egotistical desire to do good in the world changed that fact, or changed his inability to enter, actually, into the life of the poor. The poor don't want the rich to save them. Even the rioters in the Indian Federation, even the starving Australians, even they – if only they knew it – don't want to be carried by a god-like rich man into a new realm. What they want is much simpler. They want not to be poor. It's simultaneously very straightforward and very complicated. Nic's hair was, in fact, only a way of making manifest the essence of class relations. In his utopia the poor would actually become – would literally become – the vegetation of the earth. The rich would reinforce their position as the zoology to the poor's botany. Nothing could be more damaging, because it would bed-in the belief that it is natural and inevitable that the rich graze upon the poor, and that the poor are there to be grazed upon. Without even realizing it Nic was laboring to make the disenfranchised a global irrelevance; to make them grass for the rich to graze upon. I loved him, but he was doing evil. I had no choice.

X

Last night, as we lay in bed together in my new, Company-sourced secure flat in I-can't-say-where (though I'm the one paying the rent) Kate said to me: "I am cut in half like the moon; but like the moon I grow whole again." I was astonished by this. This really isn't the sort of thing she says. "What was that, sweet?" I asked her. "What did you say, my love?" But she was asleep, her red lips were pursed, and her breath slipping out and slipping in.

BEFORE MY LAST BREATH

Robert Reed

Robert Reed sold his first story in 1986 and quickly established himself as a frequent contributor to *The Magazine of Fantasy and Science Fiction, Asimov's Science Fiction,* and many other markets. Reed may be one of the most prolific of today's young writers, particularly at short fiction lengths, seriously rivaled for that position only by authors such as Stephen Baxter and Brian Stableford. And – also like Baxter and Stableford – he manages to keep up a very high standard of quality while being prolific, something that is not at all easy to do. Reed stories such as "Sister Alice," "Brother Perfect," "Decency," "Savior," "The Remoras," "Chrysalis," "Whiptail," "The Utility Man," "Marrow," "Birth Day," "Blind," "The Toad of Heaven," "Stride," "The Shape of Everything," "Guest of Honor," "Waging Good," and "Killing the Morrow," among at least a half-dozen others equally as strong, count among some of the best short works produced by anyone in the 1980s and 90s; many of his best stories have been assembled in the collections *The Dragons of Springplace* and *The Cuckoo's Boys*. Nor is he non-prolific as a novelist, having turned out eleven novels since the end of the 1980s, including *The Lee Shore, The Hormone Jungle, Black Milk, The Remarkables, Down the Bright Way, Beyond the Veil of Stars, An Exaltation of Larks, Beneath the Gated Sky, Marrow, Sister Alice,* and *The Well of Stars,* as well as two chapbook novellas, *Mere* and *Flavors of My Genius*. His most recent book is a new novel, *Eater-of-Bone*. Reed lives with his family in Lincoln, Nebraska.

Here he unravels a fascinating archaeological mystery with roots that stretch back for millions of years. . . .

Thomas

THE AFTERNOON WAS clear and exceptionally cold. An off-duty company geologist was driving across the floor of the mine when a flash of reflected light caught his gaze. He didn't particularly want to go home, and thirty-one years in the coal industry hadn't quite killed the curious boy inside him. Backing up, he saw the flash repeated, and it seemed peculiar enough that he pulled on his stocking cap and mittens and climbed slowly up over the lignite coal, taking a close, careful look at something that made no sense whatsoever.

His fingers were numb and nose frostbitten when he reached the field office. But he didn't tremble until he began to the maps, showing his superiors what patch of ground shouldn't be touched until more qualified experts could come in and kick around.

"What'd you find?" they asked.

"An unknown species," seemed like an honest, worthy answer.

Sixty million years ago, plant material had gathered inside a basin sandwiched between young mountain ranges. Then the peat was covered over with eroded debris and slowly cooked into the low-sulfur treasure that today fed power plants across half of the country. Fossils were common in Powder River country. The coal often looked like rotted leaves and sticks. But there was no way to systematically investigate what the gigantic machines wrested from the ground. Tons of profit came up with every scoop, and only one person in the room wanted the discovery preserved, no matter how unique it might be.

The geologist listened to the group's decision. Then he lifted the stakes, showing the photographs that he had taken with his cell phone camera. "This resembles nothing I've ever seen before," he added. Then mostly to himself, he muttered, "It's like nothing else in the world."

"I've seen these before," one supervisor barked. "It's nothing, Tom."

Normally an agreeable sort, the geologist nodded calmly, but then his voice showed bite when he asked, "Why can't we damn well be sure? Just to be safe?"

"No," another boss growled. "Now forget about it."

Thirty-one years of loyal service to the company brought one undeniable lesson: This argument would never be won here. So he retreated, driving into Gillette and his tiny house. His wife was sitting in the front of the television, half-asleep. He poured the last of her whiskey down the sink, and she stood and cursed him for some vague reason and swung hard at his face, and he caught her and wrestled her to bed, saying all of the usual words until she finally closed her eyes. Then he collected several dozen important names and agencies, sending out a trim but explicit e-mail that included his phone numbers and the best of his inadequate pictures. Thomas showered quickly, and he waited. Nobody called. Then he dressed and ate dinner before carrying two shotguns, unloaded, and a tall thermos of coffee out the truck, and after a few minutes of consideration, he drove back to the mine, parking as close to the fossil as possible.

Tom's plan, such as it was, involved shooing away the excavators as long as possible, first with words, and if necessary, empty threats. But these were temporary measures, and worse, he discovered that his phone didn't work down here in the pit's deepest corner. That's why he stepped out into the cold again. Navigating by the stars and carrying a small hammer, he intended to break off a few pieces of the fossil – as a precaution, in case this treasure was dug up and rolled east, doomed to be incinerated with the rest of the anonymous coal.

Mattie

Few took notice of the peculiar e-mail. Three colleagues called its author, two leaving messages on his voice mail. CNN's science reporter ordered her intern to contact the corporation's main office for reaction. The PR person on duty knew nothing about the incident, sharply questioned its validity, and after restating his employer's sterling environmental record, hung up. In frustration, the intern contacted a random astronomer living in Colorado. The astronomer knew nothing about the matter. She glanced at the forwarded e-mail, in particular the downloaded images, and then said, "Interesting," to the uninterested voice. It wasn't until later, staring at the twisted body with its odd limbs and very peculiar skull that her heart began to race. She called the geologist's phones. Nobody answered. Leaving warning of her imminent arrival, she dressed for the Arctic and grabbed the department's sat-phone, buying two tall coffees when she gassed up on her way out of Boulder.

Better than most, Mattie understood the temporary nature of life. This woman who had never before been stopped by the police earned three speeding tickets on the journey north. Approaching the mine, she slipped in behind an empty dump truck, driving almost beneath the rear axle, and because the only security guard happened to be relieving himself, she managed to slip undetected out onto the gouged, unearthly landscape.

GPS coordinates took her to a pickup truck parked beside a blackish-brown cliff. The engine was running, a stranger sleeping behind the wheel. Beside him on the seat was what looked like huge, misshapen hands cradling a large golden ring. Two shotguns were perched against the far door. For a brief moment, she hesitated. But Mattie shoved her natural caution aside. With a tap on the glass, she woke the stranger, and startled, he stared out at what must have looked like a ghost – this young woman with almost no hair and a gaunt, wasted face.

He nervously rolled down the window.

"Are you Thomas Greene? I'm Mattie Chong."

Stupid with fatigue, Tom asked, "What are you doing here?"

"I came to see your alien," she reported.

He accepted that. What bothered him more was the stranger's appearance. "Ma'am, if you don't mind my asking . . . what's wrong with you?"

"Cancer," Mattie reported amiably, throwing her flashlight's beam against the deep seam of lignite. "And if I'm alive in four months, I'll beat all of my doctors' predictions."

The President

It was rare not to be the most important man in the room. And today brought one of those exceptional occasions: a trailer crowded with scientists and Secret Service agents, mining representatives and select reporters, plus the three-person congressional delegation from Wyoming. But the hero of the moment was Dr Greene, and everybody wanted to stand beside the renowned geologist. Of course Dr Chong should have shared this limelight, but she was flown to Utah this morning, her illness taking its expected, presumably fatal turn. The president was merely another visitor, and as the lesser celebrity, it was his duty to shake hands and ask about the poor woman's health. Every researcher had to be congratulated on the historic, world-shattering work. And he insisted on smiles all around. Bullied joviality was the president's great skill, and he was at his best when he was feeling less than happy.

Today was especially miserable. The bitter wind and low leaden skies only underscored a mood that had crumbled at dawn. That's when word arrived that his former Chief of Staff – a slippery political worm on his noblest day – planned to give the Special Investigator everything, including the damned briefcase filled with cash and ten hours of exceptionally embarrassing recordings. The president's administration was wounded, and by tomorrow it might well be dead. Cautious voices wanted the Wyoming visit canceled, but that would have required an artful excuse, and what would have changed? Nothing. Besides, he understood that if enough people were fascinated with these old bones and odd artifacts, the coming nastiness might not be as awful as it promised to be.

Dr Irving Case was the project administrator, and he had been on duty for less than a week. But with a bureaucrat's instincts for what counted, he used a large empty smile and a big voice. "Mr President, sir. Would you like to go see the discovery now, sir?"

"If it's no problem. Let's have a peek at old George."

Back into the winter miseries they went. A tent-like shelter had been erected around the burial site, to block the wind and blowing coal dust. As they strolled across the barren scene, a dozen experts spoke in a competitive chorus, agreeing that the fossil was unique and remarkable, and of course immeasurably precious. The first priority was to disturb nothing, every clue precious and no one certain what constituted a clue. The president kept hearing how little was known, yet in the next moment, a dozen different hypotheses were offered to explain the creature's origins and how it might have looked in life and why it was where it was and why this wasn't where it had lived.

"It didn't live here?" the president interrupted. Aiming for humor, he said, "This splendid desolation . . . this is exactly where every movie alien roams."

Laughter blossomed – the bright fleeting giddiness that attaches itself to men of power. Then they reached the shelter, and reverent silence took hold. Dr Case mentioned rules. Politely but firmly, he reminded everybody to wear the proper masks and gloves, and nothing could be touched, and then he warned the press to stand back so that all might enjoy the best possible view.

Photographs and video had already shown the mysterious fossil to the world. The enormous stratum of coal in which he, or she, was entombed was long ago dubbed Big George, hence the fossil's popular name. Lights had been strung near the tent ceiling. The coal slag was cleared away, the flat floor littered with scientific instruments and brightly colored cables. What rose before the president was both immediately recognizable and immeasurably strange: sixty million years ago, alien hands had dug a hole deep into the watery peat, and then "George" was lowered in or climbed in, feet first. Shovels had been used in the excavation. Two archeologists pointed at nearly invisible details, describing with confidence how the metal blades must have looked and what kinds of limbs employed them, and even while they were talking, a third voice reminded everyone that conjectures were fine, but nothing was proved and might never be.

George was a big fellow, and even to the uninformed eye, he looked like something from another world. The weight of the rock had compressed him, but not as badly as the president expected. Two bent legs helped carry the long horizontal body, and two more legs were presumably buried out of sight. A fifth limb rose from behind what looked like the angular and watchful face of a praying mantis, and the arm was jointed and complicated and partially destroyed. Dr Greene had removed the matching hands and now famous gold ring. The corpse was majestic, wasn't it? But in the next moment, in the president's eyes, George looked preposterous. Pieces stolen from unrelated creatures had been thrown together, a wily hoaxer having his laugh at all this foolish, misplaced fascination.

Turning to world's most famous geologist, the president asked, "How were we so lucky, this poor fellow exposed this way?"

"The coal's weak around the edges of the grave," Dr Greene explained. His celebrity was wearing on him, puffy eyes half-closed, a dazed, deep fatigue visible in his features and slope-shouldered posture. "If the blade had cut anywhere else, I wouldn't have noticed anything."

"It was the ring you saw?"

"Yes, sir."

The president nodded. "I haven't seen that artifact yet," he mentioned.

Dr Case stepped forward. "The hands and ring have been sent to the Sandia, sir. For analysis and closer study."

The president nodded, looking up again. "So well preserved."

Dr Case enjoyed his little stage. "The corpse shows very little sign of decomposition," he explained. "And we don't know why. Maybe the acidic peat and lack of oxygen preserved it. Although it's possible that the flesh was simply too alien and our microbes couldn't find anything to chew on."

The president nodded, pretending to appreciate the vagaries of alien biology. Then he returned to one statement that had puzzled him earlier. "And why do we think George lived elsewhere?"

Somebody said, "The feet."

Each leg ended with a narrow, three-toed foot.

"They're not built for bogs," another voice volunteered. "George would have sunk in to his knees, or deeper."

Against the rules, the president stepped closer. Nobody dared correct him, but the scene grew noticeably quieter. A Clydesdale horse would have been larger, but not by much. He knelt and stared at the lead foot, moving his head back and forth to avoid his own shadow. Sixty million years in the ground, yet the corpse retained its flesh and what seemed to be its natural color, which was tan. The crushing weight had twisted the dead foot, every toe visible. But what was perhaps more remarkable lay beneath the foot – the remnants of what might be animal skin, cut and stitched to create a simple shoe.

"Is this really a moccasin?" he asked.

Dr Case joined him, kneeling and pushing his own mask closer to his mouth – making absolutely certain not to contaminate the treasure. "We have at least fifteen features that are probably remnants of clothing, Mr. President. And six metallic objects that look like knives and such, all carried on the body."

"Anything special?" the president inquired.

The administrator blinked, unsure what to make of the question.

"You know, like a laser-gun or portable reactor."

"Nothing like that, sir."

"That surprises me," the president admitted.

Dr Case stood, offering his hand. "From what we can tell, sir . . . the technology is Early Iron Age. If that."

The president rose without anyone's help.

Another few minutes of inexpert study ended when someone mentioned lunch. "A fine idea," the president agreed. "Let the scientists back to work!" Then everyone filed outside and pulled off the choking masks. The distraction was over, the show finished. The president found his previous depression waiting for him, like a black mountain bearing down on his aging frame. He wiped his mouth with a sleeve, accepted the vacuous thanks of several people, and then he dredged up another one of his patented smiles, wondering why it was that no President had killed himself in office. Considering the pressures of the job, that seemed remarkable. Almost an oversight, really. The idea was so intriguing that he spent the next several moments dancing with a lurid fantasy: He would kill himself today, people around the world would weep, and with that, he would give himself a lasting, however inglorious place in history.

Irving

He was asked to say a few words at the funeral, honoring the heroic figure that had been lost. It was a fine speech and a very pleasant day in late September, the press in full attendance and millions watching only Irving. But how does one dispose of the body of a great person, someone composed of digital images and countless memories as well as flesh and bone? That was the question he had asked himself, preparing for this moment. This opportunity. Of course he wouldn't say anything so blatant or borderline crass, but that was the crux of the situation. Most of the world's citizens were anonymous bodies with a few possessions soon to be misplaced. But one can never bury or burn the modern celebrity. Their lives were so vast, so persistent and sturdy, that it was impossible to make a suitable grave. Indeed, death could free the largest celebrities into a greater, more enduring realm where they would never age, and with luck, would only grow even more impressive with the passage of years.

What Irving did address was his great admiration for a colleague who quickly became his good friend. "A sad, tragic death," he said, "and as unexpected as the discovery inside the coal. And we are all the lesser because of it." He didn't mention the deep irony that hadn't escaped anyone's attention: Thomas Greene was killed in a minor traffic accident, while George's co-discoverer was on the rebound, her withered body responding to an experimental regime of stem cells and tailored phages.

The audience smiled as Irving left the podium.

Of course Mattie deserved the final word, and she used her public moment to beg for full funding of the ongoing Graveyard Project. It was a clumsy display of politics, and only she could get away with it. Irving was the project's administrator, far too exposed to act in such obvious ways. But he was grateful for her waving the hat, and he told her so afterwards. There was a reception back in Gillette, and another one of the endless news conferences, and the two sat close together behind a long table, fielding the same questions again and again.

Ten months after its discovery, nobody knew for sure how large the burial ground was. But evidence hinted at an enormous field of bodies, most of them deeper than George, buried over a period of many thousands of years. That was why the entire mine had been closed and made into a national monument. Power plants were sitting idle back east, but that's how important the Graveyard was. Every reporter wanted to know why the aliens had used this location. Mattie and Irving confessed that they were just as curious and as frustrated by their ignorance. To date, thirty-eight "georges" had been recovered from within the gigantic coal seam. As a rule, the deeper bodies wore better clothes and carried fancier tools, though nothing worthy of a star-traveler had been uncovered yet. Without giving details, Irving allowed that a final census might be coming, and that's when Mattie mentioned the new seismic scans – an elaborate experiment to make the lignite transparent as water.

"Don't put too much stock in success," Irving warned the reporters and cameras. "This technology is new and fickle, and we might not get results for months, if ever."

It seemed odd, a man in his position staunching excitement. But if these scans failed, he might be blamed. And what good would that do? This job was a dream, and Irving intended to remain inside the dream as long as possible. He was successful and couldn't imagine being happier, wielding power over hundreds of lives and a billion-dollar budget: emperor to an empire that had already revolutionized how humanity looked at itself and the universe.

Irving was exhilarated by the news conference; Mattie was exhausted. He made a point of walking the still-frail woman to her car, even when she claimed she could manage on her own, thank you. "I insist," he told her, and they shook hands and parted, and as he walked back into the reception hall, an associate approached quickly and whispered, "Sir, you have to see this, sir."

"See what?"

Then in the next instant, he muttered, "Results?"

"Yes, sir."

The laptop was set up in the little kitchen, linked to Base Camp's computers, and the news was astonishing enough that this man who never failed to find the right words was mute, knees bending as he stared at data that made his fondest dreams look like weak fantasies.

The screen was jammed with white marks and long numbers, each grave given a precise designation tied to estimated size and metal content and other crucial information. The graveyard covered more than a five square kilometers, and the dead were thick, particularly in the deepest layers.

"How many . . . ?" he muttered.

"At least thirty thousand, sir."

Again, Irving's voice failed him.

The assistant misread his silence, assuming disappointment. "But that's not the final number," she added. "They're so many bodies, particularly near the bottom, sir . . . the final number is sure to be quite a bit larger than this."

Badger

Why he loved the girl was a complicated business. There were so many reasons he couldn't count them – moments of bliss and the intense looks that she gave him and little touches in the dark and touches offered but then taken away. Teasing. She was an expert at the tease. She was funny and quick with her tongue, and she was beautiful, of course. Yet she carried her beauty in ways most girls couldn't. Slender and built like a boy, she had the smallest tits he'd every felt up – a fact that he foolishly admitted once. But her face had this wonderful full mouth and a perfect nose and impossibly big eyes full of an earthly blue that watched him whenever he talked and paid even closer attention when he wasn't saying anything. She was observant in ways he never would be, and she was smart about people, and even though she rarely left Wyoming, she seemed to know more about the world than did her much older boyfriend who had already traveled across the globe three or four times.

Badger had little memory for the places that he had been, but Hanna knew that if she kept asking questions, he might remember what the Sahara looked like at midnight and what he saw on a certain street in Phnom Penh and what it felt like to tunnel his way into an Incan burial chamber seven hundred years after it was sealed off from the world.

"Why Badger?" was her first question, asked moments after they met.

He sipped his beer and looked around the bar, wondering who this youngster was. "Because that's my name," he said with a shrug.

"You dig tunnels, right?"

"Who are you?" he asked.

"Hanna." She'd already settled on the stool beside his. Without another word, she pulled his glass over and took a sip, grinning as she licked the Budweiser off her upper lip. Reading his mind, she said, "I'm twenty-two."

"You aren't," he replied.

She laughed and gave back his remaining beer. "Word is, Badger, you're working at the Graveyard, digging down to the most interesting georges."

"Which high school do you go to?"

"I attend the University in Laramie," she replied. Then she put an elbow on the bar and set her delicate chin on edge of her palm, fingers curled up beneath that big wonderful smiling mouth. Without a trace of doubt, she told him, "You aren't all that comfortable with women. Are you, Badger?"

"How do you know my name?"

"I've seen you. And I've asked about you, I guess." Then she laughed at him, adding, "Or maybe I heard there was this guy named Badger digging holes for Dr Chong, and you came tromping in here, and I figured, just by looking at you, that you had to be that guy. What would you think of that?"

He didn't know what the girl was telling him, or if he should care one way or another.

"I know Mattie pretty well," she reported. "Your boss has come to school to talk . . . I don't know, maybe ten times. She's a neat, neat lady, I think."

He nodded agreeably.

"How long has she been in charge?"

"Three months," he answered. "Dr Case got pushed up to Washington – "

"I bet she drives you nuts," she interrupted.

"Why's that?"

"A feeling." Hanna shrugged and suddenly changed topics. "Does it ever make you crazy, thinking what you're working on?"

"Why would it?"

"The Graveyard!" she shouted. Down came her hand, and she sat up straight on the stool, looking around the quiet bar as if to hunt down a witness to this foolishness. "One hundred thousand dead aliens in the ground, and you're part of the team that's working their way to the bottom of the dead. Isn't that an astonishing thing? Don't you wake up every morning and think, 'God, how incredibly lucky can one burrowing weasel be?' "

"My build," he allowed.

She fell silent, watching him.

"I got the name as a kid," he reported. "My given name is Stuart, but I got the nickname because I've got short legs and a little bit of strength, I guess."

"You guess?"

"I'm strong," he said.

"I can tell."

"Yeah?"

"I like strong," she confessed, leaning in close.

Or maybe it wasn't that complicated, why he loved Hanna. She seemed to truly love him, and how could he not return the emotion? Beautiful and smart and sharp, and he was powerless to ignore her overtures. He gave her the rest of his beer and answered her questions as far as he could, admitting that the scope and importance of the Graveyard was beyond him. He was a professional digger. Using equipment designed by others, he was adept at carving his way through complicated strata, avoiding other graves and other treasures on his way to realms that hadn't seen sun since a few million years after the dinosaurs died away.

Later, Hanna asked, "What do you think of them?"

They were sitting in his truck in the open countryside, at night. So far they hadn't even kissed, but it felt as if they'd been sitting there for years. It was that natural, that inevitable.

"Think about who?" he said.

She gave him a look.

He understood. But the honest answer was another shrug and the embarrassing admission, "I don't think much. I don't know much at all. I've seen hundreds of them, but the aliens still look nothing but strange to me. What they were like when they were alive . . . I don't have any idea . . ."

"You don't call them 'georges,'" she pointed out.

"That's a silly name," he growled, "and it doesn't suit them."

She accepted the logic.

This was the moment when Badger caught himself wondering when he would ask the girl to marry him. Not if, but when.

"Everybody else has a story," Hanna told him. "I haven't met the person who doesn't think these creatures were part of some lost colony or prisoners in an alien work camp, or maybe they were wanderers living in orbit but burying themselves in the peat so we'd find them millions of years later. Just to prove to us that they'd been here."

"I don't know the answer," he said.

"And do you know why?" she asked. "Because you understand what's important." Then she lifted her face to his, and they kissed for a long while, and it was all that he could do, big strong unimaginative Badger, not to ask that girl to marry him right then.

Hanna

He called to ask, "How you doing, hon?"

"Good," she lied.

"Feel like walking around?"

"Why?"

"Dr. Chong says it's all right. I explained how the doctor wants you in bed, but for the next couple weeks you can still move—"

"Will I get to see the new one?"

"You want to?"

"I'm getting dressed now," she lied, crawling off the couch. "Are you coming to get me, Badge?"

"Pulling into the driveway right now," he reported happily.

So she got caught. Not only wasn't she close to ready, Hanna looked awful, and it took more promises and a few growls before Badger decided she was up to this adventure. Babies. Such a bother! Laying eggs would be so much easier. Drop them somewhere safe and walk away, living your own life until the kids were big enough to be fun. That's how mothering should be.

She mentioned her idea to Badger.

He was driving and laughing. "I wonder where you got that from?"

Georges had laid eggs. The younger females always had a few in some incomplete stage of development. Nobody knew if they put their basketball-sized eggs inside nests or incubators or what. Two years of research, yet the aliens' life remained mysterious, open to guesswork and wishful thinking. But somewhere in those vanished mountains, up high where the air was deliciously thin, the species had struggled mightily to replace the several friends and family being buried every year in that deep black peat.

Mattie was waiting for them at the surface. She smiled warmly and asked Hanna how she was feeling, and Hanna tried to sound like a woman in robust good health. Everybody dressed in clean gowns and masks, and then they took the long walk below ground, following one of the worm-like tunnels that Badger had cut into the deep seam. Seven other times Hanna had gotten a tour. But this visit was unique because of the age of the corpse being unearthed – one of the first generation georges, it was guessed – and because this was a privilege that not even the most connected members of the media had known.

This body lay at the graveyard's edge. To help the studies, Badger had carved an enormous room beside the fossil. The room was filled with machinery and lights, coolers full of food and drink, a portable restroom, plus several researchers busy investigating the tiniest features, making ready for the slow cautious removal of the dead alien female.

Compared to the first george, she was a giant. Hanna expected as much, but seeing the body made her breath quicken. A once-powerful creature, larger than most rhinoceroses, she now lay crumpled down by death and suffocation and the weight of the world that had been peeled away above her. She was dead, yet she was entirely whole too. The acidic peat was a perfect preservative for flesh born outside this world, and presumably the aliens understood that salient fact.

"Great," Hanna gushed. "Wonderful. Thank you."

"Step closer," Mattie offered. "Just not past the yellow line."

A pair of researchers – sexless in their gowns and masks – were perched on a short scaffold, carefully working with the alien's hands.

"The burial ring?" Hanna asked.

Mattie nodded. "An aluminum alloy. Very sophisticated, very obvious in the scans."

"How different?"

The older the corpse, the more elaborate the ring. Mattie explained, "This one's more like a cylinder than a ring, and it's covered with details we don't find in any of the later burials."

The clothing was more elaborate, Hanna noticed, legs covered with trousers held up by elaborate belts, the feet enjoying what looked like elegant boots sewn from an ancient mammal's leathery hide. A nylon satchel rode the long back, worn by heavy use, every pocket stripped of anything that would have been difficult to replace.

"Will we ever find the prize?" Hanna asked.

"That amazing widget that transforms life on earth?" Mattie shrugged, admitting, "I keep promising that. Every trip to Congress, I say it's going to happen soon. But I seriously wonder. From what I've seen, these creatures never went into the ground carrying anything fancy or difficult to make."

Those words sank home. Hanna nodded and glanced at Badger's eyes, asking, "What else did I want to ask, hon? You remember?"

"Religion," he mentioned.

"Oh, yeah." Standing on the yellow line, she asked, "So why did they go into the ground, Mattie?"

"I don't know."

Hanna glanced at the woman, and then she stared up at the alien's cupped hands, imagining that important ring of metal. "I know the story I like best."

"Which one?"

"A starship reached our solar system, but something went wrong. Maybe the ship was supposed to refuel and set out for a different star, and it malfunctioned. Maybe its sister ships were supposed to meet here, but nobody showed." Hanna liked Mattie and respected her, and she wanted to sound informed on this extraordinary topic. "Mars or the moon would have made better homes. Their plan could have been to terraform another world. I know they would have appreciated the lighter gravity. And we think – because of the evidence, we can surmise – that their bodies didn't need or want as much free oxygen as we require. So whatever the reason, earth isn't where they wanted to be."

"A lot of people think that," Mattie said.

Hanna continued. "They didn't want to stay here long. And we don't have any evidence that their starship landed nearby. But they came here. The aliens set down in the nearby mountains, and they managed to find food and built shelter, and survive. But after ten or fifty or maybe two hundred years . . . whatever felt like a long time for that first generation . . . no one had come to rescue them. And that's why they started digging holes and climbing inside."

"You believe they were hibernating," Mattie guessed.

"No," Hanna admitted. "Or I mean, maybe they slept when they were buried. But they weren't planning to wake up like normal either. Their brains weren't like ours, I know. Crystalline and tough, and all the evidence points to a low-oxygen metabolism. What I think happened . . . each of the creatures reached a point in life when they felt past their prime, or particularly sad, or whatever . . . and that's why a lady like this would climb into the cold peat. She believes, or at least she needs to believe, that in another few hundred years, another ring-shaped starship is going to fall toward our sun, dig her up and bring her back to life."

Mattie contemplated the argument and nodded. "I've heard that story a few times, in one fashion or another."

"That's how their tradition started," Hanna continued. "Every generation of georges buried itself in the peat, and after a few centuries or a few thousand years, nobody would remember why. All they knew that it was important to do, and that by holding a metal ring in your hands, you were making yourself a little easier to find inside your sleeping place."

Badger sighed, disapproving of the rampant speculation.

"That might well be true," said Mattie. "Which explains why the rings got simpler as time passed. Nobody remembered what the starship looked like. Or maybe they forgot about the ship entirely, and the ring's purpose changed. It was a symbol, an offering, something that would allow their god to catch their soul and take them back to Heaven again."

Just then, the two workers on the scaffold slipped the burial ring out from between the dead fingers. Mattie approached them and took the prize in both of her gloved hands. Hanna and then Badger stared at what everyone in the world would see in another few hours: A model of a great starship that had once crossed the vacant unloving blackness of space, ending up where it shouldn't have been and its crew and their descendants dying slowly over the next 20,000 years.

Once last time, Hanna thanked Mattie for the tour.

Walking to the surface again, she took her husband's big hand and held it tightly and said, "We're lucky people."

"Why's that?" Badger asked.

"Because we're exactly where we belong," she replied, as if it couldn't be more obvious.

Then they were in the open again, walking on a ravaged landscape dwarfed by the boundless Wyoming sky, and between one step and the next Hanna felt something change inside her body – a slight sensation that held no pain and would normally mean nothing. But she stopped walking. She stopped, but Badger kept marching forward. With both hands, she tenderly touched herself, and she forgot all about the aliens and their epic, long-extinct problems. Bleeding harder by the moment, she looked up to see her husband far ahead of her now, and to herself, with the smallest of whispers, she muttered, "Oh, no . . . not today . . ."

George

Despite night and the season, the thick air burned with its heat and choking oxygen, and the smallest task brought misery, and even standing was work too, and the strongest of the All stood on the broad planks and dug and he dug with them at the soft wet rot of the ground. Everyone but him said those good proper words saved for occasions such as this – ancient chants about better worlds and difficult journeys that ended with survival and giant caring hands that were approaching even now, soon to reach down from the stars to rescue the worthy dead. Silence was expected of the dead, and that was why he said nothing. Silence was the grand tradition born because another – some woman buried far beneath them – said nothing at her death, and the All were so impressed by her reserve and dignity that a taboo was born on that night. How long ago was that time? It was a topic of some conjecture and no good answers, and he used to care about abstract matters like that but discovered now that he couldn't care anymore. His life had been full of idle ideas that had wasted his time, and he was sorry for his misspent passion and all else that went wrong for him. Grief took hold, so dangerous and so massive that he had to set his shovel on the plank and say nothing in a new fashion, gaining the attention of his last surviving daughter. She was a small and pretty and very smart example of the All, and she was more perceptive than most, guessing what was wrong and looking at him compassionately when she said with clicks and warbles that she was proud of her father and proud to belong to his honorable lineage and that he should empty his mind of poisonous thoughts, that he should think of the dead under them and how good it would feel to pass into a realm where thousands of enduring souls waited.

But the dead were merely dead. Promised hands had never arrived, not in their lives or in his. That buoyant faith of youth, once his most cherished possession, was a tattered hope, and perhaps the next dawn would erase even that. That was why it was sensible to accept the smothering sleep now, now while the mind believed however weakly in its own salvation. Because no matter how long the odds, every other ending was even more terrible: He could become a sack of skin filled with anonymous bones and odd organs that would never again know life, that would be thrown into the communal garden to serve as compost, that the All might recall for another three generations, or maybe four, before the future erased his entire existence.

Once again, to the joy of his daughter and the others, the dead man picked up the long shovel and dug. The front feet threw his weight into the blade, and the blade cut into the cold watery muck, and up came another gout of peat that had to be set carefully behind him. Still the right words were spoken, the right blessings offered, and the right motions made, no one daring complain about the heat or the slow progress or the obvious, sorry fact that the strongest and largest of the All were barely able to manage what their ancestors had done easily.

At least so the old stories claimed.

Then came the moment when the fresh wet rectangular hole was finished and one of them had to climb inside. Odd as it seemed, he forgot his duty here. He found himself looking at the others, even at his exhausted daughter, wondering who was to receive this well-deserved honor. Oh yes, me, he recalled, and then he clicked a loud laugh, and he almost spoke, thinking maybe they would appreciate the grim humor. But no, this was a joke best enjoyed by the doomed, and these souls were nothing but alive. Leaving the moment unspoiled, the ceremony whole and sacred, he set his shovel aside and proved to each that he was stealing nothing precious. Hands empty, pockets opened, he showed them just a few cheap knives that he wanted for sentimental reasons. Then he stepped into the chilly stinking mess of water and rot, and with his feet sinking but his head exposed, he reached up with his long arm, hands opened until that good daughter placed the golden ring into his ready grip.

True to the custom, he said nothing more.

In the east, above the high snow-laced mountains, the winter sun was beginning to rise. Soon the killing heat would return to the lowlands, this brutal ground rendered unlivable. The All worked together to finish what had taken too long, shovels and muddy hands flinging the cold peat at the water and then at him – ceremony balanced on growing desperation – and he carefully said nothing and worked hard to think nothing but good thoughts. But then a favorite son returned to him, killed in a rockslide and lost, and he thought of his best mate whose central heart burst without warning, and because promises cost so little, he swore to both of them that he would carry their memories into this other realm, whatever shape it took.

When he discovered that he could not breathe, he struggled, but his mouth was already beneath the water, his head fixed in place.

With the job nearly finished, most of the All kept working. But others were standing away from the grave – those too weak to help, or too spent or too indifferent – and they decided that the dead could not hear them. With private little voices, they spoke about the coming day and the coming year, gentle but intense words dwelling on relationships forming and relationships lost, and who looked best in their funeral garb, and whose children were the prettiest and wisest, and who would die next, and oh by the way, did anyone think to bring a little snack for the journey home . . . ?

ONE OF OUR BASTARDS IS MISSING

Paul Cornell

Here's a fast-paced study of the Great Game played between nations that reads like a Ruritanian romance written by Charles Stross. . . .

British author Paul Cornell is a writer of novels, comics, and television. He's written *Doctor Who* episodes as well as episodes of *Robin Hood* and *Primeval* for the BBC, and Captain Britain for *Marvel Comics*, in addition to Doctor Who novelizations and many other comic works. His *Doctor Who* episodes have twice been nominated for the Hugo Award, and he shares a Writer's Guild Award. Of late, he's taken to writing short science fiction, with sales to *Fast Forward 2*, *Eclipse 2*, and *The Solaris Book of New Science Fiction, Volume Three*.

To GET TO Earth from the edge of the Solar System, depending on the time of year and the position of the planets, you need to pass through at least Poland, Prussia and Turkey, and you'd probably get stamps in your passport from a few of the other great powers. Then as you get closer to the world, you arrive at a point, in the continually shifting carriage space over the countries, where this complexity has to give way or fail. And so you arrive in the blissful lubrication of neutral orbital territory. From there it's especially clear that no country is whole unto itself. There are yearning gaps between parts of each state, as they stretch across the Solar System. There is no congruent territory. The countries continue in balance with each other like a fine but eccentric mechanism, pent up, all that political energy dealt with through eternal circular motion.

The maps that represent this can be displayed on a screen, but they're much more suited to mental contemplation. They're beautiful. They're made to be beautiful, doing their own small part to see that their beauty never ends.

If you looked down on that world of countries, onto the pink of glorious old Greater Britain, that land of green squares and dark forest and carriage contrails, and then you naturally avoided looking directly at the golden splendor of London, your gaze might fall on the Thames valley. On the country houses and mansions and hunting estates that letter the river banks with the

names of the great. On one particular estate: an enormous winged square of a
house with its own grouse shooting horizons and mazes and herb gardens and
markers that indicate it also sprawls into folded interior expanses.

Today that estate, seen from such a height, would be adorned with informational banners that could be seen from orbit, and tall pleasure cruisers
could be observed, docked beside military boats on the river, and carriages
of all kinds would be cluttering the gravel of its circular drives and swarming
in the sky overhead. A detachment of Horseguards could be spotted, stood
at ready at the perimeter.

Today, you'd need much more than a passport to get inside that maze of
information and privilege.

Because today was a royal wedding.

That vision from the point of view of someone looking down upon him was
what was at the back of Hamilton's mind.

But now he was watching the princess.

Her chestnut hair had been knotted high on her head, baring her neck,
a fashion which Hamilton appreciated for its defiance of the French, and
at an official function too, though that gesture wouldn't have been Liz's
alone, but would have been calculated in the warrens of Whitehall. She
wore white, which had made a smile come to Hamilton's lips when he'd
first seen it in the Cathedral this morning. In this gigantic function room
with its high arched ceiling, in which massed dignitaries and ambassadors
and dress uniforms orbited from table to table, she was the sun about which
everything turned. Even the King, in the far distance, at a table on a rise
with old men from the rest of Europe, was no competition for his daughter
this afternoon.

This was the reception, where Elizabeth, escorted by members of the
Corps of Heralds, would carelessly and entirely precisely move from group
to group, giving exactly the right amount of charm to every one of the great
powers, briefed to keep the balance going as everyone like she and Hamilton
did, every day.

Everyone like the two of them. That was a useless thought and he cuffed
it aside.

Her gaze had settled on Hamilton's table precisely once. A little smile
and then away again. As not approved by Whitehall. He'd tried to stop
watching her after that. But his carefully random table, with diplomatic
corps functionaries to his left and right, had left him cold. Hamilton had
grown tired of pretending to be charming.

"It's a marriage of convenience," said a voice beside him.

It was Lord Carney. He was wearing open cuffs that bloomed from his
silk sleeves, a big collar and no tie. His long hair was unfastened. He had
retained his rings.

Hamilton considered his reply for a moment, then opted for silence.
He met Carney's gaze with a suggestion in his heart that surely His

Lordship might find some other table to perch at, perhaps one where he had friends?"

"What do you reckon?"

Hamilton stood, with the intention of walking away. But Carney stood too and stopped him just as they'd got out of earshot of the table. The man smelled like a Turkish sweetshop. He affected a mode of speech beneath his standing. "This is what I do. I probe, I provoke, I poke. And when I'm in the room, it's all too obvious when people are looking at someone else."

The broad grin stayed on his face.

Hamilton found a deserted table and sat down again, furious at himself.

Carney settled beside him, and gestured away from Princess Elizabeth, towards her new husband, with his neat beard and his row of medals on the breast of his Svenska Adelsfanan uniform. He was talking with the Papal ambassador, doubtless discussing getting Liz to Rome as soon as possible, for a great show to be made of this match between the Protestant and the Papist. If Prince Bertil was also pretending to be charming, Hamilton admitted that he was making a better job of it.

"Yeah, jammy fucker, my thoughts exactly. Still, I'm on a promise with a couple of members of his staff, so it's swings and roundabouts." Carney clicked his tongue and wagged his finger as a Swedish serving maid ran past, and she curtsied a quick smile at him. "I do understand, you know. All our relationships are informed by the balance. And the horror of it is that we all can conceive of a world where this isn't so."

Hamilton pursed his lips and chose his next words carefully. "Is that why you are how you are, your Lordship?"

" 'Course it is. Maids, lady companions, youngest sisters, it's a catalogue of incompleteness. I'm allowed to love only in ways which don't disrupt the balance. For me to commit myself, or, heaven forbid, to marry, would require such deep thought at the highest levels that by the time the Heralds had worked it through, well, I'd have tired of the lady. Story of us all, eh? Nowhere for the pressure to go. If only I could see an alternative."

Hamilton had decided that, having shown the corner of his cards, the man had taken care to move back to the fringes of treason once more. It was part of his role as an agent provocateur. And Hamilton knew it. But that didn't mean he had to take this. "Do you have any further point, your Lordship?"

"Oh, I'm just getting – "

The room gasped.

Hamilton was up out of his seat and had taken a step towards Elizabeth, his gun hand had grabbed into the air to his right where his .66mm Webley Corsair sat in a knot of space and had swung it ready to fire –

At nothing.

There stood the Princess, looking about herself in shock. Dress uniforms, bearded men all around her.

Left right up down.

Hamilton couldn't see anything for her to be shocked at.

And nothing near her, nothing around her.

She was already stepping back, her hands in the air, gesturing at a gap – What had been there? Everyone was looking there. What?

He looked to the others like him. Almost all of them were in the same sort of posture he was, balked at picking a target.

The Papal envoy stepped forward and cried out. "A man was standing there! And he has vanished!"

Havoc. Everybody was shouting. A weapon, a weapon! But there was no weapon that Hamilton knew of that could have done that, made a man, whoever it had been, blink out of existence. Groups of bodyguards in dress uniforms or diplomatic black tie leapt up encircling their charges. Ladies started screaming. A nightmare of the balance collapsing all around them. That hysteria when everyone was in the same place and things didn't go exactly as all these vast powers expected.

A Bavarian princeling bellowed he needed no such protection and made to rush to the Princess' side –

Hamilton stepped into his way and accidentally shouldered him to the floor as he put himself right up beside Elizabeth and her husband. "We're walking to that door," he said. "Now."

Bertil and Elizabeth nodded and marched with fixed smiles on their faces, Bertil turning and holding back with a gesture the Swedish forces that were moving in from all directions. Hamilton's fellows fell in all around them, and swept the party across the hall, through that door, and down a servants' corridor as Life Guards came bundling in to the room behind them, causing more noise and more reactions and damn it, Hamilton hoped he wouldn't suddenly hear the discharge of some hidden–

He did not. The door was closed and barred behind them. Another good chap doing the right thing.

Hamilton sometimes distantly wished for an organisation to guard those who needed it. But for that the world would have to be different in ways beyond even Carney's artificial speculations. He and his brother officers would have their independence cropped if that was so. And he lived through his independence. It was the root of the duty that meant he would place himself in harm's way for Elizabeth's husband. He had no more thoughts on the subject.

"I know very little," said Elizabeth as she walked, her voice careful as always, except when it hadn't been. "I think the man was with one of the groups of foreign dignitaries – "

"He looked Prussian," said Bertil, "we were talking to Prussians."

"He just vanished into thin air right in front of me."

"Into a fold?" said Bertil.

"It can't have been," she said. "The room will have been mapped and mapped."

She looked to Hamilton for confirmation. He nodded.

They got to the library, Hamilton marched in and secured it. They put the happy couple at the centre of it, locked it up, and called everything in to the embroidery.

The embroidery chaps were busy, swiftly prioritising, but no, nothing was happening in the great chamber they'd left, the panic had swelled and then subsided into shouts, exhibitionist faintings (because who these days wore a corset that didn't have hidden depths), glasses crashing, yelled demands. No one else had vanished. No Spanish infantrymen had materialised out of thin air.

Bertil walked to the shelves, folded his hands behind his back, and began bravely and ostentatiously browsing. Elizabeth sat down and fanned herself and smiled for all Hamilton's fellows, and finally, quickly for Hamilton himself.

They waited.

The embroidery told them they had a visitor coming.

A wall of books slid aside, and in walked a figure that made all of them turn and salute. The Queen Mother, still in mourning black, her train racing to catch up with her.

She came straight to Hamilton and the others all turned to listen, and from now on thanks to this obvious favour, they would regard Hamilton as the ranking officer. He was glad of it. "We will continue," she said. "We will not regard this as an embarrassment and therefore it will not be. The Ball Room was prepared for the dance, we are moving there early, Elizabeth, Bertil, off you go, you two gentlemen in front of them, the rest of you behind. You will be laughing as you enter the Ball Room as if this were the most enormous joke, a silly and typically English eccentric misunderstanding."

Elizabeth nodded, took Bertil by the arm.

The Queen Mother intercepted Hamilton as he moved to join them. "No. Major Hamilton, you will go and talk to technical, you will find another explanation for what happened."

"Another explanation, your Royal Highness?"

"Indeed," she said. "It must not be what they are saying it is."

"Here we are, sir," Lieutenant Matthew Parkes was with the Technical Corps of Hamilton's own regiment, the 4th Dragoons. He and his men were, incongruously, in the dark of the buttery that had been set aside for their equipment, also in their dress uniforms. From here they were in charge of the sensor net that blanketed the house and grounds down to Newtonian units of space, reaching out for miles in every direction. Parkes' people had been the first to arrive here, days ago, and would be the last to leave. He was pointing at a screen, on which was frozen the intelligent image of a burly man in black tie, Princess Elizabeth almost entirely obscured behind him. "Know who he is?"

Hamilton had placed the guest list in his mental index and had checked it as each group had entered the hall. He was relieved to recognise the man. He was as down to earth as it was possible to be. "He was in the Prussian party, not announced, one of six diplomat placings on their list. Built like his muscles have been grown for security and that's how he moved round the room. Didn't let anyone chat to him. He nods when his embroidery talks to him. Which'd mean he's new at this, only . . ." Only the man had a look about him that Hamilton recognized. "No. He's just very confident. Ostentatious, even. So you're sure he didn't walk into some sort of fold?"

"Here's the contour map." Parkes flipped up an overlay on the image that showed the tortured underpinnings of spacetime in the room. There were little sinks and bundles all over the place, where various Britons had weapons stowed, and various foreigners would have had them stowed had they wished to create a diplomatic incident. The corner where Elizabeth had been standing showed only the force of gravity under her dear feet. "We do take care you know, sir."

"I'm sure you do, Matty. Let's see it, then."

Parkes flipped back to the clear screen. He touched it and the image changed.

Hamilton watched as the man vanished. One moment he was there. Then he was not, and Elizabeth was reacting, a sudden jerk of her posture.

Hamilton often struggled with technical matters. "What's the frame rate on this thing?"

"There is none, sir. It's a continual taking of real image, right down to single Newton intervals of time. That's as far as physics goes. Sir, we've been listening in to what everyone's saying, all afternoon—"

"And what are they saying, Matty?"

"That what's happened is Gracefully Impossible."

Gracefully Impossible. The first thing that had come into Hamilton's mind when the Queen Mother had mentioned the possibility was the memory of a political cartoon. It was the Prime Minister from a few years ago, standing at the dispatch box, staring in shock at his empty hand, which should presumably have contained some papers. The caption had read:

> Say what you like about Mr Patel,
> He carries himself correct for his title.
> He's about to present just his graceful apologies,
> For the impossible loss of all his policies.

Every child knew that Newton had coined the phrase "gracefully impossible" after he'd spent the day in his garden observing the progress of a very small worm across the surface on an apple. It referred to what, according to the great man's thinking about the very small, could, and presumably did, sometimes happen: things popping in and out of existence, when God, for some unfathomable reason, started or stopped looking at them. Some Frenchman had insisted that it was actually about whether people were looking, but that was the French for you. Through the centuries, there had been a few documented cases which seemed to fit the bill. Hamilton had always been distantly entertained to read about such in the inside page of his newspaper plate. He'd always assumed it could happen. But here? Now? During a state occasion?

*   *   *

Hamilton went back into the great hall, now empty of all but a group of Life Guards and those like him, individuals taken from several different regiments, all of whom had responsibilities similar to his, and a few of whom he'd worked with in the field. He checked in with them. They had all noted the Prussian, indeed, with the ruthless air the man had had about him, and the bulk of his musculature, he had been at the forefront of many of their internal indices of threat.

Hamilton found the place where the vanishing had happened, moved aside a couple of boffins, and against their protestations, went to stand in the exact spot, which felt like anywhere else did, and which set off none of his internal alarms, real or intuitive. He looked to where Liz had been standing, in the corner behind the Prussian. His expression darkened. The man who'd vanished had effectively been shielding the Princess from the room. Between her and every line of sight. He'd been where a bodyguard would have been if he'd become aware of someone taking a shot.

But that was ridiculous. The Prussian hadn't rushed in to save her. He'd been standing there, looking around. And anyone in that hall with some strange new weapon concealed on their person wouldn't have taken the shot then, they'd have waited for him to move.

Hamilton shook his head, angry with himself. There was a gap here. Something that went beyond the obvious. He let the boffins get back to their work and headed for the Ball Room.

The band had started the music, and the vast chamber was packed with people, the dance floor a whirl of waltzing figures. They were deliberate in their courses. The only laughter was forced laughter. No matter that some half miracle might have occurred, dance cards had been circulated amongst the minds of the great powers, so those dances would be danced, and minor royalty matched, and whispers exchanged in precise confidentiality. Because everyone was brave and everyone was determined and would be seen to be so. And so the balance went on. But the tension had increased a notch. The weight of the balance could be felt in this room, on the surface now, on every brow. The Queen Mother sat at a high table with courtiers to her left and right, receiving visitors with a grand blessing smile on her face, daring everyone to regard the last hour as anything but a dream.

Hamilton walked the room, looking around like he was looking at a battle, like it was happening rather than perhaps waiting to happen, whatever it was. He watched his opposite numbers from all the great powers waltzing slowly around their own people, and spiraling off from time to time to orbit his own. The ratio of uniformed to the sort of embassy thug it was difficult to imagine fitting in the diplomatic bag was about three to one for all the nations bar two. The French had of course sent Commissars, who all dressed the same when outsiders were present, but followed a byzantine internal rank system. And the Vatican's people were all men and women of the cloth and their assistants.

As he made his way through that particular party, which was scattering, intercepting and colliding with all the other nationalities, as if in the explosion of a shaped charge, he started to hear it. The conversations were all about what had happened. The Vatican representatives were talking about a sacred presence. The details were already spiraling. There had been a light and a great voice, had nobody else heard? And people were agreeing.

Hamilton wasn't a diplomat, and he knew better than to take on trouble not in his own line. But he didn't like what he was hearing. The Catholics had only come to terms with Impossible Grace a couple of decades ago, when a Papal bull went out announcing that John XXVI thought that the concept had merit, but that further scientific study was required. But now they'd got behind it, as in all things, they were behind it. So what would this say to them, that the divine had looked down on this wedding, approved of it, and plucked someone away from it?

No, not just someone. Prussian military. A Protestant from a nation that had sometimes protested that various Swedish territories would be far better off within their own jurisdiction.

Hamilton stopped himself speculating. Guessing at such things would only make him hesitate if his guesses turned out to be untrue.

Hamilton had a vague but certain grasp of what his God was like. He thought it was possible that He might decide to give the nod to a marriage at court. But in a way which might upset the balance between nations that was divinely ordained, that was the centre of all good works?

No. Hamilton was certain now. The divine be damned. This wasn't the numinous at play. This was enemy action.

He circled the room until he found the Prussians. They were raging, an ambassador poking at a British courtiers, demanding something, probably that an investigation be launched immediately. And beside that Prussian stood several more, diplomatic and military, all convincingly frightened and furious, certain this was a British plot.

But behind them there, in the social place were Hamilton habitually looked, there were some of the vanished man's fellow big lads. The other five from that diplomatic pouch. The Prussians, uniquely in Europe, kept up an actual organization for the sort of thing Hamilton and his ilk did on the never never. The Garde Du Corps had begun as a regiment similar to the Life Guards, but these days it was said they weren't even issued with uniforms. They wouldn't be on anyone's dance cards. They weren't stalking the room now, and all right, that was understandable, they were hanging back to protect their chaps. But they weren't doing much of that either. They didn't look angry, or worried for their comrade, or for their own skins –

Hamilton took a step back to let pretty noble couples desperately waltz between him and the Prussians, wanting to keep his position as a privileged observer.

They looked like they were waiting. On edge. They just wanted to get out of here. Was the Garde really that callous? They'd lost a man in mysterious circumstances, and they weren't themselves agitating to get back into that room and yell his name, but were just waiting to move on?

He looked for another moment, remembering the faces, then moved on himself. He found another table of Prussians. The good sort, not Order of the Black Eagle, but Hussars. They were in uniform, and had been drinking, and were furiously declaring in Hohenzollern German that if they weren't allowed access to the records of what had happened, well then it must be – they didn't like to say what it must be!

Hamilton plucked a glass from a table and wandered over to join them, careful to take a wide and unsteady course around a lady whose train had developed some sort of fault and wasn't moving fast enough to keep pace with her feet.

He flopped down in a chair next to one of the Prussians, a Captain by his lapels, which were virtual in the way the Prussians liked, to implicitly suggest that they had been in combat more recently than the other great powers, and so had a swift turnover of brevet ranks, decided by merit. "Hullo!" he said.

The group fell silent and bristled at him.

Hamilton blinked at them. "Where's Humph?"

"Humph? Wassay th'gd Major?" the Hussar Captain spoke North Sea Pidgin, but with a clear accent: Hamilton would be able to understand him.

He didn't want to reveal that he spoke perfect German, albeit with a Bavarian accent. "Big chap. Big big chap. Say go." He carefully swore in Dutch, shaking his head, not understanding. "Which you settle fim?"

"Settle?!" They looked amongst each other, and Hamilton could feel the affront. A couple of them even put their good hands to their waists, where the space was folded that no longer contained their pistols and thin swords. But the Captain glared at them and they relented. A burst of Hohenzollern German about this so-called mystery of their mate vanishing, and how, being in the Garde, he had obviously been abducted for his secrets.

Hamilton waved his hands. "Noswords! Good chap! No name. He won! Three times to me at behind the backshee." His raised his voice a notch. "Behind the backshee! Excellent chap! He won!" He stuck out his ring finger, offering the winnings in credit, to be passed from skin to skin. He mentally retracted the other options of what could be detailed there, and blanked it. He could always make a drunken show of trying to find it. "Seek to settle. For such a good chap."

They didn't believe him or trust him. Nobody reached out to touch his finger. But he learnt a great deal in their German conversation in the ten minutes that followed, while he loudly struggled to communicate with the increasingly annoyed Captain, who couldn't bring himself to directly insult a member of the British military by asking him to go away. The vanished man's name was Helmuth Sandels. The name suggested Swedish origins to his family. But that was typical continental back and forth. He might have been a good chap now he'd gone, but he hadn't been liked. Sandels had had a look in his eye when he'd walked past stout fellows who'd actually fought battles.

He'd spoken up in anger when valiant Hussars had expressed the military's traditional views concerning those running the government, the country and the world. Hamilton found himself sharing the soldiers' expressions of distaste: this had been someone who assumed that loyalty was an opinion.

He raised a hand in pax, gave up trying with the Captain, and left the table.

Walking away, he heard the Hussars moving on with their conversation, starting to express some crude opinions about the Princess. He didn't break stride.

Into his mind, unbidden, came the memories. Of what had been a small miracle of a kind, but one that only he and she had been witness to.

Hamilton had been at home on leave, having been abroad for a few weeks, serving out of uniform. As always, at times like that, when he should have been at rest, he'd been fired up for no good reason, unable to sleep, miserable, prone to tears in secret when a favourite song had come on the theatricals in his muse flat. It always took three days for him, once he was home, to find out what direction he was meant to be pointing. Then he would set off that way, and pop back to barracks one night for half a pint, and then he'd be fine. He could enjoy day four and onwards, and was known to be something approximating human from there on in.

Three day leaves were hell. He tried not to use them as leaves, but would find himself some task, hopefully an official one if one of the handful of officers who brokered his services could be so entreated. Those officers were sensitive to such requests now.

But that leave, three years ago, had been two weeks off. He'd come home a day before. So he was no use to anyone. He'd taken a broom, and was pushing accumulated grey goo out of the carriage park alongside his apartment and into the drains.

She'd appeared in a sound of crashing and collapse, as her horse staggered sideways and hit the wall of the mews, then fell. Her two friends were galloping after her, their horses healthy, and someone built like Hamilton was running to help.

But none of them were going to be in time to catch her –

And he was.

It had turned out that the horse had missed an inncoulation against miniscule poisoning. Its body was a terrible mess, random mechanisms developing out of its flanks and dying, with that terrifying smell, in the moments when Hamilton had held her in his arms, and had had to round on the man running in, and had imposed his authority with a look, and had not been thrown down and away.

Instead, she'd raised her hands and called that she was all right, and had insisted on looking to and at the horse, pulling off her glove and putting her hand to its neck and trying to fight the bloody things directly. But even with her command of information, it had been too late, and the horse had died in a mess.

She'd been bloody angry. And then at the emergency scene that had started to develop around Hamilton's front door, with police carriages swooping in and the sound of running boots –

Until she'd waved it all away and declared that it had been her favourite horse, a wonderful horse, her great friend since childhood, but it was just a bloody horse, and all she needed was a sit down and if this kind military gentleman would oblige –

And he had.

He'd obliged her again when they'd met in Denmark, and they'd danced at a ball held on an ice flow, a carpet of mechanism wood reacting every moment to the weight of their feet and the forces underlying them, and the aurora had shone in the sky.

It was all right in Denmark for Elizabeth to have one dance with a commoner.

Hamilton had got back to the table where his regiment were dining, and had silenced the laughter and the calls, and thus saved them for barracks. He had drunk too much. His batman at the time had prevented him from going to see Elizabeth as she was escorted from the floor at the end of her dance card by a boy who was somewhere in line for the Danish throne.

But she had seen Hamilton the next night, in private, a privacy that would have taken great effort on her part, and after they had talked for several hours and shared some more wine she had shown him great favour.

"So. Is God in the details?" Someone was walking beside Hamilton. It was a Jesuit. Mid thirties. Dark hair, kept over her collar. She had a scar down one side of her face and an odd eye as a result. Minuscule blade, by the look. A member of the Society of Jesus would never allow her face to be restructured. That would be vanity. But she was beautiful.

Hamilton straightened up, giving this woman's musculature and bearing and all the history those things suggested the respect they deserved. "Or the devil."

"Yes, interesting the saying goes both ways, isn't it? My name is Mother Valentine. I'm part of the Society's campaign for Effective Love."

"Well," Hamilton raised an eyebrow, "I'm in favour of love being—"

"Don't waste our time. You know what I am."

"Yes, I do. And you know I'm the same. And I was waiting until we were out of earshot—"

"Which we now are—"

"To have this conversation."

They stopped together. Valentine moved her mouth close to Hamilton's ear. "I've just been told that the Holy Father is eager to declare what happened here to be a potential miracle. Certain parties are sure that our

Black Eagle man will be found magically transplanted to distant parts,
perhaps Berlin, as a sign against Prussian meddling."

"If he is, the Kaiser will have him gently shot and we'll never hear."

"You're probably right."

"What do you think happened?"

"I don't think miracles happen near our kind."

Hamilton realised he was looking absurdly hurt at her. And that she
could see it. And was quietly absorbing that information for use in a couple
of decades, if ever.

He was glad when a message came over the embroidery, asking him to
attend to the Queen Mother in the buttery. And to bring his new friend.

The Queen Mother stood in the buttery, her not taking a chair having
obviously made Parkes and his people even more nervous than they would
have been.

She nodded to Valentine. "Monsignor. I must inform you, we've had an
official approach from the Holy See. They regard the hall here as a possible
site of miraculous apparition."

"Then my opinion on the subject is irrelevant. You should be addressing – "

"The ambassador. Indeed. But here you are. You are aware of what was
asked of us?"

"I suspect the Cardinals will have sought a complete record of the
moment of the apparition, or in this case, the vanishing. That would only
be the work of a moment in the case of such an . . . observed . . . chamber."

"It would. But it's what happens next that concerns me."

"The procedure is that the chamber must then be sealed, and left unob-
served until the Cardinals can see for themselves, to minimise any effect
human observers may have on the process of divine revelation."

Hamilton frowned. "Are we likely to?"

"God is communicating using a physical method, so we may," said
Valentine. "Depending on one's credulity concerning miniscule physics."

"Or one's credulity concerning international politics," said the Queen
Mother. "Monsignor, it is always our first and most powerful inclination,
when another nation asks us for something, to say no. All nations feel that
way. All nations know the others do. But now here is a request, one that
concerns matters right at the heart of the balance, that is, in the end, about
deactivating security. It could be said to come not from another nation, but
from God. It is therefore difficult to deny this request. We find ourselves
distrusting that difficulty. It makes us want to deny it all the more."

"You speak for His Royal Highness?"

The Queen Mother gave a cough that might have been a laugh. "Just as
you speak for Our Lord."

Valentine smiled and inclined her head. "I would have thought, your
Royal Highness, that it would be obvious to any of the great powers that,

given the celebrations, it would take you a long time to gather the Prime Minister and those many other courtiers with whom you would want to consult on such a difficult matter."

"Correct. Good. It will take three hours. You may go."

Valentine walked out with Hamilton. "I'm going to go and mix with my own for a while," she said, "listen to who's saying what."

"I'm surprised you wear your hair long."

She looked sharply at him. "Why?"

"You enjoy putting your head on the block."

She giggled.

Which surprised Hamilton and for just a moment made him wish he was Lord Carney. But then there was a certain small darkness about another priest he knew.

"I'm just betting," she said in a whisper, "that by the end of the day this will all be over. And someone will be dead."

Hamilton went back into the Ball Room. He found he had a picture in his head now. Something had swum up from somewhere inside him, from a place he had learned to trust and never interrogate as to its reasons. That jerking motion Elizabeth had made at the moment Sandels had vanished. He had an emotional feeling about that image. What was it?

It had been like seeing her shot.

A motion that looked like it had come from beyond her muscles. Something Elizabeth had not been in control of. It wasn't like her to not be in control. It felt . . . dangerous.

Would anyone else see it that way? He doubted it.

So was he about to do the sudden terrible thing that his body was taking him in the direction of doing?

He killed the thought and just did it. He went to the Herald who carried the tablet with dance cards on it, and leaned on him with the Queen Mother's favour, which had popped up on his ring finger the moment he'd thought of it.

The Herald considered the sensation of the fingertip on the back of his hand for a moment, then handed Hamilton the tablet.

Hamilton realized that he had no clue of the havoc he was about to cause. So he glanced at the list of Elizabeth's forthcoming dances and struck off a random Frenchman.

He scrawled his own signature with a touch, then handed the plate back.

The Herald looked at him like the breath of death had passed under his nose.

Hamilton had to wait three dances before his name came up. A Balaclava, an Entrée Grave (that choice must have taken a while, unless some Herald had been waiting all his life for a chance at the French), a Hornpipe for the sailors, including Bertil, to much applause, and then, thank the deus, a straightforward Waltz.

Elizabeth had been waiting out those last three, so he met her at her table. Maidservants kept their expressions stoic. A couple of Liz's companions looked positively scared. Hamilton knew how they felt. He could feel every important eye looking in his direction.

Elizabeth took his arm and gave it a little squeeze. "What's grandma up to, Johnny?"

"It's what I'm up to."

She looked alarmed. They formed up with the other dancers.

Hamilton was very aware of her gloves. The mechanism fabric that covered her left hand held off the urgent demand of his hand, his own need to touch her. But no, that wouldn't tell him anything. That was just his certainty that to know her had been to know her. That was not where he would find the truth here.

The band started up. The dance began.

Hamilton didn't access any guidelines in his mind. He let his feet move where they would. He was outside orders, acting on a hunch. He was like a man dancing around the edge of a volcano.

"Do you remember the day we met?" he asked when he was certain they couldn't be heard, at least, not be the other dancers.

"Of course I do. My poor San Andreas, your flat in Hood Mews – "

"Do you remember what I said to you that day, when nobody else was with us? What you agreed to? Those passionate words that could bring this whole charade crashing down?!" He kept his expression light, his tone so gentle and wry that Liz would always play along and fling a little stone back at him, knowing he meant nothing more than he could mean. That he was letting off steam through a joke.

All they had been was based on the certainty expressed in that.

It was an entirely British way to do things. It was, as Carney had said, about lives shaped entirely by the balance.

But this woman, with the room revolving around the two of them, was suddenly appalled, insulted, her face a picture of what she was absolutely certain she should feel. "I don't know what you mean! Or even if I did, I don't think—!"

Hamilton's nostrils flared. He was lost now, if he was wrong. He had one tiny ledge for Liz to grasp if he was, but he would fall.

For duty, then.

He took his hand from Princess Elizabeth's waist, and grabbed her chin, his fingers digging up into flesh.

The whole room cried out in horror.

He had a moment before they would shoot him.

Yes, he felt it! Or he thought he did! He thought he did enough –

He grabbed the flaw and ripped with all his might.

Princess Elizabeth's face burst off and landed on the floor.

Blood flew.

He drew his gun and pumped two shots into the mass of flesh and mechanism, as it twitched and blew a stream of defensive acid that discoloured the marble.

He spun back to find the woman without a face lunging at him, her eyes white in the mass of red muscle, mechanism pus billowing into the gaps. She was aiming a hair knife at his throat, doubtless with enough mechanism to bring instant death or something worse.

Hamilton thought of Liz as he broke her arm.

He enjoyed the scream.

He wanted to bellow for where the real Liz was as he slammed the imposter down onto the floor, and he was dragged from her in one motion as a dozen men grabbed them.

He caught a glimpse of Bertil, horrified, but not at Hamilton. It was a terror they shared. For her safety.

Hamilton suddenly felt like a traitor again.

He yelled out the words he'd had in mind since he'd put his name down for the dance. "They replaced her years ago! Years ago! At the mews!"

There were screams, cries that we were all undone.

There came the sound of two shots from the direction of the Vatican group, and Hamilton looked over to see Valentine standing over the corpse of a junior official.

Their gaze met. She understood why he'd shouted that.

Another man leapt up at a Vatican table behind her and turned to run and she turned and shot him twice in the chest, his body spinning backwards over a table.

Hamilton ran with the rout. He used the crowds of dignitaries and their retinues, all roaring and competing and stampeding for safety, to hide himself. He made himself look like a man lost, agony on his face, his eyes closed. He was ignoring all the urgent cries from the embroidery.

He covertly acknowledged something directly from the Queen Mother.

He stumbled through the door of the buttery.

Parkes looked round. "Thank God you're here, we've been trying to call, the Queen Mother's office are urgently asking you to come in—"

"Never mind that now, come with me, on Her Royal Highness' orders." Parkes grabbed the pods from his ears and got up. "What on Earth—?"

Hamilton shot him through the right knee.

Parkes screamed and fell. Every technician in the room leapt up. Hamilton bellowed at them to sit down or they'd get the same.

He shoved his foot into the back of Parkes' injured leg. "Listen here, Matty. You know how hard it's going to get. You're not the sort to think your duty's worth it. How much did they pay you? For how long?"

He was still yelling at the man on the ground as the Life Guards burst in and put a gun to everyone's head, his own included.

The Queen Mother entered a minute later, and changed that situation to the extent of letting Hamilton go free. She looked carefully at Parkes, who was still screaming for pity, and aimed a precise little kick into his disintegrated kneecap.

Then she turned to the technicians. "Your minds will be stripped down and rebuilt, if you're lucky, to see who was in on it." She looked back to Hamilton as they started to be led from the room. "What you said in the Ball Room obviously isn't the case."

"No. When you take him apart," Hamilton nodded at Parkes, "you'll find he tampered with the contour map. They used Sandels as the cover for substituting Her Royal Highness. They knew she was going to move around the room in a pre-determined way. With Parkes' help, they set up an open-ended fold in that corner – "

"The expense is staggering. The energy required – "

"There'll be no Christmas tree for the Kaiser this year. Sandels deliberately stepped into the fold and vanished, in a very public way. And at that moment they made the switch, took Her Royal Highness into the fold too, covered by the visual disturbance of Sandels' progress. And by old-fashioned sleight of hand."

"Propped up by the Prussians' people in the Vatican. Instead of a British bride influencing the Swedish court, there'd be a cuckoo from Berlin. Well played, Wilhelm. Worth that Christmas tree."

"I'll wager the unit are still in the fold, not knowing anything about the outside world, waiting for the room to be sealed off with pious care, so they can climb out and extract themselves. They probably have supplies for several days."

"Do you think my granddaughter is still alive?"

Hamilton pursed his lips. "There are Prussian yachts on the river. They're staying on for the season. I think they'd want the bonus of taking the Princess back for interrogation."

"That's the plan!" Parkes yelled. "Please!"

"Get him some anesthetic," said the Queen Mother. Then she turned back to Hamilton. "The balance will be kept. To give him his due, cousin Wilhelm was acting within it. There will be no diplomatic incident. The Prussians will be able to write off Sandels and any others as rogues. We will of course cooperate. The Black Eagle traditionally carry only that knowledge they need for their mission, and will order themselves to die before giving us orders of battle or any other strategic information. But the intelligence from Parkes and any others will give us some small power of potential shame over the Prussians in future months. The Vatican will be bending over backwards for us for some time to come." She took his hand, and he felt the favour on his ring finger impressed with some notes that probably flattered him. He'd read them later. "Major, we will have the fold opened. You will enter it. Save Elizabeth. Kill them all."

They got him a squad of fellow officers, four of them. They met in a trophy room, and sorted out how they'd go and what the rules of engagement would be once they got there. Substitutes for Parkes and his crew had been found from the few sappers present. Parkes had told them that those inside the fold had left a miniscule aerial trailing, but that messages were only to be passed down it in emergencies. No such communications had been sent. They were not aware of the world outside their bolt hole.

Hamilton felt nothing but disgust for a bought man, but he knew that such men told the truth under pressure, especially when they knew the fine detail of what could be done to them.

The false Liz had begun to be picked apart. Her real name would take a long time to discover. She had a maze of intersecting selves inside her head. She must have been as big an investment as the fold. The court physicians who had examined her had been as horrified by what had been done to her as by what she was.

That baffled Hamilton. People like the duplicate had power, to be who they liked. But that power was bought at the cost of damage to the balance of their own souls. What were nations, after all, but a lot of souls who knew who they were and how they liked to live? To be as uncertain as the substitute Liz was to be lost and to endanger others. It went beyond treachery. It was living mixed metaphor. It was as if she had insinuated herself into the cogs of the balance, her puppet strings wrapping around the arteries which supplied hearts and minds.

They gathered in the empty dining room in their dress uniforms. The dinner things had not been cleared away. Nothing had been done. The party had been well and truly crashed. The representatives of the great powers would have vanished back to their embassies and yachts. Mother Valentine would be rooting out the details of who had been paid what inside her party. Excommunications post mortem would be issued, and those traitors would burn in hell.

He thought of Liz, and took his gun from the air beside him.

One of the sappers put a device in the floor, and set a timer, saluted and withdrew.

"Up the Green Jackets," said one of the men behind him, and a couple of the others mentioned their own regiments.

Hamilton felt a swell of fear and emotion.

The counter clicked to zero and the hole in the world opened in front of them, and they ran in to it.

There was nobody immediately inside. A floor and curved ceiling of universal boundary material. It wrapped light around it in rainbows that always gave tunnels like this a slightly pantomime feel. It was like the entrance to Saint Nicholas' cave. Or, of course, the vortex sighted upon death, the ladder to the hereafter. Hamilton got that familiar taste in his mouth, a pure adrenal jolt of fear, not the restlessness of combat deferred, but that sensation one got in other universes, of being too far from home, cut off from the godhead.

There was gravity. The Prussians certainly had spent some money.

The party made their way forward. They stepped gently on the edge of the universe. From around the corner of the short tunnel there were sounds.

The other four looked to Hamilton. He took a couple of gentle steps forward, grateful for the softness of his dress uniform shoes. He could hear Elizabeth's voice. Not her words, not from here. She was angry, but engaged. Not defiant in the face of torture. Reasoning with them. A smile passed his lips for a moment. They'd have had a lot of that.

It told him there was no alert, not yet. It was almost impossible to set sensors close to the edge of a fold. This lot must have stood on guard for a couple of hours, heard no alarm from their friends outside, and then had relaxed. They'd have been on the clock, waiting for the time when they would poke their heads out. Hamilton bet there was a man meant to be on guard, but that Liz had pulled him into the conversation too. He could imagine her face, just round that corner, one eye always toward the exit, maybe a couple of buttons undone, claiming it was the heat and excitement. She had a hair knife too, but it would do her no good to use it on just one of them.

He estimated the distance. He counted the other voices, three . . . four, there was a deeper tone, in German, not the pidgin the other three had been speaking. That would be him. Sandels. He didn't sound like he was part of that conversation. He was angry, ordering, perhaps just back from sleep, wondering what the hell!

Hamilton stopped all thoughts of Liz. He looked to the others, and they understood they were going to go and go now, trip the alarms and use the emergency against the enemy.

He nodded.

They leapt around the corner, ready for targets.

They expected the blaring horn. They rode it, finding their targets surprised, bodies reacting, reaching for weapons that were in a couple of cases a reach away amongst a kitchen, crates, tinned foods –

Hamilton had made himself know he was going to see Liz, so he didn't react to her, he looked past her –

He ducked, cried out, as an automatic set off by the alarm chopped up the man who had been running beside him, the Green Jacket, gone in a burst of red. Meat all over the cave.

Hamilton reeled, stayed up, tried to pin a target. To left and right ahead, men were falling, flying, two shots in each body, and he was moving too slowly, stumbling, vulnerable –

One man got off a shot, into the ceiling, and then fell, pinned twice, exploding -

Every one of the Prussians gone but –

He found his target.

Sandels. With Elizabeth right in front of him. Covering every bit of his body. He had a gun pushed into her neck. He wasn't looking at his three dead comrades.

The three men who were with Hamilton moved forward, slowly, their gun hands visible, their weapons pointing down.

They were looking to Hamilton again.

He hadn't lowered his gun. He had his target. He was aiming right at Sandels and the Princess.

There was silence.

Liz made eye contact. She had indeed undone those two buttons. She was calm. "Well," she began, "this is very—"

Sandels muttered something and she was quiet again.

Silence.

Sandels laughed, not unpleasantly. Soulful eyes were looking at them from that square face of his, a smile turning the corner of his mouth. He shared the irony that Hamilton had often found in people of their profession.

This was not the awkward absurdity that the soldiers had described. Hamilton realized that he was looking at an alternative. This man was a professional at the same things Hamilton did in the margins of his life. It was the strangeness of the alternative that had alienated the military men. Hamilton was fascinated by him.

"I don't know why I did this," said Sandels, indicating Elizabeth with a sway of the head. "Reflex."

Hamilton nodded to him. They each knew all the other did. "Perhaps you needed a moment."

"She's a very pretty girl to be wasted on a Swede."

Hamilton could feel Liz not looking at him. "It's not a waste," he said gently. "And you'll refer to Her Royal Highness by her title."

"No offence meant."

"And none taken. But we're in the presence, not in barracks."

"I wish we were."

"I think we all agree there."

"I won't lay down my weapon."

Hamilton didn't do his fellows the disservice of looking to them for confirmation. "This isn't an execution."

Sandels looked satisfied. "Seal this tunnel afterwards, that should be all we require for passage."

"Not to Berlin, I presume."

"No," said Sandels, "to entirely the opposite."

Hamilton nodded.

"Well, then." Sandels stepped aside from Elizabeth.

Hamilton lowered his weapon and the others readied theirs. It wouldn't be done to aim straight at Sandels. He had his own weapon at hip height. He would bring it up and they would cut him down as he moved.

But Elizabeth hadn't moved. She was pushing back her hair, as if wanting to say something to him before leaving, but lost for the right words.

Hamilton, suddenly aware of how unlikely that was, started to say something.

But Liz had put a hand to Sandels' cheek.

Hamilton saw the fine silver between her fingers.

Sandels fell to the ground thrashing, hoarsely yelling as he deliberately and precisely, as his nervous system was ordering him to, bit off his own tongue. Then the mechanism from the hair knife let him die.

The Princess looked at Hamilton. "It's not a waste," she said.

They sealed the fold as Sandels had asked them to, after the sappers had made an inspection.

Hamilton left them to it. He regarded his duty as done. And no message came to him to say otherwise.

Recklessly, he tried to find Mother Valentine. But she was gone with the rest of the Vatican party, and there weren't even bloodstains left to mark where her feet had trod this evening.

He sat at a table, and tried to pour himself some champagne. He found that the bottle was empty.

His glass was filled by Lord Carney, who sat down next to him. Together, they watched as Elizabeth was joyfully reunited with Bertil. They swung each other round and round, oblivious to all around them. Elizabeth's grandmother smiled at them and looked nowhere else.

"We are watching," said Carney, "the balance incarnate. Or perhaps they'll incarnate it tonight. As I said: if only there were an alternative."

Hamilton drained his glass. "If only," he said, "there weren't."

And he left before Carney could say anything more.

EDISON'S FRANKENSTEIN

Chris Roberson

Chris Roberson has appeared in *Postscripts*, *Asimov's*, *Subterrranean*, *Argosy*, *Electric Velocipede*, *Black October*, *Fantastic Metropolis*, *Revolutionsf*, *Twilight Tales*, *The Many Faces of Van Helsing*, and elsewhere. He's probably best known for his Alternate History Celestrial Empire series, which, in addition to a large number of short pieces, consists of the novels *The Dragon's Nine Sons*, *Iron Jaw and Hummingbird*, *The Voyage of Night Shining White*, and *Three Unbroken*. His other novels include, *Here, There & Everywhere*, *Paragaea: A Planetary Romance*, *Set the Seas on Fire*, *Voices of Thunder*, *Cybermancy Incorporated*, *Any Time At All*, and *End of the Century*, and he has also contributed to the Warhammer, X-Men, and Shark Boy and Lava Girl series. Coming up is a new Warhammer novel, *The Hunt for Voldorius*. In addition to his writing, Robertson is one of the publishers of the lively small press MonkeyBrain Books, and edited the "retro-pulp" anthology *Adventure, Volume 1*. He lives with his family in Austin, Texas.

Here he takes us to a sideways steampunk world where many of the familiar figures from our reality have taken on new roles in life – roles that aren't always an improvement.

I T WAS LATE afternoon when Archibald Chabane finally found the boy, perched high on the steel trestle of the elevated railway. From that vantage, he could look out across the intersection of 62nd St. and Hope Avenue, over the high fence into the backstage area of Bill Cody's concession, now christened Buffalo Bill's Wild West and Congress of Rough Riders of the World.

"Mezian," Chabane called, but over the muffled roar of the crowd in Cody's 8,000 seat arena and the rumble of the Illinois Central Railroad engine coming up the track, he couldn't make himself heard.

"Mezian!" Chabane repeated, cupping his hands around his mouth like a speaking-trumpet. He glanced to the south, trying to see how close the train had come. When Chabane had been a boy, watching the 4-6-0 camel-back engines lumbering along the Algiers-Constantine line, he'd always been able to see the black smoke billowing up from their coal-fed furnaces from miles away. These new prometheic engines, though, produced nothing but steam, and virtually all of it used for locomotion, so the trains could been heard long before they could be seen.

Chabane leaned a hand against the nearest steel girder, and could feel the vibrations of the train's approach.

He shouted the boy's name once more, at the top of his lungs.

Mezian looked down, blinking, and his lips tugged up in a guilty grin. "Oh, I didn't see you there, amin."

Chabane had only to cross his arms over his chest and scowl, and the boy began clambering down the trestle like a monkey from a tree.

To the Americans, like Bill Cody – who'd already warned Sol Bloom to keep "his damned Algerians" away from the Wild West Show's Indians – Archibald Chabane was Bloom's assistant, translator, and bodyguard.

To Sol Bloom, "Archie" was just a Kabyle who'd gotten off the boat from Paris with the rest of the troupe, and threatened to throw Bloom into the waters of New York Harbor if he wasn't more polite to the performers. Bloom had offered him a cigar and hired Chabane to be his liaison with the Algerian troupe on the spot.

To the Algerians, though, Chabane was something more. At first only their guide in a foreign land, he had become their elected amin, as much the head of their "Algerian Village" concession as if he were sitting in the djemaa of a Kayble village back home.

"Careful," Chabane warned, as Mezian swung from a steel girder. "I promised your mother I'd bring you back in one piece."

The boy just grinned, and dropped a full five feet to the pavement, something colorful fluttering to the ground after him like a lost bird.

"Mother won't give me a dime to get into the show," Mezian said by way of explanation, pointing at the banners which fluttered over Cody's concession, proclaiming THE PILOT OF THE PRAIRIE.

"Mr Bloom has sworn it's my hide if any of our troupe is caught drinking with Cody's performers again," Chabane said, arms still crossed over his chest. Many of the Algerians in the troupe were not the most observant of Muslims, and even now in the final days of Ramadan they could be found passing a flask back and forth once the day's audience had cleared out. "If Cody catches one of us peaking at his show without paying, I'll never hear the end of it."

Mezian scuffed his feet against the pavement, his gaze lowered. "Sorry, amin."

"You dropped something." Chabane reached down and picked up the garishly-colored pamphlet that had fallen from the boy's pocket. It was a story-paper, what the Americans called a "dime novel." The title in oversized letters was Scientific Romance Weekly, featuring "Dane Faraday, Man of Justice, in The Electrical World of Tomorrow." Handing it back to the boy, Chabane quirked a smile. "She won't give you ten cents for the Wild West Show, but she lets you spend money on cheap fictions?"

The boy shrugged, slipping the folded pamphlet into his back pocket. "They're meant to help me practice my English." He paused, drawing himself up straight, and then in stilted tones added in English, "Hands up, the miscreant, you are the surrounded." Switching back to French, he gave Chabane a quizzical look. "What is a 'miscreant'?"

"It means unbeliever," the man explained, "or infidel. A villain, in other words." He put a hand on the boy's shoulder and gently propelled him forward. "Come along, your mother is waiting."

As they headed up 62nd to Island Avenue, they could hear the muffled applause from the crowd inside Cody's arena. Open only a little more than a week, and already the Wild West Show was drawing bigger crowds than all the concessions on the Midway Plaisance combined. In another two weeks the Columbian Exhibition proper would finally open to the public, and it remained to be seen whether there'd be crowds left over for any of the outside attractions.

"So your story-papers," Chabane said, as they turned left and headed north up Island Avenue. "Are they any good?"

Mezian shrugged. "They are alright, I suppose. Not as good as the French ones I could get back home, or in Paris."

Chabane nodded. "When I was a boy, I devoured every installment of Jules Verne's Extraordinary Voyages I could lay hands on."

The boy pulled a face. "Verne?" He shook his head. "Much too dry. No, give me Paul d'Ivoi's Eccentric Voyages, any day."

They passed 60th Street, then turned left onto the Midway Plaisance. The looming form of Ferris's still unfinished wheel dominated the horizon, even seven blocks away. Steel-bodied automata spidered up and down it on their crab-like legs, welding girders into place, stringing high tension wires. The builders promised that it would be ready to start spinning within another week, two at the most, just in time for opening day. Chabane was less than optimistic about their predictions, but knew that if not for the automata, it would not even be that far along, and would never have been ready in time.

Chabane couldn't help but think about the boy he'd once been, reading Verne in second-hand story-papers. Not yet Archibald Chabane of London, just Adherbal Aït Chabaâne of Dellys, reading about men who traveled beneath the waves, or across the skies, or to the moon in glorious machines. It had seemed a distant, ungraspable vision that he could scarcely hope to see. Then came the famine, and the oppression of the Kabyle at the hands of their French colonial masters, and finally the failure of Muhammed al-Muqrani's revolt. Chabane had been too young to fight, but his father and his uncles had not, and with the revolt put down his family name had been outlawed in Algeria, never again to be spoken in the djemaa. The young Adherbal, seeing no future in his native land, had gone instead to live among the Romni, as the Kabyles, remembering the Romans of ancient times, still thought of all foreigners across the middle sea. He ran away to the north, away from the superstitions of his

grandmothers and the traditions he had been taught. He had gone looking for the future, to reinvent himself in a rational world. In England he'd
made a new life for himself, the bodyguard to a wealthy man, and had
tried to forget the past.

In the end, though, he learned the past was something we carry with us,
and can never escape. And even though the future had arrived, it had not
been quite as he'd expected.

Chabane and the boy continued up the Midway, past the various concessions just shutting down for the day. Like the Wild West Show, they'd been
able to open early, while work on the Columbian Exhibition was still
being completed. Some of the concessions, like the Algerian Village, had
been open as early as the previous summer. And like the Algerian troupe's
"exhibit," the other concessions were all, in one way or another, caricatures
of the countries they purported to represent, pantomimes of pasts that never
existed. There were Irishmen in green felt, Germans in lederhosen, Lapps
in fur, Turks in fezzes. But as clownish as the others often seemed, it struck
Chabane that the worst indignities were always reserved for those from the
African continent. Like the natives of Dahomey, only recently conquered
by the French, being presented as "cannibal savages" for the amusement
of American audiences. A once proud people, reduced to the level of
sideshow performers.

As they neared the towering wheel, beyond which lay the Algerian
concession, Chabane heard his name called. It was one of the performers
from the Street in Cairo concession, which was proving the most popular of
the Midway's attractions.

"Another of our monkeys has been stolen, Chabane," the Egyptian
continued in Arabic. "You Kabyles haven't been breaking your Ramadan
fast with monkey stew, have you?"

"Keep your ruffians away from our women, Zewail," Chabane answered,
good naturedly, "and I'll keep my people away from your monkeys."

As they passed under the lengthening shadow of Ferris's wheel, the
Algerian Village concession coming into view, Mezian drew up short, looking behind him, a look of alarm on his face. "I've lost my story-paper." He
patted his pocket, craning his head around and twisting to look down over
his back, as though the dime novel might be clinging to his shirt-back.

Chabane turned in a slow circle, scanning the ground at their feet, looking back the way they'd come. "You must have dropped it."

Mezian looked up, his eyes wide. "My mother will kill me."

Chabane gave a sympathetic smile, but before he could answer he heard
the sound of footsteps fast approaching. He spun around, expecting trouble,
instinctually dropping into a defensive posture, but relaxed when he saw it
was only Papa Ganon, the Algerian troupe's glass-eater.

"Amin!" Ganon shouted. "Come quickly!"

Chabane tensed once more when he saw the blood darkening the front
of Papa Ganon's burnous.

"What is it?" Chabane said, rushing forward. "Are you hurt?"

Ganon responded with a confused look, then followed Chabane's gaze to his blood-stained front. He shook his head. "It isn't mine, amin. There's a stranger, badly bleeding and confused, found hiding behind the theater."

Chabane drew his mouth into a line, and nodded. "Run along and find your mother, Mezian." Then he started with long strides towards the Algerian theater, Papa Ganon following close behind.

The Algerian Village was almost identical to that which the troupe had originally set up in the Paris Exhibition four years before. It had been there that a young Sol Bloom had seen them, in the shadow of Eiffel's tower, and hired them to come perform in the United States. But when the time had come to leave Paris, the troupe had been uncertain about venturing into the unknown wilds of America.

At the time, Archibald Chabane had not heard his native tongue since leaving Dellys, years before, but traveling to Paris on business he had chanced upon the troupe on the Quai d'Orsay. After a friendly meal and reminiscences about their erstwhile home, Papa Ganon had spoken for the others in begging the assistance of the worldly, mannered Chabane. Ganon had called up Kabyle tradition, which held that a Kabyle journeying abroad was obliged to come to the aid of any Kabyle in need, even at the risk of his own fortune and life.

Chabane had thought he had put such traditions behind him. But looking into the hopeful faces of the Algerian troupe, he couldn't help but remember the sacrifices his family had made during the famine of 1867. Tradition demands that every stranger who enters a Kabyle village be treated like an honored guest, given food, lodging, whatever he requires. But even with more than ten thousand strangers from all over Algeria pouring into Dellys, not a single person died of starvation, nor had the djemaas been forced to ask aid from the government. Among the European settlers in the larger cities, police measures were needed to prevent theft and disorder resulting from the influx of strangers; in Dellys nothing of the kind was needed. The Kabyles took care of their own affairs.

There on the Quai d'Orsay, to his own astonishment, he found himself agreeing to act as the troupe's guide in America. He had tried to escape his past, but his past had eventually outrun him.

In the shuttered Algerian Theater, Chabane and Papa Ganon found the unconscious stranger being tended by two of the troupe's female performers. Though they went veiled when in the public eye, in chador or hijab, in private they favored western dress.

"I tell you, it is Salla," one of the women said, daubing blood from the stranger's face with a wet cloth. Piled on the ground were shards of glass they'd pulled from his wounds. "Look, he has Salla's eyes."

The other woman, Dihya, shook her head. "Taninna, you've gone mad. Salla is dead and buried. Besides, eyes or no, this man looks nothing like him."

Chabane crouched beside Taninna, looking closely at the man. There were cuts all over his face, arms, and hands, and underneath the wool blanket the women had thrown over him, the stranger was completely naked.

The ministrations of the two women had already staunched the flow of blood from the stranger's arms, and Chabane reached out to touch one of the scars, which looked older than the others, already healed, running like a ring around the stranger's upper arm. But when Chabane's fingers brushed the scar, he got a slight shock, like a spark of static electricity, and pulled his hand back quickly.

"What shall we do with him, amin?" Dihya asked, wiping her forehead with the back of her hand.

Chabane was thoughtful. "I'll go speak with the tin soldiers, see what they have to say."

Just opposite the Algerian Village, across the Midway Plaisance between the Old Vienna concession and the French Cider Press, was a Fire and Guard Station, manned by members of the Columbian Guard, the private police force of the Columbian Exhibition. The Guard was headed by Colonel Edmund Rice, a former infantry officer who had gained some small measure of fame during the Battle of Bull Run, where the Union army's new-minted prometheic tanks had put an end to the short-lived southern insurrection. Under Rice's command, the Columbian Guard was meant to be a model peacekeeping force, committed to the safety and security of all who strode upon the Exhibition grounds. In their uniforms of light blue sackcloth, white gloves, and yellow-lined black capes, though, they looked more like spear-carriers in a Gilbert & Sullivan production than officers of law. And their talents at peacekeeping, often, left something to be desired, more interested in presenting a dashing profile than in seeing justice done. It wasn't for nothing that the concessioneers had taken to calling them "tin soldiers."

As Chabane approached the Station, framing how best to broach the subject of the unconscious man who lay bleeding in the Algerian Theater, a trio of Columbian Guards rushed through the narrow door, the one in the lead shouldering Chabane aside.

"Out of the way, darkie," the Guard sneered in English, patting the buttoned holster at his side. "We don't have time to hear about any damned stolen monkeys."

Chabane held up his hands, palms forward, and stepped back out of the way, presenting as inoffensive a profile as possible. "My apologies," he answered, in his best drawing room English. If he'd wanted, he could have swept the legs out from under all three Guards, and taken their firearms from them as they fell. At the moment, though, he was more interested in what had stirred the normally laconic Guards to such a frenzy.

The three guards were hustling up the Midway, around the wheel and towards the Columbian Exhibition itself. A few of the other Midway concessioneers were still in the street, and Chabane could hear them muttering suspiciously to one another, like wives gossiping over a garden fence. Some had overheard the Guards within their hut, and had heard the summons to action.

There had been a murder in the park.

As he trailed behind the Columbian Guards at a discreet distance, keeping them just in sight as they hurried up the Midway, Chabane tallied up the number of deaths in the park since the previous summer, when the Algerian troupe had arrived from New York. Like the Algerian sword-swallower Salla, who had been working in a construction position in the park while waiting for the Midway to open, the deaths had all been accidents, all of them workers killed at their duties because of poor safety conditions. Salla had fallen from the airship mast and drowned in the waters of Lake Michigan, others had broken their skulls when masonry had fallen on them from improperly lashed cranes, or been crushed under piles of girders that slipped from the pincers of poorly programmed automata.

And it wasn't just the dead men buried in paupers' graves south of the park that had been affected. Even now, in the city itself, striking workers agitated for better working conditions, or for assurances that they would not lose their jobs to automation. The motto of the Columbian Exhibition was "Not Matter, But Mind; Not Things, But Men," but Chabane could not help but wonder whether such noble sentiments were any salve to men who had been replaced at their posts by "things" in recent months and years. He knew it came as no comfort to those men who had died in automata-related accidents.

But accidents were one thing. A murder was a different matter entirely. And as much as the Exhibition's Board of Directors might turn a blind eye to the loss of a few workmen, news of a murder would be bad business indeed for the fair.

It seemed a likely explanation that the bleeding and bewildered man now laying in the Algerian Theater was another victim, one who had escaped the killer's grasp. But it seemed to Chabane just as likely that the Board of Directors would be eager for a scapegoat on which to hang the crime, and a confused stranger, unable to defend himself, would suit their needs perfectly. He wasn't about to hand the stranger over to them, until he knew he wouldn't be signing the man's death warrant to do so.

Chabane followed the Guards through the 60th Street entrance and into the Columbian Exhibition itself. With only two weeks to go before the grand opening, it was clear there was still a significant amount of work to be done. The grounds were covered with litter and debris, with deep ruts cut across the greens. Lumber was piled haphazardly at the intersections of pathways, and empty crates and the discarded remains of worker's lunches were strewn everywhere.

The Guards continued east, past the Children's Building and the north end of the Horticultural Exhibition, before turning right and heading south along the western shores of the Lagoon. Chabane trailed behind, and when he rounded the corner of the Horticultural building, he could see the gentle rise of the Wooded Island in the middle of the Lagoon. Since he'd last come this way, they'd finished work on the fanciful reconstruction of the "Antediluvian" temple at the southern tip of the island. Supposedly based on archeological findings in Antarctica, it looked more like something out of Mezian's story-papers. Also new since he'd last seen the Lagoon were the miniature submersibles bobbling along on the water's surface, waiting for patrons to rent them for brief excursions to the bottom of the Lagoon once the Exhibition opened.

Chabane couldn't help wondering what Captain Nemo would have made of that.

For that matter, what might Verne himself have made of the airship now drifting at anchor atop the mast just visible on the far side of the Lagoon, past the Manufactures building, on the pier out over Lake Michigan. It was a prometheic airship, its envelope buoyed by the red vapor produced by the reaction of prometheum and charcoal.

Prometheum was such a simple substance. It looked like water and flowed like mercury. Add it to water, and it would set the water to boil. Add it to charcoal, and it turned the charcoal into still more prometheum. Put it in a vacuum and shake it, and it glowed bright white.

Now that the sun had slipped below the buildings to the west, the park's lamplighters had set to work, cranking the clockwork mechanisms at the base of each lamppost that set the cut-glass globes at the top of the posts to vibrating, agitating the prometheum within. Chabane had a pendant on his lapel, a little crystal flask, stopped with silver. If he were to shake it now, the clear, viscous liquid within would glow soft white, and not dim until almost sunrise.

Chabane watched as the Guards continued past the Transportation building, then turned left into the so-called Court of Honor, with the golden dome of the Administration building at its center. Chabane hurried his pace, so as not to lose sight of which building they entered.

As he rounded the corner of the Automata Exhibition, Chabane watched as the three Guards hurried through the massive doors of the Machinery Exhibition across the way. He followed behind at a somewhat more leisurely pace.

To Chabane's left, opposite the massive Machinery hall, were the twin Automata and Prometheum buildings. Between them stood the fifteen-foot tall statue of Cadwalader Ringgold, in one hand a sextant, in the other a model of the crab-like Antediluvian automaton he'd brought back from the South Pole.

Of course, Ringgold hadn't been the first to return with one of the automata, the first proof of the existence of the "Antediluvians." That honor had fallen to James Clark Ross, who had brought back the broken husk of a mechanism with articulated limbs from the island that now bears his name in 1843, the year after Ringgold and the rest of the Wilkes Expedition had returned from the south seas. This had set off a race to the Pole, to find other examples of this strange, unknown technology. The Ringgold Expedition had won the golden ring when they returned with another, more intact automaton from deep within an icy mountain crevasse, in whose tiny engine there still rested a few precious drops of prometheum. A few drops were enough to change history, though, since added to charcoal it quickly produced more. And in short order, the automaton itself had been reverse-engineered.

The debate still raged about just who the Antediluvians had been. Had they been some forgotten race of man? Or visitors from another world or plane of existence? Some wild-eyed savants even suggested that the Antediluvians were actually the originals of the Atlantis myth, their existence remembered only in legend. All that was known for certain was that they had left behind a scant few examples of a technology that far outstripped that of modern man in the 1850s.

It had not taken modern man long to catch up, Chabane mused, as he passed through the entrance into the Machinery Exhibition.

The interior of the building was massive, looking like three railroad train-houses side-by-side. And though many of the stalls and booths were already installed, there was still considerable work to be done before the park opened, and the massive steam-powered cranes mounted overhead still hurried from one end of the building to the other and back again, time and again, moving the heavy machinery into place.

At the far left of the building, the west end of the hall, were installations from other countries – Canada, Great Britain, Austria, Germany, France – with the rest being American products. Behind the far wall, on the southern face of the building, was the boiler-house, where tanks of lake water were impregnated with small amounts of prometheum, which set them to boil almost immediately, transforming hundreds of gallons into steam in a matter of moments.

Nearly all of the exhibits drew their power from the steam-powered line shafts spinning at between 250 and 300 revolutions a minute, running from one end of the hall to the other at fourteen feet above the ground. Pulleys were strung from the drive shafts down to the exhibit stalls, strung tight as guitar strings, powering more kinds of machines than Chabane had known existed: water pumps, bottling mechanisms, refrigerating apparatus, trip-hammers, sawmill blades, printing presses, stone-saws, refinery mechanisms, and others whose uses he could scarcely guess. All powered by prometheic steam and, according to the banners and type-written signs hung on each installation, all of them profitable, the marvels of the age.

In the south-east corner of the building, though, where Chabane could see the Columbian Guards congregating, could be found less marvelous, less profitable exhibits. And it was around the smallest of these that the Guards were now milling.

There wasn't much to the exhibit, just a shack, a banner proclaiming The Latter-Day Lazarus, a podium, a few pedestals, and a table designed to lever up on one end. The only machinery in evidence appeared to be some sort of motor, attached by a pulley to the drive shaft overhead. But the motor isn't attached to anything but a pair of long, thick cables, one of which snaked towards the shack, the other towards the levered table. It took Chabane a moment to recognize it as the same sort of device he'd seen displayed in London, years before. It was a machine for generating electricity.

Outside of Mezian's dime-novel, Chabane had heard precious little about electricity in years. It had been something of a novelty a few years back, and marketed as a new brand of patent medicine before the danger of electrocution had driven it from catalog pages all together, but aside from its use in telegraphy it was now all but abandoned. What was the product or device promoted by this "Lazarus" exhibit, and why the unnecessary risk of electricity?

The Columbian Guards he'd trailed had joined with the others already on hand, inspecting the area. Most of them were already inside the shack, which appeared to be the scene of the crime. Intent on their work, none seemed to pay any notice to Chabane. It wasn't surprising. Like many of the Americans he'd encountered since the last summer, the Guards seemed to look upon men and women with dark complexions as nothing more than menials – janitors, gardeners, busboys, maids – and so Chabane had found it possible to slip in and out of groups of them all but unnoticed, effectively invisible.

With his eyes down and an unthreatening expression on his face, Chabane slipped into the shack. He had expected to see a body, perhaps some blood or signs of violence. What he found, instead, was like something from a Grand Guignol.

On the dusty floor, covered by a sheet, was a still human form, presumably the body of the dead man. Overhead, wire cages hung empty from the tarpapered ceiling, the floor of each caked in excrement.

The center of the shack was dominated by a bed-sized bench, with casters on the legs, and straps at either end and in the middle. Affixed to the top of the bench was a boxy metal frame, from one corner of which a thick cable snaked down and under the shack's thin wooden wall. The ground around the bench was strewn with jagged bits of glass that crunched underfoot.

Beside the bench was a low table, on which were piled strange implements, saws, pliers, and clamps, along with what appeared to be various automata components. And what Chabane at first took to be strips of meat were scattered on the table and the surrounding ground, and pools of dark liquid congealing scab-like.

An abattoir stench hung thick in the air, and as Chabane stepped over to the nearest of the three barrels at the rear of the shack, he found the source of the smell. In the barrel was heaped viscera, blood, flesh, and bones. Chabane started, covering his mouth and gagging, then recognized the tiny child-like limbs as those of a monkey. Beside the limbs he saw the remains of a monkey skull, cut in half like a grapefruit, the brain scooped out. He remembered the animals missing from the Street in Cairo concession, and suppressed a shudder.

"What in god's name is this?" came a blustering voice from the shack's open door.

Chabane turned to see the chief of the Columbian Guard, Colonel Edmund Rice, shouldering into the shack, behind him another man with thinning hair and a prominent mustache.

"There's been a murder," one of the Guards explained, unnecessarily.

Rice shot the man a bewildered look, then shook his head, muttering something about the quality of officers he had at his disposal, comparing them unflatteringly to the 14th Massachusetts Infantry Regiment.

Chabane had accompanied Sol Bloom to a few meetings with Colonel Rice, but doubted the man had ever noticed he was there. Certainly, Rice hardly seemed to notice him now.

"Well, Robinson?" Rice turned to the mustached man behind him, who Chabane now recognized as L.W. Robinson, chief of the Columbian Exhibition's Machinery department. The colonel reached down and flicked the blanket off the body on the floor. "Do you know this man?"

Robinson peered down at the burnt and bludgeoned man on the floor, and with a queasy expression quickly nodded. "Yes, I know him." He straightened up and looked away. "That's Tom Edison."

Rice narrowed his eyes in concentration, and looked from Robinson to the dead man. "I know the name, but can't place it."

Robinson nodded again. "Was a bit famous for a time. He invented the phonograph, you may recall?" The colonel shook his head. "In any event, I only spoke with him briefly when he secured his spot in the hall, but it appeared that he'd sunk his fortunes into electricity years ago, and simply couldn't see a way out."

"Electricity?" the colonel repeated, disbelievingly. "Why ever for?"

Robinson shrugged. "Who can say? I tried to explain to him that there simply wasn't any call for such things, not with prometheic steam engines and lights and automation and such, that he might as well try selling butter-churns. But Edison was not to be deterred. He had that wild-eyed look you see in religious zealots, you know the type? He was determined to find a way to make his . . . now what did he call them? Oh yes, his dynamos profitable."

"That's a 'dynamo' out front, I take it?" Rice asked.

The Machinery chief nodded. "Sad, isn't it? Still, Edison wasn't the only one. I've heard of a number of inventors and investors who'd hung all their hopes on electricity, in the years before prometheum really took hold. Most ended up going off into industries or trades, sooner or later. I even heard of one, a Serbian I believe, who became a writer of cheap fictions." He looked back to the dead man on the ground, grimacing at the gruesome sight. "Clearly, though, Edison hadn't been able to adapt. And it got him in the end. Unless I'm mistaken, he shows every sign of being electrocuted."

One of the Guards stepped forward, and Chabane recognized him as the one from the Midway who was so quick with the racial epithets. "What do these dyna . . . dynami . . . dyna . . ." He shook his head. "What do these things have to do with this 'Latter-Day Lazarus' business? Was your man here intending to raise the dead with this electric thing?"

"If he was," another Guard called from the rear of the shack, "I think he was doing it one piece at a time." The Guard held aloft a severed arm, far too large to have come off any monkey.

"Jesus wept!" Rice spat, rearing back.

The Guards began muttering to one another, and Chabane distinctly heard several mentions of "grave-robbing" and "workmen's bodies."

"What?" Chabane said, stepping forward, for the first time making his presence known. "What did you say about the workmen's graves?"

The others turned to him, most of them seeming to notice him for the first time.

"You're that Jew's Arab, aren't you?" the colonel said, narrowing his gaze.

Chabane drew himself up straighter, and in perfect Queen's English replied, "I am Kabyle, sir, and not of Arab descent, but I am presently in the employ of Mr Bloom, if that is what you mean." His hands at his sides tightened into fists, but he managed to maintain a calm exterior. "What was the mention of grave-robbing and the remains of the workmen?"

Rice glanced to Robinson, who looked as confused as Chabane, and then back. "It's not public knowledge, and if the papers get word of it I'll know where from. But some of the graves to the south have been disturbed, and the bodies laid to rest there have gone missing."

"Would that include the Algerian who drowned in the lake?" Chabane asked.

Rice shrugged. "Only the Christian graves are marked, as I understand it."

Chabane ignored Rice, and looked back to the barrels, from which the Guards were still pulling cadaver parts. There were severed hands and feet, a leg, two arms, bits of skulls, even a complete torso. He barred his teeth in a snarl, and turned to look down on the dead man on the floor. "My grandmothers always said that no one is to be lamented who dies during Ramadan, during which the gates of hell are closed and those of heaven always open. It doesn't seem quite right that a man such as this should get into the gates of heaven uncontested, even if he was murdered."

"Now hold on," Rice objected, holding up his hands. "No one said anything about murder."

"They didn't?" Robinson asked, eyebrows raised.

Rice turned to the chief of Machinery, fixing him with a hard glare. "You yourself said this was an electrocution, right? An accidental electrocution?"

Robinson's hands fluttered like caged birds. "I suppose it could have been," he allowed. "But what about . . ." – he waved at the broken glass, the scattered tools, the splattered blood and viscera – ". . . all of this?"

"This," Rice said evenly, "could well be simple vandalism. And vandalism is an entirely different order of magnitude to murder. Murder will get plastered over every paper in the country, and run the risk of turning paying customers away, if they think the killer is at large. One more accidental death and a spot of vandalism, that we can handle."

"You're joking, of course," Chabane objected. "Have you no interest in seeing justice done?"

Rice glared at him. "There must be some jobs down south the automata won't do, boy. Why don't you get down there with the rest of the darkies and make yourself useful?"

Chabane bristled. There were still a few slaves in the southern United States, not yet supplanted by cheap automata. That this man could so casually dismiss their continued suffering in an off-hand slight brought Chabane's blood to boil. For an instant, he almost forgot the welfare of the troupe to whom he'd pledged himself, or the stranger who had stumbled beneath the shelter of Chaban's protection. If he'd been on his own, not responsible for anyone but himself, Chabane would have wished for nothing more than a flyssa saber in one hand and a Webley pistol in the other, and he would show these pale-skinned buffoons his worth. But he wasn't on his own, and he was responsible for many more souls than just his own.

Marshalling his last reserves of restraint, Chabane strode to the door, and left the shack of horrors behind.

As he made his way back to the Midway, the stars had come out in the darkened skies overhead, and the prometheic lamps were now bathing the park in the soft white glow that had given the exhibition its unofficial name, the White City. But as clean as the white-clad buildings looked in the pure prometheic light, Chabane knew that they were only plaster and boards, hiding the rot and void beneath.

Of course Rice and the rest of his tin-soldiers were more concerned with pay-checks than with justice, happy to paint a murder as an accident if it suited the Board of Directors, whitewashing away any chance of bad publicity. Still, Chabane wasn't sure that justice hadn't been done, anyway. He remembered another Kabyle superstition his grandmothers had taught him, that there are never any demons abroad during Ramadan, because God compels them to remain in hell throughout the sacred month. Having seen the gruesome work of the dead man, Chabane doubted any demon ever did worse.

Passing the Terminal Station, he exited the park grounds through the 64th Street entrance, heading north up Island Avenue. Just before reaching the Midway, something bright caught his eye, a splash of color on the pavement reflecting back the prometheic light from above. It was Mezian's dime-novel. Picking it up, Chabane flipped through the pages as he continued on towards the Algerian concession.

The prose was lurid, the action improbable, but there was something about the image of this future of electricity and equality presented by the author, that resonated with Chabane. This Nikola Tesla was no Jules Verne, but still Chabane was reminded of the sense of boundless potential he used to feel when reading the Extraordinary Voyages story-papers.

Before turning onto the Midway, Chabane saw a handbill posted to a lamp post, advertising the impending Opening Day celebrations for the Columbian Exhibition. In addition to the last living relative of Christopher Columbus, the duke of Veragua, the most honored guest at the ceremony would be the octogenarian Abraham Lincoln, former president of the United States, who would be on hand to cut the ribbon on the Exhibition.

The imagery of "Dane Faraday, Man of Justice" still rolling in his thoughts, Chabane tried to imagine a world in which James Clark Ross had never returned from the south seas with a broken automaton, in which Ringgold had never discovered prometheum, in which the modern age knew nothing of the forgotten Antediluvian civilization. Perhaps in such a world, there would now be an Electricity exhibit instead of a Prometheum one, with Tom Edison's dynamos at center stage. And perhaps instead of an Automata building, one devoted to some other industry, metal-working perhaps, or mining. But then, in world in which the United States army lacked prometheic tanks, perhaps they wouldn't have been able to subdue the southern insurrection, and the Union might have split in two over the question of slavery. Perhaps there might not be a Columbian Exhibition at all.

What Chabane couldn't decide was whether such a world would be better, or worse, than the one he knew.

By the time Chabane returned to the Algerian concession, the sun had long since set, and the fourth prayer of the day, Maghrib, had been completed. Now the troupe was breaking their Ramadan fast. Even the non-observant among them, like Chabane, usually had the good graces not to eat and drink in front of the others while the sun was shining in the holy month. Fast or not, though, Chabane knew that a fair number of the performers, once their meals were done, would slip off and drink spirits, perhaps swapping Algerian wines for the "firewater" favored by Cody's Indians. Perhaps tonight, instead of trying to stop them, Chabane just might join them.

The stranger sat among the Algerians, in his lap a plate of food, untouched. He had been cleaned up, his wounds bandaged, and dressed in a suit of borrowed clothes. He was awake, but unspeaking, and it was unclear what, if any, tongue he comprehended. He simply sat, watching the others silently, his expression mingling confusion and interest.

"Keep your distance, amin," Papa Ganon said, as Chabane crouched down beside the man. "My hand brushed his bare skin while we were dressing him, and I got the shock of my life. He's like a walking thundercloud, this one."

Chabane nodded, and kept his hands at his sides. In the soft white glow of the prometheic lights overhead, Chabane examined the stranger closely. His coloration, what little of it could be seen beneath the bandages, cuts, and scars, was somehow . . . off. His skin was a darker shade than his light hair would suggest, the little hairs on the backs of his hands darker than his feathery eyebrows. And his features seemed mismatched, his nose too long and narrow, his mouth a wide slash in his face, his overlarge ears too low on his head.

"What will we do with him?" Dihya asked, coming to stand beside Ganon. Taninna came with her, staring hard at the stranger's disfigured face, as though trying to find something hidden there.

Chabane thought about tradition, about the past and the future. He remembered the superstitions he'd been taught as a child, and the story-papers' fantastic futures into which he'd fled.

In many ways, the future promised by Jules Verne had arrived, but not in the way the young Adherbal Aït Chabaâne had imagined. But the future that young Mezian now dreamt of, the future promised in Nikola Tesla's colorful stories? They would never arrive. That wasn't tomorrow, but was yesterday's tomorrow. The world of Dane Faraday would never arrive, with its heavier-than-air craft, and wireless communications connecting distant nations, and incandescent lights dangling from wires, and massive dynamos. A world of phosphorescent gas tubes on lampposts, and power-lines crisscrossing the countryside, and antennas atop every house picking symphonies out of the air. Of men and women of all races and nationalities, each measured by their conduct and their character, not by their language or the color of their skins.

Chabane thought about the frisson he'd felt on flipping through Tesla's story, the familiar thrill of boundless potential. But he realized now it wasn't a hope for a new world to come, but a kind of nostalgia for a future that could never be. He thought about the dead man in the blood-covered shack in the Machinery building, so committed to a particular view of yesterday's tomorrow that he had been willing to commit horrible acts to get back to it, whatever the cost.

"Amin?" Dihya repeated, seeing Chabane lost in thought. "What will we do with the stranger?"

Chabane took a deep breath, and sighed. He had tried to escape tradition before, and now knew he never would. "We do what our grandmothers would have us do. No stranger who comes into the village for aid can ever be turned away."

Maybe it wasn't all of the tomorrows that mattered, Chabane realized. Maybe what was truly important was preserving the past, and working for a better today. Perhaps that was the only real way to choose what kind of future we will inhabit.

But Taninna was right, Chabane knew, looking back to the silent man sitting in the cool glow of the prometheic light. The stranger did have Salla's eyes.

EROSION

Ian Creasey

Here's a bittersweet look at a recently created posthuman, who, reveling in his newfound powers and abilities, says a nostalgic farewell to ordinary life on the planet before heading out forever to the stars – and who learns a few sharp lessons in the process.

Prolific short-story writer Ian Creasey has made more than forty sales since his first in 1999, to markets such as *Asimov's*, *Postscripts*, *Realms of Fantasy*, *Weird Tales*, *Paradox*, *Oceans of the Mind*, *On Spec*, *Apex Science Fiction and Horror Digest*, *Orson Scott Card's Intergalactic Medicine Show*, and elsewhere. He lives in Yorkshire, England.

L ET ME TELL *you about my last week on Earth. . . .*
       Before those final days, I'd already said my farewells. My family gave me their blessing: my grandfather, who came to England from Jamaica as a young man, understood why I signed up for the colony programme. He warned me that a new world, however enticing, would have its own frustrations. We both knew I didn't need the warning, but he wanted to pass on what he'd learned in life, and I wanted to hear it. I still remember the clasp of his fingers on my new skin; I can replay the exo-skin's sensory log whenever I wish.

My girlfriend was less forgiving. She accused me of cowardice, of running away. I replied that when your house is on fire, running away is the sensible thing to do. The Earth is burning up, and so we set forth to find a new home elsewhere. She said – she shouted – that when our house is on fire, we should stay and fight the flames. She wanted to help the firefighters. I respected her for that, and I didn't try to persuade her to come with me. That only made her all the more angry.

The sea will douse the land, in time, but it rises slowly. Most of the coastline still resembled the old maps. I'd decided that I would spend my last few days walking along the coast, partly to say goodbye to Earth, and partly to settle into my fresh skin and hone my augments. I'd tested it all in the post-op suite, of course, and in the colony simulator, but I wanted to practise in a natural setting. Reality throws up challenges that a simulator would never devise.

And so I travelled north. People stared at me on the train. I'm accustomed to that – when they see a freakishly tall black man, even the British overcome their famed (and largely mythical) reserve, and stare like scientists at a new specimen. The stares had become more hostile in recent years, as waves of African refugees fled their burning lands. I was born in Newcastle, like my parents, but that isn't written on my face. When I spoke, people smiled to hear a black guy with a Geordie accent, and their hostility melted.

Now I was no longer black, but people still stared. My grey exo-skin, formed of myriad tiny nodules, was iridescent as a butterfly's wings. I'd been told I could create patterns on it, like a cuttlefish, but I hadn't yet learned the fine control required. There'd be plenty of shipboard time after departure for such sedentary trifles. I wanted to be active, to run and jump and swim, and test all the augments in the wild outdoors, under the winter sky.

Scarborough is, or was, a town on two levels. The old North Bay and South Bay beaches had long since drowned, but up on the cliffs the shops and quaint houses and the ruined castle stood firm. I hurried out of town and soon reached the coastal path – or rather, the latest incarnation of the coastal path, each a little further inland than the last. The Yorkshire coast had always been nibbled by erosion, even in more tranquil times. Now the process was accelerating. The rising sea level gouged its own scars from higher tides, and the warmer globe stirred up fiercer storms that lashed the cliffs and tore them down. Unstable slopes of clay alternated with fresh rock, exposed for the first time in millennia. Piles of jagged rubble shifted restlessly, the new stones not yet worn down into rounded pebbles.

After leaving the last house behind, I stopped to take off my shirt, jeans and shoes. I'd only worn them until now as a concession to blending in with the naturals (as we called the unaugmented). I hid the clothes under some gorse, for collection on my return. When naked, I stretched my arms wide, embracing the world and its weather and everything the future could throw at me.

The air was calm yet oppressive, in a brooding sulk between stormy tantrums. Grey clouds lay heavy on the sky, like celestial loft insulation. My augmented eyes detected polarized light from the sun behind the clouds, beyond the castle standing starkly on its promontory. I tried to remember why I could see polarized light, and failed. Perhaps there was no reason, and the designers had simply installed the ability because they could. Like software, I suffered feature bloat. But when we arrived at our new planet, who could guess what hazards lay in store? One day, seeing polarized light might save my life.

I smelled the mud of the path, the salt of the waves, and a slight whiff of raw sewage. Experimentally, I filtered out the sewage, leaving a smell more like my memories from childhood walks. Then I returned to defaults. I didn't want to make a habit of ignoring reality and receiving only the sense impressions I found aesthetic.

Picking up speed, I marched beside the barbed wire fences that enclosed the farmers' shrinking fields. At this season the fields contained only stubble and weeds, the wheat long since harvested. Crows pecked desultorily at the sodden ground. I barged through patches of gorse; the sharp spines tickled my exo-skin, but did not harm it. With my botanist's eye, I noted all the inhabitants of the little cliff-edge habitat. Bracken and clover and thistles and horsetail – the names rattled through my head, an incantation of farewell. The starship's seedbanks included many species, on the precautionary principle. But initially we'd concentrate on growing food crops, aiming to breed strains that would flourish on the colony world. The other plants . . . this might be the last time I'd ever see them.

It was once said that the prospect of being hanged in the morning concentrated a man's mind wonderfully. Leaving Earth might be almost as drastic, and it had the same effect of making me feel euphorically alive. I registered every detail of the environment: the glistening spiders' webs in the dead bracken, the harsh calls of squabbling crows, the distant roar of the ever-present sea below. When I reached a gully with a storm-fed river at the bottom, I didn't bother following the path inland to a bridge; I charged down the slope, sliding on mud but keeping my balance, then splashed through the water and up the other side.

I found myself on a headland, crunching along a gravelled path. An ancient notice-board asked me to clean up after my dog. Ahead lay a row of benches, on the seaward side of the path, much closer to the cliff edge than perhaps they once had been. They all bore commemorative plaques, with lettering mostly faded or rubbed away. I came upon a legible one that read:

In memory of Katriona Grady
2021–2098
She Loved This Coast

Grass had grown up through the slats of the bench, and the wood had weathered to a mottled beige. I brushed aside the detritus of twigs and hawthorn berries, then smiled at myself for the outdated gesture. I wore no clothes to be dirtied, and my exo-skin could hardly be harmed by a few spiky twigs. In time I would abandon the foibles of a fragile human body, and stride confidently into any environment.

I sat, and looked out to sea. The wind whipped the waves into white froth, urging them to the coast. Gulls scudded on the breeze, their cries as jagged as the rocks they nested on. A childhood memory shot through me – eating chips on the seafront, a gull swooping to snatch a morsel. Within me swelled an emotion I couldn't name.

After a moment I became aware of someone sitting next to me. Yet the bench hadn't creaked under any additional weight. A hologram, then. When I turned to look, I saw the characteristic bright edges of a cheap hologram from the previous century.

"Hello, I'm Katriona. Would you like to talk?" The question had a rote quality, and I guessed that all visitors were greeted the same way; a negative answer would dismiss the hologram so that people could sit in peace. But I had several days of solitude ahead of me, and I didn't mind pausing for a while. It seemed appropriate that my last conversation on a dying world would be with a dead person.

"Pleased to meet you," I said. "I'm Winston."

The hologram showed a middle-aged white woman, her hair as grey as river-bed stones, her clothes a tasteful expanse of soft-toned lavender skirt and low-heeled expensive shoes. I wondered if she'd chosen this conventional self-effacing look, or if some memorial designer had imposed a template projecting the dead as aged and faded, not upstaging the living. Perhaps she'd have preferred to be depicted as young and wild and beautiful, as she'd no doubt once been – or would like to have been.

"It's a cold day to be wandering around starkers," she said, smiling.

I had forgotten I wore no clothes. I gave her a brief account of my augmentations. "I'm going to the stars!" I said, the excitement of it suddenly bursting out.

"What, all of them? Do they make copies of you, and send you all across the sky?"

"No, it's not like that." However, the suggestion caused me a moment of disorientation. I had walked into the hospital on my old human feet, been anaesthetised, then – quite some time later – had walked out in shiny new augmented form. Did only one of me leave, or had others emerged elsewhere, discarded for defects or optimised for different missions? *Don't be silly*, I told myself. *It's only an exo-skin. The same heart still beats underneath.* That heart, along with the rest of me, had yesterday passed the final pre-departure medical checks.

"We go to one planet first," I said, "which will be challenge enough. But later – who knows?" No one had any idea what the lifespan of an augmented human might prove to be; since all the mechanical components could be upgraded, the limit would be reached by any biological parts that couldn't be replaced. "It does depend on discovering other planets worth visiting. There are many worlds out there, but only a few even barely habitable."

I described our destination world, hugging a red-dwarf sun, its elliptical orbit creating temperature swings, fierce weather and huge tides. "The colonists are a mixed bunch: naturals who'll mostly have to stay back at base; then the augmented, people like me who should be able to survive outside; and the gene-modders – they reckon they'll be best off in the long run, but it'll take them generations to get the gene-tweaks right." There'd already been tension between the groups, as we squabbled over the starship's finite cargo capacity, but I refrained from mentioning it. "I'm sorry – I've gone on long enough. Tell me about yourself. Did you live around here? Was this your favourite place?"

"Yorkshire lass born and bred, that's me," said Katriona's hologram. "Born in Whitby, spent a few years on a farm in Dentdale, but came back – *suck my flabby tits* – to the coast when I married my husband. He was a fisherman, God rest his soul. *Arsewipe!* When he was away, I used to walk along the coast and watch the North Sea, imagining him out there on the waves."

My face must have showed my surprise.

"Is it happening again?" asked Katriona. "I was hacked a long time ago, I think. I don't remember very much since I died – I'm more of a recording than a simulation. I only have a little memory, enough for short-term interaction." She spoke in a bitter tone, as though resenting her limitations. "What more does a memorial bench need? Ah, I loved this coast, but that doesn't mean I wanted to sit here forever. . . . *Nose-picking tournament, prize for the biggest bogey!*"

"Would you like me to take you away?" I asked. It would be easy enough to pry loose the chip. The encoded personality could perhaps be installed on the starship's computer with the other uploaded colonists, yet I sensed that Katriona wouldn't pass the entrance tests. She was obsolete, and the dead were awfully snobbish about the company they kept. I'd worked with them in the simulator, and I could envisage what they'd say. "Why, Winston, I know you mean well, but she's not the right sort for a mission like this. She has no relevant expertise. Her encoding is coarse, her algorithms are outdated, and she's absolutely riddled with parasitic memes."

Just imagining this response made me all the more determined to fight it. But Katriona saved me the necessity. "That's all right, dear. I'm too old and set in my ways to go to the stars. I just want to rejoin my husband, and one day I will." She stared out to sea again, and I had a sudden intuition of what had happened to her husband.

"I'm sorry for your loss," I said. "I take it he was never" – I groped for an appropriate word – "memorialised."

"There's a marker in the *fuckflaps* graveyard," she said, "but he was never recorded like me. Drowning's a quick death, but it's not something you plan for. And we never recovered the body, so it couldn't be done afterwards. He's still down there somewhere. . . ."

It struck me that if Katriona's husband had been augmented, he need not have drowned. My limbs could tirelessly swim, and my exo-skin could filter oxygen from the water. As it would be tactless to proclaim my hardiness, I cast about for a neutral reply. "The North Sea was all land, once. Your ancestors hunted mammoths there, before the sea rose."

"And now the sea is rising again." She spoke with such finality that I knew our conversation was over.

"God speed you to your rest," I said. When I stood up, the hologram vanished.

I walked onward, and the rain began.

I relished the storm. It blew down from the northeast, with ice in its teeth. They call it the lazy wind, because it doesn't bother to go around you – it just goes straight through you.

The afternoon darkened, with winter twilight soon expiring. The rain thickened into hail, bouncing off me with an audible rattle. Cracks of thunder rang out, an ominous rumbling as though the raging sea had washed away the pillars of the sky, pulling the heavens down. Lightning flashed somewhere behind me.

I turned and looked along the coastal path, back to the necropolis of benches I had passed earlier. The holograms were all lit up. I wondered who would sit on the benches in this weather, until I realised that the lightning must have short-circuited the activation protocols.

The holograms were the only bright colours in a washed-out world of slate-grey cloud and gun-dark sea. Images of men and women flickered on the benches, an audience for Nature's show. I saw Katriona standing at the top of the cliff, raising her arms as if calling down the storm. Other figures sat frozen like reproachful ghosts, tethered to their wooden anchors, waiting for the storm to fade. Did they relish the brief moment of pseudo-life? Did they talk among themselves? Or did they resent their evanescent existence, at the mercy of any hikers and hackers wandering by?

I felt I should not intrude. I returned to my trek, slogging on as the day eroded into night. My augmented eyes harvested stray photons from lights in distant houses and the occasional car gliding along inland roads. To my right, the sea throbbed with the pale glitter of bioluminescent pollution. The waves sounded loud in the darkness, their crashes like a secret heartbeat of the world.

The pounding rain churned the path into mud. My mouth curved into a fierce grin. Of course, conditions were nowhere near as intense as the extremes of the simulator. But this was *real*. The sight of all the dead people behind me, chained to their memorials, made me feel sharply alive. Each raindrop on my face was another instant to be cherished. I wanted the night never to end. I wanted to be both here and gone, to stand on the colony world under its red, red sun.

I hurried, as if I could stride across the stars and get there sooner. I trod on an old tree branch that proved to be soggy and rotten. My foot slid off the path. I lurched violently, skidding a few yards sideways and down, until I arrested my fall by grabbing onto a nearby rock. The muscles in my left arm sent pangs of protest at the sharp wrench. Carefully I swung myself round, my feet groping for toe-holds. Soon I steadied myself. Hanging fifty feet above the sea, I must have only imagined that I felt spray whipping up from the waves. It must have been the rain, caught by the wind and sheeting from all angles.

The slip exhilarated me. I know that makes little sense, but I can only tell you how I felt.

But I couldn't cling there all night. I scrambled my way across the exposed crags, at first shuffling sideways by inches, then gaining confidence and swinging along, trusting my augmented muscles to keep me aloft.

My muscles gripped. My exo-skin held. The rock did not.

In mid-swing, I heard a *crack*. My anchoring left hand felt the rock shudder. Instinctively I scrabbled for another hold with my right hand. I grasped one, but nevertheless found myself falling. For a moment I didn't understand what was happening. Then, as the cliff-face crumbled with a noise like the tearing of a sky-sized newspaper, I realised that when the bottom gives way, the top must follow.

As I fell, still clinging to the falling rock, I was drenched by the splashback from the lower boulders hitting the sea below me. Time passed slowly, frame by frame, the scene changing gradually like an exhibition of cels from an animated movie. The hefty rock that I grasped was rotating as it fell. Soon I'd be underneath it. If I still clung on, I would be crushed when it landed.

I leapt free, aiming out to sea. If the cliff had been higher, I'd have had enough time to get clear. But very soon I hit the water, and so did the boulder behind me, and so too – it seemed – did half of the Yorkshire coast.

It sounded like a duel between a volcano and an earthquake. I flailed frantically, trying to swim away, not understanding why I made no progress. Only when I stopped thrashing around did I realise the problem.

My right foot was trapped underwater, somewhere within the pile of rocks that came down from the cliff. At the time, I'd felt nothing. Now, belatedly, a dull pounding pain crept up my leg. I breathed deeply, gulping air between the waves crashing around my head. Then I began attempting to wriggle free, with no success.

I tried to lift up the heavy boulders, but it was impossible. My imprisoned foot kept me in place, constricting my position and preventing me from finding any leverage. After many useless heaves, and much splashing and cursing, I had to give up.

All this time, panic had been building within me. As soon as I stopped struggling, terror flooded my brain with the fear of drowning, the fear of freezing in the cold sea, the fear of more rocks falling on top of me. My thoughts were overwhelmed by the prospect of imminent death.

It took long minutes to regain any coherence. Gradually I asserted some self-command, telling myself that the panic was a relic of my old body, which wouldn't long have survived floating in the North Sea in winter. My new form was far more robust. I wouldn't drown, or freeze to death. If I could compose myself, I'd get through this.

I concentrated on my exo-skin. Normally its texture approximated natural skin's slight roughness and imperfections. Now my leg became utterly smooth, in the hope that a friction-free surface might allow me to slip free. I felt a tiny amount of give, which sent a surge of hope through me, but then I could pull my foot no further. The bulge of my ankle prevented any further progress. Even friction-free, you can't tug a knot through a needle's eye.

Impatient and frustrated, I let the exo-skin revert to default. I needed to get free, and I couldn't simply wait for the next storm to rattle the rocks around. My starship would soon leave Earth. If I missed it, I would have no other chance.

At this point I began wondering whether I subconsciously wanted to miss the boat. Had I courted disaster, just to prevent myself from going?

I couldn't deny that I'd in some sense brought this on myself. I'd been deliberately reckless, pushing myself until the inevitable accident occurred. Why?

Thinking about it, as the cold waves frothed around me, I realised that I'd wanted to push beyond the bounds of my old body, in order to prove to myself that I was worthy of going. We'd heard so much of the harsh rigours of the destination world, and so much had been said about the naturals' inability to survive there unaided, that I'd felt compelled to test the augments to their limit.

Unconsciously, I'd wanted to put myself in a situation that a natural body couldn't survive. Then if I did survive, that would prove I'd been truly transformed, and I'd be confident of thriving on the colony world, among the tides and hurricanes.

Well, I'd accomplished the first stage of this plan. I'd got myself into trouble. Now I just had to get out of it.

But how?

I had an emergency radio-beacon in my skull. I could activate it and no doubt someone would come along to scoop me out of the water. Yet that would be embarrassing. It would show that I couldn't handle my new body, even in the benign conditions of Earth. If I asked for rescue, then some excuse would be found to remove me from the starship roster. Colonists needed to be self-reliant and solve their own problems. There were plenty of reserves on the waiting list – plenty of people who hadn't fallen off a cliff and got themselves stuck under a pile of rocks.

The same applied if I waited until dawn and shouted up to the next person to walk along the coastal path. No, I couldn't ask for rescue. I had to save myself.

Yet asserting the need for a solution did not reveal its nature. At least, not at first. As the wind died down, and the rain softened into drizzle, I found myself thinking coldly and logically, squashing trepidation with the hard facts of the situation.

I needed to extract my leg from the rock. I couldn't move the rock. Therefore I had to move my leg.

I needed to move my leg, but the foot was stuck. Therefore I had to leave my foot behind.

Once I realised this, a calmness descended upon me. It was very simple. That was the price I must pay, if I wanted to free myself. I thought back to the option of calling for help. I could keep my foot, and stay on Earth. Or I could lose my foot, and go to the stars.

Did I long to go so badly?

I'd already decided to leave my family behind and leave my girlfriend. If I jibbed at leaving a mere foot, a minor bodily extremity, then what did that say about my values? Surely there wasn't even a choice to make; I merely had to accept the consequences of the decision I'd already made.

And yet I delayed and delayed, hoping that some other option would present itself, hoping that I could evade the results of my choices.

I'm almost ashamed to admit what finally prompted me to action. It wasn't logic or strong-willed decisiveness. It was the pain from my squashed foot, a throbbing that had steadily intensified while I mulled the possibilities. And it was no fun floating in the cold sea, either. The sooner I acted, the sooner I could get away.

I concentrated upon my exo-skin, that marvel of programmable integument, and commanded it to flow up from my foot. Then I pinched it into my leg, just above my right ankle.

Ouch! Ouch, ouch, ouch, owwww!

Trying to ignore the pain, I steered the exo-skin further in. I wished I could perform the whole operation in an instant, slicing off my foot as if chopping a cucumber. But the exo-skin had limits, and it wasn't designed to do this. I was stretching the spec already.

Soon – sooner than I would have hoped – I had to halt. I needed to access my pain overrides. It had been constantly drilled into us that this was a last resort, that pain existed for a reason and we shouldn't casually turn it off. But if amputating one's own foot wasn't an emergency, I didn't ever want to encounter a true last resort. I turned off the pain signals.

The numbness intoxicated me. What a blessing, to be free from the hurts of the flesh! In the absence of pain, the remaining tasks seemed to elapse much more swiftly. Soon the exo-skin had completely cut through the bone, severing my lower leg and sealing off the wound. Freed from the rock-fall, I swam away and dragged myself ashore. There I collapsed into sleep.

When I woke, the tide had receded, leaving behind a beach clogged with fallen clumps of grass, soggy dead bracken, and the ever-present plastic trash that was humanity's legacy to the world. The pain signals had returned – they could only be temporarily suspended, not permanently switched off. For about a minute I tried to live with my lower calf's agonised protestations; then I succumbed to temptation and suppressed them.

As I tried to stand up, I discovered that I was now lop-sided. At the bottom of my right leg I had some spare exo-skin, since it no longer covered a foot. I instructed the surplus material to extend a few inches into a peg-leg, so that I could balance. I shaped the peg to avoid pressing on my stump, with the force of my steps being borne by the exo-skin higher up my leg.

I tottered across the trash-strewn pebbles. I could walk! I shouted in triumph, and disturbed a magpie busy pecking at the freshly revealed soil on the new shoreline. It chittered reprovingly as it flew away.

Then I must have blacked out for a while. Later, I woke with a weak sun shining in my face. My first thought was to return to the landslip and move the rocks to retrieve my missing foot.

My second thought was – *where is it?*

The whole coast was a jumble of fallen boulders. The cliff had been eroding for years, and last night's storm was only the most recent attrition. I couldn't tell where I'd fallen, or where I'd been trapped. Somewhere in there lay a chunk of flesh, of great sentimental value. But I had no idea where it might be.

I'd lost my foot.

Only at that moment did the loss hit home. I raged at myself for getting into such a stupid situation, and for going through with the amputation rather than summoning help, like a young boy too proud to call for his mother when he hurts himself.

And I felt a deep regret that I'd lost a piece of myself I'd never get back. Sure, the exo-skin could replace it. Sure, I could augment myself beyond what I ever was before.

But the line between man and machine seemed like the coastline around me: constantly being nibbled away. I'd lost a foot, just like the coast had lost a few more rocks. Yet no matter what it swallowed, the sea kept rising.

What would I lose next?

I turned south, back towards town, and walked along the shoreline, looking for a spot where I could easily climb from the beach to the path above the cliff. Perhaps I could have employed my augments and simply clawed my way up the sheer cliff-face, but I had become less keen on using them.

The irony did not escape me. I'd embarked on this expedition with the intent of pushing the augments to the full. Now I found myself shunning them. Yet the augments themselves hadn't failed.

Only I had failed. I'd exercised bad judgement, and ended up trapped and truncated. That was my entirely human brain, thinking stupidly.

Perhaps if my brain had been augmented, I would have acted more rationally.

My steps crunched on banks of pebbles, the peg-leg making a different sound than my remaining foot, so that my gait created an alternating rhythm like the bass-snare drumbeat of old-fashioned pop music. The beach smelled of sea-salt, and of the decaying vegetation that had fallen with the landslip. Chunks of driftwood lay everywhere.

The day was quiet; the wind had dropped and the tide was out, so the only sounds came from my own steps and the occasional cry of the gulls far out to sea. Otherwise I would never have heard the voice, barely more than a scratchy whisper.

"Soon, my darling. Soon we'll be together. Ah, how long has it been?"

I looked around and saw no one. Then I realised that the voice came from low down, from somewhere among the pebbles and the ever-present trash. I sifted through the debris and found a small square of plastic. When I lifted it to my ear, it swore at me.

"Arsewipe! Fuckflaps!"

The voice was so tinny and distorted that I couldn't be sure I recognized it. "Katriona?" I asked.

"How long, how long? Oh, the sea, the dear blessed sea. Speed the waves . . ."

I asked again, but the voice wouldn't respond to me. Maybe the broken chip, which no longer projected a hologram, had also lost its aural input. Or maybe it had stopped bothering to speak to passers by.

Now I saw that some of the driftwood planks were slats of benches. The memorial benches, which over the years had inched closer to the eroding cliff-edge, had finally succumbed to the waves.

Yet perhaps they hadn't succumbed, but rather had finally *attained* their goal – or would do soon enough when the next high tide carried the detritus away. I remembered the holograms lighting up last night, how they'd seemed to summon the storm. I remembered Katriona telling me about her husband who'd drowned. For all the years of her death, she must have longed to join him in the watery deeps.

I strode out towards the distant waves. My steps grew squelchy as I neared the waterline, and I had to pick my way between clumps of seaweed. As I walked, I crunched the plastic chip to shreds in my palm, my exo-skin easily strong enough to break it. When I reached the spume, I flung the fragments into the sea.

"Goodbye," I said, "and God rest you."

I shivered as I returned to the upper beach. I felt an irrational need to clamber up the rocks to the cliff-top path, further from the hungry sea.

I'd seen my own future. The exo-skin and the other augments would become more and more of me, and the flesh less and less. One day only the augments would be left, an electronic ghost of the person I used to be.

As I retrieved my clothes from where I'd cached them, I experienced a surge of relief at donning them to rejoin society. Putting on my shoes proved difficult, since I lacked a right foot. I had to reshape my exo-skin into a hollow shell, in order to fill the shoes of a human being.

Tomorrow I would return to the launch base. I'd seek medical attention after we lifted off, when they couldn't remove me from the colony roster for my foolishness. I smiled as I wondered what similar indiscretions my comrades might reveal, when it was too late for meaningful punishment. What would we all have left behind?

What flaws would we take with us? And what would remain of us, at the last?

Now we approach the end of my story, and there is little left. As I once helped a shadow fade, long ago and far away, I hope that someday you will do the same for me.

VISHNU AT THE CAT CIRCUS

Ian McDonald

British author Ian McDonald is an ambitious and daring writer with a wide range and an impressive amount of talent. His first story was published in 1982, and since then he has appeared with some frequency in *Interzone, Asimov's Science Fiction,* and elsewhere. In 1989 he won the Locus Best First Novel Award for his novel *Desolation Road.* He won the Philip K. Dick Award in 1992 for his novel *King of Morning, Queen of Day.* His other books include the novels *Out On Blue Six* and *Hearts, Hands and Voices, Terminal Cafe, Sacrifice of Fools, Evolution's Shore, Kirinya,* a chapbook novella *Tendeleo's Story, Ares Express,* and *Cyberabad,* as well as two collections of his short fiction, *Empire Dreams* and *Speaking In Tongues.* His novel *River of Gods* was a finalist for both the Hugo Award and the Arthur C. Clarke Award in 2005, and a novella drawn from it, "The Little Goddess," was a finalist for the Hugo and the Nebula. His most recent books are another new novel that's receiving critical raves, *Brasyl,* and a new collection, *Cyberabad Days.* Coming up is a new novel, *The Dervish House.* Born in Manchester, England, in 1960, McDonald has spent most of his life in Northern Ireland, and now lives and works in Belfast. His website is lysator.liu.se/^unicorn/mcdonald/.

In the complex novella that follows, he takes us to his evocative future India, the setting for *River of Gods* and "The Little Goddess," where ancient customs and dazzlingly sophisticated high-tech exist side by side, for a story of sibling rivalry with some very unexpected results.

They are saved by a desk.
Come Matsya, come Kurma. Come Narasimha and Varaha. By the smoky light of burning trash polyethylene and under the mad-eye moon lying drunk on its back, come run in the ring; ginger and black and tabby and grey, white and piebald and tortie and hare-legged tailless Manx. Run Varana, Pashurama, run Rama and Krishna.

I pray I do not offend with my circus of cats that carry the names of divine avatars. Yes, they are dirty street cats, stolen from rubbish dumps and high

walls and balconies, but cats are naturally blasphemous creatures. Every
lick and curl, every stretch and claw is a calculated affront to divine dignity.
But do I not bear the name of a god myself, so may I not name my runners,
my leapers, my stars, after myself? For I am Vishnu, the Preserver.

See! The trash-lamp are lit, the rope ring is set and the seats laid out,
such as they are, being cushions and worn mattresses taken from the boat
and set down to keep your fundament from the damp sand. And the cats are
running, a flowing chain of ginger and grey, the black and the white and
the part-coloured: the marvellous, the magical, the Magnificent Vishnu's
Celestial Cat Circus! You will be amazed, nay, astounded! So why do you
not come?

Round they run and round, nose to tail. You would marvel at the perfect
fluid synchronisation of my cats. Go Buddha, go Kalki! Yes, it takes a god to
train a cat circus.

All evening I beat my drum and rang my bicycle bell through the heat-
blasted hinterland of Chunar. *The Marvellous, the Magical, the Magnificent
Vishnu Cat Circus! Gather round gather round! There are few enough joys in
your life: wonder and a week's conversation for a handful of rupees.* Sand in
the streets, sand slumped against the crumbling walls of abandoned houses,
sand slumped banked up on the bare wheel rims of the abandoned cars and
minibuses, sand piled against the thorny hurdles that divided the river-edge
sandbars into sterile fields. The long drought and the flashfire wars had
emptied this town like so many others close to the Jyotirlinga. I climbed up
to the old fort, with its preview 20 kilometres up and down river. From the
overlook where the old British ambassador had built his governor's residence I
could see the Jyotirlinga spear into the sky above Varanasi, higher than I could
see, higher than the sky for it ran all the way into another universe. The walls
of the old house were daubed with graffiti. I rang my bell and beat my drum
but there was never any hope of even ghosts here. Though I am disconnected
from the deva-net, I could almost smell the devas swirling on the contradictory airs. Walking down into the town I caught the true smell of woodsmoke
and the lingering perfume of cooking and I turned, haunted by a sense of
eyes, of faces, of hands on doorframes that vanished into shadows when I
looked. *Vishnu's Marvellous Magical Magnificent Cat Circus!* I cried, ringing
my bicycle bell furiously, as much to advertise my poverty and harmlessness
as my entertainment. In the Age of Kali the meek and helpless will be preyed
upon without mercy, and there will be a surplus of AK-47s.

The cats were furious and yowling in unison when I returned, hot in
their cages despite the shade of the awning. I let them hunt by the light of
the breaking stars as I set up the ring and the seats, my lamps and sign and
alms bowl, not knowing if a single soul would turn up. The pickings were
meagre. Small game will be scarce in the Age of Kali.

My fine white Kalki, flowing over the hurdles like a riffle in a stream, it is
written that you will battle and defeat Kali, but that seems to me too big an
ask for a mere cat. No, I shall take up that task myself, for if it's your name,
it's also my name. Am I not Vishnu the ten-incarnated? Are not all of you

part of me, cats? I have an appointment down this river, at the foot of that
tower of light that spears up into the eastern sky.

Now come, sit down on this mattress – I have swept away the sand, and let
the lamps draw away the insects. Make yourself comfortable. I would offer
chai but I need the water for the cats. For tonight you will witness not only
the finest cat circus in all of India – likely the only cat circus in all of India.
What do you say? All they do is run in a circle? Brother, with cats, that is an
achievement. But you're right; running in a circle, nose to tail is pretty much
the meat of my Cat Circus. But I have other ways to justify the handful of
rupees I ask from you. Sit, sit and I will tell you a story, my story. I am Vishnu,
and I was designed to be a god.

There were three of us and we were all gods. Shiv and Vish and Sarasvati. I am
not the firstborn; that is my brother Shiv, with whom I have an appointment
at the foot of the Jyotirlinga of Varanasi. Shiv the success, Shiv the businessman, the global success, the household name and the inadvertent harbinger
of this Age of Kali; Shiv I cannot imagine what he has become. I was not the
firstborn but I was the best born and therein lies the trouble of it.

Strife, I believe, was worked into every strand of my parents' DNA. Your
classical Darwinist scorns the notion that intellectual values can shape
evolution, but I myself am living proof that middle class values can be
programmed into the genes. Why not war?

A less likely cyberwarrior than my father you would be hard-pressed to
imagine. Un-co-ordinated; ungainly; portly – no, let's not mince words, he
was downright fat; he had been a content and, in his own way, celebrated,
designer for DreamFlower. You remember DreamFlower? *Street Sumo*;
RaMaYaNa; *BollywoodSingStar*. Million-selling games? Maybe you don't. I
increasingly find it's been longer than I think. In everything. What's important is that he had money and career and success and as much fame as his
niche permitted and life was rolling along, rolling along like a Lexus, when
war took him by surprise. War took us all by surprise. One day we were the
Great Asian Success Story – the Indian Tiger (I call it the Law of Aphoristic
Rebound – the Tiger of Economic Success travels all around the globe before
returning to us) – and unlike those Chinese we had English, cricket and
democracy; the next we were bombing each others' malls and occupying
television stations. State against state, region against region, family against
family. That is the only way I can understand the War of Schism; that India
was like one of those big, noisy, rambunctious families into which the venerable grandmother drops for her six-month sojourn and within two days sons
are at their father's throats. And the mothers at their daughters, and the sisters
feud and the brothers fight and the cousins uncles aunts all take sides and the
family shatters like a diamond along the faults and flaws that gave it its beauty.
I saw a diamond cutter in Delhi when I was young – apologies, when I was
small. Not so young. I saw him set the gem in the padded vice and raise his
cutter and pawl, which seemed too huge and brutal an object by far for so

small and bright an object. I held my breath and set my teeth as he brought the big padded hammer down and the gem fell into three gems, brighter and more radiant than their parent.

"Hit it wrong," he said, "and all you have is dazzling dust."

Dazzling dust, I think, has been our history ever since.

The blow came – success, wealth, population strain – and we fell to dust but Delhi didn't know it. The loyalists resolutely defended the dream of India. So my father was assigned as Help Desk to a Recon Mecha Squad. To you this will sound unspeakably hot and glamorous. But this was another century and another age and robots were far from the shimmering rakshasa-creatures we know today, constantly shifting shape and function along the edge of human expectation. This was a squad of reconnaissance bots; two legged joggers and jumpers, ungainly and temperamental as iron chickens. And Dadaji was the Help Desk, which meant fixing them and de-virusing them and unbugging them and hauling them out of the little running circles they'd trapped themselves in, or turning them away from the unscalable wall they were attempting to leap, all the while wary of their twin flechette-gatlings and their close-defence nano-edged blades.

"I'm a games coder," he wailed. "I choreograph Bollywood dance routines and arrange car crashes. I design star-vampires." Delhi ignored his cries. Delhi was already losing as the us-too voices of national self-determination grew loud in the Rashtrapati Bhavan, but she chose to ignore them as well.

Dadaji was a Cyber Warrior, Mamaji was a Combat Medic. It was slightly more true for her than for Dadaji. She was indeed a qualified doctor and had worked in the field for NGOs in India and Pakistan after the earthquake and with *Medeçins Sans Frontieres* in Sudan. She was not a soldier, never a soldier. But Mother India needed front line medics so she found herself at Advanced Field Treatment Centre 32 east of Ahmedabad at the same time my father's recon unit was relocated there. My mother examined Tech-Sergeant Tushar Nariman for crabs and piles. The rest of his unit refused to let a woman doctor inspect their pubes. He made eye contact with her, for a brave, frail second.

Perhaps if the Ministry of Defence had been less wanton in their calling-up of cyberwarriors and had assigned a trained security analyst to the Eight Ahmedabad Recon Mecha Squad instead of a games designer, more would have survived when the Bharati Tiger-Strike-Force attacked. A new name was being spoken in old east Uttar Pradesh and Bihar; Bharat, the old holy name of India; its spinning wheel flag planted in Varanasi, most ancient and pure of cities. Like any national liberation movement, there were dozens of self-appointed guerrilla armies, each named more scarily than the predecessor with whom they were in shaky alliance. The Bharati Tiger-Strike-Force was an embryo of Bharat's elite cyberwar force. And unlike Tushar, they were pros. At 21:23 they succeeded in penetrating the Eight Ahmedabad's firewall and planted Trojans into the recon mechas. As my father pulled up his pants after experiencing the fluttering fingers and inspection torch of my mother-to-be at his little rosebud, the Tiger-Strike-Force took control of the robots and turned then on the field hospital.

Lord Shiva bless my father for a fat boy and a coward. A hero would have run out on to the sand to see what was happening when the firing started. A hero would have died in the crossfire, or, when the ammunition ran out, by their blades. At the first shot, my father went straight under the desk.

"Get down!" he hissed at my mother who froze with a look part bafflement, part wonderment on her face. He pulled her down and immediately apologised for the unseemly intimacy. She had lately cupped his testicles in her hand, but he apologized. They knelt in the kneehole, side by side while the shots and the cries and the terrible, arthritic click click click of mecha joints swirled around them, and little by little subsided into cries and clicks, then just clicks, then silence. Side by side they knelt, shivering in fear, my mother kneeling like a dog on all fours until she shook from the strain, but afraid to move, to make the slightest noise in case it brought the stalking shadows that fell through the window into the surgery. The shadows grew long and grew dark before she dared exhale, "What happened?"

"Hacked mecha," my father said. Then he made himself forever the hero in my mother's eyed. "I'm going to take a look." Hand by knee by knee by hand, careful to make no noise, disturb not the least piece of broken glass or shattered wood, he crept out from under the desk across the strewn floor to underneath the window. Then, millimetre-by-millimetre, he edged up the side until he was in a half crouch. He glanced out the window and in the same instant dropped to the floor and began his painstaking crawl back across the floor.

"They're out there," he breathed to Mamaji. "All of them. They will kill anything that moves." He said this one word at a time, to make it sound like the natural creakings and contractions of a portable hut on a Ganga sandbank.

"Perhaps they'll run out of fuel," my mother replied.

"They run off solar batteries." This manner of conversation took a long time. "They can wait forever."

Then the rain began. It was a huge thunder-plump, a forerunner of the monsoon still uncoiling across the Bay of Bengal, like a man with a flag or a trumpet who runs before a groom to let the world know that a great man is coming. Rain beat the canvas like hands on a drum. Rain hissed from the dry sand as it was swallowed. Rain ricocheted from the plastic carapaces of the waiting, listening robots. Rain-song swallowed every noise, so that my mother could only tell my father was laughing by the vibrations he transmitted through the desk.

"Why are you laughing?" she hissed in a voice a little lower than the rain.

"Because in this din they'll never hear me if I go and get my palmer," my father said, which was very brave for a corpulent man. "Then we'll see who hacks whose robots."

"Tushar," my mother whispered in a voice like steam but my father was already steadily crawling out from under the desk towards the palmer on the camp chair by the zip door. "It's only a . . ."

And the rain stopped. Dead. Like a mali turning off a garden hose. It was over. Drips dropped from the ridge-line and the never-weatherproof windows. Sun broke through the plastic panes. There was a rainbow. It was very pretty but my father was trapped in the middle of the tent with killer robots in the alert outside. He mouthed an excremental oath and carefully, deadly carefully reversed amongst all the shatter and tumbled debris, wide arse first like an elephant. How he felt the vibration of suppressed laughter through the wooden desk sides.

"Now. What. Are. You. Laughing. At?"

"You don't know this river," my mother whispered. "Ganga Devi will save us yet."

Night came swift as ever on the banks of the holy river, the same idle moon as now lights my tale rose across the scratched plastic squares of the window. My mother and father knelt, arms aching, knees tormented, side-by-side beneath the desk. My father said, "Do you smell something?"

"Yes," my mother hissed.

"What is it?"

"Water," she said and he saw her smile in the dangerous moonlight. And then he heard it, a hissing, seeping suck sand would make if it were swallowing water but all its thirst were not enough, it was too much, too fast, too too much, it was drowning. My father smelled before he saw the tongue of water, edged with sand and straw and the flotsam of the sangam on which the camp stood, creep under the edge of the tent across the liner and around his knuckles. It smelled of soil set free. It was the old smell of the monsoon, when every dry thing has its true perfume scent and flavour and colour released by the rain; the smell of water that is the smell of everything water liberates. The tongue became a film, water flowed around their fingers and knees, around the legs of the desk as if they were the piers of a bridge. Dadaji felt my mother shaking with laughter, then the flood burst open the side of the tent and dashed dazed drowned him in wall of water so that he spluttered and choked and tried not to cough for fear of the traitor mecha. Then he understood my mother's laughter and he laughed too, loud and hard and coughing up lungfuls of Ganges.

"Come on!" he shouted and leaped up, over-turning the desk, throwing himself on to it like a surfboard, seizing the legs with both hands. My mother dived and grabbed just as the side of the tent opened in a torrent and desk and refugees were swept away on the flood. "Kick!" he shouted as he steered the desk toward the sagging doorway. "If you love life and mother India, kick!" Then they were out in the night beneath the moon. The sentinel unfolded its killing-things, blade after blade after blade, launched after them and was knocked down bowled over, swept away by the flooding water. The last they saw of it its carapace was half-stogged in the sand, water breaking creamy around it. They kicked through the flotsam of the camp, furniture and ration packs and med kids and tech, the shorted, fused, sparked out corpses of the mecha and the floating, spinning swollen corpses of soliders and medics. They kicked through them all, riding their bucking desk, they kicked half-choked, shivering out into the deep green water of Mother Ganga, under the face of the full moon they kicked up the silver corridor of her river-light. At noon the next day, far far from the river beach of Chattigarh, an Indian patrol-RIB found them and hauled them, dehydrated, skin cracked and mad from the sun, into the bottom of the boat. At some point in the long night either under the desk or floating on it they had fallen in love. My mother always aid it was the most romantic thing that had ever happened to her. Ganga Devi raised her waters and carried them through the killing machines to safety on a miraculous raft. Or so our family story went.

Here a God is incarnated, and then me.

My parents fell in love in one country, India, and married in another, Awadh, the ghost of ancient Oudh, itself a ghost of the almost-forgotten British Raj. Delhi was no longer the capital of a great nation but of a geographical fudge. One India was now many, our mother goddess descended into a dozen avatars from re-united Bengal to Rajasthan, from Kashmir to Tamil Nadu. How had we let this happen, almost carelessly, as if we had momentarily stumbled on our march toward superpowerdom, then picked ourselves up and carried on. It was all most embarrassing, like a favourite uncle discovered with porn on his computer. You look away, you shun it, you never talk about it. Like we have never talked about the seisms of violence that tear through our dense, stratified society; the mass bloodletting of our independence that came with an excruciating partition, the constant threat of religious war, the innate, brooding violence in the heart of our caste system. It was all so very un-Indian. What are a few hundred thousand deaths next to those millions? If not forgotten, they will be ignored in a few years. And it certainly has made the cricket more interesting.

The new India suited my mother and father very well. They were model young Awadhis. My father, trapped by artificial intelligence once, viewed never to let that happen again and set up one of the first aeai farms breeding custom wares for low-level applications like Air Awadh, Delhi Bank and the Revenue Service. My mother went first for cosmetic surgery, then, after a shrewd investment in an executive enclave for the nascent Awadhi civil service, gave up the micro-manipulators for a property portfolio. Between them they made so much money that their faces were never out of *Delhi Gloss!* Magazine. They were the golden couple who had sailed to a glorious future over the floods of war and the interviewers who called at their penthouse asked, *so then, where is the golden son?*

Shiva Nariman made his appearance on 27 September 2025. Siva, oldest God in the world, Siva, first and favoured, Siva from whose matted hair the holy Ganga descended, generative force, auspicious one, lord of paradox. The photo rights went to *Gupshup* magazine for 500,000 Awadhi rupees. The golden boy's nursery was featured on the nightly *Nationwide* show and became quite the style for a season. There was great interest in this first generation of a new nation; the Awadh Bhais, the gossip sites called them. They were the sons not just a small coterie of prominent Delhi middle class, but of all

Awadh. The nation took them to its heart and suckled them from its breasts, these bright, bouncing brilliant boys who would grow up with the new land and lead it to greatness. It was never to be mentioned, not even to be thought, how many female foetuses were curetted or flushed out or swilled away, unimplanted, into the medical waste. We were a new country, we were engaged in the great task of nation-building. We could overlook a demographic crisis that had for years been deforming our middle classes. What if there were four times as many boys as girls? They were fine strong sons of Awadh. The others, they were only females.

So easily I say *we*, for I seem to have ended up as a impresario and story teller but the truth is that I did not exist, I didn't even exist then, not until the day the baby spoke at the Awadhi Bhai Club. It was never anything as formal as a constituted club; the blessed mothers, darlings of the nation, had fallen together by natural mutual need to cope with a media gawping into every aspect of their lives. Perfection needs a support group. They naturally banded together in each other living rooms and penthouse, and their mothers and ayahs with them. It was a gilded Mothers and Infants group. The day the baby spoke my mother had gathered with Usha and Kiran and Devi. It was Devi's baby who spoke. Everyone was talking about exhaustion and nipple softening oil and peanut allergies when Vin Johar lolling in his rocker opened his brown brown eyes, focused across the room and clearly said, "Hungry, want my bottle."

"Hungry, are we my cho chweet?" Devi said.

"Now," said Vin Johar. "Please."

Devi clapped her hands in delight.

"Please! He hasn't said 'please' before."

The rest of the penthouse was still staring, dazed.

"How long has he been talking?" Usha asked.

"Oh, about a three days," Devi said. "He picks up everything you say."

"My bottle now," demanded Vin Johar. "Quickly."

"But he's only . . ." Kiran said.

"Five months, yes. He's been a bit slower than Dr Rao predicted."

The mothers' mothers and the ayahs made furtive hand gestures, kissed charms to turn away evil. It was my Mamaji, dandling fat, content Shiv on her knee, who understood first.

"You've been, you've had, he's a . . ."

"Brahmin, yes."

"But you're a Sudra," Kiran wondered.

"Brahmin," Devi said with such emphasis that no one could fail to hear the Capital. "We've had him done, yes."

"Done?" asked Usha and then realized, "Oh." And, "Oh!"

"He'll be tall and he'll be strong and he'll be handsome – of course; that bit we didn't have to engineer – and he'll be fit and healthy. Oh so healthy – he'll never get heart disease, arthritis, Alzheimer's, Huntingdon's; with his immune system he can laugh of almost any virus or infection. His immune system will even take out malaria! Imagine that! And intelligence; well, let's just say, Dr Rao told us there isn't even a test smart enough to stretch him. He'll just need to see a thing once and he's learned it – like that! And his memory, well, Dr Rao says there is double the number of connections in the brain, or something like that: what it means is that he'll have a phenomenal memory. Like that Mr Memory on *India's Got Talent*, only even better. He won't be able to forget anything. No forgetting birthdays and phone calls to his Mata when he's off around the world with some big corporation. Look at him, look at him, isn't he just the most gorgeous thing you've ever seen; those baby baby blue eyes. Look at you, look at you, just look at you my little lord? See them all, see them your friends? They are princes each and every one, but you, you are a god. Oh, I could bite your bum, oh, just bite it like that it's so beautiful and plump and gorgeous." Devi held Vin Johar up like a trophy in a cricket match. She kissed him on his bare belly where his little vest had ridden up. "Oh you little god."

Then Shiv let out a long wail. All through Devi's song of praise to her genetically improved darling son, my mother's grip had gradually tightened in envy on golden Shiv, now hopelessly outmoded, until he cried out in pain. Her fingers had left bruises like purple carrots along his ribs.

Shiv gazed up at the mobile turning in the air-conditioning above his cot innocent and unaware of how his visual acuity was being stimulated by the cleverly designed blobs and clouds. My mother fretted and stormed by turns around the pastel-lit apartment until Dadaji returned from the office. After Shiv was born his duties at the office grew more arduous and his hours longer. He was never a terribly good father really. He was useless at cricket.

"What are you doing on Friday?" Mamaji demanded.

"Um, I'm not sure, there's something at the office."

"Cancel it."

"What?" He was never very good at manners either, but then he was a Top Geek.

"We're seeing Dr Rao."

"Dr who?"

"Dr Rao. At the Swaminathan Clinic." He knew the name. He knew the clinic. All Delhi, even Top Geeks, knew of the strange and miraculous children that came out of there. He just need a moment for his balls to unfreeze and drop from that place close to the warmth of his perineum where they had retreated in terror.

"Friday, eleven thirty, with Dr Rao himself. We are having a baby."

It wasn't Friday eleven thirty, nor the Friday after. It was not for six Fridays, after the initial consultation and the financial check and the medical assessment and the one-to-ones first Mamaji then Dadaji and only then did they get to choose from the menu. It was a menu, like in the most rarefied restaurant you can imagine. My parents blinked. Intelligence yes good looks yes enhanced concentration yes expanded memory and improved recall yes health wealth strength happiness, everything Vin Johar had. And more.

"Extended lifespan?"

"Ah yes, that is a new one. A new technique that has just been licensed."

"Does that mean?"

"Exactly what it says."

My parents blinked again.

"Your son" – for this was me they were building – "will enjoy a greatly increased span of life in full health and vigor."

"How much increased?"

"Double the current human norm; what is that? Let me think, for people like us, affluent, educated, middle-class, with access to quality healthcare, that's currently eighty years. Well double that."

A third time they blinked.

"One hundred and sixty years old."

"At the very least, you must remember that medical miracles are occurring every day. Every single day. There's no reason your son . . ."

"Vishnu."

My father stared open-mouthed ay mother. He didn't know there was a name. He hadn't yet realized that he had no say in this whatsoever. But his balls understood, cringing in his loose-and-cooling-good-for-sperm-production silk boxers.

"Vishnu, the Lord, governor and sustainer." Dr Rao dipped his head in respect. He was an old-fashioned man. "You know, I have often thought how the processes of conception, gestation and parturition are reflected in he ten incarnations of Lord Vishnu: the fish the restless sperm, the turtle of Kurma the egg, the saving of the earth from the bottom of the ocean by Varaha the fertilisation . . ."

"What about the dwarf?" my father asked. "The dwarf Brahmin?"

"The dwarf, yes," Dr Rao drawled. He was a man of slow speech, who seemed to lose the end of his sentences the closer he approached them. This led many people to make the mistake of thinking him stupid when what he was doing was shaping the perfect conclusion. As a consequence he didn't do many television or net interviews. "The dwarf's always the problem, isn't he? But your son will assuredly be a true Brahmin. And Kalki, yes, Kalki. The ender of the Age of Kali. Who's to say that he might not see this world end in fire and water and a new one be born? Yes, longevity. It's very good, but there are a couple of minor inconveniences."

"Never mind. We'll have that. Devi Johar doesn't have that."

So my father was sent with a plastic cup to catch his sacred fish. My mother went with him; to make it an act of love but mostly because she didn't trust him with Western porn. A few Fridays later Dr Rao harvested a clutch of my mother's turtle-eggs with a long needle. She didn't need my father there for that. This was an act of biology. The slow-spoken doctor did his work and called up eight blastulas from the deep ocean of his artificial wombs. One was selected: Me! Me! Little me! Here I am! See me! See me! and I was implanted into my mother's womb. It was then that she discovered the inconvenience: my doubled lifespan was bought at the price of aging at half the speed of baseline, non-Brahminic humanity. After sixteen months of pregnancy, sixteen months of morning sickness and bloating and bad circulation and broken veins and incontinence and backache but worst of all, not being able to smoke, my mother, with a great shriek of *At last At last! Get the fucking thing out of me!* gave birth on 9 August 2027 and I made my entry as a player in this story.

My Brother Hates Me

What a world, into which I was born! What times: an age of light and brilliance. Shining India truly found herself in Shining Awadh, Shining Bharat, Shining Maratha, Shining Bengal – all the shining facets of our many peoples. The horrors of the Schisming were put behind us, apart from war-maimed begging on metro platforms, gangs of undersocialised ex-teen-cyberwarriors, occasional flare-ups from hibernating combat 'ware buried deep in the city net and Concerned Documentary Makers who felt that we had not sufficiently mourned our self-mutilation and achieved reconciliation. Reconciliation? Delhi had no time for such Western niceties. Let the dead burn the dead, there was money to be made and pleasure to be savoured. Our new boulevards and maidans, our malls and entertainment zones were brilliant with the bright and the young and the optimistic. It was a time of bold new fashions, father-scandalizing hemlines and mother-troubling hairstyles; of new trends and obsessions that were old and cold as soon as they hit the gossip sites; of ten thousand shattering new ideas that disappeared as soon as they were iterated like a quantum foam of thought. It was youth, it was confidence, it was the realisation of all that old Mother India had claimed she might be but most of all it was money. As in Delhi, so in Varanasi, Kolkata, Mumbai, Chennai, Jaipur. But most of all, I think, in Delhi. In India she had been capital by whim, not by right. Mumbai, even Kolkata always outshone her. Now she truly was capital of her own nation, without rival, and she dazzled. My earliest memory, from the time when my senses all ran together and sounds had smells and colours had textures and a unified reality above those crude divisions, was of lines of light streaming over my upturned face, light in all colours and more, light that, to undifferentiated cortex, hummed and chimed like the sympathetic strings of a sitar. I suppose I must have been in our car and our chauffeur driving us somewhere through the downtown lights to some soirée or other, but all I remember is grinning up at the streaming, singing light. When I think of Delhi even now, I think of it as a river of light, a torrent of silver notes.

And what a city! Beyond Old Delhi and New Delhi, beyond the Newer Delhis of Gurgaon and the desirable new suburbs of Sarita Vihar and New Friends Colony, the Newest Delhis of all were rising. Invisible Delhis, Delhis of data and digits and software. Distributed Delhis, networked Delhis, Delhis woven from cable and wireless nodes, intangible Delhis woven through the streets and buildings of the material city. Strange new peoples lived here: the computer-constructed cast of *Town and Country*, the all-conquering soap opera that, in its complete artificiality, was more real than life itself. It was not just the characters who drew our fascinations, the genius of the production lay in the CG-actors who believed they played and had a separate existence from those characters, and whose gupshup and scandal, whose affairs and marriages meant more to us than our friends and neighbours. Other brilliant creatures streamed past and through us on our streets and squares: the aeais; the pantheon of artificial intelligences that served our immaterial needs from banking to legal services to household management to personal secretarial services. In no place and every place, these were entities of levels and hierarchies; high-end aeais cascading down through sub-routines into low-grade monitors and processors; thousands of those same daily-grind Level 0.8 (the intelligence of a street pig) scaling up through connection and associations into Level 1s – the intelligence of a monkey; those again aggregating together into the highest, the Level 2s, indistinguishable from a human seventy percent of the time. And beyond them were the rumoured, feared Level 3s: of human intelligence and beyond. Who could understand such an existence, beings of many parts that did not necessarily recognise each other? The djinns, those ancient haunters of their beloved Delhi, they understood; and older than they, the gods. They understood only too well. And in the material city, new castes appeared. A new sex appeared on our streets as if stirred out of heaven, neither male nor female, rejecting the compromises of the old hijras to be aggressively neither. The nutes, they called themselves. And then of course there were these like me; improved in egg and sperm, graced with outrageous gifts and subtle curses: the Brahmins. Yes I was an upper-middle class brat born into genetic privilege, but Delhi was laid out before me like a wedding banquet. She was my city.

Delhi loved me. Loved me, loved all of my Brahmin brothers and occasional sisters. We were wonders, freaks, miracles and avatars. We might do anything, we were the potential of Awadh. Those first-born were accidents of birth, we, the Brahmins, were the true Awadhi Bhais. We even had our own comic, of that name. With our strange genetic powers, we battled criminals, demons and Bharatis. We were superheroes. It sold pretty well.

You might think I was blithe enough, a genetically high-caste blob bouncing in my baby-rocker blinking up into the sunlight beaming through the glass walls of our tower-top penthouse. You would be wrong. As I lay giggling and blinking neural pathways were twining up through my medulla and cerebellum and Area of Broca with preternatural speed. That blur of light, that spray of silver notes rapidly differentiated into objects, sounds, smells, sensations. I saw, I heard, I sensed but I could not yet understand. So I made connections, I drew patterns, I saw the world pouring in through my senses and up the fiery tree of my neurons as relation, as webs and nets and constellations. I formed an inner astrology and from it, before I could call dog "dog" and cat "cat" and Mamaji "Mamaji," I understood the connectedness of things. I saw the bigger picture; I saw the biggest picture. This was my true superpower, one that has remained with me to this day. I never could fly to Lanka in a thought or lift a mountain by the force of my will, I was not master of fire or thunder or even my own soul, but I could always take one look and know the whole, absolute and entire.

The naming of names. That was where Mamaji first realised that Dr Rao's blessings were not unmixed. The soirée that day was at Devi Johar's house, she of the amazing Vin. There he was, running around the place with his ayah trying to keep up with him in kiddie-wear by SonSun of Los Angeles. Shiv played with the other non-Brahmins in the roof garden, happy and content at their own limited, non-enhanced activities. How fast the gilt had rubbed off him, after I was born! As for me, I sat in my bouncer, burbling and watching big-eyed the mothers of the golden. I knew Shiv's jealousy, though I didn't have the words or the emotional language for it. I saw in a thousand looks and glances, the way he sat at the table, the way he rode in the car, the way he toddled along behind Ayah Meenakshi as she pushed me through the mall, the way he stood by my cot and gazed soft-eyed at me. I understood hate.

Vin asked Devi if he could go out and play with the others on the roof garden. Please.

"All right, but don't show off," Devi Johar said. When he had toddled away, Devi crossed her ankles demurely and placed her hands on her knees, so.

"Mira, I hope you don't mind me saying, but your Vish; well, he isn't talking yet. At his age, Vin had a vocabulary of two hundred words and a good grasp of syntax and grammar."

"And shouldn't he be, well, at least crawling?" Usha asked.

"How old is he; fifteen months? He does seem a little on the . . . small side," Kiran chimed in.

My Mamaji broke down in tears. It was the crying nights and the sshing to sleep, the rocking and the cleaning and the mewling and puling, the tiredness, oh, the tiredness, but worst of all, the breast feeding.

"Breast? After a year?" Usha was aghast. "I mean, I've heard that some mothers keep them on the teat for years, but they're from the villages, or mamas who love their sons too much."

"My nipples feel like mulberries," my Mamaji wept. "You see, he's fifteen months old, but biologically, he not even eight months yet."

I would live twice as long, but age half as fast. Infancy was a huge, protracted dawn; childhood an endless morning. When Shiv started school I would only have begun toddling. When I was of university age I would still have the physiology of a nine year-old. Adulthood, maturity, old age, were points so distant on the great plain of my lifespan that I could not tell if they were insects or cities. In those great days I would come into my own, a life long enough to become part of history; as a baby, I was a mother's nightmare.

"I know breast is best, but maybe you should consider switching to formula," Devi said soothingly.

See how I recall every word? Another of Dr Rao's equivocal gifts. I forget only what I choose to unremember. I understood every word – at eighteen months my vocabulary was far in advance of your precious Vin, bitch Devi. But it was trapped inside me. My brain formed the words but my larynx, my tongue, my lips and lungs couldn't form them. I was a prisoner in a baby-bouncer, smiling and waving my fat little fists.

Four there were who understood me, and four only, and they lived in the soft-contoured plastic butterfly that hung over my cot. Their names were TikkaTikka, Badshanti, Pooli and Nin. They were aeais, set to watch over me and entertain me with song and stories and pretty patterns of coloured lights because Mamaji considered Ayah Meenakshi's sleepy-time stories far too terrifying for a suggestible Brahmin. They were even more stupid than my parents but it was because they were deeply dense that they had no preconceptions beyond their Level 0.2 programming and so I could communicate with them.

TikkaTikka sang songs.

> In a little green boat,
> On the blue sea so deep
> Little Lord Vishnu
> Is sailing to sleep . . .

He sang that every night. I liked it, I still sing it to myself as I pole my circus of cats along the ravaged shores of Mata Ganga.

Pooli impersonated animals, badly. He was a cretin. His stupidity insulted me so I left him mute inside the plastic butterfly.

Badshanti, lovely Badshanti, she was the weaver of stories. "Would you like to hear a story, Vishnu?" were the words that led into hours of wonder. Because I don't forget. I know that she never repeated a story, unless I asked her to. How did I ask? For that I must introduce the last of my four aeais.

Nin spoke only in patterns of light and colour that played across my face, an ever-wheeling kaleidoscope that was supposed to stimulate my visual intelligence. Nin-no-words was the intelligent one; because he could inter-pret facial expression, he was the one I first taught my language. It was a very simple language of blinking. One deliberate blink for yes, two for no. It was slow, it was tortuous but it was a way out the prison of my body. Nin reading my answers to Badshanti's questions, I could communicate anything.

How did my brother hate me? Let me take you to that time in Kashmir. After the third drought in a row my mother vowed never again to spend a summer in Delhi's heat, noise, smog and disease. The city seemed like a dog lying at the side of the street, panting and feral and filthy and eager for any excuse to sink its teeth into you, waiting for the monsoon. Mamaji looked to the example of the British of a hundred years before and took us up to the cool and the high places. Kashmir! Green Kashmir, blue lake, the bright houseboats and the high beyond all, the rampart of mountains. They still wore snow, then. I remember blinking in the wonder of the Dal Lake as the shikara sped us up the still water to the hotel rising sheer like a palace in one of Badshanti's tales from the water. My four friends bobbed in the wind of

our passage as the boat curved in across the lake to the landing stage where
porters in red turbans waited to transport us to our cool summer apartment.
Shiv stood in the bow. He wanted to throw them the landing rope.

The calm, the clear, the high cool of Kashmir after the mob heat of
Delhi! I bobbed and bounced and grinned in my cot and waved my little
hands in joy at the sweet air. Every sense was stimulated, every nerve vibrant.
In the evening TikkaTikka would sing, Badshanti tell a story and Nin send
stars sweeping over my face.

There was to be an adventure by boat across the lake. There was food and
there was drink. We were all to go together. It was a thing of a moment, I can
see it still, so small it looked like an accident. It was not. It was deliberate, it
was meticulously planned.

"Where's Gundi-bear? I've lost Gundi-bear," Shiv cried as my father was
about to get into the boat. "I need Gundi-bear." He launched towards the
shore along the gangplank. Dadaji swept him up.

"Oh no you don't; we'll never get anywhere at this rate. You stay here and
don't move. Now, where did you last see him?"

Shiv shrugged, innocently forgetful.

"Here, I'll come with you, you'll never find anything the way you ram
and stam around." My mother sighed her great sigh of exasperation. "Shiv,
you stay here, you hear? Don't touch anything. We'll be back in two ticks."

I felt a deeper shadow in the mild shade of the awning. Shiv stood over
me. Even if I chose to I could not forget the look on his face. He ran up
the gangplank, untied the mooring rope and let it fall into the water. He
waggled his fingers, *bye bye* as the wind caught the curve of coloured cotton
and carried me out into the lake. The frail little shikara was taken far from
the shelter of the Lake Hotel's island into the rising chop. The wind caught
it and turned it. The boat rolled. I began to cry.

Nin saw my face change. TikkaTikka awoke in the little plastic butterfly
my parents had hung from the bamboo ridge pole.

The lake is big and the lake deep
And Little Lord Vishnu is falling asleep
The wind is high and the sun is beaming
To carry you off to the kingdom of dreaming, he sang.

"Hello, Vishnu," Badshanti said. "Would you like a story today?"

Two blinks.

"Oh, no story? Well then, I'll just let you sleep. Sweet dreams, Vishnu."

Two blinks.

"You don't want a story but you don't want to sleep?"

One blink.

"All right then, let's play a game."

Two blinks. Badshanti hesitated so long I thought her software had hung.
She was a pretty rudimentary aeai.

"Not a game, not a story, not sleep?" I blinked. She knew better than to ask
"well, what do you want?" Now TikkaTikka sang a strange song I had never
heard before,

"Wind and lake water
And gathering storm,
Carry Lord Vishnu
Far into harm."

Yes. The shikara was far from shore, broadside to the wind and rolling on the chop. On gust could roll it over and send me to the bottom of the Dal Lake. I might be a hero in my own comic but Dr Rao had neglected to give me the genes for breathing underwater.

"Are we on a boat, sailing far far away?" Badshanti asked.

Yes.

"Are you out on water?"

Yes.

"Are we on our own?"

Yes.

"Is Vishnu happy?"

No.

"Is Vishnu scared?"

Yes.

"Is Vishnu safe?"

Two blinks. Again Badshanti paused. Then she started to shout. "Help aid assist! Little Lord Vishnu is in peril! Help aid assist!" The voice was thin and tinny and would not have reached any distance across the wind-ruffled lake but one of the silent aeais, perhaps stupid Pooli, must also have sent out a radio, bluetooth and GPS alarm, for a fishing boat suddenly changed course, opened up its long-tail engine and sped towards me on a curve of spray.

"Thank you thank you sirs and saviours," Badshanti babbled as the two fishermen hauled my shikara close with their hard hands and to their astonishment saw a child lying on the mattresses, smiling up at them.

A Map Drawn Inside the Skull

All my long life I have been ordained to be tied to water. My parents were delivered by the flood, my aeais saved me from the drifting boat. Even now I pick my way down the shrivelled memory of the Ganga, descended from the hair of Siva. Water it was that made me into a superhero of Awadh, albeit of a very different, non-tall-building-leaping type from the Awadhi Bhai who refused to grow up through the pages of Virgin comics.

There was of course no end of ruction after five-and-half-year old Shiv tried to expose me in an open boat. He made no attempt to deny it. He bore it stoically. The worst of it was my father's therapy-speak. I almost felt for him. At least my mother was angry, blazingly, searingly angry. She didn't try to wrap it up in swathes of *how did you find it* and *I imagine you're feeling* and *let's try and talk through this like men*. It didn't end when the monsoon finally came late and scanty and we returned to Delhi slick and greasy with rain, the wonderful, rich smell of wet dust perfuming the air more purely than any incense. Four days later it ended and Delhi became afraid. That was how my parents kept the story out of the papers. FIFTEEN MILLION THIRSTY THROATS is a more immediate headline than FIVE-YEAR-OLD TRIES TO DROWN BRAHMIN BROTHER. Just.

There was counselling, of course, long and expensive and in the end producing no better result than the child psychologist saying, "This is possibly the most intractable case of sibling rivalry I have ever seen. Your son has a colossal sense of entitlement and deeply resents what he perceives as a loss of status and parental affection. He's quite unrepentant and I fear he might make a second attempt to cause Vishnu harm." My parents took these words and reached their own solution. Shiv and I could not live together so we must live apart. My father took an apartment across the city. Shiv went with him. I stayed with Mamaji, and one other. Before they parted plump Tushar loved my mother a goodbye-time, without planning or sex selection or genetic regulation. And so Sarasvati was born, the last of the three gods; my sister.

We grew up together. We lay in our cots side by side, looking not at our stimulating and educational toys but at each other. For a blissful time she paralleled me. We learned to walk and talk and regulate our bowels together. When we were alone I would murmur the words I knew to her, the words that had roosted and chattered so long in my skull and now were free, like someone throwing open a dark and fetid pigeon loft on a Delhi rooftop. We were close as twins. Then week by week, month by month, Sarasvati outgrew me. Bigger, better co-ordinated, more physically developed, her tongue never stumbled over her few and simple words while poems and vedas rattled inarticulate inside me. She grew out of being twin to bigger sister. She was the surprise, the delight, the child free from expectations and thus she could never disappoint. I loved her. She loved me. In those murmurous evenings filled with sunset and the cool of the air-conditioning, we found a common language and knowing born of shared playing that our various and despised ayahs, even our Mother, could never penetrate.

Across the city, on his own glass tower top filled with the staggering, pollution-born sunsets of great Delhi, Shiv grew up apart. He was six and a half, he was top of his class, he was destined for greatness. How do I know this? Once a week my father came to see his other son and daughter and for a snatched evening with his darling. I had long superseded TikkaTikka, Pooli, Nin and Badshanti with more powerful (and discreet) aeai attendants, ones that, as soon as I had the words on my tongue, I found I could reprogramme to my needs. I sent them out like djinns through the apartment. Not a word was spoken, not a glance exchanged that I could not know it. Sometimes the glances would become looks, and the murmurs cease and my parents would make love to each other. I saw that too. I did not think it particularly wrong or embarrassing; I knew fine and well what they were doing but, though it made them very happy, it did not look like a thing I would ever want.

I look back now from age and loss and see those babbling days with Sarasvati as the age of gold, our Satya Yuga of innocence and truth. We stumbled together towards the sunlight and found joy in every fall and bump and grin. Our world was bright and full of surprises' delights in discovery for Sarasvati, pleasure in her evident delight for me. Then school forced us apart. What a terrible, unnecessary thing school is. I feel in it the enduring envy of parents for idle childhood. Of course it could be no ordinary school for little Lord Vishnu. Dr Renganathan Brahminical College was an academy for the elite of the elite. Education was intimate and bespoke. There were eight in my year and that was large enough for divisions. Not all Brahmins were equal in the Dr Renganathan College. Though we were all the same age we divided ourselves, quite naturally, like meiosis, into Old Brahmins and Young Brahmins, Or, as you like, Big Brahmins and Little Brahmins. Those who aged half as fast but would live twice as long and those who would enjoy all the gifts of health and smarts and looks and privilege but would still fall dead at whatever age the meditech of that era could sustain. Intimations of mortality in Miss Mukudan's reception class.

Ah, Miss Mukudan! Your golden bangles and your Cleopatra smiling eyes, your skin the soft dark of the deepest south; your ever-discreet moustache and smell of camphor as you bent over me to help my fumble-fingers with my buttons or the Velcro fastenings on my shoes. You were my first vague love. You were the undifferentiated object of affection of all of us. We loved you for your lofty remoteness, your firmness and hinted-at tetchiness and the delicious knowledge that to you we were just more children to be turned from blind and selfish little barbarians into civilized young human beings. We loved you because you were not the mother-smother of our cottonwool parents. You took no shit.

The Class of '31 was too much even for the redoubtable Miss Mukudan. At age four our engineered brains were pushing us down the strange and separate roads into strange ways of looking at the world, quasi-autistic obsessions, terrifying savant insights or just plain incomprehensibility. We were each given a personalized tutor to accompany us day and night. Mine was called Mr Khan and he lived inside my ear. A new technology had arrived to save us. It was the latest thing in comms – which has always seemed the most faddish and trivial of technologies to me. No more did you need to be trapped by screens or pictures in the palm of your hand or devices that wrote on your eyeball as delicately as a bazaar fakir writing tourists' names on a grain of rice. A simple plastic hook behind the ear would beam cyberspace into your head. Direct electromagnetic stimulation of the visual, auditory and olfactory centres now peopled the world with ghost messages and data spreads, clips from *Town and Country*, video messages, entire second-life worlds and avatars and, inevitably, spam and junk mailing. And for me, my customised aeai tutor, Mr Khan.

How I hated him! He was everything Miss Mukudan was not; irascible, superior, gruff and persistent. He was a little waspy Muslim, thin as a wire with a white moustache and a white Nehru cap. I would rip off the "hoek" in frustration and whenever I put it on again, after Miss Mukudan's ministrations – we would do anything for her – he would take up his harangue from the very syllable at which I had silenced him.

"Look and listen, you bulging pampered privileged no-right-to-call-yourself-a-proper-Brahmin brat," he would say. "These eyes these ears, use them and learn. This is the world and you are in it and of it and there is no other. If I can teach you this I will have taught you all you need to ever learn."

He was a stern moralist, very proper and Islamic. I looked at Miss Mukudan differently then, wondering what assessments she had made that assigned Mr Khan especially to me. He had been programmed just for Vishnu. How had he been built? Did he spring into being perfectly formed or did he have a history, and how did he think of this past? Did he know it for a lie, but a treasured one; was he like the self-deceiving aeai actors of *Town and Country* who believed they existed separately from the roles they played? If he masqueraded as intelligent, did that mean he was intelligent? Was intelligence the only thing that could not be simulated? Such thoughts were immensely interesting to a strange little eight-year-old suddenly becoming aware of those other strange citizens of his tight world. What was the nature of the aeais, those ubiquitous and for the most part unseen denizens of great Delhi? I became quite the junior philosopher.

"What is right to you?" I asked him one day as we rode back in the Lexus through a Delhi melted by the heat into an impermeable black sludge. It was Ashura. Mr Khan had told me of the terrible battle of Karbala and the war between the sons of the Prophet (Peace Be Upon Him). I watched the chanting, waling men carrying the elaborate catafalques, flogging their backs bloody, beating their foreheads and chests. The world, I was beginning to realize, was far stranger than I.

"Never mind me what is right to me, impudent thing. You have the privileges of a god, you're the one needs to think about right action," Mr Khan declared. In my vision he sat beside me on the back seat of the Lex, his hands primly folded in his lap.

"It's a serious question." Our driver hooted up alongside the dour procession. "How can right action mean anything to you, when anything you do can be undone and anything you undo can be done again. You're chains of digits, what do you need morality for?" Only now was I beginning to understand the existence of the aeais, which had begun with the mystery of TikkaTikka, Pooli, Badshanti and Nin living together and sharing common code inside my plastic star. Common digits but separate personalities. "It's not as if you can hurt anyone."

"So right action is refraining from causing pain, is it?"

"I think that it's the start of right action."

"These men cause pain to themselves to express sorrow for wrong action; albeit the actions of their spiritual forebears. In so doing they believe they will make themselves more moral men. Consider those Hindu saddhus who bear the most appalling privations to achieve spiritual purity."

"Spiritual purity isn't necessarily morality," I said, catching the line Mr Khan had left dangling for me. "And they choose to do it to themselves. It's something else altogether if they choose to do it to others."

"Even if it means those others may be made better men?"

"They should be left to make their own minds up about that."

We cruised past the green-draped faux-coffin of the martyr.

"So what then is the nature of my relationship with you? And your mother and father?"

My Mamaji, my Dadaji! Two years after that conversation, almost to the day, my flawless memory recalls, when I was a nine-year-old-in-a-four-year-old's body and Sarasvati was a cat-lean, ebullient seven, my mother and father very gently, very peacefully, divorced. The news was broken by the two of them sitting at opposite ends of the big sofa in the lounge with the smog of Delhi glowing in the afternoon sun like a saffron robe. A full range of aeai counselling support hovered around the room, in case of tears or tantrums or anything else they couldn't really handle. I remember feeling a suspicion of Mr Khan on the edge of my perceptions. Divorce was easy for Muslims. Three words and it was over.

"We have something to tell you, my loves," said my mother. "It's me and your father. Things haven't been going so well with us for quite some time and well, we've decided that it's best for everyone if we were to get a divorce."

"But it won't mean I'll ever stop being your Dad," plump Tushar said quickly. "Nothing'll change, you'll hardly even notice. You'll still keep living here, Shiv will still be with me."

Shiv. I hadn't forgotten him – I couldn't forget him – but he had slipped from my regard. He was more distant than a cousin, less thought of than those remote children of your parents' cousin, to whom I've never considered myself related at all. I did not know how he was doing at school or who his friends were or what sports teams he was on. I did not care how he lived his life or pursued his dreams across that great wheel of lives and stories. He was gone from me.

We nodded bravely and trembled our lips with the right degree of withheld emotion and the counsel-aeais dissolved back into their component code clusters. Much later in the room we had shared as bubbling babies and which was now our mutual den, Sarasvati asked me, "What's going to happen to us?"

"I don't think we'll even notice," I said. "I'm just glad they can stop having that ugly, embarrassing sex."

Ah! Three little letters. Sex sex sex, the juggernaut looming over our childhoods. The kiddy thrill of being naked – doubly exciting in our body-modest society – took an edge and became something I did not quite understand. Oh, I knew all the words and the locations, as Sarasvati and I played our games of doctors and patients in our den, her pulling up her little vest and pulling down her pants as I listened and examined and prodded vaguely. We knew these were grown-up things not for the eyes of grown-ups. Mamaji would have been horrified and called in squadrons of counselling ware if she had discovered our games but I had long since suborned the aeais. If she had looked at the security monitors she would have seen us watching the Cartoon Network; my own little CG *Town and Country* playing just for her. Sex games for children; everyone plays them. Bouncing up and down in the pool, pressing ourselves against the jets in the rooftop spa, suspecting *something* in the lap of artificial waves across our private places as ochre dust-smog from the failed monsoon suffocated Delhi. And when we played horsey-horsey, she riding me around like Lakshmibai the warrior Rani, there was more in the press of her thighs than just trying to hold on as I cantered across the carpets. I knew what it should be, I was mostly baffled by my body's failure to respond the way a twelve-year old's ought. My lust may have been twelve but my body was six. Even Miss Mukudan's purity and innocence lost its lustre as I began to notice the way her breasts moved as she leaned over me, or the shape of her ass – demurely swathed in a sari but no concealment was enough for the lusty curiosity of boy-Brahmins – as she turned to the smart-silk board.

"Now," said Mr Khan one day on the back seat of the Lexus. "Concerning onanism . . ." It was a dreadful realisation. By the time puberty hit me like a hammer I would be twenty-four. Mine was the rage and impotence of angels.

Now five burning years have passed and we are driving in a fast German car. I am behind the wheel. The controls have been specially modified so that I can reach the pedals, the gear-shift is a standard. If I cut you up on the Siri Ring, after the flicker of road rage, you'd wonder: that's a child driving that Mercedes. I don't think so. I'm of legal age. I passed my test without any bribery or coercion; well, none that I know of. I am old enough to drive, get married and smoke. And I smoke. We all smoke, my Little Brahmin classmates and me. We smoke like stacks, it can't do us any harm, though we are all wearing smogmasks. The monsoon has failed for the fourth time in seven years; whole tracts of north India are turning into dust and blowing through the hydrocarbon-clogged streets and into our lungs. A dam is being built on the Ganges, Kunda Khadar, on the border with our eastern neighbour Bharat. It is promised to slake our thirst for a generation but the Himalaya glaciers have melted into gravel and Mother Ganga is starved and frail. The devotees at the Siva temple in the middle of the Parliament Street roundabout protest at the insult to the holy river with felt-marker banners and three-pronged trisuls. We bowl past them, hooting and waving and up Sansad Marg around Vijay Chowk. The comics portraying us as Awadh's new superheroes were quietly dropped years ago. Now what we see about ourselves in print tends to headlines like TINY TEARAWAYS TERRORISE TILAK NAGAR, or BADMAASH BABY BRAHMINS.

There are four of us, Purrzja, Shayman, Ashurbanipal and me. We are all from the college – still the Brahminical College! – but when we are out we all have our own names, names we've made up for ourselves that sounds strange and alien, like our DNA. Strange and alien we make ourselves look too; our own style cobbled from any source that seems remote and outré: J-punk hair, Chinese bows and ribbons, French street sports fashion and tribal make-up entirely of our own design. We are the scariest-looking eight-year-olds on the planet. By now Sarasvati is a coltish, classy fifteen-year-old. Our closeness has unravelled; she has her own social circles and friends and crushing things of the heart that seem so important to her. Shiv, so I hear, is at his first year at the University of Awadh Delhi. He won a scholarship. Best marks in his school. He's followed his father into informatics. Me, I howl up and down the boulevards of Delhi trapped in the body of a kid.

We race past the open arms of the Rashtrapati Bhavan. The red stone looks insubstantial as sand in the amber murk.

"That's your home, that is, Vish," Purrzja shouts through her mask. It's well known that Mamaji Has Plans for me. Why should she not? Every other part of me is designed. A good legal job, a prominent practice, a safe parliamentary seat and a steady, planned ascent toward the top of whatever political party afforded the best chance of ambition. It's assumed that one day I will lead the nation. I'm designed to rule. I floor the pedal and the big Merc leaps forward. Traffic parts like my divine counterpart churning the soma. Their autodrive aeais make them as nervous as pigeons.

Out on the Siri Ring; eight lanes of taillights in each direction, a never ceasing roar of traffic. The car eases into the flow. Despite the barriers and warning signs police pull twenty bodies a day from the soft shoulder. The ring does not obey old Indian rules of traffic. Men race here, hedge-fund managers and data-rajas and self-facilitating media mughals; racing around the twin chambers of Delhi's heart. I flick on the auto-drive. I am not here to race. I am here for sex. I recline the driving seat, roll over and Ashurbanipal is beneath me. Her hair is drawn back behind her ear to show off the plastic curl of the 'hoek. It's part of the look.

I snap the fingers of my right hand into my palm to activate the software in the palmer glove. I hold that hand a hovering few centimetres above her fluorescent body-paint-stained belly. I don't touch. We never touch. That's the rule. Sex has rules. I move my hand in a series of gestures as gentle and precise as any classical dancer's mudras over Ashurbanipal. Not touching, never touching, never even flexing a finger. It's not about physical touch. It's our own thing. But inside her head, I am touching her, more intimately than any rubbing or pushing or chafing of *parts*. The 'hoek beams signals through the bone, stimulating those parts of the brain that correspond to my slow calligraphy. I am writing my signature across her body. As she in return maps the me drawn on the inside of my skull. How does it feel? Like a cat must feel when it's stroked. Like an otter must feel diving and turning and performing its underwater acrobatics. Like a fire must feel when the wind catches it and sweeps it up a forested mountainside. And without the poetry; like I want to cringe and melt and the same time. Like I must move in a direction I can't explain and body can't express. Like there is something in my mouth that grows bigger with every second but never changes size, like a reverse turd, only sweet and joyful, is working its way back up into my colon. Like I need need need to pee something that isn't pee that my body hasn't learned yet. Like I want this to end and never end. It goes on for a long long time and terrible little crying noises come out of our eight-year-aged lips as the aeai steers us through the howling torus of traffic on Siri Ring. We are teens and we are making out in the car.

There is a coming. Oh yes, there is a coming. Like soft fireworks, or the giggling drop at the top of a Ferris wheel or the feeling you get on those nights when the air is clear and you can see out from the roof pool all the billion lights of Delhi and you are connected to every single one. Like a djinn, made of fire. Ecstatic and guilty and dirty, like you've shouted a dirty word at a sophisticated party. My nipples are very very sensitive.

Then I start with Purrzja. And then Shayman. As I said, it's entirely our own thing. It's well into dark by the time we out up our seats and straighten our clothing and re-gel our hair and I flick off the autodrive and take us up out and over the Ring on a curving off ramp to a club. It's a bit of a freak place – nutes like it and where nutes are welcome we are usually welcome – but the door knows us – knows our money – and there are always chaati mag paps there. Tonight is no exception: we pose and pimp and preen for the cameras. I can write the society column headlines already. GENE-TWEAK FREAKS ON COCKTAIL CLUB ORGY. Except we don't drink. We're underage for that.

It's always late when we get back. Only the house steward and aeais wait for us, gently chining that it is a school day tomorrow. Don't they understand that those are the best nights? This night the lights are on in the big drawing room. I can see them from the approach to the car park. My mother waits for me. She's not alone. There's a man and a woman with her, money people, I can tell that right away from their shoes, their fingernails, their teeth, the cut of their clothes and the prickle of aeai servitors hovering around them; all those things I can assess in a glance.

"Vishnu, this is Nafisa and Dinesh Misra."

I namaste, a vision in clashing cross-cultural trash.

"They are going to be your new Mother and Father-in-law."

My Lovely Consort

My cats can do other tricks too; I feel you grow bored of them running in their ring. Cats! Cats! See, a clap of my hands and they go and sit on their little stools: Matsya and Kurma, Varaha and Narasimha, Vamana, Parashurama, Rama and Krishna and Buddha and Kalki. Good cats. Clever cats. Rama, stop licking yourself. Hah! One word from me and they do as they will. Now, please feel this hoop, just ordinary paper. Yes? Yes. And these, the same, yes? Yes.

I set them out around the ring. Tabby Parashurama is squeezing his eyes closed in that way that makes him look very very smug.

By the way, I must thank you for coming to watch the *Marvellous, the Magical, the Magnificent Vishnu Cat Circus*. Yes, that's the official name. It's on the letters of registration. Yes, and I pay whatever taxes are due. It's a small entertainment, but at least it's working. You have solar? Not hooked up to the zero point? Very long-sighted of you. Now: watch! Varaha, Vamana, Buddha and Kalki!

They flow from their painted stools like liquid and run around the inside of the ring, an effortless, cat-lazy lope. The trick with cat circuses, I have found, is to convince them they are doing it for themselves.

And lo! I clap my hands and in perfect unison my cats leap from their ordained orbits clean through the paper hoops. Your applause please, but not for me: for Varaha, Vamana, Buddha and Kalki. Now they run in a circle, hurdling through the hoops. What was that? Is there a lesson in every trick? What do you mean? The spiritual significance of the cats I call to perform? I hadn't thought of that. I don't think cats especially spiritual; quite the reverse; they are the most worldly and sensual of creatures, though the Prophet Mohammed, so it's said, was a great lover of cats and famously cut the sleeve from his robe rather than disturb a cat that had fallen asleep there.

Now, on with the story. Where am I going? Don't you know it's a terrible rudeness to interrupt the storyteller? You came here to see the cat circus, not watch some old goondah spin a yarn? You've seen cats leap through paper hoops, what more do you want? Where am I going? Very well then, to Varanasi. No, I am not. It's not just the bodhisofts who go to Varanasi. Here's the deal. I have plenty more tricks in my little ring here on the sand, but to see them you will have to listen to my story and remember, the power may be working but the broadcasters are out. Nothing on your screens tonight. But you'll like this. It's a wedding scene. What is a story without a wedding?

Elephants bore me. When I say that I don't mean that I find the pachyderm genus tedious, as if I have some special personal conversational relationship with them and knew all their conversational tics and ploys. Is Ganesh not the best-loved god in our entire profligate pantheon? I mean, simply, that elephants carried me; in a howdah like a small gilt temple through the streets of Delhi. Five elephants, with mahouts; one for my school friend Suresh Hira, one for Vin Johar, one for Syaman and one, my sole spit of defiance in the face of tradition, for Sarasvati, and one for me, Vishnu Nariman Raj, the gnarly groom. Delhi's eternal, monstrous traffic broke around the horde of musicians, drummers, dancers, merry-meeters like water. The traffic news had been reporting me as a major congestion for hours. People stopped and stared, women threw rice, ayahs pointed me out to their finger-sucking grandchildren: *there, there he is, Lord Vishnu goes to his wedding*. The chati mags had been full of little else than the first dynastic Brahmin marriage. My other break with tradition: much of the gaudy I had funded myself through the judicious auctioning of the photo rights to *Gupshup* magazine. Look here am I, in white sherwani and wrinkle-ankle pants in the very best style, the traditional veil of flowers over my face, gripping my sword with one hand (a ludicrous affectation by Sreem, Delhi's most-sought nute wedding chore-ographer; who could ever sword-fight from the broad back of an elephant?), with the other gripping white-knuckled to the gold-leaf coping of my swaying howdah. Have I said that riding an elephant is like being on a boat on unstill waters? Does what you glimpse through the cascading marigolds look afraid? Were you expecting someone larger?

Negotiations had been protracted and delicate over the winter. Hosts of aeai attorneys circled and clashed around my mother and father, temporarily unified, as they entertained the Misras to a grand vagdana. Lakshmi and I sat blandly, quietly, hands folded neatly in our laps on the cream leather sofa as relatives and relatives passed and greeted and blessed us. We smiled. We nodded. We did not speak, not to our guests, not to each other. In our years together at the Dr Renganathan Brahminical College we had said all that we could say to each other. We sat like an old married couple at a metro stop. At last the hosts of clashing attorney aeais withdrew: a pre-nuptial contract was drafted, a dowry was set. It was a brilliant match; property and ware with water, the very essence of life. Of course the price was high; we were Brahmins. It was no less than the flesh of our flesh and the seed of our loins, for all generations. Way down the list of ticky boxes on Dr Rao's shopping list was one I suspect Lakshmi's parents had tickied blindly. I know my parents had. But it was perhaps the most profound change of all that Dr Rao's nanoworkers worked on us. Our genelines were modified. The traits engineered into us were inheritable. Our children and their children, all our conceivable Nariman-Misras marching into futurity, would be Brahmins, not from the microsurgery of Dr Rao, but from our sperm and eggs.

Children, offspring, a line, a dynasty. That was our mutually contracted dowry. A match was made! Let great Delhi rejoice!

The janampatri aeais had read the stars for the most auspicious fates, the pandit had made the puja to Ganesh and the joint houses of Nariman and Misra had hired *Gupshup Girls,* Delhi's biggest and brassiest girl band to sing and flash their thighs for two thousand society guests at our sangeet sandhya. Lakshmi duetted onstage with them. Pop-girli hotpants and belly-top looked disturbing on her as she danced and skipped among the high-heels. Too small, too too young to wed. I was never much of a singer. Mamji and Dadaji had neglected to ticky that box. I boogied down in the golden circle with my classmates. Though I had still two years more at Dr Renganathan College under the tutelage of the invisible Mr Khan, our circle was broken. I was all their imminent futures.

At India Gate Sarasvati called her mahout to a halt and slipped from her elephant's back to run and dance among my parade of Baraatis. I had defied tradition by inviting her, she defied it back by coming dressed as a man in sherwani and kohl and huge, ludicrous false Rajput moustache. I watched her leap and whirl, brilliant and vivacious with the dancers and drummers and dance, laughing, with monkey-like Sreem and felt tears in my eyes behind my veil of flowers. She was so brilliant, so lovely, so lithe and free from expectation.

At Lodi Gardens the celebrity spotters were five deep. Policemen held them back with a chain of linked lathis. They had seen Rishi Jaitly and Anand Arora and ooh, isn't that Esha Rashore the famous dancer and who is that little man with the very much younger wife; don't you know, it's Narayan Mittal from Mittal Industries. Last and least to them was the seeming child perched high on the back of a painted wedding elephant. A blare of trumpets and a barrage of drums greeted us. Then the smartsilk screens draped around us woke up and filled with the characters and, in a never-before-seen-feat of CG prestidigitation, the cast of *Town and Country* singing and dancing our wedding song specially written by legendary screen composer A.H. Husayin. They were aeais; singing and dancing were easy for them. There, almost lost among the sari silk and garlands as the bridal party stepped forward to greet us, was Lakshmi.

We were swept on a wave of drum beating and brass-tootling to the pavilions arrayed across the well-watered grass like a Mughal invasion. We feasted, we danced, we were sat on our thrones, our feet not touching the ground, and received our guests.

I didn't see him. The line was long and the atmosphere in marquee stifling and I was bloated and drowsy from wedding food. I took the hand blindly, bored. I only became attentive when it held mine that moment too long, that quantum too firmly.

Shiv.

"Brother."

I nodded in acknowledgment.

"Are you well?"

He indicated his suit, the fabric cheap, the cut niggardly, the cufflinks and the jewel at the shirt-throat phoney. A budget wedding outfit. Tomorrow it would go by phatphat back to the hire shop.

"I'll be more suitably dressed when you come to my wedding."

"Are you getting married?"

"Doesn't everyone?"

I sniffed then. It was not Shiv's perfume – that too smelled cheap and phenolic. My uniquely-connected senses show me subtleties to which others are quite oblivious. In his student hire-suit and cheap Bata shoes, Shiv seemed to carry an aura around him, a presence, crackle of information like distant summer thunder. He smelled of aeais. I tilted my head to one side: did I see a momentary shifting glow? It did not take a synaesthete or a Brahmin to spot the 'hoek tucked behind his ear.

"Thank you for coming," I said and knew that he heard the lie.

"I wouldn't have missed it."

"We must meet up some time," I went on, compounding the lie. "When Lakshmi and I get back into Delhi. Have you over to the place."

"It's not going to be terribly likely," Shiv said. "I'm going to Bharat as soon as I graduate. I've a post-grad lined up at the University of Varanasi. Nano-informatics. Delhi's not a good place for anyone working in artificial intelligence. The Americans are breathing down Srivastava's neck to ratify the Hamilton Treaty."

I consumed news, all news, any news, as universally and unthinkingly as breathing. I could watch twelve screens of television and tell you what

was happening on any of them, simultaneously scan a table full of newspapers and reproduce any article verbatim; I frequently kept my newsfeeds
on brain drip waking and sleeping, beaming the happening world into my
tiny head. I knew too well of the international moves, begun by the United
States to restrict artificial intelligence by licence. Fear motivates them; that
vague Christian millennial dread of the work of our own hands rising up and
making itself our god. Artificial intelligences with a thousand, ten thousand,
infinite times our human intelligence, whatever that means. Intelligence,
when you look down on it from above, is a very vague terrain. Nevertheless
police forces had been set established, Krishna cops, charged with hunting
down and eliminating rogue aeais. Fine title, vain hope. Aeais were utterly
different from us; intelligences that could be in many places at one time,
that could be exist in many different avatars, that could only move by copy-
ing themselves, not as I moved, lugging about my enhanced intelligence
in the calcium bowl of my skull. They had very good guns, but I think
my gnawing fear was aeais today, Brahmins tomorrow. Humans are very
jealous gods.

I knew that it was inevitable that Awadh would sign up to the accord in
return for favoured nation grants from the US Neighbouring Bharat would
never accede to that; its media industry, dependent on artificial intelligence
for the success of *Town and Country* from Djakarta to Dubai, was too influential a lobby. The world's first overt soapocracy. And, I foresaw, the world's
first data-haven nation state. Stitching together stories buried way down the
business news; I was already seeing a pattern of software house relocations
and research foundations moving to Varanasi. So Shiv, ambitious Shiv, Shiv-
building-your-own-glory while I merely obeyed the imperative in my DNA,
Shiv withy our whiff of aeais around you, what is it in Bharat? Would you be
researcher into technologies as sky-blue as Lord Krishna himself, would you
be a dataraja with a stable of aeais pretending they can't pass the Turing Test?

"Not that we ever exactly lived in each other's pockets," I said prissily.
We had lived with twenty million people between us for most of our lives
but still anger boiled within me. What had I to be resentful of? I had all the
advantage, the love, the blessing and the gifts yet here he was in his cheap
hire suit smug and assured and I was the ludicrous little lordling, the boy-
husband swinging his legs on his golden throne.

"Not really no," Shiv said. Even in his words, his smile, there was an aura,
an intensity; Shiv-plus. What was he doing to himself, that could only be
consummated in Varanasi?

The line was restless now, mothers shifting from foot to foot in their
uncomfortable wedding shoes. Shiv dipped his head, his eyes meeting mine
for an instant of the purest, most intense hatred. Then he moved on into the
press of guests, picking up a glass of champagne here, a plate of small eats
there, a strangely singular darkness like plague at the wedding.

The caterers cleared away, torches were lit across the heel-trodden grass
of Lodi Gardens and the pandit tied us together in marriage. As fireworks
burst over and the tomb of Muhammad Shah and dome of Bara Gumbad

we drove away to the plane. We left the diamond stain of bright Delhi behind us and flew, far later than tots of our size should be up, through the night into morning as the private helicopter lifted us up and away to the teahouse in the cool and watered green hills. Staff discreetly stowed out baggage, showed us the lie of the rooms, the shaded verandah with its outlook over the heart-stunning gold and purple of the morning Himalayas, the bedroom with the one huge four-poster bed. Then they swept away in a rustle of silk and we were alone, together, Vishnu and Lakshmi, two gods.

"It's good isn't it?"

"Lovely. Wonderful. Very spiritual. Yes."

"I like the rooms. I like the smell of the wood, old wood."

"Yes, it is good. Very old wood."

"This is the honeymoon then."

"Yes."

"We're supposed to . . ."

"Yes. I know. Do you . . . are you?"

"Wired? No I was never into that."

"Oh. Well, I've some other stuff in my bag, it should work on you as well."

"You've tried it?"

"Sometimes. I'm finding it gets hard all on its own now, just like that, nothing in particular, so I try it then."

"Is it productive?"

"It's a bit like the 'hoek sex. Feeling you really really need to pee something that isn't pee and isn't there. To be honest, not as good. Have you tried?"

"With the fingers? Oh yes, with the whole hand. It's like you."

"Need to pee?"

"Something like that. More of a clench. It works on a swing too. I don't really think I want to use something you have on you, you know."

"I suppose not. We could . . . I could . . ."

"I don't really think so."

"Do you think they'll check? Save the sheets and show them round to all the relatives?"

"And our physical ages? Don't be stupid."

"It's part of the contract."

"I don't think anyone's going to invoke contractual obligation until I've at least had a period."

"So do you want to do anything?"

"Not particularly."

"So what will we do then?"

"The view's nice."

"There's a pack of cards in the drawer in the table."

"Maybe later. I might sleep now."

"So might I. Are you all right about the bed?"

"Of course. We're supposed too, aren't we? We are husband and wife."

We slept under the light silk cover with the ceiling fan turning slowly, each curled up like the eight-year-olds we physically were with our backs to each other, as far apart as Vish and Shiv and afterwards we invented card games of staggering complexity with the old circular Ganjifa cards on the verandah with its titanic view over the Himalayas. As Lakshmi turned over the kings and ministers our eyes met and we both knew it was more than over, it had never begun. There was nothing but contractual obligation between us. We were the hostages of our DNA. I thought of that line of offspring issuing like a rope of pearls from the end of my still-flaccid penis; those slow children toddling into a future so distant I could not even see its dust on time's horizon, and onward and onward always onward. I was filled with horror at the blind imperative of biology. I owned superhuman intelligence, I only forgot what I chose to forget, I had never known a day's illness in my life, I carried the name of a god, but to my seed all this was nothing, I was no different from some baseline Dalit in Molar Bund basti. Yes, I was a privileged brat, yes, I was a sneerer of the worst kind, how could I be anything other? I was a designer snob.

We stayed our week in the teahouse in the green foothills of Himachal Pradesh, Lakshmi and Vishnu. Lakshmi patented some of her elaborate social card games – we tested the multi-player games by each of us playing several hands at once, an easy feat for the Brahmins – and made a lot of money from licensing them. It was radiantly beautiful, the mountains were distant and serene like stone Buddhas, occasional rain pattered on the leaves outside our window at night and we were utterly utterly miserable, but even more so at the thought of what we had to face on our return to Awadh, the darlings of the Delhi. My decision had been made on the third day of our honeymoon but it was not until we were in the limo to the Ramachandra Tower where we had been given an apartment fit for gods on the floor below my Mamaji that I made the call to the very special, very discreet doctor.

Two Extraneous Aspects of Myself

"Both of them?" the nute said. Yt would have raised an eyebrow had yt possessed any hair on yts shaven head to raise.

"History is quiet on the subject of half-eunuchs," I said.

No one, alas, ever delivers such dialogue. Ticking lines, arch exchanges, loaded looks, these are things of story not real life. But I am telling you a story, my story, which is much more than just history or even memory. For if I choose to forget, I can also choose to remember and make what I chose memory. So if I wish the nute surgeon's office to be at the top of a winding, creaking flight of stairs, each level haunted by the eyes of suspicious and hostile Old Delhiwallahs, if I decide to remember it so, it will be so. Likewise, if I choose to recall that office to be a charnel house of grotesque surgical implements and pictures of successfully mutilated body-parts as a like a demon-infested hell from a Himalayan Buddhist painting: it will be so forever. Perhaps it's less strange a concept for you than for me. I more than anyone know the deceptiveness of physical appearance, but you seem young enough to have grown up in a world comfortable with universal memory, every breath and blink swarming with devas continuously writing and rewriting physical reality. And if the devas choose to rewrite that memory, who is there to say that it's not so?

But there is east light in the sky beyond the blazing pillar of the Jyotirlinga, I have far to go, you have yet to see the most astonishing my cats can achieve and the reality is that the surgery of Dr Anil was in a tastefully restored haveli in the warren of streets in the shadow of the Red Fort, the surgery elegant and discreet and fronted by the delightful Miss Modi, and Dr Anil welcoming, professional subtle and frankly surprised by my request.

"I usually deal in more, substantial surgery," yt said. The Ardhanarisvara clinic was Delhi's leading centre for nute transformation. Leading through whispers and rumours; in bright new Awadh we might claim to be urbane, global, cosmopolitan and unshockable but nute culture, those who decided to escape our desperate sex wars by choosing a third way, a neither-way it was still almost as hidden and secretive as the ancient transgendered hijras who had long ago hidden themselves away in Old Delhi. The ancient city; older than any memory, its streets convoluted like the folds of a brain, has always looked after those with needs beyond the merely average.

"I think what I'm asking is substantial enough," I said.

"True true," Dr Anil said, putting yts fingers together in a spire in that way that all doctors, male, female, transgendered or nute, seem to learn on day one of medical school. "So, both testicles."

"Yes, both."

"And not the penis."

"That would be perverse."

"You're sure you won't consider the chemical option? It's reversible, should you ever reconsider."

"No, not chemical. I don't want it to be reversible. I want to remove myself from the future. I want this to end with me. I'm more than a stud animal. Complete physical castration, yes."

"It's quite simple. Much more so than the usual kind of thing we do here." I knew well the medical procedures that flowed out from here to the anonymous godowns and grey surgery clinics beyond the Siri Ring orbital expressway. There is a video for everything somewhere in the online world and I had watched with fascination what those humans who desired another gender had done to themselves. The things strung out through the gel tanks, skin flayed, muscles laid open, organs drawn out and suspended in molecular sieve cradles, were so far from anything human as to be curious, like strange forest flowers, rather than obscene. I was much more of a coward, leaving only my two little organs on the doorstep of gender. "My only reservation would be that, as you are biologically prepubescent, it would be an internal orchidectomy. Miss Modi will draw up a consent form." Yt blinked me, a delicate, faun-like creature behind a heavy Raj desk, too too lovely to speak of such things as testicular surgery. "Forgive me for asking, I haven't met any High Brahmins before, but you are of an age to sign a consent form?"

"I'm of an age to be legally married."

"Yes, but you must understand, mine is a business that attracts scrutiny in Awadh."

"I'm of an age to pay you a profane sum of money to give me what I want."

"Profane it is then."

Surprisingly mundane it was. I did not even need to be driven out to the nasty industrial zones. In the cubicle I changed into the surgical gown, the sleeves too too long, the hem trailing on the ground, slid up onto the disinfectant-stinky operating table in the basement surgery and felt the needling suffusion of the local anaesthetic. Robot arms, finger-tips fine as insect antennae, danced in under the control of Dr Anil. I felt nothing as I blinked up into the lights and strained to hear their synaesthetic music. The dancing arms withdrew; I felt nothing. And I still felt nothing as the car spun me back through streets full of pulsing, potent, hormone-raddled people. A mild twinge from the sutures pulling against the weave of my clothes. No pain, little loss, nothing of the sense of lightnes and freedom I had read of in the literature of castration fetishists. A unique pleasure, sexual castration; an orgasm to end all orgasms. I had not even had that. The cell-weave treatments would heal the wound in three days and hide all evidence, until the passing years revealed that my voice was not significantly deepening, my hair not receding, that I was growing unusually tall and willowy and that I had singularly failed to contractually conceive any children.

"Do you want to take then with you?" Dr Anil asked as yt sat me down in yts consulting room after the short operation.

"Why should I wish to do that?"

"It was a tradition in China; Imperial eunuchs would be given their excised genitals preserved in a jar of alcohol to bury beside them on their deaths, so that they might enter heaven whole men."

"It was a tradition in Ottoman Turkey that eunuchs, after their cutting clean, would sit in a dung-heap for three days to heal their wounds, or die. I don't care for that tradition either. They're not mine, they're not me; they belong to someone else. Burn them or throw them to the pi-dogs, I don't care."

Thunder growled over me, a promise of a monsoon, the day was darkening. Lightning glowed cloud to cloud as I rode the elevator up the outside of Ramachandra Tower. Lakshmi sat curled on the sofa, the breaking storm magnificent behind her. Dry lightning, a false prophet of rain. All prophecies of rain were false these days,

"Did you do it, are you all right?"

I nodded. It was beginning to hurt now. I clenched my teeth, kicking in the analgesic nanoinfuser Dr. Anil had planted there. Lakshmi clapped her hands in joy. "I'll go tomorrow. Oh dear Lord, I'm so happy, so happy."

And then, there, in the dark apartment glowing with muter lighting, she kissed me.

We did not tell anyone. That was part of the pact. Not our parents, not our relatives, not our circle of Brahmin friends, not even our aeais. Not even dear Sarasvati; I wouldn't burden her with this. There was work we had to do before we announced to our respective families how we had so drastically denied their plans for us. Then we could sweetly and painlessly divorce.

I Nuzzle the Earlobe of Power

What is the proper work of eunuchs?

Does it make you uncomfortable, that word? Does it make you cross your legs, boys; does it give you a hollow clench in your uterus, ladies? When you hear it, do you see something other than a human being, something less? How then is it any different from other words of distinction: Kshatriya, Dalit? Brahmin? Eunuch. It is a very old and noble word, a fine and ancient tradition practised in al the great cultures of Earth. The principle is to give up the lesser to gain the greater. Of all those pitiful puffs of cock-juice, how many will ever turn into human beings? Come on, be honest. It's almost all wasted. And never imagine that the ball-less are sexless, or without desire. No, the great castrati singers, the eunuch poets and holy visionaries, the grand viziers and royal advisors all understood that greatness came at a price and that was generation. Empires could be entrusted to eunuchs, free from dynastic urges. The care and feeding of great nations is our proper work and with all the gifts my parents had endowed me I steered myself toward the political cradle of the nation.

How almost right my mother was, and how utterly wrong-headed. She had imagined me carried in through the doors of the Lok Sabha on the shoulders of cheering election workers. I preferred the servant's entrance. Politicians live and die by the ballot box. They are not there to serve, they are there to gain and hold office. Populism can force them to abandon wise and correct policies for whims and fads. The storm of ballots will in the end sweep them and all their good works from power. Their grand viziers endure. We understand that democracy is the best system by which a nation *seems* to be governed.

Months of social networking – the old-fashioned, handshake and gift type – and the setting up and calling in favours and lines of political credit, has gained me an internship to Parekh, the Minister for Water and the Environment. He was a tolerable dolt, a Vora from Uttaranchal with a shopkeeper's shrewdness and head for details, but little vision. He was good enough to seem in control and a politician often needs little more for a long and comfortable career. This was the highest he would ever rise, as soon as the next monsoon failure hit and the mobs were hijacking water tankers in the street, he would be out. He knew I knew this. I scared him, even though

I was careful to turn down the full dazzle of my intelligence to a glow of general astuteness. He knew I was far from the nine-year-old I seemed to be but he really had no idea of my and my kind's capabilities and curses. I chose my department carefully. Naked ambition would have exposed me too early to a government that was only now realising it had never properly legislated around human gene-line manipulation. Even so I knew the colour of all the eyes that were watching me, skipping through the glassy corridors of the Water Ministry. Water is life. Water, its abundance and its rarity, would sculpt the future of Awadh, of all the nations of North India, from the Panjab to the United States of Bengal. Water was good place to be bright, but I had no intention of remaining there.

The dam at Kunda Khadar neared completion, that titanic fifteen-kilometre bank of earth and concrete like a garter around the thigh of Mother Ganga. Protests from downstream Bharat and the USB grew strident but the towers cranes lifted and swung, lifted and swung day and night. Minister Parekh and Prime Minister Srivastava communicated daily. The Defence Ministry was brought into the circle. Even the PR staffers could smell diplomatic tension.

It was a Thursday. Even before, I called I Bold Thursday, to commit myself, to get myself up. The genes don't make you brave. But I had prepared as rigorously as I could; which was more than anyone in the Lok Sabha, Minister Parekh included. Srivastava was due with his entourage for a press conference from the Ministry to reassure the Awadhi public that Kunda Khadar would do its job and slake Delhi's bottomless thirst. Everyone was turned out smart as paint: moustaches plucked, slacks creased, shirts white as mourning. Not me. I had picked my spot long before: a brief bustle down the corridor as Srivastava and his secretarial team was coming up. I had no ideas what they would be talking about but I knew they would be talking; Srivastava loved his "walking briefings"; they made him seem a man of action and energy. I trusted that my research and quicker wit would win.

I heard the burble of voices. They were about to turn the corner, I went into motion, pushed myself into the wall as the press of suits came toward me. My senses scanned five conversations, lit on Srivastava murmur to Bhansal his parliamentary secretary, "If I knew we had McAuley's support."

Andrew J. McAuley, President of the United States of America. And the answer was there.

"If we could negotiate an output deal in return for Sajida Rana accepting partial ratification of the Hamilton Acts," I said, my voice shrill and pure and piercing as a bird.

The Prime Ministerial party bustled past but Satya Shetty, the Press Secretary, turned with a face of thunder to strike down this upstart, mouthy intern. He saw a nine-year-old. He was dumb-struck. His eyes bulged. He hesitated. That hesitation froze the entire party. Prime Minister Srivastava turned towards me. His eyes widened. His pupils dilated.

"That's a very interesting idea," he said and in those five words I knew he had identified, analysed and accepted the gift I had offered him. A

Brahmin advisor. The strange, savant child. The child genius, the infant guru, the little god. India adored them. It was PR gold. His staffers parted as he stepped toward me. "What are you doing here?"

I explained that I was on an internship with Minister Parekh.

"And now you want more."

Yes, I did.

"What's you name?"

I told him. He nodded his head.

"Yes, the wedding. I remember. So, it's a career in politics, is it?"

It was.

"You're certainly not backward about being forward."

My genes wouldn't allow it. My first political lie.

"Well, ideas do seem to be in short stock at the moment." With that he turned, his entourage closed around him and he was swept on. Satya Shetty dealt me a glare of pure despite, I held his eyes until he snapped his gaze away. I would see him and all his works dust while I was still fresh and filled with energy. By the time I returned to my desk there was an invitation from the Office of the Prime Minister to call them to arrange an interview.

I told my great achievement to the three women in my life. Lakshmi beamed with delight. Our plans were working. My mother was baffled; she no longer understood my motivations, why I would accept a lowly and inconspicuous civil service position rather than a high-flyer in our superstar political culture. Sarasvati jumped up from her sofa and danced around the room, then clapped her hands around my face and kissed my forehead long and hard until her lips left a red tilak there.

"As long as there's joy in it," she said. "Only joy."

My sister, my glorious sister, had voiced a truth that I was only now developing the maturity to recognise. Joy was all. Mamaji and Dadaji had aimed me at greatness, at blinding success and wealth, power and celebrity. I had always possessed the emotional intelligence if not the emotional vocabulary, to know that the blindingly powerful and famous were seldom happy, that their success and wealth often played against their own mental and physical well-being. All my decisions I made for me, for my peace, well-being, satisfaction and to keep me interested throughout my long life. Lakshmi had chosen the delicate world of complicated games. I had chosen the whirl of politics. Not economics; that was too dismal a science for me. But the state and those statelets beyond Awadh's borders with which I could see we were as inextricably entwined as when we were one India, and the countries beyond those, and the continents beyond; that fascinated me. The etiquette of nations was my pleasure. There was joy in it, Sarasvati. And I was brilliant at it. I became the hero of my childhood comics, a subtle hero, Diplomacy Man. I saved your world more times than you can ever know. My superpower was to see a situation entire, connected, and all those subtler forces acting upon it that other, less gifted analysts would have discounted. Then I would give it nudge. The smallest, slightest tap, one tiny incentive or restriction, even a hint at how a policy might be shaped, and watch how the social physics of a complex capitalist society scaled them up through power laws and networks and social amplifiers to slowly turn the head of the entire nation.

In those first few years I was constantly fighting for my own survival. Satya Shetty was my deadliest enemy from the moment our eyes had met in the corridor in the Water Ministry. He was influential, he was connected, he was clever but not clever enough to realise he could never beat me. I just let my drips of honey fall into Krishna Srivastava's ear. I was always right. Little by little his cabinet and Satya Shetty's allies realised that, more than being always right, I was essentially different from them. I didn't seek high office. I sought the greatest well-being. I was the prefect advisor. And I looked great on television: Prime Minister Srivastava's dwarf vizier, trotting behind him like some throwback to the days of the Mughals. Who isn't, at some level, unnerved by the child prodigy? Even if I was twenty two years old now, with puberty – whatever that might mean for me personally – looming on the horizon of my Brahmin generation like the rumbles of a long-delayed monsoon.

It was that treacherous monsoon that became the driver of Awadhi politics, town and country, home and away. Thirsty nations are irrational nations; nations that pray and turn to strange saviours. The great technocracy of the United States of Bengal had, in a display of national hysteria, put its faith in a bizarre plan to haul an iceberg from Antarctica into the Sundarbans with the hope that the mass of cold air would affect the shifting climatic patterns and claw the monsoon back over India. Strange days, a time of rumours and wonders. The Age of Kali was upon us and once again the gods were descending upon us, walking in the shapes of ordinary men and women. The Americans had found something in space, something not of this world. The datahavens of Bharat, boiling with aeais, had spawned Generation Three artificial intelligences; legendary entities whose intelligence as far outstripped mine as mine does the fleas crawling on my poor, harassed cats. Sajida Rana, politically embattled from resurgent Hindu fundamentalism, was preparing a pre-emptive strike on Kunda Khadar as a PR stunt. This last rumour I took seriously enough from my trawling of the Bharati press to call for a departmental level meeting between my ministry and its Bharati counterpart. Did I mention that I was now parliamentary secretary to Krishna Srivastava? A steady, not stellar, climb. It was still too easy to lose grip and fall into the reaching hands of my rivals.

My counterpart at the Bharat Bhavan was a refined Muslim gentleman, Shaheen Badoor Khan, from an excellent family and impeccably educated. Behind his pitch-perfect etiquette and a dignity I envied deeply for I was a small, scampering child next to him, I did sense a sadness; an ache behind the eyes. We recognised and liked each other immediately. We knew instinctively that we both cared deeply enough for our countries to be prepared to betray them. Such a thing could never be said, or even implied. Thus our conversation, as we walked among the Buddha's deer of old Sarnath, our security men discreet shadows among the trees, the security drones circling like black kites overhead seemed as casual and elliptical as two old dowagers on a Friday afternoon stroll.

"Awadh has always seemed to me a country at peace with itself," Shaheen Badoor Khan said. "As if it's solved some great and quintessentially Indian paradox."

"It wasn't always so," I said. Behind the security fence Western tourists on the Buddha trail tried to hold down their flapping robes in the rising wind. "Delhi's streets have run red far too many times."

"But it's always been a cosmopolitan city. Varanasi, on the other hand, always has and always will be the city of Lord Siva."

I waggled my head in agreement. I knew now what I would report to Srivastava. *Sajida Rana is under pressure from the Hindutvavadis. She will launch a pre-emptive strike at Kunda Khadar. Awadh will have the moral high-ground; we must not lose it.*

"I have a relative in Varanasi," I said casually.

"Oh, so?"

"My brother – a Shiva himself, so no surprise really that he should end up in Varanasi."

"And is he a Brahmin like yourself?'

"No, but he is very gifted."

"We do seem to attract talent. It's one of our blessings, I suppose. I have a younger brother in the United States. Terrible at keeping in contact, terrible; my mother, well, you know what they're like. Of course it's my responsibility."

You're worried that your brother has drifted into business that could adversely affect your standing, if it became public, was what this sage Mr Khan was telling me. *You want me to keep an eye on him, in return you'll open up a secure channel of communications between us to prevent war between Bharat and Awadh.*

"You know what brothers are like," I said.

The information was beaming into my head even as I stepped off the plane at Indira Gandhi airport. Shiv had opened a company, Purusa, in Varanasi. He had attracted substantial funding from a venture capital company called Odeco and match-funding from the research and development division at Bharat's mighty Ray Power. His field was nanoscale computing. Top designers and engineers were working with him. The Ghost Index, which valued companies with the potential to become global players when they went public, valued Purusa as one of their top five to watch. He was young and he was hot and he was headed for orbit. He had made some questionable friends among Bharat's datarajas and a cloud of high-level aeais hid much of Purusa's activities from its rivals and from the Bharati government. The Krishna Cops had a file on him and a deliberately clumsy team of aeai wards to keep him aware that he was known to them. My own Awadhi intelligence service surveillance aeais were of a subtler stripe than the police. They coded themselves into the very informational fabric of Purusa. The security of Awadh was a flimsy fiction; I was intensely curious as to what my brother was up to. What Shiv planned was of course monstrously ambitious. He had cracked open the prison of the skull. More prosaically, Purusa developed a prototype biochip that could interface directly with the brain. No more a tacky coil of plastic behind the ear and the soft invasion of electromagnetic radiation into the brain, like shouting in a temple. This was engineered protein, stuff of our stuff, which sent its artificial neurons through skin and bone to mesh with the threads of though. It was third eye, forever open to the unseen world. See how easily I resort to the language of the mystical? Omniscience was standard; anyone so infected had access to all the knowledge and all the bitchy triviality of the global web. Communication was no longer a click and a call, it was a thought, a subtle telepathy. Virtual worlds became real. The age of privacy, that first Western luxury that India wealth bought, was over. Where our own thoughts ended and those of others began, how would we know? We would touch the world of the aeais, in their dispersed, extended, multi-levelled perceptions. Speculation led to speculation. I could see no end to them. Lakshmi, disturbed from her mathematical games, would sense my mood and look up to see the adult anxiety on my child's face. This technology would change us, change us utterly and profoundly. This was a new way of being human, a fault-line, a diamond cutter's strike, across society. I began to realize that the greatest threat to Awadh, to Bharat, to all India, was not water. It was the pure and flawless diamond Shiv and his Purusa Corporation dangled and spun in front of each and every human. Be more, be everything. So engaged was I that I did not notice when the warning came down the Grand Trunk Road from Shaheen Badoor Khan in Varanasi and thus was caught sleeping when Sajida Rana sent her tanks to take Kunda Khadar without a shot.

The Girl with the Red Bindi

The war's names were longer than its duration. The Kunda Khadar war, the Forty-Eight Hour War, the Soft War, the First Water War. You don't remember it, though Awadhi main battle tanks manoeuvred over these very sands. You probably don't even remember it from history lessons. There have been greater and more enduring wars; war running into war, the long and, I think, the final war. The war I shall end. That grand display of arms on these river strands I now understand as its opening shot, had any shots actually been fired. That was another of its names, the Soft War. Ah! Who is it names wars? Hacks and pundits, without doubt, media editors and chati journalists; people with an interesting a good, mouth-filling phrase. It is certainly not civil servants, or cat-circus proprietors. How much better a name would "Soft War" have been for the century of unrest that followed, this Age of Kali that now seems to have run down to its lowest ebb with the arrival of the Jyotirlingas on earth?

The Water War, the War of '47, whatever we call it, for me marked the end of human history and the return of the age of miracles to earth. It was only after the smoke had cleared and the dust settled and our diplomatic teams arrived among the tall and shining towers of Ranapur to negotiate the peace that we realized the immensity of events in Bharat. Our quiet little water war was the least of it. I had received one terse communication down the Grand Trunk Road: *I am ruined, I have failed, I have resigned.* But there was Shaheen Badoor Khan, five paces behind his new Prime Minster Ashok Rana, as I trotted like a child behind our Srivastava.

"Rumours of my demise were exaggerated," he whispered as we fell in beside each other as the politicians formed up on the grass outside the Benares Polo and Country Club for the press call, each jostling for status-space.

"War does seem to shorten the political memory." A twenty-three-year-old in the body of a boy half his age may say pretty much whatever he likes. It's the liberty granted to fools and angels. When I first met Shaheen Badoor Khan, as well as his decency and intelligence, I had sensed a bone-deep sadness. Even I could not have guessed it was a long-repressed and sterile love for the other, the transgressive, the romantic and doomed, as all wrapped up in the body of young Varanasi nute. He had fallen into the honey-trap laid for him by his political enemies.

Shaheen Badoor Khan dipped his head. "I'm far from being the first silly, middle-aged man to have been a fool for lust. I may be the only one to have got his Prime Minister killed as a consequence. But, as you say, war does very much clarify the vision and I seem to be a convenient figure for public expiation. And from what I gather from the media, the public will trust me sooner than Ashok Rana. People like nothing better than the fallen mughal who repents. In the meantime, we do what we must, don't we, Mr Nariman? Our countries need us more than they know. These have been stranger times in Bharat than people can ever be let know."

Bless your politician's self-deprecation. The simultaneous collapse of major aeai systems across Bharat, including the all-conquering *Town and Country*, the revelation of the country's rampant Hindutva opposition to have been a cabal of artificial intelligences, chaos at Ray Power and the mysterious appearance of a hundred-metre hemispherical crater in the university grounds, of mirror-bright perfection and, behind all, rumours that the long-awaited, long-dreaded Generation Three aeais had arrived. There was only one who could make sense of it to me. I went to see Shiv.

He had a house, a shaded place with many trees to push back the crowding, noisy world. Gardeners moved with the slow precision up and down the rolled gravel paths, dead-heading a Persian rose there, spraying aphids there, spot-feeding brown drought-patches in the lawn everywhere. He had grown fat. He lolled in his chair at the tiffin table on the lawn. He looked dreadful, pasty and puffy. He had a wife. He had a child, a little pipit of a girl playing on the snap-together plastic fun-park on the lawn under the eye of her ayah. She would glance over at me, unsure whether to treat me as a strange and powerful uncle or invite me to whiz down the plastic slide. Yes, wee one, I was a strange creature. That scent, that pheromone of information I had smelled on Shiv the day he came to my wedding still clung to him, stronger now. He smelled like a man who has spent too much time among aeais.

He welcomed me expansively. Servants brought cool home-made sherbet. As we settled into brother talk, man-to-eleven-year-old-talk, his wife excused herself in a voice small as a insect and went to hover nervously over her daughter playing exuberantly on her brightly coloured jungle-gym.

"You seem to have had a good war," I said.

"There was war?" Shiv held my gaze for a moment, then exploded into volcanic laughter. Sweat broke out on his brow. I did not believe it for an instant. "I've got comfortable and greasy, yes."

"And successful."

"Not as successful as you."

"I am only a civil servant."

"I've heard you run Srivastava like a pimp."

"We all have our sources."

"Yes." Again that affected pause. "I spotted yours pretty early on. Not bad for government ware."

"Disinformation can be as informative as information."

"Oh, I wouldn't try anything as obvious as that with you. No, I left them there; I let them look. I've nothing to hide."

"Your investors are interesting."

"I doubt some of them will be collecting on their investment." He laughed again.

"I don't think I understand."

"It transpires that one of my key investors, Odeco, was nothing more than a front for a Generation Three aeai that had developed inside the international financial markets."

"So it wasn't just a rumour."

"I'm glad you're still listening to rumours."

"You say this all very casually."

"What other way is there to treat the end of history? You've seen what happens in India when we take things seriously." The laugh was annoying me now. It was thick and greasy.

"The end of history has been promised many times, usually by people rich enough to avoid it."

"Not this time. The rich will be the ones who'll bring it about. The same blind economic self-interest that caused the demographic shift, and you, Vish. Only this will be on a much greater scale."

"You think your biochip has that potential?"

"On it's own, no. I can see I'm going to have to explain this to you."

By the time Shiv had told his tale the gardeners were lighting torches to drive away the evening insects and wife daughter and ayah had withdrawn to the lit comfort of the verandah. Bats dashed around me, hunting. I was shivering though the night was warm. A servant brought fresh made lassi and pistachios. It was greater, as Shiv as promised. Perhaps the greatest. The gods had returned, and then in the instant of their apotheosis, departed. A soft apocalypse.

The fears of the Krishna Cops, of the scared Westerners, had of course come true. The Generation Threes were real, had been real for longer than anyone had foreseen, had moved among us for years, decades even, unresting, unhasting and silent as light. There was no force capable of extirpating truly hyper-intelligent aeais whose ecosystem was the staggering complexity of the global information network. They could break themselves into components, distribute themselves across continents, copy themselves infinitely, become each other. They could speak with our voices and express our world but they were utterly utterly alien to us. It was convenient for them to withdraw their higher functions from a world closing in on the secret of their existence and base them in the datahavens of Bharat, for they had a higher plan. There were three of them, gods all. Brahma, Shiva, Krishna. My brothers, my gods. One, the most curious about the world, inhabits the global financial market. One grew out of a massively multiple online evolution simulation game pf which I had vaguely heard. In creating an artificial world, the gamers had created its deity. And one appeared in the vast servers farms of Bharat's Indiapendent Productions, coalesced out of the cast and pseudo-cast of *Town and Country*. That one particularly impressed me, especially since, with the characteristic desire to meddle in the affairs of others mandatory in the soapi universe, it expanded into Bharati politics in the shape of the aggressive Hindutva Party that had engineered the downfall of the perceptive and dangerous Shaheen Badoor Khan and assassination of Sajida Rana.

That would have been enough to end our hopes that this twentieth first century would be a smooth and lucrative extension of its predecessor. But their plans were not conflict or the subjugation of humanity. That would have meant nothing to the aeais, it was a human concept born of a human need. They inhabited a separate ecological niche and could have endured indefinitely, caught up whatever concerns were of value to distributed intelligences. Humanity would not let them live. The Krishna Cops were cosmetic, costume cops to maintain an illusion that humanity was on the case, but they did signal intent. Humans would admit no rivals, so the Trimurti of Generation Three engineered an escape from this world, from this universe. I did not understand the physics involved from Shiv' description; neither, despite his pedantic, lecturing IT-boy tone, did he. I would look it up later, it would not be beyond me. What I did glean was that I was related to that mirrored crater on the university campus that looked so like a fine piece of modern sculpture, or an ancient astronomical instrument like the gnomons and marble bowls of Delhi's ancient Jantar Mantar observatory. That hemisphere, and an object out in space. Oh yes, those rumours were real. Oh yes, the Americans had discovered it long ago and tried to keep it secret, and were still trying, and; oh yes, failing.

"And what is it then?"

"The collected wisdom of the aeais. A true universal computer. They sent it through from their universe."

"Why?"

"Do you never give presents to your parents?"

"You're privileged to this information?"

"I have channels that even the government of Awadh doesn't. Or, for that matter, the Americans. Odeco . . ."

"Odeco you said was an avatar of the Brahma aeai. Wait." Had I balls, they would have contracted cold and hard. "There is absolutely nothing to prevent this happening again."

"None," said Shiv. It was some time since had laughed his vile, superior laugh.

"It's already happening." And we thought we had won a water war.

"There's a bigger plan. Escape, exile, partition is never a good solution. Look at us in Mother India. You work in politics, you understand the need for a *settlement.*" Shiv turned in his chair to the figures on the verandah. His wife was still watching me. "Nirupa, darling. Come over here, would you? Uncle Vish hasn't had a chance to meet you properly."

She came dashing down the steps and across the lawn, holding up the hem of her print dress, in a headlong, heedless flight that made me at once fearful for stones snakes and stumble and at the same time reminded so much of my golden years growing up alongside Sarasvati. She put her fingers in her mouth and pressed close to her father, shy of looking at me directly.

"Show him your bindi, go on, it's lovely."

I had noticed the red mark on her forehead, larger than customary, and the wrong colour. I bent forward across the table to examine it. It was moving. The red spot seemed to crawl with insect-movement, on the edge of visibility. I reeled back into my chair. My feet swung, not touching the ground.

"What have you done?" I cried. My voice was small and shrill.

"Shh. You'll scare her. Go on; run on, Nirupa. Thank you. I've made her for the future. Like our parents made you for the future. But it's not going to be the future they thought."

"Your biochip interface."

"Works. Thanks to a little help from the aeais. But like I said, that's only part of it. A tiny part of it. We have a project in development; that's the real revolution. That's the real sound of the future arriving."

"Tell me what it is."

"Distributed dust-processing."

"Explain."

Shiv did. It was nothing less than the transformation of computing. His researchers were shrinking computers, smaller and smaller, from grain of rice to sperm cell, down down to the molecular scale and beyond. The endpoint was swarm-computers the size of dust particles, communicating with each other in free flying flocks, computers that could permeate every cell of the human body. They would be as universal and ubiquitous as dust. I began to be afraid and cold in that clammy Varanasi night. I could see Shiv's vision for our future, perhaps further than he could. The bindi and the dust-processor: one broke the prison of the skull; the other turned the world into memory.

Little by little our selves would seep into the dust-laden world; we would become clouds, non-localised, we would penetrate each other more intimately and powerfully than any tantric temple carving. Inner and outer worlds would merge. We could be many things, many lives at one time. We could copy ourselves endlessly. We would merge with the aeais and become one. This was their settlement, their peace. We would become one species, post-human, post-aeai.

"You're years away from this." I denied Shiv's fantasia shrilly.

"Yes, we would be, if we hadn't had a little help."

"How?" I cried again. Now the ayah was staring concerned at me.

Shiv pointed a finger to the night sky.

"I could report you," I said. "Americans don't take kindly to having their security hacked."

"You can't stop it," Shiv said. "Vish, you're not the future any more."

Those words, of all that Shiv spoke in the garden, clung to me. Gliding silently through Delhi in the smooth-running black government car, the men in their white shirts, the woman in their coloured shoes, the cars and the buzzing phatphats seemed insubstantial. The city was still thrilled with its brilliant victory – only a drubbing in cricket would have exercised public excitement more – but the crowds seemed staged, like extras, and the lights and streets as false as a set on *Town and Country*. How would we survive without our national panacea? But Shiv had confirmed, there was nothing, absolutely nothing to prevent a new generation of Threes from arising. They could already be stirring into sentience, like my divine namesake on his scared turtle Kurma churning the sacred milk into creation. I was acutely aware of the clouds of aeais all around me, penetrating and interpenetrating, layer upon layer, level upon level, many and one. There was no place in the two Delhis for the ancient djinns. The aeais had displaced them. This was their city. Settlement was the only answer. Dust blew through the streets, dust upon dust. I had seen the end of history and still my feet did not touch the floor of the limo.

I was obsolete. All the talents and skills Mamaji and Dadaji were nothing in a world where everyone was connected, where everyone could access the full power of a universal computer, where personality could be as malleable and fluid as water. Slowly slowly I would grow up through adolescence to maturity and old age while around me this new society this new humanity, would evolve at an ever-increasing rate. I was all too aware of my choice. Take Shiv's way and deny everything I had been made for, or reject it and grow old with my kind. We, the genetically enhanced Brahmins, were the last humans. Then, with a physical force that made me spasm on the back seat of the limo, I realised my hubris. I was such an aristocrat. The poor. The poor would be with us. India's brilliant middle class, its genius and its curse, would act as it always had, in its unenlightened self-interest. Anything that would give advantage to its sons and daughters in the Darwinian struggle for succcess. The poor would look on, as disenfranchised from that post-human as they were from this fantasy of glass and neon.

I was glad, glad to tears, that I had chose to pass nothing on into this future. No endless chain of slow-aging, genetically obsolete Brahmins hauling themselves into an increasing unrecognisable and inhuman future. Had I received some premonition; had my uniquely overlapping senses seen a pattern there all those years ago that even Shiv, with his clandestine access to the collected knowledge of the Generation Threes, had not. I wept unreservedly and ecstatically in the back of the smooth-running car. It was time. As we turned into the down ramp to the underground car park at Ramachandra Tower, I made three calls. First I called Prime Minister Srivastava and tendered my resignation. Then I called Lakshmi, patient Lakshmi who had through our charade of a marriage and sterility become a dear and intimate friend, and said, *now, now's the time for that divorce*. Last of all I called my mother on the floor above and told her exactly what I had done with myself.

A Father Festooned with Memory

Wait! One more trick. You'll like this trick, the best trick of all. You haven't seen anything yet, just a bit of running on circles and jumping through hoops. Yes. I know it's very very late and the sun will soon be up the sky and you have cows to milk and fields to tend to and I appointments to keep but you will like this trick. Not a lot, but you will like it. Now, two ticks while I fix up this wire.

And anyway, I haven't finished my story. Oh no no, not by a long chalk. You thought it ended there? With the world as you see it, now you know how intimately I am involved in our history? No, it must end well, a well-made story. I must confront the villain, according to the theories on such things. There must be resolution and an appropriate moral sentiment. Then you will be satisfied.

The wire? Oh, they can walk that. Oh yes, those cats. No no no; first you must listen a little longer.

I walked away. We have a great and grand tradition of it in this great teat of divine milk hanging from the belly of Asia. Our country is big enough to swallow any soul, our orders still porous to pilgrims with a stick and a dhoti wrapped around their loins. Our society has a mechanism for disappearing completely. Anyone can walk away from the mundane world into the divine. Mine was not the orthodox spiritual path and not conventionally divine. I had seen the coming gods. I set aside my career, my clothes, my apartment, my wife – with her blessing and a farewell kiss – my family and friends, my identity, my social networks, my online presence, everything but my genetic inheritance which could not be undone and turned saddhu. Only Sarasvati knew my secret com address. I was gone from the apartment, beating through the neon-lit heat of Rajiv Circle, out along the sides of expressways, drenched in yellow light, beneath the back-throttle of aircraft coming in to the airport, past the brick and cardboard and plastic shelters of the invisible poor. Dawn saw me among the ribbed aluminium flanks of the godowns and factories of Tughluk. I crossed a city on foot in a single night. It's a great and strange thing to do. Everyone should do it. I walked along the cracked concrete spans of expressway, by the sides of country roads blasted by the grit and gust of passing trucks, along the side of the huge slow trains materialising like visions out of the heat haze, the drivers flinging me rupees for blessing as they passed. I sat down and covered my head and eyes as the high-speed shatabdi express blasted past at hundreds of kilometres per hour. Did the passengers even glance me through the darkened glass? If so I must have seemed a very strange saddhu to them. The littlest saddhu. Small but determined, beating forward with my staff at every stride.

What was I doing? Walking. What did I hope to find? Nothing. Where was I going? To see. Don't think me a coward or a failure, that I was walking away from truths I could not admit. I had been stabbed to the bone by the revelation that I was irrelevant. I was not the future. I was a dead-end, a genetic backwater. That was the natural reaction of privilege to its absolute irrelevance. I'm a brat, remember that. A spoiled Mamaji's boy. That same night I returned and dropped my progenitive bombshell; that my mother would never have the dynasty of brilliant Brahmins she desired, I woke from my sleep. It was the uncertain hour, when reality is groggy and the djinns run free. The hour when you wake in your familiar bed without the least knowledge of where the hell you are. I was woken by a sound. It was like a breath and like a roar, like traffic and air conditioners, like a distant desperate shouting and the buzz of neons and powerlines. It was the pulse of underground trains and delivery trucks; it was filmi music and item-songs playing through each other. I heard Great Delhi breath in its shallow sleep and I wanted to go to my balcony and shout as loud as my eleven-year-old glottis would allow: *wake up! Wake up!* Shiv's future might be inevitable, written into the geometry of space-time by entities outside it, but I would not allow us to sleepwalk into it. My mind was racing. I had never known anything like it before. I was thinking at a staggering rate, images and memories and ideas crashing together, shattering, fusing. Edifices of thought, huge as mountains, tumbled around me. The way was clear and bright and laid out in front of me. It was there complete and entire in two seconds. I would have to take myself away from the distractions of Delhi politics and society. My ambitions were much larger than that, I would have to become anonymous for a time, I would have to be silent and look and listen. There was a war to be fought and it was a war of mythologies.

Lakshmi kissed me and I left. I wandered for nine months, south across the border into Rajasthan, back into Bharat and to the north under the breath of the Himalayas, to the cool green ridges where I had spent my honeymoon with Lakshmi. To Dal Lake and Srinagar, to Leh and the high country. I could never grow the proper saddhu beard, but I grew the saddhu leanness and tallness. Boy eunuchs grow tall and lean. And the dreadlocks. Oh yes. They are good to have but unpleasant to get. I also gained a nickname: the Beardless Saddhu. With it I got muscles and sunburn, I grew the stamina to walk all day on a cup of rice and a cup of water. What a pulpy, unfit puppy I

had been! I begged and performed small miracles of accountancy and feats
of memory for food and shelter. Everywhere, I looked in men and women's
Third Eyes. I saw things I could never have from the top of Ramachandra
Tower or the Awadh Bhavan. I saw thirst and I saw drought. I saw good village
leaders and diligent local civil servants frustrated by government bureaucrats.
I saw clever women turn a few hundred rupees from microcredit schemes
and grameen banks into successful businesses. I saw good teachers try to lift
generations out of low expectations and the trap of caste and Awadh's soar-
away middle-class, rapidly pulling the ladder of social mobility up behind
it. I helped with harvests and rode the back of tractors and listened to farers
curse the ever-increasing price of their sterile GM seed. I chased rats with
sticks and waved my arms to set whole fields of sparrows to flight. I sat in the
community house and watched cricket on giant plasma screen powered by
stored sunlight. Oh, I was a most peculiar saddhu. I gained a new nickname
to set beside *Beardless Saddhu: Cricketing Saddhu*. I saw village weddings
and festivals, I saw funerals. I saw death. It came quite unexpectedly one
day, in a small town outside Agra. It was Holi and the streets were full of
flying colour, jets of dye, clouds of powder, stained saris and white shirts
ruined beyond the power of any laundry to save and everywhere grinning
faces stained with colours, teeth white, eye flashing, everyone shouting Holi
hai! Holi hai! as they launched jets of colour into the air. I moved through
this circus of colour, as motley as any. The phatphat was grossly overloaded,
a dozen colour-stained youth hanging off every strut and stanchion. Their
eyes were wide on ganja and they were roaring with laughter and throwing
fistfuls of dye powder at every passer-by. They caught me full in the face. The
front wheel hit a pothole, the overstrained suspension collapsed the whole
thing flipped over in a perfect somersault on to its roof, which split like an
egg. Bodies flew everywhere, many of them so relaxed on the ganja they
were still laughing as they picked themselves and skipped away. One didn't
move. He was trapped under the crushed plastic shell. He lay in his back,
his arms at odd angles. His face was stained blue and green and pink and he
seemed to be smiling but my senses realized he was dead. I had never seen
death before. It was so simple and strange, here undeniably before me yet so
subtle, an instant's transformation yet the opposite of everything that was life.
I mumbled the prayers expected of me, but inwardly I was coming to terms
with the deepest of all human truths. I was twenty-six years old with the body
of albeit-strange thirteen year-old, my lifespan was measurably in centuries,
but one day I too would lie down like this and stop moving and thinking and
feeling and be nothing forever. I saw death and began to understand.

   Village to village, town to town, temple to temple, from the huge
complexes the size of cities to white-washed roadside shrines. Then one day
outside a mall in a droyght-dusty suburb of Jaipur, as the security men were
coming to ask me politely (for one must always be respectful to saddhus) to
please move on, I saw what I had been looking for. A man turned to see the
very small kerfuffle and as I momentarily looked at him, the Eye of Shiva
looked back. I saw biotechnology move there.

I went to a community centre and wrote my first article. I sent it to Suresh Gupta, the editor of *Gupshup*, that most unashamedly populist of the Delhi's magazines, which had carried the photographs of my birth and marriage and now, unknowingly, my prophecies of the coming Age of Kali. He rejected it out of hand. I wrote another the next day. It came back with a comment: *interesting subject matter but inaccessible for our readership*. I was getting somewhere. I went back and wrote again, long into the night over the pad. I am sure I gained another nickname: the Scribbling Saddhu. Suresh Gupta took that third article, and every article since. What did I write about? I wrote about all the things Shiv had prophesied. I wrote about what they might mean for three Indian families, the Voras, the Dashmukhs and the Hirandanis, village, town and city. I created characters – mothers, fathers, sons and daughters and mad aunties and uncles with dark secrets and long-lost relatives come to call – and told their stories, week upon week, year upon year, and the changes, good and ill, the constant hammerblows of technological revolution wrought upon them. I created my own weekly soap opera; I even dared to call it *Town and Country*. It was wildly success-ful. It sold buckets. Suresh Gupta saw his circulation increase by thirty percent among those Delhi intelligentsia who only saw *Gupshup* in hair salons and beauty parlours. Questions were asked, who is this pseudony-mous "Shakyamuni?" We want to interview him, we want to profile him, we want him to appear on *Awadh Today*, we want an op-ed piece from him, we want him to be an advisor on this project, that think tank, we want him to open a supermarket. Suresh Gupta fielded all such inquiries with the ease of a professional Square Leg. There were others questions, ones I over-heard at train stations and phatphat lines, in supermarket queues and at bazaars, at parties and family get-togethers: *what does it mean for us?*

I kept travelling, kept walking, immersing myself in the village and small town. I kept writing my little future-soap, sending off my articles from a cellpoint here, a village netlink there. I watched for the Eye of Shiva. It was several months between the first and second, down in a business park Madhya Pradesh. I saw them steadily after that, but never many; then, at the turn of 2049 to 2050, like a desert blooming after rain, they were everywhere.

I was walking down through the flat dreary country south of the Nepalese border to Varanasi developing my thoughts on evolution, Darwinian and post-Darwinian and the essential unknowability of singularities when I picked up the message from Sarasvati, my first in two weeks of loitering from village to village. At once I thumbed to Varanasi and booked the first shatabdi to Delhi. My natty dreads, my long nails, the dirt and sacred ash of months on the road went down the pan in the First Class Lounge. By the time the Vishwanath Express drew into the stupendous nano-diamond cocoon of New Delhi Central I was dressed and groomed, a smart, confident young Delhiwallah, a highly eligible teenager. Saravasti picked me up in her truck. It was an old battered white Tata without autodrive or onboard or even a functioning airconditioning system. *New Delhi Women's Refuge* was painted on the side in blue. I had followed her career – or rather her careers

– while I was running the country. Worthiness attracted her; had she been a Westerner and not a Delhi girl I would have called it guilt at the privilege of her birth. Theatre manager here, urban farming collective there, donkey sanctuary somewhere else, dam protest way way down *there*. She had derided me: deep down at the grass roots was where the real work was done. People work. *And who will provide the water for those grass roots?* I would answer. It had only taken our brother's vision of the end of the Age of Kali for me to come round to her philosophy.

She looked older than the years I had spent wandering, as if those my youthfulness belied had been added to hers by some karma. She drove like a terrorist. Or maybe it was that I hadn't travelled in a car, in a collapsing Tata pick-up, in a city, in Delhi . . . No, she drove like a terrorist.

"You should have told me earlier."

"He didn't want to. He wants to be in control if it."

"What is it exactly?"

"Huntingdon's."

"Can they do anything?"

"They never could. They still can't."

Saravasti blared her way through the scrimmage of traffic wheeling about the Parliament Street roundabout. The Shaivites still defended their temple, tridents upheld, foreheads painted with the true tilak of Shiva, the three white horizontal stripes. I had seen that other mark on the forehead of almost every man and woman on the street. Sarasvati was pure.

"He would have known whenever he had the genetic checks when I was conceived," I said. "He never said."

"Maybe it was enough for him to know that you could never develop it."

Dadaji had two nurses and they were kind, Nimki and Papadi he called them. They were young Nepalis, very demure and well-mannered, quiet spoken and pretty. They monitored him and checked his oxygen and emptied his colostomy bag and moved him around in his bed to prevent sores and cleared away the seepage and crusting around the many tubes that ran into his body. I felt they loved him after a fashion.

Sarasvati waited outside in the garden. She hated seeing Dad this way, but I think there was a deeper distaste, not merely of what he had become, but of what he was becoming.

Always a chubby man, Tushar Nariman had grown fat since immobility had been forced on him. The room was on the ground floor and opened out on to sun-scorched lawns. Drought-browned trees screened off the vulgarity of the street. It was exercise for the soul if not the body. The neurological degeneration was much more advanced that I had guessed.

My father was big, bloated and pale but the machine overshadowed him. I saw it like a mantis, all arms and probes and manipulators, hooked into him through a dozen incisions and valves. Gandhi it was who considered all surgery violence to the body. It monitored him through sensory needles pinned all over his body like radical acupuncture and, I did not doubt, through the red Eye of Shiva on his forehead. It let him blink and it let him swallow, it let him breathe and when my father spoke, it did his speaking for him. His lips did not move. His voice came from wall-mounted speakers, which made him sound uncannily divine. Had I been hooked into through a Third Eye, he would have spoken directly into my head like telepathy.

"You're looking good."

"I'm doing a lot of walking."

"I've missed you on the news. I liked you moving and shaking. It's what we made you for."

"You made me too intelligent. Super-success is no life. It would never have made me happy. Let Shiv conquer the world and transform society: the super intelligent will always choose the quiet life."

"So what have you been up to, son, since leaving government?"

"Like I said, walking. Investing in people. Telling stories."

"I'd argue with you, I'd call you an ungrateful brat, except Nimki and Papadi here tell me it would kill me. But you are an ungrateful brat. We gave you everything – *everything* – and you just left it at the side of the road." He breathed twice. Every breath was a battle. "So, what do you think? Rubbish, isn't it?"

"They seem to be looking after you."

My father rolled his eyes. He seemed in something beyond pain. Only his will kept him alive. Will for what I could not guess.

"You've no idea how tired I am of this."

"Don't talk like that."

"It's defeatist? It doesn't take your superhuman intellect to work out that there are no good solutions from this."

I turned a chair around and perched on it, hands folded on the back, my chin resting on them.

"What is it you still need to achieve?"

Two laughs, one from the speakers, the other a phlegmy gurgle from the labouring throat.

"Tell me, do you believe in reincarnation?"

"Don't we all? We're Indian, that's what we're about."

"No, but really. The transmigration of the soul?"

"What exactly are you doing?" No sooner had I asked the question than I had raced to the terrible conclusion. "The Eye of Shiva?"

"Is that what you call it? Good name. Keeping me ticking over is the least part of what this machine does. It's mostly processing and memory. A little bit of me goes into it, every second."

Uploaded consciousness, the illusion of immortality, endless reincarnation as pure information. The wan, bodiless theology of post-humanity. I had written about it in my *Nation* articles, made my soapi families face it and discover its false promises. Here it was now in too too much flesh, in my own real-world soap, my own father.

"You still die," I said.

"This will die."

"This *is* you."

"There is no physical part of me today that was here ten years ago. Every atom in me is different, but I still think I'm me. I endure. I remember being that other physical body. There's continuity. If I had chosen to copy myself like some folder of files, yes, certainly I would go down into that dark valley from which there is no return. But maybe, maybe, if I extend myself, if I move myself memory by memory, little by little, maybe death will be no different from trimming a toenail."

There could never be silence in a room so full of the sounds of medicine, but there were no words.

"Why did you call me here?"

"So you would know. So you might give me your blessing. To kiss me, because I'm scared son, I'm so scared. No one's ever done this before. It's one shot into the dark. What if I've made a mistake, what if I've fooled myself? Oh please kiss me and tell me it will be all right."

I went to the bed. I worked my careful way between the tubes and the lines and wires. I hugged the pile of sun-starved flesh to me. I kissed my father's lips and as I did my lips formed the silent words, *I am now and always must be Shiv's enemy but if there is anything of you left in there, if you can make anything out of the vibrations of my lips on yours, then give me a sign.*

I stood up and said, "I love you Dad."

"I love you son."

The lips didn't move, the fingers didn't lift, the eyes just looked and looked and filled up with tears. He swam my mother to safety on an upturned desk. No. That was someone else.

My father died two months later. My father entered cybernetic nirvana two months later. Either way, I had turned my back once again on Great Delhi and walked out of the world of humans and aeais alike.

The Morning of the White Horse

What? You expected a hero? I walked away, yes. What should I have done, run around shooting like filmi star? And who should I have shot? The villain? Who is the villain here? Shiv? No doubt he could have provided you with a great death scene, like the very best black-moustached Bollywood Baddies do, but he is no villain. He is a businessman, pure and simple. A businessman with a product that has changed every part of our world completely and forever. But if I were to shoot him nothing would change. You cannot shoot cybernetics or nanotechnology; economics stubbornly refuses to give you an extended five-minute crawling death-scene, eyes wide with incomprehension at how its brilliant plans could all have ended like this. There are no villains in the real world – real *worlds*, I suppose we must say now – and very few heroes. Certainly not ball-less heroes. For after all, that's the quintessence of a hero. He has balls.

No, I did what any sensible Desi-boy would do. I put my head down and survived. In India we leave the heroics to those with the resources to play that game: the gods and the semigods of the Ramayana and the Maharabharata. Let them cross the universes in three steps and battle demon armies. Leave us the important stuff like making money, protesting our families, surviving. It's what we've done through history, through invasion and princely war, through Aryans and Mughals and British: put our heads down, carried on and little by little survived, seduced, assimilated and in the end conquered. It is what will bring us through this dark Age of Kali. India endures. India is her people and we are all only, ultimately the heroes of our own lives. There is only one hero's journey and that leads from the birth-slap to the burning-ghat. We are a billion and half heroes. Who can defeat that? So, will I yet be the hero of my own long life? We shall see.

After my father's death I wandered for decades. There was nothing for me in Delhi. I had a Buddhist's non-attachment though my wandering was far from the spiritual search of my time as a saddhu. The world was all to rapidly catching up my put-upon characters of *Town and Country*. For the first few years I filed increasingly sporadic articles with *Gupshup*. But the truth was that everyone now was the Voras and the Deshmukhs and the Hirandanis. The series twittered into nothingness, plotlines left dangling, family drama suspended. No one really noticed. They were living that world for real now. And my senses reported the incredible revolution in a richness and detail you cannot begin to imagine. In Kerala, in Assam, in the beach-bar at Goa or the game park in Madhya Pradesh, in the out-of-the-way places I chose to live, it was at a remove and thus comprehensible. In Delhi it would have been overwhelming. Sarasvati kept me updated with calls and emails. She had so far resisted the Eye of Shiva, and the thrilling instantaneousness and intimacy, and subtler death of privacy, of direct thought-to-thought communication. Shiv's Third Revolution had given firmness and vision to her gadfly career. Sarasvati had chosen and set herself among the under-class. I took some small pleasure from the television and online pundits that maybe that old fart Shakyamuni had been right in those terrible populist potboilers in *Gupshup*, and the blow of technology had cracked India, all India, that great diamond of land, into two nations, the fast and slow, the wired and the wire-less, the connected and the unconnected. The haves and the have-nots. Sarasvati told me of a moneyed class soaring so fast into the universal-computing future they were almost red-shifted, and of the eternal poor, sharing the same space but invisible in the always-on, always-communicating world of the connected. Shadows and dust. Two nations; India – that British name for this congeries of ethnicities and languages and histories, and Bharat, the ancient, atavistic, divine land.

Only with distance could I attain the perspective to see this time of changes as a whole. Only by removing myself from them could I begin to understand these two nations. India was a place where the visible and the invisible mingled like two rivers flowing into each, holy Yamuna and Ganga Mata, and a third, the invisible, divine Saraswati. Humans and aeais met and mingled freely. Aeais took shapes in human minds, humans became disembodied presences strung out across the global net. The age of magic had returned, those days when people confidently expected to meet djinns in the streets of Delhi and routinely consulted demons for advice. India was located as much inside the mind and the imagination as between the Himalayas and the sea or in the shining web of communications, more complex and connected and subtle than any human brain, cast across this subcontinent.

Bharat was poor. Bharat had cracked hands and heels, but she was beautiful. Bharat cleaned and swept and cooked and looked after children, Bharat drove and built and pushed carts through the streets and carried boxes up flights of stairs to apartments. Bharat was always thirsty. How human it is to be so engrossed by our latest crisis that we forget we have failed to solve the crisis before that. Storage was India's problem. Information was increasing exponentially, available memory only arithmetically. Data-Malthusianism was the threat to the great technological revolution. Water was Bharat's. The monsoon, ever fickle, had dispersed into a drizzle, a few thunderstorms that ran off the crusted earth as soon as it dropped it rain, a tantalising line of grey clouds along the horizon that never came closer. The Himalayan glaciers that fed the great rivers of the North India and the slow-running Brahmaputra were exhausted; grey moraines of pebbles and dry clay. The mother of droughts was coming. But what was this to a connected class? They could pay for desalinated water, wasn't India born from the waters? And if the worst came to the worst and universe ended in fire, they could, through their dazzling new technology, translate itself out of its icky physical bodies into that dream India between the real and the virtual worlds. Bodhisofts, they called these ascended creatures. Shiv would have been proud of a name like that.

From my beach bar, from my dive school, from my game reserve and bookshop and dance club and coffeehouse and walking-tour company, from my restaurant and antique shop and meditation retreat, I watched my prophecies come true. Yes, I embarked on all those enterprises. Ten of them, one for each of the dashavatara of my divine namesake. All of them on the edge of the world, all of them with that overview down onto the Age of Kali. I lost count of the years. My body grew into me. I became a tall, lean, high-foreheaded man, with a high voice and long hands and feet. My eyes were very beautiful.

I measured the years by the losses. I re-established contact with my old political counterpart in Varanasi, Shaheen Badoor Khan. He had been as surprised as any when I had vanished so abruptly from the political stage but his own career was not without a hiatus and when he discovered that I was the Shakyamuni behind the Town and Country articles (widely syndicated) we began a lively and lengthy correspondence that continued up until his death at the age of seventy-seven. He died completely, and like a good Muslim. Better the promise of paradise than the cloudy doubts of the bodhisoft. My own mother slipped from the world into the realms of the bodhisofts. Sarasvati would not say whether it was a fearful illness or just ennui at the world. Either way I never looked for her among the skyscraper-sized memory stacks that now besieged Delhi along the line of the old Siri

Ring. Lakshmi too, that almost-wife and sweetest of co-conspirators, entered the domain of the bodhisofts where she could explore the subtle mathematical games that so delighted her without limits. It was not all loss. The Age of Kali brought a friend; another great Khan, my old tutor from the Dr Renganathan Brahminical College. He would swirl out of the cloud of I-dust that had replaced the screens and 'hoeks for those who atavistically refused the Eye of Shiva and he would spend many a delightful evening lecturing me on my moral laxity.

Then the dust started to blow through the streets of Delhi. It was not the dust from the perpetual drought that burned the fields and reduced the crops to powder and sent millions from Bharat into the cities of India. It was the dust of Shiva, the sacred ash of the Purusa Corporation's nanoscale computers, released into the world. Bharat might be choking, but here! here! was the solution to India's memory problems. Shiv did have a name for these, a good name too. He called them devas.

He called me. It was decades since we had spoken last in the garden of his house in Varanasi, over lemonade. I was running the dharamshala at Pandua then. It was spacious and peaceful and cool and the only disturbance was the over-heavy feet of the Westerners who flocked to the place. They are not naturally barefooted people, I have found. The I-dust relay chimed, a call. I was expecting Mr Khan. My brother whirled out of the helix of motes instead. He had lost weight, too much weight. He looked well, too much well. He could have been anything: flesh, aeai agent, bodhisoft. We greeted each other and said how well each other looked.

"And how is Nirupa?"

His smile made me think that he was human. Aeais have their own emotions, or things like emotions.

"She's good. Very good. Twenty-eight now, would you believe?"

I confessed that I could not.

"Doing well, found an eligible boy, from a good enough family, who's not a complete gold-digger. Old-fashioned stuff like that. I'm glad she bided her time, but they can afford to take their time now."

"All the time in the world."

"She's beautiful. Vish, there's something I need to tell you. Not a warning exactly, more to prepare yourself."

"This sounds ominous."

"I hope not. You've predicted it all very well."

"Predicted what?"

"Don't be coy. I know who you were. No secrets in the transparent world, I'm afraid. No, you got it right and I'm glad you did it because I think you softened the blow, but there is something you didn't predict, maybe something you couldn't predict."

A whisper of breeze stirred the candle flames in my simple wooden room. Heavy white feet went tread tread tread on the creaking boards outside my latticed window. If they had looked through the grille they would have seen me talking to a ghost. No strange thing in this age, or most other ages.

"Whenever we last spoke, you said that you were making use of information from the legacy-device the original aeais had bequeathed us."

"Well-guessed."

"It seems logical."

"When the Trimurti left Earth, they opened a connection to a separate space-time continuum. There were several major differences from our space-time. One was that time runs much faster there than in our space-time, though it would not be noticeable to anyone in that continuum. Another was that the arrow of time was reversed. The Trimurti move backwards in time; this was how their artefact, which the Americans call the Tabernacle, seemed to have predated the solar system when it was found in space. But the more important one – and that was why they chose it – was that information was integrated into the geometrical structure of that space-time."

I closed my eyes and focused my imagination.

"You're saying that information, data – minds – form part of the basic structure of that universe. Minds without the need for bodies. The whole universe is like a cosmological computer."

"You've got it."

"You've found a way back into that universe."

"Oh no no no no no. That universe is closed. It ended with the Trimurti. Their time is gone. It was an imperfect universe. There are others, mind-spaces like that, but better. We're going to open up dozens – hundreds, eventually thousands – of portals. Our need for processing will always outstrip our available memory, and the devas are just a stopgap. A whole universe, right beside ours, only a footstep away, available for computing resources."

"What are you going to do?"

"The Jyotirlingas are coming."

The Jyotirlingas were the sacred places where, in the Vedic Age, the creative, generative energy of the Lord Siva burst from the ground in pillars of divine light, the ultimate phallic linga symbols. These would come not from the earth, but another universe. And Shiv named them after his namesake's cosmological cock. No one could accuse him of lack of hubris. His I-dust image sparkled and swirled and exploded into a billion motes of light. His smile, like that of the legendary Cheshire cat, seemed to remain. A week later, twelve pillars of light appeared in cities all across the states of India. By a slight misalignment, the Delhi jyotirlinga touched down in the middle of the Dalhousie, the city's largest slum, crowded beyond all imagining with refugees from the drought.

The simultaneous appearance, at eleven thirty-three, of twelve columns of light in cities across India paralysed the rail network. It was one of the least of the disturbances that day but for me, on an island in the middle of the Brahmaputra and needing to get to Delhi, that was the most important. That there were any flights at all was a miracle, that I could book on to one at any price at all proof indeed that the age of the gods had truly returned.

Even when alien universes open up in the hearts of our great and ancient cities, Indian grandmothers will still need to travel to see their wee darlings.

I had tried to call Sarasvati but all com channels into Delhi were down and the call-centre aeais announced indefinite delays before the network was restored. I wondered what it would be like for those accustomed to being strung out across the deva net to be back into just one head as the Air Awadh Airbus took me up over the shrivelled silver thread of the parched Ganga. In the tiny toilet I once again transformed myself back into a shaved, shorn urbane Delhi-boy. As we descended into Indira Gandhi airport the captain told those of on the right to look out and we would see the Jyotirlinga. His voice was uncertain, not a tone you want to hear from an airline captain, as if he could not believe what he was seeing. I had been studying it long before the captain's call: a line of sun-bright light rising from the hazy, grey stain of central Delhi up beyond all sight, further than I could see, craning to look up through the tiny window into the darkening sky.

Sarasvati would be there. That was Shiv's warning. When the light struck, she would have looked around and, in the same instant made her mind up. People in need. She could not refuse.

Immigration took an hour and as half. Five flights of journalists had disgorged at once. A wired world, it seemed, was no substitute for reporters on the ground. The hall buzzed with swarming fly-sized hovercams. Two hours to grind into Delhi in the limo. The highways were clogged with lines of traffic, all headed out, all moving with geological slowness. The noise of horns was appalling to one fresh from the profound, liquid silence of the dharamshala. Only military and media seemed headed into Delhi but soldiers stopped us at intersections to wave past thundering convoys of chartered refugee buses. We were held up for a motionless half an hour on the big cloverleaf on Siri Ring. In awe and leisure, I studied the wall of memory farms; towering black monoliths drinking in sunlight through their solar skins, pressed shoulder to shoulder as far as I could see. In every breath of air-conditioned air I took, I inhaled millions of devas.

Every roadside, every verge and roundabout, every intersection and car park, every forecourt and garden, was filled with the shanties and leans to the refugees. The best were three low walls of brick with plastic sacking for a roof, the worst cardboard scrapes, or sticks and rags worked together into a sun-shade. Feet had worn away all greenery and stripped the trees bare for firewood. The bare earth had blown into dust, mingling with the airborne devas. The bastis pressed right up to the feet of the memory towers. What did Sarasvati imagine she could achieve here in the face of so colossal a catastrophe? I called her again. The network was still out.

Bharat had invaded India and now India was casting it out. We drove, blaring the horn constantly, past a terrible, emaciated army of refugees. No fine cars here. Trucks, old buses, pick-ups for the better off, behind them, swarms of phatphats, more overloaded than that fatal one I had seen the Holi I discovered death. Motorbikes and mopeds almost invisible under bundles of bedding and cooking pots. I saw a chugging, home-engineered half-tractor device, engine terrifying exposed, dragging a trailer piled as high as house with women and children. Donkey carts, the donkey bent and straining at the loads. In the end, human muscle pushed the exodus onward: bicycle rickshaws, handcarts, bent backs. Military robots guided them, herded them, punished those who strayed from the approved refugee route, or fell, with shock sticks.

Before everything, over everything was the silver spear of the Jyotirlinga.

"Sarasvati!"

"Vishnu?" I could hardly hear her over the roar.

"I've come to get you."

"You've what?" It was as noisy where she was. I had a fix. The autodrive would take me there as quickly as it could.

"You've got to get out."

"Vish."

"Vish nothing. What can you do?"

I did hear her sigh.

"All right, I'll meet you." She gave me a fresh set of co-ordinates. The driver nodded. He knew the place. His uniform was crisp and his cap miraculously correct but I knew he was as scared as I.

On Mehrauli Boulevard I heard gunfire. Airdrones barrelled in over the roof of the car, so low their engines shook the suspension. Smoke rose from behind a tatty mall façade. This street, I recognized it. This was Parliament Road, that was the old Park Hotel, that the Bank of Japan. But so faded, so dilapidated. Half the windows were out on the Park. The secluded gardens around Jantar Mantar on Samsad Marg were over-run with packing-case houses, their plastic roofs pushing right against the austere marble angularities of Jai Singh's astronomical instruments. Everything was over-run with lean-tos and huts and miserable hard-scrabble shelters.

"This is as far as I am going to take you," the driver said as we ran into an immovable horde of people and animals and vehicles and military at Talkatora Road.

"Don't go anywhere," I ordered the driver as I jumped out.

"That's not likely," he said.

The press was cruel and chaotic and the most terrifying place I have ever been but Sarasvati was here, I could see her in my mind-map. A cordon of police bots tried to drive me back with the crowds from the steps of the Awadh Bhavan but I ducked under, out and away. I knew this place. I had given my balls to work in this place. Then suddenly, wonderfully, I was in the clear. My heart lurched. My vision swam. Delhi, dear Delhi, my Delhi, they let this happen to you. The gracious greens and boulevards, the airy chowks and maidans of the Rajpath was one unbroken slum. Roof after roof after roof, slumping walls, cardboard and wood and brick and flapping plastic. Smoke went up from a dozen fires. This, this was Dalhousie. I knew the name of course. I had never thought it would ever become the name of the great sink where this newest of New Delhi's condemned those driven to it by drought and want. Such disdain did new India show for old Awadh. Who needed a Parliament when universal computing made everything a consensus? From where I guessed the old Imperial India Gate had stood at the end of the gracious Rajpath, rose the Jyotirlinga. It was so bright I could not look at I for more than moments. It cast a terrible, unnatural silver shine over the degradation and dread. It abused my Brahminic sensibilities: did I smell voices, hear colour, was that prickle like cold lemon fur on my forehead the radiation of another universe?

People milled around me, smoke blew in my eyes, the downdraft of airdrones and hover cams buffeted me. I had only moments before the army would catch me and move me away with the rest of the panicked crowd. Or worse. I saw bodies on the ground and flames were coming up from a line of plastic shacks by the

"Sarasvati!"

And there she was. Oh, there she was, plunging whip-thin in combat pants and a silk blouse, but filled her wonderful energy and determination out of the pile of collapsing housing. She dragged a child in each hand, smudge-faced and tearful. Tiny mites. In this place, she had slipped from my nuptial elephant to caper with the revellers in her ridiculous man's costume and exuberant false moustache.

"Sarasvati!"

"You've got a car?"

"It's how I got here, yes."

The children were on the verge of bawling. Sarasvati thrust them at me.

"Take these two to it."

"Come with me."

"There are kids still in there."

"What? What are you talking about?"

"It's a special needs group. They get left when the sky opens. Everyone else runs and leaves the kids. Take these two to your car."

"What are you doing?"

"There are more in there."

"You can't go."

"Just get them to the car, then come back here."

"The army."

She was gone, ducking under the billowing smoke fall. She disappeared into the warren of lanes and galis. The children pulled at my hands. Yes yes, they had to get out. The car, the car wasn't far. I turned to try and find an easy way with two children through the wheeling mass of refugees. Then I felt a wave of heat across the back of my neck. I turned to see the blossom of flame blow across the top of the gali, whirling up rags of blazing plastic. I cried something without words or point and then the whole district collapsed in on itself with a roar and explosion of sparks.

The Age of Kali. I have little patience with that tendency in many Indians to assume that because we are a very old culture, we invented everything.

Astronomy? Made in India. Zero? Made in India. The indeterminate, probabilistic nature of reality as revealed through quantum theory? Indian. You
don't believe me? The Vedas say that the Four Great Ages of the Universe
correspond to the four possible outcomes of our game of dice. The Krita
Yuga, the Age of Perfection, is the highest possible score. The Kali Yuga, the
Age of strife, darkness, corruption and disintegration, is the lowest possible
score. It is all a roll of the divine dice. Probability. Indian!

Kali, Paraskati, Dark Lady, Mistress of Death and Drinker of Blood,
Terrible ten-armed one with the necklace of skulls, She Who is Seated
upon the Throne of Five Corpses. The Ender. Yet Kali is also Mistress
of Regeneration. Ruler of All Worlds, Root of the Tree of the Universe.
Everything is a cycle and beyond the Age of Kali we roll again into the Age
of Gold. And that which cannot be reasoned with must then be worshipped.

I believe I was mad for some time after Sarasvati's death. I know I have
never been sane as you would consider me sane. We are Brahmins. We are
different. But even for a Brahmin, I was crazy. It is a precious and rare thing,
to take time out from sanity. Usually we allow it to the very very young and
the very very old. It scares us, we have no place for it. But Kali understands
it. Kali welcomes it, Kali gives it. So I was mad for a time, but you could as
easily say I was divine.

How I reached the temple in the little, drought-wracked town by the
sewer of Mata Ganga, I have chosen to forget. How I came by the offering
of blood to the priest, that too I've put where I put the dis-remembered.
How long I stayed there, what I did, does any of this matter? It was time
out from the world. It is a powerful thing, to subject yourself to another
time and another rhythm of life. I was a thing of blood and ashes, hiding
in the dark sanctum, saying nothing but offering my daily puja to the
tiny, garland-bedecked goddess in her vulva-like garbigraha. I could have
vanished forever. Sarasvati, the brightest and best of us, was dead. I lolled on
foot-polished marble. I disappeared. I could have stayed Kali's devotee for
the rest of my long and unnatural life.

I was lolling on the wet, foot-polished marble when the women devotee,
shuffling forward through the long, snaking line of cattle-fences toward the
goddess, suddenly looked up. Stopped. Looked around as if seeing everything for the first time. Looked again and saw me. Then she unhooked the
galvanised railing and pushed trough the switch-back line of devotees to
come to me. She knelt down in front of me and namasteed. Above her the
single vertical line of her Shakta-tilak she wore the red Eye of Shiva.

"Vish."

I recoiled so abruptly I banged the back of my head off a pillar,

"Ooh," the woman said. "Ooh, cho chweet, that's going to smart. Vish,
it's me, Lakhsmi."

Lakshmi? My former wife, player of games? She saw my confusion and
touched my face.

"I'm temporarily downloaded into this dear woman's brain. It's rather hard
to explain if you're not connected. Oh, it's all right, it's entirely consensual.

And I'll give her herself back as soon as I'm done. I wouldn't normally do it – it's very bad manners – but these are slightly exceptional circumstances."

"Lakshmi? Where are you? Are you here?"

"Oh, you have had a bit of a nasty bang. Where am I? That's hard to explain. I am entirely bodhisoft now. I'm inside the Jyotirlinga, Vish. It's a portal as you know, they're all portals." After the initial twelve, the pillars of light had arrived all over earth, hundreds, then thousands. "It is a wonderful place Vish. It can be whatever you want it to be, as real as you like. We spend quite a lot of time debating that; the meaning of real. And the games, the number games; well, you know me. That's why I've taken this step for you Vish. It can't go on. It's destructive, the most destructive thing we've ever done. We'll burn through this world because we have another one. We have heaven, so we can do what we like here. Life is just a rehearsal. But you've seen that Vish, you've seen what that's done."

"What is it Lakshmi?" Was it memory and fond hope, the mild marble concussion, the strange nanotech possession, but was this stranger starting to look like Lakshmi?

"We have to bring this age to an end. Restart the cycle. Close the Jyotirlingas."

"That's impossible."

"It's all mathematics. The mathematics that govern this universe are different from the ones that govern yours; that's why I'm able to exist as a pattern of information imprinted on space-time. Because the logic here allows that. It doesn't where I come from. Two different logics. But if we could slide between the two a third logic, alien to either, that neither of them could recognize nor operate, then we would effectively lock the gates between the universes."

"You have that key."

"We have a lot of time for games here. Social games, language games, imagination games, mathematical and logical games. I can turn the lock from this side."

"But you need someone to turn the key on my side. You need me."

"Yes Vish."

"I would be shut out forever. From you, from Mum, from Dad."

"And Shiv. He's here too. He was one of the first to upload his bodhisoft through the Varanasi Jyotirlinga. You'd be shut out from everyone. Everyone but Sarasvati."

"Sarasvati's dead!" I roared. Devotees looked up. The sadhus calmed them. "And would this be the final answer? Would this bring around the Age of Gold again?"

"That would be up to you, Vish."

I thought of the villages that had so welcomed and amazed and blessed and watered me on my saddhu wandering, I thought of the simple pleasures I had taken from my business ventures: honest plans and work and satisfactions. India – the old India, the undying India – was its villages. Sarasvati had seen that truth though it had killed her.

"It sounds better than sprawling in this dusty old temple." Kali, Mistress of Regeneration, had licked me with her red tongue. Maybe I could be the hero of my own life. Vishnu, the Preserver. His tenth and final incarnation was Kalki, the White Horse, who at the end of the Kali Yuga would fight the final battle. Kali, Kalki.

"I can give you the maths. A man of your intelligence should be able to hold it. But you will need one of these."

The woman lifted her hand and seized a fistful of air. She threw it into my face and the air coalesced into a spray of red powder. In mid-air the cloud moiled and boiled and thickened and settled into a red circle, a tilak, on my forehead.

"Whatever you do, don't connect it to the deva net," Lakshmi said. "I'm going to have to go now. I don't want to outstay my welcome in someone else's body. Goodbye Vish, we won't ever meet again, in any of the worlds. But we were well and truly wed, for a while." For a moment I thought the woman might kiss me, then she gave a little twitch and straightened her neck just so as if shaking out a crick and I knew Lakshmi was gone. The woman namasteed again.

"Little Lord Vishnu," she whispered. "Preserve us."

I picked myself up from the marble. I dusted off the ash of the dark goddess. I walked to the edge of the temple, blinking up into the light of the real sun. I had an idea where to go to do what I had to do. Varanasi, the City of Siva, the seat of the great Jyotirlinga. How might I support myself, with nothing but the dhoti around my loins? Then I caught a sudden movement: on a window ledge on the first floor of one of the many shops that leaned in close to the temple, a cat was edging out along a waterpipe in pursuit of a bird. And I had an idea that filled me with laughter.

So here it is, here it is: at long last. The great trick, the grand Finale of the Magnificent Vishnu's Celestial Cat Circus. The wire walk. You will never, ever have seen anything like this before, unless of course you've been to a certain Kali Temple . . . See, here are the two wires. And here is our star performer. Yes, white Kalki gets his chance to shine at last. Up he goes on to the podium and . . . drum roll. Well, you'll have to provide the drum roll yourself.

Kalki! Kalki, beautiful white Kalki: do your trick!

And there he goes, carefully sliding one paw, then another out across the two wires, tail moving to keep him in balance, the whole trembling to his muscular control. Go on Kalki . . . Walking the wire. What a cat! And the final jump on to the further podium and I scoop him up to my chest and shout applause! Applause for my lovely cats! I let Kalki down and the rest of the cats run to join him, running their endless circle of fur and tails around the rope ring. Matsya, Kurma, Narasimha and Varaha; Varana, Pashurama and Rama; Krishna, Buddha and last but not least, Kalki.

I turn in the rising dawn light to savour the applause of my audience. And my cats, save your biggest cheer for Matsya, Kurma, Narasimha, Varaha, Varana, Pashurama, Rama, Krishna, Buddha and Kalki who have performed for your pleasure? And me? Just an impresario, a ringmaster: a storyteller. The light is up now and I will detain you no longer for you have your work and I have a place to go and I think now you know where that is and what I must do there. I may not succeed. I may die. I cannot see Shiv giving up without a fight. So please, will you do one thing for me? My cats. Would you look after them for me? You don't have to feed them or anything like that, just take them. Let them go, they can look after themselves. It's where I got them from in the first place. They'll be happy on a farm, in the country. Lots to hunt and kill. You might even be able to make a bit of money from them. I mean, performing cats, who ever heard of a thing like that? It's actually much easier than you think. Meat does it, every time. There, I've given away the trick. Be good to them. Well, I'll be off then.

I push the boat out into the river, run into the dawn-bright water and hop in. It rocks gently. It is a glorious morning; the Jyotirlinga ahead can hold no comparison to the sun. I touch my fingers to my forehead, to the tilak Lakshmi put there in a small salutation to the sun. Then I put my back to the narrow oars and head out into the stream.

HONORABLE MENTIONS

2009

Daniel Abraham, "Belfour and Meriwether in the Adventure of the Emperor's Vengeance," *Postscripts* 19.
_____, "The Best Monkey," *Solaris Book of SF 3*.
_____, "The Curandero and the Swede," *F&SF*, March.
_____, "The Pretender's Tourney," *Eclipse Three*.
Jim Aikin, "Leaving the Station," *Asimov's*, December.
Tim Akers, "A Soul Stitched to Iron," *Solaris Book of SF 3*.
Neal Asher, "Shell Game," *New Space Opera 2*.
Kage Baker, "Are You Afflicted with Dragons?," *The Dragon Book*.
_____, "The Green Bird," *Songs of the Dying Earth*.
_____, "The Women of Nell Gwynne's," *Subterranean Press*.
Peter M. Ball, "Horn," *Twelfth Planet Press*.
_____, "To Dream of Stars: An Astronomer's Lament," *Apex Magazine*, October.
Elliott Bangs, "This Must Be the Place," *Strange Horizons*, 2/2.
John Barnes, "The Lost Princess Man," *New Space Opera 2*.
_____, "Things Undone," *JBU*, December.
Kelly Barnhill, "Open the Door and the Light Pours Through," *Clockwork Phoenix 2*.
Laird Barron, "Catch Hell," *Lovecraft Unbound*.
_____, "Strappado," *Poe*.
William Barton, "The Sea of Dreams," *Asimov's*, October/November.
Christopher Barzak, "The Ghost Hunter's Beautiful Daughter," *Asimov's*, October/November.
Stephen Baxter, "Artifacts," *Solaris Book of SF 3*.
_____, "Earth II," *Asimov's*, July.
_____, "Formidable Caress," *Analog*, December.
_____, "Kelvin 2.0," *New Scientist*, 16 September.
_____, "The Phoebean Egg," *Postscripts* 20/21.
_____, "Starfall," *PS Publishing*.
_____, "Tempest 43," *We Think, Therefore We Are*.
_____, "The Unblinking Eye," *Other Earths*.
Peter S. Beagle, "Oakland Dragon Blues," *The Dragon Book*.
_____, "Slight of Hand," *Eclipse Three*.
_____, "Up the Down Beanstalk: A Wife Remembers," *Troll's Eye View*.
_____, "Vanishing," *OSC'sIMShow*, March.
Elizabeth Bear, "The Horrid Glory of Its Wings," Tor.com.
_____, "Snow Dragons," *Subterranean*, Summer.
_____, "Swell," *Eclipse Three*.
Chris Beckett, "Atomic Truth," *Asimov's*, April/May.
_____, "The Famous Cave Paintings on Isolus 9," *Postscripts* 19.
Gregory Benford, "Paradise Afternoon," Flurb 8.
Judith Berman, "Pelago," *Asimov's*, February.
Beth Bernobich, "Ars Memoriae," *PS Publishing*.
Terry Bisson, "Corona CenturionTM FAQ," *F&SF*, June/July.
James Blaylock, "The Dry Spell," *Subterranean*, Winter.

Michael Blumlein, "California Burning," *Asimov's*, August.
Leah Bobet, "The Parable of the Shower," *Lone Star Stories*, 1 June.
_____, "Six," Clockwork *Phoenix 2*.
Desirina Boskovich, "Celadon," *Clarkesworld*, January.
Richard Bowes, "I Needs Must Part, the Policeman Said," *F&SF*, October/November.
_____, "The Office of Doom," *Lovecraft Unbound*.
Marie Brennan, "Letter Found in a Chest Belonging to the Marquis de Monsseraille, Following the Death of That Worthy Individual," *Abyss & Apex* 29.
_____, "Once a Goddess," *Clockwork Phoenix 2*.
Damien Broderick, "Flowers of Asphodel," *Asimov's*, October/November.
_____, "The Qualia Engine," *Asimov's*, August.
_____, "The Ruined Queen of Harvest World," Tor.com.
Keith Brooke, "Sweats," *We Think, Therefore We Are*.
Eric Brown, "Cold Testing," *Asimov's*, June.
_____, "Gilbert and Edward on Mars," *PS Publishing*.
_____, "Salvage Rites," *We Think, Therefore We Are*.
_____, "Starship Fall," *NewCon Press*.
Rachel Manija Brown, "River of Heaven," *Strange Horizons*, 6/29.
Chaz Brunchley, "White Skies," *When It Changed*.
Tobias S. Bucknell, "Placa Del Fuego," *Clarkesworld* 34.
Karl Bunker, "Murder," *Abyss & Apex* 29.
Stephanie Burgis, "True Names," *Strange Horizons*, 11/9.
Chris Butler, "The Festival of Tethselem," *Interzone* 224.
Pat Cadigan, "Don't Mention Madagascar," *Eclipse Three*.
_____, "Truth and Bone," *Poe*.
Paul Carlson, "Mirror Girl," *Abyss & Apex*, 32.
Michael Cassutt, "The Last Apostle," *Asimov's*, July.
Jason K. Chapman, "Brief Candle," *Clarkesworld*, November.
_____, "The Singers of Rhodes," *Panverse One*.
Suzy McKee Charnas, "Lowland Sea," Poe.
Robert R. Chase, "Five Thousand Light Years from Birdland," *Asimov's*, January.
Catherine Cheek, "Voice Like a Cello," *Fantasy*, May.
J. Kathleen Cheney, "Early Winter, Near Jenli Village," *Fantasy*, April.
Eric Choi, "Another's Treasure," *Footsteps*.
Geffrey W. Cole, "Teaching Bigfoot to Read," *Clarkesworld*, January.
Glen Cook, "The Good Magician," *Songs of the Dying Earth*.
Brenda Cooper, "In Their Garden," *Asimov's*, September.
_____, "Sailors in a Sea of Suns," *Footsteps*.
Bruce Coville, "After the Third Kiss," *The Dragon Book*.
Albert E. Cowdrey, "Bandits of the Trace," F&SF, October/November.
_____, "The Private Eye," *F&SF*, August/September.
_____, "Seafarer's Blood," *F&SF*, January.
Dave Creek, "Zheng He and the Dragon," *Analog*, January/February.
Ian Creasey, "Digging for Paradise," *Realms of Fantasy*, August.
_____, "The Report of a Dubious Creature," *OSCIMS*, November.
Benjamin Crowell, "A Large Bucket, and Accidental Godlike Mastery of Spacetime," *Asimov's*, December.
_____, "The Rising Waters," Strange Horizons, 4 and 11 May.
Don D'Ammassa, "Duck and Cover," *Analog*, July/August.
Dennis Danvers, "Healing Benjamin," *Realms of Fantasy*, August.
Colin P. Davies, "The Certainty Principle," *Asimov's*, February.
Rebecca Day, "The Urn of Ravalos," *OSC'sIMShow*, March.
Aliette de Bodard, "After the Fire," *Apex Magazine*, November.

_____, "Dancing for the Monsoon," *Abyss & Apex*, 30.

_____, "In the Age of Iron and Ashes," *Beneath Ceaseless Skies*, 31 December.

_____, "Ys," Interzone 222.

Paul Di Filippo, "The New Cyberiad," *We Think, Therefore We Are.*

_____, "Providence," *Solaris Book of SF 3.*

_____, "Yes We Have No Bananas," *Eclipse Three.*

Cory Doctorow, "To Go Boldly," *New Space Opera* 2.

Terry Dowling, "The Copsy Door," *Songs of the Dying Earth.*

_____, "The Library," X6.

Brendan DuBois, "Illusions of Tranquility," *F&SF*, October/November.

Alexandra Duncan, "Bad Matter," *F&SF*, October/November.

Andy Duncan, "The Dragaman's Bride," *The Dragon Book.*

_____, "The Night Cache," *PS Publishing.*

Scott Edleman, "Glitch," *Solaris Book of SF 3.*

_____, "The Only Wish Ever to Come True," *Talebones*, Summer.

_____, "The World Breaks," *Postscript* 19.

Sarah L. Edwards, "Lady of the White-Spired City," *Interzone* 222.

_____, "The Tinyman and Caroline," *Beneath Ceaseless Skies*, 21 May.

Greg Egan, "Hot Rock," *Crystal Nights.*

Phyllis Eisenstein, "The Last Golden Thread," *Songs of the Dying Earth.*

Carol Emshwiller, "The Bird Painter in Time of War," *Asimov's*, February.

Gemma Files & Stephen J. Barringer, "each thing I show you is a piece of my death," *Clockwork Phoenix 2.*

Charles Coleman Finlay, "The Minuteman's Watch," *F&SF*, January.

_____, "The Texas Bake Sale," *F&SF*, February.

Michael F. Flynn, "Where the Winds Are All Asleep," *Analog*, October.

Jeffrey Ford, "The Coral Heart," *Eclipse Three.*

Eugie Foster, "Sinner, Baker, Fabulist, Priest; Red Mask, Black Mask, Gentleman, Beast," *Interzone* 220.

Karen Joy Fowler, "The Pelican Bar," *Eclipse Three.*

Ben Francisco, "Tio Gilberto and the Twenty-Seven Ghosts," *Realms of Fantasy*, October.

Gregory Frost, "The Final Act," *Poe.*

Julie Frost, "Fortune of Soldiers," *Cosmos*, April/May.

Adam Corbin Fusco, "Sails Above Greensea," *Realms of Fantasy*, April.

Diana Gabaldon & Samuel Sykes, "Humane Killer," *The Dragon Book.*

Neil Gaiman, "An Invocation of Incuriosity," *Songs of the Dying Earth.*

R. Garcia y Robertson, "SinBad the Sand Sailor," *Asimov's*, July.

_____, "Wife-Stealing Time," Asimov's, October/November.

Harry Garfield, "Stratosphere," *F&SF*, April/May.

Sara Genge, "As Women Fight," *Asimov's*, December.

David Gerrold, "Ganny Knits a Spaceship," *Jim Baen's Universe*, August.

Carolyn Ives Gilman, "Economancer," *F&SF*, June/July.

Molly Gloss, "The Visited Man," *Eclipse Three.*

Ari Goelman, "Bird of Paradise," *Talebones*, Summer.

Lisa Goldstein, "Away From Here," *Asimov's*, September.

Theodora Goss, "Ceilla's Story," *Other Earths.*

_____, "The Puma," Apex Magazine, March.

Steven Gould, "Bugs in the Arroyo," Tor.com.

Eric Gregory, "Salt's Father," *Strange Horizons*, 8/3.

_____, "The Transmigration of Aishwarya Desai," *Interzone* 223.

Christopher Green, "A Hundredth Name," *Abyss & Apex*, 31.

Dominic Green, "Coat of Many Colours," *Interzone* 223.

_____, "Glister," *Interzone* 223.

Robert Grossbach, "An Idea Whose Time Has Come," *Analog*, October.
Eileen Gunn & Michael Swanwick, "The Armies of Elfland," *Asimov's*, April/May.
Paul Haines, "Wives," *X6*.
Joe Haldeman, "Never Blood Enough," *F&SF*, October/November.
Warren Hammond, "Carnival Night," *Solaris Book of SF 3*.
Elizabeth Hand, "The Far Shore," *F&SF*, October/November.
_____, "The Return of the Fire Witch," *Songs of the Dying Earth*.
Alex Hardison, "Clouds in the Night," *Flurb 7*.
Gail Hareven, "The Slows," *The New Yorker*, 7 May.
Andy Heizler, "The Broken Hourglass," *Cosmos*, December/January.
Samantha Henderson, "Chandra's Game," *Lone Star Stories*, 1 Feburary.
_____, "East of Chula Vista," *Abyss & Apex 29*.
Howard V. Hendrix, "Monuments of Unageing Intellects," *Analog*, June.
Trent Hergenradar, "Eskhara," *Federations*.
Glen Hirshberg, "The Pikesville Buffalo," *Poe*.
M.K. Hobson, "The Warlock and the Man of the Word," *Postscripts 19*.
Nina Kiriki Hoffman, "Pranks," *Lone Star Stories*, June 1.
Cecelia Holland, "Dragon's Deep," *The Dragon Book*.
B.C. Holmes, "Glamour," *On Spec*, Winter.
Matthew Hughes, "Another Day In Fibbery," *Postscripts 20/21*.
_____, "Enemy of the Good," *Postscripts 19*.
_____, "Grolion of Almery," *Songs of the Dying Earth*.
_____, "Hell of a Fix," *F&SF*, October/November.
_____, "Hunchster," *F&SF*, August/September.
David Hutchison, "The Push," *NewCon Press*.
Simon Ings, "Zoology," *When It Changed*.
Alex Irvine, "Dragon's Teeth," *F&SF*, October/November.
_____, "Eagleburger's Lawn," *Interzone 223*.
Harvey Jacobs, "The Man Who Did Something about It," *F&SF*, October/November.
Alaya Dawn Johnson, "The Yeast of Eire," Strange Horizons, 7/1–7/14.
Kij Johnson, "The Cat Who Walked a Thousand Miles," Tor.com.
_____, "Spar," *Clarksworld*, October.
Matthew Johnson, "The Coldest War," *Asimov's*, February.
Diane Wynne Jones, "JoBoy," *The Dragon Book*.
Gwyneth Jones, "Collison," *When It Changed*.
Richard Kadrey, "Trembling Blue Stars," *Flurb 7*.
James Patrick Kelly, "Going Deep," *Asimov's*, June.
John Kessel, "The Motorman's Coat," F&SF, June/July.
Caitliln R. Kiernan, "Galapagos," *Eclipse Three*.
Alice Sola Kim, "The Ugly Zombie," *Strange Horizons*, 12/7–12/14
Swapna Kishore, "Home on the Ganges," *Ideomancer*, June.
Ellen Klages, "A Practical Girl," *Eclipse Three*.
_____, "Singing on a Star," *Firebirds Soaring*.
_____, "A Wild and Wicked Youth," *F&SF*, April/May.
Ted Kosmatka, "The Ascendant," *Subterranean*, Spring.
Mary Robinette Kowal, "At the Edge of Dying," *Clockwork Phoenix 2*.
_____, "Body Language," *OSCIMS*, November.
_____, "The Consciousness Problem," *Asimov's*, August.
_____, "First Flight," Tor.com.
_____, "Ginger Stuyvesant and the Case of the Haunted Nursery," *Talebones*, Summer.
Barbara Krasnoff, "Rosemary, That's for Remembrance," *Clockwork Phoenix 2*.
Nancy Kress, "Deadly Sins," *Asimov's*, October/November.
_____, "Exegesis," *Asimov's*, April/May.

_____, "Images of Anna," *Fantasy*, September.
_____, "Unintended Behavior," *Asimov's*, January.
Matthew Kressel, "Saving Diego," *Interzone* 221.
Naomi Kritzer, "The Good Son," *Jim Baen's Universe*, February.
Ellen Kushner, "A Wild and Wicked Youth," *F&SF*, April/May.
_____, "Dolce Domun," *Eclipse Three*.
Marc Laidlaw, "Leng," Lovecraft Unbound.
Jay Lake, "Black Heart, White Mourning," *Grant's Pass*.
_____, "Bringing the Future Home," *Global Warming Aftermaths*.
_____, "Chain of Stars," *Subterranean*, Fall.
_____, "Leopard," *Jim Baen's Universe*, June.
_____, "People of Leaf and Branch," *Fantasy*, June.
_____, "Red Dirt Kingdom," *Realms of Fantasy*, October.
_____, "To Raise a Mutiny Betwixt Yourselves," *New Space Opera* 2.
Claude Lalumiere, "Three Friends," *Clockwork Phoenix* 2.
John Lambshead, "Storming Hell," *Jim Baen's Universe*, April.
Margo Lanagan, "Ferryman," *Firebirds Soaring*.
_____, "Sea-Hearts," X6.
John Langan, "Technicolor," *Poe*.
_____, "The Wide Carnivorous Sky," *By Blood We Live*.
Joe R. Lansdale, "Hides and Horns," *Subterranean, Spring*.
Ann Leckie, "The Endangered Camp," *Clockwork Phoenix* 2.
Tanith Lee, "Clockatrice," *Fantasy*, October.
_____, "Evillo the Uncunning," *Songs of the Dying Earth*.
_____, "The Pain of Glass," *Clockwork Phoenix* 2.
_____, "The War That Winter Is," *The Dragon Book*.
Soon Ha Lee, "The Bones of Giants," *F&SF*, August/September.
_____, "Swanwatch," *Federations*.
_____, "The Unstrung Zither," *F&SF*, March.
Tim Lees, "Meeting Mr. Tony," *Postscripts 19*.
David D. Levine, "Joy is the Serious Business of Heaven," *Realms of Fantasy*, February.
Marissa Lingen, "The Calculus Plague," *Analog*, July/August.
Kelly Link, "The Cinderella Game," *Troll's Eye View*.
Jennifer Linnaea, "Second-Hand Information," *Strange Horizons*, 6/15.
Rochia Loenon-Ruiz, "59 Beads," *Apex Magazine*, December.
Richard A. Lovett, "Attack of the Grub-Eaters," *Analog*, June.
_____, "Excellence," *Analog*, January.
Ken MacLeod, "A Tulip for Lucretius," *Subterranean*, Spring.
_____, "Death Knocks," *When It Changed*.
_____, "iThink, Therefore I Am," *Solaris Book of SF* 3.
_____, "Reflective Surfaces," *New Scientist*, 16 September.
Paul McAuley, "Penance," *New Scientist*, 16 September.
_____, "Shadow Life," *Discover*, July/August.
Sharyn McCrumb, "The Mountain House," *Poe*.
Ian McDonald, "A Little School," *New Scientist*, 16 September.
Sandra McDonald, "Diana Comet," *Strange Horizons*, 3/2–3/9.
Ian McHugh, "Sleepless in the House of Ye," *Asimov's*, July.
_____, "Sundogs," *Beneath Ceaseless Skies*, October 8.
Maureen McHugh, "Useless Things," *Eclipse Three*.
Will McIntosh, "Bridesicle," *Asimov's*, January.
_____, "A Clown Escapes from Circus Town," *Interzone* 221.
Sean McMullen, "The Art of the Dragon," *F&SF*, August/September.
_____, "Mother of Champions," *Interzone* 222.

_____, "The Spiral Briar," *F&SF*, April/May.
Gregory Maguire, "Puzzle," *The Dragon Book*.
Elissa Malcohn, "Flotsam," *Asimov's*, October/November.
John Mantooth, "The Water Tower," *Fantasy*, July.
David Marusek, "Hard Man To Surprise," *Nature*, 30 July.
_____,"Timed Release," *Nature*, May.
George R. R. Martin, "A Night at the Tarn House," Songs of the Dying Earth.
John Meaney, "From the Heart," *New Space Opera 2*.
_____, "Necroflux Day," *Solaris Book of SF 3*.
Greg Meller, "Defence of the Realm," *Cosmos*, February/March.
T. J. Morganfield, "The Place That Makes You Happiest," *Paradox*, Spring.
Kris Nelscott, "Clinic," *Subterranean*, Winter.
Mario Milosevic, "Winding Broomcorn," *F&SF*, February.
Michael Moddor, "The Boy Who Sang for Others," *F&SF*, January.
Steven Mohan, Jr., "The Promise of Touch," *Ideomancer*, March.
Sarah Monette, "White Charles," *Clarksworld*, September.
Elizabeth Moon, "An Incident in Uskvesh," *Songs of the Dying Earth*.
_____, "Chameleons," *New Space Opera 2*.
Ruth Nestvold, "In the Middle of Nowhere with Company," *Abyss & Apex* 30.
_____, "On the Shadow Side of the Beast," *Apex Magazine*, January.
_____, "Woman in Abaya With Onion," *Fantasy*, June.
R. Neube, "Intelligence," *Asimov's*, March.
Kim Newman, "Illimitable Domain," *Poe*.
_____, "Moon Moon Moon," *Subterranean*, Summer 2009.
Garth Nix, "An Unwelcome Guest," *Troll's Eye View*.
_____, "The Heart of the City," *Subterranean*, Summer.
_____, "Punctuality," *New Space Opera 2*.
_____, "Stop!," *The Dragon Book*.
Naomi Novik, "Vici," *The Dragon Book*.
Charles Oberndorf, "Another Life," *F&SF*, October/November.
Mike O'Driscoll, "The Spaceman," *F&SF*, June/July.
Nnedi Okorafor-Mbachu, "On the Road," *Eclipse Three*.
Patrick O'Leary, "That Laugh," *We Think, Therefore We Are*.
Shannon Page & Jay Lake, "Bone Island," *Interzone* 225.
Suzanne Palmer, "Silence and Roses," *Interzone* 223.
Paul Park, "A Family History," *Other Earths*.
_____, "The Persistence of Memory, or, This Space for Sale," *Postscripts* 20/21.
Richard Parks, "The Mansion of Bones," *Beneath Ceaseless Skies*, 28 June.
_____, "Night, in Dark Perfection," *Clarkesworld*, December.
_____, "The River of Three Crossings," *Realms of Fantasy*, February.
Marshall Payne, "Sausages," Talebones, Summer.
Rebecca J. Payne, "By Starlight," *Interzone* 225.
Jennifer Pelland, "Minya's Astral Angels," *Solaris Book of SF 3*.
Tom Pendergrass, "Aim for the Stars," *OSCIMS*, November.
Holly Phillips, "Cold Water Survival," Lovecraft Unbound.
_____, "Thieves of Silence," *Beneath Ceaseless Skies*, 16 July.
Tony Pi, "Come-From-Aways," *On Spec*, Spring.
_____, "Silk and Shadows," *Beneath Ceaseless Skies*, 26 February.
_____, "Tokkai Exhales His Avatar," *OSCIMS*, March.
Tamora Pierce, "The Dragon's Tale," *The Dragon Book*.
Steven Popkes, "Two Boys," *Asimov's*, August.
Tim Pratt, "Another End of the Empire," *Strange Horizons*, 6/22.
_____, "Her Voice in a Bottle," *Subterranean*, Winter.

_____, "Troublesolving," *Subterranean*, Fall.
_____, "Unexpected Outcomes," *Interzone* 222.
Tom Purdom, "Controlled Experiment," *Asimov's*, June.
Cat Rambo, "Diary of a Beast's Life," *Realms of Fantasy*, December.
_____, "The Mermaids Singing Each to Each," *Clarkesworld*, November.
_____, "Ms. Liberty Gets a Haircut," *Strange Horizons*, 10/26.
Kit Reed, "Camp Nowhere," *Asimov's*, July.
Robert Reed, "Creatures of Well-Defined Habits," *Asimov's*, August.
_____, "Firehorn," *F&SF*, June/July.
_____, "Shadow Below," *F&SF*, March.
_____, "Tests," *Postscripts* 20/21.
_____, "Three Princesses," *We Think, Therefore We Are*.
_____, "True Fame," *Asimov's*, April/May.
Mike Resnick, "The Bride of Frankenstein," *Asimov's*, December.
_____, "Catastrophe Baker and a Canticle for Leibowitz," *New Space Opera* 2.
_____, "Inescapable," *Songs of the Dying Earth*.
_____& Lezli Robyn, "Soulmates," *Asimov's*, September.
Alastair Reynolds, "The Fixation," *Solaris Book of SF* 3.
_____, "The Receivers," *Other Earths*.
_____, "Scales," Guardian.co.uk, 23 June.
Chris Roberson, "All Under Heaven," *Firebirds Soaring*.
_____, "Dragon King of the Eastern Sea," *We Think, Therefore We Are*.
Adam Roberts, "Woodpunk," *Solaris Book of SF* 3.
Justina Robson, "Cracklegrackle," *New Space Opera* 2.
_____, "One Shot," *New Scientist*, 16 September.
Benjamin Rosenbaum, "Nine Alternate Alternate Histories," *Other Earths*.
Mary Rosenblum, "Dragon Storm," *The Dragon Book*.
_____, "My She," *Federations*.
Deborah J. Ross, "The Price of Silence," *F&SF*, April/May.
Rudy Rucker & Bruce Sterling, "Colliding Branes," *Asimov's*, February.
Kristine Kathryn Rusch, "Broken Windchimes," *Asimov's*, September.
_____, "Defect," *New Space Opera* 2.
_____, "Flower Fairies," *Realms of Fantasy*, October.
_____, "The Recovery Man's Bargain," *Analog*, January/February.
_____, "The Spires of Denon," *Asimov's*, April/May.
_____, "Turbulence," *Asimov's*, August.
Patricia Russo, "The Men Burned All the Boats," Fantasy, February.
_____, "Rainbows and Other Shapes," *Abyss & Apex* 32.
Geoff Ryman, "You," *When It Changed*.
Jason Sanford, "Here We Are, Falling Through Shadows," *Interzone* 225.
_____, "Sublimation Angels," *Interzone* 224.
John Scalzi, "The Tale of the Wicked," *New Space Opera* 2.
Delia Sherman, "Wizard's Apprentice," *Troll's Eye View*.
Ken Scholes, "A Weeping Czar Beholds the Fallen Moon," Tor.com.
_____, "Grail Diving in Shangrilla with the World's Last Mime," *Subterranean*, Winter.
Ekaterina Sedia, "Fungal Gardens," *Apex Magazine*,
_____, "The Mind of a Pig," *Apex Magazine*, March.
Gord Sellar, "Cai and Her Ten Thousand Husbands," *Apex Magazine*, January.
_____, "Of Melei, of Ulthar," *Clarksworld*, October.
Lucius Shepard, "Dog-Eared Paperback of My Life," *Other Earths*.
_____, "Kirikh'quru Kronkundor," *Poe*.
_____, "Sylgarmo's Proclamation," *Songs of the Dying Earth*.
Lewis Shiner, "The Death of Che Guevara," *Subterranean*, Fall.

Rachel Swirsky, "Great Golden Wings," *Beneath Ceaseless Skies*, 22 October.
_____, "Eros, Philia, Agape," Tor.com.
Robert Silverberg, "The True Vintage of Erzuine Thale," *Songs of the Dying Earth*.
Dan Simmons, "The Guiding Nose of Ulfänt Banderōz," *Songs of the Dying Earth*.
Vandana Singh, "Conservation Laws," *The Woman Who Thought She Was a Planet*.
Jack Skillingstead, "The Avenger of Love," *F&SF*, April/May.
_____, "Einstein's Theory," *On Spec*, Spring.
_____, "Human Day," *Asimov's*, April/May.
_____, "Rescue Mission," *Solaris Book of SF 3*.
Alan Smale, "Delusion's Song," *Panverse One*.
Jeremy Adam Smith, "Eko and Narkiss," *Lone Star Stories*, 1 February.
Melinda M. Snodgrass, "A Token of a Better Age," *F&SF*, August/September.
Midori Snyder, "Molly," *Troll's Eye View*.
Bud Sparhawk, "No Cord or Cable," *Abyss & Apex* 30.
Cat Sparks, "Heart of Stone," *X6*.
Katherine Sparrow & Rachel Swirsky, "No Longer You," *Interzone* 224.
William Browning Spencer, "Come Lurk with Me and Be My Love," *Lovecraft Unbound*.
Nancy Springer, "Iris," *F&SF*, October/November.
_____, "You Are Such a One," *F&SF*, August/September.
Brian Stableford, "The Great Armada," *Asimov's*, April/May.
_____, "The Highway Code," *We Think, Therefore We Are*.
_____, "Some Like It Hot," *Asimov's*, December.
Allen Steele, "The Other Side of Jordan," *Federations*.
Bruce Sterling, "Esoteric City," *F&SF*, August/September.
_____, "Join the Navy and See the Worlds," *New Space Opera* 2.
_____, "Open Source Science," *Discover*, July/August.
Jason Stoddard, "Monetized," *Interzone* 220.
Charles Stross, "Overtime," Tor.com.
_____, "Palimpsest," *Wireless*.
Jonathan Stroud, "Bob Choi's Last Job," *The Dragon Book*.
Tim Sullivan, "Inside Time," *F&SF*, October/November.
Michael Swanwick & Eileen Gunn, "Zeppelin City," Tor.com.
Rachel Swirsky, "Eros, Philia, Agape," Tor.com.
_____, "Great Golden Wings," *F&SF*, April/May.
John Alfred Taylor, "Bare, Forked Animal," *Asimov's*, June.
Steve Rasnic Tem, "The Day Before the Day Before," *Asimov's*, September.
Byron Tetrick, "The Collegeum of Mauge," Songs of the Dying Earth.
Lavie Tidhar, "Dark Planet," *Apex Magazine*, February.
_____, "The Dying World, *Clarkesworld*, April.
_____, "Funny Pages," *Interzone* 225.
_____, "Jews in Antarctica," *Fantasy*, October.
_____, "Out of the Blue," *Abyss & Apex* 32.
_____, "The Shangri-La Affair," *Strange Horizons*, 1/26.
Andrew Tisbert, "Waking the City," *Panverse One*.
Jeremiah Tolbert, "The Culture Archivist," *Federations*.
_____, "The Godfall's Chemsong," *Interzone* 224.
Harry Turtledove, "But It Does Move," *Analog*, June.
_____, "None So Blind," *The Dragon Book*.
_____, "The House That George Built," Tor.com
_____, "The Star and the Rockets," Tor.com.
_____, "We Haven't Got There Yet," Tor.com.
Lisa Tuttle, "Ragged Claws," *Postscripts* 20/21.
Garth Upshaw, "Name Day," *Realms of Fantasy*, April.

Steven Utley, "The Point," *Asimov's*, February.
Catheryene M. Valente, "Golubash, or Wine-Blood-War-Elegy," *Federations*.
_____, "The Radiant Car Thy Sparrows Drew," *Clarkesworld* 35.
Genevive Valentine, "A Brief Investigation of the Process of Decay," *Strange Horizons*, 11/16.
_____, "Carthago Delenda Est," *Federations*.
Jeff VanderMeer, "The Final Quest of the Wizard Sarnod," *Songs of the Dying Earth*.
_____, "The Goat Variations," *Other Earths*.
Greg Van Eekhout, "The Holy City and Em's Reptile Farm," *Other Earths*.
_____, "Last Son of Tomorrow," Tor.com.
James Van Pelt, "Working the Moon Circuit," *Footsteps*.
Carrie Vaughn, "Conquistador de la Noche," *Subterranean*, Spring.
Paula Volsky, "The Traditions of Karzh," *Songs of the Dying Earth*.
Juliette Wade, "Cold Words," *Analog*, October.
Howard Waldrop, "Frogskin Cap," *Songs of the Dying Earth*.
Jo Walton, "Parable Lost," *Lone Star Stories*, 1 June.
_____, "Three Twilight Tales," Firebirds Soaring.
Ian Watson, "A Virtual Population Crisis," *New Scientist*, 16 September.
K. D. Wentworth, "The Orangery," *Beneath Ceaseless Skies*, 12 March.
Ian Whates, "The Assistant," *Solaris Book of SF* 3.
Dean Whitlock, "Changeling," *F&SF*, January.
Wayne Wightman, "Adaptogenia," *F&SF*, June/July.
Kate Wilhelm, "An Ordinary Day with Jason," *Asimov's*, April/May.
_____, "Shadows on the Wall of the Cave," *F&SF*, October/November.
Liz Williams, "Caulk the Witch-chaser," *Songs of the Dying Earth*.
_____, "The Dragon of Direfell," *The Dragon Book*.
_____, "Enigma," *When It Changed*.
_____, "Under the Honey," *Subterranean*, Spring.
_____, "Winterborn," *Other Earths*.
Sean Williams, "Inevitable," *New Space Opera* 2.
_____, "Ungentle Fire," *The Dragon Book*.
Tad Williams, "A Stark and Wormy Knight," *The Dragon Book*.
_____, "The Lamentably Comical Tragedy (or the Laughably Tragic Comedy) of Lixal Laqavee," *Songs of the Dying Earth*.
_____, "The Tenth Muse," *New Space Opera* 2.
Walter Jon Williams, "Abrizonde," *Songs of the Dying Earth*.
Bill Willingham, "Fearless Space Pirates of the Outer Rings," *New Space Opera* 2.
Chris Willrich, "Sailing the Morne," *Asimov's*, June.
Robert Charles Wilson, "This Peaceable Land, or The Unbearable Vision of Harriet Beecher Stowe," *Other Earths*.
Gene Wolfe, "Donovan Sent Us," *Other Earths*.
John C. Wright, "The Far End of History," *New Space Opera* 2.
_____, "Guyal the Curator," *Songs of the Dying Earth*.
_____, "One Bright Star to Guide Them," *F&SF*, April/May.
Jane Yolen and Adam Stemple, "Mesopotamian Fire," *Eclipse Three*.
_____, "The Tsar's Dragons," *The Dragon Book*.
Marly Youmans, "The Horse Angel," *Postscripts* 20/21.
Alexsandar Ziljak, "An Evening in the City Coffeehouse, With Lydia," *Apex Magazine*, December.